Advanced Dungeons & Dragons

Monstrous Manual™

The updated *Monstrous Manual*™ for the AD&D® 2nd Edition Game

TSR, Inc.
201 Sheridan Springs Road
Lake Geneva
WI 53147
USA

TSR Ltd.
120 Church End
Cherry Hinton
Cambridge CB1 3LB
United Kingdom

Project Coordinator: Tim Beach
Editor: Doug Stewart
Editorial Assistant: Gaye O'Keefe
Cover Illustration: Jeff Easley
Interior Illustrations: Tony DiTerlizzi (pencils, inks, and colors on insects, crustaceans, faerie-folk, and miscellaneous creepy things), Jeff Butler (pencils and inks on humans, demihumans, humanoids, giants, genies, dragonets, and miscellaneous part-human creatures), Dave Simons (pencils, inks, and colors on normal animals, almost normal animals, and squishy things), Tom Baxa (pencils, inks, and colors on gith-kind and miscellaneous), Mark Nelson (pencils and inks on dragons, dinosaurs, and miscellaneous), Les Dorscheid (colors on most of the book), Tim Beach and Doug Stewart (invisible stalker)
Art Coordination: Peggy Cooper with Tim Beach
Typesetting: Gaye O'Keefe
Keylining: Paul Hanchette
Proofreading: Karen Boomgarden, Anne Brown, Andria Hayday, Thomas Reid, David Wise
Guidance: Steve Winter, Tim Brown, James M. Ward
Monster Selection Committee: Jeff Grubb, David Wise, John Rateliff, Tim Beach
Development: Tim Beach, Doug Stewart, Slade Henson, Thomas Reid, Jeff Grubb, Wolfgang Baur, John Pickens, John Rateliff
Design Concept for MONSTROUS COMPENDIUM® Appendices: David "Zeb" Cook, Steve Winter, Jon Pickens

We would like to offer special thanks to the artists and the people who helped with development, as well as Rich Baker, Carolyn Chambers, Bill Connors, Peggy Cooper, Slade Henson, Dawn Kegley, Dana Knutson, Georgia S. Stewart, and Sue Weinlein. Many people have contributed to either the original first edition monster books or to the MONSTROUS COMPENDIUM appendices. The list that follows may not be complete, but we would like to thank the following people for their contributions to the monsters described in this book: the designers and editors, Rich Baker, Jay Battista, Wolfgang Baur, Tim Beach, Scott Bennie, Donald J. Bingle, Linda Bingle, Karen Boomgarden, Grant Boucher, Al Boyce, Mike Breault, Anne Brown, Tim Brown, Dr. Arthur W. Collins, Bill Connors, David "Zeb" Cook, Troy Denning, Dale Donovan, Newton Ewell, Nigel Findley, Steve Gilbert, Ed Greenwood, Jeff Grubb, Gary Gygax, Luke Gygax, Allen Hammack, Kris & Steve Hardinger, Andria Hayday, Bruce A. Heard, Slade Henson, Tracy Hickman, Harold Johnson, Rob King, Vera Jane Koffler, Heike Kubasch, Steve Kurtz, J. Paul LaFountain, Lenard Lakofka, Jim Lowder, Francois Marcela-Froideval, David Martin, Colin McComb, Anne McCready, Blake Mobley, Kim Mohan, Roger E. Moore, Chris Mortika, Bruce Nesmith, C. Terry Phillips, Jon Pickens, Brian Pitzer, Mike Price, Louis J. Prosperi, Tom Prusa, Jean Rabe, Paul Reiche, Jim Sandt, Lawrence Schick, Rick Swan, Greg Swedburg, Teeuwynn, John Terra, Gary Thomas, Allen Varney, James M. Ward, Dori Watry, Skip Williams, and Steve Winter; the artists who helped define the monsters, Tom Baxa, Brom, Jeff Butler, Clyde Caldwell, Doug Chaffee, Tony DiTerlizzi, Les Dorscheid, Jeff Easley, Larry Elmore, Fred Fields, Jim Holloway, Daniel Horne, Mark Nelson, Keith Parkinson, Harry Quinn, Robh Ruppel, Dave Simons, Dave Sutherland, D.A. Trampier, Valerie Valusek; and the people who put the books together and make them look good, Linda Bakk, Dee Barnett, Steve Beck, Peggy Cooper, Sarah Feggestad, Paul Hanchette, Angelika Lokotz, Gaye O'Keefe, Stephanie Tabat, and Tracey Isler; and anyone who has ever asked a question, offered constructive criticism, written an article, or offered an opinion about the monsters of the AD&D® game. Special thanks to Christopher M. Carter and Seth Goodkind for spotting errors.

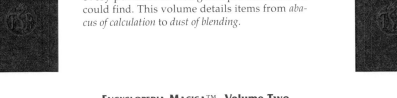

Accessories

ENCYCLOPEDIA MAGICA™ Volume One

This is the first in a series of four accessories detailing every magic item printed by TSR in every publication and game product that we could find. This volume details items from *abacus of calculation* to *dust of blending*.

ENCYCLOPEDIA MAGICA™ Volume Two

This is the second release of TSR's greatest undertaking: listing every magic item it's ever printed. This 416-page volume details *dust of decoy* through *phylactery of righteousness*. Some of the more popular items included herein are figurines, gems, lamps, maces, oils, and orbs.

Accessories

ENCYCLOPEDIA MAGICA™ Volume Three

This 416-page accessory details magic items from the *pick of earth parting* to the spellbook, *Thesis of Conditional Ruptures*. This volume includes potions, rings, robes, rods, scrolls, and shields—some of the most popular magic items.

ENCYCLOPEDIA MAGICA™ Volume Four

The last of the series, this 416-page volume details magic items from the Spellbook, *Theories on Converging Transitions*, through *Zwieback of Zymurgy*. This accessory features staves, swords, and wands. Also included are Magic Item Random Determination Tables and an extensive index.

FOR DUNGEON MASTERS

Fundamentals

DUNGEON MASTER® Guide

The single most important reference for any DM, this volume gives you the lowdown on how to create and run your own AD&D game campaign. From world-making to treasure-sorting, from role-playing to adventure generation, the *DMG* has it all.

MONSTROUS MANUAL™ Accessory

Where else can you find over 600 monsters of every sort, each with full game statistics and a full-color illustration of the beast in action? This is a fundamental reference for every DM.

DUNGEON MASTER® Screen & Master Index

This self-standing cardboard screen puts vital combat and encounter tables right before your eyes. It also hides your maps, die rolls, and secret information from players.

Accessories

DUNGEON MASTER® Guide Supplements

Add depth to your fantasy campaign and bring your adventures to greater life with these vital and comprehensive handbooks!

- Arms and Equipment Guide (handy for players, too!)
- Monster Mythology (nonhuman deities)
- The Complete Book of Villains (the best NPC book ever!)
- The Complete Book of Necromancers (the ultimate bad guys)

MONSTROUS COMPENDIUM® Annuals

One manual of monsters is not enough! Each year, a new compendium of bizarre horrors and startling creations is assembled, guaranteed to astonish the players, enliven the campaign, and please the DM.

Accessories

Book of Artifacts

This coveted collection of phenomenal devices features long-buried favorites from the original AD&D game tomes, as well as many new relics and devices native to certain TSR campaign worlds, all greatly expanded for AD&D 2nd Edition game players. You'll even learn how to create artifacts and other magical devices for your own campaign!

Adventures

The ultimate DMs' fantasies have been put together in these deluxe adventures, which can be set in any campaign world against almost any type of heroic group.

- DRAGON MOUNTAIN® Adventure
- Night Below: An UNDERDARK™ Campaign
- Temple, Tower, & Tomb
- The Rod of Seven Parts
- Labyrinth of Madness

The Rod of Seven Parts

The Rod of Seven Parts is one of the most powerful artifacts in the AD&D® game. The heroes face the incredible challenge of finding and piecing together all seven parts and harnessing the power of the Rod to defeat the Queen of Chaos and Miska the Wolf-Spider. Designed for character levels 10 to 12.

Night Below

The largest dungeon ever published! A full "generic" campaign setting for raising characters from 1st to 16th level, with hundreds of miles of underground caves, tunnels, and dungeons–even an ocean! New skills, monsters, magical items, and more will flesh out the fantasy underworld and cultures for which the AD&D game is justly famous.

How To Use This Book

This hardcover *Monstrous Manual*™ was created in response to the many requests to gather monsters into a single, durable volume which would be convenient to carry. With the *DUNGEON MASTER® Guide (DMG)* and the *Player's Handbook (PHB)*, the *Monstrous Manual* forms the core of the AD&D® 2nd Edition game.

Every monster from the MONSTROUS COMPENDIUM® Volumes One and Two are contained within, as well as a few creatures from later volumes. The monsters in the *Monstrous Manual* have been revised, edited, and updated. Statistics for many of the creatures have been corrected, new information has been added to many of the entries, and many monsters have been reclassified. There are some new beasts, as well. In cases of conflicting information, the *Monstrous Manual* supersedes all previously published data.

Certain entries have been greatly condensed from MONSTROUS COMPENDIUM entries, to make this book as complete as possible without increasing its size or price. For instance, there is a full-page description of ravens in the MONSTROUS COMPENDIUM appendix for the GREYHAWK® campaign setting; in this book, ravens are given only a few lines in the "Bird" entry. This provides enough information to use the creatures for a short encounter, and it allows a page to be devoted to another adversary.

To find a monster in this book, flip through the pages or look in the index, which contains listings for the common name(s) of every monster in the book, referenced to the correct page.

All of the monsters described here are typical for their type. DMs should note that unusual variations are encouraged, but they are most effective when they depart from the expected. Likewise, entries describe typical lairs for creatures, from the dungeon complexes they inhabit to the tree houses they build; changing the look of these can make a monster encounter unique.

Contents

This introduction describes how to interpret the monsters in this book. In addition, there are three small appendices in the back of the book. The first deals with making monsters. The second covers monster summoning and includes tables for random determination of summoned creatures; to make random encounter charts for a campaign, the DM should refer to Chapter 11 of the *DMG*. The third appendix is concerned with creating NPC parties.

Other Worlds

Several of the monsters in this book have been imported from specialized game worlds, such as the SPELLJAMMER® campaign setting, the FORGOTTEN REALMS® setting, or the DARK SUN® world. The monsters in this book may be used in any setting; if a campaign setting is noted, it simply describes where the monster was first encountered, or where it is the most common. A particular monster still may not be encountered in a specific campaign world; this is up to the DM. For monsters from one of the specific worlds, the DM should consult the appropriate MONSTROUS COMPENDIUM appendices.

The Monsters

Each monster is described fully, with entries that describe behavior, combat modes, and so on. These are explained in the following text.

CLIMATE/TERRAIN defines where the creature is most often found. Climates include arctic, sub-arctic, temperate, and tropical. Typical terrain includes plain/scrub, forest, rough/hill, mountain, swamp, and desert. In some cases, a range is given; for instance, "cold" implies arctic, sub-arctic, and colder temperate regions.

FREQUENCY is the likelihood of encountering a creature in an area. Chances can be adjusted for special areas.

Very rare	= 4% chance
Rare	= 11% chance
Uncommon	= 20% chance
Common	= 65% chance

ORGANIZATION is the general social structure the monster adopts. "Solitary" includes small family groups.

ACTIVITY CYCLE is the time of day when the monster is most active. Those active at night can be active at any time in subterranean settings. These are general guidelines and exceptions are fairly common.

DIET shows what the creature usually eats. Carnivores eat meat, herbivores eat plants, and omnivores eat either. Scavengers primarily eat carrion. If a monster does not fit any of these categories, the substances it does eat are described in the entry or in the text.

INTELLIGENCE is the equivalent of human "IQ." Certain monsters are instinctively cunning; these are noted in the monster descriptions. Ratings correspond roughly to the following Intelligence ability scores:

0	Nonintelligent or not ratable
1	Animal intelligence
2-4	Semi-intelligent
5-7	Low intelligence
8-10	Average (human) intelligence
11-12	Very intelligent
13-14	Highly intelligent
15-16	Exceptionally intelligent
17-18	Genius
19-20	Supra-genius
21+	Godlike intelligence

TREASURE refers to the treasure tables in the *DUNGEON MASTER Guide*. If individual treasure is indicated, each individual may carry it (or not, at the DM's discretion). Major treasures are usually found in the monster's lair; these are most often designed and placed by the DM. Intelligent monsters will use the magical items present and try to carry off their most valuable treasures if hard pressed. If treasure is assigned randomly, roll for each type possible; if all rolls fail, no treasure of any type is found. Treasure should be adjusted downward if a few monsters are encountered. Large treasures are noted by a multiplier (× 10, for example); this should not be confused with treasure type X. Treasure types listed in parentheses are treasures found in the creatures' lair. Do not use the tables to place dungeon treasure, since the numbers encountered underground will be much smaller.

ALIGNMENT shows the general behavior of the average monster of that type. Exceptions, though uncommon, may be encountered.

NO. APPEARING indicates an average encounter size for a wilderness encounter. The DM should alter this to fit the circumstances as the need arises. This should not be used for dungeon encounters.

Note that some solitary creatures are found in small groups; this means they are found in very small family units, or that several may happen to be found together, but do not cooperate with one another.

ARMOR CLASS is the general protection worn by humans and humanoids, protection due to physical structure or magical nature, or difficulty in hitting due to speed, reflexes, etc. Humans and humanoids of roughly man-size that wear armor will have an unarmored rating in parentheses. Listed AC does not include any special bonuses noted in the description.

MOVEMENT shows the relative speed rating of the creature. Higher speeds may be possible for short periods. Human, demihuman, and humanoid movement rate is often determined by armor type (unarmored rates are given in parentheses). Movements in different mediums are abbreviated as follows:

Fl	= flying
Sw	= swimming
Br	= burrowing
Cl	= climbing
Wb	= moving across webs

How To Use This Book

Flying creatures also have a Maneuverability Class from A to E. Class A creatures have virtually total command over their movements in the air; they can hover, face any direction in a given round, and attack each round. Class B creatures are very maneuverable; they can hover, turn 180 degrees in a round, and attack in each round. Class C creatures are somewhat agile in the air; they cannot move less than half their movement rate without falling, they can turn up to 90 degrees in a round, and attack aerially once every two rounds. Class D creatures are somewhat slow; they cannot move less than half their movement rate without falling, can turn only 60 degrees in a round, and can make a pass once every three rounds. Class E includes large, clumsy fliers; these cannot move less than half their movement rate without falling, can turn only 30 degrees in a round, and they can make one pass every six rounds. See Chapter 9 of the *DMG* for more information.

HIT DICE controls the number of hit points damage a creature can withstand before being killed. Unless otherwise stated, Hit Dice are 8-sided (1-8 hit points). The Hit Dice are rolled and the numbers shown are added to determine the monster's hit points. Some monsters have a hit point spread instead of Hit Dice, and some have additional points added to their Hit Dice. Thus, a creature with 4 + 4 Hit Dice has 4d8 + 4 hit points (8-36 total). Note that creatures with + 3 or more hit points are considered the next higher Hit Die for purposes of attack rolls and saving throws.

THAC0 is the attack roll the monster needs to hit Armor Class 0. This is always a function of Hit Dice, except in the case of very large, nonaggressive herbivores (such as some dinosaurs), or creatures which have certain innate combat abilities. A human or demihuman always uses a player character THAC0, regardless of whether they are player characters or "monsters." The THAC0 does not include any special bonuses noted in the descriptions.

NUMBER OF ATTACKS shows the basic attacks the monster can make in a melee round, excluding special attacks. This number can be modified by hits that sever members, spells such as *haste* and *slow*, and so forth. Multiple attacks indicate several members, raking paws, multiple heads, etc.

DAMAGE/ATTACK shows the amount of damage a given attack causes, expressed as a spread of hit points (based on a die roll or combination of die rolls). If the monster uses weapons, the damage done by the typical weapon will be allowed by the parenthetical note "weapon." Damage bonuses due to Strength are listed as a bonus following the damage range.

SPECIAL ATTACKS detail attack modes such as dragon breath, magic use, etc. These are explained in the monster description.

SPECIAL DEFENSES are precisely that, and are detailed in the monster description.

MAGIC RESISTANCE is the percentage chance that any magic cast upon the creature will fail to affect it, even if other creatures nearby are affected. If the magic penetrates the resistance, the creature is still entitled to any normal saving throw allowed. Creatures may have resistances to certain spells; this is not considered "magic resistance," which is effective against all spells.

SIZE is abbreviated as

    T = tiny (2' tall or less);
    S = smaller than a typical human (2 + ' to 4');
    M = man-sized (4 + ' to 7');
    L = larger than man-sized (7 + ' to 12');
    H = huge (12 + ' to 25'); and
    G = gargantuan (25 + ').

Most creatures are measured in height or length; some are measured in diameter. Those measured in diameter may be given a different size category than indicated above. For instance, while a 6-foot tall humanoid is considered size M, a spherical creature 6 feet in diameter has much more mass, so is considered size L. Similarly, a creature 12 feet long with a very slender body (like a snake) might be considered only man-sized. Adjustments like these should not move a creature more than one size category in either direction.

MORALE is a general rating of how likely the monster is to persevere in the face of adversity or armed opposition. This guideline can be adjusted for individual circumstances. Morale ratings correspond to the following range:

2-4	Unreliable
5-7	Unsteady
8-10	Average
11-12	Steady
13-14	Elite
15-16	Champion
17-18	Fanatic
19-20	Fearless

XP VALUE is the number of experience points awarded for defeating, but not necessarily killing, the monster. This value is a guideline that can be modified by the DM for the degree of challenge, encounter situation, and for overall campaign balance.

Combat is the part of the description that discusses special combat abilities, arms and armor, and tactics.

Habitat/Society outlines the monster's general behavior, nature, social structure, and goals. In some cases, it further describes their lairs (the places they live in), breeding habits, and reproduction rates.

Ecology describes how the monster fits into the campaign world, gives any useful products or byproducts, and any other miscellaneous information.

Variations of a monster are given in a special section after the main monster entry. These can be found by consulting the index. For instance, the xorn entry also describes the xaren, a very similar creature.

Psionics are mental powers possessed by many creatures in the *Monstrous Manual*. The psionic listings are explained below:
Level: How tough the monster is in terms of psionic experience level.
Dis/Sci/Dev: How many *disciplines* the creature can access, followed by the total number of sciences and devotions the creature knows. Monsters can know *sciences* and *devotions* only from the disciplines they can access.
Attack/Defense: The telepathic attack and defense modes that the creature can use. Note that defense modes are not included in the total number of powers the creature knows. Abbreviations used are as follows:

PB	Psionic Blast	M-	Mind Blank
MT	Mind Thrust	TS	Thought Shield
EW	Ego Whip	MB	Mental Barrier
II	Id Insinuation	IF	Intellect Fortress
PsC	Psychic Crush	TW	Tower of Iron Will

Power Score: The creature's usual score when using a power that is not automatically successful.
PSPs: The creature's total pool of psionic strength points (the maximum available to it).

The rest of the listing indicates, by discipline, which powers the creature has, sometimes listing the most common powers, sometimes listing only the powers that all members of the species have. Unless otherwise noted, the creature always knows powers marked by an asterisk.

For information regarding psionic powers, see PHBR5, *The Complete Psionics Handbook*. If the DM chooses not to use psionics in the campaign, the powers can be changed to magical equivalents or simply ignored, though the latter severely impedes certain monsters.

Aarakocra

CLIMATE/TERRAIN:	Tropical and temperate mountains
FREQUENCY:	Very rare
ORGANIZATION:	Tribal
ACTIVITY CYCLE:	Day
DIET:	Carnivore
INTELLIGENCE:	Average (8-10)
TREASURE:	D
ALIGNMENT:	Neutral good
NO. APPEARING:	1-10
ARMOR CLASS:	7
MOVEMENT:	6, Fl 36 (C)
HIT DICE:	1+2
THAC0:	19
NO. OF ATTACKS:	2
DAMAGE/ATTACK:	1-3/1-3 or 2-8 (weapon)
SPECIAL ATTACKS:	Dive +4
SPECIAL DEFENSES:	Nil
MAGIC RESISTANCE:	Nil
SIZE:	M (20' wing span)
MORALE:	Steady (11)
XP VALUE:	65

The aarakocra are a race of intelligent bird-men that live on the peaks of the highest mountains, spending their days soaring on the thermal winds in peace and solitude.

Aarakocra are about 5 feet tall and have a wing span of 20 feet. About halfway along the edge of each wing is a hand with three human-sized fingers and an opposable thumb. An elongated fourth finger extends the length of the wing and locks in place for flying. Though the wing-hands cannot grasp during flight, they are nearly as useful as human hands when an aarakocra is on the ground and its wings are folded back. The wing muscles anchor in a bony chest plate that provides the aarakocra with extra protection. The powerful legs end in four sharp talons that can unlock and fold back to reveal another pair of functional hands, also with three human-sized fingers and an opposable thumb. The hand bones, like the rest of an aarakocra's skeleton, are hollow and fragile.

Aarakocra faces resemble crosses between parrots and eagles. They have gray-black beaks, and black eyes set frontally in their heads that provide keen binocular vision. Plumage color varies from tribe to tribe, but generally males are red, orange, and yellow while females are brown and gray.

Aarakocra speak their own language, the language of giant eagles, and, on occasion, the common tongue (10% chance).

Combat: In aerial combat, an aarakocra fights with either talons or the heavy fletched javelins that he clutches in his lower hands. An aarakocra typically carries a half dozen javelins strapped to his chest in individual sheaths. The javelins, which can be used for throwing or stabbing, inflict 2d4 points of damage. Owing to the aarakocra's remarkable skill at throwing javelins in the air, it incurs none of the attack penalties for aerial missile fire. An aarakocra will always save its last javelin for stabbing purposes rather than throwing it. Its favorite attack is to dive at a victim while clutching a javelin in each hand, then pull out of the dive just as it reaches its target, and strike with a blood-curdling shriek. This attack gains a +4 bonus to the attack roll and causes double damage, but an aarakocra must dive at least 200 feet to execute it properly.

An aarakocra is reluctant to engage in grappling or ground combat, since its fragile bones are easily broken. Though rarely used except when cornered, an aarakocra's sharp beak can bite for 1-3 points of damage.

Habitat/Society: Aarakocra live in small tribes of about 11-30 (1d20+10) members. Each tribe has a hunting territory of about 10,000 square miles with colorful banners and pennants marking the boundaries.

Each tribe lives in a communal nest made of woven vines with a soft lining of dried grass. The eldest male serves as the tribe's leader. In tribes of more than 20 members, the second oldest male serves as the shaman, leading simple religious ceremonies involving the whistling of melodic hymns at sunset on the first day of a new month. Males spend most of their waking hours hunting for food and occasionally for treasure, such as gems and other shiny objects. Females spend eight months of the year incubating their eggs, passing the time by fabricating javelins and other tools from wood and stone. While resting on their backs, aarakocra females can use all four hands at the same time to weave boundary pennants, javelins sheaths, and other useful objects from vines and feathers.

Five aarakocra, including a shaman, can summon an air elemental by chanting and performing an intricate aerial dance for three melee rounds. The summoned air elemental will comply with the aarakocras' request for a favor, though it will not endanger its life on their behalf.

Aarakocra are extremely claustrophobic and will not willingly enter a cave, building, or other enclosed area.

Ecology: Aarakocra have little to do with other species, including neighboring aarakocra tribes, and leave their home territory only in extreme circumstances. They rarely encounter humans except for an occasional foray into a rural community to snatch a stray farm animal; this is not an intentionally malicious act, as aarakocra are unable to distinguish between domestic and wild animals. A human venturing into aarakocra territory may be able to convince one to serve as a guide or a scout in exchange for a shiny jewel or coin.

Aboleth

CLIMATE/TERRAIN:	Tropical and temperate/Subterranean
FREQUENCY:	Very rare
ORGANIZATION:	Brood
ACTIVITY CYCLE:	Night
DIET:	Omnivore
INTELLIGENCE:	High (13-14)
TREASURE:	F
ALIGNMENT:	Lawful evil

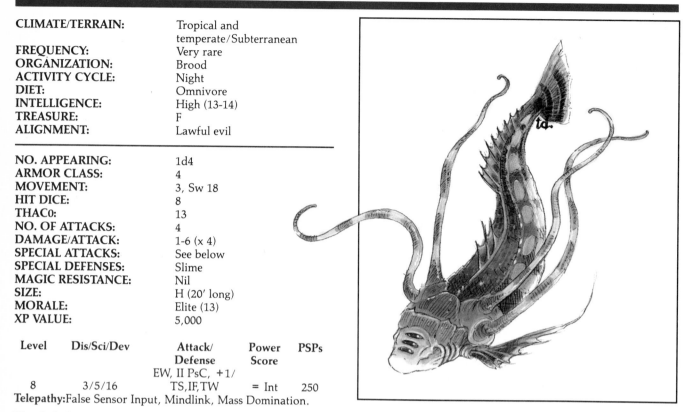

NO. APPEARING:	1d4
ARMOR CLASS:	4
MOVEMENT:	3, Sw 18
HIT DICE:	8
THAC0:	13
NO. OF ATTACKS:	4
DAMAGE/ATTACK:	1-6 (x 4)
SPECIAL ATTACKS:	See below
SPECIAL DEFENSES:	Slime
MAGIC RESISTANCE:	Nil
SIZE:	H (20' long)
MORALE:	Elite (13)
XP VALUE:	5,000

Level	Dis/Sci/Dev	Attack/ Defense	Power Score	PSPs
8	3/5/16	EW, II PsC, +1/ TS, IF, TW	= Int	250

Telepathy: False Sensor Input, Mindlink, Mass Domination.

The aboleth is a loathsome amphibious creature that lives in subterranean caves and lakes. It despises most land-dwelling creatures and seeks to enslave intelligent surface beings. It is as cruel as it is intelligent.

An aboleth resembles a plump fish, 20 feet in length from its bulbous head to its fluke-like tail. Its body is blue-green with gray splotches, and its pink-tan underbelly conceals a toothless, rubbery mouth. Three slit-like eyes, purple-red in color and protected by bony ridges, are set one atop the other in the front of its head. Four pulsating blue-black orifices line the bottom of its body and secrete gray slime that smells like rancid grease. Four leathery tentacles, each 10 feet in length, grow from its head. An aboleth uses its tail to propel itself through the water and its tentacles to drag itself along dry land.

Combat: The aboleth attacks with its tentacles for 1d6 points of damage each. If a victim struck by a tentacle fails a saving throw vs. spell, the victim's skin transforms into a clear, slimy membrane in 1d4+1 rounds. If this occurs, the victim must keep the membrane damp with cool water or suffer 1d12 points of damage each turn. *Cure disease* cast upon the victim before the membrane completely forms stops the transformation. Otherwise, *cure serious wounds* will cause the membrane to revert to normal skin.

Because its sluggish movement makes attacks difficult, the aboleth attempts to lure victims close by creating realistic illusions at will, complete with audible, olfactory, and other sensory components. The aboleth can attempt to enslave creatures within 30 feet; it can make three attempts per day, one creature per attempt. If the victim fails a saving throw vs. spell, he follows all of the aboleth's telepathic commands, although the victim will not fight on the aboleth's behalf. The enslavement can be negated by *remove curse, dispel magic*, the death of the enslaving aboleth, or, if the victim is separated from the aboleth by more than a mile, a new saving throw (one attempt per day.)

When underwater, an aboleth surrounds itself with a mucous cloud 1 foot thick. A victim in contact with the cloud and inhaling the mucus must roll a successful saving throw vs. poison or lose the ability to breathe air. The victim is then able to breathe water, as if having consumed a *potion of water breathing*, for 1-3 hours. This ability may be renewed by additional contact with the mucous cloud. An affected victim attempting to breathe air will suffocate in 2d6 rounds. Wine or soap dissolves the mucus.

Habitat/Society: An aboleth brood consists of a parent and one to three offspring. Though the offspring are as large and as strong as the parent, they defer to the parent in all matters and obey it implicitly.

Aboleth have both male and female sexual organs. A mature aboleth reproduces once every five years by concealing itself in a cavern or other remote area, then laying a single egg and covering it in slime. The parent aboleth guards the egg while the embryo grows and develops, a process that takes about five years. A newborn aboleth takes about 10 years to mature.

The aboleth spends most of its time searching for slaves, preferably human ones. It is rumored that the aboleth use their slaves to construct huge underwater cities, though none have ever been found. The aboleth are rumored to know ancient, horrible secrets that predate the existence of man, but these rumors are also unsubstantiated. There is no doubt that aboleth retain a staggering amount of knowledge. An offspring acquires all of its parent's knowledge at birth, and a mature aboleth acquires the knowledge of any intelligent being it consumes.

An aboleth's treasure consists of items taken from its slaves. The items are buried in caverns under a layer of slime resembling gray mud, recognizable by the distinctive rancid grease odor.

Ecology: The omnivorous aboleth will eat any organic matter, usually algae and micro-organisms, but they are also fond of intelligent prey so they can absorb nutrients and information at the same time. Aboleth have no natural enemies, as even the mightiest marine creatures give them a wide berth. Aboleth slime is sometimes used as a component for *potions of water breathing*.

CLIMATE/TERRAIN:	Temperate and tropical/ Plains and forests
FREQUENCY:	Rare
ORGANIZATION:	Brood
ACTIVITY CYCLE:	Any
DIET:	Omnivore
INTELLIGENCE:	Non- (0)
TREASURE:	C
ALIGNMENT:	Neutral

NO. APPEARING:	1-6
ARMOR CLASS:	Overall 2, underside 4
MOVEMENT:	12, Br 6
HIT DICE:	3-8
THAC0:	17-13
NO. OF ATTACKS:	1
DAMAGE/ATTACK:	3-18 (crush) + 1-4 (acid)
SPECIAL ATTACKS:	Squirt acid
SPECIAL DEFENSES:	Nil
MAGIC RESISTANCE:	Nil
SIZE:	L-H (10' to 20' long)
MORALE:	Average (9)
XP VALUE:	175-975

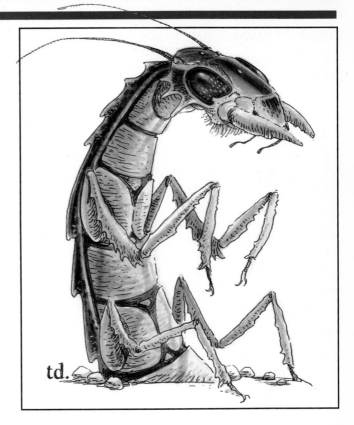

The ankheg is a burrowing monster usually found in forests or choice agricultural land. Because of its fondness for fresh meat, the ankheg is a threat to any creature unfortunate enough to encounter it.

The ankheg resembles an enormous many-legged worm. Its six legs end in sharp hooks suitable for burrowing and grasping, and its powerful mandibles are capable of snapping a small tree in half with a single bite. A tough chitinous shell, usually brown or yellow, covers its entire body except for its soft pink belly. The ankheg has glistening black eyes, a small mouth lined with tiny rows of chitinous teeth, and two sensitive antennae that can detect movement of man-sized creatures up to 300 feet away.

Combat: The ankheg's preferred attack method is to lie 5 to 10 feet below the surface of the ground until its antennae detect the approach of a victim. It then burrows up beneath the victim and attempts to grab him in its mandibles, crushing and grinding for 3d6 points of damage per round while secreting acidic digestive enzymes to cause an additional 1d4 points of damage per round until the victim is dissolved. The ankheg can squirt a stream of acidic enzymes once every six hours to a distance of 30 feet. However, since it is unable to digest food for six hours after it squirts enzymes, it uses this attack technique only when desperate. A victim struck by the stream of acidic enzymes suffers 8d4 points of damage (half damage if the victim rolls a successful saving throw vs. poison).

Habitat/Society: The ankheg uses its mandibles to continuously dig winding tunnels 30-40 feet deep in the rich soil of forests or farmlands. The hollowed end of a tunnel serves as a temporary lair for sleeping, eating, or hibernating. When an ankheg exhausts the food supply in a particular forest or field, it moves on to another.

Autumn is mating season for ankhegs. After the male fertilizes the female, the female kills him and deposits 2d6 fertilized eggs in his body. Within a few weeks, about 75% of the eggs hatch and begin feeding. In a year, the young ankhegs resemble adults and can function independently. Young ankhegs have 2 Hit Dice and an AC 2 overall and an AC 4 for their undersides; they bite for 1d4 points of damage (with an additional 1d4 points of damage from enzyme secretions), and spit for 4d4 points of damage to a distance of 30 feet. In every year thereafter, the ankheg functions with full adult capabilities and gains an additional Hit Die until it reaches 8 Hit Dice.

Beginning in its second year of life, the ankheg sheds its chitinous shell just before the onset of winter. It takes the ankheg two days to shed its old shell and two weeks to grow a new one. During this time, the sluggish ankheg is exceptionally vulnerable. Its overall AC is reduced to 5 and its underside AC is reduced to 7. Additionally, it moves at only half its normal speed, its mandible attack inflicts only 1d10 points of damage, and it is unable to squirt acidic enzymes. While growing a new shell, it protects itself by hiding in a deep tunnel and secreting a repulsive fluid that smells like rotten fruit. Though the aroma discourages most creatures, it can also pinpoint the ankheg's location for human hunters and desperately hungry predators.

Ankhegs living in cold climates hibernate during the winter. Within a month after the first snowfall, the ankheg fashions a lair deep within the warm earth where it remains dormant until spring. The hibernating ankheg requires no food, subsisting instead on nutrients stored in its shell. The ankheg does not secrete aromatic fluid during this time and is thus relatively safe from detection. Though the ankheg's metabolism is reduced, its antennae remain functional, able to alert it to the approach of an intruder. A disturbed ankheg fully awakens in 1d4 rounds, after which time it can attack and move normally.

The ankheg does not hoard treasure. Items that were not dissolved by the acidic enzymes fall where they drop from the ankheg's mandibles and can be found scattered throughout its tunnel system.

Ecology: Though a hungry ankheg can be fatal to a farmer, it can be quite beneficial to the farmland. Its tunnel system laces the soil with passages for air and water, while the ankheg's waste products add rich nutrients. The ankheg will eat decayed organic matter in the earth, but it prefers fresh meat. All but the fiercest predators avoid ankhegs. Dried and cured ankheg shells can be made into armor with an AC of 2, and its digestive enzymes can be used as regular acid.

Arcane

CLIMATE/TERRAIN:	Any
FREQUENCY:	Very rare
ORGANIZATION:	Entourage
ACTIVITY CYCLE:	Any
DIET:	Omnivore
INTELLIGENCE:	Genius (17-18)
TREASURE:	R
ALIGNMENT:	Lawful neutral

NO. APPEARING:	1 (1-6)
ARMOR CLASS:	5 (3)
MOVEMENT:	12
HIT DICE:	10
THAC0:	11
NO. OF ATTACKS:	1
DAMAGE/ATTACKS:	1-8 (weapon)
SPECIAL ATTACKS:	Nil
SPECIAL DEFENSES:	Invisibility, dimension door
MAGIC RESISTANCE:	40%
SIZE:	L (12' tall)
MORALE:	Champion (15)
XP VALUE:	3,000

The arcane are a race of merchants, found wherever there is potential trade in magical items. They appear as tall, lanky, blue giants with elongated faces and thin fingers; each finger having one more joint than is common in most humanoid life. The arcane dress in robes, although there are individuals who are found in heavier armor, a combination of chain links with patches of plate (AC 3).

Combat: For creatures of their size, the arcane are noticeably weak and non-combative. They can defend themselves when called upon, but prefer to talk and/or buy themselves out of dangerous situations. If entering an area that is potentially dangerous (like most human cities), the arcane hires a group of adventurers as his entourage.

The arcane can become *invisible*, and can *dimension door* up to three times a day, usually with the intention of avoiding combat. An arcane feels no concern about abandoning his entourage in chancy situations. They can also use any magical items, regardless of the limitations of those items. This includes swords, wands, magical tomes, and similar items restricted to one type of character class. They will use such items if pressed in combat and they cannot escape, but more often use them as bartering tools with others.

Arcane have a form of racial telepathy, such that an injury to one arcane is immediately known by all other arcane. The arcane do not seek vengeance against the one who hurt or killed their fellow. They react negatively to such individuals, and dealing with the arcane will be next to impossible until that individual makes restitution.

Habitat/Society: Nothing is known about the arcane's origins; they come and go as they please, and are found throughout the known worlds. When they travel, they do so on the ships and vehicles of other races. Finding such ships with arcane aboard is rare, and it is suspected that the arcane have another way of travelling over long distances.

Contacting the arcane is no trouble in most civilized areas: a few words spread through the local grapevine, through taverns, guilds, and barracks, are enough to bring one of these creatures to the surface. In game terms, there is a base 10% chance per day of finding an arcane, if PCs actively look for one; the chance increases or decreases depending on their location. Arcane never set up permanent "magic shops."

The arcane's stock in trade is to provide magical items, particularly *spelljamming helms*, which allow rapid movement through space. The arcanes' high quality and uniform (if high) prices make them the trusted retailers. They accept payment in gold, or barter for other magical items (as a rule of thumb, costs should be five times the XP reward of the item, or a more valuable item).

The arcane take no responsibility for the use of the items they sell. The arcane will deal with almost anyone. They often make deals with both sides in a conflict, fully aware that they might annihilate all of their potential customers in a region. The arcane have no dealings with neogi, nor with creatures from other planes, such as genies, tanar'ri, and fiends. It is unknown whether the arcane create a wide variety of magical devices, or secure them from an unknown source.

Those dealing with the arcane find them cool, efficient, and most importantly, uncaring. Trying to haggle with an arcane is a chancy business, at best. Sometimes they will engage in haggling with a bemused smirk, but just as often leave the buyer hanging and walk out on the negotiations. They do not like being threatened, insulted, or blackmailed. Those who do so will find it very difficult to purchase reliable equipment. An arcane will not raise his hand in vengeance or anger—there are more subtle ways to wreak revenge.

Ecology: It is not known what arcane do with the gold, gems, and magic they collect. One theory says they need the items for reproduction (the basis for a large number of bawdy arcane jokes), while another links it to production and acquisition of more magical items. The arcane seem sexless. No young arcane have been reported, and the arcane keep their own counsel.

CLIMATE/TERRAIN:	Space/Any Earth-based body
FREQUENCY:	Very rare
ORGANIZATION:	Solitary
ACTIVITY CYCLE:	Feed till consume 2xHD, then rest 2 hours/HD
DIET:	Omnivore
INTELLIGENCE:	Low to High (5-14)
TREASURE:	U
ALIGNMENT:	Neutral evil

NO. APPEARING:	1
ARMOR CLASS:	0
MOVEMENT:	9, Fl 3 (B)
HIT DICE:	5-10
THAC0:	5-6 HD: 15
	7-8 HD: 13
	9-10 HD: 11
NO. OF ATTACKS:	3 per victim
DAMAGE/ATTACK:	1-4
SPECIAL ATTACKS:	See below
SPECIAL DEFENSES:	See below
MAGIC RESISTANCE:	25%
SIZE:	L-G (2' per HD)
MORALE:	Champion (16)
XP VALUE:	5-6 HD: 2,000
	(+1,000 for additional HD)

Argos are found in the same regions of wildspace as the baleful beholder nations. An argos resembles a giant amoeba. It has one large, central eye with a tripartite pupil, and a hundred lashless, inhuman eyes and many sharp-toothed mouths. An argos can extrude several pseudopods, each tipped with a fanged maw that functions as a hand to manipulate various tools.

Argos move by slithering; they can cling to walls and ceilings. They can levitate and fly at the very slow rate of 3.

Argos colors tend toward shades of transparent blues and violets; they smell like a bouquet of flowers. They are huge beasts ranging in size from 10 to 20 feet in diameter, weighing about 200 pounds per Hit Die. Though they exhibit signs of being intelligent tool users, they do not wear clothes, choosing rather to carry gear stored in temporary cavities within their bodies. However, their digestive juices often ruin devices within two to three weeks (saving throw vs. acid).

Combat: An argos can attack with one to three weapons or items, or it can enfold a victim in a pseudopod and attack with 1d3 mouths for 1d4 points of damage each. It may attack as many foes in this way as it can physically reach.

If an argos rolls a natural 20 on an attack, it envelopes its victim, swallowing him whole. A swallowed victim suffers 2d8 points of damage each round from the creature's digestive juices. The victim may attempt to cut his way free from within, using only short cutting weapons. He must inflict 8 points of damage to break free.

The eyes of an argos, like those of a beholder, have a variety of special powers. An argos can bring 1d10 of its smaller eyes to bear on any target. The large, central eye can focus only on targets that are in front of the creature (within 90 degrees of the "straight-ahead point" of the central eye). Though the creature has nearly 100 eyes, only 20 special powers have been noted; therefore a number of eyes must possess the same power.

Each point of damage inflicted on an argos eliminates one eye; the DM decides which powers are reduced in the process. It is possible to target one particular eye by attacking with a −4 penalty to the attack roll.

Each ability of an argos's eye is treated as a spell effect. Use the argos's Hit Dice as the caster level. Roll 1d20 and check the following table for a particular eye's power.

1. *Blindness*	11. *Gaze Reflection*
2. *Burning Eyes (Hands)*	12. *Heat Metal*
3. *Charm Monster*	13. *Hold Monster*
4. *Clairvoyance*	14. *Imp. Phantasmal Force*
5. *Confusion*	15. *Irritation*
6. *Darkness, 15' rad.*	16. *Light*
7. *Dispel Magic*	17. *Slow*
8. *Emotion*	18. *Suggestion*
9. *ESP*	19. *Tongues*
10. *Fumble*	20. *Turn Flesh to Stone*

The central eye can use one of three different powers once per round. It can create a personal illusion (an *alter self* spell), or it can cast a *color spray* or a *ray of enfeeblement* spell.

Habitat/Society: Argos are solitary creatures, though it is not unheard of to discover an argos guardian aboard an eye tyrant ship. Argos appear capable of replenishing their own air envelope and thus may be encountered wandering asteroid rings and dust clouds alone.

Despite its relative intelligence, the argos is a ravenous creature driven by its hunger. It tries to lure prey into its grasp, feeding until it has consumed a number of creatures equal to two times its own Hit Dice. It then slips away to digest its meal for a period equal to two hours per Die. If an argos is unable to find food within a week of its last meal, it loses 1 Hit Die per week until it becomes a 5-Hit Die creature. After that point, it can hibernate for up to a year by crystallizing its outer shell and forming a chrysalis.

Ecology: Argos consume anything that moves and is digestible. Their preference is to use their abilities to lure their prey into traps and then to pick off individuals one at a time. It sorts through the tools and weapons of its victims and keeps the useful items.

Aurumvorax

CLIMATE/TERRAIN:	Temperate hills
FREQUENCY:	Very rare
ORGANIZATION:	Solitary
ACTIVITY CYCLE:	Day
DIET:	Carnivore (see below)
INTELLIGENCE:	Animal (1)
TREASURE:	Special
ALIGNMENT:	Neutral

NO. APPEARING:	1
ARMOR CLASS:	0
MOVEMENT:	9, Br 3
HIT DICE:	12
THAC0:	9
NO. OF ATTACKS:	1
DAMAGE/ATTACK:	2-8
SPECIAL ATTACKS:	2-8 claws for 2-8 each
SPECIAL DEFENSES:	See below
MAGIC RESISTANCE:	Nil
SIZE:	S (3' long)
MORALE:	Fearless (19-20)
XP VALUE:	9,000

Despite being only the size of a large badger, the aurumvorax, or "golden gorger," is an incredibly dangerous creature. The animal is covered with coarse golden hair and has small silver eyes with golden pupils. It has eight powerful legs that end in 3-inch-long copper claws. The aurumvorax's shoulders are massively muscled while its heavy jaw is full of coppery teeth.

The creature weighs over 500 pounds. This incredible density provides the animal with much of its natural protection. This, combined with its speed, power, and sheer viciousness, makes it one of the most dangerous species yet known.

Combat: The aurumvorax charges any creature that enters its territory, causing a −3 to opponents' surprise rolls if attacking from its den. A female of the species receives a +2 bonus to attack rolls when guarding her young.

The creature bites at its prey until it hits, clamping its massive jaws onto the victim and doing 2-8 hit points of damage. After it hits, the aurumvorax locks its jaws and hangs on, doing an additional 8 points of damage per round until either the aurumvorax or its enemy is dead. Only death will cause the aurumvorax to relax its grip.

Once its jaws lock, the golden gorger also rakes its victim with 2-8 of its legs, causing 2-8 hit points of damage per additional hit. An opponent who is held by an aurumvorax receives no dexterity adjustment to Armor Class.

Due to its incredibly dense hide and bones, the aurumvorax takes only half damage from blunt weapons. It is immune to the effects of small, normal fires and takes only half damage from magical fires. Neither poison nor gasses have any effect on the sturdy creature.

Habitat/Society: The aurumvorax makes its solitary home in light forests, hills, and at the timberline on mountainsides. An aurumvorax chooses a likely spot and then uses its powerfully clawed legs to create a burrow, sometimes into solid rock.

Due to their unusual dietary needs, aurumvorae make their lairs in spots that either contain rich veins of gold ore or are very near to an area where gold is readily available.

The aurumvorax is a solitary creature which jealously guards its territory, even from others of its kind. The only time adult aurumvorae willingly meet is during mating season, which occurs approximately every eight years.

The pair will stay together for a week or two before the male returns to his territory and the female prepares for the birth of her kits. A litter of 1d6 + 2 kits is born four months after mating.

For the first two weeks of life, the kits are blind and hairless. They must be fed both meat and precious ores, including gold, in order to survive. It is unusual for more than 1-2 of the strongest kits to survive. If a kit is found and "adopted" before its eyes are open, it can be tamed and trained.

Dwarves tend to dislike aurumvorae, though some communities have been known to raise one or more of the beasts for use in sniffing out veins of ore.

Ecology: In order to survive, the aurumvorax supplements its carnivorous diet with quantities of gold. The ability to digest and utilize gold and other ores makes it possible for the creature to develop the dense fur, hide, and bones that protect it so well.

If an aurumvorax is killed with a minimum of cutting damage to its hide, the hide may be turned into a garment of incredible strength and beauty worth 15,000-20,000 gold pieces. The garment will also protect its wearer as armor, the specific Armor Class depending on the size of the aurumvorax. A garment with AC 2 weighs 50 pounds, one with AC 3 weighs 40 pounds, and one with AC 4 weighs 30 pounds.

The wearer also receives a +4 bonus on saving throws vs. normal fires and a +2 bonus on saving throws vs. magical fire.

If an aurumvorax is burned in a forge, approximately 150-200 pounds of gold are left behind. This burning process is very difficult and usually takes between one and two weeks to perform. Of course, the hide may be removed before the creature is burned; if burned at the same time, the hide will provide an additional 21-40 (1d20 + 20) pounds of gold.

The aurumvorax's teeth and claws are also prized for decoration, and can bring up to 1 gp each on the open market.

	Pit Fiend	Black Abishai	Green Abishai	Red Abishai
CLIMATE/TERRAIN:	The Nine Hells	The Nine Hells	The Nine Hells	The Nine Hells
FREQUENCY:	Very rare	Common	Common	Common
ORGANIZATION:	Solitary	Solitary	Solitary	Solitary
ACTIVITY CYCLE:	Any	Any	Any	Any
DIET:	Carnivore	Carnivore	Carnivore	Carnivore
INTELLIGENCE:	Genius (17-18)	Average (8-10)	Average (8-10)	Average (8-10)
TREASURE:	G, W	Nil	Nil	Nil
ALIGNMENT:	Lawful evil	Lawful evil	Lawful evil	Lawful evil
NO. APPEARING:	1-4	2-20	2-8	1
ARMOR CLASS:	−5	5	3	1
MOVEMENT:	15, Fl 24 (C)	9, Fl 12 (C)	9, Fl 12 (C)	9, Fl 12 (C)
HIT DICE:	13	4+1	5+2	6+3
THAC0:	7	17	15	13
NO. OF ATTACKS:	6	3	3	3
DAMAGE/ATTACK:	1-4×2/1-6×2/ 2-12/2-8 or weapon	1-4/1-4/2-5	1-4/1-4/2-5	1-4/1-4/2-5
SPECIAL ATTACKS:	Fear, poison, tail constriction	Poison, dive	Poison, dive	Poison, dive
SPECIAL DEFENSES:	Regeneration, +3 or better weapons to hit	Regeneration, +1 or better weapons to hit	Regeneration, +1 or better weapons to hit	Regeneration, +1 or better weapons to hit
MAGIC RESISTANCE:	50%	30%	30%	30%
SIZE:	L (12' tall)	L (8' tall)	L (7' tall)	M (6' tall)
MORALE:	Fearless (19-20)	Average (8-10)	Average (8-10)	Steady (11-12)
XP VALUE:	57,500	21,500	23,500	25,500

General: The baatezu are the primary inhabitants of the Nine Hells. They are a strong, evil tempered race held together by an equally strong organization. The baatezu live in a rigid caste system where authority is derived from power and station.

The baatezu wish to fulfill their ancient quest to destroy the tanar'ri, their blood enemies. The baatezu also know that by infiltrating humans and entering their world they will gain power over the tanar'ri. Toward this end they constantly strive to dominate the Prime Material plane and its natives.

The baatezu are divided into three groups: greater, lesser, and least. Below are listed a few:

Greater baatezu	Lesser baatezu	least baatezu
amnizu	abishai	nupperibo
cornugon	barbazu	spinagon
gelugon	erinyes	
pit fiend	hamatula	
	osyluth	

In addition, there are the lemures, the common "foot soldiers" of the baatezu at the very bottom in station.

Combat: All baatezu except for lemures, nupperibo, and spinagon are able to perform the following magical abilities, once per round, at will: *advanced illusion, animate dead, charm person, infravision, know alignment* (always active), *suggestion,* and *teleport without error.*

Baatezu are affected by the following attack forms:

Attack	Damage	Attack	Damage
acid	full	cold	half*
electricity (lightning)	full	fire (dragon, magical)	none*
gas (poisonous, etc.)	half	iron weapon	none**
magic missile	full	poison	none
silver weapon	full***		

*the gelugon suffers half damage from fire and none from cold.
**unless affected by normal weapons.
***greater baatezu suffer half damage from silver weapons.

Pit Fiend: The most terrible baatezu of the Nine Hells, pit fiends appear to be giant, winged humanoids, very much like gargoyles in appearance, with huge wings that wrap around their bodies for defense. Pit fiend's fangs are large and drip with a vile, green liquid. Their bodies are red and scaly, often emitting flames when they are angered or excited. In the rare situations they choose to communicate, they use telepathy.

Combat: In physical combat, the pit fiend is capable of dealing out tremendous punishment, using its incredible 18/00 Strength (+6 damage adjustment). They can attack six times in a single round, dividing attacks against six different opponents. They can attack with two hard, scaly wing buffets for 1-4 points of damage per hit. Their powerful claws do 1-6 points of damage per successful attack. The bite of a pit fiend is dreadful indeed, causing any creature bitten to take 2-12 points of damage and receive a lethal dose of poison. A saving throw vs. poison is required or the victim dies in 1-4 rounds. The bite also infects the victim with a disease.

Pit fiends can also attack with their tail every round, inflicting 2-8 points of damage per hit. The tail can then hold and constrict the victim for 2-8 points of damage per round until the victim makes a successful Strength check to break free. Pit fiends can also carry jagged-toothed clubs which inflict 7-12 points of damage per hit (this replaces one claw attack).

Once per round a pit fiend can use one of the following spell-like powers, plus those available to all baatezu: *detect magic, detect invisibility, fireball, hold person, improved invisibility, polymorph self, produce flame, pyrotechnics,* and *wall of fire.*

They can, once per year, cast a *wish* spell. They may always *gate* in two lesser or one greater baatezu with a 100% chance of success, performing this action once per round. Once per day, a pit fiend can use a *symbol* of pain—the victim must save vs. rod, staff or wand or suffer a −4 penalty on attack dice, and a -2 penalty to Dexterity for 2-20 rounds.

Pit fiends regenerate 2 hit points per round and radiate a *fear* aura in a 20-foot radius (save vs. rod, staff, or wand at a -3 penalty or flee in panic for 1-10 rounds).

Baatezu

Habitat/Society: Pit fiends are the lords of the Nine Hells. They are the baatezu of the greatest power and the highest station. Pit fiends are found throughout the various layers of the Nine Hells, but are very rare on the upper layers.

Wherever they are found, these mighty lords hold a position of great authority and power. They sometimes command vast legions consisting of dozens of complete armies, leading them into battle against the tanar'ri. These huge forces are terrifying to behold, and any non-native of the lower planes, of less than 10 Hit Dice, who sees them, flees in panic for 1-3 days. Those of 10 Hit Dice or more must make a saving throw vs. rod, staff, or wand or flee in panic for 1-12 turns.

Ecology: Pit fiends are spawned from the powerful gelugons of the Nine Hells' eighth layer. When those icy fiends are found worthy they are cast into the Pit of Flame for 1,001 days after which they emerge as pit fiends.

Abishai: Abishai are common on the first and second layers of the Nine Hells, appearing much like gothic gargoyles. They are thin and reptilian with long, prehensile tails and great wings. There are three varieties of abishai. They are, in ascending order of station, black, green, and red. Abishai communicate with telepathy.

Combat: In battle, the abishai strikes with formidable claws, inflicting 1-4 points of damage per successful hit. It can also lash out with its flexible tail for 2-5 points of damage. Hidden in the end of an abishai's tail is a small stinger that injects poison on a successful hit, requiring a saving throw vs. poison (failure results in death).

Abishai can fly into the air and dive at enemies, striking with both claws. Their attack roll is made with a +2 bonus. A successful hit inflicts double damage.

In addition to the powers possessed by all baatezu, an abishai can perform the following magical powers, one at a time, once per round: *change self, command, produce flame, pyrotechnics,* and *scare.* They can also attempt to *gate* 2-12 lemures (60% chance of success, once per day) or 1-3 abishai (30% chance of success, once per day).

All abishai are susceptible to damage from holy water. If a vial is splashed on it, an abishai suffers 2-8 points of damage. All abishai regenerate 1 hit point per melee round unless the damage was done by holy water or a holy magical weapon.

Habitat/Society: Abishai are voracious and evil. They delight in tormenting those few natives of the Nine Hells that are lower in power. Abishai are fond of using *change self* and *charm person* to tempt mortals bold enough to travel to the Nine Hells.

Ecology: The abishai comprise the main body of many large, evil armies battling against the tanar'ri and intruders against the Nine Hells. In some cases, a red abishai may have proven himself worthy enough to command a force of lemures. If it is successful in this endeavor, the red abishai may be promoted to a higher form of baatezu.

Banshee

CLIMATE/TERRAIN:	Any
FREQUENCY:	Very rare
ORGANIZATION:	Solitary
ACTIVITY CYCLE:	Night
DIET:	Nil
INTELLIGENCE:	Exceptional (15-16)
TREASURE:	(D)
ALIGNMENT:	Chaotic evil

NO. APPEARING:	1
ARMOR CLASS:	0
MOVEMENT:	15
HIT DICE:	7
THAC0:	13
NO. OF ATTACKS:	1
DAMAGE/ATTACK:	1-8
SPECIAL ATTACKS:	Death wail
SPECIAL DEFENSES:	+1 or better weapon to hit
MAGIC RESISTANCE:	50%
SIZE:	M (5'-6' tall)
MORALE:	Elite (13)
XP VALUE:	4,000

The banshee or groaning spirit, is the spirit of an evil female elf—a very rare thing indeed. Banshee hate the living, finding their presence painful, and seek to harm whomever they meet.

Banshees appear as floating, luminous phantasms of their former selves. Their image glows brightly at night, but is transparent in sunlight (60% invisible). Most banshees are old and withered, but a few (10%) who died young retain their former beauty. The hair of a groaning spirit is wild and unkempt. Her dress is usually tattered rags. Her face is a mask of pain and anguish, but hatred and ire burns brightly in her eyes. Banshees frequently cry out in pain—hence their name.

Combat: Banshees are formidable opponents. The mere sight of one causes *fear*, unless a successful saving throw vs. spell is rolled. Those who fail must flee in terror for 10 rounds and are 50% likely to drop any items they were carrying in their hands.

A banshee's most dreaded weapon is its wail or keen. Any creature within 30 feet of a groaning spirit when she keens must roll a saving throw vs. death magic. Those who fail die immediately, their face contorted in horror. Fortunately, groaning spirits can keen just once per day, and then only at night. The touch of a groaning spirit causes 1d8 points of damage.

Banshees are noncorporeal and invulnerable to weapons of less than +1 enchantment. In addition, groaning spirits are highly resistant to magic (50%). They are fully immune to *charm*, *sleep*, and *hold* spells and to cold- and electricity-based attacks. Holy water causes 2d4 points of damage if broken upon them. An *dispel evil* spell will kill a groaning spirit. A banshee is turned as a "special" undead.

Banshees can sense the presence of living creatures up to five miles away. Any creature that remains within five miles of a groaning spirit lair is sure to be attacked when night falls. The nature of this attack varies with the victim. Beasts and less threatening characters are killed via a touch. Adventurers or demihumans are attacked by keening. Creatures powerful enough to withstand the groaning spirit's keen are left alone.

When attacking adventurers, the groaning spirit attacks at night with her wail. If any characters save successfully, she then retreats to her lair. Thereafter, each night, the groaning spirit returns to wail again. This routine is repeated until all of the vic-

tims are dead or have left the groaning spirit's domain, or until the groaning spirit is slain.

Habitat/Society: Banshees loathe all living things and thus make their homes in desolate countryside or ancient ruins. There they hide by day, when they cannot keen, and wander the surrounding countryside by night. The land encircling a groaning spirit's lair is strewn with the bones of beasts who heard the groaning spirit's cry. Once a groaning spirit establishes her lair she will remain there.

The treasure of groaning spirits varies considerably and often reflects what they loved in life. Many hoard gold and fine gems. Other groaning spirits, particularly those that haunt their former homes, show finer tastes, preserving great works of art and sculptures, or powerful magical items.

It is nearly impossible to distinguish the cry of a groaning spirit from that of a human or elf woman in pain. Many a knight gallant has mistaken the two sounds, and then paid for the mistake with his life. Banshees are exceptionally intelligent and speak numerous languages, including common, elvish, and other demihuman languages.

Banshees occasionally use their destructive powers to seek revenge against their former adversaries in life.

Ecology: Banshees are a blight upon wherever they settle. They kill without discretion, and their only pleasure is the misfortune and misery of others. In addition to slaying both man and beast, a groaning spirit's keen has a powerful effect upon vegetation. Flowers and delicate plants wither and die and trees grow twisted and sickly, while hardier plants, thistles and the like, flourish. After a few years all that remains within five miles of a groaning spirit's lair is a desolate wilderness of warped trees and thorns mixed with the bones of those creatures that dared to cross into the groaning spirit's domain.

Basilisk

	Lesser	Greater	Dracolisk
CLIMATE/TERRAIN:	Any land	Any land	Any land
FREQUENCY:	Uncommon	Very rare	Very rare
ORGANIZATION:	Solitary	Solitary	Solitary
ACTIVITY CYCLE:	Day	Day	Day
DIET:	Carnivore	Carnivore	Carnivore
INTELLIGENCE:	Animal (1)	Low (5-7)	Low to Average (5-10)
TREASURE:	F	H	C, I
ALIGNMENT:	Nil	Neutral	Chaotic evil
NO. APPEARING:	1-4	1-7	1-2
ARMOR CLASS:	4	2	3
MOVEMENT:	6	6	9, Fl 15 (E)
HIT DICE:	6+1	10	7+3
THAC0:	15	11	13
NO. OF ATTACKS:	1	3	3
DAMAGE/ATTACK:	1-10	1-6/1-6/2-16	1-6/1-6/3-12
SPECIAL ATTACKS:	Gaze turns to stone	See below	See below
SPECIAL DEFENSES:	Nil	Surprised only on a 1	Nil
MAGIC RESISTANCE:	Nil	Nil	Nil
SIZE:	M (7' long)	L (12' long)	H (15-20' long)
MORALE:	Steady (12)	Champion (16)	Champion (15)
XP VALUE:	1,400	7,000	3,000

These reptilian monsters all posses a *gaze* that enables them to turn any fleshy creature to stone; their gaze extends into the Astral and Ethereal planes.

Basilisk

Although it has eight legs, its sluggish metabolism allows only a slow movement rate. A basilisk is usually dull brown in color, with a yellowish underbelly. Its eyes glow pale green.

Combat: While it has strong, toothy jaws, the basilisk's major weapon is its *gaze*. However, if its gaze is reflected, and it sees its own eyes, it will become petrified itself, but this requires light at least equal to bright torchlight and a good, smooth reflector. In the Astral plane its gaze kills; in the Ethereal plane it turns victims into ethereal stone. These will only be seen by those in the Ethereal plane or who can see ethereal objects.

Greater Basilisk

The greater basilisk is a larger cousin of the more common reptilian horror, the ordinary basilisk. These monsters are typically used to guard treasure.

Combat: The monster attacks by raising its upper body, striking with sharp claws, and biting with its toothy maw. The claws carry Type K poison (saving throws vs. poison are made with a +4 bonus). Its foul breath is also poisonous, and all creatures, coming within 5 feet of its mouth, even if just for a moment, must roll successful saving throws vs. poison (with a +2 bonus) or die (check each round of exposure).

Even if a polished reflector is used under good lighting conditions, the chance for a greater basilisk to see its own gaze and become petrified is only 10%, unless the reflector is within 10 feet of the creature. (While its gaze weapon is effective to 50 feet, the creature's oddly-shaped eyes are nearsighted and it cannot see its own gaze unless it is within 10 feet.)

Dracolisk

The sages say that the dracolisk is the offspring of a rogue black dragon and a basilisk of the largest size.

The result is a deep brown, dragon-like monster that moves with relative quickness on six legs. It can fly, but only for short periods—a turn or two at most.

Combat: This horror can attack with its taloned forelegs and deliver vicious bites. In addition, it can spit a stream of acid 5 feet wide and up to 30 feet away. The acid causes 4d6 points of damage, half-damage if a successful saving throw vs. breath weapon is rolled. The dracolisk can spit up to three times per day.

The eyes of a dracolisk can petrify any opponent within 20 feet if the monster's gaze is met. Because its hooded eyes have nictating membranes, the monster is only 10% likely to be affected by its own gaze. Opponents in melee with a dracolisk and seeking to avoid its gaze fight with a −4 penalty to their to attack rolls.

	Common	Large	Huge	Azmyth	Night Hunter	Sinister
CLIMATE/TERRAIN:	Any land	Any land	Warm caves	Any land	Any land	Any land
FREQUENCY:	Common	Uncommon	Rare	Rare	Uncommon	Rare
ORGANIZATION:	Swarm	Flock	Flock	Solitary	Pack	Band
ACTIVITY CYCLE:	Night	Night	Night	Any	Night/any	Any
DIET:	Omnivore	Omnivore	Omnivore	Omnivore	Carnivore	Omnivore
INTELLIGENCE:	Animal (1)	Animal (1)	Low (5-7)	High (13-14)	Average to High (8-14)	Average to Except. (8-16)
TREASURE:	Nil	Nil	C	Nil	M, O, Z (in lair)	Nil
ALIGNMENT:	Neutral	Neutral	Neutral evil	Chaotic neutral	Neutral evil	Lawful evil
NO. APPEARING:	1-100	3-18	1-8	1	1-12 (1-30 in lair)	1d6
ARMOR CLASS:	8 (see below)	8	7 (see below)	2	6	3
MOVEMENT:	1, Fl 24 (B)	3, Fl 18 (C)	3, Fl 15 (C)	3, Fl 24 (A)	2, Fl 18 (A)	2, Fl 21 (A)
HIT DICE:	1-2 hp	1d4 hp or 1	4-6	2	2+2	4+4
THAC0:	20	19 or 20	17 (4 HD) 15 (5-6 HD)	19	19	17
NO. OF ATTACKS:	1	1	1	2	4	1
DAMAGE/ATTACK:	1	1d2 or 1d4	2d4	1/1-2	1-4/1-2/1-2/1-6 or 3-12	2-5
SPECIAL ATTACKS:	See below	Nil	See below	Magic use	Nil	Magic use
SPECIAL DEFENSES:	Nil	See below	See below	magic use	Nil	Energy field
MAGIC RESISTANCE:	Nil	Nil	Nil	40%	Nil	70%
SIZE:	T (1')	M (5'-6')	H (12'-16')	S (3')	M (7')	L (9')
MORALE:	Unreliable (2-4)	Unsteady (5-7)	Steady (11-12)	Elite (14)	Steady (11)	Champion (15-16)
XP VALUE:	15	35	420 (4 HD) 650 (5 HD) 975 (6 HD)	650	175	2,000

Bats are common animals in many parts of the world. While ordinary bats are annoying but harmless, larger varieties can be quite deadly. With almost 2,000 different species of bats known, one can find wingspans from less than two inches across to 15 feet or more. The small body of the ordinary bat resembles a mouse, while the wings are formed from extra skin stretched across its fore limbs. The larger bats are scaled up but otherwise similar in appearance.

Despite the common belief that bats are blind, nearly all known species have rather good eyesight. In the dark, however, they do not rely on their visual acuity, but navigate instead by echo-location. By emitting a high-pitched squeal and listening for it to bounce back to them, they can "see" their surroundings by this natural form of sonar.

Combat: Ordinary bats attack only if cornered and left with no other option. If startled, bats tend to become frightened and confused. This causes them to swarm around and often fly into things. The typical bat swarm ends up putting out torches (1% chance per bat encountered per round), confusing spell casting (Wisdom roll required to cast spells), inhibiting combatants' ability to wield weapons (by a −2 THAC0 penalty), and otherwise getting in the way. Under ideal flying conditions, a bat's Armor Class rating rises from 8 to 4.

Habitat/Society: While bats are found almost anywhere, they prefer warm and humid climes. Some species hibernate during the cold season and a few are know to migrate. Bats live in caves, dark buildings, or damp crevices, hanging by their toes during the day, and leaving at dusk to feed during the night. In large, isolated caverns there may be thousands of bats.

Ecology: Most bats eat fruit or insects, though some include small animals or fish in their diets. The rare vampire bat travels at night to drink the warm blood of living mammals, but its victims are rarely humans or demihumans. Care must be taken not to confuse the vampire bat with the true vampire in this regard.

Rot grubs and carrion crawlers are among the few creatures known to live in the guano on the floor of large bat-infested caverns, making any expeditions into such caves dangerous indeed. If the noxious odor from the guano is not enough to subdue the hardiest of adventurers (a single Constitution check to stay conscious), these crawling denizens are.

Large Bat
These creatures are large versions of the carnivorous variety of the ordinary bat with 3-foot-long bodies and 5- to 6-foot-long wingspans. They dwell in dark caverns, usually underground, and depend on their sonar in flight to compensate for their poor eyesight. Only 10% of giant bats are of the more powerful 1 Hit Die variety.

Extremely maneuverable in flight, large bats gain an Armor Class bonus of +3 when an opponent with a Dexterity of 13 or less fires a missile weapon at it. The creature must land (usually on its victim) to attack with its bite. The typical example of this species inflicts 1d2 points of damage with its teeth while the larger does 1d4 points of damage. Anyone bitten by a large bat has a 1% chance per point of damage done to contract rabies.

When rabies is contracted, there is a 1d4+6 day incubation period. Once this period has ended, the victim has 10 days to live. The victim cannot drink or eat anything and is overly irritable. Anything from loud noises to being awakened at night can set the victim off (the DM determines the temper triggers). If temper flares, the victim must roll a Wisdom check. If the check fails, the rabid person attacks until he is killed or knocked unconscious. When a character contracts rabies, he or she dies from the infliction, unless cured by a *wish*, *alter reality*, *limited wish*, *cure disease*, or similar spell.

Huge Bat (Mobat)
Mobats prefer warm-blooded prey that they bite to death with their fangs. They have a dim and evil intelligence that gives them a desire for shiny objects. Because the typical mobat has a wingspan of 12 to 16 feet, they must have large areas to serve as flight runways.

Bat

Because Mobats' flight is so rapid and silent, their victims suffer a −3 penalty to their surprise rolls. They can also give a piercing screech that causes such great pain that victims seek to cover their ears rather than fight, unless a saving throw versus paralyzation is successful. This screech is always used if the prey resists and it is effective in a 20-foot radius about the mobat. Note that mobile mobats have an Armor Class of 2. Under crowded flying conditions, their Armor Class suffers and raises to 7. When not in flight, mobats have an Armor Class of 10.

Azmyth

Azmyths live on flowers, small plants, and insects. They are solitary wanderers, though they do have "favorite haunts" to which they return. They often form partnerships with humanoids for mutual benefit, sometimes forming loyal friendships in the process. Azmyths have been known to accompany creatures for their entire lives, and then accompany the creatures' offspring. The life span of azmyths are presently unknown but is believed to be over 100 years. They are not familiars as wizards understand the term; no direct control can be exercised over one, except by spells.

Azmyths have crested heads and bearded chins, white, pupilless eyes, and leathery gray, mauve, or emerald green skin. They emit shrill squeaks of alarm or rage, and endearing, liquid chuckles of delight or amusement. They communicate by *telepathy* that has a range of 60 feet, and have infravision to 90 feet. They can *know alignment* three times per day, become *invisible* (self only for six rounds or less, ending when the azmyth makes a successful attack) once per day, and create *silence 15' radius*, centered on themselves, once per day.

In combat, the azmyth bites for 1 point of damage and stabs with its powerful needle-sharp tails for 1d2 points. Twice per day, an azmyth can unleash a *shocking grasp* attack, transmitting 1d8+6 points of electrical damage through any direct physical contact with another creature. This attack can be combined with a physical attack for cumulative damage.

Night Hunter

This species, know as dragazhar, is named after the adventurer who first domesticated one, long ago. Nocturnal on the surface, it is active anytime in the gloom of the underworld. It eats carrion if it must, but usually hunts small beasts. Desperate dragazhar are known to attack livestock, drow, or humans.

Night hunters swoop down to bite prey (1d4), rake with their wing claws (1d2 each), and slash (1d6) or stab (3d4) with their dexterous, triangular-shaped, razor sharp tails. They stalk their prey, flying low and dodging behind hillocks, ridges, trees, or stalactites, to attack from ambush. They have infravision to a distance of 120 feet, but rarely surprise opponents, since they emit echoing, loon-like screams when excited.

Night hunter lairs usually contain over 30 creatures. They typically live in double-ended caves, or above ground in tall, dense woods. Night hunters do not tarry to eat where they feel endangered, so their lairs often contain treasure fallen from prey carried there. Night hunters roost head-down when sleeping. They are velvet in hue, even to their claws, and have violet, orange, or red eyes.

Sinister

These mysterious jet-black creatures most closely resemble manta rays. They have no distinct heads and necks, and their powerfully-muscled wings do not show the prominent finger

bones common to most bats. A natural ability of *levitation* allows them to hang motionless in midair. This unnerving appearance and behavior has earned them their dark name, but sinisters are not evil. Above ground, they prefer to hunt at night, when their 160'-range infravision is most effective. They eat carrion if no other food is available, and regularly devour flowers and seed pods of all sorts.

Sinisters are both resistant to magic and adept in its use. In addition to their pinpoint, precision *levitation*, they are surrounded at all times by a naturally-generated 5-foot-deep energy field akin to a *wall of force*. This field affords no protection against spells or melee attacks, but missile attacks are stopped utterly; normal missiles are turned away, and such effects as *magic missile* and *Melf's acid arrow* are absorbed harmlessly. In addition, all sinisters can cast one *hold monster* (as the spell) once per day. They usually save this for escaping from creatures more powerful than themselves, but may use it when hunting, if ravenous.

Curiously, though they are always silent (communicating only with others of its kind via 20-foot-range limited *telepathy*), sinisters love music-both vocal and instrumental. Many a bard making music at a wilderness campfire has found him or herself surrounded by a silent circle of floating sinisters. Unless they are directly attacked, the sinisters will not molest the bard in any way, but may follow the source of the music, gathering night after night to form a rather daunting audience.

Sinisters are usually encountered in small groups and are thought to have a long life span. Their social habits and mating rituals are unknown.

	Black	Brown	Cave	Polar
CLIMATE/TERRAIN:	Temperate land	Temperate land	Any land	Any cold
FREQUENCY:	Common	Uncommon	Uncommon	Rare
ORGANIZATION:	Family	Family	Family	Family
ACTIVITY CYCLE:	Day	Day	Day	Day
DIET:	Omnivore	Omnivore	Omnivore	Omnivore
INTELLIGENCE:	Semi- (2-4)	Semi- (2-4)	Semi- (2- 4)	Semi- (2-4)
TREASURE:	Nil	Nil	Nil	Nil
ALIGNMENT:	Neutral	Neutral	Neutral	Neutral
NO. APPEARING:	1-3	1-6	1-2	1-6
ARMOR CLASS:	7	6	6	6
MOVEMENT:	12	12	6+6	12, Sw 9
HIT DICE:	3+3	5+5	6+6	8+8
THAC0:	17	15	13	11
NO. OF ATTACKS:	3	3	3	3
DAMAGE/ATTACK:	1-3/1-3/1-6	1-6/1-6/1-8	1- 8/1-8/1-12	1-10/1-10/2-12
SPECIAL ATTACKS:	Hug	Hug	Hug	Hug
SPECIAL DEFENSES:	Nil	Nil	Nil	Nil
MAGIC RESISTANCE:	Nil	Nil	Nil	Nil
SIZE:	M (6' + tall)	L (9' + tall)	H (12' + tall)	H (14' + tall)
MORALE:	Average (8-10)	Average (8-10)	Average (8-10)	Average (8-10)
XP VALUE:	175	420	650	1,400

A rather common omnivorous mammal, bears tend to avoid humans unless provoked. Exceptions to this rule can be a most unfortunate occurrence.

Bears are, in general, large and powerful animals which are found throughout the world's temperate and cooler climates. With dense fur protecting them from the elements and powerful claws protecting them from other animals, bears are the true rulers of the animal kingdom in the areas where they live.

The so-called black bear actually ranges in color from black to light brown. It is smaller than the brown bear and the most widespread species by far.

Combat: Although black bears are usually not aggressive, they are able fighters when pressed. If a black bear scores a paw hit with an 18 or better it also hugs for 2-8 (2d4) points of additional damage.

Habitat/Society: All bears have excellent senses of hearing and smell but rather poor eyesight. The size shown is an average for the variety and larger individuals will, of course, be correspondingly more powerful.

One common misconception people hold about bears is that they hibernate during the winter. In fact, they sleep most of the time, but their metabolism does not slow down, and they often wake up and leave their lairs during warm spells.

Bears live in small family groups. Female bears are very protective of their young, and more than one individual has been badly injured when taunting or playing with seemingly harmless bear cubs.

Ecology: All of these ursoids are omnivorous, although the gigantic cave bear tends towards a diet of meat.

Bears are fairly intelligent animals that can be trained to perform in a variety of ways, particularly if captured as cubs. Bears can thus be found dancing in circuses or accompanying "mountain men" in the wilderness.

Brown Bear
The brown bear, of which the infamous grizzly is the most well known variety, is a bear of very aggressive disposition. Brown bears are more carnivorous than their smaller cousins, the black bears. The grizzly in particular will often bring down large game such as deer and elk.

Brown bears are aggressive hunters. If a brown bear scores a paw hit with a roll of 18 or better it will also hug for 2-12 (2d6) points of additional damage. Brown bears will continue to fight for 1-4 melee rounds after reaching 0 to -8 hit points. At -9 or fewer hit points, they are killed immediately.

Cave Bear
Cave bears are quite aggressive, willing to attack well-armed parties without provocation. If a cave bear scores a paw hit with an 18 or better

it also hugs for 2-16 (2d8) points of additional damage. Cave bears will continue to fight for 1-4 melee rounds after reaching 0 to -8 hit points. At -9 or fewer hit points, they are killed immediately.

Polar Bear
These powerful swimmers feed mostly on marine animals. A paw hit of 18 or better indicates a "hug", which inflicts 3-18 (3d6) points of additional damage. These aggressive animals will fight for 2-5 rounds after being brought to 0 to -12 hit points, but beyond that they will die instantly.

Beetle, Giant

	Bombardier	Boring	Fire	Rhinoceros	Stag	Water
CLIMATE/TERRAIN:	Any forest	Any land	Any land	Any jungle	Any forest	Fresh water
FREQUENCY:	Common	Common	Common	Uncommon	Common	Common
ORGANIZATION:	Solitary	Solitary	Solitary	Solitary	Solitary	Solitary
ACTIVITY CYCLE:	Day	Night	Night	Any	Any	Any
DIET:	Carnivore	Omnivore	Omnivore	Herbivore	Herbivore	Omnivore
INTELLIGENCE:	Non- (0)	Animal (1)	Non- (0)	Non- (0)	Non- (0)	Non- (0)
TREASURE:	Nil	C, R, S, T	Nil	Nil	Nil	Nil
ALIGNMENT:	Neutral	Neutral	Neutral	Neutral	Neutral	Neutral
NO. APPEARING:	3-12	3-18	3-12	1-6	2-12	1-12
ARMOR CLASS:	4	3	4	2	3	3
MOVEMENT:	9	6	12	6	6	3, Sw 9
HIT DICE:	2+2	5	1+2	12	7	4
THAC0:	19	15	19	9	13	17
NO. OF ATTACKS:	1	1	1	2	3	1
DAMAGE/ATTACK:	2-12	5-20	2-8	3-18/2-16	4-16/1-10/ 1-10	3-18
SPECIAL ATTACKS:	Acid cloud	Nil	Nil	Nil	Nil	Nil
SPECIAL DEFENSES:	Fire cloud	Nil	Nil	Nil	Nil	Nil
MAGIC RESISTANCE:	Nil	Nil	Nil	Nil	Nil	Nil
SIZE:	S (4' long)	L (9' long)	S (2 1/2' long)	L (12' long)	L (10' long)	M (6' long)
MORALE:	Elite (13)	Elite (14)	Steady (12)	Elite (14)	Elite (13)	Elite (14)
XP VALUE:	120	175	35	4,000	975	120

Giant beetles are similar to their more ordinary counterparts, but thousands of times larger—with chewing mandibles and hard wings that provide substantial armor protection.

Beetles have two pairs of wings and three pairs of legs. Fortunately, the wings of a giant beetle cannot be used to fly, and in most cases, its six bristly legs do not enable it to move as fast as a fleeing man. The hard, chitinous shell of several varieties of these beetles are brightly colored, and sometimes have value to art collectors. While their shells protect beetles as well as plate mail armor, it is difficult to craft armor from them, and a skilled alchemist would need to be brought in on the job.

All beetles are basically unintelligent and always hungry. They will feed on virtually any form of organic material, including other sorts of beetles. They taste matter with their antennae, or feelers; if a substance tasted is organic, the beetle grasps it with its mandibles, crushes it, and eats it. Because of the thorough grinding of the mandibles, nothing eaten by giant beetles can be revived by anything short of a *wish*. Beetles do not hear or see well, and rely primarily on taste and feel.

Except as noted below, giant beetles are not really social animals; those that are found near each other are competitors for the same biological niche, not part of any family unit.

Bombardier Beetle
The bombardier beetle is usually found above ground in wooded areas. It primarily feeds on offal and carrion, gathering huge heaps of the stuff in which to lay its eggs.

Combat: If it is attacked or disturbed, there is a 50% chance each round that it will turn its rear toward its attacker and fire off an 8-foot, spherical cloud of reeking, reddish, acidic vapor from its abdomen. This cloud causes 3d4 points of damage per round to any creature within range. Furthermore, the sound caused by the release of the vapor has a 20% chance of stunning any creature with a sense of hearing within a 15-foot radius, and a like chance for deafening any creature that was not stunned. Stunning lasts for 2d4 rounds, plus an additional 2d4 rounds of deafness afterwards. Deafening lasts 2d6 rounds. The giant bombardier can fire its vapor cloud every third round, but no more than twice in eight hours.

Ecology: The bombardier action of this beetle is caused by the explosive mixture of two substances that are produced internally and combined in a third organ. If a bombardier is killed before it has the opportunity to fire off both blasts, it is possible to cut the creature open and retrieve the chemicals. These chemicals can then be combined to produce a small explosive, or fire a projectile, with the proper equipment.

The chemicals are also of value to alchemists, who can use them in various preparations. They are worth 50 gp per dose.

Boring Beetle
Boring beetles feed on rotting wood and similar organic material, so they are usually found individually inside huge trees or massed in underground tunnel complexes.

Combat: The large mandibles of the boring beetle have a powerful bite and will inflict up to 20 points on damage to the victim.

Habitat/Society: Individually, these creatures are not much more intelligent than other giant beetles, but it is rumored that nests of them can develop a communal intelligence with a level of consciousness and reasoning that approximates the human brain. This does not mean that each beetle has the intelligence of a human, but rather that, collectively, the entire nest has attained that level. In these cases, the beetles are likely to collect treasure and magical items from their victims.

Ecology: In tunnel complexes, boring beetles grow molds, slimes, and fungi for food, beginning their cultures on various forms of decaying vegetable and animal matter and wastes.

One frequent fungi grown is the shrieker, which serves a dual role. Not only is the shrieker a tasty treat for the boring beetle, but it also functions as an alarm when visitors have entered the fungi farm. Boring beetles are quick to react to these alarms, dispatching the invaders, sometimes eating them, but in any case gaining fresh organic matter on which to raise shrieker and other saprophytic plants.

Fire Beetle

The smallest of the giant beetles, fire beetles are nevertheless capable of delivering serious damage with their powerful mandibles. They are found both above and below ground, and are primarily nocturnal.

Combat: Despite its name, the fire beetle has no fire attacks, relying instead on its huge mandibles to inflict up to three times the damage of a dagger in a single attack.

Ecology: Fire beetles have two special glands above their eyes and one near the back of their abdomens. These glands produce a luminous red glow, and for this reason they are highly prized by miners and adventurers. This luminosity persists for 1d6 days after the glands are removed from the beetle, and the light shed will illuminate a radius of 10 feet.

The light from these glands is "cold"—it produces no heat. Many mages and alchemists are eager to discover the secret of this cold light, which could be not only safe, but economical, with no parts to heat up and burn out. In theory, they say, such a light source could last forever.

Rhinoceros Beetle

This uncommon monster inhabits tropical and subtropical jungles. They roam the rain forests searching for fruits and vegetation, and crushing anything in their path. The horn of a giant rhinoceros beetle extends about 6 feet.

Combat: The mandibles of this giant beetle inflict 3d6 points of damage on anyone unfortunate enough to be caught by them; the tremendous horn is capable of causing 2d8 points of damage by itself.

Ecology: The shell of this jungle dweller is often brightly colored or iridescent. If retrieved in one piece, these shells are valuable to clerics of the Egyptian pantheon, who use them as giant scarabs to decorate temples and other areas of worship. It is a representation of this, the largest of all beetles, that serves as the holy symbol for clerics of Apshai, the Egyptian god whose sphere of influence is said to include all insects.

Stag Beetle

These woodland beetles are very fond of grains and similar growing crops, and they sometimes become great nuisances when they raid cultivated lands.

Combat: Like other beetles, they have poor sight and hearing, but they will fight if attacked or attack if they encounter organic material they consider food. The giant stag beetle's two horns are usually not less than 8 feet long; they inflict up to 10 points of damage each.

Ecology: The worst damage from a stag beetle raid is that done to crops; they will strip an entire farm in short order. Livestock suffers too, stampeding in fear and wreaking more havoc. The beetles may even devour livestock, if they are hungry enough.

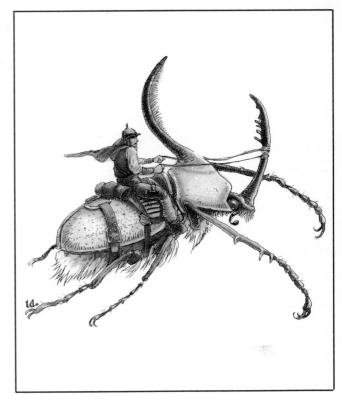

Water Beetle

The giant water beetle is found only in fresh water no less than 30 feet deep.

Combat: Voracious eaters, these beetles prey upon virtually any form of animal, but will eat almost anything. Slow and ponderous on land, they move very quickly in water. Giant water beetles hunt food by scent and by feeling vibrations.

Habitat/Society: Water beetles sometimes inhabit navigable rivers and lakes, in which case they can cause considerable damage to shipping, often attacking and sinking craft to get at the tasty morsels inside.

Ecology: Although they are air breathers, water beetles manage to stay underwater for extended periods of time by catching and holding a bubble of air beneath their giant wings. They will carry the bubble underwater, where it can be placed in a cave or some other cavity capable of holding an air supply.

Behir

CLIMATE/TERRAIN:	Any land
FREQUENCY:	Rare
ORGANIZATION:	Solitary
ACTIVE TIME:	Day
DIET:	Carnivore
INTELLIGENCE:	Low (5-7)
TREASURE:	See below
ALIGNMENT:	Neutral evil

NO. APPEARING:	1-2
ARMOR CLASS:	4
MOVEMENT:	15
HIT DICE:	12
THAC0:	9
NO. OF ATTACKS:	2 or 7
DAMAGE/ATTACK:	2-8 (2d4)/2-5 (1d4 + 1) or 2-8 (2d4)/6 x 1-6
SPECIAL ATTACKS:	Lightning bolt
SPECIAL DEFENSES:	Immune to electricity, poison
MAGIC RESISTANCE:	Nil
SIZE:	G (40' long)
MORALE:	Champion (15)
XP VALUE:	7,000

The behir is a snake-like reptilian monster whose dozen legs allow it to move with considerable speed and climb at fully half its normal movement rate. It can fold its limbs close to its long, narrow body and slither in snake-fashion if it desires. The head looks more crocodilian than snake-like, but has no difficulty in opening its mouth wide enough to swallow prey whole, the way a snake does.

Behir have band-like scales of great hardness. Their color ranges from ultramarine to deep blue with bands of gray-brown. The belly is pale blue. The two large horns curving back over the head look dangerous enough but are actually used for preening the creature's scales and not for fighting.

Combat: A behir will attack its prey by first biting and then looping its body around the victim and squeezing. If the latter attack succeeds, the victim is subject to six talon attacks next round.

A behir can discharge a 20-foot long stroke of electrical energy once every 10 rounds. This *lightning bolt* will cause 24 points of damage unless a saving throw vs. breath weapon is made. In the latter case, the target takes only half damage.

On a natural attack roll of 20 the behir swallows man-sized prey whole. Any creature swallowed will lose 1/6 of its starting Hit Points each round until it dies at the end of the sixth round. The behir will digest its meal in 12 turns, and at that time the victim is totally gone and cannot be raised from the dead. Note, however, that a creature swallowed can try to cut its way out of the behir's stomach. The inner armor class of the behir is 7, but each round the creature is in the behir it subtracts 1 from the damage each of its attacks does. This subtraction is cumulative, so on the second melee round there is a -2, on the third a -3, and so on.

Habitat/Society: Behir are solitary creatures, meeting others of their kind only to mate and hatch a clutch of 1-4 eggs. The female guards these eggs for eight months while the male hunts for the pair. When the young hatch, they are immediately turned out of the nest to fend for themselves, and the adults separate.

Newly hatched behir are about 2 feet long. Behir grow at a rate of 8 feet per year until fully mature. Interestingly enough, newly hatched behir do not have all of their legs, having instead only six or eight. Additional pairs of legs grow slowly over time until the creature has its full complement when it reaches adulthood.

Behir range over a territory of about 400 square miles, often living high up a cliff face in a cave.

Behir are never friendly with dragonkind, and will never be found coexisting in the same geographical area with any type of dragon. If a dragon should enter a behir's territory, the behir will do everything it can to drive the dragon out. If the behir fails in this task, it will move off to find a new home. A behir will never knowingly enter the territory of a dragon.

Ecology: Behir are useful to mages, priests, and alchemists for a number of concoctions. The horns of a behir can be used to brew the ink necessary to inscribe a *lightning bolt* scroll, and the sharp talons can likewise be used by a cleric to make the ink for a *neutralize poison* scroll. The heart of the behir is one of the more common ingredients for ink for a *protection from poison* scroll.

As behir sometimes swallow prey whole, there is a 10% chance that there will be some small items of value inside the monster. More often than not (60%) these will be gems (10 x Q). Otherwise, there is a 30% chance that there will be from 1-8 pieces of jewelry and a 10% chance that a single small magical object of an indigestible nature may be found. Such objects are never found in a behir's lair, because the creature expels this waste and buries it elsewhere.

The scales are valued for their hardness and color, and are worth up to 500 gp to an armorer who can use them to fashion a highly ornate set of scale mail armor.

	Beholder	Death Kiss	Eye of the Deep	Gauth	Spectator	Undead
CLIMATE/TERRAIN:	Any remote	Any remote	Deep ocean	Any remote	Any remote	Any remote
FREQUENCY:	Rare	Very rare	Very rare	Rare	Very rare	Very rare
ORGANIZATION:	Solitary	Solitary	Solitary	Solitary	Solitary	Solitary
ACTIVITY CYCLE:	Any	Any	Day	Day	Day	Any
DIET:	Omnivore	Carnivore	Omnivore	Magic	Omnivore	Nil
INTELLIGENCE:	Exceptional (15-16)	Average to high (8-14)	Very (11-12)	Exceptional (15-16)	Very to high (11-14)	Special
TREASURE:	I, S, T	I, S, T	R	B	See Below	E
ALIGNMENT:	Lawful evil	Neutral evil	Lawful evil	Neutral evil	Lawful neutral	Lawful evil
NO. APPEARING:	1	1	1	1	1	1
ARMOR CLASS:	0/2/7	4/6/8	5	0/2/7	4/7/7	0/2/7
MOVEMENT:	FL 3 (B)	Fl 9 (B)	Sw 6	Fl 9 (B)	Fl 9 (B)	Fl 2 (C)
HIT DICE:	45-75 hp	1d8 + 76 hp	10-12	6+6 or 9+9	4+4	45-75 hp
THAC0:	45-49 hp: 11 50-59 hp: 9 60-69 hp: 7 70 + hp: 5	11	10 HD: 11 11-12 HD: 9	6+6 HD: 13 9+9 HD: 11	15	45-49 hp: 11 50-59 hp: 9 60-69 hp: 7 70 + hp: 5
NO. OF ATTACKS:	1	10	3	1	1	1
DAMAGE/ATTACKS:	2-8	1-8	2-8/2-8/1-6	3-12	2-5	2-8
SPECIAL ATTACKS:	Magic	Blood drain	Magic	Magic	Magic	Magic
SPECIAL DEFENSES:	Anti-magic ray	Regeneration	Nil	Regeneration	Magic	Anti-magic ray
MAGIC RESISTANCE:	Nil	Nil	Nil	Nil	5%	Nil
SIZE:	M (4'-6' in diameter)	H (6'-12' in diameter)	S-M (3'-5' in diameter)	L (4'-6') diameter)	M (4' in diameter)	L (4'-6' in diameter)
MORALE:	Fanatic (18)	Fanatic (17)	Champion (15)	Champion to fanatic (15-18)	Elite (14)	Fanatic (18)
XP VALUE:	14,000	8,000	4,000	6+6 HD: 6,000 9+9 HD: 9,000	4,0000	13,0000

The beholder is the stuff of nightmares. This creature, also called the *sphere of many eyes* or the *eye tyrant*, appears as a large orb dominated by a central eye and a large toothy maw, has 10 smaller eyes on stalks sprouting from the top of the orb. Among adventurers, beholders are known as deadly adversaries.

Equally deadly are a number of variant creatures known collectively as beholder-kin, including radical and related creatures, and an undead variety. These creatures are related in manners familial and arcane to the "traditional" beholders, and share a number of features, including the deadly magical nature of their eyes. The most extreme of these creatures are called *beholder abominations*.

The globular body of the beholder and its kin is supported by levitation, allowing it to float slowly about as it wills.

Beholders and beholder-kin are usually solitary creatures, but there are reports of large communities of them surviving deep beneath the earth and in the void between the stars, under the dominion of hive mothers.

All beholders speak their own language, which is also understood by all beholder-kin. In addition, they often speak the tongues of other lawful evil creatures.

Combat: The beholder has different Armor Classes for different parts of their body. When attacking a beholder, determine the location of the attack before striking (as the various Armor Classes may make a strike in one area, and a miss in another):

Roll	Location	AC
01-75	Body	0
76-85	Central Eye	7
86-95	Eyestalk	2
96-00	One smaller eye	7

Each of the beholder's eyes, including the central one has a different function. The standard smaller eyes of a beholder are as follows:

1. *Charm person* (as spell)
2. *Charm monster* (as spell)
3. *Sleep* (as spell, but only one target)
4. *Telekinesis* (250 pound weight)
5. *Flesh to stone* (as spell, 30-yard range)
6. *Disintegrate* (20-yard range)
7. *Fear* (as wand)
8. *Slow* (as spell, but only a single target)
9. *Cause serious wounds* (50-yard range)

10. *Death ray* (as a *death* spell, with a single target, 40-yard range)

The central eye produces an *anti-magic ray* with a 140-yard range, which covers a 90 degree arc before the creature. No magic (including the effects of the other eyes) will function within that area. Spells cast in or passing through that zone cease to function.

A beholder may activate the magical powers of its eyes' at will. Generally, a beholder can use 1d4 smaller eyes if attackers are within a 90 degree angle in front, 1d6 if attacked from within a 180 degree angle, 1d8 if attacked from a 270 degree arc, and all 10 eyes if attacked from all sides. The central eye can be used only against attacks from the front. If attacked from above, the beholder can use all of the smaller eyes.

The beholder can withstand the loss of its eyestalks, each eyestalk/smaller eye having 5-12 hit points. This loss of hit points is over and above any damage done to the central body. The body can withstand two thirds of the listed hit points in damage before the creature perishes. The remaining third of the listed hit points are located in the central eye, and destroying it will eliminate the anti-magic ray. A beholder with 45 hit points will have a body that will take 30 points of damage, a central eye that will take 15 points, while one with 75 hit points will have a body that will withstand 50 points of damage, and a central eye that takes 25 hit points to destroy. Both beholders would have smaller eyestalks/eyes that take 5-12 (1d8 +4) points of damage to destroy, but such damage would not affect the body or central eye. Slaying the body will kill the beholder and render the eyes powerless. Destroyed eyestalks (but not the central eye) can regenerate at a rate of one lost member per week.

Habitat/Society: The beholders are a hateful, aggressive and avaricious race, attacking or dominating other races, including other beholders and many of the beholder-kin. This is because of a xenophobic intolerance among beholders that causes them to hate all creatures not like themselves. The basic, beholder body-type (a sphere with a mouth and a central eye, eye-tipped tentacles) allows for a great variety of beholder subspecies. Some have obvious differences, there are those covered with overlapping chitin plates, and those with smooth hides, or snake-like eye tentacles, and some with crustacean-like joints. But something as small as a change in hide color or size of the central eye can make two groups of beholders sworn enemies. Every beholder declares its own unique body-form to be the "true ideal" of beholderhood, the others being nothing but ugly copies, fit only to be eliminated.

Beholders will normally attack immediately. If confronted with a particular party there is a 50% chance they will listen to negotiations (bribery) before raining death upon their foes.

Beholder and Beholder-kin

Ecology: The exact reproductive process of the beholder is unknown. The core racial hatred of the beholders may derive from the nature of their reproduction, which seems to produce identical (or nearly so) individuals with only slight margin for variation. Beholders may use parthenogenic reproduction to duplicate themselves, and give birth live (no beholder eggs have been found). Beholders may also (rarely) mate with types of beholder-kin.

The smaller eyes of the beholder may be used to produce a *potion of levitation*, and as such can be sold for 50 gp each.

Death Kiss (beholder-kin)

The Death Kiss, or "bleeder," is a fearsome predator found in caverns or ruins. Its spherical body resembles that of the dreaded beholder, but the "eyestalks" of this creature are bloodsucking tentacles, its "eyes" are hook-toothed orifices. They favor a diet of humans and horses, but will attack anything that has blood. An older name for these creatures is *eye of terror*.

The central body of a death kiss has no mouth. Its central eye gives it 120-foot infravision, but the death kiss has no magical powers. A death kiss is 90% likely to be taken for a beholder when sighted. The 10 tentacles largely retract into the body when not needed, resembling eyestalks, but can lash out to a full 20-foot stretch with blinding speed. The tentacles may act separately or in concert, attacking a single creature or an entire adventuring company.

A tentacle's initial strike does 1-8 points of damage as the barb-mouthed tip attaches to the victim. Each attached tentacle drains 2 hit points worth of blood per round, beginning the round after it hits.

Like the beholder, the death kiss has variable Armor Classes. In ordinary combat, use the following table, though situations may dictate other methods (should the creature be attacking with a tentacle from 20 feet away, then no attack on the body or central eye may be made, while attacks on the stalk and mouth are still possible).

Roll	Location	AC	Hit Points
01-75	Body	4	77-84
76-85	Central Eye	8	6
86-95	Tentacle stalk	2	6
96-00	Tentacle mouth	4	See following text

A hit on a tentacle-mouth inflicts no damage, but stuns the tentacle, causing it to writhe helplessly for 1-4 rounds. If its central eye is destroyed, a bleeder locates beings within 10 feet by smell and sensing vibrations, but it is otherwise unaffected.

Tentacles must be struck with edged weapons to injure them. They can be torn free from the victim by a successful bend bars/lift gates roll. Such a forceful removal does the victim 1-6 damage per tentacle, since the barbed teeth are violently torn free from the tentacle.

If an attached tentacle is damaged but not destroyed, it instantly and automatically drains sufficient hit points, in blood, from the victim's body to restore it to a full 6 hit points. This reflex effect occurs after every non-killing hit on a tentacle, even if it is wounded more than once in a round. This cannot occur more than twice in one round. The parasitic healing effect does not respond to damage suffered by the central body or other tentacles.

A tentacle continues to drain blood, if it was draining when the central body of the death kiss reaches 0 hit points. Tentacles not attached to a victim at that time are incapable of further activity. A death kiss can retract a draining tentacle, but voluntarily does so only when its central body is at 5 hit points or less; it willfully detaches once the victim has been drained to 0 hit points.

Ingested blood is used to generate electrical energy—1 hit point of blood becomes 1 charge. A death kiss uses this energy for motor activity and healing. An eye of terror expends one charge every two turns in moving, and thus is almost constantly hunting prey. Spending one charge enables a bleeder to heal 1 hit point of damage to each of its 10 tentacles, its central body, and its eye (12 hit points in all). It can heal itself with one charge of stored energy every other round in addition to its normal attacks and activity.

Each tentacle can store up to 24 charges of drained energy, the body capable of storing 50 charges of drained energy. A severed tentacle is 70% likely to discharge its cumulative charges, when severed, into anything touching it; each charge delivers 1 hit point of electrical damage.

Finally, bleeders can ram opponents with their mass. This attack does 1-8 damage.

A death kiss may "shut itself down," remaining motionless and insensitive on the ground, and can remain alive in that state for long periods of time. To awaken from its hibernation, the creature requires an influx of

22

electrical energy, considerable heat, or the internal shock caused by a blow, fall, wound, or magical attack; any of the above stimulants must deal at least 5 points of damage to the death kiss to awaken it. Adventurers finding a hibernating death kiss usually provide such stimulation, thinking the sleeper helpless prey.

Eyes of terror are solitary hunters, fully inheriting the paranoia and ego of their cousins, the beholders. If they encounter one of their kin, the result is often a mid-air struggle to the death. The loser's body becomes an incubator and breeding ground for the death kiss' offspring. Within one day, 1-4 young will "hatch". Each new bleeder has half its parent's hit points, and fully matures in 1 month.

The death kiss has an organ in the central, upper body that is a valued ingredient in magical potions and spell inks concerned with levitation (and may be sold like beholder eyes). In addition, a brain or nerve node, deep in a bleeder's body hardens into a soft-sided, faceted red gem upon the creature's death. Called "bloodeyes," these typically fetch a market price of 70 gp each. They are valued for adornments since they glow more brightly as the wearer's emotions intensify.

Eye of the Deep (beholder-kin)

This is a water breathing version of the beholder, and dwells only at great depths, floating slowly about, stalking prey. They have two crab-like pincers which inflict 2-8 (2d4) points of damage each, and a wide mouth full of sharp teeth that does 1-6 points of damage.

The primary weapons of the eyes of the deep, however, are their eyes. The creatures large central eye emits a cone of blinding *light* 5 feet wide at its start, 30 feet long, and 20 feet wide at its base. Those in the cone must save vs. poison or be *stunned* for 2-8 (2d4) rounds.

The eye of the deep also has two smaller eyes on long stalks, and uses both to *create illusion*. Acting independently, the small eyes are able to cast *hold person* and *hold monster* spells respectively.

The eye of the deep has an Armor Class of 5 everywhere, including its eyes and eye stalks. If its eyestalks are severed they will grow back in about a week.

Gauth (beholder-kin)

The Gauth is a relative of the beholder that feeds on magic. Its spherical body is 5 feet in diameter and brown in color, mottled with purple and gray. Located in the center of the gauth's forward hemisphere is a large central eye surrounded by a ring of smaller eyes that are protected by ridges of tough flesh. These secondary body eyes provide the creature with normal vision in lighted areas and infravision to 90 feet. On the underside is the beast's fearsome mouth with its accompanying cluster of four feeding tendrils, while the top is adorned with a crown of six eye stalks. Attacks on the creature hit as follows:

Roll	Location	AC	Hit Points
01-85	Body	0	As listed
86-90	Central Eye	7	Part of Body
91-00	Eyestalk/Tendril	2	6 hit points

While the gauth is similar to the beholder, its ability to feed on the energy of magical objects makes it even more dangerous in some ways.

When a gauth moves into combat, it begins to glow, much as if it were the object of a *faerie fire* spell, to attract the attention of its foes. A creature that meets the *gaze* of the central eye must roll a successful saving throw vs. spell, with a −2 penalty, or be affected as if the victim of a *feeblemind* spell.

If a gauth chooses to bite with its great maw, the sharp fangs inflict 3d4 points of damage. The four tendrils around the mouth can grab and hold victims as if they had a Strength of 18, but they can inflict no damage.

A gauth in combat can also employ its six eye stalks. These eyes have the following powers:
1. *Cause serious wounds* (as spell, 30-foot range).
2. *Repulsion* (as spell, 10-foot wide path, 40-foot range)
3. *Cone of cold* (as spell, inflicts 3d4 points of damage and has an area of effect 5 feet wide at the start, 50 feet long, and 20 feet wide at the base; this eye can be used only three times per day)
4. *Lightning bolt* (as spell, inflicts 4d4 damage with 80' range; this power can be used up to four times per day)
5. *Paralyzation* (as wand, 40-foot range, single target; only a *dispel magic* or the beholder's death can free the victim)
6. *Dweomer drain* (see below)

Perhaps the most feared of the gauth's powers, its dweomer drain, per-

mits the gauth to drain charges from magical items. It has a 40-foot range and can be targeted on one individual per round. In addition to preventing one object from functioning for the duration of that round, this power drains one charge from one charged object. Permanent objects, such as magical swords, are rendered powerless for one round by this ability. Artifacts are not affected by the *dweomer drain*. The eye has no effect on spells that have been memorized (but not yet cast) and it will not break the concentration of a wizard. It does neutralize any spell cast by its target that round, however.

A *dispel magic* spell cast on any of the gauth's eye stalks prevents its use for 1d4 rounds. The central eye, any fully retracted eye stalks, the body's ability to glow, and the gauth's natural levitation are not subject to injury by such a spell.

If a gauth is slain, its magical energy dissipates. Usually, this is a harmless event, but there is a 2% chance that it is catastrophic, inflicting 4d4 points of damage to all creatures within 10 feet (no saving throw). Gauth are immune to their own powers and to those of other gauth. They have an unusual physiology that enables them to regenerate 1 hit point every two turns.

Although gauth are not known to fight over territories or prey, they do go to great lengths to avoid each other. Even when they encounter another of their kind in the wilderness, they often ignore them utterly.

A gauth can survive by eating meat but it greatly prefers to devour magical objects. In some unknown manner, the creature is able to absorb magical energy and feed on it. Each turn that an object spends in the gauth's stomach causes it to lose one charge. A permanent object is rendered inoperative after one day (artifacts are not affected, nor do they provide sustenance). Magical objects that cannot be entirely digested by a gauth are spat out after they have been drained of all their power.

Gauth are thought to live a century or so. Within a week of their "natural" death, two young gauth emerge from the corpse. Although smaller than their parent (each has 2+2 or 3+3 HD and a bite that causes only 2d4 points of damage), they have all the powers of a full-grown adult.

Spectator (beholder-kin)

Another relative of the beholder, the spectator is a guardian of places and treasures, and capable of limited planar travel. Once it is given a task, the spectator will watch for up to 101 years. It will allow no one to use, borrow, or examine an item or treasure, except the one who gave it its orders. The spectator has a large central eye and four smaller eye stalks protruding from the top of its hovering, spherical body.

The spectator is difficult to surprise, and has a +2 surprise modifier and a +1 initiative modifier. It is basically a passive creature, and will attempt to communicate and implant *suggestion* as its first act, unless it is immediately attacked. Striking a spectator has the following effects:

Roll	Location	AC	Hit Points
01-70	Body	4	4+4 HD
71-90	Eyestalk/Eye	7	1 hit point
91-00	Central Eye	7	1 hit point

A spectator, if blinded in all of its eyes, cannot defend its treasure and will teleport to the outer plane of Nirvana. This is the only condition under which it will leave its post. Its eyes regenerate in one day and then it returns. If the treasure is gone, the creature again leaves for Nirvana, never to return.

Spectator has a general magic resistance of 5%. As long as the central eye is undamaged, it can also *reflect* one spell cast at it, per round, sending it back against the caster. This does not apply to spells whose range is touch. Reflection occurs only if the spectator rolls a successful saving throw vs. spell. If the saving throw fails, magic resistance (and a further saving throw) must be rolled. Reflection is possible only if the caster is standing within the 60 degree arc of the central eye. Only the spellcaster is affected by a reflected spell.

All of the smaller eyes may be used at the same time against the same target. Their powers are:
1. *Create food and water* (creates the amount of food and water for a large meal for up to six people; this takes one full round)
2. *Cause serious wounds* (inflicts 2d8+3 points of damage to a single being at a range of 60 yards; a saving throw vs. spell is allowed for half damage)
3. *Paralyzation ray* (range 90 feet, one target only, for 8d4 rounds).
4. *Telepathy* (range 120 feet, only one target; communication is possible in this way, and the beast can also plant a *suggestion* if the target fails a

Beholder and Beholder-kin

saving throw vs. spell; the *suggestion* is always to leave in peace).

If properly met, the spectator can be quite friendly. It will tell a party exactly what it is guarding early in any conversation. If its charge is not threatened, it can be very amiable and talkative, using its telepathy.

Spectators move by a very rapid levitation, in any direction. They will drift aimlessly when asleep (20% likely when encountered), never touching the ground.

The treasure being guarded is 90% likely to be a magical item. If the spectator gains incidental treasure while performing its duty, this is not part of its charge and it will freely allow it to be taken. Incidental treasure can be generated as follows: 40% for 3-300 coins of mixed types, 30% for 1d6 gems of 50 gp base value, 20% for 1d4 potions, 15% for a +1 piece of armor, 15% for a +1 weapon, and 5% for a miscellaneous magical item valued at 1,000 XP or less.

Spectators are summoned from Nirvana by casting *monster summoning V* with material components of three or more small eyes from a beholder. (The chance of success is 10% per eye.) The spectator can be commanded only to guard some treasure. It performs no other duty, and if commanded to undertake some other task, it returns to Nirvana immediately. If its guarded treasure is ever destroyed or stolen, the spectator is released from service and returns to Nirvana. The summoner may take the item with no interference from the spectator, but this releases the creature.

Undead Beholder (Death Tyrant)

Death tyrants are rotting, mold-encrusted beholders. They may be shriveled, wounds exposing their internal, spherical networks of circular ribs, among the remnants of their exoskeletal plates. All sport wounds, some have eyestalks missing, or a milky film covering their eyes. They move and turn more slowly than living beholders, striking and bringing their eyes to bear last in any combat round.

An undead beholder can use all the powers of its surviving eyes, just as it did in life. The powers of 2-5 eyes (select randomly, including the central eye) are lost due to injuries or death, and the change to undeath. Although a death tyrant "heals" its motive energies through time, it cannot regenerate lost eyestalks or their powers.

Charm powers are lost in undeath. The two eyes that charmed either become useless (60%), or function as weak *hold monster* effects (40%). A being failing to save against such a *hold* remains held as long as the eye's gaze remains steadily focused on them. If the eye is turned on another being, or the victim hooded, or forcibly removed, the *hold* lasts another 1-3 rounds. Death tyrants are immune to *sleep, charm* and *hold* spells.

If not controlled by another creature through magic, a death tyrant hangs motionless until its creator's instructions are fulfilled (for example, "Attack all humans who enter this chamber until they are destroyed or flee. Do not leave the chamber."). If no instructions are given to a "new" death tyrant, it attacks all living things it perceives. Death tyrants occur spontaneously in very rare instances. In most cases, they are created through the magic of evil beings—from human mages to illithid villains. Some outcast, magic-using beholders have even been known to create death tyrants from their own unfortunate brethren.

Death tyrants have no self-awareness or social interaction; they are mindless servants of more powerful masters. "Mindless" is a relative term; the once highly intelligent brains of death tyrants still use eyes skillfully to perceive and attack nearby foes. When a death tyrant is controlled by another being, consider it to have the intelligence of its controller.

Death tyrants are created from dying beholders. A spell, thought to have been developed by human mages in the remote past, forces a beholder from a living to an undead state, and imprints its brain with instructions. "Rogue" death tyrants also exist: those whose instructions specifically enable them to ignore all controlling attempts. These are immune to the control attempts of all other beings. Beholders often leave them as traps against rivals.

Human spell researchers report that control of a death tyrant is very difficult. A beholder's mind fluctuates wildly in the frequency and level of its mental activity, scrambling normal *charm monster* and *control undead* spells. A special spell must be devised to command a death tyrant.

Saving Throws

Most beholders make saving throws according to their Hit Dice. The Death Kiss makes saving throws as a 10th-level warrior. The typical beholder and undead beholders make saving throws as follows:

Creature hit points	Saves as
45-49	10th level warrior
50-59	12th level warrior
60-69	14th level warrior
70+	16th level warrior

Beholder and Beholder-kin

	Hive Mother	Director	Examiner	Lensman	Overseer	Watcher
CLIMATE/TERRAIN:	Any remote	Any remote	Any remote	Any remote	Any remote	Any remote
FREQUENCY:	Very rare	Very rare	Very rare	Very rare	Very rare	Very rare
ORGANIZATION:	Solitary	Squad	Squad	Squad	Solitary	Solitary
ACTIVITY CYCLE:	Any	Day	Night	Day	Any	Any
DIET:	Omnivore	Omnivore	Omnivore	Insectivore	Omnivore	Scavenger
INTELLIGENCE:	Genius (17-18)	Average (8-10)	Genius (17-18)	Low (5-7)	Supra-genius (19-20)	Semi- (2-4)
TREASURE:	I, S, T	G	V × 4	R	U	Nil
ALIGNMENT:	Lawful evil	Lawful evil	Lawful neutral	Neutral evil	Lawful evil	Neutral
NO. APPEARING:	1	2-5	1-6	1-10	1	1-4
ARMOR CLASS:	0	2 (4)	5	3/7	2/7	7
MOVEMENT:	Fl 6 (A)	15, Fl 3 (A)	Fl 6 (C)	9	1	Fl 6 (A)
HIT DICE:	20	12 (8)	8	2	14	3 + 3
THAC0:	5	9	13	19	7	17
NO. OF ATTACKS:	1	2	1	1	1	1
DAMAGE/ATTACKS:	5-20	2-8/2-8	1-6 or weapon	1-8 or weapon	3-12	3-18
SPECIAL ATTACKS:	Magic	Magic	Magic	Nil	Magic	Magic
SPECIAL DEFENSES:	Anti-magic ray	Nil	Magic	Magic	Magic	Magic
MAGIC RESISTANCE:	5%	20%	25%	Nil	35%	Nil
SIZE:	H (8' in diameter)	H (8-10' in diameter)	M (4' in diameter)	M (5' tall)	H (15' tall)	L (6' in diameter)
MORALE:	Fanatic (18)	Fanatic (18)	Steady (11)	Elite (14)	Champion (16)	Average (10)
XP VALUE:	24,000	10,000	6,000	175	15,000	420

Hive Mother (beholder-kin)

The legendary hive mothers are also called the "Ultimate tyrants", or just "Ultimates". They are twice the size of typical beholders, and differ in appearance as well.

Their mouths are larger, so large that they can gulp down a man-sized target on a natural die roll of 20. Once swallowed, the prey takes 5-20 points of damage (5d4) each round until it is dead or escapes. The beholder's mouth is not very deep, so a victim can escape by making a successful attack roll.

The ultimate has no eyestalks, but its magical eyes are protected by hooded covers in the flesh of the creature's body, so that they cannot be severed. The central eye has 15 hit points.

Roll	Location	AC	Hit Points
01-90	Body	0	20 HD
91-00	Central Eye	7	15 hp

The ultimate's true ability is in controlling the actions of large numbers of beholders and beholder-kin. A hive mother may have 5-10 ordinary beholders under its command, or 5-20 abomination beholder-kin (see below), which it communicates with telepathically. A nesting hive mother spells disaster for the surrounding region, as it can apparently create a community of beholders, beholder-kin, and abominations. If destroyed, the beholders and beholder-kin will turn on each other, or seek their own lairs.

Hive mothers may be the ancestral stock of the better known beholder, the next step of its evolution, a magical mutation, or a separate species. The reality remains unknown.

Director (abomination)

Directors are a social, warrior-beholder, and breed specialized mounts. They mindlink with their mounts to better control them.

Directors resemble beholders, but their central eye is smaller. They possess only six small eyes on retractable eye stalks. Directors have a fanged mouth below the central eye and possesses three clawed, sensory tendrils on their ventral surface. These tendrils are used to cling to the mount and link with its limited mind.

Directors' eyes have their own powers:
1. *Magic Missile* (as spell , 2/round)
2. *Burning Hands* (as spell at 8th level)
3. *Wall of Ice* (as spell)
4. *Slow* (as spell)
5. *Enervation* (as spell)
6. *Improved Phantasmal Force* (as spell)

A director's central eye has the power of *deflection*—all frontal attacks on director suffer a −2 penalty to the attack roll and damage is halved. The director also gains a +2 bonus to all saving throws against spells cast by those in the field of vision of the central eye.

Director mounts seem to have derived from an insect stock, as they are covered in chitin and have simple eye spots and multiple limbs.

Directors normally possess 8 Hit Dice, but when mounted the director and mount are treated as a single creature whose Hit Dice equals the sum of those of the director and the mount. After a director/mount suffers half damage, the mount's speed is reduced to half and the director gets only one physical attack per round. A director may flee and leave his mount to fend for itself (the mount suffers a −4 penalty to its attack rolls). Directors have an AC of 4, but are AC 2 when mounted. Directors may use all of their normal powers while mounted, within the restrictions of beholder targeting angles.

Crawler (a typical mount): A crawler resembles a cross between a centipede and a spider. It has 4 Hit Dice. It has 10 legs, two pairs of frontal antennae, and two fighting spider fangs that can be used for separate stabbing attacks causing 2d4 points of damage each. Victims who fail to roll successful saving throws vs. poison are paralyzed for 1d4 rounds. Crawlers are omnivores that prefer to eat smaller creatures. Unmounted, they may roll into a ball to gain an AC of 0. They have cutting mandibles beneath their front fangs.

Examiner (abomination)

An examiner is a 4-foot diameter sphere with no central eye and only four small eyes, each at the end of an antenna, mounted atop the sphere. They have one small, lamprey-like mouth on its ventral surface. The mouth is surrounded by four multi-jointed limbs ending in gripper pads. These limbs can pick up and manipulate tools, the chief strength of the examiner.

Examiners are scholars and clerks involved in spell and magical item enhancement, research, and creation. They can use any artifact or tool as well as humans, and they can wield up to four items at a time. Examiners regenerate 1 point of damage each round. The powers of their four eyes are given below (all spell-like effects are cast at the 8th level).
1. *Enlarge* or *Reduce*
2. *Identify* or *Legend Lore*
3. *Transmute Form* (similar to a *Stone Shape* spell, but works on all types of nonmagical, nonliving material)
4. *Spell Reflection* as a *ring of spell turning*

Examiners are not the bravest of beholder-kin, but they are potentially the most dangerous with their command of artifacts. They are often the lackeys of beholders, overseers, and hive mothers.

Beholder and Beholder-kin

Lensman (abomination)

A lensman has one eye set in the chest of its five-limbed, starfish-shaped, simian body. Beneath the eye is a leering, toothy maw. Four of the five limbs end in three-fingered, two-thumbed, clawed hands. The fifth limb, atop the body, is a prehensile, whip-like tentacle. Its chitin is soft and there are many short, fly-like hairs. Lensmen are the only kin to wear any sort of garb—a webbing that is used to hold tools and weapons. Their preferred weapons are double-headed pole arms.

Lensmen are semi-mindless drones that don't question their lot in life. The eye of each lensman possesses only one of the following six special powers (all at the 6th level of ability).
1. *Emotion*
2. *Heal*
3. *Dispel Magic*
4. *Tongues*
5. *Phantasmal Force*
6. *Protections* (as scrolls, any type, but only one at a time)

Overseer (abomination)

Overseers resemble fleshy trees. They have 13 limbs, each of which ends in a bud that conceals an eye; one of these limbs forms the top spine, and three yammering mouths surround the spine. There are eight thorny, vine-like limbs that are used to grasp tools and for physical defense, inflicting 1d10+2 points of damage each. Overseers sit on root-like bases and can inch along when movement is required. They cannot levitate.

Overseers are covered with a fungus which changes color as the overseers desire, commonly mottled green, gray, and brown.

Overseers may use any physical weapons or artifacts. The powers of their 13 eyes are as follows (all magical effects are cast at 14th level).
1. *Cone of Cold*
2. *Dispel Magic*
3. *Paralysis*
4. *Chain Lightning*
5. *Telekinesis* 250 lb. weight
6. *Emotion*
7. *Mass Charm*
8. *Domination*
9. *Mass Suggestion*
10. *Major Creation*
11. *Spell Turning*
12. *Serten's Spell Immunity*
13. *Temporal Stasis*

An overseer's AC is 2, but each eye stalk is AC 7 and is severed if it suffers 10 points of damage.

Like hive mothers (that operate with them), overseers can convince similar beholders and beholder-kin to work together. Overseers are very protective of their health and always have one or two beholder guards and at least a half dozen directors protecting their welfare.

Watcher (abomination)

Watchers are 6-foot-diameter spheres with three central eyes arranged around the circumference of the sphere. These eyes are huge and unlidded. On the crown of the sphere is a compound eye and a ring of six eye spots that make it difficult to surprise a watcher. A large tentacle with a barbed prehensile pad extends from the ventral surface, right behind the small mouth with its rasp-like tongue. Watchers feed on carrion and stunned prey. They are information gatherers and are the least brave of all the eye tyrant races.

Watchers can attack with their single tentacle for 3d6 points of damage. The tentacle also inflicts an electrical shock; victims who fail a system shock roll fall unconscious.

Each of a watcher's main eyes has two powers, and the compound eye on top may draw on three different abilities. The six eye spots have no special powers.
1. *True Seeing* and *ESP*
2. *Advanced Illusion* and *Demi-Shadow Magic*
3. *Telekinesis* 1,000 lb. and *Teleport*
Compound Eye: *Message*, *Tongues*, and *Suggestion*

Watchers are not aggressive warriors; they prefer misdirection and flight to actual confrontation.

Other Beholders and Beholder-kin

The beholder races are not limited to the ones presented here. The plastic nature of the beholder race allows many mutations and abominations in the breed, including, but not limited to, the following.

Beholder Mage

Shunned by other beholders, this is a beholder which has purposely blinded its central eye, so that it might cast spells. It does so by channeling spell energy through an eyestalk, replacing the normal effect with that of a spell of its choice.

Elder Orb

These are extremely ancient beholders of godlike intelligence and power. Though they have lost the function of some of their eyestalks, they have more hit points and are able to cast spells. They can supposedly create and control death tyrants.

Orbus

This is a stunted, pale-white beholder retaining only its anti-magic eye and reputed to have great magical ability.

Doomsphere

This ghost-like undead beholder is created by magical explosions.

Kasharin

An undead beholder, it passes on the rotting disease which killed it.

Astereater

This abomination is a great boulder-like beholder-kin without eyes.

Gorbel

The gorbel is a wild, clawed beholder-kin lacking magic but with the nasty habit of exploding if attacked.

In addition, there are beholders which are in all appearances "normal" but have eyes with alternate magical abilities, such as a *detect lie* instead of a *death* ray. Such creatures are usually treated as outcasts by all the beholder and beholder-kin races.

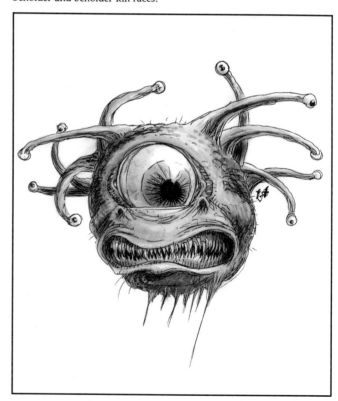

Bird	#AP	AC	MV	HD	THAC0	# AT	Dmg/AT	Morale	XP Value
Blood Hawk	4-15	7	1, Fl 24 (B)	1+1	19	3	1-4/1-4/1-6	Steady (11)	120
Boobrie	1-2	5	15, Fl 15 (D)	9	11	3	1-6(×2)/2-16	Steady (11-12)	2,000
Condor	1-2	7	3, Fl 24 (D)	3+3	17	1	2-5	Average (8-10)	175
Crow (See Raven)									
Eagle, Giant	1-20	7	3, Fl 48 (D)	4	17	3	1-6/1-6/2-12	Elite (13)	420
Eagle, Wild	5-12	6	1, Fl 30 (C)	1+3	19	3	1-2/1-2/1	Average (9)	175
Eblis	4-16	3	12, Fl 12 (C)	4+4	15	4	1-4(×4)	Champion (15-16)	650 (normal)
									1,400 (spell user)
Falcon	1-2	5	1, Fl 36 (B)	1−1	20	3	1/1/1	Unsteady (6)	65
Flightless	2-20	7	18	1-3	1-2 HD: 19	1	1 HD: 1-4	Average (8-10)	1 HD: 15
					3 HD: 17		2 HD: 1-6		2 HD: 35
							3 HD: 1-8		3 HD: 65
Hawk, Large	1-2	6	1, Fl 33 (B)	1	19	3	1-2/1-2/1	Average (9)	65
Owl	1 (2)	5	1, Fl 27 (D)	1	19	3	1-2/1-2/1	Unsteady (5-7)	65
Owl, Giant	2-5	6	3, Fl 18 (E)	4	17	3	2-8/2-8/2-5	Steady (11-12)	270
Owl, Talking	1	3	1, Fl 36 (C)	2+2	19	3	1-4/1-4/1-2	Champion (15)	975
Raven	4-32	7	1, Fl 36 (B)	1-2 hp	20	1	1	Average (8-10)	15
Raven, Huge	2-8	6	1, FL 27 (C)	1−1	20	1	1-2	Steady (11-12)	35
Raven, Giant	4-16	4	3, Fl 18 (D)	3+2	17	1	3-6	Elite (13-14)	175
Swan	2-16	7	3, Fl 18 (D)	1+2	18	3	1/1/1-2	Unsteady (6)	65
Vulture	4-24	6	3, Fl 27 (E)	1+1	19	1	1-2	Unsteady (5-7)	65
Vulture, Giant	2-12	7	3, Fl 24 (D)	2+2	19	1	1-4	Average (8-10)	120

Avians, whether magical or mundane in nature, are among the most interesting creatures ever to evolve. Their unique physiology sets them apart from all other life, and their grace and beauty have earned them a place of respect and adoration in the tales of many races.

Blood Hawk

Blood hawk hunt in flocks and are fond of humanoids. They continue to attack humans even if the melee has gone against them. Male blood hawks kill humans not only for food but also for gems, which they use to line their nests as an allurement to females.

Boobrie

The boobrie, giant relative of the stork, stands 12 feet tall. A boobrie's diet consists of giant catfish and other wetland denizens. When times are lean, the boobrie feeds on snakes, lizards, and giant spiders. Its occasional dependence on a diet of creatures that deliver a toxic bite has made the boobrie immune to all poisons. When a boobrie hunts, it finds a grove of tall marsh grass or similar vegetation and slips into it. Once in its hunting blind, it remains still for hours at a time, until prey comes within sight. When employing this means of ambush, its opponents suffer a −3 penalty to their surprise rolls.

Condor

Condors measure three to six feet and have a wingspan of 13 to 20 feet. They rarely land except to feed—they even sleep in flight. Condor eggs and hatchlings are worth 30-60 gp. They can be trained to act as spotters or retrievers. Humanoids of small or tiny size can train them as aerial mounts. Used in this way, they can carry 80 pounds, either held in their claws or riding atop their backs.

Eagle

An eagle typically attacks from great heights, letting gravity hurtle it toward its prey. If an eagle dives more than 100 feet, its diving speed is double its normal flying speed and the eagle is restricted to attacking with its claws. These high-speed attacks gain a +2 attack bonus and double damage. Eagles are never surprised because of their exceptional eyesight and hearing. Eagles mate for life and, since they nest in one spot, it is easy to identify places where eagles are normally present. On occasion, in an area of rich feeding, 1d8+4 eagles are encountered instead of the normal individual or pair. Eagles generally hunt rodents, fish, and other small animals. Eagles also feed on the carrion of recently killed creatures as well. Eagles never attack humanoids, though small creatures like brownies have to be wary of a hunting eagle.

Eagle, Giant

Giant eagles stand 10 feet tall and have wing spans of up to 20 feet. They share the coloration and fighting methods of their smaller cousins. How-

ever, if a giant eagle dives more than 50 feet, it adds +4 to its attack roll and doubles its claw damage.

Giant eagles have exceptional eyesight and hearing and cannot be surprised except at night or in their lair, and then only 10% of the time. Far more social than normal eagles, up to 20 nests can be found in the same area, one nest for each mated pair. Giant eagles can be trained, and their eggs sell for 500 to 800 gp.

Eblis

Their bodies look like those of storks, with grey, tan, or off-white plumage on their bodies and sleek black necks. Their heads are narrow and end in long, glossy-black, needle-like beaks. Eblis speak a language of chirps, whistles, and deep-throated hoots. In addition, spellcasting eblis have managed to learn a rudimentary version of common, allowing them to converse with those they encounter. Each community is led by one individual with spellcasting ability. These eblis cast 2d4 spells per day as 3rd-level casters. To determine the available spells, roll 1d8 and consult the following table. Duplicate rolls indicate the spell may be employed more than once per day.

Roll	Spell	Roll	Spell
1	Audible glamer	5	Hypnotic pattern
2	Blur	6	Spook
3	Change self	7	Wall of fog
4	Hypnotism	8	Whispering wind

Eblis love shiny objects (like gems); even the most wise and powerful of the eblis can be bribed with an impressive jewel. An eblis community consists of 2d4 huts built from straw and grasses common to the marsh around the community. Care is taken by the eblis to make these huts difficult to detect. In fact, only a determined search of the area by a ranger or someone with the animal lore proficiency is likely to uncover the community.

All eblis secrete an oil that coats their feathers and provides them with a +1 bonus to all saving throws against fire- and flame-based attacks. Any damage caused by a fire- or flame-based attack is lessened by −1 for each die of damage.

The evil nature of the eblis is best seen in the delight it takes in hunting and killing. When an eblis spots travelers who have objects it desires for its nest, it attacks. Since the eblis is cunning, these attacks often take the forms of ambushes.

Falcon

Falcons are smaller, swifter, and more maneuverable than hawks. These birds of prey are easily trained and are preferred by hunters over hawks. Trained falcons sell for around 1,000 gp each.

Bird

Flightless Bird

These avians are typified by the ostrich, emu, and rhea. Although they share many of the physiological adaptations that enable other birds to take wing and break the bonds of earth, they are unable to fly.

The ostrich is the largest and strongest, standing 8 feet tall and weighing 300 pounds. The animal's small head and short, flat beak are perched atop a long, featherless neck. The ostrich fans is able to run at 40 miles per hour. If forced to fight, an ostrich uses its legs to deliver a kick that inflicts 1d8 points of damage.

The emu reaches 6 feet high and 130 pounds. Unlike those of their larger cousins, the wings of an emu are rudimentary appendages hidden beneath their coarse, hair-like feathers.

The rhea resembles a small ostrich, standing 3 feet tall and weighs 80 pounds. The differences between the two species lie in the structure of the feet and the tail feathers. Ostriches have two toes, while rheas have three, and ostriches have elegant, flowing tail plumes, while the rhea's are far shorter. Long feathers on the bird's sides swoop down to cover the stunted tail feathers.

Hawk

Hawks have wingspans up to 5 feet. They attack in plummeting dives, usually from a height of 100 feet or more. This dive gives them a +2 attack bonus, enabling their talons to inflict double damage. Hawks cannot attack with their beaks during the round in which they use a dive attack. After the initial dive, hawks fight by biting and pecking with their beaks, tearing at their opponents with their talons. Hawks target eyes and they have a 25% probability of striking an eye whenever its beak strikes. Opponents struck in the eye are blinded for 1d10 rounds and have a 10% chance of losing the use of the eye. Because of their superior eyesight, hawks can never be surprised. Any intruder threatening the nest is attacked, regardless of size. If taken young and trained by an expert, hawks can be taught to hunt. Fledglings bring 500 gp and trained hawks sell for as much as 1,200 gp.

Owl

Owls hunt rodents, small lizards, and insects, attacking humans only when frightened (or magically commanded). They have 120' infravision and quadruple normal hearing. They fly in total silence, giving their prey a −6 penalty to their surprise rolls. Owls cannot be surprised during hours of dusk and darkness; during daylight hours, their eye sight is worse than that of humans, suffering a −3 on their surprise roll if discovered in their daylight roosting place. Owls attack with sharp talons and hooked beaks. If they swoop from a height of 50 feet or more, each attack is +2 and inflicts double damage, but no beak attack is possible.

Owl, Giant

These nocturnal creatures inhabit very wild areas, preying on rodents, large game birds, and rabbits. They are too large to gain swoop bonuses but can fly in nearly perfect silence; opponents suffer a −6 on their surprise roll. Giant owls may be friendly toward humans, though they are naturally suspicious. Parents will fight anything that threatens their young. Eggs sell for 1,000 sp and hatchlings sell for 2,000 sp.

Owl, Talking

Talking owls appear as ordinary owls, but speak common and six other languages (DM's option). Their role is to serve and advise champions of good causes on dangerous quests, which they do for 1d3 weeks if treated kindly on the first encounter; a talking owl feigns a broken wing to see how a party will react. Talking owls can *detect good*. They have a wisdom score of 21, with the appropriate spell immunities.

Raven (Crow)

Ravens and crows are often mistaken as bad omens by superstitious farmers and peasants. They attack with strong claws and their long, sharp beaks. Ravens employ a grab and peck approach to combat. These birds are 10% likely to attack an opponent's eyes. If successful, the attack causes the opponent to lose an eye. All birds of this type travel in flocks. Any encountered solo are actually scouts. As soon as they see any approaching creature, the scouts give warning cries and maintain a safe distance to keep track of them. Because of the scouts, ravens cannot be surprised during daylight conditions.

Raven, Giant

Giant ravens are both pugnacious and easily trained (if raised from fledglings), and are often used as guards and messengers. While they are too small to be used as mounts by all but small humanoids (i.e., faerie folk and PCs under the effects of a *potion of diminution*), the strength of these birds is enough to carry an adult halfling.

Raven, Huge

Huge ravens have malicious dispositions, occasionally serving evil masters. Not all raven familiars and consorts are evil—the alignment of the master is a decisive factor in such arrangements.

Swan

These aquatic birds tend to inhabit areas frequented by similar waterfowl. Such areas include rivers, ponds, lakes, and marshes. Swans posses acute senses. They are 90% likely to detect intruders. There is a 10% chance that any swan encounter includes one or more swanmays (q.v.) in avian form.

Vulture

Vultures are scavengers that search the skies for injured or dead creatures to feed upon. They measure 2 to 3 feet long with a wingspan of up to 7 feet. Greasy blue-black feathers cover the torso and wings; its pink head is bald. Vultures are cowards, and will wait until an intended meal stops moving. If six or more vultures are present, they may attack a weakly moving victim. If the victim defends itself, the vultures move out of reach but maintain their deathwatch. Creatures that are unconscious, dead, or magically sleeping or held are potential meals. If the surviving combatants are further than 20 feet from the fallen creatures, the vultures alight and begin feeding. Because of their diet, vultures kin have developed a natural resistance to disease and organic toxins.

Vulture, Giant

Giant vultures measure 3 to 5 feet. Domesticated giant vultures can be trained to associate specific species (i.e., as humanoids) with food, hence the birds concentrate on locating those creatures. Giant vulture eggs and hatchlings are worth 30-60 gp.

Brain Mole

CLIMATE/TERRAIN:	Any/ Below ground
FREQUENCY:	Very rare
ORGANIZATION:	Family
ACTIVITY CYCLE:	Night
DIET:	Psionic energy
INTELLIGENCE:	Animal (1)
TREASURE:	Nil
ALIGNMENT:	Neutral

NO. APPEARING:	1-3
ARMOR CLASS:	9
MOVEMENT:	1, Br 3
HIT DICE:	1 hp
THAC0:	Nil
NO. OF ATTACKS:	Nil
DAMAGE/ATTACK:	Nil
SPECIAL ATTACKS:	Psionic
SPECIAL DEFENSES:	Psionic
MAGIC RESISTANCE:	Nil
SIZE:	T (3" long)
MORALE:	Unsteady (5-7)
XP VALUE:	35

These small, furry animals are nearly blind, and look like normal moles. Brain moles are seldom seen, however. They live in underground tunnels, burrowing through rock as easily as through dirt. Usually, the only discernible evidence of a brain mole's presence is a network of blistered stone or mounded dirt above ground, which marks the tunnel complex. These creatures damage more than landscapes, however. Brain moles feed on psionic activity. From the protection of their tunnels, they will psionically burrow into a victim's brain, and drain his psionic energy.

Combat: A brain mole commonly attacks its victim in forests or underground; in either case, the creature is usually out of its direct line of sight. The mole waits for a psionically endowed being to appear above it, or it will burrow in search of prey.

Brain moles have an innate psionic sense and can automatically detect any psionic activity within 200 yards. However, they can only feed on psionic energy when their victim is nearby: within 30 yards if the victim is a psionicist or psionic creature, 30 feet if the victim is a wild talent. The mole can't get a fix on its prey until the victim actually uses a psionic power.

Once a brain mole locates a victim it will attempt to establish contact. If contact is made, it will attempt to feed. If the victim is a wild talent, feeding is accomplished by using mindwipe. If the victim is a psionicist (or psionic creature), feeding is accomplished through amplification.

A brain mole does not attack maliciously. It must feed at least once a week or it will die.

Psionics Summary:

Level	Dis/Sci/Dev	Attack/Defense	Score	PSPs
6	2/1/4	MT/M-	12	100

Telepathy - Sciences: mindlink, mindwipe; **Devotions:** contact, mind thrust

Metapsionics - Devotions: psychic drain (no cost), psionic sense

A brain mole can perform mindwipe up to a range of 30 feet. Strangely enough, a brain mole must establish contact before using psychic drain. Furthermore, it can only perform psychic drain upon psionicists or psionic creatures. However, it does not have to put them into a trance or a deep sleep first, it just starts siphoning away psionic energy.

Habitat/Society: Brain moles live in family units that include one male, one female, and 1d6 young (one of which may be old enough to feed by itself). Large brain mole towns of up to 3d6 family units have been reported. Of course, these only occur in places frequently traveled by the psionically empowered.

Ecology: Though brain moles can be dangerous to some, others keep them as pets. The moles are rather friendly, and easily tamed. They are favored by royalty, who enjoy the special protection which only brain moles can provide. Some sages claim that even a dead brain mole can offer protection from psionic attacks, provided the carcass is worn about one's neck as a medallion. Sometimes, nobles who have been harassed by a particular psionicist will send heroes out on quests for the little furry rodents.

On the open market, adult brain moles sell for 50 gp. Youngsters sell for 5 gp each.

Broken One

	Common	Greater
CLIMATE/TERRAIN:	Any land	Any land
FREQUENCY:	Rare	Very Rare
ORGANIZATION:	Pack	Pack
ACTIVITY CYCLE:	Any (night)	Any (night)
DIET:	Varies	Varies
INTELLIGENCE:	Low (5-7)	High (13-14)
TREASURE:	I, K, M	I, K, M (Z)
ALIGNMENT:	Neutral evil	Neutral evil
NO. APPEARING:	3-12 (3d4)	1-4 (1d4)
ARMOR CLASS:	7 (10)	5 (8)
MOVEMENT:	9	9
HIT DICE:	3	5
THAC0:	17	15
NO. OF ATTACKS:	1	1
DAMAGE/ATTACK:	1-6 (or by weapon)	1d8 (or by weapon)
SPECIAL ATTACKS:	See below	See below
SPECIAL DEFENSES:	Regeneration	Regeneration
MAGIC RESISTANCE:	Nil	Nil
SIZE:	M (4-7'tall)	M (4-7' tall)
MORALE:	Unsteady (5-7)	Steady (11-12)
XP VALUE:	175	650

Broken ones (or *animal men*) are the tragic survivors of scientific and magical experiments gone awry. While they were once human, their beings have become mingled with those of animals and their very nature has been forever altered by the shock of this event. It is rumored that some broken ones are the result of failed attempts at *resurrection, reincarnation,* or *polymorph* spells.

While broken ones look more or less human, they are physically warped and twisted by the accidents that made them. The characteristics of their non-human part will be clearly visible to any who see them. For example, a broken one who has been infused with the essence of a rat might have horrific feral features, wiry whiskers, curling clawed fingers, and a long, whip-like tail.

Broken ones know whatever languages they knew as human beings and 10% of them can communicate with their non-human kin as well. It is not uncommon for the speech of a broken one to be heavily accented or slurred by the deformities of its body.

Combat: Broken ones tend to be reclusive creatures and combat with them is rare. Still, they are strong opponents. Broken ones are almost always blessed with a greater than human stamina, reflected in the fact that they always have at least 5 hit points per Hit Die. Thus, the weakest of broken ones has at least 15 hit points. In addition, broken ones heal at a greatly accelerated rate, regenerating 1 hit point each round.

A broken one will often wield weapons in combat, inflicting damage according to the weapon used. Many broken ones have also developed claws or great strength, which makes them deadly in unarmed combat. Hence, all such creatures inflict 1d6 points of damage in melee. Unusually strong strains might receive bonuses to attack and damage rolls.

Many broken ones have other abilities (night vision, keen hearing, etc.) that are derived from their animal half. As a general rule, each creature will have a single ability of this sort.

Habitat/Society: Broken ones tend to gather together in bands of between 10 and 60 persons. Since they seldom find acceptance in human societies, they seek out their own kind and dwell in secluded areas of dense woods or rocky wastes far from the homes of men. From time to time they will attack a human village or caravan, either for supplies, in self-defense, or simply out of vengeance for real or imagined wrongs. If possible, they will try to seek out their creator and destroy him for the transformations he has brought upon them.

When a society of these monsters is found, it will always be tribal in nature. There will be from 10-60 typical broken ones with one greater broken one for every 10 individuals. The greater broken ones (described below) will act as leaders and often have absolute power over their subjects.

Ecology: Broken ones are unnatural combinations of men and animals. Their individual diets and habits are largely dictated by their animal natures. Thus, a broken one who has leonine characteristics would be carnivorous, while one infused with the essence of a horse would be vegetarian. There are no known examples of a broken one who has been formed with the essence of an intelligent nonhuman creature.

Broken ones do manufacture the items they need to survive. These are seldom of exceptional quality, however, and are of little or no interest to outsiders. Occasionally, broken ones may be captured by evil wizards or sages who wish to study them.

Greater Broken Ones

From time to time, some animal men emerge who are physically superior. While they are still horrible to look upon and cannot dwell among men, they are deadly figures with keen minds and powerful bodies. Their twisted and broken souls, however, often lead them to acts of violence against normal men.

These creatures regenerate at twice the rate of their peers (2 hit points per round) and inflict 1d8 points of damage in unarmed combat. When using weapons, they gain a +3 to +5 bonus on all attack and damage rolls. Like their subjects, they often have special abilities based on their animal natures. Such powers, however, are often more numerous (from 1-4 abilities) and may be even better than those of the animal they are drawn from. For example, a greater broken one who is created from scorpion stock might have a chitinous shell that gives it AC 2 *and* it might have a poisonous stinger.

Brownie

	Brownie	Killmoulis
CLIMATE/TERRAIN:	Temperate rural	Human areas
FREQUENCY:	Rare	Uncommon
ORGANIZATION:	Tribal	Solitary
ACTIVITY CYCLE:	Night	Nocturnal
DIET:	Vegetarian	Omnivore, scavenger
INTELLIGENCE:	High (13-14)	Average (8-10)
TREASURE:	O, P, Q	K
ALIGNMENT:	Lawful good	Neutral (chaotic good)
NO. APPEARING:	4-16	1-3
ARMOR CLASS:	3	6
MOVEMENT:	12	15
HIT DICE:	½	½
THAC0:	20	20
NO. OF ATTACKS:	1	Nil
DAMAGE/ATTACK:	1-2 (weapon)	Nil
SPECIAL ATTACKS:	Spells	See below
SPECIAL DEFENSES:	Save as 9th-level cleric	See below
MAGIC RESISTANCE:	Nil	20%
SIZE:	Tiny (2' tall)	Tiny (under 1' tall)
MORALE:	Steady (11-12)	Average (8-10)
XP VALUE:	175	35

Brownies are small, benign humanoids who may be very distantly related to halflings. Peaceful and friendly, brownies live in pastoral regions, foraging and gleaning their food.

Standing no taller than 2 feet, brownies are exceedingly nimble. They resemble small elves with brown hair and bright blue eyes. Their brightly colored garments are made from wool or linen with gold ornamentation. They normally carry leather pouches and tools for repairing leather, wood, and metal.

Brownies speak their own language and those of elves, pixies, sprites, and halflings, as well as common.

Combat: Brownies prefer not to engage in combat, and only do so if threatened. Angry brownies rarely meet their foes in hand to hand combat, relying instead on magic.

Since their senses are so keen, it is impossible to surprise brownies. They are superb at blending into their surroundings and can become all but invisible when they choose. This, combined with their great agility, gives them an AC of 3.

Brownies use spells to harass and drive away enemies. They can use the following spells, once per day: *protection from evil, ventriloquism, dancing lights, continual light, mirror image* (3 images), *confusion,* and *dimension door.* If cornered and unable to employ any spells, brownies attack with short swords.

Habitat/Society: Brownies live in rural areas, making their homes in small burrows or abandoned buildings. They often live close to or on farms, as they are fascinated by farm life.

Brownies live by harvesting wild fruits and gleaning grain from a farmer's field. Being honest to the core, a brownie always performs some service in exchange for what is taken. One might milk a farmer's cows and take only a small amount.

Some brownies go so far as to become house brownies. They observe the families in a given area, and if one meets their high moral standards, these brownies secretly enter the household. At night, while the residents are asleep, they perform a variety of helpful tasks; spinning, baking bread, repairing farm imple-

ments, keeping foxes out of the hen house, mending clothes, and performing other household tasks. If a thief creeps silently into the house, they will make enough noise to awaken the residents. Watchdogs and domestic animals consider brownies friendly and never attack or even bark at them.

All brownies ask in exchange for their labor is a little milk, some bread, and an occasional bit of fruit. Etiquette demands that no notice be taken of them. If the residents boast about the presence of a brownie, the brownie vanishes.

Brownies are not greedy, but they do have small hoards of treasure which they have taken from evil monsters or received as gifts from humans. A brownie sometimes leaves his treasure in a location where a good person in need is bound to find it.

Strangers and outsiders are constantly watched by the brownies of the community until their motives are established. If the brownies decide that a stranger is harmless, he is left in peace. If not, the brownies unite and drive the intruder out.

Brownies know every nook and cranny of the areas where they live, and thus make excellent guides. If asked politely, there is a 50% chance that a brownie will agree to act as a guide.

Ecology: Brownies are basically vegetarians who live very comfortably on the gleanings of agricultural life. They make efficient use of leftovers that are too small for humans to notice. When brownies glean from fields, they do so after harvest, gathering grains and fruits which might otherwise be wasted.

Killmoulis: The killmoulis is a distant relative of the brownie, standing under 1-foot in height but with a disproportionately large head and a prodigious nose. Killmoulis are able to blend into surroundings and are therefore 10% detectable. They live in symbiotic relationships with humans, usually where foodstuffs are handled, making their homes under the floors, and in the walls and crawlspaces.

Bugbear

CLIMATE/TERRAIN:	Any subterranean
FREQUENCY:	Uncommon
ORGANIZATION:	Tribal
ACTIVITY CYCLE:	Any
DIET:	Carnivorous
INTELLIGENCE:	Low to average (5-10)
TREASURE:	Individual: J, K, L, M, (B)
ALIGNMENT:	Chaotic evil

NO. APPEARING:	2-8 (2d4)
ARMOR CLASS:	5 (10)
MOVEMENT:	9
HIT DICE:	3+1
THAC0:	17
NO. OF ATTACKS:	1
DAMAGE/ATTACK:	2-8 (2d4) or by weapon
SPECIAL ATTACKS:	Surprise, +2 to damage
SPECIAL DEFENSES:	Nil
MAGIC RESISTANCE:	Nil
SIZE:	L (7' tall)
MORALE:	Steady to Elite (11-13)
XP VALUE:	120
Bugbear leader:	175
Bugbear chief:	175
Bugbear shaman:	175

Bugbears are giant, hairy cousins of goblins who frequent the same areas as their smaller relatives.

Bugbears are large and very muscular, standing 7' tall. Their hides range from light yellow to yellow brown and their thick coarse hair varies in color from brown to brick red. Though vaguely humanoid in appearance, bugbears seem to contain the blood of some large carnivore. Their eyes recall those of some savage bestial animal, being greenish white with red pupils, while their ears are wedge shaped, rising from the top of their heads. A bugbear's mouth is full of long sharp fangs.

Bugbears have a nose much like that of a bear with the same fine sense of smell. It is this feature which earned them their name, despite the fact that they are not actually related to bears in any way. Their tough leathery hide and long sharp nails also look something like those of a bear, but are far more dexterous.

The typical bugbear's sight and hearing are exceptional, and they can move with amazing agility when the need arises. Bugbear eyesight extends somewhat into the infrared, giving them infravision out to 60 feet.

The bugbear language is a foul sounding mixture of gestures, grunts, and snarls which leads many to underestimate the intelligence of these creatures. In addition, most bugbears can speak the language of goblins and hobgoblins.

Combat: Whenever possible, bugbears prefer to ambush their foes. They impose a -3 on others' surprise rolls.

If a party looks dangerous, bugbear scouts will not hesitate to fetch reinforcements. A bugbear attack will be tactically sound, if not brilliant. They will hurl small weapons, such as maces, hammers, and spears before closing with their foes. If they think they are outnumbered or overmatched, bugbears will retreat, preferring to live to fight another day.

Habitat/Society: Bugbears prefer to live in caves and in underground locations. A lair may consist of one large cavern or a group of caverns. They are well-adapted to this life, since they operate equally well in daylight and darkness.

If a lair is uncovered and 12 or more bugbears are encountered they will have a leader. These individuals have between 22 and 25 hit points, an Armor Class of 4, and attack as 4 Hit Die monsters.

Their great strength gives them a +3 to all damage inflicted in melee combat.

If 24 or more bugbears are encountered, they will have a chief in addition to their leaders. Chiefs have between 28 and 30 hit points, an Armor Class of 3, and attack as 4 Hit Die monsters. Chiefs are so strong that they gain a +4 bonus to all damage caused in melee. Each chief will also have a sub-chief who is identical to the leaders described above.

In a lair, half of the bugbears will be females and young who will not fight except in a life or death situation. If they are forced into combat, the females attack as hobgoblins and the young as kobolds.

The species survives primarily by hunting. They have no compunctions about eating anything they can kill, including humans, goblins, and any monsters smaller than themselves. They are also fond of wine and strong ale, often drinking to excess.

Bugbears are territorial, and the size of the domains vary with the size of the group and its location. It may be several square miles in the wilderness, or a narrow, more restricted area in an underground region.

Intruders are considered a valuable source of food and treasure, and bugbears rarely negotiate. On occasion, they will parley if they think they can gain something exceptional by it. Bugbears sometimes take prisoners to use as slaves.

Extremely greedy, bugbears love glittery, shiny objects and weapons. They are always on the lookout to increase their hoards of coins, gems, and weapons through plunder and ambush.

Ecology: Bugbears have two main goals in life: survival and treasure. They are superb carnivores, winnowing out the weak and careless adventurer, monster and animal. Goblins are always on their toes when bugbears are present, for the weak or stupid quickly end up in the stewpot.

CLIMATE/TERRAIN:	Temperate/Any terrain
FREQUENCY:	Very rare
ORGANIZATION:	Solitary
ACTIVITY CYCLE:	Any
DIET:	Carnivorous
INTELLIGENCE:	Animal (1)
TREASURE:	Nil
ALIGNMENT:	Neutral

NO. APPEARING:	1-2
ARMOR CLASS:	-2/4/6
MOVEMENT:	14 (3)
HIT DICE:	9
THAC0:	11
NO. OF ATTACKS:	3
DAMAGE/ATTACK:	4-48/3-18/3-18
SPECIAL ATTACKS:	8' jump
SPECIAL DEFENSES:	Nil
MAGIC RESISTANCE:	Nil
SIZE:	L 9$\frac{1}{2}$' tall, 12' long
MORALE:	Steady (11)
XP VALUE:	4,000

Aptly called a landshark, the bulette (pronounced Boo-lay) is a terrifying predator that lives only to eat. The bulette is universally shunned, even by other monsters.

It is rumored that the bulette is a cross between an armadillo and a snapping turtle, but this is only conjecture. The bulette's head and hind portions are blue-brown, and they are covered with plates and scales ranging from gray-blue to blue-green. Nails and teeth are dull ivory. The area around the eyes is brown-black, the eyes are yellowish and the pupils are blue green.

Combat: A bulette will attack anything it regards as edible. The only things that it refuses to eat are elves, and it dislikes dwarves. The bulette is always hungry, and is constantly roaming its territory in search of food. When burrowing underground, the landshark relies on vibrations to detect prey. When it senses something edible (i.e., senses movement), the bulette breaks to the surface crest first and begin its attack. The landshark has a temperament akin to the wolverine—stupid, mean, and fearless. The size, strength, and numbers of its opponents mean nothing. The bulette always attacks, choosing as its target the easiest or closest prey. When attacking, the bulette employs its large jaw and front feet.

The landshark can jump up to 8 feet with blinding speed, and does this to escape if cornered or injured. While in the air, the bulette strikes with all four feet, causing 3d6 points of damage for each of the rear feat as well. The landshark has two vulnerable areas: the shell under its crest is only AC 6 (but it is only raised during intense combat), and the region of the bulette's eyes is AC 4, but this is a small oval area about 8 inches across.

Habitat/Society: Fortunately for the rest of the world, the bulette is a solitary animal, although mated pairs (very rare) will share the same territory. In addition, other predators rarely share a territory with a landshark for fear of being eaten. The bulette has no lair, preferring to wander over its territory, above and below ground, burrowing down beneath the soil to rest. Since their appetites are so voracious, each landshark has a large territory that can range up to 30 square miles.

Bulettes consume their victims, clothing, weapons, and all, and the powerful acids in the stomach quickly digest the armor, weapons, and magical items of their victims. They are not above nibbling on chests or sacks of coins either, the bulette motto be-

ing eat first and think later. When everything in the territory is eaten, the bulette will move on in search of a new territory. The sole criteria for a suitable territory is the availability of food, so a bulette will occasionally stake out a new territory near human and halfling territories and terrorize the residents.

Very little is known of the life cycle of the bulette. They presumably hatch from eggs, but no young have ever been found, though small landsharks of 6 Hit Dice have been killed. It may be that the bulette is hatched from very small eggs, with few young surviving to maturity. Still other sages theorize that the bulette bears live young. There is also evidence that the bulette, like carp and sharks, grow larger as they get older, for unusually large landsharks of 11 feet tall and taller have been seen. Certainly no one has ever come upon the carcass of a bulette that died of old age.

Ecology: The bulette has a devastating effect on the ecosystem of any area it inhabits. Literally nothing that moves is safe from it—man, animal, or monster. In the process of hunting and roaming, the landshark will uproot trees of considerable size. In hilly and rocky regions, the underground movements of the bulette can start small landslides. Ogres, trolls, and even some giants all move off in search of greener and safer pastures when a bulette appears. A bulette can turn a peaceful farming community into a wasteland in a few short weeks, for no sane human or demihuman will remain in a region where a bulette has been sighted.

There is only one known benefit to the existence of the bulette: The large plates behind its head make superb shields, and dwarven smiths can fashion them into shields of +1 to +3 in value. Some also claim that the soil through which a bulette has passed becomes imbued with magical, rock-dissolving properties. Many would argue, however, that these benefits are scarcely worth the price.

Bullywug

CLIMATE/TERRAIN:	Tropical, subtropical, and temperate/Swamp
FREQUENCY:	Rare
ORGANIZATION:	Tribal
ACTIVITY CYCLE:	Any
DIET:	Carnivore
INTELLIGENCE:	Low to average (5-10)
TREASURE:	J, K, M, Q, (x5); C in lair
ALIGNMENT:	Chaotic evil

NO. APPEARING:	10-80
ARMOR CLASS:	6 (better with armor)
MOVEMENT:	3 Sw 15 (9 in armor)
HIT DICE:	1
THAC0:	19
NO. OF ATTACKS:	3 or 1
DAMAGE/ATTACK:	1-2/1-2/2-5 or by weapon
SPECIAL ATTACKS:	Hop
SPECIAL DEFENSES:	Camouflage
MAGIC RESISTANCE:	Nil
SIZE:	S to M (4'-7')
MORALE:	Average (10)
XP VALUE:	65

The bullywugs are a race of bipedal, frog-like amphibians. They inhabit swamps, marshes, meres, or other dank places.

Bullywugs are covered with smooth, mottled olive green hide that is reasonably tough, giving them a natural AC of 6. They can vary in size from smaller than the average human to about seven feet in height. Their faces resemble those of enormous frogs, with wide mouths and large, bulbous eyes; their feet and hands are webbed. Though they wear no clothing, all bullywugs use weapons, armor, and shields if they are available. Bullywugs have their own language and the more intelligent ones can speak a limited form of the common tongue.

Combat: Bullywugs always attack in groups, trying to use their numbers to surround their enemies. Whenever they can, bullywugs attack with their hop, which can be up to 30 feet forward and 15 feet upward. When attacking with a hop, bullywugs add a +1 bonus to their attack (not damage) rolls, and double the damage if using an impaling weapon. This skill, combined with their outstanding camouflage abilities, frequently puts the bullywugs in an ideal position for an ambush (-2 penalty to opponent's surprise rolls).

Habitat/Society: More intelligent than frogs, all bullywugs live in organized or semi-organized socially fascist groups, cooperating for the purpose of hunting and survival. They live primarily on fish and any other game, preferring a diet of meat. They are adept hunters and fisherman, and skilled in the use and construction of snares and nets.

Bullywug society is a savage one. Males are the dominant sex, and females exist only to lay eggs. Though females and young make up about one-half of any tribe, they count for little in the social order. The only signs of respect that bullywugs ever bestow are toward their leader and their bizarre frog god. The race is chaotic evil, and totally lacking in any higher emotions or feelings.

The leader of a bullywug community is a large individual with 8 hit points. Communities of 30 or more bullywugs have five subleaders (8 hp each) and a powerful leader (2 HD, 12+ hp, +1 to damage). Communities of 60 or more bullywugs have a chieftain (3 HD, 20+ hp, +2 to damage) and five subchieftains (2 HD, 12+ hp, +1 to damage).

All bullywugs favor dank, dark places to live, since they must keep their skin moist. Most bullywugs live in the open and maintain only loose territorial boundaries. Ordinary bullywugs do not deal with incursions into their territory very efficiently, but they kill and eat interlopers if they can. They hate their large relatives (advanced bullywugs, see below) with a passion, and make war upon them at every opportunity. Bullywugs prize treasure, though it benefits them little. They value coins and jewels, and occasionally a magical item can be found amongst their hoard.

On an individual level, bullywugs lack the greed and powerlust seen in the individuals of other chaotic races, such as orcs. Fighting among members of the same group, for example, is almost nonexistent. Some would say that this is because they lack the intelligence to pick a fight, and not from a lack of spite. The tribes are lead by the dominant male, who kills and eats the previous leader when it is too old to rule. This is one of the few instances when they fight among themselves.

Ecology: Bullywugs tend to disrupt ecosystems, rather than fill a niche in them. They do not have the intelligence to harvest their food supplies sensibly and will fish and hunt in an area until its natural resources are depleted, and then move on to a new territory. They hate men, and will attack them on sight, but fortunately prefer to dwell in isolated regions far from human beings.

Bullywug, Advanced

A small number of bullywugs are larger and more intelligent than the rest of their kind. These bullywugs make their homes in abandoned buildings and caves, and send out regular patrols and hunting parties. These groups tend to be well equipped and organized, and stake out a regular territory, which varies with the size of the group. They are more aggressive than their smaller cousins, and will fight not only other bullywugs but other monsters as well. The intelligent bullywugs also organize regular raids outside their territory for food and booty, and especially prize human flesh. Since they are chaotic evil, all trespassers, including other bullywugs, are considered threats or sources of food.

For every 10 advanced bullywugs in a community, there is a 10% chance of a 2nd-level shaman being present.

Carrion Crawler

CLIMATE/TERRAIN:	Subterranean
FREQUENCY:	Uncommon
ORGANIZATION:	Solitary
ACTIVITY CYCLE:	Any
DIET:	Carnivorous
INTELLIGENCE:	Non- (0)
TREASURE:	B
ALIGNMENT:	Neutral

NO. APPEARING:	1-6
ARMOR CLASS:	3/7
MOVEMENT:	12
HIT DICE:	3 + 1
THAC0:	17
NO. OF ATTACKS:	1 or 8
DAMAGE/ATTACK:	Special or 1-2
SPECIAL ATTACKS:	Paralysis
SPECIAL DEFENSES:	Nil
MAGIC RESISTANCE:	Nil
SIZE:	L (9′ long)
MORALE:	Special
XP VALUE:	420

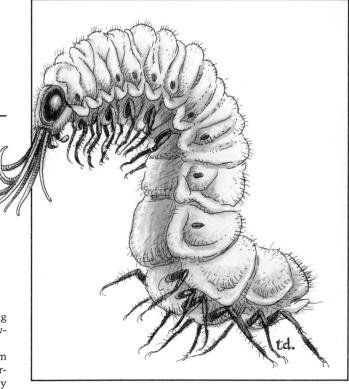

The carrion crawler is a scavenger of subterranean areas, feeding primarily upon carrion. When such food becomes scarce, however, it will attack and kill living creatures.

The crawler looks like a cross between a giant green cutworm and a cephalopod. Like so many other hybrid monsters, the carrion crawler may well be the result of genetic experimentation by a mad, evil wizard.

The monster's head, which is covered with a tough hide that gives it Armor Class 3, sprouts eight slender, writhing tentacles. The body of the carrion crawler is not well protected and has an armor class of only 7. The monster is accompanied by a rank, fetid odor which often gives warning of its approach.

Combat: The carrion crawler can move along walls, ceilings and passages very quickly, using its many clawed feet for traction.

When attacking, the monster lashes out with its 2′ long tentacles, each of which produces a sticky secretion that can paralyze its victims for 2-12 turns. A save versus paralyzation is allowed to escape these effects. They kill paralyzed creatures with their bite which inflicts 1-2 points of damage. The monster will always attack with all of its tentacles.

Carrion crawlers are non-intelligent, and will continue to attack as long as any of their opponents are unparalyzed. Groups of crawlers attacking together will not fight in unison, but will each concentrate on paralyzing as many victims as they can. When seeking out prey, they rely primarily on their keen senses of sight and smell. Clever travelers have been known to fool an approaching carrion crawler with a sight and smell illusion, thus gaining time to make good their escape.

Habitat/Society: Carrion crawlers are much-feared denizens of the underground world. They live in lairs, venturing out in search of carrion or food every few days. Some underground inhabitants such as goblins and trolls will make use of carrion crawlers by leaving the bodies of dead foes out in designated areas. This keeps the creatures at a good distance from their own homes and encourages them to "patrol" certain areas. Some orcs have been known to chain live prisoners near the lairs of these fearsome monsters.

Carrion crawlers will sometimes live with a mate or in a small group numbering no more than 6. This does not mean that they cooperate in hunting, but merely share the same space and compete fiercely for the same food. If 2 crawlers have made a kill or discovered carrion, they will often fight over the food, sometimes killing one another in the process.

The carrion crawler mates once a year. Several days after mating, the female will go off in search of a large kill. When she has found or killed an adequate food supply, she lays about 100 eggs among the carrion. The grubs hatch one week later and begin feeding.

Maternal care ceases once the eggs have been laid and it is not uncommon for eggs to later be eaten by the female who laid them. Females die a few weeks after laying their eggs, exhausted by the effort. Males live only a short time longer, having mated with as many females as possible. Grubs have been known to consume one another in feeding frenzies, and are a favorite food of adult carrion crawlers. Few of the grubs reach maturity, but those who do have eaten voraciously and will achieve their full size in a single year. When they reach maturity, the mating cycle begins again.

These monsters exist on the most basic instinctual level, having no more intelligence than earthworms or most insects. The carrion crawler is driven by two urges: food and reproduction. It has absolutely no interest in the collection of treasure.

Ecology: The carrion crawler provides the same useful, if disagreeable, function that jackals, vultures, and crows perform. Like so many other predators carrion crawlers instinctively prey on the weak, sick, and foolish. In the long run, this has a beneficial effect on the prey, strengthening its gene pool. The carrion crawler also works wonders in over crowded caverns, quickly eliminating population problems among the weaker monsters. Thus, the life cycle of the crawler is inextricably linked to those of its prey—when the prey flourishes so does the crawler.

Cat, Great

	Cheetah	Jaguar	Leopard	Common Lion	Mountain Lion	Spotted Lion	Giant Lynx	Wild Tiger	Smilodon
CLIMATE/TERRAIN:	Warm plains and grass-lands	Tropical jungle	Tropical jungle or forest	Warm plains and grass-lands	Any warm or temperate	Warm plains and desert	Subarctic forest forest	Subarctic to tropical forest	Subarctic to tropical
FREQUENCY:	Uncommon	Uncommon	Uncommon	Uncommon	Uncommon	Rare	Rare	Uncommon	Rare
ORGANIZATION:	Family group	Solitary	Solitary	Pride	Solitary	Pride	Solitary	Solitary	Solitary
ACTIVITY CYCLE:	Day	Any	Any	Day	Dawn or dusk	Day	Night	Night	Night
DIET:	Carnivorous	Carnivorous	Carnivorous	Carnivorous	Carnivorous	Carnivorous	Carnivorous	Carnivorous	Carnivorous
INTELLIGENCE:	Animal (1)	Semi-(2-4)	Semi- (2- 4)	Semi (2-4)	Semi (2-4)	Semi (2-4)	Very (11-12)	Semi (2-4)	Animal (1)
TREASURE:	Nil	Nil	Nil	Nil	Nil	Nil	Nil	Nil	Nil
ALIGNMENT:	Neutral	Neutral	Neutral	Neutral	Neutral	Neutral	Neutral	Neutral	Neutral
NO. APPEARING:	1-4	1-2	1-2	2-12 (2d6)	1- 2	2-8 (2d4)	1-4	1-4	1-2
ARMOR CLASS:	5	6	6	5/6	6	5/6	6	6	6
MOVEMENT:	15, sprint 45	15	15	12	12	12	12	12	12
HIT DICE:	3	4 +1	3+2	5+2	3+1	6+2	2+2	5+5	7+ 2
THAC0:	17	17	17	15	17	15	19	15	11(13)
NO. OF ATTACKS:	3	3	3	3	3	3	3	3	3
DAMAGE/ATTACK:	1-2/1-2/1-8	1-3/1-3/1-8	1- 3/1-3/1-6	1-4/1-4/1-10	1-3/1-3/1-6	1-4/1-4/1-12	1- 2/1-2/1-2	2-5 (1d4 +1)/ 2-5 (1d4 +1)/ 1-10	2-5 (1d4 +1)/ 2-5 (1d4 +1)/ 2-12 (2d6)
SPECIAL ATTACKS	Rear claws 1-2 each	Rear claws 2-5 (1d4 +1) each	Rear claws 1-4 each	Rear claws 2-7 (1d6 +1) each	Rear claws 1-4 each	Rear claws 2-8 (2d4) each	Rear claws 1-3 each	Rear claws 2-8 (2d)	Rear claws 2-8 (2d4)
SPECIAL DEFENSES:	Surprised only on a 1	Surprised only on a 1	Surprised only on a 1	Surprised only on a 1	Surprised only on a 1	Surprised only on a 1	See below	Surprised only on a 1	Surprised only on a 1
MAGIC RESISTANCE:	Nil	Nil	Nil	Nil	Nil	Nil	Nil	Nil	Nil
SIZE:	M (4'-4½' long)	L (5'-6' long)	M (4'-4½' long)	M (4½'-6½' long)	M (4'-5' long)	L (4½'-6½' long)	M (4½' long)	L (6'-9' long)	L (8'-12' long)
MORALE:	Average (8-10)	Average (8-10)	Average (8-10)	Average (8-10)	Average (8-10)	Average (8-10)	Average (8-10)	Average (8-10)	Steady (8-10)
XP VALUE:	175	420	270	650	270	975	175	650	1,400

The great cats are among the most efficient of all predators.

Cheetah

The cheetah is a medium-sized, lightly built cat. Its fur is sand colored and it is covered with dark spots. The cheetah is unique among cats because of its non-retractable claws.

A skilled hunter endowed with natural camouflage, victims of a cheetah attack suffer a -3 on their surprise roll. They are famed for their tremendous bursts of speed, and can run at triple speed (45 feet per round) for three rounds. The cat must rest 3 turns before sprinting again. Cheetahs can spring 10 feet upward or 20 feet forward. If both forepaws hit during an attack the cheetah is able to rake for 1-2 points of damage with each of its rear claws. If defending their young, cheetahs receive a +2 on their attack and damage rolls and will fight to the death.

Cheetahs inhabit warm plains and grasslands, often sharing their range with lions. Their favorite prey are the antelope that inhabit the plains, and they rarely attack men. Cheetahs are territorial, but may live alone, in pairs and in groups. The female raises a litter of 2-4 young alone. The young, who stay with their mother for as long as 2 years, can be completely trained and do-mesticated.

The fortunes of the cheetah rise and fall with those of its prey; when the population of antelope and other game declines, so does that of the cheetah.

Jaguar

The jaguar is a powerful cat with a deep chest and muscular limbs. Its color ranges from light yellow to brownish red, and it is covered with dark spots.

The jaguar will attack anything that it perceives as a threat. It relies on stealth to close with its prey, often pouncing from above. The jaguar can leap 30' to attack. If both of its forepaws

strike it will rake with its two rear claws for 2-5 (1d4 +1) points of damage each.

Cat, Great

The jaguar inhabits jungles, spending a great deal of time in tree tops. It climbs, swims, and stalks superbly. Jaguars are solitary and territorial, meeting only to mate. If found in a lair, there is a 75% chance there will be 1-3 cubs. Cubs do not fight effectively.

Their strength and ferocity make jaguars one of the most feared predators of the jungle.

Leopard

The leopard is a graceful cat with a long body and relatively short legs. Its color varies from buff to tawny, and its spots are rosette shaped.

Leopards prefer to leap on their prey, imposing a -3 on the surprise rolls of their victims. Leopards can spring upward 20 feet or ahead 25 feet. If they strike successfully with both forepaws, they rake with their rear claws for 1-4 points each.

Leopards are solitary, inhabiting warm deserts, forest, plains, and mountains. They hunt both day and night preying on animals up to the size of large antelopes. They swim and climb well, and will often sit in treetops sunning themselves. Leopards will also drag their prey to safety in the treetops to devour in peace. The female bears 1-3 young, and cares for them for up to two years. If found in the lair, there is a 25% chance that there will be cubs there. The young have no effective attack.

A skilled predator, the leopard is often threatened by human incursions. In areas where it is hunted, it is nocturnal.

Lion

Among the largest and most powerful of the great cats, lions have yellow or golden brown fur. The males are distinguished by their flowing manes.

Both male and female lions are fierce fighters. Lions hunt in prides, with females doing most of the actual hunting. Since their senses are so keen, lions can only be surprised on a 1. All lions can leap as far as 30 feet. Males have an Armor Class of 5 in their forequarters and 6 in their hindquarters while females are Armor Class 6 in all areas. If a lion hits with both forepaws, it can rake with its rear claws doing 2-7 points damage each.

Lions prefer warmer climates, thriving in deserts, jungles, grasslands, and swamps. They live and hunt in prides, and are extremely territorial. A pride usually consists of 1-3 males and 1-10 females. Lions frequently kill animals the size of zebras or giraffes. Lionesses will cooperate when hunting, driving their prey into an ambush. They have been known to attack domestic livestock, but will almost never attack men. A lair will contain from 1-10 cubs which are 30%-60% grown. Cubs are unable to fight. Lions are poor climbers and dislike swimming.

Lions flourish only when the supply of game is adequate. Their size and strength have made them a favorite target of human hunters.

Mountain Lion

Not a true lion, this brownish cat is lankier than its large cousins. Except for their size, males and females are difficult to tell apart.

The mountain lion is more cautious and less aggressive than its larger relatives. They can spring upward 15 feet or ahead 20 feet to attack or retreat. If they score hits with both of their forepaws, they will rake with their back ones for 1-4 points of damage each. It will not attack men unless threatened.

Mountain lions range in warm and temperate mountains, forests, swamps, and plains. They are solitary, with males and females each maintaining separate territories. Their favorite prey are deer. The female rears 2-4 cubs alone, which remain with her for 1-2 years.

The mountain lion is flexible and elusive. It is adept at surviving on the fringes of human civilization.

Spotted Lion

Spotted lions are large, fierce, dappled versions of the lion. They are generally found in the plains of the Pleistocene epoch, and rarely occur elsewhere.

Giant Lynx

The giant lynx is distinguished by its tufted ears and cheeks, short bobbed tail, and dappled coloring. It has a compact muscular body, with heavy legs and unusually large paws.

The giant lynx is the most intelligent of the great cats and uses its wits in combat. When hiding, a giant lynx will avoid detection 90% of the time. The lynx can leap up to 15 feet and imposes a -6 on the surprise rolls of its prey. It has a 75% chance of detecting traps. If a giant lynx strikes with both forepaws, it attempts a rear claw rake, causing 1-3 points of damage per claw. The giant lynx almost never attacks men.

The giant lynx prefers cold coniferous and scrub forests. They can communicate in their own language with others of its kind, which greatly increases its chances of survival. The nocturnal lynx stalks or ambushes its prey, catching rodents, young deer, grouse, and other small game. The cubs remain with their mother for 6 months.

The giant lynx has all the advantages of the great cats plus the added bonus of a high intelligence which makes it even more adaptable.

Tiger

The tiger is the largest and most feared of the great cats. Tigers have reddish-orange fur and dark vertical stripes.

A tiger is a redoubtable foe in battle and is surprised only on a 1. They are experts in stalking and often hunt in pairs or groups. They can leap 10 feet upward, and spring forward 30 feet to 50 feet to attack. If they strike successfully with both forepaws, their rear claws rake for 2-8 (2d4) points of damage per claw.

This species ranges from the subarctic to the tropics, generally inhabiting wooded or covered terrain. Tigers are nocturnal, solitary, graceful climbers and swimmers who are capable of sustained high speed. These animals rarely fight among themselves, but will protect their territories ferociously. They are also the most unpredictable and dangerous of the great cats, not hesitating to attack men. Their favorite prey includes cattle, wild pigs and deer. Females raise their 1-3 cubs alone. The cubs remain with their mother for several years. If encountered in the lair, there is a 25% chance that the cubs will be present.

Feared by men, tigers are hunted aggressively, and are threatened by the destruction of forests. In the untamed wilderness, however, the tiger occupies the top predatory niche.

Smilodon

Although not truly a member of the cat family, the so-called sabre-toothed tiger is similar to them in many ways. Smilodons are known for their 6 inches long fangs which are capable of inflicting terrible wounds. Their powerful jaws and large teeth give them a +2 on their attack rolls. They are similar to normal tigers but are found only during the Pleistocene epoch.

Cat, Small

	Domestic	Wild	Elven
CLIMATE/TERRAIN:	Any inhabited	Any non-arctic	Temperate forest
FREQUENCY:	Common	Uncommon	Rare
ORGANIZATION:	Solitary	Solitary	Solitary
ACTIVITY CYCLE:	Any	Any	Any
DIET:	Carnivore	Carnivore	Carnivore
INTELLIGENCE:	Animal (1)	Animal (1)	Semi- to low (2-7)
TREASURE:	Nil	Nil	Nil
ALIGNMENT:	Neutral	Neutral	Neutral
NO. APPEARING:	1 (1-12)	1 (2-5)	1
ARMOR CLASS:	6	5	4
MOVEMENT:	9	18	18
HIT DICE:	$1/2$	1	3+6
THAC0:	20	19	17
NO. OF ATTACKS:	3	3	3
DAMAGE/ATTACK:	1-2/1 (claws/bite)	1-2/1-2/1-2	1-2/1-2/1-3
SPECIAL ATTACKS:	Rear claw rake, 1-2	Rear claw rake, 1-2/1-2	See below
SPECIAL DEFENSES:	See below	See below	See below
MAGIC RESISTANCE:	Nil	Nil	20%
SIZE:	T (1' tall)	T (1'-2' tall)	T (1' tall)
MORALE:	Average (8-10)	Average (8-10)	Elite (13-14)
XP VALUE:	7	35	650

Cats of different sizes and colorations are common throughout the world. Some are pets, while many are wild.

Combat: Cats are efficient hunters, moving with grace and stealth; opponents suffer a −3 penalty on surprise rolls. A cat's excellent senses and agility allows it to be surprised only on a 1 or 2. Its senses also allow it to hunt efficiently at night.

Cats attack with their claws and teeth; if they hit with front claws, they rake with rear claws. A domestic cat's claws and rake each count as only one attack, rather than one per claw.

Cats have retractable claws which can be extended for climbing or drawn in for speed. They are agile climbers and can scale or move in trees at half normal movement rate. They can leap great distances to avoid obstacles or spring onto prey.

Habitat/Society: Cats are common in settled regions. Many cultures keep them as pets, and they can be found in the homes of nobles and peasants alike. Some societies worship cats as divine beings, while other nations fear and hate them as the minions of evil.

Ecology: Cats are commonly used to control rodent populations, though some hunters use them to recover downed birds and other small prey.

Domestic Cat

There are many breeds of domestic cat, all of which share basic characteristics, differing only in outward appearance. An average adult cat weighs eight to ten pounds, though some pampered specimens can weigh as much as 25 pounds.

Cats seldom attack creatures larger than themselves, though they will defend themselves. They often chase and kill mice, birds, rats, and other small creatures. A domestic cat is capable of a burst of speed, boosting its movement rate to 18 for a round and maintaining such speed for 1d10 rounds.

A well-treated cat will live for 15 years or more. The cat's gestation period is about two months, with 1d4+1 kittens in each litter. Kittens are weaned when about eight weeks old. Mother cats will fight to the death to defend kittens.

Wild Cat

Wild cats are very similar to domestic cats, and some were pets that went feral. Generally, wild cats are tougher, stronger, and more capable hunters than domestic cats.

Elven Cat

Cats kept by elves have evolved into magical creatures, possibly aided by arcane means. They are very intelligent and have their own language, and many can speak a crude form of the elven tongue. Some live with gnomes, brownies, or woodland creatures, and also speak a basic form of their keepers' language. Most have gray-brown fur with dark stripes.

Elven cats are very stealthy, imposing a −5 penalty to opponents' surprise rolls. They are surprised only on a 1. Elven cats have a 99.9% chance to move silently, and a 90% chance to hide in wilderness areas. They are excellent climbers, can leap 20 feet with ease, and enjoy swimming and playing in water.

Elven cats have magical abilities that they use to avoid enemies. They have limited *ESP* which is used to determine intent. They can use *enlarge* and *trip* once per day, and *reduce* and *tree* twice per day; for magical abilities, elven cats are treated as 9th-level spellcasters. *Enlarge* doubles an elven cat's Hit Dice and damage; *tree* allows it to assume the form of a tree's limb.

Catoblepas

CLIMATE/TERRAIN:	Any swamp
FREQUENCY:	Very rare
ORGANIZATION:	Solitary
ACTIVITY CYCLE:	Day
DIET:	Omnivore
INTELLIGENCE:	Semi (2-4)
TREASURE:	(C)
ALIGNMENT:	Neutral

NO. APPEARING:	1-2
ARMOR CLASS:	7
MOVEMENT:	6
HIT DICE:	6+2
THAC0:	15
NO. OF ATTACKS:	1
DAMAGE/ATTACK:	1-6+stun
SPECIAL ATTACKS:	Gaze causes death
SPECIAL DEFENSES:	Nil
MAGIC RESISTANCE:	Nil
SIZE:	L (6' tall at shoulder)
MORALE:	Steady (11-12)
XP VALUE:	975

The catoblepas is a bizarre, loathsome creature that inhabits dismal swamps and marshes. Its most terrifying features are its large bloodshot eyes, from which emanate a deadly ray.

The body of the catoblepas is like that of a large, bloated buffalo, and its legs are stumpy, like those of a pygmy elephant or a hippopotamus. Its long, snakey tail is swift and strong, and can move with blinding speed. The head of the catoblepas is perched upon a long, weak neck, and would be much like that of a warthog except that the catoblepas is uglier.

Combat: In combat, the catoblepas relies on two forms of attack.

First, it will use its strong, snaky tail to strike and stun its foes. Anyone struck by the tail suffers 1-6 points of damage and has a base 75% chance of being stunned for 1-10 melee rounds. The base chance of being stunned is lowered by 5% for every level above first, or for each additional Hit Die in the case of monsters and animals.

Despite the danger of a tail strike, the catoblepas' second mode of attack is by far the more fearsome of the two. The gaze of the catoblepas emanates a *deathray*, with a 60 yard range. Any creature meeting its gaze dies without a saving throw. If a party is surprised by a catoblepas, there is a 1 in 6 chance that someone in the group has met the creature's gaze. Those who close their eyes or act with their eyes averted can still be affected by the *deathray*, but a saving throw vs. death magic is allowed.

Since the neck of the creature is very weak, it has only a 25% chance of raising its head and using the *deathray* on subsequent rounds. If the catoblepas and its target are both relatively still, this increases by 15% per melee round. If the catoblepas is forced to follow quick motions it has only a 10% chance of raising its head.

If more than one catoblepas is attacking, the monsters will cooperate with one another, attempting to herd their targets into a crossfire.

Habitat/Society: For the most part, the catoblepas is a meandering creature that wanders about its swamp nibbling on marsh grasses and the like. Once a month, usually under the light of the full moon, the catoblepas seeks out meat to round out its diet. It is at this time that the catoblepas is most likely to be encountered by adventurers.

The lair of the catoblepas is usually some sort of sheltered place where the ground is firm. More often than not it is surrounded by a tall stand of reeds or other marsh plants. The creature has little fear of being disturbed in its lair, since it is frequently the most feared carnivore in the swamp.

The catoblepas mates for life and when more than one catoblepas is encountered they will be a mated pair. There is a 10% chance that the couple will have a single offspring with them. An immature catoblepas will have half the Hit Dice of an adult. It takes almost nine years for the offspring to reach youthful maturity and an adult female will bear but one child every 10 or 12 years. Both the male and the female will cooperate in raising the offspring.

When the catoblepas ventures forth to hunt it eats fish, marsh birds, eels, water rats, large amphibians, snakes, and other swamp animals. The catoblepas usually stuns its prey with its tail and then kills it with its gaze.

The catoblepas is an opportunistic predator when it hunts and it is not above eating carrion. Since it is semi-intelligent, it will treat parties of humans with respect, preferring to size them up first. As a rule, it will not attack unless it is hunting or feels that its mate or offspring is threatened. Being long-lived (150 to 200 years or so) and semi-intelligent, the catoblepas is capable of learning from the mistakes of earlier encounters and hunts.

The catoblepas has no special interest in wealth, and the listed treasure type is the result of victorious encounters with intruders. It attaches no value to the coins, gems, and occasional magical items strewn about the lair.

Ecology: The catoblepas has no natural enemies, since its gaze provides it with more than adequate protection from even the fiercest of predators.

Cave Fisher

CLIMATE/TERRAIN:	Subterranean
FREQUENCY:	Rare
ORGANIZATION:	Group
ACTIVITY CYCLE:	Night
DIET:	Carnivorous
INTELLIGENCE:	Semi- (2-4)
TREASURE:	Any
ALIGNMENT:	Neutral

NO. APPEARING:	1-4
ARMOR CLASS:	4
MOVEMENT:	1
HIT DICE:	3
THAC0:	17 or 15 (see below)
NO. OF ATTACKS:	2
DAMAGE/ATTACK:	2-8 (2d4)/2-8 (2d4)
SPECIAL ATTACKS:	Adhesive trapline
SPECIAL DEFENSES:	See below
MAGIC RESISTANCE:	Nil
SIZE:	M (7' long)
MORALE:	Steady (11-12)
XP VALUE:	175

The cave fisher is a large insectoid that has adapted to life below ground. It combines many of the characteristics of a spider and a lobster.

The cave fisher has a hard, chitinous shell of overlapping plates and eight legs. The 6 rear legs are used for movement and traction on stony walls and corridors. Because of these limbs, the fisher has no difficulty in moving up and down vertical walls. The front pair of legs are equipped with powerful pincers, which are used for killing and dismembering prey. The most unusual feature of the cave fisher is its long snout, which can fire a strong, adhesive filament. The monster can also use its adhesive to anchor itself in place on walls and ledges.

Combat: The cave fisher has two ways of hunting. Its preferred method is to string its long filament in the vicinity of its lair. The filaments are thin and strong, making them exceedingly difficult to detect or cut. There is only a 20% chance of noticing the strand at 10', and no chance at all of seeing them at a greater distance. A *detect snares and pits* spell will reveal a strand. The filament is coated with an adhesive which can only be dissolved by liquids with a high alcohol content (such as the cave fisher's blood). The filaments can only be cut by +1 or better edged weapons.

The fisher's favorite food are small, flying creatures like bats. Ever opportunistic, they are constantly trying to vary their diet by trapping a careless adventurer, foolish goblin, or orc (provided that they think that they can get away with it). If more than one fisher inhabits a lair, they will frequently pool their resources to catch larger prey. Once the victim is trapped in the filament, the cave fisher draws its prey in, reeling its filament in like a fishing line.

Should a tempting target escape the monster's neatly laid traps, the cave fisher will try another mode of attack. It will spend one round drawing its filament in and then shoot it at the prey, striking as a 6 Hit Die monster. It will try to snare its prey in this manner so long as it remains within the fisher's established territory. If the prey is hit by the filament, the monster can pull a weight of up to 400 pounds at a movement rate of 15' per round. In the event that a "tug of war" breaks out, the fisher has a strength of 18/00 with its strand.

Habitat/Society: Cave fishers prefer living on ledges and caves located above well-traveled paths, sharing their lairs with others of their kind. No more than four cave fishers will be found in one lair. Their filaments are always strung before their lair, and they attempt to kill anything they trap, often storing food for future use.

Their territories are very small, and never larger than about 300 feet to either side of the lair. Anything man-sized or smaller is considered fair game by the cave fisher and halflings are thought to be tasty treats. A single cave fisher would never attack a large, well armed party for the sake of a single meal. Still, they are cunning, and a group of the monsters might reel in their filaments and attempt an ambush if they thought they could get away with it. If hunting in one area becomes scarce, the cave fisher will simply find a new area to hunt, where the small game is more plentiful and careless.

Like all predators, the cave fisher is interested in survival. This means a steady supply of food and a mate. Females lay eggs in the vicinity of the lair, which they protect from predators. The young scatter when the eggs hatch, seeking lairs of their own.

Although the cave fisher does not collect treasure, its lair is often strewn with the possessions of its former victims.

Ecology: The cave fisher preys primarily on small flying game, and in the subterranean world this frequently means a diet of bats. It is not the top predator in its ecological niche, and has learned caution in dealing with other monsters. The cave fisher is sufficiently intelligent to know the dangers of preying on large, well-organized groups, who might grow tired of its depredations and hunt it to extinction. The monster instinctively picks the easiest route for survival, and relies on stealth and cunning to trap its prey and avoid being eaten itself.

The filaments of the cave fisher are highly prized by many thieves' guilds, for they can be made into thin and very strong rope which is nearly invisible. The filaments are wound onto reels and then specially treated to dilute the adhesive. The resulting strands are made into ropes, while the diluted adhesive is turned into a special solution, which when applied to gloves and boots, greatly increases traction for climbing.

Centaur

CLIMATE/TERRAIN:	Temperate forest
FREQUENCY:	Rare
ORGANIZATION:	Tribal
ACTIVITY CYCLE:	Day
DIET:	Omnivorous
INTELLIGENCE:	Low to average (5-10)
TREASURE:	M, Q (D, I, T)
ALIGNMENT:	Neutral or chaotic good

NO. APPEARING:	1-8
ARMOR CLASS:	5 (4)
MOVEMENT:	18
HIT DICE:	4
THAC0:	17
NO. OF ATTACKS:	3
DAMAGE/ATTACK:	1-6/1-6 and weapon
SPECIAL ATTACKS:	Nil
SPECIAL DEFENSES:	Nil
MAGIC RESISTANCE:	Nil
SIZE:	L(8'-9' tall)
MORALE:	Elite (13-14)
XP VALUE:	175
Centaur leader	270
Centaur priest	420

Centaurs are woodland beings who shun the company of men. They dwell in remote, secluded glades and pastures.

The appearance of a centaur is unmistakable: they have the upper torso, arms, and head of a human being and the lower body of a large, powerful horse.

Centaurs speak their own language and some among them (about 10%) can converse in the tongue of elves.

Combat: A band of centaurs is always armed, and the leaders carry shields. Half of the centaurs will be wielding oaken clubs (the equivalent of morning stars), one quarter will carry composite bows and have 10-30 arrows (either flight or sheaf, depending on the current state of affairs in the area). The remainder of the band will be leaders (AC4; HD5) using medium shields and medium horse lances. Centaurs make 3 attacks each round in melee: once with their weapons and twice with their hooves.

Habitat/Society: Centaurs are sociable creatures, taking great pleasure in the society of others of their kind. Their overall organization is tribal, with a tribe divided into family groups living together in harmony. The size of the tribe varies, it range from 3-4 families to upwards of 20 families. Since males have the dangerous roles of hunter and protector, females outnumber males by two to one. The centaur mates for life, and the entire tribe participates in the education of the young.

The lair is located deep within a forest, and consists of a large, hidden glade and pasture with a good supply of running water. Depending upon the climate, the lair may contain huts or lean-tos to shelter the individual families. Centaurs are skilled in horticulture, and have been known to cultivate useful plants in the vicinity of their lair. In dangerous, monster infested areas, centaurs will sometimes plant a thick barrier of tough thorn bushes around their lair and even set traps and snares. In the open area, away from the trees, are hearths for cooking and warmth. If encountered in their lair, there will be 1-6 additional males, females equal to twice the number of males, and 5-30 young. The females (3 Hit Dice) and the young (1-3 Hit Dice) will fight only with their hooves, and only in a life or death situation.

Each tribe will have a priest who is treated as a leader but has the spell abilities of a 3rd level druid.

Centaurs survive through a mixture of hunting, foraging, fishing, agriculture and trade. Though they shun dealings with humans, centaurs have been known to trade with elves, especially for food and wine. The elves are paid from the group treasury, which comes from the booty of slain monsters.

The territory of a centaur tribe varies with its size and the nature of the area it inhabits. Centaurs are also not above sharing a territory with elves. The attitude of a centaur toward a stranger in its territory will vary with the visitor. Humans and dwarves will usually be asked to leave in a polite manner, while halflings or gnomes will be tolerated, and elves will be welcomed. Monsters will be dealt with in a manner according to the threat they represent to the welfare and survival of the tribe. Were a giant or dragon to enter the territory, the centaurs would pull up stakes and relocate, while trolls and orcs and their like will be killed.

Centaurs will take the treasure of their fallen foes, and are fully aware of its value. Most male centaurs have a small coin supply, while the tribe has a treasury which may well include some magical items. Leaders will have twice the normal individual treasure. This treasure is used to buy food for the group, or to ransom (90% likely) captured or threatened members of the tribe.

While basically neutral or chaotic good, centaurs have been known to become rowdy, boorish, and aggressive when under the influence of alcohol. They are also extremely protective of their females and young. Centaurs are basically pastoral, but will react with violence if their lifestyle and survival is threatened.

Ecology: The centaur lives in close harmony with nature and spends its lifetime carefully conserving the natural resources around its lair. The race seems to have an innate knowledge of how to achieve this precious balance. If forced to chop down a tree, a centaur will plant another to replace it. Centaurs never over hunt or over fish an area as a human group might do, but choose their game with care, limiting the amount they eat.

Centipede

	Giant	Huge	Megalo-	Tunnel
CLIMATE/TERRAIN:	Any	Any	Any	Subterranean
FREQUENCY:	Common	Common	Very Rare	Rare
ORGANIZATION:	Nil	Nil	Nil	Swarm
ACTIVITY CYCLE:	Any	Any	Any	Any
DIET:	Carnivore	Carnivore	Carnivore	Carnivore
INTELLIGENCE:	Non- (0)	Non- (0)	Animal (1)	Non- (0)
TREASURE:	Nil	Nil	Nil	(M, N, Q)
ALIGNMENT:	Neutral	Neutral	Neutral	Neutral
NO. APPEARING:	2-24	5-30	1-4	1-6
ARMOR CLASS:	9	9	5	4
MOVEMENT:	15	21	18	6
HIT DICE:	2 hp	1 hp	3	9+3
THAC0:	20	20	17	11
NO. OF ATTACKS:	1	1	1	1
DAMAGE/ATTACK:	Nil	Nil	1-3	2-8
SPECIAL ATTACKS:	Poison	Poison	Poison	Lunging
SPECIAL DEFENSES:	Nil	Nil	Nil	Nil
MAGIC RESISTANCE:	Nil	Nil	Nil	Nil
SIZE:	Tiny (1')	Tiny (6")	M (5')	G (25'+)
MORALE:	Unsteady (5-7)	Unsteady (5-7)	Average (8-10)	Steady (12)
XP VALUE:	35	35	175	1,400

Giant centipedes are loathsome, crawling arthropods that arouse almost universal disgust from all intelligent creatures (even other monsters). They are endemic to most regions.

One of the things that makes the centipede so repulsive is its resemblance to the worm. Its long body is divided into many segments from which protrude many tiny feet. Hence the name "centipede" (or hundred-footed). The giant centipede is so named because it is over 1-foot long. The body is plated with a chitinous shell and it moves with a slight undulating motion. The creature has the added benefit of protective coloration, and varies in color depending on the terrain it inhabits. Those that favor rocky areas are gray, those that live underground are black, while centipedes of the forest are brown or red.

Combat: When hunting, centipedes use their natural coloration to remain unseen until they can drop on their prey from above or crawl out of hiding in pursuit of food. They attack by biting their foes and injecting a paralytic poison. The poison can paralyze a victim for 2d6 hours, but is so weak that victims are permitted a +4 bonus to their saving throw. Due to its small size, the giant centipede is less likely to resist attacks and receives a −1 penalty to all its saving throws. Although a single giant centipede rarely constitutes a serious threat to a man, these creatures frequently travel in groups. When more than one centipede is encountered, the monsters will fight independently, even to the point of fighting among themselves over fallen victims.

Habitat/Society: The centipede behaves like most other insects, roving from place to place in search of food; it has no set territory or dwelling. The centipede simply goes where its hunger leads it. It is an aggressive and hungry carnivore that must eat at least once a day to survive. Hungry centipedes often resort to cannibalism.

Ecology: Giant centipedes have several natural advantages, including poison and protective coloration, allowing them to compete with other small predators for game. Their poison bestows a certain immunity from being hunted, but hungry and skilled animals such as coyotes and large predatory birds hunt them effectively in lean times.

Their preferred targets are small mammals that are easily overcome by their weak poison. If they are very hungry, however, they have been known to attack anything that moves, including humans.

Huge Centipedes

These are identical to giant centipedes save that they are only 6 inches long. Their poison is weaker than that of their larger cousins and a failed saving throw will immobilize the victim for only 1d6 hours. Huge centipedes make their own saving throws at −2. Mice and other large insects are the favorite prey of huge centipedes. They in turn are hunted by giant centipedes.

Megalo-centipede

The megalo-centipede, because of its great size, is no longer classed as an irritant but is a threat to human and animal alike. Its acidic poison is far more potent than that of its weaker cousins. The victims of a megalo-centipede bite receive no bonuses on their saving throws and failure indicates death. If the target successfully resists the poison, the acid burns the victim's skin, inflicting 2d4 points of damage.

The megalo-centipede is more intelligent than its smaller cousins and it is a far more cunning hunter, although they still do not cooperate with each other. In the wilderness the megalo-centipede prey on animals the size of deer. In the subterranean environment, it attacks man-sized or smaller creatures, including orcs, goblins, or humans. The megalo-centipede receives no penalties to its own saving throws.

Tunnel Worm

This cousin of the giant centipede feeds upon and lays its eggs in carrion. A tunnel worm attacks by lunging out of its hidden burrow to strike with a +2 bonus to the attack roll. Success indicates the tunnel worm has seized its prey in its mandibles, but no damage is inflicted until the worm chews through the victim's armor. It takes one round for the worm to chew through leather or worse, two rounds for armor tougher than leather but no tougher than chain mail, and three rounds for armor tougher than chain mail. Once the armor is breached, the worm automatically inflicts 2d8 points of damage each round. If the worm suffers 15 or more points of fire damage or loses 60% of its hit points, it drops its victim and retreats to its lair. Tunnel worm lairs often have treasure from earlier victims.

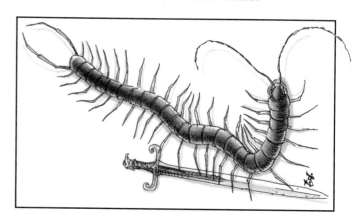

Chimera

	Chimera	Gorgimera
CLIMATE/TERRAIN:	Any temperate to tropical	Any temperate to tropical
FREQUENCY:	Rare	Very rare
ORGANIZATION:	Solitary or pride	Solitary
ACTIVITY CYCLE:	Any	Any
DIET:	Omnivore	Omnivore
INTELLIGENCE:	Semi- (2-4)	Semi- (2-4)
TREASURE:	F	F
ALIGNMENT:	Chaotic evil	Neutral
NO. APPEARING:	1-4	1
ARMOR CLASS:	6/5/2	5/2
MOVEMENT:	9, Fl 18 (E)	12, Fl 15 (E)
HIT DICE:	9	10
THAC0:	11	11
NO. OF ATTACKS:	6	5
DAMAGE/ATTACK:	1-3/1-3/1-4/1-4/ 2-8 (2d4)/ 3-12 (3d4)	1-3/1-3/2-8 (2d4) /2-12 (2d6)/ 3-12 (3d4)
SPECIAL ATTACKS:	Breath weapon	Breath weapons
SPECIAL DEFENSES:	Nil	Nil
MAGIC RESISTANCE:	Nil	Nil
SIZE:	L (5' tall at the shoulder)	L (5' tall at the shoulder)
MORALE:	Elite (13-14)	Elite (13-14)
XP VALUE:	5000	6000

How chimerae were created is a dark mystery better left unexplored. The chimera has the hindquarters of a large, black goat and the forequarters of a huge, tawny lion. Its body has brownish-black wings like those of a dragon.

The monster has three heads, those of a goat, a lion, and a fierce dragon. The goat head is pitch black, with glowing amber eyes and long ochre horns. The lion head is framed by a brown mane and has green eyes. The dragon head is covered with orange scales and has black eyes.

The chimera speaks a limited form of the foul language of red dragons. As a rule, however, it will only pause to communicate with those creatures who are more powerful than itself.

Combat: Its many heads and powerful physique make the chimera a deadly foe in combat. The monster prefers to surprise its victims, often swooping down upon them from the sky. It can attack 6 times each round, clawing with its forelegs, goring with its two horns, and biting with its lion and dragon heads. If it desires to do so, the dragon head can loose a stream of flame some 5 yards long in lieu of biting. The dragon's fire causes 3-24 (3d8) points damage, although a saving throw vs. breath weapon will cut the damage in half. The chimera will always attempt to breathe if its opponents are in range. If more than 1 chimera is encountered, they will attack in concert.

The armor classes are split as follows: Dragon, AC 2 (flank); Lion, AC 5 (front); Goat, AC 6 (rear).

Habitat/Society: The chimera, being a hybrid, combines the preferences of the lion, the goat, and the dragon in its habitat, society and ecology. The dragonish part of its nature gives the chimera a distinct preference for caves as lairs. The dragon and lion parts seem to war with one another, for some chimerae are dragon-like in their preference for solitude, while others live in small prides. Even if they mate, offspring are rare.

The monster is an omnivore. The goat head will browse on the toughest plants and shrubs and will derive nutrition from the most barren vegetation while the lion and dragon heads can only be satisfied with flesh. The chimera hunts once every 3 or 4 days, using its strength and limited intelligence to gain an advantage

over those it preys on. Having a voracious appetite, it sometimes roams over territories as large as 20 square miles.

Being chaotic evil in nature, the chimera enjoys preying upon men, elves, dwarves, and halflings. It will even gladly attack other monsters in its search for food. Anyone entering its territory becomes prey, and will be treated accordingly.

The chimera cannot resist attacking groups of travelers or monsters for another reason: its dragon nature craves the treasure that its prey might be carrying. Although it has no earthly use for it, the chimera will gather the coins of its fallen foe into a heap and roost on it like a dragon. Its hoard is nothing like that of a true dragon, however, and consists mainly of copper and silver coins, with perhaps some jewelry and a few magical items.

Ecology: The chimera fills the role of both omnivore and a top predator in its ecosystem. It is very adaptable. During times when its prey is scarce or non-existent, the chimera can make do with a vegetarian diet.

The Gorgimera

The gorgimera has the hindquarters of a gorgon, forequarters of a lion, and body and wings of a red dragon. Like the chimera, it has the heads of its three constituent creatures.

The monster can attack with its claws, bite with its lion and dragon heads, and butt with its gorgon head. In place of making its normal attack, the gorgon and dragon heads can employ their breath weapons. While the dragon's attack is similar to that of the chimera, the gorgon's breath causes petrification to any caught in its area of effect. The gorgon head can use its breath weapon twice per day to strike in a cone 3 feet long which is 1 foot wide at its base and 3 feet wide at its mouth. The gorgimera will always use one of its breath weapons if its foes are within 10 feet. A save vs. petrification will allow a victim to avoid the effects of the gorgon's breath.

The gorgon's head can see into both the Astral and Ethereal planes, and its breath weapon extends therein.

Like its relative the chimera, the gorgimera can also speak a limited form of the language of red dragons.

Cloaker

CLIMATE/TERRAIN:	Any subterranean
FREQUENCY:	Very rare
ORGANIZATION:	Solitary
ACTIVITY CYCLE:	Night
DIET:	Carnivore
INTELLIGENCE:	High (13-14)
TREASURE:	C
ALIGNMENT:	Chaotic neutral

NO. APPEARING:	1-4
ARMOR CLASS:	3 (1)
MOVEMENT:	1, Fl 15 (D)
HIT DICE:	6
THAC0:	15
NO. OF ATTACKS:	2 + special
DAMAGE/ATTACK:	1-6/1-6/ + special
SPECIAL ATTACKS:	See below
SPECIAL DEFENSES:	See below
MAGIC RESISTANCE:	Nil
SIZE:	L (8' long)
MORALE:	Elite (13-14)
XP VALUE:	1,400

Cloakers are fiendish horrors, related to trappers, that dwell in dark places far beneath the surface of the earth. They generally seek to kill those who enter their lairs, unless they can think up some other, more amusing way to punish interlopers.

When a cloaker is first seen, it is almost impossible to distinguish this monster from a common black cloak. The monster's back has two rows of black eye spots running down it that look much like buttons, and the two ivory-colored claws on its upper edge can easily be mistaken for bone clasps.

When it unfurls itself and moves to attack, however, its true nature becomes all too obvious. At this point, its white underside is clear and the monster's face is fully visible. This face, with the glow of its two piercing, red eyes and the needle-like fangs that line its mouth, is a truly horrible sight. At this point, the monster also uncurls the whip-like tail at its trailing edge and begins to swish it back and forth in anticipation.

Combat: When a cloaker strikes at its victim, it moves with blinding speed. Without warning, the cloaker flies at its target and, if the attack roll is successful, engulfs its prey within its folds. Any creature that falls victim to this attack is all but helpless and can be bitten easily (no roll required) for 1d4 points of damage plus the victim's unadjusted Armor Class. Thus, an adventurer in chain mail (AC 5) suffers 1d4 + 5 points of damage each round. Shields offer no protection from such attacks.

While it is devouring its chosen victim, the cloaker uses its two whip-like tail attacks to inflict 1d6 points of damage on those who move in to help rescue the captive. The tail is AC 1 and can be cut off if a total of 16 points of damage are inflicted upon it.

Any attacks made on the cloaker inflict half their damage to the cloaker and the other half to the trapped victim. Area effect spells, such as *fireball*, cause full damage to both the monster and its victim.

The cloaker can also emit a special subsonic moan of increasing intensities. Although this power is blocked by stone or other dense materials, it can be very effective in an open chamber. Cloakers may not moan and bite during the same round. A cloaker may emit one of four types of moan each round.

The first intensity of moaning causes unease and numbs the minds of those within 80 feet of the cloaker. The immediate effect of this moan is to cause a −2 penalty to the victims' attack and damage rolls against the cloaker. Further, any creature that is forced to listen to the moan for six consecutive rounds is tempo-

rarily forced into a trance that renders it unable to attack or defend itself as long as the moaning continues.

The second intensity of moaning acts as a *fear* spell. All creatures within 30 feet of the cloaker must roll a successful saving throw vs. spell or flee in terror for two rounds.

The third intensity of moaning causes nausea and weakness and affects all those in a cone 30 feet long and 20 feet wide at its open end. Anyone caught in this area must roll a successful saving throw vs. poison or be overcome by nausea and weakness for 1d4 + 1 rounds. During this time, those who fail their saving throws are unable to act in any manner.

The fourth and final intensity of moaning acts as a *hold person* spell. This power can be used on only one person at a time, has a range of 30 feet, and lasts for five rounds.

Each of the various effects of the cloaker's moan can be defeated by the use of a *neutralize poison* spell on a victim.

Cloakers also have the power to manipulate shadows. Known as shadow shifting, this power can be used in a number of ways, but in only one particular manner at any given time. The cloaker can employ its shadow shifting ability to obscure its opponents' vision, thus bettering its Armor Class to 1. Or the creature can produce precise images from the shadows that can be used to trick its adversaries. One common means of employing these images is to create a duplicate of the cloaker to draw away enemy attacks. If this method of shadow shifting is employed, it can be treated as a *mirror image* spell that creates 1d4 + 2 images.

A *light* spell cast directly at a specific cloaker blinds it and prevents it from using its shadow shifting powers.

Habitat/Society: The thought processes of cloakers are utterly alien to most other life forms. As such, they can only be communicated with by mages who have devoted long hours to training their minds in the arcane discipline necessary to understand these creatures.

Ecology: It is believed that cloakers are asexual, although no definitive proof of this has ever been found.

Cockatrice

	Cockatrice	Pyrolisk
CLIMATE/TERRAIN:	Temperate to tropical, any terrain	Temperate to tropical, any terrain
FREQUENCY:	Uncommon	Rare
ORGANIZATION:	Flock	Flock
ACTIVITY CYCLE:	Any	Any
DIET:	Omnivorous	Omnivorous
INTELLIGENCE:	Animal (1)	Low (5)
TREASURE:	D	D
ALIGNMENT:	Neutral	Neutral evil
NO. APPEARING:	1-6	1-4
ARMOR CLASS:	6	6
MOVEMENT:	6, Fl 18 (C)	6, Fl 18 (C)
HIT DICE:	5	6+2
THAC0:	15	13
NO. OF ATTACKS:	1	1
DAMAGE/ATTACK:	1-3	1-4
SPECIAL ATTACKS:	Petrification	Gaze
SPECIAL DEFENSES:	Nil	Immune to fire
MAGIC RESISTANCE:	Nil	Nil
SIZE:	S (3' tall)	S (3' tall)
MORALE:	Steady (11-12)	Steady (11-12)
XP VALUE:	650	1400

The cockatrice is an eerie, repulsive hybrid of lizard, cock, and bat. It is infamous for its ability to turn flesh to stone.

The cockatrice is about the size of a large goose or turkey, and has the head and body of a cock, with two bat-like wings and the long tail of a lizard tipped with a few feathers. Its feathers are golden brown, its beak yellow, its tail green, and its wings gray. The cockatrice's wattles, comb, and eyes are bright red.

Females, which are much rarer than males, differ only in that they have no wattles or comb.

Combat: The cockatrice will fiercely attack anything, human or otherwise, which it deems a threat to itself or its lair. When attacking, the cockatrice will attempt to grapple with its foe, touching exposed flesh and turning it to stone. Flocks of cockatrices will do their utmost to overwhelm and confuse their opponents, and they will sometimes fly directly into their victims' faces.

While the fatal touch of a cockatrice's beak will affect victims clothed in leather or fabric, it will not work through metal armor. The touch will, however, extend into the ethereal plane. The cockatrice is somewhat aware of the limits of its powers, and natural selection has taught it to strike only at exposed flesh. If large areas of the opponent's flesh are exposed, it should be assumed that the cockatrice automatically touches flesh. If the target is reasonably well armored, the base chance of a cockatrice striking an area which it can affect is equal to 10% times the adjusted Armor Class of the victim.

Habitat/Society: The cockatrice is immune to the petrification powers of others of its kind.

The diet of the cockatrice consists of insects, small lizards and the like. When it hunts these animals, the creature does not employ its power to petrify living things.

It is distinguished from other avians by its unusual habits and nasty temperament. Since females are rare, they are the dominant sex, and will often have more than one mate. In fact, males will often fight or strut for the privilege of joining a female's harem. These mated groups usually build their nests in caves. Nest sites are permanent, and the cockatrice constantly seeks to decorate its nesting site by lining it with shining objects like coins and gems.

Females lay 1 or 2 brownish red, rust speckled eggs per month. There is only a 25% chance that any given egg will hatch. Those that are fertile will hatch in 11-19 days. The young reach maturity and full power within 6 months. Once they achieve adulthood, the hatchlings are driven away from the nesting site by their parents. Larger groups of cockatrices encountered will frequently be young driven from the nest who have temporarily united for survival.

Ecology: The cockatrice thrives in the wilderness. Its petrification power makes it immune to most predators, and enables it to compete with other birds for food. The feathers of the cockatrice are prized by certain wizards as many magical scrolls must be inscribed with pens made from such quills. Many people also seek unhatched eggs, or even a live cockatrice, as unusual pets or guardians.

Pyrolisk

Frequently mistaken for its less malignant relative, the pyrolisk is virtually identical to the cockatrice except for the single red feather in its tail and the reddish cast of its wings. Whereas the cockatrice is motivated by instinct alone, the pyrolisk revels in spreading mayhem. Any victims who fail to save vs. death magic when meeting its gaze will instantly burst into flames, dying in agony. If the save is made, they are still burnt for 2-13 (1d12+1) points of damage. Any creature innately or magically immune to fire will not be affected by its gaze, and anyone who makes their saving throw is thereafter immune to the gaze of that particular pyrolisk.

The creature can cause any fire source within 30 yards to explode in fireworks (as a *pyrotechnics* spell) once per round.

The pyrolisk is itself immune to all fire-based spells and attacks.

The pyrolisk's mortal enemy is the phoenix, although any creature which the monster encounters is likely to be attacked.

Couatl

CLIMATE/TERRAIN:	Tropical and subtropical jungles
FREQUENCY:	Very rare
ORGANIZATION:	Solitary
ACTIVITY CYCLE:	Any
DIET:	Carnivorous
INTELLIGENCE:	Genius (17-18)
TREASURE:	B, I
ALIGNMENT:	Lawful good

NO. APPEARING:	1-4
ARMOR CLASS:	5
MOVEMENT:	6, Fl 18 (A)
HIT DICE:	9
THAC0:	11
NO. OF ATTACKS:	2
DAMAGE/ATTACK:	1-3/2-8 (2d4)
SPECIAL ATTACKS:	Poison, magic use
SPECIAL DEFENSES:	Etherealness
MAGIC RESISTANCE:	Nil
SIZE:	L (12' long)
MORALE:	Elite (13-14)
XP VALUE:	6000

Level	Dis/Sci Dev	Attack/ Defense	Power Score	PSPs
9	4/5/18	Any/All	= Int	1d100 + 110

Clarsentience: aura sight, all-round vision, see sound; **Psychometabolism:** metamorphosis, clemical simulation, ectoplasmic form; **Psychoporatation:** teleport, time shift; **Telepathy:** mindlink, ESP, invisibility.

The couatl are feathered serpents of myth and lore. It is believed that they are distant relatives of dragons, although this remains unproven.

So rare as to be considered almost legendary, the couatl is one of the most beautiful creatures in existence. It has the body of a long serpent and feathered wings the color of the rainbow. Since it has the ability to polymorph, the couatl will sometimes appear in the form of other creatures (always of good alignment).

Couatl are able to communicate via telepathy with almost any intelligent creature which they encounter. In addition, they can speak common and most serpent and avian languages.

Combat: A couatl will seldom attack without provocation, though it will always attack evildoers caught red-handed. Whenever possible, a couatl will attack from the air.

Since it is highly intelligent, the couatl will frequently use its spells from a distance before closing with its foes. If more than one couatl is involved, they will discuss their strategy before a battle. The couatl will also not hesitate to polymorph into another, more effective form in combat.

The couatl have a variety of abilities which make them more than a match for most other creatures. In addition to being able to polymorph themselves at will, a couatl can use magic. Fully 45% will be 5th level wizards, while 35% can act as 7th level priests. The remaining 20% are able to use both types of abilities.

In addition to their other magical abilities, couatl can render themselves and up to 450 pounds of additional matter ethereal at will. Further, they can *detect good/evil, detect magic*, turn *invisible*, and employ *ESP* whenever they desire to do so. The oldest and most powerful couatl can also use a *plane shift* on themselves and up to 8 others. This ability has a 90% chance of reaching the desired plane.

The couatl uses its poisonous bite and constriction when forced into melee combat. When it bites it does 1-3 points of damage and injects a deadly toxin. If the victim fails a save vs. poison it is killed instantly. If the constriction attack succeeds, the victim takes 2-8 points damage each round until it or the couatl is killed.

Habitat/Society: This winged serpent is native to warm, jungle-like regions but can also be found flying through the ether. Their intelligence and goodness have made them objects of reverence by the natives of the regions which they inhabit. Considered to be divine, there are many legends in which the couatl is the benefactor of mankind and the bestower of such precious gifts as agriculture and medicine. There are even shrines in certain areas dedicated to the couatl, and any who attack or harm a couatl are automatically viewed as the blackest of villains.

Although solitary in nature, couatl think of themselves as a single, extended clan. This clan is led by the oldest and wisest of their numbers but assembles only in dire emergencies.

Most couatl dwell alone, making their lairs in caves and abandoned buildings in remote, uninhabited regions. They hunt jungle animals for food once every fortnight or so. Many enjoy traveling, often undertaking long journeys of exploration.

On rare occasions, a pair will mate for life and establish a joint lair. Unlike many other reptiles, the couatl bear live young. Births are rare, averaging only one per couple each century. Both parents participate in the rearing and education of the single offspring, and will fight to the death if their child is threatened. Young couatl reach maturity in thirty or forty years and, though some will elect to remain with their parents for as long as a century, will eventually set off in search of the couatl's never-ending quest for wisdom.

Intellectually curious, all couatl have vast stores of information and enjoy learning more. When one of them learns some new and fascinating fact he will inevitably set out in search of his brethren to share and discuss it.

Couatl can sometimes be persuaded to help good adventurers or give sound council. If they feel that they are being sought for frivolous reasons, they will simply fly away. They are not greedy and do not seek treasure for its own sake. Aid from a couatl may well take the form of a magical item from its hoard.

Ecology: The couatl usually reigns supreme in its jungle, having little to fear from most other monsters.

Crabman

CLIMATE/TERRAIN:	Temperate to tropical sea coasts
FREQUENCY:	Rare
ORGANIZATION:	Tribal
ACTIVITY CYCLE:	Any
DIET:	Omnivore
INTELLIGENCE:	Low to average (5-10)
TREASURE:	Nil (In lair: K×5, L×5, C)
ALIGNMENT:	Neutral
NO. APPEARING:	2-12
ARMOR CLASS:	4
MOVEMENT:	9, Sw 6
HIT DICE:	3
THAC0:	17
NO. OF ATTACKS:	2
DAMAGE/ATTACK:	1-6/1-6
SPECIAL ATTACKS:	Nil
SPECIAL DEFENSES:	Nil
MAGIC RESISTANCE:	Nil
SIZE:	M-L (7'-10' tall)
MORALE:	Steady (11-12)
XP VALUE:	65

Crabmen are man-sized intelligent crabs. They walk upright on two pairs of legs. The small pincers tipping the short arms above their legs are used for fine manipulation. The two longer arms end in large claws. Two slender eyestalks bob above the beak-like collection of mandibles which makes up the crabman's mouth. Male crabmen are often brightly colored and females may be reddish-brown, green, or black.

Combat: Though generally peaceful, crabmen will fight back with their large claws if attacked, causing 1d6 points of damage per hit. Males of certain subspecies have an enlarged claw on one side which does 1d8 damage. Crabmen have never been known to wield weapons.

If severed, a crabman's limbs and eyestalks will grow back in 1-4 weeks.

At certain times, population pressure and food shortages will cause crabmen to voraciously hunt other creatures. Most such attacks are directed towards other tribes of crabmen or other coastal inhabitants. However, they will occasionally raid coastal towns for food, attacking anything that moves. Such savage frenzies last only a few days, during which the crabman population is generally reduced back to a tolerable level.

Habitat/Society: Crabmen live as simple hunter-gatherers, subsisting primarily on carrion and algae. Much of each crabman's day is spent hunting, filtering algae, or scavenging along the shore. Crabman often gather large amounts of sand into their mouths, suck out all the organic material, and spit out fist-sized pellets of sand and dirt. These hardened pellets betray the presence of a nearby crabman lair.

Crabmen generally live in coastal caves. Some tribes dig extensive burrows in seaside cliffs. Within a burrow complex, each crabman has an individual lair, situated near a large, central meeting area.

Males and females are found in approximately equal numbers in a tribe. They mate at irregular times throughout the year. The female produces about 100 eggs within two weeks. They are laid in the ocean, where they hatch into clear, soft-shelled, crablike larvae. In six months they molt, develop a stronger shell, and begin to dwell on land. The eggs and larvae are delicious, and predators greatly reduce their numbers before they reach adulthood. Larvae are almost defenseless, with AC 8, 1 HD, and weak claws which do only 1-2 points of damage per hit.

Crabmen continue to grow and molt throughout their lives, and specimens as tall as 10 feet have been reported. A crabman can live for up to 20 years.

A crabman tribe seldom has commerce with other tribes, and almost never with other intelligent races. They produce few artifacts, primarily seaweed weavings, driftwood carvings, and seashell constructions. Though these are often impermanent, some are quite beautiful. Though details of crabman religion are unknown, most artifacts are believed to be religious in nature, and are jealously guarded.

Each tribe appears to be led by a dominant, elder male or female. These leaders have maximum hit points, but are otherwise unremarkable.

Crabmen speak their own language, which consists mostly of hisses and clicks. The crabmen's xenophobia and the extreme difficulty of their language make it virtually impossible for humans and similar races to learn to speak the crabman tongue. Those few sages who know anything about the language know only a few basic words.

Crabmen are attracted to shiny metal, particularly silver-colored metal, though they seem unable to differentiate between silver, platinum, and steel. Crabman lairs often contain piles of these metals, with many pieces worked into sculptures. If the metal has rusted or tarnished, it is sometimes scraped to reveal the shine again, but often simply thrown into a refuse pile.

Ecology: Crabman artifacts can sometimes bring good prices from collectors, though they are often fragile, and readily decompose if made of plants.

Crabmen are rumored to be very tasty, especially their legs and claws. Primitive coastal inhabitants, particularly sahuagin, consider them a delicacy and often raid crabman villages. Their shells dry out and become brittle soon after they are removed or molted, so they cannot be used as armor. The claws can be used as passable clubs.

47

Crawling Claw

CLIMATE/TERRAIN:	Any
FREQUENCY:	Rare
ORGANIZATION:	Swarm
ACTIVITY CYCLE:	Any
DIET:	Special
INTELLIGENCE:	Non- (0)
TREASURE:	Any
ALIGNMENT:	Neutral

NO. APPEARING:	1-20
ARMOR CLASS:	7
MOVEMENT:	9
HIT DICE:	2-4 hit points
THAC0:	20
NO. OF ATTACKS:	1
DAMAGE/ATTACK:	1-4 (armored foes)
	1-6 (unarmored foes)
SPECIAL ATTACKS:	Nil
SPECIAL DEFENSES:	See below
MAGIC RESISTANCE:	See below
SIZE:	T (human hand)
MORALE:	Fearless (19-20)
XP VALUE:	35

The much feared crawling claw is frequently employed as a guardian by those mages and priests who have learned the secret of its creation.

No single description of a crawling claw is possible as they are not uniform in appearance. Since claws are the animated remains of hands or paws of living creatures, they are apt to be found in a wide variety of shapes and sizes.

Combat: When a claw detects a potential victim, it leaps to the attack. Although it may not appear to be capable of such a feat, its great strength enables it to do so. The maximum distance a claw can leap is 15 feet.

Once a claw lands on its victim, it attacks in one of two ways. If the victim is wearing metal armor, the claw delivers a powerful blow that inflicts 1d4 points of damage. Against those who are not armored (or only wearing leather) the claw can employ its great strength in a crushing grip. This manner of attack causes 1d6 points of damage.

In some cases, a claw may be instructed to attempt to strangle or gouge out the eyes of a victim. In any such case, the DM should consider all aspects of the situation and determine how much, if any, damage is done.

Claws are immune to any form of death magic or *raise dead* spells, although a *resurrection* spell renders them immobile for a number of turns equal to the level of the caster. Claws have the same resistance to *charm, sleep,* and *hold* spells that undead do, but claws are not subject to turning, *control undead* spells, or damage by holy water. Cold-based spells make claws brittle so that all rolls to damage them are increased by 1 point per die.

Edged weapons inflict only half damage on a claw; all magical weapons cause damage as if they were not enchanted in any way (although to hit bonuses still apply).

Society/Habitat: Crawling claws are nothing more than the animated hands and paws of once-living creatures. As such, they have no culture or society to speak of. Despite this, crawling claws do have a limited ability to communicate with each other. This takes the form of a basic telepathic link between all the claws of a single "batch." Whenever one claw finds a victim, all of the others in the area who were made at the same time move in to help it.

In addition, claws that have been instructed to do so can act in concert with each other to move large objects. The DM should use five pounds per claw as a reasonable limit to the weight that can be moved.

Ecology: Crawling claws can be created by any mage or priest who has knowledge of the techniques required to do so. To begin with, the creator must assemble the severed limbs that are to animated. The maximum number of claws that can be created at any one time is equal to the level of the person enchanting them. The hands (or paws) can be either fresh, skeletal, or at any stage of decomposition in between.

Claws can be controlled in one of two ways: directly or via programming. The manner of a claw's control must be specified when it is created and cannot be changed thereafter. All of the claws in a particular batch must be controlled in the same manner.

Programmed claws are given a single, brief instruction that they attempt to carry out to the best of their ability. The maximum length of the programming, in words, is 15 plus the level of the creator. This programming sets the conditions under which the claw attack. A sample command might be: Kill anyone except me who opens this chest.

Directly controlled claws are manipulated by the thoughts of their creator. The mental effort of controlling claws is quite tiring and cannot be maintained for more than three consecutive rounds without a one-round rest. Further, the range of such control is limited to 10 feet plus 5 feet per level of the creator. A person controlling claws cannot undertake spellcasting or any other activity. Injury to a controller does not break his control unless unconsciousness results. If direct control is broken for some reason, the claws continue to follow the last orders they were given.

Crocodile

	Crocodile	Giant Crocodile
CLIMATE/TERRAIN:	——— Subtropical and tropical/ ———	
	Saltwater swamps and rivers	
FREQUENCY:	Common	Very rare to common
ORGANIZATION:	Nil	Nil
ACTIVITY CYCLE:	Day	Day
DIET:	Carnivore	Carnivore
INTELLIGENCE:	Animal (1)	Animal (1)
TREASURE:	Nil	Nil
ALIGNMENT:	Neutral	Neutral
NO. APPEARING:	3-24	1 to 2-12
ARMOR CLASS:	5	4
MOVEMENT:	6, Sw 12	6, Sw 12
HIT DICE:	3	7
THAC0:	17	13
NO. OF ATTACKS:	2	2
DAMAGE/ATTACK:	2-8/1-12	3-18/2-20
SPECIAL ATTACKS:	Surprise	Surprise
SPECIAL DEFENSES:	Nil	Nil
MAGIC RESISTANCE:	Nil	Nil
SIZE:	L (8'-15' long)	H (21'-30' long)
MORALE:	Average (9)	Steady (11)
XP VALUE:	65	1,400

The crocodile is a large, dangerous predatory reptile native to tropical and subtropical climes. It spends most of its time submerged in swamps, rivers, or other large bodies of water.

The crocodile is one of the most feared and ugliest predators of the tropics. It has a long, squat body, ranging in size from a scant foot to well over ten feet long. Most mature specimens range from eight to 15 feet long, and some even larger. Many sages argue that crocodiles never stop growing. The crocodile has a long jaw filled with sharp, conical teeth. The powerful maw is superbly adapted for dragging prey beneath the water and dismembering it. Its four short legs are very powerful, and can propel the crocodile rapidly through the water and over the land. Its long tail is also very strong and is sometimes used on land to unbalance its foes.

The crocodile is covered with a tough horny hide, which blends in very well with the surrounding water. Its eyes and nose are placed so that when the crocodile floats, only they remain above water, enabling the beast to spot and ambush prey. The crocodile is adept at floating through the water and remaining quite still, presenting the illusion that it is nothing more than a floating log.

Combat: Ever voracious, hungry crocodiles will attack anything that looks edible, including men. They prefer to lie in wait for their prey (-2 penalty to opponent's surprise roll), and are exceedingly sensitive to movements in the water. They have been known to swiftly and silently swim up to the shore and seize a man, dragging him below the surface of the water. They prefer to attack with their powerful jaws, causing 2d4 points of damage, and lash with their tails for 1d12 points of damage. Crocodiles will fight among themselves for any prey they seize in their jaws, sometimes tearing their victim to pieces. The only thing that can slow a crocodile is cold. They become slow and sluggish (reduced to 50% of their normal movement) when the temperature falls below 40° F.

Habitat/Society: Crocodiles sometimes congregate in large numbers, but they are not by nature sociable, nor do they cooperate in hunting. They have well-concealed lairs and will often drag their prey to their lairs before eating it. When a tasty morsel comes its way, a group of crocodiles will go into a feeding frenzy, each attempting to get a part of the feast. They hunt almost daily,

primarily in the water, rarely on land. Their tastes are broad: fish, men, small mammals, aquatic birds, and even a careless lion has occasionally been known to fall into their grasp. Hungry crocodiles will sometimes upend boats to see what falls out.

Crocodiles mate once a year, and the female lays a clutch of about 60 eggs, carefully burying them in the sand. Unlike many other reptiles, the female carefully guards her eggs, protecting them from other predators. When the time comes for the eggs to hatch, the mother assists by digging the eggs out of the sand. The newly hatched young are thrown entirely on their own resources to survive. Very few of the young survive to maturity.

Swamps and rivers are not the only abode of the crocodile. In recent years there have been dreadful rumors that some of these reptiles have made their homes in the sewers of cities in tropical regions, living on waste and carrion.

Ecology: The crocodile is a formidable predator and has little competition for food from other water creatures. One of the few monsters that can compete with it is the dragonturtle. Even on the riverbanks it has little to fear from rival predators; most would prefer not to tangle with a crocodile. The only predator that the crocodile need fear is man, who hunts it for its tough hide, which can be transformed into a beautiful, gleaming leather. Crocodiles are also hunted to eliminate the danger that they represent to riverside communities.

Giant Crocodile

These creatures are far rarer than their smaller cousins. They attain sizes from 21 to 30 feet long, and they also continue to grow until death. Giant crocodiles typically inhabit salt water or prehistoric settings, where they have been know to prey upon sharks, small whales, and small seagoing crafts, such as fishing boats. When attacking a small boat, their favorite technique is to ram it, attempting to capsize and smash it open with their huge jaws. They have been known to gorge upon the catch within the fishing boats, and then to swim away, leaving the fishermen unharmed.

Crustacean, Giant

	Giant Crab	Giant Crayfish
CLIMATE/TERRAIN:	Any seashore	Temperate/ Freshwater rivers
FREQUENCY:	Rare	Uncommon
ORGANIZATION:	Nil	Nil
ACTIVITY CYCLE:	Any	Any
DIET:	Omnivore	Omnivore
INTELLIGENCE:	Non- (0)	Non- (0)
TREASURE:	Nil	Nil
ALIGNMENT:	Neutral	Neutral
NO. APPEARING:	2-12	1-4
ARMOR CLASS:	3	4
MOVEMENT:	9	6, Sw 12
HIT DICE:	3	4+4
THAC0:	17	15
NO. OF ATTACKS:	2	2
DAMAGE/ATTACK:	2-8/2-8	2-12/2-12
SPECIAL ATTACKS:	Nil	Nil
SPECIAL DEFENSES:	Surprise	Surprise
MAGIC RESISTANCE:	Nil	Nil
SIZE:	L (8'-15')	L (8' + long)
MORALE:	Elite (13)	Elite (13)
XP VALUE:	65	175

Giant crustaceans are peculiar mutations of crabs and freshwater crayfish. The first inhabits saltwater regions, while the latter is found only in fresh water.

Giant Crabs

Giant crabs look just like regular crabs except for their enormous size. They come in a variety of colors, such as reds, browns, and grays. They have eyes set on stalks, which enable them to see around corners and onto ledges. Their bodies are covered by a large, chitinous shell. Crabs are distinguished by their scuttling, sideways mode of locomotion.

Combat: Always hungry, crabs prefer to sneak up upon their prey (-3 penalty to opponent's surprise roll) and catch it in their pincers, dismembering and eating it. A successful attack by the pincers causes 2d4 points of damage. Once they have caught something edible, they stop to eat it, unless they are attacked. If a crab finds its meal in question, it attempts to scuttle off with the prize, perhaps to its den.

Habitat/Society: The giant crab lives on the shoreline, searching beaches for food and venturing into the water in search of fish and other aquatic life. It is well adapted to this sort of life, since it is able to breathe both air and water. Giant crabs frequently feed on large dead fish and other carrion washed up on the shore. They operate equally well on land and in the water. Giant crabs sometimes burrow into the sand during the day, emerging only at dusk and dawn to feed. At these times the beach is alive not only with the giant crabs, but with their tiny cousins as well. The giants may also hunt during the day and night.

The crab exists only on the most basic instinctive level, and is interested solely in survival. Crabs mate in the autumn and males attempt to mate with as many females as they can. Females bury their eggs in the sand. The eggs hatch the following spring; few hatchlings survive to reach maturity. Nature has forced the giant crabs to become flexible eaters, always willing to try new food sources.

Ecology: The giant crab performs a useful ecological function in keeping the seashores free of large carrion that would otherwise rot. On the shore, it is hunted by the ultimate predators—humans and demihumans—for its superb meat and hard chitinous shell, which is prized by some for making armor and shields.

Giant Crayfish

The crayfish is essentially a freshwater lobster. It has a similar multi-plated shell, numerous legs, eyes set on stalks, and two wicked pincers. The giant crayfish is muddy brown or sand colored, depending upon the color of the river bottom it inhabits. Some say that the giant crayfish, like the lobster, keeps growing as it gets older; certain sages even argue that the giant crayfish is really the same species as the ordinary crayfish, merely an extremely old specimen.

Combat: Like the crab, the crayfish prefers to ambush its prey (-2 penalty to opponent's surprise roll). It sits quietly on the river bottom, waiting, and then rushes forth to seize its food in its pincers. The giant crayfish does not normally represent a danger to adventurers, since it inhabits only deep rivers and spends all of its time on the river bottom. It would therefore only attack adventurers who were swimming along the river bottom, and then only if they came within its range. An attack by a giant crayfish's pincers inflicts 2d6 points of damage. The crayfish prefers to drag its catch back to its watery lair and eat in peace. Its shell is very tough, giving the creature AC 4.

Habitat/Society: The giant crayfish inhabits only wide and deep rivers, and feeds almost exclusively upon bottom-dwelling fish. Due to its great size, it can easily prey on such fish as sturgeon, carp, and large eels. It is voracious and spends most of its time hunting. On the whole it rarely crosses paths with adventurers, but it does compete with river fishermen.

Ecology: The giant crayfish is considered a delicacy by other creatures, which perhaps accounts for its rarity. Nixies especially prize the meat of the giant crayfish. Dragon turtles, giant snapping turtles, merrows, giant otters, gar, giant pike, and storm giants are just some of the monsters that hunt the giant crayfish. It is very far from being the top predator in its food chain, and must fight for its survival.

Crypt Thing

CLIMATE/TERRAIN:	Any/Tomb or grave area
FREQUENCY:	Very rare
ORGANIZATION:	Solitary
ACTIVITY CYCLE:	Any
DIET:	Nil
INTELLIGENCE:	Very (11-12)
TREASURE:	Z
ALIGNMENT:	Neutral

NO. APPEARING:	1
ARMOR CLASS:	3
MOVEMENT:	12
HIT DICE:	6
THAC0:	15
NO. OF ATTACKS:	1
DAMAGE/ATTACK:	1-8
SPECIAL ATTACKS:	Teleport
SPECIAL DEFENSES:	See below
MAGIC RESISTANCE:	Nil
SIZE:	M (6' tall)
MORALE:	Fanatic (17-18)
XP VALUE:	975

Crypt things are strange undead creatures that sometimes guard tombs, graves, and corpses. There are two types of crypt things—ancestral and summoned. The former type are "natural" creatures, while the others are called into existence by a wizard or priest of at least 14th level.

A crypt thing looks like nothing more than an animated skeleton, save that it is always clothed in a flowing robe of brown or black. Each eye socket is lit by a fierce, red pinpoint of light that is almost hypnotic in its intensity.

Combat: A crypt thing exists only to protect the bodies of those who have been laid to rest in its lair. It acts only to defend its crypt. Should grave robbers or vandals seek to enter and profane the sanctity of its tomb, the crypt thing becomes instantly animated.

A crypt thing's first line of defense is a powerful variety of teleportation, which it can cast once on any given group of adventurers. Each of those attacked with this spell must roll a successful saving throw vs. spell or be instantly transported away from the crypt. DMs should use the following table as a guideline, rolling 1d100 for each person who fails the saving throw, but they are free to use their own judgment as well:

01-20	1d10 x 100' north
21-40	1d10 x 100' east
41-60	1d10 x 100' west
61-80	1d10 x 100' south
81-90	1 dungeon level up
91-00	1 dungeon level down

Those teleported by the crypt thing cannot materialize inside solid matter, but they do not necessarily arrive at floor level. Particularly clever crypt things have been known to transport victims several hundred feet into the air or atop a vast chasm, leaving them to fall to their deaths.

Once it has employed this power, a crypt thing attacks by clawing with its skeletal hands for 1d8 points of damage.

A crypt thing can be hit only by magical weapons.

Like all undead, crypt things are immune to certain spells. It is impossible to employ a *charm*, *hold*, or *sleep* spell against a crypt thing with any chance of success. Crypt things are harmed by holy water or holy symbols, as are many undead creatures. The magic that roots them to their lairs is so powerful, in fact, that it also eliminates any chance for priests or paladins to turn them.

Habitat/Society: Crypt things are not a natural part of our world; they have no organized society or culture. They are found wherever tombs and crypts are located.

The most common crypt thing is the summoned variety. By use of a 7th-level spell (see below), any caster capable of employing necromantic spells can create a crypt thing.

Ancestral crypt things are the raised spirits of the dead that have returned to guard the tombs of their descendants. This happens only in rare cases (determined by the DM).

Ecology: The crypt thing is not a being of this world and, thus, has no proper ecological niche. It is rumored that the powdered marrow from a crypt thing's bones can be used to create a *potion of undead control*. In addition, anyone who employs the bones of a crypt thing to manufacture a set of *pipes of haunting* is 80% likely to create a magical item that imposes a -2 penalty to its victims' saving throws and has double normal effectiveness if the saving throws fail.

Create Crypt Thing

7th-level Wizard or Priest spell (necromantic)
(Reversible)

Range: Touch	Casting Time: 1 round
Components: V,S	Area of Effect: 1 corpse
Duration: Permanent	Saving Throw: None

This spell enables the caster to cause a single dead body to animate and assume the status of a crypt thing. This spell can be cast only in the tomb or grave area the crypt thing is to protect; the spell requires that the caster touch the skull of the subject body. Once animated, the crypt thing remains until destroyed. Only one crypt thing may guard a given tomb.

A successful *dispel magic* spell returns the crypt thing to its original unanimated state. Attempts to restore the crypt thing before this is done fail for any magic short of a *wish*.

The reverse of this spell, *destroy crypt thing*, utterly annihilates any one such being as soon as it is touched by the caster. The target is allowed a saving throw vs. death magic to avoid destruction.

Death Knight

CLIMATE/TERRAIN:	Any
FREQUENCY:	Very rare
ORGANIZATION:	Solitary
ACTIVITY CYCLE:	Any
DIET:	Nil
INTELLIGENCE:	Genius (17-18)
TREASURE:	Nil
ALIGNMENT:	Chaotic evil

NO. APPEARING:	1
ARMOR CLASS:	0
MOVEMENT:	12
HIT DICE:	9 (10-sided dice)
THAC0:	11
NO. OF ATTACKS:	1 with +3 bonus
DAMAGE/ATTACK:	By weapon
SPECIAL ATTACKS:	See below
SPECIAL DEFENSES:	See below
MAGIC RESISTANCE:	75% (see below)
SIZE:	M (6'-7' tall)
MORALE:	Fanatic (17)
XP VALUE:	6,000

A death knight is the horrifying corruption of a paladin or lawful good warrior cursed by the gods to its terrible form as punishment for betraying the code of honor it held in life.

A death knight resembles a hulking knight, typically taller than 6 feet and weighing more than 300 pounds. Its face is a blackened skull covered with shards of shriveled, rotting flesh. It has two tiny, glowing orange-red pinpoints for eyes. Its armor is scorched black as if it had been in a fire. The demeanor of a death knight is so terrifying that even kender have been known to become frightened.

A death knight's deep, chilling voice seems to echo from the depths of a bottomless cavern. A death knight converses in the language it spoke in its former life, as well as up to six additional languages.

Combat: A death knight retains the fighting skills it had in its former life. Since it has little regard for its own safety and an intense hatred of most living creatures, it is an extremely dangerous opponent. Still, a death knight retains a semblance of the pride it held as a good warrior and fights honorably: It never ambushes opponents from behind, nor does it attack before an opponent has an opportunity to ready his weapon. Surrender is unknown to a death knight, and it will parley only if it senses its opponent has crucial information (such as the fate of a former family member).

A death knight has a strength of 18(00). It usually attacks with a sword; 80% of the time, this is a magical sword. When a magical sword is indicated, roll 1d6 and consult the following table:

Roll	Death Knight's Sword
1	*Long sword +2*
2	*Two-handed sword +3*
3	*Two-handed sword +4*
4	*Short sword of quickness*
5	*Short sword of dancing*
6	*Short sword of life stealing*

A death knight wears the same armor it wore in its previous life, but regardless of the quality of the armor, it always has an AC of 0. Hit points for a death knight are determined by rolling 10-sided dice.

A death knight's magical abilities make it especially dangerous. It constantly generates *fear* in a 5-foot radius, and it can cast *detect magic*, *detect invisibility*, and *wall of ice* at will. Twice per day, it can cast *dispel magic*. Once per day, it can use either *power word, blind*, *power word, kill*, or *power word, stun*. It can also cast *symbol of fear* or *symbol of pain* once per day, as well as a 20-dice *fireball* once per day. All of its magical spells function at the 20th level of ability.

A death knight cannot be turned, but it can be dispelled by *holy word* spell. It has the power over undead of a 6th-level evil priest. Its magic resistance is 75%, and if an 11 or lower is rolled on the percentile roll, the spell is reflected back at the caster (the magic resistance is rerolled each time a spell is cast at a death knight).

Habitat/Society: Death knights are former good warriors who were judged by the gods to be guilty of unforgivable crimes, such as murder or treason. (For instance, Krynn's Lord Soth, the most famous of all death knights, murdered his wife so that he could continue an affair with an elfmaid.) Death knights are cursed to remain in their former domains, usually castles or other strongholds. They are further condemned to remember their crime in song on any night when the moon is full; few sounds are as terrifying as a death knight's chilling melody echoing through the moonlit countryside. Death knights are likely to attack any creature that interrupts their songs or trespasses in their domains.

Ecology: Death knights have no physiological functions. They are sometimes accompanied by skeleton warriors, liches, and other undead who serve as their aides.

Deepspawn

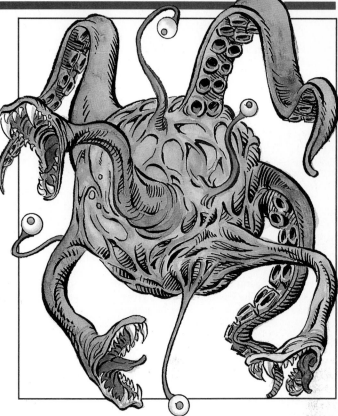

CLIMATE/TERRAIN:	Any/any
FREQUENCY:	Very rare
ORGANIZATION:	Solitary
ACTIVITY CYCLE:	Any
DIET:	Omnivorous
INTELLIGENCE:	Genius (17-18)
TREASURE:	K, L, M, Q × 2, V × 2, X
ALIGNMENT:	Chaotic evil

NO. APPEARING:	1
ARMOR CLASS:	6
MOVEMENT:	6, Sw 8
HIT DICE:	14
THAC0:	7
NO. OF ATTACKS:	6
DAMAGE/ATTACK:	3-12 × 3 (bites)/2-5 (slap) × 3 or by weapon type × 3
SPECIAL ATTACKS:	See below
SPECIAL DEFENSES:	See below
MAGIC RESISTANCE:	77%
SIZE:	H (14' diam., tentacles to 20' long)
MORALE:	Elite (15-16)
XP VALUE:	12,000

Deepspawn are infamous horrors who give birth to many other varieties of monsters; a single Deepspawn can make a vast area dangerous, even for alert, well-armed adventurers.

Deepspawn look like large, rubbery spheres of mottled grey and brown. Six arms project from their bodies; three are tentacle-arms, and three are jaw-arms, ending in mouths of many teeth. A Deepspawn also has over 40 long, retractable, flexible eye stalks it extends only three or four at a time, well away from harm.

Combat: When found, Deepspawn are usually half buried in a pile of slippery, shifting coins and other treasure. This may conceal their arms, so that tentacles and mouths erupting from the treasure may at first seem to be the attacks of separate monsters. The treasure may hamper opponents and even shield the Deepspawn from some damage (as determined by the DM).

A Deepspawn attacks by casting *hold* spells at intruders, casting spells once every three rounds. Victims under a *hold* spell are gripped by tentacle-arms and constricted, as other tentacles fight off other intruders by wielding weapons—including any magical items usable by fighters. Deepspawn love to engage prey with weapons, and then bite them from behind with a jaw-arm.

A tentacle-arm can slap for 1d4+1 points of damage, grasp items or beings and move them about (with 17 Strength), wield delicate keys or weapons, or constrict victims.

Constriction requires a successful attack roll (automatic if the victim is under a *hold* spell), and does 1d4 points of damage, plus 1d4+1 points per round thereafter. In any round in which a being gets free, it takes only 1 point of constriction damage. Constricted victims can be swung about as bludgeons—doing 1d2 damage to any others struck, ruining spellcasting, and forcing saving throws on fragile items. This action causes the constricted victim no extra damage unless driven onto points or blades (determine damage on a case-by-case basis).

Victims may only escape constriction by severing the tentacle-arm or tearing free. Tentacle-arms release their victims if severed. Each arm has 2 HD; severing occurs if damage equal to half a tentacle-arm's hit points is dealt in a concentrated area by edged or pointed weapons. To tear free, roll a d20 for both the victim and the Deepspawn on each round of constriction, adding their respective strengths (17 for the Deepspawn). If the victim has the higher total, it wins its freedom.

Deepspawn can also cast *ESP* and *water breathing* at will, and may employ a *heal* spell (self only), once a day. If a Deepspawn's life is threatened, it hurls caches of seized weapons as missiles, unleashes any magical items it has, and tries to escape by a planned route. Deepspawn seem immune to all known venoms, and regenerate lost arms and stalks, though slowly, healing 2 hp per day.

Habitat/Society: Deepspawn prefer to let their offspring fight for them. Their lairs are in caverns, dungeons, or ruins and are amply protected by traps and guardian monsters (their "spawn"). If these defenses are penetrated, the Deepspawn will usually be found in a readily-defended room or den, and it will always have at least one or more escape routes.

Deepspawn are native to the Deeps, and have successfully resisted attempts by dwarves, drow, duergar, cloakers, illithids, and aboleth to exterminate them. Deepspawn seldom make their lairs within 30 miles of each other, but individuals may be much closer together underground, on different levels.

Ecology: Deepspawn will eat anything organic, but prefer fresh meat. By some unexplained, natural means, Deepspawn can "grow" and give birth to any creature native to the Prime Material plane it has ever devoured (but not undead or other dual dimensional creatures). The "spawn" have the natural attacks, magical abilities, alignment, and intelligence of their creators. Class abilities and other learned skills are not passed on to them. A spawn "grows" in 1d4 days (varying with size and complexity) in a Deepspawn, which must ingest meat, vegetable matter, and water or blood to fuel the "birth". The Deepspawn then opens and ejects a fully active spawn. Spawn are never hostile towards their parent, and cannot be made to attack them even by magical means. Spawn can attack or defend themselves within one round of emerging. At the DM's option, they may use certain powers or abilities clumsily for a few rounds.

Dinosaur

	Ankylosaurus	Deinonychus	Diplodocus	Elasmosaurus	Lambeosaurus	Pteranodon	Stegosaurus	Triceratops	Tyrannosaurus
CLIMATE/TERRAIN:	Any land	Any land	Any swamp	Any ocean	Any land	Any	Any land	Any land	Any land
FREQUENCY:	Uncommon	Rare	Common	Uncommon	Common	Common	Common	Common	Uncommon
ORGANIZATION:	Solitary	Pack	Family	Solitary	Herd	Flock	Herd	Herd	Solitary
DIET:	Herbivore	Carnivore	Herbivore	Carnivore	Herbivore	Carnivore	Herbivore	Herbivore	Carnivore
NO. APPEARING:	2-5	1-6	1-6	1-2	2-16	3-18	2-8	2-8	1-2
ARMOR CLASS:	0	4	6	7	6	7	5	2/6	5
MOVEMENT:	6	21	6	3, Sw 15	12	3, Fl 15	6	9	15
HIT DICE:	9	4+1	24	15	12	3+3	18	16	18
THAC0:	11	17	5	5	9	17	5	5	5
NO. OF ATTACKS:	1	3	1	1	1	1	1	3	3
DAMAGE/ATTACK:	3-18	1-3/1-3/2-8	3-18	4-24	2-12	2-8	5-20	1-8/1-12/1-12	1-6/1-6/5-40
SPECIAL ATTACKS:	Nil	Jump, rake	See below	Nil	Nil	Nil	Nil	Trampling	See below
SIZE:	H (15' long)	L (12' long)	G (80' long)	G (50' long)	H (20' long)	L (30' wingspan)	H (25' long)	H (24'+ long)	G (50' long)
MORALE:	Elite (13)	Steady (11)	Steady (12)	Steady (12)	Steady (11)	Avg. (9)	Elite (13)	Elite (13)	Steady (12)
XP VALUE:	1,400	270	16,000	6,000	2,000	175	9,000	8,000	12,000

Dinosaurs are found on alternate planes of existence, or even on lost continents. The frequency figures given are for areas where dinosaurs are normally found; in all other places, they are very rare at best. All dinosaurs in this entry share the following characteristics:

ACTIVITY CYCLE:	Day
INTELLIGENCE:	Animal (1)
TREASURE:	Nil
ALIGNMENT:	Neutral
MAGIC RESISTANCE:	Nil
SPECIAL DEFENSES:	Nil

Dinosaurs, or "terrible lizards," are reptiles descended from ancestral reptiles called thecodonts. The two types of dinosaurs are saurischians ("lizard-hipped") and ornithischians ("bird-hipped"), named for terms describing their pelvic structures. Within the saurischia are the carnivorous therapods, represented here by tyrannosaurus, and the herbivorous sauropods, represented here by diplodocus. Saurischians also include ornithomimosaurs and the related dromaeosaurs, represented here by deinonychus.

Many ornithischians have armor, horns, or both. They include ceratopsians, represented by triceratops; ornithopods, such as the hadrosaurs, represented by the lambeosaurus; ankylosaurus; and stegosaurus.

Dinosaurs come in many sizes and shapes. Those presented here are generally large. Bigger species have drab colors, while smaller dinosaurs have a wide variety of markings. Most dinosaurs have a skin which is pebbly in texture; some closely related species of reptile have fur, and some may have feathers.

Combat: Dinosaurs seem to be a mixture of endothermic ("warm-blooded") and exothermic ("cold-blooded"). They regulate body temperature internally, but also depend on external heat somewhat. Though they may be slow on a cold morning, they may not be as slow as a typical reptile.

Most of these huge reptiles have comparatively small brains, but many of the predators are quite cunning. All must eat large amounts of food to maintain their huge bodies. As a result, sauropods eat almost constantly, and carnivores hunt almost constantly and also eat carrion.

Though the carnivores are both voracious and ferocious, certain plant eaters are very aggressive in their defense, usually with armor or horns. Just because they do not eat meat does not mean they will not kill other animals.

Habitat/Society: Dinosaurs can be found in almost any type of environment, except desert, high mountains, and frozen wastes. They have no society and little family life, with most species abandoning eggs before they hatch.

Ecology: Sages do not understand what has made dinosaurs extinct on certain worlds, but they do exist in the "lost lands" on several worlds. There may be places where dinosaurs have continued to evolve into different forms; they may be ancestors of modern lizard men.

Ankylosaurus
This armadillo-like ornithischian weighs four or five tons, most of this weight being its armor plating, side spines, and great, knobbed tail. If attacked or threatened, this creature lashes out with its tail, delivering blows of considerable force.

A related species is the paleocinthus, which has better plating (AC −3) and a spiked, rather than club-like, tail.

Deinonychus
This fast carnivore uses its speed, its long, grasping forearms, large teeth, and hind legs with their ripping talons in terrible combination. It hunts by running at prey, leaping, and raking with its rear claws as it claws and bites. The jump is a charge, so the creature gains a +2 on attack rolls. The rear talons count as only one attack, and cause a total of 2d6 damage. When attacking a larger creature, the deinonychus often jumps on top of it, and holds on with its front claws while continuing to rake with the rear claws. The deinonychus has a relatively large brain for a dinosaur, and its pack hunts with cunning tactics.

Despite being 12 feet long, this dinosaur is only about 6 feet tall. Its tail extends straight out behind it, held aloft by an intricate structure of bony supports, thus allowing its 150 pounds of weight to be carried entirely by the back legs.

The deinonychus is a dromaeosaur, dinosaurs which are related to ornithomimosaurs; its distant relatives include the chicken-sized night hunter, compsognathus, and the ostrich-like struthiomimus. Neither is as formidable as the deinonychus.

Diplodocus
This sauropod lives primarily on water plants, so is often found in or near lakes and marshes. It and related species can also be found on fern prairies and in open forests. It weighs about 10 tons. Though it usually ignores small things, it can step on anything in its way, or even rear up and come down on threatening creatures; this trampling causes 3d10 damage. The diplodocus

can also whip with its tail for 2d8 damage.

Related species include the huge brachiosaurus, which weighs about 90 tons and averages 75 feet in length. It causes 8d10 damage when trampling.

Elasmosaurus

The elasmosaurus looks like a snake with fins and a thick body. It is aggressive, attacking anything it notices. Its neck makes up one-half its total length. The creature is strong, fast, and highly maneuverable, able to turn quickly and lunge at prey. When hunting, the elasmosaurus travels with its head out of the water, snapping down quickly to seize prey.

This creature's relatives include many other types of plesiosaurs and pliosaurs. Females travel onto sandy beaches to lay their eggs in shallow depressions.

Lambeosaurus

This is a very common "duck-billed" dinosaur, bipedal, with a flat snout, and crests on its head. A peaceful herbivore, this hadrosaur prefers to run from attack; its only defense is its lashing tail. It has excellent senses, used to detect predators.

Its enemies include most carnivores. Related species include many other species of duck-billed dinosaurs, as well as the iguanodon. The latter has sharp thumb spikes which can cause 1-3 damage each, in addition to its tail attack.

Pteranodon

Although this flying reptile typically dives for marine prey, it attacks any creature that appears to be vulnerable. The pteranodon has no teeth, but spears victims with its beak if they are too large to swallow at a gulp. The beak of a typical pteranodon is about 4 feet long.

Despite the creature's huge wingspan, its wings are very light, and its furred body is only a little larger than a human being; the whole weighs only about 50 pounds. A pteranodon can carry off prey up to four times its own weight.

There are all sizes of related species; close relatives have crests on their heads to balance their long beak for flight.

Stegosaurus

Another of the ornithischians, the stegosaurus, or "plated lizard," is a large, stupid, herbivorous dinosaur with aggressive defenses. It thrives nearly anywhere and is often found on plains or in jungles.

A stegosaurus is about 8 feet tall at the middle of its back; its humped spine is lined with a double row of leaf-shaped plates which help the creature absorb and dissipate heat. The creature has a spiked tail, with four or more bony spikes of up to 3 feet in length. An enlarged spinal node helps relay commands to the tail and rear legs. The stegosaurus continually turns its posterior towards an enemy, while tucking its head low. It reacts in the same manner if anything near seems threatening.

Similar species include the dacentrus, which has spikes along its backbone instead of plates, and the kentrosaurus, which has bony plates along the front half of its spine, and spikes along the rear half. All have spiked tails.

Triceratops

The largest of the ceratopsians, or horn-faced dinosaurs, and by far the most aggressive, this beaked herbivore is a plains-dweller. It has a huge front plate of bone protecting its 6-foot-long head, from which project two great horns (each over 3 feet long), while a shorter horn juts from its nose. The head and neck are AC 2; its body is not armored, so is AC 6. The triceratops weighs just over 10 tons.

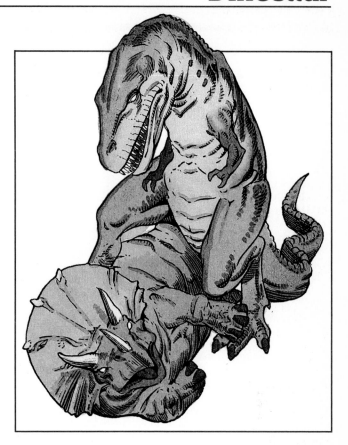

Any creature that infringes on the territory of these reptiles is likely to be charged and skewered. Smaller creatures are trampled, suffering 2d12 points of damage. The triceratops also uses its horns in fights for dominance within the herd, so it is not unusual to find specimens with past injuries on their heads.

Related species have the same bony plate which protects their necks, as well as different numbers of horns. The monoclonius has a single nose-horn; the pentaceratops has three true horns, like the triceratops, plus horn-like protrusions jutting from its cheeks; and the styracosaurus has a frill of horns located around the edge of its neck-plate.

Tyrannosaurus

This ravenous creature is one of the most fearsome and terrible of all carnivorous dinosaurs. Despite its huge size and eight-ton weight, the monster is a swift runner. Its huge head is nearly 6 feet long, and its teeth are from 3 to 6 inches in length.

Tyrannosaurus rex, the "tyrant lizard king," is a plains dweller, and so relentlessly and stupidly fierce that it will attack a small triceratops, kill it, and swallow its head in one gulp—thus killing itself in a matter of hours as the horns of the victim pierce the stomach of the victor.

This dinosaur's favorite food is any hadrosaur, such as the trachodon. The monster pursues and eats nearly anything; creatures of man-size or smaller are swallowed whole on a natural attack roll of 18 or higher. The tyrannosaurus also eats carrion, chasing away any smaller creatures to steal a meal found with its keen sense of smell.

There are many other species of carnosaur, some smaller and faster than tyrannosaurus. Some have stronger arms and more dangerous upper claws.

Displacer Beast

CLIMATE/TERRAIN:	Temperate mountains
FREQUENCY:	Very rare
ORGANIZATION:	Pack
ACTIVITY CYCLE:	Any
DIET:	Carnivorous
INTELLIGENCE:	Semi-(2-4)
TREASURE:	(D)
ALIGNMENT:	Lawful evil

NO. APPEARING:	2-5 (1d4 +1)
ARMOR CLASS:	4
MOVEMENT:	15
HIT DICE:	6
THAC0:	15
NO. OF ATTACKS:	2
DAMAGE/ATTACKS:	2-8 (2d4)/2-8 (2d4)
SPECIAL ATTACKS:	Nil
SPECIAL DEFENSES:	−2 on opponent's attack roll
MAGIC RESISTANCE:	Nil
SIZE:	L (8'-12' long)
MORALE:	Elite (13-14)
XP VALUE:	975

The displacer beast is a magical creature that resembles a puma with two powerful black tentacles growing from its shoulders. Very rare, they stay far from human habitations.

The displacer beast has the blue-black coloring of a dark panther, and a long cat-like body and head. Females range in length from 8 to 9 feet, and weigh 450 pounds; males are 10 to 12 feet long, and weigh up to 500 Lbs. They have 6 legs. Tentacles are tipped with rough horny edges that can inflict terrible wounds. Their eyes glow bright green, even after death.

Combat: The displacer beast is a fierce, savage creature that hates all forms of life. Highly aggressive, the displacer beast will attack on sight, using its tentacles to inflict 2-8 (2d4) points of damage to its victims.

Their main advantage in combat is their magical power of *displacement*, which allows them to appear to be some 3 feet from their actual location. Anyone attacking a displacer beast does so at −2 on his attack roll. In addition, the beasts save as 12th-level fighters; adding +2 to their die rolls.

To determine the true position of the displacer beast and its illusion, roll 1d10. On 1-5, the illusion is in front of the creature, 6-7 to the creature's left, 8-9, to the right. On 10, the illusion is behind the beasts actual position. Although this ability is magical, the beast's location can not be determined by *dispel* or *detect magic*. Only *true seeing* will reveal its position.

Displacer beasts will not use their claws or teeth unless near death, or when in combat with a very large opponent. If they do employ them, each claw does 1-3 points of damage, and each bite does 1-8 points of damage.

Habitat/Society: Displacer beasts are carnivores. Unless they are raising young, they usually run in packs, carving a savage swath of destruction as they go. They hate all life, and will sometimes kill purely for pleasure. Fierce and vicious as they are, however, displacer beasts never fight among themselves. The pack is a well-run and highly efficient killing machine. When encountered in packs, displacer beasts are more than a match for many large creatures and have been known to make a meal of orcs, goblins, and bands of men. Any creature entering their territory is viewed as potential prey.

Displacer beasts mate in the autumn, and the young are born in spring. A mated pair of displacer beasts makes its home in a cave, producing litters of 1-4 young. The cubs, about the size of domestic cats, are born without tentacles and reach maturity, though not full size, within 4 months. They remain in the cave until their displacement abilities are fully developed. This is followed by a two month period during which the cubs are taught how to hunt. When this is completed, the family group disbands and the monsters wander off to join separate packs. While raising young, the monsters are fiercely protective of their lairs. One adult always remains with the cubs, usually the female, while the other goes off to hunt. Dead prey is dragged back to the lair to be eaten by the family. Lairs are littered with the bones, equipment, and the treasures of its victims.

Naturally vicious and almost evil at times, displacer beasts harbor an undying hatred of blink dogs. Many theories attempt to account for this enmity. Some sages believe it springs from antipathy in temperaments—the lawful good blink dog would naturally be the enemy of a creature as savage and destructive as the displacer beast. Others argue that it is the displacement and blink abilities which cause this antipathy—the two abilities, when in close proximity, somehow stimulate the nervous system and produce hostile reactions. Encounters between the two breeds are rare however, since they do not share the same territory.

Ecology: Displacer beasts have little to fear from other large predators, save perhaps trolls or giants. Some wizards and alchemists value their hides for use in certain magical preparations, and will offer generous rewards for them. The eyes of a displacer beast are a highly prized, if uncommon, good luck charms among thieves who believe that they will protect the bearer from detection.

Dog

	Wild Dog	War Dog	Blink Dog	Death Dog
CLIMATE/TERRAIN:	Any	Any	Temperate plains	Warm deserts and subterranean
FREQUENCY:	Common	Uncommon	Rare	Very rare
ORGANIZATION:	Pack	Solitary	Pack	Pack
ACTIVITY CYCLE:	Any	Any	Any	Night
DIET:	Omnivorous	Omnivorous	Omnivorous	Carnivorous
INTELLIGENCE:	Semi- (2-4)	Semi- (2-4)	Average (8-10)	Semi- (2-4)
TREASURE:	Nil	Nil	(C)	Nil
ALIGNMENT:	Neutral	Neutral	Lawful good	Neutral evil
NO. APPEARING:	4-16 (4d4)	Variable	4-16 (4d4)	5-50 (5d10)
ARMOR CLASS:	7	6	5	7
MOVEMENT:	15	12	12	12
HIT DICE:	1+1	2+2	4	2+1
THAC0:	19	19	17	19
NO. OF ATTACKS:	1	1	1	2
DAMAGE/ATTACK:	1-4	2-8 (2d4)	1-6	1-10/1- 10
SPECIAL ATTACKS:	Nil	Nil	From the rear 75% of the time	Disease
SPECIAL DEFENSES:	Nil	Nil	Teleportation	Nil
MAGIC RESISTANCE:	Nil	Nil	Nil	Nil
SIZE:	S (3' long)	M (4'-6' long)	M (4' long)	M (6' long)
MORALE:	Unsteady (5-7)	Average (8-10)	Steady (11-12)	Steady (11-12)
XP VALUE:	35	65	270	120

Smaller than wolves, the appearance of the wild dog varies from place to place. Most appear very wolf-like, while others seem to combine the looks of a wolf and a jackal.

Combat: Wild dogs fight as an organized pack. They favor small game, and attack men and human habitations only in times of great hunger. The bite of a wild dog inflicts 1-4 points of damage.

Habitat/Society: Wild dogs are found almost anywhere. They run in packs, and are led by the dominant male. The pack usually hunts a variety of game, even attacking deer or antelope. Pups are born in the spring. Wild dogs can be tamed if separated from their pack.

Ecology: Wild dogs are omnivores which usually thrive on a combination of hunting and foraging.

War Dogs
Generally large mastiffs or wolfhounds, they have keen senses of smell and hearing, making them adept at detecting intruders. Most war dogs are not usually vicious, and will rarely attack without cause.

The status of war dogs varies greatly; some are loyal and beloved pets, some are watch dogs, others are hunting dogs, and some are trained for battle.

Blink Dogs
Blink dogs are yellowish brown canines which are stockier and more muscular than other wild dogs. They are intelligent and employ a limited form of teleportation when they hunt.

A blink dog attack is well organized. They will blink to and fro without any obvious pattern, using their powers to position themselves for an attack. Fully 75% of the time they are able to attack their targets from the rear. A dog will teleport on a roll of 7 or better on a 12-sided die. To determine where the dog appears, roll a 12-sided die: 1 = in front of opponent, 2 = shielded (or left) front flank, 3 = unshielded (or right) front flank, 4-12 = behind. When blinking, the dog will appear from 1 to 3 feet from its opponent and will immediately be able to attack.

Blinking is an innate power and the animal will never appear inside a space occupied by a solid object. If seriously threatened, the entire pack will blink out and not return.

Blink dogs are intelligent, and communicate in a complex language of barks, yaps, whines, and growls. They inhabit open plains and avoid human haunts. A lair will contain 3-12 (3d4) pups 50% of the time (1-2 hit dice, 1-2/1-3 hit points damage/attack). These puppies can be trained and are worth between 1,000 to 2,000 gold pieces.

Death dog
Death dogs are large two-headed hounds which are distinguished by their penetrating double bark. Death dogs hunt in large packs.

Each head is independent, and a bite does 1-10 points of damage. Victims must save vs. poison or contract a rotting disease which will kill them in 4-24 (4d6) days. Only a *cure disease* spell can save them. A natural roll of 19 or 20 on their attack die means that a man-sized opponent is knocked prone and attacks at a -4 until able to rise to its feet again. There is an 85% chance that death dogs will attack humans on sight.

Dog, Moon

CLIMATE/TERRAIN:	Elysium and Prime
FREQUENCY:	Rare
ORGANIZATION:	Solitary or small pack (see below)
ACTIVITY CYCLE:	Any
DIET:	Carnivore
INTELLIGENCE:	High to exceptional (13-16)
TREASURE:	Nil
ALIGNMENT:	Neutral good

NO. APPEARING:	1 or 2-8 (see below)
ARMOR CLASS:	0
MOVEMENT:	30, bipedal 9
HIT DICE:	9+3
THAC0:	11
NO. OF ATTACKS:	1
DAMAGE/ATTACK:	3-12
SPECIAL ATTACKS:	Bay, howl
SPECIAL DEFENSES:	Shadowy hypnotic pattern, +2 or better weapons to hit
MAGIC RESISTANCE:	25%
SIZE:	M (3' at shoulders)
MORALE:	Fanatic (17-18)
XP VALUE:	9,000

Often mistaken for baneful monsters, moon dogs are native creatures of Elysium and champions of the causes of good. They often appear in the Prime Material plane to fight evil wherever it shows itself.

Moon dogs look very similar to large wolf hounds. Their strange heads are slightly human in appearance, giving the animals a very intelligent look. The creatures' forepaws are adaptable, giving the moon dogs the ability to travel bipedally or on all fours. They are dark colored animals, ranging from dark gray to deep black. Moon dogs have amber eyes.

Moon dogs speak their own language, and they can communicate with all canines and lupines as well. They can speak common using a limited form of telepathy.

Combat: Woe to those who enter combat with a moon dog. These creatures of good are potent fighters and merciless against evil. Their powerful bite inflicts 3-12 points of damage.

Moon dogs prefer to attack with their keening howl. This baying is harmful to evil creatures only. Any evil creature within an 80 foot radius of a *baying* moon dog is affected as by a *fear* spell cast at 12th-level of magic use. Additional moon dogs baying have a cumulative effect. The *howling* will also cause 5-8 points of damage per round to evil creatures within 40 feet. In addition, the *howling* will cause intense physical pain to extra-planar creatures of evil alignment so much that they are 5% likely per moon dog howling to return to their plane. Moon dogs can *whine* to dispel illusions or *bark* to dispel evil, once per round.

The following spell-like powers (at 12th-level of use) are available to a moon dog one at a time, once per round, at will:

- *change self*, 3 times per day
- *cure disease*, by lick, 1 time per individual per day
- *cure light wounds*, by lick, 1 time per individual per day
- *dancing lights*
- *darkness*, 15' radius
- *detect evil*, always active
- *detect invisibility*, always active
- *detect magic*, always active
- *detect snares & pits*, always active
- *improved invisibility*
- *light*
- *mirror image*, 3 times per day
- *non-detection*

- *shades*, 1 time per day
- *slow poison*, by lick, 1 time per individual per day
- *wall of fog*

Moon dogs can become ethereal and have the ability to travel in the ethereal and Astral plane at will. They have superior vision equal to double normal vision, including 60' infravision. Combined with an unusually keen sense of smell and hearing, this grants moon dogs the detection abilities listed above, plus the ability to detect all illusions. Association with a moon dog for one hour or more removes *charms* and acts as a *remove curse*.

When in shadowy light, a moon dog is able to move in such a way as to effectively create magic equal to a *hypnotic pattern* of shadows. Only evil creatures will be affected. At the same time, each creature of good within the area will effectively gain a *protection from evil* and *remove fear* spell benefit. Moon dogs may not attack or perform any other action when weaving this pattern of shadows. It requires one full round to weave and extends to a range of 50 feet. The moon dog can *dispel magic*, but doing so will force it back to its own plane immediately.

Moon dogs may be damaged only by +2 or better magical weapons. They are never surprised (due to their keen senses) and cause opponents to subtract 3 from their surprise rolls. Moon dogs are immune to *fear* spells. They make all saving throws at a +2 bonus and takes half or quarter damage.

Habitat/Society: Moon dogs are native to the plane of Elysium. They are champions of good and will often travel about the upper planes and the Prime Material plane to challenge evil.

Moon dogs are friendly to all good and neutral races and those friendly to those races. They will not long associate with anyone because they are constantly on the move, hunting evil.

Ecology: Moon dogs will often communicate with communities of men, using telepathy, in order to locate trouble spots among them.

Dolphin

CLIMATE/TERRAIN:	Any saltwater
FREQUENCY:	Uncommon
ORGANIZATION:	School
ACTIVITY CYCLE:	Any
DIET:	Carnivore
INTELLIGENCE:	Very (11-12)
TREASURE:	Nil
ALIGNMENT:	Lawful good

NO. APPEARING:	2-20
ARMOR CLASS:	5
MOVEMENT:	30
HIT DICE:	2+2
THAC0:	19
NO. OF ATTACKS:	1
DAMAGE/ATTACK:	2-8
SPECIAL ATTACKS:	Nil
SPECIAL DEFENSES:	Save as 4th-lvl fighter
MAGIC RESISTANCE:	Nil
SIZE:	M (5'-6' long)
MORALE:	Steady (11)
XP VALUE:	120

Dolphins are intelligent seagoing mammals.

While all dolphins share a variety of common traits, the species comes in a variety of shapes and sizes. Their long, compact bodies are superbly adapted to the aquatic environment, and dolphins are among the most powerful swimmers in the oceans. All breeds of dolphins have a large fin on their backs, two flippers, a powerful tail, jaws filled with many sharp teeth, a blow hole, and are 5 to 6 feet long. Most common and well-known are the gray, or bottle-nosed dolphins, so named for their gray skin and bottle-shaped snouts. Other varieties have two-toned blue and gray coloring. The species communicates through an intricate speech consisting of high-pitched sounds, some out of the range of human hearing.

Combat: Inherently peaceful, dolphins will generally attack only if threatened. Unless outnumbered 2 to 1, dolphins always attack sharks. Whether attacking a foe or defending their school, dolphins fight as an organized unit, responding to commands from their leader. They fight with special vehemence to protect their young, and a select number of dolphins may sometimes engage in a holding action, sacrificing themselves so that the remainder of the school can swim to safety.

Habitat/Society: Dolphins are completely carnivorous, living on a diet of fish. Though they can remain submerged for several minutes at a time, they must surface regularly to breathe. Unlike most mammals, breathing is a conscious, rather than unconscious action on the part of dolphins; in other words, they literally must remember to breathe. Newborn dolphins are assisted to the surface to breathe by their mothers and a female dolphin midwife. Dolphins are by nature playful, good-tempered, and lawful good, despising evil creatures. Most roam the oceans in schools, numbering as large as 20 dolphins, swimming where their fancy suits them. They never fight among themselves or with other breeds of dolphins. Dolphins are famous for the great pleasure they take in life; when swimming they often perform dazzling aquatic stunts, leaping in and out of the water in a spectacular fashion. They will also play with objects that they find and enjoy games. Dolphins sometimes follow ships, entertaining the crews and passengers with their antics.

About 10% of all dolphins live in organized communities. These groups have 1d4+1 swordfish (AC 6, move 24, 1+1 Hit Dice, 2d6 points of damage/attack) or 1-3 narwhales (AC 6, move 21, 4+4 Hit Dice, 2d12 points of damage/attack) as guards, depending on the climatic region. If a community is found, there is a 75% possibility that there are 1d4 additional communities of dolphins within a five-mile radius. These organized communities of dolphins do not tolerate the presence of evil sea creatures in their domain, and if necessary enlist the aid of nomadic schools of dolphins to drive out evil creatures. Any region inhabited by dolphin communities is also shark and killer whale free.

Dolphins are highly intelligent and take a benign, distant interest in human doings. They will always help humans in distress, guiding them to the shore and keeping the sharks at bay. Certain solitary dolphins, known as rogues, have been known to form closer attachments to humans, accompanying them in a friendly fashion on swimming and fishing expeditions. These rogues often play dolphin games with their human companions. Dolphins are far more valuable to men in other respects. Friendly dolphins have warned sailors of the approach of pirate ships and the intentions of evil sea creatures. More than one ship owes its safe arrival in port to the timely intercession and warning of dolphins. They have come to men's aid when their ships were attacked by mermen and sahuagin. Dolphins have been known to raid sahuagin communities and destroy their eggs, for dolphins perceive these monsters as a threat to their safety.

Ecology: The dolphin is both a hunter and hunted in its marine world. Sharks and other large evil sea creatures hunt the dolphin with enthusiasm. Despite its many enemies, the dolphin has many distinct advantages that enable it to survive and even flourish. Not only is it a strong, swift swimmer, but its intelligence and organized lifestyle are highly effective defenses against its enemies.

Doppleganger

CLIMATE/TERRAIN:	Any
FREQUENCY:	Very rare
ORGANIZATION:	Tribal
ACTIVITY CYCLE:	Any
DIET:	Omnivore
INTELLIGENCE:	Very (11-12)
TREASURE:	E
ALIGNMENT:	Neutral

NO. APPEARING:	3-12
ARMOR CLASS:	5
MOVEMENT:	9
HIT DICE:	4
THAC0:	17
NO. OF ATTACKS:	1
DAMAGE/ATTACK:	1-12
SPECIAL ATTACKS:	Surprise
SPECIAL DEFENSES:	See below
MAGIC RESISTANCE:	See below
SIZE:	M
MORALE:	Elite (13)
XP VALUE:	420

The doppleganger is a master of mimicry that survives by taking the shapes of men, demihumans, and humanoids.

Dopplegangers are bipedal and generally humanoid in appearance. Their bodies are covered with a thick, hairless gray hide, which gives them a natural AC of 5. They are, however, rarely seen in their true forms.

Combat: This monster is able to assume the shape of any humanoid creature between four and eight feet high. The doppleganger chooses a victim, duplicates his form, and then attempts to kill the original and assume his place. The doppleganger is able to use *ESP* and can imitate its victim with 90% accuracy, even duplicating the victim's clothing and equipment. If unsuccessful in taking its victim's place, the doppleganger attacks, relying on the ensuing confusion to make it indistinguishable from its victim. A doppleganger is immune to *sleep* and *charm* spells and rolls all saving throws as if he was a 10th-level fighter.

Dopplegangers work in groups and act together to ensure that their attacks and infiltrations are successful. They are very intelligent and usually take the time to plan their attacks with care. If a group of the monsters spots some potential victims, the dopplegangers often trail their targets, waiting for a good chance to strike, choosing their time and opportunity with care. They may wait until nightfall, or until their victims are alone, or even follow them to an inn.

Habitat/Society: Dopplegangers are rumored to be artificial beings that were created long ago by a powerful wizard or godling. They were originally intended to be used as spies and assassins in an ancient, highly magical war. Their creator died long ago, but they live on, still working as spies for evil powers, thieves, and government. They have even been known to work as assassins.

All dopplegangers belong to a single tribe. Although this is rare, groups of dopplegangers can be found anywhere at any time, and in unexpected locations. Working as a unit, they select a group of victims, such as a family or a group of travelers. Basically lazy, dopplegangers find it easier to survive and live comfortably by taking humanoid, and especially human, shape. They prefer to take the form of someone comfortably provided for, and shun assuming the form of hardworking peasants. Since

they are only 90% accurate in their mimicry, most dopplegangers are eventually discovered and driven out, and then forced once more to assume a new shape.

Dopplegangers are found most often in their true forms in a dungeon or in the wilderness. Groups often set up a lair in an area well-suited to ambush and surprise, patrolling a regular territory. These bands make a good living by attacking weak humanoid monsters or travelers and stealing their food and treasure. If food and treasure are scarce, they hire out to a powerful wizard or thieves' guild.

A doppleganger who has been hired to replace a specific person will plan its attack with special care, learning as much about the victim and his environment as it can.

The dopplegangers' weaknesses are greed and cowardice. They spend their lives in avid pursuit of gold and other wealth. If attacking a group of adventurers, for example, they often choose the richest-looking one to attack first. If they target a party of adventurers, the dopplegangers wait until the party is on the way out of the dungeon and heading back to town. Since they are cowardly, however, they prefer to take the easiest route toward riches. A doppleganger who chooses a rich adventurer avoids risks once the treasure is safely in hand, and retreats at the earliest opportunity, making some plausible excuse for separating from the human members of the group. They sometimes hire out as spies and assassins for money as well.

Ecology: Dopplegangers are sophisticated and dangerous parasites, living off the labors of others. They must also be reckoned with as clever and effective spies and assassins who can wreak political mayhem in positions of power. Evil wizards have on rare occasions controlled entire kingdoms for short periods of time by replacing a king, prince, or councilor with a doppleganger.

Dracolich

CLIMATE/TERRAIN:	See below
FREQUENCY:	Very rare
ORGANIZATION:	Solitary
ACTIVITY CYCLE:	Night
DIET:	Special
INTELLIGENCE:	As per individual dragon
TREASURE:	B, H, S, T
ALIGNMENT:	Evil (any)

NO. APPEARING:	1
ARMOR CLASS:	See below
MOVEMENT:	As per former dragon type
HIT DICE:	As per former dragon type
THAC0:	As per former dragon type
NO. OF ATTACKS:	As per former dragon type
DAMAGE/ATTACK:	See below
SPECIAL ATTACKS:	Breath weapon and spell use
SPECIAL DEFENSES:	Spell immunities and spell use
MAGIC RESISTANCE:	See below
SIZE:	As per individual dragon
MORALE:	See below
XP VALUE:	As per individual dragon, plus 1,000 (both dracolich and host must be destroyed)

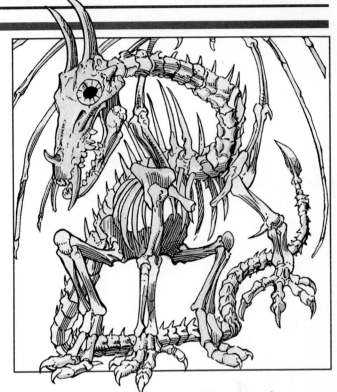

The dracolich is an undead creature resulting from the unnatural transformation of an evil dragon. The mysterious Cult of the Dragon practices the powerful magic necessary for the creation of the dracolich, though other practitioners are also rumored to exist.

A dracolich can be created from any of the evil dragon subspecies. A dracolich retains the physical appearance of its original body, except that its eyes appear as glowing points of light floating in shadowy eye sockets. Skeletal or semi-skeletal dracoliches have been observed on occasion.

The senses of a dracolich are similar to those of its original form; it can detect invisible objects and creatures (including those hidden in darkness of fog) within a 10-foot radius per age category and also possesses a natural *clairaudience* ability while in its lair equal to a range of 20 feet per age category. A dracolich can speak, cast spells, and employ the breath weapon of its original form; it can cast each of its spells once per day and can use its breath weapon once every three combat rounds. Additionally, a dracolich retains the intelligence and memory of its original form.

Combat: Dracoliches are immune to *charm*, *sleep*, *enfeeblement*, *polymorph*, *cold* (magical or natural), *electricity*, *hold*, *insanity*, and *death* spells or *symbols*. They cannot be poisoned, paralyzed, or turned by priests. They have the same magic resistance as their original forms; only magical attacks from wizards of 6th level or higher, or from monsters of 6 or more Hit Dice have a chance of affecting dracoliches.

The Armor Class of a dracolich is equal to the Armor Class of its original form, bettered by −2 (for example, if the AC of the original form was −1, the AC of the dracolich is −3). Attacks on a dracolich, due to its magical nature, do not gain any attack or damage roll bonuses.

Initially, a dracolich has the same morale rating as its original form. However, after a dracolich is successful in its first battle, its morale rating permanently becomes Fearless (19 base); this assumes that the opponent or opponents involved in the battle had a Hit Dice total of at least 100% of the Hit Dice of the dracolich (for instance, a 16-HD dracolich must defeat an opponent or opponents of at least 16 total HD to receive the morale increase). Once a dracolich receives the morale increase, it becomes immune to magical fear as well.

The dracolich has a slightly stronger ability to cause fear in opponents than it did in its original form; opponents must roll their saving throws vs. spell with a −1 penalty (in addition to any other relevant modifiers) to resist the dracolich's fear aura. The gaze of the dracolich's glowing eyes can also paralyze creatures within 40 yards if they fail their saving throws (creatures of 6th level [or 6 Hit Dice] or higher gain a +3 bonus to their saving throws). If a creature successfully saves against the gaze of a dracolich, it is permanently immune to the gaze of that particular dracolich.

The attack routine of a dracolich is similar to that of its original form; for example, a dracolich that was originally a green dragon will bring down a weak opponent with a series of physical attacks, but it will stalk more formidable opponents, attacking at an opportune moment with its breath weapon and spells.

All physical attacks, such as clawing and biting, inflict the same damage as the dracolich's original form, plus 2d8 points of chilling damage. A victim struck by a dracolich who fails a saving throw vs. paralyzation is paralyzed for 2d6 rounds. Immunity to cold damage, temporary or permanent, negates the chilling damage but not the paralyzation. Dracoliches cannot drain life levels.

All dracoliches can attempt *undead control* (as per a *potion of undead control*) once every three days on any variety of undead with 60 yards. The undead's saving throws against this power suffer a −3 penalty; if the *undead control* is successful, it lasts for one turn only. While *undead control* is in use, the dracolich cannot use other spells. If the dracolich interrupts its undead control before it has been used for a full turn, the dracolich must still wait three days before the power can be used again.

If a dracolich or proto-dracolich is slain, its spirit immediately returns to its host. If there is no corpse in range for it to possess, the spirit is trapped in the host until such a time—if ever—that a corpse becomes available. A dracolich is difficult to destroy. It can be destroyed outright by *power word, kill* or a similar spell. If its spirit is currently contained in its host, destroying the host when a suitable corpse is not within range effectively destroys the dracolich. Likewise, an active dracolich is unable to attempt further possessions if its host is destroyed. The fate of a disembodied dracolich spirit—that is, a spirit with no body or host—is unknown, but it is presumed that it is drawn to the lower planes.

Dracolich

Habitat/Society: The creation of a dracolich is a complex process involving the transformation of an evil dragon by arcane magical forces, the most notorious practitioners of which are members of the Cult of the Dragon. The process is usually a cooperative effort between the evil dragon and the wizards, but especially powerful wizards have been known to coerce an evil dragon to undergo the transformation against its will.

Any evil dragon is a possible candidate for transformation, although old dragons or older with spell-casting abilities are preferred. Once a candidate is secured, the wizards first prepare the dragon's host, an inanimate object that will hold the dragon's life force. The host must be a solid item of not less than 2,000 gp value resistant to decay (wood, for instance, is unsuitable). A gemstone is commonly used for a host, particularly ruby, pearl, carbuncle, and jet, and is often set in the hilt of a sword or other weapon. The host is prepared by casting *enchant an item* upon it and speaking the name of the evil dragon; the item may resist the spell by successfully saving vs. spell as an 11th-level wizard. If the spell is resisted, another item must be used for the host. If the spell is not resisted, the item can then function as a host. If desired, *glasssteel* can be cast upon the host to protect it.

Next, a special potion is prepared for the evil dragon to consume. The exact composition of the potion varies according to the age and type of the dragon, but it must contain precisely seven ingredients, among them a *potion of evil dragon control*, a *potion of invulnerability*, and the blood of a vampire. When the evil dragon consumes the potion, the results are determined as follows (roll percentile dice):

Roll	Result
01-10	No effect.
11-40	Potion does not work. The dragon suffers 2d12 points of damage and is helpless with convulsions for 1-2 rounds.
41-50	Potion does not work. The dragon dies. A full *wish* or similar spell is needed to restore the dragon to life; a *wish* to transform the dragon into a dracolich results in another roll on this table.
51-00	Potion works.

If the potion works, the dragon's spirit transfers to the host, regardless of the distance between the dragon's body and the host. A dim light within the host indicates the presence of the spirit. While contained in the host, the spirit cannot take any actions; it cannot be contacted nor attacked by magic. The spirit can remain in the host indefinitely.

Once the spirit is contained in the host, the host must be brought within 90 feet of a reptilian corpse; under no circumstances can the spirit possess a living body. The spirit's original body is ideal, but the corpse of any reptilian creature that died or was killed within the previous 30 days is suitable.

The wizard who originally prepared the host must touch the host, cast a *magic jar* spell while speaking the name of the dragon, then touch the corpse. The corpse must fail a saving throw vs. spell for the spirit to successfully possess it; if it saves, it will never accept the spirit. The following modifiers apply to the roll:

−10 if the corpse is the spirit's own former body (which can be dead for any length of time).

−4 if the corpse is of the same alignment as the dragon.

−4 if the corpse is that of a true dragon (any type).

−3 if the corpse is that of a firedrake, ice lizard, wyvern, or fire lizard.

−1 if the corpse is that of a dracolisk, dragonne, dinosaur, snake, or other reptile.

If the corpse accepts the spirit, it becomes animated by the spirit. If the animated corpse is the spirit's former body, it immediately becomes a dracolich; however, it will not regain the use of its voice and breath weapon for another seven days (note that it will not be able to cast spells with verbal components during this time). At the end of seven days, the dracolich regains the use of its voice and breath weapon.

If the animated corpse is not the spirit's former body, it immediately becomes a proto-dracolich. A proto-dracolich has the mind and memories of its original form, but has the hit points and immunities to spells and priestly turning of a dracolich. A proto-dracolich can neither speak nor cast spells; further, it cannot cause chilling damage, use a breath weapon, or cause fear as a dracolich. Its strength, movement, and Armor Class are those of the possessed body.

To become a full dracolich, a proto-dracolich must devour at least 10% of its original body. Unless the body has been dispatched to another plane of existence, a proto-dracolich can always sense the presence of its original body, regardless of the distance. A proto-dracolich will tirelessly seek out its original body to the exclusion of all other activities. If its original body has been burned, dismembered, or otherwise destroyed, the proto-dracolich need only devour the ashes or pieces equal to or exceeding 10% of its original body mass (total destruction of the original body is possible only through use of a *disintegrate* or similar spell; the body could be reconstructed with a *wish* or similar spell, so long as the spell is cast in the same plane as the *disintegration*). If a proto-dracolich is unable to devour its original body, it is trapped in its current form until slain.

A proto-dracolich transforms into a full dracolich within seven days after it devours its original body. When the transformation is complete, the dracolich resembles its original body; it can now speak, cast spells, and employ the breath weapon of its original body, in addition to having all of the abilities of a dracolich.

The procedure for possessing a new corpse is the same as explained above, except that the assistance of a wizard is no longer necessary (casting *magic jar* is required only for the first possession). If the spirit successfully re-possesses its original body, it once again becomes a full dracolich. If the spirit possesses a different body, it becomes a proto-dracolich and must devour its former body to become a full dracolich.

A symbiotic relationship exists between a dracolich and the wizards who create it. The wizards honor and aid their dracolich, as well as providing it with regular offerings of treasure items. In return, the dracolich defends its wizards against enemies and other threats, as well as assisting them in their various schemes. Like dragons, dracoliches are loners, but they take comfort in the knowledge that they have allies.

Dracoliches are generally found in the same habitats as the dragons from which they were created; dracoliches created from green dragons, for instance, are likely to be found in subtropical and temperate forests. Though they do not live with their wizards, their lairs are never more than a few miles away. Dracoliches prefer darkness and are usually encountered at night, in shadowy forests, or in underground labyrinths.

Ecology: Dracoliches are never hungry, but they must eat in order to refuel their breath weapons. Like dragons, dracoliches can consume nearly anything, but prefer the food eaten by their original forms (for instance, if a dracolich was originally a red dragon, it prefers fresh meat). The body of a destroyed dracolich crumbles into a foul-smelling powder within a few hours; this powder can be used by knowledgeable wizards as a component for creating *potions of undead control* and similar magical substances.

Dragons are an ancient, winged reptilian race. They are known and feared for their size, physical prowess, and magical abilities. The oldest dragons are among the most powerful creatures in the world. Most dragons are identified by the color of their scales.

There are many know subspecies of dragons, several of which fall into three broad categories: chromatic, gem, and metallic dragons. Chromatic dragons include black, blue, green, red, and white dragons; all are extremely evil and are feared by most. The metallic dragons are the brass, bronze, copper, gold, and silver dragons; these are noble and good, highly respected by wise people.

The gem dragons are the amethyst, crystal, emerald, sapphire, and topaz dragons; they are neutral with respect to good and evil, and are very charismatic and suave, masters of persuasion who delight in riddles. Though generally smaller and slower than other dragons, gem dragons are often wiser and more intelligent, and have other powers to compensate, like psionics.

In addition to the dragons in these three classifications, there are other dragons that may at first seem to be members of those categories. For instance, the steel dragon seems to be a metallic dragon, but has only one breath weapon; while each "true" metallic dragon has two. Likewise, the brown dragon seems to be a typical, evil chromatic dragon; but has no wings, so is not a "true" chromatic dragon.

Although all subspecies of dragons are believed to have come from the same roots tens of thousands of years ago, the present subspecies keep to themselves, working together only under extreme circumstances, such as a powerful mutual threat. Good dragons never work with evil dragons, however, though a few neutral dragon specimens have been known to associate with evil or good dragons. Gold dragons occasionally associate freely with silver dragons, and emerald dragons are sometimes found with sapphire dragons.

When evil dragons of different species encounter each other, they usually fight to protect their territories. While good dragons of different subspecies are more tolerant of each other, they are also very territorial. They usually try to work out differences in a peaceful manner. Gem dragons often settle inter-species disputes with riddling contests.

All subspecies of dragons have 12 age categories, and gain more abilities and greater power as they age. Dragons range in size from several feet upon hatching to more than 100 feet, after they have attained the status of great wyrm. The exact size varies according to age and subspecies. A dragon's wingspan is about equal to its body length; 15-20% of a dragon's body length is neck.

Generally, when multiple dragons are encountered they are a mated pair and young. Mated dragons are always young adults, adults, or mature adults; young dragons found with their parents are of the young adult stage or younger. To determine the age of young dragons roll 1d6: 1 = egg; 2 = hatchling; 3 = very young; 4 = young; 5 = juvenile; 6 = young adult.

During the early part of a dragon's young adult stage it leaves its parents, greed driving it on to start a lair of its own. Sometimes, although rarely, juvenile dragons leave their parents to start their own lives. As a pair of mated dragons age beyond the mature adult stage, they split up, independence and the lust for treasure driving them apart. Older dragons of either sex sometimes raise young, but only on their own—the other parent leaves when the eggs are laid.

Dragons, especially older ones, are generally solitary due to necessity and preference. They distance themselves from civilization, which they consider to be a petty and foolish mortal invention.

Dragons are fearsome predators, but scavenge when necessary and can eat almost anything if they are hungry enough. A dragon's metabolism operates like a highly efficient furnace, making use of 95% of all the food the dragon eats. A dragon can also metabolize inorganic material, and some dragons have developed a taste for such fare.

Although dragons' goals and ideals vary among subspecies, all dragons are covetous. They like to hoard wealth, collecting mounds of coins and gathering as many gems, jewels, and magical items as possible. They find treasure pleasing to look at, and they bask in the radiance of the magical items. For a dragon, there is never enough treasure. Those with large hoards are loath to leave them for long, venturing out of their lairs only to patrol the immediate areas or to get food. Dragons like to make beds of their treasure, shaping nooks and mounds to fit their bodies. By the time they mature to the great wyrm stage, hundreds of gems and coins are imbedded in their hides.

Dragon Defenses: A dragon's Armor Class improves as it gets older and the creature becomes tougher. Old dragons or older dragons are immune to normal missiles; their gem-encrusted hides deflect arrows and other small projectiles. Large missiles (from catapults, giants, etc.) and magical missiles affect them normally. Young adult and older dragons radiate a personal aura that makes them partially resistant to harmful magic. A dragon's resistance to magic increases as it ages.

Dragon Hide: Dragon skin is prized by armorers with the skill to turn it into shields and armor, valuable because of its appearance and the protection it affords. Dragon armor grants its wearer an Armor Class of 4 less than the Armor Class of the dragon it was taken from, for a minimum Armor Class of 8. For example, armor from a juvenile brass dragon (AC O) grants its wearer AC 4. Dragon armor is supple and non-bulky, weighing only 25 pounds.

The scales of gem dragons take on properties of actual gems; they are faceted and reflect light. They are slightly more brittle than those of other dragons, so armor made from them requires repair more often.

Dragon armor affords no extra protection, such as resistance to fire or cold, although the armor can be enchanted to provide such protection. A dragon's resistance to certain elements is based on its total makeup, not just its skin. Plain dragon armor is expensive to make, costing 1,000-10,000 gp, based on the workmanship and protection the armor affords. Dragon skin armor can be enchanted, just as other forms of armor can, to a maximum of +5.

Dragon shields also offer no additional protection. They are made of stretched hide over a wooden frame. Such shields weigh 3 pounds (if small) or 8 pounds (if large) and cost 20-120 or 30-180 gold pieces.

Dragon Senses: All dragons have excellent senses of sight, smell, and hearing. Their enhanced senses enable them to detect all invisible objects and creatures (including creatures or items hidden in darkness or fog) within a radius equal to 10 feet times their age category. All dragons possess a natural clairaudience ability with respect to their lairs; the range is 20 feet per age category. The dragon must concentrate on a specific section within its lair or surrounding area to hear what is going on.

Some dragons are able to communicate telepathically with any intelligent creature. The percentage chance for a dragon to speak is based on its Intelligence and age category. Refer to individual descriptions for percentages.

Dragon Lairs: All dragon lairs are far from mortal civilization, and they are difficult to find because the dragons take careful measures to cloak their coming and going. There is usually little, if any, wildlife around the lairs because neighboring creatures fear the dragons, and most dragons eat the few creatures that are foolish enough to remain.

When a young adult dragon leaves its parents in search of its own lair, it spends a few years moving from place to place to find a cave or cavern which best suits its personality. In most cases, the dragons search for increasingly larger caves which can easily accommodate them as they grow. Usually by the time a dragon has reached the mature adult stage, it has selected a large lair it plans to keep for the remainder of its life. A dragon at this stage has gathered a considerable amount of treasure and is loath to move it to a different location.

The location and character of dragon lairs vary based on each subspecies; consult individual dragons for specific information. However, one thing remains constant: any dragon considers its lair and neighboring areas its domains. A creature which violates or threatens the lair is threatening the dragon and will be dealt with harshly. Some good dragons may be more lenient than other subspecies in this matter. All dragons keep their treasure hidden deep within their lairs, and some dragons create hazardous conditions within their lain to keep unwary creatures from reaching the treasure.

Dragon Flight: Despite their large size, dragons are graceful and competent fliers; most are maneuverability class C. This is due partially to their powerful wings, and partially to the dragon's innate magic. Dragons can climb at half speed and dive at double speed.

A dragon can change direction quickly by executing a wingover maneuver. A dragon cannot gain altitude during the round it executes a wingover, but it may dive. The maneuver enables the dragon to make a turn of 120 to 240 degrees regardless of its speed or size.

Dragon, General

Diving dragons can strike with their claws with a +2 bonus to attack rolls. Dragons diving on land-bound opponents can also strike with both wings, but then must land immediately after attacking.

When engaging other flying opponents, dragons can either claw or bite, but not both. An airborne dragon must glide to cast spells (but innate abilities can be used at any time). A gliding dragon loses 1,000 feet of altitude per round, and its forward speed is equal to one half its flight speed on the round before it began gliding.

Dragon Table

Age Category	Age (in years)	Hit Die Modifier	Combat Modifier	Fear Radius	Fear Save Modifier
1 Hatchling	0-5	−6	+1	Nil	Nil
2 Very young	6-15	−4	+2	Nil	Nil
3 Young	16-25	−2	+3	Nil	Nil
4 Juvenile	26-50	Nil	+4	Nil	Nil
5 Young adult	51-100	+1	+5	15 yards	+3 (+7)
6 Adult	101-200	+2	+6	20 yards	+2 (+6)
7 Mature adult	201-400	+3	+7	25 yards	+1 (+5)
8 Old	401-600	+4	+8	30 yards	0 (+4)
9 Very old	601-800	+5	+9	35 yards	−1 (+3)
10 Venerable	801-1,000	+6	+10	40 yards	−2 (+2)
11 Wyrm	1,001-1,200	+7	+11	45 yards	−3 (+1)
12 Great Wyrm	1,200+	+8	+12	50 yards	−4 (0)

Dragon Fear: Dragons can inspire panic or fear. The mere sight of a young adult or older dragon causes creatures with fewer than 1 Hit Die (as well as all noncarnivorous, nonaggressive creatures with fewer Hit Dice than the dragon) to automatically flee in panic for 4d6 rounds.

Trained war mounts, organized military units, and single creatures with 1 Hit Die or more, but with fewer Hit Dice than the dragon are not panicked, but they may be stricken with fear if they are within the dragon's fear aura. The aura surrounds attacking or charging dragons in the specified radius and in a path along the ground directly beneath a flying dragon whose altitude is 250 feet or less. Creatures not automatically panicked are entitled to saving throws vs. petrification. Creatures failing their saving throws are stricken with fear and fight with a -2 penalty to their attack and damage rolls. The aura increases in size and power based on the age category of the dragon; creatures subjected to the aura receive a saving throw bonus or a penalty as specified on the Dragon Table. All creatures with Hit Dice equal to or greater than those of the dragon are immune to the fear effect.

Gem dragons are not as inherently fearsome as other dragons, so saving throws against their fear auras receive bonuses; the bonuses appear in parenthesis in the Dragon Table.

Dragon Hit Die Modifier: Dragon Hit Dice vary between subspecies and are modified based on age category. Refer to individual dragon entries for the base Hit Dice for each species, and to the Dragon Table for the modifier based on age. The older a dragon gets, the more Hit Dice it has. For example, a black dragon has a base of 10 Hit Dice. A hatchling black dragon subtracts 6 dice, giving it a total of 4. A great wyrm black dragon adds 8 dice for a total of 18.

Dragons' saving throws are tied to their Hit Dice. Each dragon saves as a fighter equal in level to the dragon's Hit Dice. For example, a hatchling black dragon saves as a 4th-level fighter, while a great wyrm black dragon saver as an 18th-level fighter.

Dragon Combat Modifier: A dragon's combat modifier varies with age category. The bonus or penalty applies to damage rolls for each physical attack. It does not apply to a dragon's breath weapon. The combat modifier is also applied to the dragon's base spellcasting level (age category), to determine the actual level at which the dragon casts spells (thus, a great wyrm casts spells at 24th level of ability).

Dragon Attacks: All dragons have a claw/claw/bite attack form and a breath weapon. The latter can be used once every three rounds. Dragons also employ several other attack forms which are detailed in the following text. Dragons frequently divide their attacks between opponents, using the more dangerous attacks, such as the bite, against the foes they perceive to be the toughest.

A dragon's preferred attacks are usually, in order, breath weapon, magical abilities (or spells), and physical attacks. A dragon that breathes during a round of combat cannot also attack physically. Magical abilities (but not spells) can be used in addition to any attacks, except the breath weapon.

Claws: A dragon can use its claws to attack creatures to its front and sides. If the dragon kicks with one rear leg, it can attack with only one claw (the other must be used to maintain balance).

Bite: Because of a dragon's long neck, it can bite creatures to its back and sides.

Snatch: Only young adult and older dragons can snatch. This occurs when a flying dragon dives and attempts to grab a creature in one of its claws. A creature struck by this method is taken into the air. There is a 50% chance that a snatched creature has its arms pinned, and therefore cannot physically attack the dragon. Snatched creatures are sometimes taken to great heights and dropped. The snatched creature can be squeezed in the claw for automatic claw damage each round, or transferred to the dragon's mouth (the transfer requires a successful attack roll). If the transfer succeeds, the victim automatically suffers bite damage each round; if it fails, the victim is dropped. Dragons of age old and older can carry a victim in each claw, and they can try to snatch two victims at once. Wyrms and great wyrms can carry three victims, but one of the first two snatched must be transferred from claw to mouth before the third can be snatched.

A dragon can snatch creatures two or more size categories smaller than itself. For example, a dragon that is 45' long is a Gargantuan creature, so the biggest creature it can snatch is a Large one (12' long).

Plummet: If the DM chooses to allow plummets, an airborne dragon, or a dragon jumping and descending from at least 30 feet above a target, can land on a victim. The dragon crushes and pins opponents using its claws and tail, inflicting damage equal to its bite. The dragon can crush as many creatures as its combat modifier. The dragon rolls a separate attack against each creature affected. Creatures that are missed are assumed to have escaped. Creatures that are crushed must roll successful saving throws vs. petrification or be pinned under the dragon, automatically suffering crushing damage during the next round unless the dragon moves off them. If the dragon chooses to maintain the pin, the victims must roll successful saving throws vs. petrification to get free. The dragon's combat modifier applies as a penalty to all saving throw vs. the crush. A dragon cannot take any other actions when plummeting or pinning.

Kick: Any dragon can kick creatures attacking it from behind. A kick delivers claw damage, and creatures struck must roll their Dexterity or less on 1d20 or be kicked back 1d6 feet, +1 foot per age category of the dragon. Those knocked back must make successful saving throws vs. petrification (adjusted by the dragon's combat modifier) or fall. If the dragon attacks with one claw, it can kick with only one hind leg (the other must be used for balance). It cannot slap its tail while kicking.

Wing Buffet: Young adult and older dragons can employ their wings in combat; targets must be at the dragon's sides. The damage inflicted is the same as a claw attack, and creatures struck must roll their Dexterity or less on 1d20 or be knocked prone.

Tail Slap: Adult and older dragons can use their tails to attack creatures to their rear and sides. A tail attack inflicts the same damage as two claw attacks and affects as many targets as the dragon's age category. The dragon rolls a separate attack against each creature. Creatures struck must roll successful saving throws vs. petrification (adjusted by the dragon's combat modifier) or be stunned for 1d4 +1 minutes. A tail slap can smash a light wooden structure and even damage a cube of force (one charge per two points of combat modifier, round down).

Stall: Any dragon flying near the ground can halt its forward motion and hover for one round; it must land immediately thereafter. Once stopped, the dragon can attack with its bite and all four legs. It can use its breath weapon instead, but this rarely happens since dragons can breathe on the wing. If a dragon stalls in an area with lots of trees or loose earth, the draft from its wings creates a dust cloud with the same radius as its fear aura. Creatures within the cloud are blinded, and no spell casting is possible. The dust lasts for one round.

Spells: Dragons learn spells haphazardly over the years. The DM should randomly determine which spells any particular dragon knows. The dragon can cast each spell once per day, unless random determination indicates the same spell more than once, in which case the dragon can cast it more than once a day. Dragons to not use spell books or pray to deities; they simply sleep, concentrate when they awaken, and remember their spells. Dragon spells have only a verbal component; the spells have a casting time of 1, regardless of level. Dragons cannot physically attack, use their breath weapon, use their magical abilities, or fly (except to glide) while casting a spell.

Dragon, Chromatic   Black Dragon

CLIMATE/TERRAIN:	Any swamp, jungle, and subterranean
FREQUENCY:	Rare
ORGANIZATION:	Solitary or clan
ACTIVE TIME:	Any
DIET:	Special
INTELLIGENCE:	Average (8-10)
TREASURE:	Special
ALIGNMENT:	Chaotic evil

NO. APPEARING:	1 (2-5)
ARMOR CLASS:	1 (base)
MOVEMENT:	12, Fl 30 (C), Sw 12
HIT DICE:	12 (base)
THAC0:	9 (base)
NO. OF ATTACKS:	3 + special
DAMAGE/ATTACK:	1-6/1-6/3-18
SPECIAL ATTACKS:	Special
SPECIAL DEFENSES:	Variable
MAGIC RESISTANCE:	Variable
SIZE:	G (30′ base)
MORALE:	Fanatic (17-18)
XP VALUE:	Variable

Black dragons are abusive, quick to anger, and resent intrusions of any kind. They like dismal surroundings, heavy vegetation, and prefer darkness to daylight. Although not as intelligent as other dragons, black dragons are instinctively cunning and malevolent.

At birth, a black dragon's scales are thin, small, and glossy. But as the dragon ages, its scales become larger, thicker, and duller, which helps it camouflage itself in swamps and marshes. Black dragons speak their own tongue, a tongue common to all evil dragons, and 10% of hatchling black dragons have an ability to communicate with any intelligent creature. The chance to possess this ability increases 5% per age category of the dragon.

Combat: Black dragons prefer to ambush their targets, using their surroundings as cover. Their favorite targets are men, who they will sometimes stalk for several minutes in an attempt to gauge their strength and wealth before attacking. Against a band of men or a formidable creature, older black dragons will use their special abilities first, so the very forces of the marsh can weaken the targets before the dragon joins the fight. Black dragons will also use their breath weapon before closing in melee. When fighting in heavily vegetated swamps and marshes, black dragons attempt to stay in the water or along the ground; the numerous trees and leafy canopies limit their flying maneuverability. When faced with an opponent which poses too much of a threat, a black dragon will attempt to fly out of sight, so it will not leave tracks, and hide in a deep pond or bog.

Breath weapon/special abilities: A black dragon's breath weapon is a 5′ wide stream of acid that extends 60′ in a straight line from the dragon's head. All creatures caught in this stream must save vs. breath weapon for half damage. A black dragon casts spells and uses its magical abilities at 5th level, plus its combat modifier.

Black dragons are born with an innate *water breathing* ability and an immunity to acid. As they age, they gain the following additional powers:

Juvenile: *darkness* three times a day in a 10′ radius per age category of the dragon. **Adult:** *corrupt water* once a day. For every age category a dragon attains, it can stagnate 10 cubic feet of water, making it become still, foul,

inert, and unable to support animal life. When this ability is used against potions and elixirs, they become useless if they roll a 15 or better on 1d20. **Old:** *plant growth* once a day. **Venerable:** *summon insects* once a day. **Great wyrm:** *charm reptiles* three times a day. This operates as a *charm mammals* spell, but is applicable only to reptiles.

Habitat/Society: Black dragons are found in swamps, marshes, rain forests, and jungles. They revel in a steamy environment where canopies of trees filter out most of the sunlight, swarms of insects fill the air, and stagnant moss-covered ponds lie in abundance. Black dragons are excellent swimmers and enjoy lurking in the gloomy depths of swamps and bogs. They also are graceful in flight; however, they prefer to fly at night when their great forms are hidden by the darkness of the sky. Black dragons are extremely selfish, and the majority of those encountered will be alone. When a family of black dragons is encountered, the adults will protect their young. However, if it appears the adults' lives are in jeopardy they will abandon their young to save themselves.

They lair in large, damp caves and multi-chambered subterranean caverns. Older dragons are able to hide the entrance to their lairs with their *plant growth* ability. Black dragons are especially fond of coins. Older black dragons sometimes capture and question humans, before killing them, to find out where stockpiles of gold, silver, and platinum coins are kept.

Ecology: Black dragons can eat almost anything, although they prefer to dine primarily on fish, mollusks, and other aquatic creatures. They are fond of eels, especially the giant varieties. They also hunt for red meat, but they like to "pickle" it by letting it lie in ponds within their lair for days before eating it.

Age	Body Lgt. (′)	Tail Lgt. (′)	AC	Breath Weapon	Spells Wizard/Priest	MR	Treas. Type	XP Value
1	3-6	2-5	4	2d4 + 1	Nil	Nil	Nil	4,000
2	6-15	5-12	3	4d4 + 2	Nil	Nil	Nil	5,000
3	15-24	12-19	2	6d4 + 3	Nil	Nil	Nil	7,000
4	24-33	19-27	1	8d4 + 4	1	Nil	½H	10,000
5	33-42	27-35	0	10d4 + 5	2	10%	H	12,000
6	42-51	35-43	-1	12d4 + 6	3	15%	H	13,000
7	51-60	43-50	-2	14d4 + 7	4	20%	H	14,000
8	60-69	50-57	-3	16d4 + 8	5	25%	H × 2	15,000
9	69-78	57-64	-4	18d4 + 9	6	30%	H × 2	17,000
10	78-87	64-73	-5	20d4 + 10	7	35%	H × 2	18,000
11	87-96	73-80	-6	22d4 + 11	8	40%	H × 3	19,000
12	96-105	80-87	-7	24d4 + 12	9	45%	H × 3	20,000

Blue Dragon

Dragon, Chromatic

CLIMATE/TERRAIN:	Arid deserts
FREQUENCY:	Very rare
ORGANIZATION:	Solitary or clan
ACTIVE TIME:	Any
DIET:	Special
INTELLIGENCE:	Very (11-12)
TREASURE:	Special
ALIGNMENT:	Lawful evil

NO. APPEARING:	1 (2-5)
ARMOR CLASS:	0 (base)
MOVEMENT:	9, Fl 30 (C), Br 4
HIT DICE:	14 (base)
THAC0:	7 (base)
NO. OF ATTACKS:	3 + special
DAMAGE/ATTACK:	1-8/1-8/3-24
SPECIAL ATTACKS:	Special
SPECIAL DEFENSES:	Variable
MAGIC RESISTANCE:	Variable
SIZE:	G (42' base)
MORALE:	Fanatic (17-18)
XP VALUE:	Variable

Blue dragons are extremely territorial and voracious. They love to spend long hours preparing ambushes for herd animals and unwary travelers, and they spend equally long hours dwelling on their success and admiring their trophies.

The size of a blue dragon's scales increases little as the dragon ages, although they do become thicker and harder. The scales vary in color from an iridescent azure to a deep indigo, retaining a glossy finish through all of the dragon's stages because the blowing desert sands polish them. This makes blue dragons easy to spot in barren desert surroundings. However, the dragons often conceal themselves, burrowing into the sand so only part of their heads are exposed.

Blue dragons love to soar in the hot desert air; usually flying in the daytime when temperatures are the highest. Some blue dragons nearly match the color of the desert sky and use this coloration to their advantage in combat.

Blue dragons speak their own tongue, a tongue common to all evil dragons, and 12% of hatchling blue dragons have an ability to communicate with any intelligent creature. The chance to possess this ability increases 5% per age category of the dragon.

Combat: Blue dragons prefer to fight from a distance so their opponents can clearly witness the full force of their breath weapon and so little or no threat is posed to themselves. Often blue dragons will attack from directly above or will burrow beneath the sands until opponents come within 100 feet. Older blue dragons will use their special abilities, such as *hallucinatory terrain*, in concert with these tactics to mask the land and aid in their chances to surprise. Blue dragons will only run from a fight if they are severely damaged, since they view retreat as cowardly.

Breath weapon/special abilities: A blue dragon's breath weapon is a 5' wide bolt of lightning that streaks 100' in a straight line from the dragon's mouth. All creatures caught in this stream must save vs. breath weapon for half damage. Blue dragons cast spells and use their magical abilities at 7th level, adjusted by their combat modifier.

Blue dragons are born with an immunity to electricity. As they age, they gain the following additional powers: **Young:** *create* or *destroy water* three times per day. **Juvenile:** *sound imitation* at will. **Adult:** *dust devil* once a day. **Old:** *ventriloquism* once a day. **Venerable:** *control winds* once a day. **Great wyrm:** *hallucinatory terrain* once a day.

Habitat/Society: Blue dragons are found in deserts; arid, windswept plains; and hot, humid badlands. They enjoy the bleak terrain because there are few obstacles—only an occasional rock outcropping or dune—to interrupt the view of their territories. They spend hours looking out over their domains, watching for trespassers and admiring their property. Most of the blue dragons encountered will be alone because they do not want to share their territories with others. However, when a family is encountered the male dragon will attack ferociously, protecting his property—his mate and young. The female dragon also will join in the attack if the threat proves significant.

Blue dragons' enemies are men, who kill the dragons for their skin and treasure, and brass dragons, which share the same environment. If a blue dragon discovers a brass dragon in the same region, it will not rest until the trespassing dragon is killed or driven away.

Blue dragons lair in vast underground caverns in which they store their treasure. Although blue dragons will collect anything which looks valuable, they are fond of gems—especially sapphires.

Ecology: Blue dragons are able to consume nearly anything, and sometimes are forced to eat snakes, lizards, and desert plants to help sate their great hunger. However, they are particularly fond of herd animals, such as camels, and they will gorge themselves on caravans of the creatures which they cook with a *lightning bolt*.

Age	Base Lgt. (')	Tail Lgt. (')	AC	Breath Weapon	Spells Wizard/Priest	MR	Treas. Type	XP Value
1	3-9	2-7	3	2d8 + 1	Nil	Nil	Nil	6,000
2	9-20	7-16	2	4d8 + 2	Nil	Nil	Nil	8,000
3	20-31	16-25	1	6d8 + 3	Nil	Nil	Nil	10,000
4	31-50	25-34	0	8d8 + 4	1	Nil	1/2H, S	13,000
5	50-69	34-43	-1	10d8 + 5	2	20%	H, S	15,000
6	69-88	43-52	-2	12d8 + 6	3	25%	H, S	16,000
7	88-97	52-61	-3	14d8 + 7	3 1	30%	H, S	17,000
8	97-106	61-70	-4	16d8 + 8	3 2	35%	H, S×2	18,000
9	106-115	70-79	-5	18d8 + 9	3 3	40%	H, S×2	20,000
10	115-124	79-88	-6	20d8 + 10	3 3 1/1	45%	H, S×2	21,000
11	124-133	88-97	-7	22d8 + 11	3 3 2/2	50%	H, S×3	22,000
12	133-142	97-106	-8	24d8 + 12	3 3 3/3	55%	H, S×3	23,000

Dragon, Chromatic

Green Dragon

CLIMATE/TERRAIN:	Sub-tropical and temperate forest and subterranean
FREQUENCY:	Very rare
ORGANIZATION:	Solitary or clan
ACTIVITY CYCLE:	Any
DIET:	Special
INTELLIGENCE:	Very (11-12)
TREASURE:	Special
ALIGNMENT:	Lawful evil
NO. APPEARING:	1 (2-5)
ARMOR CLASS:	0 (base)
MOVEMENT:	9, Fl 30 (C), Sw 9
HIT DICE:	13 (base)
THAC0:	7 (at 13 HD)
NO. OF ATTACKS:	3 + special
DAMAGE/ATTACK:	1-8/1-8/2-20 (2d10)
SPECIAL ATTACKS:	Special
SPECIAL DEFENSES:	Variable
MAGIC RESISTANCE:	Variable
SIZE:	G (36' base)
MORALE:	Elite (15-16)
XP VALUE:	Variable

Green dragons are bad tempered, mean, cruel, and rude. They hate goodness and good-aligned creatures. They love intrigue and seek to enslave other woodland creatures, killing those who cannot be controlled or intimidated.

A hatchling green dragon's scales are thin, very small, and a deep shade of green that appears nearly black. As the dragon ages, the scales grow larger and become lighter, turning shades of forest, emerald, and olive green, which helps it blend in with its wooded surroundings. A green dragon's scales never become as thick as other dragons', remaining smooth and flexible.

Green dragons speak their own tongue, a tongue common to all evil dragons, and 12% of hatchling green dragons have an ability to communicate with any intelligent creature. The chance to possess this ability increases 5% per age category of the dragon.

Combat: Green dragons initiate fights with little or no provocation, picking on creatures of any size. If the target creature intrigues the dragon or appears to be difficult to deal with, the dragon will stalk the creature, using its environment for cover, until it determines the best time to strike and the most appropriate tactics to use. If the target appears formidable, the dragon will first attack with its breath weapon, magical abilities, and spells. However, if the target appears weak, the dragon will make its presence known quickly for it enjoys evoking terror in its targets. When the dragon has tired of this game, it will bring down the creature using its physical attacks so the fight lasts longer and the creature's agony is prolonged.

Sometimes, the dragon elects to control a creature, such as a human or demi-human, through intimidation and *suggestion*. Green dragons like to question men, especially adventurers, to learn more about their society, abilities, what is going on in the countryside, and if there is treasure nearby.

Breath weapon/special abilities: A green dragon's breath weapon is a cloud of poisonous chlorine gas that is 50' long, 40' wide, and 30 feet high. Creatures within the cloud may save versus breath weapon for half damage. A

green dragon casts its spells at 6th level, adjusted by its combat modifier.

From birth, green dragons are immune to gasses. As they age, they gain the following additional powers: **Juvenile:** *water breathing*. **Adult:** *suggestion* once a day. **Mature adult:** *warp wood* three times a day. **Old:** *plant growth* once a day. **Very old:** *entangle* once a day. **Wyrm:** *pass without trace* three times a day.

Habitat/Society: Green dragons are found in sub-tropical and temperate forests, the older the forest and bigger the trees, the better. The sights and smells of the woods are pleasing to the dragon, and it considers the entire forest or woods its territory. Sometimes the dragon will enter into a relationship with other evil forest-dwelling creatures, which keep the dragon informed about what is going on in the forest and surrounding area in exchange for their lives. If a green dragon lives in a forest on a hillside, it will seek to enslave hill giants, which the dragon considers its greatest enemy. A green dragon makes its lair in underground chambers far beneath its forest.

The majority of green dragons encountered will be alone. However, when a mated pair of dragons and their young are encountered, the female will leap to the attack. The male will take the young to a place of safety before joining the fight. The parents are extremely protective of their young, despite their evil nature, and will sacrifice their own lives to save their offspring.

Ecology: Although green dragons have been known to eat practically anything, including shrubs and small trees when they are hungry enough, they especially prize elves. If the forest is on a hillside, hill giants will hunt the younger dragons, which they consider a delicacy.

Age	Body Lgt.(')	Tail Lgt. (')	AC	Breath Weapon	Spells Wizard/Priest	MR	Treasure Type	XP Value
1	2-7	2-5	3	2d6 + 1	Nil	Nil	Nil	5,000
2	7-16	5- 15	2	4d6 + 2	Nil	Nil	Nil	7,000
3	16-35	15- 31	1	6d6 + 3	Nil	Nil	Nil	8,000
4	35-44	31- 40	0	8d6 + 4	1	Nil	½H	11,000
5	44-53	40-48	- 1	10d6 + 5	2	15%	H	13,000
6	53-62	48-56	- 2	12d6 + 6	3	20%	H	14,000
7	62-71	56-64	- 3	14d6 + 7	4	25%	H	15,000
8	71-80	64-72	-4	16d6 + 8	4 1	30%	Hx2	16,000
9	80-89	72-80	-5	18d6 + 9	4 2	40%	Hx2	18,000
10	89-98	80-86	-6	20d6 + 10	4 3	45%	Hx2	19,000
11	98-107	86-96	-7	22d6 + 11	4 4	50%	Hx3	21,000
12	107-116	96-104	-8	24d6 + 12	5 4	55%	Hx3	22,000

Red Dragon Dragon, Chromatic

CLIMATE/TERRAIN:	Tropical, sub-tropical, and temperate hills and mountains
FREQUENCY:	Very rare
ORGANIZATION:	Solitary or clan
ACTIVITY CYCLE:	Any
DIET:	Special
INTELLIGENCE:	Exceptional (15-16)
TREASURE:	Special
ALIGNMENT:	Chaotic evil

NO. APPEARING:	1 (2-5)
ARMOR CLASS:	-3 (base)
MOVEMENT:	9, Fl 30 (C), Jp 3
HIT DICE:	15 (base)
THAC0:	7 (at 9 HD)
NO. OF ATTACKS:	3 + special
DAMAGE/ATTACK:	1-10/1-10/3-30 (3d10)
SPECIAL ATTACKS:	Special
SPECIAL DEFENSES:	Variable
MAGIC RESISTANCE:	Variable
SIZE:	G (48' base)
MORALE:	Fanatic (17-18)
XP VALUE:	Variable

Red dragons are the most covetous and greedy of all dragons, forever seeking to increase their treasure hoards. They are obsessed with their wealth and memorize an inventory accurate to the last copper. They are exceptionally vain and self confident, considering themselves superior not only to other dragons, but to all other life in general.

When red dragons hatch, their small scales are a bright glossy scarlet. Because of this, they can be quickly spotted by predators and men hunting for skins, so they are hidden in deep underground lairs and not permitted to venture outside until toward the end of their young stage when their scales have turned a deeper red, the glossy texture has been replaced by a smooth, dull finish, and they are more able to take care of themselves. As the dragon continues to age, the scales become large, thick, and as strong as metal.

Red dragons speak their own tongue, a tongue common to all evil dragons, and 16% of hatchling red dragons have an ability to communicate with any intelligent creature. The chance to possess this ability increases 5% per age category of the dragon.

Combat: Because red dragons are so confident, they never pause to appraise an adversary. When they notice a target they make a snap decision whether to attack, using one of many "perfect" strategies worked out ahead of time in the solitude of their lairs. If the creature appears small and insignificant, such as an unarmored man, the dragon will land to attack with its claws and bite, not wanting to obliterate the creature with its breath weapon, as any treasure might be consumed by the flames. However, if a red dragon encounters a group of armored men, it will use its breath weapon, special abilities, and spells (if it is old enough to have them) before landing.

Breath weapon/special abilities: A red dragon's breath weapon is a searing cone of fire 90' long, 5' wide at the dragon's mouth and 30' at the base. Creatures struck by the flames must save versus breath weapon for half damage. Red dragons cast spells at 9th level, adjusted by their combat modifiers.

Red dragons are born immune to fire. As they age, they gain the following additional powers: **Young:** *affect normal fires* three times per day. **Juvenile:** *pyrotechnics* three times per day. **Adult:** *heat metal* once per day. **Old:** *suggestion* once per day. **Very old:** *hypnotism* once per day. **Venerable:** *detect gems, kind and number* in a 100' radius three times a day.

Habitat/Society: Red dragons can be found on great hills or on soaring mountains. From a high perch they haughtily survey their territory, which they consider to be everything that can be seen from their position. They prefer to lair in large caves that extend deep into the earth.

A red dragon enjoys its own company, not associating with other creatures, or even other red dragons, unless the dragon's aims can be furthered. For example, some red dragons who have *charm* spells will order men to act as the dragon's eyes and ears, gathering information about nearby settlements and sources of treasure. When a red dragons's offspring reach the *young adult* stage, they are ordered from the lair and the surrounding territory, as they are viewed as competition.

Red dragons are quick to fight all creatures which encroach on their territory, especially copper and silver dragons which sometimes share the same environment. They hate gold dragons above all else because they believe gold dragons are "nearly" as powerful as themselves.

Ecology: Red dragons are meat eaters, although they are capable of digesting almost anything. Their favorite food is a maiden of any human or demi-human race. Sometimes the dragons are able to *charm* key villagers into regularly sacrificing maidens to them.

Age	Body Lgt.(')	Tail Lgt. (')	AC	Breath Weapon	Spells Wizard/Priest	MR	Treasure Type	XP Value
1	1-12	3-12	0	2d10+1	Nil	Nil	Nil	7,000
2	12-23	12-21	-1	4d10+2	Nil	Nil	Nil	8,000
3	23-42	21-30	-2	6d10+3	Nil	Nil	Nil	10,000
4	42-61	30-49	-3	8d10+4	1	Nil	E, S, T	12,000
5	61-80	49-68	-4	10d10+5	2	30%	H, S, T	14,000
6	80-99	68-87	-5	12d10+6	2 1	35%	H, S, T	15,000
7	99-118	87-106	-6	14d10+7	2 2	40%	H, S, T	16,000
8	118-137	106-125	-7	16d10+8	2 2 1	45%	H, S, Tx2	19,000
9	137-156	125-144	-8	18d10+9	2 2 2	50%	H, S, Tx2	21,000
10	156-165	144-153	-9	20d10+10	2 2 2 1/1	55%	H, S, Tx2	22,000
11	165-174	153-162	-10	22d10+11	2 2 2 2/2	60%	H, S, Tx3	23,000
12	174-183	162-171	-11	24d10+12	2 2 2 2 1/2 1	65%	H, S, Tx3	24,000

Dragon, Chromatic

White Dragon

CLIMATE/TERRAIN:	Arctic plains, hills, mountains, and subterranean
FREQUENCY:	Rare
ORGANIZATION:	Solitary or clan
ACTIVITY CYCLE:	Any
DIET:	Special
INTELLIGENCE:	Low (5-7)
TREASURE:	Special
ALIGNMENT:	Chaotic evil

NO. APPEARING:	1 (2-5)
ARMOR CLASS:	1 (base)
MOVEMENT:	12, Fl 40 (C), Br 6, Sw 12
HIT DICE:	11 (base)
THAC0:	9 (at 11 HD)
NO. OF ATTACKS:	3 + special
DAMAGE/ATTACK:	1-6/1-6/2-16 (2d8)
SPECIAL ATTACKS:	Special
SPECIAL DEFENSES:	Variable
MAGIC RESISTANCE:	Variable
SIZE:	H (24' base)
MORALE:	Elite (15-16)
XP VALUE:	Variable

White dragons, the smallest and weakest of the evil dragons, are slow witted but efficient hunters. They are impulsive, vicious, and animalistic, tending to consider only the needs and emotions of the moment and having no foresight or regret. Despite their low intelligence, they are as greedy and evil as the other evil dragons.

The scales of a hatchling white dragon are a mirror-like glistening white, which makes them virtually invisible against a snowy background. As the dragon ages, the sheen disappears, and by the time it reaches the *very old* stage, scales of pale blue and light gray are mixed in with the white.

White dragons speak their own tongue, a tongue common to all evil dragons, and 7% of hatchling white dragons have an ability to communicate with any intelligent creature. The chance to possess this ability increases 5% per age category of the dragon.

Combat: Regardless of a target's size, a white dragon's favorite method of attack is to use its breath weapon and special abilities before closing to melee. This tactic sometimes works to the dragon's detriment, as it can exhaust its breath weapon on smaller prey and then be faced with a larger creature it must attack physically. If a white dragon is pursuing creatures in the water, such as polar bears or seals, it will melee them in their element, fighting with its claws and bite.

Breath weapon/special abilities: A white dragon's breath weapon is a cone of frost 70' long, 5' wide at the dragon's mouth, and 25' wide at the base. Creatures caught in the blast may Save versus Breath Weapon for half damage. A white dragon casts its spells and uses its magical abilities at 5th level, plus its combat modifier.

From their birth, white dragons are immune to cold. As they grow older, they gain the following additional abilities: **Juvenile:** *ice walking*, which allows the dragon to walk across ice as easily as creatures walk across flat, dry ground. **Mature adult:** *gust of wind* three times a day. **Very old:** *wall of fog* three times a day, this produces snow or hail rather than rain. **Wyrm:** *freezing fog* three times a day. This obscures vision in a

100' radius and causes frost to form, creating a thin layer of glare ice on the ground and on all surfaces within the radius.

Habitat/Society: White dragons live in chilly or cold regions, preferring lands where the temperature rarely rises above freezing and ice and snow always cover the ground. When temperatures become too warm, the dragons become lethargic. White dragons bask in the frigid winds that whip over the landscape, and they wallow and play in deep snow banks.

White dragons are lackadaisical parents. Although the young remain with the parents from hatchling to juvenile or young adult stage, they are not protected. Once a dragon passes from its hatchling stage, it must fend for itself, learning how to hunt and defend itself by watching the parents.

White dragons' lairs are usually icey caves and deep subterranean chambers; they select caves that open away from the warming rays of the sun. White dragons store all of their treasure within their lair, and prefer keeping it in caverns coated in ice, which reflect the gems and coins and make the treasure appear even larger. They are fond of gems, especially diamonds, because they are pretty to look at.

Ecology: Although white dragons, as all other dragons, are able to eat nearly anything, they are very particular and will consume only food which has been frozen. Usually after a dragon has killed a creature with its breath weapon it will fall to devouring it while the carcass is still stiff and frigid. It will bury other kills in snow banks until they are suitably frozen.

White dragons' natural enemies are frost giants who kill the dragons for food and armor and subdue them to use for guards and mounts.

Age	Body Lgt.(')	Tail Lgt. (')	AC	Breath Weapon	Spells Wizard/Priest	MR	Treasure Type	XP Value
1	1-5	1-4	4	1d6 + 1	Nil	Nil	Nil	3,000
2	5-14	4- 12	3	2d6 + 2	Nil	Nil	Nil	4,000
3	14-23	12- 21	2	3d6 + 3	Nil	Nil	Nil	6,000
4	23-32	21- 28	1	4d6 + 4	Nil	Nil	E	8,000
5	32-41	28- 36	0	5d6 + 5	Nil	5%	E, O, S	10,000
6	41-50	36-45	- 1	6d6 + 6	1	10%	E, O, S	12,000
7	50-59	45-54	- 2	7d6 + 7	1	15%	E, O, S	13,000
8	59-68	54-62	- 3	8d6 + 8	2	20%	E, O, Sx2	14,000
9	68-77	62-70	- 4	9d6 + 9	2	25%	E, O, Sx2	16,000
10	77-86	70-78	- 5	10d6 + 10	3	30%	E, O, Sx2	17,000
11	86-95	78-85	- 6	11d6 + 11	3	35%	E, O, Sx3	18,000
12	95-104	85-94	- 7	12d6 + 12	4	40%	E, O, Sx3	19,000

Amethyst Dragon   Dragon, Gem

CLIMATE/TERRAIN:	Temperate and cold mountain lakes
FREQUENCY:	Very rare
ORGANIZATION:	Solitary or clan
ACTIVITY CYCLE:	Any
DIET:	Special
INTELLIGENCE:	Genius (17-18)
TREASURE:	Special
ALIGNMENT:	Neutral

NO. APPEARING:	1 (2-5)
ARMOR CLASS:	−4 (base)
MOVEMENT:	12, Fl 40 (C), Sw 12
HIT DICE:	14 (base)
THAC0:	7 (base)
NO. OF ATTACKS:	3
DAMAGE/ATTACK:	1-10/1-10/5-30
SPECIAL ATTACKS:	Variable
SPECIAL DEFENSES:	Variable
MAGIC RESISTANCE:	Variable
SIZE:	G (30′ base)
MORALE:	Fanatic (17-18)
XP VALUE:	Variable

Amethyst dragons are wise and regal, with a detached air, ignoring what they consider to be petty squabbles between good and evil, law and chaos. When hatched, amethyst dragons have lavender skin with small scales of a light, translucent purple. As they grow older, the scales gradually darken. Adults are a sparkling lavender in color.

Amethyst dragons speak their own tongue and the tongue common to all gem dragons, and 18% of hatchling amethyst dragons have an ability to communicate with any intelligent creature. The chance to possess this ability increases 5% per age category of the dragon.

Combat: Amethyst dragons prefer talking over combat. If parleying goes badly, the dragon attacks first with its breath weapon, then with psionics and spells. They never hide or attempt ambush. Amethyst dragons consider retreat dishonorable, but do so if faced with death.

Breath weapon/special abilities: An amethyst dragon's breath weapon is a faceted, violet lozenge, which it can spit into the midst of enemies, up to 75 feet away. The lozenge explodes with concussive force, causing the indicated damage to all creatures within 60 feet of the impact (save vs. breath weapon for half damage). In addition, all creatures size huge and smaller must save vs. paralyzation or be knocked down. Any creature taking damage from the blast has a 50% chance of being knocked unconscious for one round per age level of the dragon, plus 1d8 rounds. An amethyst dragon casts spells and uses its magical abilities at 9th level, plus its combat modifier.

Amethyst dragons are born with an innate *water breathing* ability and an immunity to poisons. They are also immune to force attacks and effects, such as those from *beads of force*, *Bigby's hand* spells, *wall of force*, and *Otiluke's resilient sphere*. As they age, they gain the following additional powers: **Young:** *water walking* six times a day. **Juvenile:** *neutralize poison* six times a day. **Adult:** *shapechange*, as a druid, into a reptile, bird, or mammal, three times a day, with each form usable only once per

day. **Old:** *Otiluke's resilient sphere* three times a day. **Very old:** *reflecting pool* once a day. **Venerable:** *control weather* once a day.

Psionics Summary:

Level	Dis/Sci/Dev	Attack/Defense	Score	PSPs
= HD	3/3/5	PB,EW,PsC/ M-,TS,TW	= Int	250

Common powers (most amethyst dragons prefer psychokinetic powers and many choose psychometabolism as an additional discipline):
- **Psychokinesis - Sciences:** detonate, project force, telekinesis. **Devotions:** control body, inertial barrier, molecular agitation.
- **Psychometabolism - Sciences:** complete healing, energy containment, metamorphosis. **Devotions:** cell adjustment, expansion, reduction.
- **Telepathy - Sciences:** domination, mindlink, mindwipe. **Devotions:** contact, ESP, identity penetration, truthear.
- **Metapsionics - Sciences:** empower, psychic surgery, ultrablast. **Devotions:** magnify, psionic sense, psychic drain.

Habitat/Society: Amethyst dragons live on the shores of isolated mountain lakes and pools, some in caves beneath the water. They are good parents, but believe their young should fend for themselves as soon as they become young adults. Amethyst dragons dislike red and white dragons, and consider silver and copper dragons to be foolish.

Ecology: Amethyst dragons prefer to eat fish and a large number of gems. They are not inherently enemies with any life form.

Age	Body Lgt.(′)	Tail Lgt.(′)	AC	Breath Weapon	Spells Wizard/Priest	MR	Treasure Type	XP Value
1	2-10	4-10	−1	2d8+1	Nil	Nil	Nil	4,000
2	10-18	10-16	−2	4d8+2	Nil	Nil	Nil	6,000
3	18-28	16-26	−3	6d8+3	Nil	Nil	Nil	7,000
4	28-38	26-36	−4	8d8+4	Nil/1	Nil	H, U, T	9,000
5	38-53	36-46	−5	10d8+5	1/1	25%	H, U×2, T	10,000
6	53-68	46-56	−6	12d8+6	1/2 1	30%	H, U×3, Tx2	12,000
7	68-80	56-66	−7	14d8+7	1/1 2 1 1	35%	H, U×4, Tx2	13,000
8	80-92	66-76	−8	16d8+8	2 1/2 2 1 1	40%	H, U×6, T×3	15,000
9	92-102	76-82	−9	18d8+9	2 1 1/2 2 2 1 1	45%	H, U×8, T×3	17,000
10	102-112	82-88	−10	20d8+10	2 2 1 1/2 2 2 2 1 1	50%	H, U×10, T×4	19,000
11	112-122	88-94	−11	22d8+11	2 2 2 2 1/2 2 2 2 2 1	55%	H, U×13, T×4	20,000
12	122-132	94-100	−12	24d8+12	2 2 2 2 2/2 2 2 2 2 2	60%	H, U×16, T×5	21,000

Dragon, Gem

Crystal Dragon

CLIMATE/TERRAIN: Temperate and cold mountains
FREQUENCY: Very rare
ORGANIZATION: Solitary or clan
ACTIVITY CYCLE: Any
DIET: Special
INTELLIGENCE: Exceptional
TREASURE: Special
ALIGNMENT: Chaotic neutral

NO. APPEARING: 1 (2-5)
ARMOR CLASS: 0 (base)
MOVEMENT: 9, Fl 24 (C), Jp 3
HIT DICE: 10 (base)
THAC0: 11 (base)
NO. OF ATTACKS: 3 + special
DAMAGE/ATTACK: 1-6/1-6/2-12
SPECIAL ATTACKS: Variable
SPECIAL DEFENSES: Variable
MAGIC RESISTANCE: Variable
SIZE: L (12' base)
MORALE: Fanatic (17-18)
XP VALUE: Variable

Crystal dragons are the friendliest of the gem dragons, always curious about the world. Though they seldom seek out company, they willingly converse with visitors who do not try to steal from them.

At birth, crystal dragons have glossy white scales. As the dragons age, their scales become translucent. Moonlight and starlight cause their scales to luminesce, while bright sunlight lends them a dazzling brilliance which makes crystal dragons almost unbearable to look at.

Crystal dragons speak their own tongue and the tongue common to all gem dragons, and 10% of hatchling crystal dragons have an ability to communicate with any intelligent creature. The chance to possess this ability increases 5% per age category of the dragon.

Combat: Crystal dragons greatly prefer conversation to combat, and often use *charm person* early in any conversation. They do not initially hide, but if visitors become hostile, a crystal dragon will retreat immediately to observe its enemies with its special abilities, and plan an attack. Often, it uses its breath weapon first, to weaken and disorient enemies. Spells and other abilities are used as needed, with claws and bite a last resort.

Breath weapon/special abilities: This dragon's breath weapon is a cone of glowing shards; the cone is 60 feet long, 5 feet wide at the dragon's mouth, and 25 feet wide at the base. Creatures caught in the blast can save vs. breath weapon for half damage, and must make a second saving throw vs. breath weapon or be blinded by the dazzling shards for one turn per age level of the dragon. The shards shine as bright as daylight, and can be seen for miles. Creatures within 60 feet must save vs. breath weapon or be dazzled, incurring a penalty of −2 to attack rolls for one turn per age level of the dragon. A crystal dragon casts spells and uses magical abilities at 5th level, plus its combat modifier.

Crystal dragons are born immune to light-based attacks and normal cold, and able to cast *charm person* at will. As they age, they gain these additional powers: **Juvenile:** *color spray* three times a day. **Mature adult:** *suggestion* three times a day. **Very old:** *luckscale* once a day. This allows the dragon to enchant one of its scales as a *stone of good luck*. The enchantment lasts one hour per age category of the dragon. Such scales are given to friendly visitors. **Wyrm:** *control winds* three times a day.

Psionics Summary:

Level	Dis/Sci/Dev	Attack/Defense	Score	PSPs
= HD	1/1/2	EW/M-	= Int	100

Common powers:
• **Clairsentience - Sciences:** clairaudience, clairvoyance, precognition. **Devotions:** any.

Habitat/Society: Crystal dragons prefer cold, open areas with clear skies, and they enjoy stargazing. They have been known to build snow forts, create beautiful snow sculptures, and throw balls of snow at various targets. They are fun-loving and mischievous. Crystal dragons are reasonably good parents, if somewhat irresponsible.

Crystal dragons are hunted by some white dragons. However, a rare crystal dragon will adopt a young white dragon, to teach it to be friendly. Though generally friendly, they bear great enmity towards all giants, who sometimes try to enslave them.

Ecology: Crystal dragons prefer gems and metal ores to all other foods.

Age	Body Lgt.(')	Tail Lgt.(')	AC	Breath Weapon	Spells Wizard/Priest	MR	Treasure Type	XP Value
1	1-4	1-6	3	1d4 +1	Nil	Nil	Nil	1,400
2	4-9	6-11	2	2d4 +2	Nil	Nil	Nil	2,000
3	9-14	11-16	1	3d4 +3	Nil	Nil	Nil	3,000
4	14-21	16-23	0	4d4 +4	Nil/1	Nil	E, Q	5,000
5	21-28	23-30	−1	5d4 +5	1/1	5%	E, Q × 2, T	6,000
6	28-38	30-40	−2	6d4 +6	1/1 1	10%	H, Q × 3, T	7,000
7	38-48	40-50	−3	7d4 +7	1/1 1 1	15%	H, Q × 4, T	9,000
8	48-56	50-60	−4	8d4 +8	1 1/1 1 1	20%	H, Q × 5, T	10,000
9	56-64	60-70	−5	9d4 +9	1 1 1/2 1 1	25%	H, Q × 6, T × 2	12,000
10	64-72	70-77	−6	10d4 +10	1 1 1/2 2 1 1	30%	H, Q × 7, T × 2	13,000
11	72-80	77-84	−6	11d4 +11	2 1 1/2 2 2 1	35%	H, Q × 8, T × 2	15,000
12	80-92	84-91	−8	12d4 +12	2 2 1/2 2 2 2	40%	H, Q × 9, T × 2	16,000

Emerald Dragon

CLIMATE/TERRAIN:	Tropical and subtropical extinct volcanoes
FREQUENCY:	Very rare
ORGANIZATION:	Solitary or clan
ACTIVITY CYCLE:	Any
DIET:	Special
INTELLIGENCE:	Exceptional (15-16)
TREASURE:	Special
ALIGNMENT:	Lawful neutral

NO. APPEARING:	1 (2-5)
ARMOR CLASS:	−2 (base)
MOVEMENT:	9, Fl 30 (C), Br 3
HIT DICE:	12 (base)
THAC0:	9 (base)
NO. OF ATTACKS:	3
DAMAGE/ATTACK:	1-8/1-8/3-18
SPECIAL ATTACKS:	Variable
SPECIAL DEFENSES:	Variable
MAGIC RESISTANCE:	Variable
SIZE:	H (20' base)
MORALE:	Fanatic (17-18)
XP VALUE:	Variable

Emerald dragons are very curious, particularly about local history and customs, but prefer to only observe. They are the most paranoid of the gem dragons, and do not like people get too close to their treasure.

Emerald dragons have translucent green scales at birth. As they age, the scales harden and take on many shades of green. They scintillate in the light, and the dragon's hide seems to be in constant motion.

Emerald dragons speak their own tongue and the tongue common to all gem dragons, and 14% of hatchling emerald dragons have an ability to communicate with any intelligent creature. The chance to possess this ability increases 5% per age category of the dragon.

Combat: Emerald dragons usually set up traps and alarms around their lairs to warn them of visitors. They often hide from intruders, using special abilities to observe, and seldom come out to speak. If intruders attack or approach the dragon's treasure, the dragon burrows underneath to surprise its victims, then use breath weapon and claws, seeking to quickly disable as many as it can. If faced with superior forces, the dragon retreats, and will wait years for revenge if necessary.

Breath weapon/special abilities: An emerald dragon's breath weapon is a loud, keening wail which sets up a sonic vibration affecting all creatures within 120 feet of the dragon's mouth. Those in the area can save vs. breath weapons for half damage from the painful vibrations. Victims must make a second saving throw vs. breath weapon or be stunned, unable to defend or attack, for three rounds per age level of the dragon, plus 1d4 rounds. Those who successfully save are deafened and disoriented instead, for a like amount of time, and at −1 to attack rolls. Deafness does not protect one from vibratory damage, but prevents stunning or additional deafness. An emerald dragon casts spells and uses its magical abilities at 6th level, plus its combat modifier.

Emerald dragons are born with an innate *flame walk* ability and an immunity to sound-based attacks. As they age, they gain the following additional powers: **Young:** *audible glamer* three times a day. **Juvenile:** *hypnotism* three times a day. **Adult:** *Melf's minute meteors* three times a day. **Mature adult:** *hold person* three times a day. **Venerable:** *animate rock* once a day. **Great wyrm:** *geas* once a day. *Hypnotism* and *geas* are effected by the dragon's skilled rippling movement of its scales.

Psionics Summary:

Level	Dis/Sci/Dev	Attack/Defense	Score	PSPs
= HD	2/2/3	PB,II/M−,TW	= Int	180

Common powers (most emerald dragons prefer telepathic powers):
• **Clairsentience - Sciences:** aura sight, object reading, precognition. **Devotions:** all-around vision, combat mind, danger sense.
• **Telepathy - Sciences:** ejection, mindlink, probe. **Devotions:** contact, ESP, life detection, sight link, sound link.

Habitat/Society: Emerald dragons are reclusive, making lairs in the cones of extinct or seldom active volcanoes. These dragons are protective parents and prefer their young to stay in the lair as long as possible for mutual protection. Emerald dragons sometimes live near sapphire dragons, and they fear the voracious greed of red dragons.

Ecology: Emerald dragons will eat anything, but prefer lizards and giants. They are actively hostile towards fire giants.

Age	Body Lgt.(')	Tail Lgt.(')	AC	Breath Weapon	Spells Wizard/Priest	MR	Treasure Type	XP Value
1	3-9	2-7	1	2d4+1	Nil	Nil	Nil	2,000
2	9-18	7-14	0	4d4+2	Nil	Nil	Nil	3,000
3	18-27	14-21	−1	6d4+3	Nil	Nil	Nil	5,000
4	27-36	21-28	−2	8d4+4	1	Nil	1/2H, Q×2	7,000
5	36-45	28-35	−3	10d4+5	1/1	15%	H, Q×4, T	8,000
6	45-54	35-42	−4	12d4+6	1 1/1	20%	H, Q×6, T	10,000
7	54-63	42-49	−5	14d4+7	1 1/1 1	25%	H, Q×8, T×2	12,000
8	63-72	49-56	−6	16d4+8	1 1 1/2 1	30%	H, Q×10, T×2	13,000
9	72-81	56-63	−7	18d4+9	2 1 1/2 1 1	35%	H×2, Q×12, Tx2	14,000
10	81-90	63-70	−8	20d4+10	2 2 1/2 2 1	40%	H×2, Q×14, Tx3	16,000
11	90-99	70-77	−9	22d4+11	2 2 1 1/2 2 1 1	45%	H×2, Q×16, Tx3	17,000
12	99-108	77-84	−10	24d4+12	2 2 1 1 1/2 2 2 1	50%	H×2, Q×18, T×3	19,000

Dragon, Gem

Sapphire Dragon

CLIMATE/TERRAIN:	Any subterranean
FREQUENCY:	Very rare
ORGANIZATION:	Solitary or clan
ACTIVITY CYCLE:	Any
DIET:	Special
INTELLIGENCE:	Genius (17-18)
TREASURE:	Special
ALIGNMENT:	Lawful neutral

NO. APPEARING:	1 (2-5)
ARMOR CLASS:	−3 (base)
MOVEMENT:	9, Fl 30 (C), Br 6
HIT DICE:	13 (base)
THAC0:	7 (base)
NO. OF ATTACKS:	3
DAMAGE/ATTACK:	1-8/1-8/5-20 (3d6 + 2)
SPECIAL ATTACKS:	Variable
SPECIAL DEFENSES:	Variable
MAGIC RESISTANCE:	Variable
SIZE:	H (24′ base)
MORALE:	Fanatic (17-18)
XP VALUE:	Variable

While not actively hostile, sapphire dragons are militantly territorial and initially distrustful of anyone who approaches.

These beautiful dragons range from light to dark blue, and sparkle in the light, even at birth. Sapphire dragons are often mistaken for blue dragons, unless someone recalls the latter's preferred arid environment.

Sapphire dragons speak their own tongue and the tongue common to all gem dragons, and 16% of hatchling sapphire dragons have an ability to communicate with any intelligent creature. The chance to possess this ability increases 5% per age category of the dragon.

Combat: Sapphire dragons generally observe intruders before deciding what to do with them, unless known enemies such as drow or dwarves are present. If others are not actively hostile the dragon attempts conversation and spell use to determine their intentions and convince them to leave. If the dragon or its treasure is threatened, it attacks immediately with breath weapon, spells, and physical attacks. It uses psionics or other special abilities to escape if its life is in jeopardy.

Breath weapon/special abilities: This dragon's breath weapon is a cone of high-pitched, almost inaudible sound, 75 feet long, 5 feet wide at the dragon's mouth, and 25 feet wide at the base. Creatures caught by the blast can save vs. breath weapon for half damage from the sound's disruption, and must make a second saving throw vs. breath weapon or be affected by fear, fleeing the dragon in panic for two rounds per age level of the dragon, plus 1d6 rounds. This is a metabolic effect, and creatures unaffected by magical *fear* still suffer from the effects if they fail their save. Deafness does not protect one from the breath weapon's damage, though it prevents fear effects. A sapphire dragon casts spells and uses magical abilities at 7th level, plus combat modifier.

Sapphire dragons are born with immunity to all forms of fear, as well as immunity to *web*, *hold*, *slow*, and *paralysis*. As they age, they gain the following additional powers: **Young:** *continual light* three times a day.

Juvenile: *stone shape* three times a day. **Adult:** *anti-magic shell* once a day. **Mature adult:** *passwall* six times a day. **Venerable:** *wall of stone* three times a day. **Great wyrm:** *sunray* three times a day.

Psionics Summary:

Level	Dis/Sci/Dev	Attack/Defense	Score	PSPs
= HD	2/2/4	PB,EW/M-,IF	= Int	200

Common powers (most sapphire dragons use psychoportive powers):
- **Clairsentience - Sciences:** clairaudience, clairvoyance. **Devotions:** know direction, radial navigation.
- **Psychokinesis - Sciences:** disintegrate, molecular rearrangement, telekinesis. **Devotions:** animate shadow, control light, molecular manipulation, soften.
- **Psychoportation - Sciences:** any. **Devotions:** any.

Habitat/Society: Sapphire dragons live deep underground and often place their treasure in caverns accessible only through magic or psionics. They sometimes share territory with emerald dragons. Sapphire dragons treat their young well, but force them to leave and find their own territory as soon as they are young adults.

Ecology: Sapphire dragons consider giant spiders a great delicacy and often hunt them. Deep dragons, drow, dwarves, mind flayers, and aboleth are great enemies of sapphire dragons.

Age	Body Lgt.(′)	Tail Lgt.(′)	AC	Breath Weapon	Spells Wizard/Priest	MR	Treasure Type	XP Value
1	4-10	2-5	0	2d6 + 1	Nil	Nil	Nil	2,000
2	10-20	5-10	−1	4d6 + 2	Nil	Nil	Nil	4,000
3	20-30	10-15	−2	6d6 + 3	Nil	Nil	Nil	6,000
4	30-40	15-20	−3	8d6 + 4	Nil/1	Nil	H, Q × 2	8,000
5	40-50	20-25	−4	10d6 + 5	1/1	20%	H, Q × 4, T	9,000
6	50-60	25-30	−5	12d6 + 6	1/1 1	25%	H, Q × 6, T	11,000
7	60-70	30-35	−6	14d6 + 7	1 1/1 1	30%	H, Q × 8, T × 2	13,000
8	70-80	35-40	−7	16d6 + 8	2 1/2 1	35%	H × 2, Q × 10, T × 2	14,000
9	80-90	40-45	−8	18d6 + 9	2 1 1/2 1 1	40%	H × 2, Q × 13, T × 3	15,000
10	90-100	45-50	−9	20d6 + 10	2 2 1/2 2 1 1	45%	H × 2, Q × 16, T × 3	17,000
11	100-110	50-55	−10	22d6 + 11	2 2 1 1/2 2 2 1 1	50%	H × 2, Q × 20, T × 4	18,000
12	110-130	55-65	−11	24d6 + 12	2 2 2 1/2 2 2 2	55%	H × 2, Q × 24, T × 4	20,000

Topaz Dragon

Dragon, Gem

CLIMATE/TERRAIN:	Temperate or cold seacoast
FREQUENCY:	Very rare
ORGANIZATION:	Solitary or clan
ACTIVITY CYCLE:	Any
DIET:	Special
INTELLIGENCE:	Exceptional (15-16)
TREASURE:	Special
ALIGNMENT:	Chaotic neutral

NO. APPEARING:	1 (2-5)
ARMOR CLASS:	−1 (base)
MOVEMENT:	9, Fl 24 (C), Sw 9
HIT DICE:	11 (base)
THAC0:	9 (base)
NO. OF ATTACKS:	3
DAMAGE/ATTACK:	2-7/2-7/2-16
SPECIAL ATTACKS:	Variable
SPECIAL DEFENSES:	Variable
MAGIC RESISTANCE:	Variable
SIZE:	H (15' base)
MORALE:	Elite (15-16)
XP VALUE:	Variable

Topaz dragons are unfriendly and selfish. Though not malevolent, but they are seldom pleasant to deal with because of their erratic behavior. Topaz dragons neither seek company nor welcome it.

At hatching, topaz dragons are a dull yellow-orange in color. As they age and their scales harden, the scales become translucent and faceted. Adult topaz dragons sparkle in full sunlight.

Topaz dragons speak their own tongue and the tongue common to all gem dragons, and 12% of hatchling topaz dragons have an ability to communicate with any intelligent creature. The chance to possess this ability increases 5% per age category of the dragon.

Combat: Topaz dragons dislike intruders, but avoid combat, often conversing to hide psionics or magic use. If intruders are hostile, or the dragon tires of them, it attacks, psionically first, if possible, using spells as needed. They enjoy using teeth and claws, and usually save their breath weapon until wounded. The dragon may pretend to surrender to buy time, and retreats if greatly threatened. It usually makes one or more false retreats, attempting to come back and attack with surprise.

Breath weapon/special abilities: This dragon's breath weapon is a cone of dehydration, 70 feet long, 5 feet wide at the dragon's mouth and 25 feet wide at the base. When directed against liquids, one cubic foot of water dries up per hit point of damage. Creatures caught by the cone can make a saving throw vs. breath weapon for half damage from water loss. Those who fail to save lose 1d6 +6 Strength points; those who succeed lose only 1d6 Strength points. Curative spells less powerful than *heal* or *regeneration* are ineffective against Strength loss, although victims who are carefully nursed back to health recover 1 Strength point per day. Any creature reduced to a Strength of 0 or less dies instantly. A topaz dragon casts spells and uses magical abilities at 5th level, plus combat modifier.

At birth, topaz dragons can breathe water and are immune to cold. As they age, they gain the following powers: Young: *protection from evil or good* three times a day. Juvenile: *blink* three times a day. Adult: *wall of fog* three times a day. Mature adult: *airy water* three times a day, 10-foot radius per age category of the dragon. Old: *part water* once a day.

Psionics Summary:

Level	Dis/Sci/Dev	Attack/Defense	Score	PSPs
= HD	1/1/3	MT,II/M-,MB	= Int	120

Common powers (most topaz dragons prefer psychometabolic powers):
- **Psychokinesis - Sciences:** telekinesis. **Devotions:** animate object, control wind, molecular manipulation, soften.
- **Psychometabolism - Sciences:** energy containment, life draining, metamorphosis. **Devotions:** biofeedback, body equilibrium, cause decay, chemical simulation.

Habitat/Society: Topaz dragons live by the sea, often building or claiming caves below the waterline; they keep their caves completely dry. These dragons enjoy sunning on rocky outcroppings, enjoying the wind and spray. They like water little and swim only to hunt or attack. They are indifferent parents at best, and abandon young to protect themselves. They dislike bronze dragons and attack them on sight.

Ecology: Topaz dragons prefer to eat fish and other aquatic creatures, especially giant squid.

Age	Body Lgt.(')	Tail Lgt.(')	AC	Breath Weapon	Spells Wizard/Priest	MR	Treasure Type	XP Value
1	2-9	2-5	2	1d6 +1	Nil	Nil	Nil	2,000
2	9-16	5-9	1	2d6 +2	Nil	Nil	Nil	3,000
3	16-23	9-13	0	3d6 +3	Nil	Nil	Nil	5,000
4	23-35	13-17	−1	4d6 +4	Nil/1	Nil	E, Q	7,000
5	35-44	17-23	−2	5d6 +5	1/1	10%	H, Q × 3, T	8,000
6	44-53	23-29	−3	6d6 +6	1/11	15%	H, Q × 5, T	10,000
7	53-59	29-33	−4	7d6 +7	1/2 1	20%	H, Q × 7, T	12,000
8	59-65	33-37	−5	8d6 +8	1 1/2 1 1	25%	H, Q × 9, T × 2	14,000
9	65-70	37-41	−6	9d6 +9	1 1 1/2 2 1	30%	H, Q × 11, T × 2	15,000
10	70-75	41-45	−7	10d6 +10	2 1 1/2 2 1 1	35%	H, Q × 13, T × 2	16,000
11	75-80	45-48	−8	11d6 +11	2 2 1/2 2 2 1	40%	H × 2, Q × 15, T × 3	17,000
12	80-92	48-50	−9	12d6 +12	2 2 1 1/2 2 2 2	45%	H × 2, Q × 17, T × 3	18,000

CLIMATE/TERRAIN:	Arid desert and plain
FREQUENCY:	Rare
ORGANIZATION:	Solitary or clan
ACTIVE TIME:	Any
DIET:	Special
INTELLIGENCE:	High (13-14)
TREASURE:	Special
ALIGNMENT:	Chaotic good (neutral)

NO. APPEARING:	1 (2-5)
ARMOR CLASS:	0 (base)
MOVEMENT:	12, Fl 30 (C), Br 6
HIT DICE:	12 (base)
THAC0:	9
NO. OF ATTACKS:	3 + special
DAMAGE/ATTACK:	1-6/1-6/4-16
SPECIAL ATTACKS:	Special
SPECIAL DEFENSES:	Variable
MAGIC RESISTANCE:	Variable
SIZE:	G (30′ base)
MORALE:	Fanatic (17 base)
XP VALUE:	Variable

Brass dragons are great talkers, but not particularly good conversationalists. They are egotistical and often boorish. They often have useful information, but will divulge it only after drifting off the subject many times and after hints that a gift would be appreciated.

At birth, a brass dragon's scales are dull. Their color is a brassy, mottled brown. As the dragon gets older, the scales become more brassy, until they reach a warm, burnished appearance.

Combat: Brass dragons would rather talk than fight. If an intelligent creature tries to take its leave of a brass dragon without talking to it at length, the dragon might have a fit of pique and try to force a conversation with *suggestion* or by giving the victim a dose of *sleep* gas. If the victim falls asleep it will awaken to find itself pinned under the dragon or buried to the neck in the sand until the dragon's thirst for small talk is slaked. Before melee, brass dragons create a cloud of dust with *dust devil* or *control winds*, then charge or snatch. Brass dragons often use *control temperature* to create heat to discomfort their opponents. When faced with real danger, younger brass dragons will fly out of sight, then hide by burrowing. Older dragons spurn this ploy.

Breath weapon/special abilities: A brass dragon has two breath weapons: a cone of *sleep* gas 70′ long, 5′ wide at the dragon's mouth, and 20′ wide at its end; or a cloud of blistering desert heat 50′ long, 40′ wide, and 20′ high. Creatures caught in the gas, regardless of Hit Dice or level, must save vs. breath weapon or fall asleep for 10 minutes per age level of the dragon. Creatures caught in the heat take damage, save vs. breath weapon for half. A brass dragon casts its spells and uses its magical abilities at 6th level, plus its combat modifier.

At birth, brass dragons can *speak with animals* freely, and are immune to fire and heat. As they age, they gain the following additional powers:

Young: *create* or *destroy water* three times a day. **Juvenile:** *dust devil* once a day. **Adult:** *suggestion* once a day. **Mature adult:** *control temperature* 3 times a day in a 10′ radius per age level. **Old:** *control winds* once a day.

Great wyrm: *Summon djinni* once a week. The dragon usually asks the djinni to preform some service. Although the djinni serves willingly, the dragon will order it into combat only in extreme circumstances, as the dragon would be dismayed and embarrassed if the djinni were killed.

Habitat/Society: Brass dragons are found in arid, warm climates; ranging from sandy deserts to dry steppes. They love intense, dry heat and spend most of their time basking in the sun. They lair in high caves, preferably facing east where the sun can warm the rocks, and their territories always contain several spots where they can bask and trap unwary travelers into conversation.

Brass dragons are very social. They usually are on good terms with neighboring brass dragons and sphinxes. Brass dragons are dedicated parents. If their young are attacked they will try to slay the enemy, using their heat breath weapons and taking full advantage of their own immunity.

Because they share the same habitat, blue dragons are brass dragons' worst enemies. Brass dragons usually get the worst of a one-on-one confrontation, mostly because of the longer reach of the blue dragon's breath weapon. Because of this, brass dragons usually try to evade blue dragons until they can rally their neighbors for a mass attack.

Ecology: Like other dragons, brass dragons can, and will, eat almost anything if the need arises. In practice, however, they eat very little. They are able to get nourishment from morning dew, a rare commodity in their habitat, and have been seen carefully lifting it off plants with their long tongues.

Age	Body Lgt. (′)	Tail Lgt. (′)	AC	Breath Weapon	Spells Wizard/Priest	MR	Treas. Type	XP Value
1	3-6	2-5	3	2d4+1	Nil/Nil	Nil	Nil	4,000
2	6-14	4-12	2	4d4+2	Nil/Nil	Nil	Nil	6,000
3	14-22	12-18	1	6d4+3	Nil/Nil	Nil	Nil	8,000
4	22-31	18-24	0	8d4+4	1	Nil	1/2H	11,000
5	31-41	24-34	-1	10d4+5	1 1	15%	H	13,000
6	41-52	34-44	-2	12d4+6	2 1	20%	H	14,000
7	52-64	44-54	-3	14d4+7	2 2	25%	H	15,000
8	64-77	54-64	-4	16d4+8	3 2/1	30%	Hx2	17,000
9	77-91	64-74	-5	18d4+9	3 3/1 1	35%	Hx2	18,000
10	91-105	74-84	-6	20d4+10	4 3/2 1	40%	Hx2	19,000
11	105-121	84-94	-7	22d4+11	4 4/2 2	45%	Hx3	20,000
12	121-138	94-104	-8	24d4+12	5 4/3 2	50%	Hx3	21,000

Bronze Dragon Dragon, Metallic

CLIMATE/TERRAIN:	Tropical, sub-tropical, and temperate subterranean, lake shore, and sea shore
FREQUENCY:	Very rare
ORGANIZATION:	Solitary or clan
ACTIVE TIME:	Any
DIET:	Special
INTELLIGENCE:	Exceptional (15-16)
TREASURE:	Special
ALIGNMENT:	Lawful good

NO. APPEARING:	1 (2-5)
ARMOR CLASS:	-2 (base)
MOVEMENT:	9, Fl 30 (C), Sw 12
HIT DICE:	14 (base)
THAC0:	8 (base)
NO. OF ATTACKS:	3 + special
DAMAGE/ATTACK:	1-8/1-8/4-24
SPECIAL ATTACKS:	Special
SPECIAL DEFENSES:	Variable
MAGIC RESISTANCE:	Variable
SIZE:	G (42' base)
MORALE:	Fanatic (17 base)
XP VALUE:	Variable

Bronze dragons are inquisitive and fond of humans and demi-humans. They enjoy *polymorphing* into small, friendly animals so they can unobtrusively observe humans and demi-humans, especially adventurers. Bronze dragons thrive on simple challenges such as riddles and harmless contests. They are fascinated by warfare and will eagerly join an army if the cause is just and the pay is good.

At birth, a bronze dragon's scales are yellow tinged with green, showing only a hint of bronze. As the dragon approaches adulthood, its color deepens slowly changing to a rich bronze tone that gets darker as the dragon ages. Dragons from the very old stage and on develop a blue-black tint to the edges of their scales, similar to a patina on ancient bronze armor or statues.

Bronze dragons speak their own tongue, a tongue common to all good dragons, and 16% of hatchling bronze dragons have an ability to communicate with any intelligent creature. The chance to possess this ability increases 5% per age category of the dragon.

Combat: Bronze dragons dislike killing creatures with animal intelligence and would rather bribe them (perhaps with food), or force them away with *repulsion*. When confronted with intelligent opponents bronze dragons use their *ESP* ability to learn their opponents' intentions. When attacking they blind their opponents with *wall of fog*, then charge. Or, if they are flying, they will snatch opponents. When fighting under water, they use *airy water* to maintain the effectiveness of their breath weapons, and to keep away purely aquatic opponents. Against boats or ships they *summon* a storm or use their tail slap to smash the vessels' hulls. If the dragon is inclined to be lenient, seafaring opponents might merely find themselves becalmed, fog bound, or with broken masts.

Breath weapon/special abilities: A bronze dragon has two breath weapons: a stroke of *lightning* 100' long and 5' wide or a cloud of *repulsion* gas 20' long, 30' wide, and 30' high. Creatures caught in the gas must save vs. breath weapon or move away from the dragon for two minutes per age level of the dragon, plus 1-6 minutes. Creatures caught in the lightning

take damage, save vs. breath weapon for half. A bronze dragon casts its spells and uses its magical abilities at 8th level, plus its combat modifier.

At birth, bronze dragons have a *water breathing* ability, can *speak with animals* at will, and are immune to electricity. As they age, they gain the following additional powers: **Young:** *create food and water* and *polymorph self* three times a day. (Each change in form lasts until the dragon chooses a different form. Reverting to the dragon's normal form does not count as a change.) **Juvenile:** *wall of fog* once a day. **Adult:** *ESP* three times a day. **Mature adult:** *airy water* three times a day in a 10' radius per age category of the dragon. **Old:** *weather summoning* once a day.

Habitat/Society: Bronze dragons like to be near deep fresh or salt water. They are good swimmers and often visit the depths to cool off or to hunt for pearls or treasure from sunken ships. They prefer caves that are accessible only from the water, but their lairs are always dry—they do not lay eggs, sleep, or store treasure under water.

Bronze dragons are fond of sea mammals, especially dolphins and whales. These animals provide the dragons with a wealth of information on shipwrecks, which the dragons love to plunder, and detail the haunts of large sharks. Bronze dragons detest pirates, disabling or destroying their ships.

Ecology: Bronze dragons eat aquatic plants and some varieties of seafood. They especially prize of shark meat. They also dine on an occasional pearl, and, like other dragons, can eat almost anything in a pinch. Evil, amphibious sea creatures (particularly sahuagin), who can invade their air filled lairs, are their greatest enemies.

Age	Body Lgt. (')	Tail Lgt. (')	AC	Breath Weapon	Spells Wizard/Priest	MR	Treas. Type	XP Value
1	5-14	3-10	1	2d8 + 1	Nil/Nil	Nil	Nil	6,000
2	14-23	10-19	0	4d8 + 2	Nil/Nil	Nil	Nil	8,000
3	23-32	19-28	-1	6d8 + 3	Nil/Nil	Nil	Nil	10,000
4	32-42	28-37	-2	8d8 + 4	1	Nil	E, S, T	12,000
5	42-52	37-44	-3	10d8 + 5	1 1	20%	H, S, T	14,000
6	52-63	44-52	-4	12d8 + 6	2 1	25%	H, S, T	15,000
7	63-74	52-60	-5	14d8 + 7	2 2	30%	H, S, T	16,000
8	74-85	60-70	-6	16d8 + 8	2 2 1/1	35%	H, S, Tx2	20,000
9	85-96	70-80	-7	18d8 + 9	2 2 2/1 1	40%	H, S, Tx2	22,000
10	96-108	80-90	-8	20d8 + 10	2 2 2 1/2 1	45%	H, S, Tx2	23,000
11	108-120	90-100	-9	22d8 + 11	2 2 2 2/2 2	50%	H, S, Tx3	24,000
12	120-134	00-110	-10	24d8 + 12	2 2 2 2 1/2 2 1	55%	H, S, Tx3	25,000

Dragon, Metallic   Copper Dragon

CLIMATE/TERRAIN:	Arid and temperate hills and mountains
FREQUENCY:	Rare
ORGANIZATION:	Solitary or clan
ACTIVE TIME:	Any
DIET:	Special
INTELLIGENCE:	High (13-14)
TREASURE:	Special
ALIGNMENT:	Chaotic good

NO. APPEARING:	1 (2-5)
ARMOR CLASS:	1 (base)
MOVEMENT:	9, Fl 30 (C), Jp 3
HIT DICE:	13 (base)
THAC0:	9
NO. OF ATTACKS:	3 + special
DAMAGE/ATTACK:	1-6/1-6/5-20
SPECIAL ATTACKS:	Special
SPECIAL DEFENSES:	Variable
MAGIC RESISTANCE:	Variable
SIZE:	G (36' base)
MORALE:	Elite (16 base)
XP VALUE:	Variable

Copper dragons are incorrigible pranksters, joke tellers, and riddlers. They are prideful and are not good losers, although they are reasonably good winners. They are particularly selfish and greedy for their alignment, and have an almost neutral outlook where wealth is concerned.

At birth, a copper dragon's scales have a ruddy brown color with a copper tint. As the dragon gets older, the scales become finer and more coppery, assuming a soft, warm gloss by the time the dragon becomes a young adult. Beginning at the venerable stage, the dragons' scales pick up a green tint.

Copper dragons speak their own tongue, a tongue common to all good dragons, and 14% of hatchling copper dragons have an ability to communicate with any intelligent creature. The chance to possess this ability increases 5% per age category of the dragon.

Combat: Copper dragons like to taunt and annoy their opponents, hoping they will give up or become angry and act foolishly. Early in an encounter, a copper dragon will jump from one side of an opponent to another, landing on inaccessible or vertical stone surfaces. If there are no such places around a dragon's lair, the dragon will create them ahead of time using *stone shape*, *move earth*, and *wall of stone*. An angry copper dragon will mire its opponents using *rock to mud*, and will force victims who escape the mud, into it with kicks. Once opponents are trapped in the mud, the dragon will crush them with a *wall of stone* or snatch them and carry them aloft. When fighting airborne opponents, a dragon will draw its enemies into narrow, stony gorges where it can use its *spider climb* ability in an attempt to maneuver the enemy into colliding with the walls.

Breath weapon/special abilities: A copper dragon's breath weapon is either a cloud of *slow* gas 30' long, 20' wide, and 20' high or a spurt of *acid* 70' long and 5' wide. Creatures caught in the gas must save vs. breath weapon or be *slowed* for three minutes per age level of the dragon. Creatures caught in the acid take damage, save vs. breath weapon for half. A copper dragon casts its spells and uses its magical abilities at 7th level, plus its combat modifier.

At birth, copper dragons can *spider climb* (stone surfaces only) and are immune to acid. As they age, they gain the following additional powers: **Young:** *neutralize poison* three times a day. **Juvenile:** *stone shape* twice a day. **Adult:** *forget* once a day. **Mature adult:** *rock to mud* once a day. **Old:** *move earth* once a day. **Great wyrm:** *wall of stone* once a day. A copper dragon can jump 30 yards forward or sideways, reaching heights up to 20' at mid jump. They can jump 30' straight up.

Habitat/Society: Copper dragons like dry, rocky uplands and mountains. They lair in narrow caves and often conceal the entrances using *move earth* and *stone shape*. Within the lair, they construct twisting mazes with open tops. These allow the dragons to fly or jump over intruders struggling through the maze.

Copper dragons appreciate wit, and will usually leave good or neutral creatures alone if they can relate a joke, humorous story, or riddle the dragon has not heard before. They quickly get annoyed with creatures who don't laugh at their jokes or do not accept the dragon's tricks and antics with good humor.

Because they often inhabit hills in sight of red dragons' lairs conflicts between the two subspecies often occur. Copper dragons usually run for cover until they can equal the odds.

Ecology: Copper dragons are determined hunters, the good sport a hunt provides is at least as important as they food they get. They are known to eat almost anything, including metal ores. However, they prize giant scorpions and other large poisonous creatures (they say the venom sharpens their wit). The dragon's digestive system can handle the venom safely, although injected venoms affect them normally.

Age	Body Lgt. (')	Tail Lgt. (')	AC	Breath Weapon	Spells Wizard/Priest	MR	Treas. Type	XP Value
1	3-8	2-6	2	2d6 + 1	Nil	Nil	Nil	5,000
2	8-16	4-12	1	4d6 + 2	Nil	Nil	Nil	7,000
3	16-27	12-20	0	6d6 + 3	Nil	Nil	Nil	9,000
4	27-38	20-30	−1	8d6 + 4	1	Nil	1/2H, S	11,000
5	38-50	30-40	−2	10d6 + 5	2	10%	H, S	14,000
6	50-59	40-50	−3	12d6 + 6	3	15%	H, S	15,000
7	59-73	50-60	−4	14d6 + 7	3 1	20%	H, S	16,000
8	73-86	60-70	−5	16d6 + 8	3 2/1	25%	H, S × 2	17,000
9	86-100	70-80	−6	18d6 + 9	3 3/2	30%	H, S × 2	19,000
10	100-114	80-90	−7	20d6 + 10	3 3 1/3	35%	H, S × 2	21,000
11	114-130	90-100	−8	22d6 + 11	3 3 2/3 2	40%	H, S × 3	22,000
12	130-147	100-110	−9	24d6 + 12	3 3 2 1/3 3	45%	H, S × 3	23,000

Gold Dragon

Dragon, Metallic

CLIMATE/TERRAIN:	Any
FREQUENCY:	Very rare
ORGANIZATION:	Solitary or clan
ACTIVITY CYCLE:	Any
DIET:	Special
INTELLIGENCE:	Genius (17-18)
TREASURE:	Special
ALIGNMENT:	Lawful good

NO. APPEARING:	1 (2-5)
ARMOR CLASS:	-4 (base)
MOVEMENT:	12, Fl 40 (C), Jp 3, Sw 12 (15)
HIT DICE:	16 (base)
THAC0:	5 (at 16 HD)
NO. OF ATTACKS:	3 + special
DAMAGE/ATTACK:	1-10/1-10/6-36 (6d6)
SPECIAL ATTACKS:	Special
SPECIAL DEFENSES:	Variable
MAGIC RESISTANCE:	Variable
SIZE:	G (54' base)
MORALE:	Fanatic (17-18)
XP VALUE:	Variable

Gold dragons are wise, judicious, and benevolent. They often embark on self-appointed quests to promote goodness, and are not easily distracted from them. They hate injustice and foul play. A gold dragon frequently assumes human or animal guise and usually will be encountered disguised.

At birth, a gold dragon's scales are dark yellow with golden metallic flecks. The flecks get larger as the dragon matures until, at the adult stage, the scales grow completely golden.

Gold dragons speak their own tongue, a tongue common to all good dragons, and 18% of hatchling gold dragons have an ability to communicate with any intelligent creature. The chance to possess this ability increases 5% per age category of the dragon.

Combat: Gold dragons usually parley before combat. When conversing with intelligent creatures they use *detect lie* and *detect gems* spells to gain the upper hand. In combat, they quickly use *bless* and *luck bonus*. Older dragons use *luck bonus* at the start of each day if the duration is a day or more. They make heavy use of spells in combat. Among their favorites are *sleep, stinking cloud, slow, fire shield, cloudkill, globe of invulnerability, delayed blast fireball,* and *maze.*

Breath weapon/special abilities: A gold dragon has two breath weapons: a cone of *fire* 90' long, 5' wide at the dragon's mouth, and 30' wide at the end or a cloud of potent chlorine gas 50' long, 40' wide, and 30' high. Creatures caught in either effect are entitled to a save versus breath weapon for half damage.

A gold dragon casts its spells and uses its magical abilities at 11th level, plus its combat modifier. Unlike other dragons, most gold dragons seek formal magical training. These dragons own spell books and always have useful spells.

At birth, gold dragons have *water breathing* ability, can *speak with animals* freely, and are immune to fire and gas. They can also *polymorph self* three times a day. Each change in form lasts until the dragon chooses a different form; reverting to the dragon's normal form does not count as a change. A gold dragon's natural form has wings. However, they sometimes choose a wingless form to facilitate swimming, gaining the higher swimming rate listed above. A gold dragon in any wingless form can fly at a speed of 6 (MC E).

As they age, they gain the following additional powers: **Young:** *bless* three times a day. **Juvenile:** *detect lie* three times a day. **Adult:** *animal summoning* once a day. **Mature adult:** *luck bonus* once a day. **Old:** *quest* once a day, and *detect gems* three times a day. (This allows the dragon to know the number and kind of precious stones within a 30' radius, duration is one minute.)

The *luck bonus* power of mature adults is used to aid good adventurers. By touch, the dragon can enchant one gem to bring good luck. The gem is usually one which has been embedded in the dragon's hide. When the dragon carries the gem, it and every good creature in a 10' radius per age category of the dragon receives a +1 bonus to all Saving Throws and similar dice rolls, cf. *stone of good luck.* If the dragon gives a gem to another creature only the bearer gets the bonus. The enchantment lasts three hours per age category of the dragon, plus 1-3 hours. The enchantment ends if the gem is destroyed before its duration expires.

Habitat/Society: Gold dragons can live anywhere. Their lairs are secluded and always made of solid stone, either caves or castles. These usually have loyal guards: either animals appropriate to the terrain, or storm or good cloud giants. The giants usually serve as guards through a mutual defensive agreement.

Ecology: Gold dragons can eat almost anything, however, they usually sustain themselves on pearls or small gems. Gold dragons who receive pearls and gems from good or neutral creatures will usually be favorably inclined toward the gift bringers, as long as the gift is not presented as a crass bribe. In the latter case, the dragon will accept the gift, but react cynically to any requests the giver makes.

Age	Body Lgt.(')	Tail Lgt.(')	AC	Breath Weapon	Spells Wizard/Priest	MR	Treasure Type	XP Value
1	7-19	6-16	-1	2d12+1	Nil	Nil	Nil	8,000
2	19-31	16-28	-2	4d12+2	Nil	Nil	Nil	9,000
3	31-43	28-38	-3	6d12+3	Nil	Nil	Nil	11,000
4	43-55	38-50	-4	8d12+4	1	Nil	E, R, T	13,000
5	55-67	50-60	-5	10d12+5	2	35%	H, R, T	15,000
6	67-80	60-70	-6	12d12+6	2 2	40%	H, R, T	18,000
7	80-93	70-84	-7	14d12+7	2 2 2	45%	H, R, T	19,000
8	93-106	84-95	-8	16d12+8	2 2 2 2/1	50%	H, R, Tx2	20,000
9	106-120	95-108	-9	18d12+9	2 2 2 2 2/2	55%	H, R, Tx2	22,000
10	120-134	108-120	-10	20d12+10	2 2 2 2 2 2/2 2	60%	H, R, Tx2	23,000
11	134-148	121-133	-11	22d12+11	2 2 2 2 2 2 2/2 2 2	65%	H, R, Tx3	24,000
12	148-162	133-146	-12	24d12+12	2 2 2 2 2 2 2 1/2 2 2 2	70%	H, R, Tx3	25,000

Dragon, Metallic

Silver Dragon

CLIMATE/TERRAIN:	Tropical, sub-tropical, and temperate mountains and clouds
FREQUENCY:	Very rare
ORGANIZATION:	Solitary or clan
ACTIVITY CYCLE:	Any
DIET:	Special
INTELLIGENCE:	Exceptional (15-16)
TREASURE:	Special
ALIGNMENT:	Lawful good

NO. APPEARING:	1 (2-5)
ARMOR CLASS:	-3 (base)
MOVEMENT:	9, Fl 30 (C), Jp 3
HIT DICE:	15 (base)
THAC0:	5 (at 15 HD)
NO. OF ATTACKS:	3 + special
DAMAGE/ATTACK:	1-8/1-8/5-30 (5d6)
SPECIAL ATTACKS:	Special
SPECIAL DEFENSES:	Variable
MAGIC RESISTANCE:	Variable
SIZE:	G (48' base)
MORALE:	Fanatic (17-18)
XP VALUE:	Variable

Silver dragons are kind and helpful. They will cheerfully assist good creatures if their need is genuine. They often take the forms of kindly old men or fair damsels when associating with people.

At birth, a silver dragon's scales are blue-gray with silver highlights. As the dragon approaches adulthood, its color slowly lightens to brightly gleaming silver. An adult or older silver dragon has scales so fine that the individual scales are scarcely visible. From a distance, these dragons look as if they have been sculpted from pure metal.

Silver dragons speak their own tongue, a tongue common to all good dragons, and 16% of hatchling silver dragons have an ability to communicate with any intelligent creature. The chance to possess this ability increases 5% per age category of the dragon.

Combat: Silver dragons are not violent and avoid combat except when faced with highly evil or aggressive foes. If necessary, they use *feather fall* to stop any missiles fired at them. They use *wall of fog* or *control weather* to blind or confuse opponents before making melee attacks. If angry, they will use *reverse gravity* to fling enemies helplessly into the air, where they can be snatched. When faced with flying opponents, a silver dragon will hide in clouds (often creating some with *control weather* on clear days), remain there using *cloud walking*, then jump to the attack when they have the advantage.

Breath Weapon/Special Abilities: A silver dragon has two breath weapons: a cone of *cold* 80' long, 5' wide at the dragon's mouth, and 30' wide at the end or a cloud of *paralyzation* gas 50' long, 40' wide, and 20' high. Creatures caught in the gas must save versus breath weapon or become *paralyzed* for one minute per age level of the dragon, plus 1-8 minutes. Creatures caught in the cold are allowed a save versus breath weapon for half damage. A silver dragon casts its spells and uses its magical abilities at 6th level, plus its combat modifier.

At birth, silver dragons are immune to cold, and can *polymorph self* three times a day. Each change in form lasts until the dragon chooses a different form and reverting to their normal form does not count as a change. They also can *cloud walk*. This allows the dragon to tread on clouds or fog as though they were solid ground. The ability functions continuously, but can be negated or resumed at will. As they age, they gain the following additional powers: **Young:** *feather fall* twice a day. **Juvenile:** *wall of fog* once a day. **Adult:** *control winds* three times a day. **Mature adult:** *control weather* once a day. **Old:** *reverse gravity* once a day.

Habitat/Society: Silver dragons prefer aerial lairs on secluded mountain peaks, or amid the clouds themselves. When they lair in clouds there always will be an enchanted area with a solid floor for laying eggs and storing treasure.

Silver dragons seem to prefer human form to their own, and often have mortal companions. Frequently they share deep friendships with mortals. Inevitably, however, the dragon reveals its true form and takes its leave to live a dragon's life for a time.

Ecology: Silver dragons prefer human food, and can live on such fare indefinitely.

Because they lair in similar territories, silver dragons come into conflict with red dragons. Duels between the two species are furious and deadly, but silver dragons generally get the upper hand since they are more capable of working together against their foes and often have human allies.

Age	Body Lgt.(')	Tail Lgt. (')	AC	Breath Weapon	Spells Wizard/Priest	MR	Treasure Type	XP Value
1	8-18	3- 6	0	2d10 + 1	Nil	Nil	Nil	7,000
2	18-30	6-12	- 1	4d10 + 2	Nil	Nil	Nil	8,000
3	30-42	12-16	- 2	6d10 + 3	Nil	Nil	Nil	10,000
4	42-52	16-21	- 3	8d10 + 4	2	Nil	E, R	12,000
5	52-63	21-27	- 4	10d10 + 5	2 2	25%	H, R	14,000
6	63-74	27-32	- 5	12d10 + 6	2 2 1	30%	H, R	17,000
7	74-85	32-37	- 6	14d10 + 7	2 2 2	35%	H, R	18,000
8	85-96	37-43	- 7	16d10 + 8	2 2 2 1/2	40%	H, Rx2	19,000
9	96-108	43-48	- 8	18d10 + 9	2 2 2 2/2 2	45%	H, Rx2	21,000
10	108-120	48-54	- 9	20d10 + 10	2 2 2 2 1/2 21	50%	H, Rx2	22,000
11	120-134	54-60	- 10	22d10 + 11	2 2 2 2/2 2 2	55%	H, Rx3	23,000
12	134-148	60-67	- 11	24d10 + 12	2 2 2 2 2 1/2 2 2 1	60%	H, Rx3	24,000

Brown Dragon

CLIMATE/TERRAIN:	Any arid/Desert
FREQUENCY:	Very rare
ORGANIZATION:	Solitary or clan
ACTIVITY CYCLE:	Any
DIET:	Special
INTELLIGENCE:	Highly (13-14)
TREASURE:	Special
ALIGNMENT:	Neutral (evil)

NO. APPEARING:	1 (2-5)
ARMOR CLASS:	2 (base)
MOVEMENT:	12, Br 24
HIT DICE:	14 (base)
THAC0:	7
NO. OF ATTACKS:	3 + special
DAMAGE/ATTACK:	1-4/1-4/3-30
SPECIAL ATTACKS:	See below
SPECIAL DEFENSES:	Variable
MAGIC RESISTANCE:	See below
SIZE:	G (54' base)
MORALE:	Fanatic (17-18)
XP VALUE:	Variable

Brown dragons, also known as great desert dragons, migrated from the desert Raurin and now frequent much of the wastes in Eastern Mulhorand. Brown dragons are ferocious beasts; while they are intelligent, they view human beings as food, and believe it peculiar to talk with one's meal. They do not have wings and cannot fly.

Brown dragons have a coloration similar to that of desert sands, ranging from dim brown at hatchling stage to almost white at great wyrm stage. They have small, webbed claws that are well developed for digging, and very large, long mouths. Their scales are leathery and not as hard as other dragon armors.

Brown dragons speak their own tongue and the language of blue dragons. They have a 5% chance per age category of being able to communicate with any intelligent creature.

Combat: Brown dragons prefer to dig deep trenches in the sand and wait for prey to appear so they may ambush them. They have a 90% chance of hearing a man-sized creature's footsteps on the desert sands from as far down as 500 feet.

Brown dragons breach the desert sand with incredible silence, imposing a −5 penalty to opponents' surprise rolls. Older brown dragons use illusions or even *invisibility* spells to conceal themselves.

When brown dragons grab their prey, they hold it in their jaws, taking it to their lairs to be eaten when it is most convenient.

The brown dragon's breath weapon is a powerful acid, which it spews in a 5-foot-wide spray that extends in a straight line from the dragon's head up to 60 feet. All creatures caught in the spray can roll a saving throw vs. breath weapon for half damage.

Brown dragons use the spray against large numbers, but not against mounted foes, since they know that horses are good eating and don't put up as much struggle as humans. Brown dragons cast spells as 8th-level wizards.

They are born immune to acid and the effects of the desert heat. They may survive in airless environments nearly indefinitely.

As they age, brown dragons gain the following abilities:

Age	Abilities
Young	Cast *create sand* to cover up their burrows
Juvenile	Cast *create water* once per day
Adult	Cast *sandstorm* (Mulhorandi spell) once per day
Venerable	Can summon a 12-HD earth elemental
Great wyrm	Cast *disintegrate* once per day

Habitat/Society: Brown dragons are found in deserts, often close to settled areas. They typically dwell in deep burrows nearly 1,000 feet beneath the sand, where they carve out vast chambers.

The brown dragon mates and raises a family for only a short period of time; all parents encountered are in the mature adult stage of development. Many brown dragons do not mate.

Man is the main enemy of brown dragons. Humans hunt them for their hides and treasure. Blue dragons also attack brown dragons.

Battles between brown and blue dragons are legendary for their ferocity. The people of the desert have a curious respect for the brown dragon, so tales often make the blue dragons more evil than the brown.

Ecology: Brown dragons are able to digest sand and other min- eral materials to sustain themselves over long periods of time. However, meat is the preferred diet, with horseflesh being a particular favorite.

Age Category	Body Lgt. (')	Tail Lgt. (')	AC	Breath Weapon	Spells (Wizard)	MR	Treasure Type	XP Value
1 Hatchling	7-19	6-16	5	2d6 + 2	Nil	Nil	Nil	2,000
2 Very Young	20-31	17-28	4	4d6 + 4	Nil	Nil	Nil	4,000
3 Young	32-43	29-38	3	6d6 + 6	Nil	Nil	Nil	6,000
4 Juvenile	44-55	39-50	2	8d6 + 8	1	Nil	Nil	8,000
5 Young Adult	56-67	51-60	1	10d6 + 10	2	20%	1/2 H	10,000
6 Adult	68-80	61-70	0	12d6 + 12	3	25%	H	11,000
7 Mature Adult	81-93	71-84	−1	14d6 + 14	3 1	30%	H	12,000
8 Old	94-106	85-95	−2	16d6 + 16	3 2	35%	H	16,000
9 Very Old	107-120	96-108	−3	18d6 + 18	3 3	40%	H × 2	18,000
10 Venerable	121-134	109-120	−4	20d6 + 20	3 3 1	45%	H × 2	19,000
11 Wyrm	135-148	121-133	−5	22d6 + 22	3 3 2	50%	H × 2	20,000
12 Great Wyrm	149-162	134-146	−6	24d6 + 24	3 3 2 1	55%	H × 3	21,000

Cloud Dragon

CLIMATE/TERRAIN:	Tropical, subtropical, and temperate/Clouds and mountains
FREQUENCY:	Very rare
ORGANIZATION:	Solitary or clan
ACTIVITY CYCLE:	Any
DIET:	Special
INTELLIGENCE:	Genius (17-18)
TREASURE:	Special
ALIGNMENT:	Neutral

NO. APPEARING:	1 (2-5)
ARMOR CLASS:	0 (base)
MOVEMENT:	6, Fl 39 (C), Jp 3
HIT DICE:	14 (base)
THAC0:	7
NO. OF ATTACKS:	3+special
DAMAGE/ATTACK:	1-10/1-10/3-36
SPECIAL ATTACKS:	Special
SPECIAL DEFENSES:	Variable
MAGIC RESISTANCE:	Variable
SIZE:	G (66' base)
MORALE:	Fanatic (17)
XP VALUE:	Variable

Cloud dragons are reclusive creatures that dislike intrusions. They rarely converse, but if persuaded to do so they tend to be taciturn and aloof. They have no respect whatsoever for creatures that cannot fly without assistance from spells or devices.

At birth, cloud dragons have silver-white scales tinged with red at the edges. As they grow, the red spreads and lightens to sunset orange. At the mature adult stage and above, the red-orange color deepens to red gold and almost entirely replaces the silver.

Cloud dragons speak their own tongue and a tongue common to all neutral dragons. Also, 17% of hatchling cloud dragons can speak with any intelligent creature. The chance to possess this ability increases 5% per age category.

Combat: Cloud dragons are as likely to avoid combat (by assuming cloud form) as they are to attack. When attacking, they use their breath weapon to scatter foes, then cast *solid fog* and use their weather manipulation abilities to blind and disorient their foes. When very angry, they conjure storms with *control weather* spells, then they call lightning. They like to use *stinking cloud* and *control winds* spells against flying opponents.

Breath Weapon/Special Abilities: A cloud dragon's breath weapon is an icy blast of air that is 140 feet long, 30 feet high, and 30 feet wide. Creatures caught in the blast suffer damage from cold and flying ice crystals. Furthermore, all creatures three size classes or more smaller than the dragon are blown head over heels for 2d12 feet, plus 3 feet per age category of the dragon. Characters who can grab solid objects won't be carried away unless they fail Strength checks; creatures with claws, suction cups, etc., can avoid the effect if they have a suitable surface to cling to.

A cloud dragon casts its spells and uses its magical abilities at 6th level plus its combat modifier.

Cloud dragons are immune to cold.

They can assume (or leave) a cohesive, cloud-like form at will, once

per round. In this form, they are 75% unlikely to be distinguished from normal clouds; when in cloud form, their Armor Class improves by −3 and their magic resistance increases by 15%. Cloud dragons can use their spells and innate abilities while in cloud form, but they cannot attack physically or use their breath weapon. In cloud form, cloud dragons fly at a speed of 12 (MC: A).

As they age, cloud dragons gain the following additional powers: **Very young:** solid fog twice a day. **Young:** *stinking cloud* twice a day. **Juvenile:** *create water* twice a day (affects a maximum of three cubic yards [81 cubic feet]). **Adult:** *obscurement* three times a day. **Mature adult:** *call lightning* twice a day. **Old:** *weather summoning* twice a day. **Very old:** *control weather* twice a day. **Ancient:** *control winds* twice a day.

Habitat/Society: Cloud dragons lair in magical cloud islands where there is at least a small, solid floor for laying eggs and storing treasure. Very rarely, they occupy cloud-shrouded mountain peaks

Cloud dragons are solitary 95% of the time. If more than one is encountered it is a single parent with offspring.

Ecology: Like all dragons, cloud dragons can eat just about anything. They seem to subsist primarily on rain water, hailstones, and the occasional bit of silver.

Because they inhabit in similar territories, cloud dragons come into conflict with silver dragons. Despite their higher intelligence, cloud dragons usually lose such confrontations because of the silver dragons' secondary breath weapons and ability to muster allies.

Age	Body Lgt. (')	Tail Lgt. (')	AC	Breath Weapon	Spells Wizard/Priest	MR	Treas. Type	XP Value
1	11-24	4-8	3	2d6+2	Nil	Nil	Nil	3,000
2	24-41	8-16	2	3d6+4	Nil	Nil	Nil	6,000
3	41-58	16-22	1	4d6+6	Nil	Nil	Nil	8,000
4	58-71	22-29	0	5d6+8	1	Nil	½R , T	11,000
5	71-87	29-37	−1	6d6+10	1 1	25%	R, T	13,000
6	87-102	37-44	−2	7d6+12	2 1	30%	R, T	14,000
7	102-117	44-51	−3	8d6+14	2 2	35%	R, T	15,000
8	117-132	51-59	−4	9d6+16	3 2 / 1	40%	R, T, X, Z	17,000
9	132-148	59-66	−5	10d6+18	3 3 / 1 1	45%	R, T, X, Z	18,000
10	148-165	66-74	−6	11d6+20	4 3 / 2 1	50%	R, T, X, Z	19,000
11	165-184	74-82	−7	12d6+22	4 4 / 2 2	55%	R, T, X, Zx2	20,000
12	184-203	82-92	−8	13d6+24	5 4 / 3 2	60%	R, T, X, Zx2	21,000

Deep Dragon

CLIMATE/TERRAIN:	Hill and mountain caverns, subterranean
FREQUENCY:	Rare
ORGANIZATION:	Solitary or clan
ACTIVITY CYCLE:	Any
DIET:	Carnivorous
INTELLIGENCE:	Exceptional (15-16)
TREASURE:	Special
ALIGNMENT:	Chaotic evil

NO. APPEARING:	1 (2-5)
ARMOR CLASS:	0 (base)
MOVEMENT:	12, Fl 30(C), Br 6, Sw 9
HIT DICE:	14 (base)
THAC0:	7 (base)
NO. OF ATTACKS:	3 + special
DAMAGE/ATTACK:	3-12/3-12/3-24
SPECIAL ATTACKS:	See below
SPECIAL DEFENSES:	Variable
MAGIC RESISTANCE:	Variable
SIZE:	H (24' base)
MORALE:	Fanatic (17-18)
XP VALUE:	Variable

Deep dragons are little known on the surface world. They are the hunters of the Underdark. Cunning and patient, they place their survival, followed by their joy of hunting, above all else. Deep dragons carefully amass and hide treasure in various caches, guarded with traps and magic. They are able to use most magical items.

Deep dragons are an iridescent maroon when they hatch, soft- scaled, and unable to change form. They keep to their birth-lair until they have mastered both of their other forms-a giant winged worm or snake and a human (or drow) form.

Combat: Deep dragons burrow and fight with powerful, stone- rending claws. They love to fight and hunt prey through the lightless caverns of the Underdark, employing their various forms. In snake form, they are AC 6, MV 9, Fl 4(D), Sw 11, losing claw attacks, but gaining a constriction attack (attack roll required, inflicts 3d8 points of damage per round, hampers movement, spellcasting, and causes -1 on attack rolls and a 1-point AC penalty).

In human form, a deep dragon is AC 10, MV 12, Sw 12, and causes damage by spell or weapon type. Armor can be worn, but it is always destroyed (inflicting 2d4 points of damage to the dragon) in any transformation of shape. A deep dragon can alter its features to resemble any humanoid of roughly human size. It is 66% likely to copy a specific being well enough to be mistaken for the actual creature.

A deep dragon's breath weapon is a cone of flesh-corrosive gas 50 feet long, 40 feet wide, and 30 feet high. Creatures in the cloud can save vs. breath weapon for half damage (if they have dry, exposed skin, they save against the flesh-eating gas at -2). Cloth, metal, and wood are not affected. Leather is treated as dry, exposed skin.

Deep dragons cast spells at 9th level, adjusted by their combat modifiers. They are born with infravision, *true seeing*, and unerring *detect magic* abilities, and immunities to *charm*, *sleep*, and *hold* magic. Deep dragons are immune to extremes of heat and cold (-3 on each die of damage taken, to a minimum of 1 hp per die).

As deep dragons age, they gain the following additional powers:

Age	Ability
Very young	assume snakeform 3 times/day
Young	assume "human" form 3 times/day
Juvenile	one more form change/day (each), regen. 1d4 hp/turn
Adult	regenerate 1d4 hp/6 rounds; *free action* at will
Mature adult	regenerate 1d4 hp/4 rounds; *levitate* 3 times/day
Old	*transmute rock to mud* and *telekinesis* 3 times/day
Very old	*move earth* 3 times/day
Venerable	*passwall* and *disintegrate* 2 times/day
Wyrm	one additional use/day of powers gained since Old age; *stone shape* 2 times/day, *tongues* once/day
Great wyrm	*repulsion* 3 times/day, affecting all except dragons. One additional use/day of *stone shape* and *tongues*

Habitat/Society: Deep dragons roam the Underdark and are great explorers. Most often deep dragons are found in well- defended lairs in the Underdark. They often use their powers to reach caverns inaccessible to most creatures. Deep dragons often work with drow.

Ecology: Deep dragons have been known to eat almost anything, but they particularly prize the flesh of clams, fish, kuo-toa, and aboleth. They view cloakers and mind flayers as dangerous rivals in the Underdark. Deep dragons avoid confrontations with other dragons and never fight or steal from others of their own kind.

Age Category	Body Lgt. (')	Tail Lgt. (')	AC	Breath Weapon	Spells (Wizard/Priest)	MR	Treasure Type	XP Value
1 Hatchling	1-5	1-4	3	2d8 + 1	Nil	Nil	Nil	3,000
2 Very Young	5-14	4-12	2	4d8 + 2	Nil	Nil	Nil	5,000
3 Young	14-23	12-21	1	6d8 + 3	Nil	Nil	Nil	6,000
4 Juvenile	23-32	21-28	0	8d8 + 4	1	Nil	H,Q	8,000
5 Young Adult	32-41	28-36	−1	10d8 + 5	2	25%	H,Q × 2,E	10,000
6 Adult	41-50	36-45	−2	12d8 + 6	2 1	30%	H,Q × 3,E,S	12,000
7 Mature Adult	50-59	45-54	−3	14d8 + 7	3 2	35%	H × 2,Q × 4,E,S	14,000
8 Old	59-68	54-62	−4	16d8 + 8	4 2 1/1	40%	H × 2,Q × 4,E,S,T	16,000
9 Very Old	68-77	62-70	−5	18d8 + 9	4 2 2/2	45%	H × 3,Q × 5,E,S,T	17,000
10 Venerable	77-86	70-78	−6	20d8 + 10	4 3 2 1/2 1	50%	H × 3,Q,E,S,T,U	18,000
11 Wyrm	86-95	78-85	−7	22d8 + 11	4 3 3 2/3 2	55%	H × 3,Q,E,S,T,U,V	19,000
12 Great Wyrm	95-104	85-94	−8	24d8 + 12	4 3 3 2 1/3 3 1	60%	H,Q,E,S,T,U,V,X,Z	20,000

Mercury Dragon

CLIMATE/TERRAIN:	Temper ate and subtropical/ Mountains
FREQUENCY:	Very rare
ORGANIZATION:	Solitary or clan
ACTIVITY CYCLE:	Any
DIET:	Omnivore
INTELLIGENCE:	Highly (13-14)
TREASURE:	See below
ALIGNMENT:	Chaotic good

NO. APPEARING:	1 (2-5)
ARMOR CLASS:	−1 (base)
MOVEMENT:	15, Fl 36(C), Jp 3
HIT DICE:	11 (base)
THAC0:	9 (base)
NO. OF ATTACKS:	3 + special
DAMAGE/ATTACK:	2-8/2-8/2-20
SPECIAL ATTACKS:	See below
SPECIAL DEFENSES:	Variable
MAGIC RESISTANCE:	See below
SIZE:	H (25' base)
MORALE:	Fanatic (17-18)
XP VALUE:	Variable

Mercury dragons are fast, highly-maneuverable creatures with relatively small bodies and long tails. Although good in alignment, they are very whimsical, making and changing decisions frequently.

At birth, a mercury dragon's scales are dull silver. As it ages, the scales become brighter and brighter, until at adult age they gain a brilliant mirror finish. Sunlight or other sources of light reflecting off the scales and wings of a mercury dragon can be blinding.

Mercuries speak the language of good dragons, but at high speed, so there's only a 75% chance of understanding a mercury dragon.

Combat: Mercury dragons are as unpredictable when it comes to combat, as they are in any other situation. They may parley, they might attack instantly, or, perhaps, they may avoid combat entirely. They never attack good-aligned creatures unless sorely provoked.

Mercury dragons always use spells in combat, if possible. They are very creative, and can always figure out some innovative way of using virtually any spell to advantage in combat.

In addition to the breath weapon and the attack modes shared by all dragons, mercury dragons can curve the mirror-bright membranes of their wings to reflect and concentrate available light (as dim as full moonlight) into a beam of dazzling brightness. They can aim the beam at one enemy per round-at the expense of not being able to use their wing buffet, and the enemy must roll a successful saving throw vs. spell or be blinded for 1d4 + 1 rounds. If not using this technique as a weapon, they can use the beam much like a search-light.

A mercury dragon's breath weapon is a beam of brilliant, yellow light. The beam is 5 feet wide and extends 60 feet from the creature's mouth. Any creature caught in the beam receives damage from heat (saving throw for half damage). The heat of the beam is intense enough to ignite flammable objects that fail saving throws vs. magical fire.

A mercury dragon casts spells and uses magical abilities at the 10th

level, plus its combat modifier. At birth, mercury dragons are immune to fire and all magical forms of blindness.

They also receive a + 3 bonus to saving throws against light-based attacks. As they age, they gain the following additional powers:

Age	Abilities
Young	*gaze reflection* at will
Juvenile	*mirror image* three times per day
Adult	*polymorph self* twice per day
Old	*telekinesis* twice per day
Wyrm	*project image* once per day

Habitat/Society: Mercury dragons are loners by nature. Their mating behavior is free-wheeling, fun loving, and generally irresponsible. If a female becomes impregnated, however, the male's protective instincts take over. Mercuries are very protective of their offspring, and will give their lives to save them. Offspring usually stay with their parents until they reach the juvenile age category.

Because of their unpredictable, sometimes almost irrational nature, mercuries very rarely have close relationships with other creatures in the area. For this reason, mercuries have to depend on magical and mechanical traps and guards to protect their lairs when they are away.

Ecology: Mercury dragons eat anything, but they prefer to feed on metal ores. Although they have no venom attacks, the flesh of mercury dragons is highly poisonous.

Age Category	Body Lgt. (')	Tail Lgt. (')	AC	Breath Weapon	Spells (Wizard/Priest)	MR	Treasure Type	XP Value
1 Hatchling	3-6	3-6	2	2d8 + 1	Nil	Nil	Nil	1,400
2 Very Young	6-11	6-11	1	4d8 + 2	Nil	Nil	Nil	3,000
3 Young	11-17	11-20	0	6d8 + 3	Nil	Nil	Nil	5,000
4 Juvenile	17-21	20-25	−1	8d8 + 4	1	10%	½ H	8,000
5 Young Adult	21-24	26-30	−2	10d8 + 5	1 1	15%	H	10,000
6 Adult	24-27	30-33	−3	12d8 + 6	2 1 1	20%	H	11,000
7 Mature Adult	27-30	33-36	−4	14d8 + 7	2 2 2	25%	H	12,000
8 Old	30-33	36-36	−5	16d8 + 8	3 2 2 1	30%	H, I	14,000
9 Very Old	33-36	39-42	−6	18d8 + 9	3 3 2 2	35%	H, I	15,000
10 Venerable	36-39	42-45	−7	20d8 + 10	3 3 3 2 1	40%	Hx2, I	16,000
11 Wyrm	39-41	45-48	−8	22d8 + 11	3 3 3 2 2 1	50%	Hx2, I, X	17,000
12 Great wyrm	41-44	48-51	−9	24d8 + 12	3 3 3 3 2 2 1	70%	Hx3, I, T, X	18,000

Mist Dragon

CLIMATE/TERRAIN:	Tropical and subtropical/Forests, lake shores, sea shores, and river banks
FREQUENCY:	Very rare
ORGANIZATION:	Solitary or clan
ACTIVITY CYCLE:	Any
DIET:	Special
INTELLIGENCE:	Exceptional (15-16)
TREASURE:	Special
ALIGNMENT:	Neutral

NO. APPEARING:	1 (2-5)
ARMOR CLASS:	1 (base) or −2 (base)
MOVEMENT:	12, Fl 39 (C), Sw 12
HIT DICE:	11 (base)
THAC0:	9 (base)
NO. OF ATTACKS:	3 + special
DAMAGE/ATTACK:	2-5/2-5/2-24
SPECIAL ATTACKS:	Special
SPECIAL DEFENSES:	Variable
MAGIC RESISTANCE:	Nil or 15%
SIZE:	G (54' base)
MORALE:	Champion (16 base)
XP VALUE:	Variable

Mist dragons are solitary and philosophical. Their favorite activity is sitting quietly and thinking. They hate being disturbed and dislike conversation.

At birth, a mist dragon's scales are shiny blue-white. As the dragon ages, the scales darken, becoming blue-gray with metallic silver flecks that sparkle in sunlight.

Mist dragons speak their own tongue and a tongue common to all neutral dragons. Also, 15% of hatchling mist dragons can speak with any intelligent creature. The chance to possess this ability increases 5% per age category.

Combat: Mist dragons try to avoid encounters by assuming mist form. In combat, they quickly use their breath weapons, then assume mist form and hide in the vapor—where they launch a spell assault.

Breath Weapon/Special Abilities: A mist dragon's breath weapon is a cloud of scalding vapor that is 90 feet long, 30 feet wide, and 30 feet high. Creatures caught in vapor suffer can roll saving throws vs. breath weapon for half damage. In still air, the vapor persists for 1d4 + 4 rounds; on the second round, it condenses into a clammy, smothering fog that blinds air-breathing creatures for 1d4 rounds and inflicts 3d4 points of drowning damage per round for as long as the creature remains in the cloud (a successful saving throw vs. breath weapon negates both effects).

A mist dragon casts its spells and uses its magical abilities at 6th level plus its combat modifier.

Mist dragons are immune to fire and heat.

Mist dragons can assume (or leave) a cohesive, mist-like form at will, once per round. In this form, they are 75% unlikely to be distinguished from normal mist; in mist form, their Armor Class improves by −3 and their magic resistance increases by 15%. They can use their spells and innate abilities while in mist form, but they cannot attack physically or use their breath weapon. Mist dragons in mist form can fly at a speed of 9 (MC: A).

As they age, they gain the following additional powers: **Very young:** *water breathing* twice a day. **Young:** *wall of fog* twice a day. **Juvenile:** *create water* twice a day (affects a maximum of three cubic yards [81 cubic feet]). **Adult:** *control winds* three times a day. **Mature adult:** *wind wall* twice a day. **Old:** *solid fog* twice a day. **Very old:** *predict weather* twice a day. **Ancient:** *airy water* twice a day.

Habitat/Society: Mist dragons live near waterfalls, rapids, coastlines, or where rainfall is frequent and heavy. Their lairs are usually large natural caverns or grottoes that are mist-filled and damp. Forest-dwelling mist dragons occasionally come into conflict with green dragons. Mist dragons greatly resent the green dragons' attempts to intimidate or dominate them; they usually spend several months vainly trying to avoid a green dragon's advances before losing all patience and launching an all-out campaign to destroy or drive away the aggressor. Likewise, coastal mist dragons might have bronze dragons for neighbors. This, however, seldom leads to conflict as both dragons are content to leave the others alone.

Mist dragons are loners, and 90% of all encounters are with individuals. Group encounters are with parents and offspring.

Ecology: Mist dragons can eat almost anything, including woody plants and even mud. However, they draw most of their sustenance directly from natural mist or spray. They often lie in misty or foggy places, thinking and basking in the moisture.

Age	Body Lgt. (')	Tail Lgt. (')	AC	Breath Weapon	Spells Wizard/Priest	MR	Treas. Type	XP Value
1	7-19	6-16	4	2d6 + 1	Nil	Nil	Nil	3,000
2	19-31	16-28	3	3d6 + 2	Nil	Nil	Nil	5,000
3	31-43	28-38	2	4d6 + 3	Nil	Nil	Nil	7,000
4	43-55	38-50	1	5d6 + 4	1	Nil	Y, Z	10,000
5	55-67	50-60	0	6d6 + 5	1 1	25%	X, Y, Z	12,000
6	67-80	60-70	−1	7d6 + 6	2 1	30%	X, Y, Z	13,000
7	80-93	70-84	−2	8d6 + 7	2 2	35%	X, Y, Z	14,000
8	93-106	84-95	−3	9d6 + 8	3 2 / 1	40%	X, Y, Zx2	16,000
9	106-120	95-108	−4	10d6 + 9	3 3 / 1 1	45%	X, Y, Zx2	17,000
10	120-134	108-121	−5	11d6 + 10	4 3 / 2 1	50%	X, Y, Zx2	18,000
11	134-148	121-133	−6	12d6 + 11	4 4 / 2 2	55%	X, Y, Zx3	19,000
12	148-162	133-146	−7	13d6 + 12	5 4 / 3 2	60%	X, Y, Zx3	20,000

Shadow Dragon

CLIMATE/TERRAIN:	Non-arctic/Ruins, subterranean, and plane of Shadow
FREQUENCY:	Very rare
ORGANIZATION:	Solitary or clan
ACTIVITY CYCLE:	Nocturnal (any on the plane of Shadow)
DIET:	Special
INTELLIGENCE:	Genius (17-18)
TREASURE:	Special
ALIGNMENT:	Chaotic evil

NO. APPEARING:	1 (2-5)
ARMOR CLASS:	−4 (base)
MOVEMENT:	18, Fl 30 (D), Jp 3
HIT DICE:	12 (base)
THAC0:	9 (base)
NO. OF ATTACKS:	3 + special
DAMAGE/ATTACK:	1-6/1-6/3-18
SPECIAL ATTACKS:	Special
SPECIAL DEFENSES:	Variable
MAGIC RESISTANCE:	Variable
SIZE:	H (21′ base)
MORALE:	Champion (16)
XP VALUE:	Variable

Shadow dragons are sly and devious. They are instinctively cunning and are not prone to taking risks.

At all ages, a shadow dragon's scales and body are translucent, so that when viewed from a distance it appears to be a mass of shadows.

Shadow dragons speak their own tongue and a tongue common to all evil dragons. Also, 17% of hatchling shadow dragons can speak with any intelligent creature. The chance to possess this ability increases 5% per age category.

Combat: Shadow dragons prefer to attack from hiding, usually employing invisibility or hiding in shadows. They use illusion/phantasm spells to confuse and misdirect foes. Older dragons are especially fond of their non-detection ability.

Breath Weapon/Special Abilities: A shadow dragon's breath weapon is a cloud of blackness that is 40 feet long, 30 feet wide, and 20 feet high. Creatures caught in the cloud are blinded for one melee round and lose 3/4 (round up) of their life energy (levels or Hit Dice); a successful saving throw vs. breath weapon reduces the loss to 1/2 (round up). The life energy loss persists for a variable number of turns, shown on the table above. Negative plane protection spells prevent this life energy loss.

A character who is reduced to 0 or fewer levels lapses into a coma for the duration of the cloud's effect.

A shadow dragon casts spells and uses its magical abilities at 6th level plus its combat modifier.

Shadow dragons are born immune to energy draining and with the ability to hide in shadows with 40% chance of success; this ability increases 5% per age category to a maximum of 95%.

As they age, they gain the following additional powers: **Juvenile:** *mirror image* three times a day (1d4 + 1 images). **Adult:** *dimension door* twice a day. **Old:** *non-detection* three times a day. **Venerable:** *shadow walk* once a day. **Great wyrm:** *create shadows* three times a day. (This ability creates a mass of leaping shadows with a radius of 100 yards, duration one hour. All magical [and normal] light and darkness sources are negated for as long as they remain in the radius. Creatures able to hide in shadows can do so in these magical shadows even if under direct observation. Shadow dragons and other creatures from the plane of Shadow can move and attack normally while hiding in these shadows, effectively giving them improved invisibility. A successful *dispel magic* spell banishes the shadows.)

Habitat/Society: Shadow dragons hate both bright light and total darkness, preferring variegated lighting with patches of diffuse light and deep, inky shadows. On the Prime Material plane, their lairs are always places that provide shadowy light for most of the day. They prefer ancient ruins, where they can hide underground when the sun is bright and still find shadows above ground during dawn and twilight. In the plane of Shadow, they live in dense thickets of trees and brambles, fortified castles, or labyrinthine caves. In either plane, they prefer to locate their lairs near colonies of other creatures that can alert them to potential foes or victims. The dragons seldom actually cooperate with these allies, however, though the dragons commonly prey on them.

Shadow dragons love dark-colored, opaque gems, and especially prize black stones. They also collect magical items that produce shadows or darkness. They use these items to turn areas filled with total darkness or light into masses of shadows.

Ecology: Shadow dragons eat almost anything. Their favorite food is rotting carrion, though they often kill for sport. Slain victims are left to decay until they become suitably foul. These dragons are equally fond of frost-killed, waterlogged, or salt-poisoned plants.

Age	Body Lgt. (′)	Tail Lgt. (′)	AC	Breath Weapon	Spells Wizard/Priest	MR	Treas. Type	XP Value
1	1-4	1-3	−1	1d4 + 1	Nil	5%	Nil	4,000
2	4-11	3-8	−2	1d4 + 2	Nil	10%	Nil	6,000
3	11-18	8-13	−3	2d4 + 1	Nil	15%	Nil	8,000
4	18-23	13-18	−4	2d4 + 2	2	20%	1/2 H, S	10,000
5	23-29	18-23	−5	3d4 + 1	2 2	25%	H, S	11,000
6	29-36	23-28	−6	3d4 + 2	2 2 2	30%	H, S	13,000
7	36-42	28-33	−7	4d4 + 1	2 2 2 2 / 1	35%	H, S	15,000
8	42-48	33-38	−8	4d4 + 2	2 2 2 2 2 / 2	40%	H, Sx2	17,000
9	48-55	38-43	−9	5d4 + 1	2 2 2 2 2 2 / 3	45%	H, Sx2	19,000
10	55-61	43-48	−10	5d4 + 2	4 2 2 2 2 2 / 3 1	50%	H, Sx2	20,000
11	61-67	48-53	−11	6d4 + 1	4 4 2 2 2 2 / 3 2	55%	H, Sx3	21,000
12	67-74	53-58	−12	6d4 + 2	4 4 4 2 2 2 / 3 3	60%	H, Sx3	22,000

Steel Dragon

CLIMATE/TERRAIN:	Temperate cities (rarely temperate hills, plains, and forests.)
FREQUENCY:	Very rare
ORGANIZATION:	Solitary
ACTIVITY CYCLE:	Any
DIET:	Special
INTELLIGENCE:	Supra-genius (19-20)
TREASURE:	Special
ALIGNMENT:	Lawful neutral (good)

NO. APPEARING:	1
ARMOR CLASS:	0 (base)
MOVEMENT:	9, Fl 30(D), Sw 6
HIT DICE:	11 (base)
THAC0:	9 (base)
NO. OF ATTACKS:	3 + special
DAMAGE/ATTACK:	1-10/1-10/3-30
SPECIAL ATTACKS:	Special
SPECIAL DEFENSES:	Variable
MAGIC RESISTANCE:	Variable
SIZE:	H (25' base)
MORALE:	Fanatic (17-18)
XP VALUE:	Variable

Steel dragons love to have human and demihuman companions, and they prefer to live amid the hustle and bustle of great cities. They often pose as sages, scholars, mages, or other intellectuals.

At birth, a steel dragon's scales are deep blue-gray with steely highlights. As the dragon approaches adulthood, its color slowly lightens to that of lustrous burnished steel. When these dragons take on human form, they always have one steel-gray feature-hair, eyes, nails, or sometimes a ring or other ornament.

Steel dragons speak their own tongue and a tongue common to all neutral dragons. Also, 19% of hatchling steel dragons can speak with any intelligent creature. This chance increases by 5% per age category.

Combat: Steel dragons favor repartee over combat. If pressed, they usually begin with a spell assault and avoid melee. If seriously harmed or threatened, they resume dragon form and use their breath weapons. They breathe on any foe they plan to engage in melee, and they seek to keep their foes within the cloud until the gas loses its potency.

A steel dragon's breath weapon is a cube of toxic gas. The dragon can monitor the amount of gas released so closely that it can make the cube as small as it wishes or as large as shown in the table below (the a side of the cube). Creatures caught in the gas must roll successful saving throws vs. poison with a −2 penalty or die instantly. The gas is quickly absorbed through the skin and is just as lethal if inhaled. Coating all exposed skin with lard or grease offers some protection (saving throw penalty negated). Victims who succeed with the save suffer the indicated amount of damage. In still air, the gas stays active for two melee rounds. Steel dragons are immune to all poisons.

A steel dragon can *polymorph self* five times a day. Each change in form lasts until the dragon chooses a different form. Reverting to the dragon's normal form does not count as a change.

Steel dragons are immune to wizard spells of 1st to 4th levels and cast spells and use their special abilities at 8th level, plus their combat modifier. As they age, they gain the following additional powers:

Age	Abilities
Young	*cantrip* twice a day
Juvenile	*friends* once a day
Adult	*charm person* three times a day
Mature adult	*suggestion* once a day
Old	*enthrall* once a day

Habitat/Society: Steel dragons prefer human lodgings that are well equipped with strong rooms or vaults to protect their treasures.

Steel dragons prefer human form to their own, and they always have mortal companions. They are endlessly curious about human and demihuman art, culture, history, and politics. They always keep their true nature secret, but they are able to recognize each other.

Ecology: Steel dragons prefer human food. Unlike other form shifting dragons, they cannot live on such fare indefinitely, as they must eat enough to maintain their true bulk. Once or twice a month, they leave their adopted cities and go into the wilderness to hunt for food. They explain their absences in a way consistent with their human identities.

Steel dragons hate chaotic creatures who seek to disrupt life in cities or despoil their hunting grounds. In the city the dragons never hesitate to report troublemakers or to use their special abilities to hunt down criminals. In the wilderness, they prefer swifter forms of justice.

Age Category	Body Lgt. (')	Tail Lgt. (')	AC	Breath Weapon	Spells (Wizard/Priest)	MR	Treasure Type	XP Value
1 Hatchling	2-8	1-4	3	15'/1d4 + 1	Nil	25%	Nil	1,4000
2 Very Young	8-14	4-9	2	20'/2d4	Nil	30%	Nil	2,000
3 Young	14-20	9-14	1	25'/2d4 + 1	Nil	35%	Nil	5,000
4 Juvenile	20-26	14-19	0	30'/3d4	4	40%	E, R	7,000
5 Young Adult	26-32	19-24	−1	35'/3d4 + 1	4 4	45%	H, R	9,000
6 Adult	32-38	24-29	−2	40'/4d4	4 4 4	50%	H, R	11,000
7 Mature Adult	38-44	29-34	−3	45'/4d4 + 1	4 4 4 4	55%	H, R	12,000
8 Old	44-50	34-39	−4	50'/5d4	4 4 4 4 4	60%	H, R × 2	16,000
9 Very Old	50-56	39-44	−5	55'/5d4 + 1	4 4 4 4 4 4	65%	H, R × 2	17,000
10 Venerable	56-62	44-49	−6	60'/6d4	5 4 4 4 4 4/2	70%	H, R × 2	18,000
11 Wyrm	62-68	49-54	−7	65'/6d4 + 1	5 5 4 4 4 4/2 2	75%	H, R × 3	19,000
12 Great wyrm	68-74	54-59	−8	70'/7d4	5 5 5 4 4 4/2 2 2	80%	H, R × 3	20,000

Yellow Dragon

CLIMATE/TERRAIN:	Desert
FREQUENCY:	Very rare
ORGANIZATION:	Solitary
ACTIVITY CYCLE:	Any
DIET:	Omnivore
INTELLIGENCE:	Very (11-12)
TREASURE:	See below
ALIGNMENT:	Chaotic evil

NO. APPEARING:	1 (1-4)
ARMOR CLASS:	0 (base)
MOVEMENT:	12, Fl 30 (C)
HIT DICE:	13 (base)
THAC0:	7 (base)
NO. OF ATTACKS:	3 + special
DAMAGE/ATTACK:	1-8/1-8/2-16
SPECIAL ATTACKS:	See below
SPECIAL DEFENSES:	Variable
MAGIC RESISTANCE:	See below
SIZE:	G (36' base)
MORALE:	Champion (15-16)
XP VALUE:	Variable

Although the existence of yellow dragons has long been predicted by sages (based on theories of primary colors), the first specimen was spotted only five or so years ago. The creatures are solitary and secretive, preferring to lay in wait for prey to stumble into carefully-prepared traps instead of hunting actively.

At birth, yellows have soft, tan scales. As they grow older, the scales harden and become lighter in color, eventually reaching the grayish yellow of desert sands. Their scales always have a dusty texture to them, giving them a finish that does not reflect light well. Even their teeth and claws have a similar finish. No part of the yellow dragon will glint in the sunlight, thereby giving away its position.

Yellow dragons speak their own tongue, which is quite different than that spoken by other evil dragons. Yellows have no interest in speaking with other races, and so they learn no other languages.

Combat: Although preferring guile to combat and ambush to attack, yellows are fierce and cunning fighters. Even if forced into a situation where direct combat is inevitable, they'll still use their spells and innate abilities so as to mislead, misdirect, and distract their opponents.

A favorite hunting tactic for a yellow is to dig a steep-walled, cone-shaped depression in the sand, and then bury itself at the bottom of this crater with just its eyes and nostrils showing. When a creature stumbles into the depression, the dragon moves its wings in the sand, causing the steep walls of the cone to collapse and drawing the prey straight to the dragon's mouth. A yellow dragon casts spells and uses magical abilities at 8th level, plus its combat modifier.

A yellow dragon's breath weapon is a high-velocity blast of scorching air mixed with sand. This affects an area 50 feet long, 40 feet wide, and 20 feet high. Creatures caught within this blast must roll successful saving throws vs. breath weapon for half damage. Regardless of the outcome of this roll, they must make another saving throw vs. breath weapon. Failure means that the abrasive sand in the breath blast has damaged their eyes, blinding them for 1d4 + 1 rounds.

Yellow dragons are immune to fire and heat and can cast *silence, 10' radius* at will. As they age, they gain the following additional powers:

Age	Abilities
Young	*create or destroy water* three times per day
Juvenile	*dust devil* three times per day
Adult	*improved invisibility* twice per day
Old	*wind wall* three times per day
Wyrm	*enervation* three times per day

Habitat/Society: Yellow dragons love deserts, preferring areas of sandy, windswept desolation. They are most comfortable in daytime temperatures of 105 degrees and up, although they can easily survive subfreezing temperatures at night. They share much the same territory as brasses; thus the species occasionally come into conflict.

Yellows are solitary, selfish creatures that form no close bonds with any other creature, including other yellows. They are highly territorial; the only time they'll let another yellow into their territory is to mate, which is actually quite rare. Immediately afterward, the dragons separate. The mother raises the offspring, but won't go out of her way to protect them from attackers. The young dragons usually leave home before they reach the juvenile age category. The main enemies of yellow dragons are brasses, which actively hunt the smaller creatures.

Ecology: Although able to eat anything, yellows favor fresh meat. (Demi)humans are considered a delicacy, as are the unhatched eggs of brass dragons. (Yellows rarely get to enjoy this latter feast.)

Age Category	Body Lgt. (')	Tail Lgt. (')	AC	Breath Weapon	Spells (Wizard/Priest)	MR	Treasure Type	XP Value
1 Hatchling	2-7	1-4	3	2d4 + 1	Nil	Nil	Nil	2,000
2 Very Young	7-16	4-12	2	4d4 + 2	Nil	Nil	Nil	3,000
3 Young	16-35	12-21	1	6d4 + 3	Nil	Nil	Nil	5,000
4 Juvenile	35-44	21-28	0	8d4 + 4	Nil	Nil	E	7,000
5 Young Adult	44-53	28-36	−1	10d4 + 5	1	Nil	E, O, S	9,000
6 Adult	53-62	36-45	−2	12d4 + 6	1 1	5%	E, O, S	11,000
7 Mature Adult	62-71	45-54	−3	14d4 + 7	2 1	10%	E, O, S	12,000
8 Old	71-80	54-62	−4	16d4 + 8	2 2 1	15%	E, O, Sx2	13,000
9 Very Old	80-89	62-70	−5	18d4 + 9	2 2 2	20%	E, O, Sx2	14,000
10 Venerable	89-98	70-78	−6	20d4 + 10	2 2 2 1	25%	E, O, Sx2	15,000
11 Wyrm	98-107	78-85	−7	22d4 + 11	2 2 2 2	30%	E, O, Sx3	16,000
12 Great wyrm	107-116	85-94	−8	24d4 + 12	2 2 2 2 1	35%	E, O, Sx4	17,000

Dragon Turtle

CLIMATE/TERRAIN:	Subtropical and temperate fresh and salt water
FREQUENCY:	Very rare
ORGANIZATION:	Solitary
ACTIVITY CYCLE:	Any
DIET:	Carnivore
INTELLIGENCE:	Very (11-12)
TREASURE:	B,R,S,T,V
ALIGNMENT:	Neutral

NO. APPEARING:	1
ARMOR CLASS:	0
MOVEMENT:	3, Sw 9
HIT DICE:	12-14
THAC0:	12 Hit Dice: 9
	13-14 Hit Dice: 7
NO. OF ATTACKS:	3
DAMAGE/ATTACK:	2-12/2-12/4-32
SPECIAL ATTACKS:	Breath weapon, capsize ships
SPECIAL DEFENSES:	Nil
MAGIC RESISTANCE:	Nil
SIZE:	G (30' diameter shell)
MORALE:	Fanatic (17)
XP VALUE:	12 Hit Dice: 10,000
	13 Hit Dice: 11,000
	14 Hit Dice: 12,000

Dragon turtles are one of the most beautiful, awesome, and feared creatures of the water. With their deadly jaws and breath weapon, and their penchant for capsizing ships, dragon turtles are dreaded by mariners on large bodies of water, both fresh and salt.

When a dragon turtle surfaces, it is sometimes mistaken for the reflection of the sun or moon on the water. The turtle's rough, deep green shell is much the same color as the deep water the monster favors, and the silver highlights that line the shell are patterned like light dancing on open water. The turtle's legs and tail are of a lighter green, and they are flecked with golden highlights. The coloration of the creature's head is similar to the legs and tail, but its crest spines are golden with dark green webbing connecting them. A dragon turtle's shell can reach to 30 feet in diameter, and an adult turtle can measure over 40 feet from its snout to the tip of its tail. Dragon turtles speak their own highly-developed language.

Combat: Though dragon turtles may be mistaken for the pleasant sight of light glinting off of water, that illusion is never maintained for long. Dragon turtles are fierce fighters and will generally attack any creature that threatens its territory or presents itself as a potential meal. In combat, dragon turtles will usually (90%) attack with their formidable claws and teeth first. Its shell provides the turtle with excellent protection, though once the dragon turtle strikes a victim, it rarely needs to rely upon this safeguard.

The dragon turtle's shell also provides the creature with a weapon to attack ships that foolishly pass through its territory uninvited. Sinking as deep as necessary, the dragon turtle will wait for the ship to pass over it and then rise up underneath the vessel, using all of its considerable bulk to capsize the unlucky target. Ships under 20 feet in length will be capsized by this attack 95% of the time, vessels from 20 to 60 feet long will be capsized 50% of the time, and ships over 60 feet will be capsized 20% of the time. Ships not capsized will sustain some damage.

In combat, when neither its bite nor its capsizing attack is enough to defeat an enemy, a dragon turtle will use its breath weapon. The turtle can belch forth a cloud of scalding steam that will cover an area 60 feet long, 40 feet wide, and 40 feet high. This attack causes 20-120 points of damage (20d6), and characters or creatures making a saving throw vs. breath weapon take half damage. Like true dragons, dragon turtles can use this deadly breath weapon three times a day.

Habitat/Society: Dragon turtles are extremely solitary creatures. Large, desolate sea caves and secret underground caverns that can be accessed only through the water are their favorite lairs. These lairs are difficult to find, but adventurers locating a dragon turtle's cave will find it filled with treasures of all types. The turtle gathers this treasure, which it will protect to the death, from the ships sunk in its territory.

A dragon turtle's territory is well-defined and may cover as much as fifty square miles of open water. Other dragon turtles are allowed into this area only during mating season, though turtles of the same sex will always fight to the death upon meeting. It is this hostility toward their own kind that keeps the number of dragon turtles relatively low.

Mariners of any experience recognize the territorial claims of dragon turtles and will often make extravagant tributes to the turtle controlling areas necessary for safe and speedy trade.

Ecology: Dragon turtles are carnivorous and will eat almost any creature, including humans or other dragon turtles, to satisfy their voracious appetite. Large fish seem to be the prefered food for dragon turtles, and the turtles can often be found lurking in the weeds and muck at the bottom of a lake or sea waiting for fish to pass. In particularly poor years for fish, dragon turtles have been known to use their breath weapon to kill large groups of sea birds that stray too close to the water for food.

Conflict often arises between dragon turtles and the many intelligent aquatic races, like the locathah or mermen, because of competition for ideal lairs. Like many of their land-based relatives, dragon turtles are considered treacherous and selfish by all creatures that share their domain.

Dragon turtle shells make outstanding shields and armor. Because of the shell's strength and natural resistance to the dragon turtle's own breath weapon, armor or a shield made out of this material gains +1 to its defensive rating. The shield or armor will also save as an item against destruction by fire or steam-based attacks at +4.

Dragonet, Faerie Dragon

CLIMATE/TERRAIN:	Temperate, tropical, and Subtropical forests
FREQUENCY:	Very rare
ORGANIZATION:	Solitary or clan
ACTIVITY CYCLE:	Any
DIET:	Herbivore
INTELLIGENCE:	Genius (17-18)
TREASURE:	S, T, U
ALIGNMENT:	Chaotic good

NO. APPEARING:	1-6
ARMOR CLASS:	5 (1 when invisible)
MOVEMENT:	6, Fl 24 (A)
HIT DICE:	See below
THAC0:	17
NO. OF ATTACKS:	1
DAMAGE/ATTACK:	1-2
SPECIAL ATTACKS:	Breath weapon, spells
SPECIAL DEFENSES:	Invisibility
MAGIC RESISTANCE:	See below
SIZE:	T (1'-1 1/2' long)
MORALE:	Steady (11)
XP VALUE:	3,000

A chaotic offshoot of the pseudodragon, the faerie dragon lives in peaceful, tangled forests and thrives on pranks, mischief, and practical jokes.

Faerie dragons resemble miniature dragons with thin bodies, long, prehensile tails, gossamer butterfly wings, and huge smiles. Their colors range through the spectrum, changing as they age, from the red of a hatchling to the black of a great wyrm (see chart). The hides of females have a golden tinge that sparkles in the sunlight; males have a silver tinge.

All faerie dragons can communicate telepathically with one another at a distance of up to 2 miles. They speak their own language, along with the language of sprites, pixies, elves, and the birds and animals in their area.

Combat: Faerie dragons can become invisible at will, and can attack, use spells, and employ breath weapons while invisible. They attack as 4-HD monsters, biting for 1-2 points of damage. Most (65%) faerie dragons employ wizard spells as a wizard of the level indicated on the accompanying chart; 35% employ priest spells of the following spheres: Animal, Plant, Elemental, and Weather. Almost all spells are chosen for mischief potential. The two most common spells of faerie dragons are *water breathing* and *legend lore*; other favorites include *ventriloquism*, *unseen servant*, *forget*, *suggestion*, *distance distortion*, *limited wish*, *obscurement*, *animal growth*, and *animate rock*.

A faerie dragon usually begins its attacks by turning invisible and using its breath weapon, a 2-foot-diameter cloud of euphoria gas. A victim failing a saving throw vs. breath weapon will wander around aimlessly in a state of bliss for the next 3d4 minutes, during which time he is unable to attack and his Armor Class is decreased by 2. Even though he is unable to attack, the victim can keep his mind on the situation if he succeeds on an Intelligence check (by rolling his Intelligence score or less on 1d20) each round; if he fails an Intelligence check, he completely loses interest in the matters at hand for the duration of the breath weapon's effect.

Faerie dragons avoid combat and never intentionally inflict damage unless cornered or defending their lairs. If attacked, however, they engage in spirited defense, ably supported by sprite and pixie friends, until the opponents are driven away.

Habitat/Society: Faerie dragons make their lairs in the hollows of high trees, preferably near a pond or stream, because they are quite fond of swimming and diving. They often live in the company of a group of pixies or sprites.

Faerie dragons take advantage of every opportunity to wreak mischief on passers-by, frequently using forest creatures to help them in their pranks. Though many of these pranks are spontaneous, months of preparation can go into a single, spectacular practical joke. A tell-tale giggle, which sounds like the tinkling of tiny silver bells, often alerts potential victims to the presence of invisible faerie dragons.

Ecology: Faerie dragons eat fruit, vegetables, nuts, roots, honey, and grains. They are especially fond of fruit pastries and have been known to go to great lengths to get a fresh apple pie.

Age Category	Hit Points	Color	Magic Resist.	Wizard Level	Priest Level
1 Hatchling	1-2	Red	10%	1	1
2 Very Young	3-4	Red-orange	16%	2	3
3 Young	5-6	Orange	24%	3	4
4 Juvenile	7-8	Orange-yellow	32%	4	6
5 Young Adult	9-10	Yellow	40%	5	7
6 Adult	11-12	Yellow-green	48%	6	8
7 Mature Adult	13-14	Green	56%	7	9
8 Old	15-16	Blue-green	64%	8	10
9 Very Old	17-18	Blue	72%	10	11
10 Venerable	19-20	Blue-violet	80%	12	12
11 Wyrm	21-22	Violet	88%	14	13
12 Great Wyrm	23-24	Black	96%	16	14

Dragonet, Firedrake

CLIMATE/TERRAIN:	Temperate/Hills and mountains
FREQUENCY:	Rare
ORGANIZATION:	Familial lair
ACTIVITY CYCLE:	Day
DIET:	Carnivore
INTELLIGENCE:	Semi- (2-4)
TREASURE:	Nil
ALIGNMENT:	Neutral

NO. APPEARING:	2-8
ARMOR CLASS:	5
MOVEMENT:	6, Fl 18(C)
HIT DICE:	4
THAC0:	17
NO. OF ATTACKS:	1
DAMAGE/ATTACK:	2-8
SPECIAL ATTACKS:	Breath weapon
SPECIAL DEFENSES:	Nil
MAGIC RESISTANCE:	Nil
SIZE:	S (4' long)
MORALE:	Average (9)
XP VALUE:	420

Although frequently mistaken on first sighting for a young red dragon, the firedrake is neither as intelligent nor as powerful as its dragon cousin. It responds with flame to any stimulus.

This small dragonet—4' long, and a bit over 2' in height—has the features and proportions of a miniature red dragon, but its scaly hide is thinner and more translucent than that of even the youngest of true dragons. The hide of the dragonet twitches and quivers almost imperceptibly, and is somewhat mottled in color, with mauve and burgundy splotches over the red undercolor. The wings beat slowly, even when the dragonet is on the ground. In this manner the firedrake provides air flow to itself, and wards off pesky insects. A shimmer of heat rises off of the dragonet at all times.

Combat: If a firedrake is disturbed, there is a 50% chance it will attack. Its primary attack is its breath weapon (fire), which it can use up to five times daily. The fire forms a cone from the snout of the dragonet to a 10' diameter circle at the extreme end of its 60' range, and causes 2-16 points on all affected (save vs. breath weapon for half damage). The firedrake's claws are not used in combat, but its bite will cause 2-8 points of damage.

The dragonet's blood burns fiercely in air, as there is a high phosphorous content to the blood. In fact, the fire-breathing of these creatures is actually the voluntary expelling of a jet of its pyrophoric blood. Because of the flammability of the dragon's blood, blunt weapons such as staves or clubs are less dangerous than those which cause blood loss. Any creature making a successful slashing or piercing attack on a firedrake must save vs. breath weapon, or take 1-2 points of fire damage.

In aerial combat, the firedrake is particularly fond of attacking airborne creatures from below and behind. The heat from the firedrake and its breath attack naturally radiates upwards, sometimes disrupting the maneuvers of creatures that depend on relatively smooth air currents for flying or gliding. The firedrake will sometimes simply ram smaller opponents in their soft underbelly in the hope of stunning them and causing them to plummet to their deaths.

Habitat/Society: Firedrakes are familial creatures, with a mated male and female taking up residence in a lair, which is generally a small cavelet or rocky shelf under a ledge or outcropping. Usually six to eight eggs are laid and tended by the pair, being kept warm by the ample heat of the bodies of the parents. The eggs,

laid in early summer, take about 60 days to hatch. The young firedrakes learn to breathe fire even before they learn to fly, and are even more nervous than the adults, spouting flames several times a day in the lair or nearby during this period. Flight first occurs about 60 days after hatching.

The parents are very protective of their lair because of the young. Although firedrakes normally only range 1-2 miles from their lair, they may patrol up to twice that distance during the times at which their young are most vulnerable to attack.

Firedrakes leave the family lair early in the spring following their hatching, flying sometimes scores of miles before encountering a firedrake of the opposite sex willing to mate for life and establish a new lair. The rare mating fights that do occur are spectacularly fiery, although one male usually concedes and retreats before the battle becomes lethal.

Firedrakes gather no treasure, although they take no special care to remove the bones or effects of any that they defeat.

Ecology: Firedrakes have a short lifespan compared with their larger cousins, the dragons, usually living only 75 to 100 years.

Firedrake blood can be kept, in its liquid state, in a sealed and airtight container, or under water or some other inert liquid. It can then be used as a firebomb, equivalent to a torched flask of oil, or used to create flaming weapons. For instance, swords dipped in the blood immediately become flaming swords for 3-6 melee rounds, although the sudden, intense heat upon the blade creates a 2% cumulative chance per round of the sword breaking upon impact with each blow struck during the period in which flame engulfs it. After the flame ends, the sword is otherwise unaffected.

The blood of the firedrake actually burns within its veins, creating the shimmer of heat that always rises from these creatures. The burning of the blood also requires a high level of oxygen, hence the constant slow beating of the dragonet's wings, even at rest. If deprived of air, it will die of suffocation in about half the time of a similarly sized creature.

CLIMATE/TERRAIN:	Temperate or subtropical forests and caves
FREQUENCY:	Very rare
ORGANIZATION:	Solitary
ACTIVITY CYCLE:	Day
DIET:	Omnivore
INTELLIGENCE:	Average (8-10)
TREASURE:	Q (x10)
ALIGNMENT:	Neutral (good)

NO. APPEARING:	1 (50% chance of 1-8 in nests)
ARMOR CLASS:	2
MOVEMENT:	6, Fl 24 (B)
HIT DICE:	2
THAC0:	19
NO. OF ATTACKS:	1
DAMAGE/ATTACK:	1-3 + special
SPECIAL ATTACKS:	Poison sting
SPECIAL DEFENSES:	Chameleon power
MAGIC RESISTANCE:	35%
SIZE:	T (1½' long)
MORALE:	Champion (15)
XP VALUE:	420

Pseudodragons are a species of small flying lizard that inhabits heavily forested wilderness areas. These playful, benign creatures have magical powers that they can share with others, so they are often sought as companions.

Pseudodragons resemble miniature red dragons. They have fine scales and sharp horns and teeth. A pseudodragon's coloration is red-brown as opposed to the deep red of red dragons. Its tail is about 2 feet long (longer than the pseudodragon itself), barbed, and very flexible.

Pseudodragons communicate via a limited form of telepathy. If one elects to take a human companion, it can transmit what it sees and hears at a distance of up to 240 yards. Pseudodragons can vocalize animal noises such as a rasping purr (pleasure), a hiss (unpleasant surprise), a chirp (desire), or a growl (anger).

Combat: The pseudodragon can deliver a vicious bite with its small, dragonlike jaws, but its major weapon is its sting-equipped tail. The creature can move it with flashing speed and strikes at +4 on attack rolls. Any creature struck must save vs. poison or go into a state of catalepsy that lasts 1-6 days. The victim appears quite dead, but at the end of that time the character will either wake up unharmed (75% chance) or die (25% chance).

Pseudodragons have a chameleonlike power that allows them to alter their coloration to blend with their surroundings. They can blend into any typical forest background with an 80% chance of being undetected by creatures which cannot see invisible objects. Pseudodragons have infravision with a 60 foot range and can see invisible objects.

A pseudodragon is highly magic resistant and can transmit this magic resistance to its human companion via physical contact (a pseudodragon likes to be perched on the top of one's head or curled around the shoulders and upper back).

Habitat/Society: These forest-dwelling creatures place their lairs in the hollows of great trees or in large caves.

A pseudodragon will very rarely take a human or demihuman as its companion. Some view these pseudodragons as the human's pet; the pseudodragon will be sure to correct this misunderstanding. There are two ways to become a pseudodragon's companion; one is to use magic to summon it (a *find familiar*

spell). Another way is to find the pseudodragon on an adventure and pursuade it to become a companion. The pseudodragon that searches for companionship will stalk a candidate silently for days, reading his thoughts via telepathy, judging his deeds to be good or evil. If the candidate is found to be good, the pseudodragon will present itself to the human as a traveling companion and observe the human's reaction. If the human seems overjoyed and promises to take *very* good care of it, the pseudodragon will accept. If not, it will fly away.

The personality of a pseudodragon has been described by some as catlike. A pseudodragon is willing to serve, provided that it is well-fed, groomed, and receives lots of attention. At times a pseudodragon seems arrogant, demanding, and less than willing to help. In order to gain its full cooperation, the companion must pamper the pseudodragon and make it feel as though it were the most important thing in his life. If the pseudodragon is mistreated or insulted it will leave, or worse, play pranks when least expected. Pseudodragons particularly dislike cruelty and will not serve cruel masters.

Ecology: Pseudodragons are omnivorous but prefer to eat meat. Their diet consists chiefly of rodents and small birds with occasional leaves, fruits, and berries. In the wild, pseudodragons live solitary lives, protecting small personal hoards in their nests. They gather to mate once per year, in early spring, when gatherings of dozens of pseudodragons are not uncommon. After mating, males and females separate; females lay speckled brown eggs in clutches of four to six which hatch in mid-summer; females raise the young by themselves. Pseudodragons hibernate in winter; the young leave the nest in spring to mate.

Pseudodragons have a lifespan of 10-15 years. Like dragons, they are attracted to bright shiny objects. Pseudodragon eggs can be resold for up to 10,000 gold pieces while a hatchling is worth as much as 20,000 gold pieces.

Dragonne

CLIMATE/TERRAIN:	Warm temperate to tropical/ Hills and desert
FREQUENCY:	Very rare
ORGANIZATION:	Solitary
ACTIVITY CYCLE:	Dusk to dawn
DIET:	Carnivore
INTELLIGENCE:	Low (5-7)
TREASURE:	B,S,T
ALIGNMENT:	Neutral

NO. APPEARING:	1
ARMOR CLASS:	6 (Flying)/2 (Ground)
MOVEMENT:	15, Fl 9 (E)
HIT DICE:	9
THAC0:	11
NO. OF ATTACKS:	3
DAMAGE/ATTACK:	1-8/1-8/3-18
SPECIAL ATTACKS:	Roar
SPECIAL DEFENSES:	Nil
MAGIC RESISTANCE:	Nil
SIZE:	M (5′ at shoulder)
MORALE:	Champion (15)
XP VALUE:	2,000

Possessing some of the most dangerous qualities of a lion and a brass dragon, the dragonne is a vicious and deadly hunter, and a threat to many who travel in warmer climates.

From a distance, a dragonne looks much like a giant lion, with the one very notable exception of the pair of small, brass-colored wings that stretch from the creature's shoulders. Upon closer inspection, other differences between the dragonne and its feline ancestor become apparent, too. The dragonne is covered with thick, brass-colored scales, much like a brass dragon, and its mane is much thicker and made of far coarser hair than a lion's. The beast also possesses huge claws and fangs, and large eyes, usually brass-colored like its scales. Dragonnes do not have their own language. Instead, they speak the languages of brass dragons and sphinxes.

Combat: Dragonnes usually attack first with their front claws, inflicting 1d8 points of damage with each set, and their terrible jaws, inflicting 3d6 points of damage. This is usually enough to slay most of the creatures the dragonne encounters. If a dragonne is in combat with an especially deadly opponent, or is wounded in a battle with a lesser opponent, however, it will use its deadly roar.

A dragonne's roar causes *weakness* (due to fear) in all creatures within 120 feet of the monster, unless they roll successful saving throws vs. paralyzation. Those creatures that save are not affected, but those that fail to save lose 50% of their Strength for 2d6 rounds. Worse still, any creature within 30 feet of the dragonne when it roars is deafened for 2d6 rounds. No save is possible against the deafening aspect of the dragonne's roar, and all affected creatures cannot hear any sound and fight with a -1 penalty to attack rolls (due to disorientation).

The dragonne's roar is like a dragon's breath weapon in that it can only be used three times a day. Creatures within the range of the dragonne's roar must roll saving throws vs. fear each time they hear it. Once a creature is deafened, however, it cannot hear the dragonne's roar, and need not save against it, until the 2d6 rounds of temporary deafness are over.

Although a dragonne's wings are useful only for short periods of time, carrying the creature for only 1-3 turns at a time, the dragonne uses its wings very effectively in battle. If any creatures attempt to charge the dragonne or encircle it, the dragonne simply takes to the air and finds a more defensible position. The dragonne prefers not to fight in the air, as it is very slow and

maneuvers poorly compared to most flying creatures. It can fight with its claws and bite, and even its roar, when airborne, so it remains almost as deadly in the air as on the ground.

Habitat/Society: Dragonnes prefer to dwell in rocky foothills and deserts. They take large, natural caves for their lairs and store their small amounts of treasure, usually taken from slain adventurers, in loose piles around their rocky homes. Their territories are usually very large, as they generally inhabit desolate areas.

They cannot bear the company of other dragonnes, and the creatures are found in pairs only during their brief mating season, late in the autumn. Dragonnes lay eggs, like their reptilian ancestors, and only one egg is produced a year by any dragonne. The female raises this young dragonne for one year, after which time even a mother and her young will be unfriendly if they meet. Male dragonnes are always antagonistic toward each other.

In fact, dragonnes get along with very few creatures, and are considered a menace by most sentient races. More than anything, however, dragonnes wish to be left alone to hunt.

Ecology: The dragonne prefers herd animals like goats for food, especially since they don't fight back as fiercely as humans. It only attacks a human or demihuman for food if no other game is available.

Dragonnes are not necessarily aggressive toward strangers, and the creature's reputation as a mindless devourer of helpless travelers is more the product of ignorance than well-researched fact. A dragonne will almost always attack any creature that invades its lair or threatens its territory. This means that adventurers who stumble across a dragonne's cave or settlers who decide to build in a dragonne's territory are often subject to fierce and immediate attack. Creatures not threatening the dragonne's lair or simply passing through its territory are usually left alone. Though the dragonne's intelligence is low, it can tell the difference between a harmless traveler and a potentially troublesome settler.

Dryad

CLIMATE/TERRAIN:	Secluded oak groves
FREQUENCY:	Very rare
ORGANIZATION:	Solitary
ACTIVITY CYCLE:	Any
DIET:	Herbivore
INTELLIGENCE:	High (13-14)
TREASURE:	M (x 100), Q (x 10)
ALIGNMENT:	Neutral

NO. APPEARING:	1 or 1-6
ARMOR CLASS:	9
MOVEMENT:	12
HIT DICE:	2
THAC0:	19
NO. OF ATTACKS:	1
DAMAGE/ATTACK:	1-4 (knife)
SPECIAL ATTACKS:	Charm
SPECIAL DEFENSES:	See below
MAGIC RESISTANCE:	50%
SIZE:	M (5' tall)
MORALE:	Steady (12)
XP VALUE:	975

Dryads are beautiful, intelligent tree sprites. They are as elusive as they are alluring, however, and dryads are rarely seen unless taken by surprise—or they wish to be spotted.

The dryad's exquisite features, delicate and finely chiseled, are much like an elf maiden's. Dryads have high cheek bones and amber, violet, or dark green eyes. A dryad's complexion and hair color changes with the seasons, presenting the sprite with natural camouflage. During the fall, a dryad's hair turns golden or red, and her skin subtly darkens from its usual light tan to more closely match her hair color. This enables her to blend with the falling leaves of autumn. In winter, both the dryad's hair and skin are white, like the snows that cover the oak groves. When encountered in a forest during fall or winter, a dryad is often mistaken for an attractive maid, probably of elvish descent. No one would mistake a dryad for an elf maid during the spring and summer, however. At these times of year, a dryad's skin is lightly tanned and her hair is green like the oak leaves around her.

Dryads often appear clothed in a loose, simple garment. The clothing they wear is the color of the oak grove in the season they appear. They speak their own tongue, as well as the languages of elves, pixies, and sprites. Dryads can also speak with plants.

Combat: Dryads are shy, nonviolent creatures. They rarely carry weapons, but they sometimes carry knives as tools. Though a dryad can use this as a weapon in a fight, she will not resort to using a knife unless seriously threatened.

Dryads have the ability to throw a powerful *charm person* spell three times a day (but only once per round). This spell is so powerful that targets of the spell suffer a -3 penalty to their saving throws. A Dryad always uses this spell if seriously threatened, attempting to gain control of the attacker who could help her most against his comrades. Dryads will only attempt to charm elves as a last resort because of their natural resistance to this type of spell.

The dryad's use of her ability to charm is not limited to combat situations, however. Whenever a dryad encounters a male with a Charisma of 16 or more, she usually tries to charm him. Charismatic victims of a dryad's attentions are taken to the tree sprite's home, where the men serve as amorous slaves to their beautiful captors. There is a 50% chance that a person charmed and taken away by a dryad will never return. If he does escape from the dryad's charms, it will be after 1d4 years of captivity.

This tree sprite also has two other powers that are very useful in defense. Unless surprised, a dryad has the ability to literally step through a tree and then *dimension door* to the oak tree she is part of. She can also speak with plants (as the 4th-level priest spell). This enables the dryad to gather information about parties traveling near her tree, and even to use vegetation to hinder potential attackers.

Habitat/Society: Some legends claim that dryads are the animated souls of very old oak trees. Whether this is really the case, it is true that dryads are attached to a single, very large oak tree in their lifetimes and cannot, for any reason, go more than 360 yards from that tree. If a dryad does wander farther away, she becomes weak and dies within 6d6 hours unless returned to her home. The oak trees of dryads do not radiate magic, but someone finding a dryad's home has great power over her. A dryad suffers damage for any damage inflicted upon her home tree. Any attack on a dryad's tree will, of course, bring on a frenzied defense by the dryad.

Although dryads are generally very solitary, up to six have been encountered in one place. This is rare, however. All this really means is that a number of dryad oaks are within 100 yards of one another and the dryads' paths cross. These dryads may come to each other's aid, but never really gather socially. Any treasure owned by a tree sprite is hidden close to her home tree. The gold and gems that make up a dryad's treasure are almost always the gifts of charmed adventurers.

These tree sprites realize that most humans and demihumans fear them for their ability to charm, so dryads only deal with strangers on rare occasions. When approached carefully, however, dryads have been known to aid adventurers. They are a useful source of information, too, as they know a great deal about the area in which they live.

Ecology: Dryads are staunch protectors of the forest and groves in which they reside. Any actions that harm the area, and especially its plant life, are met with little tolerance.

Dwarf

	Hill	Mountain
CLIMATE/TERRAIN:	Subarctic to sub-tropical rocky hills	Subarctic to sub-tropical mountains
FREQUENCY:	Common	Common
ORGANIZATION:	Clans	Clans
ACTIVITY CYCLE:	Any	Any
DIET:	Omnivorous	Omnivorous
INTELLIGENCE:	Very (11-12)	Very (11-12)
TREASURE:	M (x5)	M (x5)
	(G, Qx20, R)	(G, Qx20, R)
ALIGNMENT:	Lawful good	Lawful good
NO. APPEARING:	40-400	40-400
ARMOR CLASS:	4 (10)	4 (10)
MOVEMENT:	6	6
HIT DICE:	1	1+1
THAC0:	20	19
NO. OF ATTACKS:	1	1
DAMAGE/ATTACK:	1-8 (weapon)	1-8 (weapon)
SPECIAL ATTACKS:	See below	See below
SPECIAL DEFENSES:	See below	See below
MAGIC RESISTANCE:	See below	See below
SIZE:	S to M (4' and taller)	M (4½' and taller)
MORALE:	Elite (13-14)	Elite (13-14)
XP VALUE:	175	270

Dwarves are a noble race of demihumans who dwell under the earth, forging great cities and waging massive wars against the forces of chaos and evil. Dwarves also have much in common with the rocks and gems they love to work, for they are both hard and unyielding. It's often been said that it's easier to make a stone weep than it is to change a dwarf's mind.

Standing from four to 4½ feet in height, and weighing 130 to 170 pounds, dwarves tend to be stocky and muscular. They have ruddy cheeks and bright eyes. Their skin is typically deep tan or light brown. Their hair is usually black, gray, or brown, and worn long, though not long enough to impair vision in any way. They favor long beards and mustaches, too. Dwarves value their beards highly and tend to groom them very carefully. Dwarves do not favor ornate stylings or wrappings for their hair or their beards.

Dwarven clothing tends to be simple and functional. They often wear earth tones, and their cloth is considered rough by many other races, especially men and elves. Dwarves usually wear one or more pieces of jewelry, though these items are usually not of any great value or very ostentatious. Though dwarves value gems and precious metals, they consider it in bad taste to flaunt wealth.

Because dwarves are a sturdy race, they add 1 to their initial Constitution ability scores. However, because they are a solitary people, tending toward distrust of outsiders and other races, they subtract 1 from their initial Charisma ability scores. Dwarves usually live from 350 to 450 years.

Dwarves have found it useful to learn the languages of many of their allies and enemies. In addition to their own languages, dwarves often speak the languages of gnomes, goblins, kobolds, orcs, and the common tongue, which is frequently used in trade negotiations with other races.

Combat: Dwarves are courageous, tenacious fighters who are ill-disposed toward magic. They never use magical spells or train as wizards, though they can become priests and use the spells of this group. Because of their nonmagical nature, in fact, they get a special bonus to all saving throws against magical wands, staves, rods, and spells. Dwarves receive a +1 bonus to saving throws

against these magical attacks for every 3½ points of Constitution score they have. See Table 9 on page 21 of the *Player's Handbook* for specific bonuses.

A dwarf's nonmagical nature can also cause problems when he tries to use a magical item. In fact, if a dwarf uses a magical item that is not specifically created for his class, there is a 20% chance the item malfunctions. For example, if a dwarven fighter uses a *bag of holding*—which can be used by any class, not just fighters—there is a 20% chance each time the dwarf uses it that the bag does not work properly. This chance of malfunction applies to rods, staves, wands, rings, amulets, potions, horns, jewels, and miscellaneous magic. However, dwarves have learned to master certain types of magical items—because of an item's military nature. These objects—specifically weapons, shields, armor, gauntlets, and girdles—are not subject to magical malfunction when used by a dwarf of any class.

As with magical attacks, dwarves are unusually resistant to toxic substances. Because of their exceptionally strong Constitution, all dwarves roll saving throws against poisons with the same bonus (+1 for every 3½ points of Constitution score) that applies to saves vs. magical attacks.

In the thousands of years that dwarves have lived in the earth, they have developed a number of skills and special abilities that help them to survive. All dwarves have infravision that enables them to see up to 60 feet in the dark. When underground, dwarves can tell quite a bit about their location by looking carefully at their surroundings. When within 10 feet of what they are looking for, dwarves can detect the grade and slope of a passage (1-5 on 1d6), new tunnel construction (1-5 on 1d6), sliding/shifting walls or rooms (1-4 on 1d6), and stonework traps, pits, and deadfalls (1-3 on 1d6). Dwarves can also determine their approximate depth underground (1-3 on 1d6) at any time.

During their time under the earth, dwarves have also developed an intense hatred of many of the evil creatures they commonly encounter. Thus, in melee, dwarves always add 1 to their attack rolls to hit orcs, half-orcs, goblins, and hobgoblins. The small size of dwarves is an advantage against ogres, trolls, ogre magi, giants, and titans; these monsters always subtract 4 from their attack rolls against dwarves because of that size difference and the dwarves' training in fighting such large foes.

Dwarven armies are well-organized and extremely well-disciplined. Dwarven troops usually wear chain mail and carry shields in battle. They wield a variety of weapons. The composition of a typical dwarven army by weaponry is axe and hammer (25%), sword and spear (20%), sword and light crossbow (15%), sword and pole arm (10%), axe and heavy crossbow (10%), axe and mace (10%), or hammer and pick (10%).

For every 40 dwarves encountered, there is a 2nd- to 6th-level fighter who leads the group. (Roll 1d6 to determine level, with a roll of 1 equalling 2.) If there are 160 or more dwarves encountered, there are, in addition to the leaders of the smaller groups, one 6th-level fighter (a chief) and a 4th-level fighter (lieutenant) commanding the troops. If 200 or more dwarves are encountered, there is a fighter/priest of 3rd- to 6th-level fighting ability and 4th-to 7th-level priest ability. If a dwarven army has 320 or more troops in it, the following high-level leaders are in command of the group: an 8th-level fighter, a 7th-level fighter, a 6th-level fighter/7th-level priest, and two 4th-level fighter/priests.

The commanders of the dwarven troops wear plate armor and carry shields. In addition, the fighters and fighter/priests leading the dwarven troops have a 10% chance per level of fighting ability of having magical armor and/or weapons. The fighter/priests who lead the troops also have a 10% chance per level of priest ability of having a magical item specific to priests (and thus not subject to malfunction).

If encountered in its home, a dwarven army has, in addition to the leaders noted above, 2d6 fighters of from 2nd- to 5th-level (1d4+1 for level), 2d4 fighter/priests of from 2nd- to 4th-level (in each class), females equal to 50% of the adult males, and children equal to 25% of the adult males. Dwarven women are skilled in combat and fight as males if their homes are attacked.

Habitat/Society: Usually constructed around profitable mines, dwarven cities are vast, beautiful complexes carved into solid stone. Dwarven cities take hundreds of years to complete, but once finished they stand for millennia without needing any type of repair. Since dwarves do not leave their homes often and always return to them, they create their cities with permanence in mind. Troops guard dwarven cities at all times, and sometimes (60% chance) dwarves also use animals as guards—either 2d4 brown bears (75% chance) or 5d4 wolves (25% chance).

Dwarven society is organized into clans. A dwarven clan not already attached to a city or mine travels until it finds an outpost where it can begin to ply a trade. Clans often settle close together since they usually need the same raw materials for their crafts. Clans are competitive, but usually do not war against one another. Dwarven cities are founded when enough clans move to a particular location.

Each dwarven clan usually specializes in a particular craft or skill; young dwarves are apprenticed at an early age to a master in their clan (or, occasionally, in another clan) to learn a trade. Since dwarves live so long, apprenticeships last for many years. Dwarves also consider political and military service a skilled trade, so soldiers and politicians are usually subjected to a long period of apprenticeship before they are considered professionals.

To folk from other races, life within these cities might seem as rigid and unchanging as the stone that the dwarven houses are wrought from. In fact, it is. Above all, dwarves value law and order. This love of stability probably comes from the dwarves' long life spans, for dwarves can watch things made of wood and

other mutable materials decay within a single lifetime. It shouldn't be surprising, then, that they value things that are unchanging and toil ceaselessly to make their crafts beautiful and long-lived. For a dwarf, the earth is something to be loved because of its stability and the sea a thing to be despised—and feared—because it is a symbol of change.

Dwarves also prize wealth, as it is something that can be developed over a long period of time. All types of precious metal, but particularly gold, are highly prized by dwarves, as are diamonds and other gems. They do not value pearls, however, as they are reminders of the sea and all it stands for. Dwarves believe, however, that it is in poor taste to advertise wealth. Metals and gems are best counted in secret, so that neighbors are not offended or tempted.

Most other races see dwarves as a greedy, dour, grumpy folk who prefer the dampness of a cave to the brightness of an open glade. This is partially true. Dwarves have little patience for men and other short-lived races (since man's concerns seem so petty when seen from dwarven eyes). Dwarves also mistrust elves because they are not as serious-minded as dwarves and waste their long lives on pastimes the dwarves see as frivolous. However, dwarves have been known to band together with both men and elves in times of crisis, and long-term trade agreements and alliances are common.

Dwarves have no mixed feelings about the evil races that dwell below ground and in the Underdark, however. They have an intense hatred of orcs, goblins, evil giants, and drow. The dire creatures of the Underdark often fear dwarves, too, for the short, stout folk are tireless enemies of evil and chaos. It is a goal of the dwarves to wage constant and bitter war against their enemies under the earth until either they or their foes are destroyed.

Ecology: Since much of their culture is focused on creating things from the earth, dwarves produce a large amount of useful, valuable trade material. Dwarves are skilled miners. Though they rarely sell the precious metals and rough gems they uncover, dwarven miners have been known to sell surpluses to local human communities. Dwarves are also skilled engineers and master builders—though they work almost exclusively with stone—and some dwarven architects work for humans quite frequently.

Dwarves most often trade in finished goods. Many clans are dedicated to work as blacksmiths, silversmiths, goldsmiths, armorers, weapons makers, and gem cutters. Dwarven products are highly valued for their workmanship. In human communities, these goods often demand prices up to 20% higher than locally forged items. Many people are still willing to pay a high price for a suit of dwarven mail or a dwarven sword. Humans know that the dwarf who forged the item made it to last a dwarven lifetime, so they'll never need to worry about it wearing out in theirs.

Mountain Dwarves

Similar in most ways to their cousins, the hill dwarves, these demihumans prefer to live deep inside mountains. They tend to be slightly taller than hill dwarves (averaging 4½ feet tall) and more hearty (having 1+1 Hit Dice). They usually have slightly lighter skin and hair than their hill-dwelling relatives. In battle, mountain dwarf armies are likely to have more spears (30% maximum) and fewer crossbows (20% maximum) than hill dwarf armies. Mountain dwarves have the same interests and biases as hill dwarves, though they are even more isolationist than their cousins and sometimes consider even hill dwarves to be outsiders. Mountain dwarves live for at least 400 years.

Dwarf

	Derro	Duergar
CLIMATE/TERRAIN:	Any/ Subterranean	Subterranean
FREQUENCY:	Very rare	Very rare
ORGANIZATION:	Tribal	Tribal
ACTIVITY CYCLE:	Night	Any
DIET:	Omnivore	Omnivore
INTELLIGENCE:	Very to genius (13-18)	Average to genius (8-18)
TREASURE:	See below	M, Q Lair: B (magic only), F
ALIGNMENT:	Chaotic evil	Lawful evil (Neutral)

	Derro	Duergar
NO. APPEARING:	3-30	2-9 or 201-300
ARMOR CLASS:	5 or 4 (8)	4
MOVEMENT:	9	6
HIT DICE:	3 (see below)	1+2
THAC0:	17 (see below)	19
NO. OF ATTACKS:	1 or 2	1
DAMAGE/ATTACK:	By weapon	By weapon
SPECIAL ATTACKS:	See below	See below
SPECIAL DEFENSES:	See below	Save with +4 bonus
MAGIC RESISTANCE:	30%	Nil
SIZE:	S (4' tall)	S (4' tall)
MORALE:	Steady (12)	Elite (13)
XP VALUE:	975 and up	420
2 Hit Dice +4		650
3 Hit Dice +6		975
4 Hit Dice +8		1,400

Derro are a degenerate race of dwarven stature. They have been skulking in the Underdark for ages, but they were discovered by the mind flayers only five centuries ago, and by the drow but shortly before that. The derro have made a name for themselves by their marked cruelty. It is said that a derro lives for just two things: to witness the slow, humiliating death of surface demi-humans, and especially humans; and the perversion of knowledge to their own dark ends.

Derro are short, with skin the color of an iced over lake (white, with bluish undertones), sickly, pale yellow or tan hair (always straight), and staring eyes that have no pupils. Their features remind dwarves of humans, and vice versa. Derro have rough skin, spotted with short coarse tufts of hair. Most derro wear a loose costume woven from the hair of underground creatures and dyed deep red or brown. Their armor is leather, studded in copper and brass. Leaders wear tougher, kather armors, made from the hides of beasts far more rugged than cattle.

Combat: Derro are one of the most dexterous of humanoid races (averaging 15-18), and their Armor Class must be adjusted for this. Normally, a derro party is well-equipped with weapons and spells. All derro carry small, ornamental blades, called *secari*, which can be treated as daggers, but most use other weapons as well.

Half of all encountered derro carry a repeating light crossbow (12 maximum range, two shots each round, six-bolt capacity, 1d3 points of damage). Derro crossbowman usually coat their bolts with poison. If a derro wants to simply bring down his prey, he uses a poison that causes an additional 2d6 points of damage (successful saving throw for no additional damage). If he desires to prolong his target's suffering, he uses a poison that has the same effects as a *ray of enfeeblement* spell (asuccessful saving throw indicates no poison damage).

Twenty-five percent of derro carry a hook-fauchard, a long (6'+) pole arm that causes 1d4 points of impaling damage and can pull a man-sized or smaller creature off-balance 25% of the time. It takes one round to regain balance.

Fifteen percent of derro use only a spiked buckler. This small shield, improves the derro's AC by 1 against any one opponent. It is armed with a central spike, which can be wielded as a second weapon (no penalty because of the derro's high Dexterity) for 1d4 points of impaling damage. The derro will also have a hooked aklys, a short, heavy club that can be thrown for 1d6 points of crushing damage. It is attached to a thick leather thong so that it can be retrieved. Thanks to the hook, the aklys also pulls an opponent off-balance but it has only a 1-8 chance. These derro are considered brave by their fellows; they are awarded the rarer, heavier armors (AC 4).

The remaining 10% of the derro are the sons and daughters of derro leaders. They are given heavier armor and trained in the use of the spear and the military pick. They use bucklers (sans spikes) when not using the spear with both hands.

For every three derro encountered, there is one with 4 Hit Dice. For every six derro, there is one with 5 Hit Dice. If 10 or more, there is a 7 Hit Die leader with a 6 Hit Die lieutenant. If a party encounters 25 derro, they would be accompanied by eight 4 Hit Die derro, four of 5 Hit Die, one with 6 Hit Dice, and one with 7. The leaders always wear the thicker armor and usually wield well-made (and occasionally magical) weapons.

If 20 or more are encountered, they are accompanied by a savant and two students. Savant derro are able to use any sort of magical item or weapon. Savants know 1d4+5 of the following spells, learned at random: *affect normal fires, anti-magic shell, blink, cloudkill, ESP hypnotic pattern, ice storm, invisibility, levitate, light, lightning bolt, minor creation, paralyzation, repulsion, shadow magic, spider climb, ventriloquism, wall of fog, wall of force.* Savants have 5-8 Hit Dice, and carry two or three useful magical items. Typical magical items are any potion, any scroll, *rings of fire resistance, invisibility, protection,* and *spell storing,* any wand, *studded leather armor* +1, shields, weapons up to +3, *bracers of defense, brooches of shielding, cloaks of protection,* and so on. Savants can instinctively *comprehend languages* and *read magic* (as the spells).

Savants are capable of acting as sages in one to three areas of study. Derro raids are often inspired by a savant's research.

Student savants know only 1-3 spells, have 4-7 Hit Dice, they know only one field of study, and one minor magical item.

In combat, derro fight cunningly, with good tactics. They keep spellcasters from effectively using magic, and inflict minor wounds until they eventually kill their opponents. Savants use their powers to confuse and frustrate, rather than to simply kill. Derro have poor infravision (3-foot range) but keen hearing (treat as the blind-fighting, nonweapon proficiency).

Derro keep slaves and attempt to capture intelligent opponents, when possible.

Habitat/Society: Derro live in large underground complexes, nearer the surface than the kuo-toans and drow, but deeper than goblins and trolls. They never expose themselves to direct sunlight; it nauseates them. Sunlight will kill a derro if he is exposed to it for several days. Still, derro do visit the surface at night, raiding for humans or carrying out a savant's plans.

Derro are never encountered singly. From their combat tactics to their choice of spells, derro demonstrate a mob mentality. A lone derro is a desperate derro, seeking at all costs to return to his home.

Derro lairs always have 3d4 + 30 normal derro, plus leaders. The members of the lair are led by the resident savants (1-3 in number) and their apprentices (2-5 students). Derro obey without question the puzzling, even suicidal, dictates from their savant leaders.

Also to be found in a derro lair are 5d6 + 10 human slaves. If any of the lair's savants or students know the *charm person* spell, each slave has a 90% chance of being charmed. Derro hate humans more than any other race; they use humans for the most demeaning manual labor, and for breeding.

Derro do not appear to worship any powers, but the savants treasure knowledge and the rest seem to worship the savants.

Derro usually scour their territory for magical items, stealing them, or, if necessary, purchasing them from more powerful creatures. Derro do not share the love of gold common to their dwarven relatives, and they have been known to pay exorbitant prices for a few potions or for a magical item with a missing command word.

Every 20 years or so, the derro mount an all-out war against the other creatures of the Underdark. This is known as the Uniting War, and no savant really expects it to be won. The War is a means of winnowing out the weakest of the derro lairs, a focal point for racial identity, and a chance to really create some terror in the Underdark. It also serves the purpose of starting rumors. Humans will certainly hear that a war is being fought in the Underdark, and they will send hundreds of scouting and adventuring parties to the underground to investigate. The derro welcome this new source of slaves.

Ecology: Derro can live on a diet of underground fungi, but use it only for spice. They seek out other sustenance whenever possible. A derro hunting party usually pursues large, dangerous prey that will feed an entire lair, rather than smaller, simpler food. The derro tendency to torment prey also holds when for hunting food. They also raid other races for food.

Duergar

Duergar, or gray dwarves, are a malevolent breed that exist at extreme depths underground. Duergar may be fighters, priests, thieves, or multi-classed fighter/priests, fighter/thieves, or priest/thieves. Thieves are proficient in the use of poison.

Duergar appear to be emaciated, nasty-looking dwarves. Their complexions and hair range from medium to dark gray. They prefer drab clothing designed to blend into their environment. In their lairs, they may wear jewelry, although such pieces are kept dull.

Duergar have infravision to 120 feet. They speak the duergar dialect of the dwarven tongue, "undercommon" (the trading language of subterranean cultures), and the silent speech employed by some subterranean creatures. Intelligent duergar may speak other languages as well.

Combat: For every four, single HD duergar encountered outside a lair, there is one with 2 HD + 4 hp. If a band of nine are encountered outside a lair, there will be a tenth, with 3 HD + 6 hp or 4 HD + 8 hp always leads the group.
Duergar are armed as follows:

1st level: pick, hammer, spear, chain mail, and shield;
2nd level: pick, light crossbow, chain mail, and shield;
3rd-6th level: hammer, short sword, plate mail, and shield;
7th-9th level: hammer*, short sword*, plate mail*, and shield*;
3rd-6th/3rd-6th-level priest/thief: any usable*/any usable*;
7th-9th/7th-9th-level priest/thief: any usable*/any usable*
* 5% chance/level for magical item; for multi-class, add one-half of lower level (round up) to the higher level in order to find the appropriate multiplier.

There are noncombatant, duergar children equal to 10% of the total number of duergar fighters encountered.

The duergar's stealth imposes a −2 penalty to opponents' surprise rolls; the duergar are surprised only on a 1 on 1d10. Their saving throws vs. magical attacks gain a +4 bonus. They are immune to paralysis, illusion/phantasm spells and poisons.

All duergar possess innate magical abilities of *enlargement* and *invisibility.* They can use these spells as wizards of a level equal to their hit points. Duergar can use *enlargement* to either grow or shrink themselves, as well as anything they are wearing or carrying.

Daylight affects the duergar as follows: their enhanced ability to gain surprise is negated, Dexterity is reduced by 2, attacks are made with a −2 penalty to the attack roll, and opponents' saving throws are made with a +2 bonus. If the encounter occurs when the duergar are in darkness, but their opponents are brightly illuminated, the duergar's surprise ability and Dexterity are normal, but they still suffer a −1 penalty to their attack rolls while their opponents gain a +1 bonus to saving throws against attacks. Duergar are not adversely affected by the light given off by torches, lanterns, magical weapons, or *light* and *faerie fire* spells.

There is a 10% chance that any duergar are accompanied by 2d4 giant steeders, used as mounts (see *Spiders*).

Habitat Society: Duergar society is similar to that of other dwarven cultures, although life is much harsher because of the hostile environment deep underground. They do not venture to the surface except at night or on gloomy days. Duergar life spans can reach 400 years.

Elemental, Generic Information

Elementals are sentient beings that can possess bodies made of one of the four basic elements that make up the Prime Material plane—air, earth, fire, or water. They normally reside on an elemental Inner Plane and will only be encountered on the Prime Material plane if they are summoned by magical means. (See *Manual of the Planes* for more information on the nature of the various elemental planes.) Each elemental must adopt a shell in the Prime Material composed of the basic element it represents. and once this shell is destroyed, the elemental will return to its native plane. While there are many more powerful and more intelligent residents of the elemental planes, the common elemental is the easiest to contact, and therefore the most frequently summoned.

Their magical nature gives elementals great protection from attacks on the Prime Material plane. Elementals are not harmed by any nonmagical weapons or magical weapons of less than +2 bonus. Creatures with under four Hit Dice and without any magical abilities cannot harm an elemental either. (Magical abilities include such characteristics as breath weapons, poisons, paralysis, or even being immune to normal weapon attacks.) Orcs, for example, are powerless against a conjured elemental unless one happens to possess a weapon with +2 or better bonus to hit.

Though elementals do enjoy protection from many nonmagical attacks in the Prime Material plane, like all extraplanar and conjured creatures, elementals are affected by *protection from evil* spells. An elemental cannot strike a creature protected by this spell and must recoil from the spell's boundaries. However, the elemental can attack creatures protected by the spell as long as it doesn't touch them. For example, a fire elemental could set the ground on fire around the creature and wait for the blaze to spread.

Each of the four types of common elemental has its own particular strengths and weaknesses, attack modes and method of movement, depending on its plane of origin. These will be covered individually, by elemental type, in the next few pages. All common elementals share one major characteristic, however. They are basically stupid. This low intelligence makes it difficult for the elemental to resist a magical summons. But even the common elemental is bright enough to know it does not like being taken off of its home plane and held in the Prime Material plane.

Summoning an Elemental: There are three basic ways to call an elemental to this plane, and the strength of the conjured elemental depends on the method used to summon it:

Conjured by spell .... 8, 12, 16, or 21-24 Hit Dice
Conjured by staff .... 16 Hit Dice
Conjured by summoning device .... 12 Hit Dice

Obviously, the type of wizard or priest spell used to contact an elemental will greatly effect the size of the creature on this plane. (See *Player's Handbook* for specifics.) Also, a conjured elemental's height (in feet) is equal to its Hit Dice, so the method of summoning an elemental to the Prime Material plane will also determine its size.

Each individual's use of any spell, staff, or device in contacting the elemental planes produces a unique call. This unique summons will only be answered by the inhabitants of a particular plane once per day. Therefore, each of the methods of summoning elementals—spell, device, and staff—can be used by one person to call only one of any specific type of common elemental per day. If a staff is used four times in one day, for example, all four types of elementals must be called once.

The only exception to this is a character using more than one method to call elementals. Then, the conjurer can call a number of elementals of the same type equal to the number of methods he or she uses. This means a person with a device and a staff can summon two earth elementals. However, a person with two staffs can still summon only one elemental of any specific type in one day.

Controlling an Elemental: Because the elemental will be furious at being summoned to this plane, concentration in conjuring the creature is vital. In calling an elemental, a person must remain perfectly still and focus all of his attention on controlling the being. Any distraction to the summoner, either mental or physical, will result in a failure to control the elemental when it arrives on the Prime Material plane. Elementals that are uncontrolled and acting upon their own desires are called *free-willed*. If the party is lucky, a free-willed elemental will immediately return to its plane. However, this occurs only 25% of the time.

In most cases (75% of the time), an uncontrolled elemental will immediately attack the person or party who conjured it, also destroying anything that stands between it and its enemies. There is no way to gain control of the elemental once it is lost, and there is nothing the objects of the elemental's wrath can do but defend themselves. The elemental's intense dislike of being away from its home plane is the only safeguard those conjuring an elemental can rely upon if the elemental runs wild. Because remaining on the Prime Material plane is painful to any common elemental, the uncontrolled elemental will always return to its plane of origin three turns after control is lost, whether it has destroyed the creatures responsible for calling it away from its elemental abode or not.

There is always a 5% chance per round that an elemental is in the Prime Material (beginning with the second round) that the creature will break control and attack the person who summoned it. Also, if a person is wounded, killed, or loses concentration while controlling an elemental, the creature will become free-willed. The elemental will first attack the person who summoned it and then destroy any living thing it can find during the three turns after control is lost. The creature will then return to its home in the Inner Planes. A free-willed elemental can be sent to its home plane if a *dismissal* spell is cast upon it, but there is only a 50% chance of success for the spell in this situation.

A successfully controlled elemental will stay on the Prime Material only for the duration of the spell that summoned it, and it can be controlled from a distance up to 30 yards per level of the person who summoned it. If under control, an elemental can be dismissed by the summoner when its task is complete.

Stealing Control of an Elemental: Control of a conjured elemental can be stolen from the person who summoned it by casting *dispel magic* specifically at the magical control over the creature (not the elemental itself or the person controlling it). Most of the normal rules for dispelling magic apply (*Player's Handbook* p. 148). However, when dealing with control over an elemental, a roll of 20 by the person attempting the spell means that all control has been dispelled and the creature is now free-willed.

If control of the elemental is stolen, the creature will follow the wishes of the new person controlling it as if he or she summoned it in the first place. If the *dispel magic* fails, the elemental will immediately be strengthened to its maximum 8 hit points per die and the conjurer's ability to control the elemental will be greatly enhanced, making any new attempts to steal control of the creature impossible. Also, the elemental will recognize the person who sought to take control of its will as a threat. If the person currently guiding the creature loses control, the elemental will immediately attack the person who attempted to steal control of its will—even before attacking the person who first summoned it.

Elemental, Air/Earth

	Air	Earth
CLIMATE/TERRAIN:	Any air	Any land
FREQUENCY:	Very rare	Very rare
ORGANIZATION:	Solitary	Solitary
ACTIVITY CYCLE:	Any	Any
DIET:	Air	Earth, metal, or gem
INTELLIGENCE:	Low (5-7)	Low (5-7)
TREASURE:	Nil	Nil
ALIGNMENT:	Neutral	Neutral
NO. APPEARING:	1	1
ARMOR CLASS:	2	2
MOVEMENT:	Fl 36 (A)	6
HIT DICE:	8, 12, or 16	8, 12, or 16
THAC0:	8 Hit Dice: 13	8 Hit Dice: 13
	12 Hit Dice: 9	12 Hit Dice: 9
	16 Hit Dice: 5	16 Hit Dice: 5
NO. OF ATTACKS:	1	1
DAMAGE/ATTACK:	2-20	4-32
SPECIAL ATTACKS:	See below	See below
SPECIAL DEFENSES:	+2 weapon or better to hit	+2 weapon or better to hit
MAGIC RESISTANCE:	Nil	Nil
SIZE:	L to H (8' to 16' tall)	L to H (8' to 16' tall)
MORALE:	8-12 Hit Dice:	8-12 Hit Dice:
	Champion (15-16)	Champion (15-16)
	16 Hit Dice:	16 Hit Dice:
	Fanatic (17)	Fanatic (17)
XP VALUE:	8 Hit Dice: 3,000	8 Hit Dice: 2,000
	12 Hit Dice: 7,000	12 Hit Dice: 6,000
	16 Hit Dice: 11,000	16 Hit Dice: 10,000

Air elementals can be conjured in any area of open air where gusts of wind are present. The common air elemental appears as an amorphous, shifting cloud when it answers its summons to the Prime Material plane. They rarely speak, but their language can be heard in the high-pitched shriek of a tornado or the low moan of a midnight storm.

Combat: While air elementals are not readily tangible to the inhabitants of planes other than its own, they can strike an opponent with a strong, focused blast of air that, like a giant, invisible fist, does 2-20 points of damage. The extremely rapid rate at which these creatures can move make them very useful on vast battlefields or in extended aerial combat. In fact, the air elemental's mastery of its natural element gives it a strong advantage in combat above the ground. In aerial battles, they gain a +1 to hit and a +4 to the damage they inflict.

The most feared power of an air elemental is its ability to form a whirlwind upon command. Using this form, the air elemental appears as a truncated, reversed cone with a 10 foot bottom diameter and 30 foot top diameter. The height of the whirlwind depends on the Hit Dice of the elemental. An air elemental of 8 Hit Dice will produce a whirlwind standing 40 feet tall; a 12 Hit Dice elemental produces a whirlwind standing 60 feet tall; and a 16 Hit Dice elemental produces a whirlwind standing 80 feet tall. It takes one full turn to form and dissipate this cone.

This whirlwind lasts for one melee round, sweeps away and kills all creatures under 3 Hit Dice in the area of its cone, and does 2-16 points of damage to all creatures it fails to kill outright. If, because of overhead obstructions, the whirlwind fails to reach its full height, it can only sweep up creatures under 2 Hit Dice and do 1-8 points of damage to all others in its cone.

Earth elementals can be conjured in any area of earth or stone. This type of common elemental appears on the Prime Material plane as a very large humanoid made of whatever types of dirt, stones, precious metals, and gems it was conjured from. It has a cold, expressionless face, and its two eyes sparkle like brilliant, multifaceted gems. Though it has a mouth-like opening in its face, an earth elemental will rarely speak. Their voices can be heard in the silence of deep tunnels, the rumblings of earthquakes, and the grinding of stone on stone.

Though earth elementals travel very slowly, they are relentless in the fulfillment of their appointed tasks. An earth elemental can travel through solid ground or stone with no penalty to movement or dexterity. However, these elementals cannot travel through water: they must either go around the body of water in their path or go under it, traveling in the ground. Earth elementals prefer the latter as it keeps them moving, more or less, in a straight line toward their goal.

Combat: Earth elementals will always try to fight on the ground and will only rarely be tricked into giving up that advantage. Because of their close alliance to the rock and earth, these elementals do 4-32 points of damage (4d8) whenever they strike a creature that rests on the ground.

Against constructions with foundations in earth or stone, earth elementals do great damage, making them extremely useful for armies sieging a fortification. For example, a reinforced door, which might require a few rounds to shatter using conventional methods, can be smashed with ease by an earth elemental. They can even level a small cottage in a few rounds.

An earth elemental's effectiveness against creatures in the air or water is limited; the damage done by the elemental's fists on airborne or waterborne targets is lessened by 2 points per die (to a minimum of 1 point of damage per die).

Elemental, Fire/Water

	Fire	Water
CLIMATE/TERRAIN:	Any dry land	Large areas of water
FREQUENCY:	Very rare	Very rare
ORGANIZATION:	Solitary	Solitary
ACTIVITY CYCLE:	Any	Any
DIET:	Any combustible	Any liquid
INTELLIGENCE:	Low (5-7)	Low (5-7)
TREASURE:	Nil	Nil
ALIGNMENT:	Neutral	Neutral
NO. APPEARING:	1	1
ARMOR CLASS:	2	2
MOVEMENT:	12	6, Sw 18
HIT DICE:	8, 12, or 16	8, 12, or 16
THAC0:	8 Hit Dice: 13	8 Hit Dice: 12
	12 Hit Dice: 9	12 Hit Dice: 9
	16 Hit Dice: 5	16 Hit Dice: 7
NO. OF ATTACKS:	1	1
DAMAGE/ATTACK:	3-24	5-30
SPECIAL ATTACKS:	See below	See below
SPECIAL DEFENSES:	+2 weapon or better to hit	+2 weapon or better to hit
MAGIC RESISTANCE:	Nil	Nil
SIZE:	L to H (8′ to 16′ tall)	L to H (8′ to 16′ tall)
MORALE:	8-12 Hit Dice: Champion (15-16)	8-12 Hit Dice: Champion (15-16)
	16 Hit Dice: Fanatic (17)	16 Hit Dice: Fanatic (17)
XP VALUE:	8 Hit Dice: 2,000	8 Hit Dice: 2,000
	12 Hit Dice: 6,000	12 Hit Dice: 6,000
	16 Hit Dice: 10,000	16 Hit Dice: 10,000

Fire elementals can be conjured in any area containing a large open flame. To provide a fire elemental with an adequate shell of Prime Material flame, a fire built to house an elemental should have a diameter of at least six feet and reach a minimum of four feet into the air.

On the Prime Material plane, a fire elemental appears as a tall sheet of flame. The fire elemental will always appear to have two armlike appendages, one on each side of its body. These arms seem to flicker back into the creature's flaming body, only to spring out from its sides seconds later. The only facial features of a fire elemental are two large glowing patches of brilliant blue fire, which seem to function as eyes for the elemental. Like all common elementals, fire elementals rarely speak on the Prime Material plane, though their voices can be heard in the crackle and hiss of a large fire.

Combat: Because they resent being conjured to this plane, fire elementals are fierce opponents who will attack their enemies directly and savagely, taking what joy they can in burning the weak creatures and objects of the Prime Material to ashes. In combat, a fire elemental lashes out with one of its ever-moving limbs, doing 3-24 points of damage. Any flammable object struck by the fire elemental must save versus magical fire at a -2 or immediately begin to burn.

Fire elementals do have some limitations on their actions in the Prime Material plane. They are unable to cross water or non-flammable liquids. Often, a quick dive into a nearby lake or stream is the only thing that can save a powerful party from certain death from a fire elemental. Also, because their natural abilities give them some built-in resistance to flame-based attacks, creatures with innate fire-using abilities, like red dragons, take less damage from a fire elemental's attack. The elemental subtracts 1 point from each die of damage it does to these creature (to a minimum of 1 point of damage per die).

Water elementals can be conjured in any area containing a large amount of water or watery liquid. At least one thousand cubic feet of liquid is required to create a shell for the water elemental to inhabit. Usually a large pool serves this purpose, but several large kegs of wine or ale will do just as well.

The water elemental appears on the Prime Material plane as a high-crested wave. The elemental's arms appear as smaller waves, one thrust out on each side of its main body. The arms ebb and flow, growing longer or shorter as the elemental moves. Two orbs of deep green peer out of the front of the wave and serve the elemental as eyes. Like all other common elementals, water elemental rarely speak on the Prime Material plane, but their voices can be heard in the crashing of waves on rocky shores and the howl of an ocean gale.

Combat: In combat, the water elemental is a dangerous adversary. It prefers to fight in a large body of water where it can constantly disappear beneath the waves and suddenly swell up behind its opponent. When the elemental strikes, it lashes out with a huge wave-like arm, doing 5-30 points of damage.

Water elementals are also a serious threat to ships that cross their paths. A water elemental can easily overturn small craft (one ton of ship per hit die of the elemental) and stop or slow almost any vessel (one ton of ship per hit point of the elemental). Ships not completely stopped by an elemental will be slowed by a percentage equal to the ratio of ship's tons over the hit points of the attacking elemental.

Though the water elemental is most effective in large areas of open water, it can be called upon to serve in a battle on dry land, close to the body of water from which it arose. However, the movement of the water elemental on land is the most restricted of any elemental type: a water elemental cannot move more than 60 yards away from the water it was conjured from, and 1 point of damage is subtracted from each die of damage they inflict out of the water (to a minimum of 1 point of damage per die).

	Sylph	Aerial Servant
CLIMATE/TERRAIN:	High altitudes or treetops	Any (see below)
FREQUENCY:	Very rare	Very rare
ORGANIZATION:	Solitary	Solitary
ACTIVITY CYCLE:	Any	Any
DIET:	Omnivore	Wind
INTELLIGENCE:	Exceptional (15-16)	Semi- (2-4)
TREASURE:	Qx10, X	Nil
ALIGNMENT:	Neutral (good)	Neutral
NO. APPEARING:	1	1
ARMOR CLASS:	9	3
MOVEMENT:	12, Fl 36 (A)	Fl 24 (A)
HIT DICE:	3	16
THAC0:	17	5
NO. OF ATTACKS:	0	1
DAMAGE/ATTACK:	0	8-32 (8d4)
SPECIAL ATTACKS:	See below	See below
SPECIAL DEFENSES:	See below	+1 or better weapon to hit
MAGIC RESISTANCE:	50%	Nil
SIZE:	M (4'-5' tall)	L (8' tall)
MORALE:	Elite (14)	Elite (14)
XP VALUE:	2,000	9,000

Sylphs are beautiful, humanoid women with wings like dragon-flies. Their wings are 4-5 feet long and translucent, clear, or spotted with iridescent color. Their long, bright, hair may be any "normal" color, or blue, purple, or green. They wear flowing, diaphanous robes which accent their wings or hair.

Sylphs are related to air elementals and to nymphs, perhaps originating as a cross-breed between nymphs and aerial servants. They speak Common and their own musical language. Sylphs are friendly and may (20%) befriend adventurers and give them aid in exchange for a favor.

Combat: Sylphs defend themselves only with magical abilities. A sylph can cast spells as a 7th-level wizard, and most prefer spells of elemental air. In addition, the sylph can become *invisible at will* and summon an air elemental once each week.

Habitat/Society: Sylphs rarely touch ground in the lowlands. They are fond of travel, and it is rare to find one near its home.

Sylph nests are highly individualistic, some formed from whatever materials are available, others are elaborate retreats perched in tall trees or carved into mountains. Sylphs prefer simple and light possessions, keeping only gems and magical items as treasure. They often trade wealth for furnishings, such as light draperies, silks, and pillows.

There is a 1% chance that a sylph's home holds an egg or a child. All sylphs are female and mate with humanoid males, preferring elves, but sometimes accepting a human or halfling mate. Three months after conception, the sylph lays a pearly egg in a special nest, and summons an air elemental to guard it. Six months later, the egg hatches a baby girl with wing buds. The child grows at the same rate as a human child, gaining magical abilities at age five, and full flight by age 10.

The sylph has the innate ability to levitate; wings are needed only to provide thrust. If a sylph's wings are injured, it can only glide or hover. Anti-magical attacks may ground a sylph by negating its power of *levitation*. Sylphs live for up to 1,000 years, retaining their youthful looks throughout their lives.

Every 28 years, all sylphs gather in a grand meeting to trade, share news, renew friendships, and welcome young sylphs.

Ecology: Sylphs usually maintain their distance from the more mundane humanoid races, but associate freely with nymphs and dryads. Aerial monsters occasionally feed on them, but they are in greater danger from evil humanoid males who attempt to capture them for dark purposes.

Aerial Servant
This creature is a form of air elemental native to the plane of elemental Air, as well as the Ethereal and Astral planes, and can be summoned to the Prime Material plane by clerics.

Normally invisible, if seen on their home plane, they resemble legless humanoids of sparkling blue smoke, with empty eyes, a slash for a mouth, and long, four-fingered hands.

Aerial servants try to avoid combat on their native planes. It has a Strength of 23 and attacks by grabbing and strangling opponents, causing damage with the hit, and in each round, until the victim breaks free. A character with exceptional Strength receives a percentage chance equal to the percentage of exceptional Strength. Creatures with 18/00 Strength and above break free easily. Creatures with more hit points than the aerial servant can likewise break its grasp. Aerial servants penalize opponents surprise rolls by −5 when invisible.

A cleric who summons an aerial servant will be attacked unless behind a *protection from evil*, because the servants resent being summoned. Otherwise, the servant will complete any duty for the cleric, except fighting, as fast as possible. If the servant is prevented from completing its mission, it goes insane and returns to kill the summoning cleric.

Aerial servants are wanderers drawn to areas of extreme weather. If caught in a storm, there is a 5% chance it will be blown in two; this is the only way it can reproduce.

Aerial servants must feed on winds of their home planes at least once per month, or suffer 1d8 damage per day over 30 that they go without feeding.

Elemental, Earth Kin

	Pech	Sandling
CLIMATE/TERRAIN:	Any subterranean	Temperate or tropical, sandy or subterranean
FREQUENCY:	Rare	Rare
ORGANIZATION:	Clan	Solitary
ACTIVITY CYCLE:	Darkness	Any
DIET:	Omnivore	Minerals
INTELLIGENCE:	Average to exceptional (8-16)	Non- (0)
TREASURE:	See below	Nil
ALIGNMENT:	Neutral good	Neutral
NO. APPEARING:	5-20	1
ARMOR CLASS:	3	3
MOVEMENT:	9	12, Br 6
HIT DICE:	4	4
THAC0:	17	17
NO. OF ATTACKS:	1	1
DAMAGE/ATTACK:	By weapon +3	2- 16
SPECIAL ATTACKS:	See below	Nil
SPECIAL DEFENSES:	See below	See below
MAGIC RESISTANCE:	25%	Nil
SIZE:	S (4' tall)	L (10' diameter)
MORALE:	Average (10)	Unsteady (7)
LEVEL/XP VALUE:	1,400	420

The pech are creatures of the plane of elemental Earth, though some have extensive mines in the deepest regions of the Prime Material plane. They dwell in dark places and work stone.

Pech are thin and have long arms and legs. Their broad hands and feet are excellent for bracing and employing tools to work stone. They have pale, yellowish skin and red or reddish brown hair. Their flesh is nearly as hard as granite. Their eyes are large and have no pupils. Pech have infravision to 120 feet.

Combat: The pech use picks and peat hammers (treat as war hammers) for work and armament, and are usually equipped with equal numbers of each. Pech have 18/50 Strength.

Each pech can cast four *stone shape* and four *stone tell* spells per day. Four pech can band to together to cast a *wall of stone* spell as a 16th-level mage. Eight together can cast a *stone to flesh* spell. Group spells can be cast but once per day by any group. Pech are immune to petrification.

When fighting lithic monsters such as stone golems, gargoyles, or galeb duhr, pech are quite capable of knocking them to rubble, as their knowledge of stone allows them full attack capability against such creatures, even with nonmagical weapons. Each successful strike does maximum damage.

Habitat/Society: Pech are basically good and peaceful creatures that want to be left to themselves. They hate bright light and open skies, and they are quick to ask others to douse lights. Their lairs are constructed with numerous choke points so that *walls of stone* can quickly stop intruders. Their lair holds 10-40 individuals, with equal numbers of females and males, and young equal to 20-50% of the females.

Ecology: The pech home plane is hostile, so many travel to the Prime Material plane to search for a better life. They have few enemies there. Pech do not save large amounts of treasure; they mine for things to trade with others for food or services. They do sometimes create simple, unobtrusive ornamental objects for everyday use. A pech lair may contain 50-100 trade gems plus 5-30 dishes and utensils worked from stone and raw metal. These items are not very valuable, averaging 150 gp each.

Sandling

These creatures are composed of silicates and originated on the elemental plane of Earth. They look like piles of sand and can vary color to blend with backgrounds. Sandlings have the same temperature as their surroundings, and are immune to *sleep*, *charm*, *hold*, and other mind-affecting spells or attacks. They claim territories with boundaries recognizable only by them.

Sandlings are not aggressive unless provoked, but guard their territories from intruders. If stepped on, a sandling reflexively lunges upward, trapping 1-2 man-sized opponents; opponents receive a −2 penalty to surprise rolls when attacked in this manner. If the sandling hits its targets, they are unable to attack or defend for 1d4 rounds. Sandlings also attack by slashing with an abrasive pseudopod. If at least 10 gallons of water are poured on a sandling, it is affected as if by a *slow* spell, and its attacks cause only half normal damage.

Sandlings have no society, and their fierce defense of their territories usually precludes cooperation, even with other members of their own race. They live on minerals, but despise organic matter, always moving several hundred yards from any place they have killed an intruder.

A sandling grows until it reaches its full size, 10 feet in diameter, then reproduces by budding. Sandling buds split from their parent when they are about 2 inches long, and an adult's territory may swarm with thousands of these creatures. When an infant grows to at least 6 inches in diameter, it either moves off to find its own territory, or is hunted and killed by the parent. A group of immature sandlings forms a surface with myriad tiny bumps, which may trip the unwary.

Sandlings have little effect on an ecosystem, taking only a fraction of the minerals in any parcel of land. Dwarves sometimes seek them in hopes of finding a rich mineral deposit. They are said to be excellent ingredients for mortar, but they and many druids object to this treatment.

Elemental Fire-Kin

	Salamander	Fire Snake
CLIMATE/TERRAIN:	Special	Fires
FREQUENCY:	Rare	Uncommon
ORGANIZATION:	Pack	Pack
ACTIVITY CYCLE:	Any	Any
DIET:	Omnivore	Fire
INTELLIGENCE:	High (13-14)	Semi- (2-4)
TREASURE:	F	Q
ALIGNMENT:	Chaotic evil	Neutral
NO. APPEARING:	2-5	1-6
ARMOR CLASS:	5/3	6
MOVEMENT:	9	4
HIT DICE:	7+7	2
THAC0:	13	19
NO. OF ATTACKS:	2	1
DAMAGE/ATTACK:	2-12, 1-6 (weapon)	1-4
SPECIAL ATTACKS:	Heat 1-6	Paralyzation
SPECIAL DEFENSES:	+1 or better to hit	Immune to fire
MAGIC RESISTANCE:	Nil	Nil
SIZE:	M (7' long)	S (2'-3' long)
MORALE:	Elite (13)	Steady (11)
XP VALUE:	2,000	120

Salamanders are natives of the elemental plane of Fire, and thus they thrive in hot places. These cruel, evil creatures come to the Prime Material plane for reasons known only to them.

The head and torso of a salamander is copper-colored and has a human-like appearance. Most of the time (80%), this aspect is a male, with flaming beard and moustache. The female version has flowing, fiery red hair. Both aspects have glowing yellow eyes that sometimes switch to fluorescent green. All aspects carry a shiny metal spear, resembling highly polished steel.

The lower torso is that of a large snake, with orange coloring shading to dull red at the tail end. The entire body is covered with wispy appendages that appear to burn but are never consumed.

Combat: A salamander typically attacks with its metal spear, which inflicts 1d6 points of damage plus a like amount for the spear's heat. At the same time, it can lash out and coil around an opponent with its snake-like tail, constricting for 2d6 points of damage, plus an additional 1d6 points of damage from the heat of its body. While fire-resistant creatures do not suffer from the salamander's heat damage, they are still subject to the spear and constriction damage.

Salamanders can be affected only by magical weaponry or by creatures of a magical nature or those of 4+1 or more Hit Dice. They are impervious to all fire-based attacks. *Sleep, charm,* and *hold* spells are ineffective against them. Cold-based attacks cause an additional 1 point of damage per die of damage. The head and upper body of the salamander has an AC of 5, while the lower body is AC 3.

A favorite salamander tactic, if the creature is encountered in a lava pit or roaring fire, is to grab its opponents and hurl them into the flames. The victim would naturally take damage from contact with the salamander, then take even more from being thrown inside a roaring conflagration.

Habitat/Society: Salamanders are native to the elemental plane of Fire. They come to the Prime Material plane for reasons known only to them, though it is rumored that powerful wizards and priests of certain religions can summon them for a short time. Salamanders hate cold, preferring temperatures of 300 de-grees or more; they can abide lower temperatures for only a few hours. Their lairs are typically at least 500 degrees. Any treasure found there is the sort that can survive this heat, such as swords, armor, rods, other ferrous items, and jewels. Things of a combustible nature, such as parchment and wood, soft metals such as gold and silver, and liquids, which quickly boil away, are never found in salamander lairs.

Having a nasty disposition and an evil bent, salamanders respect only power, either the ability to resist their fire or the capability to do great damage. Anyone else is dealt a painful, slow, burning death. It is rumored that they have some sort of dealings with the efreeti.

When encountered on the Prime plane, salamanders can be found playing in forest fires, lava flows, fire pits, and other areas of extreme heat. They usually appear on the Prime plane for a purpose, and if in the middle of a task they do not take kindly to being interrupted.

Ecology: These fiery creatures' ichor is useful in the creation of *potions of fire resistance,* and the metal of their spears can be used to create *rings of fire resistance.*

Fire Snake

Some sages say that fire snakes are larval salamanders. Fire snakes, colored in shades from blood-red to orange, are always found in fires. Some large permanent fires contain 1d6 of these creatures, though in smaller, temporary fires like fire pits and oil bowls, there may be but one snake. The only treasure the snakes have is the gems they often accumulate.

Since their color matches their surroundings, they can surprise opponents easily (-4 penalty to opponents' surprise rolls). Their bite inflicts 1d4 points of damage and injects a mild venom that causes paralyzation of the victim for 2d4 turns unless a saving throw vs. poison is successful.

103

Elemental, Water Kin

	Nereid	**Water Weird**
CLIMATE/TERRAIN:	Tropical or temperate water	Any water
FREQUENCY:	Very rare	Very rare
ORGANIZATION:	Solitary	Solitary
ACTIVITY CYCLE:	Any	Any
DIET:	Clean water	See below
INTELLIGENCE:	Very (12)	Very (11-12)
TREASURE:	X	I, O, P, Y
ALIGNMENT:	Chaotic (any)	Chaotic evil
NO. APPEARING:	1-4	1-3
ARMOR CLASS:	10	4
MOVEMENT:	12, Sw 12	12
HIT DICE:	4	3 + 3
THAC0:	17	15
NO. OF ATTACKS:	0	0
DAMAGE/ATTACK:	0	0
SPECIAL ATTACKS:	See below	Drowning
SPECIAL DEFENSES:	See below	See below
MAGIC RESISTANCE:	50%	Nil
SIZE:	M (4'-5' tall)	L (10' + long)
MORALE:	Steady (11)	Elite (13)
XP VALUE:	975	420

These creatures from the elemental plane of Water, sometimes called "honeyed ones," are unpredictable and playful; half are chaotic neutral, and others tend toward good or evil. Using disguise, nereids lead sailors to their dooms.

Nereids are transparent in water, 95% undetectable except as froth and golden seaweed. Upon contact with air, they assume human form, usually as voluptuous young females with long, golden hair, pearly white skin, and sparkling green eyes. Their voices and songs are lovely. A nereid always carries a white shawl, either in its hands or over head and shoulders, and is lightly clad in white and gold. If confronted by only females, the nereid appears in a male guise, but a woman has a 65% chance to see through the disguise. All males who see a nereid are incapable of harming it (no saving throw).

Combat: Nereids can spit venom 20 feet, blinding a target for 2d6 rounds if it hits; the venom can be washed away with water. A blinded victim's attack rolls, saving throws, and AC are all worsened by 4 until the effects wear off.

Nereids can *control water* within 30 feet; it can use waves to slow movement to ¼ normal, increase chances of drowning by 10%, or crash with a roar that deafens characters within 60 feet for 3d4 rounds if precautions are not taken. Nereids can also form the water to look like a water weird, and cause it to strike as a 4 HD monster and inflict ld4 points of damage.

A nereid is 85% likely to have a pet for protection, with equal chances for a giant eel, giant otter, giant poisonous snake, giant octopus, giant squid, dolphin, giant leech, or sting ray.

If the nereid makes a successful saving throw vs. poison, she can flow like water, avoiding weapon damage or escaping a captor. The nereid's kiss causes a man to drown, unless he makes a successful saving throw vs. breath weapon, with a -2 penalty. If he lives, he finds ecstacy.

The nereid protects its shawl at all costs, for it contains the nereid's essence; if it is destroyed, the nereid dissolves into formless water. Possession of a nereid's shawl gives a character control over the creature, which will accept commands to avoid damage to the shawl. Stories tell of forlorn nereids who follow the ships of a powerful foes who have stolen their shawls. A nereid will lie and attempt anything short of violent action to regain its soul-shawl.

Habitat/Society: A nereid found on the Prime Material plane has either escaped or been exiled from its home plane. Though usually solitary, a small group of nereids with the same alignment sometimes live together, led by the eldest.

Polluted waters drain nereids' vigor, and even good nereids may attack those who pollute their lairs. Nereids do not value metals, but save any magical treasure they gain. The nereid has no goals or ambitions other than cavorting in water.

Ecology: Nereid shawls command handsome sums, but are seldom sold and are very rare. One who holds a shawl can use the enslaved nereid as a guide on the plane of Water.

Water Weird

These strange creatures from the plane of Water are hostile when encountered on the Prime Material plane, as they are usually magically kept from going home. If communication is achieved, a bargain can sometimes be struck with the creature.

Water weirds appear to be common water; a *detect invisibility* reveals something amiss, but not the nature of the threat. When a water weird detects a living being, it assumes serpentine form (this takes two rounds). It attacks as a 6 HD creature; those hit must make a successful saving throw vs. paralyzation, or be pulled into the water. Each round spent in the water requires another saving throw; failure indicates death by drowning, which releases energy that the water weird consumes. A water weird that comes in contact with a normal water elemental has a 50% chance to usurp control of it.

Water weirds take only 1 hp damage from piercing and slashing weapons. The take half damage from fire, none if they make a successful saving throw. Intense cold acts as a *slow* spell on water weirds. If reduced to 0 hp or less, a water weird is disrupted, and it reforms in two rounds. A *purify water* spell will instantly kill a single water weird.

Elemental, Composite

	Tempest	Skriaxit
CLIMATE/TERRAIN:	Any outside	Subtropical desert
FREQUENCY:	Very rare	Very rare
ORGANIZATION:	Solitary	Pack
ACTIVITY CYCLE:	Any	Any
DIET:	See below	See below
INTELLIGENCE:	Low to average (5-10)	Exceptional (15-16)
TREASURE:	K	Nil
ALIGNMENT:	Chaotic neutral	Neutral evil
NO. APPEARING:	1	3-18
ARMOR CLASS:	2	−5
MOVEMENT:	Fl 24	12, 18, or 24
HIT DICE:	9-12	16 + 16 or 24 + 24
THAC0:	9-10 HD: 11 11-12 HD: 9	5
NO. OF ATTACKS:	1	2
DAMAGE/ATTACK:	2-16	2-20/2-20
SPECIAL ATTACKS:	Whirlwind lightning	Sandstorm, dispel magic
SPECIAL DEFENSES:	+2 or better weapon to hit; see below	+2 or better weapon to hit; see below
MAGIC RESISTANCE:	Nil	50%
SIZE:	G (50′ diameter)	L (10′ tall)
MORALE:	Champion (15-16)	Fanatic (17-18)
XP VALUE:	9 HD: 6,000 10 HD: 7,000 11 HD: 8,000 12 HD: 9,000	16 + 16 HD: 16,000 24 + 24 HD: 24,000

The tempest is a living storm which appears as a dark storm cloud of comparatively small size. Human or bestial features can often be seen in the roiling vapors of the tempest. Silver veins extend across the creature and carry the electrical impulses that maintain the storm's energy.

Tempests have no language that humans may learn. They can communicate with air and water elementals and their kin, and genies, through subtle wind buffets and spatterings of precipitation. A few, perhaps 10%, have learned to speak a few words of Common. Their voices are very soft and sibilant, with a hint of malice behind the words.

Combat: Tempests are territorial and consider any violation of their airspace to be a direct challenge. They feed on moisture from animals and often hunt in and around their territories. They have a number of innate abilities which they can use to make life miserable for other creatures. Unless otherwise specified, all special abilities are used as if the tempest were a 9th-level wizard. A tempest can make two attacks each round, one using its wind powers and one using its lightning power.

Once per round, a tempest can use *wind wall* or *gust of wind*, or may attack with a strong wind buffet for 2-16 points of damage. Alternately, it may create a small whirlwind, which is conical in shape, 10 feet in diameter at the bottom, and 30 feet in diameter at the top. The whirlwind can be up to 50 feet high, and must connect to the tempest's main body.

The tempest takes one full round to create the whirlwind, which can cover an area of 100 square feet per round. Within that area, it automatically sweeps away and kills all creatures with less than 2 Hit Dice, and causes 2d6 points of damage to all creatures which it fails to kill outright.

Tempests may also use their powers over the air to penalize missile attacks by −6, or to batter down flying creatures, causing falling damage to flying creatures that fail to make a successful saving throw vs. paralyzation.

A tempest can also cast a *lightning bolt* once per round, at one victim. The *lightning bolt* causes one die of damage per Hit Die of the tempest. A victim of a lightning attack can make a saving throw vs. spells; if successful, the victim takes only half damage. The tempest's *lightning bolt* is like the 3rd-level wizard spell in other respects, having a length of 80 feet, setting fire to combustibles, melting metals, and shattering barriers. An exceptionally hungry or perturbed tempest may use lightning to destroy an entire building to reach the creatures inside.

Tempests can also use a chilling wind to affect opponents, causing damage as a *chill touch* spell, 1d4 points of damage and the loss of 1 point of Strength, unless the victim makes a successful saving throw vs. spells. This attack takes the place of either an electrical attack or another wind attack.

A tempest can produce up to 20 gallons of rain per round if it concentrates and forgoes other attacks while raining. While precipitation is usually evenly distributed throughout its area, the tempest can concentrate the fall to fill a hole, wash out a bridge, or otherwise harm its victims.

Tempests are immune to wind, gas, and water attacks, and take only half damage from electrical or cold-based attacks. They are immune to all weapons of less than +2 enchantment.

Habitat/Society: There is much speculation about the origin of these beings, who are apparently related to elementals and to genie-kind. Tempests are composed of all four basic elements, fire, earth, air, and water; fire in the form of lightning, earth in their silver "circulatory system," air in their winds, and water in the form of rain. They may be summoned accidentally when a spellcaster tries to summon an elemental, especially one of air or water. At the DM's option, when a summoning is interfered with, the caster may be given a 10%-50% chance to summon a tempest. These beings may also be attracted by a *weather summoning* spell, with a 1% (non-cumulative) chance of appearing each time a spell is cast.

Elemental, Composite

Some sages believe these creatures are jann that have been injured in some way and cannot retain human form. Whatever their origin, they do breed and reproduce as storms. Though "male" and "female" do not truly describe the different types of tempests, there are two genders. When living storms of different genders meet, they have a brief, tempestuous affair, causing a great conflagration that may last more than a week. Hurricanes or tornadoes are produced irregularly from the mass, to wreak havoc upon the surrounding area.

When the storm finally breaks, the two tempests leave the area, and the residue they leave behind forms 1d4 infant tempests. These infant storms, sometimes referred to as tantrums, often travel together until they reach maturity, one year after birth. The young storms have 6 Hit Dice each, and can use only the *gust of wind* power, besides producing rain.

Most tempests quite naturally seem to have very stormy dispositions. Their hunger for animal life goes beyond their need for the moisture contained in animal bodies. Some sages speculate that their physical form, or possibly some event in their history, causes them to hate animal life. It is quite possible that the electrical impulses produced by animal brains cause pain to the tempest.

Tempests may be related to skriaxits, the living sandstorms of some worlds' deserts. No tempest has ever been known to encounter a skriaxit, and their relationship and possible interactions are completely unknown.

Ecology: Tempests feed on the moisture found in animal bodies. Though unable to cause harm to living creatures by draining their moisture, they hover close to the ground after a battle to suck the water from dead opponents, as well as any water they may have precipitated during the battle. They are sometimes found scavenging after great battles between humans. By removing water from a corpse, they render it inviable to return to life via a *raise dead* spell, though *resurrection* and other spells work normally.

When a tempest is killed, a silver residue rains down from its form. If carefully gathered, this residue provides a mass of silver equivalent to 3d6 silver pieces. Though valuable as a precious metal, the silver can also be used as a component in making a *wand of lightning* or casting a weather-related spell. Bits of the silver are also useful for making other weather or elemental related magical items.

Genies and elementals are enemies of tempests; they often attack them, and tempests respond in like manner. However, some genies, especially djinn and marids, keep tempests as pets, training them as guards and to attack.

Tempests can be quite devastating to a local ecology if annoyed, and can cause great damage with wind, rain, and other attack forms. Living storms are never found inside buildings or underground.

Skriaxit

Skriaxits, also called blackstorms or living sandstorms, are the most feared creatures in many deserts. Spirits of retribution summoned millennia ago by ancient gods, blackstorms combine the elements of earth and air to dangerous effect. They are, fortunately, only rarely active. They speak the tongue of air elementals and their own language, a howling, shrieking tongue that frightens most humans who hear it.

Much like very large versions of the *dust devils* created by the wizard's spell, blackstorms take the sand and the dust of the desert and whirl it to create their 10-foot-tall conical forms. At rest, a skriaxit appears to be a wind-scattered pile of black dust. As a

pack, they create their greatest terror, generating high winds and a fierce sandstorm that can render a human fleshless in minutes.

Combat: Skriaxits move by generating a large vortex of wind that propels them at high speeds. If there are 1-6 skriaxits together, their speed is 12; 7-12 skriaxits have a speed of 18; if there are 13 or more skriaxits, their speed is 24. The skriaxit vortex creates a sandstorm in a 200-yard radius around them; those caught in this storm suffer 1 point of damage per round per skriaxit (so if there are 12 skriaxits in a pack, victims take 12 points of damage per round).

Within this sandstorm, the skriaxit pack constantly dispels magic as a 16th-level wizard.

Each skriaxit can form its winds into razor sharp lashes, inflicting 2d10 points of damage on a successful strike.

Though they were originally summoned from the elemental plane of Air, they have merged with earth, and the Prime Material plane is now their home. Thus, they cannot be sent to an elemental plane by a holy word or similar magic. No known magic can control them, though they are susceptible to wards against air elementals.

Each skriaxit pack is led by a Great Skriax, the most evil member of the pack. This creature has 24 + 24 Hit Dice and gains a +4 bonus to attack and damage rolls.

Habitat/Society: Skriaxits are highly intelligent, but extremely evil, elementals, combinations of the elements of air and earth. They hate and fear nothing, but simply delight in destruction. They feed on terror and destruction; once they have caused enough catastrophe, they sleep for 1d3 centuries. While asleep, they cannot be affected in any way by any being. They reawaken when hungry. They view humans, demihumans, and humanoids as playthings, with the same sadistic attitude as a human child playing with a fly. They may amuse themselves by listening to humans bargain with them, but humans have nothing of interest to offer them.

Ecology: Skriaxits feed upon the emotions of terror and fear they generate in those they destroy and kill.

Arctic Tempest

This is a variety of tempest found only in arctic regions and some of the colder temperate lands. While they are similar to tempests in most respects, their special powers differ. They cannot use the whirlwind or *lightning bolt* powers of the standard tempest. Instead, they can either cause snow to fall or cast *ice storm* spells. The arctic tempest usually uses a hail form of *ice storm*, but may use sleet instead. It can cause very cold snow to fall, inflicting 9d4 + 9 points of cold damage to those beneath it. Victims who make a successful saving throw vs. spells suffer only half damage from the attack.

Like the standard tempest, the arctic variety can make only two attacks per round, one using a wind power, such as *gust of wind* or *wind wall*, and one using a cold-based power, such as *ice storm* or *cause snow*. It may also substitute an electrical attack for either of its normal attacks, causing damage as a *shocking grasp* spell for 1d8 + 9 points of damage.

Black Cloud of Vengeance

This living storm, usually found in deserts, combines the elements of fire and air. It unleashes a fiery rain which causes 7d10 damage to all beneath it, though a successful saving throw vs. breath weapon halves the damage. It then fans the flames, and will they continue to burn as long as there is fuel.

	Elephant (African)	Mammoth	Mastodon	Oliphant
CLIMATE/TERRAIN:	Subtropical to tropical jungle and plains	Subarctic plains	Subarctic plains	Temperate to subarctic plains and tundra
FREQUENCY:	Common	Very rare (Common)	Very rare (Common)	Rare
ORGANIZATION:	Herd	Herd	Herd	Herd
ACTIVITY CYCLE:	Dawn, dusk, early morning, and early evening	Day	Any	Day
DIET:	Herbivore	Herbivore	Herbivore	Herbivore
INTELLIGENCE:	Semi- (2-4)	Semi- (2-4)	Semi- (2-4)	Low (5-7)
TREASURE:	Nil	Nil	Nil	Nil
ALIGNMENT:	Neutral	Neutral	Neutral	Neutral
NO. APPEARING:	1-12	1-12	1-12	1-8
ARMOR CLASS:	6	5	6	4
MOVEMENT:	15	12	15	15
HIT DICE:	11	13	12	8+4 (10+5)
THAC0:	9	7	9	8+4 Hit Dice: 11 10+5 Hit Dice: 9
NO. OF ATTACKS:	5	5	5	4
DAMAGE/ATTACK:	2-16/2-16/2-12/2-12/2-12	3-18/3-18/2-16/2-12/2-12	2-16/2-16/2-12/2-12/2-12	3-12/3-12/3-12/3-12
SPECIAL ATTACKS:	Nil	Nil	Nil	Nil
SPECIAL DEFENSES:	Nil	Nil	Nil	Nil
MAGIC RESISTANCE:	Nil	Nil	Nil	Nil
SIZE:	L (11' tall)	L to H (10' to 14' tall)	L (10' tall)	L (8' to 10' tall)
MORALE:	Unsteady (7)	Unsteady (7)	Unsteady (7)	8+4: Unsteady (7) 10+5: Average (10)
XP VALUE:	4,000	6,000	5,000	8+4 Hit Dice: 2,000 10+5 Hit Dice: 4,000

Elephants have thick, baggy hides, covered with sparse and very coarse tufts of gray hair. The elephant's most renowned feature is its trunk, which it uses as a grasping limb.

Combat: An elephant can make up to five attacks at one time in a battle. It can do stabbing damage of 2-16 points (2d8) with each of its two tusks; constricting damage of 2-12 points with its trunk; and 2-12 points of trampling damage with each of its front feet. No single opponent can be subject to more than two of these attacks at any one time. However, the elephant can battle up to six man-sized opponents at one time.

Creatures larger than ogre-sized are not subject to the elephant's trunk attack. Also, an elephant will never attempt to grasp anything that might harm its trunk—like an object covered with sharp spikes. Elephants greatly fear fire.

Habitat/Society: Elephants are peaceful herbivores that travel in a herd. The herd is made up of both male and female elephants, as well as their young. If a herd of 10 or more elephants is encountered, there will be 1-4 young, from 20% to 70% mature, with the group. In the herd, a clear hierarchy exists, with the older males in a clear position of dominance.

Occasionally, an older male elephant will be beaten by a rival in the herd. The defeated elephant must then leave the group, at which point it becomes a violent "rogue." Rogue elephants encountered alone are 90% likely to attack, and will have no fewer than 6 hit points per hit die.

Ecology: Elephants are commonly captured when young and trained. They make good beasts of burden, but are often used in warfare as mounts and living battering rams, as well.

Elephant tusks are worth 100 to 600 hundred gold pieces each, or about 4 gp per pound. In areas heavily populated by elephants, a substantial trade in this ivory will be common.

Mammoths: This ancestor of the elephant was common during the Pleistocene era. Mammoths are covered with thicker, woolier hair than the modern elephant, and they are considerably larger. Mammoths are much more aggressive than elephants and will attack with less provocation. Because they are heavier, a mammoth's tusks are worth 50% more than an elephant's. Mammoths are rare when encountered outside of a Pleistocene campaign, and will only be found in subarctic plains.

Mastodons: Like the mammoth, the mastodon is an ancestor of the elephant that was common in the Pleistocene era, when they roamed from subarctic to tropical plains. They are larger than the modern elephant, hairier, and somewhat greater in length. Encountered outside of a Pleistocene campaign, mastodons are rare, and found only in subarctic plains.

Oliphants: The oliphant is a modern-day mastadon, with shaggy hair and tusks that curve down. The oliphant's trunk is too short to be used in combat. This limits the number of man-sized opponents an oliphant can attack at one time to four. Oliphants are more intelligent than elephants and do not share its cousins' unreasoning fear of fire. They are also very aggressive, and when properly trained and fed, oliphants grow to greater bulk (10+5 Hit Dice) than their wild counterparts. These trained oliphants are excellent for combat duty and have a morale of 10. An oliphant's tusks are worth 100 to 400 gold pieces each, or about 4 gp per pound, but are smaller than an elephant's.

Elf

CLIMATE/TERRAIN:	Temperate to subtropical forest
FREQUENCY:	Uncommon
ORGANIZATION:	Bands
ACTIVITY CYCLE:	Any
INTELLIGENCE:	High to Supra- (14-20)
DIET:	Omnivore
TREASURE:	Individual: N; G,S,T in lair
ALIGNMENT:	Chaotic good

NO. APPEARING:	20-200
ARMOR CLASS:	5 (10)
MOVEMENT:	12
HIT DICE:	1+1
THAC0:	19 (18)
NO. OF ATTACKS:	1
DAMAGE/ATTACK:	1-10
SPECIAL ATTACKS:	+1 to hit with bow or sword
SPECIAL DEFENSES:	See below
MAGIC RESISTANCE:	90% resistance to sleep and all charm-related spells
SIZE:	M (5'+ tall)
MORALE:	Elite (13)
XP VALUE:	420

Though their lives span several human generations, elves appear at first glance to be frail when compared to man. However, elves have a number of special talents that more than make up for their slightly weaker constitutions.

High elves, the most common type of elf, are somewhat shorter than men, never growing much over than 5 feet tall. Male elves usually weigh between 90 and 120 pounds, and females weigh between 70 and 100 pounds. Most high elves are dark-haired, and their eyes are a beautiful, deep shade of green. They posses infravision up to 60 feet. The features of an elf are delicate and finely chiseled.

Elves have very pale complexions, which is odd because they spend a great deal of time outdoors. They tend to be slim, almost fragile. Their pale complexion and slight builds are the result of a constitution that is weaker than man's. Elves, therefore, always subtract 1 point from their initial Constitution score. Though they are not as sturdy as humans, elves are much more agile, and always add 1 point to their initial Dexterity scores. Elven clothing tends to be colorful, but not garish. They often wear pastel colors, especially blues and greens. Because they dwell in forests, however, high elves often wear greenish grey cloaks to afford them quick camouflage.

Elves have learned that it is very important to understand the creatures, both good and evil, that share their forest home. Because of this, elves may speak the tongues of goblins, orcs, hobgoblins, gnolls, gnomes, and halflings, in addition to common and their own highly-developed language. They will always show an interest in anything that will allow them to communicate with, and learn from, their neighbors.

Combat: Elves are cautious fighters and always use their strengths to advantage if possible. One of their greatest strengths is the ability to pass through natural surroundings, woods, or forests, silently and almost invisibly. By moving quietly and blending into vegetation for cover, elves will often surprise a person or party (opponents have a surprise modifier of -4). As long as they are not attacking, the elves hiding in the forest can only be spotted by someone or something with the ability to see invisible objects. The military value of this skill is immense, and elven armies will always send scouts to spy on the enemy, since such spies are rarely caught-or even seen.

Although their constitutions are weak, elves posses an ex-

tremely strong will, such strong wills, in fact, that they have a 90% immunity to all *charm* and *sleep* spells . And even if their natural resistance to these spells fails, they get a normal saving throw-making it unlikely an elf will fall victim to these spells very often.

Elves live in the wild, so weapons are used for everything from dealing with the hostile creatures around their camps, to such mundane tasks as hunting for dinner. The elves' rigorous training with bows and swords, in addition to their great dexterity, gives them a natural bonus of +1 to hit when fighting with a short or long sword, or when using a bow of any kind, other than a crossbow. Elves are especially proficient in the use of the bow. Because of their agility, elves can move, fire a bow, and move again, all in the same round. Their archers are extremely mobile, and therefore dangerous.

Because of limitations of horses in forest combat, elves do not usually ride. Elves prefer to fight as foot soldiers and are generally armed as such. Most elves wear scale, ring, or chain mail, and almost all high elves carry shields. Although elves have natural bonuses when they use bows and swords, their bands carry a variety of weapons. The weapons composition of a band of elves is: spear 30%; sword 20%; sword and spear 20%; sword and bow 10%; bow 15%; two-handed sword 5%.

Elven fighters and multi-class fighters have a 10% chance per level to possess a magical item of use to his or her class. This percentage is cumulative and can be applied to each major type of magical item that character would use-for each class in the case of multi-class characters. (For example, a fighter/priest of level 4 or 5 would have a 40% chance to have a magical item useful to fighters and a 50% chance of having an item useful to priests.) In addition, if above 4th level, elven mages gain the same percentage chance to gain items, but gain 2-5 magical items useful to them if a successful roll is made.

For every 20 elves in a group, there will be one 2nd- or 3rd-level fighter (50% chance of either). For every party of 40 elves, and in addition to the higher level fighter, there will be a 1st- or

2nd-level mage (again, 50% chance of either). If 100 or more elves are encountered, the following additional characters will be present: two 4th-level fighter; one 8th-level mage; and a 4th-level fighter/4th-level mage/4th-level thief. Finally, if over 160 elves are encountered, they will be led by two 6th-level fighter/6th-level mage/6th-level thief. These two extremely powerful leaders will have two retainers each-a 4th-level fighter/5th-level mage, and a 3rd-level fighter/3rd-level mage/3rd-level thief. All of these are in addition to the total number of elves in the band.

Elven women are the equal of their male counterparts in all aspects of warfare. In fact, some bands of elves will contain units of female fighters, who will be mounted on unicorns. This occurs rarely (5% chance), and only 10-30 elf maidens will be encountered in such a unit. However, the legends of the destruction wrought by these elven women are rampant among the enemies of the elves.

Habitat/Society: Elves value their individual freedom highly and their social structure is based on independent bands. These small groups, usually consisting of no more than 200, recognize the authority of a royal overlord, who in turn owes allegiance to a king or queen. However, the laws and restraints set upon elven society are very few compared to human society and practically negligible when compared to dwarven society.

Elven camps are always well-hidden and protected. In addition to the large number of observation posts and personnel traps set around a camp, high elves typically set 2-12 giant eagles as guardians of their encampments (65% of the time). For every 40 elves encountered in a camp, there will be the following high level elves, as well as the leaders noted above: a 4th-level fighter, a 4th-level cleric, and a 2nd-level fighter/2nd-level mage/2nd-level thief. A 4th-level fighter/7th-level mage, a 5th-level fighter, a 6th-level fighter, and a 7th-level cleric will also be present. Females found in a camp will equal 100%, children 50%, of the males encountered.

Because elves live for several hundred years, their view of the world is radically different from most other sentient beings. Elves do not place much importance on short-term gains nor do they hurry to finish projects. Humans see this attitude as frivolous; the elves simply find it hard to understand why everyone else is always in such a rush.

Elves prefer to surround themselves with things that will bring them joy over long periods of time-things like music and nature. The company of their own kind is also very important to elves, since they find it hard to share their experiences or their perspectives on the world with other races. This is one of the main reasons elven families are so close. However, as friendship, too is something to be valued, even friends of other races remain friends forever.

Though they are immune to a few specific spells, elves are captivated by magic. Not specific spells, of course, but the very concept of magic. Cooperation is far more likely to be had from an elf, by offering an obscure, even worthless, (but interesting) magical item, than it is with two sacks of gold. Ultimately, their radically different perspective separates the elves from the rest of their world. Elves find dwarves too dour and their adherence to strict codes of law unpleasant. However, elves do recognize dwarven craftsmanship as something to be praised. Elves think a bit more highly of humans, though they see man's race after wealth and fleeting power as sad. In the end, after a few hundred years, all elves leave the world they share with dwarves and men, and journey to a mysterious land where they live freely for the rest of their extremely long lives.

Ecology: Elves produce fine clothes, beautiful music, and brilliant poetry. It is for these things that other cultures know the folk of the forest best. In their world within the forest, however, elves hold in check the dark forces of evil, and the creatures that would plunder the forest and then move on to plunder another. For this reason alone, elves are irreplaceable.

Grey Elves (Faerie)
Grey elves have either silver hair and amber eyes, or pale golden hair and violet eyes (the violet-eyed ones are known as faerie elves). They favor bright garments of white, gold, silver, or yellow, and wear cloaks of deep blue or purple. Grey elves are the rarest of elves, and they have little to do with the world outside their forests. They value intelligence very highly, and, unlike other elves, devote much time to study and contemplation. Their treatises on nature are astounding.

Grey elves value their independence from what they see as the corrupting influence of the outside world, and will fight fiercely to maintain their isolation. All grey elves carry swords, and most wear chain mail and carry shields. For mounts, grey elves will ride hippogriffs (70%) or griffons (30%). Those that ride griffons will have 3-12 griffons for guards in their camps, instead of giant eagles.

Wood Elves
Also called *sylvan elves*, wood elves are the wild branch of the elf family. They are slightly darker in complexion than high elves, their hair ranges in color from yellow to coppery-red, and their eyes are light brown, light green, or hazel. They wear clothes of dark browns and greens, tans and russets, to blend in with their surroundings. Wood elves are very independent and value strength over intelligence. They will avoid contact with strangers 75% of the time.

In battle, wood elves wear studded leather or ring mail, and 50% of their band will be equipped with bows. Only 20% of wood elves carry swords, and only 40% use spears. Wood elves prefer to ambush their enemies, using their ability to hide in the forest until their foes are close at hand. In most cases (70%), wood elf camps are guarded by 2-8 giant owls (80%) or by 1-6 giant lynx (20%). These elves speak only elf and the languages of some forest animals, and the treant. Wood elves are more inclined toward neutrality than good, and are not above killing people who stumble across their camps, in order to keep their locations secret.

Half-Elves
Half-elves are of human stock, and have features of both the elf and human parents. They are slightly taller than common elves, growing as tall as 5 1/2 feet and weighing up to 150 pounds. Though they do not gain the natural sword or bow bonuses from their elven relatives, but they do have normal elven infravision.

A half-elf can travel freely between most elven and human settlements, though occasionally prejudice will be a problem. The half-elf's life span is their biggest source of grief, however. Since a half-elf lives more than 125 years, he or she will outlive any human friends or relatives, but grow old too quickly to be a real part of elven society. Many half-elves deal with this by traveling frequently between the two societies, enjoying life as it comes; the best of both worlds. Half-elves may speak common, elf, gnome, halfling, goblin, hobgoblin, orc, and gnoll.

Elf, Aquatic

CLIMATE/TERRAIN:	Temperate/Shallow salt water
FREQUENCY:	Very rare
ORGANIZATION:	Bands
ACTIVITY CYCLE:	Any
DIET:	Omnivore
INTELLIGENCE:	High to genius (14-18)
TREASURE:	K, Q, (I, O, X, Y)
ALIGNMENT:	Chaotic good

NO. APPEARING:	20-120
ARMOR CLASS:	6 (9)
MOVEMENT:	9, Sw 15
HIT DICE:	1+1
THAC0:	19
NO. OF ATTACKS:	1 or 2
DAMAGE/ATTACK:	1-8 (weapon)
SPECIAL ATTACKS:	+1 with spears and tridents
SPECIAL DEFENSES:	See below
MAGIC RESISTANCE:	90% to *sleep* and *charm* spells
SIZE:	M (6'+tall)
MORALE:	Elite (13)
XP VALUE:	420

Beneath the crashing waves of wild coastlines lives the sea-elf, aquatic cousin of the woodland elves in conduct and outlook.

Aquatic elves live for many centuries, and their eyes often show the effects of such great age. Otherwise, sea elves show little evidence of aging. They have gill slits on either side of their throats, and greenish-silver skin. Their hair is usually stringy, and emerald green to deep blue in color. Males usually wear their hair short, but females allow their hair to reach as much as 4 feet in length. Unlike mermen, aquatic elves have legs and usually wear clothes woven from underwater plants and reeds. Their dress is quite intricate, most often of greens, blacks, and browns woven in subtle, swirling designs. Sea elves speak elvish, sahuagin, and an oddly accented common.

Combat: Sea elves are a peaceful culture. It is a rare sight to see an aquatic elf launch an attack, and rarer still for an entire band to prepare for war. Sea elves will leave their homes to go to battle only when the entire community is in danger, or against great enemies. When forced to war, they impress all opponents with their fierce bravery and skill.

If given their choice of battlefield, aquatic elves would prefer to fight in a bed of seaweed, or on the reefs, where their natural coloration and stealth skills can give them the chance to hide from their enemies. They can become as invisible in seaweed as their woodland cousins can in the forests, imposing a −5 penalty to their opponent's surprise roll. Sea elves enjoy the ability to move unhindered through seaweed, giving them tremendous advantages in maneuverability. While they lack the infravision of their land-based cousins, they can see clearly at amazing distances. An aquatic elf can count the troops of an enemy at distances of up to 1 mile.

Their preferred weapons are the trident and the spear. These are used for hunting as well as for combat. The trident and spear are wielded so well by sea elves, that they receive a +1 bonus to their attack roll when using them. They will also use combat nets against their enemies. These off-hand weapons will bind an opponent if the wielder rolls a successful attack against AC 6. (Because of their great Dexterity, aquatic elves do not suffer a penalty to the attack roll for the nets.) Half the time, only a victim's weapon (including natural weapons, like a shark's teeth) will be entangled in the net. The rest of the time, the victim is trapped. A netted victim must either break the net (a bend bars roll) or disentangle himself (a Dexterity check with at a −3 pen-

alty) to get free. Magical gestures are impossible in a net.

On some worlds, sea elves are unable to cast spells. The reasons for this are unknown, but there is a legend among these nonmagical sea elves that the drow stole this ability from them, long ages ago.

Like their surface counterparts, aquatic elves demonstrate strong resistance to *sleep* and *charm* spells. Aquatic elves also have a 90% immunity against *charm person* spells. And even if their natural resistance to *sleep* and *charm* spells fails, aquatic elves still get a normal saving throw.

In combat, leadership is divided according to the size of the war party. For every 20 elves in a band, there is an additional 3rd-level fighter. For every 40 elves, there is an additional 4th-level fighter. In a force numbering over 100, there will be an 8th-level fighter and two 5th-level lieutenants (in addition to the 3rd- and 4th-level fighters above). A combat unit of more than 160 elves are accompanied by a 9th-level fighter and a 6th-level thief, in addition to their original numbers.

Sea elves befriend dolphins and employ them as companions and comrades-in-arms. In any party of at least 20 sea elves, there's a 50% chance for them to be accompanied by 1d3 dolphins. The dolphins are companions, however, they are neither pets nor cannon fodder. When danger threatens, dolphins join the combat as willing allies.

Battle tactics of the sea elves differ from one band to another, but common strategies include the following:

A charge from directly beneath an opponent. This is particularly effective against unwanted visitors from the surface, who are unaccustomed to being attacked from below. If the elf launched this attack from a bed of seaweed, he might well escape back to cover before his opponents could react.

A beaching, usually by more than one elf. Sea elves can survive on land for a few minutes at a time, though in a state of growing discomfort. Many of their opponents, like sharks, cannot. Several elves may attempt to wrestle an opponent to the beach, taking it well away from the ocean.

Elf, Aquatic

Traps. Beds of seaweed and coral reefs are excellent staging areas for all manner of spring-loaded booby-traps, nets, and perhaps magical entrapments designed and built by surface elves in return for favors. Predators have often decided to turn toward easier prey after encountering a sea elf band's defenses.

Habitat/Society: Small communities of 3d100 + 100 normal inhabitants are the rule of aquatic elven lifestyle. These communities are often found in heavy weed beds in sheltered waters, though the aquatic elves may fashion homes in caverns in lagoon bottoms and coral reefs. Sea elf communities keep in touch with each other through an elaborate and inefficient custom of wandering herald/messengers who travel from one band to another, much like postal carriers transmitting oral messages. In each community, there are several leader-types, as outlined earlier, ruled over by a fighter of 10th-12th level, with a personal guard of eight 7th-level elf fighters. Magical weapons would be carried by the leader or one of his guards.

Aquatic elves are an anti-social race. They avoid air-breathers as well as other races that dwell beneath the waves. Their cities are usually carved from the rock beneath beds of seaweeds, practically invisible to non-elves. A character has the same opportunity to find a sea elf community as he has to detect a secret door.

As independent as the freedom-loving elves are of each others' communities, they live in even greater isolation from the rest of the undersea races, whom they would rather not deal with. Although the aquatic elves see nothing wrong with the mermen, the tritons, and other good-aligned undersea races, the elves see no reason to involve themselves in the problems of such transitory peoples. It is part of the elven philosophy to let others go about their business with a minimum of interruption; aquatic elves would prefer it if others returned the favor.

Those aquatic elves who are willing to deal with non-elves are highly insulted if the non-elves expresses any lack of confidence in the sea elf's word. An aquatic elf who makes a promise will carry out his obligation unto death. Should he be killed before he can succeed, his entire band will work to see that the promise is fulfilled. On the other hand, aquatic elves do not accept promises from non-elven characters. The sea elves know that they are the only race with the honor to carry out the duties of its dead members. And, besides, only elves live long enough to guarantee that they will have the time to fulfill a vow.

Dolphins are one of the few creatures the sea elves genuinely like. There are 3d6 + 2 dolphins swimming about most aquatic elf bands, providing one of the few clues as to where the elven cities are located. Aquatic elves are also fairly fond of land elves. It is uncertain how closely related the two races are, although matings between land elves and aquatic elves produce elves with the coloring of high elves, but with greenish hair. As they have hidden gill slits that open up when they dive under the surface, these elves can breathe either air or water indefinitely. The attitudes and abilities of these half-breeds depend upon whether they were reared in the forests or the rich kelp beds, with individuals inclined (65%) to follow the lifestyles of their mothers.

Sea elves have an outlook on the world that comes from long lives among quiet natural beauty. Even with magical assistance to enable them to breathe air, aquatic elves are uncomfortable above the waves, and so very few have seen the forests that the high elves speak of with such enthusiasm. But there are few aquatic elves who would not like to take the impossible trip overland to see the wonders of a forest first-hand.

Sea elves hate sahuagin. This isn't much of a surprise, as almost every undersea race, with the exception of the perverse ixitachitls, hates the sea-devils. But sea elves generate a passion for conflict with the sahuagin that surprises even themselves. Aquatic elves leave their sheltered bands in war parties if they have reason to suspect that sahuagin are dwelling nearby. Should a party of sea elves encounter sahuagin, the former nearly always attack if they outnumber their hated foes. Aquatic elves also make it a point to kill any great sharks in their territory.

Sea elves have no other major enemies, but they dislike surface-dwelling fishermen, due to the numbers of sea elves snared in nets, or mistakenly killed as sahuagin by these ignorant humans.

The sea elves have legends that speak of far-away undersea elves who have learned to shapechange into sea otters or dolphins. There have been search parties motivated by these tales, but no such elves have ever been found.

Ecology: Each band of sea elves is self-sufficient, raising their kelp and hunting fish when necessary.

Sea elves scavenge. They are enchanted by the idea of magic, but they realize that land elves are more equipped to deal with it. They often trade rare or decorative items they have found to the high elves in exchange for metal weapons and tools, which they cannot forge underwater.

Aquatic elves are valuable sources of information regarding the lands beneath the sea. Their scavenging parties have uncovered artifacts and tidbits of knowledge from a vast collection of underwater ruins and sunken ships. Sea elf traders remember the histories of other races back beyond the imaginings of the current generation. The trick is to get them to reveal this information.

Malenti
There is a bond between aquatic elves and their hated enemies, the sahuagin, that neither race openly acknowledges. If sea elves are present within a mile or so of a sahuagin encampment, then approximately one out of every hundred sahuagin births resembles an aquatic elf rather than a sea-devil. Most of the time, these offspring, known as malenti, are eaten by their parents. Once in a great while, a malenti is allowed to live to adulthood because its physical resemblance to an aquatic elf, in combination with its sahuagin upbringing and attitude, make it an ideal spy in elven communities. Indeed, malenti often develop the ability to sense the presence and position of any aquatic elves within 120 feet, an invaluable skill for either a spy or a scout for an invading sahuagin force.

Few aquatic elves believe in the existence of malenti, as they suggest some disturbing possibilities about sahuagin origins.

Malenti do exist, however, and are identical to aquatic elves in most ways. They age much faster, though, with a life span of only 170 years or so. Although the sea elves themselves have a difficult time discerning malenti spies, dolphins might (20%) sense one of the changelings. malenti, understandably, aren't fond of dolphins.

It is possible for sahuagin and malenti to breed, the issue invariably being malenti. In this way, whole sahuagin communities have vanished, replaced by malenti. These extraordinarily rare bands resemble aquatic elves in nearly every way (except life span, known languages and other obvious aspects), but they are just as evil as their sahuagin parents. They often fight in that style, and they worship the same evil powers as the sahuagin.

Elf, Drow

	Drow	Drider
CLIMATE/TERRAIN:	Subterranean caves & cities	Subterranean caves & cities
FREQUENCY:	Very rare	Very rare
ORGANIZATION:	Clans, bands	Bands
ACTIVITY CYCLE:	—Any underground, night aboveground—	
DIET:	Omnivorous	See below
INTELLIGENCE:	High to Supra- (13-14)	High (14-20)
TREASURE:	Nx5, Qx2	N ×2, Q
ALIGNMENT:	Chaotic evil	Chaotic evil

NO. APPEARING:	50	1 or 1-4
ARMOR CLASS:	4 (10)	3
MOVEMENT:	12	12
HIT DICE:	2	6+6
THAC0:	19	13
NO. OF ATTACKS:	1 or 2	1
DAMAGE/ATTACK:	By weapon	1-4 or by weapon
SPECIAL ATTACKS:	See below	See below
SPECIAL DEFENSES:	See below	Nil
MAGIC RESISTANCE:	See below	15%
SIZE:	M (5' tall)	L (9' tall)
MORALE:	Elite (14)	Elite (14)
XP VALUE:	Priests: 975 Others: 650	Transformed mages: 3,000 Transformed priests: 5,000

These dreaded, evil creatures were once part of the community of elves that still roam the world's forests. Now these dark elves inhabit black caves and winding tunnels under the earth, where they make dire plans against the races that still walk beneath the sun, on the surface of the green earth.

Drow have black skin and pale, usually white hair. They are shorter and more slender than humans, seldom reaching more than 5 feet in height. Male drow weigh between 80 and 110 pounds, and females between 95 and 120 pounds. Drow have finely chiseled features, and their fingers and toes are long and delicate. Like all elves, they have higher Dexterity and lower Constitution than men.

Drow clothing is usually black, functional, and often possesses special properties, although it does not radiate magic. For example, drow cloaks and boots act as if they are *cloaks of and boots of elvenkind*, except that the wearer is only 75% likely to remain undetected in shadows or to surprise enemies. The material used to make drow cloaks does not cut easily and is fire resistant, giving the cloaks a +6 bonus to saving throws vs. fire. These cloaks and boots fit and function only for those of elven size and build. Any attempt to alter a drow cloak has a 75% chance of unraveling the material, making it useless.

In the centuries they've spent underground, drow have learned the languages of many of the intelligent creatures of the underworld. Besides their own tongue, an exotic variant of elvish, drow speak both common and the subterranean trade language used by many races under the earth. They speak the languages of gnomes and other elves fluently.

Drow also have their own silent language composed of both signed hand movements and body language. These signs can convey information, but not subtle meaning or emotional content. If within 30 feet of another drow, they can also use complex facial expressions, body movements, and postures to convey meaning. Coupled with their hand signs, these expressions and gestures give the drow's silent language a potential for expression equal to most spoken languages.

Combat: The drow's world is one in which violent conflict is part of everyday life. It should not be surprising then, that most drow encountered, whether alone or in a group, are ready to fight. Drow encountered outside of a drow city are at least 2nd-level fighters. (See Society note below.)

Drow wear finely crafted, non-encumbering, black mesh armor. This extremely strong mail is made with a special alloy of steel containing adamantite. The special alloy, when worked by a drow armorer, yields mail that has the same properties of *chain mail +1* to *+5*, although it does not radiate magic. Even the lowliest drow fighters have, in effect, *chain mail +1*, while higher level drow have more finely crafted, more powerful, mail. (The armor usually has a +1 for every four levels of experience of the drow wearing it.)

Dark elves also carry small shields (bucklers) fashioned of adamantite. Like drow armor, these special shields may be +1, +2, or even +3, though only the most important drow fighters have +3 bucklers.

Most drow carry a long dagger and a short sword of adamantite alloy. These daggers and swords can have a +1 to +3 bonus, and drow nobles may have daggers and swords of +4 bonus. Some drow (50%) also carry small crossbows that can be held in one hand and will shoot darts up to 60 yards. The darts only inflict 1-3 points of damage, but dark elves commonly coat them with poison that renders a victim unconscious, unless he rolls a successful saving throw vs. poison, with a −4 penalty. The effects last 2d4 hours.

A few drow carry adamantite maces (+1 to +5 bonus) instead of blades. Others carry small javelins coated with the same poison as the darts. They have a range of 90 yards with a short range bonus of +3, a +2 at medium, and a +1 at long.

Drow move silently and have superior infravision (120 feet). They also have the same intuitive sense about their underground world as dwarves do, and can detect secret doors with the same chance of success as other elves. A dark elf can only be surprised by an opponent on a roll of 1 on 1d10.

All dark elves receive training in magic, and are able to use the following spells once per day: *dancing lights, faerie fire,* and *darkness*. Drow above 4th level can use *levitate, know alignment,* and *detect magic* once per day. Drow priests can also use *detect lie, clairvoyance, suggestion,* and *dispel magic* once per day.

Perhaps it is the common use of magic in drow society that has given the dark elves their incredible resistance. Drow have a base resistance to magic of 50%, which increases by 2% for each level of experience. (Multi-classed drow gain the bonus from only the class in which they have the highest level.) All dark elves save vs. all forms of magical attack (including devices) with a +2 bonus. Thus, a 5th-level drow has a 60% base magic resistance and a +2 bonus to her saving throws vs. spells that get past her magic resistance.

Drow encountered in a group always have a leader of a higher level than the rest of the party. If 10 or more drow are encountered, a fighter/mage of at least 3rd level in each class is leading them. If 20 drow are encountered, then, in addition to the higher level fighter/mage, there is a fighter/priest of at least the 6th level in both classes. If there are more than 30, up to 50% are priests and the leader is at least a 7th-level fighter/8th-level priest, with a 5th-level fighter/4th-level mage for an assistant, in addition to the other high level leaders.

Dark elves do have one great weakness + bright light. Because the drow have lived so long in the earth, rarely venturing to the surface, they are no longer able to tolerate bright light of any kind. Drow within the radius of a *light* or *continual light* spell are 90% likely to be seen. In addition, they lose 2 points from their Dexterity and attack with a −2 penalty inside the area of these spells. Characters subject to spells cast by drow affected by a *light* or *continual light* spell add a +2 bonus to their saving throws. If drow are attacking a target that is in the area of effect of a *light* or *continual light* spell, they suffer an additional −1 penalty to their attack rolls, and targets of drow magical attacks save at an additional +1. These penalties are cumulative (i.e., if both the drow and their targets are in the area of effect of a *light* spell, the drow suffer a −3 penalty to their attack rolls and the targets gain a +3).

Because of the serious negative effects of strong light on the drow, they are 75% likely to leave an area of bright light, unless they are in battle. Light sources like torches, lanterns, magical weapons, or *faerie fire* spells, do not affect drow.

Habitat/society: Long ago, dark elves were part of the elven race that roamed the world's forests. Not long after they were created, though, the elves found themselves torn into rival factions + one following the tenets of evil, the other owning the ideals of good (or at least neutrality). A great civil war between the elves followed, and the selfish elves who followed the paths of evil and chaos were driven into the depths of the earth, into the bleak, lightless caverns and deep tunnels of the underworld. These dark elves became the drow.

The drow no longer wish to live upon the surface of the earth. In fact, few who live on the surface ever see a drow. But the dark elves resent the elves and faeries who drove them away, and scheme against those that dwell in the sunlight.

Drow live in magnificently dark, gloomy cities in the underworld that few humans or demihumans ever see. They construct their buildings entirely out of stone and minerals, carved into weird, fantastic shapes. Those few surface creatures that have seen a dark elf city (and returned to tell the tale) report that it is the stuff of which nightmares are made.

Drow society is fragmented into many opposing noble houses and merchant families, all scrambling for power. In fact, all drow carry brooches inscribed with the symbol of the merchant or noble group they are allied with, though they hide these and do not show them often. The drow believe that the strongest should rule; their rigid class system, with a long and complicated list of titles and prerogatives, is based on the idea.

They worship a dark goddess, called Lolth by some, and her priestesses hold very high places in society. Since most drow priests are female, women tend to fill nearly all positions of great importance.

Drow fighters go through rigorous training while they are young. Those who fail the required tests are killed at the program's conclusion. That is why dark elf fighters of less than 2nd level are rarely seen outside a drow city.

Drow often use giant lizards as pack animals, and frequently take bugbears or troglodytes as servants. Drow cities are havens for evil beings, including mind flayers, and drow are allied with many of the underworld's evil inhabitants. On the other hand, they are constantly at war with many of their neighbors beneath the earth, including dwarves or dark gnomes (svirfneblin) who settle to close to a drow city. Dark elves frequently keep slaves of all types, including past allies who have failed to live up to drow expectations.

Ecology: The drow produce unusual weapons and clothing with quasi-magical properties. Some scribes and researchers suggest that it is the strange radiation around drow cities that make drow crafts special. Others theorize that fine workmanship gives their wonderfully strong metals and superior cloth its unique attributes. Whatever the reason, it's clear that the drow have discovered some way to make their clothing and weapons without the use of magic.

Direct sunlight utterly destroys drow cloth, boots, weapons, and armor. When any item produced by them is exposed to the light of the sun, irreversible decay begins. Within 2d6 days, the items lose their magical properties and rot, becoming totally worthless. Drow artifacts, protected from sunlight, retain their special properties for ld20+30 days before becoming normal items. If a drow item is protected from direct sunlight and exposed to the radiations of the drow underworld for one week out of every four, it will retain its properties indefinitely.

Drow sleep poison, used on their darts and javelins, is highly prized by traders on the surface. However, this poison loses its potency instantly when exposed to sunlight, and remains effective for only 60 days after it is exposed to air. Drow poison remains potent for a year if kept in an unopened packet.

Driders

These strange creatures have the head and torso of a drow and the legs and lower body of a giant spider. Driders are created by the drow's dark goddess. When a dark elf of above-average ability reaches 6th level, the goddess may put him or her through a special test. Failures become driders.

Driders are able to cast all spells a normal drow can use once per day. They also retain any magical or clerical skills they had before transformation. A majority of driders (60%) were priests of 6th or 7th level before they were changed, all other driders were mages of 6th, 7th, or 8th level.

Driders always fight as 7 Hit Die monsters. They often use swords or axes, though many carry bows. Driders can bite for ld4 points of damage, and those bitten must save vs. poison with a −2 penalty or be paralyzed for 1-2 turns.

Because they have failed their goddess's test, driders are outcasts from their own communities. Driders are usually found alone or with 2d6 huge spiders (10% chance), rather than with drow or other driders. They are violent, aggressive creatures that favor blood over all types of food. They stalk their victims tirelessly, waiting for the right chance to strike.

Ettercap

CLIMATE/TERRAIN:	Heavily wooded forest
FREQUENCY:	Rare
ORGANIZATION:	Solitary or pairs
ACTIVITY CYCLE:	Any
DIET:	Carnivore
INTELLIGENCE:	Low (5-7)
TREASURE:	Nil
ALIGNMENT:	Neutral evil

NO. APPEARING:	1-2
ARMOR CLASS:	6
MOVEMENT:	12
HIT DICE:	5
THAC0:	15
NO. OF ATTACKS:	3
DAMAGE/ATTACK:	1-3/1-3/1-8
SPECIAL ATTACKS:	Poison
SPECIAL DEFENSES:	Traps (see below)
MAGIC RESISTANCE:	Nil
SIZE:	M (6' tall)
MORALE:	Elite (13)
XP VALUE:	650

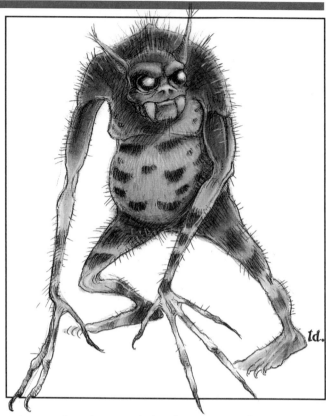

Ettercaps are ugly bipedal creatures that get along very well with all types of giant spiders. These creatures of low intelligence are exceedingly cruel, very cunning, and are skilled in setting traps—very deadly traps—much like the spiders that often live around them.

Ettercaps stand around six feet tall, even with their stooping gait and hunched shoulders. The creatures have short, spindly legs, long arms that reach nearly to their ankles, and large potbellies. The hands of ettercaps have a thumb and three long fingers that end in razor sharp claws. Their bodies are covered by tufts of thick, wiry, black hair, and their skin is dark and thick. Ettercaps' heads are almost equine in shape, but they have large reptilian eyes, usually blood-red in color, and large fangs, one protruding downward from each side of the mouth. The mouth itself is large and lined with very sharp teeth.

Ettercaps do not have a formal language. They express themselves through a combination of high-pitched chittering noises, shrieks, and violent actions.

Combat: If caught in a battle, an ettercap first strikes with its claws, causing 1-3 points of damage with each set. The creature then tries to bite its opponent, inflicting 1d8 points of damage with its teeth and powerful jaws. A successful bite attack by an ettercap enables the monster to inject its victim with a powerful poison from the glands above the ettercap's fangs.

The poison secreted by an ettercap is highly toxic and very similar to the poison of giant spiders. A creature injected with it must immediately roll a saving throw vs. poison. A failed roll means that the creature dies within 1d4 turns when the toxigen paralyzes the victim's heart.

Many adventurers never get the chance to raise a sword against ettercaps because of the devious traps they use for protection. Ettercaps prefer to ambush unwary travelers and lead them into traps rather than fight them face to face.

Like spiders, ettercaps have silk glands located in their abdomen. The thin, strong strands of silvery silk-like material these glands secrete are used by ettercaps to construct elaborate traps made up of nets, trip wires, garrotes, and anything else the monsters can make out of the strands. The traps are designed so that they often immobilize the adventurer who stumbles into it. If this is the case, ettercaps never hesitate to attack that character first,

trying to poison the victim before he escapes. Different ettercaps prefer different trap designs, so encounters with different ettercaps should expose the adventurer to new traps each time.

Habitat/Society: Ettercaps prefer to dwell in the deepest part of a forest, near paths that are frequented by game or travelers. The creatures' nests are made of a frame of strands filled with rotting leaves and moss. The lairs are often located on the ground, but can also be found up in large, sturdy trees. No treasure is to be found in ettercap lairs, but occasionally items dropped by adventurers who have fallen into ettercap traps are found nearby.

Though usually only one ettercap is encountered at any time, on rare occasions a pair of ettercaps can be found together. The pairs encountered are always mated couples, though the female and male appear to be identical. Ettercap young are abandoned as soon as they are born, so adults are never encountered with young.

Ecology: An ettercap eats any meat, regardless of the type of creature from which it comes. Upon capturing a victim, the ettercap poisons it so it cannot escape; once the creature is dead, the ettercap immediately devours as much of the corpse as possible. Typically, an ettercap can consume an entire deer or a large humanoid in a single sitting. Anything remaining after the ettercap has gorged itself is left for scavengers.

Often (40%), 2d4 spiders of some monstrous type are found cooperating with an ettercap. The ettercap uses any giant spider webs available when it designs its traps. Creatures killed by an ettercap in the web of a giant spider are shared with the spider instead of being devoured entirely by the ettercap.

Ettercap poison is highly valued, partly because of its extreme toxicity and partly because it is rather difficult to obtain. An ettercap's poison glands hold only one ounce of poison at any time, but this ounce is worth up to 1,000 gp on the open market.

Eyewing

CLIMATE/TERRAIN:	The Abyss (preferred)
FREQUENCY:	Rare
ORGANIZATION:	Band
ACTIVITY CYCLE:	Any
DIET:	None known
INTELLIGENCE:	Low (5-7)
TREASURE:	Nil
ALIGNMENT:	Lawful evil

NO. APPEARING:	1-20
ARMOR CLASS:	4
MOVEMENT:	Fl 24 (B)
HIT DICE:	3
THAC0:	17
NO. OF ATTACKS:	3 or 1
DAMAGE/ATTACK:	1-6/1-6/1-4 or eyewing tears
SPECIAL ATTACKS:	Tears
SPECIAL DEFENSES:	See below
MAGIC RESISTANCE:	Nil
SIZE:	L (15′ wingspan)
MORALE:	Steady (12)
XP VALUE:	650

Eyewings are loathsome inhabitants of the Abyss. They are obedient, loyal, and dumb—perfect servitors for the dark gods and their more powerful minions.

An eyewing's body is a fat, egg-shaped ball covered with matted black fur. The 5-foot-wide body is supported by a pair of five-foot-long leathery bat wings. Each wing is tipped with a set of three razor-sharp talons. An 8-foot-long rat's tail dangles from the back of the body. The tail ends in a small, sharp spur. It has no feet and has never been known to land.

The body is dominated by the single, bulging, 4-foot-wide eyeball. The eyeball is black with a blood-red pupil. A vile blue fluid continuously leaks from the eye, soiling its fur. Great leathery eyelids squeeze this fluid out and away from the creature. The stench is unbelievable. It gives off an acidic smell that scorches the sensitive tissues in other creatures' noses and mouths.

Combat: An eyewing has two main forms of attack. The most common form is to use its claws and tail to strike its opponents. It can either swoop down on them, or hover and slash. Its second form of attack is to bomb its enemies with a large eyewing tear that is squeezed out of the large eyeball by the leathery eyelid. It has amazing control over the release of the tear—it has the same chance to hit with a tear as with its melee attacks. It releases a tear when it is within 100 feet of its target. It can deliver this attack while hovering or diving.

An eyewing tear is a one-foot-diameter ball of poisonous blue fluid. The attack roll determines if the target dodged the tear. If the tear hits, the victim must roll a successful saving throw vs. poison or suffer 2d6 points of damage (success means only 1d6 points of damage). The tears may also splash onto anyone within ten feet of the target. The attack roll for the splash attack is made with a -2 penalty. If someone is splashed, a saving throw vs. poison must be rolled; those who fail suffer 2d4 points of damage, while those who succeed suffer 1d4 points of damage.

A tear hardens into a rubbery lump within 2d6 hours after be-

ing shed. The exact time depends upon the humidity, temperature, etc. Anybody handling a hardened tear must roll a successful saving throw vs. poison or suffer 1 point of damage.

Eyewings have extremely acute vision that enables them to see with perfect accuracy for up to 25 miles. They also have infravision out to 120 feet. They are immune to all cold-based attack forms, as are their tears.

Habitat/Society: Eyewings are supernatural creatures that exist only to serve their dark masters. When left without orders they become sluggish and listless. This should not be taken to mean that they are any less dangerous. This listlessness is their expression of boredom, but nothing relieves eyewing boredom quite like tearing apart innocent creatures.

Eyewings have no society as such. They do not have a culture. Their simple language consists of shrill squeaks. They understand other spoken languages, but cannot speak them. When in the Abyss they are found only on layers that allow for flying. Their immunity to cold makes them at home on any of the icy layers as well.

Ecology: Eyewings are sexless creatures that are not a part of nature. They kill even when they're not ordered to, just for the pleasure of it. Eyewings have been encountered on the moon, where there is no air to breathe and no water to drink. It is assumed that they do not need air or water. They have never been seen to eat; it is assumed by most who have studied them that they are sustained by magic. The more powerful creatures of the Abyss have no qualms about an eyewing snack should one be nearby, but they are not the natural prey of any creature.

Feyr

	Feyr	Great Feyr
CLIMATE/TERRAIN:	Urban	Any
FREQUENCY:	Very rare	Very rare
ORGANIZATION:	Loose band	Solitary
ACTIVITY CYCLE:	Night	Any
DIET:	Emotions	Emotions
INTELLIGENCE:	Low (5)	High (14)
TREASURE:	Nil	Nil
ALIGNMENT:	Chaotic evil	Chaotic evil
NO. APPEARING:	1-4	1
ARMOR CLASS:	2	−2
MOVEMENT:	12	12, Fl 18 (B)
HIT DICE:	4	16
THAC0:	17	5
NO. OF ATTACKS:	1	1-4
DAMAGE/ATTACK:	1-4	2-12/2-12/2-12/ 2-12
SPECIAL ATTACKS:	Fear	Emotion control
SPECIAL DEFENSES:	Nil	Invisibility
MAGIC RESISTANCE:	10%	40%
SIZE:	S (2' tall)	M (7' tall)
MORALE:	Fanatic (18)	Fanatic (18)
XP VALUE:	975	13,000

Feyrs (pronounced "fears") are created from the remnants of ordinary nightmares, mixed with residual magical energies, and unknowingly brought to life by the strong emotions of a large group of people. They are most commonly found in large cities that have a good number of mages, priests, and other spellcasters. Normal feyrs stalk the streets at night, seeking nothing more than to create havoc. Great feyrs, on the other hand, are the combination of lesser feyrs, and may be found anywhere, though they a much rarer than the common feyrs.

Common feyrs appear as humped, hunchbacked creatures, grim and inhuman in appearance. Their hide is mottled and warped like the surface of the human brain. The creature is supported by two main tentacles which act as legs, and by a handful of other tentacled limbs. Massive horizontal jaws line its underside, and the forepart of the beast has 1-5 eyes, usually the color of melted gold. The feyr's hide is a sickly rainbow of shades, like light reflected off an oil slick. There are dull blues and blacks along the body, pale reds and magentas toward the head, and deathly greens and yellows along the belly.

Combat: The horizontal jaws of the feyr slung beneath its belly are the creature's prime form of attack, inflicting 1d4 points of damage for common feyrs, 2d6 points for great feyrs. The feyr does not use its jaws to eat, but rather to strike terror into the hearts of those who witness its savage and bloody attacks. Those who witness the attack of either type of feyr must make a successful saving throw vs. *spells* or be consumed by *fear* (as the spell of the same name). This *fear* acts for 1d4 rounds for common feyrs, and 2d6 rounds for great feyrs. This form of *fear* only applies when the creature attacks. Merely sighting a common feyr does not inspire *fear*.

The great feyr has an additional power that can affect the emotions similar to the 4th-level wizard spell *emotion*. The range of this attack is 100 yards, may affect a 20-foot by 20-foot area, and the intended victim must make a successful saving throw vs. *spells* at −2 or be affected. Only the negative emotions of *fear*, *hate*, *hopelessness*, and *sadness* may be cast by the great feyr. The great feyr may cast this spell and retain its *invisibility*.

Common feyrs are slain by direct sunlight, though they have no fear of it themselves, and do not seek shelter with the coming sun, nor hesitate to venture out if they are still alive after sun-up.

Common feyrs can use a saving throw vs. spells against sunlight created by magic spells, such as *continual light*, in addition to their standard magic resistance. Greater feyrs are unaffected by sunlight.

Habitat/Society: Individual common feyrs are slain by the morning light. There are occasions when several common feyrs combine to form a great feyr, which in addition to being immune to the effects of the sun, is much more intelligent. The greater feyr seeks to inspire even stronger emotions, which it may then use to stay alive. While common feyrs do not travel far from their point of origin, great feyrs may undertake long trips, lured by strong emotional states.

While a common feyr merely slouches through the evening shadows and fogs, looking for a collection of victims to terrorize and thereby enrich itself on their emotions, a great feyr chooses to attack while *invisible*, playing the emotions of others, heightening emotional states already present, and driving mortal beings mad with terror and fear. While the great feyr is not banished by daylight, it prefers to work at night, and seeks to retreat into a hidden lair during daylight hours, preferably some abandoned area such as an old house, cavern, or underground structure.

Ecology: Common feyrs are created by the emotions of large masses of people, and great feyrs by compilations of lesser feyrs. The raw materials for such creatures may be found in any urban settlement, and when there is additional tension in the air, the feyrs stalk at night. Cities under siege, towns divided by rivalries or civil wars, oppressed peoples, and settlements baking under a merciless summer heat are all possible breeding grounds of feyrs. Guard and watch units are usually more than sufficient to handle the common feyrs, as those feyrs attack anything that moves. But the more dangerous great feyrs must be dealt with by a wizard or similar high-level individual, who can both withstand the attack of the feyr and dispatch it.

Fish	#AP	AC	MV	HD	THAC0	# of Att	Dmg/Att	Morale	XP Value
Barracuda	2-12	6	Sw 30	1 to 3	1-2 HD: 19 3 HD: 17	1	2-8	Steady (11)	1 HD: 15 2 HD: 35 3 HD: 65
Carp, Giant	1-4	6	Sw 18	8 to 12	8 HD: 13 9-10 HD: 11 11-12 HD: 9	1	2-20	Average (9)	8 HD: 3,000 9 HD: 4,000 10 HD 5,000 11 HD: 6,000 12 HD: 7,000
Catfish, Giant	1	7	Sw 18	7 to 10	7-8 HD: 13 9-10 HD: 11	1	3-12	Average (9)	7 HD: 2,000 8 HD: 3,000 9 HD: 4,000 10 HD: 5,000
Dragonfish	1	4	Sw 6	2	19	1	1-6	Unsteady (5)	270
Eel, Electric	1-3	9	Sw 12	2	16	1	1-3	Unsteady (7)	65
Eel, Giant	1-4	6	Sw 9	5	15	1	3-18	Average (8)	175
Eel, Marine	1	6	Sw 9	6 to 8	6-7 HD: 13 8 HD: 12	1 1 1	6 HD: 2-8 7 HD: 3-12 8 HD: 4-16	Average (9)	420 650 975
Eel, Weed	10-60	8	Sw 15	1-1	20	1	1	Unsteady (6)	120
Gar, Giant	1-6	3	Sw 30	8	13	1	5-20	Average (10)	2,000
Lamprey	1-2	7	Sw 12	1+2	19	1	1-2	Unsteady (7)	65
Lamprey, Giant	1-4	6	Sw 9	5	15	1	1-6	Average (9)	270
Lamprey, Land	2-12	7	12	1+2	19	2	1 hp/round	Unsteady (7)	120
Manta Ray	1	6	Sw 18	8 to 11	8 HD: 13 9-10 HD: 11 11 HD: 9	1	3-12 or 2-20	Elite (13)	3,000 4,000 5,000 6,000
Pike, Giant	1-8	5	Sw 36	4	17	1	4-16	Average (8)	175
Piranha	5-50	8	Sw 9	1/2	20	1	1-2	Unsteady (6)	7
Piranha, Giant	2-20	7	Sw 15	2+2	19	1	1-6	Average (10)	65
Pungi Ray	1-3	7	Sw 12	4	17	1-12	1-4	Unsteady (5)	975
Quipper	5-50	8	Sw 9	1/2	20	1	1-2	Unsteady (6)	7
Sea Horse, Giant	1-20	7	Sw 21	2 to 4	2 HD: 19 3-4 HD: 17	1	1-4, 2-5, or 2-8	Average (10)	2 HD: 35 3 HD: 65 4 HD: 120
Shark	3-12	6	Sw 24	3 to 8	3-4 HD: 17 5-6 HD: 15 7-8 HD: 13	1	3-4 HD: 2-5 5-6 HD: 2-8 7-8 HD: 3-12	Average (10)	3 HD: 65 4 HD: 120 5 HD: 175 6 HD: 270 7 HD: 420 8 HD: 650
Shark, Giant	1-3	5	Sw 18	10 to 15	10 HD: 11 11-12 HD: 9 13-14 HD: 7 15 HD: 5	1	10-11 HD: 4-16 12-13 HD: 5-20 14-15 HD: 6-24	Steady (11)	10 HD: 2,000 11 HD: 3,000 12 HD: 5,000 13 HD: 6,000 14 HD: 7,000 15 HD: 8,000
Sting Ray	1-3	7	Sw 9	1	20	1	1-3	Unsteady (5)	120

Giant fish are a diverse group of creatures with varying attack and defense capabilities. Many of these creatures are able to swallow victims whole. Swallowed victims take normal bite damage. Victims take 1 point of damage per round from the fish's digestive juices and have a 5% cumulative chance per round of suffocating. To escape the fish's stomach, a victim can cut free with a sharp-edged weapon. The victim may be rescued by cutting or tearing from the outside. When the fish has lost 50% of its hit points, the victim breaks free.

Barracuda
The first clue that a barracuda is in the area might be a sudden pain in the foot, as the marauder swims by and bites off a few tender toes. They are found in warm salt waters.

Carp, Giant
Giant carp attack by biting, inflicting 2-20 points of damage with their sharp, curved teeth. Additionally, if an attack causes 12 or more points of damage, the carp swallows its victim.

Catfish, Giant
A giant catfish bites for 3d4 points of damage. It swallows it prey if its attack roll is 4 points more than it needed. The fish can employ its feelers as weapons by whipping its head back and forth. These feelers secrete a

toxin that causes 2d4 points of damage. A save vs. poison limits the damage to 1d4 points. Two additional opponents can be attacked if they are within range of the feelers.

Dragonfish
Dragonfish bite for 1-6 points of damage. However, most adventurers stumble across these creatures. These encounters cause 1d6 of the fish's spines to penetrate boots, causing 1 point of damage apiece before snapping off in the wound. The spines' poison is slow-acting, and creatures injected with the toxin must make a saving throw vs. poison at a −4 or dies. If successful, the character suffers a −2 penalty on all attack rolls for the next 1d12 + 4 hours.

Eel, Electric
An attacking eel discharges a jolt of electricity with a 15-foot-radius range. Creatures less than 5 feet from the eel suffer 3d8 points of damage, creatures 5 to 10 feet away receive 2d8 points, and all others in range suffer 1d8 points. An eel must recharge itself for an hour between attacks. It is immune to electrical effects.

Eel, Giant
Giant eels have no electrical discharge attack. Instead, they attack with

Fish

their teeth. Since they strike with amazing speed, giant eels receive a +1 bonus to initiative rolls.

Eel, Marine
Marine eels have an electrical discharge with a range of 15 feet; creatures less than 5 feet from the eel suffer 6d6 points of damage, those 5 to 10 feet away receive 4d6 points, and all others in range suffer 2d6 points. Victims must roll a saving throw vs. paralyzation or be stunned for a number of rounds equal to the damage they sustained from the electrical shock. This eel, too, is immune to electrical effects.

Eel, Weed
The bite of the weed eel is poisonous; victims failing a saving throw vs. poison die in 1d4 rounds.

Weed eels are at home in both fresh and salt water, 25 to 40 feet deep. Each colony has a lair consisting of a central cave, roughly 30 feet long and 20 feet wide and high. The floor of the central cave is covered with small stones, coins, and gems that the eels have scavenged. Radiating from this central cave are a series of 6-foot-diameter tunnels, which in turn lead to a network of 6 to 8-inch-diameter holes. These are the homes of the individual eels that make up the colony. Weed eels are fiercely protective of their lairs, especially the central cave where their young are raised.

Gar, Giant
The gar attacks with its teeth, inflicting 8d4 points of damage. On a score of 20, the gar swallows its victim whole. On average, a giant gar can swallow an object up to 5 feet long. Giant gars are found in deep, freshwater lakes and rivers.

Lamprey
The lamprey feeds by biting its victims, and fastening itself by its sphincter-like mouth. Once attached, the lamprey drains 2 hit points per Hit Die of blood on the next and successive rounds. Sea lampreys are especially susceptible to fire, making their saving throws against fire-based attacks with a −2 penalty.

Lamprey, Land
Land lampreys feed as do aquatic ones. Once attached (a hit for 1 point of damage), it drains blood for three rounds, unless killed or removed, for 1 point of damage per round. In addition, while attached to a character, each lamprey encumbers an individual; this is equivalent to a loss of 1 point of Dexterity per lamprey attached.

Manta Ray
If the manta's attack roll is 2 or more greater than the number needed to hit, it swallows its prey. A manta ray can swallow one man-sized creature or three small-sized creatures. If opponents attack its rear, it uses its stinger for 2-20 points of damage; victims must save vs. paralyzation or be stunned for 2-8 rounds.

Pike, Giant
Because of its speed and natural camouflage, a pike's opponents suffer a −2 penalty to their surprise roll. Giant pike inhabit deep, freshwater lakes.

Piranha
Piranhas travel in schools of 5-50. There is a 75% chance that at least one will attack any creature that swims or wades near the school. If they attack and blood is drawn, the entire school goes berserk and each piranha attacks twice per melee round. Up to 20 piranhas can attack a single, man-sized individual simultaneously.

Piranha, Giant
Giant piranhas behave like their smaller counterparts, but only 10 can attack a single, man-sized individual simultaneously.

Giant piranhas are sometimes called sky-eaters; once per round they can charge at full speed and leap out of the water at heights of up to 10 feet; they often use this attack on water fowl that fly low over the water, but they sometimes use it against humans.

Pungi Ray
Any creature stepping on a pungi must save vs. poison or die. A footstep on a pungi ray equals one attack; if a creature fell on a pungi ray it would suffer 2-8 spinal attacks. If attacked, it swims away.

Quipper
Quippers are freshwater piranhas that live in colder waters.

Seahorse, Giant
A sea horse attacks with a head butt, but a sea horse trained as a steed can use its long tail to constrict and restrain enemies. A captured opponent can free itself with a open doors roll made with a −1 penalty. The tail of a giant sea horse is so long it can attack the same opponent its head butts, or the one its rider is attacking. The constriction causes no damage, but the sea horse can still butt the helpless victim.

Shark
Sharks attack mercilessly at the scent of blood, which they can detect a mile away. The scent of blood and the thrill of the kill sends sharks into a feeding frenzy. Since sharks move up, take a bite of flesh, and retreat, 10 normal-sized sharks can attack a man-sized opponent.

Shark, Giant
The huge megalodons (giant sharks) never reach a frenzy, since they can swallow most creatures whole on an attack roll 4 greater than minimum number needed to hit.

Sting Ray
If a creature steps on a sting ray, it lashes out with its tail spine. The creature must save vs. poison or be paralyzed for 5-20 turns.

	Giant	Killer	Poisonous
CLIMATE/TERRAIN:	Any fresh water	Any fresh water	Any fresh water
FREQUENCY:	Uncommon	Very rare	Rare
ORGANIZATION:	Pack	Pack	Pack
ACTIVITY CYCLE:	Any	Any	Any
DIET:	Carnivore	Carnivore	Insectivore
INTELLIGENCE:	Non- (0)	Non- (0)	Non- (0)
TREASURE:	Nil	Nil	Nil
ALIGNMENT:	Nil	Nil	Nil
NO. APPEARING:	5-40	3-18	2-12
ARMOR CLASS:	7	8	8
MOVEMENT:	3, Sw 9	6, Sw 12	3, Sw 9
HIT DICE:	1+3	1+4	1
THAC0:	1 HD: 19	18	19
	2-3 HD: 16		
NO. OF ATTACKS:	1	3	1
DAMAGE/ATTACK:	1-3/1-6/2-8	1-2/1-2/2-5	1
SPECIAL ATTACKS:	Tongue and swallow whole	Nil	Nil
SPECIAL DEFENSES:	Nil	Nil	Poison
MAGIC RESISTANCE:	Nil	Nil	Nil
SIZE:	T-M (2'-6' long)	S (3' long)	T (6'-1' long)
MORALE:	Average (8)	Unsteady (6)	Unsteady (6)
XP VALUE:	1 HD: 120	35	65
	2 HD: 175		
	3 HD: 270		

Giant Frogs: Giant frogs resemble their more common relatives in everything but size. Their enormous size means that they consider larger creatures as a source of food, making small creatures and even demihumans possible prey. A giant frog can range from 2 to 6 feet in length and weigh between 50 and 250 pounds (a 2-foot frog weighs 50 pounds, adding 50 pounds for each additional foot of length). Frogs with 1 Hit Die are 2 feet long, while those 2 to 4 feet long have 2 Hit Dice, and those over 4 feet long have 3 Hit Dice.

The distance that a giant frog can jump is based upon its weight, with the maximum jumping distance for a 50-pound frog being 180 feet. Subtract 20 feet for every additional 50 pounds the frog weighs. A giant frog cannot jump backward or directly to either side, but can leap 30 feet straight up.

Combat: Because of its camouflaging color, a giant frog surprises opponents easily (-3 penalty to opponents' surprise rolls) when in its natural habitat. A giant frog uses its long, sticky tongue to entrap its victim. The tongue is equal in length to three times the frog's length and strikes with a +4 bonus to the attack roll. The tongue inflicts no damage when it hits.

Once a victim is caught by the frog's tongue, it has one chance to hit the tongue before the frog attempts to reel it in. If the tongue is hit, the frog releases the victim and does not attack that creature again. Otherwise, the victim is reeled in.

If the victim weighs less than the frog, it is dragged into the frog's mouth in the same round it attacked and missed striking the tongue. If the creature weighs more than the frog, an extra round is required for the frog to draw the creature in. This grants the victim another opportunity to hit the tongue. Any creature weighing more than twice the frog's weight cannot be pulled by the frog and is released on the third round after it was caught, even if the tongue is never struck.

Once the victim has been drawn to the frog's mouth, the frog attempts to eat it. If the giant frog successfully bites its victim in the first round the creature is in range, it automatically scores maximum damage. Frogs with 1 Hit Die bite for 1-3 points of damage, those with 2 Hit Dice 1-6 points, and those with 3 Hit Dice inflict 2-8 points of biting damage.

On an attack roll result of 20, the frog can swallow whole any creature shorter than 3 feet long. Any creature swallowed whole has a chance to cut its way out of the frog with a sharp-edged weapon, but must roll an attack roll result of 18 or better. A victim has only three rounds to escape before asphyxiating. A successful escape kills the frog. Any damage inflicted upon a frog that has swallowed a creature whole has a 33% chance of also being inflicted on the swallowed victim.

Giant frogs fear fire and always retreat from it.

Habitat/Society: Giant frogs live in groups but don't have any real social structure. They are aggressive hunters and eat insects, fish, and small mammals. Large aquatic predators such as giant fish and giant turtles often prey upon them.

Killer Frogs: This smaller version of the giant frog attacks with sharp teeth and front talons. While it does not swallow victims whole, the killer frog is a vicious hunter and is especially fond of the taste of human flesh.

Poisonous Frogs: A rare type of normal frog, this breed secretes a contact poison from its skin, as well as with its bite. The weakness of the poison gives all victims a +4 bonus to their saving throws. Due to its weakness and the difficulty of collecting it, there is no market for this poison.

Fungus

	Violet	Shrieker	Phycomid	Ascomoid	Gas spore
CLIMATE/TERRAIN:	Subterranean	Subterranean	Subterranean	Subterranean	Subterranean
FREQUENCY:	Rare	Common	Rare	Very rare	Rare
ORGANIZATION:	Multicellular	Multicellular	Multicellular	Multicellular	Multicellular
ACTIVITY CYCLE:	Any	Any	Any	Any	Any
DIET:	Scavenger	Scavenger	Scavenger	Scavenger	Scavenger
INTELLIGENCE:	Non- (0)	Non- (0)	Unratable	Unratable	Non- (0)
TREASURE:	Nil	Nil	Nil	Nil	Nil
ALIGNMENT:	Neutral	Neutral	Neutral (evil)	Neutral (evil)	Neutral
NO. APPEARING:	1-4	2-8 (2d4)	1-4	1	1-3
ARMOR CLASS:	7	7	5	3	9
MOVEMENT:	1	1	3	12 (see below)	9
HIT DICE:	3	3	5	6+6	3
THAC0:	17	17	15	13	1 hp
NO. OF ATTACKS:	1-4	0	2	1	20
DAMAGE/ATTACK:	See below	Nil	3-6/3-6	See below	1
SPECIAL ATTACKS:	See below	Nil	Infection	Spore jet	See below
SPECIAL DEFENSES:	Nil	Noise	See below	See below	See below
MAGIC RESISTANCE:	Nil	Nil	Nil	Nil	See below
SIZE:	M (4'-7')	M (4'-7')	T (2' dia.)	M to L (5'-10' dia.)	Nil
MORALE:	Steady (12)	Steady (12)	Elite (14)	Champion (15)	M (4'-6' dia.)
XP VALUE:	175	120	650	1,400	Average (8)
					120

Fungi are simple plants that lack chlorophyll, true stems, roots, and leaves. Fungi are incapable of photosynthesis and live as parasites or saprophytes.

Ordinary Fungi

Ordinary fungi are well known to man: molds, yeast, mildew, mushrooms, and puffballs. These plants include both useful and harmful varieties.

Combat: Ordinary fungi do not attack or defend themselves, but they are prolific and can spread where unwanted.

Adventurers who have lost rations to mold or clothing to mildew have had unpleasant encounters with fungi.

Habitat/Society: The bodies of most true fungi consist of slender cottony filaments. Anyone who wishes to see this for himself need only leave a damp piece of bread in a cupboard for a day or two. Examining the black mold on the bread with a magnifying glass will show off not only the filaments, but also the spore bodies at the top of these. The spores are what gives mold its color.

Most fungi reproduce asexually by cell division, budding, fragmentation, or spores. Those that reproduce sexually alternate a sexual generation (gametophyte) with a spore-producing (sporophyte) one.

Fungi grow best in dark, damp environments, which they can find all too easily in a kitchen cupboard, backpack, or boot. A warm environment is preferred by some, such as yeasts and certain molds, but excessive heat kills fungi.

Proper storage and cleanliness can be used to avoid most ordinary fungi.

Ecology: Fungi break down organic matter, thus playing an important part in the nitrogen cycle by decomposing dead organisms into ammonia. Without the action of mushrooms and bracket fungi, soil renewal could not take place as readily as it does.

Fungi are also useful to man for many purposes. Yeasts are valuable as fermenting agents, raising bread and brewing wines, beers, and ales. Certain molds are important for cheese production. The color in blue cheese is a mold that has been encouraged to grow in this semisoft cheese.

Many fungi are edible, and connoisseurs consider some to be delicious. Pigs are used to hunt for truffles, an underground fungus that grows near tree roots and gives food a piquant flavor. No one has as yet managed to cultivate truffles—an enterprising botanist could make a mint by learning to grow these.

Mushrooms, the fruiting body of another underground fungus, can sometimes be eaten, but can be so poisonous that the novice mushroom hunter is allowed but one mistake in picking. The mycelium producing a single mushroom might extend beneath the ground for several feet in any direction.

Medicinally, green molds (such as penicillium) can be used as folk remedies for various bacterial infections.

An alchemist expert in the ways of fungi can produce a variety of useful substances from their action on various materials.

Violet Fungus

Violet fungus growths resemble shriekers, and are usually (75%) encountered with them. The latter are immune to the touch of violet fungi, and the two types of creatures complement each other's existence.

Combat: Violet fungi favor rotted animal matter to grow upon. Each fungus has one to four branches with which it flails out if any animal comes within range (see following). The excretion from these branches rots flesh in one round unless a successful saving throw vs. poison is rolled or a *cure disease* spell is used. The branch length of this fungi depends upon the fungi's size. Violet fungi range from four to seven feet tall, the smallest having one-foot-long branches, the five-foot-tall fungi having two-foot-long branches, and so on. Any sized growth can have up to four branches.

Shrieker

Shriekers are normally quiet, mindless fungi that are ambulatory. They are dangerous to dungeon explorers because of the hellish racket they make.

Combat: Light within 30 feet or movement within 10 feet causes a shrieker to emit a piercing shriek that lasts for 1-3 rounds. This noise has a 50% chance of attracting wandering monsters each round thereafter.

Habitat/Society: They live in dark places beneath the ground, often in the company of violet fungi. When the shriekers attract curious dungeon dwellers by their shrieking, the violet fungi are able to kill them with their branches, leaving plenty of organic matter for these saprophytic life forms to feed on.

Ecology: Purple worms and shambling mounds greatly prize shriekers as food, and don't seem to mind the noise while eating.

Shrieker spores are an important ingredient in potions of plant control.

Phycomid

The algae-like phycomids resemble fibrous blobs of decomposing, milk-colored matter with capped fungi growing out of them. They exude a highly alkaline substance (like lye) when attacking.

Combat: These fungoid monsters have sensory organs for heat, sound, and vibrations located in several clusters. When phycomids attack, they extrude a tube and discharge the alkaline fluid in small globules that have a range of 1d6+6 feet.

In addition to alkaline damage, the globs that these creatures discharge might also cause victims to serve as hosts for new phycomid growth. If a victim fails a saving throw vs. poison, the individual begins to sprout mushroom-like growths in the infected area. This occurs in 1d4+4 rounds and inflicts 1d4+4 points of damage. The growths then spread throughout the host body, killing it in 1d4+4 turns, and turning it into a new phycomid. A *cure disease* spell will stop the spread through the host.

Ascomoid

Ascomoids are huge, puffball-like fungi with very thick, leathery skin. They move by rolling.

Combat: At first, an ascomoid's movement is slow—3 for the first round, 6 the next, then 9, then finally 12—but they can keep it up for hours without tiring.

Ascomoids attack by rolling into or over opponents. Small- and medium-sized opponents are knocked down and must rise during the next round or remain prone.

The creature's surface is covered with numerous pocks which serve as sensory organs. Each pock can also emit a jet of spores to attack dangerous enemies. Large opponents or those who have inflicted damage upon the ascomoids are always attacked by spore jets. The stream of spores is about one foot in diameter and 30 feet long. Upon striking, the stream puffs into a cloud of variable diameter (five to 20 feet). The creatures under attack must roll a successful saving throw vs. poison or die from infection in their internal systems in 1d4 rounds. Even those who save are blinded and choked to such an extent that they require 1d4 rounds to recover and rejoin melee. Meanwhile, they are nearly helpless, and all attacks upon them gain a +4 bonus to attack rolls with no shield or Dexterity bonuses allowed.

Different types of weapons affect the ascomoid differently. Piercing weapons, such as spears, score double damage. Shorter stabbing weapons do damage as if against a small-sized opponent. Blunt weapons do not harm ascomoids; slashes and cuts from edged weapons cause only 1 point of damage. An ascomoid saves against magical attacks, such as magic missiles, fireballs, and lightning, with a +4 bonus to the saving throw; damage is only 50% of normal. (Cold-based attacks are at normal probabilities and damage.) As these fungi have no minds by ordinary standards, all spells affecting the brain (*charm, ESP*, etc.), unless specific to plants, are useless.

Gas Spore

At any distance greater than 10 feet, a gas spore is 90% likely to be mistaken for a beholder. Even at close ranges there is a 25% possibility that the creature is seen as a beholder, for a gas spore has a false central eye and rhizome growths atop it that strongly resemble the eye stalks of a beholder.

Combat: If the spore is struck for even 1 point of damage it explodes. Every creature within a 20-foot radius suffers 6d6 points of damage (3d6 if a saving throw vs. wands is successful).

If a gas spore makes contact with exposed flesh, the spore shoots tiny rhizomes into the living matter and grows through the victim's system within one round. The gas spore dies immediately. The victim must have a *cure disease* spell cast on him within 24 hours or die, sprouting 2d4 gas spores.

Galeb Duhr

CLIMATE/TERRAIN:	Any mountain
FREQUENCY:	Very rare
ORGANIZATION:	Family
ACTIVITY CYCLE:	Day
DIET:	Special
INTELLIGENCE:	Very (11-12)
TREASURE:	Q (x3), X
ALIGNMENT:	Neutral

NO. APPEARING:	1-4
ARMOR CLASS:	-2
MOVEMENT:	6
HIT DICE:	8-10
THAC0:	8 HD: 13
	9-10 HD: 11
NO. OF ATTACKS:	2
DAMAGE/ATTACK:	2-16, 3-18, or 4-24
SPECIAL ATTACKS:	See below
SPECIAL DEFENSES:	See below
MAGIC RESISTANCE:	20%
SIZE:	L (8'-12' tall)
MORALE:	Fanatic (17)
XP VALUE:	8 HD: 8,000
	9 HD: 9,000
	10 HD: 10,000

The galeb duhr is a curious boulder-like creature with append-ages that act as hands and feet. These intelligent beings are very large and slow-moving. They live in rocky or mountainous areas where they can feel the earth power and control the rocks around them.

A typical galeb duhr is from 8 to 12 feet tall. When not moving it looks like part of the terrain it lives in.

Combat: Galeb duhr are fairly solitary creatures, preferring to live with a few of their own kind, and none of any other kind, including earth elementals. When approached, a galeb duhr is li-able to avoid the encounter by disappearing into the ground. If chased or otherwise irritated, however, a galeb duhr does not hesitate to fight the intruder.

Galeb duhr can cast the following spells as 20th-level mages, once per day: *move earth, stone shape, passwall, transmute rock to mud,* and *wall of stone.* They can cast *stone shape* at will.

They can animate 1-2 boulders within 60 yards of them (AC 0; MV 3; HD 9; Dam 4d6) as a treant controls trees. Galeb duhr suffer double damage from cold-based attacks and save with a -4 penalty against these attacks. They are not harmed by lightning or normal fire, but suffer full damage from magical fire (though they save with a +4 bonus against fire attacks).

Habitat/Society: Galeb duhr, thought to be native to the ele-mental plane of Earth, are sometimes encountered in small family groups in mountainous regions of the Prime Material plane.

It is not known how (or whether) galeb duhr reproduce, but "young" galeb duhr have occasionally been reported—those specimens encountered being a smaller size than normal.

While galeb duhr seem to have no visible culture above ground, they are known to collect gems, which they find through their passwall ability. They sometimes have small magical items in their possession, evidently taken from those who attacked them to take their gems.

The "music" of the galeb duhr often provides the first evidence that these creatures are near—and usually the only evidence, as the unsociable galeb duhr are quick to pass into the ground when they feel the vibrations of approaching visitors.

Sitting together in groups, the galeb duhr harmonize their gravelly voices into eldritch tunes; some sages speculate that these melodies can cause or prevent earthquakes. Others argue that the low rumbling produced by these creatures is a form of warning to others in the group, but there is no conclusive evi-dence either way.

Ecology: Galeb duhr have no natural enemies, other than those who crave the gems they collect. Galeb duhr eat rock, preferring granite to other types, and disdaining any sedimentary type. The rocks they eat become part of the huge creatures; such a meal need take place only once every two or three months.

Besides the gems that they carry with them, galeb duhr are likely to know where many other gems are, as well as veins of precious metals, such as gold, silver, and platinum, though galeb duhr seem to have no interest in these minerals for themselves. A few powerful mages have been able to bargain with the galeb duhr for this information. This is a difficult agreement to con-summate, for the galeb duhr are valiant fighters, and usually have no difficulty in escaping from any harm if they are inclined to do so. Further, the galeb duhr are territorial, and would be irritated at any attempt to make use of this knowledge in their vicinity.

In some strange way, galeb duhr feel responsible for the smaller rocks and boulders around them, in much the same way that a treant feels responsible for trees in its neighborhood. A traveler who disturbs the area near a galeb duhr does so at his own peril.

	Reptilian Gargantua	Humanoid Gargantua	Insectoid Gargantua
CLIMATE/TERRAIN:	Tropical and subtropical islands	Tropical and subtropical islands, jungles, and mountains	Tropical, subtropical, and temperate mountains
FREQUENCY:	Rare	Very rare	Rare
ORGANIZATION:	Solitary or mated pair	Solitary or mated pair	Solitary or mated pair
ACTIVE TIME:	Night	Any	Any
DIET:	Special	Omnivore	Omnivore
INTELLIGENCE:	Low (5-7)	Low (5-7)	Low (5-7)
TREASURE:	Nil	Nil	Nil
ALIGNMENT:	Chaotic neutral	Chaotic neutral	Chaotic neutral
NO. APPEARING:	1-2	1-2	1-3
ARMOR CLASS:	2	4	6
MOVEMENT:	18, Sw 12	21	6, Fl 36 (E)
HIT DICE:	50	35	20-30
THAC0:	5	5	5
NO. OF ATTACKS:	3	2	1
DAMAGE/ATTACK:	3-30/3-30/6-60	4-40/4-40	3-30
SPECIAL ATTACKS:	See below	Trample	See below
SPECIAL DEFENSES:	Regeneration	Regeneration	Regeneration
MAGIC RESISTANCE:	Nil	Nil	Nil
SIZE:	G (100'-200' tall)	G (80'-100' tall)	G (60' long)
MORALE:	Elite (14)	Elite (14)	Elite (13)
XP VALUE:	43,000	28,000	20 HD: 14,000 30 HD: 24,000

Gargantua are truly monstrous species, both in size and ferocity. Whether they are throwbacks to another age, aberrations of natural processes, or results of crazed magical experiments is unknown.

Gargantua appear in many different forms, but most resemble gigantic humanoids, insects, and reptiles. Of these three types, the most common is also the largest and most dangerous: the reptilian gargantua.

The reptilian gargantua is so immense that it dwarfs virtually all of the world's creatures. Some reptilian gargantua move on all fours. Most, however, are bipedal, supported by two massive legs rivaling the width of the largest tree trunks. The creature's body is thick and bulky. Rocky scales—usually dark green with black accents—cover it from head to toe. Its smooth belly is a lighter shade of green. Certain rare types have mottled scales in shades of brown, gray, and yellow.

Its hands are almost human, though each of its four, long fingers ends in a hooked claw. Its feet are flat and broad, with webbed toes. The toes also end in hooked claws, but they're shorter and thicker than those on its fingers. A bony ridge stretches from the base of its neck, down along its spine, and extending the length of its immense tail.

The head of the reptilian gargantua is somewhat small in proportion to its body. It has two glaring eyes, usually gold or bright red. Its nostrils are flush with its head, and its ears are twin triangular projections resembling tiny wings. Its mouth is a wide slash that nearly bisects its entire head and is lined with rows of long fangs.

The reptilian gargantua cannot speak, but it emits deafening roars that sound like the trumpeting of a bull elephant amplified a thousandfold. It can breathe both air and water.

Combat: Although it has some degree of intelligence, the actions of the reptilian gargantua—along with the actions of most gargantua—are those of mindless brutes bent on destruction for destruction's sake. It attacks with sweeping rakes of its front claws and lunging bites from its powerful jaws. If moving upright, it can trample victims for 10-100 (10d10) hit points of damage. It continually sweeps the ground it with its massive tail, swinging 90 feet behind it and to each side. Any creature within range of the tail must make a successful saving throw vs. death or suffer 8-80 (8d10) hit points of damage.

A rampaging reptilian gargantua is all but oblivious to its surroundings, crushing everything—and everyone—in its path. The ground trembles under its weight when it walks. Since quaking earth always foreshadows its appearance, it never can surprise its prey. When swimming, a reptilian gargantua is similarly handicapped, as its appearance is always preceded by swirling waters or crashing waves. Additionally, its immense size makes it easy to spot from a distance. Furthermore, the squealing roars that accompany its every action make it virtually impossible to ignore.

The reptilian gargantua's tough hide gives it an Armor Class of 2, forming a strong defense against most physical attacks. When it does suffer damage, the creature can regenerate 4 hit points per round.

Fortunately, reptilian gargantua seldom bother humans. But their memories are long, and their appetite for revenge is nearly limitless. Humans who attack reptilian gargantua, disturb their lairs, or otherwise provoke the creatures will find themselves relentlessly pursued—even it means the gargantua must cross thousands of miles of ocean. This creature's hunger for revenge is seldom satisfied until it has thoroughly ravaged its attackers' villages. Sometimes, entire provinces will be laid to ruin.

The surest way to provoke the wrath of a reptilian gargantua is to threaten its offspring. Adult gargantua have remarkable mental bonds with their young, enabling them to locate their young with pinpoint accuracy at an unlimited range.

In spite of their reputation as mindless destroyers, reptilian gargantua actually possess a simple empathy that enables them to sense the emotions and desires of others, albeit on a primitive level. They seem to instinctively know which creatures bear them ill will, and direct their attacks accordingly.

Habitat/Society: A few reptilian guargantua make their home on the floors of subtropical oceans. Most, however, live on remote tropical islands, far from civilized lands. Such islands are scattered throughout the oceans of Kara-Tur, with most of them uncharted. The most notable exception is the Isle of Gargantua, one of the Outer Isles off the southwestern tip of Wa. This island is inhabited entirely by gargantua of various types.

Explorers in the arctic regions of Kara-Tur once found a maturing reptilian gargantua frozen in a block of ice. The explorers built a massive sled to haul their discovery back to civilization. The ice began to thaw en route, reviving the creature. The gargantua shattered the melting ice block, crushed his captors, and lumbered into the mountains.

Any grotto or cave that provides shelter, privacy, and sufficient room to house a reptilian gargantua can serve as its lair. Fiercely territorial, a reptilian gargantua and its family usually claim an area of several square miles as their personal property, defending it against any and all intruders. Since their eyes are sensitive to bright light, the creatures spend most of the day sleeping in their lairs, becoming active at night to search for food and patrol their territory. Their

Gargantua

thunderous roars make their presence known to all. Reptilian gargantua do not collect treasure or any other items.

Reptilian gargantua live several hundred years. They choose mates within a few years of reaching maturity, and remain with them for the rest of their lives. A female reptilian gargantua gives birth to a single offspring once per century. The birth of a reptilian gargantua is marked by shattering thunderstorms that rock the skies over the territory of its parents for 101 days.

An immature reptilian gargantua stands about 20-40 feet tall. It also has 10 HD (THAC0 11) and a movement rate of 12 (Sw 9). A youngling's claws inflict 1-10 hit points of damage each, and its bite inflicts 2-24 (2d12) hit points of damage. Its tail—not nearly as formidable as an adult's—sweeps the ground in an arch reaching 20 feet behind and to both sides, inflicting 3-18 (3d6) points of damage to all victims who fail their save vs. death.

Ecology: The reptilian gargantua is an omnivore. It primarily eats plants, swallowing whole trees in a single gulp. But it also enjoys living prey of all varieties. It can even dine on minerals, gems, and other inorganic substances in times of scarce vegetation and game.

Reptilian gargantua shun the company of other creatures. They especially dislike other types of gargantua, which sometimes compete with their reptilian cousins for the same territory.

Reptilian gargantua have two properties useful to humans:
• The petal of any flower that grows in the footprint of a reptilian gargantua can serve as a component for a *potion of growth*. Such a flower must grow naturally in the footprint; it cannot have been planted there by a human or other intelligent being.
• As noted above, thunderstorms occur when a reptilian gargantua is born. If a dead creature of any kind is struck by a lightning bolt from such a storm, the bolt acts as *resurrection* spell.

Humanoid Gargantua

Humanoid gargantua are the least intelligent type. They resemble gigantic humans, somewhat anthropoid facially, with stooped shoulders, long arms, and jutting jaws. Long, greasy hair dangles about their shoulders, though a few humanoid gargantua are completely bald. They stand 80 to 100 feet tall and are sometimes covered with black, brown, or golden fur. Their skin color ranges from pale pink to dull yellow to deep black. They have blunt noses, huge ears, and bright eyes, which are usually brown or red. Single-eyed humanoid gargantua also are rumored to exist.

Humanoid gargantua have no language of their own, but because of their strong empathy with humans, they are able to comprehend short phrases of human languages 25% of the time. The movements and other actions of humanoid gargantua are typically accompanied by thunderous bellowing and grunting.

The creature attacks with its two fists for 4-40 (3d10) hit points of damage each. It seldom uses weapons or tools, since its blunt fingers manipulate these objects with difficulty. However, reports exist of humanoid gargantua wielding trees like clubs. The creatures also can make trampling attacks on anyone (or anything) who comes underfoot, causing 10-100 (10d10) points of damage. Humanoid gargantua regenerate hit points at the rate of 4 per round.

Like reptilian gargantua, humanoid gargantua possess a simple empathy that enables them to sense the basic emotions and desires of others. Unless hungry, they tend to avoid creatures who intend them no harm, while actively seeking out and pursuing those with hostile intentions.

Humanoid gargantua live in valleys, in suitably sized caves in remote, jagged mountains, or on their own islands, far from civilized regions. They collect no treasure, spending most of their time eating and sleeping.

They live for several centuries, and mate for life. Once every hundred years or so, a female humanoid gargantua gives birth to 1-2 offspring. An immature humanoid gargantua is about 20-30 feet tall. It has 8 HD (THAC0 13) and a movement rate of 15. Its fists inflict 1-10 points of damage each. It cannot make trampling attacks.

These monsters peacefully coexist with other creatures in their environment, but humanoid gargantua compete fiercely with rival gargantua, and violent conflicts often result. Many such conflicts

continue until one of the gargantua is dead.

Humanoid gargantua eat all types of game and vegetation, preferring deer, bears, horses, and similar game.

Insectoid Gargantua

Adult insectoid gargantua resemble immense moths. Their bodies are covered with fine fur, usually gray or black, and their wings bear colorful patterns in brilliant blue, red, yellow, and green. Their movements and other actions are accompanied by a piercing screech that sounds like a warning siren.

The insectoid gargantua begins life as a gigantic egg, which hatches to reveal a gigantic larva. This larval form has 20 HD. As a larva, the insectoid gargantua can shoot a strand of cocoon silk to a range of 60 feet. This silk is exceptionally strong and sticky, adhering to whatever it hits. With this silken strand, the larva can entangle and immobilize victims. A strand can be severed in three ways: with 20 points of damage from an edged weapon, a successful "bend bars/lift gates" roll, or by monsters of 10 HD or more.

The larval insectoid gargantua grows at a phenomenal rate, increasing 1 HD per week. Upon attaining 25 HD, the larva spins a cocoon and enters the pupal stage. It remains a pupa for 2-8 (2d4) weeks, finally emerging as an immense moth with 30 HD. In this form, the creature can no longer spin silk. However, by flapping its wings, it can create a huge windstorm, 60 feet wide and extending 240 feet ahead. To remain safe, everyone and everything within the path of the storm must be solidly anchored (e.g., tied to a boulder). Unanchored victims must make a saving throw vs. death with a −4 penalty. Those who fail their saving throw are blown back 10 to 40 feet, suffering 1d6 hit points of damage for every 10 feet blown.

Insectoid gargantua establish lairs in the valleys and caverns of warm, mountainous regions. They live for several hundred years. Females lay a single egg every decade, but there is only a 20% chance that any given egg is fertile.

These mothlike creatures eat all types of game and vegetation. They prefer mulberry trees, and in just a few hours, a hungry insectoid gargantua can consume an entire grove of them.

The silk of insectoid gargantua larvae can be woven into cloth from which magical robes are created.

	Gargoyle	Margoyle
CLIMATE/TERRAIN:	— Any land, subterranean, ocean —	
FREQUENCY:	Uncommon	Rare
ORGANIZATION:	Tribe	Tribe
ACTIVITY CYCLE:	Any	Any
DIET:	Carnivore	Carnivore
INTELLIGENCE:	Low (5-7)	Low (5-7)
TREASURE:	M x 10 (C)	Q (C)
ALIGNMENT:	Chaotic evil	Chaotic evil
NO. APPEARING:	2-16	2-8
ARMOR CLASS:	5	2
MOVEMENT:	9, Fl 15 (C)	6, Fl 12 (C)
HIT DICE:	4+4	6
THAC0:	15	15
NO. OF ATTACKS:	4	4
DAMAGE/ATTACK:	1-3/1-3/1-6/1-4	1-6/1-6/2-8/2-8
SPECIAL ATTACKS:	Nil	See below
SPECIAL DEFENSES:	+1 or better weapon to hit	+1 or better weapon to hit
MAGIC RESISTANCE:	Nil	Nil
SIZE:	M (6' tall)	M (6' tall)
MORALE:	Steady (11)	Elite (13)
XP VALUE:	420	975

These monsters are ferocious predators of a magical nature, typically found amid ruins or dwelling in underground caverns. They have their own guttural language.

Combat: Gargoyles attack anything they detect, regardless of whether it is good or evil, 90% of the time. They love best to torture prey to death when it is helpless.

These winged creatures are excellent fighters with four attacks per round. Their claw/claw/bite/horn combination can inflict up to 16 points of damage, while their naturally tough hide protects them from victim's attacks.

Gargoyles favor two types of attack: surprise and swooping. Counting on their appearance as sculptures of some sort, gargoyles sit motionless around the rooftop of a building, waiting for prey to approach. Alternatively, a gargoyle may pose in a fountain, or a pair of the horrid beasts sit on either side of a doorway. When the victim is close enough, the gargoyles suddenly strike out, attempting only to injure the victim rather than to kill it all at once. (To a gargoyle, inflicting a slow, painful death is best.)

When on the move, gargoyles sometimes use a "swoop" attack, dropping down suddenly from the sky to make their attacks in an aerial ambush. In this case, they can make either two claw attacks or one horn attack. To make all four of their attacks, they must land.

Habitat/Society: Gargoyles live in small groups with others of their kind, interested in little more than finding other creatures to hurt. Smaller animals are scarcely worth the trouble to these hideous monsters, who prefer to attack humans or other intelligent creatures.

Gargoyles often collect treasure from human victims. Individuals usually have a handful of gold pieces among them, with the bulk of their treasure hidden carefully at their lair, usually buried or under a large stone.

Ecology: Originally, gargoyles were carved roof spouts, representing grotesque human and animal figures. They were designed in such a way that water flowing down gutters would be thrown away from the wall, so as to prevent stains and erosion. Later, some unknown mage used a powerful enchantment to bring these horrid sculptures to life. The race of gargoyles has flourished, spreading throughout the world.

Gargoyles do not need to eat or drink, so they can stand motionless for as long as they wish almost anywhere. The damage they do to other creatures is not for sustenance, but only for their distorted sense of pleasure.

Because they are fairly intelligent and evil, they will sometimes serve an evil master of some sort. In this case, the gargoyles usually act as guards or messengers; besides some gold or a few gems, their unsavory payment is the enjoyment they get from attacking unwanted visitors.

The horn of the gargoyle is the more common active ingredient for a *potion of invulnerability* and can also be used in a *potion of flying.*

Kapoacinth

This creature is a marine variety of gargoyle that uses its wings to swim as fast as the land-dwelling gargoyle flies. Kapoacinth conform in all respects to a normal gargoyle. They dwell in relatively shallow waters, lairing in undersea caves.

Like gargoyles, kapoacinth are eager to cause pain to others, and mermen, sea elves, and human visitors are all equally qualified candidates for this.

Margoyle

Margoyles are a more horrid form of gargoyle. They are found mainly in caves and caverns. Their skin is so like stone that they are only 20% likely to be seen when against it. They attack with two claws, a pair of horns, and a bite. They speak their own language and that of gargoyles. They are 20% likely to be found with the latter, either as leaders or masters.

Genie

	Djinni	Dao	Efreeti	Marid	Jann
CLIMATE/TERRAIN:	Air	Earth	Fire	Water	Any land
FREQUENCY:	Very rare	Rare	Very rare	Very rare	Very rare
ORGANIZATION:	Caliphate	Khanate	Sultanate	Padishate	Amirate
ACTIVITY CYCLE:	Day	Day	Day	Day	Day
DIET:	Omnivore	Omnivore	Omnivore	Omnivore	Omnivore
INTELLIGENCE:	Average to highly (8-14)	Low to very (5-12)	Very (11-12)	High to genius (13-18)	Very to exceptional (11-16)
TREASURE:	Nil	Nil	Nil	Nil	Nil
ALIGNMENT:	Chaotic good	Neutral evil	Neutral (lawful evil)	Chaotic neutral	Neutral (good)
NO. APPEARING:	1	1	1	1	1-2
ARMOR CLASS:	4	3	2	0	2 (5)
MOVEMENT:	9, Fl 24 (A)	9, Fl 15 (B), Br 6	9, Fl 24 (B)	9, Fl 15 (B), Sw 24	12, Fl 30 (A)
HIT DICE:	7+3	8+3	10	13	6+2
THAC0:	13	11	11	7	15
NO. OF ATTACKS:	1	1	1	1	1
DAMAGE/ATTACK:	2-16 (2d8)	3-18 (3d6)	3-24 (3d8)	4-32 (4d8)	1-8+Strength bonus or by weapon + Strength bonus
SPECIAL ATTACKS:	See below	See below	See below	See below	See below
SPECIAL DEFENSES:	See below	See below	See below	See below	See below
MAGIC RESISTANCE:	Nil	Nil	Nil	25%	20%
SIZE:	L (10 ½' tall)	L (8'-11' tall)	L (12' tall)	H (18' tall)	M (6'-7' tall)
MORALE:	Elite (13-14)	Champion (15-16)	Champion (15-16)	Champion (16)	Champion (15)
XP VALUE:	5,000 Noble: 11,000	5,000	8,000	16,000	3,000 (+1,000 per added Hit Die)

Genies come from the elemental planes. There, among their own kind, they are have their own societies. Genies are sometimes encountered on the Prime Material plane and are often summoned specifically to perform some service for a powerful wizard or priest. All genies can travel to any of the elemental planes, as well as the Prime Material and Astral planes. Genies speak their own tongue and that of any intelligent beings they meet through a limited form of telepathy.

Djinni

The djinn are genies from the elemental plane of Air. It should be noted that "djinn" is the plural form of their name, while "djinni" is the singular.

Combat: The djinn's magical nature enables them to do any of the following once per day: *create nutritious food* for 2d6 persons and *create water* or *create wine* for 2d6 persons; *create soft goods* (up to 16 cubic feet) or *create wooden items* (up to 9 cubic feet) of a permanent nature; *create metal*, up to 100 pounds weight with a short life span (the harder the metal the less time it lasts; gold has about a 24 hour existence while djinni steel lasts only one hour); *create illusion* as a 20th-level wizard with both visible and audible components, which last without concentration until touched or magically dispelled; use *invisibility, gaseous form*, or *wind walk*.

Once per day, the genie can create a whirlwind, which the it can ride or even direct at will from a distance. The whirlwind is a cone-shaped spiral, measuring up to 10 feet across at its base, 40 feet across at the top, and up to 70 feet in height (the djinni chooses the dimensions). Its maximum speed is 18, with maneuverability class A. The whirlwind's base must touch water or a solid surface, or it will dissolve. It takes a full turn for the whirlwind to form or dissolve. During that time, the whirlwind inflicts no damage and has no other effect. The whirlwind lasts as long as the djinni concentrates on it, moving at the creature's whim.

If the whirlwind strikes a non-aerial creature with fewer than 2 Hit Dice, the creature must make a saving throw vs. breath

weapon for each round of contact with the whirlwind, or be swept off its feet, battered, and killed. Hardier beings, as well as aerial or airborne creatures, take 2d6 points of damage per round of contact with the whirlwind.

A djinni can ride its whirlwind and even take along passengers, who (like the djinni) suffer no damage from the buffeting winds. The whirlwind can carry the genie and up to six man-sized or three genie-sized companions.

Airborne creatures or attacks receive a −1 penalty to attack and damage rolls against a djinni, who also receives a +4 bonus to saving throws against gas attacks and air-based spells.

Djinn are nearly impossible to capture by physical means; a djinni who is overmatched in combat usually takes to flight and uses its whirlwind to buffet those who follow. Genies are openly contemptuous of those life forms that need wings or artificial means to fly and use *illusion* and *invisibility* against such enemies. Thus, the capture and enslavement of djinn is better resolved by the DM on a case-by-case basis. It is worth noting, however, that a good master will typically encourage a djinni to additional effort and higher performance, while a demanding and cruel master encourages the opposite.

Djinn are able to carry up to 600 pounds, on foot or flying, without tiring. They can carry double that for a short time: three turns if on foot, or one turn if flying. For each 100 pounds below the maximum, add one turn to the time a djinni may walk or fly before tiring. A fatigued djinni must rest for an hour before performing any additional strenuous activity.

Habitat/Society: The djinn's native land is the elemental plane of Air, where they live on floating islands of earth and rock, anywhere from 1,000 yards to several miles across. They are crammed with buildings, courtyards, gardens, fountains, and sculptures made of elemental flames. In a typical djinn landhold there are 3d10 djinn of various ages and powers, as well as 1d10 jann and 1d10 elemental creatures of low intelligence. All are ruled by the local sheik, a djinn of maximum hit points.

The social structure of Djinn society is based on rule by a ca-

126

liph, served by various nobles and officials (viziers, beys, emirs, sheiks, sheriffs, and maliks). A caliph rules all the djinn estates within two days' travel, and is advised by six viziers who help maintain the balance of the landholdings.

If a landhold is attacked by a large force, a messenger (usually the youngest djinni) is sent to the next landhold, which sends aid and dispatches two more messengers to warn the next landholds; in this fashion the entire nation is warned.

Noble Djinn

Some djinn (1%) are "noble" and are able to grant three *wishes* to their masters. Noble djinn perform no other services and, upon granting the third *wish* are freed of their servitude. Noble djinn are as strong as efreet, with 10 Hit Dice. They strike for 3d8 points of damage, and the whirlwinds they create cause 3d6 hit points of damage.

Dao

A dao is a genie from the elemental plane of Earth. While they are generally found on that plane (though even there they are uncommon), the dao love to come to the Prime Material plane to work evil. Dao speak all of the languages of the genies, as well as Common and the tongue of earth elementals.

Combat: The dao's magical abilities enable them to use any of the following magical powers, one at a time, once each per day: *change self, detect good, detect magic, gaseous form, invisibility, misdirection, passwall, spectral force,* and *wall of stone.* They can also fulfill another's *limited wish* (in a perverse way) once each day. Dao can use *rock to mud* three times per day and *dig* six times per day. Dao perform all magic as 18th-level spellcasters.

A dao can carry up to 500 pounds without tiring. Double weight will cause tiring in three turns, but for every 100 pounds of weight under 1,000, the dao may add one turn to the duration of its carrying ability. After tiring, a dao must rest for one hour. Dao can move through earth (not worked stone) at a burrowing

speed of 6. They cannot take living beings with them, but can safely carry inanimate objects.

Dao are not harmed by earth-related spells, but holy water has twice its normal effect upon these monsters.

Habitat/Society: The dao dwell in the Great Dismal Delve on their own plane and in deep caves, caverns, or cysts on the Prime Material plane. Dao settle pockets of elemental matter on their own plane, bending those pockets to their will and desire. A dao mazework contains 4d10 dao, as well as 8d10 elemental and non-elemental slaves. Each mazework is ruled by an ataman or hetman who is advised by a seneschal. The loyalty of a mazework's ataman to the Great Dismal Delve is always questionable, but the seneschals are chosen by the khan of the dao, and their loyalty is to him alone.

The khan of the dao lives at the center of the great mazework called the Great Dismal Delve. The land within the delve is said to be larger than most Prime Material continents. The Great Dismal Delve is linked to all manner of elemental pockets, so the khan can call forth whatever powers he needs. The population of dao in the delve is unknown, as is the number of slaves that constantly work the tunnels and clear away damage caused by the quakes which frequently shake it.

Dao dislike servitude as much as efreet and are even more prone to malice and revenge than their fiery counterparts.

Ecology: The dao manage a thriving business of trade, driven by a desire for more power and access to precious gems. High on their list of hatreds are most other genies (except efreet, with whom they trade worked metals for minerals). They also have little use for other elemental creatures; the dao value these only if they can exploit them in some fashion.

Efreet

The efreet (singular: efreeti) are genies from the elemental plane of Fire. They are enemies of the djinn and attack them whenever they are encountered. A properly summoned or captured efreeti

Genie

can be forced to serve for a maximum of 1,001 days, or it can be made to fulfill three *wishes*. Efreet are not willing servants and seek to pervert the intent of their masters by adhering to the letter of their commands.

The efreet are said to be made of basalt, bronze, and solid flames. They are massive, solid creatures.

Combat: An efreeti is able to do the following once per day: grant up to three *wishes*; use *invisibility, gaseous form, detect magic, enlarge, polymorph self,* and *wall of fire*; create an *illusion* with both visual and audio components which will last without concentration until magically dispelled or touched. An efreeti can also produce flame or use *pyrotechnics* at will. Efreet are immune to normal fire-based attacks, and even an attack with magical fire suffers a −1 penalty on all attack and damage rolls.

Efreet can carry up to 750 pounds on foot or flying, without tiring. They can also carry double weight for a limited time: three turns on foot or one turn aloft. For each 150 pounds of weight under 1500, add one turn to either walking or flying time permitted. After tiring, the efreeti must rest for one hour.

Habitat/Society Efreet are infamous for their hatred of servitude, desire for revenge, cruel nature, and ability to beguile and mislead. The efreet's primary home is their great citadel, the fabled City of Brass, but there are many other efreet outposts throughout the plane of Fire.

An efreet outpost is a haven for 4d10 efreet and is run as a military station to watch or harass others in the plane. These outposts are run by a malik or vali of maximum normal hit points. There is a 10% chance that the outpost is also providing a temporary home for 1d4 jann or 1d4 dao (the only other genies efreet tolerate). Outpost forces are usually directed against incursions from the elemental plane of Air, but they can be directed against any travelers deemed suitable for threats, robbery, and abuse.

Efreet are neutral, but tend toward organized evil. They are ruled by a grand sultan who makes his home in the City of Brass. He is advised by a variety of beys, amirs, and maliks concerning actions within the plane, and by six great pashas who deal with efreet business on the Prime Material plane.

The City of Brass is a huge citadel that is home to the majority of efreet. It hovers in the hot regions of the plane and is often bordered by seas of magma and lakes of glowing lava. The city sits upon a hemisphere of golden, glowing brass some 40 miles across. From the upper towers rise the minarets of the great bastion of the Sultan's Palace. Vast riches are said to be in the palace of the sultan. The city has an efreet population that far outnumbers the great cities of the Prime Material plane. The sultan wields the might of a Greater Power, while many of his advisors are akin to Lesser Powers and Demi-Powers.

Ecology: Fire elementals tend to avoid the efreet, whom they feel are oppressive and opportunistic. Djinn hate them, and there have been numerous djinn-efreet clashes. Efreet view most other creatures either as enemies or servants, a view that does not endear them to other genies.

Marid

The marids are said to be born of the ocean, having currents for muscles and pearls for teeth. These genies from the elemental plane of Water are the most powerful of all genies. They are also the most individualistic and chaotic of the elemental races, and only rarely deign to serve others.

On their own plane they are rare; marids travel so seldom to the Prime Material plane that many consider marids to be creatures of legend only.

Combat: Marids perform as 26th-level spellcasters, and can use any of the following magical powers, one at a time, twice each per day: *detect evil, detect good, detect invisibility, detect magic, invisibility, liquid form* (similar to *gaseous form*), *polymorph self,* and *purify water*. Marids can use any of the following up to seven times per day: *gaseous form, lower water, part water, wall of fog,* or *water breathing* (used on others, lasting up to one full day). Once per year a marid can use *alter reality*.

Marids can always *create water,* which they may direct in a powerful jet up to 60 yards long. Victims struck by the jet take 1d6 points of damage and must make a successful saving throw vs. breath weapon or be blinded for 1d6 rounds. Marids also have the innate ability to *water walk* (as the ring).

A marid can carry 1,000 pounds. Double weight causes tiring in three turns. For every 200 pounds under 2,000, add one turn to the time the marid can carry before tiring. A tired marid must rest for one hour.

Marids swim, breathe water, are at home at any depth, and have infravision. They are not harmed by water-based spells. Cold-based spells grant them a +2 bonus to saving throws and −2 to each die of damage. Fire inflicts +1 per die of damage, with saving throws at a -1 penalty. Steam does not harm them.

Habitat/Society: Marids live in a loose empire ruled by a padisha. Each marid lays some claim to royalty; they are all shahs, atabegs, beglerbegs, or mufti at the very least. There have often been several simultaneous "single true heirs" to the padisha's throne through the eons.

A marid household numbers 2d10 and is located around loosely grouped elemental pockets containing the necessities for marid life. Larger groups of marids gather for hunts and tournaments, where individual effort is heavily emphasized.

Marids are champion tale-tellers, although most of their tales emphasize their own prowess, and belittle others. When communicating with a marid, one must attempt to keep the conversation going without continual digression for one tale or another, while not offending the marid. Marids consider it a capital offense for a lesser being to offend a marid.

Marids are both fiercely independent and extremely egoistical. They are not easily forced to perform actions; even if convinced through flattery and bribery to obey, they often stray from their intended course to seek some other adventure that promises greater glory, or to instruct lesser creatures on the glories of the marids. Most mages skilled in summoning and conjuration consider marids to be more trouble than they are worth, which accounts for the great lack of items of marid control (as opposed to those affecting efreet and djinn).

Marids can travel the Ethereal plane, in addition to those planes to which all genies can travel.

Ecology: Marids tolerate their genie relatives, putting up with jann and djinn like poor cousins, while they have an aversion to efreet and dao. Their attitude toward the rest of the world is similar; most creatures from other planes are considered lesser beings, not fit to be bothered with unless one lands in the feast hall at an inopportune time.

Janni

The jann are the weakest of the elemental humanoids known collectively as genies. Jann are formed out of all four elements and must therefore spend most of their time on the Prime Material plane. In addition to speaking Common and all the languages of genies, jann can speak with animals.

Combat: Jann often wear chain mail armor (60% chance), giving them an effective AC of 2. They typically use great scimitars which inflict 2d8 damage to small and medium creatures, and 4d4 points of damage to larger opponents. They also use composite long bows. Male jann have exceptional Strength scores; roll percentile dice for their Strengths. For female jann, roll percentile dice and subtract 50; anything above 0 indicates percentage Strength equal to that number, while anything below indicates 18 Strength.

Jann can use one the following magical powers each round: *enlarge* or *reduce*, twice each per day; *invisibility* three times per day; *create food and water* once per day as a 7th-level priest; and *etherealness* (as the armor) once per day for a maximum of one hour. Jann perform at 12th-level ability, except as noted.

Habitat/Society Jann favor forlorn deserts and hidden oases, where they have both privacy and safety. Jann society is very open, and males and females are regarded as equals. A tribe is made up of ld20 + 10 individuals and is ruled by a sheik and one or two viziers. Exceptionally powerful sheiks are given the title of amir, and in times of need they gather and command large forces of jann (and sometimes allied humans).

Many jann tribes are nomadic, traveling with flocks of camels, goats, or sheep from oasis to oasis. These itinerant jann appear human in every respect, and are often mistaken for them, unless they are attacked. Jann are strong and courageous, and they do not take kindly to insult or injury. The territory of a jann tribe can extend hundreds of miles in any direction.

While traveling, male jann live in large, colorful tents with their wives and married male children, and their families. Married daughters move away to live with their new husbands. When a family eventually grows large enough that it can no longer reside comfortably in the tent, a new tent is built, and a son takes his wife and family with him to this new dwelling. At permanent oases, the jann live not only in tents, but also in elegantly styled structures built from materials brought from any of the elemental planes.

Jann are able to dwell in air, earth, fire, or water environments for up to 48 hours. This includes the elemental planes, to which any janni can travel, even taking up to six individuals along if those others hold hands in a circle with the janni. Failure to return to the Prime Material plane within 48 hours inflicts 1 point of damage per additional hour on the jann, until the jann dies or returns to the Prime Material plane. Travel to another elemental plane is possible, without damage, providing at least two days are spent on the Prime Material plane immediately prior to the travel.

Ecology: Jann are suspicious of humans, dislike demihumans, and detest humanoids. Jann accept djinn, but shun dao, efreet, and marids. They sometimes befriend humans or work with them for a desired reward, like potent magical items.

One ethic the jann share with other nomads is the cultural demand for treating guests with honor and respect. Innocent visitors (including humans) are treated hospitably during their stay, but some day might be expected to return the favor.

Jann Leaders: Jann leaders have 17-18 Intelligence, and 10% have 19 Strength. Sheiks have up to 8 Hit Dice, amirs up to 9. Viziers have 17-20 Intelligence and the following magical powers, each usable three times per day at 12th-level spellcasting ability: *augury*, *detect magic*, and *divination*.

Ghost

CLIMATE/TERRAIN:	Any
FREQUENCY:	Very rare
ORGANIZATION:	Solitary
ACTIVE TIME:	Night
DIET:	None
INTELLIGENCE:	Highly (13-14)
TREASURE:	E, S
ALIGNMENT:	Lawful evil

NO. APPEARING:	1
ARMOR CLASS:	0 or 8 (see below)
MOVEMENT:	9
HIT DICE:	10
THAC0:	11
NO. OF ATTACKS:	1
DAMAGE/ATTACK:	Age 10-40 years
SPECIAL ATTACKS:	See below
SPECIAL DEFENSES:	See below
MAGIC RESISTANCE:	Nil
SIZE:	M (5'-6' tall)
MORALE:	Special
XP VALUE:	7,000

Ghosts are the spirits of humans who were either so greatly evil in life or whose deaths were so unusually emotional they have been cursed with the gift of undead status. Thus, they roam about at night or in places of darkness. These spirits hate goodness and life, hungering to draw the living essences from the living.

Combat: As ghosts are non-corporeal (ethereal), they are usually encountered only by creatures in a like state, although they can be seen by non-ethereal creatures. The supernatural power of a ghost is such, however, that the mere sight of one causes any humanoid being to age 10 years and flee in panic for 2-12 (2d6) turns unless a saving throw versus spells is made. Priests above 6th level are immune to this effect and all other humanoids above 8th level may add +2 to their saving throws.

Any creatures within 60 yards of a ghost is subject to attack by a *magic jar*. If the ghost fails to *magic jar* its chosen victim, it will then semi-materialize in order to attack by touch (in which case the ghost is Armor Class 0). Semi-materialized ghosts can be struck only by silver (half damage) or magical weapons (full damage). If they strike an opponent it ages him 10-40 (1d4x10) years. Note that ghosts can be attacked with spells only by creatures who are in an ethereal state. Any human or demi-human killed by a ghost is drained of its life essence and is forever dead.

If the ghost fails to become semi-material it can only be combatted by another in the Ethereal plane (in which case the ghost has an Armor Class of 8).

Ghosts can be turned by clerics after reaching 7th level and can be damaged by holy water while in their semi-material form.

Habitat/Society: In most cases, a ghost is confined to a small physical area, which the ghost haunts. Those who have heard stories of a haunted area can thus attempt to avoid it for their own safety.

A ghost often has a specific purpose in its haunting, sometimes trying to "get even" for something that happened during the ghost's life. Thus a woman who was jilted by a lover, and then committed suicide, might become a ghost and haunt the couple's secret trysting place. Similarly, a man who failed at business might appear each night at his storefront or, perhaps, at that of a former competitor.

Another common reason for an individual to become a ghost is the denial of a proper burial. A ghost might inhabit the area near its body, waiting for a passerby to promise to bury the remains. The ghost, in its resentment toward all life, becomes an evil creature intent on destruction and suffering.

In rare circumstances, more than one ghost will haunt the same location. The classic example of this is the haunted ship, a vessel lost at sea, now ethereal and crewed entirely by ghosts. These ships are most often encountered in the presence of St. Elmo's fire, an electrical discharge that causes mysterious lights to appear in the rigging of a ship.

In many cases, a ghost can be overcome by those who might be no match for it in combat simply by setting right whatever events led to the attainment of the ghost's undead status. For example, a young woman who was betrayed and murdered by someone who pretended to love her might be freed from her curse if the cad were humiliated and ruined. In many cases, however, a ghost's revenge will be far more demanding, often ending in the death of the offender.

Ecology: The dreadful fear caused by the ghost, which ages a victim 10 years, is not well understood by the common man, who often ascribes it to the fact that a ghost is "dead." If this were the case, then certainly skeletons and zombies would have the same effect, which they do not.

Common folklore further confuses this fact by relating details of the ghost's physical form: the classic example of which is the headless horseman, thought by many to be particularly frightening simply because he had no head. Under this belief, one could face a ghost if only one had the courage to stand up to him. Such a mistaken impression has cost many lives over the years. Actually, the fear is caused by the supernatural power of the ghost, and has nothing whatsoever to do with courage.

	Ghoul	Lacedon	Ghast
CLIMATE/TERRAIN:	Any land	Any water	Any land
FREQUENCY:	Uncommon	Very rare	Rare
ORGANIZATION:	Pack	Pack	Pack
ACTIVE TIME:	Night	Night	Night
DIET:	Corpses	Corpses	Corpses
INTELLIGENCE:	Low (5-7)	Low (5-7)	Very (11-12)
TREASURE:	B, T	B, T	B, Q, R, S, T
ALIGNMENT:	Chaotic evil	Chaotic evil	Chaotic evil
NO. APPEARING:	2-24 (2d12)	2-24(2d12)1-6	1-4 (with Ghoul packs)
ARMOR CLASS:	6	6	4
MOVEMENT:	9	Sw 9	15
HIT DICE:	2	2	4
THAC0:	19	19	17
NO. OF ATTACKS:	3	3	3
DAMAGE/ATTACK:	1-3/1-3/1-6	1-3/1-3/1-6	1-4/1-4/1-8
SPECIAL ATTACKS:	Paralyzation	Paralyzation	See below
SPECIAL DEFENSES:	See below	See below	See below
MAGIC RESISTANCE:	Nil	Nil	Nil
SIZE:	M (5'-6' tall)	M (5'-6' tall)	M (5'-6' tall)
MORALE:	Steady (11-12)	Steady (11-12)	Elite (13-14)
XP VALUE:	175	175	650

Ghouls are undead creatures, once human, who now feed on the flesh of corpses. Although the change from human to ghoul has deranged and destroyed their minds, ghouls have a terrible cunning which enables them to hunt their prey most effectively.

Ghouls are vaguely recognizable as once having been human, but have become horribly disfigured by their change to ghouls. The tongue becomes long and tough for licking marrow from cracked bones, the teeth become sharp and elongated, and the nails grow strong and sharp like claws.

Combat: Ghouls attack by clawing with their filthy nails and biting with their fangs. Their touch causes humans (including dwarves, gnomes, half-elves, and halflings, but excluding elves) to become rigid unless a saving throw versus paralyzation is successful. This paralysis lasts for 3-8 (2+1d6) rounds or until negated by a priest.

Any human or demi-human (except elves) killed by a ghoulish attack will become a ghoul unless blessed (or blessed and then resurrected). Obviously, this is also avoided if the victim is devoured by the ghouls. Ghoul packs always attack without fear.

These creatures are subject to all attack forms except *sleep* and *charm* spells. They can be turned by priests of any level. The magic circle of *protection from evil* actually keeps ghouls completely at bay.

Habitat/Society: Ghouls and ghasts are most frequently encountered around graveyards, where they can find plenty of corpses on which to feed.

Ecology: Ghouls (and ghasts, as described later) delight in revolting and loathsome things—from which we draw our adjectives "ghoulish" and "ghastly."

Lacedon

The lacedon is a marine form of the ghoul. Lacedons are sometimes found near marine ghosts, particularly ghost ships. Lacedons are less common than ghouls because of the fewer corpses available for them to feed on, but they can often be found swarming around recent shipwrecks in rivers, lakes, and oceans.

Ghast

These creatures are so like ghouls as to be completely indistinguishable from them, and they are usually found only with a pack of ghouls. When a pack of ghouls and ghasts attacks it will quickly become evident that ghasts are present, for they exude a carrion stench in a 10' radius which causes retching and nausea unless a saving throw versus poison is made. Those failing to make this save will attack at a penalty of -2.

Worse, the ghast shares the ghoulish ability to paralyzation, and their attack is so potent that it will even affect elves. Paralysis caused by a ghast lasts for 5-10 (4+1d6) rounds or until negated by a priest's *remove paralysis* spell.

Ghasts, like ghouls, are undead class and thus *sleep* and *charm* spells do not affect them. Though they can be struck by any sort of weapon, cold iron inflicts double normal damage. Clerics can turn them beginning at 2nd level. The circle of *protection from evil* does not keep them at bay unless it is used in conjunction with cold iron (such as a circle of powdered iron or an iron ring).

Giant, Cloud

CLIMATE/TERRAIN:	Any mountains or magical cloud islands
FREQUENCY:	Very rare
ORGANIZATION:	Tribal
ACTIVITY CYCLE:	Any
DIET:	Special
INTELLIGENCE:	Average to very (8-12)
TREASURE:	E, Q (x5)
ALIGNMENT:	Neutral (good 50%, evil 50%)

NO. APPEARING:	1-10
ARMOR CLASS:	0
MOVEMENT:	15
HIT DICE:	16 + 2-7 hit points
THAC0:	5
NO. OF ATTACKS:	1
DAMAGE/ATTACK:	1-10, or by weapon (6-24 +11)
SPECIAL ATTACKS:	Hurling rocks for 2-24
SPECIAL DEFENSES:	Surprised only on a 1
MAGIC RESISTANCE:	Nil
SIZE:	H (24' tall)
MORALE:	Fanatic (17-18)
XP VALUE:	10,000
Infant	Nil
Juvenile, -3	975
Juvenile, -2	3,000
Juvenile, -1	5,000
Spell caster, 1st	11,000
Spell caster, 2nd	11,000
Spell caster, 3rd	11,000
Spell caster, 4th	13,000

Cloud giants consider themselves above all other giants, save storm giants, whom they consider equals. They are creative, appreciate fine things, and are master strategists in battle.

Cloud giants have muscular human builds and handsome, well-defined features. The typical cloud giant is 24 feet tall and weighs 11,500 pounds. Female cloud giants can be 1 to 2 feet shorter and 1,000 to 2,000 pounds lighter. Cloud giants' skin ranges in color from a milky-white tinged with blue to a light sky blue. Their hair is silvery white or brass and their eyes are an iridescent blue. Cloud giants can live to be 400 years old.

A cloud giant's natural Armor Class is 0. Although they will wear no armor, these giants prize magical protection devices, and one in 20 will have such a device. Cloud giants dress in clothing made of the finest materials available and wear jewelry. Many of the giants consider their appearance an indication of their station; the more jewelry and the better the clothes, the more important the giant. Cloud giants also appreciate music, and the majority of giants are able to play one or more instruments (their favorite is the harp). Unlike most other giant races, cloud giants leave their treasure in their lairs, carrying with them only food, throwing rocks, 10-100 (10d10) coins, and a musical instrument.

Cloud giants speak their own tongue and the language of all other giants. In addition, 60% of all cloud giants speak common.

Combat: Cloud giants fight in well-organized units, using carefully developed battle plans. They prefer to fight from a position above their opponents. A favorite tactic is to circle the enemy, barraging them with rocks while the giants with magical abilities assault them with spells. Cloud giants can hurl rocks to a maximum of 240 yards, causing 2-24 (2d12) points of damage. Their huge morningstars do 6-24 (6d4) +11 points of damage, three times normal (man-sized) damage plus their strength bonus. One in 10 cloud giants will have a magical weapon.

Habitat/Society: Cloud giants live in small clans of no more than six giants. However, these clans know the location of 1-8 other clans and will band together with some of these clans for celebrations, battles, or to trade. These joined clans will recognize one among them to be their leader—this is usually an older cloud giant who has magical abilities. One in 10 cloud giants will have spells equivalent to a 4th level wizard, and one in 20 cloud giants will be the equivalent of a 4th level priest. A cloud giant cannot have both priest and wizard abilities.

If encountered in a lair, half will be immature giants. To determine a giant's maturity, roll 1d4. A roll of 4 indicates an infant with no combat ability and hit points of ogre. Rolls of 1-3 indicate older progeny with hit dice, damage, and "to hit" rolls equal to that of a fire giant.

The majority of cloud giants live on cloud-covered mountain peaks in temperate and sub-tropical areas. These giants make their lairs in crude castles. Only 10% of good cloud giants live in castles on enchanted clouds. All giants dwelling there are able to *levitate* their own weight plus 2,000 pounds three times a day, create a *fog cloud* three times a day, and create a *wall of fog* once a day. These abilities are performed as a 6th level wizard.

There is a 60% chance a cloud giant mountain lair will be guarded by 1-4 spotted lions, 2-5 (1d4 +1) owl bears, or 2-5 (1d4 +1) griffons (1-2 wyverns for evil cloud giants). In addition, there is a 50% chance the lairs of evil cloud giants will contain 1-20 human and demi-human slaves. There is an 80% chance that a cloud island lair will be guarded by 2-5 (1d4 +1) griffons, 2-8 (2d4) hippogriffs, or 2-5 (1d4 +1) giant eagles.

Cloud lairs are fantastic places with giant-sized gardens of fruit trees. According to legend, some giants mine their cloud islands for small chunks of the purest silver.

Ecology: Cloud giants prefer food that is carefully prepared with spices and sauces, and they relish fine, aged wines.

Good cloud giants trade with human and demi-human communities for food, wine, jewelry, and cloth. Some cloud giant clans will establish good relations with such communities, and will come to the communities' aid if they are endangered. Evil cloud giants raid human and demi-human communities to get what they want.

Giant, Cyclops

	Cyclopskin	Cyclops
CLIMATE/TERRAIN:	—Temperate/Hills and mountains—	
FREQUENCY:	Rare	Very rare
ORGANIZATION:	Clan	Clan
ACTIVITY CYCLE:	Any	Any
DIET:	Omnivore	Omnivore
INTELLIGENCE:	Low to average (5-10)	Low
TREASURE:	C	C
ALIGNMENT:	Chaotic (evil)	Chaotic evil
NO. APPEARING:	1-8	1-4
ARMOR CLASS:	3	2
MOVEMENT:	12	15
HIT DICE:	5	13
THAC0:	15	7
NO. OF ATTACKS:	1	1
DAMAGE/ATTACK:	by weapon +4 (Str bonus)	6-36
SPECIAL ATTACKS:	Nil	Hurl boulders
SPECIAL DEFENSES:	Nil	Nil
MAGIC RESISTANCE:	Nil	Nil
SIZE:	L (7½' tall)	H (20' tall)
MORALE:	Very steady (13)	Elite (16)
XP VALUE:	270	4,000

A diminutive relative of true giants, cyclopskin are single-eyed giants that live alone or in small bands.

The typical cyclopskin weighs around 350 pounds, and stands 7½ feet tall. A single large, red eye dominates the center of its forehead. Shaggy black or dull, deep blue hair falls in a tangled mass about its head and shoulders, its skin tone varies from ruddy brown to muddy yellow, and its voice is rough and sharp. Cyclopskin commonly dress in ragged animal hides and sandals. They smell of equal parts dirt and dung.

Combat: Cyclopskin are armed with either a club or a bardiche. Each will also carry a heavy hurling spear (1d6 damage) and a sling of great size (1d6 damage). They never wear armor or use shields, for their tough hide gives them ample protection from most attacks.

Cyclopskin do not bother with strategy or tactics in combat. If their opponents are out of reach, they use slings or hurl heavy spears. They can not throw boulders like their larger cousins. Since the single eye of the cyclopskin gives them poor depth perception, they suffer a -2 penalty to all missile attack rolls, but not to damage. If the opponents are close, the cyclopskin rush in to fight with their clubs or bardiches.

Habitat/Society: The single-eyed humanoids shy away from organized settlements. If left alone, they tend to leave armed groups alone, though they are not above attacking a much weaker force if they stumble across one. Cyclopskin have no regard for any form of life other than themselves. Captives are either enslaved or eaten. This doesn't happen very often, since the cyclopskin tend to live in remote rocky places. They rarely wander more than 10 miles from their caves.

Being poor hunters, most cyclopskin clans keep small herds of goats or sheep. Some clans are nomadic, while others stay put in their caves. Each spring, regional clans meet to exchange goods and slaves and to select mates. On rare occasions a charismatic cyclopskin will arise and bring together several clans to form a wandering tribe. The largest known tribe numbered around 80 fighting cyclopskin. Such a band will aggressively raid outlying areas with a boldness uncommon in a single clan. All group decisions are made by the strongest and toughest cyclopskin in the group, usually through intimidation. This in turn leads to brawls and fist fights. There are no rules in such fights, and they can lead to permanent injury or death for the loser.

A cyclopskin cave is sealed with boulders and there is but one entrance. Inside, if size permits, there will be wooden pens to house both animals and slaves. The pens always have roofs of either wooden bars or the natural cave ceiling.

At night, a large boulder or stout wooden gate is placed at the entrance of the cave to protect the cyclopskin from predators. There are no interior fire pits, since cyclopskin use fire infrequently, and then only outside their lairs. Any cyclopskin treasure will be kept in a sack in the cave.

Ecology: Cyclopskin can survive on almost any animal or plant diet. They enjoy meat of all sorts and prize it above vegetable foods. While they live off the land, they do not live with it. They have absolutely no sanitary practices, and rarely even cook their meals. They take no care to preserve their environment while hunting, and are considered to be one of the easiest creatures of their size to track.

The life of a cyclopskin is hazardous, and hence they have a short life expectancy. Besides human adventurers, there are many predators, such as tigers, giants, wyverns, and trolls, that are not above attacking a small group of these giants. However, mountain dwarves actually go out of their way to hunt cyclopskin, receiving the dwarven bonus against giants.

Cyclops: These larger versions of their slightly more common cousins are usually found in the extreme wilds or on isolated islands, where they scratch out a meager existence by shepherding their flocks of giant sheep. Cyclopes can hurl boulders up to 150 yards away, inflicting 410 points of damage.

133

Giant, Desert

CLIMATE/TERRAIN:	Desert
FREQUENCY:	Very rare
ORGANIZATION:	Tribal
ACTIVITY CYCLE:	Day
DIET:	Omnivore
INTELLIGENCE:	Average (8-10)
TREASURE:	B
ALIGNMENT:	Neutral

NO. APPEARING:	2-20
ARMOR CLASS:	1
MOVEMENT:	15
HIT DICE:	13
THAC0:	7
NO. OF ATTACKS:	1
DAMAGE/ATTACK:	1-10 or by weapon (2-12 +7)
SPECIAL ATTACKS:	Hurling spears
SPECIAL DEFENSES:	Camouflage
MAGIC RESISTANCE:	Nil
SIZE:	H (17' tall)
MORALE:	Elite (14)
XP VALUE:	5,000

Desert giants were once numerous in the scrub plains and deserts of the Land of Fate, but they have fallen victim to a divine curse which transforms them slowly but inexorably into stone. They always wander the land in the company of their cattle and their mounts. Their great civilization has long since vanished under the sands.

The weathered and craggy faces of the desert giants are scored with wrinkles. Even the youngest of desert giants are somewhat wrinkled, though this is not visible in the women, as they wear the veil. The dark hair and swarthy skin of the desert giants make their blue eyes all the more remarkable. However, it is considered a clear sign of impending fossilization when the eyes of a desert giant turn from blue to brown. The typical desert giant is 17' tall and weighs 7,000 pounds, though fossilizing giants may weigh twice that. Desert giants may live to be 400 years old.

Combat: Desert giants fight mounted when they can, though steeds of a size to suit them are rare. Battle mounts include gigantic lizards, enormous insects, huge undead horses of shifting bone, and even rocs. In the past, some desert giants took service as bodyguards and mercenaries with the most powerful of sultans. The sight of a squad of desert giants wheeling about in preparation for a charge has caused more than one desert legion to break and run.

Desert giants do not hurl rocks. Indeed, they wander many areas where there is often no ready supply of boulders, and carrying such heavy objects would tire even the strongest nomadic giant. However, they do make large throwing spears from wood they find when they pass near jungle lands. These spears are kept and cherished as heirlooms over generations. The spears have a range of 3/6/9 and cause 2-12 +7 points of damage. Desert giant chieftains sometimes carry great scimitars given to their ancestors for outstanding military service. These weapons cause 2-16 +7 when wielded by anyone with a Strength of 19 or better. On occasion, a desert giant will attack with one of its huge fists, causing 1-10 points damage on a successful attack

Some desert giants are gifted with the ability to call back their ancestors from the stones; they are called sand-shifters because of the way the summoned giants throw aside the sands when they rise again. Sand-shifters are not priests or mages; they have no other special spell abilities. One in every 10 desert giants can bring back giants who have assumed the form of stone and can command them to fight once more. Once per week, a desert gi-

ant can summon 1-6 giants from the rocks for 2-12 turns; the summoning takes one turn. These giants crumble back to rock and powder when slain. Desert giant children gifted this way can summon 2-20 stony mounts for their elders to ride into battle. Adult sand-shifters can summon 3-30 mounts instead of 1-6 giants if they so choose.

Desert giants' skin is so similar to sand and rock that they can camouflage themselves very effectively, if given one turn to prepare. This ability allows them to ambush foes and prey alike. (Desert giants who lose their herds often use this ability to become effective bandits, and the numbers of these gigantic brigands have increased as the race dwindles.) A giant so camouflaged increases chances of a surprise attack to 1-4 on a d10 and decreases the chance of being seen by search parties or soldiers to 1 in 10.

Habitat/Society: Desert giants are nomadic herdsmen and are rarely found far from their herds. Though they are responsible for stripping entire river valleys bare in fertile areas, they do not reimburse farmers or herdsmen on the edge of those territories for any damage they might do. They see the lands as theirs for the taking, and they make no apology for overgrazing or even for grazing their herds on crops. Few sultanates attempt to force them off cropland; most attempt to lure the desert giants away with promises of employment as mercenaries. Some will promise rich gifts of salt, cloth, spices, and metal if only the desert giants will return to the empty quarters of the desert.

Ecology: Desert giants wander hundreds of miles following the rains with their herds. When the rains fail, the scrub withers, and the herds and their giants starve. At these times young males among the desert giants may take up mercenary work and use the money they obtain to support the entire tribe. If a drought goes on for years, more and more giants are driven into the cities, though their absolute numbers are still tiny compared to the numbers of humans and other smaller races.

Giant, Ettin

CLIMATE/TERRAIN:	Subarctic to temperate/ Hills and mountains
FREQUENCY:	Very rare
ORGANIZATION:	Solitary
ACTIVITY CYCLE:	Night
DIET:	Carnivore
INTELLIGENCE:	Low (5-7)
TREASURE:	O, (C, Y)
ALIGNMENT:	Chaotic evil

NO. APPEARING:	1 or 1-4
ARMOR CLASS:	3
MOVEMENT:	12
HIT DICE:	10
THAC0:	10
NO. OF ATTACKS:	2
DAMAGE/ATTACK:	1-10/2-12 + weapon
SPECIAL ATTACKS:	Nil
SPECIAL DEFENSES:	Surprised only on a 1
MAGIC RESISTANCE:	Nil
SIZE:	H (13′ tall)
MORALE:	Elite (14)
XP VALUE:	3,000

Ettins, or two-headed giants, as they are often called, are vicious and unpredictable hunters that stalk by night and eat any meat they can catch.

An ettin at first appears to be a stone or hill giant with two heads. On closer inspection, however, the creature's vast differences from the relatively civilized giant races become readily apparent. An ettin has pink to brownish skin, though it appears to be covered in a dark brown hide. This is because an ettin never bathes if it can help it, and is therefore usually encrusted with a thick layer of dirt and grime. Its skin is thick, giving the ettin its low Armor Class. An ettin's hair is long, stringy, and unkempt; its teeth are large, yellowing, and often rotten. The ettin's facial features strongly resemble those of an orc—large watery eyes, turned-up piggish snout, and large mouth.

An ettin's right head is always the dominant one, and the right arm and leg will likely appear slightly more muscular and well-developed than the left. An ettin wears only rough, untreated skins, which are dirty and unwashed. Obviously, ettins smell very bad, due to their complete lack of grooming habits—good or bad.

Ettins do not have a true language of their own. Instead, they speak a mish-mash of orc, goblin, giant dialects, and the alignment tongue of chaotic evil creatures. Any adventurer who speaks orcish can understand 50% of what an ettin says.

Combat: Having two heads is definitely an advantage for the ettins, as one is always alert, watching for danger and potential food. This means that an ettin is surprised only on the roll of a 1 on 1d10. An ettin also has infravision up to 90 feet, which enables it to hunt and fight effectively in the dark.

Though ettins have a low intelligence, they are cunning fighters. They prefer to ambush their victims rather than charge into a straight fight, but once the battle has started, ettins usually fight furiously until all enemies are dead, or the battle turns against them. Ettins do not retreat easily, only doing so if victory is impossible.

In combat, an ettin has two attacks. Because each of its two heads controls an arm, an ettin does not suffer an attack roll penalty for attacking with both arms. An ettin always attacks with two large clubs, often covered with spikes. Using these weapons,

the ettin causes 2d8 points of damage with its left arm, and 3d6 points of damage with its right. If the ettin is disarmed or unable to use a weapon, it attacks empty-handed, inflicting 1d10 points of damage with its left fist and 2d6 points with its right.

Habitat/Society: Ettins like to establish their lairs in remote, rocky areas. They dwell in dark, underground caves that stink of decaying food and offal. Ettins are generally solitary, and mated pairs only stay together for a few months after a young ettin is born to them. Young ettins mature very quickly, and within eight to ten months after they are born, they are self-sufficient enough to go off on their own.

On rare occasions, however, a particularly strong ettin may gather a small group of 1d4 ettins together. This small band of ettins stays together only as long as the leader remains alive and undefeated in battle. Any major defeat shatters the leader's hold over the band, and they each go their separate ways.

Ettins collect treasure only because it can buy them the services of goblins or orcs. These creatures sometimes serve ettins by building traps around their lairs, or helping to fight off a powerful opponent. Ettins have also been known to occasionally keep 1-2 cave bears in the area of their lairs.

The sloppy caves of ettins are a haven for parasites and vermin, and it isn't unusual for the ettins themselves to be infected with various parasitic diseases. Adventurers rummaging through ettin lairs for valuables will find the task disgusting, if not dangerous.

Ecology: Because ettin society is so primitive, they produce little of any value to civilized creatures. Ettins tolerate the presence of other creatures, like orcs, in the area of their lair if they can be useful in some way. Otherwise, ettins tend to be violently isolationist, crushing trespassers without question.

Giant, Firbolg

CLIMATE/TERRAIN:	Temperate/ Hills and forests
FREQUENCY:	Very rare
ORGANIZATION:	Clan
ACTIVITY CYCLE:	Any
DIET:	Omnivore
INTELLIGENCE:	Average to genius (8-18)
TREASURE:	E, Y (M x 10, Q)
ALIGNMENT:	Neutral (chaotic good)

NO. APPEARING:	1-4 or 4-16
ARMOR CLASS:	2
MOVEMENT:	15
HIT DICE:	13 + 7
THAC0:	9
NO. OF ATTACKS:	1
DAMAGE/ATTACK:	1-10 (weapon) +7 (Str bonus)
SPECIAL ATTACKS:	Spells
SPECIAL DEFENSES:	Swat away missiles
MAGIC RESISTANCE:	15%
SIZE:	L (10½' tall)
MORALE:	Champion (16)
XP VALUE:	8,000
	Shaman: 9,000

Of all the giant-kin, the firbolg is the most powerful, due to natural intelligence and considerable magical power.

Firbolgs appear to be normal humans, except that they are over 10 feet tall and weigh over 800 pounds. They wear their hair long and keep great, thick beards. Their skin is a normal fleshy pink, with any shade of hair color, although blonde and red are most common. The flesh and skin of firbolgs are unusually dense and tough. Their voices are a smooth, deep bass, thick with rolling consonants.

Combat: Firbolgs can use any large size weapons; they disdain the use of armor or shields. Of manmade weapons, they prefer two-handed swords and halberds, both of which they may use in one hand without penalty. Weapons of their own make are double size equivalents of human weapons, for which they get a Strength bonus (19 Strength, +7 damage). However, when used with both hands, these huge weapons inflict double their normal damage, plus the Strength bonus.

If a firbolg has one hand free, it can bat away up to two missiles per round. Large missiles, such as boulders, or those with long shafts, such as javelins and spears, can be caught if desired. A catch or bat is successful 75% of the time (6 or better on 1d20). A caught weapon may be thrown at any opponent on the next round with a -2 penalty to the attack roll, for using its off hand.

All firbolgs have the following magical powers, usable once per day, on any round they are not engaged in melee combat: *detect magic, diminution* (as double the potion), *fools' gold, forget,* and *alter self.* There is a 5% cumulative chance per member of a group that one of the firbolgs is a shaman of 1st through 7th level.

Firbolgs are cautious and crafty. They have learned to distrust and fear humans and demihumans. If possible they avoid an encounter, either by hiding or with deception. If forced to fight, they do so with great strategy, utilizing the terrain and situation to best effect. They operate as a group, not a collection of individuals. Ten percent of all encounters is a large group of 4d4 members en route to an enclave of some sort.

Habitat/Society: Firbolgs live in remote forests and hills. These giant-kin distrust most other civilized races, and stay well away

from them. They keep on even terms with druids and the faerie creatures, including elves, neither asking nor giving much, but avoiding insult or injury. Strangers are met with caution, frequently in illusionary disguise as one of their own race. They do not attack or kill without reason, but do enjoy pranks, particularly those that relieve strangers of treasure.

Firbolg society is close-knit and centered around the family or clan. Each clan has 4d4 members and frequently a shaman. The level of the shaman is determined by rolling 2d4-1 if the DM doesn't wish to choose it himself. The clans live apart from each other, existing as gatherers and sometimes nomads. Their homes are huge, single-storey, wooden houses with stout walls and a central fireplace opening in several directions in the common room. When great decisions are needed, the clans involved meet in an enclave. This happens at least once a year at the fall solstice, just to celebrate if nothing else. The shamans preside over these events, and settle any disputes between clans.

Ecology: Firbolgs live off the land and with it. Their homes are built from trees cleared from around the house. The clan does keep a field for harvest, but only enough to supplement their diet. They trade tasks involving great strength for food, usually with other peaceful folk in the forests or hills. The rest of their food is obtained by gathering and hunting an area up to 20 miles from their homestead. Meat is used in small quantities for most meals, although major celebrations always include a large roast of some sort.

Although many creatures are capable of killing a firbolg, none hunt them exclusively. They are stronger than most forest beasts, and intelligent creatures know better than to mess with them. They avoid true giants, except storm giants, and aggressively repel other giant-kin from their lands.

Giant, Fire

CLIMATE/TERRAIN:	Any temperate, subtropical, tropical
FREQUENCY:	Rare
ORGANIZATION:	Tribal
ACTIVITY CYCLE:	Any
DIET:	Omnivorous
INTELLIGENCE:	Low to average (5-10)
TREASURE:	E
ALIGNMENT:	Lawful evil

NO. APPEARING:	1-8
ARMOR CLASS:	-1 (5)
MOVEMENT:	12 (15)
HIT DICE:	15 + 2-5 hit points
THAC0:	5
NO. OF ATTACKS:	1
DAMAGE/ATTACK:	1-8, or by weapon (2-20 +10)
SPECIAL ATTACKS:	Hurling rocks for 2-20 (2d10)
SPECIAL DEFENSES:	Resistant to fire
MAGIC RESISTANCE:	Nil
SIZE:	H (18′)
MORALE:	Champion (15-16)
XP VALUE:	8,000
Infant	Nil
Juvenile, -3	120
Juvenile, -2	3,400
Juvenile, -1	5,000
Shaman/Witch doctor, 1st level spells	9,000
Shaman/Witch doctor, 2nd level spells	10,000
Shaman/Witch doctor, 3rd level spells	10,000
Shaman/Witch doctor, 4th level spells	12,000

Fire giants are brutal, ruthless, and militaristic.

They are tall, but squat, resembling huge dwarves. An adult male is 18 feet tall, has a 12 foot chest, and weighs about 7,500 pounds. Fire giants have coal black skin, flaming red or bright orange hair, and prognathous jaws that reveal dirty ivory or yellow teeth. They can live to be 350 years old.

A fire giant's natural Armor Class is 5. Warriors usually wear banded mail and round metal helmets (AC -1). They carry their belongings in huge sacks. A typical fire giant's sack contains 2-5 (1d4 +1) throwing rocks, the giant's wealth, a tinderbox, and 3-12 (3d4) common items. Everything they own is battered, filthy, and smelly, making it difficult to identify valuable items.

All fire giants can speak the language of all giants and their own tongue.

Combat: Fire giants are immune to nonmagical fire and heat, as well as red dragon breath. They are resistant to all types of magical fire; such attacks inflict -1 hit point per die of damage. Adult fire giants can hurl rocks for 2-20 (2d10) points of damage. Their minimum range is 3 yards while their maximum is 200 yards. They can catch similar large missiles 50% of the time. They usually fight in disciplined groups, throwing rocks until they run out of ammunition or the opponent closes. Fire giants often wait in ambush at lava pools or hot springs, hurling heated rocks at victims for an extra 1-6 points of damage.

Warriors favor huge two-handed swords. A fire giant's oversized weapons do double normal (man-sized) damage to all opponents, plus the giant's strength bonus. Thus, a fire giant two-handed sword does 2-20 (2d10) +10 points of damage.

Habitat/Society: Fire giants live in well organized military groups, occupying large castles or caverns. When encountered in their lair there will be 13-20 (1d8 +12) giants, half of whom will be immature giants. To determine a giant's maturity, roll 1d4. A roll of 4 indicates an infant with no combat ability and the hit points of an ogre while rolls of 1-3 indicate older progeny with Hit Dice, damage, and attack

rolls reduced by 1, 2 or 3, respectively.

Their lairs are always protected by vigilant watchmen, and sometimes by traps. Fire giants favor deadfalls that can crush intruders for 5-30 (5d6) points of damage, and large crossbow devices that fire one, two, or three huge bolts for 2-16 (2d8) points of damage each.

Particularly intelligent fire giant leaders will command groups three or four times normal size. One who commands 30 or more giants usually will call himself a king. Kings always will have better than normal armor and a magical weapon of +1 to +3.

There is a 20% chance that any band of fire giants will have a shaman (80%) or witch doctor (20%). If the group is lead by a king, there is an 80% chance of a spell caster. Fire giant shamans are priests of up to 7th level. A shaman can cast normal or reversed spells from the Elemental, Healing, Charm, Protection, Divination, or Combat spheres. Fire giant witch doctors are priest/wizards of up to 7th/3rd level; they prefer spells that can detect or thwart intruders.

Fire giants often capture and tame other creatures as guards. There is a 50% chance that a fire giant lair will contain 1-4 hell hounds. Larger than normal groups check once for every 10 giants. Bands with 30 or more giants have a additional 30% chance to have 2-5 (1d4 +1) trolls, larger groups check once for every 20 giants. A king's group has a 20% chance to have 1-2 red dragons of age category 2-5 (1d4 +1) in addition to other guards. Fire giants frequently take captives to hold for ransom or use as slaves. There is a 25% chance that a lair will contain 1-2 captives, larger bands check once per 10 giants.

Ecology: Fire giants live wherever there is a lot of heat. They prefer volcanic regions or areas with hot springs. Frequently they share their lairs with other fire-dwelling creatures such as salamanders or fire elementals.

Fire giants prefer to eat meat and bread, they can hunt and kill their own meat, but raid human and demi-human settlements for grain, captives, and treasure.

Giant, Fog

CLIMATE/TERRAIN:	Temperate/Swamps, marshes, boggy forests, and coastal regions
FREQUENCY:	Very rare
ORGANIZATION:	Clan, Hunting Group
ACTIVITY CYCLE:	Day
DIET:	Omnivore
INTELLIGENCE:	Average (8-10) to highly (13-14)
TREASURE:	E, R
ALIGNMENT:	Neutral (good 50%, evil 50%)

NO. APPEARING:	1-4 (rarely 1-6)
ARMOR CLASS:	1
MOVEMENT:	15
HIT DICE:	14
THAC0:	7
NO. OF ATTACKS:	1
DAMAGE/ATTACK:	1-10, or by weapon (3-18+11)
SPECIAL ATTACKS:	Rock hurling
SPECIAL DEFENSES:	See below
MAGIC RESISTANCE:	Nil
SIZE:	H (24' tall)
MORALE:	Very steady (14)
XP VALUE:	5,000

Cousins to the cloud giants, these large rock-hurlers are more intelligent and stealthy than portrayed in story or song.

Fog giants are huge and husky, with tree-trunk sized legs, and over-developed arms muscled by constant throwing games and exercises. They have milk-white skin which aids their natural ability to blend into fog (80% chance) and gives their foes a −5 penalty to their surprise rolls when attacking in fog or mist. Their hair is silvery white and flowing, with ample hair on the arms, legs, and chest. They grow no facial hair whatsoever. They prefer to wear no armor, counting on their high natural Armor Class. However, they occasionally wear leather armor (AC −2), and at least one band wears armor made from white dragon hides studded with silver. They love massive, ornate clubs made from bleached and polished wood or bone. Fog giants speak their own tongue and Cloud Giant, and 30% speak Common.

Combat: Fog giants generally hunt in groups of 2-5 males, although they sometimes join with a cloud giant or two to form a hunting party of 3-7. They prefer to attack from cover (fog is most preferred). After some ranged rock-hurling to scatter their opponents, they will charge into melee with fists and swords flying. Adult fog giants can hurl rocks up to 3-240 yards, inflicting 2-20 points of damage to anyone struck. They also have a 45% chance of catching hurled weapons of similar size, but cannot catch fired weapons such as arrows, bolts, and sling-stones. In melee they generally fight with clubs and fists, though tales of sword-armed fog giants are common.

Because of their keen hearing and highly-developed sense of smell, fog giants are seldom surprised (+2 on surprise rolls). Access to their caves and regular hunting camps are often protected by deadfalls of rocks or logs, which can be released by a carefully thrown rock at the first sign of an attack against them.

Habitat/Society: Fog giants are proud of their strength and fighting skills, often playing games when on hunting forays in an attempt to best one another. Their favorite such game is called "copsi" and consists of the giants pairing off to toss larger and larger boulders to their partners until one of the pairs misses its throw.

The fog giant families live in caves, canyons, or thickets, in the most inaccessible areas of marsh, swamp, forest, or coast.

The men usually hunt in groups, ranging up to a dozen miles from their homes. The groups generally are formed of giants of similar alignment.

By tradition, a young giant may not mate until he has obtained at least one large ornament of silver. Usually, the young giant joins with several others in a quest to find one (or acquire enough treasure to buy one).

Fog giants do not often mix well with other creatures or races, although they can often be persuaded to perform services for a fee, or barter goods with groups of similar alignment. Fog giants will happily barter goods and services for refined silver.

Territorial disputes sometimes flare up between groups, especially in times of bad hunting. Friendly disputes can sometimes be resolved by a game of copsi or an arm-wrestling match. Fog giants fighting amongst themselves will generally throw rocks and fist-fight, rather than use swords.

Fog giants are fond of all sorts of cooked meats, particularly hoofed creatures such as horses, cows, deer, elk, and centaur. They often cook meat by building a large fire, then impaling chunks of meat on their swords and holding them over the open flame. Fog giants prefer fruits and sweets for dessert, and will also down large quantities of spirits if available to them. They do not distill their own spirits or liquors. They also sometimes smoke fresh milkweed pods in wooden pipes, though the taste is too bitter for humans and demihumans to enjoy.

Ecology: Because of their size, fog giants consume a large quantity of food, and require a considerable territory per hunting group to support themselves. The giants will often place territorial markers of boulders and logs to define the boundaries between their hunting territories. They do not look kindly on anyone who tears down or moves these markers. Their regular pathways are hard to hide, and are instead trapped with deadfalls of rocks and logs to discourage trespassers.

Giant, Fomorian

CLIMATE/TERRAIN:	Any mountain and subterranean
FREQUENCY:	Uncommon
ORGANIZATION:	Solitary
ACTIVITY CYCLE:	Any
DIET:	Omnivore
INTELLIGENCE:	Average (8-10)
TREASURE:	D, Q x 10
ALIGNMENT:	Neutral evil

NO. APPEARING:	1-4
ARMOR CLASS:	3
MOVEMENT:	9
HIT DICE:	13+3
THAC0:	9
NO. OF ATTACKS:	1
DAMAGE/ATTACK:	2 x weapon, +8 (Str bonus)
SPECIAL ATTACKS:	Surprise
SPECIAL DEFENSES:	Only surprised on a 1
MAGIC RESISTANCE:	Nil
SIZE:	H (13½' tall)
MORALE:	Elite (14)
XP VALUE:	6,000

Fomorians are the most hideous, deformed, and wicked of all giant-kin.

The fomorian giants are all grossly deformed behemoths. Each has a different set of deformities, which must be determined by the DM. A partial list of deformations includes misplaced limb, misshapen limb, misplaced facial feature, hunchbacked, bulging body part, drooping flesh, body part too big or too small, flapping ears, huge snout, large feet on short legs. Their thick, hairy hides, combined with the pelts and odd metal bits they wear for protection, give an effective AC of 3. They have scattered patches of hair as tough as wire on their pale white skin. Large warts and other growths are scattered across their bodies. There is no single odor associated with fomorians; some smell strongly due to overactive sweat glands, others have no smell. Their voices are also each different due to their unique deformities.

Combat: Fomorians use all manner of clubs and other blunt instruments. Regardless of the weapon, it inflicts double damage plus 8 points for Strength, while their fists alone inflict 2d4+8 points of damage. Their deformities prevent them from hurling boulders as true giants. They work any bits of metal they can find and scavenge into their clothing, to aid their Armor Class. The typical fomorian is AC 3, while a particularly well-armored one, or one with a shield, might get an AC as good as 1, but no better.

Typical fomorian strategy is too sneak up on an opponent and hit him as hard as it can. It works well for them since their opponents suffer a -2 penalty to their surprise rolls, because the fomorians move slowly and carefully. These giant-kin are only surprised on a 1 on the 1d10 surprise roll, because they tend to have eyes and ears in odd places on their heads. If the fomorian bothers to keep an opponent alive, he is crudely tortured until dead, and then eaten.

Habitat/Society: Fomorians live in mountain caves, abandoned mines, or other subterranean realms. They rarely modify their homes, but adapt to what is already there. These deformed giants wander throughout the underground complex, for almost any distance, stopped only by hazards they do not want to challenge. A fomorian clan picks a small, (to them) defensible alcove for a lair. Their territories are sometimes marked by the bodies of their enemies. Their treasure consists only of stolen items from enemies. Pieces of armor are added to their own patchwork protection. Since they do not care for it, this armor quickly deteriorates and becomes worthless.

Their society is ruled by depravity and wickedness. The strongest and cruelest giant rules over all the others within reach, which is usually a small number. The women and children are treated as slaves. Acts of violence are common among fomorians, sometimes resulting in permanent injury or death.

Fomorian giants have been known to work with other creatures for evil causes. Usually the other creatures must completely dominate the fomorians, or be capable of it, to form the alliance. Such an agreement lasts only as long as the fomorians fear their cohorts. Once their interests no longer coincide or the fomorians no longer feel threatened, they double-cross their partners, as quickly as possible.

Ecology: These twisted giants can live for weeks on little or no food. This is good, because their underground dwellings do not provide an abundance of it. They can eat almost any organic material, including fungi, lichens, plants of all sorts, bats, mice and fish. They particularly savor the taste of large mammals, especially those that beg not to be eaten. Preparing a meal usually involves torture rather than any efforts to improve its taste.

Giant, Frost

CLIMATE/TERRAIN:	Arctic lands
FREQUENCY:	Very rare
ORGANIZATION:	Tribal
ACTIVITY CYCLE:	Any
DIET:	Omnivorous
INTELLIGENCE:	Low to average (5-10)
TREASURE:	E
ALIGNMENT:	Chaotic evil

NO. APPEARING:	1-8
ARMOR CLASS:	0 (5)
MOVEMENT:	12 (15)
HIT DICE:	14 + 1-4 hit points
THAC0:	7 or 5
NO. OF ATTACKS:	1
DAMAGE/ATTACK:	1-8, or by weapon (2-16 +9)
SPECIAL ATTACKS:	Hurling rocks for 2-20 (2d10)
SPECIAL DEFENSES:	Impervious to cold
MAGIC RESISTANCE:	Nil
SIZE:	H (21')
MORALE:	Very Steady (13-14)
XP VALUE:	7,000
Infant	Nil
Juvenile, -3	270
Juvenile, -2	975
Juvenile, -1	4,000
Shaman/Witch doctor, 1st	8,000
Shaman/Witch doctor, 2nd	8,000
Shaman/Witch doctor, 3rd	8,000
Shaman/Witch doctor, 4th +	10,000

Like all evil giants, frost giants have a reputation for crudeness and stupidity. This reputation is deserved, but frost giants are crafty fighters.

Frost giants have muscular, roughly human builds. The typical adult male is 21' tall and weighs about 8,000 pounds. Females are slightly shorter and lighter, but otherwise identical to males. Frost giants have snow-white or ivory skin. Their hair is light blue or dirty yellow, with matching eyes. They can live to be 250 years old.

A frost giant's natural Armor Class is 5. Warriors usually wear chain mail and metal helmets decorated with horns or feathers (AC 0). They also wear skins and pelts, along with any jewelry they own.

Frost giants carry their belongings in huge sacks. A typical frost giant's sack contains 2-5 (1d4 +1) throwing rocks, the giant's wealth, and 3-12 (3d4) mundane items. Everything in a giant's bag is old, worn, dirty, and smelly, making the identification of any valuable items difficult.

Frost giants speak their own language and the language common to all giants.

Combat: Frost giants are immune to cold. Adult frost giants can hurl rocks for 2-20 (2d10) points of damage. Their minimum range is 3 yards while their maximum is 200 yards. They can catch similar large missiles 40% of the time. They usually will start combat at a distance, throwing rocks until they run out of ammunition, or the opponent closes. One of their favorite strategies is to ambush victims by hiding buried in the snow at the top of an icy or snowy slope where opponents will have difficulty reaching them.

Warriors favor huge battle axes. A frost giant's oversized weapons do double normal (man-sized) damage to all opponents, plus the giant's strength bonus. Thus, a frost giant battle axe does 2-16 (2d8) +9 points of damage.

Habitat/Society: Frost giants live in small bands consisting of a chief, his henchmen, and their camp followers. A band usually

will occupy a crude castle or frigid cavern. When encountered in their lair there will be 9-16 1d8 +8) giants; half of whom will be immature. To determine a giant's maturity, roll 1d4. A roll of 4 indicates an infant with no combat ability and hit points of ogre; rolls of 1-3 indicate older progeny with hit dice, damage, and attack rolls equal to that of a stone giant.

Particularly strong or intelligent frost giant chieftains will command bands three or four times normal size. A chieftain who commands 20 or more giants is called a jarl. Jarls always will have better than normal armor and a weapon of +1 to +3 enchantment.

There is a 20% chance that any band of frost giants will have a shaman (80%) or witch doctor (20%). If the group is led by a jarl, there is an 80% chance for a spell caster. Frost giant shamans are priests of up to 7th level. A shaman can cast normal or reversed spells from the *healing, charm, protection, divination,* or *weather* spheres. Frost giant witch doctors are priest/wizards of up to 7th/3rd level; they prefer spells that can bewilder and confound other giants. Favorite spells include: *unseen servant, shocking grasp, detect magic, ventriloquism, deeppockets, ESP, mirror image,* and *invisibility.*

Frost giants often capture and tame other creatures as guards. There is a 50% chance that a frost giant lair will contain 1-6 winter wolves. Larger than normal groups check once for every eight giants. Bands with 20 or more giants have a additional 30% chance to have 1-4 yeti, larger groups check once for every 16 giants. A jarl's band has a 20% chance to have 1-2 subdued white dragons in addition to other guards. The dragons will be age category 2-5 (1d4 +1). Frost giants also take captives to hold for ransom or use as slaves. There is a 15% chance that a lair will contain 1-2 captives, larger bands check once per eight giants. Captives can be of any race.

Ecology: Frost giants live in frigid, arctic lands with glaciers and heavy snowfall. Frost giants eat mostly meat, which they can hunt and kill themselves. They raid human and demi-human settlements for foodstuffs and other booty.

Giant, Hill

CLIMATE/TERRAIN:	Any hills and mountains
FREQUENCY:	Rare
ORGANIZATION:	Tribal
ACTIVITY CYCLE:	Any
DIET:	Omnivorous
INTELLIGENCE:	Low (5-7)
TREASURE:	D
ALIGNMENT:	Chaotic evil

NO. APPEARING:	1-12
ARMOR CLASS:	3 (5)
MOVEMENT:	12
HIT DICE:	12 + 1-2 hit points
THAC0:	9
NO. OF ATTACKS:	1
DAMAGE/ATTACK:	1-6 or by weapon (2-12 + 7)
SPECIAL ATTACKS:	Hurling rocks for 2-16 (2d8)
SPECIAL DEFENSES:	Nil
MAGIC RESISTANCE:	Nil
SIZE:	H (16' tall)
MORALE:	Elite (13-14)
XP VALUE:	3,000
Infant	Nil
Juvenile, -3	270
Juvenile, -2	650
Juvenile, -1	2,000

Hill giants are selfish, cunning brutes who survive through hunting and by terrorizing and raiding nearby communities. Despite their low intelligence, they are capable fighters.

Hill giants are oddly simian and barbaric in appearance, with overly long arms, stooped shoulders, and low foreheads. Even though they are the smallest of the giants, their limbs are more muscular and massive than those of the other giant races. The average hill giant is 16 feet tall and weighs about 4,500 pounds. Females have the same builds as males. Their skin color ranges from a light tan to a deep ruddy brown. Their hair is brown or black, and their eyes are black. Hill giants can live to be 200 years old.

Hill giants' natural Armor Class is 5. This is reduced to an Armor Class of 3 when they wear crudely-sewn animal hides, which are the equivalent of leather armor. Nearly all hill giants wear these hides, which are a symbol of esteem in some hill giant communities—the more hides a giant has, the more large kills to his credit. Only a few (5%) of the giants fashion metal armor from the armor of men they have defeated. These giants have an Armor Class of 0. Like other races of giants, hill giants carry their belongings with them in huge hide sacks. A typical hill giant's bag will contain 2-8 (2d4) throwing rocks, the giant's wealth, and 1-8 additional common items.

Hill giants speak their own language and a tongue common to all giants. In addition, 50% also speak ogre.

Combat: Hill giants prefer to fight their opponents from high rocky outcroppings where they can pelt their targets with rocks and boulders while limiting the risks posed to themselves.

Hill giants' favorite weapons are oversized clubs which do 2-12 +7 points of damage (double the damage of a man-sized club plus their strength bonus). They hurl rocks for 2-16 (2d8) points of damage. Their targets for such attacks must be between 3 and 200 yards away from the giant. They can catch rocks or other similar missiles 30% of the time.

Habitat/Society: A hill giant lair will have 9-16 (1d8 + 8) giants; usually an extended family. Sometimes these families will accept lone hill giants into their folds. If six or more giants are encountered in a lair, half of them will be male, one quarter will be female, and the remainder will be immature giants. To determine a giant's maturity, roll 1d4. A roll of 4 indicates an infant with no combat ability and hit points of gnoll; rolls of 1-3 indicate older progeny with hit dice, damage, and attack rolls equal to that of an ogre.

Occasionally a hill giant with an average intelligence can be found. Such a giant is capable of rallying bands of his peers so 2, 3, or 4 times the number of giants usually appearing can be encountered. These "giant kings," as they call themselves, stage raids on human towns or against other races of giants.

Although hill giants prefer temperate areas, they can be found in practically any climate where there is an abundance of hills and mountains. They lair in caves, excavated dens, or crude huts. Those who live in colder climates have developed more skills with preparing and using skins to keep themselves warm and to keep the harsh winds out of their lairs.

There is a 50% chance a band of hill giants will have guards in their lairs, and the guarding creatures will be 2-8 (2d4) dire wolves (50%), 1-3 giant lizards (30%), or a group of 2-8 (2d4) ogres (20%).

The majority of hill giants are suspicious of magic and will seek to destroy magic items they acquire as treasure. They ceremonially kill mages.

Ecology: Hill giants' main diet consists of meat, which they obtain by hunting. The flesh of young green dragons is considered a delicacy, and frequently giants who live on hills and mountains covered with forests will organize hunting parties in search of green dragon lairs. In turn, green dragons have been known to hunt hill giants.

Sometimes bands of hill giants will trade with each other or with bands of ogres to get foodstuffs and trinkets.

Giant, Jungle

CLIMATE/TERRAIN:	Tropical/jungle
FREQUENCY:	Uncommon
ORGANIZATION:	Tribal/cooperative
ACTIVITY CYCLE:	Day
DIET:	Carnivore
INTELLIGENCE:	Average to High (8-14)
TREASURE:	Q (A)
ALIGNMENT:	Neutral

NO. APPEARING:	1 or 1-6
ARMOR CLASS:	3
MOVEMENT:	15, Cl 6
HIT DICE:	11
THAC0:	9
NO. OF ATTACKS:	1 or 2
DAMAGE/ATTACK:	2-16 +9 or 2-12 +9/2-12 +9
SPECIAL ATTACKS:	Surprise, arrows
SPECIAL DEFENSES:	See below
MAGIC RESISTANCE:	Nil
SIZE:	H (18' tall)
MORALE:	Champion (16)
XP VALUE:	6,000

Powerful, lanky, and strictly carnivorous, jungle giants are a terror to all the animals of the tropical forests. They are great hunters and stalkers, able to clear a huge tract of forest of all game and then move on.

A typical jungle giant stands 18' tall yet weighs only 3,000 pounds—very thin for a giant. Females are generally taller than males. They can live to be 200 years old.

Jungle giants always carry everything they need with them: tools for making and maintaining their weapons, fire-starters, tinder, and spare bits of leather and sinew used to repair clothing. They also carry their valuables, and every adult jungle giant carries a quiver of arrows.

Jungle giants speak their own language and the languages of tribes of nearby humans and humanoids.

Thin and very tall, jungle giants easily blend into the vertical landscape of the tropical forest. Their wavy hair is pale green, and their skin is a rich muddy yellow, like sunlight on the forest floor. They rarely wear more clothing than strictly necessary, as they prefer complete freedom of movement when hunting. Many groups of jungle giants use ritual tattooing, colorful feather headdresses, and even filed teeth to show their fierceness. They sometimes decorate themselves with mud, sticks, and leaves when stalking especially large or wary game.

Combat: Jungle giants use 15' long bows crafted to take advantage of their tremendous size and strength. These giants are very quick with their huge bows and can fire two arrows each round. They will use poisoned arrows to bring down their prey more quickly. If these arrows are used in combat, opponents must save vs. paralyzation at −2 or be rendered immobile for 2-12 turns. Even humanoid creatures with the strength to pull a jungle giant bow cannot use it, because the arrows are over 6' long (2d6 +9 damage). Jungle giants will occasionally use the trunk of a dead tree as a club, doing 2d8 +9 points damage.

Jungle giants prefer to take their prey from ambushes, firing their bows from the treetops and then swinging down sturdy branches or thick ropes to finish off their prey. Camouflaged giants cause a −1 penalty on opponents' surprise rolls. When setting up a blind, they can camouflage themselves in jungle terrain with a 60% chance of success. Setting up a blind or decorating themselves with jungle camouflage takes three turns.

Habitat/Society: Jungle giants are friendlier than most other races of giants, and they will often cooperate with human jungle tribes on hunts. The giants provide strength and raw power, and the humans provide the numbers and skill to drive animals into ambushes.

Jungle giants have absolutely no compunctions about eating any form of meat—mammal, reptile, amphibian, or avian. They know how to stalk, kill, and prepare everything from eggs to full-grown animals, and from scavengers to predators. Their villages reflect this carnivorous tendency; the huts are made from wooden posts with roofs of greased animal hides stitched together with intestines. The smell of smoking meats and butchery hang in the air, and huge quantities of dragonflies and other insects swarm around the villages. A jungle giant village is 50% likely to shelter 1-6 giant dragonflies.

Ecology: Jungle giants think of most creatures as prey, but those they accept as fellow hunters they respect as equals, regardless of their size. Although they much prefer the jungle terrain they know so well, they are often forced to leave the trees for the savanna when their numbers become too great to survive in the jungle. They think nothing of eating every snake, antelope, cat, warthog, ostrich, and elephant they come across. Jungle giants on the savannah often return to the forest, because their great height makes stealthy hunting difficult for them on open ground.

Giant, Mountain

CLIMATE/TERRAIN:	Any/Mountains
FREQUENCY:	Very rare
ORGANIZATION:	Family
ACTIVITY CYCLE:	Any
DIET:	Omnivore
INTELLIGENCE:	Average (8-10)
TREASURE:	E
ALIGNMENT:	Chaotic neutral

NO. APPEARING:	1-4
ARMOR CLASS:	4
MOVEMENT:	12
HIT DICE:	15+3
THAC0:	5
NO. OF ATTACKS:	1
DAMAGE/ATTACK:	1-8 or by weapon (4d10+10)
SPECIAL ATTACKS:	Hurling rocks for 2-20
SPECIAL DEFENSES:	Nil
MAGIC RESISTANCE:	Nil
SIZE:	H (14' tall)
MORALE:	Champion (15-16)
XP VALUE:	Normal: 7,000
	Infant: Nil
	Juvenile: 3,000
	Shaman: 8,000
	Shaman, 3rd: 9,000

Mountain giants are huge humanoids that live in remote mountain caverns.

Standing 14 feet tall and weighing 2,000 pounds, mountain giants are impressive foes. They greatly resemble hill giants. Their skin color is a light tan to reddish brown with straight black hair. The males have heavy beards but no mustaches, and they have large pot bellies. They are typically clothed in rough hides or skins and carry huge clubs as weapons. The stale reek of a mountain giant can be detected several hundred feet downwind.

Combat: Mountain giants always attack in a straight-forward manner, not by ambush or deceit. They love to get into a high, unassailable spot with lots of boulders. When in such a position, mountain giants rarely take cover, but stand in the open to fling their missiles. They can hurl boulders down on their opponents for 2d10 points of damage each. They can catch similar missiles 30% of the time.

In melee they use huge clubs that cause 4d10+10 points of damage, including their Strength bonus. These clubs are usually just large tree limbs or logs. They usually keep several such weapons around. Mountain giants are as strong as fire giants (22).

A mountain giant can summon and control other monsters. This summoning takes a full turn to perform and 1d6 hours pass before the creatures appear. A summoning results in either 1d10+5 ogres (70%), 1d6+3 trolls (20%), or 1d4 hill giants (10%), although the giant has no idea in advance of what he will get. The control is very loose, not absolute domination. The mountain giant can give a broadly defined command and the monsters obey as they see fit. The summoned monsters stay with and fight for the mountain giant, but they value their own lives over that of the giant. The summoned creatures stay with the giant until killed, sent away, or another summoning is made.

Habitat/Society: The home of a family of mountain giants is often in a large rock cavern in a mountain. Frequently there are unexplored passages leading out of the giants' home. They rarely have any interest in anything beyond their cavern. There is a

75% chance of summoned creatures acting as guards and underlings in the cavern.

The females and young are rarely seen, since they stick close to the cavern. Mountain giants are polygamous, usually one female living with several males. Three quarters of the young are male, which accounts for their low population. If two or more mountain giants are in a lair, there is a 50% chance of a female and a 25% chance of a child. Roll 1d4 to determine the age of the child. If it is a 4, it is a helpless infant or small child. A roll of 1-3 indicates older children or teens that have the Hit Dice, damage, and attack rolls of hill giants.

There is a 20% chance that one of the giants in a family is a shaman. Roll 1d6 to determine the level of spell use, 1-4 meaning 1st level, 5-6 indicating 2nd level. This shaman can cast from the spheres of All, Animal, Charm, Combat, Elemental, and Healing. He has an innate ability to find caves and cavern entrances within half a mile, unless these are magically hidden.

While only one family is found in a given lair, several families make up a loose tribe scattered over a mountain or range. Each tribe has a 3rd-level shaman as its leader. He presides over the extremely rare gatherings of the tribe and counsels those willing to travel to talk to him. The shaman always lives with a group of summoned monsters, but never with other mountain giants.

Ecology: Mountain giants are foragers and hunters. Their favorite food is mountain sheep. They also eat nuts, tubers, and other edible mountain plants. Nothing hunts mountain giants, but sometimes they pick the wrong cave in which to set up housekeeping. Since they tend not to fully explore all the back tunnels, nasty things from underground have been known to attack and devour sleeping giants.

Since these giants are neither good nor evil, it is possible to set up peaceful relations with them. However, they are suspicious of and reluctant to deal with outsiders.

Giant, Reef

CLIMATE/TERRAIN:	Tropical or subtropical ocean/reef
FREQUENCY:	Very rare
ORGANIZATION:	Solitary
ACTIVITY CYCLE:	Day
DIET:	Omnivore
INTELLIGENCE:	Very (11-12)
TREASURE:	Z (A)
ALIGNMENT:	Neutral good

NO. APPEARING:	1 or 1-4
ARMOR CLASS:	0 or -4
MOVEMENT:	15, Sw 12
HIT DICE:	18
THAC0:	5
NO. OF ATTACKS:	1
DAMAGE/ATTACK:	1-10 or by weapon (typically 2-20 +10)
SPECIAL ATTACKS:	Boulders, whirlpool
SPECIAL DEFENSES:	Immune to water-based attacks
MAGIC RESISTANCE:	Nil
SIZE:	H (16' tall)
MORALE:	Fanatic (17)
XP VALUE:	13,000

Reef giants are the loners of giant-kind, although they often live in remarkably well-appointed mansions that seem to be no more than huts from the outside. They sometimes become sailors, but their huge mass limits them to the largest of vessels. Reef giants are typically 16' tall and weigh 4,000 pounds. Reef giants can live to be 600 years old.

Reef giants speak their own language as well as the giantish trade tongue and the languages of storm and cloud giants. In addition, 40% of the giants also speak the common tongue.

Reef giants have burnished coppery skin and pale white hair. They are barrel-chested and powerfully-muscled from the exertion of forcing their huge bodies through water. Reef giants have a Strength of 22. Reef giants wear skins or garments made of braided hair when ashore, but swim wearing no more than a belt for knives and pouches.

Combat: Reef giants prefer to fight in or under water, and they are fierce fighters when angered. They suffer no penalties when fighting in or under water. They cannot be harmed by water- or ice-based attack forms. They typically attack with giant tridents for 2-20 +10 points of damage, but have been known to lash out with a huge fist (1d10 points damage) now and again.

Once per day, a reef giant can form a whirlpool. Unless a successful Strength ability check is made, creatures within 10 yards of the giant are sucked into the whirlpool and suffer 2-16 points of battering damage plus 2-20 points drowning and choking damage (unless the creatures are able to breathe water, in which case only the battering damage applies). The whirlpool is not powerful enough to draw in ships.

Reef giants can throw boulders up to 350 yards for 3-30 (3d10) points of damage. They prefer to use thrown boulders to sink unwelcome ships. Boulders are not used against individual opponents.

Habitat/Society: Reef giants are often solitary for long periods of time, although they mate for life. When their children reach puberty, they are sent out on their own to seek an island or reef habitat to make their home.

The mansions of reef giants are sometimes built into the hills and gorges of the islands, and they are always stocked with furniture and decorations collected over generations. These mansions are passed on from one giant to another; the eldest daughter is generally reared to provide for her parents as they grow old and is usually given the mansion and all its goods upon their death. These well-dowried daughters are the objects of much competition between reef giant suitors, each of whom seeks to both prove himself to the new mistress of the mansion and undo his competitors by any means available. Diving, surfing, and fishing competitions are common in reef giant courtship.

Ecology: Reef giants are scavengers who fish and forage coral reefs for a hundred different sources of food. They can net entire schools of fish, and as accomplished divers they can retrieve hoards of pearls, sponges, and coral. Their enormous strength allows them to swim for hours at a time without tiring. In this way reef giants can amass huge amounts of goods to trade for other items.

Some reef giants keep flocks of goats or sheep on their island homes, but these giants are generally elderly and not as capable of foraging successfully.

Reef giants frequently enter into contracts or trade agreements with humans and other mercantile races. In exchange for pearls and other valuables from the sea, they are given cloth, sweets, and metal goods.

The reef giants willingness to plunder the sea has made them the enemies of merfolk, tritons, and other ocean-dwelling races.

Giant, Stone

CLIMATE/TERRAIN:	Sub-tropical and temperate mountains
FREQUENCY:	Rare
ORGANIZATION:	Tribal
ACTIVITY CYCLE:	Any
DIET:	Omnivorous
INTELLIGENCE:	Average (8-10)
TREASURE:	D
ALIGNMENT:	Neutral

NO. APPEARING:	1-10
ARMOR CLASS:	0
MOVEMENT:	12
HIT DICE:	14 + 1-3 hit points
THAC0:	7
NO. OF ATTACKS:	1
DAMAGE/ATTACK:	1-8 or by weapon (2-12+8)
SPECIAL ATTACKS:	Hurling rocks for 3-30 (3d10)
SPECIAL DEFENSES:	See below
MAGIC RESISTANCE:	Nil
SIZE:	H (18' tall)
MORALE:	16
XP VALUE:	7,000
Infant	Nil
Juvenile, -3	975
Juvenile, -2	3,000
Juvenile, -1	6,000
Elder	9,000
Spell caster	9,000

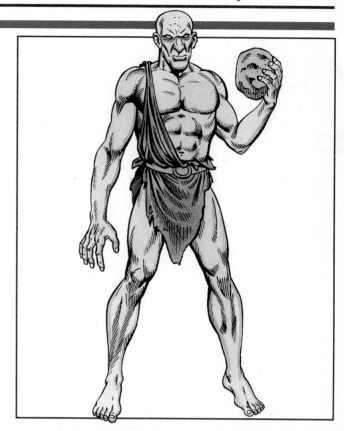

Stone giants are lean, but muscular. Their hard, hairless flesh is smooth and gray, making it easy for them to blend in with their mountainous surroundings. Their gaunt facial features and deep, sunken black eyes make them seem perpetually grim.

The typical stone giant is 18' tall and weighs 9,000 pounds because of its dense flesh. Females are a little shorter and lighter. The giants' natural Armor Class is 0. They do not wear armor to augment that, preferring to wear stone-colored garments. Stone giants can live to be 800 years old.

Stone giants, like several other giant races, carry some of their belongings with them. They leave their more valuable items in their lairs, however. A typical stone giant's bag will contain 2-24 (2d12) throwing rocks, a portion of the giant's wealth, and 1-8 additional common items.

Stone giants speak their own language, as well as those of hill giants, cloud giants, and storm giants. In addition, 50% of the giants also speak the common language of man.

Combat: When possible, stone giants fight from a distance. They are able to hurl rocks a minimum distance of 3 yards to a maximum distance of 300 yards, doing 3-30 (3d10) points of damage with each rock. These giants are able to catch stones and similar missiles 90% of the time. A favorite tactic of stone giants is to stand nearly motionless against rocks, blending in with the background, then moving forward to throw rocks, surprising their foes. Many giants set up piles of rocks near their lair which can be triggered like an avalanche when intruders get too close.

When stone giants are forced into melee combat, they use large clubs chiseled out of stone which do 2-12 (2d6) +8 points of damage; double normal (man-sized) club damage plus the giant's strength bonus.

Habitat/Society: Stone giants prefer to dwell in deep caves high on rocky, storm-swept mountains. They normally live in the company of their relatives, though such a clans usually include no more than 10 giants. Clans of giants do locate their lairs near

each other, however, for a sense of community and protection. A mountain range commonly has 2-8 clans lairing there.

Stone giants are crude artists, painting scenes of their lives on the walls of their lairs and on tanned hide scrolls. Some giants are fond of music and play stone flutes and drums. Others make simple jewelry, fashioning painted stone beads into necklaces.

If eight or more giants are encountered in a clan's lair, one quarter will be female, one quarter male, and the remainder offspring. To determine a giant's maturity, roll 1d4. A roll of 4 indicates an infant with no combat ability and hit points of an ogre; rolls of 1-3 indicate older progeny with hit dice, damage, and attack rolls equal to those of a hill giant.

One in 20 stone giants develop special abilities related to their environment. These giant elders are able to *stone shape*, *stone tell*, and *transmute rock to mud* (or mud to rock) once per day as if they were 5th level mages. One in 10 of these exceptional giants can also cast spells as if he were a 3rd level wizard. Their spells can be determined randomly or chosen to fit a specific encounter as desired. Frequently these giants are able to rise to positions of power and are considered the leaders of several clans.

Stone giants are usually found in mountain ranges in temperate and sub-tropical areas. Stone giants are fond of cave bears and 75% of their lairs will have 1-8 of them as guards. The few stone giants living in cold areas use polar bears as guards.

Stone giants are playful, especially at night. They are fond of rock throwing contests and other games that test their might. Tribes of giants will often gather to toss rocks at each other, the losing side being the giants who are hit more often.

Ecology: Stone giants are omnivorous, but they will eat only fresh food. They cook and eat their meat quickly after it has been killed. They use the skins of the animals for blankets and trade what they do not need with nearby human communities in exchange for bolts of cloth or herd animals which they use for food. Many stone giant bands keep giant goats in and near their lairs so they will have a continuous supply of milk, cheese, and butter.

Giant, Storm

CLIMATE/TERRAIN:	Special (see below)
FREQUENCY:	Very rare
ORGANIZATION:	Solitary or Tribal
ACTIVITY CYCLE:	Any
DIET:	Omnivorous
INTELLIGENCE:	Exceptional (15-16)
TREASURE:	E, Qx10, S
ALIGNMENT:	Chaotic good

NO. APPEARING:	1 (2-4)
ARMOR CLASS:	−6 (0)
MOVEMENT:	15, Sw 15
HIT DICE:	19 + 2-7 hit points
THAC0:	3
NO. OF ATTACKS:	1
DAMAGE/ATTACK:	1-10 or by weapon (3-30 + 12)
SPECIAL ATTACKS:	See below
SPECIAL DEFENSES:	Impervious to electricity
MAGIC RESISTANCE:	Nil
SIZE:	G (26' tall)
MORALE:	Fanatic (17-18)
XP VALUE:	14,000
Infant	Nil
Juvenile, -3	1,400
Juvenile, -2	4,000
Juvenile, -1	7,000
Spell caster, 1st	15,000
Spell caster, 2nd	15,000
Spell caster, 3rd	15,000
Spell caster, 4th +	17,000

Storm giants are gentle and reclusive. They are usually tolerant of others, but can be very dangerous when angry.

Storm giants resemble well-formed humans of gargantuan proportions. Adult males and females are about 26' tall and weigh about 15,000 pounds. Storm giants have pale, light green or (rarely) violet skin. Green-skinned storm giants have dark green hair and glittering emerald eyes. Violet-skinned storm giants have deep violet or blue-black hair with silvery gray or purple eyes. Storm giants can live to be 600 years old.

A storm giant's garb usually is a short, loose tunic belted at the waist, sandals or bare feet, and a headband. They wear a few pieces of simple, but finely crafted jewelry: anklets (favored by bare-footed giants), rings, or circlets being most common.

Storm giants usually carry pouches attached to their belts. These hold only a few tools, necessities, and a simple musical instrument—usually a panpipe or harp. Other than the jewelry they wear, they prefer to leave their wealth in their lairs.

They speak their own language as well as cloud giant, the tongue common to all giants, and the common tongue of humankind.

Combat: All storm giants are immune to electricity and lightning. They use weapons and special abilities instead of hurling rocks, but can catch large missiles 65% of the time.

Storm giants are born with *water breathing* ability, and can move, attack, and use magic under water as if they were on land. Juvenile and adult storm giants can cast *control weather* and *levitate* spells lifting their own weight and as much as 4,000 additional pounds twice a day. Adult storm giants also can *call lightning* (3 bolts of 15 8-sided dice each), *lightning bolt* (1 bolt of 15 6-sided dice), *control winds*, and use *weather summoning* once a day. A storm giant uses its magical abilities at 15th level. An angry storm giant usually will *summon* a storm and *call lightning*.

They employ gigantic two-handed swords in battle. A storm giant's oversized weapons do triple normal (man-sized) damage to all opponents, plus the giant's strength bonus. Thus, a storm giant's two-handed sword does 3-30 (3d10) +12 points of dam-

age. They also use massive composite bows which have a 300 yard range and do 3-18 (3d6) points of damage. There is a 10% chance that any storm giant will have enchanted weapons.

A storm giant's natural Armor Class is 0. In battle, storm giants usually wear elaborate bronze plate mail (AC -6).

Habitat/Society: Storm giants are retiring and solitary, but not shy. They live in castles built on cloud islands (60%), mountain peaks (20%), or underwater (10%). They live quiet, reflective lives and spend their time musing about the world, composing and playing music, and tilling their land or gathering food. Land- and air-dwelling storm giants usually are on good terms with neighboring silver dragons and good cloud giants, and cooperate with them for mutual defense. Aquatic storm giants have similar relationships with mermen and bronze dragons.

When two or more storm giants are encountered in lair they will be a mated couple and their children. To determine each young giant's maturity, roll 1d4. A roll of 4 indicates an infant with no combat ability and hit points of ogre; rolls of 1-3 indicate older progeny with hit dice, damage, and attack rolls equal to that of a cloud giant.

There is a 20% chance that an adult storm giant is also a priest (70%) or priest/wizard (30%). Storm giants can attain 9th level as priests and 7th level as wizards. Storm giant priests can cast regular spells from the Animal, Charm, Combat, Creation, Guardian, Healing, Plant, Weather, and Sun spheres. Storm giant wizards are generalists, and typically know spells from the Alteration, Invocation/Evocation, Conjuration/Summoning, and Abjuration schools.

Storm giant lairs are always protected by guards. Land or aerial lairs have 1-2 rocs (70%), which also serve a mounts, or 1-4 griffons (30%). Underwater lairs have 2-8 (2d4) sea lions.

Ecology: Storm giants live off the land in the immediate vicinity of their lairs. If the natural harvest is not enough to sustain them, they create and carefully till large areas of gardens, fields, and vineyards. They do not keep animals for food, preferring to hunt.

Giant, Verbeeg

CLIMATE/TERRAIN:	Temperate and arctic/Hills
FREQUENCY:	Uncommon
ORGANIZATION:	Tribe
ACTIVITY CYCLE:	Any
DIET:	Omnivore
INTELLIGENCE:	Average to very (8-12)
TREASURE:	B (K, L, M x 5)
ALIGNMENT:	Neutral (evil)

NO. APPEARING:	1-6 or 5-30
ARMOR CLASS:	4 or better
MOVEMENT:	18
HIT DICE:	5+5
THAC0:	15
NO. OF ATTACKS:	2
DAMAGE/ATTACK:	1-6 (weapon) +3 to +6 (Str bonus)
SPECIAL ATTACKS:	Nil
SPECIAL DEFENSES:	Nil
MAGIC RESISTANCE:	Nil
SIZE:	L (8½' to 10' tall)
MORALE:	Elite (13)
XP VALUE:	270

Known as "human behemoths," these human giants inhabit areas infested with hill giants and ogres.

Verbeeg vary in height from 8½ to 10 feet tall, and weigh between 300 and 400 pounds. They are unusually thin for their height, although this does not inhibit their fighting ability. Some have minor deformities, such as club foot, uneven eyes, hair lips, etc. In all other respects they appear human, including skin, hair, and eye color. They wear as much protective clothing and armor as they can obtain, which isn't much. Usually they wear furs and hides with pieces of metal armor stitched into strategic places. They almost always carry shields and have the best weapons they can steal. Typically this means clubs and spears.

Combat: Verbeeg are smart enough to let others soften up the enemy first. This does not mean that they are cowards, only selfish and practical. Since they are commonly found with hill giants and ogres, in the first few rounds of combat verbeeg drive their less intelligent companions before them into battle. This is accompanied by many curses, oaths, and highly descriptive accounts of the giants' and ogres' parentage.

Once the battle has begun, the verbeeg take on the stragglers and use their missile weapons, usually spears. The Strength of the giant determines how much further than normal the weapons can be hurled. Whatever their weaponry, the verbeeg get a Strength bonus for damage. Each giant must have his Strength determined individually (or once for the whole group, at the DM's option) by rolling 1d10 and consulting the following table. Armor is always at least the equivalent of AC 4, and sometimes better, although never better than AC 1.

Special Bonus With Spears

D10 Roll	Strength	Damage Bonus	Add to Spear Range
1-2	18/51-75	+3	30 yards
3-6	18/76-90	+4	40 yards
7-9	18/91-99	+5	50 yards
10	18/00	+6	60 yards

Habitat/Society: Verbeeg are found in the same climates as ogres and hill giants. These human behemoths are never found wandering alone. Thirty percent of wandering verbeeg encounters find 1d6 of these giant-kin with 1d4 hill giants or ogres (equal

chance), which also share their lair; 50% of the time 1d6 verbeeg are with 1d6 wolves or worgs (in polar climes winter wolves or polar bears); the rest of the time (20%) 1-2 of them are encountered with a normal sized group of wandering monsters found in that area (DM must use reasonable judgment in this case).

A verbeeg lair is usually an underground place, such as a cave or inside old ruins. There 5d6 of them can be found, an equal number of females (equal to males in combat), and 2d6 young. Half the young fight as bugbears, the other half fight as goblins. A lair usually includes 2d4 wolves (75% chance) or 1d4 worgs (25% chance). In arctic climes substitute 1-2 polar bears for wolves, and 1-3 winter wolves for wargs.

There is a 2% cumulative chance per giant of a shaman with the tribe. The verbeeg are jointly ruled by the shaman (if there is one) and a warrior chieftain. The shaman can be up to 7th level. The warrior chieftain always has 18/00 Strength and no fewer than 40 hit points. The chieftain is responsible for all activities involving hunting, war and negotiations with strangers. The shaman is responsible for all activities inside the tribe, dispensing judgments concerning law and all magic. Any magical items in the tribe belong to the shaman; he has a 90% chance of knowing how to use these. Most magical items that he does not understand are thrown into the tribal refuse heap before too long.

Ecology: Verbeeg eat almost anything, but they love flesh of all sorts. They maintain a mutually beneficial relationship with the giants and ogres that share their lair. The verbeeg provide the intelligence and direction that these giant types lack, and the giants provide protection by their greater fighting prowess. To watch a group in action can be hilarious, so long as you are not their intended victim. Hill giants and ogres are too stupid to think much on their own. They tend to follow directions too literally. This usually infuriates the verbeeg. They hop back and forth from foot to foot screaming insults at the befuddled giants that tower over them in height and size, as even the simplest instructions are misinterpreted by these denser humanoids.

Giant, Wood (Voadkyn)

CLIMATE/TERRAIN:	Temperate and subtropical/Forests
FREQUENCY:	Very rare
ORGANIZATION:	Clan
ACTIVITY CYCLE:	Day
DIET:	Herbivore
INTELLIGENCE:	High to exceptional (13-16)
TREASURE:	E
ALIGNMENT:	Chaotic good

NO. APPEARING:	1-4
ARMOR CLASS:	8 (5 in armor)
MOVEMENT:	12
HIT DICE:	7+7
THAC0:	13
NO. OF ATTACKS:	1
DAMAGE/ATTACK:	1-10 (weapon) +3 to +6 (Strength bonus)
SPECIAL ATTACKS:	-4 penalty to opponents' surprise rolls
SPECIAL DEFENSES:	Resistant to some spells
MAGIC RESISTANCE:	Nil
SIZE:	L (9½' tall)
MORALE:	Steady (11-12)
XP VALUE:	1,400

Wood giants (also known as voadkyn) are one of the smallest of the minor races of giants, looking somewhat like giant-sized wood elves. They are flighty, frivolous, and good friends with wood elves.

Standing 9½ feet tall, wood giants weigh around 700 pounds. They have the physical proportions of humans, which makes them thin and light for giants. They are completely devoid of facial and body hair, including eyebrows. Their heads seem overly large for their bodies, especially the jaws, chin, and mouth. Their ears are placed higher than on a human, almost completely above the line of the eyes.

Wood giants can be almost any shade of brown, mixed with yellow or green. They are fond of leather armor and ring mail. A wood giant carries two weapons—a two-handed sword and a giant-sized long bow with quiver. A special sheath for the sword is steel tipped, enabling it to be used as a walking stick. This does not in any way disguise the sword.

They wrap their ankles in leather strips almost up to the knee, although the foot itself is mostly bare. The only garments they wear are loose trousers or a short kilt. A wood giant always wears a leather forearm sheath to protect his arm from the bowstring. All of these items are frequently stained in forest colors of green and brown.

Combat: Voadkyn do not fight unless forced to defend themselves or allies. Their favorite weapon is their huge, non-magical long bow. They get a +1 bonus to attack rolls and 50% better range because of its unusual size. The matching arrows are over four feet long and cause 1d8 points of damage. Wood giants do not hurl rocks or boulders. If pressed into melee, they wield their two-handed swords with one hand.

When encountered, the Strength of the voadkyn must be determined by rolling percentile dice. The resulting number is the 18/(roll) value for their strength. This gives them a +3 to +6 damage bonus. They do not receive any attack roll bonus for Strength. These giant-kin are usually in the company of 1d4 wood elves (60%), 1d4 dire wolves (30%), or both (10%).

Wood giants are 90% resistant to *sleep* and *charm* spells; they have infravision up to 90 feet.

The only magical skill voadkyn have is the ability to polymorph into any humanoid figure, from 3 to 15 feet in height. They cannot become a specific individual, only a typical specimen of that race. They have been known to use this ability to join a party and trick it out of treasure.

Wood giants can move silently in a forest, despite their great height, thus imposing a -4 penalty to opponents' surprise rolls. They can blend into forest vegetation, becoming effectively invisible. Only creatures able to detect invisible objects can see them. Although they are not invisible while attacking, they are extremely quick (Dexterity 16) and can move out of hiding, launch an arrow, and move back into hiding in the same round. These arrows seem to come from nowhere unless the target is looking at the wood giants' hiding spot.

Habitat/Society: Wood giants inhabit the same forests as wood elves. They have no lairs, choosing to live under the stars or with the wood elves for a time. Wood giants encountered in the forest are mostly male (90%). Female wood giants usually remain at a makeshift camp or with the wood elves at their lair. Offspring are rare, as each female gives birth to only 1d4 children in her lifetime. The young are born and raised deep in the woods among the wood elves, away from prying eyes.

The strong bond between wood elves and wood giants goes back further than either race can remember. This may account for the elven abilities of the giants. They do not mix or treat with any other intelligent creatures, although they tolerate any good elf. Like the elves, wood giants are fond of finely cut gems and well-crafted magical items.

Humans who have had contact with wood giants describe them as friendly enough, but flighty and frivolous, and never in a great hurry to do anything other than eat and drink large amounts of wine. Treants (with whom they occasionally converse) consider them irrational, foolish, and occasionally obnoxious, but enjoyable company.

Ecology: The jaw of the voadkyn is large because of the oversized grinding teeth in it. These teeth are completely unsuited for eating meat, but they are perfect for vegetables and other plants. Wood giants can eat the leaves and roots of many plants that are inedible to humans. They especially enjoy nuts and seeds.

CLIMATE/TERRAIN:	Temperate/Forest, subterranean
FREQUENCY:	Uncommon
ORGANIZATION:	Herd
ACTIVITY CYCLE:	Night (but see below)
DIET:	Carnivore
INTELLIGENCE:	Low (5-7)
TREASURE:	Nil
ALIGNMENT:	Chaotic neutral

NO. APPEARING:	40-400
ARMOR CLASS:	10
MOVEMENT:	9
HIT DICE:	1
THAC0:	20
NO. OF ATTACKS:	1
DAMAGE/ATTACK:	1-8 (weapon)
SPECIAL ATTACKS:	Mass assault
SPECIAL DEFENSES:	Nil
MAGIC RESISTANCE:	Nil
SIZE:	S-M (4'-5' tall)
MORALE:	Irregular (5)
XP VALUE:	35

They come screaming, jabbering, and howling out of the night. Dozens, maybe hundreds, of hunchbacked, naked humanoids swarm unceasingly forward, brandishing short swords. They have no thought of safety, subtlety, or strategy, leaving others with no hope of stopping their mass assault. And then, having come and killed, the gibberlings move on randomly back into the night.

The first impression of gibberlings is of a writhing mass of fur and flesh in the distant moonlit darkness. The pandemonium is actually a mass of pale, hunchbacked humanoids, with pointed canine ears, black manes surrounding their hideous, grinning faces. Their eyes are black, and shine with a maniacal gleam. They carry short swords in their overly long arms as they lope ever faster forward.

Combat: Gibberlings attack in great numbers, uttering ghastly howls, clicks, shrieks, and insane chattering noises which cause even the boldest hirelings to check morale each round. PCs need only make a morale check if it is appropriate to their character. The screaming mob is completely disorganized in form, and random in direction.

The gibberlings attack with common swords, but such is their skill and practice in using these weapons that they are +1 to hit. Their forward motion slows only long enough to kill anything moving, then continues forward, their bloodlust apparently unabated. They always fight to the death. All food in their path is devoured, including the fallen among their own number, and any unfortified building or objects are generally wrecked.

The only true hope of survival, should a herd of gibberlings be encountered, is to take strategic advantage of their fear and detestation of bright light. The gibberlings generally frequent only dense forests and subterranean passages, loathing bright light of all kinds, and are particularly afraid of fire. Although their mass attacks would quickly overwhelm someone wielding a torch, a bright bonfire or magical light of sufficient intensity will hold them at bay or deflect their path.

Habitat/Society: It is difficult to imagine a gibberling social structure. It can be roughly compared to the social structure of lemmings throwing themselves into the sea, or of a school of pirhana in a feeding frenzy. There is no sense, no organization, and no individuality. Though they clearly have a primitive means of communicating among themselves, they have no discernable language.

Gibberlings traveling above-ground invariably burrow into the ground to hide during the daytime, and it is at such time that they are most vulnerable. They can easily be tracked by the path of chaos and destruction they leave, and can be quickly dispatched while they lie dormant just beneath the surface of the ground. If uncovered, they awake, but generally cower in fear at the bright light surrounding them, and so are easy prey. Subterranean gibberlings may burrow into the ground, or may simply lie down in a curled, fetal posture at times of rest. They awake suddenly, as a group, and burst in unison out of the ground, howling and gibbering in a most frightful way.

If captured, these strange creatures speak only their own incomprehensible gibberish, and show neither the patience nor the inclination to learn other languages or communicate whatsoever with their captors. Instead, they beat against their cages and fling themselves at barred windows and doorways in pitiful attempts to escape their captivity.

It is unclear how or when or even if gibberlings procreate.

Ecology: Attempts to find the gibberlings' lairs have inevitably led back to subterranean passages, where the trail is eventually lost in the deepest rock-floored recesses of the caverns.

Gibberlings require a prodigious amount of food to support their manic nocturnal existence, stripping to the bone anyone or anything that should fall in their path. Their fur is commonly infested with lice and other pests picked up during their burrowed slumber. Their hides are vile and worthless. Gibberlings carry no treasure or other useful items. Their swords are of the commonest variety, with no markings or decoration, and are often pitted and dull. In short, gibberlings serve no purpose and no known master, save random death in the night.

Giff

CLIMATE/TERRAIN:	Any
FREQUENCY:	Rare
ORGANIZATION:	Platoon
ACTIVITY CYCLE:	Day
DIET:	Omnivore
INTELLIGENCE:	Low (7)
TREASURE:	Nil
ALIGNMENT:	Lawful neutral

NO. APPEARING:	11-20
ARMOR CLASS:	6 (2)
MOVEMENT:	6
HIT DICE:	4
THAC0:	17
NO. OF ATTACKS:	2 or 1
DAMAGE/ATTACKS:	1-6 +7 or by weapon +7
SPECIAL ATTACKS:	Head butt
SPECIAL DEFENSES:	Can call on other giff
MAGIC RESISTANCE:	10%
SIZE:	L (9' tall)
MORALE:	Elite (14)
XP VALUE:	420

The giff are a race of powerfully muscled mercenaries. They are civilized, though they lack mages among their own race. Giff hire on with various groups throughout the universe as mercenaries, bodyguards, enforcers, and general legbreakers.

The giff is humanoid, with stocky, flat, cylindrical legs and a humanoid torso, arms, and fingers. Its chest is broad and supports a hippopotamus head with a natural helmet of flexible, chitinous plates. Giff come in colors ranging from black to gray to a rich gold, and many have colorful tattoos that leave their bodies a patchwork record of past victories. Giff speak their own language and the Common tongue.

Combat: The giff are military-minded, and organize themselves into squads, platoons, companies, corps, and larger groups. The number of giff in a platoon varies according to the season, situation, and level of danger involved. A giff "platoon" hired to protect a gambling operation may number two, while a platoon hired to invade an illithid stronghold may number well over a hundred.

The giff pride themselves on their weapon skills, and any giff carries a number of swords, daggers, maces, and similar tools on hand to deal with troublemakers.

A giff's true love in weaponry is the gun. Any giff has a 20% chance of having an arquebus and sufficient smoke powder for 2d4 shots. A misfiring weapon matters little to the giff (occasional fatalities are expected), the flash, noise, and damage is what most impresses them.

Even unarmed, the giff are powerful opponents. They are as strong as a hill giant (+7 damage adjustment for Strength). They will wade into a brawl just for the pure fun of it, tossing various combatants on both sides around to prove themselves the victors. Once a weapon is bared, the giff consider all restrictions off—the challenge is to the death.

The top of the giff's head and snout are plated with thick, chitinous plates, flexible enough to permit motion, but giving the creature a natural helmet. The giff can charge using a head butt, inflicting 2d6 points of damage.

The giff prize themselves as mercenaries, and to that end have made elaborate suits of armor (AC 2). These include full helms with other monsters on the crests, inlaid with ivory and bone

along the large plates. Armor repair is a major hobby among the giff.

Finally, giff are somewhat magic resistant. They are deeply suspicious of magic, magicians, and magical devices.

Habitat/Society: Giff of both sexes serve in their platoons, and both fight equally well. Giff young are raised tenderly until they are old enough to survive an exploding arquebus, then are inducted fully into the platoon. Every giff, male, female, and giffling, has a rank within society, which can be changed only by someone of a higher rank. Within these ranks are sub-ranks and within those sub-ranks are color markings and badges. The highest-ranking giff gives the orders, the others obey. It does not matter if the orders are foolish or even suicidal—following them is the purpose of the giff in the universe. A quasi-mystical faith among the giff mercenaries confirms that all things have their place, and the giff's is to follow orders.

Giff mercenaries are usually paid in smoke powder, though they often will accept other weapons and armor. It is purely a barter system, but to hire one giff for one standard week requires seven charges of smoke powder (one per day).

Giff are fierce fighters, despite their somewhat comical appearance and mania for weapons. They will not, however, willingly fight other giff. If forced into such a situation on a battlefield, both groups retire for at least a day of drinking and sorting out ranks. There is a 10% chance that one platoon will join another in this case, but it is more likely that both will quit their current hiring and look for work elsewhere.

Ecology: Giff live about 70 years, but do not age gracefully. As a giff grows older and begins to slow down, he is possessed with the idea of proving himself still young and vital, usually in battle. As a result, there are very, very few old giff.

Gith

CLIMATE/TERRAIN:	Arid tablelands and mountains
FREQUENCY:	Uncommon
ORGANIZATION:	Tribal
ACTIVITY CYCLE:	Day or night
DIET:	Carnivore
INTELLIGENCE:	Average (10)
TREASURE:	M (I)
ALIGNMENT:	Chaotic evil

NO. APPEARING:	10-100
ARMOR CLASS:	8
MOVEMENT:	10
HIT DICE:	3
THAC0:	17
NO. OF ATTACKS:	1 or 2
DAMAGE/ATTACK:	By weapon or 1d4/1d4
SPECIAL ATTACKS:	Springing
SPECIAL DEFENSES:	Nil
MAGIC RESISTANCE:	Nil
SIZE:	M
MORALE:	Steady (12)
XP VALUE:	175

The gith are a race of grotesque humanoids that appear to be a peculiar mixture of elf and reptile. They are extremely gaunt and lanky, with long gangling arms and spindly legs. Their hands have three fingers with no opposable thumbs, yet they are able to use tools and wield weapons. Their fingers and toes end in sharp claws. If one could get a gith to stand up straight, he would measure close to 7 feet tall. However, most gith appear to be no more than 5 feet tall, for they always stand hunched over at the shoulders, in a permanent slouch.

Combat: If possible, the gith attack in mass, usually starting with a psionic attack by one of their leaders. Then the entire party charges quickly into melee. Their main charge is often accomplished by *springing* up to 20 feet in one giant leap to close with their enemies. When they employ this spring, it gives them a +2 THAC0 bonus on the first round of combat.

The gith are usually armed with large, wicked-looking spears that have giant, razor-sharp heads of polished obsidian (1d6−1 damage). Although these spears look like thrusting weapons, they are used primarily to slash or chop. The gith often armor themselves, and especially their vulnerable backs, with inix-shell armor (AC 6) of their own manufacture.

Psionics Summary:

Level	Dis/Sci/Dev	Attack/Defense	Score	PSPs
5	2/3/10	II, MT/	16	80
		M−, TW,MB		

Gith have the following psionic powers:
- Telepathy—**Sciences:** tower of iron will, project force. **Devotions:** id insinuation, mind thrust, contact, mind blank, mental barrier.
- Psychokinesis—**Sciences:** telekinesis. **Devotions:** animate object, animate shadow, ballistic attack, control body, control flames.

Note: Only leaders commanding 25 or more gith have psionic powers. The psionics listed above are representative of these leaders, but their powers do vary greatly. Gith with more Hit Dice have correspondingly greater powers.

Habitat/Society: The gith live in tribal organizations. The individual with the most powerful psionics generally acts as the leader. All other social positions are distributed at his pleasure.

For every twenty-five gith, there will be a 5 HD leader, for every fifty, a 6 HD leader, and for every tribe of 100 or more a 7 HD leader. In addition to having hit points and THAC0 numbers appropriate to their HD, these leaders will have psionic powers approximately equal to a psionicist of an equivalent level.

Some of these leaders are priests. While little is known of the gith religion, shamans up to the 4th level are known to accompany and sometimes lead gith tribes. There have also been reports of gith wizards (defilers) ranked at the 6th level. Even if true, 6th level would be unusual for gith, but wizards of up to 4th level have been reported by reliable witnesses.

Not much is known about the reproductive cycle of the gith. It is known that they are egg layers; females lay approximately 1d6 eggs in a clutch. It is rumored that the gith operate hatcheries containing hundreds (some say thousands) of nests.

Ecology: Mountain gith live in underground lairs, claiming a particular canyon or valley as their territory. Gith inhabiting tablelands tend to organize their society more along the lines of a nomadic hunting clan, going wherever the game takes them. They do not hesitate to attack human or demihuman groups, for they view humans and demihumans as a choice food supply, preferring it over other flesh. They will even attack thri-kreen, if they are hungry enough, but the insectoids taste bad, and usually escape gith raiders.

Gith, Pirate

CLIMATE/TERRAIN:	Wildspace
FREQUENCY:	Rare
ORGANIZATION:	Ship/Military
ACTIVITY CYCLE:	Any
DIET:	Carnivore
INTELLIGENCE:	Exceptional (15-16)
TREASURE:	A (N)
ALIGNMENT:	Lawful evil

NO. APPEARING:	20-40/As ship crew
ARMOR CLASS:	0
MOVEMENT:	12
HIT DICE:	7-11
THAC0:	Special
NO. OF ATTACKS:	Varies
DAMAGE/ATTACK:	By weapon
SPECIAL ATTACKS:	See below
SPECIAL DEFENSES:	See below
MAGIC RESISTANCE:	Nil
SIZE:	M (6'-7' tall)
MORALE:	Champion (16)
XP VALUE:	Special

When the githyanki, under their liberator, Gith, freed themselves from the yoke of mindflayer slavery, this branch of the race fled not to the Astral plane, but to arcane space.

Tall, emaciated beings, the pirates of Gith appear as almost skeletal humanoids with skin varying from dirty gray to dull yellow. Long, dingy-brown hair flows down their backs and over the ornate, bejeweled arms and armor they prefer to use.

Combat: The pirates of Gith can operate as fighters, mages, or fighter/mages, with limits of 11 in each class. Typically, the highest-level fighter captains the ship. This frees all the mages (single- and multiclassed) for spelljamming or combat duty.

Clerics of Gith are occasionally encountered as well (limit of 11th level). Rarely, a fighter/cleric is encountered, almost always as the captain of its ship.

When closing with a foe, the pirates use spells and any armament their ship possesses. In melee, they use a variety of weapons, with swords predominating.

Operating from small bases hidden on asteroids, the pirates strive to capture any ship that is larger, faster, or better armed than theirs. They feverishly attempt to capture any elven-made ships that come their way (see below). As a result, many elven armadas post large bounties on the heads of Gith pirates.

The pirates' greatest fury is reserved for the illithids, however. The pirates of Gith spare no expense to kill all mindflayers they find. No Gith pirate ever uses a captured illithid ship.

A ship's complement varies, but these numbers are a general guideline:

1 Captain (highest-level fighter or fighter/cleric)
1 Mate (highest-level fighter/mage or cleric)
1 Chief Spelljammer or Warlock (highest-level mage)

The rest of the crew is evenly divided among the three common class possibilities.

Habitat/Society: The pirate philosophy carries over into all aspects of life. The strongest take what they want. Each ship is very important to its crew, as it is the primary factor in determining the pecking order in a settlement. This explains the pirates' constant quest for better ships. Each settlement is ruled by force by its best ship, or a coalition of the best ships.

Extreme isolationists, the pirates of Gith live with no other races—they may even try to commit genocide on a race that settles too close to them. Over all, despite being pirates, these Gith live a structured, militaristic lifestyle.

Every adult member of this race possesses the following magical abilities, each usable three times a day: *astral spell*, *plane shift*, and *ESP*. All function as the spell of the same name (as cast by the lowest-level caster possible). These inherent abilities also enable the pirates to pilot ships with series helms. These abilities function only in wildspace, not in the phlogiston.

The most dangerous aspect of this race is the combination of the above abilities, the properties of major and minor spelljamming helms, and the unique organic structure of the elven-made ships. When a Gith pirate is at the helm of an elven-made ship (flitter, etc.), he may use his *plane shift* and *astral spell* abilities to shunt the entire ship, and all its contents, to the Astral plane (this uses up that pirate's *astral spell* and *plane shift* abilities for the day). This gives the pirates an escape route, and it enables them to wait in known shipping lanes, astrally hidden, before returning to the Prime Material plane to launch an attack. The Gith pirates can use only elven-made ships of less than 50 tons in this manner.

This special maneuver only works in wildspace, not in the phlogiston. That is certainly the reason the Gith pirates never pursue prey into that medium.

Ecology: The Gith pirates are carnivores, pure and simple. They do not care what state, short of putrefied, the meat is in. Some of the pirate bands also engage in cannibalism.

Githyanki

CLIMATE/TERRAIN:	Astral or prime
FREQUENCY:	Very rare
ORGANIZATION:	Dictatorship/monarchy
ACTIVITY CYCLE:	Any
DIET:	Omnivore
INTELLIGENCE:	Exceptional to genius (15-18)
TREASURE:	Individuals R; Lair H
ALIGNMENT:	Any evil

NO. APPEARING:	2-8 (away from lair)
ARMOR CLASS:	Per armor
MOVEMENT:	12, 96 on Astral plane
HIT DICE:	Per class and level
THAC0:	Per class and level
NO. OF ATTACKS:	Per class and level
DAMAGE/ATTACK:	Per weapon type
SPECIAL ATTACKS:	Possible spell use, possible magical weapon
SPECIAL DEFENSES:	Nil
MAGIC RESISTANCE:	Nil
SIZE:	M (6' tall)
MORALE:	Average to elite (8-14)
XP VALUE:	Per class and level

Level	Dis/Sci Dev	Attack Defense	Power Score	PSPs
= HD	per level	All/All	= Int	1d100 + 150

Githyanki are an ancient race descended from humans. They dwell upon the Astral plane but will often leave that plane to make war on other races. They are engaged in a lengthy war with the githzerai.

Githyanki are strongly humanoid in appearance. They are approximately of human height but tend to be much more gaunt and long of limb. They have rough, yellow skin and gleaming black eyes that instantly betray their inhumanness. Like many demihuman races, their ears have sharp points and are serrated at the back. Dress for the githyanki is always an elaborate affair. Their baroque armor and weapons of war are decorated with feathers, beads, and precious metals and gems.

Githyanki speak their own tongue, and no others.

Combat: The githyanki have had long years to perfect the art of war. Their very existence attests to their battle prowess. Each individual githyanki has a character class and level from which are derived such things as THAC0, armor class, spell use, etc.

	Class		Level
01-40	Fighter	01-20	3rd
41-55	Mage	21-30	4th
56-80	Fighter/Mage	31-40	5th
81-85	Illusionist	41-60	6th
86-00	Knight	61-80	7th
		81-90	8th
		91-95	9th
		96-98	10th
		99-00	11th

The armor for each githyanki varies according to class. Mages and illusionists have AC 10. Fighters and fighter mages have differing armor—AC 5 to AC 0 (6 − 1d6). Knights have AC 0.

Githyanki have Hit Dice according to their class and level, and their hit points are rolled normally. Their THAC0 is determined per class and level, as well. Fighters, fighter/mages, and knights may receive more than one attack per round—other githyanki have one attack per round.

Githyanki knights are evil champions who take up the causes of the githyankis' mysterious lich-queen. Githyanki knights are very powerful and highly revered in their society. Githyanki knights have all of the powers and abilities of a human paladin except these are turned toward evil (e.g. *detect good* instead of *detect evil*, *command undead* instead of turning undead, etc.).

Githyanki mages, fighter/mages, and illusionists will receive all the spells available at their level of experience. Spells should be determined randomly, keeping in mind that they are by nature creatures of destruction—offensive spells should be favored.

The githyanki soldiers use arms and armor similar to humans, however these are normally highly decorated and have become almost religious artifacts. A githyanki would likely show greater care for his weapons and armor than he would toward his mate. Half of the githyanki fighters, fighter/mages, or knights that progress to 5th level receive a magical *two-handed sword +1*, the remainder using normal two-handed swords. Githyanki fighters of 7th level and above are 60% likely to carry a *long sword +2*. Knights of 7th level and above will always carry a *silver sword*—a *two-handed sword +3* that, if used astrally, has a 5% chance per hit of cutting an opponent's silver cord (see The Astral Plane, *DMG*, page 132), but *mind barred* individuals are immune. A supreme leader of a lair will carry a special *silver sword* that is +5 with all the abilities of a *vorpal weapon* that also affects *mind barred* individuals.

Githyanki will never willingly allow a *silver sword* to fall into the hands of a nongithyanki. If a special *silver sword* should fall into someone's hands, very powerful raiding parties will be formed to recover the sword. Failure to recover one of these highly prized weapons surely means instant death to all the githyanki involved at the hands of their merciless lich-queen.

All githyanki have the natural ability to *plane shift* at will. They will rarely travel anywhere besides back and forth from the Astral plane to the Prime Material plane.

Habitat/Society: History provides some information on the githyanki—their race is both ancient and reclusive. Sages believe

Githyanki

they once were humans that were captured by mind flayers to serve as slaves and cattle. The mind flayers treated their human slaves cruelly and the people harbored a deep resentment toward the illithids. For centuries these humans increased their hatred but could not summon the strength necessary to break free. So they waited for many years, developing their power in secret, waiting for an opportunity to strike out against their masters. Finally, a woman of power came forth among them, a deliverer by the name of Gith. She convinced the people to rise up against their cruel masters. The struggle was long and vicious, but eventually the people freed themselves. They had earned their freedom and become the githyanki, (which, in their tongue, means sons of Gith).

These astral beings progress through levels exactly as a human would. However, there has never been a githyanki that has progressed beyond the 11th level of experience and very few progress beyond 9th. When a githyanki advances to 9th level, he is tested by the lich-queen. This grueling test involves survival in one of lower planes for a number of weeks. Failure quite obviously results in death. Githyanki that reach 12th level of experience are immediately drawn out of the Astral plane and into the presence of the lich-queen where their life force is drawn to feed the ravenous hunger of the cruel demi-goddess.

Githyanki dwell in huge castles on the Astral plane. These ornately decorated castles are avoided by all other dwellers on the Astral plane for the githyanki are infamous for being inhospitable to strangers.

A githyanki stronghold will be ruled by a supreme leader. This leader will be a fighter/mage of 10th/8th level or 11th/9th level. The supreme leader is the undisputed overlord of the castle with the power of life and death over all who dwell there. A typical leader will be equipped with 2-8 random magical items in addition to the weapons described above.

All castles have a retinue of 20-80 knights of 9th level that serve as the supreme leader's elite shock troops. They are fanatically loyal. There will also be up to 1,000 githyanki of lesser status.

Githyanki, having the ability to *plane shift* at will, often travel to the Prime Material plane. These treks across the planes often lead to the formation of underground lairs used to mount surface raids, though their hatred is more often directed against mind flayers. Outside the war with the githzerai, these raids are conducted largely for the perverse pleasure of the kill.

A typical githyanki lair on the Prime Material plane will contain the following:

One supreme leader	11th-level fighter or 7th/8th-level fighter/mage
Two captains	8th-level fighter and 7th/6th-level fighter/mage
One knight	8th level
Two warlocks	mages of 4th/7th level
Three sergeants	fighters of 4th/7th level
Two 'gish'	fighter/mages of 4th/4th level
20-50 lower levels	determined randomly using the table above, of 1st-3rd level

On the Prime Material plane, githyanki have a pact with a group of red dragons. These proud creatures will act as mounts and companions to the githyanki. When encountered on the Prime Material plane and outside their lair, a githyanki group will typically consist of the following:

One captain	8th-level fighter
One warlock	4th to 7th-level mage
Five lower githyankis	fighters of 1st-3rd level

Such a group will have two red dragons as steeds, transporting between four and six githyanki per dragon. The dragons will fight for the safety and well-being of the githyanki but will not directly risk their lives, fleeing when the battle is turned against them. Just what the githyanki offer the red dragons in return for these services is unknown.

An interesting aspect of githyanki society is the apparent bond between military leaders and their subordinates. This bond allows a leader to give his men short, almost senseless commands (to human standards) and actually relay complex and exacting messages. Although this has no actual affect during the melee round, it often leads to more effective ambushes and attacks and allows complex military decisions to be relayed quickly.

Ecology: Githyankis have similar ecology to that of humans. However, the Astral plane does not offer the same type of environments as the Prime Material plane, so their cultural groups are much different. In a society where farmers and tradesmen are unnecessary, more unique, specialized groups have evolved.

G"lathk: The g"lathk, (admittedly nearly unpronounceable in human tongues) are the equivalent of farmers. Due to the barrenness of the Astral plane, the githyanki are forced to grow food in vast, artificial chambers. They rely upon a variety of fungi and other plants that require no sunlight to grow. The g"lathk are also experts in aquatic plantlife, sometimes tending gigantic water-gardens.

Mlar: Not all magic-using githyanki ever attain the power and self-discipline necessary to become wizards. Some use their magical talents in the field of architecture and construction. The mlar are such individuals, focusing their creative energies toward designing and constructing the buildings and structures used in day-to-day life in githyanki society. The mlar have developed their jobs into an art form.

Hr'a'cknir: The Astral plane has many strange energies moving through it. Some of these energies are obvious to the senses, such as heat and light. Others are not so easily observed. There are many psychic and strange astral energies that humans generally are not aware of. Being a psychically aware race, however, the githyanki cannot only sense these energies, but harness them too. The hr'a'cknir are the collectors of those energies. They are similar to the mlar, in that they use innate magical powers to perform their crafts.

More than humans, githyanki are hunters and predators. They will typically engage in raiding and plundering seemingly for the joy they derive from it. It is likely that the long centuries of enslavement of their race has caused the githyanki to bully those weaker than themselves.

Unlike humans, though, the githyanki never war amongst themselves. The split of the githyanki and the githzerai (*q.v.*) is the closest thing the gith races have known to civil war. Githyanki never battles githyanki. It is the unwritten rule of gith society and is never broken. This, too, may be an effect of the race's enslavement.

Githzerai

CLIMATE/TERRAIN:	Limbo
FREQUENCY:	Very rare
ORGANIZATION:	Monarchy/dictatorship
ACTIVITY CYCLE:	Any
DIET:	Omnivore
INTELLIGENCE:	Exceptional to genius (15-18)
TREASURE:	Individual P; Lair H × 2
ALIGNMENT:	Chaotic neutral

NO. APPEARING:	2-8 (away from lair)
ARMOR CLASS:	Variable
MOVEMENT:	12, 96 in Limbo
HIT DICE:	Per class and level
THAC0:	Per class and level
NO. OF ATTACKS:	Per class and level
DAMAGE/ATTACK:	Per weapon type
SPECIAL ATTACKS:	Nil
SPECIAL DEFENSES:	Nil
MAGIC RESISTANCE:	50%
SIZE:	M (6'tall)
MORALE:	Average to steady (8-12)
XP VALUE:	Per class and level

Level	Dis/Sci Dev	Attack/ Defense	Power Score	PSPs
= HD	per level	All/All	= Int	1d100 + 150

Githzerai are the monastic, chaotic neutral counterparts to the githyanki (q.v.). The two races share a stretch of time in history; the githzerai are the lesser and more repressed offshoot of the original people that the warrior Gith helped to escape the slavery of the mind flayers millennia ago.

Githzerai are very similar in appearance to their githyanki cousins, although they tend to look much more human. Their features are for the most part unremarkable, with vaguely noble countenance. Their skin tone is that of human caucasian flesh. Githzerai dress simply, wearing functional clothing and favoring conservative tones.

Combat: The githzerai are unadorned and ruthlessly straightforward with their combat and magic. Their strong resistance to magic seems to make up for their generally inferior fighting ability.

	Class		Level
			(add 3 if thief)
01-55	Fighter	01-10	1st
56-75	Fighter/Mage	11-20	2nd
76-95	Mage	21-30	3rd
96-00	Thief	31-45	4th
		46-60	5th
		61-75	6th
		76-90	7th
		91-96	8th
		97-00	9th

The armor for each githzerai varies according to class. Mages have AC 10. Fighters and fighter mages have differing armor—AC 5 to AC 0 (6 − 1d6). Thieves have AC 7.

Githzerai have Hit Dice according to their class and level, and their hit points are rolled normally. Their THAC0 is determined per class and level, as well. Fighters and fighter/mages may receive more than one attack per round—other githzerai have one attack per round.

On rare occasions, a githzerai will progress as a thief. These thieves seem to have some significance to the strange githzerai religion. Although they are never known to become leaders in any capacity, these thieves are an exception to the maximum level of 9th, often progressing up to 12th level of experience. Just what role these thieves play is unknown.

Githzerai fighters of at least 5th level have use of silver swords. These magical weapons are two-handed swords +3 that, if used in the Astral plane, have a 5% chance of cutting an opponent's silver cord upon scoring a hit (see The Astral Plane, DMG, page 132), though mind barred individuals are immune. These weapons are of powerful religious value to the githzerai and they will never willingly allow them to fall into the hands of outsiders. If this happens, the githzerai will go to great ends to recover the weapon.

All githzerai have the innate power to plane shift to any plane. This is rarely done except to travel back and forth to the Prime Material plane where the githzerai have several fortresses.

Habitat/Society: The githzerai were originally offspring of a race of humans that were freed from slavery under mind flayers by a great female warrior named Gith. These men and women did not, however, choose to follow Gith's ways after they revolted against their slavers. Instead, they fell sway to the teachings of a powerful wizard who proclaimed himself king—and later, god— of the people. The githzerai then separated themselves from the githyanki, beginning a great racial war that has endured the long millennia without diminishing.

Githzerai can progress as fighters, mages, or fighter/mages, and thieves. They will rarely attain levels above 7th and, in any case, will never progress beyond 9th. The githzerai, who worship a powerful and ancient wizard as though he were a god (he is not), are destroyed before they have enough power to become a threat to their ruler.

If encountered outside of their lair, githzerai will usually be in the following numbers:

Githzerai

One supreme leader	9th-level fighter or 4th/7th-level fighter/mage
One captain	6th-level fighter or 4th/4th-level fighter/mage
Two warlocks	mages of 3rd-5th level
Three sergeants	fighters of 3rd-5th level
Three 'zerths'	fighter/mages of 3rd/3rd level
20-50 lesser githzerai	evenly distributed between the three possible classes and of 1st-3rd level

A thief, if present (10% chance), will replace one of the lower level githzerai and will be of 6th-10th level.

The githzerai dwell primarily on the plane of Limbo. They have mighty fortresses in that plane of chaos and their position there is very strong. Typically, one of these fortresses contains approximately 3,000 githzerai led by a single supreme leader. This leader has absolute control over the githzerai, including the powers of life and death.

The githzerai hold only a few fortresses on the Prime Material plane, but these are particularly strong holdings, with walls of adamantite rising as huge squat towers from dusty plains. Each houses approximately 500 githzerai, including a supreme leader.

On Limbo, however, the githzerai presence is very strong. Living in cities typically of 100,000 or more, the githzerai enjoy total power over themselves on an otherwise chaotic and unpredictable plane. One notable example of this is the city *Shra'kt'lor*. This large githzerai capital is composed of some 2,000,000 githzerai living in great power. Shra'kt'lor serves as both a capital and as a headquarters for all githzerai military matters. The greatest generals and nobles of the race meet here to plan githzerai strategy for battling both the githyanki and the mind flayers. There is likely no force on Limbo that could readily threaten the power of Shra'kt'lor or its many inhabitants.

One of the prime motivations among the githzerai is their war with the githyanki. These offshoots of Gith's original race are obsessed with this war of extermination. They often employ mercenaries on the Prime Material plane to aid them in battling the githyanki. The evil, destructive nature of the githyanki makes the hiring of mercenaries to fight them a relatively simple task.

Legend of the Zerthimon: In githzerai lore there is a central figure that is revered above all others—Zerthimon. The githyanki believe him to be a great god that was once a man. According to githzerai lore, when the original race broke free of the mind flayers, it was Zerthimon that opposed Gith, claiming that she was hateful and unfit to lead the people.

There ensued a great battle and the people were polarized by the two powers. Those that chose to support Gith became the githyanki. Those that supported Zerthimon became the githzerai.

Zerthimon died in the battle, but in his sacrifice he freed the githzerai from Gith. The githzerai believe that someday Zerthimon, in his new godly form, will return and take the them to a place on another plane.

Zerths are special among the githzerai, acting as focal points for the attention of Zerthimon. The githzerai believe that when Zerthimon returns for them, he will first gather all of the zerths and lead them to their new paradise. It might be said that the zerths are the center of githzerai religion. Unfortunately, they are not free from religious persecution.

The wizard-king (whose name is not known) that rules over the highly superstitious githzerai would like very much to stamp out the legend of Zerthimon. The wizard-king believes that this legend challenges his authority, and very likely it does. However, he has never been able to rid the githzerai of this legend and he is now forced to tolerate it.

Rrakkma bands: Although the githzerai are not a bitter or overly violent race, they still tend to hold a strong enmity and hatred for the race of illithids that originally enslaved the gith race so many thousands of years ago. By human terms, that may be a very long time to hold a grudge, but the githzerai see the mind flayers as the cause of the split of the Gith race and much of the hardships the githzerai are forced to endure. Thus large rrakkma (in the githzerai tongue) bands are often formed to hunt mind flayers. These bands typically consist of 30-60 githzerai warriors led by the githzerai equivalent of a sergeant. For roughly three months, these bands will roam the outer and inner planes, searching for groups of illithids and destroying them utterly. The rrakkma bands are very popular in githzerai society and it is considered to be an honor to serve in one.

The githzerai fortresses on the Prime Material plane tend to be very large affairs with great, impenetrable walls. Wherever these fortresses stand, they destroy the landscape for miles. No plants or animals live within many miles of the fortresses and the land is reduced to wasteland around them. It is not known if the effect is just the land's reaction to the "other-planar" stuff of which the castles are constructed, or if githzerai mages magically produce the effect in order to keep material beings away from these fortresses.

The most likely purpose of these fortresses on the Prime Material plane is to keep tabs on the githyanki. The githzerai, not being a particularly war-mongering or violent race, have no desire to conquer the Prime Material plane like the githyanki do. However, the githzerai realize that if their enemies have a strong hold on the Prime Material plane, they will become more powerful and thus will hold power over them. The githzerai carefully monitor the progress on the githyanki and lead coordinated, focused strikes against strongpoints of the githyanki, thus hampering their ability to expand and grow in the Prime Material plane.

During these attacks, the githzerai will not intentionally attack the natural denizens of the Prime Material plane (humans, demi-humans, humanoids, etc.), but they will never sacrifice a well-planned attack on the githyanki just to preserve life. With the githzerai, the ends will always justify the means.

Like the githyanki, the githzerai really have no part in the Blood War (*q.v.*) of the fiends. They seldom venture to the lower planes, and only then for matters of absolute importance. The githzerai find the bloodthirsty, destructive nature of the fiends to be distasteful, so they will typically not deal with those creatures for any reason. They coexist with the slaadi, and githzerai are rumored to have mental powers beyond those described here.

Ecology: For as long as men have known of the ability to travel the planes, they have wondered at the natural power of the githzerai to wander from plane to plane at will. Although man and githzerai are not natural enemies, battles are frequently fought between the two races, due in part to some humans' desire to capture a live githzerai for study. To date, no such creature has been secured.

	Moth	Tenebrous Worm
CLIMATE/TERRAIN:	Any, Demi-plane of Shadow	Forests
FREQUENCY:	Rare	Uncommon
ORGANIZATION:	Solitary	Solitary
ACTIVITY CYCLE:	Night/Darkness	Any
DIET:	Carnivore	Carnivore
INTELLIGENCE:	Animal (1)	Animal (1)
TREASURE:	Nil	Nil
ALIGNMENT:	Neutral	Neutral
NO. APPEARING:	1	1
ARMOR CLASS:	1	1
MOVEMENT:	2, Fl 18 (D)	10
HIT DICE:	5+1	10
THAC0:	15	11
NO. OF ATTACKS:	3	1
DAMAGE/ATTACK:	1-3/1-3/1-8	2-16
SPECIAL ATTACKS:	Pheromone	Acid
SPECIAL DEFENSES:	Confusion	Poison Bristles
MAGIC RESISTANCE:	Nil	Nil
SIZE:	M (8')	M (6')
MORALE:	Average (8-10)	Elite (13)
XP VALUE:	1,400	5,000

The creature commonly called the gloomwing is the adult stage of the tenebrous worm (see below). These huge moths are native to the demi-plane of Shadow. Their bodies and wings are covered with shimmering, geometric patterns of black and silver. They have large, fern-like black antennae tipped with white and eight legs each ending in a pearly claw.

Combat: A gloomwing's shimmering markings make it a difficult target. Any creature viewing the moth squarely from above or below must successfully save vs. spells or be *confused*, as the 4th-level mage spell, for 5-8 (1d4+4) rounds. The markings also provide excellent camouflage, and the moth is 50% undetectable in darkness, twilight, or moonlight. Successfully camouflaged gloomwings cannot cause *confusion*.

When attacking in darkness or near darkness, a gloomwing receives a −2 bonus to its surprise roll. Gloomwings normally swoop to the attack. This gives them a +2 attack bonus and allows them to seize and carry away victims less than 3 feet tall and that weigh less than 61 pounds. Such victims are securely held in the moth's eight claws while the moth attacks each round with a +4 attack bonus and a +2 bonus to damage. When fighting creatures too large to carry away, the moth hovers, biting and flailing with its two front claws.

During the second and each successive round of combat, the moth emits a potent pheromone that can attract other gloomwings and can cause weakness in any non-insect. The weakness effect has a 25-foot radius and exposed creatures must successfully save vs. poison or lose 1 point of Strength each round they remain in the area of effect. Creatures who are successful with their initial save need not save again if exposure continues. Multiple gloomwings do not require multiple saves. Lost Strength points are recovered at the rate of 1 per turn, beginning 1d4 hours after exposure stops. Creatures reduced to 0 Strength lose consciousness until they regain at least 1 point of Strength.

There is a 20% chance each round that an additional 1d4 gloomwings will arrive at the end of any round when one or more gloomwings are emitting this strong scent. If they do arrive, they will join in combating any opponents.

Habitat/Society: Gloomwing moths are short-lived, solitary hunters. They use a variety of pheromones to ward off rivals and to find mates. They form groups, but only to attack large prey, and then only when drawn to the fray by the combat pheromone. When two gloomwings of the same sex meet they flee unless there is combat pheromone in the air.

Ecology: Gloomwing moths live only 4-9 (1d6+3) weeks. During this time they search for mates and eat voraciously. Egg-laden females (1/2 chance) use corpses of small sized or larger creatures as incubators for their eggs. The eggs hatch in 12 days, sprouting 1d6+4 small tenebrous worms. The corpse cannot be resurrected unless the infestation is removed with a *cure disease* spell first. Unless killed, the young worms completely devour the body when they emerge.

Tenebrous Worm

These natives of the demi-plane of Shadow resemble giant caterpillars. In combat, they strike with powerful mandibles and anyone bitten by the worm must roll a successful saving throw vs. poison, with a −3 penalty, or suffer double damage from the toxic bite. The head and upper body are covered with poisonous bristles that inflict 1d4 points of damage to anyone whose bare skin comes into contact with them. A successful saving throw vs. poison is required to avoid paralysis for 1d4 rounds after contact. At the end of that time, the victim dies unless a *neutralize poison* or *slow poison* spell is administered. The chance of attackers being hit by the spines is equal to 10% times their base Armor Class (before shield and Dexterity modifiers). Attacking the worm's head reduces the chance of contact by 20% (but only one character can attack the head at a time). The mandibles of this worm are attractive and worth from 1,000 to 3,000 gold pieces per set.

Gnoll

	Gnoll	Flind
CLIMATE/TERRAIN:	Any tropical to temperate non-desert	Any tropical to temperate non-desert
FREQUENCY:	Uncommon	Rare
ORGANIZATION:	Tribe	Tribe
ACTIVITY CYCLE:	Night	Night
DIET:	Carnivore	Carnivore
INTELLIGENCE:	Low (5-7)	Average (8-10)
TREASURE:	D,Qx5,S (L,M)	A
ALIGNMENT:	Chaotic evil	Lawful evil
NO. APPEARING:	2-12 (2d6)	1-4
ARMOR CLASS:	5 (10)	5 (10)
MOVEMENT:	9	12
HIT DICE:	2	2+3
THAC0:	19	17
NO. OF ATTACKS:	1	1 or 2
DAMAGE/ATTACK:	2-8 (2d4) (weapon)	1-6 or 1-4 (weapons)
SPECIAL ATTACKS:	Nil	Disarm
SPECIAL DEFENSES:	Nil	Nil
MAGIC RESISTANCE:	Nil	Nil
SIZE:	L (7½' tall)	M (6½' tall)
MORALE:	Steady (11)	Steady (11-12)
XP VALUE:	35	120
Leaders & guards	65	
Leader	120	
Chieftain	120	

Gnolls are large, evil, hyena-like humanoids that roam about in loosely organized bands.

While the body of a gnoll is shaped like that of a large human, the details are those of a hyena. They stand erect on two legs and have hands that can manipulate as well as those of any human. They have greenish gray skin, darker near the muzzle, with a short reddish gray to dull yellow mane.

Gnolls have their own language and many also speak the tongues of flinds, trolls, orcs, or hobgoblins.

Combat: Gnolls seek to overwhelm their opponents by sheer numbers, using horde tactics. When under the direction of flinds or a strong leader, they can be made to hold rank and fight as a unit. While they do not often lay traps, they will ambush or attempt to attack from a flank or rear position. Gnolls favor swords (15%), pole arms (35%) and battle axes (20%) in combat, but also use bows (15%), morningstars (15%).

Habitat/Society: Gnolls are most often encountered underground or inside abandoned ruins. When above ground they operate primarily at night. Gnoll society is ruled by the strongest, using fear and intimidation. When found underground, they will have (30% chance) 1-3 trolls as guards and servants. Above ground they keep pets (65% of the time) such as 4-16 hyenas (80%) or 2-12 hyaenodons (20%) which can act as guards.

A gnoll lair will contain between 20 and 200 adult males. For every 20 gnolls, there will be a 3 Hit Die leader. If 100 or more are encountered there will also be a chieftain who has 4 Hit Dice, an Armor Class of 3, and who receives a +3 on his damage rolls due to his great strength. Further, each chieftain will be protected by 2-12 (2d6) elite warrior guards of 3 Hit Dice (AC 4, +2 damage).

In a lair, there will be females equal to half the number of males. Females are equal to males in combat, though not usually as well armed or armored. There will also be twice as many young as there are adults in the lair, but they do not fight. Gnolls always have at least 1 slave for every 10 adults in the lair, and may have many more.

Gnolls will work together with orcs, hobgoblins, bugbears, ogres, and trolls. If encountered as a group, there must be a relative equality of strength. Otherwise the gnolls will kill and eat their partners (hunger comes before friendship or fear) or be killed and eaten by them. They dislike goblins, kobolds, giants, humans, demi-humans and any type of manual labor.

Ecology: Gnolls eat anything warm blooded, favoring intelligent creatures over animals because they scream better. They will completely hunt out an area before moving on. It may take several years for the game to return. When allowed to die of old age, the typical gnoll lives to be about 35 years old.

Flind

The flind is similar to a gnoll in body style, though it is a little shorter, and broader. They are more muscular than their cousins. Short, dirty, brown and red fur covers their body. Their foreheads do not slope back as far, and their ears are rounded, but still animal like.

Flinds use clubs (75%) which inflict 1-6 points of damage and flindbars (25%) which do 1-4 points of damage. A flindbar is a pair of chain-linked iron bars which are spun at great speed. A flind with a flindbar can strike twice per round. Each successful hit requires the victim to save vs. wands or have his weapon entangled in the chain and torn from his grasp by the flindbar. Due to their great strength, flinds get a +1 on their attack rolls.

Flinds are regarded with reverence and awe by gnolls. Flind leaders are 3+3 Hit Dice, at least 13 intelligence and 18 charisma to gnolls (15 to flinds), and always use flindbars.

	Gnome (Rock)	Svirfneblin	Tinker	Forest
CLIMATE/TERRAIN:	Hills	Subterranean	Mountains	Forest
FREQUENCY:	Rare	Very rare	Rare	Very rare
ORGANIZATION:	Clans	Colony	Colon y/Guild	Clans
ACTIVITY CYCLE:	Any	Any	Any	Day
DIET:	Omnivore	Omnivore	Omnivore	Omnivore
INTELLIGENCE:	Varies (7-19)	Varies (3-17)	Varies (8-18)	Varies (3-17)
TREASURE:	Mx3	Kx2, Qx3	Mx30	J, K, Qx2
	C, Qx20 lair	D, Qx5 lair	C, Qx20 lair	C lair
ALIGNMENT:	Neutral good	Neutral (good)	Neutral or Lawful good	Neutral good
NO. APPEARING:	4-12 (4d3)	5-8 (1d4+4)	1-12 (1d12)	1-4 (1d4)
ARMOR CLASS:	6 or better	2 or better	10 or 5	10
MOVEMENT:	6	9	6	12
HIT DICE:	1 (base)	3+6 (base)	1 (base)	2 (base)
THAC0:	19	17	19	18
NO. OF ATTACKS:	1	1	1	1
DAMAGE/ATTACK:	By weapon	By weapon	By weapon	By weapon
SPECIAL ATTACKS:	Nil	Stun darts	Nil	Traps
SPECIAL DEFENSES:	See below	See below	See below	See below
MAGIC RESISTANCE:	Special	20% (and up)	Special	Special
SIZE:	S (3½')	S (3' to 3½')	S (3½')	S (2' to 2½')
MORALE:	Steady (12)	Elite (13)	Average (8)	Elite (14)
XP VALUE:	65 (base)	420 (base)	65 (base)	120 (base)

Small cousins of the dwarves, gnomes are friendly but reticent, quick to help their friends but rarely seen by other races unless they want to be. They tend to dwell underground in hilly, wooded regions where they can pursue their interests in peace. Gnomes can be fighters or priests, but most prefer to become thieves or illusionists instead. Multi-class characters are more common among the gnomes than any other demihuman race.

Gnomes strongly resemble small, thin, nimble dwarves, with the exception of two notable facial features: gnomes prefer to keep their beards short and stylishly-trimmed, and they take pride in their enormous noses (often fully twice the size of any dwarf or human's). Skin, hair, and eye color vary somewhat by subrace: the most common type of gnome, the Rock Gnome, has skin ranging from a dark tan to a woody brown (sometimes with a hint of gray), pale hair, and eyes any shade of blue. Gnomish clothing tends toward leather and earth tones, brightened by a bit of intricately wrought jewelry or stitching. Rock gnomes have an average life span of around 450 years, although some live to be 600 years or more.

Gnomes speak their own language, and each subrace has its own distinctive dialect. Many gnomes learn the tongues of humans, kobolds, goblins, halflings, and dwarves in order to communicate with their neighbors, and some Rock Gnomes are able to communicate with burrowing mammals via a basic language of grunts, snorts, and signs.

Gnomes posses infravision to 60 feet, and the ability to detect sloping passages (1-5 on 1d6), unsafe stonework (1-7 on 1d10), and approximate depth (1-4 on 1d6) and direction (1-3 on 1d6) underground. They are highly resistant to magic, gaining a +1 bonus to their saving throws for each 3.5 points of Constitution (a typical gnome will have a bonus of +3 to +4). Unfortunately, this also means that there is a 20% chance that any magical item a gnome attempts to use will malfunction (armor, weapons, and illusionary items exempted).

Combat: Gnomes prefer the use of strategy over brute force in combat and will often use illusions in imaginative ways to "even the odds." Their great hatred of kobolds and goblins, their traditional enemies, gives them a +1 on their attack rolls when fighting these beings. They are adept at dodging the attacks of large opponents, forcing all giant class creatures (gnolls, bugbears, ogres, trolls, giants, etc.) to subtract 4 from their attack rolls when fighting gnomes.

Gnomes can use any weapon that matches their size and often carry a second (or even a third) weapon as a back-up. Short swords, hammers, and spears are favorite melee weapons, with short bows, crossbows, slings, and darts coming into play when distance weapons are called for; virtually every gnome will also carry a sharp knife somewhere on his or her person as a final line of defense.

A typical rock gnome will wear studded leather armor and use a small shield (AC 6). Their leaders will have chain mail (AC 4), and any gnome above 5th level has plate mail (AC 2). There is a 10% chance for each level above 5th that the gnome's armor and/or weapon is magical (roll separately for each). Spell casters have a 10% chance per level of having 1-3 magical items usable by their character class.

Habitat/Society: Gnomes live in underground burrows in remote hilly, wooded regions. They are clannish, with friendly rivalries occurring between neighboring clans. They spend their lives mining, crafting fine jewelry, and enjoying the fruits of their labors. Gnomes work hard, and they play hard. They observe many festivals and holidays, which usually involve games, nose measuring contests, and swapping of grand tales. Their society is well organized, with many levels of responsibility, culminating in a single chief who is advised by clerics in matters directly relating to their calling.

A gnomish lair is home to some 40-400 (4d10×10) gnomes, one-quarter of them children. For every 40 adults there is a fighter of 2nd to 4th level. If 160 or more are encountered there is also a 5th-level chief and a 3rd-level lieutenant. If 200 or more are met, there is a cleric or illusionist of 4th to 6th level. If 320 or more are present, add a 6th-level fighter, two 5th-level fighters, a 7th-level cleric, four 3rd-level clerics, a 5th-level illusionist, and two 2nd-level illusionists. Gnomes often befriend burrowing mammals, so 5d6 badgers (70%), 3d4 giant badgers (20%), or 2d4 wolverines (10%) will be present as well. These animals are neither pets nor servants, but allies who will help guard the clan.

Gnome

Ecology: Gnomes are very much a magical part of nature, existing in harmony with the land they inhabit. They choose to live underground but remain near the surface in order to enjoy its beauty.

Svirfneblin (Deep Gnome)
Far beneath the surface of the earth dwell the Svirfneblin, or Deep Gnomes. Small parties of these demihumans roam the Underdark's mazes of small passageways searching for gemstones. They are said to dwell in great cities consisting of a closely connected series of tunnels, buildings, and caverns in which up to a thousand of these diminutive creatures live. They keep the location of these hidden cities secret in order to protect them from their deadly foes, the kuo-toa, Drow, and mind flayers.

Svirfneblin are slightly smaller than rock gnomes, but their thin, wiry, gnarled frames are just as strong. Their skin is rock-colored, usually medium brown to brownish gray, and their eyes are gray. Male svirfneblin are completely bald; female deep gnomes have stringy gray hair. The average svirfneblin life span is 250 years.

Svirfneblin mining teams and patrols work together so smoothly that to outside observers they appear to communicate with each other by some form of racial empathy. They speak their own dialect of gnomish that other gnomish subraces are 60% likely to understand. Most deep gnomes are also able to converse in Underworld Common and speak and understand a fair amount of kuo-toan and drow. These small folk can also converse with any creature from the elemental plane of Earth via a curious "language" consisting solely of vibrations (each pitch conveys a different message), although only on a very basic level.

All svirfneblin have the innate ability to cast *blindness*, *blur*, and *change self* once per day. Deep gnomes also radiate *non-detection* identical to the spell of the same name. Deep gnomes have 120-foot infravision, as well as all the detection abilities of rock gnomes.

Combat: Despite their metal armor and arms, these quick, small folk are able to move very quietly. Deep gnomes are able to "freeze" in place for long periods without any hint of movement, making them 60% unlikely to be seen by any observer, even those with infravision. They are surprised only on a roll of 1 on 1d10 due to their keen hearing and smelling abilities and surprise opponents 90% of the time.

The deep gnomes wear leather jacks sewn with rings or scales of mithral steel alloy over fine chainmail shirts, giving a typical svirfneblin warrior an Armor Class of 2. They do not usually carry shields, since these would hinder movement through the narrow corridors they favor. For every level above 3rd, a Deep Gnome's Armor Class improves by one point—a 4th-level deep gnome has AC 1, a 5th-level deep gnome, AC 0; to a maximum of AC 6.

All deep gnomes are 20% magic resistant, gaining an extra +5% magic resistance for each level they attain above 3rd. They are immune to illusions, phantasms, and hallucinations. Because of their high wisdom, speed, and agility, they make all saving throws at +3, except against poison, when their bonus is +2.

Deep Gnomes are typically armed with a pick and a dagger which, while nonmagical, gain a +1 bonus to attacks and damage due to their finely-honed edges. Svirfneblin also carry 1d4+6 special *stun darts*, throwing them to a range of 40 feet, with a +2 bonus to hit. Each dart releases a small puff of gas when it strikes; any creature inhaling the gas must save vs. poison or be *stunned* for 1 round and *slowed* for the next four rounds. Elite warriors (3rd level and above) often carry hollow darts with acid inside

(+2d4 to damage) and crystal caltrops which, when stepped on, release a powerful *sleep* gas.

Habitat/Society: Svirfneblin society is strictly divided between the sexes: females are in charge of food production and running the city, while males patrol its borders and mine for precious stones. A svirfneblin city will have both a king and a queen, each of whom is independent and has his or her own sphere of responsibility. Since only males ever leave the city, the vast majority of encounters will be with deep gnome mining parties seeking for new lodes. For every four svirfneblin encountered, there will be an overseer with 4+7 Hit Dice. Groups of more than 20 will be led by a burrow warden (6+9 Hit Dice) with two 5th-level assistants (5+8 Hit Dice).

It is 25% probable that a 6th-level deep gnome will have illusionist abilities of 5th, 6th, or 7th level. Deep Gnomes who are not illusionists gain the ability at 6th level to summon an earth elemental (50% chance of success) once per day. Deep gnome clerics have no ability to turn undead.

Ecology: Stealth, cleverness, and tenacity enable the svirfneblin to survive in the extremely hostile environment of the Underdark. They love gems, especially rubies, and will take great risks in order to gain them. Their affinity for stone is such that creatures from the elemental plane of Earth are 90% unlikely to harm a deep gnome, though they might demand a hefty tithe in gems or precious metals for allowing the gnome to escape.

Tinker Gnome (Minoi)
Cheerful, industrious, and inept, tinker gnomes originated on Krynn, but they have spread to many other worlds via spelljamming ships. Physically similar to rock gnomes, even to the extent of sharing the same infravision range, magic resistance, combat bonuses, and detection abilities, their history and culture are so radically different as to qualify them for consideration as a separate subrace.

Gnome

Graceful and quick in their movements, tinker gnomes' hands are deft and sure. Tinkers have rich brown skin, white hair, and china-blue or violet eyes. Males favor oddly-styled beards and moustaches, and both sexes have rounded ears and typically large gnomish noses. Tinkers who avoid getting blown up in an experiment live for 250-300 years.

Tinker gnomes speak very rapidly, running their words together in sentences that never seem to end. They are capable of talking and listening at the same time: when two tinkers meet, they babble away, answering questions asked by the other as part of the same continuous sentence.

Combat: Tinker gnomes rarely carry weapons, although some of their ever present tools can be pressed into service at need. However, they delight in invention and are always devising strange weapons of dubious utility, from the three barrel water blaster to the multiple spear flinger. Tinkers can wear any type of armor but typically outfit themselves in a variety of mismatched pieces for an effective AC of 5.

Habitat/Society: Tinker gnomes establish colonies consisting of immense tunnel complexes in secluded mountain ranges. The largest gnome settlement on Krynn, beneath Mount Nevermind, is home to some 59,000 tinkers. Other tinker gnome colonies exist, both on Krynn and elsewhere, but their populations seldom exceed 200-400.

All tinkers have a Life Quest: to attain perfect understanding of a single device. Few ever actually attain this goal, but their individual Life Quests do keep the ever hopeful tinkers busy. Males and females are equal in tinker society, and each pursue Life Quests with similar devotion. Each tinker gnome belongs to a guild. The guild occupies the same place in a tinker's life that the clan occupies for other gnomes. Together the guildmasters make up a grand council that governs the community.

Though most tinker gnomes are content to stay home and tinker with their projects, some have Life Quests which require them to venture out into the world. Adventuring gnomes are generally unable to learn from past experience and repeat the same mistakes, yet they are often successful with quirky solutions to save the day for their companions.

Ecology: Despite their great friendliness, tinker gnomes are not well-liked by other races: their technological bent makes them quite alien to those accustomed to magic, and their poor understanding of social relations puts off many potential friends. Sages generally agree that the tinkers' indiscriminate trumpeting of technology has discouraged its development by other races who have encountered tinker gnomes.

Forest Gnome

Shy and elusive, the forest gnomes live deep in forests and shun contact with other races except in times of dire emergencies threatening their beloved woods. The smallest of all the gnomes, they average 2 to 2½ feet in height, with bark-colored, gray-green skin, dark hair, and blue, brown, or green eyes. A very long-lived people, they have an average life expectancy of 500 years.

In addition to their own gnomish dialect, most forest gnomes can speak gnome common (rock gnome), Elf, Treant, and a simple language that enables them to communicate on a very basic level with forest animals. All forest gnomes have the innate ability to *pass without trace*, *hide in woodlands* (90% chance of success), and the same saving throw bonus as their rock gnome cousins.

Combat: Forest gnomes prefer boobie traps and missile weapons to melee weapons when dealing with enemies. Due to size and quickness they receive a −4 bonus to Armor Class whenever they are fighting M- or L-sized opponents. Forest gnomes receive a +1 bonus to all attack and damage rolls when fighting orcs, lizardmen, troglodytes, or any creature which they have seen damage their forest.

Habitat/Society: Forest gnomes live in small villages of less than 100 gnomes, each family occupying a large, hollowed-out tree. Most of these villages are disguised so well that even an elf or a ranger could walk through one without realizing it.

Ecology: Forest gnomes are guardians of the woods and friends to the animals that live there. They will often help lost travellers but will strive to remain unseen while doing so.

Gnome, Spriggan

CLIMATE/TERRAIN:	Any/Wilderness
FREQUENCY:	Very rare
ORGANIZATION:	Pack
ACTIVITY CYCLE:	Any
DIET:	Omnivore
INTELLIGENCE:	Average to exceptional (8-16)
TREASURE:	A
ALIGNMENT:	Chaotic evil

NO. APPEARING:	3-12
ARMOR CLASS:	3 or 5 (10)
MOVEMENT:	9 or 15
HIT DICE:	4 or 8+4
THAC0:	17 or 11
NO. OF ATTACKS:	2
DAMAGE/ATTACK:	2-8/2-8 (weapon) +7 (Strength bonus)
SPECIAL ATTACKS:	Spells, thief abilities
SPECIAL DEFENSES:	See below
MAGIC RESISTANCE:	Nil
SIZE:	S (3' tall) or L (12' tall)
MORALE:	Champion (15-16)
XP VALUE:	Male: 3,000
	Female: 2,000

These ugly, dour cousins of gnomes are able to become giant-sized at will.

In either size, spriggans look basically the same. They are ugly, thick-bodied humanoids, with pale or dull yellow skin, brown or black hair, and red eyes. On rare occasions a spriggan may have red hair, which they believe is a symbol of good luck. Their noses are large and bulbous, but not beyond the human norm. They are very fond of mustaches and bushy sideburns, but they never clean or comb them. This same policy of uncleanliness extends to their bodies and any other possessions. Spriggans smell of dank earth, stale sweat, and grime.

Outside of their lair they always wear armor and carry weapons, usually polearms, although they have been known to carry swords or maces. Spriggans never use shields. They like to carry several nasty little daggers concealed in various places in their armor. Spriggans never wear jewelry or other ornaments. They prefer to keep these things with their hoard, where they brood over them at odd moments.

Combat: Spriggans are tricky and tough in battle. They have a wide variety of options for combat. Their major ability is to change from small to giant size at will. Weapons, armor and other inanimate objects on their person shrink and grow with them. This action takes the whole round, during which they can move up to 30 feet but not fight. When small, spriggans can use the following spell-like effects: *affect normal fires*, *shatter*, and *scare* (with a −2 penalty to the saving throw, due to their ugliness). They can perform any one of these instead of fighting, once in any round, as often as they want. When giant-sized, spriggans cannot perform magic, other than to shrink again. In this form they are as strong as hill giants (19).

In either size, they have 8th-level thief abilities like those of a gnome with an 18 Dexterity. This high Dexterity enables them to use a weapon twice each round. They can pick pockets (75%), open locks (78%), find or remove traps (70%), move silently (77%), hide in shadows (64%), hear noise (35%), climb walls (81%), and read languages (40%). Keep in mind that their size may affect these chances indirectly. For example, it is difficult for a 12-foot-tall giant to hide in a 6-foot-tall shadow. They can backstab only while in small form, and they inflict triple damage if successful.

Spriggans can never quite get organized as groups. In fact, they are sometimes encountered with part of the group giant-sized and part of them gnome-sized. On an individual level they are very clever and use their abilities to the fullest to accomplish their goals. These goals are usually to cause great havoc and mayhem amongst other races. They seem to take great pleasure in destroying property and hurting innocent creatures.

Habitat/Society: Spriggans usually travel in packs, all of them male. The females keep to dismal burrows or secret dens in forgotten ruins, rarely venturing out farther than necessary to gather food. A female has the same combat abilities as a male except that they have only 7+4 Hit Dice in giant form. The females mate with males from packs that wander nearby. The children are cast out upon reaching maturity, the males to join up with packs and the females to find a place to lair. Spriggan infant mortality is high, with the males (80%) surviving more often than the females (60%).

Spriggans hate gnomes more than any living creatures, but they truly love none but those of their own ilk. Perhaps it is the similarity of the true gnomes to their race that drives their hatred. They like to terrorize, rob, and otherwise work vile deeds. They do not hesitate to attack or steal from traveling groups or small settlements in their area. All of their possessions, including their armor and weapons, are stolen from their victims. They greatly fear large groups of organized humans and demihumans, and they avoid such parties.

Ecology: The roving packs of males tend to be meat eaters, preferring to hunt or steal their food. As such they must keep moving and establish wide areas of control. The females tend to eat fruits and grains that can be easily gathered near their dens. They eat meat only when offered by a male as part of the mating ritual.

Spriggans are too mean and nasty to have any natural predators, although gnomes attack them on sight unless faced with overwhelming odds. It usually takes a well-armed party to root out a band of spriggans.

CLIMATE/TERRAIN:	Any non-arctic land
FREQUENCY:	Uncommon
ORGANIZATION:	Tribe
ACTIVITY CYCLE:	Night
DIET:	Carnivore
INTELLIGENCE:	Low to average (5-10)
TREASURE:	C (K)
ALIGNMENT:	Lawful evil

NO. APPEARING:	4-24 (4d6)
ARMOR CLASS:	6 (10)
MOVEMENT:	6
HIT DICE:	1-1
THAC0:	20
NO. OF ATTACKS:	1
DAMAGE/ATTACK:	1-6 (by weapon)
SPECIAL ATTACKS:	Nil
SPECIAL DEFENSES:	Nil
MAGIC RESISTANCE:	Nil
SIZE:	Small (4' tall)
MORALE:	Average (10)
XP VALUE:	15
Chief & sub-chiefs	35

These small, evil humanoids would be merely pests, if not for their great numbers.

Goblins have flat faces, broad noses, pointed ears, wide mouths and small, sharp fangs. Their foreheads slope back, and their eyes are usually dull and glazed. They always walk upright, but their arms hang down almost to their knees. Their skin colors range from yellow through any shade of orange to a deep red. Usually a single tribe has members all of about the same color skin. Their eyes vary from bright red to a gleaming lemon yellow. They wear clothing of dark leather, tending toward dull soiled-looking colors.

Goblin speech is harsh, and pitched higher than that of humans. In addition to their own language, some goblins can speak in the kobold, orc, and hobgoblin tongues.

Combat: Goblins hate bright sunlight, and fight with a -1 on their attack rolls when in it. This unusual sensitivity to light, however, serves the goblins well underground, giving them infravision out to 60 feet. They can use any sort of weapon, preferring those that take little training, like spears and maces. They are known to carry short swords as a second weapon. They are usually armored in leather, although the leaders may have chain or even plate mail.

Goblin strategies and tactics are simple and crude. They are cowardly and will usually avoid a face-to-face fight. More often than not, they will attempt to arrange an ambush of their foes.

Habitat/Society: Humans would consider the caves and underground dwellings of goblins to be dank and dismal. Those few tribes that live above ground are found in ruins, and are only active at night or on very dark, cloudy days. They use no form of sanitation, and their lairs have a foul stench. Goblins seem to be somewhat resistant to the diseases that breed in such filth.

They live a communal life, sharing large common areas for eating and sleeping. Only leaders have separate living spaces. All their possessions are carried with them. Property of the tribe is kept with the chief and sub-chiefs. Most of their goods are stolen, although they do manufacture their own garments and leather goods. The concept of privacy is largely foreign to goblins.

A typical goblin tribe has 40-400 (4d10 x 10) adult male warriors. For every 40 goblins there will be a leader and his 4 assist-

ants, each having 1 Hit Die (7 hit points). For every 200 goblins there will be a sub-chief and 2-8 (2d4) bodyguards, each of which has 1 + 1 Hit Dice (8 hit points), is Armor Class 5, and armed with a battle axe. The tribe has a single goblin chief and 2-8 (2d4) bodyguards each of 2 Hit Dice, Armor Class 4, and armed with two weapons.

There is a 25% chance that 10% of their force will be mounted upon huge worgs, and have another 10-40 (1d4x10) unmounted worgs with them. There is a 60% chance that the lair is guarded by 5-30 (5d6) such wolves, and a 20% chance of 2-12 (2d6) bugbears. Goblin shamans are rare, but have been known to reach 7th level. Their spheres include: Divination, Healing (reversed), Protection, and Sun (reversed).

In addition to the males, there will be adult females equal to 60% of their number and children equal to the total number of adults in the lair. Neither will fight in battles.

A goblin tribe has an exact pecking order; each member knows who is above him and who is below him. They fight amongst themselves constantly to move up this social ladder.

They often take slaves for both food and labor. The tribe will have slaves of several races numbering 10-40% of the size of the tribe. Slaves are always kept shackled, and are staked to a common chain when sleeping.

Goblins hate most other humanoids, gnomes and dwarves in particular, and work to exterminate them whenever possible.

Ecology: Goblins live only 50 years or so. They do not need to eat much, but will kill just for the pleasure of it. They eat any creature from rats and snakes to humans. In lean times they will eat carrion. Goblins usually spoil their habitat, driving game from it and depleting the area of all resources. They are decent miners, able to note new or unusual construction in an underground area 25% of the time, and any habitat will soon be expanded by a maze-like network of tunnels.

Golem, General

CLIMATE/TERRAIN: Any
FREQUENCY: Very rare
ORGANIZATION: Solitary
ACTIVITY CYCLE: Any
DIET: Nil
INTELLIGENCE: Non- (0)
TREASURE: Nil
ALIGNMENT: Neutral

Golems are magically created automatons of great power. The construction of one involves mighty magic and elemental forces.

Background: Golems predate any known literature about their creation. The wizard who discovered the process, if indeed there was only one, is unknown. Some of the rediscoverers have written their secrets in various arcane manuals, enchanted to aid the reader in construction. It is thought that the first golem created was a flesh golem, possibly an accident of some great wizard experimenting with reanimating human bodies. Flesh golems are easier to make than any other sort because they are made of organic material that once lived. Later, the process was generalized to suit certain earthen materials, which produce much stronger golems.

Theory: Golems are all made from elemental material. So far, the great wizards have only discovered how to use various earthen materials, such as clay, stone, iron, and even glass, to make golems. The exceptions, such as the flesh golem, use organic materials as components. The animating force of the golem is an elemental spirit from the elemental plane of Earth. Since the spirit is not a natural part of the body, it is not affected by most spells or even by most weapons (see individual descriptions). The process of creating the golem binds the unwilling spirit to the artificial body, and enslaves it to the will of the golem's creator. The nature of this spirit is unknown, and has so far eluded the grasp of all researchers. What is known is that it is hostile to all Prime Material plane life forms, especially toward the spell caster that bound it to the golem.

Carving or assembling the golem's physical body is an exacting task. Most spell casters end up hiring skilled labor to do it for them, such as a stone mason or dwarf for stone golems, etc. If the maker has no experience working in that material, the construction time is doubled. The standard spells for creating golems specify the size of the creature. Anything bigger or smaller will not work, although some have investigated spells for other sizes of golems, with limited success.

The costs listed include the base physical body and the unusual materials and spell components that are consumed or become a permanent part of the golem. The rituals used to animate the golem require as much as a full uninterrupted month to complete (included in the time below), though some variants such as the necrophidius and scarecrow reduce that time by employing shortcuts. In all cases the spells used can come from devices, such as wands or scrolls. If a magical tome is used to make the golem, no spells are needed, and the level of the spell caster can be significantly lower.

Golem Creation Table
(Note: W18 = 18th-level wizard, P17 = 17th level priest, etc.)

Type of Golem	Creator	Construction Time	GP Cost
Bone	W18	2 months	35,000
Caryatid	W16	4 months	100,000
Clay	P17	1 month	65,000
Doll	P15	2 months	20,000
Flesh	W14	2 months	50,000
Gargoyle	P16	4 months	100,000
Glass	P14/W14	6 months	125,000
Guardian	W14	1 month	20,000
Iron	W18	4 months	100,000
Juggernaut	W16	3 months	80,000
Necrophidius	P9/W14	10 days	8,000
Scarecrow	P9	21 days	100
Stone	W16	3 months	80,000

Combat: All golems share several traits in common. They are all immune to all forms of poison and cannot be affected by *hold, charm, fear,* or other mindbased spells, as they have no minds of their own. Certain spells can harm golems; these are mentioned below.

Most golems are fearless and need never check morale.

Flesh Golems
The pieces of the golem must be sewn together from the dead bodies of normal humans that have not decayed significantly. A minimum of 6 different bodies must be used, one for each limb, one for the torso (with head), and a different one for the brain. In some cases, more bodies may be necessary to form a complete golem. The spells needed are *wish, polymorph any object, geas, protection from normal missiles,* and *strength*.

Clay Golems
Only a lawful good priest can create a clay golem. The body is sculpted from a single block of clay weighing at least 1000 pounds, which takes about a month. The vestments, which cost 30,000 gp, are the only materials that are not consumed and can be reused, reducing the total cost after the first golem. The spells used are *resurrection, animate object, commune, prayer,* and *bless*.

Stone Golems
A stone golem's body is chiseled from a single block of hard stone, such as granite, weighing at least 3000 pounds, which takes 2 months. The rituals to animate require another month. The materials and spell components alone cost 60,000 gold pieces and the spells used are *wish, polymorph any object, geas,* and *slow*.

Iron Golems
It takes 5000 pounds of iron, to build the body, which must be done by a skilled iron smith. The spells used in the ritual are *wish, polymorph any object, geas,* and *cloud kill*. Construction of the body requires an ornate sword which is incorporated into the monster. A magical sword can be used, in which case there is a 50% chance that it is drained of magic when the golem is animated. The golem can only use those abilities of the sword that are automatic. Any property that requires a command word and any sentient ability of the sword is lost. If the sword is ever removed from the golem, it loses all of its magic.

Variant Golems

The first golems were, undoubtedly, all traditional golems. Over the years, however, various wizards and priests examined the techniques employed by earlier designers and modified them. As they introduced changes, they documented the processes they used to create their new constructs. This process of study and modification is never-ending. Even today, the work of these mysterious scholars is being studied and revised in magical colleges around the world.

Theory: Like other golems, golem variants depend on the powerful forces of elemental magic to animate them. They have no lives of their own and are animated by a spirit from the elemental plane of Earth. In some cases this spirit is tricked, lured, or forced into animating the body while in other cases it comes willingly. In the former cases, the stone construct sometimes breaks free of the influence of its creator and becomes a freewilled entity. Because of the nature of its physical shell, constructs that break free often become berserk killers, destroying everything in their paths before being annihilated themselves.

Construction: The actual construction of any golem's physical body is a tiring and demanding task. Although the steps required to create a variant golem differ depending on the type, they do have some elements in common. The most important of these is the degree of detail that is put into the carving of the body. In the case of the caryatid column, for example, the construct must be lovingly crafted with great skill. In most cases, the wizard or priest creating a caryatid column hires a professional sculptor or stone mason to undertake this step of the animation process.

Less sophisticated golems, like the stone guardian and the primitive scarecrow, do not require the artistic perfection of the caryatid column. However, they are often covered with delicate mystical runes or glyphs that must be perfect if the creature is to be successfully animated.

Bone Golem
The body of a bone golem is assembled wholly from the bones of animated skeletons who have been defeated in combat. Any type of skeletal undead will do, but all must have been created and slain in the Demiplane of Dread. Only 10% of the bones from any given skeleton can be used, so the final product is the compilation of bones from many creatures. Often, there will be animal, monster, and human bones in the same golem, giv-

ing the creature a nightmarish appearance. The spells woven over the body must include *animate dead, symbol of fear, binding,* and *wish.*

Caryatid column

The caryatid column can be created by a priest or wizard using a special version of the manual of golems. Whenever such a tome is discovered, there is a 20% chance that it describes a caryatid column.

Doll Golem

These creatures resemble a child's toy—often a baby doll or stuffed animal. Doll golems can serve as either the guardians of children or as murdering things too foul to contemplate.

The spells needed to complete the animation are *imbue with spell ability, Tasha's uncontrollable hideous laughter, (un)holy word, bless,* and *prayer.* The first known examples of this type of golem turned up on the Demiplane of Dread in the land of Sanguinia.

Gargoyle Golem

This creature is fashioned in the image of a real gargoyle and is often placed as a warden atop buildings, cathedrals, or tombs. It is most similar to the stone golem; the body must be carved from a single slab of granite (weighing 3,000 pounds) and prepared with expensive components. Only the vestments created for the process are reusable (saving 15,000 gp on the cost of additional gargoyle golems). The spells required to complete the process are *bless, exaction, (un)holy word, stone shape, conjure earth elemental,* and *prayer.*

Glass Golem

The glass golem is composed entirely of stained glass. Perhaps the most artistic of all golems, its creation requires the following spells: *glassteel, animate object, prismatic spray, rainbow,* and *wish.* Because of the mixture of spells, this type of golem is usually built by multi- or dual-classed characters or with the aid of a powerful assistant.

The first appearance of glass golems is not recorded with certainty. It is believed that they were created by a spell-caster who fancied himself an artist (hence their eerie beauty), but no one knows.

Juggernaut

Juggernauts that can alter their form require an extra step in their creation, which normally resembles the process to make a stone golem. Prior

to animating a juggernaut, the wizard must use the mimic blood as a material component in the final spells woven over the body. This addition gives this golem variant intelligence and an alignment.

Necrophidius

A necrophidius may be created in one of three ways. The first is a special form of *manual of golems* that provides secrets of its construction. The *Necrophidicon,* as it is called, must be burnt to ashes that provide the monster's animating force. The other two arcane and priestly processes are long and complex. A wizard must cast *limited wish, geas,* and *charm person* spells. A priest requires the spells *quest, neutralize poison, prayer, silence,* and *snake charm.* Whichever method is used, the monster requires a complete giant snake skeleton (either poisonous or constrictor), slain within 24 hours of the enchantment's commencement. Each necrophidius is built for a single specific purpose (which must be in the spellcaster's mind when he creates it), such as "Kill Ragnar the Bold." The necrophidius never seeks to twist the intent of its maker, but its enchantments fade when its task is done or cannot be completed; for example, when it kills Ragnar.

The maker must want the necrophidius to serve its purpose. He could not, for example, build a death worm to "Sneak into the druid's hut and steal his staff," if he really intended for the necrophidius to merely provide a distraction. He could not build more than one death worm and assign both to kill Ragnar, since he could not imbue the second death worm with a task that he intended the first one to complete. For this reason, necrophidii almost never work as a team.

Rumors claim that there were once methods to make a necrophidius gain 1 Hit Die every century it was pursuing its purpose.

Scarecrow

Scarecrows can only be created either by using a special manual or by a god answering the plea of a priest employing the following spells: *animate object, prayer, command,* and *quest.* The final step of the process, casting the *quest* spell, is done during a new moon.

Scarecrows can be constructed to kill a specific person. To do so, the clothes worn by the scarecrow must come from the intended victim. Once the scarecrow is animated, the priest need only utter a single word—"Quest". The scarecrow then moves in a direct line toward the victim. When it reaches the victim, the scarecrow disregards all other beings and concentrates its gaze and attacks entirely on the person it has been created to kill. After slaying its victim, a quested scarecrow's magic dissipates and it collapses into dust.

Stone Guardian

A stone guardian is very similar to a traditional stone golem, but it has some unique abilities its ancestor does not. In physical appearance, the two constructs are quite similar, but the stone guardian is usually decorated with runes and magical glyphs.

A stone guardian is created with the following spells: *enchant an item, transmute mud to rock, magic mouth,* and *limited wish* or *wish.* In addition, the wizard creating the guardian may cast a *detect invisible* spell to give the creature that power.

The initial material of the body is mud around a heart of polished stone. As the various spells are woven into the body, a spirit from the elemental plane of Earth is forced to enter the body and animate it. Because the spirit is there against its will, there is a 20% chance that the golem goes berserk each time it is activated.

A special *ring of protection* can be created when the stone guardian is animated; this prevents the guardian from striking at anyone wearing it. In addition, all those within 10 feet of the ring wearer are also immune to attack. Rings of this type function only against the guardian they were made with and provide no protection from any other golem.

Golem, Greater

	Stone	Iron
CLIMATE/TERRAIN:	Any	Any
FREQUENCY:	Very rare	Very rare
ORGANIZATION:	Solitary	Solitary
ACTIVITY CYCLE:	Any	Any
DIET:	Nil	Nil
INTELLIGENCE:	Non- (0)	Non- (0)
TREASURE:	Nil	Nil
ALIGNMENT:	Neutral	Neutral
NO. APPEARING:	1	1
ARMOR CLASS:	5	3
MOVEMENT:	6	6
HIT DICE:	14 (60 hp)	18 (80 hp)
THAC0:	7	3
NO. OF ATTACKS:	1	1
DAMAGE/ATTACK:	3-24 (3d8)	4-40 (4d10)
SPECIAL ATTACKS:	See below	See below
SPECIAL DEFENSES:	See below	See below
MAGIC RESISTANCE:	Nil	Nil
SIZE:	L (9½' tall)	L (12' tall)
MORALE:	Fearless (19-20)	Fearless (19-20)
XP VALUE:	8,000	13,000

A greater golem is an artificial humanoid body which has been animated by an elemental spirit but remains under the complete control of its creator.

Stone Golem

A stone golem is 9½ feet tall, and weighs around 2000 pounds. Its body is of roughly chiseled stone, frequently stylized to suit its creator. For example it might be carved to to look like it is wearing armor with a particular symbol on the chest plate. Sometimes designs are worked into the stone of its limbs. The head may be chiseled to resemble a helmet or other head piece. Regardless of these elements, it always has the basic humanoid parts (2 arms, 2 legs, head with 2 eyes, nose, mouth etc.). It is always weaponless and never wears clothing.

Combat: Greater golems are mindless in combat, only following the simple tactics of their masters. They are completely emotionless and cannot be swayed in any way from their instructions. They will not pick up and use weapons in combat, even if ordered to, always preferring their fists. Stone golems have a strength of 22, for purposes of breaking or throwing things.

The stone golem is immune to any weapon, except those of +2 or better enchantment. A *rock to mud* spell slows a golem for 2-12 (2d6) rounds. Its reverse, *mud to rock* acts to heal the golem, restoring all lost hit points. A *flesh to stone* spell does not actually change the golem's structure, but does make it vulnerable to any normal attack for the following round. This does not include spells, except those that will cause direct damage. All other spells are ignored. Once every other round, the stone golem can cast a *slow* spell upon any opponent with 10 feet of it.

Habitat/Society: Golems are automatons, artificially created and under the direct control of their creator. They have no society and are not associated with any particular habitat. They are frequently used to guard valuable items or places. Unlike the lesser golems, the greater golems are always under the complete control of their master. A greater golem can obey simple instructions involving direct actions with simple conditional phrases. Although this is better than a lesser golem is capable of following, they still make poor servants. Any given task could take several separate commands to direct the golem to its completion.

Ecology: Golems are not natural creatures, and play no part in the ecology of the world. They neither eat nor sleep, and "live" until they are destroyed, usually in combat. Certain spells (see above) can be used to heal or repair any damage done to them in combat. This is usually done by their creators to insure long and valuable service.

Iron Golem

An iron golem is twice the height of a normal man, and weighs around 5000 pounds. It can be fashioned in any stylized manner, just like the stone golems, although it almost always is built displaying armor of some sort. Its features are much smoother in contrast to the stone golem. Iron golems are sometimes found with a short sword (relative to their size) in one hand. On extremely rare occasions this sword will be magical.

The iron golem cannot speak or make any vocal noise, nor does it have any distinguishable odor. It moves with a ponderously smooth gait at half the speed of a normal man. Each step causes the floor to tremble, unless it is on a thick, solid foundation.

Combat: The iron golem conforms to the strategies listed for the stone golem except as described here. It has a strength of 24 for the purposes of lifting, throwing or breaking objects. The iron golem is immune to any weapon, except those of +3 or better enchantment. Magical electrical attacks will *slow* it for 3 rounds, and magical fire attacks actually repair 1 hit point of damage for each hit die of damage it would have caused. All other spells are ignored. Iron golems are subject to the damage inflicted by a rust monster. Once every 7 rounds, beginning either the first or second round of combat, the iron golem breathes out a cloud of poisonous gas. It does this automatically, with no regard to the effects it might have. The gas cloud fills a 10 foot cube directly in front of it, which dissipates by the following round, assuming there is somewhere for the gas to go.

Golem, Lesser

	Flesh	Clay
CLIMATE/TERRAIN:	Any	Any
FREQUENCY:	Very rare	Very rare
ORGANIZATION:	Solitary	Solitary
ACTIVITY CYCLE:	Any	Any
DIET:	Nil	Nil
INTELLIGENCE:	Semi- (2-4)	Non- (0)
TREASURE:	Nil	Nil
ALIGNMENT:	Neutral	Neutral
NO. APPEARING:	1	1
ARMOR CLASS:	9	7
MOVEMENT:	8	7
HIT DICE:	9 (40 hp)	11 (50 hp)
THAC0:	11	9
NO. OF ATTACKS:	2	1
DAMAGE/ATTACK:	2-16 (2d8)/2-16 (2d8)	3-30 (3d10)
SPECIAL ATTACKS:	Nil	See below
SPECIAL DEFENSES:	See below	See below
MAGIC RESISTANCE:	Nil	Nil
SIZE:	L (7½' tall)	L (8' tall)
MORALE:	Fearless (19-20)	Fearless (19-20)
XP VALUE:	2,000	5,000

A golem is an artificial humanoid body which is animated by an elemental spirit and under the control of its creator.

Flesh Golem

The flesh golem stands a head and a half taller than most humans and weighs almost 350 pounds. It is made from a ghoulish collection of stolen human body parts, stitched together to form a single composite human body. Its skin is the sickly green or yellow of partially decayed flesh. A flesh golem smells faintly of freshly dug earth and dead flesh. No natural animal, such as a dog, will willingly track a flesh golem. It wears whatever clothing its creator desires, usually just a ragged pair of trousers. It has no possessions, and no weapons. The golem can not speak, although it can emit a hoarse roar of sorts. It walks and moves with a stiff jointed gait, as if it is not in complete control over its body parts.

Combat: The lesser golems are mindless in combat. They follow the orders of their master explicitly, and are incapable of any strategy or tactics. They are emotionless in combat, and cannot be easily provoked (unless they have broken control and gone berserk). They will not use weapons for combat, even if ordered to, always preferring to strike with their fists. Flesh golems have a strength of 19 for purposes of lifting, throwing or breaking down doors.

Flesh golems can only be struck by a magical weapon. Fire and cold based spells merely slow them for 2-12 (2d6) rounds. Any electrical attack restores 1 hit point for each die of damage it would normally have done. All other spells are ignored by the creature.

The elemental spirit in a lesser golem is not bound strongly, resulting in a 1% cumulative chance per round of combat, calculated independently for each fight, that it will break free of its master. The flesh golem's master has a 10% chance per round of regaining control. To do this he must be within 60 feet of the flesh golem, and the creature must be able to see and hear its master. No special spells are required to regain control, its creator just has to talk to it forcefully and persuasively, to convince it to obey.

Habitat/Society: Golems are automatons, artificially created and under the direct control of their creator. They have no society and are not associated with any particular habitat. They are frequently used to guard valuable items or places. A lesser golem can obey simple instructions involving a single, direct action. They make poor servants because each detail of a task must be given as a separate command.

Ecology: Golems are not natural creatures, and play no part in the world's ecology. They neither eat nor sleep, and "live" until their bodies are destroyed, usually in combat.

Clay Golem

The clay golem is a humanoid body made from clay, and stnds about 18 inches taller than a normal man. It weighs around 600 pounds. The features are grossly distorted from the human norm. The chest is overly large, with arms attached by thick knots of muscle at the shoulder. Its arms hang down to its knees, and end in short stubby fingers. It has no neck, and a large head with broad flat features. Its legs are short and bowed, with wide flat feet. A clay golem wears no clothing except for a metal or stiff leather garment around its hips. It smells faintly of clay. The golem can not speak, or make any noise. It walks and moves with a slow and clumsy gait, almost as if it were not in control over its actions.

Combat: Clay golems conform to the strategies listed above for the flesh golem except as noted here. A clay golem has a strength of 20 for the purposes of lifting, throwing or smashing objects. They can only be struck by magical blunt weapons such as hammers or maces. A move earth spell will drive the golem back 120 feet and inflict 3-36 (3d12) points of damage upon it. A disintegrate spell merely slows the golem for 1-6 rounds and causes 1-12 points of damage. An earthquake spell cast directly at a clay golem will stop it from moving that turn and inflict 5-50 (5d10) points of damage. After it has engaged in at least one round of combat, the clay golem can haste itself for 3 rounds. It can only do this once per day. Damage done by the golem can only be cured by a heal spell from a priest of 17th level or greater.

The elemental spirit in a lesser golem is not bound strongly, resulting in a 1% cumulative chance per round of combat, calculated independently for each fight, that it will break free of its master. If a clay golem does manage to break control, it becomes a berserker, attacking everything in sight until it is destroyed. Its first action is to haste itself, if it can. Unlike the flesh golem, there is no chance to regain control of a rampaging clay golem.

Golem, Bone, Doll

	Bone	Doll
CLIMATE/TERRAIN:	Any	Any
FREQUENCY:	Very rare	Very rare
ORGANIZATION:	Solitary	Solitary
ACTIVITY CYCLE:	Any	Any
DIET:	Nil	Nil
INTELLIGENCE:	Non-(0)	Non-(0)
TREASURE:	Nil	Nil
ALIGNMENT:	Neutral	Neutral
NO. APPEARING:	1	1
ARMOR CLASS:	0	4
MOVEMENT:	12	15
HIT DICE:	14 (70 hp)	10 (40 hp)
THAC0:	7	11
NO. OF ATTACKS:	1	1
DAMAGE/ATTACK:	3d8	3d6
SPECIAL ATTACKS:	See below	See below
SPECIAL DEFENSES:	See below	See below
MAGIC RESISTANCE:	Nil	Nil
SIZE:	M (6' tall)	T (1' tall)
MORALE:	Fearless (20)	Fearless (20)
XP VALUE:	18,000	6,000

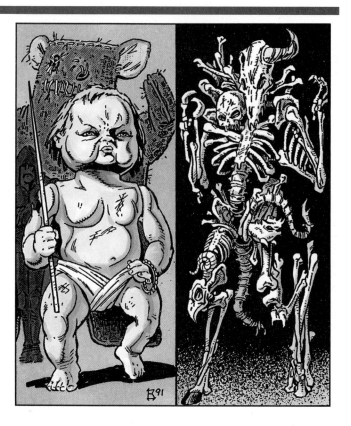

Bone Golem

The bone golem is built from the previously animated bones of skeletal undead. These horrors stand roughly 6 feet tall and weight between 50 and 60 pounds. They are seldom armored and can easily be mistaken for undead, much to the dismay of those who make this error.

Combat: Bone golems are no more intelligent than other forms of golem, so they will not employ clever tactics or strategies in combat. Their great power, however, makes them far deadlier than they initially appear to be. There is a 95% chance that those not familiar with the true nature of their opponent will mistake them for simple undead.

Bone golems attack with their surprisingly strong blows and sharp, claw-like fingers. Each successful hit inflicts 3-24 (3d8) points of damage. They can never be made to use weapons of any sort in melee.

In addition to the common characteristics of all Ravenloft golems (described previously), bone golems take only half damage from those edged or piercing weapons that can harm them.

Bone golems are immune to almost all spells, but can be laid low with the aid of a *shatter* spell that is focused on them and has the capacity to affect objects of their weight. If such a spell is cast at a bone golem, the golem is entitled to a saving throw vs. spells to negate it. Failure indicates that weapons able to harm the golem will now inflict twice the damage they normally would. Thus, edged weapons would do full damage while blunt ones would inflict double damage.

Once every three rounds, the bone golem may throw back its head and issue a hideous laugh that causes all those who hear it to make fear *and* horror checks. Those who fail either check are *paralyzed* and cannot move for 2-12 rounds. Those who fail *both* checks are instantly stricken dead with fear.

Doll Golem

The doll golem is an animated version of a child's toy that can be put to either good uses (defending the young) or evil uses (attacking them). It is often crafted so as to make it appear bright and cheerful when at rest. Upon activation, however, its features become twisted and horrific.

Combat: The doll golem is, like all similar creatures, immune to almost all magical attacks. It can be harmed by fire-based spells, although these do only half damage, while a *warp wood* spell will affect the creature as if it were a *slow* spell. A *mending* spell restores the creature to full hit points at once.

Each round, the doll golem leaps onto a victim and attempts to bite it. Success inflicts 3d6 points of damage and forces the victim to save versus spells. Failure to save causes the victim to begin to laugh uncontrollably (as if under the influence of a *Tasha's uncontrollable hideous laughter* spell) and become unable to perform any other action. The effects of the creature's bite are far worse, however. The victim begins to laugh on the round after the failed save. At this time, they take 1d4 points of damage from the muscle spasms imposed by the laughter. On following rounds, this increases to 2d4, then 3d4, and so on. The laughter stops when the character dies or receives a *dispel magic*. Following recovery, the victim suffers a penalty on all attack and saving throws of -1 per round that they were overcome with laughter (e.g., four rounds of uncontrolled laughter would equal a -4 penalty on attack/saving throws). This represents the weakness caused by the character's inability to breathe and is reduced by 1 point per subsequent turn until the character is fully recovered.

	Gargoyle	Glass
CLIMATE/TERRAIN:	Any	Any
FREQUENCY:	Very rare	Very rare
ORGANIZATION:	Solitary	Solitary
ACTIVITY CYCLE:	Any	Any
DIET:	Nil	Nil
INTELLIGENCE:	Non-(0)	Non-(0)
TREASURE:	Nil	Nil
ALIGNMENT:	Neutral	Neutral
NO. APPEARING:	1	1
ARMOR CLASS:	0	4
MOVEMENT:	9	12
HIT DICE:	15 (60 hp)	9 (40 hp)
THAC0:	5	11
NO. OF ATTACKS:	2	1
DAMAGE/ATTACK:	3d6/3d6	2d12
SPECIAL ATTACKS:	See below	See below
SPECIAL DEFENSES:	See below	See below
MAGIC RESISTANCE:	Nil	Nil
SIZE:	M (6' tall)	M (6' tall)
MORALE:	Fearless (20)	Fearless (20)
XP VALUE:	14,000	5,000

Gargoyle Golems

The gargoyle golem is a stone construct designed to guard a given structure. It is roughly the same size and weight as a real gargoyle (6' tall and 550 pounds). Although they have wings, they cannot fly. However, a gargoyle golem can leap great distances (up to 100 feet) and will often use this ability to drop down on enemies nearing any building the golem is protecting.

Gargoyle golems cannot speak or communicate in any way. When they move, the sound of grinding rock can be heard by anyone near them. In fact, it is often this noise that serves as a party's first warning that something is amiss in an area.

Combat: When a gargoyle golem attacks in melee combat, it does so with its two clawed fists. Each fist must attack the same target and will inflict 3d6 points of damage. Anyone hit by both attacks must save versus petrification or be turned to stone. On the round after a gargoyle golem has petrified a victim, it will attack that same target again. Any hit scored by the golem against such a foe indicates that the stone body has shattered and cannot be *resurrected*. *Reincarnation*, on the other hand, is still a viable option.

Gargoyle golems are, like most golems, immune to almost every form of magical attack directed at them. They are, however, vulnerable to the effects of an *earthquake* spell. If such a spell is targeted directly at a gargoyle golem, it instantly shatters the creature without affecting the surrounding area. The lesser *transmute rock to mud* spell will inflict 2d10 points of damage to the creature while the reverse (*transmute mud to rock*) will heal a like amount of damage.

On the first round of any combat in which the gargoyle golem has not been identified for what it is, it has a good chance of gaining surprise (-2 on opponent surprise checks). Whenever a gargoyle golem attacks a character taken by surprise, it will leap onto that individual. The crushing weight of the creature delivers 4d10 points of damage and requires every object carried by that character in a vulnerable position (DM's decision) to save vs. crushing blows or be destroyed. In the round that a gargoyle golem pounces on a character, it cannot attack with its fists.

Glass Golems

The glass golem is very nearly a work of art. Built in the form of a stained glass knight, the creature is often built into a window fashioned from such glass. Thus, it usually acts as the guardian of a given location—often a church or shrine.

Glass golems, like most others, never speak or communicate in any way. When they move, however, they are said to produce a tinkling sound like that made by delicate crystal wind chimes. If moving through a lighted area, they strobe and flicker as the light striking them is broken into its component hues.

Combat: When the stained glass golem attacks, it often has the advantage of surprise. If its victims have no reason to suspect that it lurks in a given window, they suffer a -3 on their surprise roll when the creature makes its presence known.

Once combat is joined, the stained glass figure (which always has the shape of a knight) strikes with is sword. Each blow that lands delivers 2d12 points of damage.

Once every three rounds, the golem can unleash a *prismatic spray* spell from its body that fans out in all directions. Any object or being (friend or foe) within 25 feet of the golem must roll as if they had been struck by a wizard's *prismatic spray* spell (see the AD&D® *Player's Handbook*).

Glass golems are the most fragile of any type of Ravenloft golem. Any blunt weapon capable of striking them (that is, a magical weapon of +2 or better) inflicts double damage. Further, a *shatter* spell directed at them weakens them so that all subsequent melee attacks have a percentage chance equal to twice the number of points of damage inflicted of instantly slaying the creature.

Anyone casting a *mending* spell on one of these creatures instantly restores it to full hit points. In addition, they regenerate 1 hit point per round when in an area of direct sunlight (or its equivalent).

Golem, Necrophidius and Scarecrow

	Necrophidius	Scarecrow
CLIMATE/TERRAIN:	Any	Any
FREQUENCY:	Very rare	Very rare
ORGANIZATION:	Solitary	Solitary
ACTIVITY CYCLE:	Any	Any
DIET:	Nil	Nil
INTELLIGENCE:	Non- (0)	Non- (0)
TREASURE:	Nil	Nil
ALIGNMENT:	Neutral	Neutral
NO. APPEARING:	1	1
ARMOR CLASS:	2	6
MOVEMENT:	9	6
HIT DICE:	2	5
THAC0:	19	15
NO. OF ATTACKS:	1	1+gaze
DAMAGE/ATTACK:	1-8	1-6+charm
SPECIAL ATTACKS:	See below	See below
SPECIAL DEFENSES:	See below	See below
MAGIC RESISTANCE:	Nil	Nil
SIZE:	L (12' long)	M (6' tall)
MORALE:	Fearless (19-20)	Fearless (19-20)
XP VALUE:	270	1,400

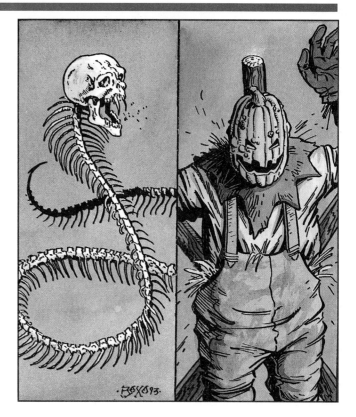

The necrophidius and scarecrow are constructs like all other golems, but they are less powerful because of the magical shortcuts employed in their construction.

Necrophidius
The necrophidius, or "death worm," is built and animated for a single task, such as protection or assassination. It has the bleached-white skeleton of a giant snake, a fanged human skull, and constantly whirling, milk-white eyes. Its bones are warm to the touch. The necrophidius is odorless and absolutely silent; the skeleton makes no noise, even when slithering across a floor strewn with leaves. A necrophidius is constantly moving with a macabre grace.

Combat: The necrophidius prefers to surprise opponents, and its silence imposes a −2 penalty to their surprise rolls. If the necrophidius is not surprised, it performs a macabre maneuver called the Dance of Death, a hypnotic swaying backed by minor magic. The Dance rivets the attention of anyone who observes it, unless a successful saving throw vs. spell is rolled. Intelligent victims are immobilized, as per the *hypnotism* spell. This allows the necrophidius to attack without opposition.

Besides taking damage as indicated, a bitten victim must make a saving throw vs. spell or be paralyzed and unconscious for 1d4 turns. This effect can be cancelled only by *dispel magic; neutralize poison* is useless.

This creature acts and reacts as if it had Intelligence 10. However, its mind is artificial, so mind influencing spells have no effect. The creature is immune to poison and requires no sleep or sustenance. It is not undead and cannot be turned.

Scarecrow
Statistics in italics above refer to conscious scarecrows.

Scarecrows are enchanted creatures made from the same materials as normal scarecrows. Though non-intelligent, they can follow simple, one- or two-phrase orders from the priest who created them. They do so to the best of their ability, without regard to their own safety.

Each scarecrow is unique, but all share several characteristics. Their bodies, arms, and legs are always made of cut wood bound with rope. Tattered rags cover the frame, and are sometimes stuffed with grass or straw. A hollow gourd with a carved face serves as head. Once animated, a fiery light burns in the scarecrow's eye sockets. Scarecrows are light but slow. Their leg and elbow joints bend both ways, so they move with an uneven, jerky gait, and the head spins freely.

Scarecrows do not speak, but cackle madly when attacking.

Combat: Once per round, a scarecrow can gaze at one creature within 40 feet. Any intelligent person meeting this gaze must make a successful saving throw vs. spells or be fascinated, standing transfixed, arms hanging limply, allowing the scarecrow to strike again and again (automatic hit each round). The charm lasts until the scarecrow either dies or leaves the area for a full turn. The scarecrow's touch causes 1d6 damage and has an effect identical to the gaze (saving throws apply). A scarecrow attacks one victim at a time, striking the first person charmed until dead. While slaying its victim, the scarecrow uses its gaze attack to charm other opponents as possible. Scarecrows attack until destroyed or ordered to stop.

Scarecrows are vulnerable to fire. Fire-based attacks gain a +1 bonus to the attack roll and a +1 damage bonus per die.

The magic that created them keeps their tattered parts from decomposing and shields them from the effects of cold.

Conscious Scarecrows
Most scarecrows disintegrate when their creators die, but a few (10%) become conscious, gaining an evil alignment, average Intelligence (8-10), and great cunning. They gain a desire for self-preservation, so their morale drops to elite (13-14). They hide by day and stalk the night, committing acts of evil. Because scarecrows hate fire and are immune to cold, conscious scarecrows try to reach colder climes. During the trek they kill everything they encounter, including those who pose no threat. Conscious scarecrows hate all life and kill humans and demihumans whenever possible.

Golem, Stone Variants

	Caryatid Column	Juggernaut	Stone Guardian
CLIMATE/TERRAIN:	Any	Any	Any
FREQUENCY:	Very rare	Very rare	Very rare
ORGANIZATION:	Solitary	Solitary	Solitary
ACTIVITY CYCLE:	Any	Any	Any
DIET:	Nil	Nil	Nil
INTELLIGENCE:	Non- (0)	Non- (0)	Non- (0)
TREASURE:	Nil	Nil	Nil
ALIGNMENT:	Neutral	Neutral	Neutral
NO. APPEARING:	1-12	1	1-4
ARMOR CLASS:	5	2	2
MOVEMENT:	6	3-12	9
HIT DICE:	5 (22 hit points)	10-13	4+4
THAC0:	15	10 HD: 11	15
		11-12 HD: 9	
		13 HD: 7	
NO. OF ATTACKS:	1	Up to 6	2
DAMAGE/ATTACK:	2-8	2-12	2-9/2-9
SPECIAL ATTACKS:	Nil	Crushing	Nil
SPECIAL DEFENSES:	See below	Immune to fire	See below
MAGIC RESISTANCE:	Nil	Nil	Nil
SIZE:	M (7' tall)	L to H (8' to 20')	M to L (6' to 8')
MORALE:	Fearless (20)	Elite to champion (13-16)	Fearless (20)
XP VALUE:	420	10 HD: 3,000	420
		+1,000 per additional Hit Die	

These variant golems are close relatives of the dreadful stone golems. They are generally created by powerful wizards and employed as guards or servants in a wide variety of settings.

Caryatid Column

The caryatid column is a beautiful and wondrous construct. Before activation, it looks like the classical architectural work it is named for, standing about 7 feet tall, and resembling a finely carved pillar in the shape of a beautiful young girl. Close examination reveals that the maiden has a slender sword in her left hand, but there is no indication that the column is anything other than what it appears to be. Once constructed and animated, it is usually assigned to keep watch over a valuable object or special places. It does so, remaining motionless, until its preset activation conditions are triggered (these depend on the creator's instructions). As soon as this happens, the column moves to take action against those who have triggered it.

When activated, the caryatid column undergoes a stunning and swift transformation. The smooth, grey stone that was once its skin changes hue to become light or dark flesh tones (depending on the nature of the carving), the eyes come alive with a gleaming white light, and the thin blade transforms into a fine weapon of gleaming steel.

In combat, the column lashes out with its gleaming sword, causing 2d4 points of damage with each hit. The column's magical nature gives it a +4 bonus to saving throws, and all nonmagical weapons inflict only half damage. Magical weapons inflict full damage, but do not receive the magical bonus normally due them. For example, a *long sword +2* does not gain its +2 bonus, but inflicts normal long sword damage.

There is a 25% chance that a weapon shatters when it successfully strikes a caryatid column. This chance is reduced by 5% for each plus of the weapon. Thus, a *sword +2* has only a 15% chance of breaking. A magical weapon with no attack bonus is considered a +1 weapon when checking for shattering.

A *stone to flesh, transmute rock to mud,* or *stone shape* spell destroys the column instantly if it fails its saving throw.

When a caryatid column has completed its task, it returns to its waiting position and reverts to stone. If it is killed in combat, it (and its sword) reverts to stone for 2d6 rounds, at the end of which time it crumbles into dust.

Juggernaut

The juggernaut generally appears as a huge, powerful stone vehicle of some sort, with wheels or rollers for locomotion.

A juggernaut is clumsy and slow moving, but it makes up for these handicaps by rolling right over opponents in a deadly crushing attack. A juggernaut has a movement rate of 3 in its first round of animation. This increases by 3 each round to a maximum of 12. A juggernaut is slow to turn, and can change direction only 90 degrees for every 30 feet of movement.

Anyone caught in the path of a juggernaut charge is run over by the thundering behemoth, though the juggernaut must make a normal attack roll if the victim can avoid the charge. A hit indicates that the victim is crushed, suffering 10d10 points of damage. In addition, every item carried by the victim must roll a saving throw vs. crushing blow to avoid destruction. A successful saving throw vs. death magic entitles the victim to only half damage, but it does not protect his equipment.

Some juggernauts are a unique crossbreed of stone golem and mimic. Once animated, these juggernauts can alter their shape as the mimics do. They can grow up to six limbs, each designed for current needs. For example, if it wishes to sound a warning, a limb may grow into a trumpet or horn. In combat, its limbs become maces or hammers that inflict 2d6 points of damage each, due to its great strength. A juggernaut can rarely bring more than two limbs to bear on a single opponent.

Stone Guardian

In combat, a guardian slams opponents with its massive arms, each of which inflicts 1d8+1 points of damage. The stone guardian suffers only 1/4 damage from edged weapons and 1/2 damage from all cold, fire, or electrical attacks. Normal missiles cause no damage. A stone guardian can be instantly destroyed by a *stone to flesh, transmute rock to mud, stone shape,* or *dig* spell; it is not entitled to a saving throw.

Gorgon

CLIMATE/TERRAIN:	Temperate or tropical/ Wilderness or subterranean
FREQUENCY:	Rare
ORGANIZATION:	Group
ACTIVITY CYCLE:	Day
DIET:	Carnivore
INTELLIGENCE:	Animal (1)
TREASURE:	(E)
ALIGNMENT:	Neutral

NO. APPEARING:	1-4
ARMOR CLASS:	2
MOVEMENT:	12
HIT DICE:	8
THAC0:	13
NO. OF ATTACKS:	1
DAMAGE/ATTACK:	2-12
SPECIAL ATTACKS:	See below
SPECIAL DEFENSES:	Nil
MAGIC RESISTANCE:	Nil
SIZE:	L (8' tall)
MORALE:	Average (8-10)
XP VALUE:	1,400

Gorgons are fierce, bull-like beasts who make their lairs in dreary caverns or the fastness of a wilderness. They are aggressive by nature and usually attack any creature or person they encounter.

Monstrous black bulls, gorgons have hides of thick metal scales. Their breath is a noxious vapor that billows forth in great puffs from their wide, bull nostrils. Gorgons walk on two hooves, when necessary, but usually assume a four-hoofed stance. Despite their great size, they can move through even heavy forests with incredible speed, for they simply trample bushes and splinter smaller trees. Gorgons speak no languages but let out a roar of anger whenever they encounter other beings.

Combat: Four times per day gorgons can make a breath weapon attack (their preferred means of attack). Their breath shoots forth in a truncated cone, five feet wide at the base and 20 feet wide at its end, with a maximum range of 60 feet. Any creature caught in this cone must roll a saving throw vs. petrification. Those who fail are turned to stone immediately! The awareness of gorgons extends into the Astral and Ethereal planes, as do the effects of their breath weapon.

If necessary (i.e., their breath weapon fails) gorgons will engage in melee, charging forward to deliver a vicious head butt or horn gore. Gorgons fight with unrestricted ferocity, slashing and trampling all who challenge them until they themselves are slain.

Habitat/Society: It is believed that gorgons can actually devour the living statues they create with their breath weapon. Whether their flat iron teeth break up and pulverize the stone or their saliva returns the victim to flesh while they eat is a matter for conjecture.

Their primary prey are deer and elk, but gorgons won't hesitate to add other meats to their diet when hungry. Their sense of smell is acute and once they get on the trail gorgons are 75% likely to track their victim successfully. Once their victim is in sight, gorgons let out a scream of rage and then charge. Unless somehow evaded, a gorgon will pursue tirelessly, for days if necessary, until the prey either drops from exhaustion or is caught in the gorgon's deadly breath.

Gorgons have no use for treasure, hence gold and gems are often left petrified on the statue of the being that once wore them. Occasionally a gorgon in his haste will devour something of value; the items will later be left in the gorgon's droppings, somewhere near the entrance to its lair.

Gorgons are usually encountered in groups of three or four—one male bull with two or three females. Gorgon calves are raised by the females to the age of two, then the young bulls are turned out to make their own way. Females remain with the dominant bull.

About 25% of the time only a single gorgon is encountered. Lone gorgons are always rogue males in search of females.

The forest around a gorgon lair is usually a crisscrossing network of trails and paths they've made. Occasionally there are clearings where the grasses were trampled down in a battle and perhaps the shattered remains of a statue can be found.

Ecology: Gorgons have no natural enemies other than themselves. Bull gorgons are often called upon to defend their positions against rogue gorgons. These battles are not usually fatal, but even a gorgon can be felled by a well-aimed horn gore. The only other creature known to hunt these fierce predators is man.

Gorgon blood, properly prepared, can seal an area against ethereal or astral intrusion; their powdered scales are an ingredient in the ink used to create a *protection from petrification* scroll.

In addition, the hide of a gorgon can be fashioned, with considerable work and some magical enhancement, into a fine set of scale mail. This armor will provide the wearer with a +2 bonus to all saving throws vs. petrification or flesh-to-stone spells.

Grell

	Worker	Philosopher	Patriarch
CLIMATE/TERRAIN:	Any	Any	Any
FREQUENCY:	Rare	Very rare	Very rare
ORGANIZATION:	Hive	Hive	Hive
ACTIVITY CYCLE:	Any	Any	Any
DIET:	Carnivore	Carnivore	Carnivore
INTELLIGENCE:	Average (8-10)	Exceptional (15-16)	Supra-genius (19)
TREASURE:	U	W	H
ALIGNMENT:	Neutral evil	Neutral evil	Neutral evil
NO. APPEARING:	1-10	1-2	1
ARMOR CLASS:	5	5 (0)	10
MOVEMENT:	Fl 12 (D)	Fl 12 (D)	0
HIT DICE:	5	7	9
THAC0:	15	13	11
NO. OF ATTACKS:	11	11	0
DAMAGE/ATTACK:	1-4(×10)/1-6 or by weapon	1d4(×10)/1-6 or by weapon	0
SPECIAL ATTACKS:	Magical items	Magical items	See below
SPECIAL DEFENSES:	Nil	Nil	See below
MAGIC RESISTANCE:	Nil	Nil	Nil
SIZE:	M (4' diameter)	M (4' diameter)	G (30' diameter)
MORALE:	Elite (13-14)	Champion (15-16)	Fanatic (17)
XP VALUE:	2,000	5,000	9,000

The grell is a fearsome carnivore that looks like a giant brain with a vicious beak and 10 dangling tentacles, each 6 feet long. Some grell are rogues, while others live in family units. The "civilized" grell is a hive or colony creature, much like an ant or a bee, but far more intelligent, arrogant, and dangerous.

Grell have a weird language composed of bird-like squawks and chirps, combined with tentacular motion and a limited telepathy with other grell. Other creatures cannot learn the grell language, and they would not deign to learn the language of "lesser beings" (a synonym for "food" in their language).

Combat: The grell's most common strategy is to use its natural levitation ability to hide in the upper reaches of large chambers. It can then drop silently on a victim, who suffers a −3 penalty to surprise rolls when attacked in this way.

A worker grell attacks with all 10 tentacles; each one that hits grips the opponent (the grip can be broken with a successful bend bars/lift gates roll). For each hit, the victim must roll a saving throw vs. paralysis, with a +4 bonus, or be paralyzed for 5d4 rounds. With two tentacles gripping the prey, the grell can lift it up toward the ceiling and devour the prey when desired. A grell automatically hits paralyzed prey each round.

Soldier grell often use weapons, including the tip-spear and the *lightning lance.* The tip-spear is an edged metal head which fits on the tip of a tentacle and is held there by suction; the weapon causes 1d6 damage if used to slash, 2d6 if used to impale. Victims hit by a tip-spear must make a saving throw vs. paralysis, as if hit by a tentacle. The *lightning lance* delivers 3d6 points of electrical damage to those hit with it, though a successful saving throw vs. spells halves the damage. A lightning lance starts with 36 charges; it can use one per round.

Any hit against a tentacle (AC 4) renders it unusable, but subtracts no hit points from the grell's total. Grell regenerate lost or damaged tentacles in 1-2 days, and are immune to electrical attacks.

Grell use strategy and tactics in their battles, and can attack more than one opponent each round. They are intelligent enough to allocate their tentacle attacks in an advantageous way. They use their beaks only against paralyzed prey.

Habitat/Society: Grell have a distinct hierarchy. Each hive is led by a patriarch, who gives orders to the philosophers, who direct the soldiers and workers in their every day tasks. A hive occupies an underground complex, or travels by ship.

Supposedly, all grell answer to a mysterious Imperator, a grell of great power who can unite all the grell for a common cause; to conquer a realm, a territory, or even a world.

A grell mates but once in its 30-40 year life span. The female later lays a clutch of 2d4 eggs. Young are born active and self-sufficient, but with only 1 Hit Die. They gain 1 Hit Die every two months until they reach adulthood.

Ecology: Arrogant and vicious, grell hunt their territories to exhaustion, then move on to more fertile places.

A grell's paralytic poison cannot be extracted from the creature's body, but parts of the monster's body can be used for spells or items relating to levitation or electricity.

Soldier/Worker: These are the common grell that form the bulk of a hive or a raiding party. Occasionally, a grell will become separated from its fellows; these become rogues. Rogues carry no weapons, collect no treasure, and avoid sunlight.

Philosopher: These grell serve as intermediaries between patriarchs and workers/soldiers. Some lead lesser grell in combat, and there is one philosopher for every 10 lesser grell encountered. Some philosophers (20%) wear powerful *rings of protection,* giving them AC 0. About 10% of philosophers can cast spells as 2nd-level wizards.

Patriarch: Each hive has a patriarch, a huge, sedentary mass of flesh that directs the lesser grell. If the patriarch is taken to a ship, it can dig its many tentacles into the ship and animate it, even make it fly to other worlds.

Gremlin

	Gremlin	Fremlin	Galltrit	Mite	Snyad
CLIMATE/TERRAIN:	Any land	Any land	Any land	Subterranean	Subterranean
FREQUENCY:	Very rare	Very rare	Very rare	Rare	Uncommon
ORGANIZATION:	Pack	Pack	Pack	Tribe	Family
ACTIVITY CYCLE:	Night	Day	Night	Any	Any
DIET:	Omnivore	Herbivore	Blood	Omnivore	Omnivore
INTELLIGENCE:	Very (11-12)	Average (8-10)	Average (8-10)	Low (5-7)	Low (5-7)
TREASURE:	Q, X	X	Q	K (C)	J (I)
ALIGNMENT:	Chaotic evil	Chaotic neutral	Chaotic evil	Lawful evil	Neutral
NO. APPEARING:	1-6	1-4	1-4	6-24	1-8
ARMOR CLASS:	4	6	2	8	−4
MOVEMENT:	6, Fl 18 (B)	6, Fl 12 (B)	6, Fl 18 (B)	3	21
HIT DICE:	4	3 + 6	2 hp	1-1	1-1
THAC0:	17	17	20	20	20
NO. OF ATTACKS:	1	1	1	1	Nil
DAMAGE/ATTACK:	1-4	1-4	1-2	1-3	Nil
SPECIAL ATTACKS:	Nil	Nil	Blood drain	Nil	Nil
SPECIAL DEFENSES:	+1 weapon needed to hit	+1 weapon needed to hit	Nil	Nil	See below
MAGIC RESISTANCE:	25%	Nil	Nil	Nil	See below
SIZE:	T (18″)	T (1′)	T (6″)	T (2′)	T (2′)
MORALE:	Unsteady (5-7)	Unsteady (5-7)	Average (8-10)	Average (8-10)	Average (8-10)
XP VALUE:	650	270	65	35	65

Often mistaken for imps, gremlins are small, winged goblinoids. There are many varieties of gremlins, and most are chaotic and mischievous. Their skin color ranges from brown to black to gray, frequently in a mottled blend. Their ears are very large and pointed, giving them a 65% chance to *hear noise*. A pair of bat-like wings enables them to fly or glide. Gremlins never wear clothing or ornamentation.

Combat: Gremlins are worthless in real combat; at every opportunity they flee rather than fight face-to-face. What gremlins like to do best is cause trouble. The angrier their victims are, the happier the gremlins. Their favorite tactic is to set up a trap to humiliate opponents and maybe even cause them to damage a valued possession or hurt a loved one. If the opponent gets hurt as well, that's just fine. For example, the gremlin may set a trip wire across a doorway that pulls down a fragile vase onto the victim's head. A building infested by a gremlin pack can be reduced to shambles in a single night.

In melee, gremlins have only their weak bite for attacks (1d4 points of damage). They can fly quite well (MC B), but they usually stay close to the ground or well over their opponents' heads, where they are difficult to reach. They can be hit only by magical weapons, and are 25% resistant to magic. Despite these defenses, they are cowards and fight only if cornered.

Habitat/Society: Gremlins are magical creatures that originated in an unknown plane of existence. They are highly susceptible to mutation and can interbreed with any goblinoid species. This has resulted in several different gremlin races, each with slightly different abilities and natures.

Gremlins travel in small packs, and they have a highly organized social order. Each gremlin knows who is above him in social rank, and who is below. As a rule, this is ordered by hit points, but an aggressive gremlin with lower hit points may be above larger gremlins in the social standing. Males and females are indistinguishable to all but other gremlins. Both sexes participate equally in all things. Offspring are left to fend for themselves from birth, which they are fully capable of doing. Within a month, the gremlin is a fully matured adult. Fortunately, they do not mate often.

These obnoxious creatures usually look for a building or estate to infest. Although they flee individual combat, they will not leave the building or grounds they infest until it is no longer fun (when everything is broken and the inhabitants have fled), or until their lives are in danger. Since the gremlins take great pains to not be seen, except as fleeting shadows, the inhabitants are frequently convinced that the place is haunted.

Ecology: Gremlins are not a natural part of the ecology. Their immunity to normal weapons protects them from normal predators. Unmolested, they live for centuries.

Fremlin
These friendly gremlins are quite harmless. They tend to be plump, whiny, and lazy, but otherwise look like small, slate colored gremlins. Occasionally, they become tolerable companions, if they take a liking to someone and are well fed and entertained. Even in this case, they never assist in combat and may in fact hinder it by giving away the location of hiding characters or making other such blunders.

Galltrit
These nasty little stone-gray creatures live in areas of dung, carrion, or offal. Because of their small size and coloration, they are detected only on a 1 in 8 chance (1 in 6 for elves). They attack anything that disturbs them. Galltrit attempt to gain surprise and bite (with a +3 bonus to the attack roll if they have surprise) somewhere unobtrusive. An anesthetic in their saliva prevents their victims from feeling the bite, rather like a vampire bat.

Once locked on, galltrits suck 1 hit point of blood per round for a full turn, if undisturbed. If challenged in any way, the galltrits flee. This loss of blood reduces the victim's Constitution by 1 point for every 4 hit points of blood lost. If the victim loses 3 or more points of Constitution, usually due to multiple galltrits, he faints from the sudden blood loss. It takes two full turns to awaken and two weeks to regain the lost Constitution points.

Mite
Mites are tiny, mischievous, wingless gremlins that waylay dungeon adventurers for fun and profit. Mites have hairless, warty skin varying in color from light gray to bright violet. Their heads are triangular, with bat-like ears and a long, hooked nose.

Male mites sport a bone ridge down the center of their skulls and short goatee beards. Many wear filthy rags stolen from previous victims. Their voices are high-pitched and twittery, conveying only the simplest ideas to each other; nongremlin races cannot make sense of their language.

Mites try to catch lone travelers and stragglers using pit traps (1d6 points of damage to the victim), nets (successful saving throw vs. paralysis or the victim is caught), and trip wires (successful Dexterity check or the victim falls prone). Mites swarm over prone or netted victims, and pummel them with weighted clubs (2% cumulative chance, per club, of stunning the victim, but only if the victim is in armor worse than splint mail). The mites bind their unconscious victims head and foot, and drag them into their lair. Once inside the lair, the victims are teased and chattered at for one to four days until the mites get bored. The mites then stun their victim again, steal all their possessions and deposit them at a random place—often one that causes the victims great discomfort or embarrassment.

Mite lairs consist of dozens of interconnecting corridors built above and below main dungeon corridors. Numerous entrances connect the mite tunnels to the dungeon, but all are hidden by carefully placed stones (check for secret doors to find a mite tunnel entrance). Mite corridors are tiny by human and demi-human standards; man-sized and larger creatures suffer a −4 attack roll penalty and a +4 Armor Class penalty when fighting in a mite tunnel.

Mites are small and quick. They scurry to and fro through their tunnels, stopping briefly to spy on the main tunnel, always chattering and twittering to themselves.

Deep inside the mite tunnel system is a single, large chamber with a low-ceiling. The mite king lives here, sitting on his tiny throne, dressed in baggy clothes stolen from previous victims. The mite king is a fierce (by mite standards) warrior with 1+1 Hit Dice. His bite causes 1d4 points of damage. Also in the chamber are 4d6 mite females and 4d6 mite children. The women have 1-2 Hit Dice and bite for 1-2 points of damage. The children are non-combatants.

The chamber itself is filthy and strewn with captured weapons, armor, and clothes. Coins and such are carelessly thrown about, but mites love bright, shiny gems. These are kept by the king, who is allowed to play with them anytime he wants. Mites are mischievous and curious. They pore for hours over every little stolen item, poking and prodding, bending and tasting, until either they grow bored, or, more likely, the item breaks. They delight in wearing clothes several dozen sizes too large. Mites are fond of bones, and they sometimes drag the skulls of great monsters into their lair.

Mites hunt vermin and other pests, but they love to eat iron rations which they consider a delicacy. Mites are viewed as bite-sized snacks by most monsters. Evil giants sometimes feature them as appetizers.

Snyad

Snyads are distant relatives of mites. Their love of treasure often compels them to steal from humans and demihumans. Snyads resemble mites, but they are slightly larger (2¹/₂ feet tall), have full, though messy, heads of hair, and are light brown in color.

Snyads speak no known language but seem to communicate with mites successfully. These two creatures sometimes team up, with the mites distracting the victim, while the snyads dart in and grab things.

Snyads steal with great skill, surprising their targets 90% of the time, often snatching items directly from a person's hand (the victim gets a successful Wisdom check to hold onto the item), then zipping back into their holes and hiding until the pursuers leave. Spotting the entrance to a snyad lair requires a successful search roll: a 1-in-3 chance for elves and a 1-in-4 chance for all others.

Snyads never attack, relying on their amazingly quick reflexes to escape combat. They are not particularly strong, and any human or demi-human character with a Strength greater than 11 can capture a snyad with a successful attack roll. Captured snyads kick and scream, squirming and twisting to get away, but never bite, (for fear that the captor might bite back). Because of their high Dexterity, snyads gain a +3 bonus to their saving throws vs. non-area-effect spells. Snyads live in immediate families, marrying for life.

Gremlin, Jermlaine

CLIMATE/TERRAIN:	Subterranean
FREQUENCY:	Uncommon
ORGANIZATION:	Clan
ACTIVITY CYCLE:	Any
DIET:	Omnivore
INTELLIGENCE:	Average (Genius cunning) (8-10)
TREASURE:	Per 10 individuals O, Q; in lair C, Q (x5), S, T
ALIGNMENT:	Neutral evil (slight lawful tendencies)

NO. APPEARING:	12-48
ARMOR CLASS:	7
MOVEMENT:	15
HIT DICE:	1-4 hp
THAC0:	20
NO. OF ATTACKS:	1
DAMAGE/ATTACK:	1-2 or 1-4
SPECIAL ATTACKS:	See below
SPECIAL DEFENSES:	See below
MAGIC RESISTANCE:	See below
SIZE:	T(1′ +)
MORALE:	Steady (12)
XP VALUE:	Normal: 15
	Elder: 65

Jermlaine are a diminutive humanoid race that dwells in tunnels and ambushes hapless adventurers. They are known by a variety of names such as jinxkin or bane-midges.

Jermlaine appear to be tiny humans dressed in baggy clothing and leather helmets. In fact the "clothing" is their own saggy skin and pointed heads. The limbs are knottily muscled. The fingernails and toenails are thick and filthy, although the fingers and toes are very nimble. Their gray-brown, warty hide blends in with natural earth and stone. When they wear rags or scraps as clothing, such items are also camouflage colored.

They speak in high-pitched squeaks and twitters. This speech may be mistaken for the sounds of a bat or rat. They can also converse with all sorts of rats, both normal and monstrous. Each jermlaine has a 10% chance to understand common, dwarvish, gnomish, goblin, or orc (roll separately for each language).

Combat: Jermlaine are cowards who have made an art of the ambush. They only attack when they feel there is no serious opposition. They prefer to attack injured, ill, or sleeping victims. They avoid directly confronting strong, alert parties, although they may try to injure them out of sheer maliciousness. Jermlaine possess weak eyes and infravision that only extends for 30 yards, but their keen smell and hearing enable them to detect even invisible creatures 50% of the time. Jermlaine move silently and quickly, with a scuttling gait (this stealth causes opponents to suffer a -5 penalty to their surprise rolls). They are 75% undetectable, even if listened or watched for, unless the jermlaine purposefully reveal their presence.

Jermlaine typically arm themselves with needle-sharp darts; they can hurl these 120 yards for 1-2 points of damage. They also carry a miniature pike; these 1¹/₂-foot-long sticks with sharp tips inflict 1d4 points of damage. If the jermlaines are out to capture a victim, they are also armed with blackjacks.

The jermlaines' favorite tactic is capturing victims with nets or pits. In little-used passages the creatures prepare pits covered by camouflaged doors or string nets overhead. In more-traveled passages, the jermlaine stretch trip cords. When a victim falls afoul of a trap, the jermlaine swarm over him. Some pummel him with blackjacks while others tie him with ropes and cords.

Such beatings have a cumulative 2% chance per blow of causing the victim to lapse into unconsciousness. If a victim is wearing splint, banded, or plate mail, these pummeling attacks are ineffective. Knowing this, the jermlaine attack well-armored victims with acid or flaming oil missiles.

Slain victims and 5% of subdued victims are later devoured by the jermlaine and their rats. Most captives are robbed, stripped, shaved totally hairless, and left trussed in a passageway. If an unsuspecting victim pauses near a lurking band of jermlaine, they dart out and cut straps, belts, packs, and pouches. Each jermlaine in the band makes one such attack before fleeing back into the shadows. Such attacks are usually not noticed till 1d12 turns later, when the slashed items begin to fall apart. They also try to steal, damage, or befoul victims' possessions.

When encountered, 25% of jermlaine are accompanied by 1d6 rats and 50% are accompanied by 1d6 giant rats (only one type of rat per group of jermlaine). Groups of 35 or more jermlaine are accompanied by an elder—a very old jermlaine with the magical ability to drain the magic from most magical items if he can handle such an object for 1d4 rounds. Artifacts and relics are immune to such attacks.

Jermlaine are treated as 4-Hit Die monsters for purposes of saving throws and magical attacks. Due to their diminutive size, they escape all damage from attacks that normally do half damage if the saving throw is successful.

Habitat/Society: Jermlaine are extremely distant relatives of the gnomes. Their deeply rooted sense of inferiority at their own diminutive size has become a malicious need to humiliate normal-sized humanoids. They make a good living preying on hapless adventurers, who provide riches, sadistic amusement, and an occasional meal. Jermlaine acquire a wide variety of treasure, although such items tend to be small objects.

The jermlaine life span is one third that of humans. Reproduction is identical to other humanoids, although cross breeding is impossible. Jermlaine females give birth to one or two babies at a time. Most (75%) of the offspring are male, although the dangers of their hostile life reduces the male numerical superiority to an even male-female mix among the adults.

Jermlaine society is divided among clans whose members are united by blood. Each clan consists of 4d4 families. The clan chief is normally the strongest or most clever of the elders. The chief both instructs the young jermlaine in the art of the ambush and leads important attacks (albeit from a secure location in the rear). The families center around the mothers, as the fathers may be unknown, off hunting, or dead. If a female jermlaine has dependent children, she normally concentrates on raising such children rather than participating in attacks. As the children mature, she and the clan chief take the young on practice attacks on potential victims and participate in the humiliation of captives.

Jermlaine lairs are cunningly hidden and physically impassable by most humanoids, as they are usually a series of small chambers and tunnels scaled to their tiny occupants. The typical jermlaine lair is a filthy cave or burrow a short distance from a larger cavern complex. The only areas that can be easily reached by a human-sized being are the areas in which living captives are held and dead victims butchered for food. Access past this area is controlled by small, one-foot-high corridors or thin, normally impassable cracks in the rock walls. The corridors lead directly to living areas and communal chambers. The living areas are furnished with crude furniture and items scavenged from past victims.

Each jermlaine family has a personal section that half resembles a nest, half a junk yard. Treasures are concealed throughout the lair. Each family maintains a series of small, personal caches, while the communal hoard is hidden in a series of small chambers at the end of cunningly concealed crawl ways. No one larger than a jermlaine can reach such treasure chambers.

Jermlaine get along well with rats of all types. They can speak all rat-related languages. They are 75% likely to be accompanied by rats and 50% likely to share their lair with rats. This cohabitation extends to all forms of mutual cooperation and defense. There is a 10% chance that the jermlaine colony has a mutual cooperation pact with osquips rather than normal rats.

The diet is an omnivorous mixture of insects, fresh meat, carrion, fungi, and molds. Humanoids are a delicacy reserved for special occasions. Lizards form the bulk of the meat intake. Jermlaine cherish foods from the surface, even the hardtack and iron rations carried by adventurers. If the jermlaine can identify which of the adventurers' bags carry food, these are stolen as enthusiastically as the treasure pouches. Jermlaine have a fondness for rarities such as sugar, candy, and preserved fruits. Such items can be used to entice the normally malevolent jermlaine to leave an adventurer alone, at least temporarily.

Ecology: Jermlaine are opportunistic brigands who prey on unwary travelers in the subterranean regions. They are well aware of any such travelers, including a party's size, composition, and general condition. Jermlaine may be persuaded, for a suitable fee, to share such knowledge with adventurers.

Jermlaine may deal with "giants" (any race bigger than they are) if they are bribed or given access to a plentiful flow of victims or riches. They never ally themselves with truly good-aligned adventurers, although they may, in a moment of craftiness, pretend to enter such an alliance. Regardless of their spoken intentions, 75% of jermlaine eventually either lie to or turn against their larger "allies." They may make their lairs near the established territories of such races as drow, trolls, or troglodytes. Although they are careful to avoid direct conflict with such evil beings, the jermlaine happily prey on the victims of their neighbors, as well as scavenging the scenes of their neighbors' battles. Jermlaine may act as watchmen for their neighbors, provided suitable terms can be agreed upon.

They unintentionally act as garbagemen, cleaning the subterranean regions. Dead animals may be used as food or supplies, while dead humanoids are taken away to be searched for valuables or used as food. Because of this, adventurers seeking the remains of a slain companion may seek out the local jermlaines since they may be aware of where the remains are located.

Griffon

CLIMATE/TERRAIN:	Temperate or subtropical/ Hills or mountains
FREQUENCY:	Uncommon
ORGANIZATION:	Pride
ACTIVITY CYCLE:	Day
DIET:	Carnivore
INTELLIGENCE:	Semi- (2-4)
TREASURE:	(C, S)
ALIGNMENT:	Neutral

NO. APPEARING:	2-12
ARMOR CLASS:	3
MOVEMENT:	12, Fl 30 (C, D if mounted)
HIT DICE:	7
THAC0:	13
NO. OF ATTACKS:	3
DAMAGE/ATTACK:	1-4/1-4/2-16
SPECIAL ATTACKS:	Nil
SPECIAL DEFENSES:	Nil
MAGIC RESISTANCE:	Nil
SIZE:	L (about 9' long)
MORALE:	Steady (11-12)
XP VALUE:	650

Half-lion, half-eagle, griffons are ferocious avian carnivores that prey upon horses and their kin (hippogriffs, pegasi, and unicorns). This hunger for horseflesh often brings griffons into direct conflict with humans and demihumans.

Adult griffons stand five feet at the shoulder and weigh over half a ton. Their head, upper torso, and forelegs are like those of a giant eagle. This eagle half is covered in golden feathers from its wing tips to its razor-sharp beak. Their powerful forelimbs end in long, hooked talons. Wings, with a span of 25 feet or more, rise out of their backs. The lower half of a griffon is that of a lion. Dusky yellow fur covers the lion half's muscular rear legs and clawed feet. A lion's tail hangs down from the griffon's powerful rear haunches. Griffons speak no languages, but emit an eagle-like screech when angered or excited (usually by the smell of horse).

Combat: Griffons hunt in groups of 12 or less, searching the plains and forests near (within 20 miles) their lair for horses and herd animals. With their superior vision and sense of smell, griffons can spot prey up to two miles distant. If the prey is horse or horse-kin, griffons are 90% likely to attack even if the horses have riders. Griffons hunt only for food, so a rider who releases one or two horses can usually escape unharmed (though in all likelihood his horse won't). Any attempt to protect a horse brings the full fury of the attacking griffons on the protector.

When attacking ground targets, griffons use their great size and weight to swoop down from above and raking their opponent with the talons before landing nearby. Griffons always fight to the death if there is horseflesh at stake.

In aerial combat, griffons are equally fierce, lunging into battle and tearing at their opponent until they or their prey are dead. Many a griffon has plummeted to its death with a struggling hippogriff caught firmly in its grasp.

Habitat/Society: Griffons prefer rocky habitats, near open plains. Once griffons establish their territory, they remain until the food supply has been exhausted.

Griffons, like lions, live in prides, with each pride comprising several mated pairs, their young, and one dominant male. The dominant male is responsible for settling territorial disputes with other prides and choosing the direction the hunt will take.

Each pair of mated griffons in the pride has its own nest, located near the pride's other lairs. Griffon nests are usually situated in shallow caves, high along a cliff face.

The nests are made of sticks and leaves, as well as an occasional bone. Griffons collect no treasure, but their caves frequently contain the remains of unfortunate travelers who tried to protect their horses from the griffons.

During spring, female griffons lay one or two eggs that hatch in the late summer. For the first three months griffon young are known as hatchlings; thereafter, until they mature the young are called fledglings. Griffon young grow rapidly for three years until they are large enough to hunt with the pride. Adult griffons are extremely protective of their young and attack without mercy any creature that approaches within 100 feet of the nest.

Ecology: If trained from a very early age (three years or less), griffons will serve as mounts. The training, however, is both time-consuming and expensive, requiring the expertise of an animal trainer for two years. Once trained, though, griffons make fierce and loyal steeds, bonding with one master for life, and protecting him even unto death. A griffon mount knows no fear in battle, but attacks any horse or horse-kin in preference to other opponents.

Acquiring a griffon fledgling is a very dangerous venture as the adults never stray far from the nest and fight to the death to defend eggs or young. Any given griffon nest is 75% likely to contain one or two fledglings or eggs. Fledgling griffons sell for 5,000 gold pieces on the open market; eggs sell for 2,000 gold pieces each.

Grimlock

CLIMATE/TERRAIN:	Any/Mountainous
FREQUENCY:	Uncommon
ORGANIZATION:	Tribal
ACTIVITY CYCLE:	Night
DIET:	Carnivorous (Human Flesh)
INTELLIGENCE:	Average (8-10)
TREASURE:	Individual K, L, M; B in Lair
ALIGNMENT:	Neutral Evil

NO. APPEARING:	20-200
ARMOR CLASS:	5
MOVEMENT:	12
HIT DICE:	2 (and see below)
THAC0:	19
NO. OF ATTACKS:	1
DAMAGE/ATTACKS:	1-6, or by weapon type
SPECIAL ATTACKS:	Nil
SPECIAL DEFENSES:	See below
MAGIC RESISTANCE:	Special
SIZE:	M (5½'-6')
MORALE:	Steady (11) (and see below)
XP VALUE:	Normal: 35
	Leader: 120
	Champion: 175

Powerfully-built humanoids clad only in dark, filthy rags, these warlike subterranean creatures emerge from their deep caverns at night to search for unlucky humans to add to their larders.

Grimlocks have thick, scaly, grey skin and long, black, filthy hair. Their teeth are white and extremely sharp. Their eyes are blank white orbs.

Grimlocks are totally blind, but have highly developed senses of smell and hearing. Their sensitive ears and noses combine to allow them to distinguish objects and creatures within 20', just as well as if they were able to see.

Combat: Grimlocks are immune to the effects of spells which affect the vision. These include *phantasmal force, darkness, invisibility, mirror image,* and many others. However, spells such as *audible glamer,* or any loud, continuous noise will partially "blind" them. This reduces their ability to perceive opponents to a 10' range and makes them −2 on their attack rolls. Substances such as snuff or strong perfumes will have much the same effect if inhaled by a grimlock or thrown in its face.

Grimlocks attack fiercely, but with little or no organization, often stopping in the middle of battle to carry off fallen foes or comrades for food. For every 10 grimlocks encountered, there will be a leader of 3 Hit Dice and AC 4, for every 40 there will be a champion of 4 Hit Dice and AC 3. These exceptional individuals will usually be the only ones to show even the most elemental strategy, usually by allowing their followers to weaken opponents before entering battle themselves.

Grimlocks will nearly always attack in darkness if possible. While not adversely affected by light, they are intelligent enough to realize that in total darkness, their unique form of perception gives them a distinct advantage.

Though able to attack with their hands (for 1-6 hp damage), grimlocks prefer edged weapons and will usually (90% chance) be armed as follows: hand-axe, 20%; battle-axe, 15%; two-handed sword, 15%; bastard sword, 15%; broad sword, 15%; long sword, 20%.

Leaders or champions will always be armed with a battle-axe or two-handed sword.

Grimlocks, whether normal, leader, or champion, make all saving throws as 6th-level fighters. Grimlocks gain a +1 on sur-prise rolls, since their acute hearing allows them to communicate in voices too faint for other races to hear. In addition, their morale is raised by 1 for every leader or champion with the group.

Habitat/Society: Grimlocks lair in vast cavern complexes in mountainous areas. They are well adapted to these environs. In any rocky terrain they blend in so well that, while motionless, they are completely undetectable—unless one actually bumps into them. In any grimlock lair, there will be nearly as many females (1 Hit Die and AC 6) as males, and at least as many young (1 hit point, AC 6 and non-combatant). Grimlock leaders and champions do wield some control over these communities. However, this control is usually effective only as long as the leader who gave the order is around to enforce his will. It is nearly impossible for those of other races to tell one grimlock from another—although leader types may appear slightly larger—but they easily tell each other apart by subtle differences in scent and movement.

Extremely xenophobic, grimlocks rarely consort with other races. However, there is a small (10%) chance that they will allow medusae to share their lairs, and a 2% chance that any wandering group will be accompanied by 1-2 mind flayers.

Ecology: Grimlocks will only eat the raw flesh of humanoid creatures, vastly preferring that of humans to all others. Foraging parties often raid the homes of other subterranean races, especially those who keep large slave populations (such as drow). They are often on good terms with mind flayers since illithids have a large supply of humanoid bodies discarded after they have devoured the brains. Grimlocks are particularly hated by githyanki for this reason. Since the slave flesh the grimlocks often consume (raw) is frequently unwholesome, whole communities are often decimated by disease.

Grippli

CLIMATE/TERRAIN:	Tropical/Swamps and jungles
FREQUENCY:	Rare
ORGANIZATION:	Tribal
ACTIVITY CYCLE:	Day
DIET:	Omnivore
INTELLIGENCE:	Very to high (11-14)
TREASURE:	Qx4, I
ALIGNMENT:	Neutral

NO. APPEARING:	1-10
ARMOR CLASS:	9
MOVEMENT:	9, leap 15
HIT DICE:	1+1
THAC0:	19
NO. OF ATTACKS:	1
DAMAGE/ATTACK:	1-4 (weapon)
SPECIAL ATTACKS:	−3 penalty to opponents' surprise
SPECIAL DEFENSES:	Nil
MAGIC RESISTANCE:	Nil
SIZE:	S (2½' tall)
MORALE:	Average (8-10)
XP VALUE:	Normal: 65
	Mates: 175
	Tribe mother: 270

Grippli resemble small, intelligent, humanoid tree frogs. They are have a primitive culture and are nonaggressive.

They stand 2½ feet tall and weigh 25 to 30 pounds. Their bodies are shaped like those of frogs, except for the human-like hands and hand-like feet. Their eyes are yellow with vertical slit pupils. Their skin is gray-green with camouflage stripes and swirling patterns. Although their skin looks wet and shiny, it is actually dry to the touch. Grippli smell of old, wet vegetation.

They love bright colors and eagerly acquire any such items. They wear clothing only for decoration or for a particular functional purpose, such as for pockets. A normal encounter with grippli outside of the village finds them wearing only thin belts or loin cloths to hold weapons or acquired items.

They speak a language of croaks, groans, clicks, and squeaks. In a tribe there is usually at least one member that can speak either common, elvish, or some other jungle humanoids' language. When speaking any language but their own, they are barely understandable because of the croaking resonances in their speech.

Combat: Because of the grippli's coloring, opponents suffer a −3 penalty to their surprise rolls. Grippli defend themselves with snares, nets, poisoned darts, and the occasional sword or dagger. Any metal weapons must be manufactured elsewhere for the grippli, so swords are rare. They can adapt to use any weapons, and they have been known to use spears and blowguns on rare occasions. They never wear armor. Generally speaking the grippli prefer small weapons that don't get in the way of climbing.

A grippli can climb trees or non-sheer rock at its normal movement rate, thanks to its unusual hands and feet. When keeping still among vegetation, a grippli's natural camouflage causes a −3 penalty to its opponents' surprise rolls. They have infravision good up to 10 yards, which means they can operate at night almost as well as during the day.

They are very capable of formulating strategies and tactics to overcome a larger, more powerful force. Grippli prefer ambushes and traps to most other strategies. By trapping their opponents in snares and nets, they can hurl darts at them safely from high in the trees. If unprovoked, they attack only to steal various brightly colored baubles.

Habitat/Society: A grippli tribal village is made of small huts of wood and mud built on the ground, in the deep shadows of large trees. On rare occasions, a grippli village is found in the strong limbs of the trees. Each village is led by a tribe mother (AC 7, HD 3, 1d6+1 points of damage with a weapon). Once per day the tribe mother can emit a musk cloud, which is treated as a *stinking cloud* spell. She looks like any other grippli, except for being almost four feet tall. She has 1d3 mates of larger than normal size (AC 8, HD 2, 1d4+1 points of damage with poisoned weapons), standing three to three-and-a-half feet tall. The tribe mother is supposed to have a touch of the blood of their god in her.

A typical village has 5d6 males capable of defending it. There are an equal number of noncombatant females and 1d6 offspring, also noncombatants. They have basic family units, just like humans, and each family has its own hut. The tribe mother's hut doubles as a temple to their small, frog-like deity. Other deities in the pantheon include evil snake gods and spider goddesses.

Their natural high intelligence enables them to learn new devices and weapons quickly and easily. As a race they have no desire to manufacture such items themselves. However, they will trade for them with other races. Trade items usually include rare fruits or other hard-to-get jungle specimens. They are extremely cautious and only develop trade relations with groups that they trust completely, such as good elves or the rare village of good humans in their area.

Ecology: Grippli's eat fruit and insects. They trap small insects in large quantities and hunt the giant varieties like humans hunt stags. They are in turn hunted by most large, ground- and tree-based predators. Giant snakes and spiders in particular are fond of grippli as meals.

Grippli are rare in the world, mostly because of their low birthrate. They live to be 700 years old, but give birth to only six or so young in that time. Because of this, the grippli defend their young ferociously.

	Annis	Green	Sea
CLIMATE/TERRAIN:	Any land	Any land or river	Any water
FREQUENCY:	Very rare	Very rare	Rare
ORGANIZATION:	Covey	Covey	Covey
ACTIVITY CYCLE:	Night	Night	Night
DIET:	Carnivore	Carnivore	Carnivore
INTELLIGENCE:	Very (11-12)	Very (11-12)	Average (8-10)
TREASURE:	(D)	(X, F)	(C, Y)
ALIGNMENT:	Chaotic evil	Neutral evil	Chaotic evil
NO. APPEARING:	1-3	1-3	1-3
ARMOR CLASS:	0	-2	7
MOVEMENT:	15	12, Sw 12	Sw 15
HIT DICE:	7+7	9	3
THAC0:	13	11	17
NO. OF ATTACKS:	3	2	1
DAMAGE/ATTACK:	9-16/9-16/3-9	7-8/7-8	7-10
SPECIAL ATTACKS:	See below	See below	See below
SPECIAL DEFENSES:	See below	See below	See below
MAGIC RESISTANCE:	20%	35%	50%
SIZE:	L (8' tall)	M (5'-6' tall)	M
MORALE:	Champion (15)	Fanatic (17)	Steady (11)
XP VALUE:	4,000	4,000	1,400

Hags are witch-like beings that spread havoc and destruction, working their magics, and slaying all whom they encounter.

Hags appear as wretched old women, with long, frayed hair, and withered faces. Horrid moles and warts dot their blotchy skin, their mouths are filled with blackened teeth, and their breath is most foul. Though wrinkled and skinny, hags possess supernatural strength and can easily crush smaller creatures, such as goblins, with one hand. Similarly, though hags look decrepit, they run swiftly, easily bounding over rocks or logs in their path. From the long, skinny fingers of hags grow iron-like claws. Hags use these claws (and their supernatural strength) to rend and tear at opponents in combat. Their garb is similar to that of peasant women, but usually much more tattered and filthy.

Combat: The combat abilities of hags vary with each type (see below for details), but all hags possess the following: 18/00 Strength or greater, some level of magic resistance, and the spell-like ability to *change self* at will. Hags use this last ability to attract victims, frequently posing as young human or demihuman females, helpless old women, or occasionally as orcs or hobgoblins. A disguised hag reveals her true form and leaps to the attack when weak opponents come near. Against well armed and armored parties, hags maintain their disguise and employ further trickery designed to place the intended victim in a more vulnerable position. This trickery can take any of several forms, including verbal persuasion, leading the victim into a prearranged trap, and so on.

The one weakness of hags is their arrogance. Hags have great disdain for the mental abilities of all humans and demihumans and, though hags are masterful employers of disguise, clever characters may be able to glean a hag's true nature through conversation.

Habitat/Society: Hags live alone or in coveys of three. They always choose desolate, out-of-the-way places in which to dwell. They sometimes coexist with ogres or evil giants. The former act as servants or guards for hags, but giants are treated with respect (for obvious reasons) and often cooperate with hags to accomplish acts of great evil against the outside world.

While individually powerful, hags are much more dangerous when formed into a covey. A covey is composed of three hags of any combination (e.g., two annis and a green hag, three annis, etc.). Coveys have special powers that individual hags don't possess.

These powers include the following spells: *curse, polymorph other, animate dead, dream, control weather, veil, forcecage, vision,* and *mind blank.* Covey spells can each be used once per day, and take effect as if they were cast by a 9th-level spellcaster. To cast one of these spells, the members of the covey must all be within 10 feet of each other and the spell being cast must be in lieu of all other attacks.

Coveys never cast these spells in combat, instead these spells are used to help weave wicked plots against neighboring human or demihuman settlements. A common ploy by coveys is to force or trick a victim into performing some heinous deed. This deed usually involves bringing back more victims, some of whom are devoured by the hags; the rest are used on further evil assignments. Any creature fortunate (or unfortunate) enough to resist a covey is immediately devoured.

A covey of hags is 80% likely to be guarded by a mixture of 1d8 ogres and 1d4 evil giants. Coveys often use one or two of their ogres as spies, sending them into the world beyond after polymorphing them into less threatening creatures.

These minions frequently (60%) wear a special magical gem called a *hag eye.* A *hag eye* is made from the real eye of a covey's previous victim. It appears to the casual observer to be no more than a low-value gem (20 gp or less), but if viewed through a *gem of true seeing,* a disembodied eye can be seen trapped in the hag eye's interior. This hidden eye is magically connected to the covey that created the *hag eye.* All three members of the covey can see whatever the *hag eye* is pointed at. *Hag eyes* are usually placed on a medallion or brooch worn by one of the hag's polymorphed servants. Occasionally *hag eyes* are given as gifts to unsuspecting victims whom the hags want to monitor. Destroying a *hag eye* inflicts 1d10 points of damage to each member of the covey that created it, and one of the three hags is struck blind for 24 hours.

Hags commonly inhabit bone-strewn glens deep within forests. There is an 80% chance that hags are keeping one or two captives in a nearby earthen pit or *forcecage.* These prisoners are held for a purpose known only to the hags themselves, though it will certainly involve spreading chaos into the outside world. Prisoners kept in a pit are guarded by an evil giant or one to two ogres; those in a forcecage are left alone.

Ecology: Hags have a ravenous appetite and are able to devour man-sized creatures in just 10 rounds. They prefer human flesh, but settle for orc or demihuman when necessary. This wanton destruc-

Hag

tion has earned hags some powerful enemies. Besides humanity in general, both good giants and good dragons hunt hags, slaying them whenever possible. Still, hags multiply rapidly by using their *change self* ability to appear as beautiful maidens to men they encounter alone. Hag offspring are always female. Legends say that hags can change their unborn child for that of a human female while she sleeps. They further state that any mother who brings such a child to term is then slain by the hag-child she carries. Fortunately, such ghastly tales have never been proven.

Hags hoard fine treasure, using the jewelry and coins to decorate the bones of their more powerful victims, and the finer gems (500 gp value or higher) to manufacture magical *hag eyes*.

Annis

The largest and most powerful of all the hags, annis stand seven to eight feet tall. Their skin is deep blue in complexion, while their hair, teeth, and nails are glossy black. The eyes of an annis are dull green or yellow. Annis have normal infravision (60-foot range), but superior hearing and sense of smell. Annis are surprised only on a 1 on 1d10.

An annis attacks using its talons and teeth to inflict horrible wounds. In melee, annis tend to close and grapple. An annis that hits an opponent with all three of its attacks in one round has successfully grappled its opponent. Next round, all attacks by the annis are automatic hits, unless the opponent is stronger, the annis is slain, or the victim uses some magical means to escape the hag. Otherwise, the annis will continue to hold the victim in its grasp, and deliver damage with its raking talons and sharpened teeth each round until the victim is slain.

In addition to normal attacks, annis have the ability to cast *fog cloud* three times per day. This spell is used to confuse resistance or to delay attack by a superior foe. Annis can also *change self* like all hags, appearing as a tall human, ogre, or even a small giant. These spells are cast at 8th level for purposes of determining spell range, duration, etc.

The skin of an annis is iron-hard; thus edged weapons cause 1 less point of damage when they hit these hags. Conversely, blunt weapons (including morning stars) cause 1 additional point of damage against an annis.

Annis speak their own language, as well as ogre, all evil giant tongues, and some common. Some of the most intelligent annis can speak common fluently and know a smattering of various demihuman languages. Annis are believed to live for 500 years.

Greenhag

These wretched creatures live in desolate countryside and amid dense forests and swamps. Greenhags, as their name implies, have a sickly green pallor. Hair color ranges from near black to olive green, and their eyes are amber or orange. Their skin appears withered but is hard and rough like the bark of a tree. Due to their coloration and their ability to move with absolute silence, greenhags impose a -5 penalty to an opponent's surprise roll when in a forest or swamp. They have superior hearing, smell, and sight, including infravision (90-foot range). They are only surprised on a roll of 1 on the 1d10 surprise roll.

Rock-hard talons grow from the long, slender fingers of greenhags. They use these talons to slash and rend their opponents. Smaller than their annis cousins, greenhags nonetheless possess Strength equivalent to that of an ogre (18/00). Because of their great Strength, all their attack rolls gain a +3 bonus and all hits receive a +6 damage bonus.

Greenhags can cast the following spells at will, one spell per round: *audible glamor, dancing lights, invisibility, pass without trace, change self, speak with monsters, water breathing,* and *weakness*. Each spell is employed at 9th level of ability.

To lure victims, greenhags typically use their mimic ability. This enables them to imitate the voice of a mature or immature

male or female, human or demihuman. Calls for help and crying are common deceptions employed by greenhags. They are also able to mimic most animals.

Greenhags speak their own language (a dialect of annis) as well as all demihuman languages and common. These are the longest lived of all hags—they can live for up to 1,000 years.

Sea Hag

These, the most wretched of all hags, inhabit thickly vegetated shallows in warm seas and, very rarely, overgrown lakes. Warts, bony protrusions, and patches of slimy green scales dot their sickly yellow skin. Their eyes are always red with deep, black pupils. Long, seaweed-like hair hangs limply from their heads, covering their withered bodies.

Sea hags hate beauty, attempting to destroy it wherever it is encountered. Sea hags can *change self* at will, and often use this ability to draw their victims within 30 feet before revealing themselves. The true appearance of a sea hag is so ghastly that anyone viewing one of these hags grows weak from fright unless a successful saving throw vs. spell is rolled. Beings that fail their saving throw lose 1/2 of their Strength for 1d6 turns. Worse still, sea hags can cast a deadly glance up to three times a day. This look affects one creature of the sea hag's choosing within 30 feet. To negate the effects of this glance, the victim must successfully save vs. poison. If the saving throw is failed, the victim either dies immediately from fright (25% chance) or falls stricken and is paralyzed for three days (75% chance). Few who survive the glance live to tell of it, for sea hags quickly devour their helpless victims.

Sea hags always use their deadly glance as their primary form of attack; they will melee, but only if they have the advantage of numbers. Unlike other hags, sea hags use daggers in combat, receiving a +3 bonus to their attack roll and a +6 damage bonus, due to their ogre-like Strength.

Sea hags speak their own language as well as common and the languages of annis, and sea elves, and live for 800 years.

	Hairfoot	Tallfellow	Stout
CLIMATE/TERRAIN:	Pastoral	Hills, forests	Hills, mountains
FREQUENCY:	Uncommon	Rare	Rare
ORGANIZATION:	Community	Community	Community
ACTIVITY CYCLE:	Day	Day	Day
DIET:	Omnivore	Omnivore	Omnivore
INTELLIGENCE:	Very (11-12)	Very (11-12)	Very (11-12)
TREASURE:	K (B)	K (B)	K (B)
ALIGNMENT:	Lawful good	Lawful good	Lawful good
NO. APPEARING:	2-12 (2d6)	2-12 (2d6)	2-12 (2d6)
ARMOR CLASS:	7 (10)	6 (10)	6 (10)
MOVEMENT:	6 (9)	6 (9)	6 (9)
HIT DICE:	1-6 hit points	1-6 hit points	1-6 hit points
THAC0:	20	20	20
NO. OF ATTACKS:	1	1	1
DAMAGE/ATTACK:	1-6 (weapon)	1-6 (weapon)	1- 6 (weapon)
SPECIAL ATTACKS:	+3 with bows and slings	+3 with bows and slings	+3 with bows and slings
SPECIAL DEFENSES:	See below	See below	See below
MAGIC RESISTANCE:	Nil	Nil	Nil
SIZE:	S (3)	S (4')	S (3)
MORALE:	Steady (11-12)	Steady (11-12)	Steady (11-12)
XP VALUE:	35	35	35

Halflings are a hard-working race of peaceful citizens. Their communities are similar to those of humans, although they usually contain many burrow homes in addition to surface cottages.

Halflings average 3 feet in height, have ruddy complexions, with sandy to dark brown hair, and blue or hazel eyes. Their dress is often colorful but serviceable, and they like to wear caps or tunics. In addition to their own language, many halflings also speak the common tongue, gnome, goblin, and orcish.

Combat: Halflings will fight with great ferocity in defense of good or their homes. They are very skilled with both the sling and the bow (receiving a +3 bonus on all attack rolls) and use these weapons to great advantage in battle. Their tactics often involve feints to draw their attackers into the open where they can be subjected to a volley of fire from cover.

When equipped for battle, halflings wear padded or leather armor. A halfling force is usually armed with short swords and hand axes. In addition, two-thirds of the halflings will be carrying either a sling or short bow.

All halflings above normal level will have Armor Class 6, while those of 3rd or 4th level wear chain mail over their leather (AC 4). Higher level halflings have a 10 percent chance per level of having a magic weapon or armor.

As all halflings are naturally resistant to magic and poisons—they save at 4 levels above their actual level. In addition, halflings are exceedingly clever at quiet movement and hiding. In combat, their opponents receive a -5 on their surprise roll. In natural terrain halflings are considered *invisible* when they are hiding in vegetation.

Habitat/Society: Halfling villages will generally have between 30 and 300 (30d10) individuals living in them. For every 30 halflings in a particular community there will be two 2nd-level fighters and a 3rd-level priest. If more than 90 halflings are encountered there will be an additional leader of 3rd-level fighting ability. If more than 150 are encountered there will also be the following additional halfling warriors in the group: one 9th-level fighter, two 4th-level fighters and three 3rd-level fighters. Further, a community of 150 halflings will have a 5th-level priest.

Cheerful and outgoing, halflings, take great pleasure in simple crafts and nature. Their fingers, though short, are very dexterous allowing them to create objects of great beauty. Halflings shun water and extremes in temperature, preferring to settle in temperate pastoral countrysides. They get along well with humans and receive a +2 bonus to all their Reaction Rolls involving human NPCs.

Ecology: Halflings hunt occasionally, but prefer breads, vegetables and fruits, with an occasional pheasant on the side. They have a life expectancy of 100 years on the average.

Tallfellow

A taller (4' +) and slimmer halfling with fair skin and hair, tallfellows are somewhat rare among the halfling folk. Tallfellows generally speak the language of elves in addition to those listed previously and greatly enjoy their company. In combat, tallfellows often ride ponies and carry spears or small lances. Tallfellows of strength 17 or more can rise to 6th level fighting ability. They live 180 years on average. Like elves, a tallfellow can recognize a secret door on a roll of 1 on a 1d6. All tallfellows receive a +2 bonus to surprise rolls when in forest or wooded terrain.

Stout

These halflings are shorter and stockier than the more common hairfoots. Stouts take great pleasure in gems and fine masonry, often working as jewelers or stone cutters. They rarely mix with humans and elves, but enjoy the company of dwarves and often speak their language fluently. Like dwarves, stouts have infravision (60'), a 75% chance to detect sloping passageways, and a 50% chance of determining direction when underground. Stouts with a strength score of 17 or better can work their way up to the 9th-level of fighting ability. Their ties with the dwarven folk have spilled over into their combat tactics, with many stouts employing hammers and morningstars in combat. Stouts also have no fear of water and, in fact, many are excellent swimmers. Stouts can reach an age of 140 or more years.

Harpy

CLIMATE/TERRAIN:	Temperate, tropical land or coast
FREQUENCY:	Rare
ORGANIZATION:	Flock
ACTIVITY CYCLE:	Day
DIET:	Carnivore
INTELLIGENCE:	Low (5-7)
TREASURE:	R (C)
ALIGNMENT:	Chaotic evil
NO. APPEARING:	2-12 (2d6)
ARMOR CLASS:	7
MOVEMENT:	6, Fl 15 (C)
HIT DICE:	7
THAC0:	13
NO. OF ATTACKS:	3
DAMAGE/ATTACK:	1-3/1-3/1-6 or 1-3/1-3/weapon
SPECIAL ATTACKS:	Singing and charm
SPECIAL DEFENSES:	Nil
MAGIC RESISTANCE:	Nil
SIZE:	M (6')
MORALE:	Elite (13-14)
XP VALUE:	975

Harpies are wicked avian beasts that prey upon nearly all creatures but prefer the flesh of humans and demihumans.

Harpies have the bodies of vultures but the upper torsos and heads of women. Their human features are youthful, but hideous, with frayed unkempt hair and decaying teeth. A foul odor surrounds all harpies and that which they touch. Harpies never bathe nor clean themselves in any way. Their dress, if anything, is limited to tattered rags and shiny trinkets taken from previous victims.

The language of harpies, in contrast to their enticing song, is a horrible collection of cackles and shrieks. Although there are instances of harpies which could speak the languages of other creatures, these are few and far between.

Combat: The song of the harpies has the ability to charm all humans and demihumans who hear it (elves are resistant to the charm). Those who fail their saving throw versus spell will proceed towards the harpy with all possible speed, only to stand entranced while the harpy slays them at its leisure. This charm will last as long as the harpy continues to sing. Harpies can sing even while engaged in melee.

It is impossible to fend off a harpy song simply by clasping hands over ears because the charm takes effect the moment the first note is heard. Characters making prior preparations to block out the sound, (wax in ears, etc.), are immune to the effects of the song. In addition, characters who make their saving throw are thereafter immune to its effect, until such time as they encounter a different group of harpies.

If forced to fight, harpies can do so quite effectively by delivering a vicious bite and raking simultaneously with their talons. About 50% of all harpies encountered will use weapons, usually a bone club (damage 1-8) which they wield surprisingly well.

The touch of a harpy upon a charmed individual has a similar, though somewhat less potent, effect. Those who are touched and miss their saving throw versus spell will stand mesmerized for 20+1d10 hours.

The effect of either charm is broken if the harpy is slain.

Habitat/Society: Harpies make their home upon coastlines in regions near shipping lanes and by well-traveled paths. There they use their song to lure travelers to their doom.

Their lair is usually a shallow cave, which they defile until no animal dare approach it. Here they remain unless hunting. Harpies often carry victims back to their lair to devour them in more familiar surroundings.

Harpies have little use for treasure, other than the shiny baubles which they often attach to their clothes. Other items, such as gold and weapons, are frequently interspersed amongst the filth and bones that litter the cave. This refuse can reach a depth of several feet in the oldest of harpy lairs.

A typical harpy lair houses about a half-dozen of these wretched creatures. No male harpies have ever been seen and it seems that harpies can reproduce at will by laying a single egg every other year. Harpies take no care of their young, which live off carcasses and cave vermin until they themselves are old enough to sing and hunt.

Harpies have no social structure, frequently quarreling over who gets what part of a victim and when to stop the torturing and start the feasting. Occasionally these quarrels will turn violent, so that more than one harpy feast has begun with the last minute addition of the losing harpy to the menu.

Harpies will occassionally agree to cooperate in evil acts with other humanoids.

Ecology: Harpies hunt all manner of beasts, remaining in an area for as long as the food supply lasts. They are despised and greatly feared by all creatures weaker than themselves.

Harpies have a voracious appetite, devouring all manner of man and beast. They take great delight in torture, and frequently kill for pleasure. Slain victims which harpies do not eat are simply left to rot.

Their life span is unknown but seems to be about 50 years.

Hatori

	Lesser	Greater
CLIMATE/ TERRAIN:	Deserts	Deserts
FREQUENCY:	Rare	Very rare
ORGANIZATION:	Solitary/Small herds	Solitary
ACTIVITY CYCLE:	Any	Any
DIET:	Carnivore	Carnivore
INTELLIGENCE:	Low (5-7)	Low (5-7)
TREASURE:	U	U (x 2)
ALIGNMENT:	Chaotic neutral	Chaotic neutral
NO. APPEARING:	1 or 2-5	1
ARMOR CLASS:	2	1
MOVEMENT:	15	12
HIT DICE:	1-5	6-20
THAC0:	Varies	Varies
NO. OF ATTACKS:	2	2
DAMAGE/ATTACK:	3-18/1-12	3-36/2-24
SPECIAL ATTACKS:	Swallow whole	Swallow whole
SPECIAL DEFENSES:	Nil	Nil
MAGIC RESISTANCE:	Nil	Nil
SIZE:	L to G (10' to 50' long)	G (60' to 200' long)
MORALE:	Average (9)	Steady (11)
XP VALUE:	Variable	Variable

Hatori, sometimes called the "crocodiles of the sands" are giant reptiles dwelling within sandy desert wastes. The hatori's hard, knobby hide ranges in color from gray-white to red-brown and is virtually indistinguishable from stone. Hatori use this semblance to great advantage, allowing the wind to partially bury them beneath the sands so that a casual observer may believe he is looking at rock outcroppings instead of behemoths of the sands.

Hatori are shaped like overgrown lizards, save that their legs have evolved into flat, flipper-like appendages that they use in conjunction with their massive tails to "swim" through the sands with astonishing speed and mobility. When forced to travel upon something more solid, such as a rocky plain, hatori move by awkwardly flopping and dragging themselves forward. Hatori eyes are normally concealed deep within dark recesses that look like small hollows. In the case of greater hatori (6 HD and over) these recesses sometimes look like cavern entrances.

Greater hatori are identical to lesser hatori in all respects save size and their ability to swallow larger prey whole (see below).

Combat: The only thing that can drive hatori into combat is hunger. Unfortunately, hatori have voracious appetites and food is rare in their home environment, so they never pass up an opportunity to make a meal out of a passing traveler—or even an entire caravan. The hatori's favorite hunting method is to position themselves along a well-used migratory trail or caravan route. When, believing the hatori to be no more than a rocky outcropping, a prospective meal passes nearby, the hatori spring into action.

Once the battle begins, hatori try to bite their victims with their toothy maws. Greater hatori swallow man-sized victims whole on a natural attack roll of 20. Such victims suffer 1d12 points of damage per round from the crushing and acid effects of the digestive tract. Swallowed victims cannot escape until the hatori is killed, for the muscular action of the esophagus prevents them from climbing out the throat.

Hatori use their bony tails to lash out at anyone attacking from the rear, or to attack fleeing victims while simultaneously trying to eat someone else.

Lesser hatori can swallow whole only opponents of kender size

or less (on a natural attack roll of 20). Experience points earned for defeating a hatori depend upon its number of HD. See Tables 31 and 32 on page 47 of the 2nd Edition *Dungeon Master's Guide* to compute the XP values.

Habitat/Society: Hatori live in the sandy regions of large deserts. Because they are constantly searching for food, however, they tend to be found near migratory paths or along busy caravan routes. They stay in a productive area until food becomes scarce.

Hatori grow very slowly, at the rate of only 1-foot per year, but they keep growing throughout their lives. They accumulate Hit Dice at the rate of 1 HD every 10 years. Therefore, young hatori of 1 HD are usually 10 feet or less in length and 10 years old or younger, hatori of 2 HD are between 10 and 20 feet and between 10 and 20 years of age, etc.

Females care for their hatchlings until the young reach 50 feet in length (5 HD). This is the only time when they are commonly encountered in groups, for adult hatori are solitary creatures. Female hatori accompanied by hatchlings seldom exceed 10 HD, for they generally stop bearing young after their 100th year.

Every 10 years, male hatori and young females without any offspring migrate to the center of the desert. Here the males engage in ferocious battles to win the right to breed with the females. Although no civilized man has ever witnessed these mating rituals, certain desert tribes speak of a "time of thunder when mountains die." These legends may refer to battles occurring during the hatori mating season.

Ecology: Hatori eat anything, though they cannot digest gems or magical armor and weaponry. These items tend to accumulate in their stomachs over their long lifetimes. Hatori have no natural predators (save for each other at mating time), though it is rumored that certain kinds of dragons have been known to attack smaller hatori in times of hunger. Legends speak of a hidden hatori burial ground where ancient hatori go to die. If such a burial ground exists, it certainly abounds with gems and magical armor.

185

Haunt

CLIMATE/TERRAIN:	Any
FREQUENCY:	Very rare
ORGANIZATION:	Individual
ACTIVITY CYCLE:	Any
DIET:	Nil
INTELLIGENCE:	Non- (0)
TREASURE:	Nil
ALIGNMENT:	Any

NO. APPEARING:	1
ARMOR CLASS:	0/victim's AC
MOVEMENT:	6/as victim
HIT DICE:	5/victim's hp
THAC0:	15
NO. OF ATTACKS:	1/1, as 5-HD monster
DAMAGE/ATTACK:	See below/by weapon
SPECIAL ATTACKS:	See below
SPECIAL DEFENSES:	See below
MAGIC RESISTANCE:	Nil
SIZE:	Variable
MORALE:	Champion (16)
XP VALUE:	2,000

(Note: Statistics separated by a slash: those to the left refer to the natural state, those to the right are for a possessed victim.)

A haunt is the restless spirit of a person who died leaving some vital task unfinished. Its sole purpose is to take over a living body and use it to complete the task, thus gaining a final release from this world.

Haunts may assume either of two forms, at will: a hovering luminescent ball of light (identical in appearance to a will-o-wisp) or a nebulous, translucent image of the haunt's former body. In the later state, haunts look like groaning spirits, spectres, or ghosts, and are often mistaken for them. Transformation from one state to the other takes one round.

Combat: A haunt must remain within 60 yards of where it died, unless it takes control of a victim's body. This 60-yard radius is called the haunt's domain.

A haunt attacks mindlessly, and always targets the first human or demihuman that enters its domain. It will continue to attack until possession is achieved or the intended victim leaves the haunt's domain.

The touch of a haunt drains 2 points of Dexterity per hit. As the character's Dexterity is drained, he suffers not only the penalties of lowered Dexterity, but increasing numbness creeps over his body. If Dexterity reaches 0, the haunt slips into the body and possesses it. Once the body is possessed, Dexterity returns to normal.

The haunt uses the host's body to complete its unfulfilled task. The task need not be dangerous, although it often is. Once the task is completed, the haunt passes on to its final rest and the victim regains control of his body. When the haunt leaves a victim, the character has a Dexterity of 3. Lost Dexterity points are regained at the rate of 1 point for each turn of complete rest. If a haunt's possessed body is slain, it will haunt the place where that body was killed.

If the victim has an alignment opposite to that of the haunt (good vs. evil), the haunt will try to strangle the victim using the victim's own hands. Unless the victim's arms are being restrained, the strangulation begins the round after the haunt takes control of the body. On the first round the victim suffers 1 point of dam-

age, on the second 2, on the third 4, and so on, doubling each round until the victim is dead or the haunt is driven off.

Attacks on a possessed character will cause full damage to the character's body. If attacked, the haunt will use whatever weapons and armor the victim carries, but it cannot use any items that would require special knowledge (spells, scrolls, rings). The only safe way to free the victim is by casting *hold person* or *dispel evil* (good). If *hold person* is cast, the haunt must make a successful saving throw vs. paralyzation or be ejected from the body; *dispel evil* (good) destroys the haunt forever.

Haunts are linked to the sites where they died and therefore cannot be turned by priests. When in the natural state (i.e., not possessing a body) haunts may be struck only by silver or magical weapons, or by fire. Weapons cause only 1 point of damage, plus the magical bonus (if any). Normal fire causes 1 point of damage per round, but magical fire inflicts full damage. If a haunt is reduced to 0 hit points, it loses control of its form and fades away. The haunt reforms in one week to haunt the same location again until its task is completed.

Habitat/Society: The exact task to be accomplished varies, but the motives are always powerful—revenge, greed, love, hate. Often great distances need to be traveled before a task can be completed, and haunts will drive their hosts mercilessly toward the goal, ignoring the need for food or sleep.

A few haunts (10%) retain some knowledge of their former lives and can be communicated with. Often these haunts feel remorse at having to prey upon the living, but the force of the uncompleted task is too powerful for the haunt to resist.

Ecology: Haunts cling to this world by force of will alone. They have no treasure of their own unless it is connected to their quest. They prey only on humans and demihumans.

Hell Hound

CLIMATE/TERRAIN:	Any land
FREQUENCY:	Very rare
ORGANIZATION:	Pack
ACTIVITY CYCLE:	Any
DIET:	Carnivore
INTELLIGENCE:	Low (5-7)
TREASURE:	C
ALIGNMENT:	Lawful evil
NO. APPEARING:	2-8
ARMOR CLASS:	4
MOVEMENT:	12
HIT DICE:	4-7
THAC0:	4 HD: 17
	5-6 HD: 15
	7 HD: 13
NO. OF ATTACKS:	1
DAMAGE/ATTACK:	1-10
SPECIAL ATTACKS:	Breathe fire
SPECIAL DEFENSES:	See below
MAGIC RESISTANCE:	Standard
SIZE:	M
MORALE:	Elite (13)
XP VALUE:	4 HD: 420
	5 HD: 650
	6 HD: 975
	7 HD: 1,400

Hell hounds are fire-breathing canines from another plane of existence brought here in the service of evil beings.

A hell hound resembles a large hound with rust-red or red-brown fur and red, glowing eyes. The markings, teeth, and tongue are soot black. It stands two to three feet high at the shoulder, and has a distinct odor of smoke and sulfur. The baying sounds it makes have an eerie, hollow tone that send a shiver through any who hear them.

Combat: Hell hounds are clever hunters that operate in packs. They do not bay like normal dogs while hunting. They move with great stealth, imposing a -5 penalty to opponents' surprise rolls. One or two of the pack sneak up on a quarry while the others form a ring around it. The first hell hound then springs from ambush, attacks the nearest victim, and attempts to drive the others toward the rest of the pack. If the prey does not run away, the rest of the pack closes in within 1d4 + 2 rounds. If hell hounds are pursuing fleeing prey, they might bay.

Hell hounds attack first by breathing fire at an opponent up to 10 yards away. The fire causes 1 point of damage for each of the hell hound's Hit Dice. A successful saving throw vs. breath weapon cuts the damage in half. The hell hound then attacks with its teeth. The hell hound can continue to exhale flame while biting. If the hell hound rolls a natural 20 on its attack roll, it grabs a victim in its jaws and breathes fire on the victim.

Hell hounds have a variety of defenses. They are immune to fire. Their keen hearing means they are surprised only on a 1 or 2 on 1d10. They can also see hidden or invisible creatures 50% of the time.

Habitat/Society: Hell hounds are native to those extradimensional planes notable for their hot, fiery landscapes. There they roam in packs of 2d20 beasts. The hell hounds on the Prime Material plane are summoned there to serve the needs of evil creatures. Most of them later escape to the wild.

Hell hounds may have 4 to 7 (1d4 + 3) Hit Dice. The more Hit Dice a hell hound has, the larger it is and the more damage it causes. Each pack is led by a 7-Hit Die hell hound. The leader

drives off other 7 HD rivals, who form their own packs.

The diet of hell hounds is similar to that of normal canines. They roam a wide area of 1d10 + 4 square miles centered on their den. Pack territories may overlap.

They do not easily reproduce on the Prime Material plane. Only 5% of encounters include puppies. Such puppies are born in litters of 2d4. They burp flame uncontrollably at least once a day. The flames are harmless aside from the tendency to set fire to anything flammable in the area. Newborn puppies are at 10% of the adult growth; they quickly grow an additional 5% each month and reach full adult growth (4 HD) in 1½ years. While growing they can attack with their incendiary bite. Hell hound puppies up to two months old inflict 1 point of damage. Older ones add an additional 1 point for each additional six months of growth.

Prey is usually eaten where it is slain, though hell hounds occasionally haul a carcass back to their den for later meals. Hell hounds are also similar to normal canines in that they may act as retrievers. Some objects are specifically sought; this is especially the case in trained hell hounds. Other hell hounds are simply playful and use the retrieved items as toys. They especially like noisy bags and pouches filled with their late victims' treasures. Flammable containers eventually burn and spill their contents in or around the den. Parchments are rarely found here unless protected by nonflammable containers.

Ecology: Hell hounds have little place in the ecology of the normal world. They are dangerous annoyances prone to cause fires wherever they hunt. Hell hounds cause more forest fires than any other creature except for humanoids. Hell hounds have their uses, though. Because of their ability to easily detect hidden or invisible creatures, hell hounds make excellent watch dogs, especially for intelligent monsters such as fire giants.

Hell hounds can be domesticated if raised from puppies, but there is a 10% chance each year that domesticated hell hounds go wild.

Heucuva

CLIMATE/TERRAIN:	Any
FREQUENCY:	Very rare
ORGANIZATION:	Solitary
ACTIVITY CYCLE:	Any
DIET:	Nil
INTELLIGENCE:	Semi- (2-4)
TREASURE:	C
ALIGNMENT:	Chaotic evil

NO. APPEARING:	1-10
ARMOR CLASS:	3
MOVEMENT:	9
HIT DICE:	2
THAC0:	19
NO. OF ATTACKS:	1
DAMAGE/ATTACK:	1-6
SPECIAL ATTACKS:	Disease
SPECIAL DEFENSES:	Hit only by silver or +1 weapons
MAGIC RESISTANCE:	See below
SIZE:	M (5'-7' tall)
MORALE:	Steady (11)
XP VALUE:	270

The heucuva is an undead spirit similar in appearance to a skeleton, but more dangerous and more difficult to dispel.

The heucuva appears to be a humanoid skeleton of normal size. The bones are covered by a robe that is little more than tattered rags.

Combat: The heucuva attacks by swiping with one of its hands; the sharp finger bones are capable of tearing into wood. A victim must roll a successful saving throw vs. poison or be afflicted with a disease. The victim suffers a daily loss of 1 point each of Strength and Constitution. A *cure disease* spell must be cast on the victim to prevent death and restore the lost points.

Heucuva are treated as wights on the Turning Undead table. They are resistant to all mind-influencing spells. Heucuva bones soon crumble once the monsters are destroyed.

Heucuva have a special hatred of priests. Once a priest uses his spells or tries to turn the heucuva, they will concentrate on attacking that priest. They may even ignore everyone else except for the priest and those defending him.

Heucuva are able to polymorph themselves up to three times a day. They may use this power to assume a nonthreatening shape in order to get close to an unsuspecting victim or avoid an undesired encounter when pursuing a specific prey. Heucuva may assume the form of people they have met in the recent past, such as a past victim or a member of the party that encounters the monsters. If the heucuva are in their lairs, they may assume their old (living) appearances. Groups encountered on the surface may appear to be pilgrims in procession. Such disguises fool only those who view the world solely via visible light; heucuva appear the same as other skeletal undead if looked at with infravision. The heucuva are incapable of speech; they can only moan or wail.

Habitat/Society: Heucuva roam the dark places of the world. They can be found in subterranean realms, as well as most temperate or tropical regions. Cold seems to prevent heucuvan activity, for they are not found in high, desolate mountains or in any cold regions.

Legends tell that heucuva are the restless spirits of monastic priests who were less than faithful to their holy vows. In punishment for their heresies, they are forced to roam the dark. Their spirits, appearance, and holy powers have become perverted mockeries of their old selves. The tatters they wear are the unrecognizable remains of their monks' robes. Instead of healing, they can kill with a diseased touch. Instead of helping others, they seek to kill all who still live. Even their old power to turn undead is now used to help them resist the efforts of others to turn them.

Heucuva retain dim memories of their old lives. Their lairs are decorated as grotesque mockeries of their old abbeys and temples. The corpses of past victims may be used to represent parishioners. These corpses may retain their original possessions, which may represent a large portion of the heucuvan treasure trove. Other accumulated treasures may be scattered around the mock altar as decorations or offerings. Such a mock temple is a chilling sight to most and an abomination that few good-aligned cleric can resist destroying.

Some heucuva are nomadic and constantly wander on a pilgrimage to nowhere. Even these are mockeries of real pilgrimages.

Ecology: Heucuva are malignant spirits that seek to destroy those who still live. They are used as examples to remind priests the fate that befalls those who stray from their devotion or use their religion as a mask to hide unpious deeds. Powdered heucuva bones may be used in the preparation of magical items intended to corrupt the spirits of living beings or to control undead.

Hippocampus

CLIMATE/TERRAIN:	Fresh or salt water depths
FREQUENCY:	Rare
ORGANIZATION:	Herd
ACTIVITY CYCLE:	Any
DIET:	Herbivore
INTELLIGENCE:	Average (8-10)
TREASURE:	Nil
ALIGNMENT:	Chaotic good

NO. APPEARING:	2-8
ARMOR CLASS:	5
MOVEMENT:	Sw 24
HIT DICE:	4
THAC0:	17
NO. OF ATTACKS:	1
DAMAGE/ATTACK:	1-4
SPECIAL ATTACKS:	Nil
SPECIAL DEFENSES:	Nil
MAGIC RESISTANCE:	Nil
SIZE:	H (18' long)
MORALE:	Steady (11-12)
XP VALUE:	120

The hippocampus is the most prized of the marine steeds, a creature that combines features of a horse and a fish.

The hippocampus has the head, forelegs, and torso of a horse. The equine section is covered with short hair. The mane is made of long, flexible fins. The front hooves are replaced by webbed fins that fold up as the leg moves forward, then fan out as the leg strokes back. Past the rib cage the body becomes fish-like. The tail tapers 14 feet into a wide horizontal fin. A dorsal fin is located on the rump. Coloration is that of seawater. Typical colors include ivory, pale green, pale blue, aqua, deep blue, and deep green.

Combat: Hippocampi are usually peaceful creatures. They do not attack unless cornered or if another hippocampus or an ally is threatened. They are fast enough to out-swim most anything that would want to attack them.

The hippocampus attacks with a strong bite. It suddenly extends its head, chomps down with a crushing bite, and then releases. Hippocampi do not hold onto their opponents.

Hippocampi also butt their heads against targets. Such attacks may stun an opponent or break his bones.

Their firm, powerfully muscled bodies provide a strong protection against attack. The blood coagulates quickly on exposure to water, thus minimizing blood loss that could both debilitate the hippocampus and attract sharks (sharks have only a 20% chance of going into a feeding frenzy if the only bleeding creature is a hippocampus).

Habitat/Society: Hippocampi are the prized steeds of the sea. They can be found in deep waters anywhere, in freshwater lakes and oceans. They are able to breathe fresh and salt water with equal ease. They can also breathe air but require frequent gulps of water to keep from drying out. They are unable to move out of water.

Despite their radically different environments, horses and hippocampi are very similar. They have approximately the same sizes, life spans, and personalities, although hippocampi are blessed with much higher intelligence.

Hippocampi are herbivores. They normally graze on seaweed and other soft vegetation. If their usual fodder is unavailable, their strong teeth can chew up mollusks and coral.

Wild hippocampi roam in herds of 2d4. These are usually a stallion, 1d4 mares, and the rest young hippocampi of either sex.

Hippocampus mares lay a single, large egg. After six months, the egg hatches a single foal. Twins are extremely rare (1% chance). The foals grow quickly in two years. The yearlings are physically the equals of the adults. Hippocampian tales speak of a "Great Herd" of hundreds or thousands of hippocampi that roams the uncharted reaches of the far seas. No non-hippocampi have ever seen this spectacle.

Hippocampi may be "domesticated" by water-breathing humanoids, especially tritons. In truth, the intelligent hippocampi cooperate with the humanoids. The hippocampi provide their services as steeds and allies while the humanoids provide protection. The benevolent hippocampi may assist surface dwellers who are visiting the aquatic world, whether voluntarily or by accident. Many a shipwrecked sailor has been saved from drowning by a passing hippocampus. Hippocampi are good judges of character; they will not assist an evil being or anyone who acts in a hostile manner toward them. Sometimes a hippocampus's offer of a ride can be more trouble than it is worth. Young hippocampi often forget that most surface dwellers breathe air, not water.

Hippocampi do not accumulate treasure. Most spurn even ornamental gifts such as collars or leg bands. They simply have no use for these gewgaws. They do appreciate delicacies, however, in the forms of tasty foods not available in the water.

Ecology: Hippocampi are one of the most successful of the intelligent, good-aligned marine monsters. They maintain ties with mermen and sea elves, as well as surface dwellers who make their living in the water. They provide valuable services as steeds, guides, and allies. Hippocampus eggs sell for 1,500 gp. Young hippocampi are worth 2,500 gp. However, surface dwellers who have been saved by hippocampi remain so grateful to their former rescuers that they may attack any merchant selling eggs or foals in a public market and attempt to return the hippocampi to the sea.

Hippogriff

CLIMATE/TERRAIN:	Unpopulated regions
FREQUENCY:	Rare
ORGANIZATION:	Herd
ACTIVITY CYCLE:	Day
DIET:	Omnivore
INTELLIGENCE:	Semi- (2-4)
TREASURE:	Q x 5
ALIGNMENT:	Neutral

NO. APPEARING:	2-16
ARMOR CLASS:	5
MOVEMENT:	18, Fl 36 (C,D)
HIT DICE:	3+3
THAC0:	17
NO. OF ATTACKS:	3
DAMAGE/ATTACK:	1-6/1-6/1-10
SPECIAL ATTACKS:	Nil
SPECIAL DEFENSES:	Nil
MAGIC RESISTANCE:	Nil
SIZE:	L (10' long)
MORALE:	Average (9)
XP VALUE:	175

Hippogriffs are flying monsters that have an equal likelihood to be predator, prey, or steed.

The hippogriff is a monstrous hybrid of eagle and equine features. It has the ears, neck, mane, torso, and hind legs of a horse. The wings, forelegs, and face are those of an eagle. It is about the size of a light riding horse. A hippogriff may be colored russet, golden tan, or a variety of browns. The feathers are usually a different shade than the hide. The beak is ivory or golden yellow.

Combat: The hippogriff attacks with its eagle-like claws and beak. Each claw can tear for 1d6 points of damage, while the scissor-like beak inflicts 1d10 points of damage.

Habitat/Society: Hippogriffs prefer the desolate sections of the temperate and tropic regions, especially rolling hills that enable them to get quickly airborne.

Hippogriffs are territorial. They have a preferred grazing and hunting area that covers 1d4 x 10 square miles. Somewhere in this territory is a naturally protected site that serves as the hippogriff nest. Here is where the young hippogriffs stay. The nest is always guarded.

The typical hippogriff herd includes 1-3 adult males, an equal number of mares, and the rest are immature young. There is a 25% chance that one or more of the mares is pregnant. Gestation takes 10 months. During the first five months, this occurs within the mare. Then she lays an egg that hatches in another five months. Twin births are rare (1% chance).

The foal is able to walk upon hatching. Its beak remains soft for the first two weeks; this enables the foal to nurse. Then its beak hardens and the hippogriff switches to regurgitated food from its mother. The colts learn to eat solid meat at four months, although they are clumsy killers (-4 penalty to attack rolls and damage). At six months they can fly (18, class D) and fight with a -2 penalty to attack rolls and damage. Yearlings are identical to adults, although they are unable to breed until they are three years old.

Wild hippogriffs are omnivorous. They feed on whatever is available, whether greenery, fruits, or wildlife. Hippogriffs are able to attack fairly large prey, such as bison, but they do not prey on carnivores. The exception is humanoids. Hippogriffs may, in the absence of other meat, attack small groups of people. Bodies are then carried back to the nest to feed the others; this is where the victim's possessions usually spill out. Hippogriffs are clean monsters; they dispose of carcasses and other debris by carrying them downhill. They like clear, sparkly things like glass, crystals, and precious gems. Males may amass a small trove kept covered by brush. As a mating ritual, he arranges these in a display to entice mares.

Ecology: Hippogriffs are closely related to griffons. Just as griffons are the result of crossing an eagle with a lion, hippogriffs resulted from the crossing of an eagle with a horse. Hippogriffs may have been created as a natural prey for the griffons. Fortunately for the hippogriff, its own formidable weapons give it a fighting chance. To make up for the griffon's superiority, hippogriffs gather in larger groups.

Hippogriffs are also related to pegasi. Because the hippogriffs eat meat, pegasi avoid their company.

Hippogriffs make excellent flying mounts. The maneuverability decreases to Class D, but their speed is unimpaired. They are less likely to eat the rider than a griffon is.

If a hippogriff is captured while still very young (under four months), it can be domesticated and trained to serve as a steed. Hippogriff eggs sell for 1,000 gp, young hippogriffs for 2,000-3,000 gp. It will probably have to be taught to fly. Domestic hippogriffs are also taught to recognize a limited number of species as food; humanoids of course are not on that list. Hippogriffs have difficulty breeding in captivity. Like flying, the wild hippogriff has to be captured before such skills are learned. Mature hippogriffs may be persuaded to voluntarily assist riders who can provide them with ample food or protection.

Hobgoblin

CLIMATE/TERRAIN:	Any non-arctic
FREQUENCY:	Uncommon
ORGANIZATION:	Tribal
ACTIVITY CYCLE:	Any
DIET:	Omnivore
INTELLIGENCE:	Average (8-10)
TREASURE:	J, M, D, (Qx5)
ALIGNMENT:	Lawful evil

NO. APPEARING:	2-20 (2d10)
ARMOR CLASS:	5 (10)
MOVEMENT:	9
HIT DICE:	1+1
THAC0:	19
NO. OF ATTACKS:	1
DAMAGE/ATTACK:	by weapon
SPECIAL ATTACKS:	Nil
SPECIAL DEFENSES:	Nil
MAGIC RESISTANCE:	Nil
SIZE:	M (6 1/2′ tall)
MORALE:	Steady (11-12)
XP VALUE: Hobgoblin	35
Sub-chief	65
Chief	120

Hobgoblins are a fierce humanoid race that wage a perpetual war with the other humanoid races. They are intelligent, organized, and aggressive.

The typical hobgoblin is a burly humanoid standing 6¹/₂′ tall. Their hairy hides range from dark reddish-brown to dark gray. Their faces show dark red or red-orange skin. Large males have blue or red noses. Hobgoblin eyes are either yellowish or dark brown while their teeth are yellow. Their garments tend to be brightly colored, often bold, blood red. Any leather is always tinted black. Hobgoblin weaponry is kept polished and repaired.

Hobgoblins have their own language and often speak with orcs, goblins, and carnivorous apes. Roughly 20% of them can speak the common tongue of man.

Combat: Hobgoblins in a typical force will be equipped with po-learms (30%), morningstars (20%), swords and bows (20%), spears (10%), swords and spears (10%), swords and morning stars (5%), or swords and whips (5%).

Hobgoblins fight equally well in bright light or virtual darkness, having infravision with a range of 60 feet.

Hobgoblins hate elves and always attack them first.

Habitat/Society: Hobgoblins are nightmarish mockeries of the humanoid races who have a military society organized in tribal bands. Each tribe is intensely jealous of its status. Chance meetings with other tribes will result in verbal abuse (85%) or open fighting (15%). Hobgoblin tribes are found in almost any climate or subterranean realm.

A typical tribe of hobgoblins will have between 20 and 200 (2d10 x 10) adult male warriors. In addition, for every 20 male hobgoblins there will be a leader (known as a sergeant) and two assistants. These have 9 hit points each but still fight as 1+1 Hit Die monsters. Groups numbering over 100 are led by a sub-chief who has 16 hit points and an Armor Class of 3. The great strength of a sub-chief gives it a +2 on its damage rolls and allows it to fight as a 3 Hit Die monster. If the hobgoblins are encountered in their lair, they will be led by a chief with AC 2, 22 hit points, and +3 points of damage per attack, who fights as a 4 Hit Die monster. The chief has 5-20 (5d4) sub-chiefs acting as bodyguards. Leaders and chiefs always carry two weapons.

Each tribe has a distinctive battle standard which is carried in-to combat to inspire the troops. If the tribal chief is leading the battle, he will carry the standard with him, otherwise it will be held by one of his sub-chiefs.

In addition to the warriors present in a hobgoblin tribe, there will be half again that many females and three times as many children as adult males.

Fully 80% of all known hobgoblin lairs are subterranean complexes. The remaining 20% are surface villages which are fortified with a ditch, fence, 2 gates, and 3-6 guard towers. Villages are often built upon ruined humanoid settlements and may incorporate defensive features already present in the ruins.

Hobgoblin villages possess artillery in the form of 2 heavy catapults, 2 light catapults, and a ballista for each 50 warriors. Underground complexes may be guarded by 2-12 carnivorous apes (60%).

They are highly adept at mining and can detect new construction, sloping passages, and shifting walls 40% of the time.

Ecology: Hobgoblins feel superior to goblins or orcs and may act as leaders for them. In such cases, the "lesser races" are used as battle fodder. Hobgoblin mercenaries may work for powerful or rich evil humanoids.

Koalinth

This marine species of hobgoblin is similar to the land dwelling variety in many respects. Koalinth dwell in shallow fresh or salt water and make their homes in caves.

Their bodies have adapted to marine environments via the evolution of gills. Their webbed fingers and toes give them a movement rate of 12 when swimming. Their bodies are sleeker than those of hobgoblins and they have light green skin. They speak an unusual dialect of the hobgoblin tongue.

They tend to employ thrusting weapons like spears and pole arms. Koalinth are every bit as disagreeable as hobgoblins, preying on every thing they come across, especially aquatic humanoid and demi-human races. They detest aquatic elves.

Homonculous

CLIMATE/TERRAIN:	Any
FREQUENCY:	Very rare
ORGANIZATION:	Solitary
ACTIVITY CYCLE:	Any
DIET:	Omnivore
INTELLIGENCE:	See below
TREASURE:	Nil
ALIGNMENT:	See below

NO. APPEARING:	1
ARMOR CLASS:	6
MOVEMENT:	6, Fl 18 (B)
HIT DICE:	2
THAC0:	19
NO. OF ATTACKS:	1
DAMAGE/ATTACK:	1-3
SPECIAL ATTACKS:	Bite causes sleep
SPECIAL DEFENSES:	See below
MAGIC RESISTANCE:	See below
SIZE:	T(18" tall)
MORALE:	Elite (13-14)
XP VALUE:	270

Homonculi are small mystical beings created by magicians for spying and other special tasks.

The average homonculous is vaguely humanoid in form. It is 18 inches tall and its greenish, reptilian skin may have spots or warts. They have leathery, bat-like wings with a span of 24 inches and a mouth filled with long, pointed teeth that can inject a potent sleeping venom.

Combat: The homonculous is a quick and agile flyer which uses this ability to great advantage in combat. It can dart to and fro so quickly that any attempt to capture it short of a net or *web* spell is almost impossible.

In combat, the homonculous will land on its chosen victim and bite with its needle-like fangs. In addition to doing 1-3 points of damage, the creature injects a powerful venom. Anyone bitten by the homonculous must save vs. poison or fall into a comatose sleep for 5-30 (5d6) minutes.

The creature's saving throws are the same as those of its creator. While most attacks against either the homonculous or creator do not affect the other, there is one exception. Any attack which destroys the homonculous causes its creator to suffer 2-20 (2d10) points of damage. Conversely, if the creator is slain, the homonculous also dies and its body swiftly melts away into a pool of ichor.

Habitat/Society: Homonculi are artificial creatures created by wizards as living tools. The process by which one is created is long, complicated, and expensive. Any wizard who desires a homonculous servant must first locate and hire an alchemist. The wizard must provide one pint of his own blood and 500-2,000 (1d4 x 500) gold pieces. The blood becomes the basis for the creature's body while the money pays for a variety of other supplies and the alchemist's time. The alchemist requires 1-4 weeks to transform the blood into the necessary magical base. The wizard is then sent for and required to cast *mending, mirror image,* and *wizard eye* spells upon the fluids. As the last of these spells is worked, the fluids spontaneously coagulate and form the body of the homonculous.

The homonculous is telepathically linked to its creator. It knows everything that its master knows and transmits everything it sees and hears to him. The creator can telepathically control the actions of the homonculous at a range of up to 480 yards. The homonculous will never willingly travel beyond the limits of contact with its master, though it can be removed from that region by force. As soon as it loses contact with its master, the creature panics and will do anything to regain contact. Contact between the two cannot be maintained across planar or dimensional barriers. If either the creator or homonculous is on another plane, the homonculous will remain near the point where it was last in contact with its master.

Homonculi are a reflection of their creator. They have the creator's alignment, basic intelligence, and even physical mannerisms. They are mute but can write if the creator is literate. They may assist their creator in a variety of tasks including magical endeavors, although they cannot themselves cast spells.

Homonculi lairs are in the homes of their creators. Indulgent wizards may provide a specially built bed, nest, or living chamber. Otherwise, the homonculous simply perches wherever it can.

Ecology: Homonculi are nothing more than tools. They have no place in the natural world and are not part of any ecological system. They provide the wizard who created them with a variety of useful services. Commonly, a homonculous is called upon to act as a spy, scout, messenger, or emissary. Because of the potential harm which the death of a homonculous inflicts on its master, they are seldom employed as body guards or living weapons.

Although they are magical creations, homonculi possess the same biological functions as non-magical creatures. They must rest and require food and drink in order to survive. When eating, they share the tastes of their masters and generally consume about as much as a typical cat.

There are rumors of magical means by which non-wizards can acquire their own form of homonculous. Although these are not widely believed to be valid, there are those who report having seen the process or its results first hand. If such a procedure exists, it would be quite valuable to its discoverer.

Hook Horror

CLIMATE/TERRAIN:	Any/Subterranean
FREQUENCY:	Rare
ORGANIZATION:	Clan
ACTIVITY CYCLE:	Any
DIET:	Omnivore
INTELLIGENCE:	Low (5-7)
TREASURE:	P
ALIGNMENT:	Neutral

NO. APPEARING:	2-12
ARMOR CLASS:	3
MOVEMENT:	9
HIT DICE:	5
THAC0:	15
NO. OF ATTACKS:	3
DAMAGE/ATTACK:	1-8/1-8/2-12
SPECIAL ATTACKS:	Nil
SPECIAL DEFENSES:	Nil
MAGIC RESISTANCE:	Nil
SIZE:	L (9′ tall)
MORALE:	Steady (11-12)
XP VALUE:	175

The hook horror is a bipedal, underground-dwelling monster that looks like a cross between a vulture and a man with hooks instead of hands.

The hook horror stands about nine feet tall and weighs almost 350 pounds. It has a tough, mottled grey exoskeleton, like that of an insect. Its front limbs end in 12-inch-long hooks. Its legs end in feet that have three small hooks, like long, sharp toes. Its head is shaped like that of a vulture, including the hooked beak. Its eyes are multifaceted. It is thought that the hook horror is distantly related to the cockroach or cave cricket.

Hook horrors do not have a smell to humans and demi-humans, but an animal would detect a dry musty odor. They communicate in a series of clicks and clacks made by the exoskeleton at their throats. In a cave, this eerie sound can echo a long way. They can use this to estimate cavern sizes and distances, much like the sonic radar of a bat.

Combat: Hook horrors have acute hearing and are surprised only on a roll of 1. They always know their territory, and they try to ambush unsuspecting travelers or denizens. Each round they swing with both hooks. If in any round both hit, during that round their beaks hit automatically. They automatically inflict 2d6 points of damage each round with the beak until at least one of the hooks is dislodged.

The eyesight of the hook horrors is very poor. They are blinded in normal light. They use their extremely acute hearing to track and locate prey. Since their eyesight is so poor anyway, they suffer no combat or movement penalties if blinded or in complete darkness. They attack silenced opponents with the penalties others suffer when attacking blind.

Hook horrors are natural climbers, as their hooks give them excellent purchase on rock surfaces. They can move at normal speed up vertical surfaces that are not sheer. Their great weight means that they cannot hang from the ceiling like other insects.

Habitat/Society: The obvious penalty for having hooks instead of hands is that hook horrors cannot use weapons or tools. They can only pick up items in their beaks. This severely restricts their ability to amass large treasures.

A clan of hook horrors most often lives in caves and underground warrens. The entrance is usually up a vertical or steeply sloped rock wall. Each family unit in the clan has its own small cavern off a central cave area. The clan's eggs are kept in the safest, most defensible place. The clan is ruled by the eldest female, who does not participate in combat. The eldest male, frequently the mate of the clan ruler, takes charge of all hunting or other combat situations and is considered the war chieftain.

Members of a clan rarely fight each other. They may quarrel or not cooperate, but they rarely come to blows. Clans sometimes fight each other, but only when there is a bone of contention, such as territorial disputes. It is rare for a clan of hook horrors to want to rule large areas or to conquer other clans.

Hook horrors have poor relationships with other races. Although they do not foolishly attack strong parties, generally other creatures are considered to be meat. They retreat when faced with a stronger group. Hook horrors do not recognize indebtedness or gratitude. Their simple language does not even have a term for these concepts. Just because a player character saves the life of a hook horror does not mean that it will feel grateful and return the favor.

Ecology: Although hook horrors are basically omnivores, they prefer meat. They can eat just about any cave-dwelling fungus, plants, lichens, or animals. Hook horrors are well acclimated to cave life. They have few natural predators, although anything that managed to catch one would try to eat it.

The hook horror's exoskeleton dries and becomes too brittle for use after a month or so.

Horses

	Draft	Heavy	Medium	Light	Pony	Wild	Riding	Mule
CLIMATE/TERRAIN:	Any non-mountainous	Any non-mountainous	Any non-mountainous	Any non-mountainous	Any non-mountainous	Any non-mountainous	Any non-mountai nous	Any non-mountainous
FREQUENCY:	Common	Uncommon	Uncommon	Uncommon	Uncommon	Uncommon	Common	Common
ORGANIZATION:	Herd	Herd	Herd	Herd	Herd	Herd	Herd	Herd
ACTIVITY CYCLE:	Day	Day	Day	Day	Day	Day	Day	Day
DIET:	Herbivore	Herbivore	Herbivore	Herbivore	Herbivore	Herbivore	Herbivore	Herbivore
INTELLIGENCE:	Animal (1)	Animal (1)	Animal (1)	Animal (1)	Animal (1)	Animal (1)	Animal (1)	Animal (1)
TREASURE:	Nil	Nil	Nil	Nil	Nil	Nil	Nil	Nil
ALIGNMENT:	Neutral	Neutral	Neutral	Neutral	Neutral	Neutral	Neutral	Neutral
NO. APPEARING:	1	1	1	1	1	5-30(5d6)	5-50(5d6)	1
ARMOR CLASS:	7	7	7	7	7	7	7	7
MOVEMENT:	12	15	18	24	12	24	24	12
HIT DICE:	3	3+3	2+2	2	1+1	2	3	3
THAC0:	17	17	19	19	19	19	17	17
NO. OF ATTACKS:	1	3	3	2	1	1	2	1 or 2
DAMAGE/ATTACK:	1-3	1-8/1-8	1-6/1-6	1-4/1-4	1-2	1-3	1-2/1-2	1-2/1-6
SPECIAL ATTACKS:	Nil	Nil	Nil	Nil	Nil	Nil	Nil	Nil
SPECIAL DEFENSES:	Nil	Nil	Nil	Nil	Nil	Nil	Nil	Nil
MAGIC RESISTANCE:	Nil	Nil	Nil	Nil	Nil	Nil	Nil	Nil
SIZE:	L	L	L	L	M	L	L	M
MORALE:	Unsteady (5-7)	Unsteady (5-7)	Unsteady (5-7)	Unsteady (5-7)	Unsteady (5-7)	Unsteady (5-7)	Unsteady (5-7)	Unsteady (5-7)
XP VALUE:	65	120	65	35	35	35	65	65

Horses are large quadrupeds often used for transportation, or as pack and draft animals, by human and demihuman races. They are frequently bred for their speed and for their beauty.

A horse can be solid white, gray, chestnut, brown, black, or various reddish tones; its hide can instead show a variation or combination of these colors. Some of the more interesting variations include the piebald, which has a coat of large, irregular patches of black and white; the palomino, with its rich yellow-gold coat and white mane and tail; and the dapple gray, which is dark gray with flecks of lighter color on the chest, belly, and hindquarters.

In addition to the coat's color, the horse may have markings of various sorts. The long hairs of the mane and tail can be lighter, darker, or of the same color as the body of the horse. Possible markings include socks (meaning the leg from the hoof, halfway to the knee, or hock, is white); a white muzzle; a blaze (a wide band of white from the top of the horse's head to the tip of its nose); and a star (a white, diamond-shaped patch set on the horse's forehead, right between its eyes).

Horses are measured in "hands." One hand equals 4 inches.

Combat: War horses will fight independently of the rider on the second and succeeding rounds of a melee. Other breeds fight only if cornered. Most attack twice per round by kicking with their front hooves.

Unless specially trained, horses can be panicked by loud noises, strange smells, fire, or sudden movements 90% of the time. Horses trained and accustomed to such things (usually warhorses) panic only 10% of the time.

Habitat/Society: The horse's gestation period is about 11 months. Mares (female horses) usually give birth to a single foal (young horse). Twins do occur, but only about 10% of the time (or less). Even triplets are possible, but are extremely rare. The foal is weaned after six months. It is mature after two to three years, and is considered adult at age five. The usual life span of a horse is 30-35 years, though rare exceptions have lived to age 50, and hard-worked horses rarely live past age 12.

Only 10% of ponies and wild horses can be trained to serve as warhorses. Of all the breeds and varieties listed here, only mules are agile enough for use in mountainous or subterranean environments.

Ecology: Modern horses evolved in temperate plains and grasslands. Domestic breeds can be found anywhere people live (even in the high mountains, if the local roads are good).

Horses can carry great weights for long periods of time, but not without tiring. The table below shows the maximum weight a horse can carry; as illustrated, greater weights cause the horse to move at slower movement rates.

Horse Table 1.

	Maximum weight in pounds at		
Type of Horse	Full speed	Half speed	One-third speed
Draft	260	390	520
Heavy war horse	260	390	520
Medium war horse	220	330	440
Light war horse	170	255	340
Pony	160	240	320
Wild	170	255	340
Riding	180	270	360
Mule	250	375	500

A horse can also move at speeds higher than those given as their base movement rates, as shown on the table below. The horse's normal movement rate is considered a trot.

Horse Table 2.

Type of Horse	Walk	Trot	Canter	Gallop
Draft	6	12	18	24
Heavy war horse	6	15	21	27
Medium war horse	9	18	27	36
Light war horse	12	24	36	48
Pony	6	12	18	24
Wild	12	24	36	48
Riding	12	24	36	48
Mule	6	12	18	24

As noted in Chapter 14 of the *Player's Handbook*, in a day of travel over good terrain, a creature can travel a number of miles equal to twice its normal movement rate. A horse's overland movement rate can be improved by pushing it to a canter or gallop. A canter can be safely maintained for two hours, or a gallop for one hour, but the horse must be walked for an hour before its speed can again be increased. For the effects of increasing a horse's speed enough to affect its overland movement rate, see Chapter 14 of the *DMG*.

A horse will not gallop when loaded with enough material to reduce its normal movement rate by half; nor will it canter or gallop if carrying a load which will reduce its normal movement rate to one-third normal (see Horse Table 1).

Draft Horse

Draft horses are large animals bred to haul very heavy loads, and are usually trained to be part of a dray team. Muscular but slow, these ponderous animals haul freight over long distances without complaint, and are frequently used by traders.

War Horse

Warhorses are bred and trained to the lance, the spear, and the sword. They have higher morale than other horses, and are not as skittish about sudden movements and loud noises. The choice of knights and cavalry, these are the pinnacle of military horses. There are three varieties; heavy, medium and light.

Heavy war horses are similar to draft animals. Large and muscular, they are relatively slow. Their size and powerful legs allow them to be armored in plate, and to carry a warrior in plate, as easily as a pony carries saddle bags. A good heavy war horse, fully trained, costs 400 or more gold pieces.

Medium war horses are lighter and smaller than their heavy cousins. They can be encumbered with leather or light plate armor and carry a rider wearing leather or light plate. The advantage of the medium war horse is its increased speed. The price of a medium war horse is 200 gp or more.

Light war horses are the fastest of the breed. They can carry warriors in leather armor, but are rarely armored themselves. They make excellent mounts for raiding parties, light cavalry, and thieves. Light war horses cost 150 gp or more.

Pony

Small horses used primarily for transportation and occasionally farm work, ponies are a lively breed. They are more excitable than the larger horses, but frequently more gentle, as well. They are sometimes trained and used as war horses by several of the smaller demihuman races. Prices vary depending on training and size, but most cost around 500 gp.

Wild Horse

Wild horses can be captured and trained to serve as mounts or work ponies. Training usually takes twice as long as training a domestic horse. Wild horses are hardy but jittery, and difficult to catch in the wild. They are sometimes hunted for food by human and demihuman tribes.

Riding Horse

Riding horses are bred to the saddle. Perhaps the most common of all horses, they are ridden, worked, and raced by humans and demihumans alike. The price of a riding horse will vary, depending on its bloodlines, training, and appearance. Fast and agile, this breed is a good choice for personal transportation and general use.

Mule

Sterile hybrids of horses and donkeys, mules are very sure-footed and exceptionally stubborn. They can be ridden by patient handlers who know how to control them, but are best used as pack animals in difficult or mountainous terrain. They are sometimes used by adventurers, for they are the only breed that can be taken into subterranean regions. The price of mules depends on how much grief they have given their current owners.

Steppe Pony

A steppe pony is not attractive, graceful, or large, but its homely, ungainly appearance disguises an animal of great endurance, speed, and strength. A steppe pony looks like a cross between a horse and a pony, but is a breed unto itself. They are small, averaging 13 hands (4'4") at the withers, and they have short necks, large heads, and heavily boned bodies. Their winter coat is shaggy and gives them the appearance of being "half-wild." They are most commonly colored copper or bronze, with a light yellow stripe running down their backs.

These horses are tough, hard to kill, and aggressive in battle. They have most of the same characteristics as a light war horse, with a few exceptions. It attacks three times per round, its third attack being a bite which causes 1-3 points of damage. The steppe pony's thick, shaggy coat and tough hide gives it an AC of 6. Its short legs are powerful and can carry horse and rider swiftly, over long distances; its small back is also very strong and it can carry as much as a medium war horse (220/330/440). The steppe pony is even-tempered and steady in battle; its morale is average (8-10), and it panics very rarely (5% chance) due to such things as fire and loud noises.

The steppe pony has remarkable endurance. It can survive by grazing alone and does not require feeding and handling by its rider, so separate supplies of grain are not needed. It can be ridden for long distances without tiring or faltering. A +3 modifier is applied to the pony's saving throws for lameness and exhaustion checks when travelling overland.

In spite of all its qualities, the steppe pony is not sought after or considered valuable. It is most commonly ridden by nomadic tribes. Outside the steppes, the animal is almost completely unknown and does not command high prices at auction. Only breeders who know the steppe pony's qualities, and who seek strength and stamina in their own horses' bloodlines, are likely to consider the steppe pony as valuable.

Human

	Aborigine/Caveman	Adventurer	Bandit/Brigand
FREQUENCY:	Rare	Very rare	Common
TREASURE:	Nil	By class	J, N, Q
ALIGNMENT:	Neutral	Any	Chaotic evil
NO. APPEARING:	10-100 (10d10)	1-8	20-200 (20d10)
ARMOR CLASS:	8	Varies	10 to 6
HIT DICE:	1-6 hp/ 2 HD	Varies	1-6 hp
THAC0:	20 (19)	Varies	20
MORALE:	Average (9)	Varies	Average (9)
XP VALUE:	15 (35)	Varies	15

	Barbarian/Nomad	Berserker/Dervish	Farmer/ Herder
	Rare	Rare	Common
	L, M	Nil	Nil
	Any	Neutral/L. good	Neutral (good)
	30-300 (30d10)	10-100 (10d10)	1-20
	10 to 6	10 to 6	10
	1-6 hp	1-6 hp	1-6 hp
	20	20	20
	Average (9)	Fearless (20)	Average (9)
	15	15	15

	Gentry	Knight	Mercenary
FREQUENCY:	Common	Very rare	Rare
TREASURE:	J,K,L,M,N,Q	L,M	L,M
ALIGNMENT:	Any	Any lawful	Any
NO. APPEARING:	1-20	1-4	10-100 (10d10)
ARMOR CLASS:	10	4 or 2	7 to 4
HIT DICE:	1-6 hp	2 +	2-8 hp
THAC0:	20	19 or less	20
MORALE:	Average (9)	Elite (14 +)	Steady (11-12)
XP VALUE:	15	Varies	15

	Merchant Sailor/Fisherman	Merchant/Trader	Middle Class
	Common	Common	Common
	10-60 sp	10-1,000 gp	J,M,N
	Any	Any	Any
	4-80 (4d20)	30-300 (3d10 × 10)	2-40 (2d20)
	10 to 8	10 to 5	10
	1-6 hp	1-6 hp	1-6 hp
	20	20	20
	Average (9)	Average (9)	Average (9)
	15	15	15

	Peasant/Serf	Pilgrim	Pirate/Buccaneer
FREQUENCY:	Common	Uncommon	Common
TREASURE:	Nil	I	J,M,N,Q
ALIGNMENT:	Any	Any	Any evil
NO. APPEARING:	1-100	10-100 (10d10)	30-300 (30d10)
ARMOR CLASS:	10	10 to 8	10 to 6
HIT DICE:	1-6 hp	1-6 hp	1-6 hp
THAC0:	20	20	20
MORALE:	Average (9)	Average (9)	Average (9)
XP VALUE:	15	15	15

	Police/Constabulary	Priest	Sailor
FREQUENCY:	Uncommon	Very rare	Common
TREASURE:	10-60 sp	J,K,M	L,M
ALIGNMENT:	Any lawful	Any	Any
NO. APPEARING:	2-20 (2d10)	1-8	4-80 (4d20)
ARMOR CLASS:	7 to 4	Varies	10 to 8
HIT DICE:	1-6 hp	1-6 hp	1-6 hp
THAC0:	20	20	20
MORALE:	Steady (10)	Varies	Average (9)
XP VALUE:	15	Varies	15

	Slaver	Soldier	Thief/Thug
FREQUENCY:	Common	Uncommon	Common
TREASURE:	Nil	I	J,M,N,Q
ALIGNMENT:	Any	Any	Any evil
NO. APPEARING:	1-100	10-100 (10d10)	1-8
ARMOR CLASS:	10	8 to 4	10 to 8
HIT DICE:	1-6 hp	1-6 hp	1 to 3
THAC0:	20	20	20
MORALE:	Average (9)	Steady (10-12)	Varies
XP VALUE:	15	15	Varies

	Tradesman/Craftsman	Tribesman	Wizard
FREQUENCY:	Common	Rare	Very rare
TREASURE:	1-100 gp	Nil	L,N,Q
ALIGNMENT:	Any	Any	Any
NO. APPEARING:	2-12 (2d6)	10-100 (10d10)	1-8
ARMOR CLASS:	10	8	10
HIT DICE:	1-6 hp	1-6 hp	Varies
THAC0:	20	20	Varies
MORALE:	Average (8-9)	Average (9)	Varies
XP VALUE:	15	15	Varies

Aborigine/Caveman

These primitive humans are found in otherwise uninhabited regions. For every 10 aborigines there will be a 3rd-level fighter. Aboriginal tribes are always led by a chief (a 5th-level fighter) and 1-4 subchiefs (4th-level fighters). For every 10 aborigines encountered there is a 10% chance that they have a shaman (3rd-level priest) with them.

Most encounters (60%) will be with predominantly male war or hunting/gathering parties. There is a 40% chance that an encounter will be in or near their lair. Aborigines make their lairs in natural shelters such as caves or forest groves. The number encountered above is for males; there will usually be an equal number of females and children in the lair.

Aborigines are typically armed with stone axes, spears, and clubs.

Adventurer

These are NPC counterparts of the PC's band, groups of fighters, thieves, priests, and wizards who band together in search of fame, fortune, and power. Typical adventuring bands consist of between two to eight members. Solitary adventurers may be separated from their group, lost, advanced scouts, or sole survivors of decimated groups.

After determining the base size of the group encountered, determine which class each belongs to:

d10	Class
1-4	Fighter
5-6	Cleric
7-8	Thief
9-10	Wizard

Determine the level of the party of adventurers; low, medium, high, or very high, and roll for each member on the table below.

Level	Level Range	Die
Low	1-3	(1d3)
Medium	4-7	(1d4+3)
High	7-12	(1d6+6)
Very high	9-20	(1d12+8)

A high level adventurer will have attracted followers who will accompany the party—1-100% of them. This can swell an encountered band's size to that of a small army.

Clerics and wizards will have 1-100% of their full spells at the time the encounter occurs (round down).

Higher level fighters and clerics will usually have plate mail and shields, and ride unbarded medium warhorses. Each level an adventurer has attained gives a cumulative 5% chance for magical items as shown below. Roll for each item marked "Y." Reroll if a cursed or otherwise undesirable item occurs, but only one reroll is allowed for each category. If no usable item is indicated, the adventurer has no item in that category.

Item	Fighter	Wizard	Cleric	Thief
Armor	Y	N	Y	N
Shield	Y	N	Y	Y
Sword	Y	N	N	Y
Misc. Weapon	Y	N	Y*	Y
Potion	Y	N	Y	Y
Scroll	N	Y	Y	N
Ring	N	Y	N	Y
Wand/Staff/Rod	N	Y	N*	N
Misc. Magic	N	Y	Y	Y

*If there is no usable miscellaneous weapon, roll again for possibility of a wand/staff/rod. If one is indicated but is unusable by a priest, there is no such item present.

In addition, such adventurers have ordinary treasure. Fighters have type L and M; clerics J, K, and M; wizards L, N, and Q; and thieves J, N, and Q.

Bandit/Brigand

Bandits are rural thieves who openly prey on travelers and isolated dwellings. They travel in groups of 20-200, usually led by high level fighters, rogues, wizards, and priests. For every 20 bandits encountered, there will be an additional 3rd-level fighter. If 100+ are encountered, the leader will be at least 8th level. Bandits are typically armed with swords, spears, and small shields. Up to 20% may be armed with bows. Bandits may wear no armor (50%), leather (35%), padded (10%), or ring mail (5%). Brigands are better equipped and will have higher morale.

Barbarian/Nomad

Barbarians belong to primitive cultures that possess rudimentary skills such as animal husbandry and simple manufacturing (weaving, carving). They may live in villages of simple buildings or in portable structures like tents, tepees, yurts, or wagons. In aquatic regions, they may live on watercraft like canoes or rafts.

Barbarians are typically armed with swords, knives, bows, spears, and clubs. Armor is limited to shields, helmets, and chestplates. They tend to be hostile toward unfamiliar wizards. Barbarians are adept at surprising opponents; such opponents have a −5 penalty on their surprise rolls.

Berserker/Dervish

Berserkers are violent war parties prone to manic behavior in battle. When encountered, berserkers drive themselves into a battle frenzy that raises their fighting skills and morale. Berserkers attack twice per round, or once at +2. Many use leather armor and shields, giving them Armor Class 7. Berserkers need never make morale checks.

Dervishes are highly religious nomads. Due to their fanatical nature, dervishes add 1 to their attack rolls and damage dice. They never check morale in combat.

If encountered during a peaceful period, berserkers may be indistinguishable from normal warrior bands; dervishes may be mistaken for armed pilgrims.

Farmer/Herder

These are simple people involved in the production of agricultural goods. About 65% of all encounters will be with farmers tilling their land. Encounters with herders may occur anywhere there is grazing land or a market for their herds. Encounters with herders also involve the herd animals, whatever they are.

Gentry

These are the upper classes. They are not the ruling nobility, but their wealth and connections make them nearly as powerful. Each member of the gentry encountered may be accompanied by 0-3 guards (d4-1) and 1-6 servants. The guards are mercenary fighters of 1st to 6th level and armed with sword and spear. The servants might fight as 0-level fighters, but are more likely to panic. The gentry themselves might be armed with daggers and short swords.

Knight

Knights are armored, mounted fighters directly serving their lord. They may be on a quest, a specific mission, or simply patrolling their lord's realm. Knights may be accompanied by their squires, hirelings, and other followers (50%). Knights are armed with sword, lance, mace or flail, and dagger. Armor includes a shield and either plate or chain mail. A knight rides a medium or heavy warhorse, usually a barded mount.

About 5% of encounters will be with a vanquished knight. Being stripped of arms and armor, the knight may be mistaken for any non-warrior class. The knight may even support this deception, at least until weaponry becomes available.

See *Adventurer* to determine level and special possessions.

Human

Mercenary Soldier

These are groups of low level fighters who hire themselves to the highest bidder. When encountered, there is an even chance they may be already hired and on their way to a war, meeting with a prospective employer, open for employment, or on their way home and not willing to take on a new task just yet.

See *Adventurer* to determine level and special possessions.

Merchant Sailor/Fisherman

Men of the sea are usually found on or near open waters. If encountered inland, sailors may be ferrymen on streams or rivers. Fishermen will either be putting out to a fishing site, fishing, or returning with their catches. Sailors may be armed with knives, short swords, cutlasses, or belaying pins (1 point of damage).

Merchant/Trader

Merchants and traders deal in goods and services. Those encountered in the wild are traveling in caravans in search of new business. Only 10% of the number encountered are actually merchants: 10% are drovers and the rest are mercenary guards. The guards are led by a fighter (6th-11th level) and a lieutenant one level lower. Each leader is accompanied by 12 guards of 2nd level. For each 50 people in the caravan there is a 10% chance of a wizard (6th-8th level) and a 5% chance of a priest (5th-7th level), as well as a 15% chance of a thief (8th-10th level) accompanied by 1-4 thieves (3rd-7th level). All such leaders, guards, and special characters are in addition to the number of merchants, drovers, and normal guards.

The treasure is mostly in trade goods (90%). The caravan has 10 pack animals or one wagon per 5,000 gp value.

Middle Class

These are travelers journeying on personal business. They are found primarily in civilized regions, although pioneers may be encountered in relatively peaceful frontier regions. Middle class travelers may be armed with knives, daggers, and short swords.

Peasant/Serf

Peasants are farmers, herders, and simple tradesmen of low social class. Unlike serfs, peasants are freemen.

Serfs are totally subject to the local lord; they are the lowest of the social classes. They farm and perform the brute labor functions on large agricultural holdings. Serfs, really, are little more than slaves.

Both peasants and serfs may be armed with daggers, clubs, quarterstaves, and farming tools. They never have any treasure except under the rarest of occasions when they are able to hoard scavenged goods.

Pilgrim

Pilgrims are groups of the devout on their way to or from a holy place. They can be found anywhere.

A group of pilgrims will always be accompanied by priests and other character classes. These people may be acting as leaders, guards, or pilgrims. Groups of pilgrims always include one to six 2nd-level priests, one to four 4th-level priests, one or two 6th-level, and one 8th-level priest (accompanied by one 3rd- and one 5th-level assistant). For every 10 pilgrims, there is a 10% chance of one to eight fighters (1st-8th level) and 1-6 thieves (2nd-7th level). There is a 5% chance per 10 pilgrims of a wizard of 6th-9th level. If the pilgrims are lawful good, the fighters will be paladins; if the pilgrims are chaotic good, the fighters will be rangers. If the party is neutral, the priests will be druids. If the pilgrims are lawful evil, they all fight as berserkers, although armed only with daggers.

Pilgrim alignment is determined below:

d100	Alignment
01-35	Lawful good
36-55	Chaotic good
56-65	Neutral
66-85	Lawful evil
86-00	Chaotic evil

About 75% of pilgrim bands encountered are on foot. There is a 5% chance that a high level priest will be carrying a religious artifact, carefully hidden and protected by traps and magic.

Pirate/Buccaneer

These are seafaring thieves and fighters. Pirates are always led by a captain of 8th or 10th level—8th if fewer than 200. The captain will have a 6th- or 7th-level lieutenant and four mates of 4th level. For every 50 pirates encountered, there will be a 3rd-level fighter, as well as a 15% chance for a cleric of 12th-15th level and a 10% chance for a wizard of 6th-9th level. For every 100 pirates, there will be a 5th-level fighter. All of these are in addition to the pirates already indicated by the dice.

Pirates wear leather armor; leaders wear chain mail. All are armed with knives, swords, and polearms. Some will be armed with crossbows, either light (20%) or heavy (10%). In addition their ships may be equipped with ballistae or catapults.

Buccaneers are similar, but are neutral with evil tendencies.

Police/Constabulary

These are the duly appointed representatives of the local government, concerned with upholding the laws, maintaining the peace, and carrying out their superior's will. If constables are encountered in the wilderness, they might be pursuing a fugitive (50%) or investigating a case on the outskirts of their jurisdiction (50%). Constables are the equivalent of fighters of 1st-4th level. Wilderness encounters include a 25% chance that the constables are accompanied by a mob. The mob is composed of citizenry temporarily deputized to assist the police; they fight as 0-level fighters.

Priest

These are typical NPC priests traveling on personal business or on a mission. The number encountered refers to the number of actual priests. If they are of high enough level, they might also have followers accompanying them (50%).

See "Adventurers" to determine level and special possessions.

Sailor

Nonmerchant sailors are the seagoing armed forces of the local government, acting as police or soldiers. They may be patrolling their home waters, pursuing a waterborne criminal, or on their way to or from a mission in other waters. Each ship is commanded by a captain (6th-level fighter) and a first officer (5th-level fighter). Sailors are armed with swords, knives, bows, and polearms. They may also be armed with heavier weapons such as catapults and ballistae.

Slaver

Slavers are usually found in control of a band of captive slaves; if no slaves are present, the slavers may be mistaken for mercenaries or brigands. The slavers' leader might be a thief, fighter, or fighter/thief (6th-11th level), assisted by a lieutenant one level lower. Each leader is accompanied by 1-12 guards of 1st or 2nd level. For each 50 slaves and slavers, there is a 10% chance of a wizard (6th-8th level) and a 5% chance of a priest (5th-7th level); these work for the slavers.

There are 10 slaves present for each 1-10 slavers. Slaves are treated the same as serfs. They may be recently acquired captives being taken from their homelands or long-time slaves being moved to a new market. Such slaves will be on foot and linked together in strings of 10-100 by ropes or chains. They will be willing to help any adventurers who try to rescue them, although they will be limited in the help they can provide. Slaves may be any class or type, but only 1% of captives belong to one of the character classes.

Soldier

These are organized militia engaged in the defense of their home region. Soldiers are led by a captain (6th level or higher) and a lieutenant (1-4 levels lower). Each leader is accompanied by 1-12 soldiers of 1st or 2nd level. Most soldiers are engaged in routine patrols of the homeland. If local wars are occurring, there is a 50% chance that the soldiers are either heading off to the war or returning from it. There is a 5% chance of a cleric (5th-7th level) for each 50 soldiers present.

See "Adventurers" to determine level and special possessions.

Thief/Thug

These are low level rogues who, if not already engaged in a crime, may attempt to rob wealthy or weak-looking adventurers. Thieves may be armed with concealed weapons such as knives, darts, blackjacks, and short swords.

See "Adventurers" to determine level and special possessions.

Tradesfolk/Craftspeople

People engaged in the trades and crafts will be about their business when encountered. They may be operating a shop, acquiring materials for their business, or traveling to or from a client's location. They are willing to do business with adventurers, provided they are properly paid. They will not attack except to defend themselves. Note that 1% of all tradesfolk may be retired adventurers. Tradesmen may be armed with knives, quarterstaves, and tools.

About 90% of their treasure is merchandise or equipment.

Tribal Culture

Tribal societies are the heart of primitive cultures; people hunt, fish, and farm near their simple villages. They are found in any climate.

For each 10 tribespeople, there will be an additional 3rd-level fighter. Tribes are led by a chief (a 5th-level fighter) and 1-4 subchiefs (4th-level fighters). For every 10 encountered, there is a 4th-level priest with them, and for each 30 tribespeople encountered, a 6th-level priest. The tribe has a shaman (8th-level priest). Tribal priests tend to be druidical in nature.

Tribal villages are made of local materials (grass, bamboo, mud, ice). In addition to the males encountered, there will also be an equal number of women and a 75% chance of 20-50 slaves.

Tribesmen's weapons are typically clubs, knives, spears, and bows. Armor is limited to shields.

Wizard

These are typical NPC wizards. They may be engaged in personal business, gathering materials, or traveling. The number encountered refers to the number of actual wizards. They may be accompanied by 0-3 (1d4-1) servants and guards for each wizard. Guards are fighters 1-4 levels lower than the wizard they protect.

See "Adventurers" to determine level and special possessions.

Hydra

	Hydra	Lernaean	Pyrohydra	Cryohydra
CLIMATE/TERRAIN:	Any swamp or subterranean	Any marsh, swamp or subterranean	Any marsh, swamp or subterranean	Any arctic
FREQUENCY:	Uncommon	Very rare	Rare	Very rare
ORGANIZATION:	Solitary	Solitary	Solitary	Solitary
ACTIVITY CYCLE:	Any	Any	Any	Any
DIET:	Carnivore	Carnivore	Carnivore	Carnivore
INTELLIGENCE:	Semi- (2-4)	Semi- (2-4)	Semi- (2-4)	Semi- (2-4)
TREASURE:	Nil	Nil	Nil	Nil
ALIGNMENT:	Neutral	Neutral	Neutral	Neutral
NO. APPEARING:	1	1	1	1
ARMOR CLASS:	5	5	5	5
MOVEMENT:	9	9	9	9
HIT DICE:	5-12	5-12	7-8	5-8
THAC0:	See below	See below	See below	See below
NO. OF ATTACKS:	5-12	5-12	5-8	5-8
DAMAGE/ATTACK:	See below	See below	See below	See below
SPECIAL ATTACKS:	Nil	Extra heads	Fire	Cold
SPECIAL DEFENSES:	Nil	Extra heads	Nil	Nil
MAGIC RESISTANCE:	Nil	Nil	Nil	Nil
SIZE:	G (30' long)	G (30' long)	G (30' long)	G (30' long)
MORALE:	Average (8-10)	Average (8-10)	Average (8-10)	Average (8-10)
XP VALUE:	2,000	3,000	3,000	3,000

Heads	THAC0	Damage		Heads	THAC0	Damage
5	15	1-6		9	12	1-8
6	13	1-6		10	10	1-8
7	13	1-8		11	10	1-10
8	12	1-8		12	9	1-10

Hydrae are immense reptilian monsters with multiple heads. For each Hit Die the hydra has, it will have one head. The chart above lists the THAC0 value for hydrae, the number of heads and the damage that they inflict each time they bite.

Hydrae are gray-brown to dark brown, with light yellow or tan underbellies. Their eyes are amber and their teeth are yellow-white. Hydrae have between 5 and 12 heads (1d8 +4).

Combat: Hydrae always have 8 points on each of their Hit Dice and all heads must be severed before the hydra dies. A hydra can bring up to four heads into action against a single foe, biting once with each of them.

Each time a hydra takes 8 points of damage, one of its heads is assumed to have been severed. When this happens, a natural reflex seals the neck arteries shut to prevent blood loss.

Hydrae attack according to the number of heads they have. Therefore, a 10-headed hydra continues to attack as a 10 HD monster even after several heads have been slain.

Attacks on the body have no effect unless a single attack inflicts damage equal to the hydra's original hit points.

Habitat/Society: Hydrae are solitary creatures who prefer dismal surroundings. They gather only to mate.

Ecology: Despite the hydra's size and multiple attacks, they are often preyed upon by dragons. They are impossible to train.

Lernaean Hydra

Although similar to a normal hydra, Lernaean hydrae will regenerate two heads for each one that is severed. A maximum of 12 heads can be grown. New heads form in 1-4 rounds and can be avoided only by the prompt application of flame to the neck following the attack which destroyed the first head. This hydra's body is immune to all attacks.

Pyrohydra

These reddish hydra have 7 or 8 heads which are able to breathe a jet of fire (5' wide and 2' long) twice per day. This attack does 8 points of damage, halved if a save vs. breath weapon is made.

Cryohydra

Each head of this purplish-brown hydra is able to breathe a stream of frost 10 feet wide and 20 feet long which does 8 points of damage. A save vs. breath weapon is allowed for half damage.

Imp

	Imp	Quasit
CLIMATE/TERRAIN:	Any	Any
FREQUENCY:	Very rare	Very rare
ORGANIZATION:	Solitary	Solitary
ACTIVITY CYCLE:	Any	Any
DIET:	Carnivore	Carnivore
INTELLIGENCE:	Average	Low
TREASURE:	O	Qx3
ALIGNMENT:	Lawful evil	Chaotic evil
NO. APPEARING:	1	1
ARMOR CLASS:	2	2
MOVEMENT:	6, Fl 18 (A)	15
HIT DICE:	2+2	3
THAC0:	19	17
NO. OF ATTACKS:	1	3
DAMAGE/ATTACK:	1-4	1-2/1-2/1-4
SPECIAL ATTACKS:	See below	See below
SPECIAL DEFENSES:	See below	See below
MAGIC RESISTANCE:	25%	25%
SIZE:	T (2' tall)	T (2' tall)
MORALE:	Average (8-10)	Average (8-10)
XP VALUE:	1,400	2,000

Imps are diminutive creatures of an evil nature who roam the world and act as familiars for lawful evil wizards and priests.

The average imp is a 2' humanoid with leathery, bat-like wings, a barbed tail, and sharp, twisted horns. Its skin is a dark red and its horns and jagged teeth are a gleaming white.

The imp can *polymorph* itself into two other animal forms. The most commonly encountered alternate forms are those of a large spider, raven, giant rat, or goat. In such forms the imp is physically identical to a normal animal.

Combat: In its natural form, the imp attacks with the wicked stinger on its tail. In addition to inflicting 1-4 points of damage, this stinger injects a powerful poison which is so deadly that those who fail their save versus poison are instantly slain by it. When it is *polymorphed*, the imp attacks with the natural weaponry of its adopted form, though the goat and raven forms lack damaging attacks.

The imp can use its special magical abilities no matter what its form. All imps are able to *detect good, detect magic,* or become *invisible* at will. Once per day they can use a *suggestion*.

Imps are immune to attacks based on cold, fire, or electricity and resist all other spell attacks as if they were 7 Hit Die creatures. They can be harmed only by silver or magical weapons and are able to regenerate one hit point per melee round.

Habitat/Society: Imps are beings of a very evil nature who originate on the darkest of evil planes. Their main purpose on the Prime Material plane is to spread evil by assisting lawful evil wizards and priests. When such a person is judged worthy of an imp's service, the imp comes in answer to a *find familiar* spell.

Once they have contacted their new "master", imps begin at once to take control of his actions. Although imps maintain the illusion that the summoner is in charge, the actual relationship is closer to that of a workman (the imp) and his tools (the master).

Although an imp's body can be destroyed on the Prime Material plane, it is not so easily slain. When its physical form is lost, its corrupt spirit instantly returns to its home plane where it is reformed and, after a time, returned to our world to resume its work.

While they are technically in the service of their master, imps retain a basic independence and ambition to become more powerful someday. They may acquire treasure from those they slay, and will often pilfer valuables encountered during their travels.

The imp confers some of its powers upon its master. A telepathic link connects the two whenever they are within one mile of each other. This enables the master to receive all of the imp's sensory impressions, including its infravision. The master also gains the imp's inherent 25% magical resistance and is able to regenerate just as the imp does. If the imp is within telepathic range, the master acts as if he were one level higher than he actually is. Conversely, if the imp is more than a mile away, the master acts as if he were one level of ability below his actual rank. If the imp is killed, the master instantly drops by four levels, though these can be regained in the usual manner.

Ecology: Imps are the errand boys of the powerful evil beings who command the darkest planes. They often act as emissaries and agents, but their primary task is to enhance the spread of evil in our world.

Quasit

Quasits are chaotic evil counterparts to imps. The chaotic evil priests and wizards which quasits "serve" gain the same benefits and disadvantages that an imp's master does. Like imps, each quasit can assume two other forms. Those most commonly chosen by quasits are bats, giant centipedes, frogs, or wolves. They can use their magic in any of their forms.

The quasit attacks with its clawed hands (doing 1-2 points each) and its deadly bite (doing 1-4 points). The quasit's claws are coated in a toxin which causes anyone struck by them to save versus poison or lose one point of dexterity for 2-12 (2d6) rounds. The effects of multiple wounds are cumulative.

Quasits can turn *invisible, detect good,* or *detect magic* at will. They regenerate 1 hit point per round and can unleash a blast of fear with a 30 foot range radius once per day. Once each week the quasit can *commune* with the lower planes (asking up to 6 questions).

Quasits can only be harmed by cold iron or magical weapons. They are able to resist magic 25% of the time, save as if they were 7 Hit Die monsters and are immune to cold, fire, and lightning.

Imp, Mephit

	Fire	Ice	Lava	Mist	Smoke	Steam
CLIMATE/TERRAIN:	Any	Any	Any	Any	Any	Any
FREQUENCY:	See below	See below	See below	See below	See below	See below
ORGANIZATION:	Solitary	Solitary	Solitary	Solitary	Solitary	Solitary
ACTIVITY CYCLE:	Any	Any	Any	Any	Any	Any
DIET:	Special	Special	Special	Special	Special	Special
INTELLIGENCE:	Average (8-10)	Average (8-10)	Average (8-10)	Average (8-10)	Average (8-10)	Average (8-10)
TREASURE:	Nx2	N	N	N	N	N
ALIGNMENT:	Any evil	Any evil	Any evil	Any evil	Any evil	Any evil
NO. APPEARING:	See below	See below	See below	See below	See below	See below
ARMOR CLASS:	5	5	6	7	4	7
MOVEMENT:	12, FL 24 (B)	12, FL 24 (B)	12, FL 24 (B)	12, FL 24 (B)	12, FL 24 (B)	
HIT DICE:	3+1	3	3	3+2	3	3+3
THAC0:	17	17	17	17	17	17
NO. OF ATTACKS:	2	2	2	2	2	2
DAMAGE/ATTACK:	1-3/1-3	1-2/1-2	1/1	1/1	1-2/1-2	2-5/2-5
SPECIAL ATTACKS:	See below	See below	See below	See below	See below	See below
SPECIAL DEFENSES:	See below	See below	See below	See below	See below	See below
MAGIC RESISTANCE:	Nil	Nil	Nil	Nil	Nil	Nil
SIZE:	M (5' tall)	M (5' tall)	M (5' tall)	M (5' tall)	M (5' tall)	M (5' tall)
MORALE:	Average (8-10)	Average (8-10)	Average (8-10)	Average (8-10)	Average(8-10)	Average (8-10)
XP VALUE:	420	420	420	420	420	420

Mephits are nasty little messengers created by powerful lower planes creatures. They are evil and malicious by nature and appear on the Prime material plane only to perform evil deeds. Six types of mephits are known: fire, ice, lava, mist, smoke, and steam. Each is created from the substance for which it is named.

Mephits appear as thin, 5-foot humanoids with wings. Their faces have exaggerated features, including hooked noses, pointed ears, wide eyes, and protruding chins. Their skin continually oozes the stuff from which they were made. Mephits speak a common mephit tongue.

Combat: In battle, mephits attack with either clawed hands or breath weapons. Damage is variable depending on the type of mephit encountered. All mephits have the ability to *gate* in other mephits; the type *gated* in and percentage chance for success varies with the mephit initiating the gating (see below for details).

Habitat/Society: Mephits love tormenting helpless creatures and bragging about their latest evil accomplishments. They wear garish, vulgar costumes in bizarre colors and outrageous designs. They give themselves pompous, impossibly long names, such as Garbenaferthal-sprite-slayer-greatest-of-all-the-steam-mephits.

Mephits assume a groveling, craven, yes-master stance around their bosses. Toward victims and each other, mephits drop their humble servant persona and take on the arrogant air of a superior being. A limited camaraderie exists between mephits of the same order. Disputes between different types are often settled by a friendly game of tug-a-demihuman.

Mephits are usually assigned to deliver some message or pick to up packages on the lower planes, but occasionally (5%) they are sent to the Prime material plane. Missions on the Prime material plane include retrieving a particular person, delivering a special magical item, or just spreading a little mayhem (so folks don't forget the lower planes are still there).

Ecology: Mephits lead brief, troublesome lives. They are quickly created and destroyed, but they have no predetermined life span. They never eat, but must return to the substance from which they were formed to heal damage (usually 1 hit point per turn in contact).

Fire Mephit
The most mischievous of all mephits, these fiends play terrible pranks on other mephits (such as pushing lava mephits into water and watching them harden) and on their victims.

Touching a fire mephit causes 1 point of heat damage (no saving throw). Their clawed hands rake for ld3 points of damage each, plus 1 hit point of heat damage per hit.

Fire mephits may use their breath weapon three times a day. It has two forms. The first is a flame jet 15 feet long and 1-foot wide. This jet automatically hits one target, of the mephit's choosing, for ld8+1 points of damage (half if saving throw is successful). The second form is a fan of flame covering a 120° arc directly in front of the mephit to a distance of 5 feet. Any creature in the arc suffers 4 points of damage, no saving throw allowed.

Fire mephits may also cast *heat metal* and *magic missile* (two missiles) spells each once per day. Once every hour a fire mephit can attempt to *gate* in another mephit. The chance for success is 25% and the summoned mephit is either fire, lava, smoke, or steam (equal probability of each).

Ice Mephit
Ice mephits are angular in form, with translucent ice-blue skin. They live on the colder lower planes and never mix with fire, lava, smoke, or steam mephits. Ice mephits are aloof and cruel, surpassing all other mephits in the fine arts of torture and wanton destruction.

In combat, ice mephits attack with two clawed hands, inflicting 1-2 points of damage each. In addition, their chilling touch has a freezing effect, reducing the victim's hit points by 1 per hit, no saving throw allowed. These effects are cumulative and last three to four turns, or until the victim is healed to full hit points (whichever comes first).

Ice mephits may breathe a volley of ice shards three times per day. This volley automatically hits a single victim within 15 feet of the mephit. Damage is 1d6, halved if the victim rolls a successful saving throw.

Once per hour an ice mephit may attempt to *gate* in one other mephit. The chance of success is 25% and the summoned mephit is either mist or ice (equal probability of each).

Lava Mephit
Lava mephits are the least intelligent of all mephits. They are slow on the uptake and frequently the brunt of fire mephit jokes. Lava mephits generate extreme heat that can be felt 30 feet away. Their claws are small and soft, causing only 1 point of damage when they hit, but each hit inflicts an additional 1d8 points of

heat damage. The touch of a lava mephit automatically melts or burns most materials. The rate of this destruction varies from one hour to burn through an inch of wood to three rounds to completely melt plate armor.

Their breath weapon is a molten blob of lava usable once every three melee rounds. This blob automatically hits one target within 10 feet of the breathing mephit (ld6 points of damage, no saving throw). A lava mephit may use this weapon a maximum of eight times, after that, the mephit must recharge by soaking in a lava pool for on hour. Mephits may recharge during battle, if they come in contact with lava during combat, they regenerate 2 hit points per melee round. This ability is, of course, lost if the mephit is brought to 0 hit points or less, at this point the mephit is dead. These fiends may shapechange into a pool of lava 3 feet in diameter by 6 inches deep. This maneuver does not recharge the breath weapon. They may still be harmed normally when in this lava pool form.

Once every hour, a lava mephit may attempt to *gate* in 1-2 other mephits. The chance of success is 25%. If two are summoned, they are of the same type (equal probability of fire, lava, smoke, or steam).

Mist Mephit

Mist mephits fancy themselves as spies par excellence and practice this ability on other mephits. They are quick to report other mephits who show mercy or any other treasonous behavior, and they never engage in idle banter with other mephits. Mist mephits have the ability to see clearly in fog or mist. Their skin is pale green. They never engage in melee unless they are trapped. Their soft claws inflict just 1 point of damage when they hit. Mist mephits may breathe a sickly, green ball of mist, every other round, up to three times an hour. This ball automatically envelopes one victim within 10 feet of the breathing mephit. The victim must roll a successful saving throw vs. poison or suffer ld4 + 1 points of choking damage and be blinded for ld4 rounds. In addition to the breath weapon, mist mephits can create a *wall of fog* (as the spell) once per day (at a 3rd level ability). They can also assume gaseous form once per day and often use this ability to spy on others or escape combat.

Once per hour a mist mephit may attempt to *gate* in 1-2 other mephits. The chance of success is 20%. If two mephits arrive, they are of the same type (either ice or mist, equal probability).

Smoke Mephit

Smoke mephits are crude and lazy. They spend most of their time lounging around invisible, smoking pipe weed, telling bad jokes about their creators, and shirking their responsibilities.

Smoke mephits' two clawed hands cause 1-2 points of damage each. Their breath weapon consists of a sooty ball usable every other melee round, with no limit on the number of times it can be used in a day. The sooty ball automatically strikes one creature of the mephit's choice within 20 feet, causing ld4 points of damage and blinding the victim for 1-2 rounds. No saving throw is permitted.

Smoke mephits may cast *invisibility* and *dancing lights* once each per day. Once per hour they can attempt to *gate* in 1-2 other mephits. The chance of success is 20%, with equal probability of the summoned mephits being fire, lava, smoke, or steam. If two mephits appear, they are of the same type.

When a smoke mephit dies, it disappears in a flash of flame. The flash causes 1 point of damage to all creatures within 10 feet (no saving throw).

Steam Mephit

Steam mephits are the self-appointed overlords of all mephits. They frequently give orders to weaker mephits. In addition to hissing steam escaping from their pores, steam mephits leave a trail of near-boiling water wherever they walk.

The hardened claws of a steam mephit cause 1d4 points of damage each, plus 1 additional point of heat damage per touch (no saving throw). In addition, the victim is 50% likely to be stunned for one round. These effects are cumulative, so a victim raked twice could be stunned for two rounds.

Steam mephits can breath a scalding jet of water every other round; no limit to the number of times per day this can be used. This jet has a 20-foot range and automatically hits its target. Damage is 1d3 points (no saving throw) with a 50% chance of stunning the victim for one round.

Once per day a steam mephit may create a rainstorm of boiling water over a 20-by 20-foot area. This storm inflicts 2d6 points of damage to all victims caught in the area of effect, with no saving throw allowed. Steam mephits may also *contaminate water* once per day (reverse of *purify water*).

Once per hour a steam mephit may attempt to *gate* in 1-2 other mephits with a 30% chance of success. There is an equal probability that the summoned mephits are either fire, lava, smoke, or steam. If two are summoned: they are of the same type.

Unlike other mephits, who will delay an attack for as long as possible, steam mephits are ruled by their oversized egos. They will even ambush even large, well-armed parties, striking first with boiling rainstorms, then concentrating their breath weapons on the nearest wizard or priest.

Insect

Insect	#AP	AC	MV	HD	THAC0	# of Att	Dmg/Att	Morale	XP Value
Ant, Giant	1-100	3	18	2 or 3	16	1	1-6 or 2-8	Average (9)	Worker: 35 Warrior: 175
Ant Lion, Giant	1	2	9, Br 1	8	12	1	5-20	Average (8)	1,400
Aratha	1	3	11	9	11	4	1-10(×4)	Elite (16)	6,000
Aspis, Cow	1	7	3	10	11	1	3-18	Elite (13-14)	2,000
Aspis, Drone	2-20	3	15	6	15	2	1d4 or weapon	Elite (13-14)	650
Aspis, Larva	6-60	6	1, Sw 6	2 to 5	2 HD: 19 3-4 HD: 17 5 HD: 15	1	2-7	2-3 HD: Steady 4-5 HD: Elite	2 HD: 65 3 HD: 120 4 HD: 175 5 HD: 270
Assassin Bug	2	5	6, Fl 18 (C)	1+1	20	1	1-4	Unsteady (5-7)	120
Bee, Worker	1-10	6	9, Fl 30 (D)	3+1	17	1	1-3+poison	Steady (11-12)	175
Bee, Soldier	1	5	12, Fl 30 (C)	4+2	15	1	1-4+poison	Champion (15-16)	270
Bumblebee	1	5	6, Fl 24 (E)	6+4	13	1	1-6+poison	Elite (13-14)	650
Cave Cricket	1-8	4	6, Hop3	1+3	20	Nil	Nil	Unreliable (2-4)	15
Dragonfly, Giant	1-6	3	3, Fl 36 (B)	7	13	1	3-12	Steady (11-12)	1,400
Dragonfly, Larva	1	3	9, Sw 3 jet 24	6+1	15	1	3-18	Steady (11-12)	650
Ear Seeker	1-4	9	1	1 hp	20	1	See below	Unsteady (5-7)	15
Firefriend	1-4	4	3, Fl 18 (B)	1+4	20	1	1-2	Unsteady (5-7)	35
Fly, Bluebottle	1-10	6	9, Fl 30 (D)	3	19	1	1-8	Unsteady (5-7)	65
Fly, Horsefly	1-4	5	6, Fl 27 (D)	6	17	1	2-16	Unsteady (5-7)	270
Fyrefly	1	5	Fl 18 (A)	1 hp	15	1	1	Steady (11)	175
Horax	3-30	3	15	4	17	1	2d8	Average (10)	Adult: 270 Young: 15
Hornet, Giant	1	2	6, Fl 24 (B)	5	15	1	1-4	Average (8-10)	650
Pernicon	4-200	3	12	1 hp	20	1	1-10	Unreliable (4)	15
Praying Mantis	1-2	5	15	2 to 12	2 HD: 19 4 HD: 17 6 HD: 15 8 HD: 13 10 HD: 11 12 HD: 9	3	2-4 HD: 1-2/1-2/1-4 6-8 HD: 1-4/1-4/1-8 10 HD: 1-6/1-6/1-10 12 HD: 1-8/1-8/1-12	Fearless (19-20) Fearless (19-20) Fearless (19-20) Fearless (19-20) Fearless (19-20) Fearless (19-20)	2 HD: 35 4 HD: 120 6 HD: 270 8 HD: 650 10 HD: 1,400 12 HD: 2,000
Termite, Giant Harvester									
King	1	5	6	6+6	15	1	3-18	Unreliable (2-4)	975
Queen	1	4	3	8+8	13	1	5-30	Unsteady (5-7)	1,400
Soldier	3-18	2/8	9	2+2	19	1	1-4	Elite (13-14)	120
Worker	6-60	2/10	9	1+2	20	1	1-2	Average (8-10)	35
Tick, Giant	3-12	3	3	2 to 4	2 HD: 19 3-4 HD: 17	1	1-4	Average (8-10)	2 HD: 35 3 HD: 65 4 HD: 120
Wasp, Giant	1-20	4	6, Fl 21 (B)	4	17	2	2-8/1-4	Average (8-10)	420

Insects are the heartiest and the most numerous of creatures. Normal insects are found almost everywhere. The giant variety, many of which are listed here, with added brawn and power, make tough opponents.

Ant, Giant
Both worker and warrior ants fight. If a warrior manages to bite, it also tries to sting for 3d4 points damage. A successful save reduces damage to 1d4. The queen has 10 HD but does not move or fight.

Ant Lion, Giant
The ant lion builds tapering pits in loose sand and waits for prey to fall in. Once the ant lion hits, all additional attacks are automatic.

Aratha
Aratha grasp and hold prey with their 8-foot clawed tentacles that can lash out 20 feet. An aratha does not bite opponents, but chews flesh torn from prey by its tentacles.

Psionics Summary:

Level	Dis/Sci/Dev	Attack/Defense	Score	PSPs
9	3/1/7	PsC,MT,PB/All	13	202

Psychokinetic - *Devotions:* molecular agitation.
Psychometabolism - *Devotions:* body equilibrium, suspend animation.
Telepathy - *Sciences:* psychic crush. *Devotions:* attraction, empathy, mind thrust, psionic blast.

Aspis, Cow
Aspis cows exude a dangerous corrosive that coats the body and adheres to the walls and floor of the chambers. This corrosive causes damage every round her opponents stay in her chamber.

Aspis, Drone
Most combat situations are handled by aspis drones. They rise on two rear legs, leaving the other four limbs to wield two weapons and two shields, increasing its AC to 2. All aspis are immune to cold and electrical damage; fire-based attacks cause only half damage.

Aspis, Larva
Aspis larvae attack with their perpetually ravenous jaws.

Assassin Bug
The male assassin bug attacks first with the female close to the battle. Those bitten must save vs. poison or that part of the body is paralyzed for one hour. The female attacks that same location the following round to inject 1d6+6 eggs. In 1d12+12 hours, the eggs hatch, and each larva causes 1 point of damage per hour. After two weeks, the larva emerge as adults. Only powerful spells like *wish* and *limited wish* will erase the infestation.

Bee, Worker
Worker bees use their stinger in combat. The victim must save vs. poison or suffer and additional 1d4 points of damage. Bees lose their stinger after one use and die in an hour. If encountered at the hive, there will be 20 times the normal number of bees.

Bee, Soldier

Soldier bees are identical to worker bees, except their sting causes more damage, and the victim must save with a −1 penalty.

Bumblebee

Bumblebee poison causes an additional 1d6 points of damage unless a save vs. poison (with a −1 penalty) is made. If encountered at or near the nest, there will be 1d6+6 bumblebees, and a combative queen. The queen has 8d4 HD and a sting that causes 1d8 points of damage. The poison from her sting causes an additional 2-8 points of damage if a save vs. poison at a −2 penalty is failed. Bumblebees do not lose their stingers after use.

Cave Cricket

If a group of people are within 20 feet of a chirping cave cricket, the noise drowns out all speech and vocal spell casting. The noise inhibits the victim's ability to hear approaching predators and enemies.

Dragonfly

Giant dragonflies gain a −3 bonus to initiative rolls and a +4 Armor Class bonus against missile weapons. A dragonfly scoops tiny- and small-sized creatures into its leg basket and devours them in midair. When captured, its victim is attacked automatically. When attacking man- or large-sized creatures, the dragonfly darts in to bite with its mandibles, and backs up, always facing its opponent.

Dragonfly, Larva

These larva surprise their prey 50% of the time. Their mandibles are covered with a rubbery organ when not in use; so even before the attack, they appear to be inoffensive, toothless creatures.

Ear Seeker

The ear seeker needs warm places to lay its eggs, favoring locations like ears. The creature lays 8+1d8 eggs that hatch in 4d6 hours. The larva eat the surrounding tissue, deafening the victim. Constantly burrowing deeper into the victim's head where food and warmth are plentiful, the host has a 90% chance of dying in 1d4 days. After this time, the ear seekers emerge from the infested ear as adults. A *cure disease* removes the infestation but does not return the loss of hearing.

Firefriend (Giant Firefly)

In addition to its mandibles, the giant firefly can brighten its abdomen once every turn, creating a beam of greenish light that causes 5d4 points of damage; one-half damage if a save vs. wands is successful.

Fly, Giant Bluebottle

This breed of giant fly prefers carrion, offal, and the like. They are, however, attracted to sweet odors, and creatures covered with blood or open wounds.

Fly, Giant Horsefly

The largest of all giant flies, the giant horsefly alights on any creature to attack for blood with its tuberous mouth. After biting, the giant horsefly causes an equal amount of damage the next round by drawing blood, unless driven off.

Fyrefly

When a fyrefly contacts flammable objects, these items must save vs. normal fire or be consumed. Persons in burning clothing suffer 1d6 points of damage. Hits that do not strike burnable material, cause 1 point of damage to the victim.

Horax

Horax attack in packs, gaining a −1 bonus to initiative rolls. Once a horax scores a hit, it maintains its hold, causing damage every round.

Hornet, Giant

The solitary giant hornet swoops down on its prey, holding with its legs while its stinger repeatedly stabs the victim. A failed save vs. poison causes an additional 5d6 points of damage and 2d6 hours of paralyzation. Hornets do not lose their stingers when they attacks.

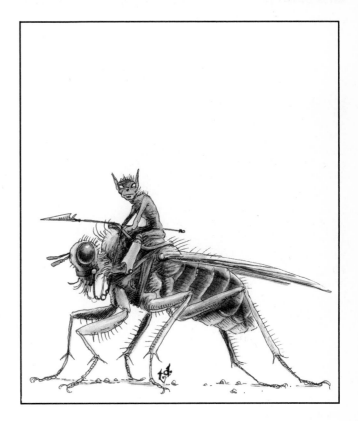

Pernicon

Pernicons attack by swarming victims and tearing at exposed flesh with their huge mandibles. Able to worm their way under clothing and armor, no one is completely safe from these creatures. When the swarm hits, the victim suffers 1d10 points of damage and 1 point of Constitution. If the Constitution dips below 3, the victim falls unconscious; below 1 and the victim dies. One point of Constitution is recovered per day, regardless of healing methods.

Praying Mantis, Gargantuan

The gargantuan praying mantis grabs prey, that inadvertently comes too close, with its front spiny arms. Besides its two claws, it bites with its strong mandibles, removing and chewing flesh with each unerring strike.

Termite, Giant Harvester

Groups of 30 or more worker termites are accompanied by soldiers. Soldier termites can spit an irritating liquid like kerosene once per turn at a range of 10 feet. This flammable liquid blinds creatures, for 5d4 rounds, that do not save vs. poison. If ignited, termite spittle causes 4d4 points of damage. King termites have double range spittle and can use this attack every other round, but the queen lacks this ability. Both the queen and king (and the eggs) are guarded by twice the number of workers and soldiers encountered normally, and who attack with a +1 to hit and a +5 bonus to morale rolls.

Tick, Giant

These creatures drop on victims from trees, stalactites, or rock formations. After the initial hit, the tick drains 1d6 hit points of blood every round until its drain total equals its hit point total. A victim has a 50% chance of contracting a fatal disease that kills the host in 2d4 days unless a *cure disease* is cast.

Wasp, Giant

These cooperative insects attack with both their bite and stinger. The venom carried by wasps is identical to that held by the giant hornet. Wasps do not lose their stingers when they attack.

Insect Swarm

	Velvet Ants	Grasshoppers and Locusts
CLIMATE/		
TERRAIN:	Tropical, sub-tropical or temperate/Forest, hills, and plains	Tropical and subtropical/Forest, hills, and plains
FREQUENCY:	Very rare	Very rare
ORGANIZATION:	Swarm	Swarm
ACTIVITY CYCLE:	Day	Day
DIET:	Omnivore	Herbivore
INTELLIGENCE:	Animal (1)	Animal (1)
TREASURE:	Nil	Nil
ALIGNMENT:	Neutral	Neutral
NO. APPEARING:	See below	See below
ARMOR CLASS:	8	8, FL6 (A)
MOVEMENT:	6	6, Fl 18 (C)
HIT DICE:	See below	1 hp/20 insects
THAC0:	See below	See below
NO. OF ATTACKS:	1	1
DAMAGE/ATTACK:	See below	See below
SPECIAL ATTACKS:	Poison	Nil
SPECIAL DEFENSES:	Nil	Nil
MAGIC RESISTANCE:	Nil	Nil
SIZE:	Individual: T (1" long); Swarm: see below	T (2" long); Swarm: see below
MORALE:	Unsteady (6)	Unsteady (6)
XP VALUE:	See below	See below

As individuals, velvet ants, grasshoppers, and locusts are relatively harmless. But in swarms, these insects can cause immense damage to fields and forests, as well as threatening the lives of all creatures in their path.

Velvet Ants

The velvet ant resembles a plump version of the common ant, except for the soft fuzz that covers its entire body. The fuzz is usually red or black, but it can also be yellow, brown, or orange.

Combat: A velvet ant swarm eats everything in its path, animal matter as well as vegetation. To determine the size of a swarm, roll 1d100 and multiply the result by 1,000. There are about 100 ants per square foot; therefore, a swarm of 10,000 ants forms a block about 10 feet per side.

If a swarm comes in contact with an obstacle, it turns 90° and continues. A victim in contact with a swarm has an 80% chance per round of being bitten and suffering 1d4 points of damage.

The victim must roll a successful saving throw vs. poison or suffer intense pain for the next 2d4 turns, making all attack and damage rolls with a -2 penalty during this time.

Each point of damage inflicted on an insect swarm kills 1d20 insects. They may be scattered with smoke or fire; immersion in water washes them off. If half of a swarm is killed, the survivors attempt to scatter and hide. If an entire swarm is killed, award 975 experience points.

Grasshoppers and Locusts

The grasshopper is about 2 inches in length and is usually green or brown in color. The grasshopper can make leaps of about four feet. Locusts are a type of grasshopper, with shorter antennae. They can rub their hind legs against their wings to produce a distinctive chirp.

Combat: Grasshopper and locust swarms fly from place to place in search of lush fields on which to settle and consume. These swarms move in straight lines and are easy to avoid.

To determine the size of a grasshopper swarm, roll 1d100 and multiply the result by 10,000. Multiply this result by 2 when determining the size of a locust swarm. There are about 20 grasshoppers or locusts per square foot (for convenience, assume there are 20 insects per cubic foot when approximating the size of flying swarm).

A victim in contact with a grasshopper or locust swarm has a 90% chance per round of being bitten and suffering 1 point of damage. Additionally, victims within a cloud of these insects have their vision reduced to 2d4 feet.

Each point of damage inflicted on an insect swarm kills 1d20 insects. They may be scattered with smoke or fire; immersion in water washes them off. If half of a swarm is killed, the survivors attempt to scatter. If an entire swarm is killed, award 2,000 experience points.

Habitat/Society: Insect swarms are migratory, sleeping at night wherever they happen to be. Females lay up to 100 eggs every year. These insects have no leaders or any specialized workers. They do not collect treasure.

Ecology: Velvet ants eat seeds, grasses, and meat, especially enjoying carrion. The poison of velvet ants renders them inedible to carnivores.

Grasshoppers and locusts prefer seeds and grains. Snakes, mice, birds, and spiders are among these insects' numerous natural enemies. Grasshoppers and locusts can be eaten by carnivores.

Intellect Devourer

	Adult	Larva
CLIMATE/TERRAIN:	Any subterranean or dark areas	Dark, moist areas
FREQUENCY:	Very rare	Rare
ORGANIZATION:	Solitary	Solitary
ACTIVITY CYCLE:	Any	During darkness
DIET:	Mental energy	Emotions
INTELLIGENCE:	Very (11-12)	Not ratable
TREASURE:	D	Qx1d20
ALIGNMENT:	Chaotic evil	Neutral (evil)
NO. APPEARING:	1-2	1-3
ARMOR CLASS:	4	5
MOVEMENT:	15	9
HIT DICE:	6+6	3+3
THAC0:	13	17
NO. OF ATTACKS:	4	1
DAMAGE/ATTACK:	1-4/1-4/1-4/1-4	2-5 (1d4+1)
SPECIAL ATTACKS:	Psionics, stalking	Psionics, poison
SPECIAL DEFENSES:	+3 weapon needed to hit; see below	Psionics
MAGIC RESISTANCE:	Nil (see below)	Nil
SIZE:	T (6" long)	T (6" long)
MORALE:	Fanatic (17-18)	Unsteady (5-7)
XP VALUE:	6,000	650

The term "intellect devourer" refers only to this creature's adult form; its larva is an ustilagor. Both resemble a brain on four legs. The body of the intellect devourer has a crusty protective covering, and its legs are bestial, jointed, and clawed. The ustilagor's body is soft and moist and usually covered with a gray fungus; it has a 3-foot-long tendril at the front, and its legs are spindly and coral-like. Though both forms are about brain-sized, the adult can use psionics to alter its size.

Combat: The ustilagor attacks by striking with its flexible tendril. The tendril secretes an alkaline substance which causes 1d4+1 damage on a successful hit, as well as another 1d4+1 damage the following round, unless the victim makes a successful saving throw vs. poison. The creature is quite agile, and can jump and dart quickly.

The ustilagor can also attack psionically, first making contact with a victim's mind. It uses aversion to give a victim an aversion to fungus or to a certain area; id insinuation to effectively paralyze the victim; or telepathic projection to increase an opponent's dislike or distrust of companions.

Despite its psionic prowess, the ustilagor cannot be attacked mentally (magically or psionically) except by psionic blast. Its fungal growth interferes with and prevents mental attacks, protects the ustilagor from drying out, prevents cerebral parasites from attacking, and makes the creature immune to fungal attacks and any power that reads or affects an aura.

The adult form also prefers to attack with psionics, though its three-taloned paws can all be used in the same round, as the creature jumps on an opponent and rakes.

Aside from its regular psionic powers (see below), the adult intellect devourer has specialized forms of three psionic powers; these are constantly in effect and cost no PSPs, but they do count as psionic activity for detection purposes. Through a special form of energy containment, the intellect devourer is immune to damage from normal and magical fires, and takes only one hit point per die of electrical damage; a form of split personality is always in effect, allowing the creature to attack with psionics and claws in the same round; and it has psionic sense with a 60 foot range.

The intellect devourer is immune to weapons with less than a +3 enchantment, and takes only 1 point of damage per hit from those weapons which can harm them. A *death spell* has only a 25% chance of success, but *power word: kill* is effective. A *protection from evil* keeps the intellect devourer at bay, and bright light (including that caused by fire) drives it away.

An intellect devourer hunts and stalks psionic creatures. After killing a psionic victim, it sometimes uses reduction to enter the body, devour the brain, and occupy its place. It reads the victim's mind as it devours it, then animates the body from within, using it to find other minds to attack and devour.

Psionics Summary:

	Level	Dis/Sci/Dev	Attack/Defense	Score	PSPs
Larva	2	2/1/5	II/M-	10	150
Adult	6	3/3/11	EW,II/M-,TS,IF	=Int	200

Intellect devourers have the following psionic powers; ustilagor have only those powers marked by asterisks:

• **Psychometabolism - Sciences:** ectoplasmic form*. **Devotions:** body equilibrium*, chameleon power, expansion, reduction.

• **Psychoportation - Devotions:** astral projection.

• **Telepathy - Sciences:** domination, mindlink. **Devotions:** aversion*, contact*, ego whip, ESP, id insinuation*, telepathic projection*.

Habitat/Society: Intellect devourers dwell beneath the ground or in dismal wilderness areas. Their reproductive method is unknown. The intellect devourer rarely protects its young, and may even devour them. Ustilagor develop a symbiotic relationship with a bizarre fungus which feeds on residual thought emanations from the ustilagor's victims. An ustilagor becomes an adult by consuming the brain of a psionic creature.

Ecology: Mind flayers raise intellect devourers, treating the ustilagor as culinary delights, and using adults as watch dogs. Both forms of the creature can be used as components in items and potions related to ESP and mind control.

Invisible Stalker

CLIMATE/TERRAIN:	Any
FREQUENCY:	Very rare
ORGANIZATION:	Solitary
ACTIVITY CYCLE:	Any
DIET:	Special
INTELLIGENCE:	High (13-14)
TREASURE:	Nil
ALIGNMENT:	Neutral

NO. APPEARING:	1
ARMOR CLASS:	3
MOVEMENT:	12, Fl 12 (A)
HIT DICE:	8
THAC0:	13
NO. OF ATTACKS:	1
DAMAGE/ATTACK:	4-16 (4d4)
SPECIAL ATTACKS:	Surprise
SPECIAL DEFENSES:	Invisibility
MAGIC RESISTANCE:	30%
SIZE:	L (8' tall)
MORALE:	Elite (13-14)
XP VALUE:	3,000

The invisible stalker is a creature from the elemental plane of Air. Those encountered on the Prime Material plane have almost always been summoned by wizards to fulfill a specific task.

The true form of the invisible stalker is unknown. On the Material, Astral, or Ethereal planes, the invisible stalker can only be perceived as a shimmering air mass which looks much like the refraction effect caused by hot air passing in front of cold.

Invisible stalkers understand the common speech of men, but can not speak it. They can converse only in their own language, which sounds much like the roaring and whooshing of a great wind storm.

Combat: Invisible stalkers attack by using the air itself as a weapon. It is capable of creating a sudden, intense vortex that batters a victim for 4-16 (4d4) points of damage. Such attacks affect a single victim on the same plane as the invisible stalker.

Due to their invisibility, these creatures impose a −6 penalty on the surprise rolls of those they choose to attack. Similarly, all opponents who are unable to see or *detect invisible* foes are at a −2 on their attack rolls. Although they are fully *invisible* on the Prime Material plane, their outlines can be dimly perceived on the Astral or Ethereal planes.

Invisible stalkers can only be killed on the elemental plane of Air. If attacked on another plane, they automatically return to their home plane when their total hit points are exceeded by the damage they suffered.

Habitat/Society: Little is known about the lives of these creatures on their home plane. It is assumed that they are similar to normal air elementals when encountered there.

Those present on the material plane are there as the result of a conjuration by some wizard. This magic causes the creature to serve its summoner for a time. The conjurer retains full command of the stalker until it either fulfills its duties or is defeated and driven back to its home plane. Once given a task, an invisible stalker is relentless. They are faultless trackers who can detect any trail less than a day old. If ordered to attack, they will do so with great fury and will cease their efforts only upon their own destruction or the direct orders of their master. Once their mission is accomplished, the creature is free to return to its home plane.

The invisible stalker is, at best, an unwilling servant. It resents any task assigned to it, although brief, uncomplicated labors

may be seen as something of a diversion and thus undertaken with little resentment. Tasks that require a week or more of its time will drive the invisible stalker to pervert the stated intent of the command. Such commands must be carefully worded and come from a powerful wizard. An invisible stalker may look for a loop hole in the command as a means of striking back at its master. For example, a simple command such as "keep me safe from all harm" may result in the stalker carrying the conjurer back to the elemental plane of air and leaving him there in a well hidden location.

Each day of the invisible stalker's indenturedness there is a 1% cumulative chance that the creature will seek a means to pervert its commands and free itself of servitude. If no option is open, the creature must continue to serve.

Ecology: Invisible stalkers are a species unwillingly transplanted to the Prime Material plane. They are slaves whose terms of servitude dominate their brief stays. Those who have been subjected to great hardship, assigned very difficult tasks, or who have faced death at the hands of humanoids, tend to retain a distrust or outright hatred of them. Those that have had an easy time during past periods of service or who are first time arrivals on the Prime Material plane may be easier to deal with. Such feelings may carry over to influence encounters with humanoids traveling in the aerial plane. Anyone who has befriended an invisible stalker in the past will find that voyages through the plane of elemental Air are far less hazardous than they might otherwise have been.

Invisible stalkers only obey those who actually summon them and few wizards can be commissioned to summon such a being on another's behalf. Some mercenary wizards have been able to construct the necessary summons onto scrolls that are usable by others. These sell for between 5,000 and 10,000 gp and are very dangerous to use. Even the slightest error can cause users of such scrolls to come to a tragic end.

CLIMATE/TERRAIN:	Shallow tropical waters
FREQUENCY:	Very rare
ORGANIZATION:	Tribe
ACTIVITY CYCLE:	Day
DIET:	Carnivore
INTELLIGENCE:	Average to High (8-14)
TREASURE:	P, R, S (in lair only)
ALIGNMENT:	Chaotic evil

NO. APPEARING:	5-12 (1d8 + 4)
ARMOR CLASS:	6
MOVEMENT:	Sw 12
HIT DICE:	1 +1 to 4 +4
THAC0:	1 +1 and 2 +2 HD: 19
	3 +3 HD: 17
	4 +4 HD: 15
NO. OF ATTACKS:	1
DAMAGE/ATTACK:	3-12
SPECIAL ATTACKS:	Spells, see below
SPECIAL DEFENSES:	Spells, see below
MAGIC RESISTANCE:	Nil
SIZE:	S-L (3'-8' wingspan)
MORALE:	Elite (13)
XP VALUE:	35
1 +1 HD priest	65
2 +2 HD priest	120
3 +3 HD guardian priest	270
4 +4 HD high priest	420
2 +2 HD vampiric	420
8 +8 HD greater vampiric	4,000

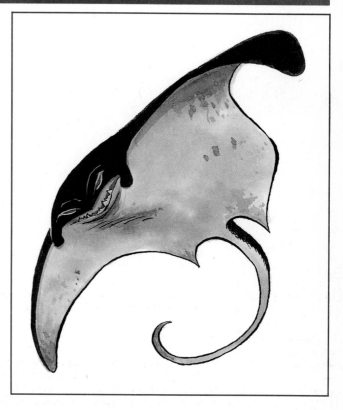

Ixitxachitl are a race of intelligent, aquatic beings that resemble small manta rays with barbed tails. They have an evil disposition and worship evil powers; they love to hunt marine humanoids, and then sacrifice or devour their catch.

Ixitxachitl is both singular and plural; it is properly pronounced ish-it-SHACH-itl, though many refer to them as icks-it-ZACH-it-ul or even icks-it-zuh-chit-ul.

Combat: A favored tactic of ixitxachitl is to hide in the sand of the ocean floor, wait for prey to pass by, then spring up and bite them. The creatures are not very stealthy, and this tactic gives them normal chances to surprise their prey.

Some ixitxachitl act as priests, learning special versions of spells which have only verbal components, from the following spheres: Charm, Divination, Elemental (Water), Necromantic, Healing, Protection, and Sun (Darkness only). For every 10 ixitxachitl encountered, there is one ixitxachitl with the abilities of a 2nd-level priest. For every 20, there is an individual with the powers of a 3rd-level priest. For every 50, there is one with 2 +2 Hit Dice and the abilities of a 5th-level priest.

When more than 50 are encountered, they are led by a high priest with 4 +4 HD and 8th-level ability. The high priest is accompanied by two guardian priests, each with 3 +3 HD and 6th-level ability. Guardian and high priests often have treasure type U, with magical items that can be used without hands.

For every 20 ixitxachitl encountered, there is a 50% chance they will be accompanied by a vampiric ixitxachitl. One in one hundred of these are greater vampiric ixitxachitl, but these are rarely encountered outside a city.

Habitat/Society: Though they are occasionally encountered in rivers, ixitxachitl live in shallow ocean depths. They usually have a community of 10-100 individuals, which lives in a maze of corridors inside a coral reef. A community usually has 20-200 humanoid slaves to do heavy labor for them, such as carving corridors. The community's entrance is hidden.

Large communities that have strong leaders, like a greater vampiric ixitxachitl, are sometimes built on the ocean floor. These large cities hold pyramids and other buildings which serve as lairs for small groups of the creatures. Rumors tell of ixitxachitl cities with populations in the thousands. The strongest ixitxachitl in the community leads its religious hierarchy, which controls the lives of the populace.

Ecology: Ixitxachitl have no natural predators, though they have many enemies, ranging from sahuagin to humans. They are vicious predators who prey on almost any living creature; they often over hunt a region, eliminating all life forms, forcing the ixitxachitl to find new hunting grounds.

Vampiric Ixitxachitl
These rare creatures are even more dangerous than the others. Each has 2 +2 HD and regenerates 3 hp per round. In addition to its normal damage, the bite of a vampiric ixitxachitl drains one life energy level. They look no different than other ixitxachitl, and often serve as guards for their leaders.

Greater Vampiric Ixitxachitl
These creatures are rare indeed; they achieve greater status only by being bitten by an existing greater vampiric ixitxachitl. These creatures have 8 +8 Hit Dice. They drain two life energy levels with a bite (except when the bite is performed on another vampiric member of their race). A greater vampiric ixitxachitl is the center of the large cities of its kind; it is their tyrannical ruler, and they worship it as the incarnation of a greater power. Captives are brought to it to be drained of life.

Jackalwere

CLIMATE/TERRAIN:	Any temperate
FREQUENCY:	Rare
ORGANIZATION:	Pack
ACTIVITY CYCLE:	Any
DIET:	Carnivore
INTELLIGENCE:	Very (11-12)
TREASURE:	C
ALIGNMENT:	Chaotic evil

NO. APPEARING:	1-4
ARMOR CLASS:	4
MOVEMENT:	12
HIT DICE:	4
THAC0:	17
NO. OF ATTACKS:	1
DAMAGE/ATTACK:	2-8 (2d4)
SPECIAL ATTACKS:	Gaze causes sleep
SPECIAL DEFENSES:	Hit only by iron and +1 or better magical weapons
MAGIC RESISTANCE:	Nil
SIZE:	S (3' long) as a jackal M (6' tall) as a human or hybrid
MORALE:	Steady (11-12)
XP VALUE:	270

The jackalwere is a terrible and savage creature which preys on unsuspecting travelers and other demihumans that it can ambush. Its ability to alter its shape at will makes it a most dangerous foe.

The jackalwere can be found in any of three forms, showing no preference for any one over the others. The first of these is that of a normal jackal. In this form it will often run and hunt with jackal packs. Its second form is a six foot tall, half-human/half-jackal hybrid which stands erect. In its third form, the jackalwere is physically indistinguishable from normal human beings. The exact physical characteristics of the jackalwere's human form varies according to the desires of the monster.

Combat: In its jackal form, the monster conforms to the statistics presented elsewhere in this volume. A careful observer, however, will find that the creature does not act in the manner typical of a normal jackal, for it is far more aggressive.

In its hybrid form, the jackalwere can attack with either its bite or with any weapons in hand. Because it has a great thirst for the blood of humans and demihumans, the jackalwere will use its bite whenever possible. Still, it will not avoid the use of weapons that will insure its victory in combat.

In its human form, the jackalwere can only attack with weapons. Although it may employ any manner of weapon, it greatly enjoys those which will cut and tear the flesh of its victims. In some cases, a jackalwere has been known to feed on the bodies of fallen enemies without reverting to its jackal or hybrid form.

In all forms, the jackalwere possesses a magical gaze. If an unsuspecting victim meets the monster's gaze, the victim must save versus spell or fall deeply asleep; the effect is identical to that of the *sleep* spell. Note that hostile, scared, or excited people are not considered to be unsuspecting.

The jackalwere's special defenses also function in all three forms. Only +1 or better magical weapons or those forged from cold iron will cause any damage to the jackalwere. Jackalweres revert to their jackal form after death.

Habitat/Society: When the jackalwere locates a victim it will assume human shape and approach its prey. It will seek to ease

the suspicions of its target, often pretending to be injured or otherwise in need, until it can employ its gaze attack. If this fails and the jackalwere is confronted with forceful resistance it will decide whether to flee or press the attack based on its estimation of its victim's strength.

The jackalwere spends its life hunting and killing any humans and demihumans it comes across. They roam the world in either the jackal or human form, seeking humanoids to kill, eat, and rob. They are sly creatures and masters of deceit.

Jackalweres are able to mate only in their jackal form. They may produce offspring either by mating with true jackals or other jackalweres, but only those young who were not of mixed blood will be jackalweres themselves. The children of a jackal and jackalwere mating will be jackals, although they will be unnaturally aggressive.

Female jackalweres give birth in five months to a litter of 1-4 pups. These are identical to jackal pups although they initially have 1 Hit Die. The pups grow quickly and add an additional Hit Die each year. Their jackal forms reach full growth at three years and pups are locked in that form for their first two years. At age two they gain the ability to assume their hybrid form and at age three they gain the ability to assume a human form which is apparently nine years of age. The human form grows at triple the normal human rate. If a parent in human form is discovered with its pups, it will often try to pass them off as pets.

Jackalweres may (20%) travel in the company of 1-6 normal jackals. Although these jackals are normal in every regard, the influence of the jackalwere tends to make them more fierce than normal. Jackals under the influence of a jackalwere will be hunters instead of scavengers.

Ecology: Jackalweres will not serve any but the most evil of humanoids, and even then only if they have the opportunity to slay more humans and demihumans than they could on their own.

Kenku

CLIMATE/TERRAIN:	Any land
FREQUENCY:	Uncommon
ORGANIZATION:	Clan
ACTIVITY CYCLE:	Any
DIET:	Omnivore
INTELLIGENCE:	Average (8-10)
TREASURE:	F
ALIGNMENT:	Neutral

NO. APPEARING:	2-8
ARMOR CLASS:	5
MOVEMENT:	6, Fl 18 (D)
HIT DICE:	2-5
THAC0:	2 HD: 19
	3-4 HD: 17
	5 HD: 15
NO. OF ATTACKS:	3 or 1
DAMAGE/ATTACK:	1-4/1-4/1-6 or by weapon
SPECIAL ATTACKS:	Nil
SPECIAL DEFENSES:	See below
MAGIC RESISTANCE:	30%
SIZE:	M (5'-7' tall)
MORALE:	Elite (13)
XP VALUE:	2 HD: 175
	3 HD: 420
	4 HD: 650
	5 HD: 975

Kenku are bipedal, humanoid birds that use their powers to annoy and inconvenience the human and demihuman races.

The typical kenku resembles a humanoid hawk wearing human clothing. Kenku have both arms and wings. The wings are usually folded across the back and may be mistaken at a distance for a large backpack. Height ranges from 5 to 7 feet. The feathers are predominantly brown with white underfeathers and face markings. The eyes are a brilliant yellow.

Combat: All kenku have the skills of 4th-level thieves. They are expert fighters and usually attack with a scimitar or quarterstaff. If unarmed, they attack with either pair of claws (two attacks for 1d4 points of damage apiece) and their beak (1d6 points of damage). If they are on foot, they use the hand claws. If in flight, the foot claws are used. They do not usually kill unless their own lives are threatened by the survival of their foe. All kenku have well-developed disguise skills. They have a 50% chance of passing for human, although their disguises often have telltale large noses.

A 3-Hit Die kenku has one 1st-level wizard spell, usually *magic missile*. Once each 30 days a kenku can shape change and retain that shape for up to seven days. A 4-Hit Die kenku has an extra 1st-level spell, often *shocking grasp*. They gain the innate ability to become invisible with no limitation on duration or frequency of use. A 5-Hit Dice kenku leader gains an additional 2nd-level mage spell, usually *mirror image* or *web*, and the innate ability to *call lightning* (the same as the 3rd-level priest spell).

Habitat/Society: Kenku are a secretive race that lives among the human and demihuman races without the bulk of the population ever being aware of their presence.

If a group of kenku is encountered, the group's size determines its composition. A group of five or fewer contains two 2-Hit Dice and three 3-Hit Dice kenku. A group of six or seven has a leader with 4 Hit Dice, three kenku with 3 Hit Dice, and the rest have 2 Hit Dice. A group of eight kenku adds a supreme leader of 5 Hit Dice.

Kenku do not speak; although they may give out bird-like squawks, these are gibberish. Kenku apparently communicate with each other telepathically. They are adept at symbols, sign language, and pantomime.

Kenku may appear to be friendly, helpful, and even generous. They freely give treasure to humans and demihumans, but it is rarely genuine and crumbles into dust within a day. They may offer nonverbal advice to humanoids, but this is carefully designed to mislead. It may actually lead the party into dangers and difficulties they might otherwise have avoided. As a rule of thumb, kenku have only a 5% chance of actually helping people.

The actual structure of kenku society is elusive. The kenku themselves either refuse to comment or lie. Those kenku lairs that have been encountered tend to be small underground chambers or cave complexes. It is believed that large caverns deep underground may hold sizeable kenku communities, including individuals of 6 Hit Dice or more and with greater magical powers.

Kenku reproduction is similar to that of large birds. The female lays a clutch of two to four eggs that hatch after 60 days. New hatchlings are featherless, helpless, and have 1 hit point each. Hatchlings grow swiftly and gain 1 hit point each month. Within six to eight months they have adult feathers and are able to function independently as 1-Hit Die kenku. At this point they can begin to learn to use the skills they need as adults (thieving, fighting, disguise). If a hatchling is captured, it either lacks this training or has whatever minimal skills it acquired before capture.

Younger kenku (3 Hit Dice or less) are reckless and prone to audacious plans. They have been known to pass themselves off as gods and collect the worshipers's offerings. Older kenku are more reserved and cunning, preferring to kidnap wealthy humans and demihumans as a source of revenue.

Ecology: Domestically raised kenku are prized as servants. Kenku eggs are commonly sold for 250 gp, hatchlings for 300-500 gp. However, this is a form of slave trade, with all the attendant complications. If a kenku discovers captive kenku, it will attempt to secretly rescue the captive and, if possible, kidnap the slave trader or owner. They will avenge slain kenku.

Ki-rin

CLIMATE/TERRAIN:	Sky
FREQUENCY:	Very rare
ORGANIZATION:	Solitary
ACTIVITY CYCLE:	Any
DIET:	Herbivore
INTELLIGENCE:	Supra-genius (19-20)
TREASURE:	I, S, T
ALIGNMENT:	Lawful good

NO. APPEARING:	1
ARMOR CLASS:	-5
MOVEMENT:	24, Fl 48 (B)
HIT DICE:	12
THAC0:	9
NO. OF ATTACKS:	3
DAMAGE/ATTACK:	2-8/2-8/3-18
SPECIAL ATTACKS:	Magic use
SPECIAL DEFENSES:	See below
MAGIC RESISTANCE:	90%
SIZE:	H (13' long)
MORALE:	Fanatic (18)
XP VALUE:	11,000

Level	Dis/Sci Dev	Attack Defense	Power Score	PSPs
9	4/5/18	All/All	= Int	200

The ki-rin is a noble creature that roams the sky in search of good deeds to reward or malefactors to punish.

The ki-rin's coat is covered with luminous golden scales like a sunrise on a clear morning. The thick mane and tail are a darker gold. The horn and hooves are gold tinged with pink. The eyes are a deep violet. The ki-rin has a melodious voice.

Ki-rin speak their own language. Since they are telepathic, they are able to mentally or verbally converse with virtually any living thing.

Combat: The ki-rin can physically attack with its powerful hooves (2d4 points of damage each) or a unicorn-like horn that gains a +3 bonus to its attack roll and inflicts 3d6 points of damage.

They can employ spells as if they were 18th-level mages. Each day they may use nine 1st-level spells, eight 2nd-level spells, seven 3rd-level spells, etc., all the way to one 9th-level spell.

The ki-rin's telepathy enables them to read conscious thoughts and are thus nearly impossible to surprise. The ki-rin also possess a variety of magical powers that can each be used once each day. They can create nutritious food and beverages for 2d12 people, as well as 32 cubic feet of soft goods or 18 cubic feet of wooden items. These are permanent creations. The ki-rin can create metal items with a total weight of up to 2,000 gp weight, but such items have very short life spans. In general, the harder the substance, the shorter the life span; for example, adamantite lasts an hour, while gold lasts 1d4+1 days.

The ki-rin can also generate illusions with audial, visual, and olfactory components. These illusions last without further concentration until the illusion is either magically dispelled or disrupted by disbelief. The ki-rin can assume *gaseous form, wind walk, summon weather,* and *call lightning* as well. When a ki-rin conjures things of the sky or things that involve the air, the creature or magic produced is at twice normal strength, including hit points and the damage inflicted by its attacks. They can enter the Ethereal and Astral planes at will.

Habitat/Society: The ki-rin are a race of aerial creatures that rarely set hoof on solid ground. Only the males ever approach the ground. No encounter with a female ki-rin has ever been recorded, although it is certain such beings exist. Likewise no young ki-rin has ever been encountered, thus details of their reproduction are unknown. Ki-rin are reticent about these topics.

Ki-rin come to the aid of humanoids if asked properly or if such beings are faced with a powerful, extremely evil being. Ki-rin believe in self-improvement, though, and do not casually come to a humanoid's aid except in the most dire of circumstances.

Ki-rin sustain themselves by creating their own food and drink. They are highly imaginative with their creations. They may establish a lair high atop a mountain or plateau. Such sites are virtually impossible to reach without resort to flight or climbing. The lairs may have an stony exterior crafted from local materials. It is enhanced by magically created wood and stout cloth. The interiors tend to be luxurious. The ki-rin are able to craft fine cloth, tapestries, pillows, and other comforts. An occupied lair is kept clean by carefully controlled winds that sweep out debris.

Although ki-rin are generous and not avaricious, they still tend to accumulate treasure. These may be their own creations, gifts from friends and allies, souvenirs of past travels and exploits, fines levied against malefactors, or booty taken from vanquished foes.

Ecology: Ki-rin spend most of their time pursuing their own affairs. They often monitor the activities of powerful evil creatures and beings. If such beings become too malevolent, the ki-rin act against them.

Ki-rin may reward allies or needy individuals by creating food and valuables.

The intact skin of a ki-rin is worth 25,000 gp. Possession of such a item is dangerous, due to the retribution that may be visited upon the possessor by other ki-rin, sympathetic humanoids, or intelligent lawful good monsters.

Kirre

CLIMATE/TERRAIN:	Forest ridge
FREQUENCY:	Rare
ORGANIZATION:	Pack
ACTIVITY CYCLE:	Day
DIET:	Carnivore
INTELLIGENCE:	Low (5-7)
TREASURE:	Nil (A)
ALIGNMENT:	Neutral

NO. APPEARING:	1
ARMOR CLASS:	7
MOVEMENT:	15
HIT DICE:	6+6
THAC0:	13
NO. OF ATTACKS:	7
DAMAGE/ATTACK:	1-4/1-4/1-6/1-8/1-4/1-4/1-6
SPECIAL ATTACKS:	Psionics
SPECIAL DEFENSES:	Nil
MAGIC RESISTANCE:	Nil
SIZE:	Large (8' long)
MORALE:	Very Steady (13-14)
LEVEL/XP VALUE:	650

PSIONICS SUMMARY:

Level	Dis/Sci/Dev	Attack/Defense	Score	PSPs
5	2/2/10	PB, II, PsC/TS, IF, TW	15	100

Psychokinesis—Sciences: project force; **Devotions:** soften, levitation.

Telepathy—Sciences: psionic blast, tower of iron will; **Devotions:** awe, psychic crush, id insinuation, thought shield, intellect fortress, life detection, contact.

The kirre is one of the more vicious animals of the forests and jungles of Athas. Resembling a tiger in many ways, the kirre is a beast not to be trifled with.

At first glance, the kirre looks like a great cat, but upon closer examination, the differences quickly become clear. The kirre is 8 feet in length and has eight legs, each ending in paws which sport very sharp claws. The kirre also has large horns on either sides of its head and a sharp barbed tail spike often used as a weapon. The mouth of the kirre is large and has sharp, canine teeth, which are used mostly for tearing food that has been killed. The kirre is a fur-covered animal with coloration similar to a tiger (both are striped). But where are a tiger is striped in black and orange, the kirre is striped in brown and grey. This coloration is consistent all over the kirre's body, with the exception of its face, which is all grey. The yellow eyes of this creature against the dark grey fur of its face create a fearsome appearance.

Combat: Being predators by nature, kirre are very well equipped for combat. This creature is very quick in melee combat, and therefore receives a −1 modifier to its initiative rolls. If the DM is using the "Optional Modifiers to Initiative", kirres are treated as small creatures, receiving only a +3 modifier, instead of the normal +6 for large creatures.

During each round of combat, a kirre can attack up to seven times, using its limbs, teeth, horns, and tail as weapons. It first attacks with its foremost claws, followed by its bite and horn attack. It then attacks with its secondary claws and its tail. Each claw does 1d4 points of damage, both the bite and tail do 1d6 points, and the horn attack does 1d8 points.

Like many of the creatures of the Athas, kirres have natural psionic powers. Instead of its multiple attacks, each round the kirre can use one of its psionic powers as can any normal psionic creature. Also, the kirre has natural psionic defense modes that are always considered to be "on." These provide the creature it with a powerful defense against psionic opponents (assuming the kirre has enough PSPs to power the defense mode being used).

Habitat/Society: Kirres are normally solitary creatures, until the approach of their mating season, at which time a male and female will join and produce offspring. Kirre litters number from three to five young. Kirres are mammals, and females produce milk for their young. Young kirres survive on milk for the first five months, at which point they begin to eat solid food such as small forest animals and other mammals.

When the female is ready to give birth, both she and her mate will make a den in a remote area of the forest where they will be unlikely to be disturbed. During the first five months after birth, both the male and female protect their den ferociously, attempting to kill any creature who threatens their young.

Ecology: Kirre are a favorite game of many hunting tribes of races who live in the forests of Athas. The meat from kirres is some of the finest on all of Athas, and it is sought after by many. Aside from a source of food, the kirre also has other uses when killed. The creature's horns can be cut off and used as spear heads; in some cases, they can be carved into ornate daggers. Also, the tail of a kirre has a sharp, bone spike at its end that can be fashioned into either an arrow head or a dart.

Kobold

	Kobold	Urd
CLIMATE/TERRAIN:	Any land	Temperate to tropical/Hills and mountains
FREQUENCY:	Uncommon	Rare
ORGANIZATION:	Tribe	Gens
ACTIVITY CYCLE:	Night	Night
DIET:	Omnivore	Omnivore
INTELLIGENCE:	Average (8-10)	Low (5-7)
TREASURE:	J,O (Q × 5)	J (Q × 5)
ALIGNMENT:	Lawful evil	Neutral evil
NO. APPEARING:	5-20 (5d4)	3-300
ARMOR CLASS:	7 (10)	8
MOVEMENT:	6	6, Fl 15 (C)
HIT DICE:	½ (1-4 hit points)	2-5
THAC0:	20	2 HD: 19
		3-4 HD: 17
		5 HD: 15
NO. OF ATTACKS:	1	1
DAMAGE/ATTACK:	1-4 or 1-6 (by weapon)	1-3 or 1-4 (weapon)
SPECIAL ATTACKS:	Nil	Rock bomb
SPECIAL DEFENSES:	Nil	Nil
MAGIC RESISTANCE:	Nil	Nil
SIZE:	S (3' tall)	S (3' tall)
MORALE:	Average (8-10)	Unsteady (7)
XP VALUE:	7	2 HD: 35
Chiefs/guards	15	3 HD: 65
		4 HD: 120
		5 HD: 175

Kobolds are a cowardly, sadistic race of short humanoids that vigorously contest the human and demi-human races for living space and food. They especially dislike gnomes and attack them on sight.

Barely clearing 3 feet in height, kobolds have scaly hides that range from dark, rusty brown to a rusty black. They smell of damp dogs and stagnant water. Their eyes glow like a bright red spark and they have two small horns ranging from tan to white. Because of the kobolds' fondness for wearing raggedy garb of red and orange, their non-prehensile rat-like tails, and their language (which sounds like small dogs yapping), these fell creatures are often not taken seriously. This is often a fatal mistake, for what they lack in size and strength they make up in ferocity and tenacity.

Kobolds speak their own language; some (75%) speak orc and goblin.

Combat: The kobold approach to combat uses overwhelming odds or trickery. Kobolds will attack gnomes on sight, but will think twice about attacking humans, elves, or dwarves unless the kobolds outnumber them by at least two to one. They often hurl javelins and spears, preferring not to close until they see that their enemies have been weakened.

Kobolds attack in overwhelming waves. Should the kobolds be reduced to only a three to two ratio in their favor, they must make a morale check. Kobolds are wary of spellcasters and will aim for them when possible.

This diminutive race also enjoys setting up concealed pits with spikes, crossbows, and other mechanical traps. They usually have view ports and murder holes near these traps so that they can pour flaming oil, missile weapons, or drop poisonous insects on their victims.

Kobold war bands are armed with spiked clubs, axes, javelins, short swords and spears. Their shields are seldom metal, but are normally wood or wicker. Chiefs and guards tend to have the best weapons available.

Kobolds have 60-foot infravision but do not see well in bright sunlight, suffering a −1 on their attack rolls.

Habitat/Society: Kobolds live in dark, damp places underground and in overgrown forests. They can be found in almost any climate. As kobolds are good miners, any area with potential for mining is fair game for settlement.

The average kobold tribe has 40 - 400 (4d10 × 10) adult males. For every 40 kobolds in a band there will be one leader and two bodyguards (AC

6; HD 1−1; hp 4 each; damage 1-6). In a lair there will be 5-20 (5d4) bodyguards, females equal to 50% of the males, young equal to 10% of the males and 30-300 (3d10x10) eggs. There will also be a chief and 2-8 guards (AC 5; HD 1+1; hp 7 each; damage 1-8). Further, there is a 65% chance there will be guard animals: (70%) 2-5 wild boars (AC 7; HD 3+3; damage 3d4 gore) or (30%) 1-4 giant weasels (AC 6; HD 3+3; damage 2d6 bite and blood drain). There may be one or more shamans.

Their society is tribal but can be further broken up into war bands based on specific clans. As many as 10 families can be part of a clan, and each clan usually is responsible for controlling the area in a 10 mile radius from the lair. Kobolds recover treasure from the bodies of their victims and often carry them back to their lair as food. In some instances, kobolds will not kill their victims, but will sell them as slaves.

Kobolds are distrustful of strangers. They hate brownies, pixies, sprites and gnomes. Gnomes are never eaten or taken prisoner.

Ecology: Perhaps kobolds are so cruel because they are easy prey for larger humanoids and hungry monsters. They have many enemies, and even the dwarves have had to admit that the numerous kobold-goblin wars have kept the number of goblins down to a safe level.

Kobolds can live 135 years.

Urd

Urds are distant relatives of kobolds. Three feet tall, with short ivory horns, their bodies are frail and covered with mottled yellow to brick red scales. Their leathery, batlike wings span 8 feet.

Urds have 60-foot infravision and prefer to hunt at night, dropping jagged stones (2-3 pounds each) from the air. Unsuspecting victims are AC 10 for the attack roll. Actively dodging opponents are considered AC 2 before modifications to Dexterity. Rocks cause 2d4 points of damage. Some urds (25%) carry light sprears (1d4 damage).

A band of 20 urds is accompanied by a subchieftain (AC 7, 7 hp). Urd flocks of 100 or more include the chieftain (10 hp, 50% have magical leather armor). Urd lairs contain 1d6 shamans able to speak with bats as per *speak with animals*.

Urd life spans can exceed 100 years, but they rarely live past 50.

Kuo-Toa

CLIMATE/TERRAIN:	Aquatic subterranean
FREQUENCY:	Very rare
ORGANIZATION:	Tribal
ACTIVITY CYCLE:	Night
DIET:	Carnivore
INTELLIGENCE:	High and up (13+)
TREASURE:	L, M, N (Z)
ALIGNMENT:	Neutral evil (with chaotic tendencies)

NO. APPEARING:	2-24
ARMOR CLASS:	4
MOVEMENT:	9, Sw 18
HIT DICE:	2 or more
THAC0:	19
NO. OF ATTACKS:	1 or 2
DAMAGE/ATTACK:	2-5 and/or by weapon type
SPECIAL ATTACKS:	See below
SPECIAL DEFENSES:	See below
MAGIC RESISTANCE:	See below
SIZE:	M (higher levels L)
MORALE:	Elite (13)
XP VALUE:	Normal: 175
	Captain: 3,000
	Lieutenant: 1,400
	Whip: 420
	Monitor: 975

Kuo-toa are an ancient race of fish-men that dwells underground and harbors a deep hatred of surface dwellers and sunlight.

A kuo-toan presents a cold and horrible appearance. A typical specimen looks much like a human body, albeit a paunchy one, covered in scales and topped with a fish's head. The huge fish eyes tend to swivel in different directions when observing an area or creature. The hands and feet are very long, with three fingers and an opposing digit, partially webbed. The legs and arms are short for the body size. Its coloration is pale grey, with undertones of tan or yellow in males only. The skin has a sheen from its slimy covering. The color darkens when the kuo-toan is angry and pales when it is badly frightened. A strong odor of dead fish follows it around.

It wears no clothing, only leather harnesses for its weapons and gear. Typically, a kuo-toan warrior carries daggers, spears, shields, harpoons and weighted throwing nets.

Kuo-toa speak the strange subterranean trade language common to most intelligent underworld dwellers. Additionally, they speak their own arcane tongue and have empathic contact with most fish. Their religious speech is a corruption of the language used on the elemental plane of Water; if a kuo-toan priest is in a group of kuo-toa, it is 75% unlikely that a creature native to the plane of Water will attack, for the priest will request mercy in the name of the Sea Mother, Blibdoolpoolp.

Combat: These creatures normally travel in well-armed bands. If more than 20 kuo-toa are encountered, it is 50% likely that they are within 1d6 miles of their lair. For every four normal warriors encountered there is an additional fighter of 3rd or 4th level. For every eight normal fighters there is an additional fighter of 5th or 6th level. For every 12 normal kuo-toa in the group there is a cleric/thief of 1d4+3 levels each. If more than 20 normal fighters are encountered, the group is a war consisting of the following:

One 10th-level fighter as Captain
Two 8th-level fighters as Lieutenants
Four 3rd/3rd-level fighter/thief Whips
One Monitor (see below)
One slave per four kuo-toa

The whips are fanatical devotees of the Sea Mother goddess of the kuo-toa. They inspire the troops to stand firm and fight without quarter for the glory of their ruler and their deity.

It is 50% probable that any kuo-toan priest above 6th level is armed with a pincer staff. This is a 5-foot-long pole topped by a three-foot-long claw. If the user scores a hit, the claw has closed upon the opponent, making escape impossible. The weapon can be used only on enemies with a girth range between an elf and a gnoll. It is 10% probable that both arms are pinned by the claw and 40% probable that one arm is trapped. If the victim is right handed, the claw traps the left hand 75% of the time. Trapped opponents lose shield and Dexterity bonuses. If the weapon arm is trapped, the victim cannot attack and the Dexterity bonus is lost, but the shield bonus remains.

The harpoon is mostly used only by higher level fighters. It is a wickedly barbed throwing weapon with a 30 yard range. It inflicts 2d6 points of damage, exclusive of bonuses. Victims must roll a successful saving throw of 13+ on 1d20 to avoid being snagged by the weapon. Man-sized or smaller beings who fail this saving throw are jerked off their feet and stunned for 1d4 rounds. The kuo-toan, who is attached to his weapon by a stout cord, then tries to haul in its victim and slay him with a dagger thrust.

Kuo-toan shields are made of special boiled leather and are treated with a unique glue-like substance before a battle. Anyone who attacks a kuo-toan from the front has a 25% chance of getting his weapon stuck fast. The chance of the victim freeing the weapon is the same as his chance for opening doors.

Hit probability for kuo-toa is the same as that of a human of similar level, but males also gain a +1 bonus to both attack rolls and damage rolls when using a weapon, due to Strength. When fighting with a dagger only, kuo-toa can bite, which causes 1d4+1 points of damage.

When two or more kuo-toan priests or priest/thieves operate together, they can generate a lightning stroke by joining hands. The bolt is two feet wide and hits only one target unless by mischance a second victim gets in the way. The bolt inflicts 6 points of damage per priest, half that if a saving throw vs. spell is successful. The chances of such a stroke occurring is 10% cumulative per caster per round.

The special defenses of these creatures include skin secretions, which gives attempts to grapple, grasp, tie, or web a kuo-toan only a 25% chance of success. Despite their eyes being set on the sides of their heads, they have excellent independent monocular vision, with a 180-degree field of vision and the ability to spot movement even though the subject is invisible, astral, or ethereal. Thus, by maintaining complete motionlessness, a subject can avoid detection. Kuo-toa also have 60-foot infravision and have the ability to sense vibrations up to 10 yards away. They are surprised only on a 1 on the 1d10 surprise roll.

Kuo-toa are totally immune to poison and are not affected by paralysis. Spells that generally affect only humanoid types have no effect on them. Electrical attacks cause half damage, or none if the saving throw is successful; magic missiles cause only 1 point of damage; illusions are useless against them. However, kuo-toa hate bright light and suffer a -1 penalty to their attack roll in such circumstances as daylight or *light* spells. They suffer full damage from fire attacks and save with a -2 penalty against them.

Sometimes kuo-toa are encountered in small bands journeying in the upper world to kidnap humans for slaves and sacrifices. Such parties are sometimes also found in dungeon labyrinths that connect to the extensive system of underworld passages and caverns that honeycomb the crust of the earth. Only far below the surface of the earth can the intrepid explorer find the caverns in which the kuo-toa build their underground communities.

Habitat/Society: Kuo-toa spawn as do fish, and hatchlings, or fingerlings as they call their young, are raised in pools until their amphibian qualities develop, about one year after hatching. The young, now a foot or so high, are then able to breathe air and they are raised in pens according to their sex and fitness. There are no families, as we know them, in kuo-toan society.

Especially fit fingerlings, usually of noble spawning, are trained for the priesthood as priests, priest/thieves, or special celibate monks. The latter are called "monitors" whose role is to control the community members who become violent or go insane. The monitor is capable of attacking to subdue or kill. A monitor has 56 hit points, attacks as a 7th-level fighter and has the following additional abilities: twice the normal movement rate, AC 1, and receives four attacks per round—two barehanded for 2d4 points of damage (double if trying to subdue) and two attacks with teeth for 1d4+1 points of damage. One hand/bite attack occurs according to the initiative roll, the other occurs at the end of the round.

Subdued creatures cannot be larger than eight feet tall and 500 pounds. Subduing attacks cause only half real damage, but when the points of damage inflicted equal the victim's total, the creature is rendered unconscious for 3d4 rounds.

Kuo-toan communities do not generally cooperate, though they have special places of worship in common. These places are usually for intergroup trade, councils, and worship of the Sea Mother, so they are open to all kuo-toa. These religious communities, as well as other settlements, are open to drow and their servants, for the dark elves provide useful goods and services, though the drow are both feared and hated by the kuo-toa. This leads to many minor skirmishes and frequent kidnappings between the peoples. The illithids (mind flayers) are greatly hated by the kuo-toa and they and their allies are attacked on sight.

The ancient kuo-toa once inhabited the shores and islands of the upper world, but as the race of mankind grew more numerous and powerful, these men-fish were slowly driven to remote regions. Continual warfare upon these evil, human-sacrificing creatures threatened to exterminate the species, for a number of powerful beings were aiding mankind, their sworn enemies. Some kuo-toa sought refuge in sea caverns and secret subter-

ranean waters, and while their fellows were being slaughtered, these few prospered and developed new powers to adapt to their lightless habitat. The seas contained other fierce and evil creatures, however, and the deep-dwelling kuo-toa were eventually wiped out, leaving only those in the underworld to carry on, unnoticed and eventually forgotten by mankind. But the remaining kuo-toa have not forgotten mankind, and woe to any who fall into their slimy clutches.

Now the kuo-toa are haters of sunlight and are almost never encountered on the earth's surface. This, and their inborn hatred of discipline, prevent the resurgence of these creatures, for they have become numerous once again and acquired new powers. However, they have also become somewhat unstable, possibly as a result of inbreeding, and insanity is common among the species.

If a kuo-toan lair is found, it contains 4d10 x 10 2nd-level males. In addition, there are higher level fighters in the same ratio as noted for wandering groups. The leader of the group is one of the following, depending on the lair's population:

A priest/thief king of 12/14th level, if 350 or more normal kuo-toa are present, or

A priest/thief prince of 11/13th level, if 275-349 normal kuo-toa are present, or

A priest/thief duke of 10/12th level, if fewer than 275 normal kuo-toa are present

There are also the following additional kuo-toa in the lair:

Eight Eyes of the priest leader—6th- to 8th-level priest/thieves
One Chief Whip—6th/6th-level fighter/thief
Two Whips of 4th/4th or 5th/5th level (see whip description)
One Monitor per 20 2nd-level kuo-toa
Females equal to 20% of the male population
Young (noncombatant) equal to 20% of the total kuo-toa
Slaves equal to 50% of the total male population

In special religious areas there are also a number of kuo-toan priests. For every 20 kuo-toa in the community there is a 3rd-level priest, for every 40 there is a 4th-level priest, for every 80 there is a 5th-level priest, all in addition to the others. These priests are headed by one of the following groups:

One 6th-level priest if the group is 160 or fewer, or One 7th-level and one 6th-level priest if the group is between 161 and 240, or

One 8th-level, one 7th-level, and one 6th-level priest if the group numbers between 241 and 320, or

One 9th-level, two 7th-level, and three 6th-level priests if the group numbers between 321 and 400, or

One 10th-level, two 8th-level, and four 6th-level priests if the group numbers over 400

Though kuo-toa prefer a diet of flesh, they also raise fields of kelp and fungi to supplement their food supply. These fields, lit by strange phosphorescent fungi, are tended by slaves, who are also used for food and sacrifices.

Kuo-toan treasures tend more toward pearls, gem-encrusted items of a water motif, and mineral ores mined by their slaves. Any magical items in the possession of a kuo-toan are usually obtained from adventuring parties that never made it home again.

Ecology: Not much is known to surface-dwelling sages about this enigmatic, violent, subterranean race, but some of the more astute scholars speculate that the kuo-toa are but one-third of the three-way rivalry that includes mind flayers and drow. It is partially because of this continuing warfare that none of the three races has been able to achieve dominance of the surface world.

	Lamia	Lamia Noble
CLIMATE/TERRAIN:	— Deserts, caves and ruined cities —	
FREQUENCY:	Very rare	Very rare
ORGANIZATION:	Solitary	Solitary
ACTIVITY CYCLE:	Any	Any
DIET:	Carnivore	Carnivore
INTELLIGENCE:	High (13-14)	High (13-14)
TREASURE:	D	D
ALIGNMENT:	Chaotic evil	Chaotic evil
NO. APPEARING:	1	1
ARMOR CLASS:	3	3
MOVEMENT:	24	9
HIT DICE:	9	10+1
THAC0:	11	11
NO. OF ATTACKS:	1	1
DAMAGE/ATTACK:	1-4 (weapon)	1-6 (weapon)
SPECIAL ATTACKS:	See below	See below
SPECIAL DEFENSES:	Nil	Nil
MAGIC RESISTANCE:	Nil	30%
SIZE:	M	M
MORALE:	Elite (14)	Elite (14)
XP VALUE:	3,000	4,000

Of all the hazards that the desert presents, few can compare with the cruel race of flesh-eating creatures known as lamias. These half-human, half-quadruped beast hybrids use deceit, speed, and spells to entrap the foolhardy adventurer who dares wander into their ruins.

Their upper torsos, arms, and heads resemble those of beautiful human women, while their lower bodies are those of beasts, such as goats, deer, or lions, with the appropriate coloration. This hybrid configuration makes lamias very fast and powerful. They are usually armed with daggers, which they use to carve up their prey for the feast. Lamias sometimes smell like perfume flowers, so as to attract unwary victims. They wear no clothing or jewelry. In communicating, they use the common tongue.

Combat: A lamia is able to use the following spells once per day: *charm person*, *mirror image*, *suggestion*, and *illusion* (as a wand). For purposes of duration, effect, etc. assume that the lamia casts its spells at 9th-level spell ability. These spells are typically used to lure persons to the lamia and then hold them there for the creature to devour at its leisure.

The lamia's touch permanently drains 1 point of Wisdom from a victim, and when his Wisdom drops below 3, he willingly does whatever the lamia tells him do. These orders often involve having the victim attack his compatriots while it continues whittling down their ranks. If it has a chance to drain the Wisdom of more than one victim, it will certainly do so. It may even use its *charm* spell to supplement its control over party members.

Among a lamia's favorite illusions to cast upon itself are the following: a lovely damsel in distress, a tough but beautiful female ranger, or an elf maiden. At times, it simply may cast an illusion of a lost child in distress or a group of peasants being attacked by a large beast, while hiding itself, awaiting the right moment to attack from the rear.

Habitat/Society: Lamias dwell in ruined cities or caves, places situated in desert or wasteland areas. These evil creatures are solitary beasts, sustaining themselves on the flesh of those who walk too close to their territories. During lean times, they supplement their diet by stalking game animals. Lamias hardly ever venture more than 10 miles from their lairs.

Ecology: Lamias are legendary monsters that prey upon travelers or guard hidden places or objects of power. They are mysterious creatures that seem devoted to the spreading of chaos and evil in their dwelling places.

Lamia Noble

These beings rule over the lamias and the wild, lonely areas they inhabit. They differ from the normal lamias in that the lamia nobles' lower bodies are those of giant serpents and their upper bodies can be either male or female. It is rumored that the normal female lamia is born from the union of two nobles.

The males wield short swords and have 1d6 levels of wizard spells, plus the inherent spells *charm person*, *mirror image*, *suggestion*, and *illusion*. The females are unarmed and only attack with magic; they are more experienced magically and have 2d4 levels of wizard spells plus the usual inherent spells.

Like normal lamia, lamia nobles have the Wisdom-draining touch.

All lamia nobles are able to assume human form. In this guise they attempt to penetrate human society and wreak evil. They speak all of the languages of humans and demihumans. When in human form, they are recognizable as lamias by humans and demihumans only if the characters are of 7th level or higher, with a 5% cumulative chance per level above 6th. Priests and paladins receive an additional 15% chance (i.e., a 10th-level priest has a 35% chance). Lamia nobles are given to outbursts of senseless violence.

Lammasu

	Lesser	Greater
CLIMATE/TERRAIN:	— Warm, with visits to other climes —	
FREQUENCY:	Rare	Very rare
ORGANIZATION:	Pride	Solitary (Pride)
ACTIVITY CYCLE:	Day	Day
DIET:	Herbivore	Herbivore
INTELLIGENCE:	Genius (17-18)	Supra-genius (19-20)
TREASURE:	R, S, T	Nil
ALIGNMENT:	Lawful good	Lawful good
NO. APPEARING:	2-8	1-2
ARMOR CLASS:	6	3
MOVEMENT:	12, Fl 24 (C)	15, Fl 30 (B)
HIT DICE:	7+7	12+7
THAC0:	13	7
NO. OF ATTACKS:	2	2
DAMAGE/ATTACK:	1-6/1-6	2-12/2-12
SPECIAL ATTACKS:	See below	See below
SPECIAL DEFENSES:	See below	See below
MAGIC RESISTANCE:	30%	40%
SIZE:	L	L (5' high at shoulder)
MORALE:	Elite (14)	Champion (16)
XP VALUE:	4,000	8,000

The lammasu, a winged leonine figure with a human head, aids and protects lawful good persons. They are generally kind and friendly to all good creatures.

Lammasu resemble golden-brown lions with the wings of eagles and the heads of men with shaggy hair and beards. Their formidable appearance is softened by their regal, compassionate, and beneficent expressions. They communicate in their own tongue, in common, and through a limited form of telepathy.

Combat: Since lammasu are concerned for the welfare and safety of good beings, they almost always enter combat if they see good creatures being threatened, in the way least likely to cause harm to the good beings.

Lammasu are able to become invisible or dimension door at will. They radiate a *protection from evil, 10' radius* (-2 penalty to all evil attacks, +2 bonus to saving throws against evil attacks). Additionally, they are able to use priest spells up to 4th level, at 7th-level proficiency. Lammasu can employ four 1st-level spells, three 2nd-level spells, two 3rd-level spells, and one 4th-level spell. They have *cure serious wounds* (4d8+2) and *cure critical wounds* (6d8+6), and 10% of lammasu can speak a *holy word* as well.

If all else fails, lammasu can attack with their two razor-sharp front claws, inflicting 1d6 points of damage each. If they choose to swoop down from the sky on a target, this damage is doubled.

Habitat/Society: The lammasu have a very structured and lawful society, reflecting their alignment. They are organized in prides, just like lions. They dwell in old, abandoned temples situated in warm regions. These temples have not lost their consecration, and in some way, the lammasu are the self-appointed resident guardians of these high and holy places. As a rule, only one pride of lammasu is ever found in a 25-mile area; they spread themselves out so they can respond quickly to any evil outburst.

Lammasu females fight as effectively as the males; for every four lammasu encountered, one is a female. When found in their lair, there are young equal to 25% of the adult population. Female lammasu have the heads of women, with long, hair.

Once a month, the pride leaders gather together to consort about how the war on evil goes. This grouping is called the Whitemoon, since it takes place on the first night of the full moon. There are usually 6d6 lammasu and 2d4 greater lammasu, with the latter presiding over the meeting. Such a gathering of lawful good causes the entire temple where they meet to glow in a pure light, until it breaks up at dawn. There is perhaps no safer place in all the world that night.

Though they dwell in warm areas, they occasionally visit every clime. They speak their own tongue as well as common. At times they use a limited form of telepathy.

Good-aligned strangers are always well received. Neutrals are watched carefully, but are treated politely unless the outsiders begin causing trouble. Evil beings are firmly asked to leave, and if they fail to do so, they are attacked by the pride. In case of trouble, there is a cumulative 10% chance per turn that a neighboring pride picks up a telepathic summons and come to help out the original pride. Lammasu harbor an especially strong dislike for lamias and manticores. Some foolish people confuse lammasu for manticores, which does little to improve the lammasu disposition toward them.

Ecology: Lammasu keep the wastelands from being completely overrun by evil creatures. Their aid to frontier settlements is beyond measurable value.

Greater Lammasu
These creatures are slightly larger than a lesser lammasu and one or two may be found dwelling with a pride of six or more lesser lammasu. Greater lammasu can travel the Astral and Ethereal Planes, become invisible, teleport without error and dimension door, all at will. They radiate *protection from evil* in a 20' radius (-4 penalty to evil attacks and +4 bonus to saving throws) and have the curative powers of their lesser cousins. Their priest spells consist of five 1st-level, four 2nd-level, three 3rd-level, two 4th-level, and one 5th-level spell. Fifty percent of greater lammasu can speak a *holy word* as well. They cast spells as 12th-level priests.

Greater lammasu have empathy, telepathic communication, and speak their racial speech and the common tongue. Despite their greater stature, these lammasu are just as gentle and humble as their lesser brethren.

Leech

	Giant	Throat	Swarm
CLIMATE/TERRAIN:		Temperate/Swamps and marshes	
FREQUENCY:	Uncommon	Common	Uncommon
ORGANIZATION:	Group	Group	Swarm
ACTIVITY CYCLE:	Any	Any	Any
DIET:	Carnivore	Carnivore	Carnivore
INTELLIGENCE:	Non- (0)	Non- (0)	Non- (0)
TREASURE:	Nil	Nil	Nil
ALIGNMENT:	Neutral	Neutral	Neutral
NO. APPEARING:	4-16	1-6	200-500
ARMOR CLASS:	9	10	10
MOVEMENT:	3, Sw 3	1, Sw 1	Sw 1
HIT DICE:	1-4	1 hp	Special
THAC0:	1-2 HD: 19	20	NA
	3-4 HD: 17		
NO. OF ATTACKS:	1	1	1
DAMAGE/ATTACK:	1-4	1-3	Special
SPECIAL ATTACKS:	Drain blood	Choke	Drain blood
SPECIAL DEFENSES:	Nil	Nil	Nil
MAGIC RESISTANCE:	Nil	Nil	Nil
SIZE:	S to M (2'-5')	T (1")	L (10' wide)
MORALE:	Unsteady (7)	Unsteady (6)	Unsteady (5)
XP VALUE:	1 HD: 65	35	15
	2 HD: 120		
	3 HD: 175		
	4 HD: 270		

Giant leeches are horrid, slug-like creatures that dwell in wet, slimy areas and suck the blood of warm-blooded creatures.

These disgusting parasites range from 2 to 5 feet long. Their slimy skin is mottled brown and tan with an occasional shade of gray. Two antennae protrude from atop the head.

Combat: Leeches wait in the mud and slime for prey. The initial attack attaches the sucker mouth of the giant leech. On the next round, and on each round thereafter, it drains blood for 1 point of damage per Hit Die of the leech. There is only a 1% chance that the victim is aware of the attack if it occurs in the water. The leech has anesthetizing saliva, and its bite and blood drain are not usually felt until weakness (the loss of 50% of hit points) sets in and makes the victim aware that something is amiss.

They can be killed by attack or by salt sprinkled on their bodies. There is a 50% chance that the bite of one of these creatures causes a disease that is fatal in 1d4+1 weeks unless cured.

Habitat/Society: These creatures are found only in the waters of swamps and marshes. Giant leeches range from 1 to 4 Hit Dice in size; various sized creatures usually are found in a group.

Throat Leech
This leech is about one inch long and resembles an inconspicuous twig. It is found in pools, lakes, and streams.

Anyone drinking water containing a leech has a 10% chance of taking it into his mouth unless the water is carefully filtered (such as through a sheet of gauze) before drinking. The leech sucks blood at the rate of 1-3 points of damage per round, until it becomes completely distended. After ten rounds of sucking, the leech is bloated and will not suck any more blood.

Each round that the leech is in the victim's throat, there is a 50% chance that the victim chokes, causing an additional 1d4 points of damage. A victim who chokes on three successive rounds dies on the third round.

Apart from magical means that may suggest themselves, the only way to kill a throat leech in a victim's throat is to place a thin, heated metal object, such as a wire, into the bloated leech;

the hot metal causes the leech to burst and no further damage is inflicted on the victim.

Leech swarm
This is merely a massive swarm of small leeches, found only in the water. They move in a cloud 10 feet in diameter. Anyone caught in the swarm receives 1d10 points of damage per round from blood drain. Area-effect attacks that inflict 10 or more points of damage will disperse the swarm.

Leprechaun

CLIMATE/TERRAIN:	Temperate/Green lands, sylvan glens
FREQUENCY:	Uncommon
ORGANIZATION:	Clans
ACTIVITY CYCLE:	Any
DIET:	Omnivore
INTELLIGENCE:	Exceptional (15-16)
TREASURE:	F
ALIGNMENT:	Neutral

NO. APPEARING:	1-20
ARMOR CLASS:	8
MOVEMENT:	15
HIT DICE:	2-5 hp
THAC0:	20
NO. OF ATTACKS:	0
DAMAGE/ATTACK:	Nil
SPECIAL ATTACKS:	See below
SPECIAL DEFENSES:	See below
MAGIC RESISTANCE:	80%
SIZE:	T (2' tall)
MORALE:	(Steady) 11
XP VALUE:	270

Leprechauns are diminutive folk who are found in fair, green lands and enjoy frolicking, working magic, and causing harmless mischief.

Rumored to be a cross between a species of halfling and a strong strain of pixie, leprechauns are about 2 feet tall. They have pointed ears, and their noses also come to a tapered point. About 30% of all male leprechauns have beards. Pointed shoes, brown or green breeches, green or gray coats, and either wide-brimmed or stocking caps are the preferred dress of the wee folk. Many leprechauns also enjoy smoking a pipe, usually a long-stemmed one.

Combat: These fun-loving creatures of magical talent are by nature noncombative. They can become invisible at will, polymorph nonliving objects, create illusions (with full audio and olfactory effects), and use *ventriloquism* spells as often as they like. Their keen ears prevent them from ever being surprised. Being full of mischief, they often (75%) snatch valuable objects from adventurers, turn invisible and dash away. There is a 75% chance that the attempt is successful. If pursued closely, there is a 25% chance per turn of pursuit that the leprechaun drops the stolen goods. The chase never leads to the leprechaun's lair.

If caught or discovered in its lair (10% chance), the leprechaun attempts to mislead his captor into believing that he is giving over his treasure while he actually is duping the captor. It requires great care to actually obtain the leprechaun's treasure.

Habitat/Society: Leprechauns live in families of up to 20, though they call this unit a clan. They use first names and surnames, and it is fairly certain that these names are a good indicator of which clan one is dealing with. A lair usually consists of a warm, dry cave with a hearth, rugs, and furniture. Strangely, word travels fast between clans of the same surname, and a clan that a group of adventurers runs into may already know the adventurers' names from another clan the party encountered several days prior.

There is a rumor that a King of the Leprechauns exists, but there seems to be no official political hierarchy. There are no communities or villages of leprechauns.

It is rare to see leprechaun offspring, but they do exist, born with the full magical powers of an adult. For every 10 adults encountered in a lair, one child will be found.

Leprechauns enjoy eating the same sorts of foods that humans and demihumans eat, with a special fondness for wine. This weakness may be used to outwit them.

Gold is the one treasure found in every leprechaun's hoard. If an intruder secures this treasure, a leprechaun will bargain and beg to get it back. As a last desperate measure, he will grant the intruder three wishes (very limited), but only if the intruder gives over the treasure first. When this is done, the leprechaun will indeed grant the three wishes. After all three wishes, the leprechaun will flatter the intruder and declare that the three wishes were so well-phrased that he will give a fourth wish. If the fourth wish is pronounced, the leprechaun will cackle with glee, the results of all the wishes will be reversed, and the intruder plus his group will be teleported (no saving throw) to a random location 2d20 miles away. No member of that party will never be able to find that particular leprechaun again.

Leprechauns are naturally distrustful toward humans and dwarves, since these races have greedy tendencies. They get along well with elves, gnomes, and halflings.

A leprechaun will not sit idly by while a helpless creature is attacked, since they have a soft spot for weaker creatures. In general, if a leprechaun senses that a stranger means no harm, he can be quite civil, but he will not bring visitors to his lair. If the leprechaun finds someone hurt, he might take the victim to his lair, but only after making sure that the stranger is not followed and cannot see where he is being taken.

Ecology: The best times and places to observe leprechauns are called borderlines. Dawn and dusk (which are neither all light nor dark), the shore (which is neither all earth nor all water), or the equinoxes and solstices (which are neither one season nor another), are the best times and places to see leprechauns and their ilk frolicking and celebrating.

Leucrotta

CLIMATE/TERRAIN:	Temperate/Wasteland, broken terrain
FREQUENCY:	Rare
ORGANIZATION:	Pack
ACTIVITY CYCLE:	Any
DIET:	Carnivore
INTELLIGENCE:	Average (8-10)
TREASURE:	D
ALIGNMENT:	Chaotic evil

NO. APPEARING:	1-4
ARMOR CLASS:	4
MOVEMENT:	18
HIT DICE:	6+1
THAC0:	15
NO. OF ATTACKS:	1
DAMAGE/ATTACK:	3-18
SPECIAL ATTACKS:	See below
SPECIAL DEFENSES:	Kick in retreat
MAGIC RESISTANCE:	Nil
SIZE:	L (7' at shoulder, 9' long)
MORALE:	Elite (14)
XP VALUE:	975

The leucrotta is a creature of ugly appearance and temperament that haunts deserted places in search of prey.

The average leucrotta stands 7 feet tall at the shoulder and can reach a length of 9 feet in its mature form. The body of the leucrotta resembles that of a stag, with a leonine tufted tail and cloven hooves. Its head resembles that of a huge badger, but instead of teeth it has sharp, jagged bony ridges. Its body is tan, with the neck gradually darkening until it turns black at the head. The so-called teeth are sickly gray, and its eyes glow with a feral red light. The smell of animals, decomposing on a hot humid day follows the leucrotta, and its breath is especially bad.

Combat: This monster is very sly and can imitate a range of noises and voices, the most common ones being a man, a woman, a child, or domestic animals in pain. It uses these noises in order to trick its prey into approaching within attack distance. It hunts humans, demihumans, humanoids, and even other animal predators. Leucrotta are intelligent and can speak their own language as well as the common tongue.

Leucrotta attack by biting for 3d6 points of damage. It is rumored that their bony ridges and jaws are so powerful that they can even bite through metal. If a leucrotta scores a hit against someone with a shield or armor, the target must roll a saving throw vs. crushing blow for the shield. If the roll fails, then in addition to scoring the regular damage, the beast managed to also bite through the shield. Once the shield is gone, the armor must go through the same routine with subsequent successful bites.

Once an opponent is rendered helpless, a leucrotta will leave its prize and attack any other intruders if the melee is still going on. It will give chase to an enemy, but will never pursue beyond sight of any prey it has managed to already capture.

When a leucrotta retreats, it turns its back on its opponent and kicks with its hind legs, causing 1d6 points of damage with each hoof.

Note to trackers: It is almost impossible to identify leucrotta tracks, since they look exactly like a stag's.

Habitat/Society: This ugly creature haunts deserted and desolate places because most other creatures cannot bear the sight of it. Its ugliness is legendary. Leucrotta lair in treacherous ravines and rocky spires, because they are as surefooted as a mountain goat. Caves, old abandoned towers, or a hollowed out deadfall are the preferred lairs for this disgusting beast.

For every four leucrotta found in a lair, there is a 10% chance that an extra one, an immature leucrotta of half strength, is also present. Leucrotta are not a very family oriented species, as their nasty tempers extend sometimes to each other. The beasts range over a 20-mile area.

Since the leucrotta is not a very social creature, all strangers are nothing more than sources of food. Sometimes, a powerful chaotic evil person may entrap a leucrotta and force it to serve as a guardian, but such beasts rebel at the first opportunity.

Those brave enough to venture into a leucrotta lair must first roll a successful saving throw vs. poison with a -1 penalty, due to the horrendous stench, or gag helplessly for 1d4 rounds. Once inside, the money and possessions of past victims await.

Though the leucrotta prefer freshly killed meat, they are not above eating carrion. This serves to enhance their already bad reputation.

Ecology: Leucrotta distance themselves from the grand picture of nature, preferring to lurk on the fringes. They serve no practical use and one would be hard pressed to find a druid that would try to protect a member of this species. Some sages speculate that the leucrotta is an unnatural abnormality, an aberration spawned by some demented power or archmage.

Still, some mages prize the leucrotta hide for creating *boots of striding and springing*, hoping that the surefootedness of the beast passes down to the boots themselves. There are rumors that leucrotta saliva is an effective antidote to love philters, but so far there have been no volunteers to test this theory.

Lich

	Lich	Demilich
CLIMATE/TERRAIN:	Any	Any
FREQUENCY:	Very rare	Very rare
ORGANIZATION:	Solitary	Solitary
ACTIVITY CYCLE:	Night	See below
DIET:	Nil	Nil
INTELLIGENCE:	Supra-genius (19-20)	Supra-genius (19-20)
TREASURE:	A	Z
ALIGNMENT:	Any evil	Any evil
NO. APPEARING:	1	1
ARMOR CLASS:	0	See below
MOVEMENT:	6	See below
HIT DICE:	11+	See below
THAC0:	9	9
NO. OF ATTACKS:	1	See below
DAMAGE/ATTACK:	1-10	See below
SPECIAL ATTACKS:	See below	See below
SPECIAL DEFENSES:	+1 or better magical weapon to hit	See below
MAGIC RESISTANCE:	Nil	See below
SIZE:	M (6' tall)	M (6' tall)
MORALE:	Fanatic (17-18)	Fanatic (17-18)
XP VALUE:	8,000	10,000

The lich is, perhaps, the single most powerful form of undead known to exist. They seek to further their own power at all costs and have little or no interest in the affairs of the living, except where those affairs interfere with their own.

A lich greatly resembles a wight or mummy, being gaunt and skeletal in form. The creature's eye sockets are black and empty save for the fierce pinpoints of light which serve the lich as eyes. The lich can see with normal vision in even the darkest of environments but is unaffected by even the brightest light. An aura of cold and darkness radiates from the lich which makes it an ominous and fearsome sight. They were originally wizards of at least 18th level.

Liches are often (75%) garbed in the rich clothes of nobility. If not so attired, the lich will be found in the robes of its former profession. In either case, the clothes will be tattered and rotting with a 25% chance of being magical in some way.

Combat: Although a lich will seldom engage in actual melee combat with those it considers enemies, it is more than capable of holding its own when forced into battle.

The aura of magical power which surrounds a lich is so potent that any creature of fewer than 5 Hit Dice (or 5th level) which sees it must save vs. spell or flee in terror for 5-20 (5d4) rounds.

Should the lich elect to touch a living creature, its aura of absolute cold will inflict 1-10 points of damage. Further, the victim must save vs. paralysis or be utterly unable to move. This paralysis lasts until dispelled in some manner.

Liches can themselves be hit only by weapons of at least +1, by magical spells, or by monsters with 6 or more Hit Dice and/or magical properties. The magical nature of the lich and its undead state make it utterly immune to charm, sleep, enfeeblement, polymorph, cold, electricity, insanity, or death spells. Priests of at least 8th level can attempt to turn a lich, as can paladins of no less than 10th level.

A lich is able to employ spells just as it did in life. It still requires the use of its spell books, magical components, and similar objects. It is important to note that most, if not all, liches have had a great deal of time in which to research and create new magical spells and objects. Thus, adventurers should be prepared to face magic the likes of which they have never seen before when stalking a lich. In addition, liches are able to use any magical objects which they might possess just as if they were still alive.

Defeating a lich in combat is difficult indeed, but managing to actually destroy the creature is harder still. In all cases, a lich will protect itself from annihilation with the creation of a phylactery in which it stores its life force. This is similar to a magic jar spell. In order to ensure the final destruction of a lich, its body must be wholly annihilated and its phylactery must be sought out and destroyed in some manner. Since the lich will always take great care to see to it that its phylactery is well hidden and protected this can be an undertaking fully as daunting as the defeat of the lich in its physical form.

Habitat/Society: Liches are usually solitary creatures. They have cast aside their places as living beings by choice and now want as little to do with the world of men as possible. From time to time, however, a lich's interest in the world at large may be reawakened by some great event of personal importance.

A lich will make its home in some ominous fortified area, often a strong keep or vast subterranean crypt.

When a lich does decide to become involved with the world beyond its lair, its keen intelligence makes it a dangerous adversary. In some cases, a lich will depend on its magical powers to accomplish its goals. If this is not sufficient, however, the lich is quite capable of animating a force of undead troops to act on its behalf. If such is the case, the lich's endless patience and cunning more than make up for the inherent disadvantages of the lesser forms of undead which it commands.

Although the lich has no interest in good or evil as we understand it, the creature will do whatever it must to further its own causes. Since it feels that the living are of little importance, the lich is often viewed as evil by those who encounter it. In rare cases, liches of a most unusual nature can be found which are of any alignment.

The lich can exist for centuries without change. Its will drives it onward to master new magics and harness mystical powers not available to it in its previous life. So obsessed does the monster become with its quest for power that it often forgets its former existence utterly. Few liches call themselves by their old names when the years have drained the last vestiges of their humanity from them. Instead, they often adopt pseudonyms like "the Black Hand" or "the Forgotten

Lich

King." Learning the true name of a lich is rumored to confer power over the creature.

Ecology: The lich is not a thing of this world. Although it was once a living creature, it has entered into an unnatural existence.

In order to become a lich, the wizard must prepare its phylactery by the use of the *enchant an item, magic jar, permanency* and *reincarnation* spells. The phylactery, which can be almost any manner of object, must be of the finest craftsmanship and materials with a value of not less than 1,500 gold pieces per level of the wizard. Once this object is created, the would-be lich must craft a potion of extreme toxicity, which is then enchanted with the following spells: *wraithform, permanency, cone of cold, feign death,* and *animate dead.* When next the moon is full, the potion is imbibed. Rather than death, the potion causes the wizard to undergo a transformation into its new state. A system shock survival throw is required, with failure indicating an error in the creation of the potion which kills the wizard and renders him forever dead.

Demilich

The demilich is not, as the name implies, a weaker form of the lich. Rather, it is the stage into which a lich will eventually evolve as the power which has sustained its physical form gradually begins to fail. In most cases, all that remains of a demilich's body are a skull, some bones, and a pile of dust.

When it has learned all that it feels it can in its undead life, the lich will continue its quest for power in strange planes unknown to even the wisest of sages. Since it has no use for its physical body at this point, the lich leaves it to decay as it should have done centuries ago.

If the final resting place of a demilich's remains are entered, the dust which was once its body will rise up and assume a man-like shape. In the case of the oldest demiliches (25%), the shape will advance and threaten, but dissipate without attacking in 3 rounds unless attacked. Younger demiliches (75%) still retain a link to their remains, however, and will form with the powers of a wraith. This dust form cannot be turned. In addition, it can store energy from attacks and use this power to engage its foes. If the dust form is attacked, each point of damage which is delivered to it is converted to an energy point. Since the demilich will fall back and seem to suffer injury from each attack (though none is actually inflicted), its attackers are likely to press on in their attempts to destroy it. Once the demilich has acquired 50 energy points, it will assume a manifestation which looks much like the lich's earlier undead form and has the powers and abilities of a ghost, but which cannot be turned.

If anyone touches the skull it will rise into the air and turn to face the most powerful of the intruders (a spell user will be chosen over a non-spell user). Instantly, it unleashes a howl which acts as a *death ray*, affecting all creatures within a 20' radius of the skull. Those who fail to save vs. death are permanently dead.

On the next round, the demilich will employ another manner of attack. In order to attain the status of a demilich, a lich must have replaced 5-8 (1d4+4) of its teeth with gems. Each of these gems now serves as a powerful magical device which can *trap the soul* of its adversaries. The physical body of someone hit with the demilich's spell collapses and rots away in a single round. Once it has drained the life essence from the most powerful member of the party, the skull sinks back to the floor. If it continues to be challenged, the demilich can repeat this attack until all of its gems are filled. An *amulet of life protection* will prevail over the gem, but the character's body will perish regardless.

In addition to the attacks mentioned above, a demilich can also pronounce a powerful *curse* on those who disturb it. These can be so mighty as to include: always being hit by one's enemies, never making a saving throw, or the inability to acquire new experience points.

Demilich *curses* can be overcome with a *remove curse*, but the victim loses one point of charisma permanently when the curse is removed.

The skull of a demilich is Armor Class −6 and has 50 hit points. It can be affected by spells in only a few ways: a *forget* spell will cause it to sink down without attacking (either by howling or draining a soul), a *dispel evil* will do 5-8 (1d4+4) points of damage to it, a *shatter* spell will inflict 3-18 (3d6) points of damage to it, a *holy word* pronounced against it will deliver 5-30 (5d6) points of damage, and a *power word kill* spell cast by an ethereal or astral wizard will cause the skull to shatter (destroying it).

Most weapons will be unable to harm the skull of a demilich, but there are exceptions. A fighter or ranger with a *vorpal sword, sword of sharpness, sword +5,* or *vorpal weapon* can inflict normal damage on the skull, as can a paladin with a vorpal or +4 weapon. Further, any character with a +4 or better weapon or a *mace of disruption* can inflict 1 point of damage to the skull each time he strikes it.

Upon the destruction of the skull, those who have been trapped inside the gems must make a saving throw vs. spell. Those who fail are lost forever, having been consumed by the demilich to power its magical nature. If the character survives, the gem glows with a faint inner light, and *true seeing* will reveal a tiny figure trapped within. If the throw is made the soul can be freed by simply crushing the gem. A new body must be within 10 yards for the soul to enter or it will be lost. Such a body might be a clone or simulacrum. (See spells of those names.)

If the fragments of the destroyed skull are not destroyed by immersion in holy water and the casting of a *dispel magic* the demilich will reform in 1-10 days.

Archlich

From time to time, sages have heard rumors of liches having alignments other than evil, and even lawful good liches apparently have existed. There have even been reports of priests who, in extreme circumstances, have become liches. These reports have recently been verified, but the archlich is as rare as Roc's teeth.

Living Wall

CLIMATE/TERRAIN:	Any
FREQUENCY:	Very Rare
ORGANIZATION:	Solitary
ACTIVITY CYCLE:	Any
DIET:	Assimilation (see below)
INTELLIGENCE:	Variable (3-18)
TREASURE:	Variable
ALIGNMENT:	Chaotic evil

NO. APPEARING:	1
ARMOR CLASS:	8 (Base)
MOVEMENT:	Nil
HIT DICE:	8 (Base)
THAC0:	Variable
NO. OF ATTACKS:	Variable
DAMAGE/ATTACK:	Variable
SPECIAL ATTACKS:	See below
SPECIAL DEFENSES:	See below
MAGIC RESISTANCE:	20%
SIZE:	L to G + (Rectangular area)
MORALE:	Fearless (20)
XP VALUE:	2,000 to 100,000 +

Living walls appear to be normal walls of stone or brick, although they radiate both evil and magic if detected. Infravision will not detect any peculiar patterns. However, a character who casts a *true seeing* spell or who peers through a *gem of seeing* will see past the illusion: the wall actually consists of greying and sinewy flesh—of faces, hands, broken bones, feet, and toes jutting from the surface. Characters within 5 yards of the wall can hear low moans of horror, pain, and sorrow issuing from it. Even if a silence spell is cast, the moans still rise.

A living wall contains the melded bodies of humanoids and monsters who died within 100 yards of the wall since its creation. Those who die fighting a living wall are absorbed into it and actually strengthen it. Characters and monsters captured by the wall retain all the abilities they had in life; as part of the wall, they become chaotic evil and fight any creature that approaches it to the best of their abilities.

If a wizard becomes melded with a living wall, his spellcasting abilities are retained and can immediately be used for attacks. The wizard retains any spells that were memorized at the time he was absorbed into the wall; these are renewed each day. If a warrior loses his life in combat with a living wall, his fighting abilities and his weapons come under control of the beast: the weapons are hidden within the wall until the wall attacks, then are pushed through the mass of graying flesh to the surface. A hand attaches itself to the weapon, and eyes jutting from the wall guide the attack of the weapon. If the wall absorbs characters with ranged weapons, the weapons become useless once arrows, quarrels, or other necessary projectiles are expended.

Combat: A living wall never initiates combat, except against its creator, whom it despises. When such a wall is attacked, every creature that is part of the wall returns one attack, per strike against the wall. If a wall is made up of 12 creatures and one creature lands a blow on the wall, the attacker is subject to a dozen return blows from the wall.

All creatures in the wall fight according to their normal attack modes. These attacks can be magical, physical, or mental in origin. The type of attack and its damage often depend upon who or what is melded into the wall.

If a 10th-level fighter and a 6th-level fighter are absorbed into the wall, the wall attacks as one 6th-level fighter and one 10th-level fighter. For every mage or priest absorbed, the wall gains spell attacks. The only spells that can be used, however, are those that the mage or priest had memorized (and had material components for) at the time of absorption. Each of these spells may be cast once per day. The material components of the spells are not consumed. If one absorbed mage has three *fireball* spells memorized and a second mage has one *fireball* in memory, the living wall can attack with four *fireballs* per day. If the wall assimilates a paladin or a lawful good priest, all his special powers are reversed (e.g., *detect good* rather than *detect evil*, harm by laying of hands rather than *heal*, etc.).

Magical items absorbed with characters grant the wall their spell effects, though items that grant AC improvements are less effective because of the wall's size. The wall gains 1 point improvement in Armor Class for every 3 points of magical improvement to AC. Thus, a *ring of protection* +3 lowers the wall's AC by 1.

When a character is absorbed, his hit points, at full health, are added to the wall's base hit point total of 64.

Nonmagical armor, packs, and purses are lost by absorbed characters. The piles of loot at the base of the wall often attracts bystanders, bringing them close enough to be seized by one of the wall's hands.

Though a living wall will not initiate an attack, characters who come within 2 feet of the wall may be weakly grabbed by its many beseeching hands, tugging at them and imploring them for deliverance. (Any character, regardless of Strength, may break the hold.). Sometimes PCs who hear voices imploring, "help me! pull me free, help me!" grope about until they grab a hand. In this case, the character must roll a save vs. spell or become absorbed. If another character is holding onto the first character, he must also roll a saving throw vs. spell or become absorbed into the wall. If the save vs. spell succeeds, the character is able to break free. A character who views the absorption of any creature into the wall must make a horror check.

Once absorbed, characters are lost forever. A *wish* spell, worded carefully, can remove one or more trapped characters.

Passwall spells do not allow individuals to go through a living wall. Characters must either cut through or blast through using magic. This, however, allows the wall to return attacks. When cutting or blasting though the living wall, the stench that rises from the exposed underflesh is nauseating and horrifying. A saving throw vs. poison is required to avoid passing out from the smell. A successful saving throw indicates the character is only nauseated.

Living walls are immune to all planar and temporal spells. *Speak with dead, ESP* and similar spells reveal a cacophony of tortured minds and voices. The caster learns nothing and must make a horror check.

Habitat/Society: Living walls never reproduce and always remain active until they are killed. Living walls encountered in the lairs of malevolent creatures often serve as part of a torture chamber, or to cover the true openings to secret passageways or corridors.

No one knows whether these monstrosities are limited in size or longevity. Walls as large as 15 feet high, 30 feet long, and 10 feet thick have been reported. Living walls do, however, seem to be limited to one section of wall. Thus, a cemetery or castle could not be surrounded by one large living wall.

Nor can a wall section spread beyond itself: a house with a living wall in its basement will not slowly become a living house.

The wall desires, above all else, to slay the creature who created it. If it does so, or the creature meets its end within 100 yards of the wall, the corpse of the hated creator is assimilated and the beings trapped in the wall are freed to return to the peace of death. The wall reverts to being a structure of stone, with the corpse of its creator entombed within.

Ecology: Chaotic evil mages occasionally create these monoliths. The exact method is unknown, but several years of preparation and spellcasting are required. A minimum of three corpses are necessary for the spells.

A fact known only to one or two inhabitants of Ravenloft, is that living walls also arise as rare manifestations of Ravenloft's power, as responses to despair and dread. These walls are born in curses, midwived by death, and nursed on massacre.

The seed for such a living wall is planted when one sapient creature willfully entombs another in a wall. The hapless victim may be bound and walled alive in a rock niche on a windswept mountain trail, a sill in a fetid catacomb, a corner in an asylum, a cave wall, a mausoleum facade, or any other stone or brick wall. Once entombed, the victim will suffocate, dehydrate, or starve in utter darkness and solitude. But even this agony is not sufficient

to wake the land's attention—the entombed creature, in his terror, must curse his slayer, screaming loudly enough for his voice to carry beyond his tomb of stone. Only then does the land hear his agony.

When the victim dies, his life force is trapped within the wall. As he struggles to escape, his life energy becomes soiled by the soot of his screams and curses, which thickly coat the inside of his stone sarcophagus. In a matter of days, madness corrupts the trapped life force, changing it to chaotic evil.

At this point, the bodies of any creatures that have died within 100 yards of the wall within the last month rise, shamble to the wall, and meld into it. Even corpses that have been buried will dig their way to the surface and converge upon the wall. Although the wall retains its previous appearance, it is no longer stone, but a gray and rotting bulwark of limbs, ribs, hands, bones, and faces, twisted and fused together. Bodies of any subsequent deaths occurring within 100 yards also rise and wander to the wall for assimilation.

Most cultures, and all good-aligned characters, attempt to destroy these creations wherever they are found. But many of these assaults merely strengthen the wall with deposits of more corpses.

Lizard

	Fire	Giant	Minotaur	Subterranean
CLIMATE/TERRAIN:	Any warm land	Any warm land	Tropical hills and mountains	Any subterranean
FREQUENCY:	Very rare	Uncommon	Rare	Uncommon
ORGANIZATION:	Solitary	Solitary	Solitary	Solitary
ACTIVITY CYCLE:	Day	Day	Day	Day
DIET:	Carnivore	Carnivore	Carnivore	Carnivore
INTELLIGENCE:	Animal (1)	Non- (0)	Non- (0)	Non- (0)
TREASURE:	B, Q (x10), S, T	Nil	J-N, Q, C (magic)	O, P, Q (x5)
ALIGNMENT:	Neutral	Neutral	Neutral	Neutral
NO. APPEARING:	1-4	2-12 (2d6)	1-8	1-6
ARMOR CLASS:	3	5	5	5
MOVEMENT:	9	15	6	12
HIT DICE:	10	3+1	8	6
THAC0:	11	17	13	15
NO. OF ATTACKS:	3	1	3	1
DAMAGE/ATTACK:	1-8/1-8/2-16	1-8	2-12/2-12/3-18	2-12
SPECIAL ATTACKS:	See below	See below	See below	See below
SPECIAL DEFENSES:	See below	Nil	Nil	Nil
MAGIC RESISTANCE:	Nil	Nil	Nil	Nil
SIZE:	G(30')	H(15')	G(40')	H(20')
MORALE:	Steady (11-12)	Average (8-10)	Average (8-10)	Average (8-10)
XP VALUE:	3,000	175	975	650

Fire Lizards

Fire lizards resemble wingless red dragons and are sometimes called "false dragons." They are gray-colored with mottled red and brown back and reddish undersides. Hatchlings are light gray in color, and darken as they age.

Combat: Fire lizards attack with a combination of raking claws and bite. They can simultaneously breathe a fiery cone 5 feet wide at the mouth, 10 feet wide at the end, and 15 feet long which inflicts 2-12 points of fire-based damage (half if saving throw vs. breath weapon is made). Fire lizards are immune to fire-based attacks.

Habitat/Society: Fire lizards prefer subterranean lairs but come out every fortnight to hunt fresh game. Prey is hauled back to the lair for a leisurely meal; the debris forms the treasure trove. Fire lizards are slow moving and sleep 50% of the time. Their lairs may have 1-4 eggs (10% chance, market value 5,000 gp each). Hatchlings immediately leave to hunt on their own. Shiny objects attract fire lizards; gems and metals form the bulk of treasure found in their dens.

Ecology: Fire lizards are perhaps an ancestral dragon type or offshoot of a common ancestor. Real dragons avoid these "false dragons," which live to be 50-100 years old. Fire lizard eggs are worth 5,000 gp, hatchlings 7,500 gp.

Giant Lizards

This lizard is relatively normal, albeit large, and lives in marshes and swamps. An attack score of 20 means the giant lizard's victim is trapped in the mouth and suffers double damage (2-16 points). The giant lizard inflicts 2-16 points of damage each round thereafter. Giant lizards are lazy hunters and tend to attack anything edible that wanders by. While their great size protects them from most predators, it renders them a sumptuous feast to the black dragons who share their swamps. Giant lizards are sometimes domesticated by lizard men, who use them as mounts, beasts of burden, and food. Their lairs may be home to a wide range of lizards, from eggs to century-old adults.

Minotaur Lizards

This huge, aggressive lizard derives its name from its horns. While these horns look like those of a minotaur, the male's horns are not used in combat—rather, they are believed to be a means of attracting a mate. The minotaur lizard attacks with sharp claws and teeth. They are adept at ambushes; others are -5 on their surprise roll. An attack roll of 20 means the lizard has trapped its victim within its jaws and can automatically inflict 3-18 points of damage each round thereafter until the victim escapes or dies. The victim is unable to attack the following round. Minotaur lizards are found in tropical hills and mountains near copper and red dragons.

Subterranean Lizards

This aggressive lizard is able to run across walls or ceilings with the help of its suction cup-tipped feet. An attack roll of 20 means the lizard has clamped its jaws on its victim and does double damage (4-24 points). The victim automatically suffers an additional 2-12 points of damage each round thereafter. These lizards never leave their caves voluntarily. Some species are albino; these shun light and attack at -1 in daylight or its equivalent. Other species have tongues up to 20 feet long. Any man-sized or smaller prey seized by the tongue will be drawn into the mouth and bitten the next round unless a *bend bars* roll is made.

Lizard Man

	Lizard Man	Lizard King
CLIMATE/TERRAIN:	Tropical, sub-tropical and temperate swamp	Tropical, sub-tropical and temperate swamp
FREQUENCY:	Rare	Very rare
ORGANIZATION:	Tribal	Tribal
ACTIVITY CYCLE:	Any	Any
DIET:	Special	Special
INTELLIGENCE:	Low (5-7)	Average (8-10)
TREASURE:	D	E
ALIGNMENT:	Neutral	Chaotic evil
NO. APPEARING:	8-15 (1d8 + 7)	1
ARMOR CLASS:	5	3
MOVEMENT:	6, Sw 12	9, Sw 15
HIT DICE:	2 + 1	8
THAC0:	19	13
NO. OF ATTACKS:	3	1
DAMAGE/ATTACK:	1-2/1-2/1-6	5-20 (3d6 + 2)
SPECIAL ATTACKS:	Nil	Skewer
SPECIAL DEFENSES:	Nil	Nil
MAGIC RESISTANCE:	Nil	Nil
SIZE:	M (7' tall)	L (8' tall)
MORALE:	14	16
XP VALUE:	65	975
Patrol leader	65	
Subleader	120	
War leader	270	
Shaman, 3rd	175	
Shaman, 5th	650	
Shaman, 7th	975	

Lizard men are savage, semi-aquatic, reptilian humanoids that live through scavenging, raiding, and, in less hostile areas, by fishing and gathering.

Adult lizard men stand 6 to 7 feet tall, weighing 200 to 250 pounds. Skin tones range from dark green to gray to brown, and their scales give them a flecked appearance. Their tails average 3 to 4 feet long and are not prehensile. Males are nearly impossible to distinguish from females without close inspection. Lizard man garb is limited to strings of bones and other barbaric ornament. Lizard men speak their own language.

Combat: In combat, lizard men fight as unorganized individuals. If they have equality or an advantage over their opponents, they tend toward frontal assaults and massed rushes. When outnumbered, overmatched, or on their home ground, however, they become wily and ferocious opponents. Snares, sudden ambushes, and spoiling raids are favored tactics in these situations. While individually savage in melee, lizard men tend to be distracted by food (such as slain opponents) and by simple treasures, which may allow some of their quarry to escape. They occasionally take prisoners as slaves, for food, or to sacrifice in obscure tribal rites.

For every 10 lizard men encountered, there will be one patrol leader with maximum hit points (17 hp) and a 50% chance for a shaman with 3 Hit Dice and the abilities of a 3rd-level priest. If one or more tribes are encountered, each tribe will also have a war leader of 6 Hit Dice, two subleaders with 4 Hit Dice, and a shaman of either 4 or 5 Hit Dice (50% chance of each). Any group of two or more tribes has a 50% chance for an additional shaman of 7 Hit Dice. Furthermore, each such group has a cumulative 10% chance per tribe to be led by a lizard king. If a lizard king is present, a shaman of 7 Hit Dice will always be present, and all patrol leaders from each tribe (i.e., 10% of the male warriors) will be combined into a single fanatical bodyguard for the lizard king.

Habitat/Society: Lizard men are typically found in swamps, marshes, and similar places, often (35%) dwelling totally underwater in air-filled caves. A tribe rarely numbers more than 150 individuals, including females and hatchlings. It is not uncommon for several tribes in an area to forge an informal alliance against outsiders, including other lizard man tribes.

Lizard men are omnivorous, but are likely to prefer human flesh to other foods. In this regard they have been known to ambush humans, gather up the corpses and capture the survivors, and take the lot back to their lair for a rude and horrid feast.

Ecology: Lizard men have few natural enemies. They prey on human, demihuman, or humanoid settlements if these are nearby. Lizard man eggs are bitter and inedible, as is their flesh, but their skin is sometimes worked as scale armor (Armor Class 6). Lizard men produce no art, artifacts, or trade goods.

Advanced Lizard Men
About 1 tribe in 10 has evolved to a higher state. These lizard men dwell in crude huts, use shields (thus Armor Class 4) and hurl barbed darts (30 yard range, 1-4 points damage) or javelins (1-6 points damage) before closing with the enemy. These lizard men use clubs (treat as morning stars, 2-8 points damage), and the leaders may use captured swords or other weaponry. The chance of these advanced lizard men having a lizard king is doubled, i.e., 20% cumulative chance per tribe.

Lizard King
A lizard king is a lizard man of above average height and intelligence, leading one or more loosely organized tribes of lizard men. The lizard king is most often armed with a great trident, which it wields with great skill and ferocity. In the hands of the lizard king, the weapon inflicts 5-20 (3d6 + 2) points of damage. If the attack roll is 5 or more greater than the score needed to hit, the lizard king inflicts double damage (with a minimum of 15 points).

A lizard king usually demands two humans each week. If no humans are available, demihumans and other humanoids will be sought. If none are available, two of the lizard king's bodyguards will be killed and eaten instead.

Locathah

CLIMATE/TERRAIN:	Tropical and subtropical/ Coastal waters
FREQUENCY:	Rare
ORGANIZATION:	Clan
ACTIVITY CYCLE:	Any
DIET:	Omnivore
INTELLIGENCE:	Very (11-12)
TREASURE:	A
ALIGNMENT:	Neutral
NO. APPEARING:	20-200
ARMOR CLASS:	6
MOVEMENT:	1, Sw 12
HIT DICE:	2
THAC0:	19
NO. OF ATTACKS:	1
DAMAGE/ATTACK:	By weapon
SPECIAL ATTACKS:	Nil
SPECIAL DEFENSES:	Nil
MAGIC RESISTANCE:	Nil
SIZE:	M (5' + tall)
MORALE:	Average (9)
XP VALUE:	35

The locathah are a humanoid race of aquatic nomads that roams warm coastal waters.

A typical locathah stands 5 to 6 feet tall and weighs 150 to 200 pounds. The skin is covered in fine but tough scales. The scales vary in color from a ivory yellow on the stomach and neck to a pale yellow on the rest of the body. The fins of their ears and spine are ocher. The ear fins enhance hearing while the large eyes are designed to enhance underwater vision. The only way to distinguish males from females is a vertical ocher stripe marking the egg sac. On the surface, locathah have a typically fish-like smell. They speak their own language; 10% also speak merman, koalinth, or other aquatic languages.

Combat: The intelligent locathah have developed tactics that enable them to beat their deadlier rivals. They always operate in teams, the larger the better. Furthermore, when away from their homes they ride giant eels that act as both mounts and allies.

A typical locathah force is armed as follows:

Lance	20%
Crossbow	30%
Trident	30%
Short sword	20%

Since a locathah lacks claws or teeth, it cannot do damage if it is disarmed. If that happens, it will either grapple a foe (if armed locathah are present), look for weapons, or flee. Locathah only battle to the death if cornered or if their home is threatened.

Habitat/Society: Locathah have developed a society similar to that of surface humans. They have a well-developed hunter-gatherer society and a strong sense of territory. Locathah make their lairs in rocks carved into castle-like strongholds. These aquatic castles are very similar to their surface counterparts. Openings are protected by stout doors, shutters, or coral bars. Often 4d4 moray eels are used as guardbeasts. There is a 50% chance that Portuguese man-o-war jellyfish may be used as traps. A herd of giant eels is kept at the edge of each stronghold.

Locathah have a communal society organized in tribes of 20 to several hundred. Each band of forty locathah has a leader (18 hit points, treat as a 4th-level fighter) and four assistants (14 hit

points, treat as 3rd-level fighters). Clans of more than 120 locathah are led by a female chieftain (22 hit points, treat as a 5th-level fighter) accompanied by 12 guards (12-14 hit points, treat as 3rd-level fighters).

Clan chieftains are prolific egg layers. Eggs are gathered into well-guarded nurseries where they hatch after five to six months. Hatchlings are raised communally but each is assigned a "parent", a nonwarrior adult that takes personal responsibility for that hatchling.

Locathah shamans are priests of up to the 3rd level.

Ecology: Locathah are omnivorous. They have both aquatic farmers and hunter-gatherers that provide a varied diet for their clan brethren. The locathah's stone-age technology is limited to manufacturing weapons, tools, and ornaments from available materials. More advanced or magical items are scavenged from sunken wrecks, invaders, and drowning victims. Although they defend their territories against hostile invaders, locathah cooperate with nonhostile visitors, especially traders. Locathan coral carvings and jewelry are highly valued by art collectors and are traded for forged metals, ceramics, and durable magical items. Locathah can be hired to assist travelers in their realm. They also collect tolls from fishermen using locathah territorial waters.

Locathah never voluntarily leave the water. They are almost helpless on land. They are limited to slow crawls because they are unused to supporting their own weight. The use of magic to fly or levitate will negate this helplessness. They risk swift suffocation as their gills dry out; after ten turns, a surfaced locathah suffers 1 point of damage each round. If the locathah immerses itself in water, the damage is halted.

Locathah always try to recover captive locathah or their bodies. If such are detected aboard a ship, other locathah might first demand the return of their kin or simply sink the boat by carving into its bottom.

	Lurker	Trapper	Trapper, Forest
CLIMATE/TERRAIN:	Subterranean	Subterranean	Forest
FREQUENCY:	Uncommon	Rare	Rare
ORGANIZATION:	Solitary	Solitary	Solitary
ACTIVITY CYCLE:	Any	Any	Any
DIET:	Omnivore	Carnivore	Carnivore
INTELLIGENCE:	Non- (0)	Highly (13-14)	Highly (13-14)
TREASURE:	C, Y	G	G
ALIGNMENT:	Neutral	Neutral	Neutral
NO. APPEARING:	1 (1-4)	1	1
ARMOR CLASS:	6	3	4
MOVEMENT:	1, Fl 9 (B)	3	3, Br 6
HIT DICE:	10	12	10
THAC0:	11	9	11
NO. OF ATTACKS:	1	4 +	See below
DAMAGE/ATTACK:	1-6	See below	See below
SPECIAL ATTACKS:	See below	See below	See below
SPECIAL DEFENSES:	Nil	Nil	Nil
MAGIC RESISTANCE:	Nil	Nil	Nil
SIZE:	H (20' diam.)	H (20'-30' diam.)	H (20' diam.)
MORALE:	Steady (11)	Steady (11)	Steady (11)
XP VALUE:	2,000	3,000	3,000

The lurker is a carnivorous scavenger found only in subterranean settings. It resembles a large manta ray; its grayish belly is textured like stone. The lurker typically attaches itself to a ceiling, where it is very difficult to detect (only 10% chance) unless actually prodded.

Combat: Lurkers are slow-moving creatures that must wait for their prey to come into range. Lurkers wait on the ceiling, then drop and wrap themselves around their prey. Lurkers cause a -4 penalty to opponents' surprise rolls. The constriction causes 1d6 points of damage per round and suffocation within 1d4+1 rounds, regardless of the damage suffered by the victim. This damage is automatic each round unless the victim breaks free or the lurker dies. Lurkers do not stop attacking until dead. Prey can only fight with short weapons that were in hand when the lurker attacked.

Habitat/Society: Lurkers are solitary creatures. The females lays eggs in a glutinous clutch near the ceiling. The hatchlings fall to the ground and feed on vermin until they become large enough to fly. Young resemble rectangular patches of moss.

Ecology: Lurkers are opportunistic feeders that make do with whatever wanders by. The lurker flies by means of gases generated into sacs. These gases may be used in the preparation of a *potion of levitation*. Lurker eggs or hatchlings may be sold as living defenses for those who want them. Lurker, trapper, and miner eggs can all be sold for 900 gp, hatchlings for 1,100 gp.

Trapper

The subterranean trapper is found only in caves and other dark places. It can alter its shape and color to resemble the local floor and to form a protuberance in the center that resembles a box. A trapper is difficult to detect (95%) once it has settled into a disguise. When prey wanders into the trapper's center, the creature's edges rise up and wrap around the victim. The victim suffers damage per round equal to 4 points plus his Armor Class (a victim with AC 2 suffers 6 points of damage per round). The constriction prevents breathing; victims smother in six rounds regardless of the damage suffered. A trapper does not release a victim unless the trapper is reduced to 1 hit point or killed.

Trappers are immune to heat- or cold-based attacks. Trappers remain wrapped in a ball for 1d8 hours while digesting a victim. The remains of their victims are excreted below and form the trappers' treasure troves. A typical trapper can cover about 400 square feet, while large ones can cover up to 600 square feet.

Eggs are laid in a pebble-like mass. Hatchlings resemble flat rocks. Trapper skin may be used to make nonmagical +1 leather armor.

Forest Trapper (Miner)

The forest trapper, or miner, resembles a tailless manta ray mottled brown or green-brown. Its frontal and dorsal ridges are hard bone.

It preys primarily on small forest animals but traps larger creatures by burrowing beneath paths or roads, then extending the 1d20+5 poisonous, twig-like barbs on its back through the surface. Passers-by have a 25% chance (75% if surprised) of unknowingly stepping on one. If not surprised, druids or rangers have a 5% chance per level of spotting and identifying the barbs. Victims must roll successful saving throws vs. poison or be paralyzed for 2d20 turns. A miner will not surface until all surface movement stops. Then it attacks in the same manner as a subterranean trapper.

Miners travel slowly on the surface by rippling like a snake. Burrowing is faster but travel is limited to soil, sand, and gravel.

Because a miner is always underground unless attacking, it is rarely attacked. The miner's toxin is located in sacs at the base of the barbs. The toxic barbs can be used in a blowgun or as a hand weapon by small creatures, provided the grip is wrapped.

Eggs are laid in a clutch several feet below the surface. The young feed on burrowing animals for their first year.

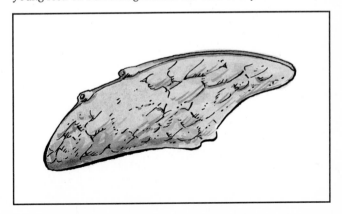

Lycanthrope, General

Lycanthropes are humans who can transform themselves to resemble normal animals or monsters. The term "lycanthrope" is actually a misnomer, coming from the roots *lycos* (wolf), and *anthropos* (man). A more correct term is "therianthrope," from *therios* (animal) and *anthropos.* However, since werewolves are the most common therianthropes, the term lycanthrope has gained much more popularity, and more common usage.

To further confuse the issue, there are creatures like the wolfwere and jackalwere, animals which can assume human form. These creatures ("antherions" for lack of a better term) pass on their condition genetically (that is, by having offspring), not by biting and infecting other creatures. Other differences between the two classes of creature include their vulnerabilities: antherions can be struck by cold iron, lycanthropes by silver. Antherions hate lycanthropes, and always attack their counterparts (wolfweres attack werewolves, etc.). Likewise, most lycanthropes feel enmity for antherions, and attack on sight as well.

In addition, there are many subspecies of some lycanthropes, beyond the differences in animal type. For instance, there are three distinct subspecies of werewolf, differing in their secondary form: one has fangs, a furred body, a tail, wolf-like legs, and lupine features (but without the snout); another has a very wolf-like face and body, with human hands, and is easily mistaken for a wolf when down on all fours; and the third secondary form is that of a huge wolf, as big as a bear.

The condition of being a lycanthrope, often referred to as a curse, is called lycanthropy. A distinction must be made between true lycanthropes and infected lycanthropes. True lycanthropes are those to whom lycanthropy is a genetic trait; they breed with other lycanthropes and produce baby lycanthropes. Only true lycanthropes can infect others with lycanthropy. Infected lycanthropes are those whose lycanthropy results from being wounded by a true lycanthrope.

There are also creatures known by some as "induced lycanthropes," whose shape changes are effected by magical items; these creatures cannot infect others with lycanthropy, though the magical items can be transferred to new owners. Some of the items are cursed, so that once they are worn, they cannot be removed without the application of a *remove curse* spell. Induced lycanthropes include swanmays and anyone using a *cloak of the manta ray.*

Finally, there are "cursed lycanthropes" created by a certain spell, *curse of lycanthropy* (see boxed text).

True lycanthropes and induced lycanthropes seldom hate their "curse." They see themselves as being like any other creature, with the same right to survival. Those bitten and infected, or those affected by the *curse of lycanthropy* spell, are generally unhappy with their fate. These unfortunates seek cures and occasionally try to hunt down the lycanthrope who infected them (or the wizard who cursed them).

Description: Most lycanthropes have three forms; some have only two. See the individual descriptions for more details. The first form is always the natural humanoid form, which over time becomes more and more reminiscent of the lycanthrope's animal form. The second form is a hybrid, combining both animal and humanoid features; the size of this hybrid tends to lie between the humanoid size and the size of the creature replicated. The third form of the lycanthrope is externally identical to that of a normal creature of the replicated species; the only visual clue is that the eyes may glow in the dark. A slain lycanthrope always reverts to its natural humanoid form within one round of being killed.

Curse of Lycanthropy (Necromancy, Alteration)
6th-level Wizard spell

Range: Touch	Casting Time: 6
Components: V, S, M	Area of Effect: Creature touched
Duration: Special	Saving Throw: Negates

This spell causes a temporary case of lycanthropy in the victim touched by the caster. A normal attack roll is required for the wizard to touch the victim, who must then roll a saving throw vs. spell. Failure indicates that the victim is affected by lycanthropy. Every month, the victim's condition manifests with the full moon; after each attack, the victim can make another saving throw vs. spell to see if the spell's effects wear off.

Almost any type of standard lycanthropy can be induced with this spell. By using the blood of a normal animal as a spell component, the wizard can cause the victim to assume that were-form.

Lycanthropy manifests the night of the full moon, as well as the night immediately before, and the night immediately after, the full moon. During those nights, the character gains no benefits from sleep or normal healing, and loses all memory of events which happen while in animal form. In all respects, the character gains the abilities, immunities, defenses, and bloodlust of an infected lycanthrope; it cannot transmit lycanthropy. When the three-night attack is over, the victim can make another saving throw, with a −3 penalty, to throw off the spell's effects.

A *remove curse* allows the character to roll a saving throw vs. polymorph; success means the curse is broken. A *wish* also dispels the curse. No other spells can remove the curse.

Contracting lycanthropy: Although the forms of attack vary with each species, all true lycanthropes can transmit their dreadful affliction. Any humanoid creature injured by a lycanthrope but not actually killed (and presumably eaten) has a chance to contract lycanthropy. This chance equals 1% per point of damage caused by the lycanthrope. Some lycanthropes transmit their affliction only through their bite, others through any natural attack, and some even through the weapons they use. For ease of bookkeeping, if a character suffers 24 points of damage (from all attacks) from a true werewolf, the character has a 24% chance to become an infected werewolf.

If the character eats belladonna within an hour of the attack, there is a 25% chance this will cure the affliction; it definitely incapacitates the character for 1d4 days. Note that only a sprig of belladonna need be eaten, and it must be reasonably fresh (picked within the last week). If too much is eaten, the character may still be cured, but is incapacitated for 2d4 days.

The only other way to lift the affliction is to cast a *remove curse* on the character, on the night of a full moon, or the night immediately preceding or following the full moon. After *remove curse* is cast, if the character makes a successful saving throw vs. polymorph, the curse is broken. Otherwise the changes take place and the spell has no effect. *Cure disease* and other healing spells and abilities have no effect against lycanthropy.

Only infected lycanthropes can be cured. To a true lycanthrope, lycanthropy is as natural as breathing, and the condition cannot be altered. True lycanthropes have complete control over their physical states; they are not affected by darkness, phases of the moon, or any of the other situations which traditionally affect infected lycanthropes.

Combat: In human form, the lycanthrope uses weapons to attack. They tend to use natural attack abilities in other forms.

In lycanthrope form, the monster can be struck only by silver or magical weapons. Wounds from any other weapon heal too quickly to cause actual damage. Damage from spells, acid, fire, and other special effects apply normally. Because of their vulnerability to silver, some lycanthropes have a psychological aversion to the metal and refuse to handle it; in some cases, the psychosomatic effect is so great that touching silver actually burns the lycanthrope.

Habitat/Society: True lycanthropes can change shape at will, regardless of the time of day or phase of the moon. Infected lycanthropes are usually humanoid during the day. When darkness falls on the night of a full moon, or on the night immediately preceding or immediately following a full moon, the infected lycanthrope unwillingly changes shape and is overcome by bloodlust. During this time, an infected PC is beyond the player's control; the DM takes over the character.

The character's Strength increases temporarily to 19. Armor Class, number of attacks, movement rate, and immunities, become identical to those of the type of lycanthrope that bit the character. The transformed character wants only to hunt and kill, and usually selects either personal friends or enemies as victims. The werecreature makes no distinction between friends and enemies; all that matters is the Strength of the emotion binding them.

When the character returns to normal form, 10% to 60% (1d6 × 10) of any wounds suffered while in animal form heal instantly. The character also has hazy, haunting memories of performing terrible acts.

Each type of lycanthrope has its own language as well as its humanoid language; some may be able to speak the languages used by the animals they imitate.

True lycanthropes tend to avoid human society unless attacking or on an errand. Lycanthropes travel alone or in packs. The packs are usually of similar lycanthropes, but may also include normal animals or monsters whom the lycanthropes resemble. Some lycanthropes have the ability to summon such creatures.

Ecology: Lycanthropes fit a variety of roles, depending on the type of creatures they become, scavengers act as scavengers, predators as predators. See individual descriptions for more details.

Designing New Types of Lycanthrope
Described here is a process for creating variant lycanthropes, either as true lycanthropes, one-shot opponents, or for the results of a *curse of lycanthropy.*

Animal Type: Virtually any predator between the size of a small dog and a large bear can be the basis for a type of lycanthrope. Most (but not all) true lycanthropes are mammals; most (but not all) are carnivores. An animal type used by the DM to create a race of true lycanthropes should be a carnivorous mammal with animal Intelligence (1), or rarely, a reptile, bird, or even fish with animal Intelligence. There has never been a reliable report of a were-amphibian of any type.

Induced lycanthropes, by spell or item, can be created using a wide variety of animal types, and even monstrous creatures.

Appearance: In humanoid form, the lycanthrope has subtle indications of the curse, ranging from hair color like that of the animal, to general facial type, to voice and actions. In animal form, the lycanthrope resembles a large version of the normal animal (but not so large as to be immediately noticeable). On close inspection, the animal form's eyes show a faint spark of unnatural intelligence, and often glow red in the dark.

The lycanthrope may also have a third form, part human and part animal. This form is usually humanoid in general shape, and the body has the same covering as the animal (usually fur, sometimes scales or feathers). Facial features and body shape change somewhat, gaining more characteristics of the animal (fangs, whiskers, claws, animal leg structure, etc.).

Statistics and Attributes: To determine the new lycanthrope's statistics, extrapolate from those of the base animal and from existing lycanthrope types. If the base animal is more powerful than a wolf, the new lycanthrope should have more Hit Dice than a werewolf; if the base animal is similar to a giant rat, the new werecreature should have about the same Hit Dice as a wererat. In almost every case, the new lycanthrope should have at least 1-2 Hit Dice more than the base animal.

The lycanthrope gets the same attack forms as the base animal type, such as claws, bite, tail slap, head butt, or whatever. The damage should be very similar to that caused by the base animal. Many lycanthropes associate with animals of their base type, and the werebeast should be able to dominate such a group.

Armor Class depends on the base animal's natural toughness, speed, and dexterity. The lycanthrope should have a slightly better AC than the base animal, perhaps by 1 or 2 places.

Movement rate should be the same as that of the base animal, as should diet and habitat. Morale should be about one category better than that of the base animal.

The creature's alignment tends to be an extrapolated version of the base animal's alignment. Since most base animals are neutral, the DM must look at the animal's tendencies. If the animal is a vicious predator and a strong fighter, the lycanthropic version is probably evil; it tries to stay out of the way of other creatures, it may be good or neutral. If the animal is very independent, the lycanthrope should be chaotic; if the animal is very methodical and has regular habits, the lycanthrope is probably lawful.

Vulnerability: True lycanthropes share a vulnerability to silver weapons, possibly because of the metal's mystical relationship with the moon, or the inherent qualities or powers of the metal itself. Extremely rare variants might have no such vulnerability, but instead may have developed a weakness for another precious metal (gold and copper being the most likely), or perhaps for bronze, obsidian, or even wood.

Special Abilities: In addition to their abilities of shapeshifting, calling normal animals to their aid, and so forth, some lycanthropes have other special powers. These should not be rolled randomly for a new lycanthrope type, but chosen to fit with the attitude and style of the base animal. A few samples are listed below.

- Thief skills, level 1-6
- *Charm person* by gaze or voice
- Regeneration (except for damage from silver weapons)
- Wizard spells, casting level 1-6
- *Cause fear*
- Psionicist abilities, level 1-6
- Cast *sleep*, once per day
- Poison

Lycanthrope, Seawolf

	Lesser	Greater
CLIMATE/TERRAIN:	Saltwater	Saltwater
FREQUENCY:	Very rare	Very rare
ORGANIZATION:	Pack	Pack
ACTIVITY CYCLE:	Any	Any
DIET:	Carnivore	Carnivore
INTELLIGENCE:	Average (8-10)	Low to high (5-14)
TREASURE:	Nil	Nil
ALIGNMENT:	Neutral evil	Chaotic evil
NO. APPEARING:	3-18	4-16
ARMOR CLASS:	6 (7)	5
MOVEMENT:	Sw 12, 30	Sw 27, 9
HIT DICE:	2+2	9+2
THAC0:	19	11
NO. OF ATTACKS:	1 (3)	1 or 2
DAMAGE/ATTACK:	2d4 (1-2/1-2/1-4)	3-12 or 1-2 and by weapon type
SPECIAL ATTACKS:	Nil	Nil
SPECIAL DEFENSES:	Nil	Hit only by silver, cold iron, or +1 or better magical weapons
MAGIC RESISTANCE:	Nil	Nil
SIZE:	M(6'-7')	L(12'-15' long) or M
MORALE:	Steady (11-12)	Elite (13-14)
XP VALUE:	120	1,400

The seawolves are humans who can assume a form combining aspects of a seal and a wolf. Their packs roam the seas in search of ships to attack.

The monstrous form of the lesser seawolf has the 6 to 7 foot long body of a seal. The head and shoulders are those of a wolf. In human form the lesser seawolves stand 5 to 6 feet tall. All are thickly muscled and have tiny ears and long hair that covers their head and shoulders like a mane. The lesser seawolf has a hybrid form of a wolfman, a humanoid shape that retains the seawolf's teeth, claws, and fur; statistics for this form are given in parentheses above.

Combat: Lesser seawolves approach a ship in seawolf form, then change into the hybrid form and climb aboard. There they use their teeth and claws to kill their opponents. If the ship looks too heavily defended, the seawolves may gnaw holes in the hull in order to sink the ship.

Unlike most other lycanthropes, lesser seawolves have no special protection against normal weapons. Dead seawolves revert to their human form in a single round.

Habitat/Society: Most seawolves were formerly fishermen or sailors; as such, they also tend to be male and human. They travel in packs with those of their own kind. Their fierce hatred of their former coworkers drives them to seek to kill them or pass on the lycanthropic curse. Victims who acquire the disease become seawolves in 2-5 days. Once night falls, the new seawolf slips into the water and goes off in search of a pack.

Seawolves are nomads constantly roaming the cooler sections of the seas. They neither build lairs nor keep treasure. During the day, they sleep on beaches or in caves or appropriated houses. If surprised on a beach, they pretend to be shipwreck victims, then kill the intruders and take their clothing. If at sea, the seawolves are still able to sleep during the day by floating on their backs; in this case they may be mistaken for a cluster of drowning victims. If a ship moves close to investigate, the seawolves wait for the best opportunity to attack and take over the ship.

Seawolves breathe air. They can remain submerged for 17-24 (1d8+16) minutes. Failure to surface after that time causes them to suffer 1-6 points of damage each round until they drown.

Female seawolves give birth to single cubs. These may appear to be human infants during the day or baby seals at night. Seawolves lack parental feelings and abandon the cubs. Although the cubs are able to swim and hunt from birth, they have difficulty keeping up with adults and often drown during the day if they are at sea. Only 5% of cubs reach adulthood. The offspring of a seawolf and a human are good swimmers who feel mysteriously drawn to the sea, but few (25%) become seawolves upon reaching adolescence.

Seawolves may ally themselves with other evil aquatic lycanthropes. They hate selkies, whom they consider allies of the humanoids. Lesser seawolves attack selkies on sight.

Their diet includes a variety of foods, such as shellfish, fish, seabirds, sea mammals, and anyone they can sink their teeth into. Occasionally, packs may wander into a town and take over a tavern for a round of drinking and wenching.

Seawolf personalities are a twisted version of their original, human personalities. It is as if the seawolf persona is a savage, magnified version of all the original person's bad traits. Seawolves periodically return to their original home port. This may be a subconscious longing for their old life or a means to renew their hatred of those still humanoid. If a seawolf spots his old self's mate or child, he may attempt to make contact.

Ecology: Seawolves are the sworn enemies of any humanoid who makes his living in the sea. They live to destroy shipping, spread terror, and spread their curse further.

Greater Seawolves

The monstrous form of the greater seawolf has a 12 to 15 foot long body, but is otherwise identical to the lesser seawolf. In human form, greater seawolves stand 6 to 7 feet tall.

Combat: Greater seawolves assume their human forms to get close to their opponents. The typical plan is to bite or strangle one or two deckhands, take their weapons, and begin a general assault.

In seawolf form, greater seawolves can be harmed only by silver, cold iron, or magical weapons of +1 or better. Steel weapons have no effect. Dead seawolves revert to their human form in one round.

Lycanthrope, Werebat

CLIMATE/TERRAIN:	Temperate woodlands
FREQUENCY:	Rare
ORGANIZATION:	Flock
ACTIVITY CYCLE:	Night
DIET:	Blood
INTELLIGENCE:	Average (8-10)
TREASURE:	B
ALIGNMENT:	Neutral evil

NO. APPEARING:	1-4
ARMOR CLASS:	5
MOVEMENT:	9, Fl 15 (D)
HIT DICE:	4+2
THAC0:	17
NO. OF ATTACKS:	3
DAMAGE/ATTACK:	1d4/1d4
SPECIAL ATTACKS:	See below
SPECIAL DEFENSES:	See below
MAGIC RESISTANCE:	Nil
SIZE:	M (6' tall)
MORALE:	Steady (11-12)
XP VALUE:	420

Like the other species of lycanthrope found in Ravenloft, two varieties of werebat exist—natural (or true) and infected. True werebats are those creatures who have been born to werebat parents. The parents may be either true or infected werebats themselves, but the offspring of any two werebats is a true werebat. In those rare cases when a child is born with one werebat and one human parent, there is a 50% chance that it will be a true werebat and a 25% chance that it will be an infected werebat.

True werebats have three forms: normal human, vampire bat, or hybrid. In the first form, it is marked by bat-like features and traits (an aversion to bright lights, keen night vision, a taste for blood or raw meat, etc.). In its vampire bat form, it looks just like a common vampire bat. By far the most feared of its forms, however, is that of the hybrid. In this form, it retains its humanoid shape but takes on the added features of a bat. The arms extend to become willowy and leather wings form under them, the teeth sharpen into deadly fangs, and the snout protrudes from the face. The nails stretch into deadly claws and the eyes spawn an inner glow when light hits them.

Infected werebats have only two of the three forms listed above. Most (75%) have a human and hybrid form, while the rest have only a human and true bat form.

Combat: The type of attacks employed by a werebat depend upon its form. In human form, it will depend upon weapons to inflict damage, for its bare hands inflict but 1d2 points per attack. If at all possible, the creature will avoid combat in this form.

In bat form, they attack just as if they were bats. Each round, they may attack once and inflict but a single point of damage with any successful strike. The bitten victim, of course, stands a chance of contracting lycanthropy (see below), even from this meager wound. Opponents of a werebat in this form will find that it is unusually resilient, for it has its full human-form hit points.

In hybrid form, the werebat does not have the manual dexterity to employ weapons effectively. However, its deadly sharp claws and needle-like teeth make it far from helpless. In each round it may strike twice with its claws (inflicting 1d4 points of damage each). If both of these attacks hits, it may follow with a vicious bite that does 2d4 points of damage. Werebats can fly in their hybrid form and often use this ability to their advantage in combat.

Anyone who takes damage from a werebat's natural attacks stands a chance of contracting the disease of lycanthropy and becoming an infected werebat. Every point of damage done indicates a flat 2% chance per point that the victim will become infected. The procedures for curing an infected lycanthrope are given in Chapter 5 of the *Ravenloft Boxed Set*.

Werebats can be harmed only by silver or +1 or better magical weapons. Any wound inflicted by another type of weapon knits as quickly as it is inflicted, hinting at the creature's true nature.

Habitat/Society: Werebats favor caves in lightly wooded, temperate regions as their homes. From here, they can fly out and seek prey from which they can draw the blood necessary to satisfy their thirst.

Werebat caves are commonly home to only one family of werebats (two parents and 1-4 young). The young remain in true bat form until they reach 3 years of age. A this time, they mature into adults and, within a single year, become fully grown. This time of transformation brings out a great hunger in the creature, which forces it to spend most of its time hunting and feeding. Human villages near a werebat cave will certainly lose many citizens to the feasting of the ravenous creature at this time.

In addition to the werebat family, each cave will contain 20-200 (20d10) common bats and 1-10 giant bats. All of these lesser are under the command of the adult werebats and will act as their sentinels and companions.

Ecology: Although werebats favor humans and demihumans as prey, they have been known to feed on the blood of other mammals (like cattle and horses) when preferred prey is not available. Interestingly, such animals seem to be immune to the lycanthropy that these dark creatures spread.

While werebats do look upon humans and demihumans as animals to be devoured, they are not cruel or evil in their attacks. They simply regard such beings as having a lower place in the food chain. Werebats will, typically, refer to themselves as "predators of the night."

Lycanthrope, Werebear

CLIMATE/TERRAIN:	Cold or temperate regions
FREQUENCY:	Rare
ORGANIZATION:	Solitary
ACTIVITY CYCLE:	Nocturnal
DIET:	Omnivore
INTELLIGENCE:	Exceptional (11-12)
TREASURE:	R, T, X
ALIGNMENT:	Chaotic good

NO. APPEARING:	1-4
ARMOR CLASS:	2
MOVEMENT:	9
HIT DICE:	7+3
THAC0:	13
NO. OF ATTACKS:	3
DAMAGE/ATTACK:	1-3/1-3/2-8
SPECIAL ATTACKS:	Hug for 2-16
SPECIAL DEFENSES:	Hit only by silver or +1 or better magical weapons
MAGIC RESISTANCE:	Nil
SIZE:	L (6'-9')
MORALE:	Elite (13-14)
XP VALUE:	1,400

Werebears are humans who can transform themselves into large brown bears. They are the best known good-aligned lycanthropes. The ursine form most often resembles a brown bear. Some have blond, reddish, black, or ivory fur (the latter is common in frozen regions).

In human form they are large, stout, well-muscled, and hairy. Their brown hair is thick; males usually wear beards. Some have reddish, blond, ivory, or black hair; this matches the color of the ursine form. They dress in simple cloth and leather garments that are easily removed, repaired, or replaced.

Combat: In human form, the werebear uses available weapons, preferring axes, spears, and knives, since these have practical applications suitable for woodland life. If attacked in daylight, the werebear usually remains human unless death is likely. The shapechange renders the werebear helpless for a round. In ursine form, the werebear attacks with two swiping claws and a bite. If both claws hit, during the next round the werebear can hug for an additional 2-16 points of damage. This subsequent damage continues automatically each round thereafter.

Like those of other lycanthropes, the werebear's defenses function only in the bear form. Weapons used against the werebear must be either silver or magical weapons of +1 or better. Werebears can summon 1-6 brown bears within 2-12 turns, provided such animals are within one mile. Werebears heal at three times the normal human rate and can *cure disease* in another creature in 1-4 weeks if they so desire.

If a werebear dies, he reverts to his human form in one round.

Habitat/Society: Werebears are normally solitary creatures. As humans, they build cabins far from settled areas, preferably in a deep forest near well-stocked waters. Werebears do not marry although they may have preferred mates they meet on a very irregular basis. Females bear 1-2 children in human form. Such children are very stout and grow quickly. Within eight years they gain adolescence and the ability to change into werebears. Shortly after, the mother drives the children out and seeks a mate to start the cycle anew. The newly independent young are discreetly guided and assisted by older werebears. Despite their apparent isolationism and rugged individualism, werebears have a sense of community. They never attack each other and aid any werebear threatened by another lycanthrope species.

Werebears are closest to forest-dwelling classes like rangers, druids, and wildlife-oriented priests. They rarely enter villages and never enter cities except in dire emergencies or to help other good-aligned people, especially those threatened by evil lycanthropes. Werebears hate wererats and werewolves.

The average werebear claims a territory 1 to 4 square miles in size. Fishing areas are open to all werebears. A werebear feels a close bond to its home region, acting as a game warden to protect its territory and the animals therein from the ravages of intruders.

Werebears do not travel a great deal. Only the rare individual (usually young) can be coaxed into joining a band of adventurers. Werebears may join an adventuring group as guides, provided the money is right and the job is agreeable.

Treasure is usually limited to small, valuable commodities like gold, platinum, gems, and jewelry. Werebears rarely carry any treasure and instead hide it near their homes. They also collect scrolls, potions, and other magical items, often as fees or rewards for past services. Werebears destroy any magical items that specifically affect lycanthropes or bears, since such items might be used against themselves.

Ecology: Werebears are omnivorous, preferring fish, small mammals, and a honey-rich mead. This mead is extremely intoxicating to normal humans. Werebears have few natural enemies. Their closest enemies are the werewolves who share their preferred wilderness regions.

Lycanthrope, Wereboar

CLIMATE/TERRAIN:	Any dry land
FREQUENCY:	Rare
ORGANIZATION:	Tribal
ACTIVITY CYCLE:	Any
DIET:	Omnivore
INTELLIGENCE:	Average (8-10)
TREASURE:	B, S
ALIGNMENT:	Neutral

NO. APPEARING:	2-8
ARMOR CLASS:	4
MOVEMENT:	12
HIT DICE:	5+2
THAC0:	15
NO. OF ATTACKS:	1
DAMAGE/ATTACK:	2-12 or by weapon
SPECIAL ATTACKS:	Nil
SPECIAL DEFENSES:	Silver or +1 or better to hit
MAGIC RESISTANCE:	Nil
SIZE:	M (5'-6' tall)
MORALE:	Elite (13)
XP VALUE:	650

Wereboars are humans who are able to transform themselves into a form combining human and boar features. Their tempers are as ugly as their features.

In human form wereboars tend to be stocky, muscular people of average height. Their hair is short and stiff. They dress in simple garments that are easy to remove, repair, or replace.

The boar form stands slightly taller than the human form, but the hunchbacked posture thrusts the head forward. The head is identical to a boar's head, complete with short tusks. The torso's diameter is doubled, the neck shortened, and the feet become hoof-like. Stiff, black hair like wire bristles covers the skin.

Combat: The wereboar combines his hands and tusks for deadly effect. The wereboar seizes a target and pulls it toward his head. He stabs his tusks into the victim, then pulls his victim to one side while swinging his head in the other direction, which tears the wound further. He then tosses the victim aside and attacks someone else. A wereboar will gladly wade into the center of a group of opponents and then fight his way out.

In human form the wereboar attacks with whatever weapon he has. Wereboars prefer bludgeoning or chopping weapons, such as axes and maces, rather than stabbing or missile weapons such as swords, spears, or bows.

In either form the wereboar is immune to damage from nonmagical and nonsilver weapons. Such wounds are little more than scratches that quickly heal.

Habitat/Society: Wereboars are ill-tempered, easily angered, and almost as prone to attack their few friends as they are to attack an enemy. As humans they are rude, crude, and vulgar. However, they are invaluable allies in a fight. A wereboar does not give his friendship easily, but when he does it is a special bond he will not break. The problem is, due to the wereboar's peculiar personality, it is difficult to tell whether he is being friendly or hostile.

Wereboars prefer dense woodlands, ideally far from towns and cities. Like werebears, they live in caves or build cabins for their homes. Their homes tend to be ill-kept and slovenly. Wereboars don't repair things, they replace them.

Despite their personalities, wereboars have close-knit families. Females give birth to litters of 1d4+2 offspring. Newborns are very small by human standards but are strong and able to crawl hours after birth. The offspring mature quickly. When they reach adolescence at eight years, they gain the ability to become wereboars themselves. A wereboar father appears to be distant and aloof, but a staunch protector who will attack any foe who threatens his family, no matter how uneven the odds. Females are aggressive when defending their young (+2 bonus to attack roll). Neither males nor females check morale when defending their young.

The diet is a mixture of small game, vegetables, and fungi. Their favorite food is the subterranean fungus called truffles; even in human form they can detect the truffles growing several feet underground. Wereboars aren't very good gardeners. A typical garden is a cleared field strewn with a variety of seeds and bulbs in the hope that something edible will grow. Wereboar cuisine is equally haphazard; it can be summed up as burned meat and stews.

Wereboars avoid normal hogs and boars. They are suspicious of strangers. Wereboars assume everyone is hostile. In human form they may wait for the first attack, but when in boar form they usually (75% chance) chase the intruders away and attack any who defend themselves.

Ecology: Wereboars produce little of value, whether trade goods or services. Their main desire is simply to stay away from everyone else. In the wild, they defend their territories against any intruders. Wereboars fit into orcish society as well as they do into human society, and might sometimes assist or ally themselves with orcish forces. Wereboars can tolerate half-orcs.

Lycanthrope, Werefox (Foxwoman)

CLIMATE/TERRAIN:	Any
FREQUENCY:	Very rare
ORGANIZATION:	Solitary
ACTIVITY CYCLE:	Nocturnal
DIET:	Carnivore
INTELLIGENCE:	Average to Exceptional (8-16)
TREASURE:	E, Q (x5), S
ALIGNMENT:	Chaotic evil

NO. APPEARING:	1 (see below)
ARMOR CLASS:	2, 4, or 6
MOVEMENT:	24, 18, or 12
HIT DICE:	8 + 1
THAC0:	13
NO. OF ATTACKS:	1
DAMAGE/ATTACK:	1-2, 2-12, or by weapon
SPECIAL ATTACKS:	Charms, spells
SPECIAL DEFENSES:	Silver or +1 weapons to hit
MAGIC RESISTANCE:	Special (see below)
SIZE:	M
MORALE:	Elite (13)
XP VALUE:	2,000

A foxwoman is an elven-appearing woman who is able to transform herself into a silver fox form or a silver-furred humanoid (vixen) form with a fox's head. They are extremely self-centered.

The female elven form of the foxwoman is extremely beautiful. She has silver or silver-streaked hair, including a widow's peak. She dresses attractively in loose garments. A pouch holds valuables and spell components.

The vixen form is a hybrid of elven and fox-like features. The body and limbs are those of the elven form but covered with silvery fur. The head and tail are fox-like. The vixen may wear elven clothing. The vixen can run very quickly (18).

The silver fox form appears to be a normal, large fox. It moves extremely fast (24), can *pass without trace*, and is 90% undetectable in undergrowth if it passes out of view for a moment.

Combat: The silver fox's bite inflicts 1-2 points of damage but is otherwise harmless. The vixen's more savage bite causes 2d6 points of damage. Human or elven women who are bitten by a vixen for 50% or more of their hit points become foxwomen within three days unless both a *cure disease* and a *remove curse* spell are cast upon the victim by a priest of at least 12th level.

In elven form, the foxwoman relies on weapons. She gains a +1 bonus with bow or sword. Her best weapon is her incredible beauty. Any human, humanoid, or demihuman males whose Wisdoms are 13 or less are effectively caught by a *charm* spell. Those whose Wisdoms are 14 or greater are not charmed but still find the foxwoman extremely attractive. In elven form, the foxwoman has magic use as a wizard of level 1d4. She is 90% resistant to *sleep* and *charm* spells.

In any form, the foxwoman is able to see by infravision (60-foot range). They can only be harmed by silver or +1 or better magical weapons. Scars from nonfatal wounds vanish within a month.

Habitat/Society: Foxwomen dwell in lonely woodlands far from humanoid communities. Their homes may be hidden cottages or comfortably furnished cave complexes; in either case their homes are filled with typical human comforts. Foxwomen are solitary in regard to their own kind. They are self-serving, vain, and hedonistic. Foxwomen serve their vanity by enslaving humanoid males. Those males become servants and companions.

Werefoxes do not keep dwarves, gnomes, or halflings; such males are slain quietly as soon as the opportunity arises.

Each foxwoman is always accompanied by 1d4 + 1 charmed males. At least one of the males is a fighter (70%) or ranger (30%) of level 1d4 + 1. There is a 50% chance that any one of the other males is also a fighter of level 1d4. There is a 10% chance that one of the remaining males is a cleric (10%), druid (45%), mage (10%), thief (25%), or some other class (10%) of level 1d4. Of her elven or half-elven companions, 25% are multi-class characters. All males who do not fit into any of the above categories are 0-level fighters and elves or half-elves of 1 Hit Die. The males may use such magical items as they possessed prior to being charmed into the foxwoman's service.

Foxwomen are barren. They must kidnap or adopt their children. There is a 10% chance that a foxwoman has a "daughter." The foxwoman has stolen an elven girl, infected her with lycanthropy, and is raising her as a foxwoman. Such a child is be 1d8 + 5 years old. If she is 12-13, she is treated the same as a normal foxwoman; otherwise she is a noncombatant.

Non-elven women who are afflicted with lycanthropy undergo a slow transformation that alters their normal form. Over a period of one to two years, such women turn into elven women; only their faces and odd marks (tattoos, birthmarks) provide faint proof of their old identities.

Ecology: Foxwomen are unique among the lycanthropes. They have no major goals or desires aside from pampering themselves and feeding their vanity. They have little contact with other foxwomen (whom they see as rivals), real foxes (irrelevant beasts), or other lycanthropes (crude, unattractive, and uncharmable).

Lycanthrope, Wererat

CLIMATE/TERRAIN:	Any
FREQUENCY:	Uncommon
ORGANIZATION:	Pack
ACTIVITY CYCLE:	Nocturnal
DIET:	Scavenger
INTELLIGENCE:	Very (11-12)
TREASURE:	C
ALIGNMENT:	Lawful evil

NO. APPEARING:	4-24 (4d6)
ARMOR CLASS:	6
MOVEMENT:	12
HIT DICE:	3+1
THAC0:	17
NO. OF ATTACKS:	1
DAMAGE/ATTACK:	By weapon
SPECIAL ATTACKS:	Surprise
SPECIAL DEFENSES:	Hit only by silver or +1 or better weapons
MAGIC RESISTANCE:	Nil
SIZE:	S-M (3'-6')
MORALE:	Steady (11-12)
XP VALUE:	270

Wererats, also called ratmen, are humans who can transform themselves into three forms—human, human-sized ratman, and giant rat. They are sly and evil, and usually inhabit tunnel complexes beneath cities.

The wererat's human form tends to be a thin, wiry individual of shorter than average height. His eyes constantly dart around, and his nose and mouth may twitch if he is excited. Males often have thin, ragged moustaches.

The ratman form is somewhat shorter than the human form. The head, torso, and tail are identical to those of a rat, but the limbs remain human.

The third form is that of a giant rat 2 feet from nose to rump. This form is identical to that of the giant rat (q.v.). This is the preferred form for travel and spying on potential victims.

Wererats are often followed by 1-6 mice or rats that are instinctively drawn to them but are not controlled by them.

Combat: In all three forms, wererats rely on weapons for their attacks, preferring shortswords and daggers. Anyone who is injured by a true wererat has a 1% chance per point of damage of becoming a wererat. In their ratman and giant rat forms, wererats can be hurt only by silver or magical weapons.

Wererats prefer to attack from ambush. A favorite tactic is to assume human shape and lure unsuspecting victims into a trap. This is the only time wererats are voluntarily alone. Victims are then robbed, held for ransom, or eaten.

Each wererat is able to summon and control 2-12 giant rats.

Habitat/Society: Wererats live in packs, regardless of form, never being alone if they can help it. Solitary wererats are either sole survivors or engaged in mischief. They do not form interpersonal bonds like love or marriage. In fact, wererats rarely mate with their own kind. Offspring of a wererat and a human woman are human, although they are small, like their fathers. Offspring of a female wererat resemble giant rats with human-like paws. These ratlings grow to maturity in two years and gain the ability to transform themselves into human children with an apparent age about three times that of the ratling's actual age.

Wererats prefer subterranean lairs hidden among the sewers and catacombs beneath cities. Nothing can pass through the sewers and escape their attention. Unfortunately for the wererat, the sewer's stains and smells do not vanish when it assumes human form. This effectively limits wererats to the less savory sections of town as well as reducing the number of humans who might unknowingly mate with a wererat.

Wererats see cities as their hunting grounds. They delight in matching their superior intellects and meager physical skills against the more powerful and numerous humans. But they are no fools; they will not attack unless they are sure they can win. If a battle is going against them, wererats will scatter, transform to rat form, and head for the sanctuary of the sewers. They won't even defend their own lairs. Their attitude is that since they had stolen most of their belongings in the first place, they can always replace them.

Wererats are greedy and collect anything they think might have worth. The resulting trove usually has more junk than treasure, but a thorough search may reveal a wide variety of valuables.

Wererats frequent sleazy taverns, both for the cheap alcohol and to follow drunks into the streets to drag them away for the next day's meal.

Ecology: Wererats are parasites. They recognize that they are physically weaker than most species that dominate the surface. They have found and exploited the one niche where they have a chance to dominate, the world beneath the cities. They feed on humans and steal their riches. Humans unknowingly protect the wererats from both surface dwelling creatures and those who might burrow up from far below. Besides, the humans pay for the upkeep of the wererat's sewer realm.

Psychologically, wererats remind humans that no matter how strongly defended they think they are, monsters can still get in. Mothers describe wererats as bogeymen to scare unruly children.

Lycanthrope, Wereraven

CLIMATE/TERRAIN:	Temperate Woodlands
FREQUENCY:	Uncommon
ORGANIZATION:	Flock
ACTIVITY CYCLE:	Day
DIET:	Omnivore
INTELLIGENCE:	Genius (17-18)
TREASURE:	Qx10
ALIGNMENT:	Neutral good

NO. APPEARING:	2-8 (2d4)
ARMOR CLASS:	6
MOVEMENT:	1, Fl 27 (C)
HIT DICE:	4+2
THAC0:	17
NO. OF ATTACKS:	1
DAMAGE/ATTACK:	2-12 (2d6)
SPECIAL ATTACKS:	See below
SPECIAL DEFENSES:	See below
MAGIC RESISTANCE:	Nil
SIZE:	M (5' tall)
MORALE:	Elite (13-14)
XP VALUE:	420

Wereravens are a race of wise and good-aligned shapechangers who seem to have migrated to Ravenloft from another realm (probably Greyhawk) centuries ago. While they are no longer found on their plane of origin, they have managed to survive in Ravenloft.

Natural wereravens have three forms, that of a normal human, a huge raven, and a hybrid of the two. Infected wereravens can assume only two of the above forms. While all infected wereravens can take the human form, roughly half are able to turn into hybrids while the others can transform into huge ravens.

The hybrid form of these creatures looks much like that of a werebat. The arms grow long and thin, sprouting feathers and transforming into wings. The mouth hardens and projects into a straight, pecking beak, and the eyes turn jet black. A coat of feathers replaces the normal body hair of the human form.

Combat: Wereravens are deadly opponents in close combat, although they seldom engage in it. Because they can be hit only by silver weapons or those with a +2 or better magical bonus, these creatures do not fear most armed parties.

When in human form, a wereraven retains its natural immunities to certain weapons, but has no real attack of its own. If forced to fight unarmed, it inflicts a mere 1-2 points of damage. For this reason, wereravens in human form often employ weapons, doing damage appropriate to the arms they wield.

In raven form, the wereraven attacks as if it were a common example of that creature. Thus, it inflicts but 1-2 points of damage but has a 1 in 10 chance of scoring an eye peck with each successful attack. Any eye peck will cause the target to lose the use of one eye until a *heal* or *regeneration* spell can be cast on the victim. Half-blinded persons (those who have lost 1 eye) suffer a −2 on all attack rolls. A second eye peck results in total blindness until the above cure can be affected.

In hybrid form, the wereraven's arms have grown into wings, making them almost useless in combat. However, the muscles in their mouths/beaks strengthen, giving them a savage bite. Each attack made with the creature's beak inflicts 2d6 points of damage.

Anyone bitten or pecked by the wereraven has a 2% chance per point of damage inflicted of becoming an infected wereraven. Infected lycanthropes are discussed in the *Ravenloft Boxed Set*.

Wereravens are strong flyers and often use this ability to their advantage in combat.

Habitat/Society: A wereraven family will be found only at the heart of a dense forest. Here, they live in the hollowed out body of a great tree. Entrance to their lair is possible only from above (if one does not wish to cut or break through the trunk itself). Curiously, the wereravens are able to keep the tree in which they nest from dying even after they have hollowed it out, so it is difficult to distinguish from the normal trees around it.

Wereravens recognize that they are bastions of good in a land dominated by evil. They have managed to survive by avoiding large populations or overt acts of good that would draw the attention of the reigning lords to them. Thus, a wereraven flock will generally have no more than 2-8 adults in it. Of course, such groups have young with them (1-4 per 2 adults), but these are seldom encountered for they remain in a true raven state until they are old enough to fend for themselves. In addition, a typical wereraven lair will draw 10-100 (10d10) common ravens to nest in the trees about it. These wise birds will serve the wereravens, doing their bidding and striving to protect them from harm.

Wereravens are not opposed to helping out the cause of good in Ravenloft, but they do so reluctantly. This is not because they do not wish to do good, but because they fear the wrath of the Dark Powers. It is said that the wereravens have come to the aid of endangered Vistani clans on several occasions and that close ties exist between these two races, but neither will admit this openly.

Ecology: Wereravens are omnivores who prefer to maintain a vegetarian diet. They enjoy berries and nuts, but will eat carrion or kill for fresh meat from time to time in order to maintain good health.

Lycanthrope, Weretiger

CLIMATE/TERRAIN:	Any wilderness
FREQUENCY:	Very rare
ORGANIZATION:	Solitary
ACTIVITY CYCLE:	Nocturnal
DIET:	Carnivore
INTELLIGENCE:	Average (8-10)
TREASURE:	D, Q(x5)
ALIGNMENT:	Neutral

NO. APPEARING:	1-6
ARMOR CLASS:	3
MOVEMENT:	12
HIT DICE:	6+2
THAC0:	15
NO. OF ATTACKS:	3
DAMAGE/ATTACK:	1-4/1-4/1-12
SPECIAL ATTACKS:	Rake for 2-5/2-5
SPECIAL DEFENSES:	Hit only by silver or +1 or better magical weapon
MAGIC RESISTANCE:	Standard
SIZE:	M or L (6'-9')
MORALE:	Elite (13-14)
XP VALUE:	975

Weretigers are humans, usually female, that have the ability to transform into tigerlike forms. They have a strong affinity for all felines.

The human form tends to be sleekly muscular, taller than average, and very agile. The voices of weretigers are husky and they tend to roll their r's.

The weretiger form is a hybrid between a human and a tiger. It is about 25% larger than the human form, and is covered by tiger-striped hide. A 3-foot tail extends from the spine. The legs are more feline than human; this form walks on its toes. The head is also a mixture of features. The ears, nose, muzzle, and teeth are tigerlike, but the eyes and overall shape are human. If the human form's hair is long, it is still present. The fingernails grow into claws. Despite the changes, the hybrid form can pass for human at a distance if properly disguised.

The third form is that of a fully grown tiger without any trace of human features.

Weretigers speak the languages of all feline breeds, so normal felines, including the great cats, have a 75% chance of being friendly toward a weretiger. Even feline monsters have a 25% chance of being automatically friendly. However, weretigers are rarely found in the company of real tigers, being only 5% likely to be accompanied by them.

Combat: In either tiger form, the weretiger attacks with a variety of punches, raking claws, and bites. The weretiger's punches are so strong that they cause 1-4 points of damage. Otherwise the claws can be raked across an opponent, causing 2-5 points of damage. The teeth are the most dreadful weapon. They can tear a victim apart or crush a windpipe. Weretigers usually bite only in their full tiger form.

In human form, the weretiger uses a wide variety of weapons with which it is adept. A weretiger is also good at unarmed combat; it retains its deadly punch in this form, as well as an enhanced sense of smell and night vision.

Habitat/Society: For various reasons weretigresses outnumber weretigers five to one.

Weretigers travel alone or in small prides. They do not marry but have preferred mates, which may be either humans or tigers.

Weretigers give birth to one or two cubs. The cubs are the hybrid form; they look like fuzzy human babies with tails. Cubs mature quickly. They can crawl within days, walk within a month, and hunt within a year. Their physical size matches that of a human child of three times the same age. At age six, they reach adolescence and gain the ability to transform into a fully human form. At age 12, they gain the ability to assume a full-tiger form; this is considered the mark of adulthood.

If a male weretiger mates with either a real tigress or human woman, the offspring initially has the same appearance as the mother. Lycanthropic transformations do not begin until the hybrid reaches adolescence.

Weretigers are omnivorous. In the wild they roam a territory of 7-10 (1d4 + 6) square miles. Their homes are usually near human settlements. These tend to be well kept cabins with small herb and vegetable gardens. The only livestock will be a variety of cats and some poultry.

Weretigers rarely live in confined settings such as cities or large towns because their lycanthropic nature would be hard to conceal. If found in such a setting, one or two weretigers in human form will be on an errand, such as a mission, a revel, or a simple shopping trip. In any form, weretigers are very confident and not prone to attack unless provoked.

Treasure varies widely, acquired as payment for past services, plunder from past adventures, or scavenged from the remains of past opponents. Weretigers have an affinity for gems and often keep a small cache hidden somewhere near their homes.

Ecology: Weretigers are the most adaptable of the lycanthropes. They are equally at home in human, feline, or monster company.

Lycanthrope, Werewolf

CLIMATE/TERRAIN:	Any
FREQUENCY:	Common
ORGANIZATION:	Pack
ACTIVITY CYCLE:	Nocturnal
DIET:	Carnivore
INTELLIGENCE:	Average (8-10)
TREASURE:	B
ALIGNMENT:	Chaotic evil

NO. APPEARING:	3-18 (3d6)
ARMOR CLASS:	5
MOVEMENT:	15
HIT DICE:	4+3
THAC0:	15
NO. OF ATTACKS:	1
DAMAGE/ATTACK:	2-8
SPECIAL ATTACKS:	Surprise
SPECIAL DEFENSES:	Hit only by silver or +1 or better magical weapon
MAGIC RESISTANCE:	Standard
SIZE:	M (6' tall)
MORALE:	Steady (12)
XP VALUE:	420

Werewolves are the most feared of the lycanthropes, men who can transform into wolflike beasts. They should not be confused with *wolfweres* (q.v.)—wolves who turn into men. Great enmity exists between werewolves and wolfweres.

The human forms of werewolves have no distinguishing traits. The werewolf form is equally varied. Many have a bipedal form that is a hybrid of human and lupine features. These creatures are about 1-foot taller and stronger than their human forms. The bodies are fur-covered and have short tails, wolflike legs, and heads that are combinations in varying degrees of human and lupine features.

A second form of hybrid is more wolflike, and may be mistaken for a large wolf when it runs on all four legs. This hybrid can also walk erect and has humanlike hands.

Another type of werewolf (about 20%) looks exactly like a large wolf about the size of a bear. This creature has no human features, although the eyes may glow red in the dark.

Combat: In their human forms, werewolves attack with a variety of weapons, generally those common to their human identity and class. In the werewolf or wolflike forms, the creature attacks with its fearsome teeth. If the form has hands, the werewolf may grab its prey for a better bite.

In the wolf form, the werewolf can be harmed only by silver or magical weapons of +1 or better. Wounds from other weapons heal too quickly to actually injure the werewolf.

Werewolves attack in packs; packs including females and young drive the adults to hit harder. If the female is attacked, the male fights at +2 to hit and does full damage with each blow. If the young are attacked, the female attacks at +3 to hit and does full damage. Cubs with 60% full growth are -4 to hit, cubs with 70% are -3 to hit, and so on. All cubs inflict 2-5 points of damage.

Habitat/Society: Werewolf packs roam the wilderness in search of human or other prey. True werewolves tend to be nomadic, although infected werewolves often continue to live the life to which they were accustomed. Werewolves retreat to their dens during the winter months or the years when the females are raising the helpless cubs. As humans, werewolves do not build homes, although they may take over existing dwellings, some-

times the home of past victims. Caves and burrows are the dens most commonly used in the wild. These sparsely furnished retreats are used mostly as a sleeping area and a place to store their human possessions. Many werewolf families roam the countryside in wagons, much like gypsies. In fact, this has caused many gypsies to be accused of being werewolves.

Werewolves live in packs, generally related by bloodlines. Werewolf packs of five to eight individuals are single family groups consisting of a male, female, and three to six cubs, six to nine years old. Cubs under six years old are kept in secluded dens and never encountered by hostile humans.

When pregnant, the female retreats with her mate and an older female who will act as midwife. In a very secluded area they prepare a special den that will be home for the mother and her cubs for the next six years. The female gives birth to a litter of 5-10 cubs. The cubs are born in the hybrid form; they resemble fuzzy human babies with wolflike faces. Infant mortality is high; 2-4 cubs of each litter never reach 60% growth. Cubs grow at the same rate as humans for their first five years. By the sixth year they attain 60% of their full growth. At this point they develop the ability to transform into their other forms. Each following year brings an increase of an additional 10% growth. Werewolves are considered mature at age 10.

If a werewolf mates with a woman, the offspring is completely human. The temperament reflects the father; such children are violent, combative, and prone to mental illness. There is a 10% chance each year from the onset of adolescence that such a child will spontaneously transform into a true werewolf.

Ecology: Werewolves are a peculiar hybrid of human and lupine personalities. They are savage killers, yet they are devoted to their close-knit families. Werewolves are hostile toward lycanthropes who oppose them, especially werebears.

Mammal

Mammal	#AP	AC	MV	HD	THAC0	# of Att	Dmg/Att	Morale	XP Value
Ape, Carnivorous	2-8	6	12, 9 in trees	5	15	3	1-4/1-4/1-8	Steady (11-12)	175
Baboon, Wild	10-40	7	12, 12 in trees	1+1	19	1	1-4	Unsteady (5-7)	35
Badger	2-5	4	6, Br 3	1+2	19	3	1-2/1-2/1-3	Average (8-10)	35
Banderlog	4-24	6	6, 12 in trees	4	15	1	2-5	Average (8-10)	120
Bhaergala	1	6	15	4+4	15	3	1-6/1-6/1-8	Elite (13-14)	650
Boar, Wild	1-12	7	15	3+3	17	1	3-12	Average (8-12)	175
Chattur	2-24	7	12	1-1	20	1	1-4 (or weapon)	Average (8-10)	15
Cooshee	1-8	5	15, sprint 24	3+3	17	3	1-4/1-4/2-8	Steady (11-12)	270
Dakon	6-60	5	6	1+1	20	2	1-10/1-10	Champion (15-16)	65
Debbi	1-8	7	15, climb 6	1+1	19	1	1-4	Unsteady (5-7)	65
Goat	5-20	7	15	1+2	19	1	1-3	Average (8-10)	35
Gorilla	1-4	6	12	4+1	17	3	1-3/1-3/1-6	Average (8-10)	175
Hsing-sing	2-20	6	6, Sw 9	2+1	19	1	1-6 (or weapon)	Average (8-10)	65
Hyena	2-12	7	12	3	17	1	2-8	Unsteady (5-7)	65
Jackal	1-6	7	12	1/2	20	1	1-2	Unreliable (2-4)	7
Losel	3-30	7	6, 9 in trees	2	19	3	1-3/1-3/1-4	Unsteady (5-7)	120
Monkey Spider	20-60	6	18, climb 18	1hp	18	1	1	Fanatic (17-18)	1
Porcupine, Black	1-2	6	9, climb 2	1/2	20	1	1-3	Unreliable (2-4)	15
Porcupine, Brown	1-2	6	9, climb 2	1/2	20	1	1-4	Unreliable (2-4)	15
Rothé	2-20	7	9	2	19	3	1-3/1-3/1-8	Elite (13-14)	35
Skunk	1-6	8	12	1/4	20	1	1	Unsteady (5-7)	35
Sleek	1-10	3	36	2+1	19	3	1-4/1-4/2-12	Steady (11-12)	65
Stag, Wild	1-4	7	24	3	17	1 or 2	1-3/1-3 or 2-8	Unsteady (5-7)	65
Stench Kow	15-60	2	15	3+3	17	1	2-8	Average (8-10)	175
Taer	10-40	4	18	3+6	17	3	1-6/1-4/1-4	Steady (11-12)	270
Tyrg	1-10	5	18	5-8	5-6 HD: 15 / 7-8 HD: 13	1	1-12	Elite (13-14)	5 HD: 270 / 6 HD: 420 / 7 HD: 650 / 8 HD: 975
Warthog	1-6	7	12	3	17	2	2-8/1-8	Average (8-10)	120
Weasel	1-2	6	15	1/4	20	1	1	Steady (11-12)	7
Wolverine	1	5	12	3	17	3	1-4/1-4/2-5	Steady (11-12)	120

Mammals are the most common of the vertebrate. Generally born alive, mammals possess hair. Warm-blooded, mammals maintain a single body temperature, regulated by an internal thermostat. Most mammals are harmless to humanoids and they are often trained to perform a specific function.

Ape, Carnivorous: Carnivorous apes gain a +2 to their surprise rolls. They eat anything they can kill.

Baboon, Wild: Wild baboons are large, herbivorous primates that are characterized by long arms and legs, large dog-like muzzles, and sharp canine teeth.

Badger: Badgers are vicious little creatures that prefer to run from danger than fight. If cornered, the badger will fight, attempting to bite the tender throat of its opponent.

Banderlog: Banderlogs resemble baboons with green skin and brown fur. They throw retch plant fruit or coconuts at enemies. Coconuts cause 1d4+1 points damage while retch plant fruit splash a 5-foot radius area with nauseating fluids. Those caught in the splash, retch for three rounds and their Strength is reduced by half for the next hour+no saving throw allowed.

Bhaergala: This predator jumps its prey from great heights. It can drop from as high as 60 feet, causing maximum damage plus 1d6 for every 10 feet dropped. This beast heals 2 hit points every day and gains a +3 to all saving throws vs. poison. Four times a day, the bhaergala can turn spells as the *ring of spell turning*.

Boar, Wild: Wild boar continue to attack until they are reduced to −7 hit points. The giant boar is often called an alothere.

Chattur: Chatturs, called space bandits, are small mammals that exhibit traits of both primates and rodents. Not very combative, they fight in defense of their nests, kin, or friends.

Cooshee: Known as elven dogs, they only bark to warn their elven masters of danger. They can strike bipedal opponents with front paws to knock man-sized or smaller creatures down.

Dakon: Dakons are intelligent apes with a reasonable grasp of the common tongue. When attacking it gains a +2 bonus.

Debbi: This desert scavenger, a baboon-hyena crossbreed, can *cause fear* by stamping its feet in a slow, rhythm and calling forth magical power that makes its fur crackle and spark. This fear lasts for two rounds.

Goat: When a goat charges, it gains a +2 attack bonus and does an additional 1-2 points damage.

Gorilla: The gorilla is non-aggressive and shy, but fights fiercely when threatened or cornered.

Hsing-sing: The hsing-sing are a recluse ape-like race believed to personify the principles of pacifism and harmony with nature. However, once a year, for 2d6+4 days, the males gather into raiding bands and complete the "war season." Their bands attack humanoid settlements on the edge of their territory. Such attacks are impartial; pillaging good and evil creatures alike. To maximize the advantage of surprise, the hsing-sing rarely attack the same settlement two years in a row.

Hyena: Often confused as a canine, the hyena taunts enemies with its nervous, high-pitched howl.

Mammal

Jackal: Jackals are timid scavengers that run from the threat of other predators. When attacking, the jackal darts in to bite its victim and quickly retreats to a safe distance. If more than one jackal is trying to down an animal, they attack in a haphazard fashion with little or no coordination of effort.

Losel: An arboreal orc/baboon cross, losel resemble primitive humans in many respects. They can throw stones up to 20 yards for 1d4 points damage.

Monkey Spider: Measuring 1-inch in length, monkey spiders fight creatures their own size, avoiding combat with larger creatures. If forced to battle such creatures, the monkeys jump and bite at an eye. The bite causes extreme pain and the victim must hold his eye and take no other action for a round, giving the monkey a chance to run away. Monkey spiders can jump 10 feet down or 5 feet forward and can climb anything a typical spider can.

Porcupine: Porcupines are covered with long barbed quills. The creature is unable to throw its quills. Generally, a predator who chases the fleeing creature gets a mouthful of quills which causes the damage cited above.

Rothé: The rothé (pronounced "roth-AY") is a musk ox-like creature with an aversion to light. It prefers to live underground near lichen and moss.

Skunk: Anyone within a skunk's 10x10x10-foot cloud of musk must save vs. poison or be nauseated for 1-4 rounds, losing 50% of Strength and Dexterity.

Sleek: This ermine-like mammal surprises opponents on 1-5 on 1d6. On an attack roll of 19 or 20, the sleek opens a major vein, causing 2d6 points of damage. Every round thereafter, the victim suffers 1d6 more points damage until the wound is wrapped with a tourniquet, direct pressure, or magical healing.

Stag, Wild: Wild stags are the aggressive males of the deer herds. Normally docile and passive, they defend their herds against all but the most fearsome opponents.

Stench Kow: Stench Kine are the cattle of the lower planes. They are immune to all forms of cold, fire, and poison. In close quarters, their breath and bodies are so foul, a save vs. poison must be made or the character is affected as if struck by a *stinking cloud* spell. The save must be made every three rounds of exposure.

Taer: These vile primates live in cold mountain caves. They throw spears before closing in for hand-to-hand.

Tyrg: When in melee, tyrgs emit fierce howls that mildly stun their victims (+2 penalty to initiative and −2 penalty to attack rolls) for the next three rounds + no saving throw allowed. These are tiger-dog crossbreeds that move silently 75% of the time and have a +2 bonus to avoid surprise.

Warthog: The warthog is so aggressive, it continues to attack until it reduced to −7 hit points.

Weasel: Weasels, related to minks and stoats, are common predators, though they are hunted for their pelts, or for pets.

Wolverine: When engaged in battle, the wolverine becomes a most fearsome adversary, giving it a +4 bonus to its attack roll.

Minimal Mammals: Minimals are half-sized breeds of otherwise normal animals. They have the same physical and behavioral traits of their full-sized relatives, although most are not dangerous. Minimals generally have one-half the number of Hit Dice with a corresponding drop in THAC0, a +2 Armor Class penalty, and a −2 Morale penalty. The damage caused by a minimal is one-half that of the full-sized relative.

Giant Mammals: Giant mammals are double-sized breeds of otherwise normal animals. They have the same physical and behavioral traits of their full-sized relatives. These giants generally have double the number of Hit Dice, a corresponding rise in THAC0, a −2 AC bonus, and a +2 Morale bonus. The damage caused by the attacks of a giant mammal is twice that of the full-sized relative.

Mammal, Herd

	Camel	Cattle	Buffalo	Antelope	Sheep
CLIMATE/TERRAIN:	Any land	Any land	Tropical and temperate plains	Tropical and temperate plains	Any land
FREQUENCY:	Common	Common	Uncommon	Common	Common
ORGANIZATION:	Herd	Herd	Herd	Herd	Herd
ACTIVITY CYCLE:	Day	Day	Day	Day	Day
DIET:	Herbivore	Herbivore	Herbivore	Herbivore	Herbivore
INTELLIGENCE:	Animal to semi- (1-4)	Semi- (2-4)	Semi- (2-4)	Animal (1)	Animal (1)
TREASURE:	Nil	Nil	Nil	Nil	Nil
ALIGNMENT:	Nil	Neutral	Nil	Nil	Nil
NO. APPEARING:	1-12	20-200	4-24 (4d6)	4-24 (4d6)	10-100
ARMOR CLASS:	7	7	7	7	7
MOVEMENT:	21	15	15	24	12
HIT DICE:	3	1-4	5	2	2
THAC0:	17	17	15	19	19
NO. OF ATTACKS:	1	1	2	1	1
DAMAGE/ATTACK:	1-4	1-4	1-8/1-8	1-4	1-4
SPECIAL ATTACKS:	Spitting	Stampede	Charge	Stampede	Charge
SPECIAL DEFENSES:	Nil	Nil	Head is AC 3	Nil	Nil
MAGIC RESISTANCE:	Nil	Nil	Nil	Nil	Nil
SIZE:	L (8' tall)	L (8' long)	L (5' at shoulder)	M (5' tall)	M (5' long)
MORALE:	Unreliable (3)	Unreliable (4)	Average (10)	Unreliable (3)	Unreliable (3)
XP VALUE:	65	15-120	175	35	35

Herd animals live in all climates and terrain, from freezing tundra (bactrian camel) to temperate hills (wild cattle) to tropical plains (antelope). Though normally passive, herd animals can be dangerous when angered or frightened.

Herd animals are four-legged hoofed mammals covered with hair—thick fur for buffalo, curly wool for sheep, and short, coarse hair for camels, antelope, and sheep. Male cattle, buffalo, antelope, and sheep have sharp horns. A camel's humps (one hum for dromedaries, two for bactrian) enable it to go without food or water for up to two weeks.

Combat: Most herd animals attack by biting. Buffalo defend themselves with their horns, usually attacking if approached too closely (6' or less); if charging from a distance of at least 40', a buffalo does 3-18 hp of impaling damage plus 1-4 hp of trampling damage. Nasty-tempered camels have a 50% chance of spitting at persons attempting to ride them or use them for pack animals; the victim of a spit attack has a 25% chance of being blinded for 1-3 rounds. Cattle, antelope, and sheep generally flee from danger, but will attack if cornered or threatened. A male antelope or sheep defending his herd will charge, inflicting 1-4 hp of butting damage if charging from at least 40'. Male cattle are 75% likely to attack if intruders approach before the herd has a chance to escape.

If frightened by intruders, there is a 25% that the entire herd will stampede. If a herd stampedes, roll 2d4 for each creature in the path of the stampede who does not take cover (such as by hiding in a tree or behind a rock pile or wall). This is the number of herd animals trampling the exposed creature. Trampling causes either 1-4 hp of damage (camel, cattle, antelope, and sheep) or 1-6 hp of damage (buffalo) per herd animal trampling.

Habitat/Society: Herd animals graze on open terrain, migrating to a new territory when the food supply of the old has been depleted. Herd size varies from a family of four buffalo to a commercial flock of 1,000 sheep. The largest and oldest male usually serves as the leader, directing the movement his herd and watching for predators. Herd animals do not collect treasure.

Ecology: Herd animals eat grass, grains, and shrubbery. They are the favored prey of carnivores, including lions, tigers, and dragons. Man often domesticates herd animals for their meat, milk, fur (blankets and clothing), and skin (shoes and tents). Dried droppings of herd animals can be burned for fuel.

Mammal, Small

Mammal	HD	AC	No. App.	No. of Attacks	Damage/ Attack	Mv	XP Value	Notes
Beaver	1-4 hp	9	10-40	1	1	4, Sw 12	7	
Chipmunk	1 hp	7	1-6	1	1	12, Br 1	0	
Ermine	1	6	1-2	1	1	15	15	
Ferret	1	6	1-2	1	1	15	15	
Fox	1	7	1-2	1	1-3	15	15	
Gopher	1-3 hp	8	1-20	1	1	12, Br 2	7	
Hedgehog	1-2 hp	8	1-2	nil	nil	4	7	
Mink	1	6	1-2	1	1	15, Br 1	15	
Mole	1 hp	10	1	nil	nil	1, Br ½	0	
Monkey	1+1	8	1-50	1	1	9	35	
Mouse	1 hp	7	1-100	nil	nil	15, Br ½	0	
Muskrat	1-3 hp	10	1-2	1	1	4	7	
Opossum	1-3 hp	10	1-8	1	1	4	7	
Otter	1-1	5	1-4	1	1-2	12, Sw 18	7	
Otter (sea)	1+1	5	1-4	1	1-3	12, Sw 18	35	
Otter (giant)	5	5	2-5	1	3-18	9, Sw 18	175	
Pig (domestic)	2	10	1-20	1	1-4	12	35	
Pig (wild)	2	9	1-8	1	1-4	12	35	
Rabbit	1-3 hp	6	1-12	1	1	18	7	
Raccoon	1-6 hp	9	1-4	1	1-2	5	7	
Squirrel	1 hp	8	1-6	1	1	12	0	
(Flying)	1 hp	8	7	1	1	12, Fl 15 (E)	0	Gliding
(Giant black)	1+1	6	1-12	1	1+3	12	35	
Woodchuck	1-6 hp	9	1-2	1	1	5, Br 2	7	

CLIMATE/TERRAIN: Various
FREQUENCY: Common
INTELLIGENCE: Animal (1)
ALIGNMENT: Neutral
MAGIC RESISTANCE: Nil
MORALE: Unreliable to Average (2-9)

Most small mammals are harmless to humans. Some have useful traits or abilities. Most animals have only rudimentary languages that humanoids cannot use except with the aid of magical spells. All have THAC0 20, except where noted below.

Beavers quickly chew trees and construct homes in ponds. Adult pelts are worth two gp.

House cats are small, domesticated breeds.

Chipmunks have excellent hearing and eyesight.

Ermines are related to weasels. The white, spotted pelt is worth four gp.

Ferrets are related to weasels. If captured as cubs or raised domestically, ferrets may be trained to perform simple tricks, retrieve objects, or hunt small burrowing game.

Foxes have superb vision, hearing, and noses. Their pelts are worth three to five gp.

Gophers live in large colonies burrowed into the soil of the plains. They have acute senses of hearing and smell. For each gopher encountered, another 1d10 are hiding in the burrows nearby.

Hedgehogs are covered with sharp but harmless quills.

Moles have an excellent ability to detect tastes and vibrations, but very poor vision.

Monkey refers to a variety of small, non-hostile species (rhesus, spider, tamarind, lemurs, and others). THAC0 19.

Mice infest virtually any human structure.

Minks are related to weasels. The pelt is worth three gp.

Muskrats have a moderately valuable pelt worth five sp.

Opossum are woodland marsupials with good hearing.

Otters are fast runners (12) and swimmers (18). They are friendly and only attack if cornered or if their young are threatened. Pelts are worth two to three gp. Giant otters are identical except for their size (10'-15' long). Pelts are worth 1,000-4,000 gp. THAC0 19 (sea and giant otters).

Pigs may bite or attempt to stun, then crush a victim by butting. Domestic pigs are normally harmless unless angered or magically controlled. Wild pigs are domestic pigs that have escaped to the wild. They are smaller (2 feet long) and nonaggressive unless provoked. THAC0 19.

Rabbits are difficult to surprise or catch due to their sensitive eyesight, hearing, nose, and natural paranoia.

Raccoons only attack if cornered or rabid (10% chance). The pelts are worth one gp.

Squirrels have good vision and hearing.

Flying Squirrels have furry membranes that enable them to glide five feet for each one foot they drop.

Giant black squirrels are 2-foot-long residents of evil-dominated forests. They steal loose, small valuables (rings, gems, vials) to decorate their nests. THAC0 19.

Woodchucks are capable of quickly gnawing through trees or wood. The pelts are worth 1 gp.

Manscorpion

CLIMATE/TERRAIN:	Tropical or subtropical desert or caves
FREQUENCY:	Rare
ORGANIZATION:	Squad, swarm, and city
ACTIVITY CYCLE:	Any
DIET:	Carnivore
INTELLIGENCE:	Low to genius (5-18)
TREASURE:	J, K, M, Q (F, Ux10)
ALIGNMENT:	Neutral evil

NO. APPEARING:	8 or more
ARMOR CLASS:	5
MOVEMENT:	12
HIT DICE:	8-12
THAC0:	8 HD: 13
	9-10 HD: 11
	11-12 HD: 9
NO. OF ATTACKS:	3
DAMAGE/ATTACK:	2-5/2-5/1-4 (claw/claw/tail), or by weapon and 2-5/1-4
SPECIAL ATTACKS:	Poison, possible spell use
SPECIAL DEFENSES:	Nil
MAGIC RESISTANCE:	20%
SIZE:	L (6' tall, 4' long plus 10' tail)
MORALE:	Champion to fanatic (15-18)
XP VALUE:	4,000

9 HD squad leader: 5,000	11 HD noble: 7,000
9 HD squad spellcaster: 6,000	11 HD sorcerer: 9,000
10 HD swarm leader: 6,000	12 HD king or queen: 8,000
10 HD swarm spellcaster: 8,000	12 HD high cleric: 10,000

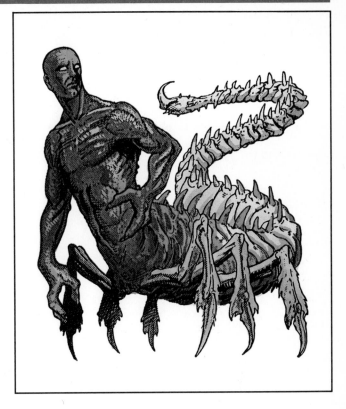

These horrors, sometimes called *tlincallis*, are part human and part scorpion. A manscorpion has a dark-skinned human torso, its abdomen is protected by bony plates, and its ribs and backbone protrude from the body. Their hands have two thick fingers and a long thumb; the hands are often mistaken for scorpion-like claws. The creatures are hairless, and their faces are handsome and noble, except for the red, glowing eyes which have no pupils.

The creature's torso sits atop a 4-foot-long, bony-plated, arachnoid body which is supported by six legs. Bony plate completely covers the strong legs. The protruding spine continues along the abdomen and forms a tail 10 feet long. The lower body, legs, and tail are usually sand-colored, and blend easily with the desert. Observers rarely see anything but the muscular human torso until the manscorpions are close.

The origins of these creatures is thought to lie in an ancient curse placed on evil humans. They speak their own language, and 20% also speak some locally spoken tongue.

Combat: Most manscorpions have low to average intelligence; they patrol their territory in squads of six warriors. A squad leader and a spellcaster, each with 9 HD and greater intelligence, are also present. The spellcaster has the abilities of a 4th-level cleric or mage. Fully 50% of them carry obsidian-studded clubs (treat as a battle axe) and bolas or javelins. The rest use only their natural weapons.

When directed by the squad leader, manscorpions attack in an organized manner. They use long-range attacks before closing for melee. In close combat, they attack with weapon, claw, and tail, or with tail and two claws. The tail can strike anywhere nearby, including in front of the creature. When not being used for attack, the tail sweeps the area behind the manscorpion, checking for obstacles and assailants. Anyone struck by the tail's spur must make a successful saving throw vs. poison or die in 2d4 rounds. Victims suffer weakness for one round (−2 attack penal-

ty), start to shake in the next round (−3 attack penalty and no Dexterity bonus to AC), then convulse (AC 10 and no attacks possible) until they die.

Common manscorpions lose organization and their morale is reduced without a leader. When morale is reduced to 1 or 2 hit points, common manscorpions go into a stinging frenzy, making two tail attacks per round, but no other attacks.

Patrols are more common near the manscorpion lair, which is guarded by a swarm consisting of three squads. A swarm leader and a spellcaster, each with 10 Hit Dice, accompany a swarm. The spellcaster is the equivalent of a 7th-level priest or wizard. These leaders stay out of combat, directing the action and casting spells. Swarms are sent on patrol in times of trouble.

For every two swarms, there is a noble and a sorcerer. They stay near the lair unless an army of manscorpions is marching, then they will lead two swarms. These leaders have 11 HD, and sorcerers cast spells at 9th-level ability.

Finally, every lair has a king or queen, or both, with 12 Hit Dice. A high cleric, also with 12 HD, aids these rulers with the abilities of an 11th-level priest. They always remain in the lair and will only fight if directly threatened.

Habitat/Society: Manscorpions live under the desert sands in burrows connected by tunnels, all situated above underground cities of 40-400 individuals. These often mirror great human cities, with pits instead of buildings, and great chasms like inverted pyramids.

Manscorpions often hold humans and dwarves as slaves, using them to mine and create weaponry. A manscorpion's fingers are not very dexterous, but they are fine sculptors with hammer and chisel, and many sculptures decorate their cities.

Ecology: Manscorpions eat practically any meat, including carrion. No normal creatures prey on them.

Manticore

CLIMATE/TERRAIN:	Any
FREQUENCY:	Uncommon
ORGANIZATION:	Solitary
ACTIVITY CYCLE:	Any
DIET:	Carnivore
INTELLIGENCE:	Low (5-7)
TREASURE:	E
ALIGNMENT:	Lawful evil

NO. APPEARING:	1-4
ARMOR CLASS:	4
MOVEMENT:	12, Fl 18 (E)
HIT DICE:	6+3
THAC0:	13
NO. OF ATTACKS:	3
DAMAGE/ATTACK:	1-3/1-3/1-8
SPECIAL ATTACKS:	Tail spikes
SPECIAL DEFENSES:	Nil
MAGIC RESISTANCE:	Nil
SIZE:	H (15')
MORALE:	Elite (13-14)
XP VALUE:	975

The manticore is a true monster, with a leonine torso and legs, batlike wings, a man's head, a tail tipped with iron spikes, and an appetite for human flesh.

The manticore stands 6 feet tall at the shoulder and measures 15 feet in length. It has a 25-foot wingspan. Each section of the manticore closely resembles the creature it imitates. The leonine torso has a tawny hide, the mane is a lion's brown-black color, and the batlike wings are a dark brown with sparse hair. All manticores have heads that resemble human males; the mane resembles a heavy beard and long hair.

Combat: The manticore first fires a volley of 1-6 tail spikes (180 yard range as a light crossbow). Each spike causes 1-6 points of damage. The manticore can fire four such volleys each day (the spikes regrow quickly). Next, the manticore closes with its prey and attacks with its front claws and sharp teeth. In an outdoor setting, the manticore tries to stay in the air to minimize its chance of being attacked. It is a clumsy flier, however, and cannot use its teeth in the air.

Habitat/Society: Manticores are found in any climate but prefer warm lands to cool ones. This reflects the wide climate range of their favorite food, humans. A manticore's territory may cover 20 or more square miles and includes at least one human settlement. Such territories usually overlap with those of other manticores and other man-eating predators like dragons.

Manticores mate for life. The male remains with the female during gestation and hunts for her. Manticores bear one or two cubs which grow rapidly to adulthood in five years. Cubs are born with 1 Hit Die and gain an additional one each year. In their first year, cubs lack flying ability, but they are still small enough for an adult to grasp in its forelegs. There is a 20% chance a she-manticore's lair holds cubs under one year old. Cubs up to two years inflict one point of damage per front paw and 1-2 points with their bite. Cubs 3-4 years old inflict 1-2, 1-2, and 1-6 points of damage.

Manticore cubs can be caught and trained to assist evil humans. Such training is difficult and dangerous, especially since domesticated adults have an 80% chance of reverting to a wild state. Manticores will not allow themselves to be used as mounts. Wild adults may voluntarily ally themselves with evil humans, provided such allies can provide them with a steady, ample food supply.

Manticores normally eat their prey where they kill it. Males sometimes haul slain prey back to their mates or drag still-living prey to their lairs for the cubs to practice killing.

Manticores collect their victims' valuables for a variety of reasons, including curiosity, emulation of other monsters who collect treasure, the man-scent on the things, or because they know humans value the things and therefore might come looking for them. Their lack of real hands prevents most manticores from using what magical items fall into their possession. However, manticores that have allied with evil humans may possess magical items designed specifically for their use. Examples include magical collars or bracelets that are, in effect, oversized magical rings.

Ecology: Manticores are wide-ranging carnivores that have successfully survived in every region inhabited by humans, whether in the wilderness or underground. They are nightmarish opponents but invaluable allies if conditions are right. A manticore's pelt is a mark of the most powerful hunters and warriors. An intact, cured manticore hide complete with wings is worth 10,000 gp.

Medusa

	Medusa	Greater Medusa
CLIMATE/TERRAIN:	Any	Any
FREQUENCY:	Rare	Rare
ORGANIZATION:	Solitary	Solitary
ACTIVITY CYCLE:	Any	Any
DIET:	Omnivore	Omnivore
INTELLIGENCE:	Very (11-12)	Very (11-12)
TREASURE:	P, Q(x10), X, Y	P, Q(x10), X, Y
ALIGNMENT:	Lawful evil	Lawful evil
NO. APPEARING:	1-3	1-3
ARMOR CLASS:	5	3
MOVEMENT:	9	12
HIT DICE:	6	8
THAC0:	15	13
NO. OF ATTACKS:	1	1 + weapon
DAMAGE/ATTACK:	1-4	1-4
SPECIAL ATTACKS:	Petrification, poison	Petrification, poison
SPECIAL DEFENSES:	Nil	Poisonous blood
MAGIC RESISTANCE:	Nil	20%
SIZE:	M (6'-7')	M (6'-7')
MORALE:	Elite (13-14)	Elite (13-14)
LEVEL/XP VALUE:	2,000	4,000

Medusae are female humanoids with hair of swarming snakes. They are hateful creatures that can petrify any creature that meets their gaze.

The typical medusa has a pale-skinned, very shapely woman's form. It stands 5 to 6 feet tall with the snakes adding up to another foot. At distances farther than 30 feet, the medusa is easily confused with a normal woman. Its red-glowing eyes are visible up to 30 feet. At distances of 20 feet or closer, the medusa's true nature is revealed. Its face is horrible—the snakes writhe constantly, especially if the medusa is excited.

Medusae wear human clothing such as loose dresses or robes. They seldom wear armor and cannot easily wear helmets. Medusae may carry a knife, dagger, or short bow. Medusae speak their own tongue and the common one.

Combat: The medusa tries to get close to a victim before it reveals its true nature. It will use its attractive body to lure males nearer while staying in the shadows. Once the medusa is within 30 feet, it strikes, trying to get its victim to look into its eyes. Any creature within 30 feet must make a saving throw versus petrification or turn instantly to lifeless stone. If an opponent averts his eyes, the medusa rushes up so that its serpentine growths can attack. The range of such attacks is only 1 foot, but the victim must save versus poison or die.

The medusa is able to see creatures in the Ethereal and Astral planes, and its petrifying gaze is equally as effective against creatures there. It retains its petrifying gaze after death. Creatures looking at a freshly-dead medusa's head make a saving throw at +1. The saving throw increases +1 each day the head decays.

If the medusa cannot easily use its normal tactics, it may resort to normal weapons such as knives and shortbows.

Habitat/Society: Medusae dwell in dark caves or the lower regions of large abandoned buildings. They arrange the lighting such that their homes are filled with flickering shadows.

The presence of petrified victims is a sure indicator of the occupant's true nature. For this, aesthetic, and other reasons, the medusa usually removes most of its victims. Those that resemble interesting statues may be retained; the rest are often broken into unrecognizable (and unrevivable) chunks.

The one form of treasure never found in a medusa's lair is a mirror. If a medusa sees its own reflection in a mirror, it turns to stone itself. Reflection in nonmetallic reflectors such as water or polished stone have no such effect. Medusae are immune to the petrifying effect of another medusa.

Medusae are infrequently driven to mate with humanoid males. The act always ends in the male's death, usually by petrification when the medusa reveals its previously hidden visage. Two to six eggs are laid one month later and hatch eight months after that. The female hatchlings appear as baby girls with stubby green tendrils. The hatchlings are revolting to look at but cannot petrify. Medusae grow at the same rate as humans. At about age two the serpentine hair becomes alive and gains its poisonous bite. The medusa can petrify with the onset of adolescence.

Greater Medusa (Serpentine)
Rare medusae (10%) have serpentine bodies in place of the lower torso and legs. The entire body is covered with fine scales and measures 10 to 20 feet. The poison of these medusae is so deadly that saving throws are made at -1, and they are known to use bows and poisoned arrows. Their blood is so poisonous, in fact, that even after one has been killed, touching its body still requires a saving throw versus poison. They seldom venture far from their lairs, since they are immediately recognizable. Greater medusae have a morale bonus of +1.

Medusa, Maedar

	Maedar	Glyptar
CLIMATE/TERRAIN:	Subterranean	Any
FREQUENCY:	Very rare	Very rare
ORGANIZATION:	Solitary	Solitary
ACTIVITY CYCLE:	Any	Any
DIET:	Carnivore	Not applicable
INTELLIGENCE:	Very (11-12)	Very (11-12)
TREASURE:	P,Q(x10),X,Y	See below
ALIGNMENT:	Lawful Evil	Lawful evil
NO. APPEARING:	1	1
ARMOR CLASS:	5	5
MOVEMENT:	9	Fl 9 (A)
HIT DICE:	6	1-4 hp
THAC0:	15	See below
NO. OF ATTACKS:	2	1
DAMAGE/ATTACK:	2-8/2-8	1 hp or by animated weapon
SPECIAL ATTACKS:	See below	Nil
SPECIAL DEFENSES:	See below	See below
MAGIC RESISTANCE:	Nil	Nil
SIZE:	M (5'-7')	T (under 6")
MORALE:	Elite (13-14)	Elite (13-14)
XP VALUE:	975	65

Maedar

Maedar are male counterparts to medusae, though they lack the petrifying gaze of the females.

The typical maedar is a muscular, hairless humanoid male, usually dressed in a kilt or tunic.

Combat: Maedar attack with powerful fists that each cause 2d4 points of damage. One every three turns, the maedar can turn stone to flesh by touch. Maedar can pass through stone at their normal movement rate. They require one round of concentration before this; no other activity can be undertaken that round. Maedar struck by a *phase door* spell while passing through stone are killed instantly.

Maedar are immune to petrifaction and paralyzation (including related spells, such as *hold* and *slow*). They are immune to the poisonous bite of a medusa's serpentine hair. In addition, maedar can see into and extend their stone into flesh power into the Astral and Ethereal planes.

Habitat/Society: Maedar are the little-known male version of the medusae. They are extremely rare, however (far more rare than the frequency would indicate), and few medusae ever find a maedar spouse. Most medusae typically mate with human males. This cross produces two to six eggs that hatch into fledgling, human-like females, who mature into medusae. The cross insures the continuation of the medusae species.

When a medusa finds and mates with the extremely rare maedar, the eggs hatch into human infants, 25% male and 75% female. Only 1% of the males born of these matings are actually maedar; the remaining males and all the females are normal human infants who die at the sight of their mother.

The typical maedar is a monogamist who mates for life; he is fiercely devoted to his mate and will go to any length to assist or avenge her. A widowed maedar will pursue his mate's killer for years.

Because of the Maedar's rarity and natural reclusiveness, even most sages are unaware of their existence. Maedar are rarely seen; generally they remain in the lair they share with a medusa

mate. A maedar's magical power provides food for him and his mate. He smashes her petrified victims, then transforms them into meat.

Ecology: Maedar may cooperate with lawful evil creatures, such as kobolds and orcs, in exchange for security or reward. If forced to aid another creature, maedar seek revenge at the first opportunity.

Glyptar

Glyptars are rock crystals animated by the spirits of maedar. When a maedar has foreknowledge of his death, he can transfer his life force into the rocks. An extremely evil maedar retains his consciousness as it drifts through the ground. When such a life force encounters gemstones, such as feldspar or amethyst, it is trapped within and cannot leave voluntarily. Eventually the maedar goes mad. (Note that once a maedar is trapped within a glyptar crystal, his life force cannot be trapped in a second crystal.)

If this glyptar is removed intact from the ground, the maedar's spirit is now able to animate the crystal and anything inorganic attached to it. Thus if the glyptar is set in the eye of a stone statue, the maedar's life force animates it as a golem. This can affect a maximum of 1,000 pounds.

Similarly, if the glyptar is set in the pommel of a sword, the sword can be animated to strike as though it were wielded by the living maedar. The weapon gains a +1 bonus to its attack roll, strikes as if it were wielded by a 6th-level fighter, and gains a +2 bonus to its damage roll. Note that the glyptar's *stone to flesh* power enables the weapon to sink harmlessly into stone as the glyptar uses its power.

The glyptar retains its other powers as well. The glyptar and its attachments may pass through stone at will at the normal movement rate. It is immune to *phase door* spells. Once every three turns the glyptar can perform a *stone to flesh* attack against a target touched by the glyptar or its setting. Glyptars remain immune to paralyzation and petrification attacks of all sorts.

Merman

CLIMATE/TERRAIN:	Temperate/Oceans
FREQUENCY:	Uncommon
ORGANIZATION:	Community
ACTIVITY CYCLE:	Any
DIET:	Omnivore
INTELLIGENCE:	Average-Very (8-12)
TREASURE:	C, R
ALIGNMENT:	Neutral

NO. APPEARING:	20-200
ARMOR CLASS:	7
MOVEMENT:	1, Sw 18
HIT DICE:	1+1
THAC0:	19
NO. OF ATTACKS:	1
DAMAGE/ATTACK:	By weapon type
SPECIAL ATTACKS:	Grapple ship
SPECIAL DEFENSES:	Nil
MAGIC RESISTANCE:	Nil
SIZE:	M (5'-6' long)
MORALE:	Average (10)
XP VALUE:	1 HD: 65
	2 HD: 120
	3 HD: 175
	4 HD: 270
	5 HD: 420
	6 HD: 650
	Shaman: 420

Mermen are marine-dwelling, amphibious humanoids with the upper torso of a human and the lower torso of a fish.

Mermen were once human but were transformed by unknown powers into their current forms. They live by herding fish, but during times of need they attack other sea-peoples or ocean-going vessels. They live underwater but surface to sun themselves on large rocks.

Adult mermen are 5 to 6 feet long (tall) and weigh between 150 and 225 pounds. Their skin tone is fair to tan, hair color is usually dark brown (occasionally fair), while their scale color ranges from green to silver. Females, also known as mermaids, are 6 inches shorter than the males and weigh between 100 to 150 pounds. Mermen adorn themselves with coral and shell decorations. Mermen speak their own language (with different dialects spoken by communities that are separated over wide distances), and 50% of all communities also speak locathah.

Combat: Mermen communities are well-armed. The arms used by mermen are as follows:

> Trident, dagger (50%) *
> Crossbow, dagger (30%)
> Javelin, dagger (20%)

* 20% of all trident wielders are also armed with a hook and grappling line (50 feet long).

Mermen crossbows have a range of 30 yards underwater. They use grapples to attack ships; the grapples can be thrown up to 50 feet. Each grapple held by 10 mermen slows a ship by 1. Once stopped, the ship is attacked and a hole is knocked in its hull in 4d4 rounds, after which the ship slowly sinks, to be looted by the mermen.

Merman suffer double damage from fire attacks.

Habitat/Society: For every 20 mermen encountered, there is a patrol leader (2-3 HD) and 1-3 barracuda (AC 6; Move 30; HD 3; #AT 1; Dmg 2d4). For every 40 mermen, there is a leader (4 HD). For every 120 mermen encountered, there is one chief (6 HD) and two guards (4 HD). For every ten mermen, there is a 10% chance of a shaman (3 HD, with the spells of a 3rd-level priest).

Mermen have regular undersea communities, usually a reef or cliff honeycombed with passages. Rarely (10% of the time) they construct a village from sea shells and coral. An average community has between 100 and 600 males. Females and sub-adults each equal 100% of the males in a village. The communities are usually guarded by 3d6 trained barracudas.

Mermen society is heavily patriarchal. They prefer to be left to themselves and usually reject proposals of friendship or trade. They have strong territorial instincts and, while closely related to humans, they have no love for them. Males hunt and herd fish and protect their territory. Females raise children and tend to domestic affairs. Mermaids are also known for their creativity, and they produce works of art for the community (shell carvings, seaweed tapestries, and songs).

Ecology: Mermen are omnivorous, but they prefer a diet of fish, lobster, crab, and shellfish. They do not cook these creatures, but must fillet them before eating. They can survive out of water for one hour before they begin to dehydrate. When dehydrated, they lose 2 hit points per hour and will die when they reach zero; immersion in fresh or salt water immediately restores these lost hit points.

Mermen have an average life expectancy of 150 years. Mermen have many natural enemies but particularly hate the sahuagin and ixitxachitl. They often clash with tritons over territory.

Mimic

	Common	Killer
CLIMATE/TERRAIN:	Subterranean	
FREQUENCY:	Rare	Rare
ORGANIZATION:	Solitary	Solitary
ACTIVITY CYCLE:	Any	Any
DIET:	Carnivore	Carnivore
INTELLIGENCE:	Average (8-10)	Semi- (2-4)
TREASURE:	Incidental	Incidental
ALIGNMENT:	Neutral	Neutral (evil)
NO. APPEARING:	1	1
ARMOR CLASS:	7	7
MOVEMENT:	3	3
HIT DICE:	7-8	9-10
THAC0:	13	11
NO. OF ATTACKS:	1	1
DAMAGE/ATTACK:	3-12 (smash)	3-12 (smash)
SPECIAL ATTACKS:	Glue	Glue
SPECIAL DEFENSES:	Camouflage	Camouflage
MAGIC RESISTANCE:	Nil	Nil
SIZE:	L	L
MORALE:	Champion (15)	Elite (13)
XP VALUE:	7 HD: 975	9 HD: 2,000
	8 HD: 1,400	10 HD: 3,000

Mimics are magically-created creatures with a hard rock-like outer shell that protects their soft inner organs. Mimics can alter their form and their pigmentation; they use this talent to lure victims into close range, where they attempt to feed on them. They usually appear in the form of treasure chests. There are two varieties, the smaller, more intelligent common mimic, and the larger, less intelligent killer mimic.

Mimics are large. Common mimics occupy about 150 cubic feet (a 3' x 6' x 8' chest, or a large door frame). Killer mimics occupy about 200 cubic feet. Mimics' natural color is a speckled grey that resembles granite. Mimics can alter their pigmentation to resemble varieties of stone (such as marble), wood grain, and various metals (gold, silver, copper); it takes one round to make the desired alteration. They cannot lose mass in this transformation (they must remain the same size, though they may radically alter their dimensions).

Common mimics have their own tongue (corruptions of the original language spoken by their wizard creators) and can also be taught to speak in common and other languages. Killer mimics are incapable of speech.

Combat: A mimic can surprise its victims easily (-4 penalty to victims' surprise rolls). When a creature touches a mimic, it lashes out with a pseudopod that inflicts 3d4 points of damage. Furthermore, the mimic covers itself with a glue-like substance. Any creature or item that touches a mimic is held fast. Alcohol will weaken the glue in three rounds, enabling the character to break free, or the character may attempt to make an open doors roll to break free. Only one attempt may be made per character, and no other action, offensive or defensive, may be performed during the round that the attempt is being made. A mimic may neutralize its glue at any time that it desires; the glue dissolves five rounds after the mimic dies. The mimic is immune to acid attacks and is unaffected by molds, green slime, and various puddings.

Habitat/Society: Mimics live underground, where they can avoid sunlight. They are solitary creatures; this is to ensure that each mimic has a large grazing area. They have no culture; their primary concerns are survival and food. Common mimics are quite intelligent and will gladly offer information in exchange for food. Killer mimics attack regardless of attempts at communication. Mimics have no moral code and no interest in culture or religion. Wizards who use them as guardians have sometimes found them to be less than enthusiastic about obeying their commands.

Ecology: Mimics were originally created by wizards to protect themselves from treasure hunters. A good meal (one or two humans) can sustain them for weeks. They reproduce by fission and grow to full size in several years. Mimics pose as stonework, doors, statues, stairs, chests, or other common items made from stone, wood, and metal. Their skin is covered with optical sensors that are sensitive to heat and light in a 90-foot radius, even in pitch darkness. Any powerful light source can easily blind them, including direct sunlight. Along with glue, they can excrete a liquid that smells like rotting meat; this attracts smaller, more common prey (usually rats). Mimic ichor is useful in the creation of *polymorph self* potions, and their glue and solvent sacs can be sold to alchemists. Other internal organs are useful in the manufacture of perfumes. The mimic's internal organs are considered tasty delicacies in some cultures.

Mind Flayer (Illithid)

CLIMATE/TERRAIN:	Any subterranean
FREQUENCY:	Rare
ORGANIZATION:	Community
ACTIVITY CYCLE:	Any
DIET:	Carnivore (brains)
INTELLIGENCE:	Genius (17-18)
TREASURE:	S, T, × (B)
ALIGNMENT:	Lawful evil

NO. APPEARING:	1-4
ARMOR CLASS:	5
MOVEMENT:	12
HIT DICE:	8 + 4
THAC0:	11
NO. OF ATTACKS:	4
DAMAGE/ATTACK:	2; see below
SPECIAL ATTACKS:	Mind blast, see below
SPECIAL DEFENSES:	Magical powers
MAGIC RESISTANCE:	90%
SIZE:	M (6' tall)
MORALE:	Champion (15) + special
XP VALUE:	9,000 (7,000 for psionic version)

The illithid, or mind flayer, is an evil and feared creature of the Underdark; its powers are formidable and it feeds on the brains of any creature it encounters. Using arcane powers, it enslaves or destroys its foes, which include such powerful creatures as drow and kuo-toa.

Mind Flayers stand about 6 feet tall and have hideous mauve skin that glistens with slime. The head resembles an octopus, with white eyes (no pupils are evident) and four tentacles around its mouth, a round, many-toothed orifice like that of a lamprey. The creature has three reddish fingers and a thumb on each hand.

Illithids have infravision. They can communicate with any creatures via innate telepathy; they have no spoken language, although they often accompany their thoughts with hissing, and the eager lashing of their tentacles. Mind flayers dress in flowing robes, often with high, stiff collars, adorned with symbols of death and despair.

Combat: A mind flayer's preferred method of attack is the *mind blast*, projected in a cone 60 feet long, 5 feet wide at the mind flayer, and 20 feet wide at the opposite end. All within the cone must make a saving throw vs. wands or be stunned and unable to act for 3d4 rounds. The illithid tries to grab one or two stunned victims (requiring normal attack rolls if others try to prevent this) and escape with them.

The illithid keeps some victims as slaves and feeds on the brains of the others. When devouring the brain of a stunned victim, it inserts its tentacles into the victim's skull and draws out its brain, killing the victim in one round. A mind flayer can also use its tentacles in combat; it does so only when surprised or when attacking a single, unarmed victim. A tentacle which hits causes 2 hp damage and holds the victim. A tentacle does no damage while holding, and can be removed with a successful bend bars/lift gates roll. Once all four tentacles have attached to the victim, the mind flayer has found a path to the brain and kills the victim in one round. If preferred, the DM can simply roll 1d4 for the number of rounds required to kill a struggling victim.

A mind flayer can also use the following arcane powers, one per round, as a 7th-level mage: *suggestion, charm person, charm monster, ESP, levitate, astral projection,* and *plane shift.* All saving throws against these powers are made at a −4, due to the creature's mental prowess.

If an encounter is going against a mind flayer, it will immediately flee, seeking to save itself regardless of its treasure or its fellows.

Habitat/Society: Mind flayers hate sunlight and avoid it when possible. They live in underground cities of 200 to 2,000 illithids, plus at least two slaves per illithid. All the slaves are under the effects of a *charm person* or *charm monster,* and obey their illithid masters without question.

The center of a community is its elder-brain, a pool of briny fluid that contains the brains of the city's dead mind flayers. Due to the mental powers of illithids, the elder-brain is still sentient, and the telepathic union of its brains rules the community. The elder-brain has a telepathic range of 2 to 5 miles, depending on its age and size. It does not attack, but telepathically warns the mind flayers of the presence of thinking crea-

tures, so a mind flayer within its telepathic radius can be surprised only by non-intelligent creatures. The range of the elder-brain determines the territory claimed and defended by the community, though raiding parties are sent far beyond this limit.

Mind flayers have no family structure. Their social activities include eating, communicating with the elder-brain, and debating on the best tactics to conquer the Underdark. For amusement, they inflict pain on their captives and force slaves to fight in gladiatorial games.

Mind flayers are arrogant, viewing all other species only as cattle to be fed upon. They prefer to eat the brains of thinking creatures.

Ecology: Mind flayers live about 125 years. They are warm-blooded amphibians, and spend the first 10 years of life as tadpoles, swimming in the elder-brain pool until they either die (which most do) or grow into adult illithids. On an irregular basis, adult illithids feed brains to the tadpoles, which do not molest the elder-brain. Illithids are hermaphroditic; each can produce one tadpole twice in its life.

Mind flayer ichor is an effective ingredient in a *potion of ESP.*

Psionic Illithids

Psionic flayers, considered the only true illithids by some (including themselves), have most of the same statistics and abilities as other mind flayers. Instead of magic-based abilities, however, theirs are purely psionic. Psionic mind flayers have a beak-like mouth and disdain the stiff-collared robes preferred by their cousins.

Psionics Summary:

Level	Dis/Sci/Dev	Attack/Defense	Score	PSPs
10	4/5/15	EW, II/All	= Int	1d100 + 250

Illithids use psionics for attack, mind control, and travel. All psionic illithids have at least the following powers:
- **Psychokinesis - Devotions:** control body, levitation.
- **Psychometabolism - Sciences:** body equilibrium (their only psychometabolic power).
- **Psychoportation - Sciences:** probability travel, teleport. Devotions: astral projection.
- **Telepathy - Sciences:** domination, mindlink. Devotions: awe, contact, ESP, ego whip, id insinuation, post-hypnotic suggestion.

Minotaur

CLIMATE/TERRAIN:	Temperate and subtropical labyrinths
FREQUENCY:	Rare
ORGANIZATION:	Clan
ACTIVITY CYCLE:	Night
DIET:	Carnivore (man-eater)
INTELLIGENCE:	Low (5-7)
TREASURE:	(C)
ALIGNMENT:	Chaotic evil

NO. APPEARING:	1-8
ARMOR CLASS:	6
MOVEMENT:	12
HIT DICE:	6+3
THAC0:	13
NO. OF ATTACKS:	2
DAMAGE/ATTACK:	2-8/2-8 or 1-4/by weapon type
SPECIAL ATTACKS:	Grapple, charge
SPECIAL DEFENSES:	+2 bonus on surprise roll
MAGIC RESISTANCE:	Nil
SIZE:	L (7½' tall)
MORALE:	Elite (13) +Special
XP VALUE:	1,400
Elder	3,000

Minotaurs are either cursed humans or the offspring of minotaurs and humans. They usually dwell in underground labyrinths, for they are not confused in these places, which gives them an advantage over their prey.

Minotaurs are huge, well over 7 feet tall, and quite broad and muscular. They have the head of a bull but the body of a human male. Their fur is brown to black while their body coloring varies as would a normal human's. Clothing is minimal, usually a loin cloth or skirt.

Combat: Minotaurs are very strong (equivalent human Strength of 18). Against man-sized opponents (minimum 6 feet tall) they may butt for 2-8 points of damage. Against smaller opponents, they bite for 1-4 points of damage. If a minotaur is 30 feet or more from its opponent, it can lower its head and charge against any creature that is at least 6 feet tall. If successful, the charge causes double head-butt damage. In addition to these attacks, most minotaurs also carry weapons—a huge axe (treat as a halberd) or flail, with which it inflicts normal damage +2.

Minotaurs are not particularly intelligent, but are extremely cunning and have excellent senses. They have a +2 bonus on their surprise rolls, have infravision, and can track prey by scent like a ranger, with 50% accuracy. They always pursue an unfamiliar scent. Minotaurs are immune to *maze* spells. They attack any intruder without fear, and will retreat only if the creature is obviously beyond their ability to defeat (+3 to morale score in combat).

Habitat/Society: Minotaurs live in communities of up to eight members. If the community contains more than six minotaurs, one will be an elder minotaur with 18/50 Strength and 8+4 Hit Dice. The minotaur elder is the clan leader; he remains in the center of the labyrinth and raises young minotaurs while others hunt. He is always encountered in the center of a labyrinth.

A minotaur's labyrinth is rarely natural. Often an evil wizard or a tyrant will construct a labyrinth and place the minotaur family there, feeding it prisoners and slaves on a regular basis.

Occasionally this tyrant will be killed and the minotaurs forced to fend for themselves; since creatures rarely enter a labyrinth on their own accord, these minotaurs will usually be ravenously hungry.

Minotaurs speak their own primitive language and are 25% likely to speak a halting form of common. They have little culture; their lives resemble animals more than humans. Their culture venerates physical strength above all else and particularly strong human fighters have been known to earn their respect. They worship crude gods and have weak clerics (maximum 3rd-level shaman). Rumors persist of more intelligent minotaurs with developed societies.

Ecology: The curse which creates minotaurs is unknown, but sages suspect it involves "crimes against the natural order." Minotaurs are always male. It is also said that the first minotaur was originally a great and ill-tempered human fighter; he wanted to be as strong as a bull and his wish was granted in the most hideous manner possible. Minotaurs breed with human females to produce offspring, which are male minotaurs. Minotaurs have a lifespan of 200 years. They can live without food for years at a time, but are always hungry unless they are fed regularly. They are meat-eaters, but their curse causes them to prefer a diet of human flesh. Those transformed into minotaurs by curses may be restored to human form by a *wish*, but those who were born as minotaurs cannot be made human. Gnolls are their natural enemies; they will kill each other on sight.

Minotaur components are sometimes used in spells and potions, and might be used in magical items involving strength, location, and misdirection.

Mist, Crimson Death

CLIMATE/TERRAIN:	Bogs, swamps
FREQUENCY:	Very rare
ORGANIZATION:	Solitary
ACTIVITY CYCLE:	Night
DIET:	Carnivore
INTELLIGENCE:	Genius (17-18)
TREASURE:	Z
ALIGNMENT:	Neutral evil

NO. APPEARING:	1
ARMOR CLASS:	0 (4)
MOVEMENT:	Fl 12, Fl 6 after feeding (B)
HIT DICE:	13
THAC0:	7
NO. OF ATTACKS:	1
DAMAGE/ATTACK:	3-30
SPECIAL ATTACKS:	See below
SPECIAL DEFENSES:	See below
MAGIC RESISTANCE:	95%
SIZE:	M (6')
MORALE:	Champion (15-16)
XP VALUE:	9,000

The crimson death is a malevolent, vaporous creature that feeds on the bodily fluids of its victims.

The body of the crimson death is a humanoid-shaped cloud of pale color. It is difficult to distinguish if seen against fog and nearly invisible to infravision. During this time, the creature has an initiative bonus of +4. When the creature is fed, it develops a crimson flush that is easily visible by normal or infravision. The cloud possesses humanoid features. The fingers elongate into tentacles when it is feeding. Because of its behavior, sages believe that a Crimson Death Mist is the result of the actual death of a vampire.

The crimson death's language is a barely audible series of whispers. It can communicate with other vaporous beings such as air elementals. It communicates with humanoids only if it is their captive.

Combat: The monster attacks only to feed or defend itself. It surrounds its victim with vaporous tentacles. Whenever it hits, the tentacles drain bodily fluids and cause 3d10 points of damage.

The creature is normally immaterial (AC 0) and can be struck only by magical weapons of +2 or better. After feeding, the creature attains solidity (AC 4) for six turns. At this time the creature turns red, moves more slowly (Fl 6), and can be struck by magical weapons of +1 or better.

When a crimson death dies, it immediately dissipates into the air while its undigested fluids fall to the ground in a grotesque shower.

The crimson death is able to carry loads by levitating anything surrounded by its vaporous mass. Despite its vaporous nature, the crimson death possesses strength equal to a normal human. It is able to carry a passive weight equal to an adult human. If it attempts to pick up a struggling victim, it must make a successful attack roll for each round it carries the person. Failure means the person drops to the ground (suffering damage appropriate to the height of the fall).

Habitat/Society: The crimson death dwells in the bogs and marshes where chill and damp prevail. The creature is nearly invisible in its native habitat.

The crimson death is a secretive creature. It prefers to feed on solitary beings, since these are easy to sneak up on and have no allies to lend them support. If several people are present, the crimson death tries to pick off the guard while the others sleep; it then feeds on the others at its leisure. In order to conceal its presence, the crimson death disposes of corpses in its lair or a deep bog.

It maintains a lair in a thicket, undercut bank, or a hollow space under a windfall. There the monster stores the valuables it collects from its victims. These can be used as bribes for humanoid allies or bait for intended victims. The lair may also contain the remains of past victims.

The crimson death prefers to feed on humanoids. It normally requires one victim per week. If more people are available, the monster may feed continuously until destroyed or driven off.

Legends tell of a connection between crimson deaths and vampires. One tale suggests that, when an undead vampire is destroyed, its spirit is transformed into a crimson death. Another tale suggests that, when a vampire is created, the monster's lost soul is reborn elsewhere as a crimson death. This legend also suggests that a vampire may be restored to normal life if it is rejoined by its crimson death counterpart. A third legend says that extremely evil air elementals are condemned and cast out into the Prime Material plane in the forms of crimson deaths.

Ecology: The crimson death is a dangerous predator that roams the swamps like a living ghost. A crimson death can be collected and imprisoned in an airtight container. This does not harm it. A crimson death in such a container may be mistaken for, or mislabeled as, a bottled djinn or magical vapor. If someone releases the crimson death, the starving creature immediately attacks its unwitting rescuer.

Crimson deaths are aware of the advantages of alliances. They may agree to cooperate with evil humanoids who can provide them with a steady supply of victims. They make excellent allies for those dwelling in or near their lairs.

Mist, Vampiric

CLIMATE/TERRAIN:	Non-arctic/Swamps and subterranean
FREQUENCY:	Rare
ORGANIZATION:	Solitary
ACTIVITY CYCLE:	Night
DIET:	Blood
INTELLIGENCE:	Average (8-10)
TREASURE:	(D)
ALIGNMENT:	Neutral evil

NO. APPEARING:	1-3
ARMOR CLASS:	4 (8 when substantial)
MOVEMENT:	12 (6 when substantial)
HIT DICE:	3
THAC0:	See below
NO. OF ATTACKS:	1
DAMAGE/ATTACK:	1-8
SPECIAL ATTACKS:	See below
SPECIAL DEFENSES:	See below
MAGIC RESISTANCE:	See below
SIZE:	M (5'-8' tall)
MORALE:	Elite (13-14)
XP VALUE:	270

These gaseous monsters prey on all living creatures, enveloping them with their gaseous tendrils, then draining their blood for food.

Vampiric mists appear as thick, billowing clouds, 5 to 8 feet in diameter. Color ranges from pale pink when hungry to crimson red when sated. Vampiric mists speak no language, but they communicate through a limited form of telepathy. These creatures reek of old blood and are often smelled before seen.

Combat: Vampiric mists automatically sense the presence of any warm-blooded creature within 50 feet. Hungry mists take the shortest route possible to the victim, navigating by touch, flowing easily over water or through narrow cracks. Their path can be blocked by nonporous obstacles, but vampiric mists are intelligent and if any reasonable path exists they will find it.

All vampiric mists have maximum hit points (8 per die) when full, but they are almost never encountered in this state. For each 12 hours a mist goes unfed, it loses 1 hit point. Vampiric mists whose hit point totals reach 0 due to starvation die. To regain hit points, vampiric mists must drain fresh blood from living victims (hence the mist's name). For each 2 hit points of blood drained, the mist regains 1 hit point.

A vampiric mist may attack one victim per round by reaching out with a gaseous tendril. Targets of a vampiric mist are treated as AC 10. Modify this number by the victim's Dexterity, and by the magical protection worn (+1, +2, etc.) but ignore magical shields. The touch of a vampiric mist drains 1d8 points of blood. A hit 4 above the needed to hit number means the mist has enveloped its victim. Enveloped victims are automatically hit each round until either the mist dies, finishes feeding, or retreats. Attacks by other characters against an enveloping vampiric mist divide their damage evenly—half against the mist, half against the victim. Only the enveloped victim may attack the mist without harm to himself, However, because of the disorienting effect of rapid blood loss, enveloped victims may not use any spells or magical devices that require concentration.

While blood draining is mainly used to feed, the ability can also be used in defense by sated vampiric mists. Extra blood is simply dumped upon the ground.

Normally, a vampiric mist is damaged only by magical weapons or by spells that effect air. *Lightning bolt* and *magic missile* are also effective. However, immediately after reaching maximum hit points a vampiric mist takes on substance. This substantial stage last 1d6 turns. During this time the mist's movement rate slows to 6, its AC drops to 8, and it may be hit by normal weapons.

Blood draining is not a form of regeneration; a mist that loses hit points in combat must heal those points normally. Keep track of a mist's current hit points and its maximum possible for that combat (this total starts at 24 and goes down with damage caused to the mist). Each time the mist is wounded, reduce both the current hit points and the maximum. If the current hit point total ever reaches 0, the mist dies. Hit points gained by draining blood are added to the current hit points, which cannot exceed the maximum total (24 minus damage to the mist). Hit points lost due to starvation are subtracted from the current hit points only. The current hit points may never exceed the mist's maximum hit point total. (After the current battle is over, the maximum hit point totals for any surviving mists return to 24.)

Habitat/Society: These dread monsters inhabit both swamps, where they creep along mixing in with morning and night fog, and subterranean caverns, where they stalk prey in absolute darkness. Vampiric mists attack at night or early morning, flowing over the ground in search of warm-blooded victims. They prefer lone victims, but hungry mists sometimes raid towns at night, slaying livestock and draining victims in their sleep, before slipping out at dawn.

Ecology: First thought to be immature forms of crimson death, it is now known that these fiends were deliberately created by a powerful vampire wizard.

Vampiric mists reproduce via division. A mist is 10% likely to divide during its substantial stage immediately after feeding. The two mists created have 3 Hit Dice each, but only 4 hit points per die (thus they are born ravenously hungry).

Vampiric mists prey on all warm-blooded creatures. No animals hunt vampiric mist deliberately, though stirges, leeches, and other bloodsuckers are sometimes drawn (fatally) to their smell. Vampiric mists have no known life span. They live until they starve, are slain, or reproduce.

Mold

	Brown	Russet	Yellow
CLIMATE/TERRAIN:	Subterranean	Subterranean	Subterranean
FREQUENCY	Very rare	Very rare	Uncommon
ORGANIZATION:	Patch	Patch	Patch
ACTIVITY CYCLE:	Any	Any	Any
DIET:	Heat	Moisture	Mental Energy
INTELLIGENCE:	Non- (0)	Non- (0)	Not Ratable (0)
TREASURE:	Nil	Nil	Nil
ALIGNMENT:	Neutral	Neutral	Neutral
NO. APPEARING:	1 patch	1 patch	1 patch
ARMOR CLASS:	9	9	9
MOVEMENT:	0	0	0
HIT DICE:	N/A	N/A	N/A
THAC0:	N/A	N/A	N/A
NO. OF ATTACKS:	0	0	1
DAMAGE/ATTACK:	N/A	N/A	N/A
SPECIAL ATTACKS:	Freezing	Spores	Poison Spores
SPECIAL DEFENSES:	Absorb Heat	Immune to weapons, cold, fire	Affected only by fire
MAGIC RESISTANCE:	Nil	Nil	20%
SIZE:	S-L	S-L	S-L
MORALE:	N/A	N/A	N/A
XP VALUE:	15	35	65

Molds are a variety of spore-producing fungi that form in decaying food or in warm, moist places. These fungi usually have a woolly or furry texture. While most molds are harmless, there are (at least) three varieties of monstrous molds that pose a deadly threat to adventurers: brown, russet, and yellow mold.

Brown Mold

Brown mold is found in damp subterranean areas, such as caverns and caves. It is light to golden brown in color. Brown mold feeds by absorbing heat, even body heat; where brown mold grows, the temperature is below average. Direct sunlight or ultraviolet light kills it.

If a warm-blooded creature comes within 5 feet of a brown mold, the mold drains heat equal to 4d8 points of damage from its victim, per round. A *ring of warmth* provides complete protection against this attack. Brown mold grows instantly from heat. If a torch is used in its vicinity, it doubles in size; if flaming oil is used, it quadruples, and fireball-type spells cause it to grow eight-fold.

Brown mold is not fed by cold light sources (e.g., *light, faerie fire*). The only magic that affects it are *disintegrate* (which destroys it), plant-affecting magic, and cold spells. Ice storms or walls of ice cause it to go dormant for 5d6 turns. A *cold wand*, white dragon breath, or a *cone of cold* kills it. Brown mold does not affect cold-using creatures such as white dragons, winter wolves, ice toads, etc.

Russet Mold

Russet mold is golden-brown to rust red in color. It has a lumpy texture similar to cold porridge; it is covered by short, hair-like growths that stand upright and wave as if they were in a cold breeze. It resembles rust at distances beyond 30 feet (70% chance of error). It is immune to weapons and most spells; it is affected only by alcohol, acid, and salt, which kill it; a *cure disease* or a *continual light* spell also destroys it.

Russet mold continuously emits a cloud of spores in a three-foot radius. All creatures in this cloud suffer 5d4 points of damage (per round in the cloud) and must roll a successful saving throw vs. poison or become infected with spore sickness. Victims of spore sickness are instantly paralyzed and die in 5d4 minutes unless a *cure disease* spell is cast on them.

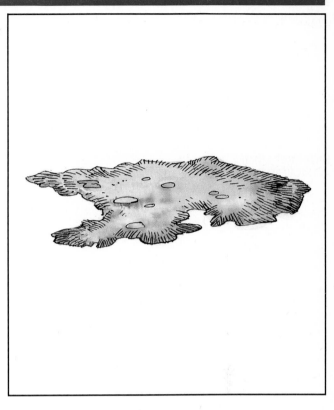

Anyone who dies from spore sickness undergoes a transformation and begins to sprout russet mold growths; when completely covered in mold (1d4 + 20 hours), he becomes a mold man or vegepygmy. A *hold plant* spell will halt the growth of the mold for the duration of the spell, while a *cure disease* spell destroys it within an hour after death; after that, a *wish* is necessary to destroy it.

Yellow Mold

This mold is pale yellow to golden orange in color. If touched roughly, it may (50% chance) emit a cloud of spores in a 10-foot radius. Any creature caught in this cloud must roll a successful saving throw vs. poison or die. A *cure disease* spell and a *resurrection* spell within 24 hours are necessary to restore life.

Fire of any sort destroys yellow mold. A *continual light* spell renders it dormant for 2d6 turns.

Yellow mold colonies of over 300 square feet are sometimes sentient (1 in 6 chance). These molds sense creatures within 60 feet, and may project their spores that distance. Twice per day, they may use a *suggestion* on someone within that radius; in addition to the saving throw, the victim must successfully roll an Intelligence check or lose 1 point of Intelligence permanently (it is devoured by the mold).

Level	Dis/Sci Dev	Attack Defense	Power Score	PSPs
1	2/0/2	II/Nil (special)	15	1d10×5

Telepathy: mindwipe, id insinuation.
Metapsionics: psionic sense (1d100 + 20' range, no cost).

Only sentient yellow molds (1 in 6 chance) have psionic powers. Such creatures are also immune to psionic attacks unless the creature is being aided by one who aan communicate with plants.

Mold Man (Vegepygmy)

CLIMATE/TERRAIN:	Tropical or subtropical moist forests and caverns
FREQUENCY:	Very rare
ORGANIZATION:	Tribe
ACTIVITY CYCLE:	Any
DIET:	Carnivore
INTELLIGENCE:	Low (5-7)
TREASURE:	O, P
ALIGNMENT:	Neutral

NO. APPEARING:	6-24 or 30-300
ARMOR CLASS:	4
MOVEMENT:	12
HIT DICE:	1 to 6
THAC0:	1 or 2 HD: 19
	3 or 4 HD: 17
	5 or 6 HD: 15
NO. OF ATTACKS:	1
DAMAGE/ATTACK:	1-6 or by weapon
SPECIAL ATTACKS:	See below
SPECIAL DEFENSES:	See below
MAGIC RESISTANCE:	Nil
SIZE:	S-M (2'-4½')
MORALE:	Average (8-10)
XP VALUE:	1 HD: 120
	2 HD: 175
	3 HD: 270
	4 HD: 420
	5 HD: 650
	6 HD: 2,000

Mold men, sometimes derogatorily called vegepygmies or even moldies, are short, bipedal fungus creatures. They have sharp, thorn-like claws, and leaf-like tendrils form a fringe on their shoulders, abdomens, and limbs. A topknot of these tendrils sits at the apex of a vegepygmy's head.

The coloration of mold men matches their surroundings; forest mold men have brown skin and green tendrils, while those found underground might have gray skin and black tendrils. Mold men are 1½ feet tall, plus 1/2-foot per Hit Die.

Although they do not have a spoken language, vegepygmies are capable of vocalized cries. They normally communicate by tapping on their chests and on trees or stones.

Combat: Parties of mold men hunt near their lairs. In their home territory, mold men blend into their surroundings, so opponents receive a −2 penalty to surprise rolls.

Mold men will attack any form of animal life for food. Though capable of using their natural camouflage for ambush, they seldom use other tricks or traps, preferring direct assault.

Half of the mold men in a group have 1 HD, while 25% have 2 HD. The rest are 3 or 4 HD (equal chances). For every 50 mold men, there is a subchief with 5 HD and 1d4+1 bodyguards with 3 HD each. Each tribe of mold men is led by a chief with 6 HD and 2d4 bodyguards with 4 HD each.

Half of the mold men encountered carry spears, while the others use clubs or go without weapons (equal chances).

Chiefs also attack with spores; victims must make a saving throw vs. poison or be paralyzed, dying in 5d4 minutes unless treated by a *cure disease* spell. Victims who die in this manner are reborn 1d4+20 hours later as mold men with 4 HD. These individuals generally become the chief's bodyguards.

Attacks from piercing weapons cause only 1 point of damage to mold men. They are immune to electrical attacks, as well as all charm spells except those which affect plants. Mold men always receive saving throws vs. enchantments, even if one is not normally allowed.

About half of all of their hunting parties are accompanied by a pack of thornies as well. Mold men settlements always hold 1-4 packs of thornies (see thorny, under Plant, Dangerous).

Habitat/Society: Mold men form primitive, settled tribes. Their lairs are usually found in warm underground areas, though some tribes have lairs in the underbrush of deep, dark forests and jungles. Tribes are very territorial.

Mold men co-exist well with plant and fungus life. They often use shriekers to guard their lairs, and mold men native to the lair can pass by those shriekers unnoticed. Russet mold is usually found in the vicinity of a mold man lair as well.

New mold men are created by russet mold, by their leaders' spore attacks, or by budding. The latter occurs only if food is plentiful. Russet molds produce 5 HD mold men, while leaders create 4 HD mold men, and normal budding produces 1 HD mold men.

Mold men have been known to associate with myconids, which view them as rustic cousins.

Ecology: Mold men live by scavenging and hunting. They will eat meat in any condition, from fresh to carrion. In times of great need, they have been known to eat other mold men, or even myconids, though they seldom attack members of their own or an allied tribe.

Mongrelman

CLIMATE/TERRAIN:	Any
FREQUENCY:	Rare
ORGANIZATION:	Tribal
ACTIVITY CYCLE:	Night
DIET:	Omnivore
INTELLIGENCE:	Low to Average (5-10)
TREASURE:	(C)
ALIGNMENT:	Lawful neutral

NO. APPEARING:	1-100
ARMOR CLASS:	5
MOVEMENT:	9
HIT DICE:	1-4
THAC0:	1-2 HD: 19
	3-4 HD: 17
NO. OF ATTACKS:	1
DAMAGE/ATTACK:	1-4 (1 HD), 1-6 (2 HD), 1-8 (3 HD), 1-10 (4 HD) or by weapon type
SPECIAL ATTACKS:	Nil
SPECIAL DEFENSES:	Camouflage, Mimicry
MAGIC RESISTANCE:	Nil
SIZE:	M (5' to 7' tall)
MORALE:	Steady (12)
XP VALUE:	1 HD: 35
	2 HD: 65
	3 HD: 120
	4 HD: 175
	Leader: 270

Mongrelmen are a mixture of the blood of many species: humans, orcs, gnolls, ogres, dwarves, hobgoblins, elves, bugbears, bullywugs, and many others. Their appearance varies greatly, combining the worst features of their parent stocks. They are usually clad in dirty rags; they are ashamed of their appearance and try keep their bodies concealed, especially among strangers. They have no distinct tongue of their own, but speak a debased common, mixed with grunts, whistles, growls, and gestures. Their names often mimic animal noises.

Combat: Mongrelmen have three special abilities that help them to survive: mimicry, pickpocketing, and camouflage.

Mimicry enables them to imitate the sounds made by any monster or creature they have encountered except for special attack forms (groaning spirits' death wail, for instance), which they cannot imitate.

Pickpocketing enables them to acquire items that they could not otherwise obtain (they have a 70% chance of success).

Camouflage enables them to hide themselves and their items with great skill. The base chance of being unnoticed is 80%, and it requires one turn for camouflage to be performed. Each additional turn spent preparing the camouflage increases the chance by 1%, to a maximum of 95% (after 16 turns). Successfully camouflaged persons or items are not noticed unless they are moved or touched (or move themselves, in the case of creatures). Camouflaged buildings are usually unnoticeable or unrecognizable at ranges greater than 50 feet (this varies with size and type of structure).

Mongrelmen normally fight with clubs and swords, but 5% of the members of any group encountered are armed with blowguns and poison or paralyzing darts.

Habitat/Society: For every 10 mongrelmen encountered, there is at least one with 2 Hit Dice; for every 30, there is one with 3 Hit Dice; and for every 40, there is one with 4 Hit Dice. In a community where they are not held as thralls, there are usually a leader (AC 4, Move 12, HD 5, Dmg 1d12, +1 bonus to attack roll) and five bodyguards (HD 4).

Because of their appearance, mongrelmen are seldom welcome in any lawful or good society, and are usually enslaved or abused by evil or chaotic groups. Thus mongrelmen are found as either slaves or serfs, working long hours for evil humans or humanoids in a dismal community, or as refugees living in abandoned ruins. Enslaved mongrelmen are not willing to rebel, but wait patiently for their masters to be destroyed by outside forces. They prefer to live an orderly day-to-day existence.

A mongrelman prides itself in the ability to survive; they consider the title "The Survivor" to be more esteemed than "The Great." For them, patience is a greater virtue than being good at the arts of war. A mongrelman performs acts of violence only in self-defense or (in the case of slaves) on the orders of their masters; free mongrelmen do not hesitate to kill anyone they believe threatens their community. They prefer to avoid contact with other creatures except in times of great need, when they try to steal what they require (food, tools, etc.).

Free mongrelmen raise domestic game and grow fruits and vegetables. They have a long tradition of art, music, and literature. Their songs are a bizarre cacophony of animal songs mixed with mournful dirges and wails; a few sages consider them to be beautiful, but most disagree.

Ecology: Mongrelmen are omnivorous, but their teeth are most efficient at eating meat. The life span of a free mongrelman is between 25 and 35 years; the average slave lives only 15 to 20 years. Their infant mortality rate is very high. Their major enemies are tribes of wandering humanoids that hunt them for sport.

Morkoth

CLIMATE/TERRAIN:	Any aquatic
FREQUENCY:	Very rare
ORGANIZATION:	Solitary
ACTIVITY CYCLE:	Night
DIET:	Carnivore
INTELLIGENCE:	Exceptional (15-16)
TREASURE:	(G)
ALIGNMENT:	Chaotic evil

NO. APPEARING:	1
ARMOR CLASS:	3
MOVEMENT:	Sw 18
HIT DICE:	7
THAC0:	13
NO. OF ATTACKS:	1
DAMAGE/ATTACK:	1-10
SPECIAL ATTACKS:	Hypnosis
SPECIAL DEFENSES:	Spell reflection
MAGIC RESISTANCE:	Nil
SIZE:	M (6' long)
MORALE:	Elite (14)
XP VALUE:	1,400

Of all the creatures that inhabit the deep, only the kraken exceeds the morkoth in malice and cruelty. Also known as the "wraith of the deep", the morkoth lurks in tunnels hoping to lure its victims into a trap from which they cannot escape.

The descriptions given by those who have encountered morkoths contain considerable variation, so no one is certain what they really look like. They are usually said to resemble an intelligent fish with an octopus's beak. They are most frequently described as being between 5 to 6 feet long, inky black in color, with faint luminescent silver patches. They may have fins for arms and legs that vaguely resemble those of humans, and a number of fins for navigation and propulsion in the depths. Morkoths have infravision with a 90-foot range. They speak their own language.

Combat: A morkoth attacks by snapping with its squid-like beak, which inflicts 1d10 points of damage. A morkoth lives at the center of six spiraling tunnels, each of which leads to a central chamber. These tunnels are narrow (only one size M creature may enter at a time, and no size L). As a victim passes over a tunnel, he is drawn in by a hypnotic pattern, which leads him toward the central chamber. As the victim is drawn into the central chamber, he approaches the morkoth without realizing it and must roll a successful saving throw vs. spell with a -4 penalty or be charmed. A charmed victim is devoured at the morkoth's leisure. If the morkoth doesn't charm the victim before he comes within 60 feet, the hypnotic effect of the tunnels is broken.

A morkoth is highly resistant to magic. It reflects any spell that is cast at it back to the caster, including spells with an area of effect. If a *dispel magic* is simultaneously cast with a spell, there is a 50% chance the morkoth will be unable to reflect it, though it is entitled to a saving throw vs. the dispel.

Habitat/Society: Morkoths are normally solitary creatures. They sometimes make alliances with kraken, offering their help in exchange for an occasional slave. If approached by evil sea humanoids for assistance, morkoths may strike a bargain but often betray their "allies" at the most opportune moment.

Morkoths rarely leave their tunnels. The tunnels are originally natural, but are slowly carved over the course of centuries by the morkoths so that the central chamber grows larger. Morkoths sometimes build their tunnels near hot air vents, so the water in morkoth lairs may be warmer than normal.

Morkoths realize that other intelligent creatures like treasure, so they collect belongings from the creatures they kill to use in bargaining with other creatures. They place no value on gold or gems or even magical items. Morkoths enjoy deception above all else. They do not enslave their victims, if only because their appetites are so fierce that slaves would not survive long.

Ecology: According to the most popular theories, morkoths are a species of fish with human and squid influences. Sages are unsure if this species occurred by chance or design. Morkoths are carnivorous and will eat nearly any sea creature. Their usual diet is deep-water creatures such as sharks, octopi, kuo-toans, and sahuagin. The life spans of male morkoths are about 80 to 100 years, while females die after egg-laying.

Once every ten years, a morkoth leaves its tunnels and wanders the seas searching for a mate, leaving a distinctive odor trail that is easy for morkoths to identify and follow. After mating, the male morkoth returns to its tunnels and the female lays a clutch of about 25 eggs, which she buries in the ocean floor. She then dies. The eggs hatch in two months, and the immature morkoths struggle to survive, instinctively searching for vacant tunnels. Most hatchlings die on this journey.

After six months, a young morkoth is mature enough to survive (it now has 2 hp/HD, for 14 hit points). It grows into a full-sized, exceptionally intelligent morkoth adult by its fifth year.

Muckdweller

CLIMATE/TERRAIN:	Temperate or tropical/ Swamp
FREQUENCY:	Rare
ORGANIZATION:	Tribal
ACTIVITY CYCLE:	Day
DIET:	Omnivore
INTELLIGENCE:	Average
TREASURE:	Q, (J, K, L, M, N)
ALIGNMENT:	Lawful evil

NO. APPEARING:	5-20
ARMOR CLASS:	6
MOVEMENT:	3, Sw 12
HIT DICE:	$1/2$
THAC0:	20
NO. OF ATTACKS:	1
DAMAGE/ATTACK:	1-2
SPECIAL ATTACKS:	Water jet
SPECIAL DEFENSES:	Nil
MAGIC RESISTANCE:	Nil
SIZE:	T (1' high)
MORALE:	Average (10)
XP VALUE:	15

Muckdwellers are a species of small intelligent bipedal amphibians that lurks in swamps, marshes, or still, mud-bottomed waters. They have been known to serve lizard men and kuo-toa.

Muckdwellers are only 1-foot tall and resemble upright gila monsters with large, partially webbed rear feet. Their forepaws are prehensile, but very small and weak. Their backs are colored a mottled gray and brown, and their underbellies are yellow. They have short tails that are used for swimming and keeping their balance on land. They speak their own hissing language and possibly (50% chance) the lizard man tongue.

Combat: Muckdwellers use ambush techniques. Packs of muckdwellers wait for a victim; when one arrives, several squirt water (at up to a ten-yard range) into the victim's eyes, which temporarily blinds it (a successful saving throw vs. wands negates this, but surprised creatures get no saving throw). A blinded victim cannot act in that round, loses all Dexterity bonuses, and all attacks against the victim gain a +2 bonus to the attack roll. Furthermore, if the muckdwellers lure the victim into knee-deep muddy waters, the victim loses all Dexterity bonuses and fights with a -1 penalty to its attack roll, due to unsteady ground. If the water is waist-high, the penalty increases to -2; if the water is chest-high, the penalty is -3. A *ring of free action* or equivalent magic negates these penalties. These disadvantages do not apply to the amphibious muckdwellers. Usually, a muckdweller fights only if it is cornered or if it is certain it can score an easy kill.

Habitat/Society: The lair of these creatures is underwater, but they always have a muddy, above-water area for resting, sunning themselves, and eating. There are 5d4 muckdwellers in each lair. They keep shiny-things (gold, gems, etc.) in hoards in their above ground lairs. If 16 or more monsters are encountered in this lair, they have double the given type Q treasure.

Muckdwellers are an intelligent species, but they have very little culture. They have a very primitive nature worship that em-phasizes the supremacy of water over land. They like shiny things because they gleam like the sea. Due to the weakness of their hands, they do not use or produce tools and use their back paws for burrowing and their teeth for cutting. They occasionally build tiny rafts of cut reeds and mud to float on the surface of the water, and propel themselves quickly with their hind legs (movement 18). They infrequently build crude shelters of reeds, twigs, and mud. These shelters are designed to protect them from predators, not to shelter them, as weather doesn't bother them very much.

Because of the size difference between muckdwellers and lizard men, muckdwellers consider lizard men to be a superior species and occasionally serve them. Muckdwellers believe in the "survival of the fittest" and have no room for love, mercy, or compassion. Scoring the deathbite on a much larger creature gives the individual elite status in the community, while being killed by a bigger creature is a mark of shame, for it demonstrates poor hunting ability.

Ecology: Omnivorous muckdwellers will eat plants, insects, and aquatic animals, but fresh, warm-blooded meat is their preferred diet.

Muckdwellers are amphibians that spend their larval stage in the water but their adult stage on land. Their average life span is 9 to 12 years. It takes three years to grow to full-size. Muckdwellers in temperate climates hibernate during the winter months. Their natural enemies are snakes and certain giant carnivorous fishes. A muckdweller community has a hunting range of about two miles' radius.

Mudman

CLIMATE/TERRAIN:	Any pool
FREQUENCY:	Very rare
ORGANIZATION:	Pack
ACTIVITY CYCLE:	Any
DIET:	Dweomer
INTELLIGENCE:	Non- (0)
TREASURE:	Nil
ALIGNMENT:	Neutral

NO. APPEARING:	2-12 (2d6)
ARMOR CLASS:	10
MOVEMENT:	3
HIT DICE:	2
THAC0:	19
NO. OF ATTACKS:	1
DAMAGE/ATTACK:	Special
SPECIAL ATTACKS:	Mud-throwing, suffocation
SPECIAL DEFENSES:	See below
MAGIC RESISTANCE:	Nil
SIZE:	S (4' high)
MORALE:	Special
XP VALUE:	175

Mudmen are formed in pools of mud where enchanted rivers (even mildly enchanted ones, such as a stream eroding a magical structure) collect and evaporate and concentrate the dweomer. Because they are creatures of magic, mudmen are sometimes called *dweomerlings*. Mudmen are unintelligent life forces with but one goal—to protect their pools against intruders.

When aroused into a physical form, mudmen take on the appearance of animated mud in a stocky humanoid shape, about 4 feet tall. Their coloration varies between a dirty brown and tar black. They have four thick fingers on each hand. Their legs stay submerged within the pool, and are not usually visible. Their eyes are pools of jet black shadow.

Mudmen speak no languages and are incapable of communicating with any living creature.

Combat: In their dormant state, mudmen wait beneath the surface of the pool, spread on the bottom, feeding on the dweomer. In this state they are immune to all weapons, even magical ones. Spells that normally harm a mudman will still affect it, although damage is divided evenly among all the mudmen in the pool (the entire group counts as one creature for these effects, and fractions are rounded down). When a creature enters the pool the mudmen immediately sense its presence and take but a single round to draw their substance together and rise to the surface, ready to attack on the following round. Once fully formed and standing, a mudmen can be harmed by magical weapons.

Mudmen attack by hurling mud at their opponents, who are considered AC 10 (modified by Dexterity) for the purpose of determining hits. Mud hardens on impact and slows the creature's movement rate by 1 if it hits. While hurling mud, a mudman will also advance on its victim at its full movement rate. Once within 10 feet, it will hurl itself (literally) at the victim. A sucessful hit means the death of the mudman, but slows the victim's movement by 4. A miss means the mudman must spend the next round re-forming in order to attack again.

Once a victim's movement is brought to 0, he becomes immobilized and suffocates, suffering 1-8 points of damage per round until the mouth or nose is clear. The victim will die of suffocation

in five consecutive rounds unless rescued. Hardened mud can be cleared from a character's nose and mouth in one round. Movement can be restored at a rate of 1 per five rounds.

If the creature flees the pool, the mudmen will not pursue, as their senses do not extend beyond the pool. Instead, they sink into the depths, return to their dormant state, and wait until the next time someone enters the pool.

Mudmen are affected by all spells that cause damage to living creatures (e.g., *cause light wounds, magic missile, fireball, flame strike*). *Dispel magic* and *dig* act as *fireballs* cast at the same level as the mage.

Transmute mud to rock kills all mudmen within its area of effect, with no saving throw allowed.

Mudmen are immune to all poisons, natural and magical, and are unaffected by spells that affect the mind (e.g., *hold, charm,* and *sleep*).

Habitat/Society: Mudmen have two states: rest and activity, the latter of which solely involves killing intruders. A mudman's pool varies in size between 20 and 200 feet in diameter. Such pools are often found near waterfalls.

Ecology: Mudmen are not natural creatures and not part of the ecosystem. They try to kill all natural creatures that encounter them and have no natural enemies. Over a long period of time they absorb flesh, wood, and bone, extracting whatever dweomer they can get from it, so they rarely possess any treasure—only if they were attacked within the last month by someone who was bearing treasure. Though no uses have been recorded for a mudman's mud, it is logical that mages would not ignore its magical properties.

Mummy

CLIMATE/TERRAIN:	Desert subterranean
FREQUENCY:	Rare
ORGANIZATION:	Pack
ACTIVITY CYCLE:	Night
DIET:	None
INTELLIGENCE:	Low (5-7)
TREASURE:	P, (D)
ALIGNMENT:	Lawful evil

NO. APPEARING:	2-8 (2d4)
ARMOR CLASS:	3
MOVEMENT:	6
HIT DICE:	6+3
THAC0:	13
NO. OF ATTACKS:	1
DAMAGE/ATTACK:	1-12
SPECIAL ATTACKS:	Fear, disease
SPECIAL DEFENSES:	See below
MAGIC RESISTANCE:	Nil
SIZE:	M (6')
MORALE:	Champion (15)
XP VALUE:	3,000

Mummies are corpses native to dry desert areas, where the dead are entombed by a process known as mummification. When their tombs are disturbed, the corpses become animated into a weird unlife state, whose unholy hatred of life causes them to attack living things without mercy.

Mummies are usually (but not always) clothed in rotting strips of linen. They stand between 5 and 7 feet tall and are supernaturally strong.

Combat: Mummies are horrific enemies. A single blow from one's arm inflicts 1-12 points of damage, and worse, its scabrous touch infects the victim with a rotting disease which is fatal in 1-6 months. For each month the rot progresses, the victim permanently loses 2 points of Charisma. The disease can be cured only with a *cure disease* spell. *Cure wounds* spells have no effect on a person inflicted with mummy rot and his wounds heal at 10% of the normal rate. A *regenerate* spell will restore damage but will not otherwise affect the course of the disease.

The mere sight of a mummy causes such terror in any creature that a saving throw versus spell must be made or the victim becomes paralyzed with fright for 1 to 4 rounds. Numbers will bolster courage; for each six creatures present, the saving throw is improved by +1. Humans save against mummies at an additional +2.

Mummies can be harmed only by magical weapons, which inflict only half damage (all fractions round down). *Sleep, charm, hold,* and cold-based spells have no effect. Poison and paralysis do not harm them. A *resurrection* spell will turn the creature into a normal human (a fighter at 7th level ability) with the memories of its former life; or will have no effect if the mummy is older than the maximum age the priest can resurrect. A *wish* will also restore a mummy to human form but a *remove curse* will not.

Mummies are vulnerable to fire, even nonmagical varieties. A blow with a torch inflicts 1-3 points of damage. A flask of burning oil inflicts 1-8 points of damage on the first round it hits and 2-16 on the second round. Magical fires are +1 damage/die. Vials of holy water inflict 2-8 points of damage per direct hit.

Any creature killed by a mummy rots immediately and cannot be raised from death unless both a *cure disease* and a *raise dead* spell are cast within six rounds.

Habitat/Society: Mummies are the product of an embalming process used on wealthy and important personages. Most mummies are corpses without magical properties. On occasion, perhaps due to powerful evil magic or perhaps because the individual was so greedy in life that he refuses to give up his treasure, the spirit of the mummified person will not die, but taps into energy from the Positive Material plane and is transformed into an undead horror. Most mummies remain dormant until their treasure is taken, but then they become aroused and kill without mercy.

A mummy lives in its ancient burial chamber, usually in the heart of a crypt or pyramid. The tomb is a complex series of chambers filled with relics (mostly nonmagical). These relics include models of the mummy's possessions, favorite items and treasures, the bodies of dead pets, and foodstuffs to feed the spirit after death. Particularly evil people will have slaves or family members slain when they die so the slaves can be buried with them. Because of their magical properties, mummies exist on both Prime and Positive Material planes.

Ecology: To create a mummy, a corpse should be soaked in a preserving solution (typically carbonate of soda) for several weeks and covered with spices and resins. Body organs, such as the heart, brain, and liver, are typically removed and sealed in jars. Sometimes gems are wrapped in the cloth (if the treasure listing for the mummy indicates it possesses gems, a few may be placed in the wrappings). Mummies are not part of the natural ecosystem and have no natural enemies.

Mummy dust is a component for rotting and disease magical items.

Mummy, Greater

CLIMATE/TERRAIN:	Any desert or subterranean
FREQUENCY:	Very rare
ORGANIZATION:	Solitary
ACTIVITY CYCLE:	Night
DIET:	Nil
INTELLIGENCE:	Genius (17-18)
TREASURE:	V (Ax2)
ALIGNMENT:	Lawful evil

NO. APPEARING:	1
ARMOR CLASS:	2
MOVEMENT:	9
HIT DICE:	8+3 (base)
THAC0:	11 (base)
NO. OF ATTACKS:	1
DAMAGE/ATTACK:	3d6
SPECIAL ATTACKS:	See below
SPECIAL DEFENSES:	See below
MAGIC RESISTANCE:	Nil
SIZE:	M (6' tall)
MORALE:	Fanatic (17-18)
XP VALUE:	8,000 See below

Also known as *Anhktepot's Children,* greater mummies are a powerful form of undead created when a high-level lawful evil priest of certain religions is mummified and charged with the guarding of a burial place. It can survive for centuries as the steadfast protector of its lair, killing all who would defile its holy resting place.

Greater mummies look just like their more common cousins save that they are almost always adorned with (un)holy symbols and wear the vestments of their religious order. They give off an odor that is said to be reminiscent of a spice cupboard because of the herbs used in the embalming process that created them.

Greater mummies are keenly intelligent and are able to communicate just as they did in life. Further, they have an inherent ability to telepathically command all normal mummies created by them. They have the ability to control other mummies, provided that they are not under the domination of another mummy, but this is possible only when verbal orders can be given.

Combat: Greater mummies radiate an *aura of fear* that causes all creatures who see them to make a fear check. A modifier is applied to this fear check based on the age of the monster, as indicated on the Age & Abilities table at the end of this section. The effects of failure on those who miss their checks are doubled because of the enormous power and presence of this creature. The mummy's aura can be defeated by a *remove fear, cloak of bravery,* or similar spell.

In combat, greater mummies have the option of attacking with their own physical powers or with the great magic granted to them by the gods they served in life. In the former case, they may strike but once per round, inflicting 3d6 points of damage per attack.

Anyone struck by the mummy's attack suffers the required damage and becomes infected with a horrible rotting disease that is even more sinister than that of normal mummies for it manifests itself in a matter of days, not months. The older the mummy, the faster this disease manifests itself (see the Age & Ability table at the end of this entry for exact details). The disease causes the person to die within a short time unless proper medical care can be obtained. Twenty four hours after the infecting blow lands, the character loses 1 point from his Strength and Constitution due to the effects of the virus on his body. Further, they lose 2 points of Charisma as their skin begins to flake and whither like old parchment. No normal healing is possible while the disease

is spreading through the body, and the shaking and convulsions that accompany it make spell casting or memorization impossible for the character. Only one form of magical healing has any effect—a *regenerate* spell will cure the disease and restore lost hit points, but not ability scores. All others healing spells are wasted. A series of *cure disease* spells (one for each day that has passed since the rotting was contracted) will temporarily halt the infection until a complete cure can be affected. Regaining lost ability score points is not possible through any means short of a *wish.*

The body of a person who dies from mummy rot begins to crumble into dust as soon as death occurs. The only way to *resurrect* a character who dies in this way is to cast both a *cure disease* and a *raise dead* spell on the body within 6 turns (1 hour) of death. If this is not done, the body (and the spirit within it) are lost forever.

Greater mummies can be turned by those who have the courage and conviction to attempt this feat; however, the older the mummy, the harder it is to overcome in this fashion. Once again, the details are provided on the Age & Abilities Table. They are immune to damage from holy water, but contact with a holy symbol from a non-evil faith inflicts 1d6 points of damage on them. Contact with a holy symbol of their own faith actually *restores* 1d6 hit points.

Perhaps the most horrible aspect of these creatures, however, is their spell casting ability. All greater mummies were priests in their past lives and now retain the spell casting abilities they had then. They will cast spells as if they were of 16th through 20th level (see below) and will have the same spheres available to them that they did in life. Greater mummies receive the same bonus spells for high Wisdom scores that player characters do. Dungeon Masters are advised to select spells for each greater mummy in an adventure before the adventure starts. For those using *Legends & Lore* in their games, greater mummies are most often priests of Osiris, Set, and Nephythys. For those using *The Complete Priest's Handbook,* they are usually associated with

Mummy, Greater

the worship of ancestors, darkness, death, disease, evil, guardianship, and revenge. (If neither of these works is being used in the campaign, simply assign the mummy powers as if it were a standard high-level cleric.)

Greater mummies can be harmed only by magical weapons, with older ones being harder to hit than younger ones. Even if a weapon can affect them, however, it will inflict only half damage because of the magical nature of the creature's body.

Spells are also less effective against greater mummies than they are against other creatures. Those that rely on cold to inflict damage are useless against the mummy, while those that depend on fire inflict normal damage. Unlike normal mummies, these foul creatures are immune to non-magical fire. The enchanting process that creates them, however, leaves them vulnerable to attacks involving electricity; all spells of that nature inflict half again their normal damage. In addition, older mummies develop a magic resistance that makes even those spells unreliable.

Greater mummies, like vampires, become more powerful with the passing of time in Ravenloft. The following table lists the applicable changes to the listed statistics (which are for a newly created monster) brought on by the passing of time:

Age & Ability Table

Age	To Hit	AC	HD	THAC0
99 or less	+1	2	8+3	11
100-199	+1	1	9+3	11
200-299	+2	0	10+3	9
300-399	+2	-1	11+3	9
400-499	+3	-2	12+3	7
500 or more	+4	-3	13+3	7

Age	Align	Wis	Magic	Disease
99 or less	LE	18	Nil	1d12 days
100-199	LE	19	5%	1d10 days
200-299	LE or CE	20	10%	1d8 days
300-399	CE or LE	21	15%	1d6 days
400-499	CE	22	20%	1d4 days
500 or more	CE	23	25%	1d3 days

Age	Level	XP	Fear	Mummies
99 or less	16	8,000	-1	1d4
100-199	17	10,000	-2	2d4
200-299	18	12,000	-2	3d4
300-399	19	14,000	-3	5d4
400-499	20	16,000	-3	6d4
500 or more	20	18,000	-4	7d4

Notes:

To Hit indicates the magical plus that must be associated with a weapon before it will inflict damage to the mummy.

AC is the Armor Class of the monster.

HD are the number of hit dice that the mummy has. Greater mummies are turned as if they had one more Hit Die than they actually do, so a 250 year old (10+3) is turned as if it had 11 Hit Dice. Any mummy 300 years old or older is turned as a "special" undead.

THAC0 is listed for the various Hit Dice levels of the mummy to allow for easy reference during play.

Alignment As the mummy grows older, it becomes darker and more evil. In cases where two alignments are listed, there is a 75% chance that the mummy will be of the first alignment and a 25% chance that it will be of the second. Thus, a 300 year old mummy is 75% likely to be of chaotic evil.

Wisdom is the creature's Wisdom score. When employing their spells, greater mummies receive all of the bonus spells normally

associated with a high Wisdom. Further, as they pass into the higher ratings (19 and beyond) they gain an immunity to certain magical spells as listed in the *Player's Handbook*.

Magic is the creature's natural magic resistance. As can be seen from the table, old mummies can be very deadly indeed.

Disease is the length of time it takes for a person infected with the mummy's rotting disease to die.

Level indicates the creature's level as a priest. Older mummies have access to far greater magics than younger ones and are thus more dangerous than younger ones.

XP lists the number of experience points awarded to a party for battling and defeating a greater mummy of a given age.

Mummies indicates the number of normal mummies that the creature will have serving it when encountered.

Fear indicates the penalty to those making fear checks due to the evil influence of the greater mummy's foul aura.

Habitat/Society: Greater mummies are powerful undead creatures that are usually created from the mummified remains of powerful, evil priests. This being the case, the greater mummy now draws its mystical abilities from evil powers and darkness. In rare cases, however, the mummified priests served non-evil god in life and are still granted the powers they had in life from those gods.

Greater mummies often dwell in large temple complexes or tombs where they guard the bodies of the dead from the disturbances of grave robbers. Unlike normal mummies, however, they have been known to leave their tombs and strike out into the world—bringing a dreadful shroud of evil down upon every land they touch.

When a greater mummy wishes to create normal mummies as servants, it does so by mummifying persons infected with its rotting disease. This magical process requires 12-18 hours (10+2d4) and cannot be disturbed without ruining the enchantment. Persons to be mummified are normally *held* or *charmed* so that they cannot resist the mummification process. Once the process is completed, victims are helpless to escape the bandages that bind them. If nothing happens to free them, they will die of the mummy rot just as they would have elsewhere. Upon their death, however, a strange transformation takes place. Rather than crumbling away into dust, these poor souls rise again as normal mummies. Obviously, this process is too time consuming to be used in actual combat, but the greater mummy will often attack a potential target in hopes of capturing and transforming it into a mummy. All mummies created by a greater mummy are under its telepathic command.

Ecology: The first of these creatures is known to have been produced by Anhktepot, the Lord of Har'akir, in the years before he became undead himself. It is believed that most, if not all, of the greater mummies he created in his life were either destroyed or drawn into Ravenloft with him when he was granted a domain. A number of these creatures are believed to serve Anhktepot in his domain, acting as his agents in other lands he wishes to learn what is transpiring in other portions of Ravenloft.

The process by which a greater mummy is created remains a mystery to all but Anhktepot. It is rumored that this process involves a great sacrifice to gain the favor of the gods and an oath of eternal loyalty to the Lord of Har'akir. If the latter is true, then it may lend credence to the claim of many sages that Anhktepot can command every greater mummy in existence to do his bidding. If this is indeed the case, it makes the power of this dark fiend far greater than is generally supposed.

Myconid (Fungus Man)

CLIMATE/TERRAIN:	Subterranean
FREQUENCY:	Rare
ORGANIZATION:	Communal
ACTIVITY CYCLE:	Day
DIET:	Herbivore
INTELLIGENCE:	Average (8-10)
TREASURE:	S (x2)
ALIGNMENT:	Lawful neutral

NO. APPEARING:	1-12; 20-200 in lair
ARMOR CLASS:	10
MOVEMENT:	9
HIT DICE:	1-6
THAC0:	1-2 HD: 19
	3-4 HD: 17
	5-6 HD: 15
NO. OF ATTACKS:	1
DAMAGE/ATTACK:	1d4 x HD
SPECIAL ATTACKS:	Spore Clouds
SPECIAL DEFENSES:	Poisonous Skin
MAGIC RESISTANCE:	Nil
SIZE:	T-L (2' per HD)
MORALE:	Steady (12) to Elite (13)
XP VALUE:	1 HD: 65
	2 HD: 120
	3 HD: 175
	4 HD: 270
	5 HD: 420
	6 HD: 650

Myconids, or fungus men, are a race of intelligent fungi that live in the remote reaches of the Underdark. They are cautious creatures that deplore violence; myconids have no desire to conquer anybody and would prefer to be left alone.

Myconids resemble walking toadstools in human form. Their flesh is bloated and spongy and varies in color from purple to gray. Their wide feet have vestigial toes and their pudgy hands have two stubby fingers and a thumb on either side. Myconids' Hit Dice determine their social status and abilities. They have no spoken language.

Combat: Fungus men fight by clubbing with their clasped hands, causing 1d4 points of damage per Hit Die. Thus a 1-Hit Die myconid inflicts 1d4 points of damage, a 2-Hit Die myconid causes 2d4 points of damage, etc., up to the 6-Hit Dice king that inflicts 6d4 points of damage on a hit.

Myconids also have the ability to spew forth clouds of special spores. The number and kind of spores increase as they grow. As each myconid advances to another size level, it gains the ability to spray another type of spores, and the number of times per day that each spore type can be emitted also increases. A myconid can emit each of its spore types a number of times per day equal to its Hit Dice. For example, a 3-HD myconid (6 feet tall) can spray three types of spores, and it may use each type three times per day. These spore types include the following:

Distress: This spore type is used to alert other myconids to danger or a need for aid. The cloud expands at a rate of 40 feet per round, expanding to its maximum of 120 feet in three rounds. This ability is gained at the 1-Hit Die level.

Reproducer: These spores are only emitted at the proper time for growing new myconids so the population can be rigidly controlled. They are also automatically ejected by a dying myconid. This ability is gained at the 2-Hit Die level.

Rapport: These spores are primarily used in the melding process. However, they can be used by the myconids to communicate with other species, since the fungus men do not talk. A small cloud of spores is aimed at one person; if the person fails a saving throw vs. poison (it can choose to fail), it can go into telepathic rapport, speaking mind-to-mind with the myconid as if it were normal speech. The range of this effect is 40 feet. The duration is a number of turns equal to the Hit Dice of the myconid. This ability is gained at the 3-Hit Dice level.

Pacifier: This type of spore cloud may be spewed at a single creature. If the creature fails its saving throw vs. poison, it becomes totally passive, unable to do anything. The affected creature only observes; it is unable to perform any action even if attacked. The range of this effect is 40 feet. The duration of this effect is a number of rounds equal to the Hit Dice of the myconid. This ability is gained at the 4-Hit Dice level.

Hallucinator: This type of spore is usually used in the melding ritual, but a myconid can project them at an attacker. The spore cloud may be shot at one creature, and if that creature fails its saving throw vs. poison, it suffers violent hallucinations for a number of turns equal to the Hit Dice of the myconid. Hallucinating creatures react as follows (roll 1d20):

D20 Roll	Reaction
1-10	Cower and whimper
11-15	Stare into nothingness
16-18	Flee shrieking in a random direction
19-20	Try to kill the closest creature

The range of this effect is 40 feet. This ability is gained at the 5-Hit Dice level.

Animator: This ability is gained at the 6-Hit Dice level, the level only the king may achieve. The king uses these spores to infect a dead animal or creature. A purple fungus quickly covers the corpse, taking over the dead body systems and putting it to work, animating the corpse to resemble a zombie (AC 10, Move 9, HD 1, hp 4, #AT 2, Dmg bony claws for 1-3/1-3). It is not undead and cannot be turned by priests. It always strikes last in a round. The body continues to rot and the fungus gradually replaces the missing parts, becoming specialized to take over their

Myconid (Fungus Man)

functions. Eventually, however, the decay proceeds too far, and the body stops functioning, able to rest at last. Animation takes place 1d4 days after infection, and the corpse is animated for 1d4+1 weeks before it decays. Animated creatures will follow simple orders given by the animator (with rapport spores) to the best of their ability. Orders take priority over self-preservation.

A myconid has a deathly fear of sunlight and will not willingly travel to the surface world. The exact effects of sunlight on a myconid are unknown, but they must be highly detrimental for the fungus men to fear sunlight as they do.

Habitat/Society: Myconid society is based on "circles," extremely tight social groups that are linked by group work and melding sessions. Myconid circles usually consist of 20 members: four of each size from 1-5 Hit Dice (i.e., four 1-HD, four 2-HD, etc.). Each community consists of 1d10 circles.

Each circle's day is rigidly structured: eight hours of rest, followed by eight hours of farming the fungus crops, followed by eight hours of melding. For the myconids, melding is entertainment, worship, and social interaction combined. The fungus men gather in a tight circle and the elder myconid release rapport and hallucinatory spores. The entire group then merges into a collective telepathic hallucination for eight hours. Myconids consider this melding to be the reason for their existence. Only distress spores will bring a circle out of its meld before the eight hours have elapsed.

The myconid king is always the largest member of the colony and is the only member at the 6-Hit Dice level. It is also the only myconid that is not the member of a circle. The other myconids regard separation from the circles with horror and pity the lonely king. The leadership role is thought of as an unpleasant duty, almost a condemnation. However, when the old king dies, the strongest 5-Hit Dice myconid always assumes the role of the new king. The king must remain outside of circles to retain objectivity and to pay close attention to the duties of leadership. The king animates guardians for the colony so the myconids need not commit violence. It coordinates the work schedule and pays attention to affairs outside the colony that could affect the fungus men. The king also practices fungal alchemy, brewing special potions that may be useful in times of trouble.

In general, myconids are a peaceful race, desiring only to work and meld in peace. There are no recorded instances of disharmony, or any sort of violence or disagreement between myconids. If forced into combat, they avoid killing if at all possible; violence adversely affects their melding.

Accord has never been reached between fungoid and humanoid. Each views the other as a disgusting threat; humanoids see myconids as ugly monsters. Myconids view humanoids as a violent, insane species out to conquer anything in their path, destroy anything they can't conquer, then go back down the path to make sure there isn't anything they forgot to destroy or conquer. Myconids find it difficult to believe that humanoids are not going to immediately use violence against them, and so they are very reluctant to deal with them. Given population pressures in the underworld in which the myconids live, further conflicts seem inevitable. If the myconids are approached in peace, it is possible that they will communicate, though they will be suspicious.

Myconids live in Underdark regions, which are large cavernous underground areas that range in size form a large cavern complex to an entire secret continent beneath the ground. Myconids try to find isolated spots away from civilized areas. These communities will usually be near water, for they like dampness. Work details sometimes patrol the Underdark, looking for signs of battles and unburied dead, which they bring to the king to animate; these are the only myconids that will be found outside of their lair. A myconid community is arranged around mounds of moss-covered stones, on which the circle members sit when they meld, and on which they sleep. There will also be a large garden area; the myconids feed on water and small fungi, and the king uses the garden ingredients to make his potions. Dead myconid kings are buried with honor beneath the mounds, while dead myconids are buried near the gardens.

Ecology: Myconids are an unusual species of fungi. They grow fungi, which later decay, and the myconids feed from these soil nutrients.

A myconid has a life span of 24 years. It requires four years to grow to each Hit Die, thus a 1-Hit Die myconid is four years old, a 2-Hit Die myconid is eight years old, etc., to a maximum of 5 Hit Dice at 20 years of age. It requires a special regimen for a myconid to reach 6 Hit Dice (king).

A myconid king has the ability to brew magical potions from fungi. In addition to standard magical potions, a myconid king can brew the following:

Potion of Fungus Growth: This is used in times of population shortage, when myconid circles need their young members to grow quickly. This potion increases a myconid's Hit Dice by 1. It can only be used on a myconid once in its lifetime; repeated doses have no effect.

Potion of Fungus Healing: This potion only works on fungi. It heals 1d6+1 lost hit points.

Potion of Decay: This poison affects a humanoid creature as if it were a dead creature infected with purple fungi spores. The victim must roll a successful saving throw vs. poison or die, replaced within 1d4+1 days by a fungal intelligence friendly to the myconids, which lasts for 1d4+1 weeks before permanently decaying. A *cure disease* spell will prevent the victim's death if cast within three minutes of the infection. The combination of a *cure disease* spell and a *raise dead* spell will bring back victims of the fungus disease after 48 hours. This potion is rarely used by the fungus men.

Powders of Hallucination: This is used when hallucinatory spores are in short supply due to the death of 4- and 5-Hit Die members of the circles. It is also used as a defensive measure when myconids are certain they are going to be attacked; a powder is bundled and placed on a spider-silk film inside the entrance to their circle. Creatures of size M will break the powder free, affecting all creatures in a 20-foot radius as hallucinatory spores.

Potion of Anointment: This is the special regimen that enables a 5-Hit Die fungus to grow to 6 Hit Dice and become king. Growth is immediate and painful. It affects a myconid only once. It is poisonous to humans (successful saving throw vs. poison or die).

There is always one *potion of anointment* in the community. If other potions are indicated, consult the following table:

01-10	Another *potion of anointment*
11-20	*Potion of fungi growth*
21-30	*Potion of fungus healing*
31-40	*Powder of hallucination*
41-45	*Potion of decay*
46-00	Roll on standard potion table

Alchemists have found a number of uses for myconid spores, typically in poisons and potions of delusion. Other than their potions, myconids produce little of value to humanoid creatures.

Naga

	Guardian	Spirit	Water
CLIMATE/TERRAIN:	Any land	Subterranean	Freshwater
FREQUENCY:	Very rare	Rare	Uncommon
ORGANIZATION:	Solitary	Solitary	Solitary
ACTIVITY CYCLE:	Day	Night	Any
DIET:	Omnivore	Carnivore	Omnivore
INTELLIGENCE:	Exceptional(16)	Highly (13)	Very (11)
TREASURE:	X (H)	X (B,T)	X (D)
ALIGNMENT:	Lawful good	Chaotic evil	Neutral
NO. APPEARING:	1-2	1-3	1-4
ARMOR CLASS:	3	4	5
MOVEMENT:	15	12	9, Sw 18
HIT DICE:	11-12	9-10	7-8
THAC0:	9	11	13
NO. OF ATTACKS:	2	1	1
DAMAGE/ATTACK:	1-6/2-8	1-3	1-4
SPECIAL ATTACKS:	See below	See below	See below
SPECIAL DEFENSES:	Nil	Nil	Nil
MAGIC RESISTANCE:	Nil	Nil	Nil
SIZE:	H (20' long)	H (15' long)	L (10' long)
MORALE:	Champion (15)	Elite (14)	Steady(11)
XP VALUE:	7,000	5,000	3,000

Possessing high intelligence and magical abilities, naga are snake-like creatures with human heads. They prefer warmer climates and tend not to wander far from their lairs.

The cold-blooded naga have glittering scales and grow to an adult length of 10 to 20 feet. Their lidless eyes are bright and wide, almost luminescent, and their spines are armored with sharp triangular extensions that grow in a line from the napes of their necks to the tips of their tails. Wise and patient, these creatures can stay still for hours but move swiftly when alarmed. They favor resting in a semi-aware state that conserves their energy and makes them very hard to surprise. Occasionally, naga fashion a pouch to carry items under their chins. Both land types have a distinctive smell that pervades their lair and nearby areas.

Naga can usually speak four or more languages.

Combat: Naga often set traps to snare trespassers. Magical spells are always attempted first, since naga have few melee skills. Once their magic is expended, naga rely on their poisonous bites—only the largest of these creatures can actually constrict victims like a giant snake.

Habitat/Society: Naga live solitary lives, hunting or foraging over an area usually only a quarter mile square. They favor dwelling in a deep hole, but sometimes are found curled up in ruins or in a darkened room. While the sexes are impossible to tell apart, there is a 10% chance that an encounter includes one or more mates. These matings are temporary, as a pregnant naga quickly leaves the male to hide her eggs in a secluded spot. Young naga resemble giant snakes until they reach adulthood; then their human-like head emerges after a long and painful molting.

Ecology: While naga do not produce trade goods, their lives span many human generations and they keep a detailed oral history, so they are good sources of information. They are often protectors of treasures or artifacts for centuries. Their hides can be fashioned into *scale mail +2*, and their eyes and teeth have been sold for use in arcane spells.

Guardian Naga
Surrounded with a flowery sweet scent, the guardian naga is marked by green-gold scales, silvery spines, and flashing golden eyes. It is so called because its lawful good nature makes it a perfect sentinel over a like-aligned being's treasure or some evil. This naga always warns off trespassers, and often buries those defeated in battle. The guardian naga can spit poison at an individual attacker at up to 30-foot range, and the poison kills all who fail their saving throws vs. poison. In addition to a poisonous bite and constriction, these naga have the ability to use priest spells as 6th-level priests.

Spirit Naga
These black-and-crimson-banded naga have a most human-like head, with stringy hair and deep brown eyes, and they smell of rotting flesh, which happens to be their preferred food! Hiding in deserted ruins or caverns, these evil and cunning spirit naga seek to cause harm to any creature that passes through their domains. They set traps and frequently attack without warning. While they are not big enough to constrict their prey, they have a poisonous bite, a gaze that charms (as a *charm* spell) all those who look into their eyes and fail a saving throw vs. paralyzation, and can use wizard spells at 5th-level ability and priest spells at 4th-level ability.

Water Naga
The beautiful water naga are emerald green to turquoise in reticulated patterns with chocolate brown and pale jade green or dark grey and olive, and their spines have red spikes that raise like hackles when they are angry. Their eyes are pale green to amber. These naga are found in clear, fresh water. Curious but neutral in attitude, water naga seldom attack unless threatened. In addition to their poisonous bite that inflicts 1d4 points of damage, these naga have 5th-level wizard spell abilities. They never know spells that deal with fire.

Naga, Dark

CLIMATE/TERRAIN:	Any except arctic/any land
FREQUENCY:	Very rare
ORGANIZATION:	Trios, pairs, alone or work with other lawful evil creatures
ACTIVITY CYCLE:	Any
DIET:	Carnivore
INTELLIGENCE:	Exceptional (16)
TREASURE:	S, T, W
ALIGNMENT:	Lawful evil
NO. APPEARING:	1-3 (usually 1)

ARMOR CLASS:	6
MOVEMENT:	13
HIT DICE:	9
THAC0:	11
NO. OF ATTACKS:	2
DAMAGE/ATTACK:	1-4/2-8
SPECIAL ATTACKS:	See below
SPECIAL DEFENSES:	Nil
MAGIC RESISTANCE:	Nil
SIZE:	L (up to 12' long)
MORALE:	Champion (15)
XP VALUE:	4,000

Dark nagas are fey creatures who have human-like faces (with fanged mouths) on leathery, snake-like bodies. They usually work with other evil beings for mutual gain or survival. Dark nagas tend to be black, purplish-black, or very dark blue in hue, and their crested heads and smooth, almost invisible scales make them look like gigantic eels more than snakes.

Combat: Dark nagas have natural *ESP* powers (80' range), and use this ability constantly.

Dark nagas have a (non-poisonous) bite and a poisonous tail-sting; the barbed stinger does physical damage, and any struck being must save vs. poison or take 1-2 hp additional damage and fall into a drugged sleep (onset time 1 round, sleep lasts 2d4 rounds).

The most feared ability of dark nagas is their power to wield magic. A dark naga casts spells as a 6th-level wizard (4,2,2), and employs only verbal spells. It may learn these spells from dragons, Phaerimm, or other creatures who can cast spells with but a word or thought (act-of-will spells, as opposed to spell-like natural powers, can easily be altered into verbal-release magics . . . but the devising of a verbal-only version of a spell that normally has somatic and material components is not nearly so simple a matter). It may devise new spells, or verbal-only spell versions, itself by means of experimentation. Either means of acquiring new magics is slow and expensive, and this can often force dark nagas into servitude to a stronger evil creature or anyone who hires them, or into the life of an adventurer.

Dark nagas are immune to the effects of all known (normal and magical) acids, venoms, and poisons. Some have been known to swallow poisons and act as a courier, spitting up the dangerous liquid when they deliver it to its destination. They can spit poison so that they are so carrying up to 10' distant at any opponent; this requires a successful attack roll, and takes the place of their bite, though a naga can elect to bite and then release the poison as it does so, combining the damage.

In battle, a dark naga may use its sting and either a spell or a bite in the same round. If space permits, the naga can direct its sting and bite against the same foe, but it is quite intelligent enough to direct attacks at multiple opponents, even attacking foes in front of and behind it, simultaneously, if caught between them in a narrow passage.

Dark nagas cannot be mind-read; their *ESP* ability somehow renders them immune to the *ESP*-like probes of others. They are subject but resistant to *charm*, *sleep*, *hold* and similar enchantment/charm spells, receiving a +2 bonus to all saving throws against this school of magic.

Habitat/Society: Dark nagas lair in rocky places, such as caverns or ruins; they like to have a home where they can hide things (such as treasures and spellbooks), that has more than one entry or exit, and at least one place narrow enough that they can block it with their body, and singlehandedly fight off intruders. Dark nagas are fond of traps, and will devise these (or hire other creatures to install them) whenever possible.

Dark nagas tend to be loners, but can form stable family groups of two or three; they are bisexual, and give birth to a squirming mass of many wormlike young which they promptly abandon to fend for themselves. Intelligent enough to know they can prevail against few creatures in the Realms alone, dark nagas work with other evil creatures, such as orcs, hobgoblins, drow, phaerimm, beholders, and the like. They like to fill a "commander and magical strike force" role, perhaps in a sergeant-like intermediary rank, under a more powerful ruler—but they are wise enough to adopt the faith, beliefs, and rules of whatever group they join.

Ecology: Dark nagas do not willingly eat other dark nagas, but they will eat just about anything else, both alive and dead. They eat a few lichens and the occasional green plant, but their main diet is meat. They especially prize hot, still-fresh blood.

Dark nagas spend their lives outwardly working with, or serving, others. Whenever possible, however, they also pursue private goals, which may be as whimsical and odd as some human goals ("cover this desert valley with trees," for instance), but always include increasing their personal power by acquiring new spells and magical items. Dark nagas are quick to plunder fallen foe, swallowing items, scrolls, and spellbooks to spit forth later—for all dark nagas have a bag-like internal organ that they can use to carry things. This organ has thick, rubbery air-sac walls to protect the naga against sharp points and the like, but it also protects the cargo against digestive juices, and has the unusual side-effect of shielding magic from all detection spells.

Neogi

	Neogi	Great Old Master
CLIMATE/TERRAIN:	Any	Any
FREQUENCY:	Rare	Very rare
ORGANIZATION:	Tribal	Solitary plus feeders
ACTIVITY CYCLE:	Any	Any
DIET:	Carnivore	Carnivore
INTELLIGENCE:	Highly (13-14)	Low (5-7)
TREASURE:	Q	Nil
ALIGNMENT:	Lawful evil	Lawful evil
NO. APPEARING:	1-8	1
ARMOR CLASS:	3	5
MOVEMENT:	6	3
HIT DICE:	5	20
THAC0:	15	Nil
NO. OF ATTACKS:	3	0
DAMAGE/ATTACKS:	1-3/1-3/1-6	0
SPECIAL ATTACKS:	Slowing poison	Digestion, young
SPECIAL DEFENSES:	Possible magic	Young
MAGIC RESISTANCE:	Nil	10%
SIZE:	S (3' high)	H (20' high)
MORALE:	Steady (12)	Unsteady (6)
XP VALUE:	650	14,000

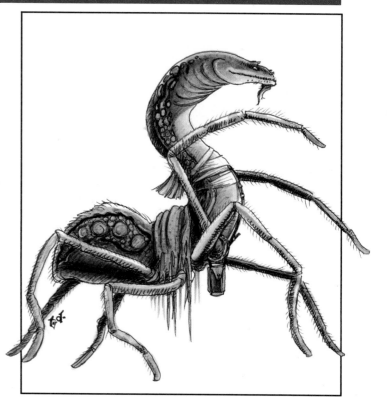

The neogi appear as a cross between a wolf spider and a moray eel. The short, furry, eight-limbed body is topped by a lithe, bare, fleshy neck with a serpentine head, its mouth filled with needle-sharp teeth. The ends of its limbs are tipped with small claws. The fur of the neogi is a light tan, but dyed a variety of colors to signify power, rank, accomplishments, and warnings to other neogi. The older a neogi grows, the more colorful its hide becomes.

The neogi are ruthless slayers and plunderers, and think nothing of eating their enemies, servants, or fallen comrades. They are a hateful, xenophobic race.

Neogi can communicate in their own language and in Common. Many speak 1-4 other languages to help facilitate their slaves taking orders correctly.

Combat: The neogi have a number of defenses, the first, and most obvious being their enslavement of umber hulks (see entry). Each neogi has a personal umber hulk slave who is a combination bodyguard, manservant, and useful set of hands. Second, the bite of the neogi is poisonous. Those bitten and failing a saving throw vs. poison are affected as by a *slow* spell for 1d8 rounds. Multiple bites will extend this period by an additional 1d8 rounds per bite. Lastly, 1 in 10 neogi has some magical ability, equal to human spell use of levels 1-8.

Habitat/Society: The hated neogi are only found in very remote locations, deep beneath the earth, or among the farthest stars. Their lives revolve around their communities and their slaves.

Neogi are a slaving race with an inborn sense of property: all is either owned or owner, slave or neogi. Even neogi are slaves to other neogi, but slave-neogi may have their own slaves. The neogi tattoo their non-neogi slaves with symbols of ownership, usually on the left shoulder in the front and back.

Captive umber hulks are trained from birth to follow their "small lords," caring for their every need. Any neogi can command another umber hulk (the effect of this command is akin to the effect of the *charm monster* spell).

The neogi world view of "own or be owned" has resulted in a paranoid outlook that borders on xenophobia, and their relentless attacks on other races result in their being universally hated.

The only "normal" race with ties to neogi are the mind flayers, who make a profit on the neogi slave trade.

Ecology: As a neogi grows older and his mind fades, his orders become confused and his slaves become disobedient. His fellow neogi may choose to poison the older one at once. The different poisons moving through its body overload the old neogi's system, and it begins its change into a Great Old Master.

The neogi making the transformation swells to 20 feet in height and a similar girth. Its legs and arms become useless, and its intelligence fades; it now lives only to eat. Live flesh is preferred, but the dead will sustain it. A Great Old Master inflicts 1d12 points of damage per round to any creature it is fed.

After 2 months of eating, the skin of the Great Old Master bursts and a new crop of mature neogi spill forth. These are unmarked and barely sentient at birth, and for the next week the brood area resounds with combat as the young neogi kill each other for food. Of the 20-40 neogi that eat their way out, only about 3-6 survive. These are considered slaves of the community, until such a time as they claim an umber hulk as their personal slave.

If a Great Old Master is attacked and its flesh pierced, it releases 2d4 neogi to defend itself. These are taken from the future brood, and are not replaced. Blunt weapons will not pierce the skin and therefore do not bring forth young. Edged or piercing weapons, or magical spells that pierce or burn, will produce this defensive reaction.

Reaver

These rogue neogi have rebelled and are seeking to escape the other neogi and their poisons that will transform them into Great Old Masters. Rogue neogi are little better than their fellows, and are, if anything, more desperate, due to being pursued by their former fellows, all eager to start the process of producing more neogi.

Nightmare

CLIMATE/TERRAIN:	Lower planes
FREQUENCY:	Very rare
ORGANIZATION:	Solitary
ACTIVITY CYCLE:	Any
DIET:	Carnivore
INTELLIGENCE:	Very (11-12)
TREASURE:	Nil
ALIGNMENT:	Neutral evil

NO. APPEARING:	1
ARMOR CLASS:	−4
MOVEMENT:	15, Fl 36 (C)
HIT DICE:	6+6
THAC0:	17
NO. OF ATTACKS:	3
DAMAGE/ATTACK:	4-10/4-10/2-8
SPECIAL ATTACKS:	Burning hooves
SPECIAL DEFENSES:	Paralyzing cloud
MAGIC RESISTANCE:	Nil
SIZE:	L (6' at shoulder)
MORALE:	Elite (13-14)
XP VALUE:	2,000

Nightmares are the evil steeds of the lower planes, often serving as mounts for baatezu, tanar'ri, night hags, liches, and powerful undead lords.

They look like large, powerful horses with a jet black coat. Nightmares have glowing red eyes, flaming orange nostrils, and hooves that burn like embers. Their flowing manes and great tails are ragged and wild.

Nightmares can understand commands from evil riders. They communicate among themselves by empathy.

Combat: Nightmares are hateful of material life. They will often attack any non-lower planar creature they encounter (and will sometimes attack the lower planar creatures, too). They have vicious fangs that inflict 2-8 points of damage on a successful bite. Their burning hooves each inflict 4-10 (1d6+4) points of damage per attack and will set any combustibles on fire.

During combat, the excitement and fervor of the fight will cause nightmares to emit a smoking, hot cloud of noxious vapors. It blinds and chokes all those within 10 feet of the evil steed. Victims must make a saving throw vs. paralyzation or be at a −2 penalty on their attack and damage dice.

Although they have no wings, nightmares are able to magically propel themselves through the air at an impressive rate. They may fly through the Astral and Ethereal planes at will.

Habitat/Society: Nightmares are the servitor steeds of many lower planar creatures. They are intelligent, however, and cannot be treated as casually as a simple horse. They will willingly and gleefully serve as a mount for any mission involving evil. However, for the unwary rider, a nightmare's own ambitions can prove to be insurmountable. These hateful steeds will often do what *they* want rather than follow the wishes of their "master." In many ways, nightmares pose the same problems as magical weapons with large egos.

Anyone on the lower planes who is not a native thereof can attract the attention of a nightmare to secure it as a mount. The process involves several spells, as well as an offering for the creature's service. The summoning requires a mage or specialist wizard of at least 5th level. The following spells must all be cast by the same spell-user. First, the mage must cast a *mount* spell. This conjuration is used to attract the attention of the nightmare. Next, a *monster summoning III* spell must be cast to bind the

nightmare into service. When that is complete, a *wall of fog* spell is cast. If all of this is done properly, the nightmare will come galloping through the fog, nostrils flaring and eyes gleaming, ready to perform in the service of evil. Lastly, an offering is required. This may be given by anyone, not just the spell caster. The offering must be oat-like flakes made from platinum that the nightmare will eat. The flakes must be of at least 200 gp value. Whoever feeds the oats to the nightmare will be its master for 72 hours.

Creatures of the lower planes do not perform these steps to summon a nightmare. It is unknown what dark agreement they make for a nightmare's service.

Once per decade, on the plane of Hades, there is a dark and sinister time called *Gloom Meet*. At this time the various lower planar denizens will meet and decide how they will spread their will for the next decade. The nightmares play a special role in *Gloom Meet*, for they spread the word that the meeting is about to begin. As the *Gloom Meet* approaches, there is a higher concentration of nightmares and their frequency changes from very rare to uncommon. This is the first indication that *Gloom Meet* is to occur, and lasts for approximately two weeks. Immediately prior to the meeting, the nightmares ride the planes in a terrifying charge that notifies all that the *Gloom Meet* has started.

Ecology: Nightmares are the wild steeds of the planes. It is their place in the lower planes to act as mounts for missions of evil and dread. They have no biological link to true horses. A nightmare is merely a foul minion of evil, without need of food or air, that through some unknown pact has taken the form of a huge, terrible steed. Nightmares are listed as carnivores, based solely on their habit of eating fallen foes whenever possible. However, there is nothing to indicate that the nightmares derive any of their sustenance from the flesh of animals—they more likely gain all their strength through their service to evil.

Nymph

CLIMATE/TERRAIN:	Any
FREQUENCY:	Very rare
ORGANIZATION:	Solitary
ACTIVITY CYCLE:	Day
DIET:	Nil
INTELLIGENCE:	Exceptional (16)
TREASURE:	Q (Qx10, X)
ALIGNMENT:	Neutral (good)

NO. APPEARING:	1-4
ARMOR CLASS:	9
MOVEMENT:	12
HIT DICE:	3
THAC0:	17
NO. OF ATTACKS:	0
DAMAGE/ATTACK:	Nil
SPECIAL ATTACKS:	See below
SPECIAL DEFENSES:	See below
MAGIC RESISTANCE:	50%
SIZE:	M (4'-6')
MORALE:	Unsteady (7)
XP VALUE:	1,400

So beautiful that a glimpse can blind or even kill a man, the nymphs are the embodiment of loveliness, a triumph of nature.

A nymph's beauty is beyond words—an ever-young woman with sleek figure and long, thick hair, radiant skin and perfect teeth, full lips and gentle eyes. A nymph's scent is delightful, and her long robe glows, hemmed with golden threads and embroidered with rainbow hues of unearthly magnificence. A nymph's demeanor is graceful and charming, her mind quick and witty. Nymphs speak their own musical language and the common tongue.

Combat: Neutral in their alliances and cares, nymphs do not fight, but flee if confronted by an intruder or danger. Nymphs are able to cast *dimension door* once per day, and can employ druidical priest spells at 7th ability level, giving a nymph four 1st, two 2nd, two 3rd, and one 4th level spell once per day. Looking at a nymph will cause permanent blindness unless the onlookers save versus spell. If the nymph is nude or disrobes, an onlooker will die unless a saving throw versus spell is successful.

Habitat/Society: These beautiful females inhabit only the loveliest of wilderness places, clear lakes and streams, glacier palaces, ocean grottoes, and crystalline caverns. Nymphs prefer a solitary existence, but very occasionally a few will gather together in a place of spectacular charm, though these rendezvous seldom last for more than a few months. Animals of all types flock to a nymph to be petted and caressed, forgetting their natural enemies to gather around the lovely creature.

There is a 10% chance that a nymph will be friendly if approached by a good creature without the latter first glimpsing the nymph, by calling or other prior notice. On the other hand, if a nymph sees a human male with 18 Charisma and good alignment before he sees her, it is 90% probable that the nymph will be favorably inclined toward the man. It is still necessary to make saving throws upon sighting the nymph.

Nymphs hate ugliness and evil and sometimes will help to defeat it. Any treasure they possess has usually been given to them by some lovesick man.

Ecology: Like a druid, a nymph believes in the sanctity of nature and her environment and will try to keep her lair safe and pure. She will heal wounded animals and mend broken trees and plants. Sometimes she will even help a human in distress (5% chance). Since nymphs live for many generations, they can provide a wealth of information on the history of an area and often know secret places, hide-outs, and entrances long forgotten. If a man is kissed by a nymph, all painful and troubling memories are forgotten for the rest of the day—this may be a boon to some and a curse to others. A lock of nymph's hair can be used to create a powerful sleeping potion or, if enchanted and woven into a cloth and sewn into a garment, will magically add one point to the wearer's Charisma. The tears of a nymph can be used as an ingredient in a *philter of love*. If a woman bathes in a nymph's pool, her Charisma is increased by two points until she bathes again.

Octopus, Giant

CLIMATE/TERRAIN:	Any salt water
FREQUENCY:	Rare
ORGANIZATION:	Solitary
ACTIVITY CYCLE:	Nocturnal
DIET:	Carnivore
INTELLIGENCE:	Animal (1)
TREASURE:	(R)
ALIGNMENT:	Neutral (evil)

NO. APPEARING:	1-3
ARMOR CLASS:	7
MOVEMENT:	3, Sw 12
HIT DICE:	8
THAC0:	13
NO. OF ATTACKS:	7
DAMAGE/ATTACK:	1-4 (x6)/2-12
SPECIAL ATTACKS:	Constriction
SPECIAL DEFENSES:	Ink, color change
MAGIC RESISTANCE:	Nil
SIZE:	Large (9'-12' across)
MORALE:	Elite (13)
XP VALUE:	2,000

The dreaded "cuttlefish" are the scourge of ocean-going sailors and fishermen. Malicious and cunning, giant octopi have been known to attack ships, sinking smaller craft and stealing crew members from the larger ships.

Giant octopi change their color to blend into their surroundings, and the range of colors and patterns available to them is extensive, from green to deep black, blue speckles and red stripes. Tentacles are often disguised as seaweed. Once camouflaged, there is only a 10% chance to detect them, and usually it is their eyes that give them away. Normal coloration is grey to brown, and their vicious beaks are a deep yellow with a bright orange mouth and tongue.

Combat: An octopus will readily attack swimmers or small vessels in order to eat the crew. Several have been known to cooperate in order to overwhelm a larger ship, and any craft seized by these monsters loses way and comes to a full stop in three turns.

A giant octopus generally attacks with six of its eight tentacles, using two to anchor itself. Each striking tentacle causes 1d4 points of damage, but unless the member is loosened or severed, it constricts for 2d4 points of damage every round after striking. If a victim is dragged close enough to the beak, the monster can bite for 2d6 points of damage.

Any victim under 8 feet tall or long can be struck by only one tentacle at a time, and the chance that both upper limbs are pinned on a successful strike is 25%, while the chance that both upper limbs are free is also 25%. When both upper limbs are held, the victim has no attack; if only one limb is held the victim attacks with a -3 penalty to its attack roll; if both limbs are free (i.e., the tentacle is wrapped around the victim's body) then the victim attacks with a -1 penalty to its attack roll. Tentacles grip with a Strength of 18/20. Any creature with a Strength equal to or greater than 18/20 can grasp the tentacle and negate its constriction. This does not free the victim, and the octopus will immediately seek to drag the victim to its mouth to eat it. To break free, a tentacle must be severed; this requires 8 points of damage. (These hit points are in addition to those the octopus gains from its 8 Hit Dice.)

Once three or more tentacles are severed, it is 90% probable that the octopus will retreat, ejecting a cloud of black ink 40 feet high by 60 feet wide by 60 feet long. This ink cloud completely obscures the vision of any creature within it. The wounded octopus then camouflages itself in its lair or a nearby hiding place. It takes the monster two to three months to grow back severed tentacles.

Habitat/Society: While octopi cooperate to attack a food source, they live a solitary existence, preferring to shelter in warm water of medial to shallow depth. Lairs are made in wrecked ships and undersea caves; any treasure found there is just an incidental leftover from previous meals. Consummate hunters, these monsters have great patience and cover a very small area, waiting for their food to come to them. Mating season comes every spring. Like most marine animals, octopi leave their eggs in a reef to fend for themselves.

Ecology: When prey is scarce, or if it has been wounded, an octopus turns to scavenging, eating everything from small crustaceans to seaweeds. Survival is paramount with this monster. It prefers to hunt at night, and often a man missing during the late night watch has been grabbed by a giant octopus, pulled quickly over the side, and eaten.

Giant octopi's leathery hide is tough and waterproof, and it is worked into fine rain ponchos by sailors lucky enough to catch and kill one. Another byproduct of these monsters is their ink—they are most often hunted for this commodity. Giant octopus ink can be used to pen magical scrolls.

Ogre

	Ogre	Ogre Mage	Merrow
CLIMATE/TERRAIN:	Any land	Any oriental land	Any water
FREQUENCY:	Common	Very rare	Uncommon
ORGANIZATION:	Tribal	Tribal	Tribal
ACTIVITY CYCLE:	Any	Any	Any
DIET:	Carnivore	Carnivore	Carnivore
INTELLIGENCE:	Low (8)	Average to exceptional (9-16)	Average (8-10)
TREASURE:	M(Q, B, S)	G (R, S, magic)	M (A)
ALIGNMENT:	Chaotic evil	Lawful evil	Chaotic evil
NO. APPEARING:	2-20 (2d10)	1-6	2-24 (2d12)
ARMOR CLASS:	5	4	4
MOVEMENT:	9	9, Fl 15 (B)	6, Sw 12
HIT DICE:	4+1	5+2	4+4
THAC0:	17	15	15
NO. OF ATTACKS:	1	1	3 or 1
DAMAGE/ATTACK:	1-10 (or by weapon +6)	1-12	1-6/1-6/2-8 (or by weapon +6)
SPECIAL ATTACKS:	+2 to damage	Magic spells	See below
SPECIAL DEFENSES:	Nil	Nil	Camouflage
MAGIC RESISTANCE:	Nil	Nil	Nil
SIZE:	Large (9'+)	Large (10½')	Large (9')
MORALE:	Steady (11-12)	Elite (13-14)	Steady (11-12)
XP VALUE:	270	650	420
Leader	650	—	650
Chieftain	975	975	975

Ogres are big, ugly, greedy humanoids that live by ambushes, raids, and theft. Ill-tempered and nasty, these monsters are often found serving as mercenaries in the ranks of orc tribes, evil clerics, or gnolls. They mingle freely with giants and trolls.

Adult ogres stand 9 to 10 feet tall and weigh 300 to 350 pounds. Their skin colors range from a dead yellow to a dull black-brown, and (rarely) a sickly violet. Their warty bumps are often of a different color—or at least darker than their hides. Their eyes are purple with white pupils. Teeth and talons are orange or black. Ogres have long, greasy hair of blackish-blue to dull dark green. Their odor is repellent, reminiscent of curdled milk. Dressing in poorly cured furs and animal hides, they care for their weapons and armor only reasonably well. It is common for ogres to speak orc, troll, stone giant, and gnoll, as well as their own guttural language. A typical ogre's life span is 90 years.

Combat: In small numbers, ogres fight as unorganized individuals, but groups of 11 or more will have a leader, and groups of 16 or more usually include two leaders and a chieftain. Ogres wielding weapons get a Strength bonus of +2 to hit; leaders have +3, chieftains have +4. Females fight as males but score only 2-8 points of damage and have a maximum of only 6 hit points per die. Young ogres fight as goblins.

Habitat/Society: Ogre tribes are found anywhere, from deep caverns to mountaintops. Tribes have 16-20 males, 2-12 females, and 2-8 young. Shamans, if present, will be of 3rd level, and have access to the spheres of combat, divination, healing, protection, and sun (darkness only). Ogres live by raiding and scavenging and they will eat anything. Their fondness for elf, dwarf, and halfling flesh means that there is only a 10% chance that these will be found as slaves or prisoners. There is a 30% chance that an ogre lair will include 2-8 slaves. Captured prisoners are always kept as slaves (25%) or food (75%). Extremely avaricious, ogres squabble over treasure and cannot be trusted, even by their own kind.

Ogre Leader
When more than 11 ogres are encountered, a leader will be present. He is a 7 Hit Dice monster with 30-33 hit points and Ar-

mor Class 3. He inflicts 5-15 (2d6+3) points of damage per attack, +6 with weapon.

Ogre Chieftain
If 16 or more ogres are encountered, they will be led by two patrol leaders and a chieftain. The chieftain is a 7 Hit Dice monster with 34-37 hit points and Armor Class 4. He inflicts 8-18 (2d6+6) points of damage per attack, +6 with weapon. Chieftains are usually the biggest and smartest ogres in their tribes.

Ogre

Ecology: Ogres consistently plague mankind, lusting for gold, gems, and jewelry as well as human flesh. They are evil-natured creatures that join with other monsters to prey on the weak and favor overwhelming odds to a fair fight. Ogres make no crafts nor labor.

Ogre Mage

The oriental ogre has light blue, light green, or pale brown skin with ivory horns. The hair is usually a different color (blue with green, green with blue) and is darker in shade; the main exception to this coloration is found in ogre magi with pale brown skin and yellow hair. They have black nails and dark eyes with white pupils. The teeth and tusks are very white. Ogre magi are taller and more intelligent than their cousins and they dress in oriental clothing and armor.

Combat: Ogre magi can perform the following feats of magic: *fly* (for 12 turns), become *invisible*, cause *darkness* in a 10-foot radius, *polymorph* to a human or similar bipedal creature (4 feet to 12 feet tall), and *regenerate* one hit point per round (lost members must be reattached to regenerate). Once per day they can do the following: *charm person*, *sleep*, assume *gaseous form*, and create a *cone of cold* 60 feet long with a terminal diameter of 20 feet, which inflicts 8-64 (8d8) points of damage (save vs. spell for half damage). Oriental ogres attack with magic first and resort to physical attacks only if necessary. They are +1 on morale.

In battle, ogre magi prefer the naganata (75%) or scimitar and whip (25%). Those found in oriental settings might (25%) possess ki power or have mastered a martial arts form. As ogre magi are intelligent, they will not fight if faced with overwhelming odds, but will flee to gather their forces or hide.

Habitat/Society: These monsters live in fortified dwellings or caves and foray to capture slaves, treasure, and food. Ogre magi priests of up to 7th level have been reported. Tribes are small, with 2-5 females and 1-3 children that will not fight, but rather seek to escape in *gaseous form*. These monsters are extremely protective of their young and will battle with savage abandon to save one's life. If a young ogre mage is captured, these creatures will pay high ransom for its return, but they will seek revenge and will never forget the insult of the kidnaping.

If encountered in their lair, ogre magi will be led by a chief of great strength (+2 on each Hit Die, attacking and saving as a 9 Hit Dice monster). Treasure is divided by this chief and his trove is always the richest. The tribe will have their own clan symbol typical to the oriental lands, and this symbol will be stitched on its war banners and flags as well as on armor and headdresses. The chief will often have the tribe's symbol tattooed on his forehead or back.

Ogre magi speak the common tongue, their own special language, and the speech of normal ogres.

Ecology: Ogre magi magical armor is too large to fit a man. This monster's lair is usually a powerful structure that can be expanded into a mighty fortress if it can be rid of its original owners.

Merrow (Aquatic Ogre)

Faster and fiercer than their land kin, the freshwater merrow are greenish and scaled with webbed hands and feet. Their necks are long and thick, their shoulders are sloping, and they have huge mouths and undershot jaws. Merrow have black teeth and nails and deep green eyes with white centers, and their hair resembles slimy seaweed. About 10% grow ivory horns, especially the more powerful males.

Aquatic ogres are very fond of tattoos, and females may have their entire bodies inked with scenes of death and destruction as a

sign of status. Merrow speak their own dialect and the language of other ogres.

Combat: Using their green coloration, aquatic ogres can hide, becoming effectively invisible 10-80% of the time, depending on terrain. They attack from cover, so others are -5 on their surprise roll. Merrow typically attack with a large piercing spear (inflicting 2-12 points of damage) in a swimming charge at +1 to hit, followed by melee with talons and teeth.

Habitat/Society: A typical merrow tribe consists of:
- 1 chief, AC3, 6+6 Hit Dice, +2 on damage
- 2 patrol leaders, AC3, 5+5 Hit Dice, +1 on damage
- 2-24 standard merrow
- 2-24 females, AC5, 3+3 Hit Dice, 1-2/1-2/1-6 damage
- 1-12 young, AC6, 2+2 Hit Dice, 1-2/1-2/1-4 damage
- 1 shaman of 3rd level ability

Merrow dwell in caves in shallow, fresh water (50-250 feet deep), often with scrags (see Troll). They can live out of water for about two hours, so they often forage on land. Merrow usually control an area with a radius of 10-15 miles, hunting and foraging throughout this territory. In times of scarcity, or when the lure of treasure becomes too great, a war party will attack the coastal villages of man. Merrow prefer gold and jewels and often overlook dull magical items in search of glittering prizes. The goals of a merrow chieftain rule the tribe, and these power-hungry monsters seek to completely control their "kingdoms," often leading to attacks on intruding ships.

Ecology: Merrow are ignorant and superstitious and have no skills but plundering and murder. Areas of the freshwater lakes and seas where they have influence are avoided by sailors and fishermen. These monsters are carnivores, preying on all who enter their regions, often emptying the seas of life with their voracious appetites.

Ogre, Half-

	Half-Ogre	Ogrillon
CLIMATE/TERRAIN:	Any/Land	Any/Land
FREQUENCY:	Very rare	Rare
ORGANIZATION:	Tribal	Tribal
ACTIVITY CYCLE:	Any	Any
DIET:	Omnivore	Carnivore
INTELLIGENCE:	Semi- to High (3-14)	Low (5-7)
TREASURE:	B, M (Q, B, S)	M (B, S)
ALIGNMENT:	Chaotic evil	Chaotic evil
NO. APPEARING:	1-4	1-4 (5-30)
ARMOR CLASS:	5 (9)	6
MOVEMENT:	12	12
HIT DICE:	2+6	2+4
THAC0:	17	17
NO. OF ATTACKS:	1	2
DAMAGE/ATTACK:	2-8 (by weapon)	2-7/2-7
SPECIAL ATTACKS:	Nil	Nil
SPECIAL DEFENSES:	Nil	Nil
MAGIC RESISTANCE:	Nil	Nil
SIZE:	L (8'-9' tall)	M (6'-7' tall)
MORALE:	Steady (12)	Average (10)
XP VALUE:	270	175

Half-Ogre

When adventuring companies journey into the wilderness they often run into ogres; big, ugly humanoids. Occasionally, an ogre party will include one or two individuals that are a little shorter, but significantly smarter, wielding a weapon with more skill than might have been expected. They have a better understanding of their opponents, and they grunt commands that anticipate the adventurers' moves. In this way half-breeds, the issue of ogres and humans, earn the respect of their kind.

Half-ogres range from 7 to 8 feet in height and weigh from 315 to 425 pounds. Skin and hair color are variable, but tend toward brown, gray, black, dull yellow (skin only), or any of the above with a slight gray-green tint. Teeth and nails are always orange. Most half-ogres have human-like eyes, though about one in five have the white pupils common to ogres. Their odor is noticeable, but it is not as overpowering as that of a full-blooded ogre. The half-ogre traditionally wears heavy skins and furs, bringing his Armor Class up to that of his ogre brethren, but rare individuals have the ability to make a shirt of chain-mail, for an AC of 3. Half-ogres speak common (more clearly and unimpeded than ogres), ogrish, orcish, troll, and one other, usually human, language. They live about 110 years.

Half-ogres posses infravision out to 60 feet. Their sense of smell is better than an ogre's, but it falls short of a human's.

Combat: Half-ogres of any sort suffer −2 penalties to their attack rolls against dwarves and −4 against gnomes, since those smaller races are so skilled at battling bigger folk.

Half-ogres in combat are often found with full-blooded ogres. If so, the half-ogre will most likely be leading the ogre party. The ogres fight more wisely when led by a half-ogre that concentrates assaults on characters it recognizes as spellcasters, and teaming up against skilled fighters. Ambushes are better-planned and more carefully baited.

To earn command privileges, particularly when ogre leaders are present, a half-ogre must show himself quick to battle and fierce in combat. Half-ogres' usual weapon of choice is a huge sword (use the statistics for a two-handed bastard sword, save that half-ogres can employ it one-handed, with a large shield in the other), or a war spear capable of causing 2d4 points of damage. A half-ogre inflicts an additional 2 points of damage, due to his mass.

Half-ogres sometimes gather together to form their own tribes. In this case, they will be encountered in bands of 2d10 and will expend as much energy choosing and preparing an ambush as on the combat itself.

For every five half-ogres in an encounter, there is an additional veteran with 5+3 Hit Dice. For every 10 half-ogres, there is a kader with 6 Hit Dice. If more than 15 half-ogres are encountered, they will have a shaman, a fighter/priest with 5 + 3 Hit Dice and the spells of a 4th-level priest, and two acolyte shamans, with 4+6 Hit Dice and the spells of a 2nd-level priest.

Half-ogres are inclined to intimidate others. A broad, fang-filled smile and perhaps a slamming fist, often encourages an NPC to suddenly remember appointments, or perhaps faint dead away. Kobolds will clutch their spears and cringe in unison when 7'6'' of solid muscle smashes their door to splinters and storms in; even larger monsters have serious reservations about attacking half-ogres. They will also terrify local human populations into leaving a half-ogre and his companions alone.

Habitat/Society: Half-ogres have no society of their own. If they live with ogres, they are the quick-thinking members of the tribe, ever on their toes to prove themselves worthy. If a half-ogre is reared in a human community, he learns to live with suspicion and fear, and often turns to a military or solitary occupation.

Occasionally, half-ogres join with half-orcs, orogs, ogrillons, and other humanoids. These communities are small (5-200 residents) and usually isolated, but can appear in virtually any terrain. Half-ogres fill a middle niche—more powerful than half-orcs or orogs, but smarter than ogrillons, trolls, and other humanoids. As a whole, these communities are chaotic evil, with neutral tendencies stemming from the level of cooperation necessary in a "half-caste" situation. They prefer others of their own kind, and are tolerant of orcs and ogres. Enough of them have human blood that they regard humans with neutrality. Indeed, chaotic evil humans often find their most enthusiastic followers in such a hybrid tribe. They also tolerate monstrous humanoids such as trolls and giants, but all other races are treated with undisguised hostility.

Hybrid settlements raid civilized territories for prisoners and loot. A settlement may be found holding prisoners. It is also likely for treasure to be found in a hybrid camp. Half-ogres are usually cheated out of most of their rightful treasure shares by the more cunning orogs and half-orcs.

Ecology: Sages have expressed much concern over the years, wondering why ogres can interbreed with humans but not with elves or halflings. When the actual answer was discovered, the sages' concerns proved unfounded. The explanation had nothing to do with any supposed common origin of humans and ogres, but rather in a unusual characteristic that ogres share with orcs: rapidly adaptive biology. Just as orcs and ogres can adapt quickly to any terrain, from forests to the highest mountains, their genetic construction allows them breed with any humanoid race.

This ability to breed easily is frequently passed on to their progeny. Half-ogres can also breed successfully with most other humanoid races. If this process continues for many generations, the result is a horrible hybrid known as a *mongrelman*. Many mongrelmen have strong strains of orc and ogre in their bloodlines, which may account for their chaotic evil attitudes.

The half-ogre shares the ogre's place in the ecosystem: that of a plague upon demihumans and humans, lusting for treasure and making neither crafts nor good labor. The beginnings of half-ogre poetry have been around for many years, but it is exceptionally ugly and disturbing.

Half-Ogres as NPCs or PCs

Half-ogres may be NPCs or even PCs, with DM's consent. If so, they have statistics determined in the following fashion. Strength is ld6 +13, with a roll of 6 being treated as 18(00) strength. Characters with a Strength roll of 5 (18 strength) should roll normally for extraordinary strength. Dexterity is 3d4. Constitution is ld6 +13, with a roll of 6 being treated as an 18. Intelligence is 3d4. Wisdom is 2d6. Charisma is 2d4, doubled for effective Charisma with respect to ogres, half-ogres, orcs, orogs, and other humanoids. Half-ogres reared outside of the tribes do not gain the languages mentioned earlier. Player character half-ogres may not be exclusively priests, but may practice any other class allowed half-ogres. Starting Hit Dice are doubled at 1st level, progressing normally at 2nd level and above.

As NPCs, shaman half-ogres are fighter/priests. Also possible are half-ogres that function solely as priests, rising to 8th level, and rarely seen fighter/thieves (3 +9 Hit Dice with the skills of 1st- or 2nd-level thieves). Half-ogre thieves are always self-taught, and accept the following racial adjustments: Pick Pockets -20%, Open Locks +5%, Find/Remove Traps +0%, Move Silently -5%, Hide in Shadows +5%, Detect Noise +0%, Climb Walls -30%, Read Languages -25%.

Ogrillon

The ogrillon is a fiercer species of the half-ogre, being the fruit of a union between ogres and orcs. The ogrillon displays the general tendencies of its larger cousin with some exceptions. It is even more brutish and violent, and it normally learns to speak only ogrish and a handful of words in common.

The ogrillon is the size of an orc, and closely resembles one. One in every ten is born with features and coloration very similar to those of ogres: purple eyes with white pupils, black teeth, yellowish skin with dull, dark green hair. The skin of an ogrillon of either type is covered with small horn plates, giving it a superior Armor Class and enabling it to fight without weapons. An ogrillon disdains armor and most other material items, retaining only a handful of gold pieces as treasured belongings. It is uncertain why they would keep gold, except perhaps as good luck charms.

They love mayhem. In combat they disdain weapons and plunge in with both fists. Due to their great strength and horn-reinforced fists, each punch delivers ld6 +1 points of damage. An ogrillon out of combat is restless and troubled, but it will be seen chuckling merrily to itself during a good fight.

Because of their single-mindedness, ogrillons are often approached by orcs when they need good fighters against some enemy. Ogrillons are happy to join and fight, sometimes for the love of combat and destruction, but often for more lucky gold pieces. In combat, there is only a 10% chance that a typical ogrillon can be distinguished from an orc. Ogrillons that resemble ogres, of course, clearly stand out.

Ogrillons are the issue of a female orc mated with a male ogre. Thankfully, it is sterile. The union of a male orc and a female ogre yields an orog, a better class of humanoid monster detailed in the "Orc" entry.

Ooze/Slime/Jelly

	Olive Slime	Olive Slime Creature	Mustard Jelly	Jelly, Stun-
CLIMATE/TERRAIN:	Any subterranean	Any damp	Any subterranean	Any subterranean
FREQUENCY:	Very rare	Rare	Rare	Rare
ORGANIZATION:	Colony	Colony	Solitary	Solitary
ACTIVITY CYCLE:	Any	Any	Night	Night
DIET:	Scavenger	Carnivore	Scavenger	Scavenger
INTELLIGENCE:	Non- (0)	Animal (1)	Average (8-10)	Animal (1)
TREASURE:	Nil	Nil	See below	See below
ALIGNMENT:	Neutral	Neutral	Neutral	Neutral
NO. APPEARING:	1-4	1-20	1	1
ARMOR CLASS:	9	9	4	8
MOVEMENT:	0	6	9	4
HIT DICE:	2+2	See below	7+14	17
THAC0:	19	17, 15, or 13	13	17
NO. OF ATTACKS:	0	1	1 or 2	1
DAMAGE/ATTACK:	Nil	See below	5-20	2-8
SPECIAL ATTACKS:	See below	Olive slime	See below	Paralyzation
SPECIAL DEFENSES:	See below	See below	+1 or better to hit	Nil
MAGIC RESISTANCE:	See below	See below	10%	Nil
SIZE:	S (4' radius)	Special	L (9'-12' diam.)	L (10' on a side)
MORALE:	Average (10)	Average (9)	Elite (13-14)	Average (9)
XP VALUE:	420	420, 975, or 2,500	4,000	420
			(1/2 if half slain)	

There are many different varieties of ooze, slime, and jelly. More are being discovered all the time, as warped wizards seek to create life or fashion efficient dungeon scavengers. The unifying feature of these creatures is a dissolving touch that consumes flesh as well as weapons and armor.

Olive Slime

Olive slime is a strain of monstrous plant life, closely related to green slime, that grows while clinging to ceilings. More dangerous than green slime, olive slime favors moist, subterranean regions. It feeds on whatever animal, vegetable, or metallic substances happen to cross its path. The vibrations of a creature beneath it are sufficient to cause it to release its tendrils and drop. Olive slime ignores armor for purposes of determining hit probability. It also negates Dexterity bonuses unless its target is aware of the presence of the slime and takes steps to avoid the stuff. Contact with olive slime causes a numbing poison to ooze from the creature. The slime then spreads itself over the body of its victim, sending out parasitic tendrils to feed upon the body fluids of the host. For humans and demihumans, the point of attachment is usually along the spinal area. The feeding process soon begins to affect the brain of the host as it changes the host's body. An unobservant victim must roll a saving throw vs. poison, failure indicating that the victim has not noticed that the olive slime has dropped upon him. Any group of characters in the vicinity will have a 50% chance of noticing the slime's attachment with a casual glance. This percentage may be adjusted only by magical items. A thorough search by wary individuals reveals the olive slime without difficulty.

Within 2d4 hours, the host's main concern becomes how to feed, protect, and sustain the growth of the olive slime. Naturally, this includes keeping the slime's presence a secret from any companions. If an affected character's companions become suspicious, or if they demonstrate any desire to destroy olive slime, the affected character will escape at the first opportunity. The host's food intake must double or the character wastes away (10% of the character's hit points per day, rounding up, and no natural healing can take place while a character is wasting away. After 1d6+6 days, the host suddenly and painfully metamorphoses into a vegetable creature. The olive slime gradually replaces skin and muscle tissue, and it forms a symbiotic brain link.

The new creature has no interest in its former form or fellows. It exists as a new species more akin to plants than any other life form. Feeding then becomes photosynthetic, paralytic, or, most likely, both. When slain, an olive slime creature dissolves into a new patch of olive slime.

Olive slime is harmed only by acid, freezing cold, fire, or by a *cure disease* spell. Spells that affect plants will work on olive slime, although *entangle* will have no practical effect. Green slime and olive slime are complete opposites—when they encounter each other, the attack of one neutralizes the other.

If an affected character has been transformed into an olive slime creature, there is very little short of a *limited wish* that can return him to normal.

Olive Slime Creature

Olive slime creatures, popularly known as "slime zombies," are the end result of the metamorphosis upon the host. The newly formed vegetable creature is linked symbiotically with the olive slime patch that created it. The symbiotic bond is a secure link within 200 miles, but not from one plane of existence to another. The olive slime can call its zombies to defend it from attack, and they will immediately and mindlessly obey.

Regardless of their former existence, and despite their general form, slime creatures are only differentiated by size:

Size	HD	DAMAGE/ATTACK
Tiny	1+2	1-3
Small	3+2	1-4
Man-sized	5+2	2-8
Larger	8+2	3-12
Huge	12+2	4-16
Gargantuan	16	4-24

Slime creatures have a telepathic bond, effective at a range of 200 yards, and gather together for mutual assistance while feeding or for defense. Their former identities can be discovered only upon close examination.

Habitat varies from well-populated subterranean places to damp forests, swamps, and fens. Slime creatures are equally at home on land or in warm, shallow water. Slime zombies seek out animal hosts for their slime; they attack man-sized creatures on sight. When they attack, olive slime zombies have a 10% chance, per successful hit, to infect an opponent with slime. If they succeed in doing so, they either change targets or flee combat before killing their target—they certainly do not want to kill the new host.

Olive slime zombies are harmed by acid, freezing cold, fire and *magic missile* spells. Spells that affect plants will also affect them, although the effects of *entangle* are minimal at best. No other attacks, by weapons, lightning, or spells that affect the mind will kill a slime creature. An olive slime zombie, however, can suffer only as much physical damage as it has hit points, before its skeleton collapses and it becomes nothing more than a puddle of olive slime. When green slime is applied to an olive slime zombie, it neutralizes the olive slime, delivering 2d4 points of damage per round until the body is reduced to a (non-animate) skeleton.

The vegetable intelligence of slime zombies is no greater than that of common animals, but does enable them to learn from experience. This innate intelligence extends to the use of simple traps, and they will lie in wait at the bottom of hidden shafts.

Mustard Jelly

Mustard jelly originated when a young wizard attempted to *polymorph* herself into an ocher jelly. Her spell failed, and she became a mustard jelly. The stuff has multiplied rapidly in the years since her accident, and it is now a serious threat in many areas.

The monstrous amoeboid mustard jelly is far more dangerous than the ocher jelly. Mustard jelly is translucent, and very hard to see until it attacks. The only clue to its presence is a faint odor, similar to blooming mustard plants. Once it does attack, it may be seen as yellowish brown in color.

Normally, mustard jelly attacks by forming an acidic pseudo-pod of its own substance and thrusting. The jelly monster secretes a vapor over a 10-foot radius. Those near the jelly must roll a saving throw vs. poison each round. Those who fail the saving throw become lethargic and move at half-normal speed, due to the effects of the vapor. The toxic effects last for two rounds and they are cumulative.

This large creature can divide itself at will into two smaller, faster halves (movement rate 18). Each is capable of attacking, but has only half the hit points the creature had before dividing. A mustard jelly can, for example, flow into a room, divide itself into independent halves to attack, and then reform into a torus in order to surround a pillar its prey has climbed. Unlike the ocher jelly, mustard jelly cannot move through tiny spaces, nor can it move along ceilings, although it will eat through wooden doors. It cannot climb walls either, and so most of its bulk must remain on the floor, stretching up only 4 or 5 feet.

Although intelligent, mustard jelly is not known to value treasure of any sort, except as a lure for greedy adventurers. Of course, it is possible that some treasure might remain after a victim has been devoured.

Mustard jelly is impervious to normal weapons (and can eat wooden ones) and electrical attacks. A *magic missile* spell will only cause it to grow; mustard jelly gains hit points equal in number to the damage rolled. Cold causes only half damage, and other attacks have normal effects.

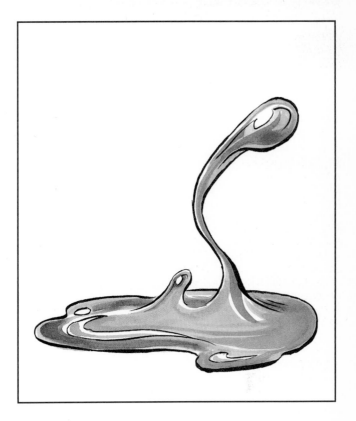

Stunjelly

This relative of the gelatinous cube was designed by some forgotten mage to resemble a section of ordinary stone wall. They are usually about 10 feet square by 2 1/2 to 5 feet thick, and somewhat translucent. If a bright light is shone on one side of the stunjelly, it will be seen on the other. Illumination equal to a *continuous light* spell will reveal whatever treasure a stunjelly might be carrying. Stunjellies make no noise when they move, but they do produce a faint odor of vinegar.

The stunjelly has many features in common with the gelatinous cube. Like the cube, the stunjelly paralyzes creatures who venture too close! Adventurers walking near a stunjelly may be attacked by an anaesthetic pseudopod; those struck must roll a saving throw vs. paralyzation. Those who succeed suffer no ill effects. Those who fail are paralyzed for 5d4 rounds, during which time the stunjelly tries to surround the victim and digest him. Like the gelatinous cube, it is immune to electrical attacks, mind-influencing spells, paralyzation, and *polymorph* spells. Unlike the gelatinous cube, stunjelly is affected normally by cold attacks.

Stunjellies reproduce by fission, as one extremely thick jelly splits into two smaller ones. This process is accompanied by a horrible, rending sound, audible throughout the vicinity.

A stunjelly might mindlessly carry undigested metals around with it for days. These would include treasure types J, K, L, M, N, and Q, as well as potions, daggers, or similar objects.

Stunjellies are tolerated in many dungeons as traps for unwary intruders, or as janitorial monsters sweeping the passages of digestible litter. For this duty, they are preferred over other breeds of slime and ooze, since they cannot slither through doors into areas where they would be unwelcome.

Ooze/Slime/Jelly

	Ochre Jelly	Gray Ooze	Crystal Ooze	Gelatinous Cube	Green Slime
CLIMATE/TERRAIN:	Subterranean	Subterranean	Dimly lit water	Subterranean	Subterranean
FREQUENCY:	Uncommon	Rare	Rare	Uncomm on	Rare
ORGANIZATION:	Solitary	Solitary	Solitar y	Solitary	Colony
ACTIVITY CYCLE:	Any	Any	Any	Any	Any
DIET:	Omnivore	Omnivore	Omnivore	Omn ivore	Omnivore
INTELLIGENCE:	Non- (0)	Animal (1)	Animal (1)	Non- (0)	Non- (0)
TREASURE:	Nil	Nil	Nil	Nil (incidental)	Nil
ALIGNMENT:	Neutral	Neutral	Neutral	N eutral	Neutral
NO. APPEARING:	1-3	1-3	1-2	1	1- 6
ARMOR CLASS:	8	8	8	8	9
MOVEMENT:	3	1	1, Sw 3	6	0
HIT DICE:	6	3 + 3	4	4	2
THAC0:	15	17	17	17	19
NO. OF ATTACKS:	1	1	1	1	0
DAMAGE/ATTACK:	3-12	2-16	4-16	2- 8	Nil
SPECIAL ATTACKS:	Nil	Corrodes metal	Poison	Paralyzation, surprise	See below
SPECIAL DEFENSES:	See below	See below	See below	See below	See below
MAGIC RESISTANCE:	Nil	Nil	Nil	Nil	Nil
SIZE:	M (4-7')	M to L (4-12')	M to L (4-12')	L (10' cube)	S (2-4')
MORALE:	Average (10)	Average (10)	Average (10)	Average (10)	Average (10)
XP VALUE:	270	270	420	650	65

Psionic Summary, Gray Ooze only

Level	Dis/Sci Dev	Attack/ Defense	Power Score	PSPs
1	2/1/1	Psc/M-	13	1d100 + 20

The oozes, slimes and jellies of the underworld are hideous, amorphous creatures that are the bane of all that lives, dissolving the weapons, armor, and flesh of their victims.

Ochre Jelly

This monster resembles a giant amoeba, seeping through darkened corridors, through cracks and under doors, searching for flesh or cellulose to devour. Their form allows them to travel on walls and ceilings and drop on unsuspecting prey.

Combat: The ochre jelly attacks by attempting to envelop its prey. Its secretions dissolve flesh, inflicting 3-12 (d10 + 2) points of damage per round of exposure. While a *lightning bolt* will divide the creature into one or more smaller jellies, each doing one-half normal damage, fire- and cold-based attacks have normal effects.

Habitat/Society: An asexual creature, the ochre jelly is a solitary beast that is occasionally found with its own divided offspring. It lives only to eat and reproduce.

Ecology: Voraciously dissolving all types of carrion and trash, this monster is sometimes tolerated in inhabited subterranean areas for its janitorial services, but this activity is difficult to organize and is usually not appreciated by the inhabitants because of its danger.

Gray Ooze

A slimy horror that looks like wet stone or a sedimentary rock formation, the gray ooze is rarely thicker than six or eight inches, but sometimes grows to a length of 12 feet. It cannot climb walls or ceilings, so it slides, drips, and oozes along cavern floors.

Combat: The gray ooze strikes like a snake, and can corrode metal at an alarming rate (chain mail in one round, plate mail in two, and magical armor in one round per each plus to Armor Class). Spells have no effect on this monster, nor do fire- or cold-based attacks. Lightning and blows from weapons cause full

damage. Note that weapons striking a gray ooze may corrode and break.

Habitat/Society: After a large meal, a gray ooze reproduces by "budding:" growing a small pod that is left behind in a corridor or cavern. This pod takes two to three days to mature and then the little gray ooze absorbs its leathery shell and begins slithering about, searching for a meal. Sometimes more than one of these monsters are found together, but this is just a random event because they are not intelligent.

Ecology: The gray ooze is a dungeon scavenger. It is rumored that metalworkers of extraordinary skill keep very small oozes in stone jars to etch and score their metal work, but this is a delicate and dangerous practice.

Crystal Ooze

This creature is a variety of gray ooze which has adapted to living in water. It is 75% invisible when immersed in its natural element. It is translucent, mostly glassy clear, with an occasional milky white swirl in its substance.

Combat: Crystal ooze strikes like a snake, then attempts to flow over a victim and exude its paralyzing poison. Unlike its cousin, the gray ooze, this creature does not corrode metal, but its poisons attack wood, cloth, and flesh. Unless a victim successfully saves vs. poison, he becomes paralyzed and will be consumed by the crystal ooze in a short time. When prey is reduced to -20 hit points, it is totally consumed. Crystal ooze cannot be harmed by acid, cold, heat, or fire attacks, but electricity and *magic missiles* inflict full damage. Blows from weapons inflict only 1 point of damage per hit. A wooden weapon must save vs. acid or it will dissolve and break.

Habitat/Society: Crystal oozes live in any dim or dark body of water, though they can exist out of water for several hours. They reproduce by budding, like the gray ooze, but the crystal pods usually take seven to 10 days to hatch. Crystal oozes will eat their offspring, but occasionally, if the body of water is large enough and food is not scarce, a few of them might be found living in the same water.

Ecology: Crystal oozes are scavengers that leave metal and stone objects in their wake, so incidental treasure can often be found around and in their lairs.

Gelatinous Cube

So nearly transparent that they are difficult to see, these cubes travel down dungeon corridors, absorbing carrion and trash along the way. Their sides glisten, tending to leave a slimy trail, but gelatinous cubes cannot climb walls or cling to ceilings. Very large cubes grow tall to garner mosses and the like from ceilings.

Combat: A gelatinous cube attacks by touching its victim with its anesthetizing slime. A victim who fails to save vs. paralyzation is paralyzed (anesthetized) for 5-20 (5d4) rounds. The cube then surrounds its prey and secretes digestive fluids to absorb the food. All damage is caused by these digestive acids. Because gelatinous cubes are difficult to see, others are -3 on their surprise roll. Electricity, fear, holds, paralyzation, *polymorph*, and sleep-based attacks have no effect on this monster, but fire and blows from weapons have normal effects. If a cube fails its saving throw against a cold-based attack, the cube will be slowed 50% and inflicts only 1-4 points of damage.

Habitat/Society: Possessing no intelligence, gelatinous cubes live only for eating. They prefer well-traveled dungeons where there is always food to scavenge. These creatures reproduce by budding, leaving clear, rubbery cubes in dark corners or on heaps of trash. Young are not protected and are sometimes reabsorbed by the parent. Treasure is sometimes swept up by a gelatinous cube as the creature travels along a cavern floor; any metals, gems, or jewelry are carried in the monster's body until they can be ejected as indigestible. Items found inside a cube include treasure types J, K, L, M, N, Q, as well as an occasional potion, dagger, or similar object.

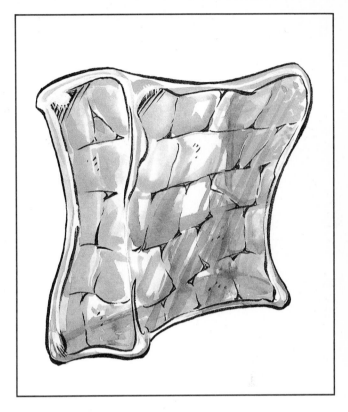

Ecology: The gelatinous cube is sometimes encouraged to stay in a certain area for its scavenging abilities, and is preferred over other jellies and oozes since its square shape does not allow it to slither under doors and into areas in which it is not desired.

Green Slime

A hideous growth, green slime is bright green, sticky, and wet. It grows in dark subterranean places on walls, ceilings and floors.

Combat: This slime cannot attack but is sensitive to vibrations and often drops from the ceiling onto a passing victim. Green slime attaches itself to living flesh and in 1-4 melee rounds turns the creature into green slime (no resurrection possible). Green slime eats through one inch of wood in an hour, but can dissolve metal quickly, going through plate armor in three melee rounds. The horrid growth can be scraped off quickly, cut away, frozen, or burned. A *cure disease* spell kills green slime, but other attacks, including weapons and spells, have no effect.

Habitat/Society: Green slime hates light and feeds on animal, vegetable, and metallic substances in dark caverns. Since it cannot move, this slime grows only when food comes to it. Sunlight dries it out and eventually kills it. Occasional huge slimes or colonies of dozens have been reported.

Ecology: Green slime is an infestation that all creatures avoid; it is burned out of caverns or mines if found. Once it has infected an area, it has a tendency to grow back, even after being frozen or burned away, because dormant spores can germinate years later.

Ooze/Slime/Jelly

	Slithering Tracker
CLIMATE/TERRAIN:	Subterranean
FREQUENCY:	Rare
ORGANIZATION:	Solitary
ACTIVITY CYCLE:	Any
DIET:	Living plasma
INTELLIGENCE:	Average (8-10)
TREASURE:	C
ALIGNMENT:	Neutral

NO. APPEARING:	1
ARMOR CLASS:	5
MOVEMENT:	12
HIT DICE:	5
THAC0:	15
NO. OF ATTACKS:	0
DAMAGE/ATTACK:	Nil
SPECIAL ATTACKS:	Paralyzation
SPECIAL DEFENSES:	Transparency
MAGIC RESISTANCE:	Nil
SIZE:	S (3' long)
MORALE:	Champion 15
XP VALUE:	975

Slithering trackers are transparent, plasma-draining jellies found in many dungeons and other dark places.

They are not invisible per se, but are instead made of a transparent jelly-like material. Thus they are almost impossible to detect normally (only a 5% chance of happening to notice one).

Combat: The unique nature of slithering trackers gives them the distinct advantage of being able to slip through cracks and holes as small as a rat hole. They move completely silently across all surfaces, simply oozing slowly over all bumps and turns. They prefer to attack sleeping, solitary, or unconscious creatures, as their main weakness lies in the extended duration of their attack form. They secrete a paralyzing substance that immobilizes the victim on contact for 12 hours if a saving throw vs. paralyzation fails. The slithering tracker then covers the entire body of its victim and slowly draws all of the plasma from the creature (killing the victim in the process, of course). It can drain a man-sized creature in one hour.

Habitat/Society: Slithering trackers are solitary beasts. Since they possess no attack form capable of harming other trackers, territoriality is a question of first-come, first-serve. Being the most intelligent of all slimes and jellies, it would seem natural that slithering trackers would establish themselves as the leaders of the rest. But jellies and slimes lack both the means of communication and the intelligence to band together. They remain on the lower end of the monster food chain, serving as scavengers that kill the weak and stupid, leaving the larger creatures for major predators in the dungeons they inhabit.

In fact, slithering trackers often hide themselves in the lairs of large monsters, which are known to kill far more than they can eat at a sitting. The tracker waits until the beast goes to sleep or departs and then it sucks dry the morsels left over. Many times the victims are merely unconscious instead of dead—at least until the tracker gets to them. And on more than one occasion, monster-slaying players have left a hoard guarded by a comrade, while they go for help, only to return to find their friend mysteriously dehydrated, with all of the treasure still in the lair.

Ecology: There are two theories regarding the origin of slithering trackers. The first and most likely one is that slithering trackers are just advanced forms of the other jellies, fortunate enough to have developed a transparent plasma body and a modicum of intelligence. Like most jellies, they reproduce asexually when the time and quantity of food allow for it.

The second, more dubious theory, is that slithering trackers were created, not born. Their high intelligence seems to lead many knowledgeable sages to believe that the creation of a slithering tracker is a hideous process, involving the transformation of a living human being. Certain legends seem to support this assertion, as there are many accounts of dark wizards removing the bones of their enemies, turning them into hulking masses of jelly-like flesh. While it is certain that no respectable wizard (good or neutrally aligned) would resort to creating such horrors, it is just as certain that there are many practitioners of the darker arts who have performed much worse experiments.

It is possible that somewhere deep in the bowels of some long-deserted wizard's dungeon, there lies an ancient diary, with a detailed account of the terrifying curse of the tracker.

There are tales of abnormally large slithering trackers that live in the deep recesses of the Underdark. Such monsters are often said to lurk around the edges of great underground civilizations, growing to vast size on the abundance of prey.

Orc

	Orc	Orog
CLIMATE/TERRAIN:	Any land	Any land
FREQUENCY:	Common	Uncommon
ORGANIZATION:	Tribe	Tribe
ACTIVITY CYCLE:	Night	Night
DIET:	Carnivore	Carnivore
INTELLIGENCE:	Average (8-9)	High (10- 12)
TREASURE:	L (C, O, Qx10, S)	L (C, O, Qx10, S)
ALIGNMENT:	Lawful evil	Lawful evil
NO. APPEARING:	30-300 (3d10x10)	20-80 (2d4x10)
ARMOR CLASS:	6 (10)	4 (10)
MOVEMENT:	9 (12)	6 (12)
HIT DICE:	1	3
THAC0:	19	17
NO. OF ATTACKS:	1	1
DAMAGE/ATTACK:	1-8 (weapon)	1-10 (weapon)
SPECIAL ATTACKS:	Nil	+1 to damage
SPECIAL DEFENSES:	Nil	Nil
MAGIC RESISTANCE:	Nil	Nil
SIZE:	M (6' tall)	M (6'-7')
MORALE:	Steady (11-12)	Elite (13-14)
XP VALUE:	15	65
Subchief, leader	35	120
Guards	35	
Chief	65	175
Bodyguard	65	
Shaman, 1st	35	
Shaman, 3rd	175	
Shaman, 5th	650	

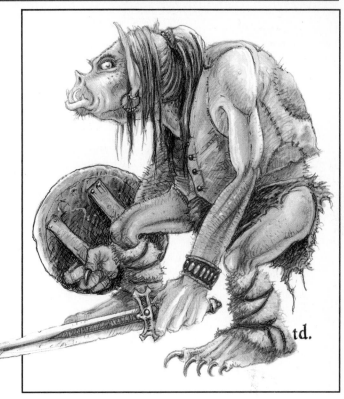

Orcs are a species of aggressive mammalian carnivores that band together in tribes and survive by hunting and raiding. Orcs believe that in order to survive they must expand their territory, and so they are constantly involved in wars against many enemies: humans, elves, dwarves, goblins, and other orc tribes.

Orcs vary widely in appearance, as they frequently crossbreed with other species. In general, they resemble primitive humans with grey-green skin covered with coarse hair. Orcs have a slightly stooped posture, a low jutting forehead, and a snout instead of a nose, though comparisons between this facial feature and those of pigs are exaggerated and perhaps unfair. Orcs have well-developed canine teeth for eating meat and short pointed ears that resemble those of a wolf. Orcish snouts and ears have a slightly pink tinge. Their eyes are human, with a reddish tint that sometimes makes them appear to glow red when they reflect dim light sources in near darkness. This is actually part of their optical system, a pigment which gives them infravision. Male orcs are about 5^1/$_2$ to 6 feet tall. Females average 6 inches shorter than males. Orcs prefer to wear colors that most humans think unpleasant: blood red, rust red, mustard yellow, yellow green, moss green, greenish purple, and blackish brown. Their armor is unattractive besides—dirty and often a bit rusty. Orcs speak Orcish, a language derived from older human and elvish languages. There is no common standard of Orcish, so the language has many dialects which vary from tribe to tribe. Orcs have also learned to speak local common tongues, but are not comfortable with them. Some orcs have a limited vocabulary in goblin, hobgoblin, and ogre dialects.

Combat: Orcs are constantly in battle. They use the following weapons.

sword and flail	5%
sword and spear	10%
axe and spear	10%
axe and polearm	10%
axe and crossbow	10%
axe and bow	10%
sword and battleaxe	5%
spear	10%
axe	10%
polearm	20%

Polearms are typically either halberds, pikes (set to receive charge), or glaives. Leaders typically possess two weapons. If a subchief is present, there is a 40% chance the orcs will be fighting around a standard. The presence of this standard increases attack rolls and morale by +1 for all orcs within 60 yards. Orcs typically wear studded leather armor and a shield (AC 6).

Orcs hate direct sunlight and fight at -1 penalty to their attack rolls in sunlight. Their morale decreases by 1 under these circumstances as well. Orcs employ sniping and ambush tactics in the wild. They do not obey the "rules of war" unless such is in their best interests; for example, they will shoot at those who attempt to parlay with them under a white flag unless the orc leader feels it is advantageous to hear what the enemy has to say. They abuse human rules of engagement and chivalry to their best advantage. They have a historic enmity against elves and dwarves; many tribes will kill these demihumans on sight.

It is often believed that orcs are so bloodthirsty and cruel that they are ineffective tacticians and that they would rather be vicious than victorious. Like most stereotypes, this is highly misleading; it is true for some orc tribes but not for all. Many orc tribes have waged wars for decades and have developed a frightening efficiency with battle tactics.

Habitat/Society: For every three orcs encountered, there will be a leader and three assistants. These orcs will have 8 hit points each, being the meanest and strongest in the group. If 150 orcs or more are encountered there will be the following additional figures with the band: a subchief and 3-18 guards, each with Armor

Orc

Class 4, 11 hit points, and +1 damage due to Strength on all attacks. They fight as monsters of 2 Hit Dice (THAC0 19). For every 100 orcs encountered, there will be either a shaman (maximum 5th level priest) or a witch doctor (maximum 4th-level mage). Shamans and witch doctors gain an extra 1d4 hit points for each level above 1st and fight as a monster of 1 Hit Die for every two levels (round fractions up) of spell-casting ability (e.g., a 5th-level shaman has d8+4d4 hit points and fights as a 3 Hit Dice monster.)

If the orcs are not in their lair, there is a 20% chance they will be escorting a train of 1-6 carts and 10-60 slave bearers bringing supplies, loot, or ransom and tribute to their orc chief or a stronger orc tribe. The total value of the goods carried by all of the carts will vary between 10 and 1,000 silver pieces, and each slave bearer will bear goods valued between 5 and 30 silver pieces. If the orcs are escorting a treasure train, double the number of leaders and assistants and add 10 orcs for each cart in the train; one subchief with 5-30 guards will always be in charge.

Orc lairs are underground 75% of the time, in a wilderness village 25% of the time. Orc communities range from small forts with 100-400 orcs to mining communities with 500-2,000 orcs to huge cities (partially underground and partially above ground) with 2,000 to 20,000 orcs. There will always be additional orcs when the encounter is in a creature's lair: a chief and 5-30 bodyguards (AC 4, 13-16 hit points, attack as monsters with 3 Hit Dice (THAC0 17) and inflict an extra +2 damage on all attacks due to Strength). If the lair is underground, there is a 50% chance that 2-5 ogres per 200 orcs will be living with them. Most lairs above ground are rude villages of wooden huts protected by a ditch, log rampart and log palisade, or more advanced constructions built by other races. The village will have 1-4 watch towers and a single gate. There will be one ballista and one catapult for every 100 adult male orcs.

Orcs are aggressive. They believe other species are inferior to them and that bullying and slavery is part of the natural order. They will cooperate with other species but are not dependable: as slaves, they will rebel against all but the most powerful masters; as allies they are quick to take offense and break agreements. Orcs believe that battle is the ideal challenge, but some leaders are pragmatic enough to recognize the value of peace, which they exact at a high price. If great patience and care are used, orc tribes can be effective trading partners and military allies.

Orcs value territory above all else; battle experience, wealth, and number of offspring are other major sources of pride. Orcs are patriarchal; women are fit only to bear children and nurse them. Orcs have a reputation for cruelty that is deserved, but humans are just as capable of evil as orcs. Orcs have marriage customs, but orc males are not noted for their faithfulness.

Orcs worship many deities (some who have different names among different tribes); the chief deity is usually a giant, one-eyed orc. Orcish religion is extremely hateful toward other species and urges violence and warfare. Orc shamans have been noted for their ambition, and many tribes have suffered because of political infighting between warriors and priests.

Ecology: Orcs have an average lifespan of 40 years. They have a gestation period of 10 months and produce two to three offspring per birth. Infant mortality is high. Orcs are carnivores, but prefer game meats or livestock to demihumans and humanoids.

It is said that orcs have no natural enemies, but they work hard to make up for this lack. Orc tribes have fearsome names such as Vile Rune, Bloody Head, Broken Bone, Evil Eye, and Dripping Blade.

Orcs are skilled miners who can spot new and unusual constructions 35% of the time and sloping passages 25% of the time. They are also excellent weaponsmiths.

Orogs

Elite orcs, or orogs, are a race of great orcs, possibly mixed with ogre blood. Orogs range between 6 and 6½ feet tall. They are highly disciplined warriors and have their own standards and banners which they display prominently—it is usually easy to tell when orogs are present among common orcs. Orogs can be found at the vanguard of large orc armies, but rarely on patrol. There is a 10% chance that an orc tribe will have orogs, whose number equals 10% of the male population. (Thus a community of 3,000 male orcs has a 10% chance of having 300 additional orogs.) Small bands of elites (20-80 orogs) will hire themselves out as mercenaries. Orogs have 3 Hit Dice, plate mail (AC 3), and have a +3 Strength bonus on damage dice. For every 20 orogs, there will also be one leader with 4 Hit Dice (THAC0 17). There is but one orog chief, who has 5 Hit Dice (THAC0 15). Orogs use weaponry common to orcs, but will typically possess two weapons apiece.

Half-orcs

Orcs will crossbreed with virtually every humanoid and demihuman species except elves, with whom they cannot. The mongrel offspring of orcs and these other species are known as half-orcs. Orc-goblins, orc-hobgoblins, and orc-humans are the most common. Half-orcs tend to favor the orcish strain heavily, and as such are basically orcs, although 10% of these offspring can pass as ugly humans. They are treated as humans with levels instead of Hit Dice. If multi-classed, they have these maximums: priest, 4th level; fighter, 10th level; thief, 8th level.

If half-orcs remain single-classed, these maximums increase to: priest, 7th level (Wisdom 15 required for 5th, Wisdom 16 for 6th, Wisdom 17 for 7th); fighter, 17th level (Strength 18/00 required for 11th, Strength 19 for 12th, Strength 20 for 14th, and Strength 21 for 17th); thief, 11th level (Dexterity 15 required for 9th, Dexterity 16 for 10th, and Dexterity 17 for 11th).

Half-orcs are distrusted by both human and orc cultures because they remind each of the other's racial stock. Half-orcs advance in orc culture by flaunting their superior ability and in human culture by associating with people who don't care about appearance. Most tend toward neutrality with slight lawful and evil tendencies, but lawful good half-orcs are not unknown. Some half-orcs have split from both cultures to form their own societies in remote areas. These half-orcs worship their own gods and (like most hermits) are extremely suspicious of strangers.

	Otyugh	Neo-otyugh
CLIMATE/TERRAIN:	Subterranean	Subterranean
FREQUENCY:	Uncommon	Rare
ORGANIZATION:	Solitary	Solitary
ACTIVITY CYCLE:	Any	Any
DIET:	Omnivore	Omnivore
INTELLIGENCE:	Low-Average (5-10)	Average-Very (8-12)
TREASURE:	See below	See below
ALIGNMENT:	Neutral	Neutral

NO. APPEARING:	1 (2)	1
ARMOR CLASS:	3	0
MOVEMENT:	6	6
HIT DICE:	6-8	9-12
THAC0:	6 HD: 15 7-8 HD: 13	9-10 HD: 11 11-12 HD: 9
NO. OF ATTACKS:	3	3
DAMAGE/ATTACK:	1-8/1-8/2-5	2-12/2-12/1-3
SPECIAL ATTACKS:	Grab, disease	Grab, disease
SPECIAL DEFENSES:	Never surprised	Never surprised
MAGIC RESISTANCE:	Nil	Nil
SIZE:	M-L (6'-7' diam.)	L (8' diam.)
MORALE:	Elite (14)	Fanatic (17)
XP VALUE:	6 HD: 650 7 HD: 975 8 HD: 1,400 9 HD: 2,000 10 HD: 3,000 11 HD: 4,000 12 HD: 5,000	

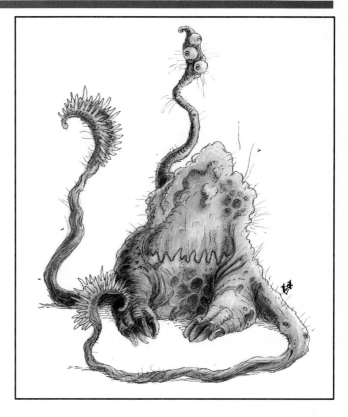

Otyughs (Aw-tee-ug), also known as the gulguthra, are terrifying creatures that lurk in heaps of dung and decay, waiting for something to disturb it. There are two varieties, the regular otyugh, and its larger, more intelligent offshoot, the neo-otyugh. They feed on dung and wastes from other dungeon creatures (gulguthra means "dung eaters") but also enjoy an occasional snack of fresh meat.

Otyughs have huge, bloated bodies covered with a rock-like skin that is brownish gray in color, which is in turn covered with dung. They stand on three thick legs that give them slow ground movement but enable them to pivot quickly. They have three eyes on a leaf-like stalk that moves quickly from side to side, enabling them to scan a large area. The eye stalk is also a receiver/transmitter for their telepathic abilities. Otyughs have a huge mouth with very sharp teeth in the center of their mass. They also have two tentacles with leaf-like ridges that they use to smash and grapple their opponents. The tentacles are covered with rough thorn-like projections. Neo-otyughs have smaller mouths than otyughs.

Otyughs and neo-otyughs speak their own language, much of which is non-verbal (movements of eye stalk and tentacles, or emission of certain smells); they also have limited telepathy that enable them to communicate with other creatures. Otyughs reek of dung and decay.

Combat: Otyughs lurk under piles of offal with only their eyes exposed. They usually attack if they feel threatened, or if they are hungry and there is fresh meat nearby. They attack with their two ridged tentacles, which either smash an opponent or grapple it. Grappled opponents suffer 2-4 points of damage per round. Otyughs' bite attacks gain a +2 bonus to the attack roll when biting grappled opponents. Otyughs smash grappled opponents to the ground, while the more intelligent neo-otyughs use their victims as shields, bettering their Armor Class by 1. Neo-otyughs may also force attackers to hit the grappled character with a suc-

cessful attack roll of its own (vs. the grappled character's AC); to do this the neo-otyugh forgoes its squeeze attack. Characters with a Strength of at least 18 can struggle for one round and automatically break free; others must make a successful open doors roll to escape.

Both types of gulguthra are disease-ridden; their bite is 90% likely to infect the character with a debilitating (80%) or fatal (20%) disease. Otyughs are immune to these diseases.

Habitat/Society: All gulguthra have limited telepathic ability. An otyugh can communicate with creatures up to 40 feet away, while a neo-otyugh can communicate with creatures as distant as 60 feet. Communication is usually limited to simple feelings and emotions such as hunger, temperature conditions and associated discomforts, its dislike of bright lights, and imminent death for its prey. Gulguthra also have infravision with a 90-foot range.

Otyughs and neo-otyughs live in ruins and dungeons. They make deals with other dungeon denizens, agreeing not to attack them in exchange for their dung and body wastes, which they then devour. To keep the supply of waste coming (and to get fresh meat) they will agree to help defend their home against intruders, which includes many adventurers. Otyughs may be persuaded not to attack creatures in exchange for promises of friendship and food. Neo-otyughs are less trusting (and more vicious), and usually attack intruders on sight. An otyugh's dungeon allies will sometimes ask it to guard treasure for them. Most gulguthra live alone; 10% of the time, during mating season, two gulguthra can found in its lair.

Ecology: Otyughs and neo-otyughs live underground in heaps of offal and refuse. They hate bright sunlight, preferring the comfortable darkness of dungeons. They mate each year for one month, with one offspring produced. It takes the newborn four months to mature (immature gulguthra have 3-5 HD, damage 1-6/1-6/1-2, and a Strength of 16 is required to break free of their grasp). Otyughs are so disgusting that no alchemist or wizard would want to touch their components, so the corpses of the gulguthra have no known use or value.

Owlbear

CLIMATE/TERRAIN:	Temperate forest
FREQUENCY:	Rare
ORGANIZATION:	Pack
ACTIVITY CYCLE:	Late afternoon/early evening
DIET:	Carnivore
INTELLIGENCE:	Low (5-7)
TREASURE:	(C)
ALIGNMENT:	Neutral

NO. APPEARING:	1 (2-8)
ARMOR CLASS:	5
MOVEMENT:	12
HIT DICE:	5+2
THAC0:	15
NO. OF ATTACKS:	3
DAMAGE/ATTACK:	1-6/1-6/2-12
SPECIAL ATTACKS:	Hug
SPECIAL DEFENSES:	Nil
MAGIC RESISTANCE:	Nil
SIZE:	L (8' tall)
MORALE:	Steady (11-12) +Special
XP VALUE:	420

Owlbears are probably the crossbred creation of a demented wizard; given the lethality of this creation, it is quite likely that the wizard who created them is no longer alive. Owlbears are vicious, ravenous, aggressive, and evil tempered at all times.

Owlbears are a cross between a giant owl and a bear. They are covered with a thick coat of feathers and fur, brown-black to yellow-brown in color. The 8-foot-tall males, which weigh between 1,300 and 1,500 pounds, are darker colored. The beaks of these creatures are yellow to ivory and their terrifying eyes are red-rimmed. Owlbears speak their own language, which consists of very loud screeches of varying length and pitch.

Combat: The owlbear attacks prey on sight, always fighting to the death (ignore morale rating for purposes of determining retreat). It attacks with its claws and snapping beak. If an owlbear scores a claw hit with a roll of 18 or better, it drags its victim into a hug, subsequently squeezing its opponent for 2-16 points of damage per round until either the victim or the owlbear is slain. The owlbear can also use its beak attack on victims caught in its grasp, but cannot use its claws. A single attempt at a bend bars/lift gates roll may be made to break from the grasp of an owlbear. Note that if the Armor Class of a victim is high enough that 18 is insufficient to hit, the hug is not effective and no damage is taken.

Habitat/Society: Owlbears inhabit the depths of tangled forests in temperate climes, as well as subterranean labyrinths, living in caves or hollow stumps.

Owlbears live in mated pairs; the male is slightly larger and heavier than the female. If encountered in their lair there is a 25% chance that there will be 1-6 eggs (20%) or young (80%) in addition to the adults. The offspring will be 40% to 70% grown and fight as creatures with three or four Hit Dice, depending on their growth. They have hit points based on their adjusted Hit Dice. Immature offspring inflict 1-4/1-4/2-8 points of damage with their attacks and a character has a +20% to his bend bars/lift gates roll to escape the hug of an immature owlbear.

An owlbear pair claims a territory of one or two square miles and will vigorously defend this territory against all intruders.

An owlbear's main weakness is also its greatest strength—its ferocity. Because owlbears are so bad-tempered, they stop at nothing to kill a target. It is not difficult to trick an owlbear into hurling itself off a cliff or into a trap, provided you can find one.

Ecology: Owlbears have a lifespan of 20 years. They are warm-blooded mammals, but lay eggs. They prey on anything, from rabbits to bears, to trolls, to snakes and reptiles. Owlbears prefer temperate climates, but some thrive in subarctic environments. As a hybrid of two animals, one diurnal and the other nocturnal, they have an unusual active time, waking at noon, hunting animals active during the day, then hunting nocturnal creatures before going to sleep at midnight. Owlbears are active in the summer months and hibernate during the cold season. There are rumors of white arctic owlbears, a cross between arctic owls and polar bears, but no specimens have ever been captured.

An owlbear does not actively seek treasure but the remains of victims may be found buried in shallow holes around an owlbear lair. Owlbear eggs are worth 2,000 silver pieces and hatchlings are worth 5,000 silver pieces on the open market. These are typically bought by wizards; while they are impossible to domesticate, they make formidable guardians and wizards sometimes place them in locations of strategic importance (it has been said that an owlbear is a less subtle version of a "keep out" sign). Owlbears in dungeons and ruins almost always have been placed there by someone.

Pegasus

CLIMATE/TERRAIN:	Temperate and subtropical forests
FREQUENCY:	Very rare
ORGANIZATION:	Herd
ACTIVITY CYCLE:	Day
DIET:	Herbivore
INTELLIGENCE:	Average (8-10)
TREASURE:	Nil
ALIGNMENT:	Chaotic good

NO. APPEARING:	1-10
ARMOR CLASS:	6
MOVEMENT:	24, Fl 48 (C, D mounted)
HIT DICE:	4
THAC0:	17
NO. OF ATTACKS:	3
DAMAGE/ATTACK:	1-8/1-8/1-3
SPECIAL ATTACKS:	Dive, rear kick
SPECIAL DEFENSES:	Nil
MAGIC RESISTANCE:	Nil
SIZE:	L (5½' at the shoulder)
MORALE:	Steady (11)
XP VALUE:	175
Greater	650

Pegasi are magnificent winged steeds that often serve the cause of good. These intelligent creatures are very shy and wild, not easily tamed. They serve only good characters, and when they do, they will serve their master with absolute faithfulness for the rest of his life.

A pegasus is a thoroughbred which resembles an Arabian horse (though slightly larger) with two large feathered wings. Pegasi are usually white, but brown pegasi are not unknown, and rumors persist of black pegasi. As should be expected, alignments do not vary according to color (all pegasi are chaotic good). Pegasi are 17 hands tall (5 feet at the shoulder) and weigh over 1,500 pounds. Pegasi must be ridden bareback; they will not accept saddles.

Pegasi speak their own language and can communicate with horses. They can understand common, and will obey their master's commands if they are given in that language.

Combat: A pegasus attacks with its hooves and teeth. It can attack an opponent who is behind it with its rear hooves, inflicting 2-12 points of damage, but it cannot use any of its other attacks in that round. A pegasus can also dive at an opponent from heights of 50 feet or higher and use its hoof attacks; each attack roll is +2 and does double damage.

In battle, a pegasus will try to lure larger opponents (such as dragons) into tight spaces. As the opponent struggles to maneuver into attack range, the pegasus climbs and attacks with its hooves from above. Against creatures their own size, such as griffons, pegasi use their superior speed to outrun them. If griffons are close to a pegasus nest (especially if there are young present), one parent will attack aggressively, get the griffon's attention, and then fly away. By doing this, they hope to lure enemies away from the nest and tire them out over a long distance before returning home.

Habitat/Society: Pegasi are egg-laying mammals. If encountered in their lair, there will be one nest for every pair of pegasi. There is a 20% chance per nest that there will be 1-2 eggs (30% chance) or young (70%) of 20-50% maturity. Each egg is worth 3,000 silver pieces, while the young are worth 5,000 silver pieces per head on the open market.

A pegasus can be used as a warhorse; a male can carry weight as a medium warhorse (220/330/440), while a female can carry weight as a light warhorse (170/255/340).

Pegasi are intelligent creatures. They can *detect good* and *detect evil* at will (60 yard range). They use these powers on those who would ride them; they try to throw anyone of non-good alignments who would tame them. If provoked, pegasi will not hesitate to attack creatures whom they perceive as evil.

To tame a pegasus, a person of good alignment must locate a pegasus herd. Then, at night, he can try to sneak up on a pegasus and surprise it. The character must have the airborne riding proficiency. There is an initial +10 penalty to the roll; pegasi do not like to be tamed. A magical bridle enchanted for the purpose will remove this penalty. If the character successfully makes his roll, then the pegasus will be tamed.

A tamed pegasus will obey the commands of its master for as long as it lives, if the master remains of good alignment.

Ecology: Pegasi feed on grass, fruits, and other plants. Griffons and hippogriffs are the natural enemies of a pegasus. Pegasi have a lifespan of about 40 years.

Greater Pegasus
Legend has it that if a medusa is slain and beheaded, there is a small (5%) chance that a greater pegasus will be born, springing fully born from the medusa's cloven neck. These pegasi have the same attacks and movement rate of a normal pegasus but are worth 6 Hit Dice and have 20% magic resistance. They also have a +1 bonus to their morale rating. There is a 5% chance that the leader of a herd of pegasi will be a greater pegasus. Greater pegasi can be tamed only by the noblest and greatest of heroes, and have a lifespan of 100 years.

Peryton

CLIMATE/TERRAIN:	Any/Mountains
FREQUENCY:	Rare
ORGANIZATION:	Nest
ACTIVITY CYCLE:	Day
DIET:	Omnivore
INTELLIGENCE:	Average (10)
TREASURE:	B
ALIGNMENT:	Chaotic evil

NO. APPEARING:	2-8
ARMOR CLASS:	7
MOVEMENT:	12, Fl 21 (C)
HIT DICE:	4
THAC0:	17
NO. OF ATTACKS:	1
DAMAGE/ATTACK:	4-16
SPECIAL ATTACKS:	+ 2 to attack roll
SPECIAL DEFENSES:	+ 1 or better to hit
MAGIC RESISTANCE:	Nil
SIZE:	M (5' tall)
MORALE:	Champion (16)
XP VALUE:	270

High above the mountains and rocky hills of most lands flies a sharp-eyed monster known as the peryton. Intelligent, patient, and malevolent, it watches and waits for prey—to pluck their hearts out.

The peryton resembles a giant, dark green eagle, except that its head is that of a blue-black stag, its horns glitter as ebon as obsidian, its eyes glow a dull red-orange. The chest feathers of a male peryton are light blue; those of the female are drab brown. Perytons normally cast the shadow of an adult human being, rather than those of their own form.

Perytons do not adorn themselves with trinkets, nor arm themselves with weapons. Their language is a collection of roars and screeches, and often sounds as if a peryton were either injured or enraged. Some creatures, with a keen sense of smell, claim that a peryton smells like a human, while others are filled with an irrational fear upon catching first scent.

Combat: A peryton has only a secondary interest in prey as food. Its main interest in humans and humanoid creatures is the heart of its prey. It is unnaturally accurate in combat. In game terms a peryton receives a +2 bonus to its attack roll.

It attacks with its sharp horns, since its claws are too weak to use in melee. When a peryton chooses a target for combat, it locks itself into a duel that nearly always ends in either the peryton's death or that of its target. A peryton will never switch targets during combat, no matter the tactical situation. On rare occasions, the creature can be driven off, but it will continue to stalk its prey, and return at a later time.

Perytons are immune to all weapons but those of at least +1 enchantment.

Some perytons choose to swoop at a target. In this form of attack, the peryton climbs several hundred feet in the air and then plunges at the target, dropping with awesome speed. This attack is made at an additional +2 bonus to its attack roll. If the attack succeeds, the peryton delivers double damage. This is an extreme maneuver that the peryton will only attempt if combat is going poorly, or if it believes it has a chance to achieve total surprise.

Another common tactic is for the peryton to seize a human-sized target and then lift off with the prey in its talons. The peryton climbs so rapidly that most targets do not react until they are at least 100 feet in the air and facing a 10d6 plummet if they manage to escape the peryton's grasp.

Habitat/Society: Perytons roost in caves high atop cliffs or on mountain peaks. They settle in nests of 2d4 creatures, each nest independent of any other, and no two nests being within several miles of one another, except for unusual circumstances—like a dwarven community in the mountains providing them with plentiful prey.

Perytons sometimes take humans and humanoid creatures alive and hold them captive in their nests until they are needed as food (90% likely for nonhumans, 25 % the case for humans) or for reproduction (see below). Because of this, the peryton nests may have treasure scattered about, as well as 1d4 unhatched eggs.

Ecology: The peryton is a predator, with no natural enemies (few could pierce its magically resistant skin). Humanoids, and especially humans, are its selected prey. A female peryton requires a fresh, beating heart to reproduce, and human hearts are the preferred variety. Once a peryton has eaten a heart, its shadow changes into that of its normal form and the creature becomes fertile for 3d6 hours.

Unhatched peryton eggs can be sold for 10d12 gp apiece.

Phantom

CLIMATE/TERRAIN:	Any/Land
FREQUENCY:	Very rare
ORGANIZATION:	Solitary
ACTIVITY CYCLE:	Any
DIET:	Nil
INTELLIGENCE:	Nil
TREASURE:	Nil
ALIGNMENT:	Neutral

NO. APPEARING:	1
ARMOR CLASS:	Nil
MOVEMENT:	9
HIT DICE:	Nil
THAC0:	Nil
NO. OF ATTACKS:	Nil
DAMAGE/ATTACK:	Nil
SPECIAL ATTACKS:	Fear
SPECIAL DEFENSES:	Nil
MAGIC RESISTANCE:	See below
SIZE:	Varies, usually M
MORALE:	Nil
XP VALUE:	Nil

Phantoms are images left behind by particularly strong death traumas. A phantom is like a three-dimensional movie image filmed at the time of death, in the place where it died.

The standard phantom may appear as almost anything. It often appears as the character who experienced the trauma-a transparent image re-enacting the death scene. Alternatively, it could represent whatever was foremost in the victim's mind at the time of death; an attacker, or some goal left unachieved. Phantoms are experienced in faded colors, by all senses.

Combat: It is difficult to fight phantoms, since they are merely images and have no power to directly cause harm. They cannot themselves be harmed. Swinging weapons or casting spells into the area of the image does not interfere with the projection, and they cannot be reasoned with. A phantom is not intelligent and does not exist for any real reason; tracking down its killer or completing its quest will not get rid of a phantom.

Phantoms are often mistaken for ghosts, haunts, or groaning spirits, but they can not be turned as undead. Only a priest spell *remove curse*, cast at 12th level, can dispel a phantom.

Although a phantom cannot directly do any actual harm, it is the very essence of magic and calls up a superstitious awe in anyone who sees one. The enchantment is such that the phantom affects both the mind and the senses of the observer. Creatures without minds (such as undead) are immune to the effects of phantoms, as are those rare beings who are somehow unable to experience them (since the phantom is present to all senses, blindness is not normally protection against one).

Characters witnessing a phantom must roll a successful saving throw vs. death magic, with a −2 penalty, or immediately panic and run away as per the effects of a *fear* spell. Particularly vivid phantoms may require those who fail their saving throw to make a system shock roll, with a +10 bonus to the roll. Failure results in death for the unfortunate victim. Such a character can be raised normally, however.

There are other difficulties with the fear effect; the cause of the phantom's death might still be around. Even after centuries, traps and undead monsters can be just as effective and deadly, and running away in panic is usually not the best defense.

Of course, a phantom may provide characters with important information, either forewarning careful characters of an upcoming danger, or finding a lost and treasured object.

There is a slight chance that a character's death may engender a phantom. This chance should be minuscule to nonexistent for 0-level or very low-level characters, or for those who were expecting to die-those dying of natural causes or in war. However, characters of 4th level or above, dying suddenly or by surprise might have a 1-2% chance of becoming phantoms. If those characters were on an important mission or were subject to *geas* or *quest* spells, this chance might rise to 5-6 percent. The percentage chance for generating a phantom should never be higher than the level of the character at the time of death. (Characters killed by energy-draining undead rarely produce phantoms.) It is up to the DM to decide what the precise image presents. A character who is murdered and generates a phantom may also return as a revenant.

There are nonstandard types of phantoms that affect only one of the senses. Often, these are purely visual images, but they can also manifest themselves as sounds (explosions, moaning, or quiet whispering) or smells. Most of these phantoms require saving throws, but the effects of failure may differ. A gloomy whispering of danger might produce despair (as per the *symbol* spells) effects. A foul stench might induce the retching effects of a ghast. Suffocating pressure, temperature extremes, the sounds of a swarm of bats, might all carry different consequences of failing the saving throw.

Of greater concern, however is that there are some phantoms that are actually evil, created when powerful evil creatures from other planes are "slain" (forced to return to their home planes) in the Prime material plane. These phantoms appear at the will of the evil creature 35% of the time, and can seriously misinform or endanger any character it meets. These phantoms can be detected with a *detect evil* spell; *dispel evil* can neutralize the phantom for a number of turns equal to the caster's level.

Phoenix

CLIMATE/TERRAIN:	Elysium
FREQUENCY:	Very rare
ORGANIZATION:	Solitary
ACTIVITY CYCLE:	Any
DIET:	Omnivore
INTELLIGENCE:	Genius (17-18)
TREASURE:	O
ALIGNMENT:	Neutral good
NO. APPEARING:	1-3
ARMOR CLASS:	−3
MOVEMENT:	6, Fl 39 (D)
HIT DICE:	20
THAC0:	5
NO. OF ATTACKS:	1 or 2
DAMAGE/ATTACK:	2-12 or 1-8/1-8
SPECIAL ATTACKS:	Shriek
SPECIAL DEFENSES:	+3 or better weapons to hit, never surprised
MAGIC RESISTANCE:	50%
SIZE:	L (40+' wing span)
MORALE:	Champion (15-16)
XP VALUE:	19,000

The phoenix is a great, extra-planar bird thought to represent the spirit of freedom and rebirth. It is a mortal creature that displays the ultimate in godlike detachment.

A phoenix appears as a large bird with a 40' wingspan and bright, multi-colored feathers. The plumage includes bright violet, scarlet, crimson and flaming orange. Its beak and claws are of blue-violet. A phoenix's eyes are a deep, glowing ruby color.

In addition to its own language, a phoenix can speak with all avians. It otherwise communicates with a limited telepathy or by empathy.

Combat: The phoenix is a free and benevolent spirit and does not derive pleasure from attacking others. But if the need for combat arises, a phoenix is a swift and powerful foe. It can attack in the air with two powerful claws inflicting 1-8 points of damage per strike. When on the ground it attacks with its great beak for 2-12 points of damage per hit. The phoenix is an intelligent and magical beast, however, so it usually opts for more effective measures of attack and defense.

A phoenix will always open up each round of combat with a piercing shriek that gives the creature an edge in the combat round. All opponents of 12 hit dice or less within 30 feet of a shrieking phoenix receive a +3 penalty on their initiative dice. The shriek does not affect the phoenix's combat roles in any way.

Every phoenix has the following spell-like powers, at 20th level of magic use, usable once per round, one at a time, at will:

- *affect normal fires*
- *audible glamer*
- *blindness*
- *blink*
- *blur*
- *call woodland beings*, 1 time per day
- *color spray*, 3 times per day
- *continual light*
- *control temperature, 10' radius*
- *dancing lights*
- *detect charm*, always active
- *detect evil*, always active
- *detect magic*, always active
- *duo-dimension*, 1 time per day
- *find traps*
- *find the path*, 1 time per day

- *fire charm*
- *fire seeds*, 1 time per day
- *incendiary cloud*, 1 time per week
- *invisibility*
- *misdirection*
- *neutralize poison*, 1 time per day
- *polymorph self*, 3 times per day
- *produce fire*
- *protection from evil, 10' radius*, always active
- *pyrotechnics*
- *reincarnate*, 1 time per day
- *remove fear*, within a 10-foot radius
- *remove curse*
- *snake charm*
- *veil*, 1 time per day
- *wall of fire*, 1 time per day

Also, by spreading its wings and performing a ritual dance, the phoenix can perform the following spell-like abilities at 40th level of magic use:

- *dismissal*
- *dispel evil*
- *dispel magic*

Any of these three abilities can be used by a phoenix as many times as desired, but can only be done one at a time and each takes a full round to complete. No other activities—such as a shriek—can be done in conjunction with these three powers.

A touch of its wing is equal to a *cure light wounds* spell, with 2 touches possible per individual per day per phoenix. A touch of the comb gives an effect equal to *cure disease*, but only once per day per person.

When hard-pressed, the phoenix is able to cause spilled droplets of its own blood to act as *fire seeds* of the holly berry type, one being created for every five points of damage taken by the phoenix.

In extreme situations, the phoenix can create a 40th-level combination of *fire storm* (20' high × 5' wide × 8' deep) and *incendiary cloud*, even if it has already used these powers previously. This destroys the adult phoenix but leaves behind a young phoenix with all the powers and abilities of its predecessor.

The phoenix can travel astrally or ethereally at will. They are hit only by +3 or better magical weapons. The phoenix can never be surprised. It has infravision to 120 feet.

Habitat/Society: Phoenixes are strange and enigmatic creatures. They are held in very high regard in the legends of many tribes of barbarians and in other, primitive cultures. It is said that the phoenix is the embodiment of rebirth. This is symbolized in the classic imagery of the self-immolation of the phoenix from which a new bird is formed. This is seen as the ultimate sacrifice for the cause of good and thus the phoenix are considered noble creatures.

Legend states that the phoenix has an extremely long lifespan. Some reports claim they can live to be over 1,000 years old, while others suggest it to be as high as 12,000 years. When it is time for the phoenix to die, it goes far into the mountains away from civilization. At the very top of these peaks, the phoenix builds a great nest made of straw and various herbs. The phoenix will lie in the nest, taking its last look at the world it knows. Satisfied that its work in the world is at an end, it then immolates itself in a flash of great flame and light. When the flames die down, there in the nest, which remains untouched by flames, is a young phoenix arrayed in bright colors like its parent before it. Legend then suggests that the phoenix must fly away to the temple of the sun and there bury the mummified corpse of its parent.

In general, phoenixes are reclusive creatures, tending to make their lairs away from the worlds of humanoid beings. Though they have the ability to travel through the Astral and Ethereal planes (and thus to any inner and outer plane), they will generally tend to stay on Elysium or in a secluded place on the Prime Material plane.

There are as many legends of the phoenix as there are cultures, each with its own slightly differing viewpoint. Some believe the phoenix to be the benevolent symbol of death, only appearing when someone's time is up among the living. Other cultures—primarily evil—see the phoenix as the symbol of destruction and rage, bringing fiery devastation in its wake. Still other cultures record their phoenix to be a friend and benefactor of good beings.

Although a wealth of mystery surrounds the phoenix, still there are some things that are known for sure. It is obvious that the phoenix is a champion of good. Although is seems these creatures do not actively seek out evil to destroy, they will rarely pass up such an opportunity when it presents itself. Also, despite the vast differences in ideology, belief, and philosophy in the various cultures that revere the phoenix, one thing remains constant: the phoenix is the symbol of creation by destruction. Some cultures believe that fire is the one great purifier, cleansing all that it touches. Others believe that fires merely destroys. With the phoenix, both are true. In its own reproduction, fires destroys the old bird, taking with it many centuries of life and wisdom, yet it creates a new phoenix with a new mind, thus purifying the line.

Ecology: Of all magical or enchanted creatures, the phoenix is perhaps most sought after by alchemists and sages alike. There is almost no part of a phoenix that cannot be used in a magical potion or for research.

The feathers of the phoenix have a great many uses. They can be used to adorn a *staff of healing*, they can be used to make *potions of extra-healing*, and have many other healing, magic uses. The eyes, beak, and talons of a phoenix are very valuable in the open market, often commanding 5,000 gp and up. Of course it is not always easy to find a buyer on the open market, because many cultures consider it a bad omen or taboo violation to kill a phoenix.

The exact nature of the phoenix can only be guessed at by scholars. All phoenixes are male and the reproduction cycle consists entirely of the self-immolation. Whether this is a natural biological reproduction cycle or a magical birth is unclear.

Call Phoenix (Conjuration/Summoning)
6th-level Priest Spell, Animal Sphere

Range: 0
Components: V, S, M
Duration: 1 round per level of caster
Casting Time: 2 rounds
Area of Effect: Special
Saving Throw: None

This potent priest spell enables the caster to actually summon a phoenix that will come and aid him. The most stringent restriction to this is that the caster must be of good alignment or a druid. Evil or nondruid neutral priests cannot summon a phoenix.

When cast, a phoenix will *always* come to aid. However, depending on how far away the nearest phoenix is, it may take some time for it to appear. One of these powerful creatures will appear in 1d8 − 1 rounds. A modified roll of '0' indicates that a phoenix will appear right away in a huge burst of smoke and flame.

Because the caster must be good or be a druid, there is seldom a conflict of interest between the phoenix and the summoner. However, a phoenix will never attack beings of good alignment (unless there is an *extremely* good reason for it). It will, however, risk its own life if the cause mandates such action and will further the aims of good that the summoner has undertaken.

When the spell has expired, the phoenix does not disappear, but it is then free to do what it will. This may in fact be what the caster summoned it for, or it may leave if it feels the reasons for its summoning were insufficient.

The material components for this spell are three diamonds of at least 500 gp value (which are consumed by the energies of the spell) and a red hot coal.

Piercer

CLIMATE/TERRAIN:	Any subterranean
FREQUENCY:	Uncommon
ORGANIZATION:	Colony
ACTIVITY CYCLE:	Any
DIET:	Carnivore
INTELLIGENCE:	Non- (0)
TREASURE:	Nil
ALIGNMENT:	Neutral

NO. APPEARING:	3-18 (3d6)
ARMOR CLASS:	3
MOVEMENT:	1
HIT DICE:	1-4
THAC0:	19 (1-2 HD),
	17 (3-4 HD)
NO. OF ATTACKS:	1
DAMAGE/ATTACK:	1-6 (1 HD),
	2-12 (2 HD),
	3-18 (3 HD),
	4-24 (4 HD)
SPECIAL ATTACKS:	Surprise
SPECIAL DEFENSES:	Nil
MAGIC RESISTANCE:	Nil
SIZE:	T-M (1-6' tall)
MORALE:	Average (8-10)
XP VALUE:	
1 HD	35
2 HD	65
3 HD	120
4 HD	420

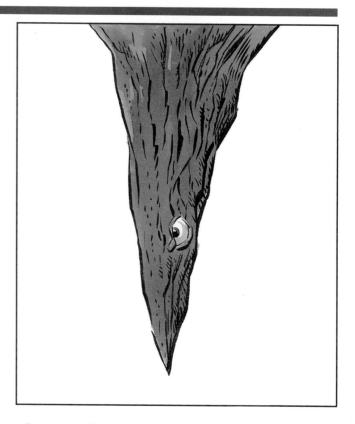

Piercers resemble stalactites found on cave roofs. They are actually a species of gastropods that, without their shells, resemble slugs with long tails. A piercer climbs onto the ceiling of a cavern and waits patiently; when it detects prey beneath it, it drops from the ceiling and impales the victim with the sharp end of its shell.

Piercers look like limestone growths on the ceiling of a cavern, just like ordinary stalactites. They come in the following sizes: one foot long (1 Hit Die), three feet long (2 Hit Dice), four and one-half feet long (3 Hit Dice), and six feet long (4 Hit Dice). Piercers can be identified on very close inspection by a pair of tiny eyestalks that curl along the side of the stalactite.

Combat: Piercers have only one chance to hit; if an attack fails to score a kill, the piercer cannot attack again until it slowly scales a wall to resume its position. Piercers can hear noises and detect heat sources in a 120-yard radius; these heat sources include humans. If the noise and light are stationary for many minutes at a time, piercers will slowly edge into attack position over the source of the stimulus. Piercers are virtually indistinguishable from natural phenomena. A group of characters has a -7 modifier on its surprise roll against a piercer (this guarantees that the group will be surprised unless it has some positive modifiers).

A piercer, after it has fallen, is slow and fairly easily slain. Its soft underbelly has one defense mechanism; when exposed to air it covers itself in a corrosive acid which inflicts 1 point of damage on contact with flesh. This is usually enough to dissuade natural predators from disturbing it.

Habitat/Society: While piercers are nonintelligent, the piercers in a colony are aware of each other. They often fall simultaneously, to feed on those killed by other piercers (which makes the area suddenly very dangerous).

Piercers dwell in caverns, where they live in groups of about 10 members. They prefer to hang over high traffic areas, so they will usually be found near cave entrances. Aside from mating, the piercers are not social creatures. There are rumored to be great caverns deep underground that contain colonies of hundreds of piercers. Piercers are not attracted to treasure, only to food.

Ecology: The piercer is a mollusk, hatched from a hen-sized egg which the parent lays in clutches of six to eight in isolated areas of the cavern. When they hatch, the young appear to be slugs feeding on fungi. After several months, they climb the cavern walls, secrete a chemical that hardens into the familiar stalactite shape, and then wait for prey to come.

A piercer has a lifespan of four years and grows one Hit Die per year. In any group of piercers, the number of creatures with one, two, three, and four Hit Dice will be nearly evenly divided (e.g., in a group of 12 piercers, there will be three one Hit Die piercers, three with two Hit Dice, three with three Hit Dice, and three with four Hit Dice).

A piercer can go without food for months. It stores food in a second stomach that can preserve food for long periods of time; some alchemists seek out piercers to extract a substance from this organ and refine it for human use, as it can keep foodstuffs and precious ingredients fresh for weeks. Piercers also store large supplies of water, extracted from their victims. Piercers can maintain this water supply for months.

The taste of a piercer is said to resemble that of a snail, but with a bitter aftertaste. Their eggs and offspring are not traded on the open market.

Plant, Dangerous

	Choke Creeper	Mantrap	Retch Plant	Snapper-saw	Thorn-Slinger	Tri-flower Frond	Yellow Musk Creeper	Yellow Musk Zombie
CLIMATE/TERRAIN:	Temperate forest	Tropical hills or forest	Any warm land	Any land	Any land	Tropical forest	Temperate forest or subterranean	Temperate forest or subterranean
FREQUENCY:	Rare	Very rare	Rare	Very rare	Rare	Very rare	Rare	Rare
ORGANIZATION:	Solitary	Pair	Cluster	Solitary	Cluster	Stand	Solitary	Squad
ACTIVITY CYCLE:	Day	Day	Any	Any	Any	Day	Any	Any
DIET:	Carnivore	Carnivore	Sun, soil	Carnivore	Carnivore	Carnivore	Carnivore	Nil
INTELLIGENCE:	Non- (0)	Non- (0)	Non- (0)	Non- (0)	Non- (0)	Non- (0)	Non- (0)	Animal (1)
TREASURE:	Nil	J-N (×5), Q	Nil	Nil	Nil	Nil	B	Nil
ALIGNMENT:	Neutral	Neutral	Neutral	Neutral	Neutral	Neutral	Neutral	Neutral
NO. APPEARING:	1	1-2	2-20	1-2	3-12	1-10	1	1 per 2 flowers
ARMOR CLASS:	6/5	6	8	4/7/9	8	9	7	10 or better
MOVEMENT:	1/2	0	0	0	0	0	0	6
HIT DICE:	25	4-9	5-8	5	4	2+8	3	2 (special)
THAC0:	7	Nil	5-6 HD: 15 7-8 HD: 13	15	Nil	17	17	19
NO. OF ATTACKS:	8 or more	0	1 or 1d4+1	1d4+2	1 volley	1	2-12	1
DAMAGE/ATTACK:	1-4	0	0	2-5	2-8	0	Nil	1-8 or by weapon
SPECIAL ATTACKS:	Strangling	See below	See below	Trapping	Dew	See below	Pollen	Nil
SPECIAL DEFENSES:	See below	Nil	See below	Nil	Nil	Nil	Immunities	Immunities
MAGIC RESISTANCE:	Nil	Nil	Nil	Nil	Nil	Nil	Nil	Nil
SIZE:	G (20'-160' long)	L-G (4' per Hit Die)	H (20' tall)	H (15' radius)	M (4' radius)	M (5'-8' tall)	L (20' square)	M (4'-7' tall)
MORALE:	Elite (14)	Steady (12)	Average (8-10)	Steady (11-12)	Average (8-10)	Average (10)	Fearless (20)	Fearless (20)
XP VALUE:	18,000	4 HD: 650 5 HD: 975 6 HD: 1,400 7 HD: 2,000 8 HD: 3,000 9 HD: 4,000	5 HD: 270 6 HD: 420 7 HD: 650 8 HD: 975	3 saws: 270 4-5 saws: 420 6 saws: 975	270	420	650	120

Of the many hazards in the wilds, these plants are among the most frightening. They feed on animals, perhaps as nature's revenge on animals for their habit of feeding on plants.

Choke Creeper
The choke creeper, or strangler vine, is a long, thick vine with many branch vines, each capable of attacking. The vine is olive green in color, and the main vine is almost 1-2 feet thick. Branch vines have flexible tendrils, allowing them to creep at 5 yards per round. They are attracted to light and heat.

For each 20 feet of main vine, it has the 1 hp per HD; branch vines have 2 hp per 20 feet of the main vine (branch vine hit points are in addition to those of the main vine, not part of the total). In each 10-foot section of the main vine, there are four branch vines. The smallest choke creeper is 20 feet long, has 1 hp/HD (25 hp total), and has eight branch vines, each with 2 hp. The largest choke creeper is 160 feet long, has 8 hp/HD (200 hp total), and has 64 branch vines, each with 16 hp. The main vine is AC 6, the branches AC 5.

A maximum of four branch vines can attack a single target. They appear to be normal vegetation and can usually grab unsuspecting victims. Victims can break free with a successful bend bars/lift gates roll; if the roll fails, they are held fast until the vine that holds them is severed. Seized victims suffer 1d4 points of damage per round, with a 10% chance per round (noncumulative) that the choke creeper achieves a strangling grip. The victim dies after one round of strangulation.

A choke creeper is immune to torch fire, but takes normal damage from hotter fires such as those caused by burning oil; hot fires make the vine move away. The creeper takes only 1 hp damage per die of cold damage, but cold stuns the all plant sections struck for 1d4+1 rounds. Electrical attacks do no damage; instead, they double the creeper's movement rate for 1d4+1 rounds.

Mantrap
This insidious relative of the much smaller Venus flytrap attracts prey by scent, entrapping and dissolving its victims in acidic secretions. It is a gigantic bush with towering stalks of purple blossoms, and huge green leaves at ground level.

During daylight hours the mantrap releases pollen continuously; all creatures who approach to within 60 feet must make a successful saving throw vs. poison or become attracted to the odor. Those attracted proceed to the body and voluntarily climb into one of the 1d4+1 leaf traps on the plant. Once entered, a leaf trap closes, firmly entrapping the victim (no chance of escape). The victim cannot be pulled free until the plant is destroyed. Its acidic secretions destroy the victim quickly, inflicting damage per round equal to the victim's AC (discounting Dexterity bonuses). Regardless of the adjusted AC, the victim takes at least 1 point of damage per round. Items exposed to the acid must roll a saving throw once per round against the effects; all metal items receive a +2 bonus.

The fascination with the mantrap is so strong that, once a being is enthralled, it takes 24 hours for the effect to wear off. The fumes from burning the plant counteract the effect. Because of its powerful attractive ability, the nectar of mantrap flowers is an ingredient in a *philter of love.*

Retch Plant
The retch plant, or globe palm, appears to be a typical palm tree, except that each always has 1d4+4 globe-like, coconut-sized fruit growing at its top. Each globe is membranous, taut, and blue, violet, or lilac in color.

Walking under a retch plant makes it 20% likely that one of the globes will fall. If there is solid contact against the tree trunk (banging against it, running into it, or climbing it) 1d4+1 of the noisome fruits plop down. Randomly choose the target attacked;

291

Plant, Dangerous

they are AC 10 against this attack. When the globes strike, they burst, and a nauseating fluid is splashed over a 5-foot radius. Those 5-9 feet from the impact have a 25% chance of being splashed. The sticky, foul fluid causes creatures to vomit and retch for the next three rounds. In addition to being nauseated, victims are at half normal Strength for one hour. No saving throw is allowed against either effect of the fluid.

Creatures splashed must be washed in alcohol (including drinkable types) or they are more likely to attract carnivores in the area, doubling the frequency and chance for success of encounter checks. The odor is discernible within a 50-foot radius, and it persists for 1d4 hours unless removed as above.

Snapper-Saw

This plant, also called foresters' bane, has a central bush with several greenish-white berries that are plump, smell delicious, edible, nutritious, and rich in protein. Several broad, dark green, ribbed leaves radiate out 5-7 feet from the bushy center, which hides 1d4+2 tough, purple, saw-like stalks with thorny projections. A healthy plant has six saw-stalks, while damaged specimens have less.

Creatures stepping into the radius of the low-growing ribbed leaves risk attack. The leaves snap up one or two victims; armor is ignored for this attack, though dexterity and magical bonuses to AC are counted. A victim must make a successful Strength check to pull free.

A creature caught by the snapper leaves is attacked by the saw-stalks, even if the victim breaks free in the same round in which it was caught. Each saw-stalk attacks once per round for 1d4+1 points of damage, shredding the victim so its flesh and blood feed the snapper-saw. Clutched prey does not receive Dexterity adjustments to AC, though armor and magical protection apply normally.

Saw-stalks are AC 4 and require 1d8+16 points of damage a piece to sever. Each snapper leaf is AC 7 and takes 1d8+8 points of damage to sever. These hit points do not count toward the total of the central bush's Hit Dice. The central bush is AC 9, but it is completely protected from outside attack when the snapper leaves are up. A victim held by the snapper leaves can attack the saw-stalks or the central bush, but only with small piercing weapons. Lost leaves and stalks grow back in 2d4 weeks unless the central plant is slain.

Thornslinger

Thornslingers are carnivorous, spidery, white plants with dew-covered, pale yellow blossoms. They average about 8 feet in diameter and lie very close to the ground.

Thornslingers attack living creatures by firing thorns. Each thorn has a range of 30 feet and causes 1 point of damage. Since a large number of thorns are shot in a spread pattern at intended targets, being hit by one or more thorns is automatic. Damage from the thorns is 2d4 to any creature within 30 feet, once per round. They have virtually inexhaustible supplies of thorns, and are found in close clusters. Since the shower of thorns is their only defense, thornslingers are often found in out-of-the-way places, such as pits or inaccessible caves, or growing on brick and stone walls.

The leaves and central stem of a thornslinger are covered with a strong adhesive sap. Those who touch it are held fast if they have Strength 13 or less, until they are freed or digested. Characters with Strength 13 or greater can break free in 1d4 rounds.

Once a victim is caught by the dew, the thornslinger secretes digestive acids, causing 1-3 hp damage per round.

Thornslingers are not very flammable, but flame causes normal damage. Open flame is extinguished after one round and oil burns for only two rounds.

Tri-flower Frond

The deep green stalks of this plant are topped by trumpet-shaped flowers of vivid orange, bright yellows, and intense red; other color combinations are possible, but rare.

Each flower has its own function. The orange one shoots 2d4 pollen-covered tendrils, each 3 feet long; any creature struck must make a successful saving throw vs. poison or fall into a coma for 1d4 hours. The plant's sensitive rootlets tell the yellow blossom where to find the slumbering victim; the yellow bloom bends over and shakes down a shower of sticky enzyme that causes 2d4 points of damage per round until washed off (damage is reduced by 1 point per flask of water; complete immersion in water removes the sap in one round). The red blossom extends tendrils into the victim, draining body fluids at a rate of 1d6 points of damage per round.

Yellow Musk Creeper and Zombie

The yellow musk creeper is a plant that attacks humanoids, draining Intelligence and turning them into yellow musk zombies. Both creeper and zombie are immune to *charm*, *hold*, *illusion*, *sleep*, and other mind-affecting attacks.

The creeper is a large, light green climbing plant with leaves like ivy, 1d4 dark green buds, and 2d6 bright yellow flowers with splashes of purple. It can cover an area up to 20 feet square from its single bulbous root. Damage done to the plant is disregarded unless the root is attacked, for the vine eventually grows back from the main root. The creeper has a sweet, entrancing odor while dormant.

Creepers are dormant until a creature approaches within 10 feet; then the nearest flowers turn toward the prey and puff musky pollen. A victim hit by the pollen must make a successful saving throw vs. spell or be *entranced* and walk toward the plant, resisting all those who try to prevent it. When the victim reaches the creeper, a green bulb extends its roots into the victim's head, and reach the brain in two rounds. The victim loses 1d4 points of Intelligence per round after that.

A victim reduced to 0 Intelligence or less dies instantly; a victim reduced to Intelligence 1 or 2 becomes a yellow musk zombie under the creeper's control. If the plant dies before reducing its prey to zombie status, 1 point of Intelligence is regained per day, or a *heal* spell will restore lost Intelligence instantly. If the mother plant is destroyed first, a zombie can be cured by a *neutralize poison* followed by a *heal* spell and four weeks of complete rest.

Only man-sized humanoids become yellow musk zombies; the creeper can control one zombie for every two flowers. A zombie acquires yellow skin and a glazed look, but otherwise looks as it did before, wearing the same clothes and armor and wielding any weapon it had held at the time of its conversion. It has the same hit points as before, but attacks as a 2 HD monster. It can cast no spells, nor receive bonuses for high ability scores. The zombie can move up to 100 feet from the creeper. Yellow musk zombies are not true undead and cannot be turned. A zombie serves the creeper for about two months before moving off at least 200 feet and dying; the seedling that has been growing in its head quickly sprouts, flowers, and becomes a new creeper.

Plant, Intelligent

	Hangman Tree	Kelpie	Obliviax	Quickwood	Shambling Mound	Strangle-weed	Sundew, Giant	Thorny
CLIMATE/TERRAIN:	Temperate or subtropical forest	Temperate or tropical saltwater	Any warm land	Any forest with oaks	Swamps or wet subterranean	Subtropical or tropical ocean	Temperate or tropical forest	Warm, wet forests or caves
FREQUENCY:	Very rare	Very rare	Rare	Very rare	Rare	Common	Uncommon	Very rare
ORGANIZATION:	Solitary	Solitary	Colony	Solitary	Solitary	Bed	Solitary	Pack
ACTIVITY CYCLE:	Day	Any	Any	Any	Any	Any	Day	Any
DIET:	Carnivore	Carnivore	Soil, water, memories	Soil, water	Omnivore	Carnivore	Carnivore	Carnivore
INTELLIGENCE:	Low (5-7)	Low-Avg. (5-10)	Average (8)	Very (11-12)	Low (5-7)	Animal (1)	Semi- (2-4)	Animal (1)
TREASURE:	Incidental	D	Nil	Special	B, T, X	J-N, Q, C	Nil	Nil
ALIGNMENT:	Neutral (evil)	Neutral evil	Neutral evil	Neutral	Neutral	Neutral	Neutral	Neutral
NO. APPEARING:	1	1-4	2-12	1 (90%) or 2-4 (10%)	1-3	3-12	1-4	2-20
ARMOR CLASS:	3/5	3	10	5	0	6	7	3
MOVEMENT:	0; see below	9, Sw 12	0	1 (roots 3)	6	0	1	15
HIT DICE:	6, +1 hp per year	5	1-2 hp	5-10	8-11	2-4	8	4
THAC0:	7	Nil	20	5-6 HD: 15 7-8 HD: 13 9-10 HD: 11	8 HD: 13 9-10 HD: 11 11 HD: 9	2 HD: 19 3-4 HD: 17	13	17
NO. OF ATTACKS:	3	0	0	1	2	1	6 per target	1
DAMAGE/ATTACK:	1-3	0	0	3-12	2-16/2-16	See below	1-3	2-5
SPECIAL ATTACKS:	See below	See below	See below	Roots	Suffocation	Crushing	Suffocation	Thorn rake
SPECIAL DEFENSES:	See below	See below	See below	See below	See below	Nil	See below	Nil
MAGIC RESISTANCE:	See below	Nil	Nil	Nil	Nil	Nil	Nil	Nil
SIZE:	H-G (20'+ tall)	M (6'-7' tall)	T (6" square)	L (12'+ tall)	L (6'-9' tall)	L (7'-12' long)	M (3'-4' tall)	M (4' long)
MORALE:	Champion (15)	Elite (13)	Average (9)	Champion (15-16)	Fanatic (17-18)	Average (9)	Steady (11)	Steady (11-12)
XP VALUE:	1,400	420	35	5 HD: 2,000 (+1,000 for each added Hit Die)	8 HD: 6,000 (+1000 for each added Hit Die)	2 HD: 120 3 HD: 175 4 HD: 270	2,000	175

Like other breeds of dangerous plants, these are not at all defenseless. Some are the unnatural results of arcane influences, while others may have evolved naturally.

Hangman Tree

This tree is named for its noose-like vines. Hangman trees are deciduous, resembling thick oaks with few branches and sparse foliage. Knot-like sensory organs are usually located high on the trunk. In the area where the tree's main branches split off, there is an opening which leads to the creature's acid-filled "stomach." The lower trunk has a slash-like opening for the expulsion of indigestibles. Saplings can move at 6 feet an hour, while older trees can move only 2 feet an hour.

Their shallow root systems and small number of leaves require them to supplement their diet by direct ingestion of protein, so each tree traps prey. During freezing weather, a taproot is put down and the tree is dormant.

A hangman tree can release a hallucinatory perfume at will, and it does so when prey is 30-80 feet away. Those who inhale the perfume believe the hangman tree to be a normal tree, or even a treant, depending on the mood of the tree. Mature and older hangman trees can speak halting Common.

The tree attacks by dropping noose-like vines around prey. Although each tree has 1d4+5 appendages, it can control only three of them at any one time. It takes 1d8+12 points of damage to sever a vine; this is in addition to the damage needed to kill the tree. Vines are AC 5, while the main tree is AC 3. When in contact with a victim, the tree inflicts 1-3 points of damage per round as the vine tightens and lifts its prey (1,000-pound limit) to the opening in the upper trunk. This requires four rounds. One attempt at a bend bars/lift gates roll can be made to break free;

victims who fail the roll cannot escape. On the fifth round after being picked up, the victim is dropped into the hangman tree's stomach. The victim suffers 3d4 points of acid damage per round until dead, and is then digested. Escape from the stomach is impossible. Many sharp growths surround the top of the opening, they point inward and down. About three man-sized victims can fit in the tree's stomach at one time.

A hangman tree draws power from its environment. It has 5% resistance to magic per decade of age, up to a maximum of 95%. However, the tree is vulnerable to elemental attacks. *Lightning* that passes its magic resistance inflicts double damage; extreme cold shocks the tree into dormancy until it thaws. Darkness also causes it to slow its activities, so it functions at half efficiency (three attacks per two rounds).

Hangman trees have no interest in treasure and, because they move constantly, it is unlikely that treasure would be found near one, although they do expel undigestible items periodically.

Age guide: 0-4 years, non-combatant sprout, 1 hp/HD, no attacks; 5-20 years, sapling, 2-3 hp/HD; 21-75 years, mature tree, 4-5 hp/HD; 76-150 years, old tree, 6-7 hp/HD; 151+ years, ancient tree, 8 hp/HD.

Kelpie

The kelpie is a mass of animate seaweed, able to alter its form to resemble a green-clad woman, a hippocampus, or a green horse. It lives to drown the foolish., and can communicate telepathically with those in its embrace.

When a humanoid male approaches, the kelpie reshapes to appear as a woman or a mount; its imitation is a grotesque mockery, 95% detectable in daylight. Once per day, however, the kelpie can cast a *charm* on a humanoid male, who suffers a −2

293

Plant, Intelligent

penalty to his saving throw. If he fails to save, he perceives the kelpie as a desirable woman or mount, leaps into the water, and swims on to possess the kelpie. The kelpie wraps itself around the charmed victim, who happily drowns, taking 2d10 points of damage per round until he surfaces for air, is protected from drowning, or dies. The kelpie takes the body back to her lair to devour.

Victims who can breathe water or who otherwise do not drown, happily entwine themselves in the kelpie's embrace, which confuses her, though she may welcome the victim's continued activity.

A kelpie in the form of a woman or horse can travel onto land for 1-3 hours. She tries to charm a victim to protect her until she returns to the water. He will do anything he can to protect his beloved kelpie, though he may be enraged by his companions' perceived treachery. The effect of this charm ends, only if the kelpie dies, freeing any victims still alive.

Kelpies maintain body temperature equal to that of their surroundings. Due to their water-drenched forms, they take only half damage from fire (none if a saving throw is made).

There are various legends about the creations of kelpies. They are said to have been created by a sea god to punish sailors, in a time before women were sailors; or created by a female elemental princess of water, Olhydra, who made those of her own gender immune to kelpies' powers.

Kelpies reproduce by increasing in size to 7 feet, then breaking into two or four smaller kelpies. They can do this once a month, if victims are plentiful and the local fish do not feed on them too much.

Obliviax

Obliviax, or memory moss, is an evil black moss with the ability to steal memories, even memorized spells. It grows in small patches and must have sunlight to spur reproduction by spores, though it needs no light for growth. It prefers a balance of wet and dry, and cannot abide cold temperatures.

The moss senses intelligent creatures within 60 feet; it chooses one, preferring wizards, then other spellcasters. This victim must make a saving throw vs. spells or lose all memory of the last 24 hours. The obliviax continues to attack once per round until it succeeds and then makes no more attacks for 24 hours. If an obliviax with stolen memories is attacked, it forms part of itself into a tiny moss imitation of the creature whose memories it stole. This mossling remains attached to the parent moss and defends it by casting stolen spells.

To regain stolen memories, a victim must eat the living obliviax, which takes one round. If a saving throw vs. poison is successful, the eater regains all stolen memories and spells; if the saving throw fails, the eater becomes very ill for 3d6 turns. Extra memories and spells can be gained by eating obliviax which has fed on someone else recently. Spells can be used by the eater, but all such memories fade within a day.

A *potion of forgetfulness* can be distilled from obliviax, and its spores can be used to make an elixir to restore the memories of the forgetful or senile.

Quickwood

Also called the spy tree, this plant appears to be an oak, although close examination reveals that it has a visage and sensory organs that resemble a distorted human face. It is 90% unlikely that the "face" is noticed unless the observer is within 10 feet of the quickwood. The creature has excellent senses, with 120-foot infravision and the ability to detect vibrations through its roots, and aerial movements through its leaves.

The quickwood seldom moves, but it sends its roots up to 90 feet, through loose topsoil, to seize and hold immobile any creature weighing under 1,000 pounds. Roots cause no damage. They

are too strong to be broken and take no damage from blunt weapons, and only 1 point of damage from piercing weapons. Edged weapons can sever roots, which are treated as large creatures with 10 hp each; damage inflicted to the roots does not count toward the tree's total. The quickwood will allow up to six of its roots to be severed before it withdraws the other 1d6+6 to safety. The roots pull prey to the quickwood's mouth, which can clamp down to cause 3d4 points of damage to anything touching it.

The quickwood can perspire and drench itself, so it is immune to fire; it is immune to lightning, poisons, and gasses. It is also immune to most other spells which do not affect plants specifically, including all mind-affecting spells. If attacked by a spell, the quickwood absorbs some or all of the spell's energy, and uses it to radiate *fear* in a radius of 10 feet per spell level absorbed. The spellcaster must make a saving throw vs. spells; if the save fails, all the spell's energy is siphoned into the *fear* effect. Otherwise, the spell has normal effects, and *fear* is simply a side effect.

The quickwood can control up to 2d4 normal oaks within one mile, using them to gather information.

Although it gathers no treasure, it may be *charmed* or otherwise convinced to guard treasure, which may be placed in the quickwood's trunk. If acting as a guardian for some other being, a quickwood can make a hollow drumming sound which can be heard for a mile or more.

Shambling Mound

Shambling mounds, or shamblers, appear to be heaps of rotting vegetation. They are actually an intelligent form of plant life, with a roughly humanoid shape, and a brain-like control center in its "chest" area. A shambler has a 6-foot girth on its lower half, tapering to about 2 feet at its "head."

Shambling mounds are found only in regions of dense rainfall and vegetation. Dismal swamps, marshes, and rain forests are their favorite living areas, but some wet, subterranean places also serve as shambler lairs. They are solitary beasts, rarely living in the same area with other shamblers—usually only in areas where the food source is constant, near famous ruins, or abandoned gold mines.

Shamblers are almost totally silent and invisible in their natural surroundings; opponents suffer a −3 penalty to surprise rolls. A shambler often lies in a shallow bog, waiting for some creature to walk onto it, then it attacks. The creatures are excellent swimmers as well, and they have been known to sneak into the camps of unsuspecting travelers at night.

A shambling mound attacks with huge, arm-like appendages; a victim hit by both arms in the same round is entangled in the creature's slimy vines and rotting vegetable matter. Entangled creatures suffocate in the slime in 2d4 rounds unless the shambler is killed, or the victim breaks free with a successful bend bars/lift gates roll.

Because of the vegetation which covers its critical inner body, the shambling mound is immune to blunt weapons, and takes only half damage from piercing and slashing weapons. The creature is immune to fire, and takes half or no damage from cold, depending on whether it makes its saving throw. Lightning actually causes a shambler to grow, adding 1-foot to its height, as well as 1 HD and appropriate hit points, for each lightning-based attack used against it.

Because of the location of its brain, the shambler cannot be killed by lopping off its head or limbs. The remaining vines along the torso join together to form a new extremity within one round. Only when enough of the shambling mound has been hacked away, will it finally die. A wounded shambler need only rest in a damp clump of foliage to heal; it rises again in 12 hours, fully healed, and probably angry.

Since shamblers gain power from electrical attacks, there are rumors of shambling mounds with 20 or more Hit Dice. Since they often live in the same areas as will-o'-wisps, there may be truth to such rumors, and giant shamblers may inhabit deep, dark swamps and jungles.

Strangleweed

Strangleweed is an intelligent kelp found in relatively warm sea water. A bed of these carnivorous plants are indistinguishable from normal seaweed. A strangleweed patch will cover an oval area of 3d4 square feet, on the sea's surface; 3d4 fronds of varying lengths (1d6 + 6 feet) hanging downward from the patch.

Any creature near enough is attacked, a hit indicating that the frond has entwined about its victim. Any victim entwined suffers a −2 penalty to attack rolls. Each frond has 4d4 Strength points, and the other fronds add their Strength to the total. A victim compares Strength with the strangleweed; Strengths of 18/51 to 18/00 are rounded up to 19. If the victim is stronger, each point of difference in Strength gives a 10% chance of escape, which can be attempted each round.

If the frond is stronger than the victim, the victim cannot escape alone, and the fronds crush the victim for 1 point of damage, per point of Strength difference. If the two are of equal Strength, the victim cannot escape, but takes no damage.

Giant Sundew

A giant sundew appears to be a 3- to 4 foot-mound of grayish green, tarry ropes or rags. The air around one is fly infested and holds a thick odor like sweet syrup. Preferring shaded places in which to grow, the sundew has only hair-like roots that anchor it

lightly in place. It can pull itself slowly along the ground using sticky tendrils. Due to the plant's sticky exterior, missiles and fire-based attacks inflict only half damage.

The sundew detects moving creatures by vibrations. When anything moves within 5 feet of it, it lashes out with its tendrils. Its body is covered with hundreds of tendrils, and a maximum of six can attack each creature in range, each round. The tendrils exude sticky globs of sap. For every three tendrils that attach to a victim, the victim suffers a −1 penalty to attack rolls. The sap contains a mild enzyme that inflicts 1 point of damage per round for each tendril striking the victim, regardless of whether or not the tendril is still attached. A successful open doors roll breaks a tendril; each tendril must be checked separately, up to once per tendril, per round.

If a sundew's attack roll is an unmodified 20, it has struck the victim's mouth and nose, clogging them with sap; suffocation occurs in 1d3 + 1 rounds unless the sap is removed. The sap may be dissolved by vinegar or alcohol.

Thorny

Thornies are dog-like plant creatures trained as guards by mold men. They are covered by a spiky bark. A thorny attacks first with its bite; if the bite hits, the creature tries to roll its body against its victim, causing 3d4 points of damage with a successful hit. Thornies reproduce by laying egg-like seeds in the ground. A small tree sprouts from the seed, eventually producing buds which grow into small thornies. Thornies can be trained if raised from buds.

Poltergeist

CLIMATE/TERRAIN:	Subterranean
FREQUENCY:	Rare
ORGANIZATION:	Group
ACTIVITY CYCLE:	Night
DIET:	None
INTELLIGENCE:	Low (5-7)
TREASURE:	Nil
ALIGNMENT:	Lawful evil

NO. APPEARING:	1-8
ARMOR CLASS:	10
MOVEMENT:	6
HIT DICE:	$1/2$
THAC0:	15
NO. OF ATTACKS:	1
DAMAGE/ATTACK:	Nil
SPECIAL ATTACKS:	Fear
SPECIAL DEFENSES:	Invisibility, silver or magical weapon to hit
MAGIC RESISTANCE:	Nil
SIZE:	M (6' tall)
MORALE:	Average (10)
XP VALUE:	120

Poltergeists are the spirits of restless dead. They are similar to haunts but are more malevolent. They hate living things and torment them constantly, by breaking furniture, throwing heavy objects, and making haunting noises. They are often, but not always, attached to a particular area.

Poltergeists are always invisible. Those who can see invisible objects describe them as humans whose features have been twisted at the sight of horrors. They wear rags and are covered with chains and other heavy objects that represent a multitude of evil deeds that these creatures have committed against themselves as well as others.

Combat: A poltergeist attacks by throwing a heavy object—any nearby object that a strong human can throw will suffice. It has the same chance to hit as a 5-HD monster (hence its adjusted THAC0 in the statistics given above). If the victim is struck he suffers no damage (treat the use of deadly weapons such as knives and swords as terrifying near misses), but he must roll a successful saving throw vs. spell or flee in terror in a random direction (choose available exits away from the poltergeist and determine randomly) for 2d12 rounds before recovering. There is a 50% chance that the victim drops whatever he was holding (he drops it at the start of his flight). Once a person rolls a successful saving throw, he is immune to further *fear* attempts by the poltergeist in that area.

Those who try to hit a poltergeist but cannot detect invisible objects suffer a -4 penalty to their attack roll. A poltergeist is harmed only by silver or magical weapons. Sprinkled holy water or a strongly presented holy symbol drives back a poltergeist but cannot harm it. Poltergeists that are bonded to the area of their death are hard to dispel; these are treated as if they were ghouls on the Turning Undead table. Wandering poltergeists may be turned or destroyed by a priest as if they were skeletons.

Habitat/Society: Some say that poltergeists are the spirits of those who committed heinous crimes that went unpunished in life. Whatever their origins, poltergeists are malevolent spirits whose activities can be anything from annoying to deadly. Their purpose in existence is to haunt and disrupt the lives of those who still live.

Poltergeists often haunt families and partnerships. In the latter case, they haunt their place of business, striking almost as much terror in death as they did in life.

A poltergeist is often strongly bonded to a particular place, the place where its corporeal existence ended. Bonded poltergeists almost never wander more than 100 feet from this place. A few are wandering spirits, doomed never to find their way home. Bonded spirits are stronger than wandering spirits (wanderers never have more than 3 hit points).

Places where poltergeists are particularly strong have been known to have *phantom shifts*. These extremely rare and terrifying illusions take the character encountering the poltergeist back in time, to the time when the poltergeist was still alive. They often reveal why the being was transformed into a poltergeist. Characters in a *phantom shift* may interact freely with the illusion, but any attempt to harm the illusion shatters it and returns the characters to the present time; likewise, any attempt on the part of the illusion to attack the characters also shatters the illusion without any harm being done. The illusion may continue at different times, or may repeat itself endlessly. No one can predict exactly when a place will experience a *phantom shift*, but they seem to occur on the anniversary of the poltergeist's death.

Ecology: These spirits, which are terrifying and pitiable at the same time, do not consume food and do not collect treasure. Poltergeists dissolve when slain or laid to rest.

	Black	White	Dun	Brown
CLIMATE/TERRAIN:	Any underground	Arctic plain	Arid desert	Any marsh
FREQUENCY:	Uncommon	Rare	Rare	Uncommon
ORGANIZATION:	Solitary	Solitary	Solitary	Solitary
ACTIVITY CYCLE:	Any	Any	Any	Any
DIET:	Any	Any	Any	Any
INTELLIGENCE:	Non- (0)	Non- (0)	Non- (0)	Non- (0)
TREASURE:	Nil	Nil	Nil	Nil
ALIGNMENT:	Neutral	Neutral	Neutral	Neutral
NO. APPEARING:	1 (1-4)	1 (1-4)	1 (1-4)	1 (1-4)
ARMOR CLASS:	6	8	7	5
MOVEMENT:	6	9	12	6
HIT DICE:	10	9	8+1	11
THAC0:	11	11	13	9
NO. OF ATTACKS:	1	1	1	1
DAMAGE/ATTACK:	3-24	7-28	4-24	5- 20
SPECIAL ATTACKS:	See below	See below	See below	See below
SPECIAL DEFENSES:	See below	See below	See below	See below
MAGIC RESISTANCE:	Nil	Nil	Nil	Nil
SIZE:	S-L (3'-8')	S-L (3'- 8')	S-L (3'-8')	S-L (3'-8')
MORALE:	Special	Special	Special	Special
XP VALUE:	2,000	1,400	1,400	2,000

Puddings are voracious, puddinglike monsters composed of groups of cell colonies that scavenge and hunt for food. They typically inhabit ruins and dungeons. They have the ability to sense heat and analyze material structure from a distance of up to 90 feet to determine if something is edible. Deadly puddings attack any animals (including humans) or vegetable matter on sight.

All deadly puddings are immune to acid, cold, and poison. Lightning bolts and blows from weapons divide them into smaller puddings, each able to attack exactly as the original pudding. Fire causes normal damage, as do *magic missiles*. Puddings can ooze through cracks that are at least 1 inch wide and can travel on ceilings and walls (falling on victims as a nasty surprise) at the same speed as on a level surface.

Puddings reproduce by fission. They are adapted to live in a wide variety of climates.

Puddings starting with 11-30% of maximum possible hit points are 3 feet to 4 feet in diameter; with 31-50% of full hit points, 5 feet wide; with 51-70% of full hit points, 6 feet wide; with 71-90% of full hit points, 7 feet wide; and with 91-100% of full hit points, 8 feet wide. If a pudding is split up so it becomes less than 3 feet wide, it becomes thinner but retains its 3-foot diameter. Because puddings do not use all of their mouth openings (which cover their exposed surfaces), the smallest pudding does the same damage as the largest.

Black Puddings

Black pudding acid is highly corrosive, inflicting 3-24 points of damage per round to organic matter and dissolving a 2-inch thickness of wood equal to its diameter in one round. Black puddings also dissolve metal. Chain mail dissolves in one round, plate mail in two; each magical "plus" increases the time it takes to dissolve the metal by one round (thus *plate mail +3* takes two rounds to dissolve for being plate mail, plus three rounds for having a +3 magical bonus, for a total of five rounds).

White Puddings

These cold-loving creatures are 50% likely to be mistaken for ice and snow (guaranteeing surprise) even under the best of conditions. White puddings haunt polar regions or icy places in order to find prey, although they can live by devouring any animal or vegetable matter; even ice provides them with enough nutrition to exist. White puddings cannot affect metals but dissolve animal and vegetable materials in a single round, inflicting damage to flesh at an astonishing rate.

Dun Puddings

Adapted to dwell in arid regions, these monsters scavenge barrens and deserts and feed on silicates (sand) if animal and vegetable matter is unavailable. They dissolve leather in a single round, regardless of magical pluses. Metals are eaten at a rate half that of black puddings; chain takes two rounds to dissolve, plate four rounds, with an additional two rounds per magical plus.

Brown Puddings

This type dwells principally in marsh areas. It has a tough skin but its attack is less dangerous than other types of puddings. Brown puddings cannot affect metals but dissolve leather and wood in a single round, regardless of magical pluses.

Other pudding types are possible, at the DM's option.

Quaggoth

CLIMATE/TERRAIN:	Subterranean caves
FREQUENCY:	Rare
ORGANIZATION:	Tribal
ACTIVITY CYCLE:	Any
DIET:	Carnivore
INTELLIGENCE:	Low (5-7)
TREASURE:	Nil (O, R)
ALIGNMENT:	Neutral

NO. APPEARING:	2-24
ARMOR CLASS:	6
MOVEMENT:	12
HIT DICE:	2+2
THAC0:	19
NO. OF ATTACKS:	2 or 1
DAMAGE/ATTACK:	1-4/1-4 or by weapon
SPECIAL ATTACKS:	Berserk rage
SPECIAL DEFENSES:	Immune to poison
MAGIC RESISTANCE:	Nil
SIZE:	L (7′ + tall)
MORALE:	Elite (15-16)
XP VALUE:	Normal: 175
	Jald: 270
	Thonot: 1,400

Quaggoths are humanoids with long, shaggy, white hair covering their entire bodies. They wear no clothing. Warlike and vicious, they roam the Underdark looking for prey. Drow sometimes enslave them as guards and spider handlers.

Quaggoths speak a halting form of Undercommon, and can grasp only simple concepts. More intelligent quaggoths may also speak a few words of Duergar, Drow, or Common.

These aggressive beasts have infravision with a range of 120′. They are immune to all poisons.

Combat: Quaggoth tribes claim a certain territory as theirs and patrol it, hunting for food. Any detected animals or creatures (such as a party of adventurers) invite certain attack.

Most tribes (70%) of quaggoths do not carry weapons, and attack with their claws for 1-4 hit points of damage per hit. The remainder of quaggoth tribes carry stone clubs or axes. Those quaggoths which are or have been drow slaves carry superior weapons, such as steel battle axes or two-handed swords.

If a quaggoth is reduced to 25% or less of its original hit points, it enters a berserk fury and receives a +2 bonus to its attack and damage rolls. This rage lasts until the quaggoth dies or all enemies are dead or out of sight.

For every 12 quaggoths encountered, there will be a leader, or jald. The jald has 3+3 Hit Dice and wears leather or skins, making it AC 5. In addition, it gains a +1 bonus to damage rolls. Jalds direct combat; if no jald is present, the quaggoths will fall upon their prey, whatever it is, in an unorganized manner

Any quaggoth tribe has a 20% chance of having one or two thonots. A thonot is the quaggoth equivalent of a shaman. Instead of magic, however, thonots use psionics. A thonot will use its abilities to aid the tribe in combat, escape, or healing.

If quaggoths win combat, they take all bodies, including those of dead quaggoths, to their lair and devour them.

Psionics Summary (Thonots only):

Level	Dis/Sci/Dev	Attack/Defense	Score	PSPs
3	2/2/5	MT/MBl	15	50

Only have:
- **Psychokinesis** – **Sciences:** telekinesis. Devotions: control flames, molecular agitation.

- **Psychometabolism** – **Sciences:** shadow-form. Devotions: cell adjustment, expansion, reduction.

Habitat/Society: Quaggoths are nomadic hunters. They change territories periodically. In each new territory, they claim a central cave as a lair, leaving treasure with a few guards. The rest of the tribe hunts, returning periodically to rest and change guards.

Females are equal to males in numbers and abilities in a quaggoth tribe. For every adult quaggoth, there will be one young. Half of these young are unable to attack or defend; the other half have 1+1 HD and the same AC and attacks as adults.

Thonots control what passes for religious life among quaggoths. They oversee what few rituals there are; those rituals which are known include the daily preparation for hunting, coming of age, and death (a brief whistling to send the spirit away before the rest of the quaggoths eat the body).

Quaggoths can mate at any time of the year. They are not known to have any courtship or mating rituals. Young are born about 10 months after mating. Births are usually singular, but twins are not uncommon.

The origin of quaggoths is unknown. Some sages claim that they were once a semi-civilized race which dominated much of the Underdark through conquest and ritual sacrifice, until the drow, duergar, and other races broke their power. Others speculate they had some sort of civilization on the surface and were driven underground; this theory is supported by the quaggoths' hatred for surface-dwelling dwarves and elves.

Ecology: Quaggoths produce a few artifacts, mostly crudely carved stone items. A few seem to be talented at making necklaces with wooden, bone, or stone beads

Quaggoths fear no creature. Though they are dangerous hunters, they are just as often prey for other predators of the Underdark. Quaggoths can be trained as servants and guards if captured early.

Rakshasa

	Rakshasa	Rakshasa, Greater
CLIMATE/TERRAIN:	Tropical or sub-tropical forest, jungle, or swamp	Tropical or sub-tropical forest, jungle, or swamp
FREQUENCY:	Rare	Very rare
ORGANIZATION:	Solitary	Solitary
ACTIVITY CYCLE:	Night	Night
DIET:	Carnivore	Carnivore
INTELLIGENCE:	Very (11-12)	High (13-14)
TREASURE:	F	B,F
ALIGNMENT:	Lawful evil	Lawful evil
NO. APPEARING:	1-4	1
ARMOR CLASS:	-4	-5
MOVEMENT:	15	18
HIT DICE:	7	8+16
THAC0:	13	11
NO. OF ATTACKS:	3	3
DAMAGE/ATTACK:	1-3/1-3/2-5	1-6/1-6/2-10
SPECIAL ATTACKS:	Illusion	Illusion
SPECIAL DEFENSES:	+1 or better magical weapon to hit	+2 or better magical weapon to hit
MAGIC RESISTANCE:	Special	Special
SIZE:	M (6' tall)	M (6½' tall)
MORALE:	Champion (15-16)	Fanatic (17-18)
XP VALUE:	3,000	
Ruhk	7,000	
Rajah	7,000	
Maharajah	11,000	

Rakshasas are a race of malevolent spirits encased in flesh that hunt and torment humanity. No one knows where these creatures originate; some say they are the embodiment of nightmares.

Rakshasas stand 6 to 7 feet tall and weigh between 250 and 300 pounds. They have no uniform appearance but appear as humanoid creatures with the bodily features of various beasts (most commonly tigers and apes). Hands whose palms curve backward, away from the body, seem to be common. Rakshasas of the highest standing sometimes have several heads. All rakshasas wear human clothing of the highest quality.

Combat: Rakshasas savor fresh human meat and use illusions to get it. They have a limited form of *ESP* which allows them to disguise themselves as someone the victim trusts; the rakshasa uses this illusion as a lure and strikes when the victim is most unprepared. The rakshasa must drop the illusion when it attacks. Normally rakshasas can have magical abilities, up to the following limits: four 1st level wizard spells, three 2nd level wizard spells, two 3rd level wizard spells, and three 1st level priest spells. These are cast at 7th level ability. Rakshasas are immune to all spells lower than 8th level. An attacker needs at least a +1 magical weapon to harm a rakshasa; any weapon below +3 inflicts only half damage. However, a hit by any *blessed* crossbow bolt kills a rakshasa instantly.

Habitat/Society: Rakshasa society is bound by rigid castes. Each rakshasa is born into a particular role in life and cannot advance. Females (known as rakshasi) are fit to be consorts, honored only by their faithfulness and the fighting ability of their children. There are 1-3 females per male.

Rakshasa society is led by a rajah or maharajah, whose commands are to be obeyed without question.

Rakshasas wage war on humanity constantly, not only to feed themselves but because they believe that battle is the only way to gain honor. If confronted by humans who recognize their true appearance, they are insufferably arrogant.

A rakshasa's life varies in cycles of wild self-indulgence in times of prosperity and strict fasting and sacrifice in times of trouble or before battle. They are honorable creatures but will twist the wording of an agreement to suit their purposes. They prefer to deal with humanity by using their illusion powers to deceive and manipulate them, but are brave and forthright in battle.

Ecology: As spirits, rakshasas are virtually immortal. They produce a new generation every century to replace the rakshasas that have been slain in battle. No creatures prey on rakshasas except those who would avenge their victims. Rakshasa essence can be an ingredient in a *potion of delusion*.

Rakshasa Ruhks
About 15% of all rakshasas are greater rakashasas or ruhks, (*knights*). These warriors are the guardians of a rakshasa community. They are hit only by magical weapons of +2 or better; any weapon below +4 inflicts only half damage against them. Their spells are cast at 9th level of ability.

Rakshasa Rajahs
About 15% of all rakshasa ruhks are rakshasa rajahs, or lords. Each rajah is the leader (patriarch) of his local clan. These rulers of rakshasadom have the same abilities as a ruhk, but also have the spell casting abilities of both a 6th level priest and an 8th level wizard, cast at 11th level of ability.

Rakshasa Maharajahs
About 5% of all rakshasa rajahs are rakshasa maharajahs, or dukes. Maharajahs have the same abilities as a ruhk, but have 13+39 Hit Dice, and the spell casting abilities of a 13th level wizard and 9th level priest. A maharajah is the leader of either several small, related clans, or a single powerful clan. Maharajahs reside on the outer planes, where they rule island communities of hundreds of rakshasas, and serve as minions to even greater powers.

Rat

	Rat (Giant)	Osquip
CLIMATE/TERRAIN:	Any	Subterranean
FREQUENCY:	Common	Uncommon
ORGANIZATION:	Pack	Pack
ACTIVITY CYCLE:	Night	Night
DIET:	Scavenger	Carnivore
INTELLIGENCE:	Animal (1)	Animal (1)
	Semi- (2-4)	
TREASURE:	Nil (C in lair)	D in lair
ALIGNMENT:	Neutral (evil)	Neutral
NO. APPEARING:	1-100 (5-50)	2-24
ARMOR CLASS:	7	7
MOVEMENT:	15 (12, Sw 6)	12, Br ½
HIT DICE:	¼ (½)	3+1
THAC0:	20	16
NO. OF ATTACKS:	1	1
DAMAGE/ATTACK:	1 (1-3)	2-12
SPECIAL ATTACKS:	Disease	Nil
SPECIAL DEFENSES:	Nil	Nil
MAGIC RESISTANCE:	Nil	Nil
SIZE:	T (1' long)	S (2' at
	T (2' long)	shoulder)
MORALE:	Unreliable (2-4)	Unsteady (7)
	Unsteady (5-7)	
XP VALUE:	7 (15)	120

Rats are long-tailed rodents 5-12 inches long. They are aggressive, omnivorous, and adaptable, and they often carry diseases. Statistics in italics above refer to the giant rat. Stats without an italicized entry apply to both varieties.

The black rat is about 8 inches long, with a tail at least that long, a lean body, pointed nose, and long ears. The "black" rat is dark gray with brownish patches, and a gray or white belly. It is a good climber (climb 3) and jumper, but cannot swim.

The brown rat, also known as the sewer rat or the wharf rat, is 5-10 inches long, and its tail is shorter than the black rat's. Its eyes and ears are also smaller, but it has a larger, fatter body. Brown rats may be gray, white, black, or piebald in color. They cannot climb, but are excellent swimmers (swim 3) and burrowers. If rats infest a building, black rats inhabit the upper floors, and brown rats occupy the lower floor and the cellars.

Combat: Rats normally flee anything bigger than themselves, but a trapped rat will do anything to survive and a pack of starving rats will attack anything in order to feed. Rats attack with their sharp front teeth and often carry diseases, so that a rat bite has a 5% chance of infecting its victim with a serious disease unless the victim makes a successful saving throw vs. poison. Normal rats fear fire, but brave it when very hungry.

A swarm of rats can be treated as a single monster having an assigned number of Hit Dice and automatically causing damage each round to small creatures in the swarm's area. A typical pack might cover a 10-× 10-foot area, have 4 HD, and inflict 4 points of damage per round. Weapons have little effect on a pack, but area effect spells and some other attacks (such as flaming oil) are effective. When the pack has lost its hit points, it is considered dispersed and unable to inflict mass damage.

Habitat/Society: The chief purpose of rats is to find food. Packs often burrow into and eat food stores. Rats nest almost anywhere, chewing cloth, paper, or wood to make a nest.

Ecology: Rats are very prolific, breeding three to five times a year. Brown rats produce 2d4+6 young per litter, while a black rat litter contains only 5-6 young. Both types of rats are omnivorous. Brown rats are considered to be more aggressive than black rats. Their teeth are extremely powerful; they have been known to gnaw holes in lead pipes. Rats have a lifespan of two to four years.

Brush Rats

Brush rats (also known as trade rats and pack rats) belong to a much less aggressive family of rats known as wood rats. They are slate gray above and white on their underbellies. They are nearly the size of brown rats. Brush rats build nests or burrows in forested areas. They are attracted to small, shiny objects and sometimes steal them and carry them to their hoard. Pack rats are herbivores and will not attack humans. They do not carry diseases. Brush rats can be trained.

Giant Rats

These vile beasts plague underground areas such as crypts and dungeons. Their burrows honeycomb many graveyards, where they cheat ghouls of their prizes by tunneling to newly interred corpses. Giant rats are brown/black in color with white underbellies, and are related to the brown rat, with fatter bodies and shorter tails. As with normal rats, any creature bitten by a giant rat has a 5% chance per wound of catching a debilitating disease; a successful saving throw vs. poison prevents catching the disease. Giant rats avoid attacking strong parties unless driven by hunger or commanded by creatures such as vampires and wererats. Giant rats are fearful of fire and flee from it except if driven by hunger or magic. They are excellent swimmers and can attack in water as well as on land.

Osquip

The osquip is a multi-legged rodent the size of a small dog. It is hairless, with a huge head and large teeth. Most have six legs, but some (25%) have eight, and a few (5%) have 10. The creatures' leathery hides are pale yellow in color.

Osquips build small, carefully hidden tunnels, and their teeth are sharp enough to dig through stone. If someone enters an area in which there are osquip tunnels, the creatures can emerge quickly, and opponents receive a −5 to surprise rolls. The osquip are territorial and attack fearlessly and ferociously. Osquips are not afraid of fire, but are poor swimmers (50% drown, 50% paddle with a movement rate of 1).

Osquips are difficult to domesticate, but jermlaine and a few wizards have succeeded by giving the creatures gems, for they collect shiny objects. Osquip leather is soft and water-resistant, and their teeth can be used in digging magic.

Remorhaz

CLIMATE/TERRAIN:	Arctic plain
FREQUENCY:	Very rare
ORGANIZATION:	Solitary
ACTIVITY CYCLE:	Day
DIET:	Carnivore
INTELLIGENCE:	Animal (1)
TREASURE:	D
ALIGNMENT:	Neutral

NO. APPEARING:	1
ARMOR CLASS:	Overall 0, head 2, underbelly 4
MOVEMENT:	12
HIT DICE:	7-14
THAC0:	13 (7-8 HD),
	11 (9-10 HD),
	9 (11-12 HD),
	7 (13-14 HD)
NO. OF ATTACKS:	1
DAMAGE/ATTACK:	Bite: (7-8 HD) 4-24; (9-12 HD) 5-30;
	(13-14 HD) 6-36
SPECIAL ATTACKS:	Swallow whole, heat lash
SPECIAL DEFENSES:	Melt metal
MAGIC RESISTANCE:	75%
SIZE:	G (21'-42' long)
MORALE:	Elite (13-14)
XP VALUE:	
7 HD	5,000 (+1000 per Hit Die over 9)

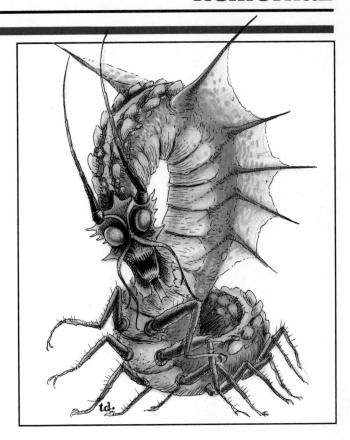

Remorhaz, sometimes known as *polar worms*, inhabit only chill arctic wastes. They are very aggressive predators that devour any animal matter, including humans, demihumans, and humanoids; they have even been known to attack frost giants.

A remorhaz has a segmented body with a winged head and neck, standing on dozens of chitinous legs. Remorhaz have an ice blue color everywhere except on their backs, where a streak of white sets off the many protrusions located there. The size of a remorhaz is determined by its Hit Dice: a 7 Hit Dice remorhaz is 21 feet long, an 8 Hit Dice creature is 24 feet long, etc. Their language consists of roaring, bellowing, and howling.

Combat: In combat the remorhaz beats its small wings, raising up the front quarter of its body. It then snaps itself forward, striking with blinding speed. They are able to swallow prey whole on an unmodified attack roll of 20; any victim swallowed is killed instantly by the intense heat inside the creature. When aroused, the remorhaz secretes a substance that causes its intestines to become very hot and its back protrusions actually glow cherry red from excess heat. Any nonmagical weapon melts from contact with its back and any creature touched by these surfaces suffers 10-100 points of damage.

To determine where a blow has struck a remorhaz, consider where the attacker is in respect to the remorhaz. While the remorhaz is rearing to attack, a blow from the front hits the relatively soft underbelly. When the remorhaz is attacking a creature, any blow inflicted hits the head unless the underside is specifically stated as the object of the attack. In all other cases, the body is the object of the attack, subject to adjudication by the DM.

Remorhaz are slower than most polar dwellers, so they prefer to burrow into the snow and surface when they hear prey nearby, hoping to achieve surprise. Remorhaz have infravision to 60 feet.

Habitat/Society: A remorhaz lair usually consists of a number of large, smoothly rounded tunnels in ice and snow or rock, gradually descending to a large central chamber. Tunnels in ice and snow will be very slippery, as the remorhaz's hot back repeatedly melts the snow, leaving it to refreeze. The central chamber is only about twice the size of a remorhaz, while the central chamber of a nesting pair is about four times their size and may contain icy stalactites.

Remorhaz have a hunting range of 60 miles. Except where the game has been hunted to extinction, these creatures tolerate the presence of other remorhaz in their hunting grounds.

Ecology: Remorhaz are carnivores, sustaining themselves with a diet of deer, elk, and even polar bears. They mate in late summer and stay together for two months before departing to live solitary existences. Remorhaz mate every year but can produce offspring only three or four times in a lifetime; the female lays a clutch of one or two grey-blue eggs, remaining with the eggs at all times, coiling around them to keep them warm; if the eggs are left in the freezing cold for only one minute, they will never hatch. Young remorhaz have 1 Hit Die at birth and grow to 7 Hit Dice after four months, when they leave the nest. Immature remorhaz have weaker armor (+2 AC in all locations); 1-3 Hit Dice remorhaz can only bite for 2-12 points of damage, while 4-6 Hit Dice creatures inflict 3-18 points of damage. From birth, the young remorhaz have all the powers of an adult.

Remorhaz have lifespans of 30 years. Their eggs are valued at 500 gold pieces and are eagerly sought because these creatures can be trained to be excellent guards. However, a remorhaz can be trained to obey only one or two masters, and will attack its master if hungry enough. The heat secretion of a rhemorhaz, thrym, is valuable as a component for heat-related magical items and can be sold to alchemists for 5-10 gold pieces per flask. The remorhaz will contain 10 flasks worth of thrym per Hit Die.

Revenant

CLIMATE/TERRAIN:	Any
FREQUENCY:	Very rare
ORGANIZATION:	Solitary
ACTIVITY CYCLE:	Night
DIET:	Not applicable
INTELLIGENCE:	See below
TREASURE:	Nil
ALIGNMENT:	Neutral

NO. APPEARING:	1
ARMOR CLASS:	10
MOVEMENT:	9
HIT DICE:	8
THAC0:	13 (base)
NO. OF ATTACKS:	1
DAMAGE/ATTACK:	2-16
SPECIAL ATTACKS:	Paralyzation
SPECIAL DEFENSES:	See below
MAGIC RESISTANCE:	See below
SIZE:	M (5'-6')
MORALE:	See below
XP VALUE:	3,000

Revenants are vengeful spirits that have risen from the grave to destroy their killers.

The revenant appears as a spectral, decayed version of its appearance at the time of its death. Its pallid skin is drawn tightly over its bones. The flesh is cold and clammy. The sunken eyes are dull and heavy-lidded but, when the revenant faces his intended victim, the eyes blaze with unnatural intensity. The revenant bears an aura of sadness, anger, and determination.

Combat: A revenant attacks by hooking its claw-like hands around its victim's throat. This strangulation causes 2d8 points of damage each round. It will not release its grip until either the revenant is destroyed or its victim is dead. It never uses weapons.

If the revenant stares into its victim's eyes, that person must roll a successful saving throw vs. spell or be paralyzed with terror for 2d4 rounds. This power affects only the revenant's killer.

If a revenant is dismembered, the severed parts act independently, as though guided by the revenant's mind. The revenant's willpower causes the parts to reunite. It can also regenerate 3 hit points of damage each round, except for fire damage. It is immune to acid and gas. Although a revenant's body can be cut apart by normal or magical weapons, the damage is temporary and does not destroy the revenant. Only burning destroys a revenant—the original body must be completely consumed and reduced to ash.

Although it is undead, the revenant is motivated entirely by self-will. Therefore, as it is not inherently evil, it is not affected by holy water, holy/unholy symbols, or other religious paraphernalia. It cannot be turned by priests nor can it be raised or resurrected.

Habitat/Society: Under exceptional circumstances, a character who has died a violent death may rise as a revenant from the grave to wreak vengeance on his killer(s). In order to make this transition, two requirements must be met. The dead character's Constitution must be 18 and either his Wisdom or Intelligence must be greater than 16. Also, the total of his six ability scores must be 90 or more. Even if these conditions are met, there is only a 5% chance that the dead character becomes a revenant.

If *both* Intelligence and Wisdom are over 16, the chance increases to 10%. If Intelligence, Wisdom, and Constitution are all 18, the creature can shift at will into any freshly killed humanoid, if the revenant rolls a successful saving throw vs. death.

If the character died a particularly violent death, it may be unable to reoccupy its original body. In this case, the spirit occupies any available, freshly-dead corpse. However, the revenant's killer and associates always see the revenant as the person they killed.

The revenant retains all the abilities it possessed in its previous life and has at least the hit points and saving throws of an 8-Hit Die creature. Its alignment is neutral, regardless of its alignment in life. It can converse fluently in its original language, although the stiffness of its vocal cords deters it from speaking except under extreme circumstances, such as when casting a spell at its killer.

The sole purpose of the revenant's brief existence is to wreak vengeance on its killer, together with anyone who may have aided in the murder. It stops at nothing to achieve its purpose and can locate its intended victim wherever he may be. Accomplices are also tracked down if they are in the company of the killer, but if they are elsewhere they are ignored until the killer is dealt with. If the associates of the killer are with him in a party, they are dealt with after the killer is dead.

The revenant's body does decay, though at a slower rate than normal. Within three to six months, the corpse decomposes rapidly and the revenant's spirit returns to the plane from which it came. When the revenant has completed its mission, the body immediately disintegrates and its spirit finally rests in peace.

A revenant does not attack innocents except in self-defense. If necessary, the revenant can use cunning to get to its prey.

Ecology: Revenants give murder victims a chance to avenge their own murders. They pursue their goals alone without desire or need for allies. However, if the revenant faces a powerful foe able to destroy the revenant's new form, the revenant may decide to use adventurers as pawns in its quest.

Roc

CLIMATE/TERRAIN:	Subtropical/Mountains
FREQUENCY:	Rare
ORGANIZATION:	Solitary
ACTIVITY CYCLE:	Day
DIET:	Omnivore
INTELLIGENCE:	Animal (1)
TREASURE:	C
ALIGNMENT:	Neutral

NO. APPEARING:	1-2
ARMOR CLASS:	4
MOVEMENT:	3, Fl 30
HIT DICE:	18
THAC0:	5
NO. OF ATTACKS:	2 or 1
DAMAGE/ATTACK:	3-18/3-18 or 4-24
SPECIAL ATTACKS:	Surprise
SPECIAL DEFENSES:	Nil
MAGIC RESISTANCE:	Nil
SIZE:	G (60' long + wingspan)
MORALE:	Steady (11)
XP VALUE:	10,000

Looking almost too big to be real, rocs are huge birds of prey that dwell in warm mountainous regions and are known for carrying off large animals (cattle, horses, elephants) for food.

Rocs resemble large eagles, with either dark brown plumage or all golden feathers from head to tail. In a few rare instances, rocs of all red, black or white are sighted, but such sightings are often considered bad omens. These giant birds are 60 feet long from beak to tail feathers, with wingspans as wide as 120 feet.

Combat: The roc swoops down upon prey, seizes it in powerful talons, and carries it off to the roc's lair to be devoured at leisure. The resulting damage is 3d6 per claw. Most of the time (95%), a roc carries off its prey only if both claws hit. If the prey was hit by only one claw, the roc usually lets go, then turns around and attempts another grab. Once the prey has been secured, the roc flies back to its nest. If the creature resists, the roc strikes with its beak, inflicting 4d6 points of damage per hit.

Should a human, humanoid, or demihuman be captured, there is a 65% chance that the victim's arms are both pinned to his sides, making impossible melee weapon attacks or spellcasting that requires hand gestures. A roc will let go of its prey if it suffers damage equal to a quarter of its hit points. A roc can pick up two targets simultaneously if they are within 10 feet of each other.

A roc usually cruises at a height of about 300 feet, seeking out likely prey with its sharp eyes. When a good target is found, it swoops down silently. The stealth of this first attack imposes a -5 penalty to its opponents' surprise rolls.

Habitat/Society: Roc lairs are vast nests made of trees, branches, and the like. They inhabit the highest mountains in warm regions. Rocs are not given to nesting close to each other, with a nest rarely being located within 20 miles of another nest. There is a 15% chance of finding 1d4 +1 eggs in a roc nest. These eggs sell for 2d6 x 100 gp to merchants specializing in exotic items. As may be expected, rocs fight to the death to protect these nests and their contents, gaining a +1 bonus to their attack roll.

The treasure of a roc is usually strewn about and below the nest, for the creature does not value such. It is the residue from its victims. If the roc has been seizing pack horses and mules, some of that treasure may be merchant's wares such as spices, rugs, tapestries, perfume, rich clothing, or jewels.

The roc ranges for food three times a day; about an hour after sunrise, at noon, and an hour before sunset. If there are young in the nest, a fourth feeding, approximately two hours after noon, is added to keep the young strong and well-fed.

Ecology: Rocs are occasionally tamed and used by cloud or storm giants. Good-aligned giants do not allow their rocs to attack civilized areas and the animals therein.

As mentioned before, rocs do not nest too closely together, since such a high concentration of these hungry predators would deprive entire regions of its animal population. Rocs serve to keep down the number of large predators, as they are fond of ankheg, purple worms, and harpies. Thanks to the rocs' prodigious appetites, these creatures are not swarming about with impunity.

It is said that roc feathers can be used in the manufacture of *Quaal's feather tokens*, as well as *wings* and *brooms of flying*.

One race that has little love for rocs is dwarves. Dwarven mines located in remote mountains often have to contend with unruly rocs intent on protecting their territory. Attempts by the dwarves to tame rocs have all met with failure, so the accepted manner of dealing with rocs is to kill them and smash their eggs. Adventurers who happen on a community of mountain dwarves may find employment as roc hunters. Such groups would do well not to allow any druids to find this out.

Roper

CLIMATE/TERRAIN:	Subterranean
FREQUENCY:	Rare
ORGANIZATION:	Solitary
ACTIVITY CYCLE:	Darkness
DIET:	Carnivore
INTELLIGENCE:	Exceptional (15-16)
TREASURE:	See below
ALIGNMENT:	Chaotic evil

NO. APPEARING:	1-3
ARMOR CLASS:	0
MOVEMENT:	3
HIT DICE:	10-12
THAC0:	10 HD: 11
	11-12 HD: 9
NO. OF ATTACKS:	1
DAMAGE/ATTACK:	5-20
SPECIAL ATTACKS:	Strands, strength drain
SPECIAL DEFENSES:	See below
MAGIC RESISTANCE:	80%
SIZE:	L (9' long)
MORALE:	Champion (15)
XP VALUE:	10 HD: 10,000
	11 HD: 11,000
	12 HD: 12,000

A roper resembles a rocky outcropping. The creature's hide is yellowish gray and rough, and its body very malleable. They are usually pillar-like in shape, 9 feet tall, about 3 feet in diameter at the base, and about 1 foot in diameter at the top. The roper has a single yellow eye, and a maw ringed with sharp teeth. Halfway up its body are small bumps which are the sources of the strands it fires at opponents (see below). Ropers have the same body temperature as their surroundings.

Combat: A roper can stand upright to resemble a stalagmite, lie on the ground to imitate a boulder, or even flatten itself to look like a lump on a cavern floor. They can change color a little, enough to blend into rocky backgrounds. Opponents suffer a −2 penalty to surprise rolls when faced by a roper.

Ropers attack by shooting strong, sticky strands at opponents. They can shoot a total of six strands, one per round, as far as 50 feet; each strand can extend (1d4 + 1) × 10 feet and pull up to 750 pounds. Each time a strand hits (requiring a normal attack roll), the victim must make a successful saving throw vs. poison or lose half its Strength (round fractions down). Strength loss occurs 1d3 round after a hit, is cumulative for multiple hits, and lasts for 2d4 turns.

If a roper's prey cannot break free, it is pulled 10 feet closer per round; when it reaches the roper, the creature bites the victim for 5d4 points of damage (automatic hit against a victim held by a strand). A strand can be pulled off or broken by a character who makes a successful open doors roll. A strand can also be cut; it is AC 0, and it must take at least 6 points damage from a single hit of an edged weapon to be severed.

Ropers are unaffected by lightning and take only half damage from cold-based attacks. They have a −4 penalty to saving throws vs. fire.

Habitat/Society: Ropers are not social and rarely cooperate with one another, though a group of them may be found in a good hunting spot. A group of ropers has been named a "cluster" by scholars with nothing better to do.

Ropers reproduce asexually by shedding some of their material in the form of a seed. Drawing nutrients from the cavern floor

(and perhaps siphoning magical energies from deep within the earth), the infant roper grows to maturity in 2d4 weeks. Until that time has passed, the roper is indistinguishable from a boulder.

Ropers move using large, cilia-like appendages on their undersides, which also allow them to cling to walls and ceilings. They seldom leave the caverns, but may migrate to a new feeding ground when prey population drops too low in its current home. Migration usually occurs through underground tunnels, but when this is not possible, ropers travel late at night, sometimes giving rise to stories of walking stones.

Ecology: Ropers eat any meat but prefer demihumans and humans. Gnomes, dwarves, and other mining races often serve as prey for ropers.

A roper has a gizzard-like organ which often holds undigested treasure. Platinum and gems cannot be digested by a roper, so its gizzard holds 3d6 platinum pieces, and has a 35% chance of holding 5d4 gems. The glue from a roper's strands is prized by alchemists, as are its digestive acids, which must be stored in platinum vials.

Storoper

A "stone-roper" is a roper with a more stony, less flexible exterior; it resembles a statue of a roper. Its rocky tentacles are always extended at least 20 feet, and can shoot to 50 feet to attack prey. The storoper can attack with all its tentacles at the same time, preferring to attack two victims with three tentacles each. Twice per day, the storoper can inject venom through its tentacles. Victims must make a successful saving throw vs. poison or be paralyzed for one round, then fight to aid the storoper; the venom lasts for 10 turns. Storopers' stony exteriors give them total protection from normal missiles. Storopers have 6 HD, but have all the other abilities and statistics of a 10 HD roper.

Rust Monster

CLIMATE/TERRAIN:	Subterranean
FREQUENCY:	Uncommon
ORGANIZATION:	Solitary
ACTIVITY CYCLE:	Night
DIET:	Metalavore
INTELLIGENCE:	Animal (1)
TREASURE:	Q
ALIGNMENT:	Neutral

NO. APPEARING:	1-2
ARMOR CLASS:	2
MOVEMENT:	18
HIT DICE:	5
THAC0:	15
NO. OF ATTACKS:	2
DAMAGE/ATTACK:	Nil
SPECIAL ATTACKS:	See below
SPECIAL DEFENSES:	Nil
MAGIC RESISTANCE:	Nil
SIZE:	M (5' long)
MORALE:	Average (9)
XP VALUE:	270

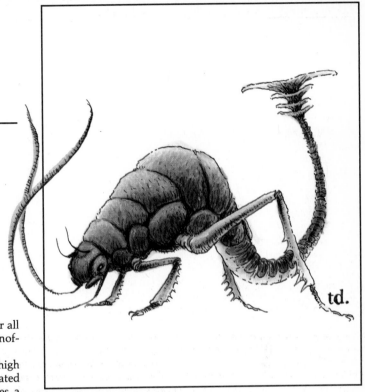

Rust monsters are subterranean creatures with an appetite for all sorts of metals. These unique creatures, though generally inoffensive, are the bane of fighters everywhere.

The average rust monster measures 5 feet long and 3 feet high at the shoulder. It has a strange tail that appears armor plated and ends in an odd-looking bony projection that resembles a double-ended paddle. Two prehensile antennae are located under the thing's two eyes. The hide of the rust monster is rough, covered with lumpy projections. Coloration varies from a yellowish tan on the underside and legs, to a rust red upper back. Rust monsters smell like wet, oxidized metal.

Combat: Rust monsters are placid by nature, but when they get within scent range of metal, they become excited and immediately dash toward the source. Rust monsters can smell metal up to 90 feet away. If the rust monster's antennae touch metal (determined by a successful attack roll), the metal rusts. Magical items have a chance of being unaffected equal to 10% for each plus (a +2 weapon or armor has a 20% chance of not being affected). Any affected metal rusts or corrodes and immediately falls to pieces that are easily eaten and digested by the creature. Metal weapons striking a rust monster are affected just as if the creature's antennae had touched them. Should a nonweapon metallic magical item happen to make contact with a rust monster, treat it as a +2 magical weapon for purposes of determining whether or not it breaks up.

Rust monsters, being none too bright, stop pursuing a fleeing party for one round to devour metallic items, such as a handful of iron spikes, a mace or a hammer, if the party throws them behind. Rust monsters go after ferrous metals such as iron, steel, and magical steel alloys, such as mithril and adamantite. They choose such metals over valuable metals such as copper, gold, silver, or platinum. In fact, they would continue to pursue a party that just dropped a fistful of copper coins, for example, in hopes of getting the much-preferred ferrous metal of armor and weapons.

Sometimes (30% chance), a rust monster will even pause for one round during combat in order to eat. Rust monsters are not known for being tacticians, just ravenously hungry metal-eaters. Feeding time always takes one round regardless of the size of the metal meal.

Habitat/Society: Rust monsters dwell only in dark, subterranean places such as caverns and underground structures. They are not disposed to groups; often a lair comprises one or two rust monsters, with a 5% chance of encountering a single offspring, which acts as a half-strength rust monster with a full-strength appetite. These creatures have been known to range the length and breadth of an underground complex, searching for supplies of metal. Though it will eat raw ore, a rust monster always prefers the refined, forged metal (just as a human would prefer fresh, filtered water over swamp water).

The creature's relatively inoffensive nature makes it an unlikely target. There have been many accounts of mages approaching a rust monster and the only reaction from the beast was a cursory sniff, then a leisurely departure. Dwarves and gnomes, known for metalworking and mining, have no sympathy for rust monsters, and will do anything to get rid of them.

The only treasure to be found in a rust monster lair is gems, usually the sort used for decoration on armor or sword pommels. Rust monsters have no grand designs, only the wish to keep well-fed.

Ecology: Rust monsters help in removing metallic junk and clutter from underground fastnesses. In fact, it is not unusual to find a rust monster and a carrion crawler working in a symbiotic relationship, with the latter eating the organic litter and the former consuming the metal castoffs.

Sahuagin

CLIMATE/TERRAIN:	Temperate/Salt water
FREQUENCY:	Uncommon
ORGANIZATION:	Tribal
ACTIVITY CYCLE:	Night
DIET:	Carnivore
INTELLIGENCE:	High (13-14)
TREASURE:	N (I, O, P, Q (x10), X, Y)
ALIGNMENT:	Lawful evil

NO. APPEARING:	20-80
ARMOR CLASS:	5
MOVEMENT:	12, Sw 24
HIT DICE:	2+2
THAC0:	19
NO. OF ATTACKS:	1 or see below
DAMAGE/ATTACK:	1-2/1-2/1-4/1-4 or weapon type
SPECIAL ATTACKS:	See below
SPECIAL DEFENSES:	See below
MAGIC RESISTANCE:	Nil
SIZE:	M (6'), some L (9')
MORALE:	Steady (12)
XP VALUE:	175
	Lieutenant: 270
	Chieftain: 420
	Priestess: 650
	Baron: 975
	Prince: 2,000

Sahuagin are a vicious, predatory race of fish-men that live in warm coastal waters. They are highly organized and greatly enjoy raiding shore communities for food and sport.

Typical sahuagins are blackish green on their backs, shading to green on their bellies, with black fins. Their great, staring eyes are deep, shining black. They have scaly skin, with webbed fingers and toes, and their mouths are filled with sharp fangs. About 1 in 216 sahuagin is a mutation with four usable arms. These specimens are usually black shading to gray. Females are indistinguishable from males, except that they are slightly smaller. Hatchlings are a light green color, but they darken and attain full growth approximately one to two months after hatching.

Sahuagin speak their own tongue.

Combat: Though they wear no armor, their scales are tough and equal to AC 5. Sahuagin wear a harness to carry their personal gear and weapons. A group of these creatures is typically armed as follows:

Heavy crossbow & dagger	20%
Spear & dagger	30%
Trident, net & dagger	50%

Spears are used only as thrusting weapons. Nets are set with dozens of hooks that make escape virtually impossible for unarmored victims or creatures not able to grasp and tear with a Strength of 16 or greater. Nets are replaced by three javelins when the band forays onto land. The crossbows fire a maximum of 30 feet underwater and normal ranges on the surface. Tridents have three uses—to spear small prey, to pin prey trapped in nets, and to hold threatening opponents at bay.

Sahuagin are well-equipped to attack even without weapons, for their webbed hands each end in long, sharp claws that can inflict 1-2 points of damage per attack. Their powerful rear legs are likewise taloned, and if they kick an opponent with them, they inflict 1d4 points of damage with each hit from either foot. The sharp teeth of the sahuagin cause 1d4 points of damage if a bite is scored on a victim. Thus, it is possible for an unarmed

sahuagin to attack three or five times in a melee round causing 1-2/1-2/1-4 and an extra 1-4/1-4 if the legs can rake.

The eyes and ears of these monsters are particularly keen. They can see for 300 feet underwater at depths of up to 100 feet. For each 100 feet of greater depth, their vision is reduced by 10 feet (e.g., when 500 feet deep they can see 260 feet; when 1,000 feet deep they can see 210 feet). Their ears are so sharp as to be able to detect the clinking of metal at one mile, or a boat oar splashing at twice that distance.

A band of sahuagin is always led by a chieftain. He has one lieutenant for every ten members of the group. The chieftain has 4+4 Hit Dice, and his lieutenants have 3+3 Hit Dice. All are in addition to the normal sahuagin in the group.

When raiding villages, sahuagin attack en masse, with leaders in the second rank. As long as there is no truly spirited resistance, they continue in their plunder and violence.

Underwater, in their natural element, the sahuagin are far more confident. Using the three-dimensional aspect of underwater fighting, they sometimes dive down on a group of underwater explorers, coming in from behind, and swooping down and past them, dropping nets on their intended victims.

When sahuagin attack ships, they swarm up from all sides and try to overwhelm with numbers. They often grab their opponents and hurl them into the sea, where at least a fourth of the raiding party lurks, waiting for such an action or as reinforcements. Some leaders carry a conch shell, which when sounded gives the signal for the group of sahuagin in reserve to enter the fray.

Sahuagin have an almost paralyzing fear of spellcasters. They direct their strongest attacks toward anyone who uses spells or spell-like powers, such as the functions of some magical items. Their saving throws vs. fire-based spells suffer a -2 penalty, and they receive an additional point of damage per die of damage from such attacks.

Habitat/Society: The sahuagin are sometimes referred to as "sea devils" or "devil men of the deep." They dwell in warm salt waters at depths of 100 to 1,500 feet. Sahuagin are predatory in the extreme, and they pose a threat to all living things because they kill for sport and pleasure as well as for food. They abhor fresh water. They dislike light, and bright light such as that created by a *continual light* spell is harmful to their eyes.

The social structure of the sahuagin is based upon rule by a king who holds court in a vast city deep beneath the waves. This overlord's domain is divided into nine provinces, each ruled by a prince. Each prince has 2d10 + 10 nobles underneath him. Each noble controls the small groups of sahuagin dwelling in his fief. The sahuagin worship a great devil-shark. Sahuagin priests above 5th level are very rare.

The king is supposed to dwell in a city somewhere at the greatest depth that a sahuagin can exist. This place is supposedly built in an undersea canyon, with palaces and dwellings built along either face. There, fully 5,000 of these monsters live, not counting the king's retinue of queens, concubines, nobles, guards, etc., said to number 1,000 or more. The sahuagin king is reported to be of enormous size (10 Hit Dice + 10 hit points), and of greatest evil. The king is always accompanied by nine noble guards (9 + 9 Hit Dice) and the evil high priestess of all sahuagin (9 + 9 Hit Dice) with its retinue of nine underpriestesses (7th-level clerics).

If sahuagin are encountered in their lair, there are the following additional sahuagin:

1 baron (6 + 6 Hit Dice)
Nine guards (3 + 3 Hit Dice)
3d4 x 10 females (2 Hit Dice)
1d4 x 10 hatchlings (1 Hit Die)
2d4 x 10 eggs

Also, there is a 10% chance per 10 male sahuagin that there is an evil priestess and 1d4 assistant priestesses, for the religious life of these creatures is dominated by the females. If a priestess is with the group in the lair, it is of 1d4 + 1 level ability, and the lesser clerics are 3rd or 4th level.

There are always 2d4 sharks in a sahuagin lair. Sahuagin are able to make these monsters obey simple one- or two-word commands. Whenever a sahuagin lair is encountered, there is a 5% chance that it is the stronghold of a prince. The prince has 8 + 8 Hit Dice plus nine guards of chieftain strength. There are also one 8th-level sahuagin evil high priestess and four 4th-level underpriestesses. The numbers of males, females, hatchlings and eggs in a prince's lair are double the numbers given above. There are 4d6 sharks present at all times.

Sahuagin lairs are actual villages or towns, constructed of stone. The buildings are domed, and the seaweed and similar marine plants growing around and on these buildings make them hard to detect.

Few persons have survived capture by the sahuagin, for prisoners are usually quickly tortured and eaten. Any creatures taken alive from raids or intercepting unwelcome visitors are brought to the sahuagins' lair and confined in cells. Although sahuagin are able to stay out of water for up to four hours, there is no air in the confinement areas in the typical village, but in the towns of the nobles there are special quarters to maintain air-breathing creatures. The sahuagin set aside a few prisoners to torture and provide sport—typically a fight to the death between two different creatures in an arena. The bulk of captives are simply killed and eaten. It is seldom that any prisoner escapes, although the sahuagin find sport in allowing captives to think that they have found freedom, only to be encircled by sadistic guards while a school of sharks moves in for the kill.

The sahuagin are cruel and brutal, and the strongest always bully the weaker. Any injured, disabled, or infirm specimen is slain and eaten by these cannibalistic monsters. Even imperfect hatchlings are dealt with in this fashion. This strict law has developed a strong race, however, and any leader is subject to a challenge. Sahuagin never stop growing, although they grow very slowly, and death comes to most before the years allow growth to large size. Leaders are always the largest and strongest. It is reported that the nine sahuagin princes are each of the four-armed sort, as is the king. In any event, the loser of a challenge is always slain, either during combat or afterward. Sometimes the loser winds up as the main course at the victory feast.

Duels are fought without weapons, only fang and claw being permitted.

The sahuagin are chronicled because of their great evil, having time and again raided the land, desolating whole coasts, and destroying passing ships continually. The exact origin of the sahuagin is unknown. It is suggested that they were created from a nation of particularly evil humans by the most powerful lawful evil gods in order to preserve them when the great deluge came upon the earth. Some sages claim that they are degenerate humans who formerly dwelt on the seacoasts, whose evil and depravity was so great that they eventually devolved into fish-folk and sought the darkness of the ocean depths. The tritons however, are purported to have believe that sahuagin are distantly related to sea elves, claiming that the drow spawned the sahuagin.

Sahuagin range as far as 50 miles from their lairs. Most of their lairs are located 2d10 + 20 miles from coastal shores. Some of these creatures enjoy collecting pearls and coral formations, fashioning them into jewelry. This jewelry is worn as a status symbol. They are fond of wealth, which they use as a measure of influence, and for sacrifice to the deities that they worship in exchange for granted powers and other favors. Most of the treasure found in a sahuagin lair belonged to former victims. There is usually a high concentration of water-related items, such as magical boats, tridents, helms, potions, necklaces, etc. These were gained from adventurers who explored underwater too close to the sahuagin community.

These creatures want nothing less than full control of the sea coasts, collecting as much wealth and power as possible in the process while maintaining the secrecy of their lairs' locations. Those who attempt escape are obsessively hunted down, for fear that the former prisoners may reveal the location of the sahuagins' city.

Ecology: Sahuagin venture ashore on dark, moonless nights to raid and plunder human coastal towns. They hate even the evil ixitxachitl, and only sharks are befriended by them.

The feuds and outright warfare between the sahuagin and ixitxachitl have indirectly contributed to preventing the ascendancy of the spellcasting, manta ray-like race. Sahuagin are also fond of eating giant squid and kraken. Their hunting of these monsters of the deep has kept the squid and kraken numbers down to a safe level. Conversely, these beasts enjoy eating sahuagin, which prevents the sahuagin from overrunning coastal areas.

Of all the sea-dwelling races, tritons, sea elves, dolphins, and hippocampi are the most implacable enemies of the sahuagin. In fact, the few air-breathers that have escaped the sahuagin owe their freedom to such beings that bravely aided the captives.

Satyr

	Satyr	Korred
CLIMATE/TERRAIN:	Temperate sylvan woodlands	Temperate forest and sylvan settings
FREQUENCY:	Uncommon	Very rare
ORGANIZATION:	Band	Clan
ACTIVITY CYCLE:	Any	Any
DIET:	Omnivore	Omnivore
INTELLIGENCE:	Very (11-12)	Very (11-12)
TREASURE:	I, S, X	E
ALIGNMENT:	Neutral	Chaotic Neutral
NO. APPEARING:	2-8 (2d4)	1-4
ARMOR CLASS:	5	5
MOVEMENT:	18	9
HIT DICE:	5	6+1
THAC0:	15	15
NO. OF ATTACKS:	1	1
DAMAGE/ATTACK:	2-8 or by weapon	3-6 (1d2+4) or by weapon +4
SPECIAL ATTACKS:	See below	See below
SPECIAL DEFENSES:	See below	See below
MAGIC RESISTANCE:	50%	25%
SIZE:	M (5' tall)	S (3' tall)
MORALE:	Elite (13)	Elite (13-14)
XP VALUE:	975	1,400

Also called fauns, satyrs are a pleasure loving race of half-human, half-goat creatures. They symbolize nature's carefree ways. Satyrs have the torso, head, and arms of a man, and the hind legs of a goat. The human head is surmounted by two sharp horns that poke through the satyr's coarse, curly hair. The skin of the upper body ranges from tan to light brown, with rare individuals (1%) with red skin. A satyr's hair is medium, reddish, or dark brown. The horns and hooves are black.

Satyrs have their own tongue and can speak elven and Common. Satyrs living near centaurs are 80% likely to be friendly with them and speak their language. Rarely (5%), satyrs are found with korred.

Combat: Satyrs have keen senses, so they gain a +2 bonus on surprise rolls. They can be almost silent, and can blend with foliage so as to be 90% undetectable; this gives opponents a −2 penalty to surprise rolls. Satyrs have infravision to a distance of 60 feet.

A satyr attacks by butting with its sharp horns. Some (20%) use +1 magical weapons, especially long or short swords, daggers, or short bows. Before resorting to combat, a satyr often plays a tune on its pipes, an instrument only a satyr can use properly. Using these pipes, the satyr can cast *charm, sleep,* or *cause fear,* affecting all within 60 feet, unless they make a successful saving throw vs. spell.

Usually, only one satyr per band has pipes. If comely females (Charisma 15+) are in a group met by satyrs, the piping will be to *charm.* Should the intruders be relatively inoffensive, the piping casts *sleep,* and the satyrs steal all of the victims' choice food and drink, as well as weapons, valuables, and magical items. If intruders are hostile, the piping is used to *cause fear.* The effects of the piping lasts 1d6 hours or until dispelled. Any creature that saves vs. piping is not affected by additional music from the same pipes in that encounter. A bard's singing can nullify the pipe's music before it takes effect.

Habitat/Society: Satyrs are interested only in sport: frolicking, piping, chasing wood nymphs, and other pleasures. They resent intrusions and drive away any creature that offends them. A lucky wanderer may stumble on a woodland celebration, which will contain an equal number of dryads and fauns plus 3d8 other woodland creatures and a 25% chance of 2d6 centaurs. Strangers are welcomed only if they contribute some good food and drink, especially superior (10+ gp per bottle) wines. Such wine can also be used to lure or bribe satyrs. If a group includes elves, they have a better chance of being welcomed.

These celebrations last all night in warm months, with newcomers waking up the next morning with massive headaches, minus a few valuables, and not a woodland creature (nor their tracks) to be found.

Shying away from the trappings of an organized society, a colony of satyrs usually includes young numbering 50% of the adults. Satyrs live in comfortable caves and hollow trees. There are no female satyrs and sages believe that dryads are the female counterparts of the satyr, and that satyrs mate with dryads to produce more satyrs and dryads. Satyrs share the dryads' affection for humans of the opposite sex, but a female charmed by a satyr might return after 1d4 weeks (10% chance).

Satyrs are an inoffensive, fun-loving race. They rarely venture more than 10 miles from their homes, most often doing so to gather food. They are fond of venison and small game but also eat plants and fruits.

Ecology: Satyrs in sylvan woodlands keep game animal populations at normal levels; they never hunt to excess or despoil plants.

Korred

This small, dance-loving relative of the satyr looks much like its cousins, but lacks horns, and has wildly flowing beard and hair. Korred smell like pine trees and fresh earth. They usually wear leather britches, carry large leather pouches, and wield oaken cudgels. They have loud voices and speak their own language, plus those of satyrs, dryads, centaurs, and elves; a few even speak druidic.

Korred have 18/76 Strength. They hurl boulders up to 100 feet (damage 2d8), or use cudgels (1d6 damage), shears (1d4 damage), or fists (1d2 damage), gaining a +4 to damage because of their Strength.

Korred can weave their hair into entangling ropes and snares in 1d4 rounds. Such ropes have AC 1, 5 hp, and a movement rate of 3. Anyone attacked by the ropes must make a saving throw vs. spells or be entangled. The ropes sometimes guard special areas.

A korred may use its magical *laugh* three times per day; unless it is nullified by a bard's singing, all within 60 feet must roll above their Charisma score or be stunned for 1d4 rounds. Korred can also use the following abilities at will, one per round: *stone shape, animate rock, stone door* (teleport 30'), *shatter rock, transmute rock to mud,* and *stone tell.*

Korred do not have structured communities; families in a common clan live within 5 miles of one another. Korred do not tolerate outsiders, except for rare rangers, druids, and elves. Even these must not interrupt the weekly korred dance. Those who interrupt must make a saving throw vs. spells or dance themselves, losing 1d4 hp per round until dead or restrained, or until the korred stop playing and dancing.

Korred pouches contain hair, shears, and other items. These items turn to gold (5d4 × 10 gp value) if sprinkled with holy water. A korred will not voluntarily give up this pouch.

Scorpion

	Large	Huge	Giant
CLIMATE/TERRAIN:	Warm wilderness and subterranean areas	Warm wilderness and subterranean areas	Warm wilderness and subterranean areas
FREQUENCY:	Uncommon	Common	Uncommon
ORGANIZATION:	Swarm	Swarm	Swarm
ACTIVITY CYCLE:	Any	Any	Any
DIET:	Carnivore	Carnivore	Carnivore
INTELLIGENCE:	Non- (0)	Non- (0)	Non- (0)
TREASURE:	D	D	D
ALIGNMENT:	Neutral	Neutral	Neutral
NO. APPEARING:	1-6	1-4	1-4
ARMOR CLASS:	5	4	3
MOVEMENT:	9	12	15
HIT DICE:	2+2	4+4	5+5
THAC0:	19	15	15
NO. OF ATTACKS:	3	3	3
DAMAGE/ATTACK:	1-4/1-4/1	1-8/1-8/1-3	1-10/1-10/1-4
SPECIAL ATTACKS:	Poison sting	Poison sting	Poison sting
SPECIAL DEFENSES:	Nil	Nil	Nil
MAGIC RESISTANCE:	Nil	Nil	Nil
SIZE:	S (2' long)	M (4' long)	M (5'-6' long)
MORALE:	Average (8)	Average (10)	Steady (11)
XP VALUE:	175	420	650

Giant scorpions are vicious predators that live almost anywhere, including relatively cold places such as dungeons, though they favor deserts and warm lands. These creatures are giant versions of the normal 4-inch-long scorpion found in desert climes.

The giant scorpion has a green carapace and yellowish green legs and pincers. The segmented tail is black, with a vicious stinger on the end. There is a bitter smell associated with the scorpion, which probably comes from the venom. They make an unnerving scrabbling sound as they travel across dungeon floors.

Combat: The giant scorpion is 95% likely to attack any creature that approaches. The creature has a hard, chitinous carapace that gives it Armor Class 3. This monster attacks by grabbing prey with its two huge pincers, inflicting 1-10 points of damage each, while it lashes forward with its tail to sting. Thus, it can fight three opponents at once. If a giant scorpion manages to grab a victim in a pincer, it will automatically inflict 1-10 points of damage each round until it releases the victim. The victim has but one chance to escape. If he can make his *bend bars/lift gates* roll, he will escape the claw. However, this can be the character's only action that round and it can be tried only once per combat. If the sting is employed against an untrapped victim, an attack roll is required for a successful attack, but a trapped character is automatically struck by any sting attack directed at him with no attack roll required.

The sting inflicts 1-4 points of damage and the victim must save versus poison or die the next round (type F). Note that scorpions are not immune to their own poison. If a scorpion is reduced to 1 or 2 hit points, it will go into a stinging frenzy, stinging everything in sight, gaining two attempts to hit per round with only the tail. Slain creatures are dragged to the scorpion's burrow to be eaten.

Habitat/Society: Giant scorpions live in underground burrows or dungeons. Each lair may (20%) have 5d4 scorpion eggs. These beasts eat any living creature that is unfortunate enough to stray too close to their lair. Any treasure found comes from the bodies of human or demihuman victims that have been dragged here to be consumed. Armor is rarely found intact, since the scorpion will surely have used its pincers to cut up its prey.

Ecology: These bizarre insects contribute to the ecosystem by feeding on other giant versions of insects such as spiders and ants. They themselves are prey for purple worms and other huge, subterranean creatures. Alchemists and assassins prize the scorpion's venom because of its potency.

Large and Huge Scorpions

Often found in dungeons and wildernesses, these creatures are merely smaller versions of the giant scorpion. Colors range from tan to brown to black, and rumors persist of rare white scorpions deep underground. All attack with pincers and tail stinger. If struck by the stinger, the victim must save versus poison or die the next round. However, the poison of the large scorpion is weaker than normal (type A, 15/0 points damage), giving the victim a +2 on his saving throw. Huge scorpions have deadly (type F) poison and can pin a victim in a way similar to the giant scorpion, but with the huge scorpion, the victim can still fight back. It is not unusual to see scorpions of various sizes fighting with each other.

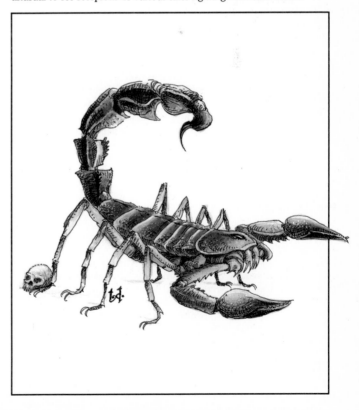

Sea Lion

CLIMATE/TERRAIN:	Coastal marine
FREQUENCY:	Uncommon
ORGANIZATION:	Packs
ACTIVITY CYCLE:	Day
DIET:	Carnivore
INTELLIGENCE:	Semi- (2-4)
TREASURE:	B
ALIGNMENT:	Neutral

NO. APPEARING:	3-12
ARMOR CLASS:	5/3
MOVEMENT:	Sw 18
HIT DICE:	6
THAC0:	15
NO. OF ATTACKS:	3
DAMAGE/ATTACK:	1-6/1-6/2-12
SPECIAL ATTACKS:	Mauling
SPECIAL DEFENSES:	Nil
MAGIC RESISTANCE:	Nil
SIZE:	L (15' long with tail)
MORALE:	Steady (12)
XP VALUE:	420

A sea lion is a fearsome creature with the head and forepaws of a lion and the body and tail of a fish.

Combat: Sea lions are ferocious and difficult to deal with. They are very territorial and usually attack anything that enters their domains, no matter what the size. Their vicious teeth and huge paws are a match even for most sharks, which they hate above all other creatures. Sea lions must attack the same opponent with paws and teeth and cannot divide attacks. Any creature hit by both paw attacks in the same round is being mauled. Mauled creatures cannot attack if they have not already done so that round and must roll a successful open doors roll to free themselves. When mauling a creature, the lion follows up with a bite attack with a +4 bonus to the attack roll, causing double damage if successful.

The head of a sea lion, with its thick mane, is treated as AC 5, while the rest of its scaly body is AC 3.

Sea lions are very difficult to raise in captivity, but can become the best and most loyal of steeds. In fact, they are arguably the most powerful mountable creature beneath the waves. They are very useful as guarding and hunting beasts, since their tremendous roar can be heard for up to 10 miles underwater, providing ample time to prepare for an attack or to send help. They are not as skillful swimmers as are sea horses—they are the underwater equivalents of Maneuverability Class B creatures.

Habitat/Society: Sea horses and sea lions almost never encounter one another as sea lions prefer to dwell in the shallow coastal regions, while sea horses delve the deeps. This is primarily due to their respective dietary differences. Sea horses eat plankton, while sea lions eat any type of meat, be it a fish, dinosaur, or wandering herd animals caught drinking at the water's edge. Sea lions are not afraid of land and it is not unheard of for sea lions to drag themselves a few dozen yards up the beach in search of meals. While these attacks are rare indeed, the reports of sea lions in the vicinity does tend to foster more fear among the general populace than a simple shark attack does. But in a world of krakens, dinosaurs, and vampires, sea lions are a relatively minor threat.

Sea lions roam the seas in packs, what might be called a pride of lions on land. The strongest one (usually with maximum hit

points) is the leader. In a sea lion pack, both sexes hunt and care for young, but the males are superior hunters, something that differentiates them from their land-based cousins.

While sea lions rarely travel anywhere with specific goals in mind, they do sometimes team up to aid other packs of lions, usually when they roam close enough to hear the collective bellowing of their comrades. But territoriality comes into play immediately after the kill is made, and rarely does the reigning leader allow the helpful newcomers to share in the spoils of the victory. Often a new battle for power ensues between the two leaders. If the resident leader wins, the newcomers leave without a taste of meat. If the newcomer wins, he and his pack remain just long enough to take first choice of flesh, and then depart for home. The remaining leader, vanquished and weakened before his peers, rarely lives long enough to enjoy the spoils.

Ecology: Sea lions hate sharks, often going to great lengths to hunt them down. The taste of sharks is apparently abhorrent to sea lions and they always leave the carcass uneaten, so it is something of a mystery why this rivalry exists. Some sages claim that it is the result of conflicts between the lesser deities of nature, but it is more likely two strong predators vying for supremacy of the seas.

Because of the water-proofing qualities of their thick scales, sea lions can remain out of water for up to 24 hours before their gills dry out and become incapable of removing oxygen from the water. If a sea lion is fed a constant source of water into its mouth, it can survive for an entire week before disease enters the cracking scales and starvation takes its toll. It is theoretically possible to keep a sea lion in captivity but, like most aquatic carnivores, the restriction of space is often psychologically too much for the creature and death slowly takes the once-proud beast.

Selkie

CLIMATE/TERRAIN:	Cold to subarctic waters
FREQUENCY:	Very rare
ORGANIZATION:	Solitary or tribal
ACTIVITY CYCLE:	Any
DIET:	Omnivore
INTELLIGENCE:	Average to exceptional (8-16)
TREASURE:	A (magic only), R
ALIGNMENT:	Neutral (good)

NO. APPEARING:	1 or 12-30
ARMOR CLASS:	5 (10 base in human form)
MOVEMENT:	12, Sw 36
HIT DICE:	3+3
THAC0:	17
NO. OF ATTACKS:	1
DAMAGE/ATTACK:	1-6 or by weapon type
SPECIAL ATTACKS:	Nil
SPECIAL DEFENSES:	Can change into human form
MAGIC RESISTANCE:	Nil
SIZE:	M (5'-6' in either form)
MORALE:	Steady (11-12)
XP VALUE:	175
Leader	420

Selkies are seal-like beings that have the ability to change into human form for a few days at a time.

When in their true, seal-like forms, they are nearly indistinguishable from normal seals. Close inspection of their arms, however, will reveal the presence of slightly webbed hands instead of fore flippers and legs instead of a tapering body and rear flippers. Once a month, each selkie is able to assume human form for about a week. Usually selkies prefer to briefly visit the realm of men (which they call the "overworld") out of curiosity, but sometimes they are ordered to go forth and purchase desperately needed supplies or information. When in human form, selkies are very attractive indeed and their fine looks have broken more than a few overworlders' hearts. Their eyes are particularly noticeable as they are always either a bright emerald green or startling light blue. Since the selkie transformation is not a spell or magical effect, only spells like *true seeing* will reveal a selkie's true nature, although their peculiar mannerisms and predilection for seafood also might.

Combat: Since selkies are unable to swim quickly while carrying weapons, 90% of selkies encountered underwater will be unarmed. They use their sharp teeth whenever they are cornered but prefer to use their impressive speed underwater to escape superior odds. If encountered on land, selkies are wise enough to bear human weapons, most likely swords scavenged from the wrecks of ships (see below).

Habitat/Society: Selkie communities are divided between male and female, with females usually outnumbering males, as male selkies are the hunter/gatherers throughout the often dangerous waters nearby. However, both aspects of selkie "community" (domestic and provider) are equally respected within the lair, and no sex is accorded undue privileges.

Selkies inhabit only colder waters and there are both saltwater and freshwater varieties. Selkies almost always build their lairs in huge, underwater caverns and grottos containing both air and water-filled regions— selkie young must be raised in an air-filled environment for about their first year.

As mentioned earlier, selkies often find and explore wrecks of sunken treasure. Most selkie communities have hoarded at least some booty (especially pearls), keeping those otherwise useless trinkets only for purposes of trade with the overworld. Only selkies who have visited the overworld many times have ever acquired a taste for ornamenting themselves like overworlders, and can be distinguished from more traditional selkies immediately. For obvious reasons, these more experienced selkies are often the best representatives to deal with if one is an overworlder. Selkies can be hired and have a limited knowledge of overworlder customs. All magical treasure recovered by selkies is immediately commandeered for the good of the community and the lair's defense.

Ecology: Selkies are omnivorous, preferring to eat fish, shellfish, crustaceans, and various forms of seaweed. Those that have visited the surface are often partial to human fare as well. Selkies are particularly susceptible to fine wine, which is to be expected since these intoxicants are unknown below the seas.

Selkies are sensitive about their environment and harvest only what they need to survive. It is worth noting that selkie representatives lobby heavily whenever local overworlder environmental issues threaten selkie existence. Most selkie communities have learned the value of dropping a few pearls here and there in order to get what they want from men.

While selkies in human form are quite beautiful, they are fortunate indeed that their pelts have little value in overworlder markets. They are, therefore, without any special enemies besides those common to seals and all ocean dwelling beings.

Selkie, Leader

Each venerable leader of a selkie community can cast the following spells once per day, one spell per round: *augury*, *cure light wounds*, and *cure disease*. Leaders can also cast *weather summoning* and *control weather* once per week. Selkies fear the wrath of the sea should they ever use their powers for ill.

Shadow

CLIMATE/TERRAIN:	Any ruins or subterranean chambers
FREQUENCY:	Rare
ORGANIZATION:	Roving bands
ACTIVITY CYCLE:	Night or darkness
DIET:	Living beings
INTELLIGENCE:	Low (5-7)
TREASURE:	F
ALIGNMENT:	Chaotic evil

NO. APPEARING:	2-20 (2d10)
ARMOR CLASS:	7
MOVEMENT:	12
HIT DICE:	3+3
THAC0:	17
NO. OF ATTACKS:	1
DAMAGE/ATTACK:	2-5+special
SPECIAL ATTACKS:	Strength drain
SPECIAL DEFENSES:	+1 or better weapon to hit
MAGIC RESISTANCE:	See below
SIZE:	M (6' tall)
MORALE:	Special
XP VALUE:	420

Shadows are shadowy, undead creatures that drain strength from their victims with their chilling touch.

Shadows are 90% undetectable in all but the brightest of surroundings (*continual light* or equivalent), as they normally appear to be nothing more than their name would suggest. In bright light they can be clearly seen.

Combat: As shadows exist primarily on the Negative Material plane, they have the ability to drain the life force of their victims. The chilling touch of a shadow inflicts 2-5 points of damage to its victim as well as draining one point of Strength. Lost Strength points return 2-8 turns after being touched. If a human or demi-human opponent is reduced to zero Strength or zero hit points by a shadow, the shadow has drained the life force and the opponent becomes a shadow as well. The newly formed shadow is then compelled to join the roving band and pursue a life of evil. Other living creatures simply collapse from fatigue (if taken to zero Strength) or fall unconscious (if taken to zero hit points), where they are left to die or are hounded again upon waking.

Shadows are immune to *sleep, charm,* and *hold* spells and are unaffected by cold-based attacks. They can be turned by clerics.

Habitat/Society: Shadows travel in loosely organized packs that freely roam ancient ruins, graveyards, and dungeons. They specialize in terrifying their victims.

Shadows have no leaders and thus spend much of their time roaming aimlessly about their chosen surroundings. Contrary to popular belief, shadows do not hoard treasure. In fact, such earthly baubles only help to remind the creatures of their former lives. Instead, the furious undead throw all of the treasure they find away, in the same location (often at the bottom of a well or deep pit), where it is out of sight of the band. It is therefore speculated that the removal of a shadow hoard would be quite easy (even welcomed), were it not for the fact that shadows attack living beings without hesitation, regardless of their intent or threat.

Ecology: According to most knowledgeable sages, shadows appear to have been magically created, perhaps as part of some ancient curse laid upon some long-dead enemy. The curse affects only humans and demihumans, so it would seem that it affects the soul or spirit. When victims no longer can resist, either through loss of consciousness (hit points) or physical prowess (Strength points), the curse is activated and the majority of the character's essence is shifted to the Negative Material plane. Only a shadow of their former self remains on the Prime Material plane, and the transformation always renders the victim both terribly insane and undeniably evil.

Attempts to remove the curse from captured shadows have all failed, thus providing more clues into the nature of the disorder. A *limited wish* spell proved only partially successful as the victim returned for an hour but remained insane for the duration. It has been recently speculated that a full *wish,* followed by a *heal* spell, might be capable of restoring a shadow to his former state, but again it must be emphasized that this is only a theory.

Fortunately, shadows rarely leave their lairs, and a bold party wishing to rescue a lost fighter or wizard should have plenty of time to venture forth and recover their friend, provided that no one else explores the lair and slays the unfortunate character while the shadows are absent.

The original body of a victim is destroyed when changed to a shadow whether by the curse itself or by unprotected exposure to the Negative Material plane. In any case, killing a shadow is merely a case of severing the bond between the Prime Material and Negative Material forms.

Shedu

	Lesser	Greater
CLIMATE/TERRAIN:	Any (prefer hot)	/Any open region
FREQUENCY:	Rare	Very rare
ORGANIZATION:	Herd	Herd Leader
ACTIVITY CYCLE:	—Hottest part of the day—	
DIET:	Herbivore	Herbivore
INTELLIGENCE:	Exceptional (15-16)	Genius (17-18)
TREASURE:	G	Nil
ALIGNMENT:	Lawful good	Lawful good
NO. APPEARING:	2d4	1-2
ARMOR CLASS:	4	2
MOVEMENT:	12, Fl 24 (C)	15, Fl 30 (B)
HIT DICE:	9+9	14+14
THAC0:	11	5
NO. OF ATTACKS:	2	2
DAMAGE/ATTACK:	1d6/1d6	3d6/3d6
SPECIAL ATTACKS:	Psionics	Psionics
SPECIAL DEFENSES:	Psionics	Psionics, invisibility
MAGIC RESISTANCE:	25%	50%
SIZE:	L (as a mule)	L (as a draft horse,
MORALE:	Champion (15-16)	Fearless (19-20)
XP VALUE:	8,000	15,000

Shedu are native to hot, arid climates. They have powerful, stocky equine bodies with short, powerful feathered wings. Their heads are large and humanoid, and rather dwarven in appearance. They always have beard sand mustache.s Shedu hair is very bristly, and curls into tight waves or bands.

All shedu wear a simple headband made of braided cloth or rope, with a single button for adornment. The button is centered on the forehead, and its material represents the bearer's status. From the lowest rank to the highest, a button may be made of silver, gold, platinum, sapphire, ruby, or diamond. Lesser shedu almost never have a button above the platinum level, greater shedu almost never wear one below sapphire status.

Shedu wander the Prime material, astral, and ethereal planes. They further the cause of law and goodness, help allied creatures in need, and combat evil. Greater shedu typically lead herds of six or more lesser shedu.

Combat: All shedu attack with powerful front hooves. However, both forms of shedu prefer to use their psionic powers whenever possible.

LESSER SHEDU
Languages: Lesser shedu speak shedu, lamia, lammasu, and most human tongues (although not common). Of course, they can always use empathy (a limited form of telepathy, see below).

Psionics Summary:

Level	Dis/Sci/Dev	Attack/Defense	Score	PSPs
9	4/4/13	All/ALL	= Int	100

Lesser shedu always have the five powers listed below (within three disciplines), and they can use them without expending PSPs. In addition to these powers, a lesser shedu knows any three sciences and five devotions desired (from these disciplines, or others). Each creature tends to specialize in a particular discipline to complement the herd (each takes a different discipline).

Psychometabolism - Devotions: ectoplasmic form.
Telepathy - Devotions: contact, empathy, mindlink.
Psychoportation - Devotions: astral projection.

GREATER SHEDU
Greater shedu radiate *protection from evil, 10' radius.*

Languages: Greater shedu speak shedu, lamia, lammasu, common, and root languages (i.e. most human tongues). However, they can always rely upon telepathy, which they have mastered so well that they can even make rudimentary contact can be made even with plants.

Psionics Summary

Level	Dis/Sci/Dev	Attack/Defense	Score	PSPs
14	5/12/15	All/ALL	= Int	200

Common powers (* denotes powers they always have, † denotes innate abilities that are like the psionic powers, but require no point expenditures):
Defense - mind bar*†
Clairvoyance - Sciences: aura sight, clairaudience, clairvoyance, object reading, precognition Devotions: danger sense, sensitivity to psychic impressions
Psychometabolism - Sciences: energy containment, metamorphosis Devotions: body control, ectoplasmic form*†
Psychokinesis - Sciences: telekinesis Devotions: molecular agitation, molecular manipulation
Telepathy - Sciences: domination, mass domination, mindlink*+ Devotions: contact*, invisibility*†, post-hypnotic suggestion
Psychoportation - Sciences: probability travel*†, teleport*† Devotions: dimensional door, dimension walk*†

Sirine

CLIMATE/TERRAIN:	Temperate or tropical salt or fresh water, in wilderness areas
FREQUENCY:	Rare (salt water) or very rare (fresh water)
ORGANIZATION:	Solitary or family
ACTIVITY CYCLE:	Any
DIET:	Omnivore
INTELLIGENCE:	High to genius (13-18)
TREASURE:	L, M, N, Q; X
ALIGNMENT:	Any
NO. APPEARING:	1 (2d4)
ARMOR CLASS:	3
MOVEMENT:	12, Sw 24
HIT DICE:	4-7
THAC0:	4 HD: 17
	5-6 HD: 15
	7 HD: 13
NO. OF ATTACKS:	1
DAMAGE/ATTACK:	By weapon type
SPECIAL ATTACKS:	Song, spell powers
SPECIAL DEFENSES:	Spell powers, water-breathing
MAGIC RESISTANCE:	20%
SIZE:	M (5'-6' tall)
MORALE:	Steady (11-12)
XP VALUE:	4 HD: 2,000 (+1,000 for each additional Hit Die)

Sirines are beautiful, human-like females, at home in any aquatic environment. They have human skin tones ranging to a light yellow-green, and their hair can be almost any color, though silver and dark green are the most common. Sirines have beautiful figures and wear scanty clothing at best.

Most sirines are antisocial, so they try to drive intruders away, with evil sirines taking stronger measures. Other sirines are hungry for social interaction, and try to lure male humans or demihumans to join them for a time.

Sirines speak their own language and the language of the nearest intelligent races. They can breathe water and air, and they have infravision to a range of 120 feet.

Combat: A lone sirine will always have 6 or 7 HD; each member of a group has an equal chance for 4, 5, or 6 HD. All members of a group have the same basic alignment (all evil, all good, or all neutral in regards to good and evil). All sirines can defend their solitude with some skill.

Sirines have a Dexterity of 18; combined with their innate magic, this grants them an exceptional Armor Class. Most (90%) sirines carry a short sword or a dagger, and 30% carry missile weapons, javelins or slings, as well. Each weapon has a 10% chance of being magical, and *javelins of lightning* are common.

Sirines also have several spell-like abilities, each usable once per day as an 11th-level wizard: *charm person, fog cloud, polymorph self,* and *improved invisibility.* The charm ability is used through the sirine's song, and all people within 30 feet are subject to it, even if they are hostile or attacking.

If the sirine touches an opponent, the victim must make a saving throw vs. poison; those failing to save are reduced to an Intelligence of 2. The touch is automatic for charmed individuals, but requires a normal attack roll for others. A successful *dispel magic* (against 11th-level casting) will restore the victim's intelligence, as will a sirine's touch, if she so wills it. Any sirine can restore intelligence taken by another sirine.

Sirines make saving throws as 11th-level wizards, with a +2 bonus vs. poison. They are immune to all gas attacks.

Habitat/Society: Sirines are encountered only in lonely places that are otherwise uninhabited. Most live near rocky outcroppings or small islands in the sea. Some choose to live in fresh water, but tend to avoid these areas because they are usually populated and sometimes difficult to reach.

Young sirines often live with their sisters; these sirines are the more social type. As a sirine grows older, she becomes more reclusive and contemplative, however, and eventually looks for a home of her own where she can think and sing in solitude. Even then, they have a rare desire for companionship.

Sirines usually mate with male humans. Some sirines choose elves, tritons, or merfolk as mates, producing children with some of their parents' traits (pointed ears from elves, green skin from aquatic elves, scales and webbed fingers and toes from merfolk and tritons). Sirines never form lasting relationships, for the call of the sea is too great to bind them.

After a gestation period of nine months, they give birth to 1d4 baby sirines, which are cared for by their mother until they are five years old. After that, they fend for themselves, living on the bounty of the sea. Reaching adulthood at 10 years, they live for about 50 years, and yet their beauty never leaves them.

Sirines live to sing, and to think about the sea. If deprived of their voices, or confined away from water, they will slowly wither away until they die. Sirines often have great knowledge regarding the history of their area and any current events. They sometimes trade this knowledge for companionship.

Ecology: Sirines are not harmful to their environment in any manner. They kill only enough to eat, and never take too much from the sea. They have few natural enemies, and they are more than able of taking care of themselves. Though they make beautiful garments from sea shells, fish skin, and seaweed, they gain other belongings and treasure by scavenging shipwrecks.

	Skeleton	Animal	Monster
CLIMATE/TERRAIN:	Any	Any	Any
FREQUENCY:	Rare	Very rare	Very rare
ORGANIZATION:	Band	Band	Band
ACTIVITY CYCLE:	Any	Any	Any
DIET:	Nil	Nil	Nil
INTELLIGENCE:	Non- (0)	Non- (0)	Non- (0)
TREASURE:	Nil	See below	Nil
ALIGNMENT:	Neutral	Neutral	Neutral
NO. APPEARING:	3-30 (3d10)	2-20 (2d10)	1-6
ARMOR CLASS:	7	8	6
MOVEMENT:	12	6	12
HIT DICE:	1	1-1	6
THAC0:	19	20	15
NO. OF ATTACKS:	1	1	1
DAMAGE/ATTACK:	1-6 (weapon)	1- 4	Special
SPECIAL ATTACKS:	Nil	Nil	Nil
SPECIAL DEFENSES:	See below	See below	See below
MAGIC RESISTANCE:	See below	See below	See below
SIZE:	M (6' tall)	S-M (3'- 5')	L-H (7'-15')
MORALE:	Special	Special	Special
XP VALUE:	65	65	650

All skeletons are magically animated undead monsters, created as guardians or warriors by powerful evil wizards and priests.

Skeletons appear to have no ligaments or musculature which would allow movement. Instead, the bones are magically joined together during the casting of an *animate dead* spell. Skeletons have no eyes or internal organs.

Skeletons can be made from the bones of humans and demi-humans, animals of human size or smaller, or giant humanoids like bugbears and giants.

Combat: Man-sized humanoid skeletons always fight with weapons, usually a rusty sword or spear. Because of their magical nature, they do not fight as well as living beings and inflict only 1-6 points of damage when they hit. Animal skeletons almost always bite for 1-4 points of damage, unless they would obviously inflict less (i.e., skeletal rats should inflict only 1-2 points, etc.). Monster skeletons, always constructed from humanoid creatures, use giant-sized weapons which inflict the same damage as their living counterparts but without any Strength bonuses.

Skeletons are immune to all *sleep, charm,* and *hold* spells. Because they are assembled from bones, cold-based attacks also do skeletons no harm. The fact that they are mostly empty means that edged or piercing weapons (like swords, daggers, and spears) inflict only half damage when employed against skeletons. Blunt weapons, with larger heads designed to break and crush bones, cause normal damage against skeletons. Fire also does normal damage against skeletons. Holy water inflicts 2-8 points of damage per vial striking the skeleton.

Skeletons are immune to *fear* spells and need never check morale, usually being magically commanded to fight to the death. When a skeleton dies, it falls to pieces with loud clunks and rattles.

Habitat/Society: Skeletons have no social life or interesting habits. They can be found anywhere there is a wizard or priest powerful enough to make them. Note that some neutral priests of deities of the dead or dying often raise whole armies of animated followers in times of trouble. Good clerics can make skeletons only if the dead being has granted permission (either before or after death) and if the cleric's deity has given express permission to do so. Otherwise, violating the eternal rest of any being or animal is something most good deities disapprove of highly.

Skeletons have almost no minds whatsoever, and can obey on-ly the simplest one- or two-phrase orders from their creators. Skeletons fight in unorganized masses and tend to botch complex orders disastrously. It is not unheard of to find more than one type of skeleton (monsters with animals, animals with humans) working together to protect their master's dungeon or tower.

Ecology: Unless the skeleton's remains are destroyed or scattered far apart, the skeleton can be created anew with the application of another *animate dead* spell. Rumors of high-level *animate dead* spells which create skeletons capable of reforming themselves to continue fighting after being destroyed have not been reliably comfirmed.

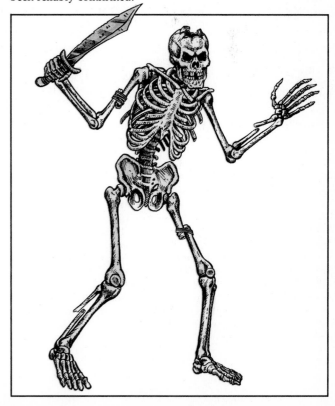

Skeleton, Giant

CLIMATE/TERRAIN:	Any
FREQUENCY:	Rare
ORGANIZATION:	Solitary
ACTIVITY CYCLE:	Any
DIET:	Nil
INTELLIGENCE:	Non-(0)
TREASURE:	Nil
ALIGNMENT:	Neutral

NO. APPEARING:	2-8 (2d4)
ARMOR CLASS:	4
MOVEMENT:	12
HIT DICE:	4+4
THAC0:	15
NO. OF ATTACKS:	1
DAMAGE/ATTACK:	1d12
SPECIAL ATTACKS:	Nil
SPECIAL DEFENSES:	See below
MAGIC RESISTANCE:	Nil
SIZE:	L (12' tall)
MORALE:	Fearless (20)
XP VALUE:	975

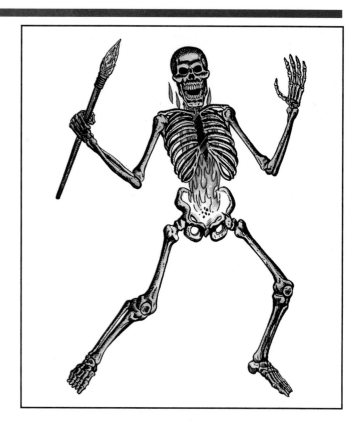

Giant skeletons are similar to the more common undead skeleton, but they have been created with a combination of spells and are, thus, far more deadly than their lesser counterparts.

Giant skeletons stand roughly 12 feet tall and look to be made from the bones of giants. In actuality, they are simply human skeletons that have been magically *enlarged*. They are normally armed with long spears or scythes that end in keen bone blades. Rare individuals will be found carrying shields (and thus have an Armor Class of 3), but these are far from common. A small, magical fire burns in the chest of each giant skeleton, a by-product of the magics that are used to make them. These flames begin just above the pelvis and reach upward to lick at the collar bones. Mysteriously, no burning or scorching occurs where the flames touch the bone.

Giant skeletons do not communicate in any way. They can obey simple, verbal commands given to them by their creator, but will ignore all others. In order for a command to be understood by these animated skeletons, it must contain no more than three distinct concepts. For example, "stay in this room, make sure that nobody comes in, and don't allow the prince to leave,". would be the type of command these creatures could obey.

Combat: In melee combat, giant skeletons most frequently attack with bone-bladed scythes or spears. Each blow that lands inflicts 1d12 points of damage.

Once per hour (6 turns), a skeleton may reach into its chest and draw forth a sphere of fire from the flames that burn within its rib cage. This flaming sphere can be hurled as if it were a *fireball* that delivers 8d6 points of damage. Because these creatures are immune to harm from both magical and normal fires, they will freely use this attack in close quarters.

Giant skeletons are immune to *sleep, charm, hold,* or similar mind-affecting spells. Cold-based spells inflict half damage to them, lightning inflicts full damage, while fire (as has already been mentioned) cannot harm them. They suffer half damage from edged or piercing weapons and but 1 point of damage per die from all manner of arrows, quarrels, or missiles. Blunt melee weapons inflict full damage on them.

Being undead, giant skeletons can be turned by priests and paladins. They are more difficult to turn than mundane skeletons, however, being treated as if they were mummies. Holy water that is splashed upon them inflicts 2d4 points of damage per vial.

Habitat/Society: The first giant skeletons to appear in Ravenloft were created by the undead priestess Radaga in her lair within the domain of Kartakass. Others have since mastered the spells and techniques required to create these monsters; thus, giant skeletons are gradually beginning to appear in other realms where the dead and undead lurk.

Giant skeletons are employed as guards and sentinels by those with the power to create them. It is said that the Dark Powers can see everything that transpires before the eyes of these foul automatons, but there is no proof supporting this rumor.

Ecology: Like lesser animated skeletons, these undead things have no true claim to any place in nature. They are created from the bones of those who have died and are abominations in the eyes of all who belief in the sanctity of life and goodness.

The process by which giant skeletons are created is dark and evil. Attempts to manufacture them outside of Ravenloft have failed, so it is clear that they are in some way linked to the Dark Powers themselves. In order to create a giant skeleton, a spell caster must have the intact skeleton of a normal human or demihuman. On a night when the land is draped in fog, they must cast an *animate dead, produce fire, enlarge,* and a *resist fire* spell over the bones. When the last spell is cast, the bones lengthen and thicken and the creatures rises up. The the creator must make a Ravenloft Powers check for his part in this evil undertaking.

Skeleton, Warrior

CLIMATE/TERRAIN:	Any
FREQUENCY:	Very rare
ORGANIZATION:	Solitary
ACTIVITY CYCLE:	Any
DIET:	Nil
INTELLIGENCE:	Exceptional (15-16)
TREASURE:	A
ALIGNMENT:	Neutral evil

NO. APPEARING:	1
ARMOR CLASS:	2
MOVEMENT:	6
HIT DICE:	9+2 to 9+12
THAC0:	11
NO. OF ATTACKS:	1
DAMAGE/ATTACK:	By weapon (+3 to attack roll)
SPECIAL ATTACKS:	See below
SPECIAL DEFENSES:	See below
MAGIC RESISTANCE:	90%
SIZE:	M (6'-7' tall)
MORALE:	Champion (15)
XP VALUE:	4,000

Formerly powerful fighters, skeleton warriors are undead lords forced into their nightmarish states by powerful wizards or evil demigods who trapped their souls in golden circlets. The sole reason that skeleton warriors remain on the Prime Material plane is to search for and recover the circlets that contain their souls.

A skeletal warrior appears as a cracked and yellowing skeleton covered with shards of decaying flesh. Its eyes are black holes containing pinpoints of reddish light. It is clad in the blackened armor and rotted trappings it wore in its former life.

Combat: Anyone possessing a skeleton warrior's circlet can control its actions, so long as the controller remains within 240 feet of the warrior. The controller is either in active control of the warrior or in a passive mode. When in active control, the controller can see whatever the skeleton sees, and he can mentally command it to fight, search for treasure, or take any other actions; however, the controller himself is unable to cast spells, move, or take any other actions while in active control. When in the passive mode, the controller can take any normal actions, but he is unable to see through the warrior's eyes; the skeleton warrior remains inert while the controller is in passive mode. The controller can change between the passive mode and active control at will.

The controller must have the warrior's circlet on his head in order to control the warrior. If the circlet is removed from the controller's head, he can no longer control the warrior; likewise, if the controller and the warrior are separated by more than 240 feet, the controller can no longer control the warrior. If the circlet remains in the controller's possession, he can resume control at a later time. But if the controller loses the circlet, either by accident or by a deliberate act, the warrior immediately proceeds toward the controller at twice its normal movement rate (12) to attack and destroy him. The warrior does not rest until it destroys its former controller or until control is re-established. If the warrior holds the circlet to its head, both the warrior and the circlet turn to dust, never to reappear.

When a character first comes into possession of a circlet, he is unlikely to be aware that the skeleton warrior is tracking him, unless he recognizes the circlet's significance. To establish control for the first time, the character not only must hold the circlet to his head, he must be able to see the warrior and concentrate on the establishment of control for one round and then roll a successful Wisdom check; if he fails the Wisdom check, he can try again in subsequent rounds. Meanwhile, the skeleton warrior continues to approach, attempting to destroy the character and gain possession of the circlet. If his concentration is broken before control is established—for instance, if he has to defend himself against an attack—he must concentrate again for three rounds. Once control has been established for the first time, it can only be broken as indicated above. To be effective, the circlet cannot be worn with any other headgear; placing it in a helm, for instance, nullifies its powers, though the skeleton warrior is still aware of the circlet's presence.

Skeleton warriors usually fight with two-handed swords, but they can use other weapons as well. Skeleton warriors make all weapon attacks with a +3 bonus to their attack roll; this is an innate ability, the weapon itself is not magical.

Only magical weapons affect skeleton warriors. They have a 90% magical resistance. The mere sight of a skeleton warrior causes any creature with fewer than 5 Hit Dice to flee in panic. Skeleton warriors cannot be turned by priests.

Habitat/Society: Skeleton warriors are usually found near the areas where they died in their former lives, or where they were buried. A skeleton warrior usually has a sizeable collection of treasure, the remnants of a lifetime of adventure. Since a skeleton warrior is preoccupied with recovering its circlet, protecting its treasure is not a priority.

Ecology: Skeleton warriors are used by their controllers as bodyguards, servants, or workers. Since skeleton warriors are obsessed with their circlets and are therefore undependable, evil creatures and other undead seldom associate with them. Skeleton warriors do not eat, sleep, or perform any other physiological functions.

Slaad

	Red	Blue
CLIMATE/TERRAIN:	Limbo	Limbo
FREQUENCY:	Uncommon	Rare
ORGANIZATION:	Group	Group
ACTIVITY CYCLE:	Any	Any
DIET:	Carnivore	Carnivore
INTELLIGENCE:	Low(5-7)	Low (5-7)
TREASURE:	K,Q	K,Q
ALIGNMENT:	Chaotic neutral	Chaotic neutral
NO. APPEARING:	3-18	2-12
ARMOR CLASS:	4	2
MOVEMENT:	6	6
HIT DICE:	7+3	8+4
THAC0:	13	13
NO. OF ATTACKS:	3	5
DAMAGE/ATTACK:	1-4/1-4/2-16 2-12/2-16	2-12/2-12/ 2-12/
SPECIAL ATTACKS:	Stun, egg-pellet	Disease
SPECIAL DEFENSES:	See below	+ 1 or better weapons to hit
MAGIC RESISTANCE:	30%	40%
SIZE:	L (8' tall)	L (10' tall)
MORALE:	Average (8-10)	Steady(11-12)
XP VALUE:	7,500	16,500

The slaadi are great frog-like beings, who dwell on the outer plane of Limbo. Their form is that of a large bipedal frog, though some of the more powerful slaadi have *polymorph self* or shape change abilities and sometimes appear as men. In frog form their heads are huge and their claws are extremely sharp. There are powerful symbols embedded into their foreheads signifying rank. They speak their own language and, occasionally, some additional evil languages. Telepathy allows them to understand and converse with all things.

Red Slaad

Slaadi are vicious combatants and quick to attack all other creatures. They can be ruthless when encountered in numbers, often surrounding smaller groups of beings and bullying and tormenting them before finally slaying the lot.

Combat: Red slaadi attack with two claws for 1-4 points of damage per hit and bite for 2-16 points. They are not terribly intelligent, so they choose predictable, uninspired tactics.

Red slaadi have a special gland under the skin of each claw. When one hits with a claw attack, there is a 25 % chance that an egg pellet is planted in its opponent's body. The egg pellet begins to move through the victim's body, often without the victim even knowing he has been infected until it reaches the chest cavity. There it gestates for three months, forming a baby red slaad that will eats it way out of the victim's body, killing him. The victim falls very ill 24 hours before the baby slaad eats its way out. An egg pellet can only be detected by a *detect evil* spell, and destroyed by a *remove curse* or similar spell.

Red slaadi regenerate at a rate of 3 hit points per melee round. They can attempt to *gate* in 1-2 additional red slaadi twice per day with a 35% chance of success. Once per day, red slaadi may stun by emitting a loud croak that affects all opponents within 20 feet of the slaad. Victims must make a saving throw vs. petrification or be disabled for two rounds.

Blue Slaad

Blue slaad are ruthless warriors that specialize in mass combat.

Combat: Blue slaadi have two razor-sharp bone rakes sticking out from the back of each hand. These potent weapons inflict 2-12 points of damage on a successful hit. They have perfected their fighting style with these rakes, which give them two attacks per hand. Their bite does 2-16 points of damage per hit and has a 10% chance of infecting the slaad's opponent with a rotting disease. Blue slaadi have the following magical abilities: *hold person*, one person only, *passwall*, and *telekinesis*.

They may attempt to *gate* in either 1-4 red slaadi or 1-2 blue slaadi, four times per day, with a 40% chance of success.

Green Slaad

Very rarely seen, they are the highest form of lesser slaadi. They attack with claws for 3 to 8 (1d6+2) points of damage.

Gray Slaad

Known as *executioners*, and very rare, gray slaadi are great slaadi. They use a claw/claw/bite routine for 4 to 10 points of damage from their wicked claws, and 2 to 16 points of damage from the vicious bite they inflict upon opponents.

Death Slaad

The greatest of all the slaadi, and the absolute masters of their race. Their claws strike for 3 to 18 points of damage and their bite inflicts 2 to 20 points of damage.

Habitat/Society: Slaadi have a hierarchial society. Their caste system is rigid because the strong will simply destroy the weak for disobedience; lesser slaadi are forced to be their servants. Reds and blues aid each other only in extreme emergencies.

Ecology: Although slaadi are inhabitants of the outer planes, and are frequently found travelling the lower planes, they have little or nothing to do with the Blood War between the baatezu and the tanar'ri.

Slug, Giant

CLIMATE/TERRAIN:	Subterranean and wet
FREQUENCY:	Uncommon
ORGANIZATION:	Solitary
ACTIVITY CYCLE:	Any
DIET:	Omnivore
INTELLIGENCE:	Non- (0)
TREASURE:	Nil
ALIGNMENT:	Neutral

NO. APPEARING:	1
ARMOR CLASS:	8
MOVEMENT:	6
HIT DICE:	12
THAC0:	9
NO. OF ATTACKS:	1
DAMAGE/ATTACK:	1-12
SPECIAL ATTACKS:	Spits acid
SPECIAL DEFENSES:	Immune to blunt weapons
MAGIC RESISTANCE:	Nil
SIZE:	H-G (25'-50' long)
MORALE:	Steady (12)
XP VALUE:	5,000

Giant slugs are huge, omnivorous mutations of the small and benign garden slugs. Their highly developed mouths are capable of chewing flesh and well as plants, and they spit a highly corrosive acid on their food. Most giant slugs are pale gray, with dead white underbellies.

Combat: Giant slugs can bite for 1d12 points of damage, but their main attack form is their corrosive acid saliva. The acid is spat at a single target and corrodes any organic tissue (plants or animals). It will also destroy equipment (saving throw vs. acid). The acid inflicts 4d8 points of damage (successful saving throw vs. breath weapon for one-half damage). Giant slugs can use this breath weapon every round (its acid stores are never used up). Slugs are not very accurate with this attack; the first shot has only a 10% chance of hitting. The success of subsequent shots depends on the distance to the target—the base chance of hitting is 90% at a distance of ten yards, with a -10% penalty per additional ten yards. If the slug misses, the acid hits 10 feet from the desired target (determine randomly which direction). Note that giant slugs are impervious to this acid spittle.

Giant slugs are immensely strong and can batter down doors and wooden buildings in seconds. They have no bones and can squeeze through holes and crevasses normally impassible to much smaller predators. For example, a party of adventurers might seek cover in a large stone building, while taunting the slowly approaching slug behind them. To their astonishment, the huge creature enters through the same doorway the party did and begins to send acid everywhere.

The rasping tongue of a giant slug enables it to burrow through 1 foot of earth or 6 inches of wood per round, making most standard barricades useless against it.

Because of their lack of bones and their thick, rubbery hides, giant slugs are not harmed by blunt weapons or spells that cause crushing or impact damage. Only edged and pointed weapons and magical attacks, can harm a giant slug.

Habitat/Society: Giant slugs can be found in any wet and dark environment, including deserted dungeons, swamps, and rain forests. Giant slugs are solitary creatures and speak no language. They are barely sentient, exhibiting only rudimentary instinctive reactions when confronted.

Ecology: No one has ever found a good use for giant slugs, except maybe as huge garbage disposals. They have no known predators. They will eat anything—plants, carrion, garbage—but prefer warm, living flesh when they can catch it. Since giant slugs have such huge appetites, they rarely attack smaller creatures, such as squirrels and monkeys, which they have a hard time seeing anyway. Even on a good day, they must usually supplement their feedings with some vegetation.

Normal slugs have a nasty reaction to salt when it is sprinkled on them. They dry up and die in 1d4+1 rounds. It is unlikely that this technique is adaptable to the giant variety, but some fabrication and summoning spells might be adaptable if there ever seemed to be a need for it.

For now, giant slugs remain a very real danger in jungles, forests, and dungeons everywhere.

Snake

	Amphis-baena	Boalisk	Constrictor (Normal)	Constrictor (Giant)	Heway	Poison (Normal)	Pois on (Giant)	Sea, Giant	Spitting
CLIMATE/TERRAIN:	Any temperate	Any tropical	Any warm	Any warm	Desert oases	Any land	Any land	Tropical marine	Tropical land
FREQUENCY:	Very rare	Rare	Uncommon	Uncommon	Uncommon	Uncommon	Uncommon	Uncommon	Rare
INTELLIGENCE:	Animal (1)	Animal (1)	Animal (1)	Animal (1)	Low (5-7)	Animal (1)	Animal (1)	Animal (1)	Animal (1)
NO. APPEARING:	1-3	1-3	1-2	1-2	1-2	1-6	1-6	1-8	1-4
ARMOR CLASS:	3	5	6	5	7	6	5	5	5
MOVEMENT:	12	12	9	9	12, Sw 6	15	15	12, Sw 12	12
HIT DICE:	6	5+1	3+2	6+1	1+3	2+1	4+2	10	4+2
THAC0:	15	17	17	15	19	19	17	11	17
NO. OF ATTACKS:	2	2	2	2	1	1	1	2	2
DAMAGE/ATTACK:	1-3/1-3	1-3/2-7	1/1-3	1-4/2-8	1-3	1	1-3	1-6/3-18	1-3
SPECIAL ATTACKS:	Poison	Gaze and constrict	Constrict	Constrict	Poison and hypnotic stare	Poison	Poison constrict	Poison,	Spit poison
SPECIAL DEFENSES:	See below	Nil	Nil	Nil	Nil	Nil	Nil	Nil	Nil
SIZE:	M (13' long)	L (25' long)	M (10'-20' long)	L (30' + long)	M (12' long)	S (5' long)	M (12' long)	G (50' + long)	M (8' long)
MORALE:	Average (9)	Steady (10)	Average (8)	Average (9)	Unsteady (6)	Average (8)	Average (9)	Steady (11)	Average (9)
XP VALUE:	650	975	175	650	175	175	420	3,000	650
Elder:	1,400	2,000	420	1,400	420	420	975	5,000	1,400
Jaculi:	975	1,400	270	975	N/A	270	650	N/A	975

Snakes are long, slender reptiles that can be found anywhere in the entire world, even in the coldest arctic regions.

There are basically two types of snakes, in all manner of sizes. The poisonous snakes make up for their relatively smaller size with deadly venoms, while the larger constrictors squeeze their victims to death. Both types sleep for days after eating. All snakes shed their skin several times each year. All snakes in this entry share the following characteristics:

ORGANIZATION:	Solitary
ACTIVITY CYCLE:	Day
DIET:	Carnivore
TREASURE:	Nil
ALIGNMENT:	Neutral
MAGIC RESISTANCE:	Nil

Snakes fear fire and will retreat from open flames, suffering a −6 morale modifier when flames are used against them.

Amphisbaena
These monsters have heads at both ends, and both heads are armed with poisonous fangs. The creature travels by grasping one of its necks and rolling like a hoop. It can attack with both heads, each head attacking a separate target. Victims failing to make a saving throw vs. poison when bitten die instantly. Amphisbaena are immune to cold-based attacks.

Boalisk
The boalisk is a tropical constrictor snake with a *gaze* attack. Any creature meeting its *gaze* (failing a saving throw vs. petrification) is infected with a magical rotting disease, identical to that inflicted by a mummy. Characters refusing to look at the boalisk automatically avoid its *gaze* but suffer a −4 penalty to their AC. Surprised victims always meet its *gaze* and gain no saving throw. The boalisk can use its *gaze* on a single victim each round in addition to normal biting and constriction attacks.

Constrictor Snake
Constrictors of all sizes hide in the branches of trees, waiting patiently until they can slowly lower themselves or suddenly drop onto their unsuspecting victims. Once they strike, the victim is constricted automatically, suffering damage every round. Constricted humanoid creatures can escape the coils of normal con-

strictors with a successful open doors roll (at a −1 penalty). Anyone who attempts to free a captive by hacking at the constrictor has a 20% chance of striking the victim instead (roll normal damage and apply it to the victim). Area spells like *fireball* will likewise affect both combatants, but target-specific spells like *charm monster* and *magic missile* are more precise.

Common constrictor species include anacondas, boas, and reticulate pythons, all of which can reach lengths of 30 feet. Their skin is valuable, with an unblemished skin selling for as much as 100 gp.

Some constrictor snakes are known as birdcharmers; these innately magical snakes can mesmerize their prey by swaying slowly and steadily while staring down their victims. Creatures of animal intelligence or less must make a saving throw against paralyzation or be effectively paralyzed for as long as the snake continues to sway, and for 2d6 rounds thereafter.

Giant Constrictor Snake
Giant constrictor snakes are larger and much stronger than their smaller cousins. It requires the combined efforts of 60 total points of Strength (the coiled victim plus outside help) to extricate someone from a giant constrictor's steel grasp.

The skin of a giant constrictor snake is too thick and stiff to be workable, and is valuable only as armor, not for decoration. An uncured hide can fetch 20 gp.

Snow serpents are a particularly large and dangerous form of giant constrictor snake, one adapted to life in a sub-arctic climate. These furred white snakes hide their 100-foot bodies in the snow bodies and wait for prey to pass by. When it does, they spring up and coil their loops around the victims. After that, snow serpents automatically bite for 2d10 points of damage each round. Those in its coils are helpless. Snow serpents are very rare and have the following statistics: AC 6, MV 9, HD 10, THAC0 11, SZ G (100' long), ML average (8-10), XP 2,000. Their pelt is worth 2,000 gp. In all other respects they are similar to other giant constrictor snakes.

Heway
These intelligent snakes have slimy, poisonous skins that they use to foul wells and oases. After swimming in a body of water for several hours and releasing its poison, it slinks off to wait for its prey to arrive. A creature drinking water poisoned by a heway must make a successful saving throw vs. poison at +2 or suffer

30 points damage within 3d6 minutes and be paralyzed for 1d6 hours. Creatures that make their saving throws suffer 15 points of damage. Even animals that survive the initial effects are often doomed to die of dehydration.

Many humans and animals attack heways on sight, but it can defend itself with its hypnotic stare, which has a powerful effect; any creature failing a saving throw vs. paralyzation will follow the heway to its lair and allow itself to be devoured. The heway sometimes uses this stare simply to immobilize a menacing creature. It then leaves the area while the hypnotized creature remains stationary for 1d6 turns.

Heway are innate cowards and avoid contact with other animals. It is a weak fighter, its bite is not venomous, and its jaws are weak. Its preferred food is small animal carrion. Simply touching heway skin has no effect; the poison must be ingested.

Poisonous Snake

All poisonous snakes deliver toxins automatically through their bite. Roll on the table below (or choose) to determine what type of poison is present.

Die Roll	Modifier to Save	Onset Time	Result of Failed Saving Throw*
1-4	+3	1-4 turns	Incapacitated for 2-8 days
5-6	+2	2-5 rounds	Death
7-11	+1	2-12 rounds	2-8 points of damage
12-14	None	1-6 rounds	3-12 points of damage
15-17	-1	2-8 rounds	Incapacitated for 1-4 days
18-19	-2	1-4 rounds	Incapacitated for 1-12 days
20	-3	1 round	Death

* A successful saving throw means no damage.

Typical varieties of poisonous snakes include the asp, cobra, copperhead, coral snake, death adder, krait, mamba, puff adder, rattlesnake, sidewinder, and water moccasin.

Some cobras and sidewinders hunt by night and can track warmblooded prey by body heat as well as by sight. They have the equivalent of 30-foot infravision. Black mambas are the fastest known snakes and can reach 30 across open ground.

Giant Poisonous Snake

Giant poisonous snakes cause death in one round if their victims fail a saving throw vs. poison. Some varieties inflict 3-18 points of damage even if the saving throw is made.

The giant cobra is an example of a variant, giant poisonous snake. Its venom results in death 2-8 rounds after a successful strike; if the victim makes a saving throw at −2 he suffers only 10 points of damage. Giant cobras mesmerize prey as birdcharmer snakes do (see above). They can kill and eat an entire goat or a demihuman up to halfling or gnome size. Some varieties of giant weasel can hunt them successfully, and jungle giants consider giant cobras a delicacy, as do some elven tribesmen.

Giant Sea Snake

Found only in tropical waters, the giant sea snake is the only type of snake that is both constricting and poisonous. Its constricting grasp on small ships can crush them in 10 rounds. Sea snakes attack ships only when they are hungry (20% chance). Their poisonous bite is deadly in 1-4 rounds. Sea snakes are fully capable of diving to great depths, and their nostrils (on the top of their snouts) have membranes that automatically seal them underwater.

From time to time giant sea snakes gather in huge floating masses of hundreds or thousands of snakes, often 100 yards wide and 30 miles long. These may be mating rituals or they may be seasonal migrations; the actual reason is unknown.

Spitting Snake

Spitting varieties of snakes bite their victims and can shoot poisonous spittle at a single target within 30 feet. Their poison is identical to normal poisonous snakes (see above). Typical species include the African spitting cobra, which can spit up to 15 feet. Its spittle can blind victims that fail a saving throw vs. poison. The blindness wears off after 2-12 hours.

Jaculi (Tree Snakes)

Many of the above land snakes can be encountered as tree snakes, also known as jaculi. These subspecies are simply arboreal varieties of other types of snakes that have adapted to life in a forest canopy. They have chameleon-like camouflage abilities and can leap onto their prey from 50 feet above ground; opponents suffer a −4 penalty to surprise rolls.

Some tree snakes have broad, flat heads with razor spines or barbs that make their initial impact particularly potent (double normal bite damage). After their initial flying attack, they must depend on biting or constriction attacks or climb back into the trees to leap again.

Jaculi snakes include the poisonous boomslang and the emerald tree boa. Many jaculi species prey on other snakes.

Elder Serpents

Ancient snakes are said to gain wisdom with age, giving them Semi- to Low intelligence (2-7). They gain an additional Hit Die and the ability to speak (with a lisp). Elder serpent venom is more concentrated than that of its younger cousins (death in 1-4 rounds maximum, saving throws at −4). They suffer no modifier to morale when faced with open flames. Elder serpents have a measure of cunning and value glittering objects; they have treasure, type W.

Elder serpents can paralyze prey as birdcatchers do (see constrictors above). In the case of elder boalisks, their *gaze* has two simultaneous effects and victims are entitled to two saving throws. All elder serpents can hypnotize people as well as animals with their paralyzing stare.

The largest elder serpent is called the Grand Snakemaster, and is said to be immortal. When it sheds its skin, the discarded skin is rumored to possess healing powers. Those who eat it are said to gain wisdom, but since the Grand Snakemaster has never been seen, the truth of these rumors is questionable.

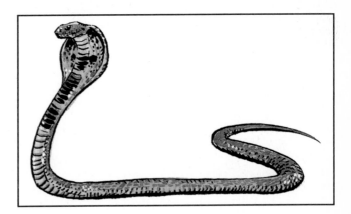

Snake, Winged

CLIMATE/TERRAIN:	Tropical/Forests
FREQUENCY:	Rare
ORGANIZATION:	Flocks
ACTIVITY CYCLE:	Any
DIET:	Herbivore
INTELLIGENCE:	Semi (2-4)
TREASURE:	Nil
ALIGNMENT:	Neutral

NO. APPEARING:	2-8
ARMOR CLASS:	5
MOVEMENT:	12, Fl 18 (B)
HIT DICE:	4+4
THAC0:	15
NO. OF ATTACKS:	1
DAMAGE/ATTACK:	1-4
SPECIAL ATTACKS:	Poison, spark shower
SPECIAL DEFENSES:	Immune to electricity
MAGIC RESISTANCE:	Nil
SIZE:	L (8-10' long)
MORALE:	Average (9)
XP VALUE:	1,400

Winged serpents, sometimes called spark snakes, are colorful reptiles that dwell in Zakhara's forests and jungles. Winged serpents come in many colors, ranging from sky blue and emerald green to raspberry red. They are supported by invisibly swift, gossamer wings, making them resemble reptilian hummingbirds. When their delicate wings are folded back, winged serpents can *spider climb* at will.

Combat: Winged serpents move with liquid grace and devastating speed. They always receive a −3 bonus to initiative.

The bite of a winged serpent inflicts 1d4 points of damage and injects the victim with a corrosive, acidic fluid. This poison has an onset time of 1 round and inflicts an additional 2d8 points of damage for the following 2 rounds (half damage if a save vs. poison is made).

By far the most dangerous attack of these reptiles is their sparking breath weapon. Their wings beat so quickly that they build up a static charge from the ambient air (especially in the humid forest). A winged serpent can discharge this static electricity from its mouth in a spark shower, a cloud of dancing sparks and electrical energy 10 feet in diameter. Those caught in the area of effect take 2d8 (2-16) points of damage (half if a save vs. breath weapon is made). The spark shower will also ignite any exposed flammable objects, like clothes, hair, dry wood, or lamp oil. Once it has been discharged, it takes one turn for a winged serpent to build its static charge back up. All winged serpents are immune to electricity.

Winged serpents are vulnerable to fire-based attacks (especially their delicate wings), against which they save at penalty of −2. If a winged serpent fails its saving throw against a fire attack, assume that its wings are incinerated. Although this won't affect its ability to bite a victim, the serpent cannot use its breath weapon until the wings grow back.

Habitat/Society: Winged serpents must eat constantly in order to survive. They flit about the jungle in small flocks, searching for tropical fruits, from which they draw their nourishment. A winged serpent will fly up to one and inject it with corrosive venom. The venom breaks down the fruit into a soft, juicy mixture, partially digesting the fruit while it still remains in its skin. The serpent will then suck out the fruity pulp through the incisions made by its fangs. A typical winged serpent will eat roughly 10 times its weight in fruit each day, just to stay alive.

Winged serpents mate as often as they eat (i.e., incessantly), although they do not care for their young, which are born live and wingless. They are born with their spider climbing ability, which helps them climb fruit trees and search for food. The young are dark green in color to help them blend in better with the foliage, gaining their chromatic hues only after their wings mature. During the first few months of life, winged serpents are extremely vulnerable to an entire host of predators that roam the jungle heights (including mundane snakes, monkeys, and giant insects). Vestigial wings appear after a month of life, and become fully functional after three months.

Winged serpents have no permanent lair and hoard no treasure.

Ecology: Winged serpents play an important role in the jungle ecology. Like giant bees, they transport pollen from fruit tree to fruit tree and help with the distribution of seeds throughout the jungle. As adults, they have no natural enemies.

If captured during their first month of life before their wings have matured, they make excellent (if expensive) pets. They must consume a great quantity of fruit to survive, eating on average 100 gp worth of fruit each month (this cost might be reduced if a large orchard is available). A skilled animal trainer can teach a winged serpent up to three tasks or tricks per point of intelligence, which the creature will gladly perform (provided a supply of fresh fruit is constantly at hand). They can even be trained as guardians, although rogues have quickly discovered that unless they are extremely well-trained, they can be easily distracted by a decoy of aromatic, fresh fruit.

Few useful by-products can be obtained from a winged serpent. Their poison decomposes almost immediately after exposure to air, and their hide is too thin and fragile to serve as good leather. Their wings, however, if powdered and mixed with ink, can be used to inscribe a *protection from lightning* scroll.

Spectre

CLIMATE/TERRAIN:	Desolate dungeons and ruins
FREQUENCY:	Rare
ORGANIZATION:	Solitary
ACTIVITY CYCLE:	Darkness and night
DIET:	Nil
INTELLIGENCE:	High (13-14)
TREASURE:	Q(x3), X, Y
ALIGNMENT:	Lawful evil

NO. APPEARING:	1-6
ARMOR CLASS:	2
MOVEMENT:	15, Fl 30 (B)
HIT DICE:	7+3
THAC0:	13
NO. OF ATTACKS:	1
DAMAGE/ATTACK:	1-8
SPECIAL ATTACKS:	Energy drain
SPECIAL DEFENSES:	+1 or better weapon to hit
MAGIC RESISTANCE:	See below
SIZE:	M (6' tall)
MORALE:	Champion (15)
XP VALUE:	3,000

Spectres are powerful undead that haunt the most desolate and deserted of places. They hate all life and light.

Spectres appear as semitransparent beings and are often mistaken for haunts or ghosts. Unlike most undead, spectres retain the semblance and manner of dress of their former life and can be recognized by old friends or through paintings of the persons they used to be.

Combat: Spectres exist primarily on the Negative Material plane and can therefore be attacked by beings on the Prime Material plane only with magical weapons. Daylight makes spectres powerless by weakening their ties to the Negative Material plane.

The chilling touch of a spectre drains energy from living creatures. A successful attack inflicts 1-8 points of damage and drains two life energy levels from the victim. Any being totally drained of life energy by a spectre becomes a full-strength spectre under the control of the spectre which drained him. The victim loses all control of his personality and may become more or less powerful than before, depending on his level and class before becoming a spectre.

Spectres are immune to all *sleep, charm, hold,* and cold-based spells, as well as poisons and paralyzation attacks. Holy water inflicts 2-8 points of damage when it strikes a spectre. The water can be splashed on a spectre successfully. A *raise dead* spell apparently reverses the undead status, destroying the spectre immediately if a saving throw versus spell is failed.

Habitat/Society: Most spectres are solitary, but some enclaves exist where a particularly powerful or lucky spectre has managed to drain mortals of life. This lead spectre is known as the master spectre (always with maximum hit points per die), while the others are known collectively as the followers. In this arrangement, the master spectre almost never engages enemies personally, but instead sends his minions in for the kill. Mortals drained of life by follower spectres are subservient to the master spectre, not the followers. Note that if the master spectre is slain, all followers become independent and can travel anywhere they wish in hopes of becoming master spectres themselves. Once a character becomes a spectre, recovery is nearly impossible, requiring a special quest.

Spectres hate light and all life, as both remind them of their undead existence. They are therefore encountered only in places of extreme darkness and desolation, like long-abandoned ruins, dungeons, and subterranean sewers.

Contrary to popular mythology, spectres remain highly intelligent and generally rational after the transformation to undeath. Life makes them lament their unlife, and they bear a strong hatred for all those lucky enough to live and truly die.

Spectres have enough cunning to plan their attacks, and rival vampires in their skill at remaining hidden from the general populace.

Ecology: No one knows who the first spectre was or how it came to be; the few facts detailed above are all that is known with any degree of certainty.

Sphinx

	Androsphinx	Criosphinx	Gynosphinx	Hieracosphinx
CLIMATE/TERRAIN:	Warm lands	Warm woodlands	Warm lands	Warm hills
FREQUENCY:	Very rare	Rare	Rare	Rare
ORGANIZATION:	Solitary	Solitary	Solitary	Solitary
ACTIVITY CYCLE:	Day	Day	Day	Day
DIET:	Carnivore	Carnivore	Carnivore	Carnivore
INTELLIGENCE:	Exceptional (15-16)	Average 9-10)	Genius (17-18)	Low (5-7)
TREASURE:	U	F	R, X	E
ALIGNMENT:	Chaotic good	Neutral	Neutral	Chaotic evil
NO. APPEARING:	1	1	1-4	1-6
ARMOR CLASS:	−2	0	−1	1
MOVEMENT:	18, Fl 30 (D)	12, Fl 24 (D)	15, Fl 24 (D)	9, Fl 36
HIT DICE:	12	10	8	9
THAC0:	9	11	13	11
NO. OF ATTACKS:	2	3	2	3
DAMAGE/ATTACK:	2-12/2-12	2-8/2-8/3-18	2-8/2-8	2-8/2-8/1-10
SPECIAL ATTACKS:	See below	Nil	See below	Nil
SPECIAL DEFENSES:	Nil	Nil	Nil	Nil
MAGIC RESISTANCE:	Nil	Nil	Nil	Nil
SIZE:	L (8′ tall)	L (7¹/₂′ tall)	L (7′ tall)	L (7′ tall)
MORALE:	Fanatic (17)	Champion (16)	Fanatic (17)	Elite (13)
XP VALUE:	7,000	5,000	3,000	1,400

Androsphinx

Androsphinxes are huge, winged mythological creatures with the bodies of male lions and man-like facial features. They can speak the languages of common and all sphinxes.

Combat: The male, or andro-, sphinx is the most powerful of the sphinxes. Its huge paws can kill a normal man with just one swipe. If brute force is not successful, an androsphinx can cast spells as if a 6th-level priest. Note that most androsphinxes use these spells for healing and defense rather than damage and attack.

The androsphinx has another special weapon as well—his bellowing roar. It can roar three times per day, but must be very angry to do so. The first time an angry androsphinx roars, all creatures within 360 yards must roll successful saving throws vs. wands or flee in panic for three turns. When an already angry androsphinx is continually molested, even after bellowing once, it can roar even louder, causing all creatures within 200 yards to roll successful saving throws vs. petrification or be paralyzed with fright for 1d4 rounds. In addition, any creatures within 30 yards of this second roar are automatically deafened for 2d6 rounds (unless they are deaf already or have protected hearing organs). Any creature foolish enough to anger an androsphinx further will unleash his third and final roar with devastating effects. All creatures within 240 yards must successfully roll saving throws vs. spell or lose 2d4 points of Strength for 2d4 rounds (use −1 point equals −10% for characters with exceptional Strength). In addition to the weakness effects, any creature within 30 yards of the androsphinx is knocked over unless it is 8 feet tall or larger. Creatures knocked over suffer 2d8 points of damage and must roll a successful saving throw vs. breath weapon to avoid being stunned for 2d6 rounds. The force of this third roar is so powerful that stone within 30 yards cracks under the strain, unless it successfully saves vs. crushing blow.

Habitat/Society: Androsphinxes are the most solitary of the sphinxes. They shun gynosphinxes because they are jealous of the higher intelligence of their female counterparts, and find their neutral disposition a bit hard to deal with. However, most androsphinxes eventually succumb to the advances of a gynosphinx at least once in their lives.

Ecology: What is strangest about androsphinxes is not their combination lion/human appearance (as there are many such cross-mutations found in the world), but their apparent lack of purpose. They are by far the strongest of the sphinxes, but unlike their counterparts, have no true pattern of behavior universal to all androsphinxes. They despise communicating with humans and hate riddles (mostly because gynosphinxes love them so much). It is therefore suggested by those knowledgeable in mythological beasts and desert lore that androsphinxes are the guardians of the sphinxes, evil (hieraco-), neutral (gyno- and crio-), and good (andro-).

Certainly, androsphinxes are the lifelong adversaries of the hieracosphinxes, but they almost always let the defeated enemy go free instead of finishing the kill (often with a roar or two at the fleeing sphinxes' behinds).

In short, androsphinxes are free-roaming sphinxes sworn to defend other sphinxes against other races, namely men and their ilk. They have been known to bargain with men on occasion, but are the least greedy of the sphinxes, and are the only sphinxes likely to take offense at such offerings if made by characters with low Charismas or evil alignments.

Criosphinxes

Criosphinxes have the bodies of winged lions, but they have the heads of rams. They are always male. They can speak their own dialect of sphinx, as well as that spoken by andro/gynosphinxes and the languages of animals.

Combat: Criosphinxes attack with their two paws or with a head butt with their ram's horns. Because they cast no spells and are not the brightest of sphinxes, their bargains with other beings are limited to "safe passage or die." They love treasure and lust after gynosphinxes constantly. Plenty of wealth, or knowledge of the location of a gynosphinx's lair, is always enough for adventurers to avoid confrontation with criosphinxes.

Habitat/Society: Criosphinxes prize wealth and usually seek to extort passers-by for safe passage in exchange for a hefty bribe. They are sometimes found in packs of two or more, but only because all of these sphinxes are looking for the same gynosphinx. They often follow other criosphinxes, even if they have no idea whether or not the leader really knows where he's going. When a number of criosphinxes find a gynosphinx, the first order of business is to restrain their prey. Usually pushing boulders in front of the lair with their huge horns is sufficient. Then the criosphinxes butt horns like rams, except these creatures do their fighting in the air. The winner gets the prize.

More often than not, however, criosphinxes begin their combat immediately upon finding their quarry, and inevitably the victor strides forth to find the gynosphinx gone. While the criosphinxes often find themselves richer for their trouble, as the gynosphinx rarely sees the need for material wealth while it is fleeing, it is only a poor reward indeed for their often decades-long quest.

Ecology: Criosphinxes are obviously just further mutations of the already mysterious sphinx form. Their ability to speak with animals seems to be an evolutionary necessity, as criosphinxes are particularly fond of warm wooded areas, often bordering on the desert lands preferred by gynosphinxes.

Gynosphinxes

The gynosphinx is the female counterpart of the androsphinx, having a winged lion's body and human-like facial features. Gynosphinxes are not nearly as powerful as androsphinxes, but they are much more knowledgeable, clever, and wise. Gynosphinxes speak all sphinx languages as well as common.

Combat: Gynosphinxes can attack with two paws, but prefer to bargain with their opponents. They help strangers only if they are paid. They accept payment for services rendered or knowledge and advice given, in the form of gems (preferred), jewelry, magic, or knowledge. Knowledge that would be of special interest to a gynosphinx is the location of an androsphinx, but they accept fine prose, poetry, lore, or a good riddle.

If anyone breaks a bargain with a gynosphinx, he is subject to attack and the gynosphinx won't hesitate to devour the victim if it wins the fight. The gynosphinx can cast the following spells once per day: *detect magic, read magic, read languages, detect invisibility, locate object, dispel magic, clairaudience, clairvoyance, remove curse,* and *legend lore.* It can also use each *symbol* once per week. Note that a gynosphinx is very intelligent and can use these spells in many ways. If a bargaining group of adventurers steps back to discuss their plans among themselves, the gynosphinx will growl a little and cast *clairaudience* to listen in.

Habitat/Society: Gynosphinxes are solitary by nature, but not by choice. They spend most of their lives avoiding the advances of criosphinxes (which they detest) and hieracosphinxes (which they fear), and searching high and low for an androsphinx.

Gynosphinxes are intelligent enough to actively seek out ruins and mystical places, like forgotten temples and such, which they immediately occupy. Using their many spells to learn as much as possible about the setting, they then wait for the next group of travelers, pilgrims, or adventurers to come by and hope that they've encountered an androsphinx in their travels or have spells or magical items that might be usable for just such a purpose.

Ecology: Gynosphinxes own the dubious distinction of being the only female sphinx. A gynosphinx mated with an androsphinx will produce another androsphinx or gynosphinx (even chances for both). A gynosphinx mated with a criosphinx only produces another male criosphinx, while mating with a hieracosphinx produces similarly displeasing results.

Fortunately, gynosphinxes are much smarter than all of their counterparts and can avoid otherwise compromising situations through trickery and outright deceit. Unfortunately, they are among the slowest of the sphinxes when flying or running, and the lustful criosphinx and vicious hieracosphinx rarely give up the chase once a gynosphinx has been located.

Hieracosphinxes

Hieracosphinxes are the only evil members of their breed. They have the bodies of lions, but the wings and head of hawks. They are always males. They speak the languages of the other sphinxes, and some (20%) also speak common.

Combat: Hieracosphinxes do not cast spells, much like the criosphinxes, but make up for their weaknesses with tenacious evil and viciousness. Their paws and sharp beaks are deadly in combat, and they have been known to swoop down on victims.

Habitat/Society: Hieracosphinxes live in hilly regions exclusively, dwelling in caves overlooking the nearby deserts. They delight in evil and sometimes gather in bands of as many as six to do their vile business. Most often when a band of hieracosphinxes is encountered, it is hot in pursuit of an androsphinx, which they hate with all of their beings. Only in numbers can they hope to defeat so powerful an adversary, and these sphinxes never believe in honor or playing fair. While it is true that a victorious androsphinx sometimes lets the defeated flee (in the vain hope that the battle may change the losers' dispositions), a defeated androsphinx is always ripped to pieces when the hieracosphinxes are numerous and lucky enough to win the fight.

Hieracosphinxes also spend much of their time searching for a gynosphinx to mate with, but prefer to kill an androsphinx and inhabit his lair until a gynosphinx eventually arrives (usually by following old rumors and legends). It is worthwhile to note that there are more hieracosphinxes than criosphinxes.

Ecology: Hieracosphinxes are belligerent mutations of unknown origin. It is believed that they were created by elder gods of evil merely to wreak havoc on the other, more pleasant sphinxes described above.

Spider

	Hairy	Large	Huge	Giant	Phase	Sword	Gargantuan
CLIMATE/TERRAIN:	Any non-arctic land	Any non-arctic land	Any non-arctic land	Any non-arctic land	Any	Any (prefers jungles)	Any non-arctic land
FREQUENCY:	Common	Common	Common	Uncommon	Rare	Very rare	Very rare
ORGANIZATION:	Swarm	Swarm	Pack	Nest	Solitary	Solitary	Nest
ACTIVITY CYCLE:	Any	Any	Any	Any	Any	Any	Any
DIET:	Omnivore	Carnivore	Carnivore	Carnivore	Carnivore	Carnivore	Carnivore
INTELLIGENCE:	Low (5-7)	Non-(0)	Animal (1)	Low (5-7)	Low (5-7)	Avg. (8-10)	Low (5-7)
TREASURE:	Nil	J-N	J-N, Q	C	E	Nil	C
ALIGNMENT:	Neutral evil	Neutral	Neutral	Chaotic evil	Neutral	Chaotic evil	Chaotic evil
NO. APPEARING:	1-20	2-20	1-12	1-8	1-4	1	1-6
ARMOR CLASS:	8	8	6	4	7	3	4
MOVEMENT:	12, Wb 9	6, Wb 15	18	3, Wb 12	6, Wb 15	6, Wb 8, Cl 8	9, Wb 12
HIT DICE:	1-1	1+1	2+2	3+3 or 4+4	5+5	5+5	7+7 or 8+8
THAC0:	20	19	19	3+3 HD: 17 4+4 HD: 15	15	15	7+7 HD: 13 8+8 HD: 11
NO. OF ATTACKS:	1	1	1	1	1	2	1
DAMAGE/ATTACK:	1	1	1-6	1-8	1-6	2-8 (bite)/ 2-12 per leg	2-12
SPECIAL ATTACKS:	Poison	See below	See below	See below	See below	See below	See below
SPECIAL DEFENSES:	Nil	Nil	Nil	Nil	Phasing	Nil	See below
MAGIC RESISTANCE:	Nil	Nil	Nil	Nil	Nil	Nil	Nil
SIZE:	T (6" or less diameter)	S (2' diameter)	M (6' diameter)	L (8'-12' diameter)	H (14' diameter)	H (12' diameter)	G (10' long, 20' diameter)
MORALE:	Average (10)	Unsteady (7)	Average (8)	Elite (13)	Champion (15)	Elite (13)	Elite (14)
XP VALUE:	65	175	270	3+3 HD: 420 Flying: 650 4+4 HD: 650 Steeder: 975 Trap door: 975	1,400	2,000	7+7 HD: 1,400 8+8 HD: 3,000

Spiders are aggressive predators, dwelling both above and below ground. Most listed here are poisonous and bite prey first, because unconscious victims are easier to carry to a lair.

Spiders have eight legs and eight eyes. They usually fit into two categories: web-spinners, which have bulbous abdomens and thin, sleek legs; and hunting spiders, which have smaller bodies, larger heads and fangs, and hairy bodies and legs.

Hairy Spider

These are the vicious, black, hunting spiders that are found in jungles, tombs, caverns, and throughout the Underdark. Though spin no webs, they can move readily in the webs of other spiders, and they are immune to all known spider venoms.

Hairy spiders hunt in groups, swarming over victims to bite. Up to 40 hairy spiders can swarm a human-sized victim, and bite with a +5 bonus to attack rolls once they are attached. Hairy spiders are remarkably resistant to crushing damage; rolling or crashing into walls is ineffective at removing or destroying hairy spiders. They must be individually struck or torn away.

Hairy spiders are sometimes used as familiars, especially by drow wizards. They can carry small items and walk on walls and ceilings; they have 60-foot infravision and are not afraid of fire. Some (40%) of these spiders can *detect invisibility*; they have a 4 in 6 chance, once per round. These familiars are sometimes given treasure by their masters.

Victims receive a +2 bonus to saving throws vs. the hairy spiders' weak poison. If the saving throw fails, the victim's AC and attack rolls are penalized by 1, and Dexterity is penalized by -3 with respect to Dexterity checks. These effects begin one round after the bite and last for 1d4+1 rounds.

Large Spider

Large spiders are web-spinners that build strong, sticky webs, and often lurk nearby waiting for victims to get stuck while examining the beautiful constructions of their own spinning. A being with Strength 19 or more is unaffected by the webs. For each point of Strength less than 19, it takes one round to break free of the webs (for exampie, a PC with Strength 15 can break free in four rounds). As many spiders as possible will attack the defenseless victim during its struggle to free itself. Entangled characters can be attacked with a +4 bonus to hit, and lose all Armor Class adjustments due to Dexterity.

The large spider's poison is Type A, the onset time is 15 minutes. Victims take 15 points of damage, or no damage if a saving throw vs. poison (with a +2 to the roll) is successful.

Huge Spider

Huge spiders are hunting spiders that prefer to hide in camouflaged tunnels and holes and wait to leap as much as 30 feet through the air at unsuspecting victims. Their opponents suffer a -6 to surprise rolls when attacked in this manner.

Huge spiders also posses Type A poison, with the same effects as that of a large spider. Victims receive a +1 to saving throws vs. the poison of the huge spider.

The **watch spider** is a specially bred, huge spider used as a guard animal in cellars, warehouses, and some drow homes. It has Low Intelligence (5-7) and can be trained to obey a master, not attack beings designated by the master, and to disable spellcasters. Their venom has an onset time of 1-2 rounds and causes paralysis for 2d4 turns, unless the victim makes a successful saving throw vs. poison (with a +1 on the roll). If starved for long periods, they often eat paralyzed prey.

Giant Spider

Most giant spiders are simply much bigger versions of the web-spinning large spiders. Their poison is Type F, which causes immediate death if the victim fails the saving throw.

The **giant water spider** is a small version (8-foot diameter, 3+3 HD) of the giant spider. It lives in a burrow in a body of fresh water, and fills its burrow with bubbles of air. These spiders drag prey underwater to their lairs, where they can safely wrap it in cocoons for later repasts. It is faster than a normal giant spider

Spider

(movement rate 15), but cannot travel through webs. It is only semi-intelligent (2-4) and has treasure as a huge spider; its bite causes only 1d4 damage plus poison.

The **flying spider**, sometimes just called a hunting spider, is a giant, winged, hunting spider. They are sometimes trained as guard animals, especially by the drow. They are 10 feet in diameter and have 3+3 Hit Dice. Its normal movement rate is 9, and its great gossamer wings allow it to fly at the same rate (MC: D). These spiders can also leap up to 70 feet, and fall any distance without harm upon landing, as long as they use their wings. Hunting spiders have Type A poison, just as a large spider, with the same damage and saving throw adjustment.

The **giant trap door spider** is a hunting spider which builds tunnels and surprises prey like a huge spider; it is brown or golden, with red strips around its legs. On a successful attack roll, the spider can grab a victim and attempt to drag it into its lair. A victim can get free by making a successful Strength check, with a −2 penalty, or be freed by companions, if their Strength totals 20 or more. The victim can make no attacks.

A giant trap door spider has 4+4 Hit Dice and causes 2d4 damage per bite. Its poison causes an additional 1d6 points of damage if the victim fails a saving throw vs. poison. Though it does not build webs, it can travel through webs of other spiders, and it can shoot web strands up to 3 feet. The web strands require normal attack rolls to hit; they cause no damage, but entangle a victim for 1d4 rounds.

The **steeder** is a giant hunting spider with tarantula markings, 4+4 Hit Dice, and a movement rate of 12. It does not spin webs and cannot move in them, but its feet exude a sticky substance which allows it to cling to precarious surfaces, even if only one foot is touching the surface. The steeder also uses the secretions (50% of the time) to cling to prey; this requires an attack roll from the steeder, against AC 10 for the victim, adjusted only for magic and Dexterity. A victim can escape by making a successful Strength or Dexterity roll with a −10 penalty. While held, the victim suffers a −2 penalty to attack and damage rolls and is automatically bitten once per round.

Duergar dwarves use steeders as mounts, fitting the spiders with complex saddles and control straps. A steeder can leap 240 feet, even with a rider. Leaps are considered charging attacks. A steeder moves on walls and ceilings at half its normal rate; duergar saddles are built for this kind of motion.

Phase Spider

Phase spiders are web-spinners with a raised thorax and a human-like head; they are often confused with neogi or driders. They have a unique ability to phase in and out of the Prime material plane. They phase in, attack, and phase out, all in a single round. This gives them a −3 modifier on initiative rolls; if a phase spider wins initiative by more than 4, it attacks and phases out before its opponent has a chance to strike back. Then too, a phase spider usually phases into existence behind its chosen victim, so they get a +4 modifier for attacking from behind. Phase spiders flee to the Ethereal plane when outmatched; there, they gain only a −1 modifier to initiative and can be attacked every round, regardless of the initiative result.

Phase spiders have Type F poison, and victims receive a −2 penalty on saving throws against it.

Sword Spider

This giant hunting spider is native to jungles, but has been introduced into the Underdark by drow traders. It has a sleek, hairy, black body with brown stripes. Its legs have bony plates with sharp, raised ridges that cut like sword blades.

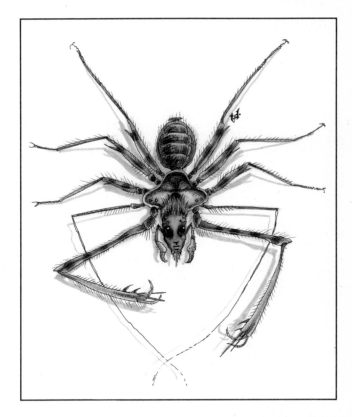

Against formidable prey, a sword spider leaps horizontally as far as 30 feet, and lands legs forward, impaling its prey. Only one attack roll is made for the creature. If the attack is successful, the victim is struck by a number of legs based on its size: size S, three legs; size M, four legs; size L, five legs; size H, six legs; size G, all eight legs. If the spider's leap is greater than 20 feet, each leg receives a +1 bonus to damage. Any upward attack against the leaping spider receives a −4 to the attack roll, due to the impaling blades which protect the spider.

Gargantuan Spider

The gargantuan spider, also called a whisper spider, is a hunting spider with red eyes, a black body, and two gray stripes along its abdomen. They usually live in huge webs in a forest or a cave, keeping treasure from prey in a small hole, or in the bole of a tree. The whisper spider has 8+8 Hit Dice. It can flatten itself to become 80% undetectable; it is so silent that opponents suffer a −5 penalty to surprise rolls.

Using its webbing, it can make a false spider, a flapping banner, a filmy veil, or any shape it has ever seen; it uses these to mislead prey. The spider can make a web net to trap prey, or it can shoot web strands up to 2 feet to bind a foe. Either attack treats the spider's opponent as AC 10 and prevents the spider from making a melee attack that round. A victim caught by webbing is treated as if caught in a *web* spell. When bitten, a victim must make a successful saving throw vs. poison, with a penalty of −2, or fall into a coma for 2d4 turns.

Giant marine spiders are gargantuan spiders with 7+7 Hit Dice, which live in burrows near bodies of saltwater. Like their freshwater cousins, they carry prey to their lairs; though they collect no treasure, their lairs may contain incidental items from victims. They have type F poison, and do not share the whisper spider's special abilities.

Sprite

	Sprite	Sea Sprite	Pixie	Nixie	Atomie	Grig
CLIMATE/TERRAIN:	Meadows and woods	Tropical coral reefs	Temperate forests	Temperate lakes	Temperate forests	Temperate forests
FREQUENCY:	Rare	Rare	Very rare	Rare	Rare	Very rare
ORGANIZATION:	Tribe	Community	Community	Tribe	Tribe	Band
ACTIVITY CYCLE:	Day	Day	Night	Day	Night	Night
DIET:	Omnivore	Omnivore	Herbivore	Fish	Herbivore	Herbivore
INTELLIGENCE:	Very (11-12)	Very (11-12)	Exceptional (15-16)	Very (12)	Average to very (8-12)	Low to average (5-10)
TREASURE:	C	(D)	R, S, T, X	Q (C)	M (X)	M (X, Y)
ALIGNMENT:	Neutral (good)	Chaotic neutral	Neutral	Neutral	Chaotic neutral	Neutral (good)
NO. APPEARING:	10-100	5-40 (5d8)	5-20	20-80 (2d4 × 10)	30-120 (3d4 × 10)	2-12
ARMOR CLASS:	6	6	5	7	4	2
MOVEMENT:	9, Fl 18 (B)	6, Sw 24	6, Fl 12 (B)	6, Sw (12)	12, Fl 24 (A)	6, leap 12
HIT DICE:	1	1	$^1/_2$	1/2	1/2	1/2 +1
THAC0:	19	19	20	20	18 (see below)	20
NO. OF ATTACKS:	1	1	1	1	2	3 (darts) or 2 (swords)
DAMAGE/ATTACK:	By weapon	By weapon	By weapon	By weapon	By weapon	By weapon
SPECIAL ATTACKS:	See below	See below	See below	Charm	See below	See below
SPECIAL DEFENSES:	See below	See below	See below	See below	See below	See below
MAGIC RESISTANCE:	Nil	Nil	25%	25%	20%	30%
SIZE:	S (2′ tall)	T (2′ tall)	S (2 ½′ tall)	S (4′ tall)	T (1′ tall)	T (1 ½′ tall)
MORALE:	Steady (11-12)	Elite (13-14)	Steady (11)	Average (8-10)	Steady (11-12)	Steady (11-12)
XP VALUE:	270	270	650	270	270	270

Sprites are shy and reclusive faerie people, related to other faerie-folk, like brownies and leprechauns. There are several varieties, including pixies and nixies. Most have small, semitransparent wings, and elven features.

Normal sprites have distinctly elven features and live in meadows and wooded glens. The wingless sea sprites make their homes on colorful coral reefs, living in harmony with the sea creatures, protecting the reefs' delicate environment, and frolicking in the waves. The naturally invisible pixies are perhaps the most intelligent and mischievous of the faeries; they dwell in idyllic woodlands and delight in harassing travelers with their pranks. Nixies are water sprites that live in freshwater lakes, and, while they harbor no grudges against humankind, they delight in enslaving men as their beasts of burden. Other sylvan creatures related to sprites include the swift atomies and the mischievous grigs, both forest-dwellers.

Combat: Sprites hate evil and ugliness, and are capable of stout militancy, should their secluded homes be invaded by orcs or worse. They fight with long, slim swords which do damage as a human-sized dagger, or their own special bows. Bows have a range half that of a human short bow and do only half as much damage (1-3 points). The tips of their arrows are coated with a special ointment concocted by the sprites. Any creature struck by the drugged arrows, regardless of level, race, or magic resistance, must make a saving throw vs. poison or fall into a deep sleep lasting 1d6 hours. Normally sprites do nothing more than take their victims to safe a place very far away (often confiscating their weapons in the process), though evil creatures may be slain.

Habitat/Society: Sprites prefer to avoid other intelligent beings and live in places where they can have many celebrations, parties, and gatherings. They gather on most moonlit nights for singing and dancing, land sprites in the glens, and water sprites in the surf. Land sprites live in sylvan woodlands, they monitor and protect forests and secluded glens. Water sprites protect their watery territories equally well.

Most land-dwelling species of sprite are immortal, and never die unless killed. The sprites' diminutive size and their dangerous environments keep sprite populations low.

Sprite (standard)

Sprites usually speak only their own language, common, and elven, but seem to get along with woodland mammals and other creatures anyway. Humans often mistake sprites for butterflies at a distance, and it is guessed that the majority of forest creatures also think of the fair sprites in this way.

Combat: Sprites can become *invisible at will* and *detect good/evil* within 50 yards, so they are hard to deceive, evade, or capture. When invisible, sprites get +2 to attack rolls against opponents, who suffer a −4 penalty to hit the sprites.

Habitat/Society: Sprites are very flighty, and find even elves much too serious about most woodland affairs.

Only druids deal with sprites regularly. Some druids even receive a little of their training in the company of a few sprites. Most sprites love druids, for their neutral alignment and love for nature make them see the forest in much the same way. On rare occasions, sprites associate with rangers as well.

Sprites are loosely tribal, electing the best warrior among the group (male or female) as the group spokesperson. This leader is recognized as the one who makes major decisions and bargains with druids and elves. Sprites rarely wait for their leader's decision, often attacking an evil creature before the leader can issue any command.

Ecology: Sprite sleep ointment is concocted from forest mushrooms. The ointment must be left to cure in the sun for seven days. Sprites hollow out tree stumps to serve as containers for this rare substance.

Sprites keep watch on their fellow sprites, so they know who to invite to their frequent gatherings. A deserted meadow or glen is never empty for more than a decade before a new clan of sprites moves in.

Sea Sprites

Sea sprites have fine, cheerful faces, with rounded cheeks and wide, fish-like eyes. Their hair is the color and texture of seaweed, and reaches down to the gills on their necks, which enable sea sprites to breathe water as well as air. Their skin is light blue, smooth, and slick. Sea sprites have no wings, but webbing grows between their toes and fingers. Sea sprites wear bright, eelskin jerkins, and often adorn themselves with ornaments crafted from treasures found in the ocean.

Combat: About half of the sea sprites encountered carry special crossbows. In the hands of sea sprites, these crossbows function like light crossbows above and below water. Sea sprites coat their crossbow bolts in *sprite sleep ointment*.

Sea sprites hate and fear sahuagin, and kill those they put to sleep. Air breathers are left on a nearby beach provided they have neither harmed nor attempted to harm the coral reef.

Sea sprites can turn *invisible at will* and *detect good/evil* within 50 yards. Three times per day, a sea sprite may cast *slow*, by touch, at the 5th level of ability. Once per day, a sea sprite can cast *airy water* as a 10th-level spellcaster.

Sprite

Sea sprites are 45% likely to be accompanied by ld6 large carnivorous fish, such as barracudas. These fish act as guards and pets, attacking any creature that threatens the sprites.

Habitat/Society: Sea sprites live in natural caves in coral reefs, or amid large wrecks. Though sea sprites can breathe air, they rarely set foot on land. Their homes are cheerfully decorated with a mishmash of seashells, bones, pearls, free-swimming and colorful pet fish, and artifacts taken from sunken ships. Sea sprites live in small communities of four or five families.While each community is led by the eldest male, the true power often rests in the hands of his mate.

Ecology: Sea sprites eat seaweeds, small crustaceans, and fish. They raise fish and never deplete the reefs where they live. The only natural enemies of sea sprites are sahuagin. Sea sprites usually live for several centuries. They sometimes trade with sea elves but never mix socially with them.

Pixie

Pixies stand about 2 1/2 feet tall. When visible, they resemble small elves, but with longer ears. Pixies have two silver wings, like those of moths. They wear bright clothing, often with a cap and a pair of shoes with curled and pointed toes. Pixies speak their own language, Common, and the language of sprites.

Combat: Pixies carry sprite-sized swords and bows. They use three types of arrows, and shoot them with a +4 bonus to the attack roll. Besides standard sprite sleep-arrows, pixies use a war arrow, which inflicts ld4+1 points of damage, and an arrow which does no physical harm to the target. Those hit by this arrow must make a successful saving throw vs. spell, or suffer complete loss of memory which can be restored only by a *heal* or a *limited wish*.

Pixies can, once per day, use each of the following magical powers, as if they were 8th-level mages: *polymorph self, know alignment, dispel magic, dancing lights,* and *ESP*. They can also do the following once per day: become visible for as long as they desire; create illusions with both audial and visual components; and cause *confusion* by touch. Their illusions require no concentration and last until magically dispelled. A creature attacked with *confusion* must make a successful saving throw vs. spell, or suffer its effects until a *remove curse* is applied. One pixie in 10 can use *Otto's irresistible dance,* also once per day.

Because pixies are normally invisible, opponents suffer a −4 penalty to attack rolls. A successful *dispel magic* against 8th-level magic makes any pixies, in its area of effect, visible for one round, then they automatically become invisible again. They attack while invisible without penalty.

Habitat/Society Pixies live in deep forest caves, dancing in moonlit glades to the music of crickets and frogs. They are pranksters and they love to lead travelers astray. They use their illusion powers to accomplish this, hence the expression "pixie-led" for one who has lost his way. They like to frighten maidens, rap on walls, blow out candles, and play in water.

Pixies love to trick misers into giving away their treasure, especially by convincing them that something horrible will happen to them if they do not. Pixies carry no treasure, but sometimes have a hoard in their lair to impress visitors. Pixies use treasure to taunt greedy people, and then play merciless pranks on them until they abandon their search for the pixies' fortune. If the victim shows no greed and exhibits a good sense of humor about their pranks, the pixies may allow that individual to choose one item from their hoard.

Pixies dwell together in a community of clans or families that seem to mimic human customs. Each family has a last name, and family and community loyalty is very important to pixies. Their life span is about 300 years.

Ecology: Pixies eat fruits and nectar. The most famous by-product of pixies is pixie dust, also known as *dust of disappearance.* Crushing 50 pixie wings into a fine powder creates one dose of *dust of disappearance.* Naturally, pixies frown on this use of their wings.

Nixie

Nixies have webbed fingers and toes, pointed ears, and wide silver eyes. Most are slim and comely, and they have lightly scaled, pale green skin and dark green hair. Females are attractive, often twining shells and pearl strings in their thick hair, and they modestly dress in tight-fitting wraps woven from colorful seaweeds. Males wear loincloths of the same

materials. Nixies can breathe both water and air; travel on land is possible, but they prefer not to leave their lakes. Nixies speak their own language and the Common tongue.

Combat: If one or more men approach within 30 feet of a group of nixies, the nixies pool their magic to create a powerful *charm* spell, one such spell per every 10 nixies. The victim must make a saving throw vs. spell at −2 on the die roll. Before a charmed man enters the water, there is a 75% chance that a *dispel magic* will break the charm. Once the victim is in the water, the chance of dispelling the magic drops to 10%. Nixies keep each charmed slave for one full year, forcing him to do all their heavy labor, but thereafter the charm wears off and the victim is set free. During this enslavement, the nixies keep a *water breathing* spell on the human captive. Nixies can cast this spell on any creature, or dispel it, once per day; the spell's duration is one day.

Male nixies carry daggers and javelins. The javelins are used to spear things in the water, or can be thrown. A group of 10 nixies can use a large fishing net against adversaries who are in the water with them. Nixies make one net attack against AC 10 to ensnare a single man-sized creature, −2 AC for each additional victim, up to five total victims (and AC 0). Nixies sometimes employ guardian fish in battle.

Even with 25% magic resistance, nixies fear fire and very bright lights, so a *flaming sword* or a *light* spell keeps them at bay. Nixies try to negate a *continual light* spell by summoning small fish to crowd around the light and dim it.

Habitat/Society: Nixie dwellings are woven from living seaweed and difficult to detect (5% chance within 20 feet, impossible from farther away). Nixies keep giant fish as guards, either 1-2 gar (20%) or 2-5 pike (80%); these are taught to obey simple commands. Small bright, ornamental fish are kept as pets and trained to perform elaborate tricks. Trout, bass, and catfish are herded as food. Nixies can also summon 10-100 small fish, which takes 1-3 rounds.

Nixie tribes have 20-80 members, about one third are youth. Families have 4-8 members, and the tribe usually includes 10-15 families, all related through common ancestors. A nixie tribe controls an area with a radius of 3-5 miles; when a tribe gets too large, 2-3 families split off to form a new tribe. Nixies live for several centuries.

Nixie tribes are ruled by the Acquar (water mother), a hereditary position held by a direct descendant of the original founding ancestor. She

329

Sprite

decides major disputes and chooses the most apt warrior to be the S'o-quar, the warlord responsible for hunting and defense. The Acquar is advised by a council of elders, whose spokesperson is called the L'uquar, the keeper of the tribe's oral history. Treasures, whether the spoils of war or the results of work or luck, are divided equally by the Acquar. Intertribal rivalries are often fierce, and females are sometimes kidnapped as brides, for nixies are polygamists, keeping 2-3 wives. Nixies worship water and nature powers.

Ecology: Lakes with nixie tribes are kept clean and well stocked; often, human slaves work to improve the environment through the removal of trash and obstructions. Nixie artifacts include jewelry of shells, pearls and opals, silk from water spiders, and *potions of water breathing.*

Atomie

Atomies avoid most serious-minded creatures, but mix freely with grigs, and are 20% likely to be found in their company. The lightest and quickest of all the sprites, atomies are less than 1-foot tall. Atomies have four dragonfly-like wings. Their features are elven, their skin is pale with a hint of woodland green. Atomie clothing is innately magical, bright and festive while at the same time blending with woodland surroundings.

Atomies have twice the hearing range of humans, and they have infravision to 90 feet. Their voices are high-pitched, almost a bee-like buzz. Atomies speak their own language and often the languages of sprites, pixies, and some broken Common. They can also speak with plants and animals.

Combat: Atomies attack as 3rd-level fighters. About 20% of atomies carry tiny crossbows and spears. Atomie crossbows have a 3-foot range and inflict 1d3 points of damage. Atomie spears cause 1d4 points of damage. The remaining atomies are armed with either spears (40%) or sprite swords (40%). Atomies have the following magical abilities, usable once per round at 5th-level ability: *blink, invisibility, pass plant, speak with animals,* and *summon insects.*

Atomies are surprised only on a 1; opponents suffer a −6 penalty to surprise rolls. Upon hearing an intruder, atomies hide and try to make the intruder go away, using false lights, clattering voices, and pesky, summoned insects. Repeat intruders are warned with crossbow bolts. If combat is inevitable, or the intruders are orcs, the atomies regroup and attack. Atomies with spears fly in and dive on surprised opponents (usually aiming at their posteriors). Diving attacks inflict double damage (2d4).

Habitat/Society: Atomies live in the upper branches of old hardwood trees (usually oaks), one family per tree. Each family hollows out a series of tiny rooms, decorating with walnut chairs, woven pine needle rugs, acorn dishes, and the like. A network of balconies, landings, and rope bridges connects the dwellings, forming a village high above the forest floor. A typical atomie village houses 3d4 × 10 adults and 4d6 children.

Atomies seldom bother with outsiders, even standard sprites (whom they view as tedious and too serious), but they will sometimes help a lost child. A rescued child is well cared for and entertained before being returned to the outside world.

The concept of pets is unknown, but atomies often grow mushroom "friends" in their living rooms.

Atomies have loose leadership, choosing a chieftain based on storytelling and singing ability.

Ecology: Atomies are herbivores and find the eating habits of their cousins repulsive. They favor nuts above fruit, and prefer honey when they can trick bees into giving them some.

Atomies make a perfect, bite-sized morsels for most creatures, and sometimes fall prey to evil animals, such as worgs.

Atomies view magic as a force connected with life and are fascinated by inanimate magical items. Atomies collect magical items and display them in their homes or communities. Non-magical treasures are considered clutter and are either thrown away or given to forest creatures who value such things.

Grigs

Grigs are mischievous and lighthearted. They have no fear of big people and take great joy in playing tricks upon them.

A grig has the head, torso, and arms of a sprite, with the wings, antennae, and legs of a cricket. They can leap great distances. Grigs have light blue skin, forest green hair, and brown hairy legs. They usually wear tunics or brightly colored vests with buttons made from tiny gems. Grigs speak atomie, brownie, pixie, sprite, and Common. They have double normal hearing range and 180-foot infravision. The origin of the grigs remains a mystery.

Combat: Fierce (by sprite standards), each grig carries six small darts and a sprite sword. Grigs gain a +2 bonus to attack rolls with darts. Darts and swords do normal damage when used by grigs, but only 1 point of damage when used by non-grigs.

Grigs have the following spell-like abilities, usable once per round at 6th-level ability: *change self, entangle, invisibility, pyrotechnics, trip,* and *ventriloquism.* Grigs move silently in woodlands; they are surprised only on a 1, while opponents suffer a −6 penalty to surprise rolls. Some grigs throw darts, while others leap to attack, and one grig fiddler (grigs never go anywhere without a fiddle), plays a song with the same effect as *Otto's irresistible dance.* All non-sprites within 30 feet of the fiddler must make a successful saving throw vs. spell or dance until the grig ceases playing. Grigs can play for hours.

Habitat/Society: Grigs roam the forests in small bands. They have no permanent homes but often sleep in the limbs of treants, or near unicorns (who protect grigs even unto death).

Grigs are cautious but trusting. They delight in playing pranks on big people. Common ploys include stealing food, collapsing a tent, and using *ventriloquism* to make objects talk. Once a prank is set, the grigs sit back and watch, laughing at the unfortunate person. People who make fools of themselves are apt to be plagued by harmless jokes until they reach the forest edge. At that point, one of the grigs comes out of hiding and makes amends with a gift, either a harmless bauble such as a 1d6 × 100 gp gem (25%) or a precious jar of really fresh honey (75%).

Ecology: Grigs live on nuts, berries and honey.

	Squid, giant	Kraken
CLIMATE/TERRAIN:	Any deep waters	Very deep oceans
FREQUENCY:	Rare	Very rare
ORGANIZATION:	Solitary	Solitary
ACTIVITY CYCLE:	Any	Any
DIET:	Carnivore	Carnivore
INTELLIGENCE:	Non- (0)	Genius + (19-20 +)
TREASURE:	A	G, R, S (+ A)
ALIGNMENT:	Neutral	Neutral evil
NO. APPEARING:	1	1
ARMOR CLASS:	7/3	5/0
MOVEMENT:	Sw 3, Jet 18	Sw 3, Jet 21
HIT DICE:	12	20
THAC0:	9	5
NO. OF ATTACKS:	9	9
DAMAGE/ATTACK:	1-6 (x8)/5-20	3-18(x2)/2-12(x6)/7-28
SPECIAL ATTACKS:	Constriction	See below
SPECIAL DEFENSES:	See below	See below
MAGIC RESISTANCE:	Nil	Nil
SIZE:	G (60' + long)	G (90' + long)
MORALE:	Elite (13)	Fanatic (18)
XP VALUE:	5,000	14,000

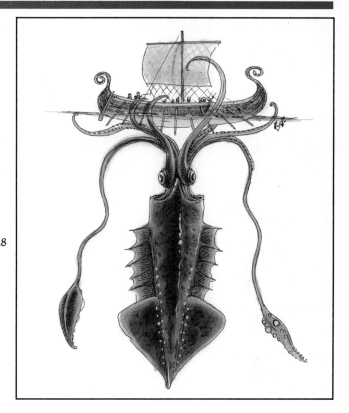

Giant squids are huge varieties of the normal, peaceful, tentacled cephalopods (unshelled invertebrates).

They have ten long tentacles, two of which are always used to maintain stability when attacking or defending, and long, protected heads with two eyes. Their beak-like mouths are located where the tentacles meet the lower portion of their bodies.

Combat: Giant squids prefer to grab their opponents in their tentacles and constrict them, while they bring the thrashing victims into their huge jaws. As many as eight tentacles can attack one opponent, but only one at a time can constrict a man-sized opponent (the rest are free to attack anything else within reach). The rubbery tentacles are so strong they cannot be broken by force and must be severed. A giant squid's tentacles hit for 1d6 points of damage and constrict for 2d6 points of damage every round after the initial strike. The beak of a giant squid inflicts 5d4 points of damage.

Any character who is constricted may have one arm (01-25% left, or 26-50% right), no arms (51-75%), or both arms (76-100%) pinned. A constricted character cannot cast any spells, but he can grab a weapon and attack the tentacle (if only one arm is free, he attacks with a -3 penalty to the attack roll; if both arms are free, the penalty is -1). A giant squid's tentacle requires 12 points of damage from sharp or edged weapons to sever (these hit points are in addition to the hit points from Hit Dice).

If a giant squid has four or more tentacles severed, the monster is 80% likely to squirt out a cloud of jet-black ink 60 feet high by 60 feet wide and 80 feet long. The squid then jets away and retreats to its lair. The ink completely obscures the vision of all within the cloud.

A giant squid can drag ships of small size to the bottom and can halt the movement of larger ones in one turn of dragging. After six or more tentacles have squeezed the hull of the ship for three consecutive rounds, the vessel suffers damage as if it had been rammed and it begins to take on water and sink.

Kraken

A kraken is a rare form of gargantuan squid. It is one of the most deadly monsters in existence.

Combat: Krakens attack as huge varieties of giant squid. Two of their tentacles are barbed and cause 3d6 points of damage when they hit. They then try to drag prey toward their gaping maws for a bite

of 7d4 points of damage. The other six free tentacles inflict 2d6 points of damage when they hit and constrict for 3d6 points each round thereafter. A kraken's tentacle must suffer 18 points of damage from sharp or edged weapons to be severed (these hit points are in addition to those the kraken gets from its Hit Dice).

If three of more of its tentacles have been severed, the monster is 80% likely to retreat, leaving behind a cloud of ink to discourage pursuit. The kraken is 50% likely to retreat to its den if four or more of its tentacles have victims. It leaves behind an ink cloud in this case also. The ink cloud of a kraken is 80 feet high by 80 feet wide by 120 feet long and is poisonous (it dissipates in 2-5 rounds). Those within the cloud receive 2d4 points of damage every round they remain. Krakens jet away to their lairs at a movement rate 21.

Krakens can drag ships of 60 feet long down in the same way as normal giant squids attack. They have the innate power to cause airy water in a sphere 120 yards across or in a hemisphere 240 yards across (they can do this continuously). They can employ the following spell-like powers, one at a time, at will: *faerie fire* for up to eight hours, *control temperature* in a 40-yard radius continuously, *control winds* once per day, *weather summoning* once per day, and *animal summoning III* (fish only) three times per day (note that this spell does not grant control of the fish once summoned).

Krakens are not affected by the conch horns of tritons.

Habitat/Society: Krakens have Intelligences of genius or higher and often control entire regions of the underwater world. Their lairs lie thousands of feet below the surface and they maintain huge complexes of caverns where they keep and breed human slaves to serve and feed them.

Ecology: Krakens can breathe either air or water and are aggressive hunters. Many tropical islands have been completely stripped of all inhabitants (animal and human) by krakens.

It is said that krakens retreated to the depths when the forces of good thwarted their attempt to rule the seas, but it is also said that in the future krakens will rise again.

Stirge

CLIMATE/TERRAIN:	Forests or subterranean
FREQUENCY:	Uncommon
ORGANIZATION:	Clusters
ACTIVITY CYCLE:	Night
DIET:	Blood
INTELLIGENCE:	Animal (1)
TREASURE:	D
ALIGNMENT:	Nil

NO. APPEARING:	3-30
ARMOR CLASS:	8
MOVEMENT:	3, Fl 18 (C)
HIT DICE:	1+1
THAC0:	17
NO. OF ATTACKS:	1
DAMAGE/ATTACK:	1-3
SPECIAL ATTACKS:	Blood drain
SPECIAL DEFENSES:	Nil
MAGIC RESISTANCE:	Nil
SIZE:	S (2' wingspan)
MORALE:	Average (8)
XP VALUE:	175

Stirges are bird-like creatures that drink the blood of their victims for sustenance. They have four small, pincer-like legs that they use to clamp onto the necks of their victims. They are rusty-red to reddish brown in color, and their eyes and feet are yellowish. The dangling proboscises of stirges are pink at the tip, fading to gray at the base (near their heads).

Combat: Due to an instinctive ability to find and attack weak points, stirges attack as 4-Hit Die creatures, rather than 1+1. Their long proboscis inflicts 1-3 points of damage when it hits, and drains 1d4 points of blood every round thereafter. When a stirge drains a total of 12 points of blood from a victim, it becomes bloated and flies off to digest its protein-rich meal.

Stirges must be killed to be removed, due to their strong grip. If an attack against an attached stirge misses, make another attack roll against the victim's Armor Class to see if the attack hits the victim instead. Caution is advisable when attempting to remove an attached stirge.

Habitat/Society: Stirges form nest-like colonies in attics, dungeons, and copses of trees. Although they resemble birds, they hang upside down when sleeping, indicating that stirges may be closely related to vampire bats.

Stirges can breed in captivity, but a constant supply of blood is needed. Stirges mostly kill low-level humans, animals and children, so the arrival of these predators in any civilized territory is always a cause for alarm. Fortunately, even a low-level group of adventurers or town militia is usually capable of ending the menace with little or no loss of life.

Ecology: Stirges have an acute sense of smell, can see in the dark, and can sense heat sources within 200 feet. These senses keep stirges informed when living creatures enter their habitat. Creatures with a natural AC of 3 or better are usually immune to a stirge's blood draining attack, since their hides are too thick to penetrate. As a consequence, huge nests of stirges live symbiotically with some evil dragons. Characters who protect their entire bodies with special leather or better armor (this special armor costs two to three times more than normal armor) can safely approach a stirge. Even the slightest gap in the protection is seen and smelled by the creature, and a successful attack roll means the creature has broken through the weakness and locked on.

After a stirge has gorged itself by draining blood, it sleeps for one day, plus one day for every 2 points of blood it drank (the maximum sleep period is after drinking 12 points of blood—seven days). During this period of rest, silent attackers can impose a −2 penalty to the stirges' surprise roll, as the beasts wake slowly and remain drowsy for a few moments. They are most vulnerable at this time. While certain species of stirges prefer to dine on human blood, most are content with any large mammal, like cows, moose, and deer. Experienced druids and rangers usually recognize the traces of a stirge colony by the occurrences of mysteriously drained and dead animals in the vicinity.

A stirge colony's territory extends for only a mile in diameter, so stirges move around a lot after they've drained a region of the available blood. Often, the presence of stirges is only discovered long after the colony has departed, making it very difficult to track them.

Jungle Stirges

There are rumored to be exceptionally large varieties of stirges deep in the densest tropical jungles. Though they are only 2+2 Hit Die creatures, they attack as 8 Hit Die monsters. Purportedly, they have a paralyzing poison in the tips of their sharp snouts that is highly prized by local tribesmen. Jungle stirges have been known to mingle with giant vampire bats. None of these larger versions have ever been captured or examined by sages, so nothing else is known about their strengths or weaknesses. What little of them is known came from the cannibals and head hunters of the jungle regions.

CLIMATE/TERRAIN:	Dark areas/
	Wilderness and subterranean
FREQUENCY:	Uncommon
ORGANIZATION:	Family/clan
ACTIVITY CYCLE:	Dawn and Sunset
DIET:	Omnivorous
INTELLIGENCE:	Average (8-10)
TREASURE:	C, Y
ALIGNMENT:	Chaotic (evil)

NO. APPEARING:	1d12
ARMOR CLASS:	6
MOVEMENT:	9
HIT DICE:	5+5
THAC0:	15
NO. OF ATTACKS:	5
DAMAGE/ATTACK:	1d4/1d4/1d4/1d4/2d4
SPECIAL ATTACKS:	Psionic, ambush
SPECIAL DEFENSES:	Psionic
MAGIC RESISTANCE:	Nil
SIZE:	M (large ape)
MORALE:	Average (8-10)
XP VALUE:	650

Su-monsters look like big gray monkeys, 4 to 5 feet tall. They have large bones and muscular limbs, but they always appear a bit underfed, because their ribs and vertebrae show prominently. Their long, prehensile tails can easily support their weight. Their hands and feet are virtually alike, each having three long, thick fingers and an opposable thumb, all equipped with claws. Like the tail, their hands and feet are very strong, allowing them to hang by one limb for several hours. Short, dirty gray fur covers most of their body. Their face and tail are black, while their paws are always bloody red (making them look like they just finished killing something, which is the case more often than not). They frequently grin, but this is usually a sharp-toothed threat rather than a gesture of friendliness.

Combat: Su-monsters attack with all four legs when possible, raking their extremely sharp nails across their victim. They can also deliver a powerful bite with their canine-like mouth. These creatures like to hunt in small packs (1d12 members). Their favorite hunting grounds are well-traveled trails through the jungle/forest. They search for a sturdy branch overhanging a trail, and perch in the trees, waiting patiently. When a victim passes beneath them, they an swing down, using their tails as anchors. This way they can attack with all four claws plus the bite. Victims of this kind of ambush suffer a −4 penalty to their surprise rolls.

What really makes these beasts ferocious is their tribal protectiveness. Half the time (50% chance), the entire family takes part in the hunt: male, female, and two young. If the young are attacked or threatened, the females fight as if under a *haste* spell (i.e., double movement and number of attacks). Likewise, if the they females are attacked, the males appear to fight with *haste*. A surge of adrenaline accounts for this ferocity. Females can maintain the effect for up to 6 turns (an hour), and males can maintain it for up to 4 turns. Psionically these creatures can be deadly. They know three attack modes. They are also impervious to telepathic attacks. When su-monsters are using enhancement, they can attack both psionically and physically if they choose (instead of a double attack rate).

Psionics Summary:

Level	Dis/Sci/Dev	Attack/Defense	Score	PSPs
2	3/1/3(2/5)	PsC,MT,PB/Nil	= Int	120

Su-monsters always know the following powers, and there is a 10% chance that they will have one more science and two more devotions in the psychometabolic discipline.
- **Psychometabolism - Devotions:** enhancement (no cost, see above).
- **Metapsionics - Devotions:** psionic sense (always on, no cost) .
- **Telepathy - Sciences:** psychic crush. Devotions: mind thrust, psionic blast.

Habitat/Society A su-monster family is composed of two parents (adult male and female) and two young. When two or more families live together, they form a clan. Su-monsters are very territorial and have a particular hatred for the psionically empowered.

According to legend, su-monsters were created by a powerful evil cleric or mage, who wished to guard his forest from intruders (especially psionic ones). The creatures do make a formidable attack force, which tends to support this theory. According to some sages the creatures are magical hybrid of humanoids and apes. In any event, many evil wizards and priests employ su-monsters as forest guards today.

Ecology: Su-monsters keep their valuables well hidden in the high boles of the trees in their territory. They have no food value, since their meat is mildly poisonous. Characters who eat su-monster meat must save vs. poison or become ill, and no natural healing is possible for 1 week.

Swanmay

CLIMATE/TERRAIN:	Swanmay	Bird Maidens
	Temperate wetlands	Tropical mountains
FREQUENCY:	Very rare	Very rare
ORGANIZATION:	Flock	Solitary
ACTIVITY CYCLE:	Any	Day
DIET:	Omnivore	Omnivore
INTELLIGENCE:	Highly to Genius (13-18)	Average to Genius (8-18)
TREASURE:	See below	
ALIGNMENT:	As ranger	Any
NO. APPEARING:	1 or 2-5	1
ARMOR CLASS:	7	7
MOVEMENT:	3 or 15, Fl 19 (D)	12, or 3, Fl 36 (C)
HIT DICE:	2 to 12	2 to 8
THAC0:	As ranger	As kahina
NO. OF ATTACKS:	3 or as ranger	2 or as kahina
DAMAGE/ATTACK:	1/1/1-2 or by weapon	1/1-3 or by weapon
SPECIAL ATTACKS:	See below	Spells
SPECIAL DEFENSES:	+1 or better weapon to hit	+2 or better weapon to hit
MAGIC RESISTANCE:	2% per HD	5% per HD
SIZE:	M	M
MORALE:	Champion (15)	Elite (13)
XP VALUE:	120 to 3,000	420 to 3,000

Swanmays are human females who can assume swan form. In human form, swanmays are indistinguishable from other people. They normally wear light armor and carry rangers' gear, as well as a sword, dagger, bow, and arrows. These items are unaffected by a swanmay's shapeshifting, so they must be hidden. Swanmays may be recognized by a feather token, feathered garment, or signet ring. Such items are transformed into part of the swans' plumage or worn on a leg.

Combat: In human form, the swanmay functions as a ranger. To determine the level and Hit Dice of a swanmay, 2d6 are rolled. She attacks with whatever weapons she possesses.

In swan form, a swanmay is harmed only by +1 or better weapons. She attacks with buffeting wings, a flying leap, and a bite.

Habitat/Society: Swanmays are members of a special sorority of lycanthrope rangers. Unlike other lycanthropes, their shapeshifting ability is gained voluntarily from a special token: a feather token, a feather garment, or a signet ring. Such items reveal their magical auras when exposed to a *detect magic* spell. Without the item, she is forced to remain in her current form. Tokens only function for swanmays.

Swanmays are extremely secretive about their sorority. Only human women are admitted; the other requirements are unknown. It is suspected that women are invited to join when they unknowingly perform a great service for another swanmay. If a PC is invited to join, it is 50% likely that she will retire from casual adventuring to devote herself full time to her new responsibilities.

Swanmays are guided by their swan personalities. They dislike noisy, brash creatures, ferocious beasts, and anything of an evil alignment. They are friendly with forest folk, such as sylvan elves and dryads. They tend to avoid normal humanoids. Only nature priests are known to regularly associate with swanmays; such alliances are generally initiated by swanmays when they need help against a common evil.

Swanmays build communal lodgings near bodies of water, deep in the forest. Such lodgings are lightly fortified against land attack. They usually contain two means of escape—a secret tunnel to the lake and a ceiling hatch. Swanmays in swan form can use either route. Swanmay lodgings may be recognized by the number of waterfowl living nearby. The remains of poachers may also be left here as a warning to others.

Ecology: Swanmays are independent protectors of the forests and wildlife. They actively oppose evil races or monsters that might otherwise decimate wildlife and the countryside. They protect swans more out of sympathy for their similarity than out of any kinship.

Bird Maidens

In the mountains and cool valleys of the lands of Zakhara lives a race of bird maidens, related to the swanmays. Just like their sisters, they depend on a token to change forms: a colorful shawl or veil of feathers. They can assume many bird shapes, including falcons, swallows, parrots, and even (at 8th level) giant eagles.

Though they have no sorority, bird maidens are loosely united by their faith. All bird maidens are kahina, idol priestesses who believe in the divinity of all things. They live as wandering teachers, protecting the land from those who despoil it. They get along best with those who respect the land: desert riders, mystics, and fisherfolk. In the fertile river valleys, they preach the faith and maintain the fertility of the land and livestock. Some tribesmen believe bird maidens are *hama*, spirits of the departed, who return to help the living. Bird maidens deny this and may cut themselves to prove that they are flesh and blood.

Bird maidens' Hit Dice are equal to their priestly level, from 2-8. They have major access to the All, Animal, Divination, Elemental, Healing, Plant and Weather spheres and minor access to the Creation, Protection, and Sun spheres. They carry spears, darts, and slings, but may not wear armor or shields (even magical) heavier than hide. If they do, they cannot use spells. Bird maidens cannot turn undead.

In bird form, bird maidens can peck and claw, but most don't fight as birds. Only a bird maiden's shawl or veil changes with her when she shifts form. All other equipment is unchanged and must be hidden or cared for by others until the bird maiden again changes her form.

Bird maidens are sometimes forced to marry men who steal their shawls; if they ever recover them, they leave their husbands, killing their sons and taking the daughters with them to become bird maidens. If the feathered garment is destroyed, the bird maiden dies as well.

Rumors tell of a great wooden fortress among the clouds of the high hills, called the Crown of All Feathers, where young bird maidens are taught the rituals and duties of kahinas by the aaracockra.

	Tabaxi	Tabaxi Lord
CLIMATE/TERRAIN:	— Tropical or subtropical jungle —	
FREQUENCY:	Rare	Very rare
ORGANIZATION:	Clan	Clan or solitary
ACTIVITY CYCLE:	Any	Nocturnal
DIET:	Carnivore	Carnivore
INTELLIGENCE:	Average to High (8-14)	High to genius (13-18)
TREASURE:	U	U
ALIGNMENT:	Chaotic neutral	Chaotic evil
NO. APPEARING:	2-8	1
ARMOR CLASS:	6	3
MOVEMENT:	15	15
HIT DICE:	2	8
THAC0:	19	13
NO. OF ATTACKS:	3	3
DAMAGE/ATTACK:	1-3/1-3/1-3 or by weapon	1-4/1-4/1-10
SPECIAL ATTACKS:	Rear claw rake for 1d4+1/1d4+1	Magic use, rear claw rake for 1d6+1/1d6+1
SPECIAL DEFENSES:	— Surprise, surprised only on a 1 —	
MAGIC RESISTANCE:	Nil	Nil
SIZE:	M (6'-7' tall)	L (10'-12')
MORALE:	Steady (11-12)	Average (8-10)
XP VALUE:	420	5,000
	Clan leader: 975	
	Shaman, 3rd: 975	
	Shaman, 5th: 3,000	

Tabaxi have spotted coats ranging in color from light yellow to brownish red. These graceful feline humanoids are tall and slender, with retractable claws, and eyes of green or yellow.

Some tabaxi have solid spots and are also called leopard men; they pronounce their name ta-BAX-ee. Tabaxi in other regions have roseate spots, are called jaguar men, and pronounce their race's name tah-BAHSH-ee.

Combat: Tabaxi are great hunters, combining quick, stealthy movements with natural camouflage to surprise prey. Enemies suffer a −2 penalty to surprise rolls. Tabaxi are clever and organized, often driving prey into an ambush (though some play with prey before killing it). Tabaxi climb and swim, and can use those abilities in combat. Because of their cleverness and acute sense of smell, tabaxis are almost impossible to trap.

Tabaxi often use weapons of wood, bone, and stone, including bolas, slings, obsidian studded clubs (treat as battle axes), and javelins with atlatl. They are as likely to use claws and teeth as any other weapon. If both forepaws hit, a tabaxi rakes with its rear claws. A group encountered in the wild will include a Hunt Leader with maximum hit points, and may (50% chance) include a 3rd-level priest with appropriate Hit Dice and spells.

Habitat/Society: Tabaxi clans contain equal numbers of males and females, and a full clan has 1d6+1 Hunts of 2d4 tabaxi. The Hunts work the area around the clan lair. Some lairs are temporary, but most are small villages of ramadas (huts with grass roofs supported by tall poles, and no walls). In a lair, 3d4 young with 1 HD each will be found. An elder with 4 HD leads the clan, and 50% of the leaders are aided by a 5th-level shaman. A clan has a 10% chance of owing allegiance to a tabaxi lord; these clans tend toward evil, warlike ways, and their shamans worship evil powers. Shamans of other clans worship powers related to sunlight, rain, or animals.

Tabaxi are reclusive and avoid other intelligent beings, even other tabaxi clans. They do not engage in trade, which they consider demeaning, but some few have agents who trade for them. Tabaxi speak their own ancient language. Legends tell of a great tabaxi civilization that was supplanted by other races.

Ecology: Tabaxi have few natural enemies. For food, they prefer the boar-like peccaries and huge rodents called capybaras; only a very degenerate clan attacks members of another intelligent species for food. Tabaxi are sometimes hunted for their pelts, worth up to 250 gp each. Their skins and claws are also useful in some types of natural magic.

Tabaxi Lord
A tabaxi lord appears as a huge jaguar or leopard, depending on where it is found. They are intelligent, malicious, and cunning. They speak tabaxi and languages commonly used by nearby societies. The antithesis of couatls, tabaxi lords hate them (the feeling is mutual) and attack couatl on sight.

Tabaxi lords use trickery, ambush, allies, and spells to weaken foes before closing for combat. Some 55% are 7th-level wizards, while 40% are 7th-level priests of a dark power known as Zaltec. Five percent are both wizard and priest. Wizard spells are chosen from the schools of illusion, enchantment/charm, or necromancy; spells from the schools of alteration and invocation/evocation are never used. In addition to spells that require only verbal components, they can use the following powers at will: *detect good/evil*, *detect invisibility*, *bind*, and *hypnotism*. The bravest and cruelest tabaxi lords can use *dimension door* three times per day.

Tabaxi lords are closely related to tabaxi, perhaps a cursed version. All tabaxi lords are male and must take a tabaxi mate to produce offspring (always a male tabaxi lord). Although usually solitary, a tabaxi lord sometimes takes leadership of a tabaxi clan for the purpose of mating and insuring offspring. Some choose to stay with the clan even after the offspring is born and sent off to make its way in the jungle.

Tako

	Male Tako	Female Tako
CLIMATE/TERRAIN:	Tropical, subtropical, and temperate ocean	Tropical subtropical, and temperate ocean
FREQUENCY:	Rare	Very rare
ORGANIZATION:	Tribe	Tribe
ACTIVITY CYCLE:	Any	Any
DIET:	Carnivore	Carnivore
INTELLIGENCE:	Average (8-10)	Average (8-10)
TREASURE:	J, Q	J, Q
ALIGNMENT:	Lawful neutral	Lawful neutral
NO. APPEARING:	3-12	1-2
ARMOR CLASS:	3	2
MOVEMENT:	3, Sw 9	3, Sw 9
HIT DICE:	4	6
THAC0:	17	15
NO. OF ATTACKS:	7	7
DAMAGE/ATTACK:	1-2 (x7)/3-6 or by weapon	1-3 (x7)/2-8 or by weapon
SPECIAL ATTACKS:	Constriction	Constriction
SPECIAL DEFENSES:	Camouflage	Camouflage
MAGIC RESISTANCE:	Nil	Nil
SIZE:	M (6′ diameter)	L (7′ diameter)
MORALE:	Steady (12)	Steady (12)
XP VALUE:	270	650

The tako are a race of intelligent octopi who can move onto land and use weapons and other tools.

Tako have no bones; their plump bodies are protected by tough mantles of leathery skin. They have eight supple tentacles, similar to those of octopi, lined with circular muscles that act as suction cups. They have a single golden eye centered in their heads, and sharp, protruding jaws that resemble the bill of a parrot. Although tako can change color with ease, a mature male's normal color is light green, while a mature female's is orange-red. Young tako appear in a variety of colors, including black, brown, white, blue, and golden.

Tako have their own language based on tentacle movements and skin-color changes. Characters with an Intelligence of at least 17 (or with the reading/writing proficiency) have a 25% chance of understanding the tako's language.

Combat: Though normally docile, tako attack any creature who invades their territory. In addition, they have a strong sense of honor, and will avenge attacks and ally with members of other races who assist them. They are crafty opponents. Tako can change their color and pattern to match any natural terrain in a single round. This camouflage makes them 90% undetectable, and modifies the surprise rolls of opponents by −3.

Most tako war parties are exclusively male. The tako attack with their beaks. They also can anchor themselves with a single tentacle, leaving the remaining seven tentacles free to make attacks. Usually, the tako carry seven weapons—one spear or hand axe in each free tentacle.

Tako can make constriction attacks similar to octopi. Any victim under 7 feet tall (or 7 feet long) can be grappled by one tentacle at a time. Male tako have a 10% chance of pinning both of the victim's arms with a single strike; females have a 15% chance. The chance of pinning only one upper limb is the same. If both

limbs are pinned, the victim has no attack. If only one limb is pinned, the victim attacks with a −3 penalty to his attack roll. If no limbs are pinned, the victim attacks with a −1 penalty.

Tako tentacles grip with a Strength of 18/00; a victim with a Strength equal to or greater than 18/00 can grasp the tentacle and loosen it, negating the constriction. To break completely free, a tentacle must be severed; males have 4 hit points per tentacle, females have 6 hit points per tentacle. Unless loosened or severed, tentacle constriction automatically inflicts 1-4 hit points of damage per round from males, or 2-8 (2d4) points from females.

Young tako cannot perform constriction attacks. Their AC is 7, and they have 1 HD. Their THAC0 is 20. They inflict 0-1 hp of damage per tentacle attack, and 1-3 hp with their beak. Otherwise, they're just small, feisty versions of their parents, with an MR of 1 (Sw3) and XP value of 35.

Habitat/Society: A tako tribe comprises 3-12 (3d4) males, half as many young, and 1-2 females. Females make all decisions for the tribe, while the males act as defenders and hunters. The creatures establish their lairs in coastal underwater caves, making occasional raids on land for food, weapons, and treasure items. In some areas, tako coexist with humans, cooperating to attack sea monsters and to help fishermen, but such cases are extremely rare.

Ecology: Tako eat oysters, crabs, lobsters, and other shell fish, which they crack open with their powerful jaws. They can eject small clouds of rich blue ink, but the clouds are too limited to serve as a defense. Humans greatly prize the ink, however, and use it to create calligraphy.

	Balor	Marilith
CLIMATE/TERRAIN:	The Abyss	The Abyss
FREQUENCY:	Very rare	Very rare
ORGANIZATION:	Solitary	Solitary
ACTIVITY CYCLE:	Any	Any
DIET:	Carnivore	Carnivore
INTELLIGENCE:	Supra-genius (19-20)	Genius (17-18)
TREASURE:	H×3	C, F
ALIGNMENT:	Chaotic evil	Chaotic evil
NO. APPEARING:	1	1-2
ARMOR CLASS:	-8	-9
MOVEMENT:	15, Fl 36 (B)	15
HIT DICE:	13	12
THAC0:	7	9
NO. OF ATTACKS:	1 or 2	7
DAMAGE/ATTACK:	by weapon or 2-12	4-24 and 6 by weapon
SPECIAL ATTACKS:	Terror, body flames, death throes, explosion	Magical weapons, constriction
SPECIAL DEFENSES:	+3 or better weapons to hit	+2 or better weapon to hit, never surprised, spell immunity
MAGIC RESISTANCE:	70%	70%
SIZE:	L (12' tall)	L (7' tall)
MORALE:	Fanatic (17-18)	Fanatic (17-18)
XP VALUE:	46,000	45,000

Tanar'ri are, in the broadest terms, chaos and evil defined. The less intelligent often attack without question and fight until slain. True and greater tanar'ri often roam the Astral and Ethereal Planes—their attention is attracted by those in an ethereal state.

Combat: In addition to the separate abilities of each sort of tanar'ri, they all share the following magical powers:

Attack	Damage	Attack	Damage
acid	full	gas (poisonous, etc.)	half
cold	half	iron weapon	full
electricity (lightning)	none	magic missile	full
fire (magical)	half	poison	none
fire (nonmagical)	none	silver weapon	full*

* greater tanar'ri suffer half damage from silver weapons.

All tanar'ri with average or above average intelligence have a form of telepathy that enables them to communicate with any intelligent life form, regardless of any language barriers.

Frequently, the Abyss-forged, magical weapons of the tanar'ri dissolve upon the death of the creature. When one doesn't, it is likely that the weapon in question originated somewhere else.

Habitat/Society: There are five classifications of tanar'ri, listed in ascending order of power, and with species, below:

Least: dretch, manes, rutterkin
Lesser: alu-fiend, bar-lgura, cambion, succubus
Greater: babau, chasme, nabassu
True: balor, glabrezu, hezrou, marilith, nalfeshnee, vrock
Guardian: molydeus

Balor (True Tanar'ri): The greatest and most terrible of the true tanar'ri, the balors are the undisputed terrors of the Abyss. They are the very motivation behind the tanar'ri involvement in the *Blood War*. In every sense of the word, balors are the quintessential tanar'ri. They derive great pleasure from the suffering of others and go out of their way to torment lesser beings and cause them pain.

Balors are repulsive and loathsome to behold. They are towering humanoids with deep, dark red skin. They have huge wings that propel them with unnatural speed and agility. They have long, wicked claws and grotesque fangs that drip with venom. Balors are commonly surrounded by searing flames.

Combat: Balors attack with their great fists for 2-12 points of damage. Anyone struck by a balor's fists must roll a saving throw vs. spells with a −6 penalty or flee in terror for 1-6 turns.

Balors much prefer weapons to fists in combat. Each carries a great sword that looks like a bolt of lightning. In the hands of a balor, these swords are vorpal and can *detect evil/good* in a 30 foot radius. Any creature that picks up a balor's sword, regardless of whether its skin actually touches it, immediately suffers 10-60 points of damage and must roll a saving throw vs. spells, or die immediately.

Balors also use a great whip with many tails. These whips will inflict but 1-4 points of damage per hit. However, they magically wrap the victim, allowing the balor to draw the victim into his ever-present bodily flames. Once dragged into the flames, the victim suffers 4-24 points of damage per round. Escaping the whip requires a successful one-half strength check. When the whip holds a victim, it cannot be used in other attacks.

Balors may use one of the following additional magical powers at the 20th level of spell use per round at will: *detect invisibility* (always active), *detect magic* (always active), *dispel magic*, *fear*, *pyrotechnics*, *read magic*, *suggestion*, *symbol* (any type), *telekinesis*, and *tongues*.

They may also gate 1-8 least, 1-6 lesser, 1-4 greater, or 1 true tanar'ri to their location. The gate is always successful but may only be used once per hour.

Balors are completely immune to gas. If a balor is slain in the Abyss, it explodes in a blinding flash of light, inflicting 50 points of damage to everything in a 100-foot radius around the creature (saving throw vs. spell for half damage).

Tanar'ri

Habitat/Society: Balors exist for one purpose only: to wage the *Blood War.* They are driven by the strongest primal desire to fight and will command whole legions of beings into battle.

Balors also recognize a subtle but important aspect of the War: the prime material plane. They will often make pacts with mortals to perform services for the purpose of gaining power in the prime material plane. Balors know that the more followers or allies they can gain in the prime material, the more power they will have there.

There are at least 24 balors known to exist. The creatures do not inhabit any particular area of the Abyss, but wander about forming armies for battle with the baatezu (q.v.).

Ecology: There is nothing more important in the Abyss than the *Blood War.* The balor, in a sense, *are* the Blood War from a tanar'ri perspective, the ecology of the Abyss, driving the creation of new beings and mandating their survival.

Marilith (True Tanar'ri): Bold and cunning, marilith are the generals and tacticians for the *Blood War.* Where the balors are the influence and energy behind the war effort, the marilith are the brains and tactics.

Terrible to behold, these creatures have the bodies of giant snakes, with huge, green, scaly coils. From the waist up, they are beautiful, comely females. Besides her obvious snake body, the feature that reveals the true nature of this tanar'ri is her six arms. They are commonly adorned with precious jewelry and highly decorated weapons—marilith most often carry a different weapon in each of their six hands.

Combat: Although marilith are strategists and tacticians, they love to join combat and do so whenever the opportunity presents itself. They can attack with each of their six arms and constrict a victim with their snaky tails as well.

Marilith always carry a different weapon in each hand, favoring exotic swords and axes. The DM should assign specific weapons; 90% of them should be enchanted versions of the common variety, and 15% of those should be a special weapon. Marilith favor their weapons highly. If one should ever be lost or stolen, marilith go to great lengths to see that the weapon is recovered.

A marilith can also constrict with her deadly tail. If the tail hits in combat, it wraps around a victim, automatically inflicting 4-24 points of crushing damage each round. Additionally, due to the constriction of air, the victim must roll a successful Constitution check every round or fall unconscious. No opponent with less than a 15 Strength score can even hope to break free of the marilith's coils. There is a 10% chance per round, per point of Strength over 14, that the victim can escape. Marilith have the following additional magical powers that they can use once per round, one at a time, at will: *animate dead, cause serious wounds, cloudkill, comprehend languages, curse, detect evil, detect magic, detect invisibility, polymorph self* (7 times per day), *project image, pyrotechnics,* and *telekinesis.*

They may also attempt to gate in 2-20 least tanar'ri, 1-6 lesser tanar'ri, 1-4 greater tanar'ri, or 1 true tanar'ri once per hour with a 35% chance of success.

Weapons of +1 or less magical enchantment cannot harm a marilith. These creatures are never surprised. They cannot be fooled by illusions and are immune to mind-affecting spells.

Habitat/Society: As noted, marilith are the strategists of the *Blood War.* They are in charge of devising all tactics to be used during the battles and coordinate the activities of all true tanar'ri (save the mighty balors, of course). Due to the chaotic nature of the tanar'ri, it is not really possible to coordinate their activities, but the marilith are charged with it, nonetheless.

These stunningly powerful creatures have a hatred for the glabrezu. They feel that the subtle warfare of the glabrezu is a children's game and inferior to proper warfare. A marilith will attempt to discredit the workings of the glabrezu any chance it gets. They would completely destroy the subtle beasts, but the all powerful balors favor the glabrezus' tactics and would have them continue their ways.

Ecology: Marilith are true tanar'ri, which makes them a part of the driving force behind the *Blood War.* Moreover, they are the coordinators and generals of the war effort. Marilith feel that they are the true force behind the war. Secretly, they feel that the balors have their place only because of their great power, but are not absolutely necessary. They may be right in their belief, but the power of the balors remains unchallenged.

Tarrasque

CLIMATE/TERRAIN:	Any land
FREQUENCY:	Unique
ORGANIZATION:	Solitary
ACTIVITY CYCLE:	See below
DIET:	Omnivore
INTELLIGENCE:	Animal (1)
TREASURE:	See below
ALIGNMENT:	Nil

NO. APPEARING:	1
ARMOR CLASS:	-3
MOVEMENT:	9, Rush 15
HIT DICE:	300 hp (approx. 70 HD)
THAC0:	−5
NO. OF ATTACKS:	6
DAMAGE/ATTACK:	1-12/1-12/2-24/5-50/1-10/1-10
SPECIAL ATTACKS:	Sharpness bite, terror
SPECIAL DEFENSES:	See below
MAGIC RESISTANCE:	Nil
SIZE:	G (50' long)
MORALE:	Champion (15)
XP VALUE:	107,000

The legendary tarrasque, for there is fortunately only one known to exist, is the most dreaded monster native to the Prime Material plane. The creature is a scaly biped with two horns on its head, a lashing tail, and a reflective carapace.

Combat: The tarrasque is a killing machine and when active (see below) eats everything for miles around, including all animals and vegetation. Normal attacks are with its two forelimb claws (1d12 points of damage each), a sweeping tail lash (2d12 points of damage), a savage bite (5d10 points of damage plus acts as a *sword of sharpness*, severing a limb on a natural attack roll of 18 or better), and two thrusting horn attacks (1d10 points of damage each).

Once every turn, the normally slow-moving tarrasque can rush forward at a movement rate of 15, making all horn attacks cause double damage and trampling anything underfoot for 4d10 points of crushing damage.

The mere sight of the tarrasque causes creatures with less than 3 levels or Hit Dice to be paralyzed with fright (no saving throw) until it is out of their vision. Creatures of 3 or more levels or Hit Dice flee in panic, although those of 7 or more levels or Hit Dice that manage to succeed with a saving throw vs. paralyzation are not affected (though they often still decide to run away).

The tarrasque's carapace is exceptionally tough and highly reflective. Bolts and rays such as lightning bolts, cones of cold, and even magic missiles are useless against it. The reflection is such that 1 in 6 of these attacks actually bounces directly back at the caster (affecting him normally), while the rest bounce off harmlessly to the sides and into the air.

The tarrasque is also immune to all heat and fire, and it regenerates lost hit points at a rate of 1 hit point per round. Only enchanted weapons (+1 or better) have any hope of harming the tarrasque. The Tarrasque is totally immune to all psionics.

Habitat/Society: It is fortunate that the tarrasque is active only for short periods of time. Typically, the monster comes forth to forage for a week or two, ravaging the countryside for miles around. The tarrasque then seeks a hidden lair underground and

lies dormant, sleeping for 5d4 months before coming forth again. Once every decade or so, the monster is particularly active, staying awake for several months. Thereafter its period of dormancy is 4d4 years unless disturbed. The ratio of active to dormant states seems to be about 1:30.

Ecology: Slaying of the tarrasque is said to be possible only if the monster is reduced to -30 or fewer hit points and a *wish* is then used. Otherwise, even the slightest piece of the tarrasque can regenerate and restore the monster completely. Legend says that a great treasure can be extracted from the tarrasque's carapace. The upper portion, treated with acid and then heated in a furnace, is thought to yield gems (10d10 diamonds of 1,000 gp base value each). The underbelly material, mixed with the creature's blood and adamantite, is said to produce a metal that can be forged by master dwarven blacksmiths into 1d4 shields of +5 enchantment. It takes two years to manufacture each shield, and the dwarves aren't likely to do it for free.

It is hoped that the tarrasque is a solitary creation, some hideous abomination unleashed by the dark arts or by elder, forgotten gods to punish all of nature. The elemental nature of the tarrasque leads the few living tarrasque experts to speculate that the elemental princes of evil have something to do with its existence. In any case, the location of the tarrasque remains a mystery, as it rarely leaves witnesses in its wake, and nature quickly grows over all remnants of its presence. It is rumored that the tarrasque is responsible for the extinction of one ancient civilization, for the records of their last days spoke of a "great reptilian punisher sent by the gods to end the world."

Note: Creatures with a minus THAC0 can only be hit on a 1.

Tasloi

CLIMATE/TERRAIN:	Tropical/Jungles
FREQUENCY:	Rare
ORGANIZATION:	Tribal
ACTIVITY CYCLE:	Night
DIET:	Omnivore
INTELLIGENCE:	Low to average (5-10)
TREASURE:	Q (x5)
ALIGNMENT:	Chaotic evil

NO. APPEARING:	10-100
ARMOR CLASS:	5 (6)
MOVEMENT:	9, Cl 15
HIT DICE:	1
THAC0:	19
NO. OF ATTACKS:	2 or 1
DAMAGE/ATTACK:	-3/1-3 or by weapon type
SPECIAL ATTACKS:	Surprise
SPECIAL DEFENSES:	Nil
MAGIC RESISTANCE:	Nil
SIZE:	S (2'-3' tall)
MORALE:	Average (10)
XP VALUE:	Normal: 35
	Chieftain: 270
	Shaman: 420

Tasloi are long-legged, flat-headed humanoids. They walk in a crouching posture, touching their knuckles to the ground from time to time. Their skins are a lustrous green and are thinly covered with coarse black hair. Their eyes are similar to a cat's and are gold in color.

Often they can be heard at night, speaking in their high, whispery voices. Tasloi speak their own tongue and can also speak the languages of monkeys and apes. About 5% of their kind have learned a pidgin common that they use when trading.

Combat: Tasloi like to hide in tree tops and drop down on the weak and unwary. They are quick and nimble in the trees, but slow and clumsy on the ground. When they are in jungle, their stealthy movements impose a -4 penalty to opponents' surprise rolls. They also hide in shadows, like a thief, with 75% effectiveness. Their infravision enables them to see up to 90 feet in darkness, but they hate daylight and suffer a -1 penalty to their attack roll when fighting in broad daylight.

Tasloi carry the following weapons: small shield (AC 5) and javelin—20%, club and javelin—40%, short sword and small shield (AC 5)—10%, javelin and net—15%, short sword and net—10%, or javelin and lasso—5%. Tasloi without shields are AC 6. They customarily carry all javelins and shields on their backs when they travel through the trees.

Tasloi eat anything, but they enjoy all kinds of flesh, especially humans and elves. They normally attack from above, trying to capture if possible. If they gain surprise, they use their 10-foot-diameter nets to trap their prey (the nets totally entangle those of less than 15 Strength; those of 15 or greater Strength need a successful open doors roll to rip the net and escape). If a party is too vigilant or prepared, the tasloi attempt to wear down the group through short, sudden attacks followed by retreat. If possible, tasloi try to steal the enemy's dead after an attack.

Habitat/Society: The tasloi live in loosely-structured bands of several families. In every band of 70 or more, there is a chief of 5 Hit Dice. There is a 30% chance that any band has a shaman. Tasloi shamans may advance up to 5th level.

When found in their lair, in addition to the males, there are females and young equal to 70% and 50% of the number of males, respectively. Females fight as males, but the young do not fight at all. The lair consists of a series of 1d6 large trees with 4d6 platforms 50-100 feet above the ground. All the trees are connected by vines and ropes. There is a 60% chance that the tasloi have 1d6 trained giant spiders and a 20% chance that they have 2d4 trained giant wasps. Tasloi are able to ride these wasps for great distances, and the spiders aid in the construction, protection, and overall maintenance of the tree-village.

Ecology: It is not known where and how tasloi originated. It is likely they have been around for many millennia, interbreeding in deep isolated jungles. Their primitive lifestyle has probably existed in much the same fashion for thousands upon thousands of years.

While certainly among the least fearsome of all jungle creatures, tasloi are perhaps worth worrying about in numbers, or after fleeing encounters with nastier jungle denizens. Tasloi know the location of such lairs and often set up obvious escape routes for any creature that foolishly finds itself confronting the beast. The tasloi then lay their traps along the escape path and wait for the weakened, unsuspecting creatures to run through blindly. This strategy is highly successful, apparently, as the tasloi boast many more trophies than their small size and limited prowess might otherwise indicate.

Thought-Eater

CLIMATE/TERRAIN:	Ethereal Plane
FREQUENCY:	Rare
ORGANIZATION:	Solitary
ACTIVITY CYCLE:	Any
DIET:	Mental energy
INTELLIGENCE:	Not ratable
TREASURE:	Nil
ALIGNMENT:	Neutral
NO. APPEARING:	1-3
ARMOR CLASS:	9
MOVEMENT:	6 (ethereal plane only)
HIT DICE:	3
THAC0:	Nil
NO. OF ATTACKS:	0
DAMAGE/ATTACK:	Nil
SPECIAL ATTACKS:	Psionics, absorb: psionics, spells, and intelligence
SPECIAL DEFENSES:	Ethereal existence
MAGIC RESISTANCE:	absorb (See below)
SIZE:	S (3' long)
MORALE:	Unsteady (5-7)
XP VALUE:	1,400

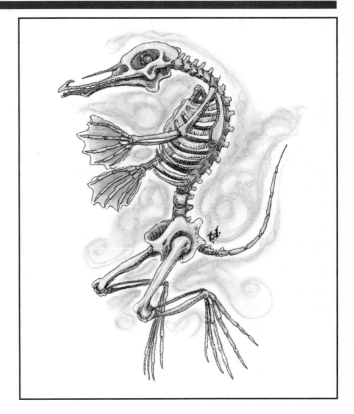

Thought eaters are natives of the Border Ethereal, and they only survive in ethereal form. They appear as sickly gray skeletal bodies with oversized platypus heads. They have webbed skeletal paws, suited to swimming through the ether.

A thought eater has only one desire—to avoid death. For some reason, they die almost instantly on the Prime material plane. Fortunately for them, they have several psionic powers which help to prevent this.

Combat: Thought eaters are unique. They have no combat abilities except their innate psionic talents, even on the Border Ethereal, so they can be easily slain if encountered there.

Thought eaters are far from harmless, however. Although they cannot survive outside the Border Ethereal, their psionic powers extend into the Prime material plane. This is one of the few known examples of transplanar extension.

The thought eaters' psionic sense is always operating. Because of their unique abilities, they can sense psionic activity in the Prime material plane, as well as the Border Ethereal. When they detect psionic activity of any kind, they will shift to the location of the emanations.

Their only "attack" is their innate ability to absorb psionic energy. They can absorb psionic energy within 60 feet of a true psionicist or psionic creature, or within 10 feet of a wild talent. Thought eaters drain 10 psionic points per round and they will also absorb any spell cast in the area as well as memorized spells (5 points per spell level). Finally, they can feed upon Intelligence, with each point converted to 10 PSPs that they absorb. They will feed until all victims die or escape, or until they themselves are sated. This occurs when they reach a number of points equal to their PSPs.

Although they feed on brain power, thought eaters are essentially stupid. Because they lack intelligence, they are immune to all telepathic attacks and controls (psionic or otherwise). Their preferences and the order in which they feed are always the same: 1) psionic points being expended (causes power to fail); 2) magical energy being expended (causes spell to fail; 3) PSPs; 4) memorized spells; 5) Intelligence. Note that if a thought eater consumes all of someone's Intelligence, the victim will become a vegetable (effectively dead). The Intelligence loss is permanent, unless it is relieved by *restore* or psychic surgery. Spells can be re-memorized and drained PSPs can be recovered naturally

The thought eaters' feeding frenzy has the sole purpose of maintaining thought eaters in the ether. Their bodies process PSPs the way humanoids process food, at a rate of 3 PSPs/hour. If they run out of points, they drop out of the ether into the Prime material plane and meet an instant death.

Note that ethereal beings are invisible to creatures on the Prime material plane, it is probable that a thought eater will attack and feed unnoticed and uncontested until sated, or until its victims are out of range. Although it only has a movement rate of 6, this is ethereal movement, allowing passage through walls, trees, etc. as if they didn't exist.

Any defense mode except those with a 0 maintenance cost will prevent the thought eaters from feeding. This includes spells like *mind blank*, and magical devices that thwart psionic attacks

Psionics Summary: Thought eaters have 1d100 + 100 (101-200) PSPs. Their score is 18. They boast a natural, innate form of psionic sense (in a metapsionic power), which operates continuously at no cost to PSPs. They also absorb PSPs-see *Combat*.

Habitat/Society: Little is known about thought eaters, except that they exist solely in the ethereal plane and are very solitary beings. Magical research has indicated that they are not malevolent; their attacks are for the sole purpose of staying alive, the same as any humanoid hunter. Some sages believe that though eaters are the final fate of psionisists, once they die.

Ecology: Thought eaters carry no treasure. When one dies, it automatically drops out of the ether and materializes on the Prime material plane. Of course, they are usually dismissed as platypi that died from starvation.

Thri-Kreen

CLIMATE/TERRAIN:	Temperate or tropical arid land	
FREQUENCY:	Uncommon	
ORGANIZATION:	Pack	
ACTIVITY CYCLE:	Constant	
DIET:	Carnivore	
INTELLIGENCE:	Average to high (8-14)	
TREASURE:	Varies	
ALIGNMENT:	Chaotic neutral	

NO. APPEARING:	2d12
ARMOR CLASS:	5
MOVEMENT:	18
HIT DICE:	6+3
THAC0:	13
NO. OF ATTACKS:	5 or 2
DAMAGE/ATTACK:	1d4(×4)/1d4+1, or
	1d4+1 and by weapon
SPECIAL ATTACKS:	Paralyzation
SPECIAL DEFENSES:	Missile dodge
MAGIC RESISTANCE:	Nil
SIZE:	L (11' long)
MORALE:	Fanatic (17-18)
XP VALUE:	1,400

The figures given above are for mature adult thri-kreen. Others have the following abilities, based on their age (they age one age category per year until they reach mature adult):

	HD	THAC0	XP	Claw/bite damage	Special ability gained (see below)
Larva	1+3	19	65	1/1	—
Child	2+3	17	120	1/1	—
Young	3+3	17	175	1d3/1d3	leap
Young adult	4+3	15	270	1d3/1d3	—
Adult	5+3	15	975	1d4/1d4+1	venom, chatkcha
Mature adult	6+3	13	1,400	1d4/1d4+1	dodge missiles

Thri-kreen are a race of large, intelligent insects often referred to as "mantis warriors." They roam the deserts and savannahs, where they have marked-out hunting territories. They have no need of sleep and can remain active through the day and night.

Mature adult thri-kreen are roughly 7 feet tall at the shoulder and 11 feet long. Of the six limbs protruding from their midsection, two are used for walking; the other four end in four-fingered hands. The tough, sandy-yellow exoskeleton is extremely hard. A thri-kreen has two compound eyes, usually black with highlighted eyespots, two antennae, and a complicated jaw structure that manipulates food as the thri-kreen chews. The antennae help the individual to maneuver through brush and grasslands in the darkness (they also reduce any melee combat penalty from darkness or blindness by 1; missile combat is not affected). Thri-kreen often wear harnesses and even some forms of clothing, but they never wear armor.

The native thri-kreen language is made up of clicks and the grinding of its jaw appendages. While it is difficult for other creatures to speak this tongue, it is just as difficult for a thri-kreen to imitate more standard speech patterns. Thri-kreen speak their own language, but some understand the Common tongue.

Thri-kreen seldom live more than 35 years.

Combat: A thri-kreen's chitinous exoskeleton gives it AC 5 naturally. Unarmed, it can attack with four claws and one bite attack per round. If using a weapon, the thri-kreen can attack with its weapon and bite. The *gythka*, a pole arm with a blade at each end, can slash for 1d6 hp damage against man-sized or smaller targets, or 1d10 hp damage against a larger target. The gythka can be thrown as a spear to inflict 1d6+2 hp damage. Thri-kreen also learn special combat maneuvers as they grow older, learning all by the time they are mature adults.

Leap: This ability allows a thri-kreen to leap 20 feet straight up or up to 50 feet forward. They cannot leap backward.

Chatkcha: This is a crystalline throwing wedge. A thri-kreen can throw

two chatkcha per round, up to 90 yards. A chatkcha causes 1d6+2 damage when it hits, and returns to the thrower when it misses.

Venom: This venom is delivered through an older thri-kreen's bite. Anyone bitten must make a successful saving throw vs. paralyzation or be paralyzed. Smaller than man-sized creatures are paralyzed for 2d10 rounds, man-sized for 2d8 rounds, large creatures for 1d8 rounds, and huge and gargantuan creatures for only one round.

Dodge missiles: A mature thri-kreen can dodge missiles fired at it on a roll of 9 or better on 1d20; they cannot dodge magical effects, only physical missiles. Magical physical missiles (arrows, thrown axes, etc.) modify this roll by their magical bonus.

Psionics: Some thri-kreen have psionic wild talents. There is a 50% chance that any thri-kreen will have a psionic wild talent, described in the *Complete Psionics Handbook*.

Magical Items: Thri-kreen can use most magical items, though those designed for humanoid creatures cannot be worn properly, so will not function for a thri-kreen.

Habitat/Society: Thri-kreen organize into hunting packs; there are no permanent thri-kreen communities. Packs range over wide territories that they call their own. Small groups consist only of mature adults. Groups of more than eight thri-kreen are two-thirds mature adults, and one-third other age categories (in about equal numbers).

Ecology: Thri-kreen are carnivores. They seldom hunt other intelligent creatures for food, but will do so in times of need. Mantis warriors have a well-known taste for elves, which keeps both races at an uneasy peace at best.

Related Species

The **tohr-kreen**, or mantis nobles, are larger, more cultured versions of thri-kreen. Though many of them wander their world to gain knowledge, they sometimes build cities as well. They regard thri-kreen as somewhat barbaric cousins, though there have been incidences of a tohr-kreen creating a permanent settlement of thri-kreen, or teaching a pack more civilized ways.

The **xixchil** are spacefaring mantis. These creatures are skilled surgeons and artificers, who enjoy replacing lost limbs with "more efficient" substitutes.

Titan

CLIMATE/TERRAIN:	Olympus
FREQUENCY:	Uncommon
ORGANIZATION:	Group
ACTIVITY CYCLE:	Any
DIET:	Omnivore
INTELLIGENCE:	Supra-genius to godlike (19-21 +)
TREASURE:	E, Q (×10), R
ALIGNMENT:	Chaotic good

NO. APPEARING:	1-10
ARMOR CLASS:	0
MOVEMENT:	36
HIT DICE:	20
THAC0:	5
NO. OF ATTACKS:	2
DAMAGE/ATTACK:	7-42 (7d6) weapon +14 (strength bonus)
SPECIAL ATTACKS:	See below
SPECIAL DEFENSES:	See below
MAGIC RESISTANCE:	50%
SIZE:	G (25 +' tall)
MORALE:	Fanatic (17-18)
XP VALUE:	21,000 (see below)

Titans are gargantuan, almost godlike men and woman. They, quite simply, look like 25' tall people of great physical strength and beauty. They are commonly dressed in traditional Greek garb, favoring togas, loincloths, and such. They wear rare and valuable jewelry and in other ways make themselves seem beautiful and overpowering.

In addition to speaking their own language, titans are able to speak the six main dialects of giants. All titans are also conversant in the common tongue as well as that commonly spoken by forest creatures, as these giants have close ties with nature.

Combat: The basic attack of titans is their great maul (*maul of the titans*). These monstrous beings are capable of attacking twice in a melee round and inflicting 7-42 points of damage per hit.

Titans may choose to make a single other attack in a round. This form of special attack is so destructive and deadly, that a titan will use it only if there are no other options left open. The form of each titan's attack will be different (some kick, some punch, others use a breath attack, lightning, etc.), but the effect is the same for each. The special attack inflicts 10-60 points of damage per hit and can be used every other round. These mighty attacks have been known to destroy buildings and sink ships.

Titans can become ethereal twice per day. All titans are able to employ both mage or priest spells (dependent on the individual titan—only one, not both) as a 20th-level spell caster. In addition, all titans have the following spell-like powers, at 20th level of spell use, usable once per round, one at a time, at will:

- *advanced illusion*
- *alter self*
- *animal summoning II*
- *astral spell*
- *bless*
- *charm person or mammal*
- *commune with nature*
- *cure light wounds*
- *eyebite*
- *fire storm*
- *hold person*
- *hold monster*
- *hold undead*
- *invisibility*

- *levitate*
- *light*
- *mirror image*
- *pass without trace*
- *produce fire*
- *protection from evil, 10' radius*
- *remove fear*
- *remove curse*
- *shield*
- *speak with plants*
- *summon insects*
- *whispering wind*

Titans are not affected by attacks from nonmagical weapons.

Habitat/Society: Titans are livers of life, creators of fate. These benevolent giants are closer to the well springs of life than mere mortals and, as such, revel in their gigantic existences. Titans are wild and chaotic. They are prone to more pronounced emotions that humans and can experience godlike fits of rage. They are, however, basically good and benevolent, so they tend not to take life. They are very powerful creatures and will fight with ferocity when necessary.

To some, titans seem like gods. With their powers they can cause things to happen that, surely, only a god could. They are fiery and passionate, displaying emotions with greater purity and less reservation than mortal beings. Titans are quick to anger, but quicker still to forgive. In fits of rage they destroy mountains and in moments of passion will create empires. They are in all ways godlike and in all ways larger than life.

And yet is should be noted that titans are not gods. They are beings that make their home in Olympus and walk among the gods. Yet they are not omnipotent, omniscient rulers of the planes. Sometimes their godlike passions and godlike rages make them seem like deities, however, and it is common for whole civilizations to mistake them for deities.

Titan

In one society, Jeuron, a titan with dominion over knowledge, was revered as a god for centuries. Those mortals built their whole civilization around him and Jeuron revelled in the worship. He even walked among them occasionally to see their love and admiration. But Odin, of the Norse mythos, discovered his deception and punished Jeuron by shackling him to the bottom of the deepest sea for 100 years.

Titans have a natural affinity for storm giants. Those giants are the closest beings the titans have found to peers and they will readily befriend them. In any group of titans, there is a 35% chance that they will be accompanied by one or more storm giants. Although titans can sometimes be condescending by nature, they never treat the storm giants as subordinates or inferiors.

On Olympus, titans have developed a culture similar to what they found there. They wear similar clothing, eat similar foods, play similar music, etc. It is unclear why this has occurred. Perhaps the titans, in a godlike whim, adopted their favorite mortal lifestyle. Such would not be unusual for these great beings.

Titans primarily dwell in great palaces and mansions in Olympus where they live their lives whimsically. There they will dance, sing, study, debate and engage in all other manner of activities with titanic proportion. If a titan finds something that interests him, it would not be unusual for him to study it in great detail for many weeks, only to leave it when his interest has waned. They may also engage in debates or arguments that last literally for weeks at a time. These debates might end in a jovial laughter and good spirits or in thunder and rage. Such are the whims of titans.

Ecology: Titans are basically identical to humans, except much larger. What makes them immortal is not known. Perhaps it is their enchanted existence in the halls of Olympus.

These giants are commonly known to experience the same range of emotions as humans do. They develop idiosyncrasies as humans do, also. In fact, titan mannerisms emulate those of humans very closely. Again, it is difficult to tell if the titans are whimsically copying humans, or vice versa.

Titans, being godlike creatures, tend to be very diverse and unique. Each individual titan (or sometimes group of titans) have a special power is that related to their personality or sphere of influence. These powers are very different, and usually very strong. Some examples of the powers of a titan are explained below:

Algorn, a titan that has influence over the seas, has the ability to *create water* whenever he chooses to. This water can be vast as he desires, up to the volume of a medium-sized lake. Algorn can simply cause the water to flow, he can cause it to jet out from his hands (washing away everything in its path away), or he can even cause the water to be frozen.

Mane, a titan with dominion over felines, has the ability to change into a giant form of any cat. When he transforms, he is instantly cured of all wounds, poisons, and diseases. Mane may change into a cat and back again five times per day.

Porphyl is a titan with the power of growth. He may cause any immature life to grow to maturity. Thus, he can cause crops to grow, he can make a boy grow to manhood, etc. Porphyl is very wise and would never abuse his ability.

Malephus, a titan with influence over law and justice can unerringly detect any spoken lie and any bad intention. He is often used by many greater powers in trials of justice. Malephus is totally honest; he is incapable of lies or deception.

Syllia, a titan with power over love, can remove any negative feelings from any being (except deities and powers). She has the ability to remove hatred, unhappiness, depression, etc. Syllia cannot remove the feeling permanently, but for at least a day or so. The deities of the upper planes often employ her power when trying to stop wars.

Girzon, a titan with dominion over death, can take the life from any living being. It should be noted that Girzon has never used this ability unless commanded to by a deity. Girzon's restraint and self-control is revered by other titans.

Greater Titans: Rumors exist of a race of titans more powerful still than common titans. These *greater* titans are said to be very close to the gods and always accompany one (with some deities and powers being attended by more than one greater titan). Perhaps greater titans were formally common titans who have grown so great in power that the gods brought them closer to themselves. Such matters are not common knowledge.

It is very difficult to provide combat statistics for greater titans. Like the gods themselves, greater titans are simply not subject to aggression from nondivine beings. They are never harmed by such attacks.

Toad, Giant

	Giant Toad	Fire Toad	Ice Toad	Poisonous Toad
CLIMATE/TERRAIN:	Non-arctic or subterranean	Non-arctic or subterranean	Arctic, subarctic land or subterranean	Non-arctic or subterranean
FREQUENCY:	Common	Rare	Rare	Uncommon
ORGANIZATION:	Colony	Colony	Colony	Colony
ACTIVITY CYCLE:	Any	Any	Day	Any
DIET:	Carnivore	Carnivore	Carnivore	Carnivore
INTELLIGENCE:	Animal (1)	Low (5-7)	Average (8-10)	Animal (1)
TREASURE:	Nil	C	Q, (C)	Nil
ALIGNMENT:	Neutral	Chaotic neutral	Neutral	Neutral
NO. APPEARING:	1-12	1-6	1-4	1-8
ARMOR CLASS:	6	10	4	7
MOVEMENT:	6, hop 6	6, hop 6	9, hop 9	6, hop 6
HIT DICE:	2+4	4+1	5	2
THAC0:	17	17	15	19
NO. OF ATTACKS:	1	1	1	1
DAMAGE/ATTACK:	2-8	Variable	3-12	2-5
SPECIAL ATTACKS:	See below	See below	See below	See below
SPECIAL DEFENSES:	Nil	Nil	Nil	Nil
MAGIC RESISTANCE:	Nil	Nil	Nil	Nil
SIZE:	M (5' length)	S (4' length)	L (8' length)	M (5' length)
MORALE:	Unsteady (7)	Average (8-10)	Steady (11-12)	Unsteady (7)
XP VALUE:	120	270	270	175

Giant toads are found in most regions. Although their smaller cousins are beneficial insect eaters, the large toads devour (or at least attempt to devour) any creature which appears edible.

Their exact appearance varies from species to species, but these beasts are all just what their name implies, giant versions of toads. Coloration runs the gamut from weak brown to iron red, but their skin is always dry, rough to the touch, and warty.

Combat: All giant toads can jump up to their movement distance. This hop will clear any object up to one-third as high as the length of the leap and requires but a single round to accomplish. A jumping toad can attack in midair or at the end of the leap.

When hunting, giant toads remain motionless until likely prey walks or slithers within range. The toad then leaps to the attack; the victim has a -3 penalty on its surprise roll.

Habitat/Society: Giant toads often make their homes underground, where they enjoy both the damp air and the steady supply of food. They prefer temperate zones, near water where they can lay their eggs, but often survive in surprisingly cool or dry regions.

Toads are often attracted to settled areas where they prey upon livestock (goats, chickens, and even sheep). Cities often have problems with sewer toads, giant monstrosities which have grown fat on vermin, house pets, and, occasionally, civil engineers.

Ecology: Giant toads keep no treasure, but worthwhile indigestibles are occasionally found in their droppings. Their skin can be fashioned into suitable leather armor, but its odor will be at least as distinctive as its appearance.

Fire Toad

These large, red toads are about 4 feet long and covered with rough, purple warts. Fire toads shun water, preferring drier surroundings. Fire toads are so named because of their ability to exhale small fireballs. These fireballs are their only form of attack; a single fireball can travel up to 30 feet and has a blast radius of 5 feet. Damage is equal to 2-16 points, half that if a saving throw vs. spell is made. Fire toads rarely attack unless threatened, molested, or defending their lairs. Fire toads subtract 1 point of damage on all dice for fire-based attacks against them, but cold- or water-based attacks inflict an additional point of damage per die. Throwing liquid—even water—at a fire toad will cause it to retreat, though it will immediately breathe twice at its assailant in the round of its retreat.

Ice Toad

Fully intelligent, ice toads dwell in cold climes or far beneath the surface of the ground. In addition to its vicious bite, the creature can radiate cold in a 10-foot radius from its body. Ice toads can generate this special attack once every other round. All noncold-using creatures within this sphere of cold suffer 3-18 points of damage. Characters making a saving throw vs. spell suffer only half damage. Ice toads speak their own weird language and actively collect gems and jewelry, particularly diamonds.

Poisonous Toad

These toads, indistinguishable from common giant toads, secrete a weak, hemotoxic poison. A creature bitten by a poisonous toad must save vs. poison at +2. Failure means the victim falls comatose and will die within 24 hours unless treated.

Treant

CLIMATE/TERRAIN:	Any forest
FREQUENCY:	Rare
ORGANIZATION:	Grove
ACTIVITY CYCLE:	Any
DIET:	Photosynthesis
INTELLIGENCE:	Very (11-12)
TREASURE:	Q (x5), X
ALIGNMENT:	Chaotic good

NO. APPEARING:	1-20
ARMOR CLASS:	0
MOVEMENT:	12
HIT DICE:	7-12
THAC0:	13 (7-8 HD),
	11 (9-10 HD),
	9 (11-12 HD)
NO. OF ATTACKS:	2
DAMAGE/ATTACK:	Variable
SPECIAL ATTACKS:	See below
SPECIAL DEFENSES:	Never surprised
MAGIC RESISTANCE:	Nil
SIZE:	H (13'-18')
MORALE:	Champion (15-16)
XP VALUE:	
7 HD	2,000 (+1000 per Hit Die)

Treants are strangely related to both humans and trees, combining features of both species. Peaceful by nature, treants can cause great damage when roused to anger. They hate evil things and the unrestrained use of fire.

Treants are almost indistinguishable from trees. Their skin is a thick, textured, brown bark. Their arms are gnarled like branches and their legs fit together when standing like the trunk of a tree. Above the eyes and along the head are dozens of smaller branches from which hang great leaves. In winter the leaves of a treant change color but rarely fall out. Treants are very intelligent and often speak a number of languages including their own, elf, dwarf, common, and a smattering of just about all other humanoid tongues (at least enough to say "Get out of my trees!").

Combat: The combat ability of treants varies with their size. Young treants (13 or 14 feet) have 7 or 8 Hit Dice and inflict 2-16 points of damage per attack. Middle-aged treants (15 or 16 feet) have 9 or 10 Hit Dice, respectively, and inflict 3-18 points of damage per attack. Elder treants (17 or 18 feet) have 11 or 12 Hit Dice and inflict 4-24 points of damage per attack.

Due to their tough, barklike skin, treants have a superior Armor Class rating against almost all weapons. Their only weakness is fire. Any fire-based attack against a treant is at +4 to hit and +1 damage. In addition, treants save against all fire-based attacks at -4. This weakness to fire also applies to animated trees controlled by a treant.

Treants have the ability to animate normal trees. One treant can animate up to two trees. It takes one round for a normal tree to uproot itself. Thereafter the animated tree can move at a rate of 3 per turn and fights as a full-grown treant (12 Hit Dice, two attacks, 4-24 points of damage per attack). A treant must be within 60 yards of the tree it is attempting to animate. Animated trees lose their ability to move if the treant who animated them is incapacitated or moves more than 60 yards away.

Treants (regardless of size) and treant-controlled trees can inflict structural damage when attacking a building or fortification.

Habitat/Society: Treants live in small communities, usually amidst old hardwood forests (oak, maple, mahogany, etc.). In the forest treants rarely reveal themselves, preferring not to interact with the more transient lifeforms (anything with a lifespan of 500 years or less). Humans and demihumans have only a slight chance of spotting a treant who is trying to blend in with the trees. Rangers have a fair chance of spotting a treant (10% per level).

Treants are intolerant of evil, particularly when fire and the wanton destruction of trees is involved. They hate orcs and goblins with a passion and tend to be suspicious of anyone carrying an ax.

Treants have no use for treasure, and usually place all such items somewhere out of sight, such as under a great rock. Occasionally a treant can be convinced to give up his treasure but only when some great good will be accomplished by this generosity.

Ecology: Treants, like all trees, gain sustenance via photosynthesis. Treants often sleep for long periods of time (anywhere from a few days to several years) during which short roots grow into the ground beneath them gathering water and minerals from the soil. Reproduction is via off-shoot stalks which the female treants then protect and care for until the stalks are grown.

The lifespan of a treant is not known, but is several thousand years at least. As they grow older, treants become slower and less agile, sleeping for longer periods and talking less of things that are and more of things that were. Eventually an old treant will not wake up, taking permanent root in the spot where he sleeps and living out the rest of his life as a normal tree.

CLIMATE/TERRAIN:	Any sea
FREQUENCY:	Rare
ORGANIZATION:	Community
ACTIVITY CYCLE:	Day
DIET:	Omnivore
INTELLIGENCE:	High and up (13+)
TREASURE:	M, Q (C, S, T)
ALIGNMENT:	Neutral (good)

NO. APPEARING:	6-60
ARMOR CLASS:	5
MOVEMENT:	Sw 15
HIT DICE:	3
THAC0:	17
NO. OF ATTACKS:	1
DAMAGE/ATTACK:	By weapon
SPECIAL ATTACKS:	See below
SPECIAL DEFENSES:	See below
MAGIC RESISTANCE:	90%
SIZE:	M (7' tall)
MORALE:	Elite (13)
XP VALUE:	Normal: 270
	Exceptional (4-6 HD): 650
	Exceptional (7-8 HD): 2,000
	Mage: 2,000
	+1,000 per level over 7th
	Priest: 2,000
	+1,000 per level over 7th
	Triton leader: 4,000

Tritons are rumored to be creatures from the elemental plane of Water that have been placed on the Prime Material plane for some purpose unknown to man. They are sea dwellers, inhabiting warmer waters principally but equally able to live at shallow or great depths.

The lower half of a triton ends in two finned legs, while its torso, head, and arms are handsomely human. Tritons have a silvery skin that fades into silver-blue scales on the lower half of their bodies. Their hair is deep blue or blue-green. Triton speak their own language as well as those of sea elves and locathah.

Combat: Tritons carry either tridents (60%) or long spears (40%). Some 25% are also armed with heavy crossbows. When equipped for battle, tritons wear armor made of scales (AC 4).

Outside their lair, tritons are 90% likely to be mounted, either on hippocampi (65%) or giant sea horses (35%). These mounts fight in defense of their riders.

Exceptional tritons (see below) and triton leaders always carry conch shells with them. Not magical, their sounds are well known to all marine creatures. When blown properly by an exceptional triton, a conch summons 5d4 hippocampi, 1d10 sea lions, or 5d6 giant sea horses. These creatures swim to the aid of the summoning triton, arriving 1d6 rounds after the conch is first sounded. The conchs can also be sounded to frighten aquatic animals as the *fear* spell. This latter noise causes all marine creatures within 60 feet and with animal Intelligence or less to flee in panic. Creatures are allowed a saving throw vs. spell to avoid the fear effect, but even those who succeed with their saving throws have a -5 modifier on their attack rolls against the tritons.

Triton are reclusive and nonviolent. They normally attack to capture. If a triton is killed in a battle, however, the fight immediately becomes one of retribution. Should the fighting go poorly, the tritons withdraw to their lair to either gather reinforcements or make a last stand.

In addition to their other abilities, tritons are nearly impervious to magic with a natural magic resistance of 90%.

Habitat/Society: Tritons live either in great undersea castles (80% chance) or in finely sculpted caverns (20%). While tritons lean toward good alignment, they are very suspicious of outsiders and have no love for land dwellers in general.

Tritons rarely kill, unless provoked, but they are quick to apprehend those who intrude upon their seas. Trespassers found guilty of intentionally entering triton waters or treasure seeking are left "to the fate of the seas." This means being stripped of all belongings and set adrift at least 10 miles from any shoreline. Characters ruled innocent by the triton court awaken the next day on some distant shore. Tritons never aid land dwellers unless their own interests are involved in the matter.

For every 10 tritons encountered there is an exceptional triton of 4-6 Hit Dice. For every 20 encountered there is an exceptional triton with 7-8 Hit Dice. Groups of 50 or more are always accompanied by a triton leader (AC 2, 9 Hit Dice). There is a 10% chance for every 10 tritons encountered that they are accompanied by a triton mage of 1d6 levels.

At a triton lair, the following additional tritons are always found:

> 60 males (with related exceptional tritons)
> One mage of 7th- to 10th-level ability
> One priest of 8th- to 11th-level ability
> Four priests of 2nd- to 5th-level ability
> Female tritons equal to 100% of males (2 HD, AC 6)
> Young equal to 100% of males (noncombatants)

There is also a 75% chance that the lair contains 2d6 sea lions as pets/guards.

Ecology: Tritons are omnivorous and live on fish, shellfish, and sea weed. They have no natural enemies save the giant squid, which is immune to the effects of their conch shells. Normal triton live approximately 300 years while their leaders and spellcasters have life expectancies of 500 years or more.

Troglodyte

CLIMATE/TERRAIN:	Subterranean and mountains
FREQUENCY:	Common
ORGANIZATION:	Clan
ACTIVITY CYCLE:	Any
DIET:	Carnivore
INTELLIGENCE:	Low (5-7)
TREASURE:	A
ALIGNMENT:	Chaotic evil

NO. APPEARING:	10-100
ARMOR CLASS:	5
MOVEMENT:	12
HIT DICE:	2
THAC0:	19
NO. OF ATTACKS:	3 or 1
DAMAGE/ATTACK:	1-2/1-2/2-5 or 2-8 weapon
SPECIAL ATTACKS:	See below
SPECIAL DEFENSES:	See below
MAGIC RESISTANCE:	Nil
SIZE:	M (6' tall)
MORALE:	Steady (11)
XP VALUE:	Normal: 120
	Guard: 175
	Subchieftain: 270
	Chieftain: 650

Troglodytes are a warlike race of carnivorous reptilian humanoids that dwell in natural subterranean caverns and in the cracks and crevices of mountains. They hate man above all other creatures and often launch bloody raids on human communities in search of food and steel.

Troglodytes stand about 6 feet tall, are covered in roughened leathery scales, and have a toothy lizard-like head. Males are easily distinguished from females by the fin-like crest that runs across their heads and down their necks. Coloration for both sexes varies due to the troglodyte's chameleon-like ability to change skin tone, but grayish brown is most common. Most troglodytes wear little more than a leather weapons belt, with perhaps a small bag of semi-fresh meat. Leaders adorn their belts with pieces of steel, a sign of power in troglodyte culture. Troglodytes have excellent infravision (90-foot range). They speak their own language and no other.

Combat: Fifty percent of a troglodyte force use their teeth and claws. The remaining 50% use weapons: swords (5%), stone battle axes (10%), stone morning stars (10%), or two troglodyte javelins (25%). Of special note is the troglodyte javelin. These great darts grant a +3 bonus to the attack roll when thrown by a troglodyte; they cause 2d4 points of damage. This bonus reflects the troglodytes' great skill with these darts. About 25% of troglodytes carry two such darts apiece.

Troglodytes prefer ambushes to frontal assaults. Their favorite tactic is to pick a well-trod mountain or subterranean path and then use their chameleon power to blend in with the surrounding rocks. When a likely target walks by, the troglodytes hurl a volley of javelins (this attack gives opponents a -4 penalty to their surprise rolls, but only for the initial round). After a second volley, the troglodytes descend upon their hapless victims.

When angered or engaged in melee, troglodytes secrete an oil that smells extremely disgusting to all humans and demihumans. Those failing their saving throws vs. poison are so revolted as to lose 1d6 points of Strength. This loss remains in effect for 10 rounds.

Habitat/Society: Troglodyte society is organized into clans, with each clan led by a chieftain (usually the biggest and most

fearsome troglodyte). A number of subchieftains also are present, chosen from those troglodytes that most distinguished themselves in battle. Rank is loose and internal squabbles common. Most chieftains lead only as long as the clan stays fed (and not one meal longer).

For every 10 troglodytes encountered there is one leader with 3 Hit Dice. For every 20 there are two subchieftains each with 4 Hit Dice. Groups of 60 or more always include the clan chieftain. The chieftain stands 7 feet tall, has 6 Hit Dice, and is accompanied by 2d4 guards with 3 Hit Dice each.

Troglodytes usually set their lair near a human or demihuman settlement. This enables them to prey on both the settlers and their livestock. The lair itself is typically a large cave or cavern with a number of smaller chambers adjoining it for the females and hatchlings. Troglodyte lairs contain a number of females equal to 100% of the males. Females have 1+1 Hit Dice each and fight to the death in defense of the hatchlings. Hatchlings number about 50% of the male population and are noncombatants.

Troglodytes value steel above all else, using it to make javelins and as a form of wealth. Individual troglodytes carry nothing of real worth, but their lair may contain considerable treasure amassed from their raids on the outside world. Often this wealth is carelessly strewn about, mixed in with half-eaten food, or just shoved into some out-of-the-way corner.

On moonless nights, raiding parties of 50 or more troglodytes venture forth in search of steel and food. These attacks usually target human settlements, where the troglodytes can use their infravision and their chameleon power to maximum advantage.

Ecology: Strict carnivores, troglodytes prefer human flesh over all others, but they won't hesitate to devour practically anything they can catch, including members of other troglodyte clans. Few creatures hunt troglodytes, for their taste is said to be even more vile than their odor.

	Troll	Two-headed	Freshwater	Saltwater	Desert	Spectral	Giant	Ice
CLIMATE/TERRAIN:	Any land	Any land	Lakes/rivers	Any coast	Any desert	Any forest	Any land	Arctic
FREQUENCY:	Uncommon	Very rare	Rare	Uncommon	Rare	Very rare	Rare	Rare
ORGANIZATION:	Group	Group	Group	Group	Solitary	Solitary	Tribe	Tribe
ACTIVITY CYCLE:	Night	Any	Day	Night	Any	Night	Any	Any
DIET:	Carnivore	Carnivore	Carnivore	Carnivore	Carnivore	Carnivore	Carnivore	Carnivore
INTELLIGENCE:	Low (5-7)	Average (8-10)	Low (5-7)	Low (5-7)	Average (8-10)	Very (11-12)	Low (5-7)	Average (8-10)
TREASURE:	Q (D)	Q (D)	Q×4 (C)	(D)	C	C	C	Q (D)
ALIGNMENT:	Chaotic evil	Chaotic evil	Chaotic evil	Chaotic evil	Chaotic evil	Chaotic evil	Chaotic evil	Chaotic evil
NO. APPEARING:	1-12	1-3	1-6	1-8	1 (10% 1-6)	1	1-12	2-12
ARMOR CLASS:	4	4	3	2	4	0	4	8
MOVEMENT:	12	12	3, Sw 12	3, Sw 12	12	12	12	9
HIT DICE:	6+6	10	5+5	6+12	7+7	8	8	2
THAC0:	13	11	15	13	13	13	13	19
NO. OF ATTACKS:	3	4	3	3	3	3	1 weapon	2
DAMAGE/ATTACK:	5-8/5-8/5-12	5-8/5-8/ 1-12/1-12	2-5/2-5/3-12	1-4/1-4/9-16	3-6/2-6/3-10	3-6/3-6/3-10	2d6+7	1-8/1-8
SPECIAL ATTACKS:	See below	See below	See below	See below	Surprise	Nil	Nil	Nil
SPECIAL DEFENSES:	Regeneration	Regeneration	Regeneration	Regeneration	Regeneration	See below	Regeneration	See below
MAGIC RESISTANCE:	Nil	Nil	Nil	Nil	Nil	Nil	Nil	Nil
SIZE:	L (9')	L (10')	L (8')	L(10')	L (9')	L (10')	L (10')	L (8')
MORALE:	Elite (14)	Champion (15-16)	Elite (14)	Champion (16)	Fanatic (17-18)	Champion (15)	Fanatic (17-18)	Steady (11)
XP VALUE:	1,400	3,000	650	1,400	1,400	1,400	1,400	175

Trolls are horrid carnivores found in all climes, from arctic wastelands to tropical jungles. Most creatures avoid these beasts, since trolls know no fear and attack unceasingly when hungry. Their frame appears thin and frail, but trolls possess surprising strength. Their arms and legs are long and ungainly. The legs end in great three-toed feet, the arms in wide, powerful hands with sharpened claws. The trolls' rubbery hide is colored a moss green, mottled green and gray, or putrid gray. A writhing hairlike mass grows out of their skulls and is usually greenish black or iron gray in color. Their dull, sunken black eyes possess 90-foot infravision. Females are easily distinguished from males; they are both larger and more powerful than their male counterparts.

Trolls walk upright but hunched forward with sagging shoulders. The trolls' gait is uneven and, when running, the arms dangle free and drag along the ground. For all this seeming awkwardness, trolls are very agile. They are masterful climbers and can scale even sheer cliffs with an 80% chance of success. Trolls have a poor hearing, but their sense of smell is superior.

Trolls have no language of their own, using "trollspeak", a guttural mishmash of common, giant, goblin, orc, and hobgoblin. Trollspeak is highly transient and trolls from one area are only 25% likely to be able to communicate with trolls from another.

Combat: Trolls attack with two clawed hands and their bite, and they can attack at multiple opponents. In the rare case that a troll wields a weapon, it attacks with a +8 damage bonus. Trolls regenerate at an amazing rate. Starting three rounds after first blood, the creatures recovers 3 hit points per round until healed. Trolls reduced to 0 or fewer hit points fall to the ground, incapacitated but not slain. Incapacitated trolls continue to regenerate and stand up to fight as soon as they have a positive number of hit points.

When using an edged weapon, it is possible to sever the thin limbs of a troll (a natural 20 with an edged weapon is needed). Severed limbs continue to fight after separation from the body (hands squeeze, heads bite if stepped on, etc.). Attacks by severed limbs are at normal chances to hit. Separated limbs fight for the remainder of the battle, then scuttle back and rebind with the body once the battle is over. Limbs unable to reach the body to die within 24 hours, but this is of little consequence since trolls regenerate lost body parts (including the head) within a week. If a troll is dismembered and scattered, the largest surviving piece regenerates. The others die within one day if they cannot rejoin that piece. Only fire and acid cause permanent damage to trolls. These forms of attack destroy its regenerative ability. A troll reduced to 0 or fewer hit points and immersed in acid or burned with fire is killed.

Trolls have no fear of death, and launch themselves into combat, flailing wildly at their opponents and biting whoever comes closest. They occasionally (25%) throw stones before closing with their victims.

Thrown stones have a maximum range of 20 yards, weigh 10 to 20 pounds, and inflict 1d8 points of damage. If confronted by a large natural or magical fire, trolls try to find some way around the flames. Trolls combine a ravenous appetite with limited intelligence, so they are frequently distracted and break off pursuit 50% of the time to pick up food dropped by fleeing prey.

Habitat/Society: Trolls can survive in all climes, but prefer dense forests and subterranean locales, since bright sunlight hurts their eyes; trolls suffer no combat penalties because of this. They usually make their lairs in caves, using great boulders to block the entrances. Inside a troll cave are a number of rough nests made of straw and grass, plus scattered bones and treasure from victims. If there are no caves in an area, trolls dig themselves a trollhole and cover its opening with twigs and leaves. Trollholes are usually built near trees and are 90% undetectable. Anyone who steps on a trollhole is 75% likely to fall through the leafy door and tumble into the den below.

Trolls live in small packs of 3 to 12 trolls led by a dominant female who acts as shaman/chieftain. She casts priest spells at 7th level; spheres typically include Charm, Divination, Sun (Darkness only), and Weather. Leadership is only retained by combat, so fights for pack control are frequent. Often heads rend each other limb from limb, but these battles are never fatal. Still, it is the custom of trolls to toss the loser's head a great distance from the fight scene, and frequently losers must sit and stew for a week until their new head grows in.

The pack chieftain's duties are few. She leads the trolls on nightly forages, loping along, sniffing the air for prey. If a scent is found, the trolls charge, racing to get there first, and letting out a great cry once prey is spotted. In return for being the hunt leader, the shaman gets her choice of mates in the pack. Females give birth to a single troll about once every five years.

Trolls have ravenous appetites, devouring everything from simple grubs to bears and humans. Their lairs are often located near human settlements or along well traveled roads, but not too near, for even trolls respect organized resistance by fire-bearing humans. Wandering trolls, in search of a new lair, travel by night and sleep by day. Ravenous from walking, these packs, on occasion, attack and devour entire humanoid villages.

Ecology: Trolls prey on all but the most powerful of creatures. They respect and fear dragons, but they hate giants of good alignment and wage war with them frequently. The troll's green blood is used to manufacture both poison antidotes and healing potions. The blood from one troll, worth 400 gp, can make three such potions.

Troll

Giant Two Headed Troll

These ferocious troll/ettin crossbreeds posses a mottled greenish brown skin tone, and their dress is usually moth-eaten rags or animal skins. Two-headed trolls use trollspeak as their language. Though part ettin, these monsters retain many of the abilities of trolls. They regenerate like trolls, but only 1 hit point a round, and severed limbs cannot reattach (their thicker limbs are not cleaved on a roll of 20). Two-headed trolls attack with two claws and two bites. Both bite attacks are against one opponent, but the claws may be directed against different foes. The troll can, though rarely, wield a weapon with a +6 damage bonus. Like ettins, two-headed trolls are surprised only on a 1. These creatures live in damp, underground caverns and can be found leading groups of their smaller troll cousins.

Freshwater Troll (Scrag)

These gilled trolls, also called scrags or river trolls, are the most loathsome of all the trolls. River trolls, as their name implies, travel the waterways in search of victims. Their arms are thin and frail but their mouths are wide and lined with dozens of needle-sharp fangs. Their color ranges from blue-green to olive. Scrags have all of the abilities of normal trolls, but they only regenerate when immersed in fresh water. Scrags can survive out of water for one hour and often come ashore in search of prey. River trolls devour anything they catch, but prefer humanoids and have a fondness for dwarves.

Scrags are devious hunters and often carry a few baubles with them. They lay gems near the water's edge and wait for someone to spot them and reach down. Other traps include burying themselves in the sand, in shallow water, and waiting to be stepped on or tangling the rudders of small boats. River trolls occasionally nest beneath bridges or near ferry boats, demanding a toll in exchange for passage. The toll varies, but averages the equivalent of one cow per week, per troll. Livestock and children frequently disappear when river trolls are near. Scrag shamans also have access to Elemental (water) spells.

Saltwater Troll (Marine Scrag)

Like freshwater scrags, marine scrags can breathe air for one hour and have all of the abilities of normal trolls, except they regenerate only when immersed in saltwater. Large, green, and pot-bellied, marine scrags are thick-skinned and heavily scaled. Limp hair, the color of seaweed, hangs down to their shoulders. Their feet are wide and webbed to aid them in swimming. While their limbs are shorter and weaker than those of ordinary trolls, their mouths are larger and filled with hundreds of needle-sharp teeth. Marine scrags can subsist on fish and shellfish, but crave human flesh. They create their lairs in shallow ocean caves or beneath city docks. They emerge from their caves at night, climbing over ship railings in search of sailors or hunting the piers for a strolling couple or a lone drunk. Their attacks are quick and stealthy; they usually hunt in packs of four to six, but occasionally, several dozen may attack a large ship. Marine scrag shamans also have access to Elemental (water) spells.

Desert Trolls

Desert trolls are usually tan, but can modify their color from bleached tan to mottled rock brown, causing a −2 penalty to opponents' surprise rolls. Their keen senses and animal cunning reduce their chances of being surprised to 1-in-10. Like normal trolls, the desert variety usually attacks with two claws and a bite.

Desert trolls are immune to normal fire, heat, and cold. They do not regenerate acid damage, damage from magical fire, or fire breath weapons. In addition, they suffer damage from normal water that cannot be regenerated. Normal water inflicts 1d4 points of damage per vial, 2d4 points per flask, and 4d4 points per skin. A *decanter of endless water* aimed directly at a desert troll (successful attack roll required) causes 25 points of damage per round. Purified water (including normal and holy water) causes double damage. A *potion of sweet water* causes 6d6 points of damage and the troll must make a saving throw vs. poison or die.

These trolls are tougher and more tenacious than their more common counterparts, but they are also more solitary. They skulk at the edges of settled areas, waylaying travelers and polluting sources of pure water.

Spectral Troll (Troll Wraith)

Spectral trolls, taking material form only in darkness, are tormented by the memory of life. They try to slay all living creatures they encounter. Resembling normal trolls in all respects except color, their jet black skin and hair make them easily distinguishable from other trolls. Spectral trolls have the same attacks as regular trolls and can divide them among

many opponents. A silver or magical weapon is needed to attack them, making the final disposition of a spectral troll an even trickier prospect.

Being undead, spectral trolls can be turned by priests as though they were specters. It is noted that a humanoid slain by a spectral troll becomes one itself in three days, unless a proper burial ceremony is performed by a priest of the victim's religion. Spectral trolls vanish in direct sunlight. They do not take damage from sunlight, they merely fade from view and reappear at the same spot at nightfall. Even those captured, unconscious, or trapped in *temporal stasis* have escaped permanent imprisonment in this manner.

Giant Trolls

Giant Trolls are hideous hill giant/troll crossbreeds. They resemble normal trolls in all respects, except for their unnatural size. Their skin is reddish brown and they have red-rimmed eyes.

Despite their pot-bellied appearance, giant trolls are immensely strong and inflict damage like a hill giant when they are using their favorite weapon of attack—a large spiked club made from a tree trunk or a house timber. These clubs cause 2d6 +7 points of damage. In those rare instances when a giant troll has no weapons, its claws inflict 1d6 +1 points of damage; as with all trolls, the claw attacks can be divided among different opponents as necessary.

Instead of using their claws to attack, weaponless giant trolls are more likely to grab medium-sized prey in their large hands and wield the struggling victim like a club, beating a new target with the body. Refer to the rules on hand-to-hand combat in the *Dungeon Masters Guide* for guidelines.

Giant trolls who are overwhelmed by many small- and medium-sized opponents take time to grab and hurl the warriors into nearby trees, leaving more time to deal with the softer, weaker enemies. Note that, like hill giants, giant trolls can catch missiles 25% of the time, if in reach, and can hurl boulders that cause 2d8 points of damage.

Unlike normal trolls and their closer relatives, giant trolls never attack with their bite. This is due to the fact that they are much taller than the meals they like best (humanoids, of course), and they find it difficult to bend forward with the flexibility normal trolls enjoy. Then too, the head of a giant troll, more than any other part of the cross-breed anatomy, is almost identical to that of a hill giant, except that their skin is reddish brown. The giant troll also lacks the razor sharp teeth of normal trolls that strike fear in so many.

Giant trolls regenerate damage as normal trolls, but at the rate of 2 hit points per round. They cannot reattach severed limbs. Before a giant troll can be killed, at least 10 points of damage must be inflicted on it by fire. If this condition is not met, and the giant troll is reduced to a single hit point, further damage has no effect, except to prevent regeneration.

They have a very acute sense of smell and 90-foot infravision. Giant trolls are feared throughout the world, for not only do they possess the horrible ability to regenerate damage inflicted upon them, but they also possess the power and strength of hill giants (fearsome in their own right). The combination is a deadly one, and, even worse, giant trolls travel in loose tribal bands of 1d12 members. They are rarely encountered alone. Lairs of giant trolls are always served by 2d6 normal trolls who act as simple lackeys (and sometimes food) for their larger cousins.

Giant trolls are found in nearly every clime. Giant trolls are on good terms with strong hill giant tribes, for which they serve as elite personal guardians for the ruling chief.

Ice Troll

The ice troll is a smaller, more intelligent relative of the normal troll, and is probably the result of magical experimentation. It closely resembles its more common cousin, but has semitransparent, very cold skin. Ice trolls are famous for being cunning, evil creatures which keep humans and demi-humans as livestock. Because ice trolls need water to regenerate, they never leave their lakes and rivers, and will create elaborate traps to lure their prey to them.

Ice trolls are organized and intelligent enough to know their weaknesses, and rarely start a fight at a disadvantage. Unlike their larger and less intelligent cousins, they do not wade into combat blindly, but will try to pick off weaker opponents one by one, hoping to bring back live prey. Ice trolls generally attack with claws for 1d8 hit points of damage each, but have been known to use weapons on rare occasions (10%), at an additional +4 to each weapon's damage due to Strength. Attacks may be directed against different opponents.

The regenerative powers of ice trolls are not as great as normal trolls. An ice troll must be immersed in water to be able to regenerate 2 hit points per melee round. The creatures often make their stand in a shallow pool of water to keep this advantage.

Because of the thin, brittle nature of the ice troll, it is possible to sever one of the creature's limbs with an edged weapon, on a natural attack roll of 20 with an edged weapon. Severed limbs also regenerate 2 hit points per turn, as long as they are immersed in water. If a severed limb is not in contact with water, it will move up to 30 feet in search of water, always moving toward it, if it is in range.

Fire and acid are the only attack forms which negate the ice troll's ability to regenerate.

Because of the ice troll's physiology, fire-based attacks do double damage. Ice trolls are unaffected by cold or cold-based spells, and because of their magical nature, can only be hit by magical weapons or missiles.

Ice trolls live in groups of 7-12 in arctic and sub-arctic regions, near open water. Because they are smaller and less resilient than their larger cousins, they have developed a higher sense of cooperation to stay alive. Each group has a leader, usually the most intelligent. Leaders are responsible for keeping the group safe and well-fed.

Ice trolls live near settled regions, hoping to waylay and capture humans and demi-humans. Ice trolls will frequently bait traps for adventurers, using treasure they have salvaged from previously waylaid groups. Settlements also provide more common livestock, which, although less preferable than human flesh, is considered edible in times of need. Ice trolls establish their lairs near lakes or rivers. Here the ice trolls will have gathered all their treasure, as well as 5-20 human or demi-human captives. These prisoners are kept well-fed on grains and vegetables, so that the ice trolls need never go too long without food.

Ice trolls mate in the spring and give birth to one baby ice troll in the late fall. When an ice troll tribe gets too large, it splits, one group wandering off to find a new lair. Ice trolls that live in arctic regions often hunt remorhaz, and will even pick off a solitary frost giant. Ice troll blood is frequently used in the manufacture of *frost brand swords*, and *rings of cold resistance*.

Spirit Trolls

The spirit troll is an odious mutation of the spectral troll. Several schools of thought completely separate this creature from the spectral variety, presenting evidence that the spirit troll is a perverted magical interbreeding of trolls and invisible stalkers. The spirit troll is invisible; characters able to see invisible objects observe it to be very similar to a troll, slightly shorter and with diffused features. The spirit troll can only be hit by magical weapons. Fire inflicts full damage, but it is invulnerable to cold-based attacks. It regenerates as does a troll, and at the same rate.

It attacks with its fangs and two sharp claws, against three different opponents if it so desired. The damage inflicted by its fangs (2d4+2) is normal damage, except that the spirit troll adds the damage to its own hit points—in effect healing itself! The damage inflicted by the spirit troll's claws (1d4+2) is taken not only from the victim's hit points but also from Strength. Strength points lost in this way are recovered in 2d4 turns. If a character's Strength is reduced to 0, the PC dies. If the Strength is reduced to 1 or 2 points, the PC is rendered comatose, only recovering when (and if) sufficient hit points are recovered to raise the Strength to 3 or more. The spirit troll has an acute sense of smell and superior, 120 foot-range, infravision.

Umber Hulk

	Umber Hulk	Vodyanoi
CLIMATE/TERRAIN:	Subterranean	Freshwater aquatic
FREQUENCY:	Rare	Rare
ORGANIZATION:	Solitary	Solitary
ACTIVITY CYCLE:	Any	Any
DIET:	Carnivore	Carnivore
INTELLIGENCE:	Average (8-10)	Average (8-10)
TREASURE:	G	G
ALIGNMENT:	Chaotic evil	Chaotic evil
NO. APPEARING:	1-4	1-3
ARMOR CLASS:	2	2
MOVEMENT:	6, Br 1-6	3, Sw 6
HIT DICE:	8+8	8
THAC0:	11	13
NO. OF ATTACKS:	3	3
DAMAGE/ATTACK:	3-12/3-12/1-10	3-12/3-12/1-10
SPECIAL ATTACKS:	See below	Nil
SPECIAL DEFENSES:	Nil	See below
MAGIC RESISTANCE:	Nil	Nil
SIZE:	L (8' tall, 5' wide)	L (8' tall, 5' wide)
MORALE:	Elite (13)	Elite (13)
XP VALUE:	4,000	2,000

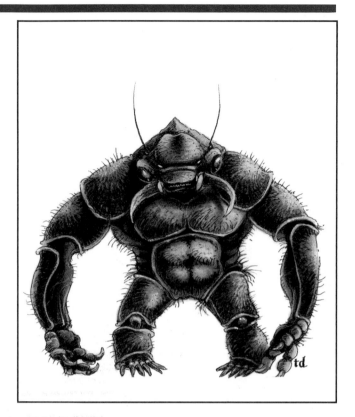

Umber hulks are powerful subterranean predators whose iron-like claws allow them to burrow through solid stone in search of prey.

Umber hulks are tremendously strong, standing nearly 8 feet tall and over 5 feet wide. Muscles bulge beneath their thick, scaly hides and their powerful arms and legs all carry great claws. They have no necks to speak of, but the head features a powerful maw with rows of triangular teeth and 8-inch mandibles capable of biting through any hide or bone. Most peculiar of all are the four round eyes, spaced evenly across each umber hulk's forehead. Umber hulks are black, shading to a lighter shade of yellowish gray on the front. Their eyes are mere blackened dots each the size of a small coin. Umber hulks have their own language.

Combat: For all of their monstrous features, umber hulks are intelligent opponents. They usually dig to a point adjacent to a main corridor, then wait, peeking through a crack they've made, until likely prey walks by. The umber hulk then springs out upon its startled victim. When using this technique, opponents have a -5 modifier on their surprise rolls. Other tactics involve planned cave-ins and dead-end tunnels where an umber hulk can wait for victims to come to him. Their burrowing rate varies from 10 feet per turn in solid stone to 60 feet per turn in soft earth.

In melee, umber hulks can deliver a vicious bite but, understandably, their main weapon is their great claws. Worse, looking into an umber hulk's eyes causes *confusion*, as per the spell, unless a saving throw versus spell is made. In addition to this special confusion attack the outer eyes of an umber hulk provide the creature with infravision to a distance of 90 feet.

The one saving grace when fighting an umber hulk is their speed. Their gait is slow and ponderous and their balance is poor in wide spaces.

Umber hulks never fight to the death unless cornered (which is rare, since the creature can dig through stone). If hard pressed, an umber hulk won't hesitate to cause a cave-in (25% chance of success per round) and then dig his way to freedom.

Habitat/Society: Umber hulks dwell in the depths of the earth. They raid dungeons for food, much the way anteaters raid ant colonies, eating their fill and then moving on to let the "colony" recover.

Umber hulks are usually solitary hunters. Males and females mate, then go their separate ways. One to three young are born about a year later in a special nursery which has been hollowed out by the female. Two years later, once the hulklings are big enough, the female begins taking them with her when hunting. It is during this period that unfortunate victims may stumble across more than one umber hulk at a time.

No umber hulk culture is known, but it is rumored that there may be entire cities of these beings underground with tunnels that radiate out, like threads in a spider's web, toward the nearer dungeons and mountain ranges. If true, this would explain much, for umber hulks seem to disappear or spring up in a region at will and always take great care in hiding their tunnels behind them.

Ecology: Umber hulks eat young purple worms, ankhegs, and similar creatures. Their favorite prey, however, is humankind.

Vodyanoi

These aquatic predators are closely related to the umber hulk. Vodyanoi live in deep bodies of fresh water. They are similar in appearance to umber hulks but have only two eyes and thus lack the ability to confuse opponents. Their skin is green and slimy to the touch, but beneath it is a thick, knobby hide. Their claws are webbed. Vodyanoi prey upon all manner of creatures but prefer human flesh. They can rend the hulls of small vessels and frequently sink or overturn small boats. Once per day a vodyanoi can attempt to summon 1-20 electric eels with a 50% chance of success. The existence of a saltwater variety of vodyanoi of twice the size and greater ferocity is rumored but unconfirmed.

Unicorn

CLIMATE/TERRAIN:	Temperate sylvan woodlands
FREQUENCY:	Rare
ORGANIZATION:	Family
ACTIVITY CYCLE:	Day
DIET:	Herbivorous
INTELLIGENCE:	Average (8-10)
TREASURE:	X
ALIGNMENT:	Chaotic good

NO. APPEARING:	1-6
ARMOR CLASS:	2
MOVEMENT:	24
HIT DICE:	4+4
THAC0:	15
NO. OF ATTACKS:	3
DAMAGE/ATTACK:	1-6/1-6/1-12
SPECIAL ATTACKS:	Charge
SPECIAL DEFENSES:	See below
MAGIC RESISTANCE:	Nil
SIZE:	L
MORALE:	Elite (14)
XP VALUE:	650

Unicorns dwell only in temperate woodlands, away from human habitation. These fierce but good creatures shun contact with all but sylvan creatures (dryads, pixies, sprites, and the like); however, they will show themselves to defend their woodland home.

Powerful steeds with gleaming coats of pure white hair, unicorn eyes are usually deep sea blue or fiery pink. Long, silky white strands of hair hang down from the mane and forelock. A single ivory-colored horn, 2 to 3 feet in length, grows from the center of each unicorn's forehead. Males are distinguished by the white beard beneath the chin; females by their more elegant and slimmer musculature. The hooves of a unicorn are cloven and yellow-ivory in color. Unicorns speak their own language as well as those of other sylvan creatures and elves.

Combat: Unicorns can sense an enemy from 240 yards away. Likewise, unicorns move very silently, so opponents are penalized -6 on their surprise rolls. Unicorns can kick with their front hooves and thrust with the horn each round. Due to the horn's magical nature, it always has a +2 bonus to hit. Unicorns can charge into battle, using the horn like a lance. To make this charge, there must be at least 30 feet of open space between the unicorn and his opponent. Opponents struck by a charging unicorn suffer 3-36 points of damage from impaling. Unicorns may not attack with their front hooves in the round they charge.

Once per day a unicorn can use a *teleport* spell of limited range. This spell will transport the unicorn (and its rider) to any place that the unicorn desires, up to 360 yards away. Unicorns often use this ability as a last resort to avoid death or capture.

In addition, unicorns can never be *charmed* or *held* by magic. They are immune to death spells and make all saving throws against spells as if they were wizards of 11th level. Unicorns are immune to poison.

Habitat/Society: Unicorns mate for life and make their home in an open dell of the forest they have chosen to protect. There, in the boles of the trees, unicorns etch a glyph, recognizable to sylvan creatures, indicating that the forest is under unicorn protection. Rangers have a 10% chance per level of determining

correctly whether a forest is guarded by unicorns. Once a woodland has a unicorn protector, no other unicorn will enter that forest unless the forest is very large. Each family of unicorns stakes out a territory approximately 400 square miles (20 miles by 20 miles).

Travelers may pass through a unicorn's forest freely and even hunt there, but anyone killing for sport or damaging the forest maliciously will be attacked if the unicorn is nearby (10% chance). The ferocity of this attack is determined by the evil of the trespasser. Truant youths throwing stones at animals, for example, would be driven off with just a few bruises as a reminder, while pillaging orcs would be hunted down and slain.

Lone unicorns occasionally allow themselves to be tamed and ridden by a human or elf maiden of pure heart and good alignment. A unicorn that submits once and is treated kindly will act as the maiden's steed for life, even carrying her beyond the realm of his forest if she so desires. Unicorns make exceptionally loyal mounts and will protect their riders even unto death.

Ecology: Unicorns are herbivores, living on tender leaves and grasses. Their only enemies are griffons and those creatures who destroy forests, in particular red dragons and orcs.

The life span of unicorns has never been recorded but is known to surpass 1,000 years. They are believed to maintain their youth until death is only weeks away. The secret to this longevity is the strong magical nature of the horn. Unicorn horns are highly sought after, since possession of one is a sovereign remedy against all poisons. Alternately, a single horn can be used, by an alchemist, to manufacture 2-12 potions of *healing*. Unicorn horns sell for 1,500 gold pieces or more on the open market.

Urchin

	Black	Green	Red	Silver	Yellow	Land
CLIMATE/TERRAIN:	Sea bed, coast	Sea bed, coast	Sea bed, coast	Sea bed, coast	Sea bed, coast	Any temperate to tropical land
FREQUENCY:	Uncommon	Rare	Rare	Very rare	Very rare	Rare
ORGANIZATION:	Bed	Group	Group	Pair	Group	Pair
ACTIVITY CYCLE:	Any	Any	Any	Any	Any	Day
DIET:	Scavenger	Scavenger	Scavenger	Scavenger	Scavenger	Scavenger
INTELLIGENCE:	Semi- (2-4)	Semi- (2-4)	Semi- (2-4)	Semi- (2-4)	Semi- (2-4)	Animal (1)
TREASURE:	10 x 1d10 gp	40 x 1d10 gp	90 x 1d10 gp	250 x 1d10 gp	160 x 1d10 gp	See below
ALIGNMENT:	Neutral	Neutral	Neutral	Neutral	Neutral	Neutral
NO. APPEARING:	1-6	1-4	1-4	1-2	1-3	1-2
ARMOR CLASS:	4	3	2	0	1	3
MOVEMENT:	6, Sw 6	6, Sw 6	6, Sw 6	6, Sw 6	6, Sw 6	12
HIT DICE:	1+1	2+1	3+1	5+3	4+2	3+3
THAC0:	19	19	17	15	17	17
NO. OF ATTACKS:	2	2	3	5	4	6
DAMAGE/ATTACK:	1-4	2-7	2-5	2-5	1-6	1-2
SPECIAL ATTACKS:	See below	See below	See below	See below	See below	See below
SPECIAL DEFENSES:	Nil	Nil	Nil	Nil	Nil	Nil
MAGIC RESISTANCE:	Nil	Nil	Nil	Nil	Nil	Nil
SIZE:	S (3')	S (3')	S (3')	S (3')	S (3')	S (3')
MORALE:	Steady (11)	Steady (11)	Steady (11)	Steady (11)	Steady (11)	Steady (11)
XP VALUE:	65	120	420	975	650	420

Urchins are a family of marine creatures that, like oysters, are hunted for the value of the stones found in their bodies.

They resemble 3-foot-diameter balls covered with thousands of 3-inch-long, needle-sharp spines. There are several species of urchins, which can be distinguished from each other by their distinctive colors.

Combat: Urchins can fire their spines with the distance and accuracy of light crossbows. An urchin can fire multiple spines per round as listed above under "No. of Attacks." Urchins have no eyes with which to see their opponents; instead they possess an innate clairvoyance ability. This ability gives all spines fired by urchins a +2 bonus to the attack roll. Damage from an urchin spine varies from species to species and many spines contain paralytic or even lethal poisons. Since urchins are covered with thousands of spines, they have a virtually unlimited supply of ammunition.

Habitat/Society: Urchins are primarily scavengers, scouring the ocean floors for remains of shellfish. Occasionally they hunt fish, but they never attack man-sized beings unless threatened or approached within 10 feet.

Urchins live in the shallows and upon shoals near the coast. They occasionally (10% chance) remain on land during low tide to scavenge for food. While on land, urchins move via rolling. They are capable of surprisingly high speeds when moving this way.

Ecology: Inside each urchin is a crystalline organ-gem that seems to have some connection to their innate clairvoyance ability. While this gem has little value as a stone, it is highly prized by alchemists. The exact value of the organ-gem depends on quality and the type of urchin it was taken from. To determine a stone's value, consult the "Treasure" entry above.

Land Urchin

These distant cousins of sea urchins live strictly on land. Land urchins move on five spindly legs. They are shy creatures and only attack if approached within ten feet. Their paralytic poison lasts for six turns. Land urchins have no organ-gem but often (80% chance) form pearls inside their bodies. Old urchins contain 2d6 such pearls, each valued at 1d6 x 100 gold pieces.

Vampire

CLIMATE/TERRAIN:	Any land
FREQUENCY:	Rare
ORGANIZATION:	Solitary
ACTIVITY CYCLE:	Night
DIET:	Special
INTELLIGENCE:	Exceptional (15-16)
TREASURE:	F
ALIGNMENT:	Chaotic evil

NO. APPEARING:	1-4
ARMOR CLASS:	1
MOVEMENT:	12, Fl 18 (C)
HIT DICE:	8+3
THAC0:	11
NO. OF ATTACKS:	1
DAMAGE/ATTACK:	5-10
SPECIAL ATTACKS:	Energy drain
SPECIAL DEFENSES:	+1 or better magical weapon to hit
MAGIC RESISTANCE:	See below
SIZE:	M (5$\frac{1}{2}$'-6$\frac{1}{2}$')
MORALE:	Champion (16)
XP VALUE:	
Western	8,000
Eastern	9,000

Of all the chaotic evil undead creatures that stalk the world, none is more dreadful than the vampire. Moving silently through the night, vampires prey upon the living without mercy or compassion. Unless deep underground, they must return to the coffins in which they pass the daylight hours, and even in the former case they must occasionally return to such to rest, for their power is renewed by contact with soil from their graves.

One aspect that makes the vampire far more fearful than many of its undead kindred is its appearance. Unlike other undead creatures, the vampire can easily pass among normal men without drawing attention to itself for, although its facial features are sharp and feral, they do not seem inhuman. In many cases, a vampire's true nature is revealed only when it attacks.

There are ways in which a vampire may be detected by the careful observer, however. Vampires cast no reflection in a glass, cast no shadows, and move in complete silence.

Combat: When engaging in combat, vampires are savage and fearsome opponents. They are physically very powerful, with a Strength score of 18/76, receiving a bonus of +2 to hit and +4 to damage. The crushing blows of a vampire's attack are so fierce that they inflict 5-10 points of damage.

The gaze of a vampire is one of its most powerful and dangerous weapons. Any person who allows the vampire to look into his eyes will be affected as if by a *charm person* spell. Due to the power of this enchantment, a -2 is applied to the victim's saving throw vs. spell. In this manner, vampires are often able to pass posted sentries and surprise their chosen victims.

Like all undead creatures, vampires exist in both the Positive Material and Negative Material planes at the same time. Their powerful negative essence allows them to drain two life energy levels from anyone they strike. If the vampire is making use of some form of weapon in the attack, it cannot employ this power.

Weapons of less than +1 enchantment pass through vampires without harming them in any way. Even if attacked with and harmed by magical weapons, vampires regenerate 3 hit points per round. If reduced to zero hit points, a vampire is not destroyed, but is forced to assume *gaseous form*. Once in this state, it will attempt to flee and return to its coffin where, after eight hours of rest, it regains its corporeal form. If the defeated vampire is unable to reach its coffin within 12 turns, however, its essence breaks up and the creature is truly destroyed.

Sleep, charm, and *hold* spells do not affect vampires. Similarly, they are unharmed by poisons and immune to paralysis. Spells that are based on cold or electricity cause only half damage.

At will, vampires are able to disperse their bodies into clouds of elemental vapor and assume *gaseous form*. In this state, they are all but immune to attack and can escape from almost any confinement. In addition, vampires can *shape change* so as to take on the form of a large bat (hence the flying movement rate given above).

Vampires can summon lesser creatures for aid. In a subterranean environment, they will typically call forth a swarm of 10-100 rats or bats. In the case of the latter, these do not physically attack but serve to confuse and obscure the vision of the vampire's foes. In the wilderness, a vampire will normally call upon 3-18 wolves for assistance. In all cases, the summoned animals arrive in 2-12 rounds.

At will, a vampire can use a *spider climb* ability and scale sheer surfaces. Often, they will employ this power to gain access to rooms on upper floors without alerting those on watch downstairs. This power also permits the vampire to seek refuge in places which are all but beyond the reach of mortal men.

Despite the great powers which vampires obviously possess, they are not without weaknesses of their own. The odor of strong garlic repels them and they will not approach it. Further, they will recoil from the face of a mirror or lawful good holy symbol if either of these is presented to them with courage and conviction. It is important to understand, however, that this will not actually harm the vampire in any way nor drive it off. Garlic will prevent the creature from attacking or entering the area, while mirrors and holy symbols force the vampire to find some means of removing the offending object before it can be bypassed. In most cases, the vampire will seek to overcome these hazards with the aid of its minions. For example, a *charmed* person might be called upon to attack someone who is holding the vampire at bay with a holy symbol. Another important point to keep in mind is that a lawful good holy symbol will affect the vampire regardless of the vam-

Vampire

pire's original religious background. Vampires which are splashed with a vial of holy water or struck with lawful good holy symbols are burned by them, suffering 2-7 points of damage.

Just as vampires can be kept at bay, so too can they be slain by those who have the knowledge to do so. Any vampire which is exposed to direct sunlight is instantly rendered powerless and, after one round, utterly annihilated. If the vampire can be immersed in running water, it loses one-third of its hit points each round, until destroyed on the third round. Last, a vampire can be killed by having a wooden stake driven through its heart. In this case, however, the creature can be restored simply by removing the stake if further measures are not taken to ensure the fate of the vampire. In order for it to be completely destroyed, the vampire's head must be cut off and its mouth stuffed with holy wafers (or their equivalent).

In addition to its aversion to items like garlic and holy symbols, the vampire acts under many other limitations. One of the most powerful of these is the creature's inability to enter a home without being first invited to do so by a resident of the dwelling. This does not apply to public buildings and places of business which, by their very nature, extend an "invitation" to all. Once a vampire has been invited to enter a residence, it may come and go freely afterward. A common manner for obtaining permission to enter a home is the use of the vampire's gaze to *charm* a servant or other inhabitant.

Any human or humanoid creature slain by the life energy drain of a vampire is doomed to become a vampire himself. Thus, those who would hunt these lords of the undead must be very careful lest they find themselves condemned to a fate far worse than death. The transformation takes place one day after the burial of the creature. Those who are not actually buried, however, do not become undead and it is thus traditional that the bodies of a vampire's victims be burned or similarly destroyed. Once they become undead, the new vampire is under the complete control of its killer. If that vampire is destroyed, the controlled undead are freed from its power and become self-willed creatures.

In most cases, vampires do not lose the abilities and knowledge which they had in life when they become undead. Thus, it is possible for a vampire to have the powers of, for example, a wizard, thief, or even priest. In all cases, of course, the new vampire becomes chaotic evil.

Habitat/Society: Vampires live in areas of death and desolation where they will not be reminded of the lives they have left behind. Ruined castles or chapels and large cemeteries are popular lairs for them, as are sites of great tragedies or battles. Vampires often feel a strong attachment to specific areas with some morbid significance, like the grave of a suicide or the site of a murder.

When deciding on a course of action or planning a campaign, vampires move very slowly and meticulously. It is not uncommon for a vampire to undertake some scheme which may take decades or even centuries to reach its conclusion. Because of the curse of immortality that has fallen upon them, they feel that time is always on their side and will often defeat foes who might otherwise overcome them; the vampire can simply go into hiding for a few decades until the passing of the years brings down its enemies.

Vampires are normally solitary creatures. When they are found in the company of others of their kind, the group will certainly consist of a single vampire lord and a small group of vampires which it has created to do its bidding. In this way, the vampire can exert its power over a greater range without running

the risk of exposing itself to attack by would-be heroes.

In general, vampires feel only contempt for the world and its inhabitants. Denied the pleasures of a true life, they have become dark and twisted creatures bent on revenge and terror. When a vampire creates another of its kind, it considers the new creature a mere tool. The minion will be sent on missions which the vampire feels may be too dangerous or unimportant for its personal attention. If the need arises, these pawns will gladly be sacrificed to protect or further the ends of their master.

Ecology: The vampire has no place in the world of living creatures. It is a thing of darkness that exists only to bring about evil and chaos. Almost without exception, the vampire is feared and hated by those who dwell in the regions in which it chooses to make its home. The vampire's unnatural presence is all-pervasive and will cause dogs and similar animals to raise a cry of alarm at the presence of the creature.

Vampires sustain themselves by draining the life force from living creatures. Unless they have a specific need to create additional minions, however, they are careful to avoid killing those they attack. In cases where the death of a victim is desired, the vampire will take care to see that the body is destroyed and thus will not rise as an undead.

Eastern Vampires:
This breed of vampire is, if anything, even more frightful than its western cousin. Although they share many of the western vampire's strengths and weaknesses, they have the ability to fade from sight at will. Once they have become *invisible*, they receive all of the normal bonuses which such a state normally bestows, including being attacked at -4. These monsters are unable to *charm* their victims, however, and cannot assume *gaseous form* at will as western vampires can.

CLIMATE/TERRAIN:	Temperate plains
FREQUENCY:	Very Rare
ORGANIZATION:	Prides
ACTIVITY CYCLE:	Day
DIET:	Carnivore
INTELLIGENCE:	Average (8-10)
TREASURE:	B
ALIGNMENT:	Neutral

NO. APPEARING:	2-16
ARMOR CLASS:	Males 6(5), females 7
MOVEMENT:	12
HIT DICE:	5+8
THAC0:	15
NO. OF ATTACKS:	2 or 3
DAMAGE/ATTACK:	1-4/1-4 and weapon
SPECIAL ATTACKS:	Nil
SPECIAL DEFENSES:	−2 initiative modifier
MAGIC RESISTANCE:	Nil
SIZE:	L (7′)
MORALE:	Steady (11-12)
XP VALUE:	Normal: 270
	Chief/Chieftain: 420
	Witch Doctor/King: 975

Wemics are leonine counterparts to centaurs.

A wemic's body consists of a leonine body with a humanoid torso extending from what would be a lion's neck. The typical wemic measures ten feet from head to rump. When standing erect in centaurian posture, the wemic stands 6 to 7 feet tall.

Most of the body is covered in dusky golden fur. The tail is tipped by a brush of long, black hair. Adult males also have a mane of long black hair; the mane covers the top and back of the head and extends to the neck and shoulders. Male cubs develop this mane in their third year. The underbelly is covered in short, white fur. The nose may be black or russet. The eyes are gold with vertically slit pupils. The digits on all limbs end in claws. The claws on the forelegs are retractable.

Wemics speak their own leonine language and a highly accented dialect of the common tongue.

Combat: Wemics use forepaws and weapons to attack. A claw delivers a vicious swipe that inflicts 1d4 points of damage. Normally the wemic uses his forelegs to claw and employs his hands to wield a weapon.

Wemic males carry javelins and either a stone club or short sword. They often carry a tough leather shield (AC 5) for protection. Females are AC 7 and do not use weapons; however, they gain a +2 bonus to attack rolls if their cubs are attacked. Cubs under 2 years do not attack.

Wemics possess keen senses. They are masters of ambushes and hunting strategy. If they cannot surprise an intended victim, 1-3 wemics move to outflank prey.

Wemics possess powerful leg muscles. They can leap 10 feet upward or 30 feet forward.

Habitat/Society: Wemic society is a blend of leonine and aboriginal human cultures. They live in groups called prides. A typical pride consists of 4d4 adult males, 2d12 adult females, and 1d12 cubs.

Up to 3d10 prides often band together into a tribe that is led by a chief. The chief has an Armor Class of 5, 6+4 Hit Dice, and its claws inflict 1d6 points of damage. It gains a +1 bonus to its attack rolls with any weapon.

Sometimes 2d4 tribes join together into a clan or nation. Such a grand gathering is led by a king and 2d4 chieftains. The king has an Armor Class of 3, 9 Hit Dice, and claws that inflict 1d8 points of damage. It has a +2 bonus to its attack rolls with any weapon.

Some wemics are able to use magic. There is a 70% chance that any tribe includes a witch doctor. Such wemics may attain a maximum level of 7th-level priest and 4th-level wizard.

Mating occurs at any time of year. The female bears a litter of one to three cubs in ten months. The cubs are born with a camouflage pattern of black spots; these fade within two months. Wemic cubs are playful and curious; they possess few instincts and thus must learn everything. Cubs are born with 1 HD and gain 2 HD each year. They reach maturity at age 3.

Wemics have human-level intelligence. They possess a Stone age culture, using fire and possessing modest manufacturing skills with which they can create stone weaponry, pottery, and ornaments. They can be taught more complex skills. They are excellent trackers and guides. They may hire out their services in exchange for treasure and tools, such as weapons and magical items. They may also charge travelers a toll for safe passage through their nation's territory.

Ecology: Wemic cubs are worth 500 gp. They can be trained as servants or allies.

Whale

	Common	Giant	Leviathan	Killer	Narwhal
CLIMATE/TERRAIN:	Oceans	Oceans	Oceans	Oceans	Oceans
FREQUENCY:	Common	Very rare	Very rare	Common	Rare
ORGANIZATION:	Pod	Pair	Solitary	Pod	Pod
ACTIVITY CYCLE:	Any	Any	Any	Any	Any
DIET:	Plankton	Omnivore	Omnivore	Carnivore	Fish
INTELLIGENCE:	Low (5-7)	Average (8-10)	Exceptional (15-16)	Average (8-12)	Animal (1)
TREASURE:	Nil	See below	See below	Nil	Nil
ALIGNMENT:	Neutral	Neutral	Neutral	Neutral	Neutral
NO. APPEARING:	1-8	1-2	1	5-40	1-6
ARMOR CLASS:	4	3	1	4	6
MOVEMENT:	Sw 18	Sw 18	Sw 18	Sw 30	Sw 21
HIT DICE:	12 to 36	18 to 54	36 to 72	9 to 12	4+4 to 6+6
THAC0:	12 HD: 9	5	5	9-10 HD: 11	4+4 - 5+5 HD: 15
	13-14 HD: 7			11-12 HD: 9	6+6 HD: 13
	15+ HD: 5				
NO. OF ATTACKS:	1	1	1	1	1
DAMAGE/ATTACK:	See below	See below	See below	5-20	2-24
SPECIAL ATTACKS:	Tail	See below	See below	See below	Nil
SPECIAL DEFENSES:	Nil	Nil	Nil	Nil	Nil
MAGIC RESISTANCE:	Nil	Nil	Nil	Nil	Nil
SIZE:	G	G	G	H-G	H-G
MORALE:	Champion (15)	Champion (15)	Champion (15)	Elite (14)	Steady (12)
XP VALUE:	2,000 + 1,000	8,000 + 1,000	26,000 + 1,000	9 975	4 + 4 175
	per HD over 12	per HD over 18	per HD over 36	10 1,400	5 + 5 270
				11,12 2,000	6 + 6 420

Whales are the largest sea mammals. They are highly intelligent creatures that occupy a number of ecological niches. The common whales include plankton eaters like blue or hump-backed whales and carnivores like sperm whales.

Common whales range in size from a 10-foot-long calf to 110-foot-long blue whales. The skin is normally blue-gray. Whales share a common language that is difficult for land creatures to learn since it uses tones below human hearing.

Combat: All common whales can attack with their tails. These can deliver a crushing blow that inflicts damage equal to half the whale's Hit Dice.

Plankton-feeding whales can attack with either of their flukes (fins). Whales of 12-17 HD cause 1d8 points of damage, those of 18-24 HD inflict 3d8 points, and those of 24-36 HD cause 5d8 points.

Carnivorous whales can bite. Whales of 12-17 HD inflict 5d4 points of damage, those of 18-24 HD cause 1d4x10 points, and those of 24-36 HD inflict 3d4x5 points.

Whales are vulnerable to surface ships only when the whales are on the surface.

Habitat/Society: Whales live in tribal gatherings called pods. They maintain strong personal and family ties. Their culture is based on complex songs that can be heard for miles underwater. Whales are curious about humanoids but if attacked they can become deadly foes. Whales rarely initiate combat. Whales are curious about other intelligent beings. They welcome communication with other beings. They do not lie, but they may not reveal everything they know.

Most whales feed on a variety of plankton, shrimp, and small fish that they suck up as they swim along. Sperm whales feed on larger fish, octopi, and especially giant squids.

Whale cows normally give birth to a single calf. Twins occur in 5% of births. The calf remains with the cow for the next five to ten years, depending on the species. After five years, the cow may give birth again. The calves are protected and taught by all members of the pod.

Ecology: Although they are neutral in alignment toward humanoids, their alignment toward sea life is generally lawful good. With their great size, power, and diversity, they are the masters of the sea. They preserve order through their conflicts with evilly inclined sea monsters.

Unfortunately, their relations with seafarers are less certain. Because of the value placed on parts of the whale's body, the creatures are hunted to excess by greedy whalers. Despite the hostil-

Whale

ity of the humanoids, whales remain curious and basically friendly toward non-whaling seafarers.

The carcass of a common whale is worth 100 gp per Hit Die, both for its meat and blubber. Whales possess a stinking, yellow mass called ambergris that is valuable for making perfumes; they vomit this up when ill. The ambergris is worth 1d20 x 1,000 gp.

Giant Whale

Giant whales are immense versions of sperm whales, 100' to 400' long. In the cetacean culture, they serve functions similar to knights or barons by protecting common whales against evil sea monsters and whalers. Giant whales are attended by 2d4 common whales.

Giant whales attack by biting or crushing. Whales of 18-25 HD inflict 1d4x10 points of damage, those of 26-35 HD cause 2d4x10 points, and those of 36-54 HD inflict 3d4x10 points. The tail can deliver a crushing blow that inflicts damage equal to half the whale's Hit Dice. Giant whales can ram the sides of surface ships, delivering a crushing blow that, if successful, sinks the ship. They can also leap halfway out of the water and fall onto a target vessel (50% chance of success). If successful, the ship is immediately driven under the surface. If a giant whale is facing an opponent under 20 feet long, it can swallow the target intact on an attack roll that is 4 or more greater than it needs to hit.

Their stomachs contain large air chambers in which a victim might survive until he escapes or is digested. The stomach acid is diluted by seawater; characters or objects trapped in the stomach gain a +1 bonus to saving throws vs. this acid. A swallowed character suffers 2 points of damage per round (1 if the saving throw is successful each round) from the acid. The stomach might contain undigested possessions of previous meals. Each type of treasure has a 1% chance per Hit Die (of the whale) of being present in the giant whale's gullet. There may be 1,000-3,000 coins of each type, 1d20 gems, or 1d4 magical items.

The carcass of a giant whale is worth 100 gp per Hit Die. The ambergris is worth 2d20 x 1,000 gp.

Leviathan

The leviathan is an almost unimaginably immense whale, 500 to 1,000 feet long. It is the lord of all whales and the intermediary between cetaceans and the gods. Under normal conditions, only one leviathan dwells in each ocean. The leviathan is not always active. It may hibernate for years on the ocean floor. During these long sleeps, the leviathan is attended and protected by its entourage of other whales. The leviathan awakens if summoned by the needs of other whales or in answer to a divine request. Leviathans are awesome foes with a variety of attacks. Their bite damage is determined by their Hit Dice. Leviathans of 24-35 HD inflict 3d4x5 points of damage, those of 36-47 HD cause 3d4x10 points, and those of 48-72 HD inflict 3d4x15 points. The tail can deliver a crushing blow that causes damage equal to half the whale's Hit Dice. On an attack roll that is 4 or more greater than it needs to hit, a leviathan is capable of swallowing a target up to 80 feet long. When attacking a mass of surface vessels, the leviathan creates a powerful wave by swimming deep, rushing to the surface, and leaping halfway out of the water. The resulting wave causes every ship within 500 feet to roll a saving throw vs. crushing blow and every ship within 500 to 2,000 feet to roll a saving throw vs. normal blow. Ships that fail a saving throw immediately sink.

Once each century, leviathans gather in arctic waters to confer and to mate. This gathering lasts six months. Each leviathan is attended by 2d10 giant whales and 10d10 whales of other species.

The stomach of a leviathan contains air pockets that are capable of sustaining a victim until he escapes or is digested. The stomach may also contain undigested possessions of previous meals or even sea vessels. Each type of treasure has a 1% chance

per Hit Die (of the whale) of being present in the giant whale's gullet. There may be 2,000-6,000 coins of each type, 5d20 gems, or 1d8 magical items.

The carcass of a leviathan is worth 100 gp per Hit Die. The ambergris is worth 4d20 x 1,000 gp. However, the killing of a leviathan will result in every whale within that ocean converging on the killer to avenge their lord's death.

Killer Whale (Orca)

The killer whale is one of the largest predatory sea mammals. It is a deadly killer able to hold its own against all but the most powerful sea monsters. A killer whale is likely to attack humanoids; it is capable of swallowing a man whole, should the need arise.

Killer whales measure 15 to 30 feet long. Their black bodies are marked by a brilliant white belly and markings that vary from individual to individual.

Killer whales are not inherently hostile and do not attack unless hungry or provoked. There is a 20% chance that encountered killer whales are hungry. If they are communicated with rather than attacked, killer whales may prefer to talk rather than feed.

The killer whale's diet consists of both fish and warm-blooded animals. It is a crafty hunter that can recognize the shadows and sounds made by animals atop ice floes. It will break through the ice to visually confirm the presence of prey. Smaller ice floes are rammed and shattered to force the prey into the water. When the killer whale smashes into the ice, every being on the ice must roll a saving throw vs. paralyzation. Failure means the being has slipped into the water and can be attacked the following round.

When a killer whale makes a successful hit, its prey is held in its jaws where it can automatically bite each round. Victims risk drowning in two to four rounds and the loss of 1 point of Strength and Dexterity per round, due to the numbing effect of the icy water. When either Strength or Dexterity reaches 0, the victim dies.

The killer whale's main weapon is its terrible bite. Killer whales of 9-10 HD inflict 4d6 points of damage, while those of 11-12 HD cause 6d4 points.

When hunting larger creatures, the pod acts together to bring down prey of up to 100 feet in length.

Most pods consist only of adults, but 25% of encountered pods also have 1d8 calves (2-5 HD, swim 15, bite for 2d4). Adults defend their calves to the death. They also assist each other.

Although killer whales prey on other whales, they also act as their protectors by battling other sea monsters that might decimate the entire cetacean family. Killer whales may enter into alliances with aquatic elves.

The carcass of a killer whale is worth 100 gp per Hit Die. The ambergris is worth 1d10 x 500 gp.

Narwhal

The narwhal is common to cold, subarctic waters. It is called the "unicorn of the sea" because of the 6- to 12-foot-long spiral horn that the narwhal uses to dig into the sea floor for shellfish. If a narwhal is provoked, the horn can also be used like a lance to attack. When a narwhal attacks with its horn, its Hit Dice determine the damage caused. A narwhal of 4+4 HD inflicts 2d12 points of damage, one of 5+5 HD causes 6d4 points, and one of 6+6 HD inflicts 7d4 points. Only a male can develop this horn. A female attacks by ramming headfirst into its target, inflicting 2d4 points of damage.

Narwhals are basically peaceful creatures. They may serve as companions or guards for dolphins. They may also be trained and used by aquatic elves.

The carcass of a narwhal is worth 100 gp per Hit Die. The ivory is worth 1d4x10 gp. The ambergris is worth 1d10 x 200 gp.

Wight

CLIMATE/TERRAIN:	Any land
FREQUENCY:	Uncommon
ORGANIZATION:	Solitary
ACTIVITY CYCLE:	Night
DIET:	See below
INTELLIGENCE:	Average (8-10)
TREASURE:	B
ALIGNMENT:	Lawful evil

NO. APPEARING:	2-16 (2d8)
ARMOR CLASS:	5
MOVEMENT:	12
HIT DICE:	4+3
THAC0:	15
NO. OF ATTACKS:	1
DAMAGE/ATTACK:	1-4
SPECIAL ATTACKS:	Energy drain
SPECIAL DEFENSES:	Hit only by silver or +1 or better magical weapon
MAGIC RESISTANCE:	See below
SIZE:	M (4'-7')
MORALE:	Elite (14)
XP VALUE:	1,400

In ages long past, the word "wight" meant simply "man." As the centuries have passed, though, it has come to be associated only with those undead that typically inhabit barrow mounds and catacombs.

From a distance, wights can easily be mistaken for any number of humanoid races. Upon closer examination, however, their true nature becomes apparent. As undead creatures, wights are nightmarish reflections of their former selves, with cruel, burning eyes set in mummified flesh over a twisted skeleton with hands that end in sharp claws.

Combat: Wights are fierce and deadly foes in combat. When attacked, they are unharmed by any weapons that are not forged from silver or enchanted in some manner.

The wight attacks with its jagged claws and powerful blows, inflicting 1-4 points of damage with each successful strike. In addition to this physical harm, the wight is able to feed on the life essence of its foes. Each blow that the wight lands drains one level from the victim, reducing Hit Dice, class bonuses, spell abilities, and so forth. Thus, a 9th-level wizard struck by a wight loses 1-4 hit points and becomes an 8th-level wizard; he has the spells and hit points of an 8th-level wizard and he fights as an 8th-level wizard.

Persons who are slain by the energy draining powers of a wight are doomed to rise again as wights under the direct control of their slayer. In their new form, they have the powers and abilities of a normal wight but half their experience levels, class abilities, and Hit Dice. If the wight who "created" them is slain, they will instantly be freed of its control and gain a portion of its power, acquiring the normal 4+3 Hit Dice of their kind. Once a character becomes a wight, recovery is nearly impossible, requiring a special quest.

Wights are unaffected by *sleep, charm, hold* or cold-based spells. In addition, they are not harmed by poisons or paralyzation attacks.

Wights can be engaged and defeated by individuals who are well prepared for battle with them. Physical contact with holy water is deadly to wights and each vial splashed on one burns it

for 2-8 points of damage. In addition, a *raise dead* spell becomes a powerful weapon if used against the wight. Such magic is instantly fatal to the creature, utterly annihilating it.

Wights cannot tolerate bright light, including sunlight, and avoid it at all costs. It is important to note, however, that wights are not harmed by exposure to sunlight as vampires are.

Habitat/Society: Like the other undead that infest the world, wights live in barrow mounds, catacombs, and other sepulchral places. They despise light and places which are vibrant with living things. As a rule, the wight is hateful and evil, seeking to satisfy its hatred of life by killing all those it encounters.

Although wights are often found in small groups, they are actually solitary creatures. Without exception, encounters with multiple wights will be a single leader and a number of lesser creatures which it has created to serve it. In these cases, the leader of the group will be more than willing to sacrifice some or all of its minions to assure its own survival or victory.

Ecology: Like all undead, wights exist on both the Prime Material and Negative Material planes simultaneously. It is this powerful link to the negative world that gives them their fearsome level-draining ability. Further, it is this draining which provides them with sustenance.

As they are not living creatures and have no rightful place in our world, many animals can sense the wight's presence. Dogs will growl or howl with alarm, horses will refuse to enter an area which wights inhabit, and birds and insects will grow silent when the creature passes near them. In addition, their presence will gradually cause the plant life around their lairs to wither and die, marking the region as unclean.

CLIMATE/TERRAIN:	Any swamp
FREQUENCY:	Uncommon
ORGANIZATION:	Solitary
ACTIVITY CYCLE:	Night
DIET:	See below
INTELLIGENCE:	Exceptional (15-16)
TREASURE:	Z
ALIGNMENT:	Chaotic evil

NO. APPEARING:	1 or 1-3
ARMOR CLASS:	-8
MOVEMENT:	Fl 18 (A)
HIT DICE:	9
THAC0:	11
NO. OF ATTACKS:	1
DAMAGE/ATTACK:	2-16
SPECIAL ATTACKS:	See below
SPECIAL DEFENSES:	See below
MAGIC RESISTANCE:	See below
SIZE:	S (2'-4')
MORALE:	Fanatic (17)
XP VALUE:	3,000

The will o'wisp is a malevolent entity that makes its home in swamps, bogs, and moors. It subsists by luring unsuspecting creatures to their deaths amid the natural hazards of such places and feeding on the energies which their death struggles release.

When encountered in the wild, will o'wisps normally appear as faintly glowing balls of light. They can alter their own color, shape, and size to some extent and can be easily mistaken for lanterns, *light* spells, and similar sources of artificial illumination.

If they do not attack, will o'wisps are able to utterly blank out their glows, rendering them invisible to all those who cannot spot invisible objects, for 2-8 melee rounds.

The will o'wisp language is a most unusual one, being purely optical in nature. All communication between will o'wisps is by means of changes in color or brightness, many of which are far too subtle for the average observer to notice. Because this form of exchange is almost impossible to mimic, it is very difficult for travelers to communicate with these creatures. Exceptional examples of this race have mastered a very simple sound-based language. They produce sounds by vibrating very rapidly and thus have a shallow and ghostly-sounding voice when they "speak."

Combat: As a rule, will o'wisps seek to avoid physical combat with other creatures, preferring to lead them to their deaths in the swamps around them instead. When pressed, however, they are dangerous adversaries who must be attacked with the greatest care. In combat, they glow blue, violet, or pale green.

Will o'wisps are very versatile flyers. They can hover in place without effort, often looking like lanterns or similar beacons to lure others toward them. When they decide to move, they can do so with rapid bursts of speed or slow drifting movements.

A will o'wisp's main weapon in combat is its ability to manifest a powerful electric charge. In melee, it swoops at its foe and attempts to brush against the victim, discharging the stored energy. A successful strike by one of these creatures will cause 2-16 points of damage.

Those attacking a will o'wisp with any form of physical weapon are able to inflict damage normally. Persons making use of magical attacks, however, will find their powers almost ineffective against them. As a rule, the only spells which have any effect on the will o'wisp are *protection from evil, magic missile,* and *maze*. A will o'wisp which is reduced to 5 or fewer hit points will attempt to escape. If it is unable to flee, the creature will surrender to its attackers and attempt to buy its safety by offering up any treasure which it may have. It is important to note, however, that the chaotic alignment of the will o'wisp can make any agreement with the creature uncertain.

Habitat/Society: For the most part, will o'wisps will be found on their own. On rare occasions (10% of the time) groups of up to three may be found near a particularly fertile hunting ground. In the latter case, they will work together to trick victims into the traps which they have arranged.

Ecology: Although difficult to say with certainty, evidence indicates that the will o'wisp feeds on the fury of electrical activity given off by the brains of panic stricken individuals as they realize that death is inescapable. In order to prolong the suffering of their victims and increase the amount of "food" which they give off, will o'wisps will typically lure their victims into areas like quicksand pits which promise a slow and frightening death.

It seems certain that the unusual environment found in bogs and swamps is important to the creature's existence in some way, but the exact nature of this link is uncertain. It seems probable that the ominous and haunting nature of these places increases the fear and dread which their victims feel, and thus the energy which they give off prior to death.

Wolf

	Wolf	Worg	Dire	Winter
CLIMATE/TERRAIN:	Non-tropical	Any forest	Any forest	Arctic
FREQUENCY:	Uncommon	Rare	Rare	Very rare
ORGANIZATION:	Family	Pack	Pack	Pack
ACTIVITY CYCLE:	Any	Any	Any	Any
DIET:	Carnivore	Carnivore	Carnivore	Carnivore
INTELLIGENCE:	Low (5-7)	Low (5-7)	Semi-(2-4)	Average (8-10)
TREASURE:	Nil	Nil	Nil	I
ALIGNMENT:	Neutral	Neutral Evil	Neutral	Neutral evil
NO. APPEARING:	2-12 (1/1%)	3-12	3-12	2-8
ARMOR CLASS:	7	6	6	5
MOVEMENT:	18	18	18	18
HIT DICE:	3	3+3	4+4	6
THAC0:	18	17	15	15
NO. OF ATTACKS:	1	1	1	1
DAMAGE/ATTACK:	2-5	2-8	2-8	2-8
SPECIAL ATTACKS:	Nil	Nil	Nil	Frost
SPECIAL DEFENSES:	+1 versus *charm*	Nil	Nil	Nil
MAGIC RESISTANCE:	Nil	Nil	Nil	Nil
SIZE:	S (3'-4')	M (4'-7')	L(7'-12')	L (7'-12')
MORALE:	Average (10)	Steady (11)	Average (10)	Elite (13)
XP VALUE:	120	120	175	975

The wolf is a very active, cunning carnivore, capable of surviving in nearly every climate. Shrouded in mystery and suspicion, they are viewed as vicious killers that slaughter men and animals alike for the lack of better things to do. The truth is that never in recorded history has a non-rabid or non-*charmed* wolf attacked any creature having an equal or higher intellect than itself. (The chance of encountering a rabid wolf that would attack anything is 1%, if a lone wolf is encountered.)

Northern wolves exhibit colors from pure white, to grey, to black. Southern wolves are reddish and brown in color. Although fur coloration vary with climate, all wolves have various features in common. They are characterized by powerful jaws; wide strong teeth; bushy tails; tall, strong ears; and round pupils. Their eyes, a gold or amber color, seem to have an almost *empathic* ability.

Combat: Wolves hunt in packs during winter and late fall when only large herbivores are available. Wolves prefer small prey over the larger variety, because of the amount of energy required to run them down. Even then, they catch only the weak and sickly animals. Wolves usually hunt only one large quarry per week, per pack, going without food for days at a time. During summer months, a single wolf can consume over 30 mice in a single day.

If a wolf or wolf pack is attacked by humans, they run away, looking back momentarily to make sure they are not being followed. If backed into an inescapable location, they will attack by tearing at clothing or legs and arms until they have an opening to escape.

Habitat/Society: Wolves, like humans and demi-humans, are social animals. They live, hunt and play in families. There is a very strict social structure in these family groups that is continually followed. Each pack is led by an *alpha male*; his mate is the *alpha female*. Only the alpha male and alpha female breed, but the second ranking female often helps in whelping and nursing duties.

Wolves prefer areas not inhabited by other large predators. Their domain has many terrain features in which they can play. Large rocks, fallen trees, and brooks play an important part in their recreational activities. Wolves will leave an area once humans move in.

Ecology: Wolves are valuable hunters in the wild. Fear of the wolf has resulted in their extinction in many areas. This genocide results in a marked increase in rodents and deer population that has nearly demolished the surrounding ecosystems.

Dire Wolves
The dire wolf is an ancestor of the modern species. Though larger in size, they are otherwise similar to their descendants.

Worgs
Worgs are an offshoot of dire wolf stock that have attained a degree of intelligence and a tendency toward evil. Worgs have a primitive language and often serve as mounts of goblins.

Winter Wolves
The most dangerous member of the species, the winter wolf is known for its great size and foul disposition. Living only in chill regions, they can unleash a stream of frost from their lungs once every 10 rounds, causing 6d4 points of damage to everything within 10 feet. A save vs. breath weapon is allowed for half damage. Cold-based attacks to not harm the winter wolf, but fire-based attacks cause an additional point of damage, per die of damage. Winter wolves are more intelligent than their cousins and, in addition to being able to communicate with worgs, have a fairly sophisticated language of their own. The winter wolf is beautiful, with glistening white or silver fur and eyes of pale blue or silver. If in good condition, a pelt is worth 5,000 gold pieces.

Wolfwere

CLIMATE/TERRAIN:	Any forest
FREQUENCY:	Rare
ORGANIZATION:	Solitary
ACTIVITY CYCLE:	Any
DIET:	Carnivore
INTELLIGENCE:	High to exceptional (13-16)
TREASURE:	B, 50% of S, T
ALIGNMENT:	Chaotic evil

NO. APPEARING:	1-3
ARMOR CLASS:	3
MOVEMENT:	15
HIT DICE:	5+1
THAC0:	15
NO. OF ATTACKS:	1 or 2
DAMAGE/ATTACK:	2-12 and weapon
SPECIAL ATTACKS:	Singing brings on lethargy
SPECIAL DEFENSES:	Iron or +1 or better weapon to hit
MAGIC RESISTANCE:	10%
SIZE:	M (4'-7')
MORALE:	Elite (14)
XP VALUE:	1,400

The wolfwere is an evil and hateful creature that delights in the brutal slaying of humans and demihumans alike. In many cases, the wolfwere is able to attack its victims with utter surprise because of its ability to assume the shape of a human of exceptional charisma.

The wolfwere is able to assume a wide variety of shapes at will. Transformation from one form to another takes only a single round. Its true shape, and that in which it prefers to spend the vast majority of its time, is that of a large wolf. When in this state, it is almost indistinguishable from a dire wolf.

When a wolfwere is attempting to lure humans or demihumans into an ambush, it will assume the shape of member of their race. Almost without exception, the new persona will not be of the same sex as the potential victim. Thus, a wolfwere which is stalking a male elf will transform itself into a female elf. In all cases, the newly disguised wolfwere will have exceptional physical beauty.

Combat: The wolfwere is a sly and dangerous adversary. In addition to its great fury and fighting prowess, its high intelligence must not be overlooked or underestimated.

When a wolfwere first spots unsuspecting humans or demihumans in its territory, it will change into its fully humanoid form and assume the guise of a pilgrim, minstrel, or similar wanderer. The wolfwere will normally carry some form of stringed instrument which it seems to absent-mindedly play at while it travels. The true nature of its song, however, is terrible and often fatal. Anyone who hears the wolfwere's song and then fails a saving throw vs. spell will be overcome with *lethargy*. The effects of this enchantment are the same as those of the *slow* spell. Once this effect begins, it cannot be countered and lasts for 5-8 rounds.

When a wolfwere is ready to attack, the creature again changes its shape. Now, in a form which is half-wolf and half-human (or demihuman), it strikes. The wolfwere will almost always change into this form when it engages in combat because it has the ability to bite like a wolf and also wield a weapon of some type.

In any form but its fully humanoid one, the creature can deliver a savage bite with its powerful jaws. It is this mode of attack which the monster prefers to employ above all others.

When in its humanoid or half-humanoid state, it is also able to carry and employ weapons. Although the exact type of weapon used will depend upon the specific tastes of the creature encountered, wolfweres tend toward axes, swords, and similar cutting edges.

If the creature is forced to engage in battle while in its humanoid form, it will be forced to rely wholly on its weapons for defense. In such cases, it normally seeks to escape and transform into its half-humanoid state before returning to battle.

The magical nature of the wolfwere makes it immune to damage inflicted by any weapon which is not made from cold wrought iron or enchanted to +1 or better. All other weapons are simply turned aside by the creature's hide.

It is possible to protect oneself from attacks by wolfweres, however, for they are disgusted by wolfsbane and will avoid it whenever possible.

Habitat/Society: The wolfwere is generally fairly solitary in nature. When encountered in the wild, it is rare that more than three of these creatures will be found. In almost all cases, encounters with more than one wolfwere will be with a mated pair or a group which has decided to work together to increase the success of their hunting.

Ecology: There is a 75% chance that any encountered wolfwere will be running with a pack of wild wolves. In such cases, the animals will be worgs 70% of the time. If they are not worgs, they will be common wolves. In all cases, the influence of the wolfwere will make the creatures far more vicious and evil than they might normally be.

Despite their fondness for wolves and worgs, wolfweres loathe the company of werewolves. The enmity between these two monsters is so great that they will often attack each other on sight.

Worm

	Purple Worm	Giant Bloodworm	Bookworm	Rot Grub
CLIMATE/TERRAIN:	Subterranean	Subterranean pools	Any land (books)	Any land (refuse)
FREQUENCY:	Rare	Rare	Rare	Uncommon
ORGANIZATION:	Solitary	Solitary	Solitary	Swarm
ACTIVITY CYCLE:	Any	Any	Any	Any
DIET:	Carnivore	Blood	Books	Scavenger
INTELLIGENCE:	Non-(0)	Non-(0)	Non-(0)	Non-(0)
TREASURE:	(B, Q×5, X)	Q	Nil	Nil
ALIGNMENT:	Neutral	Neutral	Neutral	Neutral
NO. APPEARING:	1	1-4	1-2 (10-40)	5-20
ARMOR CLASS:	6	4	2	9
MOVEMENT:	9, Br 9	6, Br 1	12, Br 3	1, Br 0
HIT DICE:	15	6	$1/4$	1 hp
THAC0:	5	15	Nil	Nil
NO. OF ATTACKS:	2	1	0	0
DAMAGE/ATTACK:	2-24/2-20	1-8	0	0
SPECIAL ATTACKS:	See below	Blood drain	Nil	See below
SPECIAL DEFENSES:	Nil	Nil	Camouflage	Nil
MAGIC RESISTANCE:	Nil	Nil	Nil	Nil
SIZE:	G (25' long)	H (20' long)	T (1" long)	T ($1/2$"-2" long)
MORALE:	Steady (12)	Fanatic (17-18)	Unreliable (2-4)	Uns teady (5)
XP VALUE:	13,000	420	15	15

Though they vary widely in size, all the worms in this listing have some common characteristics. They are all burrowers with long, cylindrical shapes.

Purple Worm

A constant threat to subterranean explorers, the purple worm burrows through the earth in search of prey. The worm is sensitive to minute vibrations in the earth, and can sense prey at a range of 60 feet. Adult purple worms as large as 8-9 feet in diameter and 140-150 feet long have been reliably reported.

The worm attacks by biting; an attack roll that exceeds the required score to hit by 4 or more indicates the victim has been swallowed whole. This worm can devour creatures up to 8 feet tall and 6 feet wide. A swallowed creature dies in six rounds, is digested in two hours, and cannot be raised from the dead. Anyone trapped inside a purple worm may attempt to cut their way out. The interior is AC 9, but digestive juices weaken the victim, causing a cumulative -1 penalty to the damage the victim can cause. This worm has a stinger on its tail. Anyone hit by the stinger suffers 2d4 points of damage and must make a successful saving throw vs. poison or be slain instantly.

The purple worm is solitary and seeks a companion only to mate. The moment a new worm hatches, it burrows into the ground, never to be seen by its siblings again. As the worm tunnels, it consumes vast amounts of material that are excreted when it returns to its lair. Among the discharged substances are precious metals and gems.

The **mottled worm** is an aquatic variety of the purple worm. It inhabits shallow bottom muck, but it often surfaces to search for prey. Otherwise, it is the same as a purple worm.

The **thunderherder** is desert variety of the purple worm; they travel in herds of 10-100, several feet under the sands. They feed on small creatures in the sand, their bodies ejecting sand. They are 3-5 feet in diameter and 5-10 feet long, and have 7 Hit Dice. Their mouths are unable to cause damage, but their passage beneath an area causes an earthquake-like effect.

Giant Bloodworm

These worms are mottled green in color, with a dark, slimy, brown underbelly. A giant bloodworm attacks when hungry or when stepped on, by trying to fasten its mouth to its victim. If it hits, it causes 1d8 damage, and continues to cause 1d8 damage per round from blood drain, until killed or removed (removal requires a successful open doors roll).

These worms are especially vulnerable to fire, taking double normal damage from such attacks, or full damage when they make a successful saving throw despite a −2 penalty to the roll.

Bookworm

This worm can change its normal gray color to match its surroundings; opponents suffer a −6 to surprise rolls. Bookworms inhabit libraries, eating through the pages and bindings found there. They cannot eat living matter, but they will burrow through dead wood, leather, and other normal book materials at a rate of 3 inches per round. They are very fast and seek to avoid capture and combat when discovered.

Rot Grub

These maggot-like creatures live in refuse. If they touch exposed skin (they have a percentage chance to do this equal to the victim's AC, not counting shield), they burrow into the flesh and secrete a mild poison that deadens the burrowing area; a victim must make a successful Wisdom check to notice the burrowing; one check is allowed each round. Fire kills 2d10 grubs per application to infested flesh, but after 1d6 rounds they are too deep to be burned. A *cure disease* will kill the rot grubs. If the worms are not stopped, they reach the heart in 1d3 turns, killing the victim.

Wraith

CLIMATE/TERRAIN:	Any
FREQUENCY:	Uncommon
ORGANIZATION:	Pack
ACTIVITY CYCLE:	Night
DIET:	Special
INTELLIGENCE:	Very (11-12)
TREASURE:	E
ALIGNMENT:	Lawful evil

NO. APPEARING:	2-12 (2d6)
ARMOR CLASS:	4
MOVEMENT:	12, Fl 24 (B)
HIT DICE:	5+3
THAC0:	15
NO. OF ATTACKS:	1
DAMAGE/ATTACK:	1-6
SPECIAL ATTACKS:	Energy drain
SPECIAL DEFENSES:	Hit only by silver or +1 or better magical weapon
MAGIC RESISTANCE:	Nil
SIZE:	M (6' tall)
MORALE:	Champion (15)
XP VALUE:	2,000

The wraith is an evil undead spirit of a powerful human that seeks to absorb human life energy.

These horrible creatures are usually seen as black, vaguely man-shaped clouds. They have no true substance, but tend to shape themselves with two upper limbs, a torso, and a head with two glowing red eyes. This shape is a convenience born from the habit of once having a human body.

Combat: The touch of a wraith does damage in two ways. First, the chilling effect of the touch inflicts 1-6 points of damage, even to creatures immune to cold. Second, such a hit drains a level of experience from its victim. This includes hit points and all abilities associated with that level, such as spell casting or combat ability. The damage from the chill can be healed normally, but the experience points are gone forever and must be earned again or magically *restored*.

Wraiths are immune to normal weapons. An attack with such a weapon merely passes through its body with no effect. Silver weapons cause only half normal damage. Magical weapons inflict their full damage, causing a black vapor to boil away from the body of the wraith. A wraith slowly regains its full hit points if left alone for at least a week (recovering one point every eight hours). Like most undead, wraiths are immune to *sleep, charm, hold, death* and cold-based spells. They are immune to poison and paralyzation. A vial of holy water causes 2-8 points of damage (as acid) upon striking the body of a wraith. A *raise dead* spell will utterly destroy one if a saving throw vs. spell is failed.

Wraiths attack humans or demihumans in preference to other creatures. However, animals will sense their presence within 30 feet and refuse to advance further, panicking if forced. A pack of wraiths will try to get surprise when attacking, and will wait and position themselves for the most advantageous moment to attack. Wraiths are very intelligent and tend to cluster around the weaker members, or stragglers, when attacking. Any human killed by a wraith becomes a half-strength wraith under its control (e.g., a 10th-level fighter will become a 5 Hit Die wraith under the control of the wraith that slew him).

This foul creature has no power in direct sunlight and will flee from it. Sunlight cannot destroy the wraith, but the undead creature cannot attack in sunlight. It shuns bright (e.g., *continual*) light sources in general, but will occasionally attack if the compulsion to do so is strong.

Habitat/Society: A wraith is an undead spirit of a powerful, evil human. As such, it is usually found in tombs or places where such men and women would have died. Since such men and women are frequently buried together, in the case of the wealthy, or with their families, wraiths are most commonly encountered in packs. Those that died or were buried alone might still be encountered in packs, because a human who dies from the touch of a wraith becomes a wraith under the sway of its slayer. The treasure of the wraith is usually its possessions in life, now buried with it, or those of its victims. Wraiths exist only to perpetuate evil by absorbing the life force of as many people as possible. A character who becomes a wraith is nearly impossible to recover, requiring a special quest.

The wraith cannot communicate, except through a *speak with dead* spell. They do not even seem to communicate with each other, except as master to slave for combat strategy. Any attempt to speak to a wraith is met with scorn, unless by a very powerful party. In that case, the wraith desires only to flee. Wraiths can be dominated by powerful evil creatures, particularly other undead, priests, and wizards, and made to serve their will.

Ecology: The wraith has no proper niche, serving no useful purpose in nature and providing no byproducts that others can use. It requires no nourishment, killing only for the sheer hatred of life. All creatures close to nature will shun the presence of a wraith. It exists more in the Negative Material plane than in the Prime Material plane, and thus is not a natural part of this world.

Wyvern

CLIMATE/TERRAIN:	Temperate mountain forests and jungles
FREQUENCY:	Uncommon
ORGANIZATION:	Solitary
ACTIVITY CYCLE:	Dusk and dawn
DIET:	Carnivore
INTELLIGENCE:	Low (5-7)
TREASURE:	E
ALIGNMENT:	Neutral (evil)

NO. APPEARING:	1-6
ARMOR CLASS:	3
MOVEMENT:	6, Fl 24 (E)
HIT DICE:	7 + 7
THAC0:	13
NO. OF ATTACKS:	2
DAMAGE/ATTACK:	2-16/1-6
SPECIAL ATTACKS:	Poison
SPECIAL DEFENSES:	Nil
MAGIC RESISTANCE:	Nil
SIZE:	G (35' long)
MORALE:	Very steady (14)
XP VALUE:	1,400

A distant cousin to the dragon, the wyvern is a huge flying lizard with a poisonous stinger in its tail.

The 35-foot-long dark brown to gray body of the wyvern is half tail. Its leathery batlike wings are over 50 feet from tip to tip. The head alone is 4 feet long and filled with long, sharp teeth. Unlike the dragon, it has only hind legs, using them the same way a hunting bird would. The tip of the tail is a thick knot of cartilage from which a 2- foot-long stinger protrudes, very much like that of a scorpion. The eyes are red or orange. A wyvern does not have a strong odor, although its lair might smell of a recent kill. These beasts can make two sounds: a loud hiss, which sounds like a hot sword plunged into water, and a low, deep-throated growl, much like that of a bull crocodile.

Combat: Rather stupid, but aggressive, wyverns will nearly always attack. In combat, the wyvern always prefers to be flying, and will seize any opportunity to take flight and continue combat. If trapped on the ground it will bite (2-16 points of damage) and use its stinger (1-6 points of damage), attacking the most convenient target or targets. The tail is very mobile, easily striking over the back of the wyvern to hit an opponent to its front. The stinger injects poison (type F) into the wound, against which the victim must make a save vs. poison or die. Even if the saving throw is successful, the victim suffers 1-6 points of physical damage from the sting.

From the air the wyvern is a far more deadly opponent. It dives upon ground targets, attempting to snatch them up in its two taloned claws (1-6 points of damage each) and fly off. Man-sized victims are snatched if at least one talon hits for damage. Large victims require both talons to hit in order to snatch them up. The wyvern cannot fly while carrying anything bigger. After a dive, it takes the wyvern a full round to circle around. On the next round it can dive again. Once airborne with prey in its talons, the wyvern stings and bites each round, both at +4 to hit, until the victim is motionless. In aerial combat, the wyvern will make a pass during which it will either bite or sting. Then it will land and feast, not hunting again until the next day.

As a hunter, the wyvern is cunning. It will avoid letting its shadow fall across its prey as a warning. The final approach of the dive is done in complete silence, imposing a -2 surprise modifier on the target. It trails its prey from downwind whenever possible. A mature wyvern often waits for the right moment to strike, and is willing to let prey go that is too powerful or within easy reach of cover. Such a wyvern understands that men, particularly those armed in bright metal, are stronger than their size would indicate. Given a perfect opportunity, it will attempt to snatch up an unarmored member and fly out of range.

Habitat/Society: The wyvern is a solitary creature, nesting only with its mate and young. It tends to lair on mountainsides that overlook forests, jungles, or sometimes plains. A wyvern makes its lair in large caverns that can be found in such places, staking out a territory about 25 miles across. If game is sparse, it will hunt with a small group of its own kind. Only young wyverns attack others of their kind, usually to establish new territory. Older wyverns settle disputes in an unknown manner without actual combat.

Some wyverns have been known to work with evil dragons. Usually these dragons completely dominate the weaker and smaller wyverns.

Ecology: An adult wyvern consumes the equivalent of a man-sized to large creature once per day. This could translate to a horse, pig, or a handful of sheep. While it eats them whole, the bones are not digested, and neither are metal objects. The wyvern eats carrion only if desperate.

The wyvern has no natural enemies, although it would not be a match for certain powerful creatures. It is noted for the foul taste of its flesh. No one has found a way to cure its hide and the bones are light and brittle to aid in flying. Certain body parts are used by spell casters as spell components, for which they will pay a reasonable price.

	Xorn	Xaren
CLIMATE/TERRAIN:	Subterranean	Subt erranean
FREQUENCY:	Very rare	Very rare
ORGANIZATION:	Solitary	Solitary
ACTIVITY CYCLE:	Any	Any
DIET:	Minerals	Minerals and magical metal
INTELLIGENCE:	Average (8-10)	Average
TREASURE:	OO, P, Q(×5), X,	YO, P, X, Y
ALIGNMENT:	Neutral	Neutral
NO. APPEARING:	1-4	1
ARMOR CLASS:	-2	1
MOVEMENT:	9, Br 9	9, Br 3
HIT DICE:	7+7	5+5
THAC0:	13	15
NO. OF ATTACKS:	4	4
DAMAGE/ATTACK:	1-3(×3)/6-24	1-3(×3)/4-16
SPECIAL ATTACKS:	Surprise	Surprise
SPECIAL DEFENSES:	Spell immunities	Spell immunities
MAGIC RESISTANCE:	Nil	Nil
SIZE:	M (5′ tall)	M (4′ tall)
MORALE:	Champion (16)	Champion (15)
XP VALUE:	4,000	3,000

The xorn (zorn) are natives to the elemental plane of Earth.

The wide body of a xorn is made of a pebbly, stone-like material. It has a large, powerful mouth on top of its head with three long arms, tipped with sharp talons, symmetrically positioned every 120 degrees around it. Between the arms are large, stone-lidded eyes that see in all directions. At its base are three thick, short legs, each directly beneath an eye. The whole body is designed for burrowing, mouth first.

Combat: Xorn do not attack flesh creatures except to defend themselves or their property, since they can not digest flesh. Xorn have no excessive love or hate for creatures of the Prime Material plane. The sole exception to this is anyone carrying a significant amount of precious metals or minerals, which it can smell up to 20 feet away. The normally peaceful xorn can become quite aggressive when after food, especially on the Prime Material plane, where such sustenance is harder to find than it is on its native plane. Xorn expect to be given a reasonable portion in exchange for peaceful passage, or else they attack (90% chance) to get food.

In combat, xorn have two different methods of fighting. Against a single opponent, they bend the two legs nearest the opponent deeply, angling their bodies toward the enemy. In this way all four attacks can be brought to bear. Against several opponents, they attack with arms in all directions, each striking at a different target. One of the targets suffers a second attack, as the xorn angles its body down to bite.

If necessary, a xorn can use its ability to blend into the surrounding stone to impose a −5 penalty to opponents' surprise rolls when it attacks. This incorporates a blending of coloration and its physical ability to pass into and through stone. This does not happen very often, since a xorn is more likely to ignore a party, or openly demand metals. However, once combat begins, it can use a variation on this theme. The xorn may pass through the nearest stone (usually the floor) and vanish for 1-3 rounds. It then lunges out of a stone surface to gain surprise, often at the feet of an opponent, attacking with three arms and its mouth. This guerrilla warfare can continue indefinitely. During any round that it passes through stone, a *phase door* spell kills it instantly. If fight goes against it, the xorn retreats to the nearest stone surface.

A xorn is immune to fire and cold, both magical and normal. Electrical attacks cause half damage if the xorn fails its saving throw, and no damage if the saving throw is successful. Edged weapons cause only half damage to xorn, though blunt and piercing weapons do full damage. A *move earth* spell flings a xorn back 30 feet, and the creature is stunned for one round. A *stone to flesh* or *rock to mud* spell lowers its AC to 8 for one round. During that round the xorn will

attack, as it is readjusting its substance back to stone. Lastly, a *passwall* spell inflicts 1d10+10 points of damage on a xorn.

Habitat/Society: A xorn is normally found on the elemental plane of Earth. It is only on the Prime Material plane if forcibly summoned or if it was the victim of an interplanar accident.

On their native plane, xorn are as peaceful as Prime Material plane herbivores. While xorn are intelligent, their society is limited to small clans of mineral gatherers. These clans wander from place to place, leaving behind open pockets where they have eaten out a vein of mineral. On the Prime Material plane they always seek wide regions of stone underground. What humans would consider treasures, xorn consider food. They keep their store of food in a nearby air pockets.

Ecology: On the Prime Material plane, they are visitors that serve no ecological function. On their own plane, they are gatherers, eating only stone and minerals. The empty pockets in the stone are quickly inhabited by various creatures of the plane. Dao have been known to hunt them for sport. Equally as often, xorn serve dao as slaves.

Xaren

Xaren are relatives of the xorn, with identical abilities in combat. Xaren resemble xorn closely, though they are slightly smaller and their hides are shinier, almost metallic. Unlike ordinary xorn, they crave magical metal as food. For each plus of enchantment they eat, they permanently gain 1 hit point, up to their maximum of 45. Even after reaching their maximum growth, they still require magical metal to maintain their health. They can smell magical metal up to 40 feet away.

Like xorn, xaren expect handouts. They demand magical metal from creatures with enchanted weapons or armor, and attack if they are denied. They prefer iron, copper, silver, gold and electrum (in that order), though they will also snack on metallic ore.

If attacked with a magical weapon, xaren can make an attack roll against AC −2 to bite an opponent's weapon. If they hit, the weapon must save vs. crushing blow or be destroyed.

Xaren and xorn are indifferent to one another and rarely cooperate. Dao do not enslave xaren, though they do hunt them.

Yeti

CLIMATE/TERRAIN:	Arctic hills and mountains
FREQUENCY:	Very rare
ORGANIZATION:	Clan
ACTIVITY CYCLE:	Day
DIET:	Carnivore
INTELLIGENCE:	Average (8-10)
TREASURE:	D
ALIGNMENT:	Neutral

NO. APPEARING:	1-6
ARMOR CLASS:	6
MOVEMENT:	15
HIT DICE:	4 + 4
THAC0:	15
NO. OF ATTACKS:	2
DAMAGE/ATTACK:	1-6/1-6
SPECIAL ATTACKS:	Squeeze
SPECIAL DEFENSES:	Immune to normal cold, invisible in snow and ice
MAGIC RESISTANCE:	Nil
SIZE:	L (8' tall)
MORALE:	Elite (13)
XP VALUE:	420

Sometimes confused with the abominable snowman, the yeti is a distant cousin to the great carnivorous apes of warmer climates.

An adult yeti stands 8 feet tall and is covered in long, white fur. Their feet and hands are wide and flat, which helps to disperse their great weight (about 300 pounds) on treacherous snow fields. They travel on all fours like the apes, but fight very comfortably standing erect. Unlike most apes and gorillas, the yeti does not have an opposable toe on its feet. They wear no clothing or ornamentation. The spoor, or smell, of a yeti is very subtle in cold climates, but in confined or warm areas, they have a strong, musky odor. The eyes of a yeti are icy blue or almost colorless. Their claws and flesh are ivory white. Unlike many arctic creatures, the yeti does not have a thick layer of body fat to keep it warm. Instead, it relies upon the special properties of its thick, warm fur. It has a transparent second eyelid, which allows the creature to see in blowing snow, and prevents its eyes from freezing in extreme temperatures.

Combat: The yeti is a fierce hunter of the polar regions. It stalks its prey and lays an ambush, attempting to gain surprise. A favorite trick is to get ahead of its prey and lie in a depression in the snow, or dig a shallow pit and cover itself with snow. Such works can be detected only by natives of the arctic regions, and then only 25% of the time. Against the snow, the yeti is invisible due to its coloration until its prey is 10 yards away. Under a thin layer of snow it is completely invisible.

Any opponent surprised by a yeti must save vs. paralyzation or go rigid with fright for three rounds, indicating that he has looked into the icy blue depths of the yeti's eyes. Any opponent that is paralyzed in this way can be automatically hit by both claws and squeezed.

Although the yeti does have fangs (1-4 points of damage), it does not usually attack with them, preferring to use its formidable claws. If any hit with claws is made with a natural 20, the victim is pulled in for a chilling squeeze. The creature's fur actually absorbs heat, making it extraordinarily cold if contacted (2-16 points of damage if squeezed). The heat-absorbing property of the yeti's fur can work against it; damage from heat is 50% greater than normal.

Habitat/Society: Although the yeti is of average intelligence, it has no civilization. They can use simple tools, including man-made weapons, but will not make any themselves. Yeti live in ice caves in hills and mountains. Sometimes these are natural, sometimes they are excavated by the yeti or enlarged to accommodate the family. Most yeti treasure consists of items recovered from the bodies of explorers.

Life is harsh in the arctic, and friends and food are hard to find, making survival and reproduction the yeti's only goals. The yeti will associate only with its immediate family, the young leaving to fend for themselves as soon as they mature. A family usually consists of an adult male with one to three females and a 50% chance of 1-6 young if females are present. In an attacking group, the largest yeti is the male, the next largest ones are his mates. Any others are small males or females that are due to leave the family soon.

Ecology: Any living creature not of its family is considered potential food, including other yeti. This does not make them foolhardy; only a starving yeti will attack an obviously stronger party. Their typical diet consists of herd creatures, such as caribou, bears, wolves, and other creatures inhabiting the snowy mountains in which they live. The yeti may turn to scavenging in hard times. They range across a wide area in search of food, usually 15 miles in all directions from their lair.

Yeti claws and teeth have value only because of the rarity of the creature. They sell for about a gold piece a tooth or claw on the open market. Yeti fur is another story. It is prized by those living in cold climates for its extraordinary ability to keep its wearer warm. A full grown yeti pelt can fetch up to 300 gold pieces on the open market.

Yuan-ti

CLIMATE/TERRAIN:	Tropical jungles
FREQUENCY:	Very rare
ORGANIZATION:	Tribe or nation
ACTIVITY CYCLE:	Any
DIET:	Carnivore
INTELLIGENCE:	Genius (17-18)
TREASURE:	C
ALIGNMENT:	Chaotic evil

NO. APPEARING:	1-4
ARMOR CLASS:	4/0
MOVEMENT:	12, slither 9
HIT DICE:	6-9
THAC0:	15 (6 HD),
	13 (7-8 HD),
	11 (9 HD)
NO. OF ATTACKS:	2
DAMAGE/ATTACK:	See below
SPECIAL ATTACKS:	Spells
SPECIAL DEFENSES:	Nil
MAGIC RESISTANCE:	20%
SIZE:	M or L (10' long)
MORALE:	Elite (14)
Abominations	Champion (15)
XP VALUE:	Variable

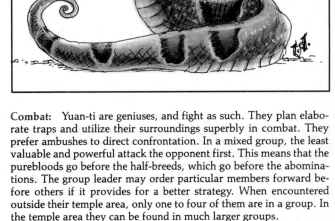

Psionics Summary

Level	Dis/Sci/Dev	Attack/Defense	Power Score	PSPs
HD-2	3/level	MT, II/M-, IF, TW	= Int	15 × Mult

Clairsentience - danger sense, feel sound, poison sense*. **Psycometabolism** - Animal affinity* (snake), metamorphosis (snake), chameleon power*, chemical simulation*, flesh armor.
Telepathy - attraction (to snakes), aversion* (to snakes), false sensory input, inflict pain, invincible foes, life detection, phobia amplification*, post-hypnotic suggestion, repugnance (to snakes), taste link*.

Descendants of humans whose blood has been fouled, yuan-ti have varying degrees of snakelike body parts. They are highly intelligent and evil, always plotting to advance their causes.

There are three major varieties of yuan-ti: *purebloods, halfbreeds,* and *abominations*. A pureblood can pass for human 80% of the time. It has only slight differences from true humans, such as slit eyes, or a forked tongue, maybe even small fangs. Halfbreeds are part human and part snake. Roll a d6 twice on the table below; a duplicate roll produces no result, but is not rerolled. Ignore unworkable combinations. This is a general guide; the DM can invent his own combinations of snake and human.

Roll	Feature	Effect
1	Snake head	Bites for 1-10 points damage
2	Flexible torso	+1 to saves using Dexterity
3	No legs, snake tail	Constricts for 1-4 points of damage
4	Snakes instead of arms	Each bites for 1-6 points damage
5	Scales instead of skin	Armor Class 0
6	Legs and a snake tail	Constricts for 1-4 points of damage

Abominations are either all snake (50%) or have only a single human feature, either head or arms, and are of large size (10 feet long). Halfbreeds and abominations disdain wearing human clothing or armor, while purebloods do not. All yuan-ti use weapons and other items. Yuan-ti do not give off an odor that humans can detect. However, animals will detect a dry, musty smell on them. The snake features of these foul creatures vary greatly from simple green and brown scales to wild patterns of stripes, diamonds, and whorls in reds and blues. Yuan-ti speak their own language. They can also speak with any snake or snakelike creature. Those with human heads speak common besides.

Combat: Yuan-ti are geniuses, and fight as such. They plan elaborate traps and utilize their surroundings superbly in combat. They prefer ambushes to direct confrontation. In a mixed group, the least valuable and powerful attack the opponent first. This means that the purebloods go before the half-breeds, which go before the abominations. The group leader may order particular members forward before others if it provides for a better strategy. When encountered outside their temple area, only one to four of them are in a group. In the temple area they can be found in much larger groups.

Purebloods have 6 Hit Dice, half-breeds have 7 or 8 Hit Dice, and abominations have 9 Hit Dice. All yuan-ti, if they have hands, always use weapons, preferring those with an edge. They use poison, particularly slow acting types, but in traps, not on weapons.

Any yuan-ti with a human head can cast the following spells once per day; *cause fear, darkness* (15 foot radius), *snake charm, sticks to snakes, neutralize poison, suggestion,* and *polymorph other.*

Habitat/Society: Yuan-ti are devout worshippers of evil. They also hold all reptiles in high esteem. The center of yuan-ti life is the temple. They tend toward old ruins far away from man, but have even been known to build underneath human cities. Their own works tend toward circles, with ramps and poles replacing stairs. In all cases they are secretive about the location of their city or temple. The abominations rule over the yuan-ti, and are the leaders of the temple, with the high priest (human-headed) ruling over all. Their rituals often involve bloody sacrifices. The purebloods take care of all outside negotiations, always pretending to be human. Yuan-ti speak their own language and common.

Ecology: Ages ago, a cult of humans worshiping a reptilian elder god recieved a "blessing" from their dark lord: their offspring all were part snake. Since then the breeding line has been polluted and mixed, producing purebloods (those least favored), half-breeds, and abominations (the truly blessed). They are strictly carnivorous, eating any warm-blooded creature they can catch. They have a special taste for birds and human flesh. They are clever enough about their ecology not to overhunt any particular region. Larger groups keep captive herds of wingless birds or other warm-blooded creatures.

Yuan-ti, Histachii

CLIMATE/TERRAIN:	Tropical jungles
FREQUENCY:	Very rare
ORGANIZATION:	Tribe
ACTIVITY CYCLE:	Any
DIET:	Carnivore
INTELLIGENCE:	Low (5-7)
TREASURE:	Nil
ALIGNMENT:	Chaotic evil

NO. APPEARING:	2-20
ARMOR CLASS:	8
MOVEMENT:	12
HIT DICE:	2+2
THAC0:	19
NO. OF ATTACKS:	3
DAMAGE/ATTACK:	1-2/1-2/1-3
SPECIAL ATTACKS:	See below
SPECIAL DEFENSES:	See below
MAGIC RESISTANCE:	See below
SIZE:	M (5'-6' tall)
MORALE:	Average (10)
XP VALUE:	120

Once human, yuan-ti histachii are near-mindless abominations who have been transformed into reptilian humanoids to serve their yuan-ti masters. Most often, they are found guarding yuan-ti brood chambers.

Histachii are hairless creatures. Their clothing, little more than filthy rags, hangs limply over their emaciated bodies. Their gray or yellow-green skin is tough and scaly, and smells faintly of rotting meat. They have beady, bloodshot eyes, and their forked tongues continually dart in and out of their mouths. Their dull yellow teeth are like tiny hooks, razor-sharp. Their fingernails are black and twisted, resembling the claws of a lizard.

Histachii speak in short, hissing phrases. They know the languages of yuan-ti and all snakes and snakelike creatures, as well as the languages they spoke in their original human lives.

Combat: Histachii attack any nonreptilian creature or humanoid on sight, unless their yuan-ti masters give them orders to the contrary. Unsophisticated fighters, most histachii charge directly at their opponents, attacking with their claws and teeth. To protect their yuan-ti masters, histachii will fight to the death.

Regardless of their abilities in their former lives, histachii do not wield weapons or use magic. Once per day, they can become *berserk*. In this state, they are so enraged that they gain a +2 bonus to their attack rolls. The *berserk* condition persists for 2-12 (2d6) rounds.

Unlike yuan-ti, histachii have no natural magic resistance. However, they are immune to all types of *hold* and *charm* spells.

Habitat/Society: Yuan-ti create most histachii servitors from human prisoners. They also may transform human worshippers who voluntarily agree to become histachii. Humans become histachii by drinking a distillation of yuan-ti venom mixed with certain herbs and roots. (The yuan-ti prepare this special concoction.) If a human is unwilling to drink, the yuan-ti pin their captive to the ground and pour the mixture down his throat.

Any human who drinks this mixture, whether by choice or by force, must make a saving throw vs. poison with a −4 penalty. If the saving throw fails, the victim becomes a histachii in 7-12 (1d6+6) days. If the save is successful, the victim immediately lapses into a coma; death will follow in one hour. A comatose victim can be revived with a *slow poison* or *neutralize poison* spell, presuming the spell is cast within 1 hour after the mixture

has been swallowed. Human-headed yuan-ti have the ability to *neutralize poison*, and they may save a comatose victim themselves. It is not for the victim's benefit. A human who fails his save after drinking the mixture may suddenly find himself alive again, only to face another flask of the mixture when the yuan-ti attempt another transformation.

Only humans can become histachii. Nonhumans who drink the yuan-ti mixture must also make a save vs. poison with a −4 penalty, however. If the save is successful, the nonhuman will be violently ill, unable to take any action for 1-4 turns. If the save throw fails, the nonhuman becomes comatose and dies in 2-5 rounds.

If a human fails his saving throw after consuming the mixture, a few desperate measures may prevent his transformation into a histachii. If *neutralize poison*, *dispel magic*, *remove curse*, and *heal* are cast on the victim, in precisely this order, the transformation process will be reversed. However, the victim will permanently lose 1 point of Intelligence. A *wish* or a *limited wish* will reverse the transformation with no loss of Intelligence. Once the transformation is complete, only a *wish* can restore the victim to his former self. Histachii live 20-80 (2d8 x 10) years after their creation. They cannot breed; histachii only can be created from human beings.

Histachii are completely submissive to their yuan-ti masters, carrying out their every order without hesitation. The servants share the lairs of their yuan-ti masters. Usually, these lairs are in ancient ruins deep in tropical jungles, but sometimes yuan-ti dwell in subterranean caverns beneath human cities. A histachii's duties include hunting, caring for the yuan-ti's reptile menageries, guarding prisoners, and various custodial chores. In rare moments of leisure, the servants enjoy soaking in pools of cool water. Histachii do not collect treasure.

Ecology: Like yuan-ti, histachii are strictly carnivorous, feasting on rats, worms, and other vermin. They also eat yuan-ti leftovers.

	Least	Lesser	Greater
CLIMATE/TERRAIN:	Any	Any	Any
FREQUENCY:	Rare	Very rare	Very rare
ORGANIZATION:	Solitary	Solitary	Solitary
ACTIVITY CYCLE:	Any	Any	Any
DIET:	Nil	Nil	Nil
INTELLIGENCE:	Average (8-10)	Very (11-12)	High (13-14)
TREASURE:	See below	See below	See below
ALIGNMENT:	Neutral	Neutral (evil)	Neutral (evil)
NO. APPEARING:	1	1	1
ARMOR CLASS:	3	1	-1
MOVEMENT:	9	9	9, Fl 9 (D)
HIT DICE:	6	8	10
THAC0:	15	13	11
NO. OF ATTACKS:	3	3	3
DAMAGE/ATTACK:	1-4/1-10/1-10	1-6/1-12/1-12	1-10/1-12/1-12
SPECIAL ATTACKS:	See below	See below	See below
SPECIAL DEFENSES:	See below	See below	See below
MAGIC RESISTANCE:	Nil	Nil	25%
SIZE:	Variable	Variable	L (9' tall)
MORALE:	Elite (14)	Champion (16)	Fanatic (18)
XP VALUE:	2,000	4,000	11,000

These yugoloths are summoned by evil wizards or priests to guard something of importance. Yugoloth guardians always defend their charge with great ferocity.

There are three types of yugoloth guardians—least, lesser, and greater. The least and lesser yugoloth guardians vary in size and form, often being horned and frog-like (least) or ape- or boar-like (lesser). Greater yugoloth guardians always appear as gigantic, winged bears with ram horns protruding from their foreheads, and eagle talons for hands.

yugoloths guardian have the ability to speak all languages.

Combat: yugoloth guardians can breath fire three times per day in a cone 30 feet long with a 10-foot base diameter. Damage depends upon the type of daemon breathing. Least and lesser yugoloths cause 3d6 and 5d6 points of damage, respectively, while greater yugoloths inflict 7d6 points per breath attack. A successful saving throw vs. breath weapon reduces damage by half. Yugoloth guardians never use their fire breath if the fire might damage whatever they are assigned to protect.

All yugoloth guardians are immune to *charm, hold, sleep, polymorph,* and *fear* spells. Lesser and greater yugoloths are also impervious to weapons with less than a +2 bonus. Many of these creatures are invulnerable to one or more additional forms of attack (e.g., sword, cold, fire, electricity).

Habitat/Society: Yugoloth guardians must remain at all times within 90 yards of the object they have been summoned to protect. Within this 90-yard radius, yugoloth guardians prefer to remain at a distance in battle, using their breath weapon to maximum advantage.

Ecology: Summoning a guardian daemon is a dangerous affair. There is a 10% chance for each level the summoner is over 7th level of having his request for a guardian daemon granted (maximum chance of 90%). Conversely, if the summoning fails, there is a 30% chance (-2% per level of the summoner over 10th) that the daemon takes offense and gates in to slay the spellcaster.

Least Yugoloth
These creatures are often summoned to protect treasures valued at less than 25,000 gold pieces. Least yugoloths have a 50% chance of being immune to one additional type of attack.

Lesser Yugoloth
Lesser yugoloths are usually found guarding treasures of 25,000 gold pieces or more. They have a 80% chance of being impervious to one additional attack form.

Greater Yugoloth
These yugoloths are dispatched only to protect objects of exceedingly great value. Greater yugoloth guardians are resistant to magic (25%) and are always immune to two additional forms of attack. They can make a *suggestion,* as the spell, once per round, even when engaged in combat.

Zaratan

CLIMATE/TERRAIN:	Tropical/Fresh and salt water
FREQUENCY:	Very rare
ORGANIZATION:	Solitary
ACTIVITY CYCLE:	Any
DIET:	Omnivore
INTELLIGENCE:	Average (8-10)
TREASURE:	See below
ALIGNMENT:	Neutral

NO. APPEARING:	1
ARMOR CLASS:	−6/0
MOVEMENT:	1, Sw 2
HIT DICE:	51-70
THAC0:	5
NO. OF ATTACKS:	1
DAMAGE/ATTACK:	10-100
SPECIAL ATTACKS:	Swallow
SPECIAL DEFENSES:	Immune to poison, magic weapon needed to pierce shell
MAGIC RESISTANCE:	Nil
SIZE:	G (200-350′ diameter)
MORALE:	Fearless (19)
XP VALUE:	46,000 + 1,000 per HD over 51

The zaratan is an enormous, passive turtle found in the warm currents of Zakhara's seas, in the Al-Qadim campaign setting. Thankfully, the zaratan spends most of its existence in a profoundly deep slumber.

The shell of a zaratan (plural, zaratani) looks like a sloped, rocky mound several hundred feet in diameter. The zaratan's head, over 50 feet across, is often mistaken for a partially-submerged, barnacle-encrusted boulder. The zaratan usually keeps its eyes shut, covered with stony lids that blend with the rest of its head in texture and color. The zaratan's four flippers, each over a hundred feet long, appear to be small reefs, supporting a variety of corals, barnacles, and small fish. The zaratan's rocky shell is considered AC −6, while its head and flippers are only AC 0. In its dormant state, a zaratan appears to be a small, floating island.

Combat: More often than not, once wakened from its slumber, a zaratan will react to an enemy by withdrawing into its rocklike shell, against which nonmagical weapons have absolutely no effect. In addition, no known poison will effect a zaratan with its incredibly slow metabolism. A zaratan will remain in its shell for 1-10 years (if not further provoked) before re-emerging.

However, if pestered and wounded for more than 5% of its total hit points, a zaratan becomes a terrible opponent. Although it attacks last in every round, a single bite from its 40′ maw delivers 10-100 points of damage and will swallow any beings within a 10′ radius of its target (no save), should its attack roll succeed by 4 more than needed.

The stomach of a zaratan is a tough, tube-shaped cave. Usually there is enough stale, trapped air for a creature to survive indefinitely (if they survived the bite attack), but creatures trapped within also suffer 2 points of damage per day unless they can figure out a way to protect themselves from the stomach's corrosive digestive juices. The stomach lining is AC 5. Damage equal to 5% of the zaratan's total hit points (a case of painful indigestion) will result in the victims' regurgitation. A zaratan's stomach might contain just about anything, depending upon the whim of the DM, from pieces of driftwood and chunks of ships, to weapons, armor, and even a small amount of treasure (suggested type Z).

After a battle, a zaratan will immediately fall into a deep slumber, which typically lasts 1-100 years.

Habitat/Society: The slow metabolism of the zaratani assure them incredibly long (if uneventful) lives, measured in millennia. The zaratani are said to have been floating in the sea long before the genies first visited the Land of Fate.

At any given time, a zaratan is 99% likely to be sleeping. As it slumbers, it keeps its mouth wide open. Any small to man-sized creatures stupid enough to swim inside (large fish mostly) are reflexively swallowed. The zaratan spends the rest of its time either mating or conversing with others of its own kind.

Every few centuries, by sheer coincidence, a pair of zaratani will drift into each other. Should they awake (and be of the opposite sex), they will mate. The courtship ritual may take decades, and the mating itself lasts as long as a year.

The zaratani communicate with one another in a language similar to that of the whales. Conversations between the zaratani often last decades. On rare occasions, they have been known to communicate with other beings via telepathy.

Ecology: The older a zaratan gets, the longer it sleeps. As a result, many actually become indistinguishable from a floating island or reef, supporting their own mini-ecosystems on their broad, rocky carapaces and underbellies. Many sport stunted palm trees and vegetation on their shells.

The older and wiser zaratani are perfectly content to be attended by lesser symbiotic beings, provided the symbiotes are not too bothersome and don't interfere with a zaratan's sleep. A few are known to support small, uncivilized villages, while others have even been used as a mobile base for pirates and corsairs!

Visitors will find most inhabitants of a zaratan highly superstitious. Many revere their island home as a god. They believe (rightly) that were their deity to awaken due to hunger, their island might sink beneath the sea, destroying their village. As a result, these villagers strive at every opportunity to keep the zaratan well-fed and content, sacrificing large quantities of caught fish and even visitors to placate their floating deity.

	Common	Monster	Ju-ju	Lord	Sea
CLIMATE/TERRAIN:	Any	Any	Any	Any	Shallow water
FREQUENCY:	Rare	Very Rare	Very Rare	Very rare	Rare
ORGANIZATION:	Nil	Nil	Nil	Solit ary	Pack
ACTIVITY CYCLE:	Night	Night	Night	Night	Night
DIET:	Nil	Nil	Nil	Carrion	Scave nger
INTELLIGENCE:	Non-(0)	Non-(0)	Low (5-7)	Average (8-10)	Low (5-7)
TREASURE:	Nil	Nil	Nil	A	M
ALIGNMENT:	Neutral	Neutral	Neutral evil	Neutral evil	Chaotic evil
NO. APPEARING:	3-24	1-6	1-4	1	2-24
ARMOR CLASS:	8	6	6	6	7
MOVEMENT:	6	9	9	6	6, Sw 12
HIT DICE:	2	6	3 + 12	6	5
THAC0:	19	15	15	15	15
NO. OF ATTACKS:	1	1	1	2	1
DAMAGE/ATTACK:	1-8	4-16	3-12	2-8/2-8	1-10
SPECIAL ATTACKS:	Nil	Nil	See below	See below	Stench, disease, spell use
SPECIAL DEFENSES:	Spell immunity	Spell immunity	Spell immun ity	Spell immunity	Spell immunity
MAGIC RESISTANCE:	See below	See below	See below	Nil	N il
SIZE:	M (6')	L (8'-12')	M (6')	M (6')	M (6')
MORALE:	Special	Special	Special	Average (8-10)	Fearle ss (19-20)
XP VALUE:	65	650	975	650	420

Zombies are mindless, animated corpses controlled by their creators, usually evil wizards or priests. The condition of the corpse is not changed by the animating spell. If the body was missing a limb, the zombie created from it would be missing the same limb. Since it is difficult to get fresh bodies, most zombies are in sorry shape, usually missing hair and flesh, and sometimes even bones. This affects their movement, making it jerky and uneven. Usually zombies wear the clothing they died (or were buried) in. The rotting stench from a zombie might be noticeable up to 100 feet away, depending upon the condition of the body. Zombies cannot talk, being mindless, but have been known to utter a low moan when unable to complete an assigned task.

Combat: Zombies move very slowly, always striking last in a combat round. They are given only simple, single-phrase commands. They always fight until called off or destroyed, and nothing short of a priest can turn them back. They move in a straight line toward their opponents, with arms out-stretched, seeking to claw or pummel their victims to death. Like most undead, zombies are immune to *sleep, charm, hold, death magic, poisons,* and cold-based spells. A vial of holy water inflicts 2-8 points of damage to a zombie.

Habitat/Society: Zombies are typically found near graveyards, dungeons, and similar charnel places. They follow the spoken commands of their creator, as given on the spot or previously, of limited length and uncomplicated meaning (a dozen simple words or so). The dead body of any humanoid creature can be made into a zombie.

Ecology: Zombies are not natural creations and have no role in ecology or nature.

Ju-Ju Zombie
These creatures are made when a wizard drains the life force from a man-sized humanoid creature with an *energy drain* spell. Their skin is hard, gray, and leathery. Ju-ju zombies have a spark of intelligence. A hateful light burns in their eyes, as they realize their condition and wish to destroy living things. They under-

stand full-sentence instructions with conditions, and use simple tactics and strategies. Since they became zombies at the moment of death, their bodies tend to be in better condition. Ju-ju zombies use normal initiative rules to determine when they strike. They are dexterous enough to use normal weapons, although they must be specifically commanded to do so. These zombies can hurl weapons like javelins or spears, and can fire bows and crossbows. Their Dexterity allows them to climb walls as a thief (92%) and they strike as a 6 Hit Die monster. Ju-ju zombies are turned as specters.

The animating force of a ju-ju zombie is more strongly tied to the Negative Material plane. The result is that only +1 or better magical weapons can harm them. Regardless of the magic on the weapon, edged and cleaving weapons inflict normal damage, while blunt and piercing weapons cause half damage. In addition to normal zombie spell immunities, ju-ju zombies are immune to mind affecting spells and psionics, illusions, and to electricity and magic missiles. Fire causes only half damage.

Zombie Lord
The zombie lord is a living creature that has taken on the foul powers and abilities of the undead. They are formed on rare occasions as the result of a *raise dead* spell gone awry. Zombie lords look as they did in life, save that their skin has turned to the pale grey of death, and their flesh is rotting and decaying. The odor of vile corruption and rotting meat hangs about them, and carrion feeding insects often buzz about them to dine on the bits of flesh and ichor that drop from their bodies.

The zombie lords can speak those languages they knew in life and they seem to have a telepathic or mystical ability to converse freely with the living dead. Further, they can *speak with dead* merely by touching a corpse. Zombie lords are turned as vampires.

When forced into combat, it relies on the great strength of its two crushing fists. The odor of death surrounding the zombie lord is so potent it causes horrible effects in those who breathe it. On the first round a character comes within 30 yards, he must save vs. poison or be affected in some way. The following results are possible:

Zombie

1d6 Roll	Effect
1	*Weakness* (as the spell).
2	*Cause disease* (as the spell).
3	-1 point of Constitution.
4	*Contagion* (as the spell).
5	Character unable to act for 1d4 rounds due to nausea and vomiting.
6	Character dies instantly and becomes a zombie under control of the zombie lord.

All zombies within sight of the zombie lord are subject to its mental instructions. Further, the creature can use the senses of any zombie within a mile of it to learn all that is happening within a very large area. Once per day, the zombie lord can *animate dead* to transform dead creatures into zombies. This works as described in the *Player's Handbook* except that it can be used on the living. Any living creature with fewer Hit Dice than the zombie lord can be attacked in this manner. A target who fails a saving throw vs. death is slain. In 1d4 rounds, the slain creature rises as a zombie under the zombie lord's command.

Zombie lords seek out places of death as lairs. Often, they live in old graveyards or on the site of a tremendous battle—any place there may be bodies to animate and feast upon. The mind of the zombie lord tends to focus on death and the creation of more undead. The regions around their lairs are often littered with the decaying bodies, half eaten, of those who have tried to confront the foul beast.

The zombie lord comes into being by chance, and only under certain conditions. First, an evil human must die at the hand of an undead creatures. Second, an attempt to *raise* the character must be made. Third, the corpse must fail its resurrection survival roll. Fourth and last, a deity of evil must show "favor" to the deceased, and curse him or her with the "gift of eternal life." Within one week of the *raise* attempt, the corpse awakens as a zombie lord.

Sea Zombie

Sea zombies (also known as drowned ones) are the animated corpses of humans who died at sea. Although similar to land-dwelling zombies, they are free-willed and are rumored to be animated by the will of the god Nerull the Reaper (or another similar evil deity).

The appearance of drowned ones matches their name: they look like human corpses that have been underwater for some time; bloated and discolored flesh dripping with foul water, empty eye-sockets, tongue frequently protruding from between blackened lips. Their visage and the stench of decay surrounding them are so disgusting that anyone seeing a drowned one or coming within 20 feet of one must roll a saving throw vs. poison. A failed saving throw indicates that the character is nauseated, suffering a −1 penalty to his attack roll and a +1 penalty to his AC for 2d4 rounds. On land, drowned ones move slowly, with a clumsy, shambling gait. In water, however, they can swim with frightening speed.

Drowned ones have an abiding hatred for the living and attack them at any opportunity. These attacks often show surprising cunning (for example, luring ships onto the rocks and attacking the sailors as they try to save themselves from the wreck). Drowned ones take advantage of their swimming speed by attacking ships as they lie at anchor—climbing aboard the vessel and trying to drive the sailors overboard, where they can deal with them more easily.

Drowned ones attack with the weapons typical of sailors: short swords, daggers, hooks, clubs, belaying pins, etc. Because of the unnatural strength of the creatures, these weapons all inflict 1d10 points of damage. The putrid water that drips from the drowned ones contains many bacteria, so any successful hit has a 10% chance of causing a severe disease in the victim. The water-logged condition of the creature's flesh means that fire and fire-based magic cause only half damage. Lightning, electrical, and cold-based attacks inflict double damage. Drowned ones are immune to *sleep*, charm spells, illusions, and other mind-altering spells. Because they are created by the direct will of a deity, they cannot be turned.

Many of the humans who become drowned ones were priests while alive, and they retain their powers as undead. There is a 50% chance that each drowned one encountered is a priest of level 1d4. These creatures are granted their spells directly from Nerull (or similar deity), receiving only baneful spells.

Drowned ones congregate in loose packs. Their only motivation is their hatred for the living. They have no need to eat, although they rend and chew the flesh of their prey (this is probably just to strike terror in others). Underwater, drowned ones are active around the clock and are often found in the sunken wrecks of the ships in which they drowned. They are active above the surface during the night. Drowned ones normally stray no more than 100 yards from the water. If the wind drives the fog onto the coast, however, they can roam inland as far as the fog reaches. When the fog retreats, or when the sun is about to rise, they must return to the water.

Drowned ones communicate among themselves by a form of telepathy; they have no need of a spoken language (other than for spellcasting). The verbal components for spells are spoken in unintelligible whispers.

Appendix I: Instructions for the Blank Monster Form

When designing a monster, avoid extremes. It is a common mistake to make a monster incredibly tough for no reason. Really tough monsters are very rare! If a monster has an extreme ability or combat statistic, there should be a good reason. In the same light, fit the monster's abilities to its description. Players need a fair chance to anticipate what the monster might do. For example, a monster that can fly should have wings, or else usually be encountered aloft. If a monster will have a surprising ability, keep it to just one, and have a good reason for the surprise.

Not all monsters have to be evil. There are many other reasons a monster can be dangerous without arbitrarily making it evil. For example, any creature will fight to protect its family or territory whether it is good or evil.

Characters should be able to negoitate with or intimidate many creatures, but negotiating with a monster does not always mean giving it treasure. Most animals will put off an attack if tossed a free meal they can eat in peace; intelligent creatures have many different motivations. Try not to force characters into having to kill every monster they meet. If a monster is left alive after an enounter, it might be encountered again, and become a regular part of the campaign.

CLIMATE/TERRAIN: Restrict your monsters reasonably. As a rule, only tool-making creatures can be found in every climate or every terrain. Remember that the physical design of a monster should make sense for the climate and the terrain.

FREQUENCY: Monsters should not dominate the landscape unless your campaign plot requires them to. Most monsters avoid settled areas because organized groups of humans and demihumans tend to kill them.

ORGANIZATION: Give a lot of thought to this entry; it determines the group tendencies of the monster. A pack can be controlled by controlling its leader. A flock, on the other hand, has no leader, but it does have a pecking order.

ACTIVITY CYCLE: Most monsters need to rest. When are they out and about? When are they sleeping? These habits should make sense with the diet and climate/terrain of the monster.

DIET: What does the monster eat? Not every monster is a man-eater. A wild bull is just as dangerous as a tiger, but it does not eat meat. Remember, fangs and claws imply carnivores, tusks and horns imply herbivores.

INTELLIGENCE: Avoid the tendency to make monsters too intelligent or too stupid. A creature living in the middle of the jungle with no manipulative organs is not likely to be intelligent. Really high intelligence usually implies civilization, or at least sophisticated tools. On the other hand, monsters that must fight to survive must have enough intelligence or other natural ability to conquer their foes.

TREASURE: Treasure is usually collected only by intelligent creatures. An animal type may guard a treasure for another creature, but the treasure itself belongs to the intelligence that set it there as a guard. Monsters that care little for riches and magical items might still have some as a result of encounters, but things will be scattered and ill-kept, often rusting away to worthlessness. Intelligent monsters, on the other hand, will use their magical treasures to their best advantage—which may be no help at all to the characters!

ALIGNMENT: This is a broad description of the moral and ethical tendencies of the monster. A creature of animal intelligence has no morals or ethics, and hence is of neutral alignment. In general, try to avoid extremes, unless these fit the monster.

NO. APPEARING: The number of monsters typically encountered should correspond to the other facts about the monster. A solitary monster does not travel in a pack of 20! In general, carnivores travel in small groups, herbivores travel in large groups. This number is also a good way to keep things balanced; weak monsters are dangerous in large numbers, while a strong monster all alone is easy prey to a well-organized group of heroes.

COMBAT STATISTICS: This includes such values as Hit Dice and Armor Class. They should match the physical description of the monster. A well-designed monster fights the way it looks. A small, fuzzy creature with big, soft eyes should not have 25 Hit Dice, an Armor Class of -8, and swoop through the air to attack. The amount of damage done should reflect the weapon being used. Avoid the tendency to give monsters excessive Hit Dice and damage capabilities. The DM is the only person who gets a kick from seeing a PC suffer 40 points of damage in one round; players don't find that amusing at all.

See Chapter 9 of the *DMG* to determine THAC0 for monsters.

APPEARANCE: Include in the physical description of the monster its size, weight, color (skin, hair, eyes, etc.), smell, noises, type of movement (graceful walk, shambling gait, etc.), typical clothing, and preferred weapons.

COMBAT: Include any special combat abilities or disabilities. Be sure to cover any basic strategies or tactics the monster might use. Remember, smart monsters use smart tactics. The strategies should reflect their natural advantages and disadvantages.

HABITAT/SOCIETY: How does the monster relate to others of its kind, and to strangers? When do they work together and when do they fight? How do they choose leaders and how do these leaders rule? What are the goals of these monsters? Where do they live and how does this affect their behavior? Do they use or make tools? If so, what types and how are they made? Why does this monster have treasure? How does it get it? What is the nature of the family, and how many live together? Does the monster have special guards or allies and how frequently are they found together?

ECOLOGY: This should include the types of food eaten—as well as what eats them, if anything. Any useful by-products should be listed, such as fur or edible parts. You may list uses for magical items or spells. On the other hand, don't turn your monster descriptions into shopping lists. The PCs are heroes, not butchers or fur trappers. List other creatures that live in harmony with the monster or compete against it, along with information about the size and nature of its territory.

VARIANTS: If there are major subraces, they should be detailed here. This may be a stronger leader type, an inferior servant race, or a DM special, such as skeletons that hurl their finger joints like *magic missiles*.

XP VALUE: Guidelines for awarding experience are found in Chapter 8 of the *DMG*. Hit Dice Value Modifiers for psionic monsters are +1 if the creature has access to only devotions, +2 if the creature has both sciences and devotions.

In addition to the Hit Dice Value Modifiers listed for monsters in the *DMG*, consider the following optional modifiers: +1 for any special movement which gives an advantage, not just flying; +2 for magic resistance over 50%, +1 for magic resistance of 50% or under; +2 for breath weapons which can cause more than 20 points damage per attack, +1 for other breath weapons.

CLIMATE/TERRAIN: _____
FREQUENCY: _____
ORGANIZATION: _____
ACTIVITY CYCLE: _____
DIET: _____
INTELLIGENCE: _____
TREASURE: _____
ALIGNMENT: _____

NO. APPEARING: _____
ARMOR CLASS: _____
MOVEMENT: _____
HIT DICE: _____
THAC0: _____
NO. OF ATTACKS: _____
DAMAGE/ATTACK: _____
SPECIAL ATTACKS: _____
SPECIAL DEFENSES: _____
MAGIC RESISTANCE: _____
SIZE: _____
MORALE: _____
XP VALUE: _____

Appearance: _____
_____
_____
_____
_____
_____

Combat: _____
_____
_____
_____
_____
_____
_____
_____
_____
_____
_____
_____

Habitat/Society: _____
_____
_____
_____
_____
_____
_____

Ecology: _____
_____
_____
_____
_____
_____
_____
_____

Variants: _____
_____
_____
_____

Appendix II: Monster Summoning Tables

Monster Summoning I

1. Ant, giant
2. Bat, huge
3. Beetle, fire
4. Bullywug
5. Goblin
6. Hobgoblin
7. Jermlaine (3d4 appear)
8. Kobold (3d4 appear)
9. Leech, giant (1 HD)
10. Muckdweller
11. Orc
12. Rat, giant (3d4 appear)

Monster Summoning II

1. Beetle, bombardier
2. Centipede, giant
3. Frog, giant or killer
4. Gnoll or flind
5. Lamprey, land
6. Lizard man
7. Mongrelmen (2 HD)
8. Mudmen
9. Spider, large
10. Stirge
11. Toad, giant
12. Troglodyte

Monster Summoning III

1. Ankheg (3-4 HD)
2. Bat, giant (mobat)
3. Beetle, boring
4. Bugbear
5. Centipede, megalo-
6. Crab, giant
7. Crocodile, wild
8. Dog, death
9. Gelatinous cube
10. Ghoul
11. Lizard, giant
12. Lyc., rat
13. Orc, orog
14. Osquip
15. Sandling
16. Scorpion, large
17. Snake, constrictor
18. Spider, huge
19. Weasel, giant
20. Urchin, land

Monster Summoning IV

1. Ankheg (5-6 HD)
2. Ape, carnivorous
3. Banderlog
4. Ettercap
5. Gargoyle
6. Ghast
7. Hell hound
8. Huecuva
9. Hydra, 5 heads
10. Lyc., wolf
11. Ogre
12. Ooze, gray
13. Owlbear
14. Scorpion, huge
15. Snake, giant const.
16. Toad, poisonous
17. Toad, fire
18. Wasp, giant
19. Wolf, worg
20. Yeti

Monster Summoning V

1. Ankheg (7-8 HD)
2. Cockatrice
3. Displacer beast
4. Doppleganger
5. Hornet, giant
6. Hydra, 7 heads
7. Hydra, 5 heads, cryo- or pyro-
8. Leucrotta
9. Lizard, subterranean
10. Lyc., boar
11. Margoyle
12. Minotaur
13. Ochre jelly
14. Rust monster
15. Slithering tracker
16. Snake, giant, pois. or spitting
17. Spider, giant
18. Giantkin, verbeeg
19. Wolf, winter
20. Zombie, ju-ju

Monster Summoning VI

1. Basilisk
2. Beetle, stag
3. Carrion crawler
4. Dracolisk
5. Drider
6. Griffon
7. Hydra, 8 heads
8. Lizard, minotaur
9. Lyc., tiger
10. Manticore
11. Ogre mage
12. Otyugh
13. Pyrolisk
14. Salamander
15. Spider, phase
16. Troll
17. Wolfwere
18. Wraith
19. Wyvern
20. Yuan-ti, halfbreed

Monster Summoning VII

1. Basilisk, greater
2. Behir or tunnel worm
3. Bulette
4. Chimera
5. Ettin or hill giant
6. Golem, flesh
7. Gorgon
8. Hydra, 10 heads
9. Hydra, 8 heads (pyro- or cryo-)
10. Lizard, fire
11. Mummy
12. Neo-otyugh
13. Pudding, black
14. Roper
15. Shambling mound
16. Slug, giant
17. Sphinx, hieraco-
18. Troll, 2-headed
19. Umber hulk
20. Xorn

Monster Summoning VIII

1. Beetle, rhinoceros
2. Giant, fire or frost
3. Giant, fomorian
4. Golem, stone
5. Gorgimera
6. Hydra, 12 heads
7. Hydra, lernaean, 8 heads
8. Pudding, brown
9. Remorhaz
10. Rust monster
11. Will o'wisp
12. Worm, purple

Conjured Animals

HD	Roll	Animal	Value
1	01-10	Baboon	$1\frac{1}{4}$
	11-25	Dog, wild	$1\frac{1}{4}$
	26-35	Hawk, large	1
	36-40	Hawk, blood	$1\frac{1}{4}$
	41-50	Jackal	$\frac{1}{2}$
	51-55	Mammal, small	varies
	56-60	Minimal	varies
	61-65	Otter	$\frac{3}{4}$
	66-70	Otter, sea	$1\frac{1}{4}$
	71-80	Owl, common	1
	81-90	Rat, giant	$\frac{1}{2}$
	91-00	Skunk	$\frac{1}{4}$
2	01-70	Animal, herd	2
	71-80	Badger	$1\frac{1}{2}$
	81-00	Horse, wild	2
3	01-05	Badger, giant	3
	06-10	Boar, warthog	3
	11-15	Cattle, wild	$2\frac{1}{2}$
	16-20	Cheetah	3
	21-30	Dog, war	$2\frac{1}{2}$
	31-35	Hyena, wild	3
	36-45	Lion, mountain	$3\frac{1}{4}$
	46-50	Lynx, giant	$2\frac{1}{2}$
	51-60	Mule	3
	61-70	Camel	3
	71-80	Stag	3
	81-90	Wolf	$2\frac{1}{2}$
	91-00	Wolverine	3
4	01-10	Bear, black	$3\frac{3}{4}$
	11-25	Boar, wild	$3\frac{3}{4}$
	26-40	Eagle, giant	4
	41-50	Jaguar	$4\frac{1}{4}$
	51-60	Leopard	$3\frac{1}{2}$
	61-75	Owl, giant	4
	76-90	Weasel, giant	$3\frac{3}{4}$
	91-00	Wolf, dire	$3\frac{3}{4}$
5	01-15	Ape, carnivorous	5
	16-25	Buffalo	5
	26-40	Hyena, giant	5
	41-55	Otter, giant	5
	56-70	Skunk, giant	5
	71-85	Stag, giant	5
	86-00	Wolverine, giant	5
6	01-25	Bear, brown	$6\frac{1}{4}$
	26-50	Lion	$5\frac{1}{2}$
	51-75	Porcupine, giant	6
	76-00	Tiger	$6\frac{1}{4}$
7	01-50	Boar, giant	7
	51-00	Lion, spotted	$6\frac{1}{2}$
8	01-50	Bear, cave	$7\frac{1}{2}$
	51-00	Tiger, sabre-tooth	$7\frac{1}{2}$
9	—	Oliphant	$8\frac{1}{2}$
10	—	Bear, polar	10
11	—	Elephant (African)	11
12	—	Mastodon	12
13	—	Mammoth	13
14+	—	Whale	(to 36)

Stag: This is a large male deer that can butt for 2-8 or strike with its hooves for 1-3/1-3.

Giant stag: A very large stag, 7' at the shoulder and weighing about 1,500 pounds. It can butt for 4-16 (4d4) or strike with its hooves for 1-4/1-4.

Terrain Guide

Plain: downs, heath, meadow, moor, prairie, savanna, steppe, tundra
Scrub: brackens, brush, bush, thickets, veldt
Forest: copses, groves, jungle, rain forest, woods
Rough: badlands
Hills: bluffs, dunes, ridges (gorge, rift, valley, canyon)
Mountains: glacier, mesa, tor
Desert: barrens, flat, waste
Swamp: bog, fen, marsh, mire, morass, quagmire, slough
Pond: lake, pool, tarn

Monster Summoning

Special Encounters: Roll on the appropriate table. If the encounter is not suitable, then none occurs.

Surface Encounters: Unintelligent monsters are 75% likely to be driven off by flaming oil nearby, 90% if actually burned by it. Large amounts of food thrown overboard are 50% likely to end such an encounter.

Fish School: This is a large group of one type of fish, the aquatic version of herd animals. They usually do not attack unless commanded by magical means. If panicked, they might mill about, obstructing vision and movement. If large enough, they might cause buffeting damage (1-2 to 1-8, depending on size).

Ghost Ship: This is a lost ship manned by undead. Although it can be seen at any time, it usually attacks only at night, when its masters are at full power. Roll percentile dice once for the crew and once for their leaders. *Crew:* 01-40 = 10-40 skeletons; 41-80 = 10-40 zombies; 81-00 = 10-20 ju-ju zombies. *Leaders:* 01-30 = 1-4 wights; 31-60 = 1-3 wraiths; 61-80 = 1-2 spectres; 81-95 = 1-2 ghosts; 95-00 = 1 lich.

Hazard (ice): This can be a single huge ice mountain or 10-20 smaller, grinding floes. Hard contact with ice reduces seaworthiness by 5% and is 10% likely to require a seaworthiness check to avoid sinking.

Seaweed: This includes both floating masses of weed and beds on the bottom. The former slows ships by 50%. The latter are 30-300' high and provide a 40% chance for another encounter if moved through or investigated.

Sunken Ship: This is a victim of a storm, ice, or hostile action. Sometimes these have their original cargo, and may be inhabited. Roll percentile dice: 01-10 = Has merchant treasure (see Men, merchant); 11-20 = No treasure; 21-60 = 2-24 lacedons (original crew); 61-00 = Monster (roll on appropriate encounter table).

Special Encounters: These can include morkoth, mottled worms, shipwreck survivors, an eye of the deep, sudden storms, seaweed that allows underwater breathing when eaten, giant clams, aquatic versions of carnivorous plants, storm giants, and so on.

Aquatic Monster Summoning, Salt Water

Monster Summoning I

1. Barracuda (1 HD)
2. Lamprey, common
3. Merman
4. Otter, sea
5. Piranha (3d4 appear)
6. Urchin, black

Monster Summoning II

1. Barracuda (2 HD)
2. Dolphin
3. Locathah
4. Ray, ixitxachitl
5. Ray, sting
6. Sea horse
7. Seawolf, lesser
8. Urchin, green

Monster Summoning III

1. Barracuda (3 HD)
2. Crab, giant
3. Lacedon (ghoul)
4. Sahuagin
5. Selkie
6. Urchin, red

Monster Summoning IV

1. Hippocampus
2. Kapoacinth (gargoyle)
3. Lobster, giant (crayfish)
4. Merrow, ogre
5. Otter, giant
6. Shark (3-5 HD)
7. Triton
8. Urchin, yellow

Monster Summoning V

1. Crocodile, giant
2. Lamprey, sea
3. Scrag (troll)
4. Sea lion
5. Selkie
6. Shark (5-6 HD)
7. Spider, giant marine
8. Water weird
9. Urchin, silver
0. Roll again with 1d8

* This creature has a 10% chance to become free-willed for the duration of the spell if ordered to act against its nature or inclinations.

Monster Summoning VI

1. Eel, marine
2. Narwhal
3. Octopus
4. Seawolf, greater
5. Shark (7-8 HD)
6. Snake, giant sea (8 HD)

Monster Summoning VII

1. Ray, manta
2. Slug, giant sea
3. Snake, giant sea (10 HD)
4. Squid, giant

Monster Summoning VIII

1. Eye of the deep
2. Dragon turtle (12 HD)
3. Kraken*
4. Shark, giant
5. Vodyanoi (16 HD)*
6. Whale, killer
7. Whale, small herbivore (12 HD)
8. Worm, mottled (purple)

Special Encounters: Roll on the appropriate table. If the encounter is not suitable, then none occurs.

Surface Encounters: Unintelligent monsters are 75% likely to be driven off by flaming oil nearby, 90% if actually burned by it. Large amounts of food thrown overboard are 50% likely to end such an encounter.

Fish School: This is a large group of one type of fish, the aquatic version of herd animals. They usually do not attack, unless commanded by magical means. If panicked they might mill about, obstructing vision and movement. If large enough, they might cause buffeting damage (1-2 to 1-8, depending on size).

Ghost Ship: This is a lost ship manned by undead. Although it can be seen at any time, it will usually attack only at night, when its masters are at full power. Roll percentile dice once for the crew and once for their leaders. *Crew:* 01-40 = 10-40 skeletons; 41-80 = 10-40 zombies; 81-00 = 10-20 juju zombies. *Leaders:* 01-30 = 1-4 wights; 31-60 = 1-3 wraiths; 61-80 = 1-2 spectres; 81-95 = 1-2 ghosts; 95-00 = 1 lich.

Hazard (navigational): This can ground or damage a vessel that does not have aboard a pilot familiar with the waters. Such hazards as sandbars and submerged logs often change position.

Seaweed: This includes both floating masses of weed and beds on the bottom. The former slows ships by 50%. The latter are 30-300' high and reduce vision to 10 feet. Both provide a 40% chance for another encounter if moved through or investigated.

Special Encounters: These can include morkoth, mottled worms, shipwreck survivors, an eye of the deep, pearl beds, sudden storms, seaweed that allows underwater breathing when eaten, giant clams, aquatic versions of carnivorous plants, storm giants, and so on.

Aquatic Monster Summoning, Fresh Water

Monster Summoning I

1. Frog, giant (1 HD)
2. Koalinth (hobgoblin)
3. Lamprey, common
4. Nixie (3d4 appear)
5. Otter, common
6. Piranha (3d4 appear)

Monster Summoning II

1. Eel, electric
2. Frog, giant (2 HD)
3. Kuo-toa
4. Leech, giant (2 HD)
5. Lizard man
6. Piranha, giant

Monster Summoning III

1. Crab, giant
2. Crocodile, common
3. Frog, giant (3 HD)
4. Lacedon (ghoul)

Monster Summoning IV

1. Beetle, giant water
2. Crayfish, giant
3. Kapoacinth (gargoyle)
4. Kelpie
5. Merrow, ogre, ogre
6. Otter, giant
7. Pike, giant
8. Spider, giant water

Monster Summoning V

1. Crocodile, giant
2. Eel, giant electric
3. Scrag (troll)
4. Water weird

Monster Summoning VI

1. Eel, marine
2. Gar, giant
3. Octopus
4. Seawolf, greater
5. Snake, giant sea (8 HD)
6. Vodyanoi (8 HD)

Monster Summoning VII

1. Catfish, giant
2. Greenhag
3. Naga, water
4. Snake, giant sea (10 HD)

Monster Summoning VIII

1. Slug, giant sea
2. Dragon turtle (12 HD)
3. Kuo-toan monitor
4. Worm, mottled (purple)

NPC Parties

To avoid delays, create NPC parties before play. The tables allow such parties to be set up quickly and impartially, and the DM is encouraged to make any changes that will enhance play. The tables should be considered a starting point.

A typical NPC party has 2-12 members—2-5 major characters and the rest henchmen or men-at-arms.

Characters: The Character Subtable provides a typical party structure by limiting number and classes of the NPC characters encountered. Determine character race (20% demihuman) and demihuman multiclasses on the Racial Subtable (multiclass results can exceed the Character Subtable limits).

Character Level and Equipment: These will usually be comparable to those of the player characters, but NPC level will rarely exceed 12th. Arms, armor, and equipment will be typical: a 1st level warrior would have scale or chain armor and minimal gear. At 2nd level, banded or plate mail is typical, weapons profuse, and equipment complete (much oil, holy water, mirrors, etc.). NPC magic will be used if a fight breaks out. Note that if the NPCs are defeated, their magical items will enter your campaign.

Character spells: These are selected by the DM according to those most suited to the NPC party. Wizards are subject to the limits of spells known. Henchmen spellcasters are treated likewise.

Henchmen: The major NPCs will have a total of 2-5 henchmen, up to the party size, with any remainder men-at-arms. If the encounter is below the 3rd dungeon level, all those with the major NPCs will be henchmen.

Henchman class and race is determined as for the major characters. Major NPCs are assigned henchmen in order of Charisma, allowing for compatibility (e.g., a paladin would not follow a thief, nor would a ranger below 8th level have henchmen). A henchman's level is one-third of that of his master (round up or down). If the master's level is above 8th, the henchman has 1 additional level per 3 full levels of the master. Thus, a 5th level mage would have a 2nd level henchman, while an 11th level mage would have a 5th level henchman (4 + 1). Henchmen are armed much as

major NPCs, though they are not as heavily armored. Their magic is assigned as for major NPCs, but is usually less powerful.

Men-at-Arms: Little detail is needed for these other than hit points. They often have poor armor and few weapons: for example, studded leather, crossbow and dagger, or (at best) scale mail, shield, spear, long sword, and backpack. They are seldom found underground below the 3rd dungeon level.

Character Subtable

Dice Score	Character Type*	Maximum Number in Party
01-17	Cleric	3
18-20	*Druid*	2
21-60	Fighter	5
61-62	*Paladin*	2
63-65	*Ranger*	2
66-86	Wizard	3
87-88	*Specialist*	1
89-98	Thief	4
99-00	*Bard*	1

* Typically, 20% of these will be non-human.

Race Subtable

Dice Score	Race	% of Multiclass
01-30	Dwarf*	15%
31-55	Elf	85%**
56-65	Gnome*	25%
66-90	Half-Elf*	85%**
91-00	Halfling*	10%

* In an evilly aligned party, these will be half-orcs (elves will be renegade drow). The chance for a multiclass half-orc is 50%: fighter-thief (01-33), fighter-cleric (34-45), or cleric-thief (45-50).

** If the roll for multiclass is 01-20, the character is triple-classed.

Multiclass levels: For two classes, subtract 1 level; for three classes, subtract 2 levels. Adjust each class downward to the racial maximum, if applicable.

Magical Items for NPC Parties

Level	Chance/No. of Items/Table
1st	10% / 1 / I
2nd	20% / 2 / I
3rd	30% / 2 / I
	10% / 1 / II
4th	40% / 2 / I
	20% / 1 / II
5th	50% / 2 / I
	30% / 1 / II
6th	60% / 3 / I
	40% / 2 / II
7th	70% / 3 / I
	50% / 2 / II
	10% / 1 / III
8th	80% / 3 / I
	60% / 2 / II
	20% / 1 / III
9th	90% / 3 / I
	70% / 2 / II
	30% / 1 / III
10th	* / 3 / I
	80% / 2 / II
	40% / 1 / III
11th	* / 3 / I
	90% / 2 / II
	50% / 1 / III
	10% / 1 / IV
12th	* / 3 / I
	* / 2 / II
	60% / 1 / III
	20% / 1 / IV
13th +	* / 3 / I
	* / 2 / II
	* / 1 / III
	60% / 1 / IV

* Automatically has this with no roll needed. Use random determination only when any general magical item would be suitable to the individual. Note that some items are in groups or multiples.

Magical Items for Character Encounters

TABLE I

Die Item (d20)
1. 2 Potions: *flying, healing*
2. 2 Potions: *extra-healing, polymorph (self)*
3. 2 Potions: *fire resistance, speed*
4. 2 Potions: *healing, hill giant strength*
5. 2 Potions: *heroism, invulnerability*
6. 2 Potions: *human control, levitation*
7. 2 Potions: *animal control, diminution*
8. 1 Scroll: *1 spell, level 1-6*
9. 1 Scroll: *2 spells, level 1-4*
10. 1 Scroll: *protection from magic*
11. 1 Ring: *mammal control*
12. 1 Ring: *protection +1*
13. 1 Armor: *leather +1*
14. 1 Shield: *+1*
15. 1 Sword: *+1 (no special abilities)*
16. 10 Arrows: *+1*
17. 4 Bolts: *+1*
18. 1 Dagger: *+1*
19. 1 Javelin: *+2*
20. 1 Mace: *+1*

TABLE II

Die Item (d20)
1. 2 Potions: *oil of etherealness, superheroism*
2. 2 Potions: *ESP, gaseous form*
3. 1 Scroll: *3 Spells, level 2-9 or 2-7*
4. 2 Rings: *fire resistance, invisibility*
5. 1 Ring: *protection +2*
6. 1 Staff: *striking*
7. 1 Wand: *magic missiles*
8. 1 Wand: *wonder*
9. 1 bracers of defense AC 4
10. 1 brooch of shielding
11. 1 cloak of elvenkind
12. 1 dust of appearance
13. 1 figurine: *serpentine owl*
14. 3 javelins of lightning
15. 1 jar Keoghtom's ointment
16. 1 robe of useful items
17. 1 set: *chain mail +1, shield +2*
18. 1 set: *chain mail +3*
19. 1 Sword: *+2 (or +1 with abilities*)*
20. 2 Weapons: *crossbow of speed, hammer +1*

TABLE III

Die Item (d20)
1. 1 Ring: *spell storing*
2. 1 Ring: *mind shielding*
3. 1 Rod: *cancellation*
4. 1 Staff: *command*
5. 1 Wand: *fear*
6. 1 Wand: *negation*
7. 1 bag of tricks
8. 1 boots of speed
9. 1 boots of striding and springing
10. 1 cloak of displacement
11. 1 necklace of missiles
12. 1 pipes of the sewers
13. 1 rope of climbing
14. 1 rope of entanglement
15. 1 scarab of protection
16. 1 set: *plate mail +2, shield +3*
17. 1 Shield: *+5*
18. 1 Sword: *+3 (or +2 with abilities*)*
19. 1 Mace or hammer: *+2*
20. 1 Spear: *+2*

TABLE IV

Die Item (d20)
1. 1 Ring: *djinni summoning*
2. 1 Ring: *human influence*
3. 1 Ring: *spell turning*
4. 1 Rod: *smiting*
5. 1 Rod: *terror*
6. 1 Wand: *lightning or fire*
7. 1 Wand: *illusion*
8. 1 Staff: *thunder & lightning*
9. 1 amulet of life protection
10. 1 cube of force
11. 1 deck of illusion
12. 1 eyes of charming
13. 1 helm of teleportation
14. 1 horn of blasting
15. 1 robe of blending
16. 1 stone of good luck
17. 1 set: *plate mail +3, shield +4*
18. 1 Sword: *+4 (or +3 with abilities*)*
19. 1 Arrow: *of slaying (character class)*
20. 1 Net: *of entrapment*

* Intelligence, if any, will not exceed 16.

Monstrous Manual Index

Monstrous Manual Index

Monstrous Manual Index

Birthright™ Campaign

Experience the thrill of playing rulers of legend who command mighty armies and wield the power of kingdoms! The Birthright Campaign setting for the AD&D® game makes this possible as never before. Role-play warriors, wizards, priests, and thieves descended from royal bloodlines, command imperial powers, and control the destinies of far-reaching lands. But be prepared to battle enemies who are equally as powerful, as well as millennia-old monstrous abominations that will stop at nothing to steal your kingly power - your birthright.

Forgotten Realms® Campaign

Well met, and welcome to the most popular, most detailed fantasy campaign world ever created! Here gods walk the earth, and fantastic armies clash. Visitors explore a vast frontier filled with fascinating folk, from bold heroes and whimsical characters to shadowy villains and clandestine societies. This is the home of Elminster the sage and Drizzt the dark elf—two heroes featured in TSR's best-selling Forgotten Realms novel line. No setting can match the grand scope of the Forgotten Realms campaign world.

Ravenloft® Campaign

Whether you journey to Ravenloft for an evening of terror or an extended nightmare, the experience will haunt you forever. The Ravenloft campaign is a horrific realm of dread and desire, rooted in the Gothic tradition. The misty fingers of this world can reach into any other campaign setting to draw unsuspecting travelers into its midst. Once it holds them in its icy embrace, it may never let them go. In a shadowy world filled with vampires, werewolves, and ghosts, only the strong of heart may survive!

Dark Sun® Campaign

The Dark Sun world is the AD&D® game's most savage game setting—a desert realm scorched by a relentless sun, blasted by the destructive magic of generations of evil wizards. It is a land of evil sorcerer-kings and powerful psionicists who command astounding mental powers. In this wild and brutal landscape, a single adventurer can alter the course of history and forever change the world. One of those heroes could be yours!

Planescape™ Campaign

Until now, only the most powerful wizards could peek into the magnificent wealth of the multiverse, but no longer! Now every adventurer can enter the mighty planes—but surviving them is another matter entirely. Infinite universes of infinite variety and danger lie beyond the portal, beginning with Sigil, the City of Doors, where all worlds in existence meet.

Dragonlance® Saga Campaign

Enter Krynn, a world of romance and high adventure. Discover tinker gnomes, gully dwarves, gleeful kender, nefarious villains, noble heroes . . . and dark, deadly dragons. Draconian thugs patrol the streets, evil red dragons fill the skies, and beautiful dragons of gold and silver do battle on the side of good. This world struggles to regain its lost honor and glory, and unlikely adventurers can become legendary heroes!